THE GREAT MARTIAN WAR

AMERICA IN FLAMES

BY SCOTT WASHBURN

**ZMOK
BOOKS**

The Great Martian War: America In Flames
By Scott Washburn

Cover with permission of Robot Peanut Studio

Zmok Books an imprint of

Winged Hussar Publishing, LLC,
1525 Hulse Road, Unit 1,
Point Pleasant, NJ 08742

This edition published in 2018 Copyright ©Winged Hussar Publishing, LLC

ISBN 978-1-945430-58-9
Library of Congress Number 2018942064

Bibliographical references and index
1.
Fantasy 2. Epic Fantasy 3. Action & Adventure

For more information on Winged Hussar Publishing, LLC, visit us at: https://www.
WingedHussarPublishing.com
Twitter: WingHusPubLLC
Facebook: Winged Hussar Publishing LLC

CONTENTS

INVASION

INVASION

PROLOGUE

CYCLE 597,838.2, INVASION SITE 1.3

The city was *burning*.

Bajnatrus had never visualized anything like this. The Homeworld's atmosphere had thinned to the point that it could no longer sustain combustion, but the target world's air was thick and rich with oxygen and things would burn.

The merest touch of the heat rays would ignite any combustible object, and the prey-creatures' structures were filled with combustibles. Some appeared to actually be *built* of combustibles!

The results were… amazing. The super-heated gases leaping skyward glowed brightly in a number of wavelengths, producing patterns unique to Bajnatrus' experience. None of its clanmates would ever have accused it of having aesthetic sensibilities, but Bajnatrus found itself strangely moved by the spectacle.

Or maybe it was just the fever.

It was growing worse. No doubt. Bajnatrus had first noticed it two local days earlier; a strange overheated sensation, as if it had been involved in intense physical activity, even though it was at rest. Then had come an irritation in its throat and a collection of fluid in its breathing sacs. At first the symptoms were manageable, but now there was a growing numbness in its manipulating tendrils. Communications with its clanmates confirmed that they were experiencing similar difficulties.

The inescapable conclusion was that some sort of contagion from the local environment had infected them. All such threats had been eliminated from the Homeworld so long ago that no one had considered this possibility. No provisions had been made…

A small group of the prey-creatures emerged from the space between two structures. They were carrying large bundles and clearly had not realized that Bajnatrus' fighting machine was nearby. The moment they saw it, they dropped their bundles and attempted to flee. Bajnatrus gripped the controls more tightly and brought the heat ray to bear. The targeting reticule moved across the creatures and Bajnatrus activated the ray—but too late! The beam swept jerkily to the left, incinerating several large plant-growths and an unoccupied vehicle of some sort. It brought the ray back, blasting a glowing trench in the ground, and this time caught the intended targets. The creatures disappeared in blasts of flame and steam, leaving nothing but a few charred patches on the ground. The ray continued on for a distance before Bajnatrus could regain control. Yes, this was getting worse; much worse. How much worse would it get? For the first time the idea that this could lead to its death entered its thoughts.

What a ridiculous notion! It had existed for over a hundred thousand cycles, budding off replacement bodies every few hundred cycles as necessary. It had survived the Clan Wars; it had survived the perilous journey to the target world; it had defeated the prey-creature warriors in battle! To be brought low like this! An unfamiliar sensation flooded it. It was a sensation Bajnatrus had no word to describe, but suddenly it was firing the heat ray again. The urge to destroy *everything* was irresistible. Back and forth it swung the ray; structures exploded into flames... *beautiful* flames!

It sent its machine lurching forward, through the pathways between the infernos, colliding with walls and tall plant-growths. For some reason, it could not control the machine properly. Its vision was blurred and its manipulators were so numb it could scarcely feel the control studs anymore. It reached an open circular space and stopped. In the center stood a tall stone pillar with an effigy of one of the prey-creatures, several times life-size, on the top.

A worthy target!

It took three attempts to align the heat ray, but at last the beam leaped out. The effigy cracked and several pieces broke off, but it remained mostly intact as it began to glow. Hotter and hotter until it began to melt. White hot droplets splattered off and it slowly slumped down into a featureless lump of slag.

Still not satisfied, Bajnatrus turned the ray against the base of the pillar and left it there until the entire thing came crashing down. An alarm came on in the control cockpit, but it ignored it until the heat ray suddenly stopped firing. Checking the status, it saw that the device was overheated. It released the firing control as the need to destroy seeped away. *I am so tired...*

Ulla! Ulla! Ulla!

The 'general alert' siren took it by surprise. It could hear it faintly through the hull of the fighting machine and a duplicate signal lit up on the control panel. With clumsy tendrils, Bajnatrus located the source of the alarm—Hadjrubal's machine—and saw that it was not far off. Slowly it turned the machine and moved in that direction. It had to detour several times because of the structures and mounds of rubble that often blocked its path; once it almost fell when a leg tangled with an obstruction.

Eventually, Bajnatrus emerged in another open space and saw that a fighting machine was standing on a small rise. The device was lowered into the loading position and the hatch stood open. As Bajnatrus neared, it saw the body of Hadjrubal lying beneath the hatch. It was clearly dead.

As I will soon be.

The knowledge wasn't so shocking as it had been earlier. It now seemed inevitability rather than an outrage. A great sense of loss filled it, though. The mission had failed. And that failure would doom its clan back on the Homeworld. Such an expenditure of resources could only be justified with success. So its clan would die.

But the Race could still live!

That thought filled it with a new sense of urgency. Its tendrils were nearly useless now, but somehow it activated the long-range communicator. A door on the top of the machine slid open and the transmission antenna deployed. By great good fortune—when had it stated to believe in such things as fortune?—the Homeworld was above the horizon and a clear line of sight existed. The link was established and Bajnatrus painfully composed its last message.

Expedition... failed. Infected... by... local... microorganisms. Lethal. With... precautions... success... still... possible. Repeat... success... still... possible...

SEVEN YEARS LATER...

MARCH, 1907, UNITED STATES MILITARY ACADEMY, WEST POINT, NEW YORK

The mournful strains of 'Taps' echoed off the cliffs overlooking the Hudson River and slowly faded away. A misty rain dripped from the bare branches and beaded on the clothing of the watchers. Cadet Andrew Comstock shivered beneath his greatcoat, but the chill March wind blowing off the river had nothing to do with that.

The words had been spoken, the flag had been folded and given to his mother, but Andrew continued to stand and stare at the open grave and the coffin that lay within. The honor guard and bugler marched away and the mourners began to disperse, but still he stood there. The thing in the box in the hole could not possibly be his father, could it? Not the big, strong man with the bushy mustache and out-of-style mutton-chop sideburns? The man who had taught him to shoot and to fish, and who had dragged him and his mother from post to post all over the country? Not him!

It still all seemed like a dream. The news from England; his father had been sent there to observe some experiment with the fantastic devices the British had captured from the Martian invaders seven years earlier. An explosion. Several city blocks leveled. And then the telegram; his mother in tears. Finally, this trip to West Point's cemetery. A dream.

His aunt was leading his mother away, saying something to him about it being time to go. But he could not bring himself to move. The crowd was almost all gone now, but he dimly became aware of someone standing beside him.

"He always loved this place," said a voice. "I'm glad we could bring him back here."

Andrew finally forced himself to move, turning his head slightly to the left. An officer stood there, the silver oak leaves of a lieutenant colonel on his uniform. It was Benjamin Hawthorne, his father's commanding officer. "Yes, sir," he heard himself say.

"It's a hell of a shame, and I can't tell you how truly sorry I am, Andy. He was a very good man."

"Thank you, sir."

"And..." Hawthorne hesitated. "I'm also very sorry on a personal level."

Now Andrew turned to face the man. "Sir?"

"I was the one who sent your pa over there. I should have gone myself, but I was busy with things and your pa was so eager to volunteer. I let him go. I'm very sorry."

Andrew blinked in surprise. A tiny bit of anger flared up in him, followed by embarrassment. Because he *had* raged silently over the fate—or the idiot—who had put his father in the midst of the accident. He hadn't realized it was Hawthorne, a man he'd met many times and rather liked. "I... you couldn't possibly have known, sir."

"No... no, none of us can ever know, can we? I mean what might come from the decisions we make. We live our lives walking through a fog and we can never know what lies more than a few feet ahead."

"I suppose not." Why did Hawthorne keep talking? Why wouldn't he just leave him be?

"You're graduating this spring, aren't you?"

The change in subject caught him by surprise. "Y-yes, sir, June Week."

"Have you given any thought to where you'll go after that?"

"Uh, I suppose I'll go wherever they send me, sir. That's the army, after all."

"Well, that's true, but if you're interested, I can find a place for you in my office, Andy."

11

Now he really was surprised. "The Ordnance Department, sir? I... my grades aren't really good enough for a posting like that, sir. I'm sure to be put in the infantry, with my class ranking and all." The class ranking, a combination of grades and demerits—he had quite a lot of demerits—would usually determine what branch of the service a cadet was assigned to upon graduation. The highest being sent to the prestigious branches, like the engineers; the lowest found themselves in the infantry.

Hawthorne smiled. "I have a bit of pull and a lot of people admired your father. I think I could make it happen—if you want me to." Andrew hesitated, unsure what to say. "I'm sure your father would be proud to have you follow in his footsteps, son. He really believed in what we are doing."

"The Preparedness Movement, sir? He talked about that a lot."

Hawthorne nodded. "Most people think that the invasion was a one-shot thing and that the Martians will never return. Or if they do, they will just die off again like the first batch. Well, maybe that's true. But we'd be fools to make that assumption. We need to be ready if they come back, and what we do in the Ordnance Department is vital to being ready. That's why your father went to England."

"I see, sir. I... I'll have to think about it, sir."

"Of course. But come on, let's not stand here. It's freezing!"

* * * * *

OCTOBER, 1907, WASHINGTON, D.C.

"Theodore, there is no one in the country happier than I that you've made this decision. But are you sure you want to build your platform and run on *this* foundation?"

The President of the United States turned to look at his old friend, Major General Leonard Wood, and fixed him in his unwavering gaze. "It's the foundation I've been running on all along, Leonard." he said sharply. "And it's the only issue that could bring me to break my promise and run for a third term. Who else can be trusted to do what needs to be done? Everyone seems to think that Taft will be the Republican candidate if I don't run. He's a fine fellow, but he doesn't truly understand the need. Worse, he won't be able to convince the country of the need. And Bryan! He and half the Democrats don't believe there even *are* any Martians! No. It has to be me—and this platform."

Wood sighed. "Theodore, I know you're fond of the Preparedness Movement, but..."

"Fond! *Fond!* You make it sound like some pet cat that's followed me home! You didn't see London after the invasion; I did! A great city laid prostrate; women and children slaughtered in the streets! Do you want to see that in our own cities?"

"Not many people think that can happen here..."

"And why not?" demanded Roosevelt. "Because we are special somehow? That the Martians will spare us simply because we are Americans? Nonsense!"

"I'm not doubting the seriousness of the threat, Theodore," said Wood. "I've been a soldier most of my life and I know how starved the army has been, but it's been seven years and nothing further has happened. People are asking that if they were going to come back, wouldn't they have done so by now?"

"How can anyone know? Do you know what monumental effort must be required to cross the fantastic gulf of space between the planets? I surely don't! But it would make the effort of building a canal across Panama shrink to insignificance in comparison! Perhaps the first invasion was just a scouting mission. Even now they may be massing their forces for the real invasion!"

"But we have no evidence of that…"

"What about the recent sightings made by those Harvard astronomers with their new 60-inch telescope?" interrupted Roosevelt. "Bright flares seen on Mars! Just as happened before they started seeing the gas eruptions that heralded the first invasion. Scientists thought that was the casting of the great launching gun. If they are casting more of them, they must be getting ready to launch more cylinders!"

"Theodore, *I'm* not doubting you, but other people will," Wood said soothingly. "Those flares were only seen by a few men—and they could mean anything. I'm not saying don't prepare—far from it! But to make it the central plank of your platform could lose votes. People are suspicious of the expense, of the sums already spent…"

"What sums?!" snorted the President. "A few millions in the first panic after the invasion. We added a few regiments to the army, built a few new ships, constructed a few additional forts, and then—nothing! People forget what's happened and what could happen! And their congressmen vote what they think their constituents want rather than what they know is needed. In the last few years we haven't accomplished a damn thing beyond a few research projects. I need to remind people of the danger, Leonard."

"Your opponents will remind people of the *expense*. With what we are paying on the canal, we can hardly ask for even more money for something with even less tangible benefits. I know you are disappointed that you haven't been able to accomplish all that you'd wish, but if you are not reelected, you won't be in a position to accomplish anything."

Roosevelt opened his mouth as if to deliver a blistering reply, but then thought better of it. "What's the matter with you, Leonard? Have you been talking with Cortelyou?"

Wood shrugged. "He did ask me to have a word with you. He will be managing your campaign, after all."

"He worries too much."

"So that you can worry about other things—like the Martians."

"Be that as it may, Leonard, this is what I will run on."

Wood spread his hands in acquiescence. "All right then. But it will make a much harder campaign for you."

"So be it," said the President.

"Theodore, Cortelyou expected that to be your answer, but he begs you to at least wait until after the new year to make the announcement. That will give him some time to prepare people and smooth the way."

"Very well, but no longer than that."

* * * * *

CYCLE 597,842.6, AJAKANTHAS

It had done this hundreds of times over the long centuries, and at each *awakening*, the being known to its fellows as Qetjnegartis went through the same routine. First, it opened its eyes and regarded the dead body that until moments ago had hosted its consciousness. Then, closing its eyes again, it searched its memories, going back, back to that first *awakening* when its progenitor had budded it off during a rare time of plenty, when offspring had been permitted.

Qetjnegartis knew that this self-examination was illogical. Hundreds of studies over many years had concluded again and again that the Transference did not produce any loss of memory. It was

13

doubly illogical since if any of its memories *were* missing, how would it know? Nevertheless it searched the nearly endless caverns of its mind housing all the experiences that were the total of its being.

The Homeworld of that first *awakening* was much different than the one it would soon be leaving. The air was warm and thick, the water in the canals flowed deep and strong, nourishing vast croplands that grew under the open sky, as did the food-animals that fed off those crops. And the memories went even farther, for it held some of its progenitor's experiences as well, and they stretched back to times so remote as to be nearly incomprehensible. The vast low deserts which had covered most of the Homeworld even at Qetjnegartis' first *awakening* had held seas of water instead. The higher elevations had been thick with vegetation that grew free and un-ordered and held creatures just as wild. No such things existed at the time of its first *awakening*. Even then, the People had realized that their world was slowly dying and that only by strictly ordering the use of resources could that death be postponed.

Century by century and millennium by millennium Qetjnegartis had helped fight that losing battle. The croplands and animals had been moved underground as the thinning air made growing them above ground impossible. The cities moved underground as well. The canals were dry except for short periods during the spring melts. The ability of the People to make *changes* during the budding process allowed them to still survive on the surface, but there were limits even to that.

As the crisis deepened, logic had been sorely tested. Drawn by some instinct that predated even the most ancient memories, the People had started to draw into groups that had sprung from the same progenitors—*clans*, the academics had called them. Instead of working for the common good, many had worked for the good of their clan alone, even if that caused harm to others. Illogical. Self-destructive. They all knew it, but few were able to defeat it. It was a hard truth that animal instinct could still overrule their minds.

From competing for resources, they had eventually started to fight for them. Conflict! Something unimaginable had become reality. Wars had swept the Homeworld. Weak clans were destroyed; stronger clans expanded their numbers to fill the space. Qetjnegartis remembered the novel experience of budding off new beings—*offspring*—rather than just copies of itself as its old body died. The experience of slaying a fellow being had been novel, too…

At last a new equilibrium was formed and logic reasserted itself. Further wars would accomplish nothing except to hasten the death of all. The Council of Five Hundred, the heads of the clans, was formed. An uneasy peace returned.

And it was a peace that could not last for long. Despite all of their efforts, the Homeworld's ability to support the People had dropped and dropped. The population had to be reduced, and reduced again. At first this was done by culling out the youngest, a certain proportion from each clan. But then the larger and stronger clans began to refuse. They made up their deficits by destroying the smaller and weaker clans. The Five Hundred had dropped to Four Hundred. And then Three. A cycle of new wars, with each interval of peace shorter and grimmer, seemed inevitable. On and on until no one was left. The logic of the situation was all too clear.

But then someone—and it was so very odd that no one seemed able to put a name to that someone—had proposed a new logic: If the Homeworld was doomed to die, then leave it before it did.

It was an idea so radical that few listened at first. Oh, it had been known for centuries that the second and third planets supported life, but no one, except a few damaged individuals, had wasted thought on the idea of traveling to them. But imminent extinction made radical ideas seem far less radical. The notion gained supporters and minds turned to the task.

14

But it was an enormous task and many opposed spending the vast resources that would be necessary. If the effort was made and then it failed, it would only hasten the end for everyone. Despite this, one clan began to build the machines that would be necessary.

This very nearly brought on a war in its own right as clans who opposed the idea prepared to use force to prevent it. Qetjnegartis suspected that war, indeed, would have broken out, but then the scientists who had been studying the third planet made the remarkable announcement that the world was inhabited by thinking beings! Powerful telescopes had seen what appeared to be cities. Further observations had concluded that these beings were becoming industrialized at a frightening pace. Weak radio signals were detected. Fear swept through all the clans that the faint hope that so many had scoffed at would soon be lost altogether as these new beings developed the means to defend themselves.

Caution had been abandoned to panic. All the major clans began to prepare to launch colonization missions. The clan who had started first was ready first and they refused to wait for the others. They launched their mission—which met with disaster.

But the disaster had brought back the information needed for the following missions to succeed. The third planet was teeming with life, both micro and macro. Ironically, the micro was the more dangerous, although the thinking beings posed a danger, as well. But the scientists said that the *change* could be used to overcome the threat of the microbes. The engineers said that their machines could overcome the rest.

And so…

Qetjnegartis opened its eyes again and regarded its old body. *That* was certainly different from the hundreds of other *awakenings* it had undergone. Its old body was not all that old; it would have lasted for many more cycles. But Qetjnegartis would soon be departing for the third planet and it was determined that all those making the journey should begin it with bodies which were as young and strong as possible. It flexed its tentacles and drew in breath.

That done, it pulled itself toward its machine.

There was much work to do.

CHAPTER ONE

NOVEMBER 1907, PHILADELPHIA, PENNSYLVANIA

The huge metal box lurched, made a horrible screeching sound, and then ground to a halt, wrapped in a hissing cloud of steam. Lieutenant Andrew Comstock was quite proud of the fact that he was able to refrain from laughing, although one look at Colonel Hawthorne's face told him it would be a good idea to not even smile.

"Mr. Schmidt," said Hawthorne to one of the civilians standing nearby. "The Baldwin Locomotive Works does, in fact, make locomotives, does it not?"

"Well of course, Colonel…"

"Then why is this… *device*, not locomoting?"

"Colonel," replied the man, his face a bit redder than the sharp November wind could account for, "this is an entirely new type of vehicle! You have to expect minor setbacks. I'm sure our people will have this fixed in no time."

But despite Mr. Schmidt's assurances, the Baldwin mechanics who swarmed over the vehicle were unable to get it running again as the morning slipped by. All Andrew could do was stamp his feet to try and keep from freezing to death. Finally, Schmidt admitted defeat and suggested that they return the next day and try again.

"I'm afraid that won't be possible," said Hawthorne in a voice as chilling as the wind. "We'll be taking the train back to Washington. I have a conference with my superiors tomorrow. I had hoped to be able to report a success here today."

"Colonel, we will get this working! We just need a little more time."

"Time? You've had what? Two years? I fail to see why this is proving so difficult for you. Steam engines have existed for a century. Railroad locomotives for nearly as long. Steam powered tractors that don't need rails are no new thing, either. Even the system of caterpillar tracks is not new. As I understand it, the basic design of this is based on the Holt Steam Tractor, which has been around for years. Why can't you put all of those things together and make them work, sir?"

Schmidt's face was getting red again. "It's not just a matter of putting the components together! We have to keep them within the size limitations which you have established. The weight of the components—and the armor you've insisted on—puts a huge strain on the driving mechanism. An unprecedented strain!"

"I'll remind you that the design also calls for mounting a three-inch quick-firing gun and all of its ammunition. If your machine can't handle the weight now, how will it handle that addition?"

"We'll make it work!"

"I sincerely hope so." Hawthorne shook his head. "Very well, we will return next week. Perhaps you'll have your… your… *tank* working by then. Come along, Lieutenant, let's go."

17

They left the huge Baldwin plant, which was located in the northern part of Philadelphia, and caught the street car heading south on Broad Street. Some of the other passengers took note of their uniforms, but none of them said anything. Once away from the plant, the street was lined with once-fashionable brownstones, now looking a bit sad and worn. The city's well-to-do had moved their residences a mile or so farther north these days. The street, which was indeed very wide, as its name indicated, was crowded with horse-drawn carriages, delivery wagons, and even an automobile or two. The very impressive city hall rose up ahead of them.

"Don't worry, sir," said Andrew. "I'm sure they'll get their tank working soon."

"Their what?" asked Hawthorne, looking at him in confusion.

"Tank, sir. It's what you just called it."

"Did I? Well, it's a good name for the thing."

"A lot easier than 'steam-propelled, armored gun tractor', that's for sure."

"Yes," chuckled Hawthorne.

They had expected to spend considerably longer at Baldwin, so their train wasn't for some hours yet. The colonel decided to take the street car all the way to the end of its run, which was at the naval shipyard on the Delaware River. William Cramp & Sons was building the new battleship *South Carolina* there and Hawthorne wanted a look at it. It was of a new design, larger and more powerful than any previous class. The British had just completed a similar ship, which they were calling *Dreadnought*. Sadly, work had not advanced that far and there was little to look at except the nearly completed hull and huge piles of steel plates.

"The sister ship, *Michigan*, is being built across the river in Camden," said Hawthorne. "They'll each mount eight twelve-inch guns, Andy. Imagine what that could do to a Martian fighting machine."

"Blow it to smithereens, I'd expect, sir. Assuming it could get close enough to hit it."

"Yes, that's the thing, isn't it? The navy can go anywhere and beat anything as long as there's enough water to float their boats. But beyond that, they're helpless. While we, on the other hand, can't even get a *tank* capable of moving itself, let alone a gun! I'm telling you, Andy, if it does come to another invasion, we will be depending on guns. Guns that can get to where they are needed and which can survive long enough to get the job done. The old notions about masses of infantry and cavalry and horse-drawn field guns will all be in the dust bin. The British found that out in the first invasion."

"Yes, sir. It's shame we can't put wheels on battleships."

Hawthorne laughed. "Not a bad idea, that! Perhaps you should suggest that at the meeting tomorrow!"

"Not me, sir! General Crozier would bite my head off!" Which, sadly, was probably true. The chief of the Ordnance Department had no sense of humor at all that Andrew had ever noticed.

They headed back to the station and caught the train south to Washington. It was dark by the time they passed through Baltimore and they bought sandwiches for dinner from a vendor at the station there. Hawthorne paid for Andrew's dinner and he was grateful for that. A second lieutenant's pay didn't go very far, and he was already sending a portion of it to his mother. On their way again, they rode in silence for a while. He was about ready to doze off when the Colonel asked: "So how do you like the job, son?"

"Oh!" he said coming awake. "It... it's fine, sir."

"More interesting than drilling a platoon of infantry at some fort in North Dakota?"

"Oh yes, sir! Much! Thanks so much for getting me the assignment."

"My pleasure. And you've been a big help. Frankly, I'm not as young as I used to be and all of this running around the country is starting to wear me out. Once you become a bit more seasoned, I might start sending you on some of these inspection trips on your own."

"Really sir?" exclaimed Andrew in genuine surprise. "That would be grand, sir... if you think I could do the job..." Doubts welled up in him.

"You just need to learn to growl properly. You saw how I growled at Schmidt there today, didn't you? Nothing to it!"

"If you say so, sir. But I've been taught that second lieutenants don't growl, they get growled *at*. A *first* lieutenant on the other hand... that might have some real growling potential, sir. Or even a captain."

Hawthorne guffawed. "Andy, you are quite the wiseacre, aren't you? You try to hide it, but it pops out every now and again."

"So I've been told, sir. The Commandant at the Academy told me that several times—although not quite so politely."

"Hence all those demerits."

"Uh, yes, sir. The Commandant did not appear to appreciate my sense of humor."

"Yes, Howze is a bit of a curmudgeon. He tried to dismiss that entire class over a simple hazing incident, didn't he? But I did look at your records before I made you the offer, you know. Your grades were not bad at all; it was all the demerits that dragged you down."

"Yes, sir, my father pointed that out a number of times before..."

"Well, out here in the real world, we don't worry so much about demerits. What matters is that a man can do the job. What I've seen of you in the last five months makes me think that you can. First lieutenant, eh? Something might be done, I suppose. I'm due to be promoted to full colonel in a few months, and a colonel really needs an aide of appropriate rank."

Andrew didn't know what to say. He'd just been joking, but if a promotion was offered, he surely wouldn't turn it down! "Thank you for all your kindness, sir."

"Just doing my duty to a fallen comrade. How's your mother these days?"

"She took it very hard at first, but I think she's recovering. My aunt thinks so, anyway."

"She's staying with her now, correct? In Lynn?"

"Saugus, sir,"

"Ah, right. Well, the next time our duty takes us up to Boston, you make sure to see her, right?"

"Yes, sir." Andrew had no desire to talk about his mother or his aunt, so he said: "Why do you think the Martians haven't come back, sir?"

Hawthorne took the change of subject in stride. "Hard to say. But these days everyone thinks things have to happen quickly. If they were here last year, they'll certainly be back by next year; and if they're not back by next year that must mean they aren't coming at all. Nonsense! Remember your American history? The first English colony was established in Roanoke in 1585. It vanished, of course, but the next attempt at a colony wasn't until 1607, twenty-two years later. And the Pilgrims didn't reach Plymouth until thirteen years after that. Perhaps to the Martians, crossing the space to Earth is like crossing the Atlantic was to our ancestors. And those first colonies were all private ventures, too. Maybe the invasion in England was like that first Roanoke Colony, just a private venture which failed. It might be a while before they try again. But I'm certain they will try again. And we have to be ready."

"I never really thought about it in those terms before, sir. So… so you're equating us with the Indians?"

"Well, I'd never say so in public," snorted Hawthorne. "But that's about the case. Think about it: the first Europeans to arrive here had muskets and cannons—terrifying and magical weapons to the Indians—metal armor, ships, horses, and all the poor Indians had were stone-tipped arrows and spears. Now think metal fighting machines and heat rays against rifles. Seem similar?"

"A bit…" conceded Andrew, not much liking the comparison. "So do you think we're destined to go the same way as the Indians, sir?"

"Who can say? But we do have one advantage that the Indians also had—but never made use of: our numbers. Each of the European colonies started out as tiny things. If the Indians had recognized the danger and just *cooperated*, they could have massed thousands of warriors against each colony as it arrived and wiped it out. Their inferior weapons wouldn't have mattered all that much."

"At least we do recognize the danger, sir."

"Some of us do, but far too many won't admit that it exists until those cylinders start landing in their gardens. But until we can understand the Martian machines and learn to build our own, we need to do what the Indians didn't: use our numbers to stamp out each colony as it lands. Don't allow them to get established!"

"Yes, sir."

"Of course, that's the job of the General Staff. Our job is to make sure that our men have the best weapons that we can provide."

"The new guns, the things that Mr. Edison and Mr. Tesla are working on, the… uh, tanks."

"Yes, exactly," said Hawthorne. He took a deep breath and gave off an enormous yawn. "But it's been a long day. I'm going to try to get some sleep."

* * * * *

CYCLE 597,842.7, GUERKADAN

Qetjnegartis regarded the massive construction in satisfaction. Through the observation blister, it could see ten huge cylindrical tubes stretching up the side of the ancient volcano, the largest on the planet. One of the ten appeared somewhat sand-worn compared to the other nine. That was the one first built by the now-extinct clan which had made the first failed attempt to colonize the third planet. The other nine were new and represented an outpouring of resources and effort not seen since the cities were moved underground an age ago. As satisfying as the accomplishment might be, Qetjnegartis could see the argument of the naysayers: if this attempt failed, it could dramatically hasten the downfall.

The resources expended were truly enormous. Each tube was 15 quel wide and almost 180 telequel in length, from the underground loading breech, where the transport capsules would be inserted, to the muzzle, which projected almost completely above the planet's thin atmosphere. Almost a hundred secondary breeches angled off the main tube at intervals, each one holding additional propellants to further accelerate the capsule. Each capsule would be flung away at a velocity that would allow it to escape the gravity of the Homeworld. The launch angle would also be in almost exactly the opposite direction in which the Homeworld orbited the sun. Once free of the planet's gravity, each capsule would begin a long slow fall sunward—until it intersected the third planet slightly more than a quarter of a cycle later.

Assuming all went well.

All *should* go well, of course. The calculations had been checked and checked again. Qetjnegartis, itself, had checked them and found them accurate. And the other clan had succeeded in reaching the third planet. Despite their ensuing failure, the launcher and the capsules had worked as anticipated. They worked before, and they would work again.

It was nearly time. The first salvo would be launched shortly. Qetjnegartis' capsule was in the second salvo, which would not be launched until the following day. The reloading process was lengthy and since the launch had to take place when the planet was pointed in the proper direction, only a single salvo could be launched each day. Thus it could linger here to watch the first salvo. A small group of the clan had also gathered there.

At the proper moment, a noticeable tremor passed through the structure that went on and on until a dazzlingly bright flash appeared far up the mountain. Moments later, a concussion thumped against the observation port. Dust boiled up all along the length of the launcher and an enormous plume of gas billowed outward as though the long-extinct volcano had come back to life.

There was a short wait while the final checks of the next gun were made, and also to allow the high-altitude winds to pull the first gas plume away. Then the procedure was repeated and another flare and plume appeared.

Qetjnegartis did not wait to watch the rest; things were clearly going as expected. It needed to get to its own capsule and make sure all was in order before it entered hibernation. It turned and made its way to the elevator.

* * * * *

NOVEMBER 1907, WASHINGTON, D.C.

It was very late by the time they reached Washington. They were lucky to find a cab willing to take them from Union Station to the State, War, & Navy Building; a huge Second Empire-style structure just across the street from the White House. There were a few small sleeping rooms in the basement meant for the use of visiting officers, and Andrew had stayed in them before on previous visits. Still groggy from trying to sleep on the train, he flopped down on the narrow bed and was asleep immediately.

The next morning, he helped Hawthorne collect all their notes for the upcoming meeting with General Crozier, which was only a preparation for a joint meeting with the Navy Ordnance Board in the afternoon. Ultimately, whatever reports were generated would go on up the chain of command to the Chief of Staff and the President. In the six months he'd been working for Colonel Hawthorne, Andrew had slowly become acquainted with the way the bureaucracy worked in the War Department. At the top, of course was the President. Beneath him was the Secretary of War and reporting to him was the Chief of Staff, technically the top military officer. Assisting him was the General Staff, which, among other things, was in charge of planning. And beneath this were all the various bureaus: Artillery, Infantry, Engineers, Quartermaster, and all the rest of the things an army needed to function, including Ordnance.

Up until a few years ago, all of those bureaus were quasi-independent organizations, ruled like medieval fiefs by their various chiefs, and they in turn were ruled by the Adjutant General. They cooperated with each other and with their supposed superior, the Commanding General, if and when it pleased them. All of the bureau chiefs, and the Commanding General, had gained their posts based strictly on seniority, rather than merit. Andrew could remember his father complaining about it at dinner on numerous occasions. Apparently, the system didn't work very well and this became all too obvious during the war with Spain and then in the panic after the first Martian invasion.

21

Reform had been attempted, first by McKinley and later by Roosevelt. Elihu Root, a lawyer, had been made Secretary of War. He had diligently educated himself in military matters and been won over by some reform-minded officers to the merits of the German staff system, which was the envy and model for the rest of the world. Root had slowly and carefully attempted to introduce the system to the American Army. The Commanding General at the time, Nelson Miles, had fought him every step of the way. It wasn't until Miles had been forced into retirement that change was finally accomplished.

But then, before Root's reforms could really take hold, the President decided he needed him more urgently as Secretary of State and William Taft had taken over at the War Department. Taft was also a lawyer, but he had far less interest in military matters and he did not press the Root reforms. Things began to backslide and the bureau chiefs now had nearly as much independence as before. The Adjutant General, Major General Fred Ainsworth, had reasserted his dominion over the bureaus and the Chief of Staff, currently Major General J. Franklin Bell, had little control over what they did.

The only bright spot was that nearly all of the bureau chiefs were more than willing to embrace President Roosevelt's Preparedness agenda as it meant more money coming to their departments. Or at least more money coming to the War Department—which the bureaus chiefs could then fight over.

From what Andrew could tell, the Ordnance Department had made out pretty well in the scramble for funds. Congress and the American People viewed any further expansion of the army with great suspicion, but they were far more willing to accept the development of new weapons. So, in the years since the end of the Spanish War and the Insurrection in the Philippines, the Ordnance Department in the army and the navy's corresponding department had been using their resources to create weapons capable of dealing with another Martian invasion—which would also be perfectly effective against human foes if the Martians did not appear.

Some of these efforts had been directed at improving existing types of weapons, principally artillery, while others had been focused on innovative ways of using the weapons, like the balky 'tank' being developed by Baldwin Locomotives. Working in parallel with this were groups of inventors and scientists around the country trying to unravel the secrets of the Martian machines. Sadly, the Americans were hampered by the fact that the British had been extremely reluctant to part with any of the devices they had captured after the invasion, for fear that other countries might use the knowledge gained against them. The Americans, thanks to the huge outpouring of help they had given the British in the aftermath of the invasion, had been given much greater access to the devices and the discoveries of British scientists than had other countries, but it was a poor substitute for having the devices here in American laboratories. American scientists were obliged to travel to England for any first-hand information. Andrew still felt considerable resentment that his father was killed in one of those expeditions.

Colonel Hawthorne was General Crozier's chief liaison between the Department and all of those scientists and industrialists. That meant a lot of traveling about, visiting laboratories all over the country, and then reporting back to General Crozier. Andrew found it interesting work. He also found it a bit thrilling to be included in some of the high level meetings that took place. Even though he never had to say anything or do much besides have copies of reports handy, he was rubbing elbows with generals and admirals and sometimes high-ranking civilian officials. Yes, definitely more interesting than drilling infantry in North Dakota!

The morning's meeting was routine. Major Waski reported on the successful test-firing of a new high-velocity cannon at the Sandy Hook Proving Grounds and Captain Phillips updated everyone on the program to develop armor-piercing ammunition for the rifles and machine guns. Colonel Hawthorne's report on the steam-propelled armored gun tractor was met with considerable disappointment on the part of General Crozier.

"Do you think they'll ever get it sorted out, Ben?" he asked.

"I'm sure they will, sir. I plan to stop there again next week on our way up to Long Island to talk with Tesla. I hope the Baldwin people will have the thing running by then. They really have made quite a bit of progress."

"For what we're paying them, they should be. Oh, that reminds me, do they have any figures yet on the coal and water consumption of the darn contraption? The Quartermaster Department is wanting to know what they'll be expected to supply if we ever manage to deploy any of these things."

"Not yet, sir. We'll need to make some tests once we have a working prototype."

"Well, keep on them about it."

"Yes, sir."

The morning meeting wrapped up and they had lunch and then walked over to the navy wing of the building, where they met with Rear Admiral Nathan Twining and his staff. Twining was the head of the Navy Ordnance Bureau. For this meeting, Andrew had no real duty at all beyond helping serve the coffee. He shared this with a navy ensign, Drew Harding, whom he had met before.

General Crozier summarized the things they had discussed that morning, glossing over the problems with the tanks. Andrew stifled his yawns and tried to stay awake. He perked up a bit when it was the navy's turn. Admiral Twining let one of his subordinates make the presentation, which had mostly to do with a new type of aiming system being pioneered by the British which would allow the guns on a moving ship to hit a moving target at unprecedented ranges. Twining, himself, commented at this point that if the system was a success, it would need to be installed in the coastal defense forts. He also hinted that perhaps those forts ought to be under navy control as was the case in most European countries. This produced a rumble among the army officers. Colonel Hawthorne had told Andrew that this argument had been going on pretty much forever, but the army clung to its coast artillery with a very tight fist.

They also mentioned a new 14-inch gun being considered for future classes of battleship and an improved design for the 5-inch guns. Then there was a bit of stir among the navy types and a large portfolio filled with drawings was produced. Most of the drawings were for proposed classes of monitors and river gunboats which could operate in very shallow water, allowing the navy to project force far up the country's waterways.

"We can't assume that the Martians will be so obliging as to confine their invasion to areas near the coast," said Twining. "These ships would allow us to operate on the Mississippi, the Missouri, the Ohio, and a number of other smaller rivers."

General Crozier's response was politely non-committal, but Andrew suspected that he didn't particularly like the idea of the navy expanding its role into what ought to be army territory. But if the gunboats disturbed the Ordnance Chief, what came next was even worse. A new set of plans was laid out on the table and Andrew craned his neck to try and see what they were. At first glance they looked like another gunboat or maybe a small cruiser, but wait, what were those things on the bottom? They sort of looked like...

"What is this, Admiral?" asked Crozier.

"We're calling it a land ironclad, General," replied Twining proudly. "As you can see, it is much like a standard warship, but it also has two sets of huge caterpillar tracks, which will allow it to travel over land, as well. An amphibious creature, as it were."

"You can't be serious!" exclaimed Crozier.

"Entirely serious, I assure you. Vessels such as these could travel easily by water to the point nearest the enemy and then move overland the rest of the way. Naturally, we would operate in cooperation with any army forces in the vicinity, although we are looking into the possibility of strengthening our Marine landing parties to provide whatever escort is needed."

"But... but the cost..."

"Only slightly more than a conventional warship of comparable size. The naval secretary has already broached the idea to the President and he was quite enthusiastic."

"Oh, God, he would be," moaned Crozier before he could stop himself.

"Admiral," said Colonel Hawthorne, "you do realize what a challenge those caterpillar tracks are going to be, don't you? They are on a scale far beyond anything ever attempted. The strain on them would be stupendous. Considering the problems we've encountered with our much more modest gun tractors, you might find these insurmountable."

Twining smiled. "The navy is quite used to large scale engineering, Colonel. There's probably more steel in one of our battleships than in all the army's artillery combined. We are quite confident we can make this work."

There were some more half-hearted objections from the army officers in the room, but navy smugness snuffed them out.

"Battleships with wheels, eh?" whispered Hawthorne to Andrew. "I *should* have made you tell that idea to Crozier!"

"And *I* should have gone to Annapolis, sir," replied Andrew.

"A wiseacre, just like I said."

It was the navy's turn to host the dinner that night, although Andrew doubted that many of the army men had much of an appetite. But they dutifully allowed themselves to be transported down to the officers' club at the Navy Yard. Andrew found himself in a carriage with General Crozier, Colonel Hawthorne, and Major Waski. Crozier was fuming.

"Blast the man! How dare he spring something like that on us with no warning! And to take it to the President in secret! Damnation! Did you hear what he was saying about the Marines? If they're allowed to build a fleet of those things, the army is going to be out of business, gentlemen!"

"I don't think it's that serious, sir," said Hawthorne. "The navy is going to find it a lot harder to build those things than they believe."

"Well, what if they accomplish it anyway? You know how Roosevelt loves big, grand ideas! He'll look at the navy's monstrosities and then look at our gun tractors and you can just bet which one he'll like best!"

"You could be right, sir." said Major Waski. "So what do we do?"

"What do we do? We damn well have some big, grand ideas of our own! Even if it's just our version of the same land ironclad as the navy! So I want all of you to get to work on this. Ben, contact Baldwin and see what they can do. Waski, you make some quiet inquiries with the New York ship builders up your way and find out just what's involved with constructing something like this."

"Yes, sir," they both answered, but then Hawthorne asked: "We aren't giving up on the gun tractors though, are we, sir? Despite the problems we've had, they'll be ready years before any of these behemoths."

"No, no, we'll go ahead on all fronts."

They completed the trip in silence and then had to act pleasant with their navy hosts. But it was a fine dinner and the wine flowed freely. Andrew, having none of the weighty concerns of his superiors, was enjoying himself, sharing drinks with Drew Harding and drawing sketches of land-going battleships on a napkin when an officer burst into the room.

"Sir! Sir!" the man exclaimed breathlessly. "They're coming! The Martians are coming again!"

Fortunately, they were in a private room rather than the main bar or who knows what sort of panic the man's cry might have produced. Everyone was shocked, of course, but Admiral Twining took it very calmly. "What the devil are you talking about, man?" he growled. "Pull yourself together and report to me properly!"

The young man, an ensign as young as Andrew, did as he was told. "Yes sir! Sorry sir! There's a report from the Naval Observatory, sir! Gas eruptions on Mars!"

The silence in the room was like a living thing, clutching at the throat of each man. After over seven years of waiting, the hope had begun to grow in everyone that the Martians would not be back; that they'd given up. That the first invasion had been all they had the resources for. They had shot their bolt and that was the end of it. All those hopes dashed in an instant. Andrew felt a shiver go down his spine.

"Indeed?" rumbled Twining as if the ensign had just informed him that it was raining. "Well, let's go and see for ourselves. Gentlemen?"

And so they bundled themselves into several motor staff cars and chugged up Massachusetts Avenue to where the navy had its observatory northwest of the city. This facility, like many observatories around the world, had been greatly expanded since the first invasion. The older telescope had been replaced with a new marvel with a diameter no less than fifty inches. There were bigger ones elsewhere in the world, but this was the biggest in the vicinity of Washington. As the last invasion had been launched during the time in which the two planets were relatively close in their orbits, the opposition as it was called, a special watch was kept on Mars at that time. Andrew vaguely recalled that the actual time of closest approach had been several months earlier.

The weather was typical for November and it was a crystal clear night. As they walked up the hill toward the observatory, Andrew noted that all the lights were on in all the buildings and people were dashing about and talking loudly. The admiral was the ranking officer present, so they managed to get a reasonably precise report from the head of the facility, a navy captain who also held a doctorate in astronomy.

"We observed the first eruption about an hour ago, sir…" he began.

"The first?" interrupted Twining. "You mean there have been more?"

"Yes sir, four more after the first…" A cry from a man who was at the eye-piece of the great telescope interrupted the captain again. "Uh, make that five more, sir. Mars will be setting soon and we'll lose our view, but we've cabled other observatories further west to continue the watch."

"Six eruptions in only an hour?" exclaimed the admiral incredulously. "My God! The first time there was a full day between them!"

"Yes, sir. I'm afraid so, sir."

A long silence enveloped the other group that was eventually broken by Colonel Hawthorne:

"It would appear that the Martians have not been idle, either, sir."

CHAPTER TWO

JANUARY 1908, WASHINGTON, DC

"Well, Theodore, I have to admit that I wish I hadn't convinced you to delay the announcement as Cortelyou asked me to," said Leonard Wood. "If we'd done this in October, like you wanted, you'd look like a genuine soothsayer now."

"Now, now, Leonard," said the President, grinning ear to ear, "if people start to believe I can predict the future, they'll expect me to do it every time! But if the prospects weren't so dire, I'd almost want to thank the Martians for the timing. At least this came soon enough for me to cancel the battle fleet's cruise around the world; would have been damned embarrassing to have them halfway to Japan."

Wood nodded. "Your reelection is almost guaranteed now. If all you were facing was the robber barons and the problems with the Canal, some people might balk at giving you a third term. But with war on the horizon, there's no one the people would rather see in the White House than you."

"Assuming the Martians show up on time. We're going to look damn silly if they don't, after all the fuss we're making."

"And when are they expected?"

Roosevelt scratched at his mustache. "That's the big question and unfortunately, I'm getting a lot of different answers. The so-called experts can't seem to make up their minds. The last time, the gas eruptions preceded the arrival of the cylinders by four months. But things seem to be different this time."

"The newspapers are predicting everything from next year to about five minutes from right now. But you are saying it won't be four months like last time?"

"*I'm* not saying anything. But the experts have been telling me all sorts of things." He rummaged in a drawer and pulled out a sheaf of papers which he spread out on the polished desktop. Some sheets were covered with mathematical equations and others had drawings and diagrams. He found one particular sheet and picked it up. "With the first invasion, the gas eruptions were spotted about two months prior to the closest approach at opposition with Mars and the cylinders began falling two months after the opposition. Apparently the Martians were firing ahead of us, leading us like a man shooting at a grouse with a shotgun, so that the cylinders would intersect the Earth as we caught up and passed them in our faster orbit."

"That makes sense," said Wood. "But they are saying they didn't do that this time?"

"No, this time, the eruptions were seen almost four months *after* the opposition, after we'd already gone by."

"Well, that seems odd—not that I can claim to know anything about such things. What do they think that means?"

"There's no consensus there. Some seem to think that the Martians aren't coming here at all. That they're headed for Venus or even Mercury. Maybe they've decided that Earth is a bad deal and they are trying somewhere else."

"They are sending, what? Two hundred cylinders this time?"

Roosevelt nodded. "That's the best guess. We couldn't keep them under continuous observation, but it appears they launched ten times each day for twenty days."

"Then I'd consider it a relief if they weren't coming here—even though it would be politically embarrassing for us."

"I'll swallow all the embarrassment in the world if it would spare our country the horrors of an invasion," said Roosevelt firmly.

"Certainly, certainly. But you were saying, not all agree they aren't coming here?"

"No, the majority still think they are on their way to Earth." He picked up another paper. It was larger than a normal sheet of paper and had elaborate calligraphy on it and it didn't appear to be written in English.

"Is that… Russian?" asked Wood.

"Yes, their ambassador delivered it on Tuesday—fortunately he also brought a translation. Direct from the Tsar. It seems he feels he still owes us for helping settle his war with Japan. He sent a report from one of their scientists, a man named… Tsiolkovsky, apparently a renowned expert in this sort of thing. He has calculated that if the cylinders were launched with a lesser force than last time, they would fall in toward the sun slowly and still intersect with Earth in about nine months—this coming September. In other words, the Martians are still leading us, except they are waiting for us to come around the sun again. I showed all this to the captain up at the observatory and he agrees that it might be so."

"But why would they do that? Why deliberately make it a longer trip?" demanded Wood.

"A fine question. They are only of two minds on that question, which is better than on most of the other questions. The first possibility is that if they are using the same sort of launching gun, then a slower velocity would allow them to fire a bigger cylinder with a bigger crew and more cargo."

"Good God, and there are two hundred of them on their way."

"Yes, and the other possibility isn't much more comforting. This Tsiolkovsky fellow points out that with the oppositions about twenty-six months apart, if the Martians launched their cylinders like they did the first time, that is, two months prior to the opposition, then it would, naturally, be twenty-six months between salvos, as it were. But by doing it this way, that is, delaying the arrival of the first salvo, and then launching the next one as they first did, then it will only be about fifteen months between arrivals. Maybe the Martians don't want to wait so long for reinforcements."

"This is all… very disturbing, Theodore. But perhaps these new invaders will just die off like the last batch."

"A lot of people are hoping that, but I wouldn't count on that, Leonard. They clearly aren't stupid creatures. If they have some sort of long-range wireless transmitters, then the first batch may have warned their fellows back on Mars just what was killing them. We poor, stupid Earthlings have managed to figure out how to inoculate ourselves against certain diseases; we must assume the Martians can do the same."

"Yes, I suppose…"

"And even if they *do* die off like last time, we saw how much damage only ten cylinders were able to do in the short time they had. We can't just stand by and let them devastate our cities while we wait. We must be prepared to fight them!"

"Of course, of course; the preparations must go on."

"So!" Roosevelt slapped his large hands on the desk, scattering some of the papers. "Whenever they arrive we have to be ready for the rascals! And that's what I wanted to talk to you about."

"Oh?"

"Yes! I'm going to replace Taft as Secretary of War. He's a capable administrator in peacetime, but I need someone with fire in his belly to run a real war. He has quite the belly, but no fire that I can see. Hate to say that; we've been friends for a long time, but there it is." Roosevelt frowned. "And I don't know that I can work with him anymore. He's not happy with me running again. He really had his heart set on being the next president. Or perhaps I should say that his *wife* had set his heart on being the next president."

"Yes, she's quite a determined lady. Well, the good of the country comes before his—or her—personal ambition."

"Well, he's always wanted a spot on the Supreme Court, so I may be able to soften the blow."

"Yes, that would do it. Who did you have in mind to replace him?"

"My first choice would be Root. He's done it before and I trust him completely. But he's already begged off. Claims he's more valuable where he is as Secretary of State, and that he doesn't have the energy to be War Secretary."

"It's hard to argue with that. Someone younger might be a better choice."

"Who? Do you have any ideas? Unless you want the job."

"No thank you!" Wood thought for a moment. "How about Henry Stimson? He's a protégé of Root, as I recall."

"Yes… yes! He might do! I'll have a talk with him."

"But Theodore," said Wood, "no matter who you decide on, the task is enormous. Do you think we can be ready?"

"We must be! I've got all our best people working on it night and day."

* * * * *

MARCH, 1908, SHOREHAM, LONG ISLAND, NY

The wind blowing off Long Island Sound cut right through Andrew Comstock despite several layers of heavy wool. *Why do they always do these things in the coldest weather?* He'd never liked the cold and some of his fondest memories of his childhood were from when his father was stationed at Fort Sam Houston in Texas. But this bleak stretch of coastline was a long way from sunny Texas.

In front of him stood a tall metal tower which for some reason was called Wardenclyffe. It rose from a low brick building and looked to be nearly a hundred feet high and was made entirely of iron struts and girders. The lower portion looked rather like an oil-drilling derrick, but the upper part was an open dome, bristling with metal tubes and rods. It looked, he suddenly realized, like one of the Martian fighting machines—except with far too many legs. Another, much thinner tower, was about fifty yards away.

Andrew was there with Colonel Hawthorne and another man, Nikola Tesla. The famous—and notoriously eccentric—scientist, engineer, and inventor did not appear to be bothered by the cold at all. He was tall, very thin, and his deep-set eyes fairly blazed with enthusiasm as he described the tower in front of them. The man had come to America from Hungary or Serbia or some such place and still spoke with a noticeable accent.

"This was originally built to transmit wireless messages across the Atlantic," he explained. "But as I worked, I became convinced that in addition to messages, it would be possible to transmit electrical power over long distances without the use of wires. Naturally, my original intentions were that these transmissions would be for peaceful purposes, to provide electricity to all." He waved an arm around in a broad arc, nearly slapping Andrew, who took a step sideways. "But then in the aftermath of the first Martian invasion, I came to realize that my device could also have military potential."

"Yes, Mr. Tesla, we are aware of that," said Colonel Hawthorne patiently. "You also convinced influential people in the government of that potential. You have been contracted to turn that potential into reality and we are here today to observe what progress you have made."

"Of course! Of course!" said Tesla. "I only wanted to be sure you understood the genesis of my creation."

"I think we do, sir. But it is rather cold out here today. Can we get on with the demonstration?"

"Certainly, certainly! I will start the generators. Excuse me, please." Tesla walked off toward the building with long strides.

"What's going to happen, sir?" asked Andrew.

"I guess we'll find out shortly."

"They say Mr. Tesla is a genius."

"Perhaps. Others say he'd make the world's greatest snake-oil salesman. Genius or not, he has a flair for salesmanship. He failed to mention that John Jacob Astor and J. P. Morgan sunk close to a quarter million dollars into this thing when he was still trying to build a transoceanic wireless transmitter. When Marconi beat him to the punch, he was left with this tower and a lot of empty promises."

Tesla reappeared from the building and hastened to rejoin them. He wasn't even wearing a hat and Andrew shivered at the thought of going bareheaded in this weather. "All right," he declared, "the generators are building up the charge. Direct your attention to the space between the Wardenclyffe tower and the smaller one over there." They did as instructed, but nothing was happening that Andrew could see. A minute or more went by.

"What are we supposed to be seeing?" asked Hawthorne.

"Patience, Colonel, patience. Just a few more seconds."

Andrew was thinking about several snake-oil salesmen he'd seen during his life when he realized that *something* was happening. He felt a tingling and prickling all over his skin and scalp. Tesla's thick, dark hair was actually standing straight up! A strange humming, like some gigantic bumblebee, was filling the air.

"Watch!"

Sparks began jumping between the rods and tubes on top of the big tower and a blue nimbus shimmered around them. Suddenly, a dazzlingly bright light, like a lightning bolt, jumped from the large tower to the smaller one. An ear-splitting thunderclap rent the air. The light twisted and writhed like a dying snake and then a new bolt branched off to strike a nearby tree and then a smaller one leaped to a workman's wheelbarrow a dozen yards further on. Both the tree and the barrow burst into flames.

As quick as it came, the lighting vanished, although a bright afterimage was left in Andrew's eyes. The thunder rolled and reverberated across Long Island Sound before slowly fading away.

"Wow!" he cried, rubbing at his eyes. Both the tree and the wheelbarrow were still burning, and the smaller tower had partially melted and was leaning drunkenly to one side. Tesla was grinning like a maniac and fairly bouncing up and down on his feet.

"See? Did you see?"

"Yes, we did," said Hawthorne. "That was... that was most impressive, Mr. Tesla. What sort of range do you estimate this device to have?"

Tesla's enthusiasm abated somewhat. "Well, right now it is about... about what you see here."

"Two hundred feet? The Martian heat rays are effective for a mile or more, Mr. Tesla. You are going to have to do better than that!"

"Yes, yes, I know that, of course! There is still much work to do, but for an entirely new type of weapon, that is to be expected. The range will improve!"

"I hope so. And the power source? Am I to understand that the generators required fill that large building there?"

"Not entirely, no. But yes, they are bulky. That needs to be worked upon, too!" Telsa's enthusiasm was giving way to irritation, it seemed to Andrew. "More compact power sources will be needed. Such as the Martians themselves use. I have requested repeatedly that I be allowed to examine some of the samples the British possess." Andrew stiffened at the mention of those murderous devices.

"Yes, I know," said Hawthorne. "You and about a thousand other people. The British have refused. They claim they are too dangerous." Hawthorne glanced at Andrew.

"Ah!" spat Tesla. "To them, maybe! What do the British know about physics? Give one to me and I will learn its secrets!"

"We may have all the samples you could want before too much longer."

"Uh, how do you *aim* your weapon, sir?" asked Andrew.

Tesla stared at him like he'd never seen him before. "Well, uh, you see, the bolt travels from the greater potential to the lesser, naturally, and the target tower, being the nearest tall object with a clear grounding path, becomes the most attractive target..."

"Sir, are you saying that if there had been a second tower, an equal distance away, that the bolt might have jumped there just as easily as to the first?"

"Uh, well, that would be a possibility..."

"So when the bolt jumped from the tower to the tree and then to the wheelbarrow, you didn't intend for that to happen?"

"Not precisely, no..."

"So you are *saying*," said Hawthorne, jumping in, "you can't aim the blasted thing at all?"

"Such refinements will come as I further develop the device, Colonel! We are in uncharted waters!" Tesla was becoming angry and Hawthorne managed to calm him down before they left. They walked back to the local station and caught the train to New York City.

They rode in silence for quite a while before Hawthorne said: "Good job catching the aiming problem, Andy. I must admit I hadn't even thought about that. I just assumed the bolt went where Tesla wanted it."

"I did, too, at first, sir. The thought just stuck me."

"Well, it was a good thought." Hawthorne laughed. "And here I was worried about the range! If he can't aim the damn thing, it's just as well that it *will* only go two hundred feet! Imagine the havoc it could do with a longer range!" He looked out the train window and pointed. They were just

31

passing the Oyster Bay station. "He might have set fire to the President's home on Sagamore Hill!"

"Wouldn't that have taken the cake, sir? But what are you going to recommend about Mr. Tesla's machine? It might still have some value."

"Yes, it might, I suppose."

"When they first invented gunpowder, they must have had all sorts of problems making it an effective weapon."

"True. Well, I'll tell the general what we saw today. He can decide if we keep funding it."

"Mr. Tesla's device might not be practical out in the field, but maybe it could be installed as part of some permanent defenses, sir. That way it could draw its power from some big generator."

"Yes, that's a possibility." Hawthorne looked at him. "So how do you like being a first lieutenant, Andy?"

"Sir? It's great, sir, thanks for putting it through." It was rather nice. He was quite proud of those silver bars on his uniform. The extra pay was very nice, too. Hawthorne was sporting new insignia of his own: the eagles of a full colonel.

With the threat of a new invasion, the President's Preparedness Movement had roared back to life. Congress had authorized an expansion of the Regular Army and the mobilization of the National Guard along with the funds to train and equip them. This had led to a wave of promotions throughout the army to provide the officers needed for the new formations, but that was not enough and many more officers would be needed. A large training camp had been constructed in Plattsburg, New York to train new officers. It had been set up by private individuals, but the army had agreed to make use of what it turned out. Two of President Roosevelt's own sons were currently there.

As they neared New York City, their car clattered past one of the new camps. A sea of canvas tents filled a muddy field. Troops were out drilling in the cold and Andrew didn't envy them. Dozens of such camps had sprung up all over the country. Men were flocking to the recruiting stations, factories were gearing up to produce the new weapons which would be needed, and everyone had been gripped with a patriotic fervor. There were rallies and parades and recruiting drives. John Phillip Sousa had composed a new march titled: 'Solid Humans to the Front', and a popular tune called 'The Martian Three-Step' was sweeping the dance halls.

And just as during the war with Spain in '98, the government had authorized the raising of separate volunteer regiments. The President, of course, was famous for his exploits with the 1st United States Volunteer Cavalry, the 'Rough Riders', and had been all in favor of the idea. The army was less enthusiastic since many of these organizations, while high on enthusiasm, were of questionable military utility. Many were brain-children of politicians and businessmen who were more interested in the publicity than in actually commanding a unit in the field. The results had ranged from good to ridiculous.

On a more serious note, the General Staff was refining its plans, and troops were being moved to assembly points. Earthwork fortifications were being built around cities big and small. Most of these were the initiatives of the local authorities and their military value was questionable. Much more formidable concrete structures were also being built and fitted with artillery. The army had always maintained a powerful series of forts and batteries protecting the coasts from seaborne invaders, but now forts were planned to protect the landward approaches as well. Nothing like this had been seen since the Civil War.

Baldwin Locomotive Works had finally gotten their tanks running and several prototypes were at Sandy Hook being fitted with 3-inch guns for firing tests. Assuming all went well, they would go into full production. It was hoped that several battalions would be ready before the September date when the Martians were expected. Baldwin was also working on the first designs for a land ironclad for the army. The navy was moving ahead with theirs as well. As a stop-gap until the tanks were ready, a new program to develop some armored cars using commercial automobile chassis was in the works.

There were problems, of course. The states were wrangling over the exact provisions of the Dick Act, as the Militia Act of 1903 was usually called. The army wanted full control over the National Guard units and the governors didn't want to give it to them. Congress was debating how to pay for everything and stalling several important appropriation bills. And the army was quite capable of creating its own troubles, too. There was a savage fight going on between the Chief of Staff and the Adjutant General over jurisdiction. Even the new tanks were causing problems. Both the Cavalry and Artillery branches were laying claim to them and Andrew had no clue who would win that battle; he could see both points of view.

Not much of that affected him personally. He was busy doing interesting and important work; what more could a person want? Granted that it was tiring; he probably didn't spend more than one night a week in his tiny room in the Bachelor Officers' Quarters at Fort Myer. But the colonel made it a point to get home to his family on Sundays whenever possible and he often had Andrew there for dinner. That was very pleasant because not only was the food good, but the colonel's daughter, Victoria, a sweet girl of sixteen, had been making eyes at him for months now. The colonel's wife seemed to be encouraging this, but he wasn't sure exactly how Hawthorne felt about it. Well, nothing much could happen on *that* front until the Martians were dealt with.

"Andy," said the colonel, jolting him out of his ruminations.

"Sir?"

"I'm going to send you off to Dayton by yourself next week. Crozier wants several reports finished and there's no way I can do both. Do you think you can handle it?"

"Uh, yes, sir," replied Andrew. "The meeting with the Wright brothers?"

"What else is in Dayton? Yes, of course. Take a look at their latest flying machine and report back."

"Yes sir, I can do that."

"It should be an easy mission, Captain."

Andrew blinked. "Sir?"

"Brevet promotion, effective on Monday. Crozier approved it." Hawthorne was grinning.

"Thank… Thank you, sir!" He glanced at his lieutenant's bars. "Do I…?"

"You wear the rank. They haven't decided about the pay yet."

"That's wonderful, sir."

"Well, don't throw away your old bars. Brevet rank can disappear as fast as it comes. If this crisis blows over, you'll be a lieutenant again before you can blink."

They changed trains in New York and Andrew was so bemused over his new rank, he nearly fell off the platform. *Captain!* And him not even a year out of the Academy! Of course it wasn't unprecedented, not in the least. In war time all sorts of strange things could happen. During the Civil War, there had been men his age who were colonels commanding regiments. George Custer had been jumped from captain to brigadier general in one day. Hawthorne was right, of course, the rank wouldn't last much longer than the war. Of course, who knew how long the war would last?

The following week found him on a series of trains taking him to Dayton, Ohio, home of the famous Wright brothers. There were a lot of other men in uniform on the trains now, quite a difference from the journeys he used to make with Colonel Hawthorne. It felt very strange being on his own, but the captain's bars on his uniform gave him more confidence than he expected. He'd started growing a mustache to try and look older, but so far it just looked like he'd forgotten to shave.

Several times his train was forced onto a siding to make way for other trains moving troops or munitions. The call up of the National Guard was requiring a great deal of shuffling about. The widely scattered Guard companies were being shipped from their local armories and drill halls to regimental assembly areas, and the equipment they would need had to be sent there, too. Materials to build those assembly areas and the new fortifications were also on the move, and except for those close to rivers, it all had to go by rail.

He spent the night in a Dayton hotel and felt very important when he showed the desk clerk the document that allowed him to charge the room to the War Department. The next morning he rented a cab to take him to the Wrights' demonstration area, which was an open field called Huffman Prairie, about a dozen miles north of the town. There was a small crowd gathered there and, to Andrew's surprise, another army officer; a lieutenant from the Signal Corps' newly formed Aeronautical Division, named Frank Lahm.

"Good morning... Captain," said Lahm. The man looked to be at least ten years older than Andrew and suddenly those captain's bars on his uniform felt more an embarrassment than a confidence builder. "I didn't know the Ordnance Department had taken an interest in aeroplanes."

"Uh, I'm just here to observe the flights, s-... Lieutenant. Like, you, I guess?"

"Oh, more than just observe. Orville will be taking me up with him today!" the man grinned.

"Really?" asked Andrew in surprise. "They can carry passengers now?"

"Yes, their new model has two seats. There it is." He pointed to a low shed at the near end of the field. A small group of men were wheeling out the flying machine. Lahm started walking in that direction and Andrew followed along. "I met the Wrights last year in France during the demonstration tour they made. Remarkable fellows, both of them. If today's flights go well, the Signal Corps plans to buy a few of the machines."

Lahm was good enough to introduce Andrew to the Wrights, but the men, both around forty years old, seemed distracted by their machine and little interested in someone half their ages—even if he was a captain. Andrew wasn't offended; he imagined he'd be getting a lot of that. He walked around the machine while Lahm pointed out its features enthusiastically. Andrew felt much less enthusiasm. It was the flimsiest looking collection of wood, wires, and canvas he'd ever seen. It scarcely seemed capable of supporting its own weight, much less lifting people into the air! The only solid part of it was the gasoline-powered motor which turned the air screws.

"Hard to believe this can really fly," he said quietly.

"Yes," agreed Lahm. "Do you know that until they went over there and showed them, the Europeans thought the Wrights were frauds? Four years after they first flew at Kitty Hawk, the Frenchies still didn't believe it! Their faces were as red as the trousers of their soldiers when the Wrights showed them! At least the French do know how to apologize properly."

It took nearly an hour of tinkering before the Wrights were satisfied that their machine was ready. Orville Wright and Lieutenant Lahm climbed aboard and several men yanked on the air screws, causing the engine to roar to life. And then, to Andrew's amazement, the machine lurched forward on its launching rail and jumped into the air! He stood with his mouth hanging open as the craft rose to a height of about a hundred feet and then flew in graceful circles and figure-eights around the field. Then it straightened out and headed off to the north, until it was lost to sight behind some trees. The noise of the motor faded and died.

The watching crowd had grown and they started chatting noisily. Andrew reclaimed his wits and managed to gain the attention of the remaining Wright. If the one flying was Orville, this one must be Wilbur. "Sir, how long can your craft stay up and how far can it go?"

"The best we've done so far is a little over an hour and close to thirty miles," replied the inventor. "But we are improving that all the time."

"And how much weight can it carry?"

"Well, you see that it can carry the weight of the operator and a passenger."

"Could it carry any more than that, do you think?"

"Perhaps another thirty or forty pounds. But we are improving on that, too."

"I see. Thank you, sir." Wright moved away to talk to someone else and Andrew made a few short notes on paper.

After what seemed quite a while, the noise of the aeroplane was heard again and then people began to shout and point at it coming back from the northwest. It circled the field several times, and as it flew overhead, he saw Lieutenant Lahm throw something down: a small object trailing a ribbon of some sort. One of the Wrights' assistants dashed over and picked it up. He looked it over and brought it to Wilbur Wright. The man chuckled and handed it to Andrew. "It's for you," he said.

Sure enough, it was a tiny bundle of paper with his name scrawled on it. He opened it up, detaching the ribbon and a small rock that had been added for weight. Inside was a short message:

> *March 28, 1908*
> *10:35 AM*
> *No Martians Sighted!*
> *Lt. Lahm*

"What is it?" asked Wilbur.

Andrew handed it back to him. "The first official scouting report by an American officer from an aeroplane."

They all had a good laugh over that, but quickly became serious as the machine descended to land. It got lower and lower and then touched down on its ski-like skids. It lurched to a rather abrupt halt, but machine and passengers appeared unhurt. Lahm came bounding over, his face flushed with wind and excitement.

"So, what do you think?" he cried, reclaiming his message.

"Amazing," said Andrew honestly. "I could see it being very valuable for scouting."

"Yes! The view from up there is incredible!"

"But not much use as a weapon, I'm thinking. It can't carry very much, and the merest touch of a heat ray would send the thing up like a torch."

Lahm's excitement wasn't diminished in the slightest. "This is still all brand new! Give them time!"

"We haven't got much time."

On the long trip back to Washington, Andrew had plenty of time to think. He was seeing some amazing things, steam powered gun-tractors, Tesla's lighting device, the Wrights' flying machine, but they were all devices in their infancy. The Martians were going to arrive in less than six months.

Would any of these things be ready by then? He doubted it. The war would have to be fought and won by the men and guns they had right now.

The weeks and months that followed found him being sent off again and again to observe and report. He grew into his new rank and grew out his mustache; he scarcely thought about either anymore, although he was pleased when he started getting a captain's pay. He didn't see much of Victoria, but they began to write each other letters.

The most exciting thing to happen that summer came in late June when a report from Russia indicated that a huge fireball had been sighted falling from the sky. This was followed by a stupendous explosion which was recorded on seismographs and barometers thousands of miles away. The obvious conclusion was that this was first of the expected Martian cylinders, even though it was several months ahead of the expected date. Newspaper headlines around the world shouted that the Martians were here, and many militaries began to mobilize. But after a few weeks it was determined that the explosion had taken place in an extremely remote part of Siberia and no additional fireballs had been observed anywhere else. The Russians dispatched a military expedition to investigate, but many experts began to suggest that perhaps this was some natural phenomenon, rather than the Martians. There were more than a few red faces, and after a few more weeks, the excitement died down and the troops went back to their barracks.

In July, a major conference was held in Washington with all the high commanders and bureau chiefs, along with the Secretary of War and the President, to review the plans and preparations which had been made to repel the Martians—now only a few months away. Normally, Andrew wouldn't have been included in such a high-level meeting, but Colonel Hawthorne was quite ill and General Crozier had grabbed Andrew to take his place. Washington was usually almost deserted this time of year due to the summer heat, but with the threat of war looming, the place was nearly as busy as ever.

The meeting was held in a large room in the State, War, & Navy Building. The walls were hung with dozens of maps and a world globe sat in one corner. Stewards bustled about providing coffee, and junior officers, like Andrew, clustered in the corners and along the walls, carrying any documents their chiefs might want. Andrew's friend, Drew Harding, now a lieutenant, junior grade, was there with the navy contingent.

A few minutes after nine, the President bustled in, with the War and Navy Secretaries, and General Wood in tow. Andrew had seen the President at a distance on several other occasions and he'd always been dressed in appropriate fashion, but today Roosevelt was wearing an outfit that harked back to his days with the famous Rough Riders: a blue jacket, buff trousers tucked into tall boots, and a broad-brimmed hat. A holstered pistol hung from his belt. Everyone not already standing got to their feet.

"Morning gentlemen! Morning!" boomed the President. "Please! Be seated, be seated!" He proceeded to shout greetings to nearly everyone above the rank of major, and Andrew was impressed that he could remember so many names—but the President's amazing memory was legendary. The long, long table had the President at the head, naturally, flanked by his two secretaries. On the right was the Chief of Staff, Major General J. Franklin Bell, and then the General Staff officers trailing away in order of rank. On the left was Major General Fred C. Ainsworth, the Adjutant General, and then the various bureau chiefs, including General Crozier, Andy's boss today. The navy people, under Admiral Robley Evans, seemed content to huddle near the far end of the table—out of the line of any possible fire between the feuding Bell and Ainsworth.

"Let's get started, shall we? So, are we ready, General?" he asked, looking to Bell. "Not much time left and we must be ready!"

General Bell got to his feet and gave Ainsworth a little smile, clearly pleased that the President had addressed him first. "Yes, Mr. President, our preparations are well along and will be complete by the end of August." He then proceeded to point to various maps and charts and tables of organization showing how the Regular Army and the National Guard had been integrated into brigades and divisions and how they had been assembled to protect all the major cities in the east and midwest. "Our strategy is based upon the idea of rapid response, sir. During the first invasion, the British, being unaware of what they were dealing with or the danger it posed, reacted very slowly to the arrival of the Martian cylinders. This gave the Martians the time they needed to assemble their war machines. By the time the British did bring up their army, it was too late. We, however, will take full advantage of the Martians' period of vulnerability after they land. The moment a cylinder is spotted, we will rush forces to the location and immediately attack."

"Bully!" cried the President. "Catch the rascals with their pants down!"

"Yes, sir, that's the idea."

"And how will you know where to rush your forces, General?" asked Henry Stimson, the new Secretary of War. "These creatures could land anywhere, could they not?"

"Yes, Mr. Secretary," replied Bell, "and that was a major challenge we had to deal with. But under the direction of the General Staff, the Signal Corps has set up a system of observation posts across large sections of the country—thousands of them. Some of these are manned by military personnel, and many more are staffed by civilian volunteers. They are maintaining a watch on the skies around the clock, sir. Each station has either direct telegraphic connections or quick access to a telegraph. The commercial telegraph companies are all cooperating with this effort. At the first sign of a landing, a warning will be sent to one of the six regional communications centers we have established. Once the sighting has been confirmed, it will be sent on to our headquarters here. We will then determine the forces closest to the site and dispatch them. We have tested this system and from the sighting to the dispatch of the force is less than one hour."

"And how will the force get to the landing site?"

"That will depend on where the landing site is in relation to the force or forces we dispatch, Mr. Secretary. If the distance is short, then the force will march on the site directly, sending its mounted and motorized elements ahead. If the distances are longer, we will make use of rail transport. All of our assembly areas are on rail lines and trains will be standing by at all of them."

"I see," nodded Stimson.

"Once our forces reach the site, we will attempt to rush the Martians before they can debouch from their cylinders. We have men trained to use explosives and will blow our way into the cylinders if necessary. If our first rush is repulsed, we will bring up our artillery and place the site under a constant bombardment until we assemble the forces needed for another assault."

"That's excellent work, General!" exclaimed Roosevelt. "My compliments to you and your staff, and the Signal Corps, too!"

"Thank you, Mr. President."

"Excuse me, Mr. President," said General Ainsworth. "While I agree that General Greely of the Signal Corps has done an excellent job in this situation, I'm gravely concerned by the manner in which this was brought about."

"What do you mean, General?"

"It is vital in any organization—especially any military organization—that the established chain of command be respected and followed. In this case, and in a number of other cases in recent months, the Chief of Staff and his subordinates have ignored the chain of command and issued orders directly to the bureau chiefs. Sir, this must stop or the results will be chaos!"

There was a stir around the table and Harding nudged Andrew. "Oh boy, Ainsworth has stepped in it for sure!" he whispered. "TR won't put up with hogwash like that!"

From the expression on Roosevelt's face, Andrew suspected that Harding was right. "Really, General?" he said. "I refreshed my memory on the details of the General Staff Act just this morning and it appears to me that the Chief of Staff has full authority to deal directly with anyone he wants to in the army."

"Sir, that is *not* how the Act has usually been interpreted! The bureau chiefs have *always* reported to the Adjutant General! If the Chief of Staff has requests, they should be directed through my office."

"Seems like an unnecessary extra step, General. The General Staff, which is responsible for making plans, decided they needed this warning system. They need the Signal Corps' help to set it up. So they go to the Signal Corps and get what they need. The Adjutant General's Office is, as I recall, concerned with personnel, promotions, pension records, things like that, not signals. The last thing we need right now is more red tape, General!"

"But Mr. President…"

Roosevelt waved away Ainsworth's protests. "But speaking of the Bureaus, why don't we go around the table and listen to their reports? Since we're already talking about the Signal Corps, we'll start with you, General Greely."

With only the slightest glance at Ainsworth, Greely made his report. From there it went down the table. The chief engineer talked about the construction of the new camps and the new fortifications which were being constructed in great numbers, and consequently, creating a general shortage of building materials—especially concrete. The quartermaster reported a number of problems concerning the equipping and supplying of all the new troops. In particular, the troops absolutely hated the changes which had been made to the uniforms in order to protect them from the deadly black dust the Martians had used in England. "They're throwing away the leggings and the gloves almost as fast as we issue them, sir! Even the breathing masks! We are barely keeping up with the demands of the new formations; we cannot keep up with this sort of wastage!"

"Hard to blame the men," said the Inspector General. "I tried those things on, and in hot weather, they're torture."

"Hot?" snorted Roosevelt. "You should have been in Cuba! Now *that* was hot! Still, soldiers will do what they can to stay comfortable. Surely they aren't expected to wear those things all the time?"

"No, sir, but as you say, the men try to ease their burdens and carrying unused items is a burden. If you follow a unit on its first long march, you'll see the roads strewn with gloves, leggings, and masks. Right now the usual penalty is the same as it's always been: dock the men the cost of the lost equipment from their pay. But most of 'em don't care."

"We may have to resort to harsher methods," said the Army Provost. "It is a serious offense to render oneself unfit for duty and I suppose that getting yourself killed by not having the protective gear would fall under that category. Commanders should be instructed to punish the men who discard their gear."

"Perhaps, perhaps," said Roosevelt. "But don't punish them too hard. They'll resent it. The spirit of the American fighting man is legendary! Appeal to their reason first. Explain how important the gear is, not just to them but to their comrades and their country. They'll understand."

"Uh, yes, sir. We'll try."

The reports went on and Andrew came to full attention when it was General Crozier's turn to report on what the Ordnance Department was doing. Crozier had a brief summary of the various projects his department was overseeing; the tanks, several new artillery pieces, Tesla's lighting machine, a few interesting ideas Thomas Edison was working on, and the Wrights' flying machine. To Andrew's horror, he was called upon to answer a few questions that the President had.

"Captain, you say that Tesla's device made a noise like a thunderbolt?"

"Y-yes, sir. Like a very close lightning strike. Very loud and then it reverberated off into the distance."

"Ha!" cried Roosevelt, slapping the table. "Some of my neighbors up that way have been asking if the navy has been doing gunnery practice out on the Sound! So this is what it was!"

Crozier finished up and then it was the turn of the navy. Andrew gladly retreated to his spot along the wall. Admiral Evans gave a concise listing of the navy's ships and where they would be stationed, mostly guarding important coastal cities. Sadly, their newest and most powerful ships, the *North Carolina* and *Michigan*, which Andrew had seen under construction, would not be ready.

"We are rushing them ahead as much as possible," said Evans, "and we'll have them launched next month, but I'm afraid they won't be ready for action until next year."

"God willing, we won't need them," said Roosevelt.

Evans also talked about the new classes of monitors now under construction and his hopes for an expanded Marine Corps. The President seemed noncommittal about that. To Andrew's surprise, the admiral made no mention of the land ironclads that had been revealed at that fateful meeting the previous year. For that matter, General Crozier hadn't asked him to produce the crude sketches of an army version which had been hastily put together. Were both services assuming that the war would be over before any such new devices could be constructed? A hopeful thought!

Finally, everyone had had their say and the President thanked them for their efforts. It was at this point that Secretary Stimson spoke up.

"This is all very impressive, gentlemen," he said waving his hand at the maps. "But all of our defenses seemed to be concentrated in the east. What if they don't land there? You have almost nothing west of Saint Louis."

General Bell got to his feet. "Sir, since we don't know where the enemy will land, we must position our limited resources to protect our most vital locations. The cities of the east, with their large civilian populations and nearly all of our vital industries, must be given first priority."

"And we have no way to predict where the enemy will land?"

"No sir. The astronomers have no means of locating objects as small as the Martian cylinders while they are in flight. We won't know where they are going until they arrive."

"Root tells me that the British are in a quiet panic over the idea that all two hundred of the things are going to land in England," said Roosevelt. "They might be right, I suppose, since that's where the first batch landed."

"So we might see a hundred cylinders landing in America or none at all?" persisted Stimson.

"Yes, sir, that's true."

"Let's pray it's none."

"Prayer won't save us this time, Henry!" said Roosevelt. "Or we can't assume that it will. Good old American steel and lead will have to do the job this time!" He slapped the pistol on his belt.

With that, the meeting broke up. In the evening, Andrew dropped in at Colonel Hawthorne's house to fill him in on what had happened. He was pleased that the colonel was recovering. He was even more pleased when Mrs. Hawthorne suggested he and Vickie take a stroll down by the Potomac after dinner. He was amazed that she let them go without a chaperone.

They tried to go down to the river, but the mosquitoes were much too active and they retreated back up the hill to escape them. They strolled for a while along the paved paths of Fort Myer, and after a while he dared to take her hand.

"Your father is looking much better," he ventured.

"He works too hard," she replied. "So do you."

"There is so much to do, and we must be ready."

"You're just like him." He wasn't sure if that was a compliment or a complaint, so he just nodded his head. The long evening was coming to an end and the first stars could be seen. "They'll be here soon?"

"A month or so, if the experts are right."

"I hope they are right. This waiting is unbearable."

"Don't worry, Vickie; it will all be over soon."

She squeezed his hand. "I hope so."

The last days of August sped by. The final preparations were completed. Troops were put on alert; warships patrolled on their stations. The first of the new tank battalions was activated, although the crews still needed a lot of training. It was kept near Philadelphia, where it could quickly be moved north, south, or west by rail.

By all reports, the Europeans were doing the same thing, and the American military men envied them their huge armies, much smaller territories, and their superb rail networks. England was a bristling armed camp, although most of the leaders there were more worried about how to defend their sprawling empire than the home islands. No one was quite sure what the Russians were up to. Still smarting from their humiliation by Japan and with a colossal amount of territory to defend, their shaken military had an impossible task. The Japanese issued careful statements that they were prepared for any eventuality. Most of the rest of the world: South and Central America, China, Southeast Asia, seemed to feel that all the fuss did not concern them at all.

September arrived and millions of eyes scanned the skies; each person looking for the fiery streak of a descending cylinder. They watched and they waited.

And waited.

The days turned to weeks and still they waited. There were hundreds of alerts and everyone tensed, only to laugh or curse when it turned out to be another false alarm. The news from around the world was the same: nothing. The Russians had reached the site of the June explosion and while they had found an area of unprecedented devastation, with whole forests being flattened, there was no sign of Martians.

September was nearly over and the question on every lip was the same:

Are they coming?

CHAPTER THREE

SEPTEMBER 1908, NEW MEXICO TERRITORY

The sparkling waters of Quemado Lake met Rebecca Harding's eyes as her horse turned the bend in the narrow dirt road. She loved this time of year; the heat of mid-summer was giving way to the cooler days of autumn here in the mountains of western New Mexico. The aspen and cottonwood trees were a soothing rest to the eyes, covering the slopes of the surrounding hills with a green blanket. Purple Bull Thistles and yellow Sneezeweed dappled the fields with bright colors. She caught the sound of a wild turkey in the brush off to her left.

Her horse, Ninny, snorted as they passed the Jensen place. Probably smelled some of his friends in the corral. She waved at Mrs. Jensen out in her vegetable garden, but the woman didn't see her and it was just too nice a day to shout. So she kept on going, following the road as it went around the north side of the lake toward home.

The Harding Ranch covered about 2,000 acres bordering the eastern end of Quemado Lake. Rebecca's grandfather had laid claim to the land right after the war and made a real go of it. With the good water and grasslands, it was the perfect place for raising cattle and horses. Her father had been born here, as had she. Grandpa had died three years ago of a fever, but Grandma was still going strong. The ranch had prospered, and while she would never think of her family as being rich, they certainly weren't poor, either.

The ranch came into view now: the big house; old abode walls and new metal roof, added on to several times; the long, low barn, the house for the hired hands, the stables, the fenced in corrals, all so familiar. She steered Ninny into the closest stable and took off his saddle. She rubbed him down and made sure he had plenty of fodder at hand. He was her favorite, but she loved all the other horses, too. She looked over the others that were there, although there were a number of empty stalls since it was still a working day and most of the men were out watching over the herds.

"Rebecca!"

She sighed when she heard her mother calling. She briefly considered sneaking out the back door, but instead she answered: "In here, Ma!" Her mother appeared almost instantly.

"There you are! Where have you been? I've been calling for half an hour!"

"Out riding. But I'm back." She refrained from adding that she'd been back for fifteen minutes and had not heard her mother calling at all.

"And just in time! Did you forget the Andersens are coming for dinner tonight? Get out of those filthy clothes, wash the dust off your face, and put on something nice!"

"Yes, Ma." She gave Ninny a last hug and followed her mother back to the house and then got a pitcher of water before heading to her room. Cleaning up and dressing didn't take long at all, but then Ma and Grandma decided that her hair needed a proper brushing and braiding and that took far longer. Only the arrival of the Andersens saved her from further fussing.

41

"Grandma?" she said after her mother left the room.

"What is it, dear?"

"When you and Grandpa first settled here, you didn't spend all this time botherin' over dresses and hair and entertainin' the neighbors did you?"

"Heavens no!" laughed the woman. "First off, we didn't have any neighbors, 'cept for a few Indians. The nearest white folks were in Quemado, ten miles away. I had two dresses to my name and, for the first year, we lived in our wagon and an old army tent your Grandpa took with him when he mustered out."

"So why does Ma worry so much about stuff like this? About bein' respectable?"

"Well, dear, your ma grew up in Santa Fe. She's used to a bit more... civilized society. I guess she's just tryin' to bring a little civility way out here. And that might be a good thing."

"Civility don't shoe no horses or brand no cattle, Grandma."

"True enough. But we got hands to do that sorta thing now."

"Are you sayin' civilized folk don't do no work?"

"Not sayin' any such thing, girl. Just different sorts of work. But enough of this! Let's go help with the dinner."

The Andersens were an older couple with grown children. They were nice and Rebecca liked them. The dinner, mostly prepared by the cook, Rosita, was very good and Mr. Andersen told several funny stories that had them all laughing. Afterward, her father and Mr. Andersen retired to one end of the big room to smoke cigars, while the ladies clustered in the other.

"I understand you had a birthday last week, Becca," said Mrs. Andersen. "Fifteen, are you?"

"Yes ma'am."

"Well, next year, we'll have to throw a special party when you turn sixteen, right, Katherine?"

"Well, normally we would," replied her mother, smiling. "But I'm afraid Rebecca won't be here for that."

"What?" cried Rebecca. "Why?"

"Heavens, where are you going, Becca?" asked Mrs. Andersen.

"Rebecca will be going east—to school in Hartford, Connecticut."

"But Ma!" cried Rebecca in dismay.

"We talked about this, dear..."

"But just talked! We never decided anything!"

"I received the acceptance letter last week. But don't make such a face, dear! You won't be leaving until next summer; nearly a year."

"But, Ma, I don't want..."

"Sounds like quite an adventure, Becca," said Mrs. Andersen. "You should be excited."

"And grateful," said Grandma. "Not many girls from around here get the chance to go to school."

"I go to school!"

"A real school," said her mother. "With proper teachers. And a chance to meet other proper young ladies."

"And some proper young men," added Grandma with a smile.

42

Rebecca looked from face to face and realized that there wasn't a sympathetic soul among them. Well, Grandma, maybe, but she was siding with the others. She opened her mouth for further protests, but realized it would do no good. She looked to where her father was sitting and knew that if Ma had already made the arrangements, there was no way he was going to overrule her now.

"Excuse me," she said icily.

She got up and went out the front door. She heard her Grandma say: "Don't worry, she'll get over it."

It was fully dark by now and she stalked off toward the corral. *But I don't want to go to school in the east! I don't! I don't! I don't!* Her mother had been talking about the possibility for years, but she never thought she would actually make it happen! And without even telling her! How could she do that?!

The East. To Rebecca it was some mythical place with huge crowds of people, buildings as tall as mountains, clouds of dirty smoke filling the skies, and no freedom. She supposed they must have horses, but only a carriage would be fit for a proper lady. She wouldn't be able to saddle up and ride off when she wanted. Classes on literature and manners, dances she'd have to practice forever for, and poofy, fancy clothes she wouldn't want to wear—phooey! She leaned against the corral fence muttering to herself and using some words she'd heard the farmhands using.

But what could she do? She'd hoped her mother would forget about the idea, but here she was, already accepted and expected. Short of running away—which she realized was a stupid idea— what could she do to escape this trap?

"Becca? What are you doing out here?" The voice from off to her left startled her. She looked and saw that it was Pepe, a mestizo boy of uncertain parentage who hung around the ranch doing odd jobs. He was about thirteen and Rebecca's most frequent playmate while growing up—despite her mother's obvious disapproval. He was sitting on the top rail of the fence.

"Oh, hi, Pepe. I'm just… thinkin'."

"What about?"

"About how… unfair the world can be."

"The world's always unfair. But who's being unfair to you?"

"Ma. She wants to send me off east to go to school."

"East? You mean to Albuquerque?"

"Further than that. A *lot* further."

"And you don't want to go?"

"No."

"I've never been to school."

Rebecca looked at her friend with his bare feet and ragged clothes and realized that she was being stupid. Unfair? She had a fine house and nice clothes and parents who did love her. Even if they made her do stupid things. Pepe had… nothing. Why hadn't she ever thought about that before? She climbed up on the fence, unmindful of her dress and sat next to him.

"When are you leavin'?"

"Oh, not 'til next summer."

"Oh good! Not for a long time. I would have missed you, Becca."

"I'll come back." *I will come back! They are not going to marry me off to some rich easterner who'll keep me there forever!* She sat there for a minute and then asked: "What are you doing out here?"

"Watchin' the falling stars. They are very bright!"

"What? Where?" She looked up at the sky, but only saw the usual stars.

"They were over there," said the boy, pointing south. "I've seen two of them and... look! There's another!"

Rebecca jerked her head around and instantly saw what Pepe was shouting about. Off to the west, a bright light had appeared in the sky. It was much brighter than any star and it seemed to be getting brighter! As she stared in wonder, she realized that the reason it was getting bright was because it was getting closer! It was coming toward her! But not directly toward her. Years of hunting birds had taught her to judge the path of flying objects. It was coming toward her, but would pass to the south.

It got closer and brighter; the light had a strange green color to it and every few seconds it would give off a puff of sparks which quickly faded. She also realized that it was getting lower, too. The light from it was brighter than a full moon and caused objects to cast distinct shadows on the ground. It was briefly obscured by a hill on the far side of the lake, but reemerged before disappearing for good behind Slaughter Mesa off to the southeast. A second later, a bright flash lit up the sky, silhouetting the mesa briefly. A minute went by and then she heard a rumble like distant thunder, traveling across the sky from right to left until it ended in a low boom which she could actually feel through the ground.

"What... what was that?" asked Rebecca.

"A... shooting star, I think," replied Pepe. "You should make a wish."

"It wasn't like any shooting star I've ever seen!"

"No, me neither."

"And I think that one hit the ground!"

"The first two fell over there, too."

"I wonder if we could find it?"

"Maybe we could, but... oh! Look! Another one!"

The second looked to be just like the first, growing brighter by the moment. "My Pa should see this!" cried Rebecca. She jumped off the fence and dashed toward the house. But by the time she could convince the adults that there was something to see worth leaving their comfortable chairs for, and drag them outside, the star was gone. "It came down just where the other ones did!" cried Pepe.

"They were very bright, Pa! Brighter than any I've ever seen before!"

"I've seen a few really bright ones," said Mr. Andersen. "Did it leave a glowing trail?"

"Yes! And it was green!"

"Green? Really? Wish I'd seen it. Think there will be any more?"

"Maybe," said her father. "Sometimes they come in groups." But they watched for a while longer and didn't see any more.

"It really looked like they came down beyond Slaughter Mesa, Pa! We could hear the boom when it hit! D'you think maybe we could ride over there tomorrow and look for 'em?"

44

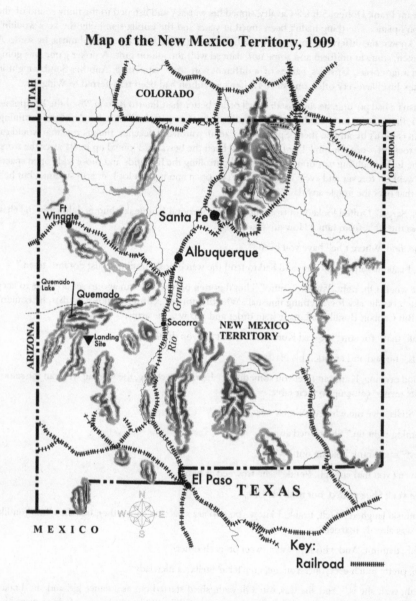

Map of the New Mexico Territory, 1909

Key:
Railroad ⊢⊢⊢⊢⊢⊢

"Don't be silly, Rebecca!" exclaimed her mother. "You have school tomorrow!"

"And if it's where you say, you are looking at twenty miles of hard riding to get there," pointed out her father.

"But…"

"We'll hear no more about it!" said her mother, scowling at Pepe. "Now come along inside!"

* * * * *

SEPTEMBER 1908, FORT WINGATE, NEW MEXICO TERRITORY

Sergeant Frank Dolfen, 5th US Cavalry, sipped his whiskey and listened to the tinny sound of the saloon's piano. The thing hadn't been tuned in years and the gorilla slamming the keys wouldn't have known the difference anyway. The resulting noise might have been called music by some. A few men, some in uniform and some not, danced with the saloon girls. A poker game was going on in a far corner. Upstairs, games of a different sort were happening. Another Sunday night in Gallup. Just like every other one since Dolfen's squadron had been transferred to Wingate.

It wasn't a bad posting, he supposed. A hell of lot better than Puerto Rico in '98 or the Philippines in '01, that was for sure! God, he'd hated both of those tropical hellholes. Jungle, close, confining; a man couldn't breathe in there. Spiders the size of your hand, leeches, fungus rots that would eat your toes off—not for him! The Dakotas had been the best. He'd joined up in '91 after the worst of the Indian fighting was done, so it was just patrolling the badlands and those wide open spaces that went on forever and ever. Wingate wasn't so open and it got a lot hotter in summer, but he'd take that over the jungle any day.

"Hey, Sarge!" Dolfen looked up from his glass as Corporal Kuminski thumped down in the chair across the table from him. "How are you doing?"

"Fine, fine. Where t'hell have you been?"

"Ah, I caught some extra duty and had to tend the watch posts until ten. Just got into town."

"The what? Oh, right. Waste of time." They'd gotten orders a month ago to set up posts to keep a watch on the sky for 'anything unusual'. Why the normal sentries couldn't do that, he couldn't see. But Captain Bonilla had made it an order and this was the army.

"Yeah, that's for sure," agreed Kuminski. "What are you drinking?"

"This," he said and emptied his glass.

"Good evening, Karl, can I get you something?" Estelle Freehling, the woman who ran the saloon for its owner, came up to their table.

"Hi Stella, give me whatever Frank was drinking."

"Coming right up." She turned away.

"Hey!" said Frank holding out his glass.

"Haven't you had enough, Frank?" she frowned at him.

"Not yet." She snorted, but took his glass.

Kuminski laughed. "Hell, Frank, I know you two are sweet on each other, but she treats you like you was already married!"

"Yeah, dammit. And who says we're sweet on each other?"

"Oh, pretty much everyone. You are, aren'tcha? Stella's a nice lady."

"Yeah, yeah she is." And she was, too. Oh yeah, she'd started out as a dance girl and she'd taken plenty of turns in those rooms upstairs, but so what? Wasn't like either one of them were high class. His dad had come over from Germany as a kid during the troubles in '48, fought in the war, got married, and had Frank. Or 'Franz' as his legal name was. Then his father had gotten himself killed in one of the Pennsylvania miners' riots and Frank decided there was no way he was spending the rest of his life in one of those holes. So it had been the army. Seventeen years of it. "Three more years until retirement. If we're both still here then, well, maybe."

"Maybe you shouldn't wait. If there's a war, we could get pulled out of here, right quick!"

"War? War with who? The Martians?"

"That's what everyone's saying."

Dolfen snorted. "Hey, Stell, you believe in Martians?" he asked as she returned with their drinks.

"Nope, and I won't until one of them comes through that door and orders a drink." They all laughed.

"See?" said Dolfen, "If Stell don't believe in 'em, they don't exist."

"What about what they done in England?"

"Stories. Made 'em up t'sell newspapers."

"But I've seen pictures…"

"Made them up, too. Now shut up about 'em and drink your drink."

"Sure, Sarge, sure."

Quite some time later, he staggered his way down the street, Stella helping to hold him upright. She wasn't happy with him for how much he'd had to drink. But then she was usually mad at him for that exact reason. But she'd let him stay at her place and make sure he made it back to the fort before formation. Yeah, she was a good woman.

The town was mostly dark and the night air very clear, so he had no trouble seeing the bright green spark streaking along, just above the southern horizon. Stella had no distance vision so she didn't see, but he stopped and stared for a moment. *Something unusual…* Maybe he should…

"Frank, come on! I'm tired!" Stella pulled at his arm.

"Okay, okay." What had he been thinking about? Bed? Yeah, definitely bed.

* * * * *

CYCLE 597,843.1, LANDING SITE 32

Qetjnegartis opened its eyes and then contracted its lateral muscles to eject a stream of thick liquid from its mouth. It repeated the process several times until it was able to take in air to fill its breathing sacs. Once it could breathe, it proceeded to empty its feeding sac in a similar fashion. The liquid had served to fill every space which normally held air in its body, rendering Qetjnegartis an incompressible mass. This allowed it to survive the enormous pressures of launch and landing. It had no memory of either event, of course, since it had entered a hibernation cycle prior to launch and left it just now, presumably, after landing.

It tried to pull itself out of the acceleration vat, but slipped and fell back in. High gravity. The target world had a gravitational pull over twice that of the Homeworld. Qetjnegartis exerted itself and this time succeeded, flopping heavily on the deck of the transport vessel. Its two subordinates were doing the same. The transport appeared undamaged to a brief visual inspection, but Qetjnegartis needed a more detailed report. It pulled itself to the main control position and grasped the interface with its tendrils. Information flowed and it confirmed that all was well with the vessel itself.

It extended its examination to the outside. The vessel was embedded in a small crater, obviously on the target world—the gravity confirmed that. Locational beacons established that the landing was in the planned position on the second continent. Transports 2, 3, and 5 were nearby, but where was Transport 4? Expanding its search, it could find no trace of the missing transport. A mishap of some sort? Unfortunate. But not critical. Contingencies had been made and would be enacted.

Its subordinates completed their inspection of the stored equipment and reported that all was well. Assembly of the machines could commence at once. There was no time to waste.

* * * * *

OCTOBER, 1908, WASHINGTON, D.C.

There were times when Leonard Wood regretted ever introducing the game of 'singlesticks' to Theodore Roosevelt. The game was supposed to teach swordsmanship, but when played by the President, it soon devolved into an endurance match with the players beating the stuffings out of each other with the heavy ash rods. The padded helmets and surcoats helped, but Wood invariable found himself covered with bruises after an evening with Roosevelt.

Wood darted to one side and landed a blow on the President's chest. A good solid blow, too, Theodore always resented it if he felt someone was holding back. Wood retreated a pace and, as usual, Roosevelt forgot the rules and struck at him. He barely deflected the blow. "Dammit, Theodore! I've told you a thousand times that after a hit both men have to go back to the guard position before proceeding!"

"Yes, yes, I know. Sorry, I was just getting into a rhythm."

"You were just letting out your frustrations—on me."

"Yes, you're right," said the President, pulling off his helmet. "God forgive me, Leonard, how can the leader of any civilized nation find himself wishing for war? It keeps me up at night."

"You're not wishing for a war, Theodore; we already have a war. You're just wishing for the Martians to get on with it. It's the waiting that's the hard part."

"I suppose you're right. Yes, by God, you are right! And if the beasties don't come, I'll laugh and thank God—even if it does cost me the presidency!"

Wood nodded, but didn't reply. Yes, it could cost Roosevelt the presidency. After all the enormous build-up, the new taxes, the spending, and the rush to prepare, if the Martians did not show up soon, it would be very bad at the polls. Some critics were already saying that it had all been a hoax. Some plot by Theodore Rex to further increase hisown power. No one of any standing with the Democrats had gone quite that far yet. But in another few weeks, it would begin. And if they still weren't here by November 3rd, William Jennings Bryan would be the next president of these United States. Wood shuddered at the thought. The American people might tolerate a president who made a mistake, but they would never tolerate one who tried to make fools of them—and that is what the Democrats would say he did.

And what if the Martians landed the next day?

Roosevelt laid aside his stick and began peeling off his surcoat. He was sweating profusely and Wood noticed his bulging waistline. Theodore continued to gain weight despite all the exercise he got. He ate prodigiously and exercised prodigiously, but never wisely. He was nearly blind in his left eye from a boxing injury years before. He tried to conceal it—as he did every human weakness—but those close to him knew. Seven years as president had taken its toll; he wasn't a young man anymore.

They cleaned up and went back upstairs. Roosevelt started to put on his coat, but Wood stopped him. "Take a rest, Theodore."

"I was just going to take a little stroll…"

"Across the street to the War Department to read the latest telegrams."

"Well, I thought I might…"

"The operators don't need you looking over their shoulders. If anything happens, you'll know within…"

"Mr. President! Sir!"

The shout spun them both around. A young officer, flanked by two secret service men, fairly sprinted into the room, waving a scrap of paper.

"What is it, son?" asked Roosevelt, gently, but Wood could see that he was coiled like a spring.

"They're here! The Martians, sir!"

Roosevelt turned and peered out one of the windows. "Really? I don't hear anything."

"Uh, Russia, sir! Kaz… Kazakhstan!"

"Indeed? Has this been confirmed?"

"I… I don't know, sir!"

"Let me have that," said Wood, taking the paper. "'Russian Imperial cavalry report metal war machines near Turgay', that's all."

"Let's have a look at my globe," said Roosevelt, leading the way to his office. The large, ornate globe revealed Kazakhstan, but much squinting could not find any town labeled Turgay. "It's certainly the middle of nowhere, isn't it? Why would they land there? There's not a major city within a thousand miles."

"I'm afraid that's exactly why they did land there," said Wood.

"What do you mean?"

"I mean that they aren't stupid, Theodore. They must know that we would be prepared this time, and I'm afraid they've guessed our strategy: rush them before they're ready to fight. So they've landed somewhere where we can't get at them before they're ready."

"Damnation," muttered Roosevelt. He went over to the huge map of the United States that he'd had hung on one wall. It was studded with colored pins and flags, but nearly all of them were in the east. There were huge areas in the west with hardly a pin to be seen. "If they do the same thing here…" He swept a large hand across the map from the Dakotas down to the Mexican border. There was an awful lot of empty space out there.

"We do have observers with the system the Signal Corps set up," said Wood.

"But not enough! I lived in the Dakotas in the '90s and I was through there in the '04 campaign and there are hundreds of places where a cylinder could land and no one would see!"

"We need to get the word out there—and send some more troops."

"Yes! And right away!"

* * * * *

OCTOBER, 1908, QUEMADO LAKE, NEW MEXICO TERRITORY

"There it is again!" Rebecca Harding pointed. A faint flash lit the sky for an instant. Off to the south, beyond Slaughter Mesa—where all the other flashes had come from. It had become almost a nightly ritual for her and Pepe to watch the southern skies. Over the weeks since spotting the falling stars, they'd seen dozens—hundreds—of the strange flashes.

"What do you think they are?" asked Pepe. They'd both asked that question many times. Neither had an answer.

"We need to ride over there and find out!"

"Your father won't let you." It was true, she'd asked him a half-dozen times about it and he always said no. He'd seen the flashes, but he still said no.

"Yeah…" She leaned against a fence rail and tapped her fingers in frustration. Another flash. "But…"

"What?"

49

"Ma and Pa are going into Quemado tomorrow. They're leaving early and won't be back until late. If we hurried, we could get over there and get back before them!"

"It's a long ride," pointed out Pepe. "I've never been that far."

"Neither have I. But if we follow Largo Creek, it will take us up to that high meadow. From there we can cut over to Dead Horse Canyon. That ought to take us around the Mesa and right down to the San Augustin Plains. That's got to be where those flashes are coming from!"

"Your pa will be angry."

"Only if he finds out!" They both laughed at that and then set to work. Even though they would only be gone for a day, they would need food and water and other supplies. They had to get two horses ready to go and they had to do it without anyone knowing they were doing it. Rebecca felt a vague sense of guilt about disobeying her father, but she could see no real harm in what she was doing, and something in the back of her head was telling her that this was important. If they didn't find anything, then they'd come home and no one would be the wiser. And if they did find something... well, she'd deal with that when it happened.

It took them the whole afternoon to get everything ready and it was actually a lot of fun doing it all secretly. For some reason, it made her feel very grown up and wickedly rebellious. Her parents wanted to send her two thousand miles to the east to have her finish growing up, but she could do it right here!

She said very little at dinner for fear of giving something away and her parents didn't appear to notice anything, although her grandmother gave her a few odd looks. She went to bed early, but hardly slept at all. Everyone was up before dawn; her parents wanted to get an early start. Breakfast was eaten, the buckboard was brought out, and a horse harnessed to it. Goodbyes were said and her parents drove away. Rebecca was already wearing the clothes she planned to use that day so, leaving the breakfast dishes to Rosita and Grandma, she snuck out to the stables.

Pepe was waiting for her. He had Ninny and another horse named Star saddled and all the stuff they'd agree to take already packed. They led the horses out, checked to see no one was watching, and then climbed into the saddles and trotted off into the growing dawn.

At first they made good time. Riding along the creek bed was easy and the ranch was soon out of sight. But then the land began to rise sharply and the going was slower. Even so, they reached the high meadow by mid-morning and stopped to let the horses rest. She'd been up here dozens of times, but had never gone any farther south. The land got rougher and dryer in that direction.

"I think if we go that way, we'll hit Dead Horse Canyon," she said, pointing.

After a while they got moving again. It was a beautiful day with a brisk breeze blowing. A few more weeks and it would start getting cold at these high altitudes, but right now it was marvelous. As they left the meadow, the spruce and ponderosa pines closed in around them and they had to search for a passable route. They reached several dead ends and had to double back. Rebecca was getting worried about how much time they were wasting. They weren't even at the halfway point of the trip and it was nearly noon. But finally they found a narrow path that seemed to be leading in the right direction. Her father had a few maps of the region and she'd studied them often. Another hour and they were definitely in the canyon, with Slaughter Mesa rearing up to their left. It ought to lead them right where they wanted to go. They stopped and ate lunch. While they sat there, Pepe kept looking around with a worried expression on his face.

"What's wrong?" she asked.

"It's so quiet. Except for the wind. No animals making noise at all."

She realized that he was right. Even the horses seemed uneasy. When they got ready to move again, she took the rifle out of its saddle holster. It was a Henry that her grandfather had brought back from the war. She'd always liked this one because of its pretty brass frame. She'd learned to shoot when she was six; she checked the action and put it back. "Come on, another hour and we'll be there. We'll look around and then head back."

"We will be lucky to make it home before dark."

"So let's move!"

They quickened their pace as much as the ground would allow and in a shorter time than she'd expected, they rounded a bend and the flat, dusty plain of San Augustin stretched out below them. It was a sandy depression about five miles north to south and four times that east to west. Higher elevations surrounded it. The eastern end was invisible from where they were. The land was worthless for farming or grazing and as far as Rebecca knew no one lived in the area. They both shaded their eyes and scanned the plain. Whatever had been making those flashes had to be here somewhere.

"What is that?" asked Pepe, pointing.

"Where?"

"That dark patch on the ground."

Rebecca leaned over to look down the boy's arm. Sure enough, there was a circular splotch of dark earth in the midst of the lighter plain. It looked like another streak of dark soil led off for a distance toward the west before stopping. It was at least four or five miles away.

"Maybe… maybe that's where the shooting star came down."

"There were four of them; do you see any more?"

They strained their eyes and thought they could make out another one farther east. Then, a flash of light, like sunlight reflecting off metal, flickered for a few moments beyond the first patch and they saw another bit of darkness there. Try as they might, they couldn't spot a fourth. As they continued to watch, a cloud of smoke or mist surged up from the nearest dark patch and then suddenly lit up briefly.

"That's what's been causing those flashes!" cried Rebecca.

"But what are they?" asked Pepe.

"I don't know. We should get closer."

"Maybe we should go back."

"Not until we get a better look. Come on!" She led the reluctant Pepe further down the canyon. They lost sight of the plain for a while as they worked their way through some very narrow spots where the canyon's sides loomed up over them. But then they came to a place where they could see out again. The nearest dark patch was just a couple of miles away, although being lower down, they couldn't spot the other patches at all. But the near patch was much more distinct now; it looked as though earth had been piled up in a ring surrounding a hole in the ground.

"Look! There's something moving there!" cried Pepe. Sure enough, something appeared to be moving on the edge of the ring. It was still too far to see clearly, but it must have been pretty large, much bigger than a man. After a moment, it disappeared below the lip of the ring.

"What was it?" asked Rebecca.

"Can't see it now! I'm going to climb up and see if I can spot it!" There was a tall rock outcrop thirty feet high to their right. Pepe jumped off Star, threw the reins to Rebecca, and began scrambling up the rocks.

"Pepe, wait!" She was suddenly very nervous. Whatever was going on here, it wasn't right. The horses began to jerk about and whinny. "Pepe! We should go!" But the boy kept climbing. He reached the top and stood up. And froze.

"Can you see anything?" she called.

Pepe didn't move.

"Pepe!"

Something huge loomed up just beyond him. Rebecca couldn't begin to describe it. Part of it was blocked by the stone outcropping, but the rest towered at least twenty feet higher than Pepe. It had a head of sorts and arms, thuds and crunching rocks hinted at legs. A single baleful red eye glowed in the middle of the head. And it was made of metal, all metal. A thin snake-like arm darted out and wrapped itself around Pepe. Only then did the boy react. He screamed as he was lifted into the air.

"Pepe!" shrieked Rebecca.

She fumbled for the rifle, but the horses were going mad. Ninny turned and fled back up the canyon, Star was right behind. She twisted to look back and gasped. The thing was chasing her! Three metal legs were propelling it after her; Pepe was still caught in its grasp, his legs kicking madly.

Every thought except to escape left her mind. Blind panic seized her and she urged Ninny on, though he needed no urging. Just ahead the canyon narrowed; if she could just make it past, she would be safe! The thing couldn't fit through the gap! She reached it! They were through!

From behind her an enormous noise shook the air: "Ulla! Ulla! Ulla!" It was like some colossal horn. She dared to look back. Star was just galloping through the gap when suddenly the horse was engulfed in flames. He gave off one hideous shriek before being consumed. A blast of scorching air swirled around her. She buried her face in Ninny's mane and rode on.

* * * * *

CYCLE 597,843.2, LANDING SITE 32

The machine sucked the last bit of nourishment from the prey-creature. The empty husk was disposed of and the nourishment was conveyed through a system of filters before being delivered to Qetjnegartis. It drank deeply, filling its food sacs. The technique was different from normal and unsettling somehow, but it greatly lessened the chance of infection from the pathogens which teemed on this world. If the scientists were right, its body ought to last many times longer than those who came in the first expedition. Still, sooner or later this body would succumb. But it was growing a replacement. The new bud was already large enough to be visible along its flank. The bud could either become a replacement body for Qetjnegartis or an actual offspring, a new being. It would not be necessary to decide which for some time. If its body was still healthy, then it would be an offspring. If not, a replacement. An offspring would be best, of course, since it would quickly be able to contribute to the efforts here. But only time would tell which it would be.

Finished feeding, it turned its attention to more serious matters. One of the creatures had escaped and it must be assumed it would alert its fellows to their presence here. How quickly they might react was unknown. The landing site was far from any major habitations, nor were any of the crude transport systems the prey used nearby. It might be many rotations before any response arrived. They still had time to prepare, but they had to be ready to move on short notice. Several of the landing groups on the first continent had already been forced to engage in battle. But this had been expected. Under ideal conditions, all groups would wait until the planned time before attacking, but it was always understood that the ideal was unlikely to be met and each group must respond to the local circumstances.

Qetjnegartis took hold of the command interface and reviewed the status of its own group. All twelve of the battle machines had been assembled and were ready. There should have been fifteen, but with the loss of Lander Four, they had but twelve. Four constructors had also been assembled. Initial probes could find no significant metal deposits in the immediate vicinity. This was unfortunate, but not unexpected. But it did rule out building a permanent holdfast in this location. They would have to move to find a better area.

Under the plan, it was too soon to move. So in the meanwhile, the constructors would salvage the landers themselves and begin constructing additional machines to be ready for the new offspring.

But the time to move was fast approaching. The conquest of this world would soon begin.

* * * * *

NOVEMBER, 1908, WASHINGTON, D.C.

Leonard Wood could not help thinking about just how strange a day this was. It was Election Day of what was certainly the most important presidential election since 1864 and the President was ignoring it completely. Aides were coming in periodically with results and predictions and Roosevelt just waved them away. His attention was completely focused on the maps and stacks of reports that he and his top military advisors were poring over.

"New Mexico for sure..."

"What about that report from Idaho?"

"There's only the one sighting from that. No confirmation..."

"Two reports from the Mexicans..."

"A possible sighting in Alberta..."

The low babble had been going on for hours—days, really. Ever since first the report of Martians in Kazakhstan, more sightings had been coming in from all over the world. Asia, Africa, the Middle East, Australia, and South America. Only a fraction of the sightings had been confirmed, but that fraction was enough to prove that the Martians had landed. As feared, they were coming down in out-of-the-way locations, apparently all over the planet. So far, Europe was the only area with no sightings at all.

After an agonizing delay, reports had finally started coming in from American territory. The official spotting network had been terribly thin west of the Mississippi, but sighting were now being received from local sheriffs and ordinary citizens. They were confusing, sometimes contradictory, and lacking in important details, but they could not be ignored.

"Mr. President." A naval officer, an expert in navigation, stood up from the map he'd been working on with protractors and calipers for nearly an hour.

"Yes? What have you got?" Roosevelt moved to stand beside him.

"Sir, the New Mexico sighting seems very solid. We have independent sightings of the falling cylinders from six different locations; three in New Mexico and three in Arizona which the cylinders passed over. By using their descriptions, I've managed to lay out approximate courses and they all seem to converge in this area here." He moved his hand over a portion of the map of the southwest. "This region of western New Mexico between Socorro and the border with Arizona."

"That's really desolate country," said another officer. "Hardly a town or a road within fifty miles."

"Well, we need to get someone out there to take a look!" said the President. "What troops do have in the area?"

53

"I'll check, sir."

"Theodore? Theodore?" Wood looked up to see Elihu Root come into the room. The Secretary of State looked tired, but he was smiling. He pushed through the crowd to Roosevelt's side. "Theodore? You've won Ohio. You are re-elected, Mr. President."

The news brought a round of applause and congratulations from the others in the room, but Roosevelt seemed unaffected.

"That's fine, that's fine, bully. Write up some sort of message for me will you, Root? Now what can we get to this spot, gentlemen?"

Root shook his head and moved away. One of the staff officers pointed to the map, to a spot well north of the area the naval officer had denoted. "Fort Wingate, sir. It's the nearest post. One squadron of the 5th Cavalry's there. But it's on the railroad so we can get more there in less than a week."

"Good! Good! Send everything you can! Let's get moving, gentlemen!"

CHAPTER FOUR

NOVEMBER, 1908, QUEMADO LAKE, NEW MEXICO TERRITORY

Rebecca Harding could hear voices.

"Well good God, Katherine, something surely happened!"

"It was that filthy boy she's always hanging around with. He tricked her with wild tales, just so he could steal that horse!"

"Oh come now! What about the burns on the back of her head—and on her horse? Where did those come from?"

"I don't know. But don't tell me you believe her story? She was hysterical! Probably so ashamed that she let the boy trick her that she made up the story out of guilt."

"And then burned her hair off? I could hardly believe her doing that to herself, but she would never hurt that horse of hers! No, something really happened and I'm going to tell the sheriff."

"And make us the laughing stock of the whole valley?"

"Katherine! You've heard the stories, read the newspapers! What if this is the Martians?"

"Out here? In the middle of nowhere? Why on Earth would they come here…?"

The voices faded away and Rebecca slowly became aware that she was lying on something soft. A faint clicking noise, rhythmic and persistent, was coming from her left. She cracked open an eye.

"Ah, waking up, Honey?" It was her grandmother. The clicking noise had been her knitting needles. The woman set them aside and came over to her. "How are you feeling, dear?"

"How… how did I get here?"

"Ninny brought you home. Smart critter that one. Can you tell me what happened?"

She tried to think back. What had happened? She was going to try to find the shooting stars. Her and… "Pepe!" she cried. "It got Pepe!"

"Calm down, Dearie!" soothed her grandmother.

"It got Pepe!"

"Gently, gently, what got Pepe?"

"That… that *thing*!" She looked around wildly. She was in her bedroom. Somehow she'd gotten away, gotten back here. She couldn't remember anything after… after…

"What thing? What got Pepe?"

"It… it… I don't know!" she sobbed. "It was huge! Taller than the barn…than the windmill! It was all metal with a red eye in its head! It had arms like snakes and one of them grabbed Pepe!

Grandma! We have to save him!" She tried to sit up in the bed, but there was pain in her head and she felt dizzy. Her grandmother gently forced her to lie back down.

"Take it easy. You have a nasty burn on the back of your head, Becca. How did that happen?"

"After… after it got Pepe, I… the horses bolted. But the thing was chasing me! I made it through a narrow point and it couldn't follow… but then everything was on fire… Star burned up! Oh, Grandma, Star *burned up!* And then… and then… I don't remember any more!" She was crying uncontrollably now and her grandmother stroked her brow until she settled down. Then the woman got up and left the room. Rebecca could hear the voices again.

"She's awake and her story hasn't changed at all. Bob, your daughter is not making this up! It really happened and you better let someone know!"

"All right, all right, I'll go talk to the sheriff tomorrow."

* * * * *

NOVEMBER, 1908, GETTYSBURG, PENNSYLVANIA

The line of tanks rumbled across the field, churning up mud with their caterpillar tracks, black smoke belching from their stacks. The practice field had been totally stripped of vegetation and was a sea of mud after recent rains. Captain Andrew Comstock could feel his boots slowly sinking into the goo. The place was called Camp Colt and it had been set up on the edge of the historic Civil War battlefield as a training camp for tank crews. The first two battalions of steam tanks had been delivered from the Baldwin Works in Philadelphia and their crews were learning how to use them. Andrew was here to report on their progress.

So far, what he was seeing didn't fill him with a lot of confidence. One of the battalions, some thirty tanks, had lined up at one edge of a field about a half mile across. They had clanked and lurched to the other end and nearly a third of them were stuck, broken down, or in one case turning in random circles, spewing clouds of steam. Baldwin had sent a team of their own mechanics to help train the soldiers and these men were now wearily shouldering their tool kits and wading out to see what they could do with the stragglers. It looked like a ritual they were all too familiar with.

"Well, we're improving," said the camp commander, a Major Wainwright. "Last time, we lost over half of them."

"This is an entirely new type of vehicle," said the head Baldwin man, a fellow named Klein, who Andrew had met before. "You have to expect some initial problems."

"This sort of performance would be unacceptable in the field, Mr. Klein," said Andrew. He was getting pretty good at growling, he thought.

"As the crews get used to them, they'll be able to prevent these breakdowns. And what we are learning here will allow us to make the next model even more reliable."

"Next model?"

"Yes, we're calling this the Mark 1. We're already working on the Mark 2."

Major Wainwright snorted. "The *men* call this one the *Stumbler.*"

"Why Tumbler?"

"With the gun and ammunition, the thing is seriously front-heavy. A few weeks ago one of them tried to go down a steep slope and it flipped over completely. It was miracle that none of the crew were scalded to death."

Klein made a note in a small book he was carrying. "You could try moving the ammunition farther to the rear."

"Right next to the firebox for the boiler? Oh, good idea!"

While they watched, several of the tanks got moving again and managed to rejoin their comrades at the far end. The rest remained where they were and did not look like they'd be moving soon. So much for the demonstration. While Andrew, Wainwright, and Klein were slogging their way back to the headquarters area, a courier on a motorcycle splattered to a stop next to them and handed a dispatch to the Major.

"They can't be serious!" he exclaimed after reading it.

"'Fraid so, sir," said the courier.

"What is it?" asked Andrew.

"We've been ordered to move out!"

"Move out? Where?"

"Doesn't say. Just pack up everything, lock, stock, and barrel and be ready to load aboard trains in three days. This is crazy! We're not ready!"

"Sorry to hear that, Major," said Klein sympathetically. "We'll give you whatever help we can before you go."

"Excuse me, sir" said the courier, "Are you…" He was holding another envelope and read from it. "… Douglas Klein?"

"Yes. What is that?"

"Dunno, sir, but it's for you." He handed it over and Klein opened it and looked it over. He stiffened suddenly and his face paled.

"What! They… they can't do this!"

"What is it?" asked Wainwright.

"They've drafted me! Me and my men! I'm going with you!"

"Really? Hadn't heard that Congress had enacted a draft yet."

"It amounts to the same thing!" snarled Klein in disgust. "The Army wants us to go along and Baldwin has agreed to lend us to you! If we want to keep our jobs, we're going! Hell's bells!"

Andrew decided that this was a good time to take his leave. He made his way back to the Gettysburg station and caught the next train to Harrisburg. From there he returned to Washington. He had a pretty good idea where Major Wainwright and Mr. Klein were headed with two battalions of steam tanks. He'd been to enough meetings recently to know that the Martians had landed and they'd landed where no one expected them. Alarming reports were being received from all over the world of landings in remote areas, areas far away from where the armies had been massed. Everyone from Buenos Ares to Vladivostok was scrambling to redeploy their forces to meet the threat. And it was no different in the United States. Reports of a landing in New Mexico were being taken the most seriously, although there might be another in Idaho. Troops were being shipped west as quickly as the trains could get them there. Civilian authorities in the east were screaming that they were being left defenseless. The President was calling for more men and more equipment. A draft really was being discussed.

Despite several delays, he made it back to Fort Myer in time for dinner at the Hawthorne residence. He filled the colonel in on what he'd seen. "And you should have seen the look on Klein's face when he found out he was going with them!" laughed Andrew.

For some reason the colonel wasn't smiling. "I wouldn't be so quick to laugh, Andy," he said. "You see, you'll be going along, too."

"What?" exclaimed Andrew, a jolt passing through him like an electric shock.

"Oh, Dad, no!" cried Victoria.

"Yes, I'm afraid so. General Crozier wants one of his people out there. Not just to observe how the tanks perform, but also to be on hand to collect any Martian equipment that might fall into our hands. I offered to go, but he wants me here. So you win the prize, Andy. Sorry about that."

"When do I leave, sir?" He glanced at Victoria and the poor girl looked stricken. He wasn't sure how he felt about this. It would be uncomfortable and possibly dangerous, but a part of him was excited at the prospect.

"Oh, probably a week or so. We are going to give you a team of enlisted men to assist you and that will take a little time to assemble. Then you'll be off to Santa Fe or maybe Albuquerque. They are collecting everything they can there, including the steam tanks. It will probably be at least a month before they are ready to move. In the meanwhile, they are going to send out a scratch force of cavalry to try and locate the Martian landing area."

"Sir… I'll try to do a proper job of it, sir."

"I know you will, son. You've been doing some fine work and that's why Crozier is willing to give you this responsibility."

"I won't let you down, sir."

Hawthorne suddenly smiled. "I know you won't. And by the way, the general is brevetting you major for this mission."

Andrew was stunned. "T-thank you, sir!"

"Well, he wanted you to have enough clout to make sure that if any Martian equipment is salvaged that you'll be able to keep it from falling into enemy hands."

"Enemy hands, sir?"

"You know, the Corps of Engineers, or even worse, the Navy!"

* * * * *

NOVEMBER, 1908, FORT WINGATE, NEW MEXICO TERRITORY

"Prepare to mount… MOUNT!" Sergeant Frank Dolfen swung into the saddle and automatically looked to check on his squad. They were all in order, but not looking terribly military. Each man was bundled up against the bitter wind as he saw fit and they were wearing a collection of issue overcoats, civilian coats, blankets, gloves, and a variety of hats. Veterans.

"Fours left—MARCH!" came the order, and the troopers swung from line into a column four men abreast. A bugle echoed the command down the line to make sure everyone had heard—a needless precaution really, since everyone knew what to do. But this was the Army and the forms had to be followed.

The column that rode out of Fort Wingate looked impressive; well over two hundred troopers plus a gaggle of hangers-on and a supply train of pack animals almost as big as the rest of the column. Despite his and Stella's denial, apparently the Martians were real after all. Or at least that's what the officers were saying. A batch of them had landed eighty or ninety miles to the south and the 5th had been ordered to go find them. Or half of the 5th, anyway. The 1st Squadron had been joined by the 2nd and they were being sent off. The rest of the regiment had been too widely scattered to get here in time. Rumor had it that a much bigger force was being assembled at Santa Fe and would follow along in time—assuming the 5th found anything.

Colonel O'Dell had arrived to take command and this was the first time Dolfen had actually seen his colonel in the flesh. He was a bit surprised by how young the man looked. At the time Dolfen had first enlisted, all the regimental commanders in the whole army had been veterans of the Civil War, and with a static peacetime army with no hope of promotion to higher rank, and no mandatory retirement for officers, those men had hung on and on. By the time of the Spanish War they were getting pretty ancient. But the campaigns in Cuba and Puerto Rico and the Philippines had weeded them all out—they simply couldn't stand the pace. So a new generation had taken charge and that was a good thing in Dolfen's opinion.

But O'Dell was saddled with a gaggle of other officers sent out from Washington. Engineers and Signal Corps people and even some from the General Staff. Everyone wanted a look at the Martians! Dolfen had to admit that he was a trifle curious himself. He'd been skeptical, but surely all these people couldn't be wrong! Well, they could, he supposed, but there must be something to it.

They rode due south for an hour or so, the land climbing gently but steadily, the trees getting thicker. Then they angled a bit to the southwest and managed to strike the road to San Lorenzo about noon. A long, tree-covered ridge to their west gave them some protection from the wind, and with the sun on them, things warmed up quite a bit. Dolfen smiled in satisfaction. This was the sort of thing he loved. Riding with the troops, a clear road stretching before them, beautiful country all around. There was already some snow on the tops of the Zuni Mountains off to the east.

He dropped back a bit to ride next to Corporal Kuminski and the second squad for a while. He was responsible for both squads, while Lieutenant Hopkins commanded the whole troop.

"So whaddaya think, Sarge?" asked Kuminski. "We gonna shoot some Martians?"

"Oh yeah," he said slapping the saddle holster for his rifle. "Think I'll have mine stuffed and mounted. Then when I retire, I can take it back east and charge people a nickel each to see it." They both laughed.

"You won't get anything with that Krag of yours! Can't believe you're still carrying that thing around!"

Dolfen patted the butt of his Krag-Jorgensen lovingly. Everyone else was carrying the '03 Springfields, but he'd kept the Krag.

"How do you get ammo for it anyway? Won't take the thirty-ought-sixes, will it?"

"No, but I laid in a stock of ammo when I could. She took good care of me in the Philippines and she'll serve me well against any damn Martian, too!"

He thought back to his time in the Philippines fighting the insurrectionists there. Bloodthirsty bastards. Didn't seem to appreciate the Americans freeing them from the Spanish and giving them democracy. Well, they learned! He started humming a song that all the men were singing back then. It was set to the tune of the Civil War song *Tramp! Tramp! Tramp!* but the men had made up their own words:

> *…And beneath our starry flag,*
> *We'll civilize 'em with a Krag,*
> *And return us to our own beloved home…*

They rode south.

* * * * *

NOVEMBER, 1908, QUEMADO LAKE, NEW MEXICO TERRITORY

"Grandma, what's happening?" asked Rebecca Harding. "When are Pa and the sheriff going to *do* something! It's been a week since that thing got Pepe!" She strode back and forth across her room and thumped her fist against the wall. "It could be coming here next! We can't just sit around!"

"They have been doing things, dear," said her grandmother soothingly. "Your pa talked to the sheriff and the sheriff sent a wire to Albuquerque. They've also talked to most of the folks hereabout to warn them."

"But… but what about Pepe? Aren't they going to go look for him? There's no telling what that thing might be doing to him!"

"I believe the sheriff sent a few men to take a look, but they didn't find anything. I'm sorry, Honey."

"Did they go all the way down to San Augustin like we did?"

"I don't know, dear."

"Of course they didn't! They probably didn't go any farther than the meadow! The cowards!"

"Becca! That is no way to speak about your elders!"

She slumped down on her bed and started to cry. "This is all my fault! I never should have gone out there! And Pepe wanted to turn back when we saw those holes. But I made him keep going and now… now… Oh, Grandma! He's my friend and I got him into awful trouble!"

Her grandmother sat down next to her and put an arm around her. "I'm sorry dear. But… well, the plain fact is that folks are scared to go down there. If it really is the Martians. All those stories about what happened in England the last time. If cannons and battleships couldn't stop 'em, what are a few men with rifles going to do?"

Rebecca stopped crying and looked at her grandmother in surprise. She hadn't thought about that at all. She'd told the grown-ups and she'd expected them to make things right. That was their job, after all! But what had she really expected? The sheriff to go and arrest the Martians? She suddenly felt very insecure, even in her own bedroom. She looked out the window. "What… what if they come here?"

Grandma frowned. "The sheriff wired for help and they say the Army will be coming. Meanwhiles, your pa is making plans to move the herds, and me and your ma have been packing some things in case we have to leave. Just in case. We didn't want to worry you until you were well."

Rebecca ran her hand along the back of her head. "I'm fine and my hair is growin' back! I can help!"

Her grandmother smiled. "That would be good, dear."

* * * * *

CYCLE 597,843.25, LANDING SITE 32

Qetjnegartis contemplated the message from the Expedition Conclave. Attack. The command had come earlier than planned, but not so early that it would cause major difficulty. Apparently the prey-creatures were reacting aggressively in many areas. So many landing forces had been forced into battle already that holding the others back made little sense. So all would go forth together now.

The early move and the loss of Lander 4 would leave Qetjnegartis with a weakened command. The original plan would have had fifteen war machines and five constructors. Given time, the salvage of the landers would have allowed the construction of fifteen additional war machines. These would not have been able to fight without operators, but could have followed along in slave-mode until the new buds were sufficiently developed to operate them.

Now, however, it had only twelve war machines, four constructors, and the salvage of the landers was not complete. It was unwilling to abandon the salvaged materials, so it would have to take a risk. It would attack with only nine of the war machines. Three subordinates would be left to complete the salvage and the construction of the twelve additional war machines. They would then follow along when they were able. The danger would be if a strong enemy arrived to attack the landing site while Qetjnegartis and the others were beyond supporting range. Loss of the constructors and the materials would be a serious blow. But analysis of the surrounding area put the probability of such an attack at an acceptably low level—especially if Qetjnegartis and the attack force were acting aggressively elsewhere.

So they would attack—aggressively.

The master plan called for them to strike north to link up with other forces, cutting the second continent into two. Holdfasts would be established, materials mined, more war machines built, and buds grown to pilot them. The conquest would then proceed.

Qetjnegartis contacted its subordinates and gave the orders.

* * * * *

NOVEMBER, 1908, VANDALIA, ILLINOIS

Brevet Major Andrew Comstock surveyed the wreck and shook his head. What a mess. In fact, the entire attempt to transport the 1st and 2nd Steam Tank Battalions across the country could probably be described as a mess, too. The only way to do it, of course, was by rail and the railroads weren't really up to it. The problem wasn't the weight of the tanks, they didn't weigh as much as a gondola car full of coal, after all, but their size. They were over two feet wider than a standard railroad flat car and they hung out over the edges dangerously. They didn't dare to pass another train on double-tracked sections and Andrew couldn't count the number of telegraph poles they'd clipped off. It made for a slow trip.

And now this. They were about sixty miles east of St. Louis and the tracks crossed over a stream on a small bridge. A party had been sent ahead of the trains to make sure that things were clear. They'd promised that the bridge here was wide enough.

They'd been wrong.

The engine had passed through with no problem, but the first tank had collided with the bridge girders on either side. It had become wedged and torn loose from the first flat car. The tank on the second car smashed into it. Fortunately, the train hadn't been going all that fast and the next few cars had simply derailed and turned over on their sides. It looked as though only the first two tanks had been seriously damaged. But the way was blocked and the bridge too damaged to take any more traffic. They would have to back up and find another route. From what the railroad men were saying, that would mean going practically back to Ohio.

"So what do we do, Major?" Andrew turned and saw that Lieutenant Robert Frye and some of the other men had come up behind him. Frye was part of the little team that had been given to him for this mission. It included an ordnance sergeant named McGill and twenty additional enlisted men. They had easily caught up with the tank convoy and had been accompanying it ever since.

So what *were* they going to do? Good question. The information he had was that the expedition assembling at Santa Fe had been put under the command of General Samuel S. Sumner. Sumner had a reputation as a fire-eater and he doubted that he'd delay his advance to wait for the steam tanks. Andrew had been given two missions: observe and report on how the steam tanks performed and also try to salvage any Martian devices that might fall into their hands during the campaign. Clearly, the second part was more important and he had to be there, with Sumner's force, to do that.

"Sir?" persisted Frye.

Okay, you're a major now! Time to make some decisions, kid!

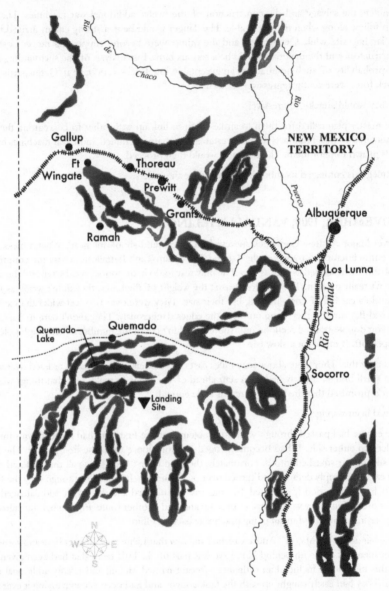

"Lieutenant, I am detaching you and two enlisted men to stay with the tanks. You will accompany them wherever they go, making a complete record of any and all problems you observe. Clear?"

"Yes, sir, but…"

"I will take Sergeant McGill and the rest of the men ahead to join General Sumner's force. We will rendezvous there when you arrive with the tanks. Understood?"

"Y-yes, sir." Frye didn't look too happy with his orders, but that was just too damn bad.

"Good. Sergeant McGill, round up the men. We're moving out."

* * * * *

DECEMBER, 1908, QUEMADO LAKE, NEW MEXICO TERRITORY

The dogs woke her up.

A half dozen of them were barking madly in the distance and Rebecca jerked awake in her bed. She pushed the curtains on the window aside and looked out. It must be nearly dawn, she thought blearily. The horizon was all streaked with red. *Red? But my window looks south! Not east!*

That thought had just penetrated when there was a pounding on her door. Her father shouted through it: "Becca! Get up! Get dressed!" She fell out of her bed and started fumbling for her clothes in the red-tinted light coming through the window. Underthings, shirt, jeans, boots; she pulled on her heavy leather coat and grabbed a hat and then went out the door. Her mother and grandmother were already up with a few lighted lanterns. They were gathering piles of things and setting them on the table. Her father dashed past and out the door with a rifle in his hand. "Get the buckboard loaded! I'll be back!"

"Becca!" cried her mother. "Get the horse for the buckboard!"

Fully awake now, she sprinted for the stables. The dogs were still barking and there were people shouting and the growing sound of frightened cattle and horses. There was a smell of smoke in the air and she realized the red glow was from a fire—a big one. She threw open the doors and grabbed the first horse she came to, an even-tempered roan named Sandy. She led it back to where the women were throwing things into the buckboard. In the distance she heard a rifle shot and then a bunch more. Sandy's even temper disappeared abruptly and it took all three of the women to get her harnessed up. As soon as they were finished, she ran back to the stables.

"Becca! Come back!" screamed her mother.

"I need to get Ninny!" She dashed inside and opened all the stalls she came to until she found Ninny. Fortunately, the saddle and blanket were right there and she threw them up on the horse in one motion. Loud rumbles were coming from outside, followed by shouts that now sounded like screams. She hurried. Ninny was snorting in alarm and trying to follow the other horses out of the stable, but Rebecca kept him under control and got the saddle and tack into place and then led him out.

The world was on fire.

The trees on the hill across the lake were burning, the flames reflecting off the water. As she watched in horror, the Jensen place exploded, bits of the house tumbling across the dark sky, leaving fiery tracks. Closer at hand, the roof of the long shed where the hands lived was blazing. Small, dark shapes fled in all directions. The pasture itself seemed to be ablaze. Smoke stung her eyes and her lungs as a terrible roaring filled her ears.

And in the midst of the fire, tall dark shapes were moving. Nightmare shapes; half ogre and half spider. They strode on long, thin legs with a strange but rapid gait. There was one down the lake by the Jensens', two more out in the pasture, and maybe another one on the hill. Flames erupted wherever they went.

Someone, one of the hands, she thought, galloped past, screaming something at the top of his lungs. Horses and cattle, neighing and bellowing, thundered along after him. But where was her father? He'd gone out with his gun, those shots…where was he?

"Rebecca!"

A shrill cry pierced the other noise and she saw her mother standing in the buckboard, waving frantically at her. Shaking off her paralysis, she leaped into the saddle and urged Ninny forward. But the horse only went a few paces before it stopped and reared. Another shape had appeared; right on the road leading around the lake—right in path of where they wanted to go! The glowing red eye in the center of its head seemed to be staring right at her.

A bright light sprang from one of its arms. The light struck the far end of the house, which erupted in flames. The light swept down the length of her home, turning it into an inferno in seconds. But the light didn't stop there; it swept onward—toward the buckboard and…

"Ma! Grandma!"

For an instant the buckboard, the horse, and the two women were silhouetted in flames; then they melted, dissolved into nothing, and only the fire remained.

Rebecca screamed and screamed.

Suddenly, a hundred cattle were all around her, stampeding in terror. Ninny was pulled along with them—right toward the shape! Rebecca, sobbing hysterically, yanked on the reins desperately, trying to get out of the herd, to turn aside before the shape melted her, too! A cow slammed into Ninny's side and the horse stumbled and nearly fell, but somehow he recovered and they were free of the stampede. The slopes of Escondido Mountain rose up in front of her, seemingly the only thing left in the world that wasn't on fire. It was steep and rough and no place to take a horse, but there was no choice; no choice at all.

"Go on!" she cried, digging her heels into the horse's flanks. Ninny needed no urging; he wanted out as badly as she did. He surged forward and up the slope. Trees closed in around them, blocking out most of the red light from the fire. What did leak through made it harder to see, not easier. Patches of red and inky black shadows, splattered in random shapes like spilled paint, turned the familiar into nightmares. Low branches nearly knocked her out of her saddle more than once, but somehow she hung on and somehow Ninny kept going. The roar of the fire slowly faded, but clouds of choking smoke drifted up the mountainside. The smell… not just burning wood… burning flesh. Rebecca nearly vomited.

Finally, Ninny came to a halt, wheezing and shaking. Rebecca was shaking, too, her throat raw from the smoke and from her screams. She dared to look back. They were in a small clearing and she could look down the mountain. She was amazed at how high they were. The lake and the valley were far below. She couldn't see anything much because of the smoke, but the red glow was still there. Swiveling her head around, she could see the first faint traces of the true dawn off to the southeast.

She was gasping for breath and still crying. Her mother! Grandma! They had… they had burned up! Just like Star! And her father; where was he? Dead like the others? Burned up just like them? The numbing awareness that she was completely alone filled her. Everything, her whole world, was gone.

"Oh, Ninny, what am I going to do?" she moaned. Ninny didn't answer. "We have to get away! Away from here!"

She let Ninny rest for a little while longer and then they headed the only way to go—north.

* * * * *

DECEMBER, 1908, WASHINGTON, D.C.

"Mr. President, the Prime Minister and His Majesty share your concerns, but until the situation becomes clearer, they cannot authorize the release of any forces from the home islands. I'm sorry."

Major General Leonard Wood sat in his usual spot in Roosevelt's office and watched the British ambassador, James Bryce, 1st Viscount Bryce, tell Theodore that he couldn't have what he wanted—something few people dared to do. But not only did Bryce represent the most powerful empire in the world, he was also an old friend of Roosevelt's.

"Damn it, James," said Roosevelt, clearly annoyed, "there hasn't been a single landing in the British Isles, have there?"

"None that we know of, no."

"And with that tiny little postage stamp of an island you live on, it's hard to believe any could have landed without your noticing! Nearly all the scientists agree that there won't be another wave of cylinders for over a year. England is safe and so is all of Europe from what it seems. You, the French, and the Germans have militaries that dwarf all the rest of the world combined; it makes no sense to have them all sitting idle!"

"Theodore," said Bryce, "you have to realize I can't speak for the French or the Germans. And while Britain has a powerful navy, our army is relatively small. And we already have enormous overseas responsibilities. South Africa, India, and Australia are all in danger, to say nothing of Suez! The canal must be kept open."

"Well, what about Canada? You're responsible for that, too, aren't you? Our forces are already stretched too thin. We can't push west and guard our northern flank at the same time. Can't you send some help to Canada?"

"There have been no confirmed landings in Canada," observed Bryce.

"The railroad and telegraph to the Pacific have been cut, haven't they?"

"Could just be the weather. Happens about two winters out of three."

"So you'll do nothing?" demanded Roosevelt, looking angrier than ever. "After all we did to help you after the first invasion?"

Now Bryce looked peeved. "It's a little early to be accusing us of ingratitude, Theodore. England owes a debt to America, what with the help you gave us after the first invasion, and we all realize that. But it makes no sense to send our forces haring off around the globe until we are sure where the main threat lies. We have confirmed sightings in Asia, Africa, the Middle East, and Australia. While you aren't sure if any Martians have even landed in North America yet. The rumors of landings in Central and South America may be nothing more than that: rumors. Perhaps the Martians are ignoring the Western Hemisphere."

"We expect to have confirmation of the New Mexico sightings within a few days," said Wood.

"And you've sent a substantial force to deal with it, I understand."

"Hardly substantial!" snapped the President. "A couple of brigades and some artillery; all we could get there quickly in this weather."

"Should be enough," said Bryce with a wave of his hand. The man was in his seventies with thick white hair and a patriarchal air. He was clearly very fond of Roosevelt and respected him, but they were from different generations. "You know, we were horribly unprepared for the first invasion, but in spite of that, we did manage to destroy five of their damned machines before they succumbed to the microbes. Five out of thirty. Our generals have determined that given another month we probably would have gotten them all, germs or no germs. Your forces are vastly better prepared, Theodore, they'll do fine." He rose from his chair. "I have to go. But don't worry, once we have a better picture of what's happening, His Majesty's Government will send whatever aid we can." They shook hands and Bryce left.

"Well, that was disappointing," said Roosevelt.

"But not really unexpected," replied Wood. "And he does have a point: until we know where they really are and what they're threatening, it's risky to deploy forces."

"Yes, yes, I know, and I shouldn't have expected too much. And it's true the British Army isn't much bigger than our own—if you discount their colonial troops. The ones we really need to help are the French and Germans!"

"Have you talked to their ambassadors?"

"Root did. And they were the same charming fellows they always are. They did offer to help, but I don't know if we can trust them."

"The Caribbean?"

"Yes, and Mexico, damn them. Jusserand says that France might be willing to send an expedition to Mexico to 'shore up our southern flank'. Von Bernstorff was practically drooling over the prospect of sending troops to Venezuela. We almost went to war with the Germans in '02 over Venezuela! And now they want us to invite them back!"

"We may have to take them up on it, Theodore. I can't see us having the resources to send armies to South America. Not for a long time, anyway. There might be a few hard years coming up for the Monroe Doctrine." Wood stopped and then laughed. "Ha! I hadn't thought of that: the Martians are *clearly* in violation of the Monroe Doctrine!"

Roosevelt laughed, too. "Yes! The rascals are in *real* trouble now!" The President quickly became serious again. "French and German help would be wonderful, but I wish we could get them to commit their strength somewhere else."

"Like where?"

"Oh, I don't know, Africa, the Middle East; somewhere that would free up British resources. I'd feel a lot better about the British coming west than them."

"Ah, so you'd rather they threaten *British* interests?"

"Of course." Roosevelt smiled. "But as for us sending forces south, I'm afraid that we will have to send some. There is one absolutely vital spot that we must hold on to down there."

"Panama?"

"Yes. If the Martians are landing in our heartland, we have to face the prospect that they could cut the east-west rail lines. If that happens, we must have the canal."

"Theodore, it's not finished yet. It's got what? Another five years by the schedule?"

"We are going to get it done in three, Leonard. The war funding bill I've sent to Congress doubles expenditures on the canal. It is a vital war resource. And we must protect the site in the meantime. I'm ordering the Navy to send its biggest ships—the ones that will be of no use on the rivers— down there. Once we have ships on both sides, their guns can control practically the entire length. We'll be sending more troops, as well. And guns. We'll fortify the whole region."

Wood raised his eyebrows. "Will Congress approve something that ambitious? They're still balking at any sort of conscription act. I mean, there hasn't been a shot fired yet."

Roosevelt walked over to one of the huge maps that covered one wall of his office. He put his finger on a part of New Mexico.

"The shooting is going to start very soon."

* * * * *

DECEMBER, 1908, SAN LORENZO, NEW MEXICO TERRITORY

The bugle woke up Sergeant Frank Dolfen. He groaned and painfully crawled out of his tiny dog tent. He'd pitched it on the lee side of the old mission where they'd halted the day before, so he'd had some protection from the wind, but he was still thoroughly chilled. He stood up, shivering, and stamped his feet and flapped his arms to try and warm up. It didn't work. He shuffled over to one of the fires and tried to absorb some of the heat. That didn't work, either. Damn, it was cold! There was frost on the ground and it covered the tents. More men began clustering around the fires and they scrounged for firewood to build them up higher. Coffee was soon boiling and

66

Dolfen got his tin cup and filled it with the scalding black liquid. Ah! Now *that* helped a bit! The warmth travelled out from his belly and he stopped shivering. He let the men warm up and then had them fall in for morning roll call. With numb fingers he filled in the roster book with a pencil. He reported the results to the orderly sergeant, who would fill out the morning report for the troop and give it to the adjutant. It was a routine they'd all done thousands of times before and it didn't change even when hunting Martians.

They'd been moving too fast for cook wagons to follow, so they were left to their own devices for cooking meals. Hard tack and some bacon had to do for breakfast. When he'd first joined the army, the veterans joked that the cracker-like hard tack was left-over from the Civil War. Sometimes Dolfen thought that was still the case. A man could break a tooth on some of that stuff. They had some of the new canned rations, but they usually saved those for supper. They were a little better, but not much.

He had just finished a visit to the hastily dug sinks when the bugler sounded Sergeants Call, and he hurried over to the squadron command tent. Captain Bonilla was there with all the 1st Squadron's officers and he led the whole lot of them to the regimental headquarters where all the officers and sergeants of the 2nd Squadron were assembling, too. The colonel had them gather around so they could all hear. "Morning gentlemen."

"Morning, sir!"

"All right, the easy part is over. From this point, heading south, we will be entering the area where the experts think the Martians may have landed. We are going to have to spread out to cover the widest front that we can manage. So, starting today, the 1st Squadron will deploy to the east, and the 2nd Squadron to the west. I want about a mile between each squad, so the squads near the end of the line will have the most riding to do. Each morning we will stretch out the line and each afternoon we will pull it back in again. Each troop will form its own camp. With the extension and contractions, we'll probably only advance about fifteen miles a day. Regimental headquarters will be in the center and I'll expect to receive reports from each troop each day. Understood?" Everyone made affirmative noises.

"We'll continue in this fashion until we hit the road that runs from Socorro through Quemado. South of there, the country becomes a lot rougher and we'll probably have to break up into separate columns. We'll address that when we get there. Questions?"

"What do we do if we spot any of these critters, sir?" The question came from a lieutenant in 2nd Squadron. Dolfen didn't know him, but he'd been wondering the same thing.

"Your primary duty is to get word back," answered O'Dell. "We are here to scout, people. Find the Martians and report their position back to higher headquarters. Each squad will have their best rider and fastest horse detailed as a courier. You spot something, get the courier off immediately, and then continue to watch whatever you've found. We're not here to fight them unless we can do so at a clear advantage. There's a big force assembling at Albuquerque. We find them, they kill them. Clear?"

"Yes, sir!"

The colonel turned things over to the adjutant and the quartermaster who gave out the details for the movement and the supplies. They had a substantial pack train carrying ammunition, food, and fodder for the horses. A winter expedition like this made feeding the horses a real challenge. The pack animals would be split into three groups, one for each squadron and a reserve with the headquarters.

Once all the details had been worked out, the officers and sergeants returned to their commands. It was time to get moving. The buglers sounded 'boots and saddles' and the men quickly broke camp and got their gear packed. Dolfen grimaced to find that the canvas of his tent was still stiff and frozen. He folded it up as best he could and strapped it onto his horse with the rest of his kit. The sun was well up by the time they were all mounted and ready to move. The bugles sounded and they moved out, leaving the crumbling mission of San Lorenzo behind them.

1st Squadron's orders were to stretch a line to the east, but for this first day, they couldn't stretch very far. They were still hard up against Oso Ridge. It would be a day or two before they left that behind. So they had an easy day of it. The poor sods in 2nd Squadron had open country all the way to Arizona, so they would have a much harder time. Captain Bonilla had put A Troop on the right of the squadron's line so Dolfen's squad was fairly close to the center of the whole regiment. From time to time during the day, he could spot the headquarters group off to the west. But that was all he spotted and no one else found anything, either. The only significant occurrence was that the wind shifted around to the southwest, bringing a much welcome improvement in the weather. It wasn't warm, but it was a lot warmer than it had been. He slept much better that night.

The next day was much like the previous one. Oso Ridge bent away to the east and the squadron's line stretched out to follow it. But around midday, they began to encounter small groups of Indians heading north. There were never more than a dozen in any band, mostly Navaho, but there were a few Pueblos, too. They were family groups, usually on foot, carrying bundles of possessions. When asked why they were moving, they said there was trouble to the south. What sort of trouble? Bad trouble. But when pressed, no one seemed to know what sort of trouble. None of them had actually seen anything themselves, they'd just heard about the trouble, and the word was that it was time to move. Each encounter was reported to headquarters. They'd already gotten a dozen or more similar reports. Trouble to the south, but nothing specific.

"So what do you think, Sarge?" asked Kuminski that night as they sat around the fire. One of the men had a bottle and Dolfen gratefully took a pull on it. He had one bottle, himself, stashed with his things, but he was rationing it carefully. He knew where he could get more if he needed it, but he didn't drink so much when they were on patrol.

"About what?" he replied, just to annoy Kuminski.

"About what's going on! The Indians on the run! They gotta know something! Think it's the Martians?"

"How t'hell should I know? Damn Indians are always gettin' spooked by somethin'. Don't mean nothin'."

"Come on! You don't really believe that, do ya? They ain't gonna pull up stakes in the middle of winter over nothing!"

Dolfen glared at the corporal, but he knew that he was right. Whatever it was, it had to be serious. And what else could it be? Martians! It didn't seem possible. What would they be doing in New Mexico? It made no sense. The territory had no big cities, no industry, not all that many people, actually. Why come here?

"So what are we gonna do when we find 'em?" persisted Kuminski.

"We're gonna do exactly what we've been ordered to do: report in and then watch 'em. Now hand me that bottle!"

The next day was still fairly mild, but there were clouds building. It would probably rain that night or tomorrow. Dolfen made sure he had his gum blanket where he could get to it. The squadron spread out to its maximum extent with the extreme left on the edge of what the map said were ancient lava flows from some volcano. The squads were now barely in sight of each other. The ground they passed over was fairly flat, although there were numerous bits of rough terrain that had to be avoided or negotiated. The grass, which could be quite luxuriant in summer, was brown and shriveled in the cold. Clumps of leafless trees grew here and there. Tomorrow would bring them to the town of Quemado and the east-west road. Their ride was uneventful, although about noon they realized that they had seen no more parties of Indians. Dolfen wasn't sure if that was good or bad. But then an hour later, they saw a smudge of black smoke on the horizon to the southwest. That ought to be the direction of Quemado… He didn't bother to send a messenger with that information, because everyone else would have to be blind not to see it.

The men had been relaxed, but now everyone was much more serious, much more alert. Dolfen pulled out his Krag and checked the magazine, even though he knew full well it was loaded. Another hour and smoke could no longer be seen against the dark clouds that had been piling up to the south all day. He checked the time and saw that they needed to start pulling in the line. He gave the order and they began sidling to the left to close on the squadron headquarters.

"Hey Sarge!" shouted Private Urbaniak. "There's a rider over there!" He looked and saw that indeed, someone on a horse was about a mile away to the south. He squinted, but he couldn't tell who or what it was. Whoever it was, didn't seem to be in any hurry, though.

"All right, let's go find out who they are," he said. "Follow me." He nudged his horse into a brisk trot and headed for the rider. They closed the distance quickly, but the rider seemed oblivious to their approach. He was slumped over in his saddle, leaning against the neck of his horse. And the horse could barely hold its head up. As he got closer, Dolfen could see that the poor beast had been ridden to exhaustion and was just plodding along, one hoof in front of the other.

"Hey there!" he cried as they got close. He didn't want to startle them because he'd spotted the butt of a rifle in a saddle holster. No telling how they might react. But the rider—it looked to just be a kid from the size—didn't react at all. He reined in alongside and at that point realized…

"Hey! It's a girl!" cried Urbaniak. And indeed it was. A teenage girl with dirty blonde hair falling out from under a floppy hat. She was wearing jeans and a heavy leather coat. Aside from the rifle, there was nothing else attached to her saddle. No blankets, food, or water.

"Miss? Miss?" said Dolfen. Her horse had come to a stop and stood there quivering and snuffling. "Miss? Are you all right?"

The girl finally raised her head. Strange, glassy, blue eyes met his and then she closed them again and started to fall off her horse. Dolfen lunged out and managed to grab her coat, preventing her from hitting the ground. He slid out of his saddle and gently lowered her down.

"Get me a canteen!" he snapped. His troopers clustered around and someone offered a canteen. He took it and poured a few drops on the girl's mouth. From the look of her dry and cracked lips, she hadn't had any water in a while. Her mouth moved and she swallowed some of the water, before coughing and drinking a little more. Her eyes fluttered open and stared at him.

"Who…? Who…?" she said in a raspy voice.

"Sergeant Frank Dolfen, 5th Cavalry, miss. What's your name?"

"Becca… Rebecca Harding."

"What are you doing out here, Becca? Where you from?"

"Quemado Lake…"

"Quemado? The town up ahead?"

"N-not the town, the lake…'bout ten miles farther south…" The girl started turning her head, looking around, eyes getting wider, wilder.

"How'd you get way out here? What happened?"

She suddenly grabbed him by the arm hard enough to hurt. "G-giants! Metal giants! Fire! Oh, God, they burned everything!" Her eyes darted around, wide with terror.

"What? You mean the Martians?"

"They burned *everything!*" she shrieked, thrashing her legs. "Everything! My Ma and Grandma and the house! Everything!" She made one lunge to break free of him and then collapsed back, crying convulsively.

"Jesus Christ," muttered Urbaniak.

"Miss? Becca?" said Dolfen, but the girl just kept crying. *Hell.*

"All right, Cordwainer!" he snarled, looking to their designated messenger. "Get to the colonel! Tell him we've found someone who's seen the Martians! We're taking her to the squadron headquarters. Have them send the surgeon; she's in a bad way. Move it, man!"

"Right, Sarge!" Cordwainer leapt back onto his horse and was gone in an instant.

"We've got to get her to the camp site. She needs food and water and warmth. Here, take her and pass her up to me." He handed the girl off to two of the men and then climbed on his own horse. They lifted her up and he cradled her in front of him as best he could. "All right, let's go."

They started moving and suddenly the girl cried: "Ninny!"

"It's all right, miss, I'll take it as easy as I can." *I know you're hurting, but no need to call me names!*

"Ninny! M'horse!" she flung out one of her hands, pointing toward her horse.

"Oh! Jones! Bring the horse!"

"Right, Sarge, but he ain't gonna be able to keep up."

"I know; catch up to us when you can."

It was about four miles to where the squadron HQ would be camping and it took about an hour to get there. The girl curled up in front of him and just shivered. He tried to talk to her, but she either didn't respond at all or her replies were gibberish. When they got close, he sent another man on ahead to warn command what was coming and to have food and a bedroll ready.

By the time they arrived, quite a crowd had gathered. Captain Bonilla tried to take the girl from Dolfen, but she clutched at his coat so tightly that he was obliged to dismount, still carrying her, and set her down on some blankets set inside the Captain's small tent (which was still much larger than a soldier's dog tent). They had used some of the fodder they'd brought along for the horses to provide some padding and a fire had been built just outside. They propped her head up with some more blankets and someone had provided tea, so she didn't have to endure army coffee. Captain Bonilla contributed some of his own rations, so before long they could offer her soup. This, along with the tea, she sipped tentatively at first, but then wolfed down like she was starving—which she probably was. Dolfen tried to slip off during all of this, but she made such a fuss, he was obliged to stay.

"Seems she trusts you, Sergeant," said Bonilla.

"First friendly face she's seen in a while, I guess, sir. Just luck of the draw."

"And she claims to have seen the Martians?"

"Metal giants, she said, sir. Said they were burning up everything."

"Their heat rays," said the captain, nodding. "Just like in England."

"I think they destroyed her farm, sir. I... she saw her mother and grandma killed, I think."

"Damn. Well, people from headquarters will be here soon and I'm sure they'll have a thousand questions. No point in us pestering her now and then having to do it all over again when they get here. You stay with her since she trusts you. Try and get her settled down."

"Yes, sir."

Dolfen did what he was told and made sure the girl had as much food and drink as she wanted. She did seem to be recovering, and the arrival of trooper Jones with her horse did much to revive her spirits. He had Jones rub the critter down, then had it fed and watered where she could see it through the open tent flaps. Mindful of what Bonilla had said, he made no more attempts to ask her what had happened. Overall, the girl didn't seem to be in too bad shape. She was actually quite pretty, with a pleasant face, dusted with freckles. But there were dark circles under her eyes. She didn't have any obvious injuries, although for some reason the hair on the back of her head was only a couple of inches long, while the rest of it was long enough to braid. But she clearly was in need of food and drink and some rest. They should let the kid rest.

But it wasn't long before a party arrived from headquarters, led by Colonel O'Dell, himself. Bonilla explained the situation and the colonel came and sat down just inside the tent, while several other officers, including some of the staff officers from Washington, clustered around just outside. The surgeon came in and did a brief examination and confirmed that everything that needed to be done was already being done. Dolfen was obliged to stay.

"Good evening, Miss Harding, I'm Colonel Henry O'Dell," said the colonel after the surgeon withdrew, as though he was simply passing the time of day. "I'm terribly sorry to inconvenience you, but I was wondering if you'd be willing to have a few words with me?" Dolfen was impressed with the colonel's wits. Yes, this was the right tack to take. No intense, 'you must tell me this now!' nonsense. Slow and easy.

"O-okay," said the girl warily.

"Can I call you Becca?"

"Okay."

"Good. You told the sergeant, here, that you come from a place near Quemado Lake?"

"Yes. Our ranch." The girl's eyes grew wide. She knew what was coming.

"And why are you all the way out here?" She didn't answer. "Were you running away from something?" She dipped her head ever so slightly in a tiny nod. For some reason, Dolfen found himself getting angry. *Leave the kid alone!* But that was crazy; they needed to know what she knew!

"Becca, the Army is here now and you are safe. We will protect you. You told the sergeant you saw metal giants. Did you see metal giants?"

"Y-yes."

"Where?"

"T-the first time was down by the San Augustin Plains. I saw one there... it took Pepe." The colonel looked at Dolfen and mouthed: *who's Pepe?* Dolfen shrugged and shook his head.

"The first time? When was this?"

"A couple of months ago... September." She struggled upright. "We saw the shooting stars! I tried to tell people! But no one believed me! My Ma wouldn't believe me! It took Pepe and they wouldn't believe me!"

"Easy! Easy, Becca! It's all right, it's all right." He made soothing gestures with his hands, but he didn't touch her.

"Martians were sighted two and half *months* ago and this is the first we hear of it?" exclaimed one of the staff officers. O'Dell angrily waved at him to shut up. The girl was sniffling and huddling down in her blankets.

"It's all right, Becca. No one's angry at you. But September, you haven't been running since September, have you?"

71

"N-no. I went home and told everyone what happened. But my Ma wouldn't believe me. My Pa and my Grandma did—a little. Pa told the sheriff. He said the sheriff wired for help."

"Yes, he did. That's' why we're here, Becca," said O'Dell, smiling. "You did just fine. But did you see the metal giants again?"

She nodded her head. "A few days ago. They came to the ranch. Everything... everything was burning."

"How many of them were there?"

"I don't know... four or five. Everything was burning."

"But you got away?"

"Ninny and I, we went up the mountain and they didn't follow."

"Ninny's her horse," supplied Dolfen at the colonel's puzzled look.

"Where did you go then?"

"It... it took most of the next day to get across the mountain. Then I tried t'go to Quemado, but... but it was all on fire an' there were more of the giants there." She paused and sobbed for a moment. "All the houses, everything. All I could think t'do was head east, to Socorro, but there were more of them that way. They're so tall you can see 'em a long way off. The only way left was t'go was north. So I rode... we rode... I don't know. We rode and rode and then... then we were here."

O'Dell watched her for a while and gently patted her knee. "Thank you, Becca. You rest. You're safe now." He got up and left the tent. But he started talking with the other officers and Dolfen—and the girl—could hear them plainly.

"Well, there isn't any doubt, is there? They're here, and we're too late to catch them before they could build their machines."

"Yes, sir. We need to get word back right away."

"Yes, you take a party and get moving immediately; don't wait for dawn, ride at once."

"Yes, sir."

"The rest of us will continue on in the morning to make contact. We need to know how many of these things there are and where they are going. Alert your men."

The officers dispersed to their duties, but Bonilla returned in a moment and stuck his head in the tent. "Sergeant, looks like you've got a new assignment." He nodded at the girl. "Watch over her. She trusts you. In the morning you and your squad will escort her back to Fort Wingate."

"What? But sir!"

"No arguments, Frank! You found her, you take care of her."

"Yes sir," he sighed. *Great, just great!*

He set up his dog tent outside the captain's tent and then he had the men build a little 'outhouse' for the girl's use with a couple of blankets on sticks for privacy. She managed to use it and then came back to her blankets and was asleep in moments. After that, he saw to his own supper and that of his men. It was fully dark by then and stepping away from the light of the campfires, he looked south. There were a number of red glows in that direction, reflecting off the low clouds. It wasn't long before a cold rain started falling and the night became very dark. He retreated to his own tent and wrapped himself in his wool blanket with the gum blanket around that. He should have fallen asleep immediately, but he lay awake for a while listening to the rain on the canvas. He thought he heard a moan or two from the girl. Eventually he slept.

It was still raining the next morning and Dolfen was soaked nearly through. He roused his men and spoke through the canvas of the girl's tent. "Miss? Miss Becca? Are you awake?"

After a few moans and groans, she answered: "Uh, yeah, I'm awake… what's happening?"

"We'll be moving soon, miss. We have some breakfast for you."

"All right, I'll be out in a few minutes."

"It's raining pretty hard. Let me know when you're ready and I can hand your breakfast in to you."

"Thank you."

Several minutes passed and then when she said she was ready, he handed a tin plate and cup full of tea in to her. The girl seemed to be recovering quickly from her ordeal. At least she seemed able to function. Hopefully she'd be able to ride on her own when they moved out. He ate his own breakfast and saw about getting the horses saddled. They had a spare horse ready for the girl, transferring her own saddle to it, and a pack horse to carry the supplies they'd need to get back to Wingate. They also had her own horse ready to lead along—he knew she'd make trouble if they tried to leave it behind. He wasn't sure if it would make it. Dolfen was still angry at being made nursemaid to the kid, but he supposed someone had to do it. She couldn't go along to hunt Martians and they couldn't just turn her loose out here. Still, he wished he would be going with his troop. He looked to the south, but in spite of being well after dawn, the thick clouds and heavy rain made it impossible to see more than half a mile or so.

Finally the girl emerged from the tent and he offered her a rain poncho to go over her coat. Her wide-brimmed hat would have to do to keep the rain off her face. "Where are we going?" she asked.

"I've got orders to take you back to Fort Wingate, miss. That's up north a few days ride and…"

Two faint gunshots interrupted him and he whipped his head around to look south, but he couldn't see anything. Several more shots came and then a bugle, sounding recall.

"Sounds like it's from the picket line, Sarge," said Urbaniak.

A moment later the bugler in the camp sounded assembly and the men began scrambling for their horses. Dolfen saw Captain Bonilla and ran toward him.

"Sir!"

"Sergeant," snapped his captain. "You will carry out your orders and get that girl out of here! Now move it, soldier!"

Dolfen halted in his tracks and said: "Yes, sir."

More shots were coming and then a new sound: a strange buzzing, like an angry bee. He looked south and there was a red flare of light, glimmering through rain and mist. "Shit!" he hissed. "They're coming!" He ran back to his squad. "Get mounted! Miss Becca! Get on your horse!" The girl looked around in confusion, so Dolfen seized her and lifted her bodily onto the animal. He swung up onto his own mount.

"Hell's Bells! Look at that!" cried one of his men.

Emerging from the mist, maybe a half mile away was a tall, dark shape. A bulbous head sat atop a small body from which three long legs descended. Several arms waved about it. A single red eye glowed faintly in the center of the head. As Dolfen looked on in amazement, a beam of light sprang out from one of the arms. A blast of flame erupted from the ground and a cloud of steam nearly obscured the strange machine for a moment.

They didn't wait for us to go find them—they came to find us!

73

"There's another one!"

"And another off to the west!"

Two more had appeared and they were all coming on—fast! They moved with an awkward gait, unlike anything Dolfen had ever seen from man or beast, but somehow the long legs were eating up the distance very rapidly.

"They're coming," whimpered the girl.

"Sergeant Dolfen! Get out of here! *Now!*" Captain Bonilla was screaming at him as the squadron formed up.

"Sarge! We gotta move!" cried Private Urbaniak.

Muttering a curse, he turned his horse and spurred it into a gallop. He looked behind to make sure the others were with him. The girl was right there, riding, like she was born in the saddle. A flurry of rifle fire erupted from behind him and he heard the angry bee again. More shooting and then, incredibly, a bugle sounding the charge.

"Damn fools!" cried Private Jones. "They were just supposed to watch 'em!"

"They're buying time for us! Keep going!"

They thundered on for a couple of miles, the driving rain lashing them in the face, and then halted on a small hill. Dolfen looked back. There were three of the machines where they'd been camped. They were striding about, with their heat rays lashing out now and then. Flames leapt up from the remains of the camp.

"Look! Some of the boys are coming back... No! The bastards have seen them! They're chasing... Oh God!" The figures were just specks in the distance, but after the heat rays passed over them, there was nothing left to see at all. Dolfen clutched the reins of his horse, his lips drawn back in a snarl. Those were his comrades! And he was abandoning them! It took every ounce of willpower to keep from riding back.

"Bastards! Oh, the stinkin' bastards!" The boys were swearing. The girl covered her eyes with her hand and looked away.

The Martians continued to slaughter the 5th Cavalry, but they were also moving steadily northward.

Sergeant Dolfen looked for one moment longer and then turned his horse.

"Come on, we have to keep moving."

* * * * *

CYCLE 597,843.3, NORTH OF LANDING SITE 32

Qetjnegartis swung the heat ray in an arc and obliterated four more of the prey. It felt a distinct sense of satisfaction. This latest group clearly consisted of warriors of some sort. The earlier groups had made no attempt to fight and tried to flee as soon as they sighted the war machines. This group had been different. They had held their ground and even advanced briefly, firing their crude chemical projectile weapons.

Of course they had died the same as the others, and that was a good thing. Reports from the first expedition indicated that once the prey-warriors had been defeated several times, the others tended to break up and flee like the non-warriors, and resistance would crumble. This group had probably only been a scouting party, so its destruction would have little effect. But it was a start. The last of the enemy within range had been destroyed and it was time to move on. These prey-creatures had come from the north. Perhaps there were more in that direction.

Qetjnegartis gave the orders and they moved forward.

CHAPTER FIVE

DECEMBER, 1908, ALBUQUERQUE, NEW MEXICO TERRITORY

Dear Victoria,

Well, we have finally arrived in Albuquerque. But without the tanks. As near as I can tell, they are back near St. Louis. Albuquerque is not what I expected. I suppose I was expecting something out of a dime novel western, a place overrun with cowboys and saloons with swinging doors. That sort of thing. But honestly, it's like a lot of towns back east. Nice houses, hotels, a city hall, library, there's even a small college up on a hill. The bigger places have electricity and running water. There's even an electric street car system.

The hotels are all packed due to the influx of troops here. The higher ranking officers have grabbed all the best places, but I was able to find a room in a small boarding house near the college that isn't too bad. I use my room here as my office as I have nowhere else to work. My men are lucky in that they are staying in a warehouse near the rail yard. Nearly all the other troops are in tents outside the town since there are nearly as many of them here as the usual inhabitants. The weather has been cold and wet, so I don't envy them. Trains are arriving every day with more troops and artillery and supplies. No idea when we will be moving.

I miss you very much, Vickie, and I hope I'll be able to see you again soon. Please pass on my fond regards to your mother and father.

Most Sincerely,
Andrew

Brevet Major Andrew Comstock carefully folded the letter, put it into an envelope, which he addressed and sealed. Fortunately, by sending it through Colonel Hawthorne, he could put it in the military mail pouch and be sure it would get there quickly. He wasn't sure that sending love letters to a girl by way of her father was the best idea, but he trusted that Hawthorne would not stoop to reading them. Sadly, the mail coming the other direction wasn't finding him nearly as fast. He supposed that was to be expected; Washington stayed in one spot, while he was constantly on the move. Only one letter from Victoria had caught up to him so far. He took it out and read for about the thirtieth time, sighed, and then put it away. He really did miss her. When he got back from this trip, perhaps it would be time to ask her.

But, he had no idea when he'd be getting back. Despite the build-up of troops in Albuquerque, there was no sign that they would soon be moving anywhere. General Sumner was having a meeting later in the day to discuss the situation. As the Ordnance Department's official representative, Andrew would be allowed to attend. But that wasn't until the afternoon and he had a lot of work to do before then.

Or rather, he had a lot of work to try to do before then. He had rather abruptly discovered the other side of that shiny coin that had major's oak leaves on the front side: He had a job to do and he had to do it himself. He had a party of men with orders to accompany the army to observe the Martian equipment and try to secure samples of it. How, exactly, was he supposed to do that? Well, first, they needed transport. They had taken the train to get to Albuquerque, and presumably they could take the train a bit further, but what happened when the army left the railroad behind? They'd need horses. Okay, where to get horses? The army was buying up every horse it could get its hands on locally to provide remounts for the cavalry and draft animals for the quartermaster's supply wagons. Andrew had put in a requisition to General Sumner's logistics officer, but so far he hadn't gotten any horses. And then if he was going to bring back any captured Martian equipment, he was going to need wagons and more horses. Another requisition to the logistics officer. And then he needed men to drive those wagons since none of his ordnance men had any experience as teamsters. And he had to feed his men. And once they left their cozy warehouse they'd need tents and bedrolls and coffee pots and frying pans and canteens and… The list went on and on. The sad fact was that their day-to-day activities in Ordnance hadn't prepared him, or his men, for duty in the field.

If they had been part of one of the combat formations this wouldn't be a problem. They could just put in the normal requests and eventually they would get what they needed. But they weren't. They were an independent formation operating under orders directly from the Ordnance Department. And unfortunately, Andrew Comstock was the Ordnance Department in the territory of New Mexico.

He hadn't counted on that.

Oh, he had copies of his orders and a letter from General Crozier requesting that General Sumner give him his full cooperation, and the general had promised him that he'd get that cooperation, but promises had not conjured up any horses or wagons or canteens. The general and his staff had a huge job getting their force ready to move and they really had no time to spare for some whippersnapper brevet major from Washington! So, after a few days of run-arounds and delays, he'd come to the conclusion that he had two options: he could send telegrams back to Washington asking General Crozier to fix his problems, or, he could fix them himself. The first option would be a lot easier, but he had a sneaking suspicion that option two would be a much better career move.

With a sigh of anticipated frustration, he pushed himself up from the small table in his room that he used as a desk. He looked out the window to confirm it was still raining and took his rain slicker off the hook on the back of the door. A rainstorm had come up from the southwest two days ago and while it had brought a welcome rise in the temperature, it had also turned the unpaved roads to mud. He went down the steps, said goodbye to the woman who ran the boarding house, and proceeded out onto the street. The rain was much lighter than yesterday and the clouds looked to be breaking up. Good.

He made his way down to the warehouse where his men were staying. This was by the railroad tracks, and even this early in the morning the place was bustling. Trains arrived at all hours and had to be unloaded and their cargoes sent off to the right place. Many of the box cars full of supplies were just shunted off to sidings prepared to follow the army when it moved. This particular morning there was a troop train unloading. Hundreds of soldiers were spilling out of the cars and lining up beside them. Sergeants were shouting at them to hurry and officers stood by watching. Andrew asked a captain who they were and he told him they were the 19th infantry, regulars, but Andrew could already tell that just from the professional manner of the troops. "Where you coming from?" he asked.

"Charleston," replied the captain. "We got orders to pull out of there a week ago and have been on these damn trains ever since. Damn shame, Charleston was a nice posting."

"Yeah, a shame the Martians couldn't have landed there and saved you the trip and—Good God, what are *they*?" Andrew had caught sight of a new batch of… well, he supposed they were soldiers, getting off the train. They were wearing uniforms, but unlike any uniform Andrew had seen before. They were basically khaki, like the regulars, but they had red piping on the collars and cuffs, little chainmail epaulets like the British sometimes wore, red leather leggings, and all of it topped off by an Australian-style bush hat with one side pinned up.

The captain turned and saw them and laughed. "Oh, those are the Charleston Fencibles." His smile faded. "One of those damnable volunteer units they authorized. Made up of Charleston's finest young men, you know. They were attached to our regiment so that we could get them trained as soldiers. We tried, but it doesn't seem to be taking. Damn fools want to fight, but aren't the least interested in learning how."

"Well, they better learn fast. They may not have much more time."

"Really? So are there any Martians around here, sir?"

"That's what they say. Haven't seen any myself so far. But good luck—with everything." He left the captain to his duty and pushed through the crowd to the warehouse he wanted. The warehouse was packed with stuff, but they'd found a small attic space that was barely large enough for the men. It was cramped but dry. Sergeant McGill had them all up and ready for him. McGill was a crusty old Scotsman twice his age, but he knew how to get things done. From what some of the other men had told him, McGill had deserted from a British regiment stationed in Canada decades ago, crossed the border, and enlisted in the US Army. It wasn't that uncommon a thing, actually.

"So what's on the agenda today, sir?" asked McGill. He still had a bit of a brogue after all these years, but it was faint.

"Well, Sergeant, I've decided that we'll leave the horses and wagons until last. If we did manage to get them now, we'd just have to take care of them—and guard them—until we were ready to leave. Let's concentrate on getting all the rest of our gear first."

"Yes, sir, although if we got some horses now, we could get some practice ridin'. Some o' these sods have never had their legs over a horse in their lives."

"Have you, Sergeant?" asked Andrew with a grin.

"Oh, a time or two, sir. A bit out o' practice, though, I must admit."

"Well, we'll see what we can do." It was a good point, he realized. Most of the men probably didn't have any riding experience. Andrew, himself, was a competent rider, having had instruction at West Point, but he'd never had to ride anywhere very far. This was going to be a challenge. "Let's go and see what we can find, shall we?"

"Begging your pardon, sir, but it might be wise to leave a few o' the lads here to keep hold of our claim to this place. We all go out an' there might be someone else sleepin' here by the time we get back. There were a couple o'gits snooping around here last night."

"Good point, Sergeant. Leave Gallagher and a couple of others. He's big enough to scare off just about anyone."

So, they set out. Andrew realized it was slightly ridiculous for a major to be scrounging tents and blankets, but the truth was he didn't have a blessed thing to do other than that. If his rank could smooth the path, then it was time well spent. Prior reconnaissance had at least revealed where they needed to go. They found the chief quartermaster's office in one of the other warehouses and then waited and waited to see him. His men waited outside the building. When he and McGill were finally allowed into his office, the man looked extremely harried and though he feigned sympathy, he told them there was simply nothing he could do without a signed requisition allowing the release of the items they wanted. Andrew showed him Crozier's letter and relayed the verbal promise of assistance from General Sumner and his logistics officer, but none made any impression on the quartermaster. Sadly, the man was a lieutenant colonel, so Andrew couldn't even attempt to pull rank.

"Well, I suppose I'll have to go back to Sumner's logistics officer and try to squeeze a signed requisition out of him," sighed Andrew after they were ushered out. "God knows how long that will take. You may as well take the men back to their quarters."

"Wait a minute, sir," said McGill. He gestured to a score of enlisted men working on stacks of paper at desks set up on part of the warehouse floor. "Why don't we have a word with the folks who actually make this all work?"

"What do you mean?"

"Armies run on paper work, sir. And while the brass might think they're runnin' the show, it's really run by these gits who fill out the forms."

"Huh," said Andrew, looking at the pack of scribbling scribes. "What do you suggest?"

"Let's ask 'em." McGill strolled over to an especially busy-looking individual. "'Scuse me, Corporal, we're with General Sumner's staff and we need to requisition some equipment. But we can't remember which form to use for that. Can you help us out a wee bit?"

The man looked up, annoyed at first, but when he spotted Andrew's oak leaves, he suddenly became very cooperative. "Uh, it would be the QM-423 form, sir—uh, Sergeant."

"Excellent! Would you happen to have some of those forms?"

"Uh, I think I can find some…"

"Well, done! Give us a dozen or so!" The man got up from his chair and started rummaging around in a stack of boxes and eventually returned with a fistful of paper. "And once we've filled out the forms, Corporal, how do we actually get the items we need?"

"Uh, well, you can bring them back here and give them to Lieutenant Gilchrist and he'll send it through channels, or if it's an emergency…"

"It is, actually."

"Oh. Well, then, you can go right to the warehouses where the stuff is stored. There'll be someone there you can give the form and get the gear."

Andrew was looking the form over. "Each item needs a requisition code. Where can we find that?"

"Oh, they're all on those lists posted on the wall over there, sir," said the man, pointing. "We use those all the time." Indeed, there were dozens of sheets of paper tacked to the wall. Several of the clerks were referring to them as they watched.

"I see. Well, thank you very much, Corporal. What's your name? I'll be sure to tell the general how helpful you were."

"Wenger, sir! Joshua Wenger! Thank you, sir!"

"Don't mention it. Come on, Sergeant, let's take a look at this." They found a crate that they could use as a desk and puzzled their way through the form. "By the way, Sergeant, that was very smart thinking on your part. Thank you."

"Glad to do it, sir. Once you've been in the Army for a few decades you come to know how things work. Don't worry, sir, you'll get the hang of it."

"Can I assume you've used similar methods in your normal job, Sergeant?" Andrew asked, grinning.

"Oh, maybe a time or two, sir. See? You're catching on already!"

Moving between their impromptu desk and the list of items on the wall, they filled out what they wanted on the first form: *Haversack, M1908, 20 ea. Haversack straps, M1908, 40 ea. Waist Belt M1903, 20 ea.* And so on until they ran out of room. "Uh, oh," said Andrew as they got to the bottom of the form. "What about this authorization signature they want here?"

McGill looked at it for a moment and then took the pen and wrote: *By Order of General Samuel S. Sumner.* "There you go, sir. You just sign your name under this and we're legal."

"Legal?" said Andrew skeptically.

"Certainly. You asked the general for this stuff and he promised that you'd get it, right?"

"Well, yes…"

"So he wanted you to have the stuff, right?"

"I suppose…"

"So there you go, sir! We're just carrying out his orders!"

"If you say so, Sergeant." He took the pen and signed his name. *What am I getting myself into here?*

"Good! One down! Looks like we're gonna have to fill out about ten of these to get everything we need."

Andrew pulled out his pocket watch. "I have to go to a meeting with the general and his staff in less than an hour."

"Well, you go right ahead, sir. I can handle getting the rest of this. Me and the lads will go and collect it. You just sign all these blank forms and I can fill in the rest." With a certain amount of misgiving, Andrew did so and left McGill to his task.

General Sumner had made his headquarters in the largest mansion in the city; its owner had graciously given him the use of the place. Naturally, it wasn't anywhere near the railroad yards, so Andrew had quite a walk to get there. He could have taken the trolley, but the rain had stopped and he felt like walking. The streets were packed with soldiers and this close to the railroad there were plenty of establishments that catered to their needs. He supposed that in normal times they must have catered to the needs of cattlemen and railroad men, but the influx of soldiers was creating boom times in Albuquerque. He'd been told that women of questionable virtue were flocking here from all over the southwest. From what he'd seen, he could believe it.

Eventually, he left most of the crowds behind and reached more respectable neighborhoods. The architecture was a strange mix of Spanish-style adobe-and-tile buildings, with Victorian styles which would not have been out of place in Boston or Washington. Unlike the area near the railroad, the streets here were nearly deserted and he didn't think the poor weather could all be to blame.

There was a considerable crowd around the headquarters, but they were all military, of course. He went in the front door, still a little bit startled that his major's rank entitled him to a present arms from the two sentries. The meeting was held in the large dining room. Even his major's rank wasn't enough to earn him a chair at the table, but he was very used to standing against one of the walls from all his time as a lieutenant back in Washington. Sumner was already there, a distinguished gentleman with a bushy mustache. The hair of the mustache and that on his head was mostly gray, but there were still a few startlingly black strands evident. Sumner was in his mid-sixties. He'd barely been old enough to have served in the Civil War where his father had been a corps commander. Now, a veteran of service on the plains, Cuba and the Philippines, he was just a year short of the mandatory retirement age.

A few last officers scurried in and found places before the meeting began. "Well, gentlemen," said Sumner, "we've finally got some news. A wire came in this morning from Fort Wingate. The 5th Cavalry, moving south from Wingate, encountered a civilian near the town of Quemado who has seen the Martians and fled from them when they attacked her ranch. We have more information that the initial landing site may have been in a desert region about thirty miles to the south of Quemado. In addition, testimony from the civilian and sighting of smoke by the 5th indicate that

Quemado itself has been destroyed." The general's words produced a stir in the room and men began pulling out maps to pinpoint the locations mentioned. Andrew craned his neck to get a look.

"So," continued Sumner, "we have a decision to make, gentlemen. As you can see from the map, we could either move south along the railroad to Socorro and then west overland toward Quemado and the supposed landing site. Or we can take the railroad west to Fort Wingate and then proceed south from there toward Quemado. The overland distance is about the same either way, although there is a better road going west from Socorro. Opinions, gentlemen?"

"Sir," said Sumner's chief of staff, "our orders are to find the Martian landing site and destroy it. Even if the Martians have constructed their machines, the landing site could still be an important objective. The Socorro option brings us closer to the reported landing site. Also, Socorro would provide us with a good base of operations. The town of Gallup near Fort Wingate is little more than a whistle stop."

"But the indications are that the Martians are moving north," said another officer; one of the brigade commanders, Andrew thought. "They've gone almost due north from this San Augustin Plains region over some very rough territory to reach Quemado. If they continue north they'll reach Fort Wingate and cut the railroad to Flagstaff."

"Yes," said Sumner, "the east-west railroad is critical, much more so than the railroad south to El Paso that runs through Socorro. We have to keep that in mind for our future operations."

"But we don't know they'll continue north, sir. They might turn east."

"But they might not…"

The discussion became general with many people expressing opinions or concerns. Andrew wasn't even tempted to venture an opinion—not that he really had one. He didn't care which way they decided to go as long as they managed to bag some Martians. The discussion lasted several hours but in the end it was decided to send another cavalry regiment, the 3rd, south by rail to Socorro and have it push west to make contact with the enemy and also take a look at the suspected landing site. In the meantime, more reports were expected from the 5th Cavalry. The rest of the army would make preparations to move out in whichever direction seemed best. The meeting ended and Andrew walked back to check on how Sergeant McGill and the others were making out.

The clouds were breaking up and the setting sun cast long shadows as the short winter day came to an end. Andrew realized, that it was, in fact, the shortest day of the year. The wind was shifting around to the northwest and it would probably get cold again in the coming days.

He reached the warehouse where his men were staying and was surprised to see several wagons parked outside the door which led to the stairs going up to the attic. He was even more surprised to see his own men swarming over them, hauling away piles of stuff under the direction of Sergeant McGill. When he got closer he saw that the 'stuff' was just the sort of equipment they'd been trying to get!

"Sergeant! What's all this?"

McGill grinned a huge grin. "An early Boxing Day gift, sir."

"You did it!"

"Yes sir! And tomorrow we'll go and get the horses!"

* * * * *

80

DECEMBER, 1908, NEW MEXICO TERRITORY

"They're still following us, Sarge."

Sergeant Dolfen looked back over his shoulder and saw that Private Jones was correct: the Martians were still following them. The ugly shape of one of the war machines could be faintly seen four or five miles behind them. As he watched, it caught the rays of the setting sun and briefly glowed red. There were times when he could spot more of the machines far off to the east and west. They appeared to be spread out in a long skirmish line, sweeping all the country—just like the 5th had done going the other way. The damn things had been following them all day, since the nightmarish slaughter that had taken place that morning.

He had no way to know if it was actually following them or if it was just travelling in the same direction. It didn't really matter because if it caught up with them, he and the others would die just the same. Part of him still couldn't believe that this was happening. The 1st Squadron wiped out! Probably 2nd Squadron, too. The colonel, the captain, Lieutenant Hopkins, and probably Corporal Kuminski, too. His home… his family, reduced to piles of ash. He'd lost comrades before, but never like this. Burned away with no hope of fighting back. Like jack rabbits stalked by a hunter with a shotgun. Some of the rabbits might escape, but they could do nothing to hurt the hunter. And oh, how he wanted to hurt those bastards!

He'd felt rage like this only a few times before. In the Philippines when an insurgent ambush had killed a buddy and then the ambushers had fled before they could be caught and killed. It was like that—only different. This time the killers were right there, in plain sight, but he couldn't strike back. It wasn't right.

"Whadda we gonna do, Sarge?" demanded Jones. "The horses are about finished and those things don't ever seem to get tired! Another hour and they'll have us."

It was true. After the first mad rush to get away, they had proceeded at an easier pace until they realized the Martians were catching up. At a gallop or even a fast canter, they could pull away for a while, but the horses couldn't stand that pace forever. They'd had to slow down, dismount, and walk the horses for a while and the Martians would start to gain on them. Indeed, they would have overtaken them already if it weren't for the fact that the country they were passing through wasn't completely deserted. There were ranches and homesteads scattered about, even a few tiny villages. The Martians would turn aside to destroy them and that allowed them to open up the distance again.

When they came close to such places they would shout warnings for the people to flee. Sometimes they listened. Usually it didn't make any difference. The people would try to load wagons and take their possessions with them, despite the soldiers' warning to run at once. By the time they realized their mistake, it was too late. A handful had taken their warnings to heart and escaped on horseback, swelling Dolfen's party to about twice its original size. Three men, four women, and five children now accompanied them. He wasn't sure he wanted the extra civilians, but there really wasn't much choice. At least their horses were fresher.

But now none of the horses could be pushed much farther. They had already lightened the load as much as they could, tossing away their tents and their sabers and any other thing not absolutely needed, but the horses were still nearly spent. And if the Martians came on, they would be done. He looked ahead. They had covered a lot of ground today, as much as they'd covered in three days going the other way. The mass of Oso Ridge loomed up in front of them, the tallest peaks blazing gold in the last of the sunlight. If they could make it there, maybe they could find some place to hide. There was no place to hide where they were. He wasn't exactly sure where they were. Probably not too far from San Lorenzo where they'd camped… how many days was it ago? It seemed like in some other lifetime now.

"It'll be dark soon," said Jones. "Maybe we can lose them in the dark."

"They… they can see in the dark," gasped the girl, Becca. "They attacked our ranch at night."

"Great," muttered Dolfen.

They splashed through a creek, swollen with the recent rains. It had been nearly dry when they'd crossed it before; now it was halfway up the horses' legs and the banks muddy and treacherous. The horse of one of the civilians nearly fell and the children were shrieking and crying. "Come on! Keep moving!"

"We're not gonna make it, Sarge," said Private Urbaniak in a near-whisper.

"I know. When that thing gets a bit closer, I'm going to veer off and double back and see if I can get it to chase me. When I do, you're in charge. Keep moving and try to find cover. If it catches up, then the only thing left to do is scatter. Maybe some of you will get away."

"Sarge!" priested Urbaniak. "You'll be killed!"

"Yeah? And if we just try to keep running we'll all be killed. Whaddaya want me to do? Order one of the other guys to go back and get himself killed? It's my job."

"Well, don't do anything yet! It's still a good ways back."

"Yeah, yeah." But it was closing fast. And he had no idea what the range on its heat ray was. If he waited too long they could all get fried.

The ridge got closer but at an agonizingly slow pace. The short winter evening closed in around them and all that could be seen of the Martian was the red light in the middle of its head. It was definitely getting brighter as it closed on them. He'd have to make his move pretty soon. *Will it even notice me in the dark? Well, if it doesn't, then maybe they can't see in the dark and we'll all get away.* It was a comforting thought—sort of.

The ground was rising now as they neared the ridge. Just about time…

"Hey! It's stopped!" cried Private Johnson.

Dolfen jerked around to look back. It was nearly dark now and it was hard to see. The waning moon wouldn't be up for hours yet, but there was still some sky glow off in the west. The shape of the Martian machine could be faintly seen, but its glowing eye flickered on and off as if it were turning from side to side. A tiny gleam of reflected light showed that it was stopped by the creek they'd crossed.

"Maybe it's afraid to get its feet wet!" quipped Private Friswell.

"Well, let's not wait for it to start moving again!" snapped Dolfen. "Let's go!"

They urged their exhausted horses onward, down into a little valley at the foot of the ridge, and the Martian was lost to sight. They pressed on for another mile or so, looking back every few seconds, fearful to see the red eye. But it didn't appear, and the ridge was suddenly very close. Now, if they could just find some place to hide…

"There's someone up ahead there, Sarge!" shouted Private Cordwainer, who was in the lead.

For the first time in his Army career, the sudden appearance of strangers in the dark didn't send Dolfen's heart racing or his hand grabbing for a weapon. Whoever they were, they were only people. Only *people*. Dolfen moved forward.

"Indians, Sarge," said Cordwainer. "Pueblos, I think." A dozen dark shapes stood huddled a few yards away.

"Hola!" said Dolfen. He knew a fair amount of Spanish and the Pueblos often knew that language. Dolfen had picked up some Sioux when he was up on the northern plains, but Pueblo had defeated him. At least these weren't Navajo—their language was impossible. He had to repeat the greeting three times before someone answered his greeting—in Spanish.

"Quien estan y donde vamos?" he asked, wanting to know who they were and where they were going.

The reply was hard to understand, but he thought they said they were fleeing the troubles to the south. But as for where they were going, the words didn't mean anything to him.

"Donde?" he demanded, but again the reply meant nothing.

"They… they say they are going to an old… dwelling in the cliffs ahead." Dolfen whipped his head around and was surprised to see that it was Becca Harding who had spoken. She'd scarcely said a word all day.

"You speak their language?"

"A little."

"How far is it? Can we hide there?"

She spoke to the Indians and got a reply. "They say it is two or three miles. And there are places for all to hide."

"Well let's go then! Tell 'em the 'trouble' is right on our heels!" The whole group of them moved off. Dolfen ordered all the riders to dismount and lead their horses since they could move no faster than the foot-bound Indians.

It was fully dark and despite their urgent need to find cover, they could not move very fast. They tripped and stumbled their way forward, following the Pueblos. They had been going on for what seemed hours, but probably wasn't nearly that long when one of the civilians cried: "Look! It's coming!"

Everyone looked back and to their dismay they could see a faint red light in the distance. Not that close, but not nearly far enough. "Keep moving!" snarled Dolfen. "We're almost there!" He hoped he was right.

Another ten minutes and the dark wall of a cliff loomed up in front of them. Their destination? The Indians began talking again. "They say there's a little box canyon over there where we can leave the horses," said Harding. "There's a path leading up the cliff to the refuge right here."

The Indians started up immediately, but the rest had to drag their exhausted mounts into the canyon and make sure they couldn't wander out again. Then it was back to the path leading upward. Dolfen looked south but couldn't spot the Martian. Where was it?

They scrambled up the path as quickly as they could, but it was difficult and treacherous. One wrong step could send a person falling into the blackness. By the time he reached the top he was going on all fours, gasping for breath. The Indians were waiting and half-dragged them into an opening in the rock. Dolfen hung back to make sure everyone was up.

When the last person was inside, he looked back and flung himself flat on the ground. The Martian was there, maybe half a mile away. Dolfen was much higher now and looking down on the machine. Was it still on their trail? He watched, holding his breath, but then slowly let it out again. The Martian was moving, but not toward him. It was hard to tell, but it looked to be going northwest. Yes! Minute by minute it was sliding by him to the west; not getting any closer. Finally, an outthrust portion of the ridge blocked the view and it was gone. He closed his eyes and rested his forehead against the cold rock.

"Sarge? Sarge?" It was Urbaniak. "What's happening?"

"It's gone," he replied getting to his feet. He went through the opening in the rock into pitch blackness. He could hear all the people around him, but couldn't see them. "Okay, I think we're safe. But we can't risk a fire. So everyone settle down and try to get some sleep."

* * * * *

83

CYCLE 597,843.3, NORTH OF LANDING SITE 32

Qetjnegartis was beginning to have doubts about this world. It was… *wet*. There was water everywhere; in the soil, standing in open pools, even falling from the sky! During the destruction of the enemy warriors there was a heavy precipitation which reduced the effective range of the heat rays by nearly half. At longer ranges, the ray merely created clouds of steam.

Of course it was well known from prior observations that the planet had huge amounts of water—three-quarters of the surface was covered by seas, and much of the planet was often obscured by clouds of water vapor. But even so, all the implications of this had not been considered. Precipitation, in particular—the water moved around.

And once the water had fallen, it reduced the soil to a slippery, sticky… muck. Just now Qetjnegartis' machine had become almost completely mired in an especially deep patch of the stuff. It was quickly becoming obvious that there were flaws in the design of the war machines. The bottoms of the lower limbs had narrow cross sections which created a great deal of ground pressure. The limb would simply sink into the water-softened soil. Qetjnegartis' machine had sunk in deeper than the first joint on one leg and it took a great deal of time and effort to extricate itself. For a few moments it thought that it was going to have to call for help from its clanmates. Once free, it had attempted to stay on rocky ground—further slowing its pace.

And the lost time had allowed a band of prey to escape. They were of no consequence in their own right, and it would not waste more time searching, but it was still… irritating.

No matter. There would be more opportunities ahead.

* * * * *

DECEMBER, 1908, NEW MEXICO TERRITORY

Becca Harding opened her eyes and saw the dim shapes of people all around her. The long night had finally come to an end and a grey light was leaking through the opening into the cave. She didn't need her sight to know about all those people. She had heard them snoring and weeping, grunting and groaning all night. And the smell of wet leather, wet wool, and sweat-soaked people filled the air.

Shifting slightly, she found she was leaning against a rock wall, wedged between one of the soldiers and a little Pueblo boy, both still sound asleep. She was so tired she wanted to follow their example, but a growing pressure in her bladder forced her to move. Just trying to stand produced waves of pain from her muscles. The ordeal of the last few days had taken its toll and she hurt from head to toe.

Picking her way over and around the other people in the room—cave?—she made it to the entrance and breathed in a lungful of cold, clean air, bringing her fully awake. She carefully peered out the opening in the rock, fearful of spotting a metal giant waiting for her to reveal herself. But there was a commanding view from the cliff dwelling and the plain below seemed empty of threats.

"Don't worry, miss, they're gone."

Only now did she see the blanket-wrapped figure sitting with his back against the rock and his knees drawn up to his chest. A rifle was leaning next to him. It was the sergeant, the one who had taken care of her. He was staring at her now with red-rimmed eyes, his face gray with fatigue. "Are… are you sure?"

"As sure as I can be from here. Nothing moving down there at all—and those things are hard to miss. But what are you doing up so early? You should sleep."

"I need to… uh… you know…" She felt herself blushing.

"Oh. There's a room, two doors down, with a pit in it. I think that's what it's for. Be careful you don't fall in." He smiled slightly.

"Thank you." She moved down the ledge in the direction he'd indicated. To her left was a frightening drop-off and the ledge was only a few feet wide. She stayed close to the rock wall on her right. She came to one opening in the rock, like a doorway, but she couldn't see anything within. She kept going and found the second door and edged inside. It took a few moments for her eyes to adjust but she eventually found the pit and made use of it. She went back the way she'd come and after a slight hesitation, she sat down next to the Sergeant. Dolfen, his name was Dolfen.

"What are we going to do now?" she asked. "Do you think the… the Martians have gone?"

"I think they all kept moving north," he replied. "They aren't going to waste time looking for a little group like us—I hope."

"North, but didn't you say that's where your fort is?"

"Yeah. I'm a bit worried about that. But we sent riders back there as soon as we found you. They'll be there by now. There's a telegraph and the railroad. They'll have sent for help and maybe it's there now, or on the way."

"So will we be going on; to your fort?"

"Not for a few days. Our horses are shot. We'll have to let them rest for a while. As soon as the others are awake, we'll go down and do what we can for them—and haul our gear up here. We've got enough food on the pack horse to last us all a couple of days. After that we can get moving again."

She stared at the man. He had a strong face, but the skin was tanned and creased like old leather. He'd spent a lot of time outdoors in the sun. "Thank you… thank you for taking care of me, Sergeant."

He looked embarrassed by her thanks. "Don't mention it. M'job."

"And thanks for bringing my horse along. Ninny's… my friend." Dolfen just grunted. "I hope… I hope some… most of the other soldiers got away. They were very brave."

"I'm sure some got away. They're probably out there somewhere, hiding like we are. Rifles just aren't no damn good against those bastards. Beggin' your pardon. Need to bring up some heavier stuff."

"My pa… my pa only had a rifle."

Dolfen didn't say anything, but she could feel him staring at her.

"Maybe… maybe he got away." She choked a little bit and swallowed. "I didn't see… maybe he got away."

"I hope so, miss."

She nodded, but in her heart she knew her father was dead, too. Burned up just like her mother and grandmother. Just like the ranch and all the hands and livestock. Everything. *It's all gone. Everything.* Her whole world. She sniffled, but she clenched her fist and bit on her tongue so she wouldn't cry again. This wasn't the time for it!

"Do… do you have any kin anywhere?" asked Dolfen. "If… when we get you back to the fort, you can send a wire to 'em. Maybe find somewhere we can send you."

"I've got an aunt and uncle in Santa Fe." Her mother's sister and husband; she'd never liked them much.

"Good. You'll be safe there. We can send you on the train."

"Uh huh."

They sat there for a while until the others started getting up. Then she went down the very frightening path—it hadn't seemed nearly so bad coming up in the dark! At the bottom, she looked back up and was amazed at the complex of dwellings built or carved out of the cliff. The place where they had spent the night was on one of three different levels. She could scarcely imagine the amount of work it must have taken.

The horses were all where they'd left them and they spent a good deal of the morning hauling up their gear and caring for the animals. Poor Ninny seemed better than she'd feared, but he could have been better. She was particularly concerned by the lack of forage. There was a trickle of water at the rear of the canyon, but there wasn't nearly enough stuff growing there, in the dead of winter, for all those horses to eat. If they couldn't find something, they were going to die. That thought almost had her crying. Ninny was the only one left; she couldn't stand the thought of losing him, too. She mentioned her concern to Sergeant Dolfen and he agreed that they'd have to search around to find some forage.

But first they had to see to their own forage. They found enough really dry wood to make a fire that wouldn't create much smoke and managed to cook a passable breakfast. Becca discovered that she was ravenous, having eaten nothing since the morning before. But they didn't dare use too much of their food, so she was still hungry afterward.

Then they went back down and scoured the area for fodder. They found enough for the day and laboriously cut it and hauled it back to the canyon. But it had taken a lot of work and tomorrow they'd have to go even farther to find anything.

As the short day drew to a close, they built a fire in a sheltered location, where the light wouldn't show, and had their supper. It was pretty meager, but there was nothing for it. As they sat around the fire, trying to keep warm, one of the soldiers suddenly laughed.

"Hey, everyone! Merry Christmas!"

This brought forth cries of amazement from the other soldiers, but some cries of woe from the little children. Becca had totally lost track of the days, but the others confirmed that it was indeed Christmas Day. Several of the people started praying. Becca tried, but no words came. The only things she wanted were not the sort of things that God miraculously took care of. *He did that sort of stuff in the old days, why doesn't He anymore?* Someone tried to get them singing a hymn, but it fell flat and they gave up. After that, there was nothing left to do but try to sleep.

By some unspoken agreement, all the Indians went off to another room in the complex. The soldiers all stayed in the same one as the previous night and the other civilians picked a third. Becca wasn't sure which group to stay with. One of the women suggested she go with them, and Sergeant Dolfen seemed to encourage that choice, but after hesitating a while, she went with the soldiers, instead. The woman seemed scandalized, but she was a stranger and the soldiers were not anymore.

The weather had been turning cold again all day and the small fire they dared build didn't do much to warm up the cold stone. They piled up some of the gear to block a bit of the air from coming in the doorway, but it was still cold. Becca wrapped herself in a blanket that a soldier provided and fell asleep at once, but woke many times during the night.

The next day was much the same except it was getting colder, the sky was clouded over, and looked and felt like snow was on the way. They found enough forage for the horses again, but if it snowed, things could get very bad. And they only had enough food for themselves for two more days. The other people decided that they would go back to their homes the following day. Sergeant Dolfen argued against that, pointing out that their homes had probably been destroyed by the Martians.

"So what do you suggest?" demanded one of the men angrily. "Stay here until we all starve?"

"While we were out today, I spotted the mission of San Lorenzo off in the distance. It looked like it was still standing. The town of Ramah is just beyond. Tomorrow we can go over there and see what we can find. Even if the Martians have been through there, we might be able to find some food and forage. After that, we can head north to Fort Wingate."

"That's where the Martians went! Are you crazy?"

"That's also where the army is going to be!" said Dolfen. "They're the only ones who can protect you!"

They argued back and forth for a while, but in the end all of the other people decided they would go back to their homes. Only one woman with a little boy decided to go with the soldiers. Becca had less trouble sleeping that night; she was so tired she almost fell asleep during dinner.

Dawn revealed a gloomy sky with light snow falling and the threat of much more. One man changed his mind about going back to his home, but the others quickly saddled their horses and rode off south. Sergeant Dolfen made sure his men were ready almost as quickly.

"Come on! It's at least six miles to Ramah and we need to get there before the storm really hits!"

The days of rest had done the horses quite a bit of good and Becca rode Ninny. The Indians refused to come and she had no idea what they planned to do, but they couldn't waste time arguing. They headed west, eight soldiers and four civilians.

The land seemed sad and empty—and frightening. She told herself that the tall Martian machines would be visible for miles and that they couldn't catch them by surprise, but she wasn't sure if she really believed that. After an hour or so, the snow got heavier and they couldn't see very far at all. Would one of the machines suddenly appear out of the snow, too close to run?

Fortunately, the only things that appeared out of the snow were some stray cattle. The soldiers quickly roped them and towed them along, boasting that they'd have steak that night. At least they'd have food for a while, even if this Ramah place had none at all. Nothing else hindered their march and they arrived at the town by mid-morning. It wasn't much of a town, maybe thirty or forty adobe buildings; not even half the size of Quemado.

The Martians had clearly been through here and fire had swept the settlement. But adobe didn't burn and with all the rain the previous days, things were well-soaked. There had been a lot of destruction, but it wasn't total. The soldiers spread out and searched and even though they didn't find a single person, they did find food and forage. The general store had an underground storage room to keep things cool during the summer months and there were bags of flour and canned goods down there, untouched by the fires. There was also a livery stable with a sodden pile of hay in the back which had only been a little scorched.

The snow was much heavier now, so they quickly got the horses under shelter with plenty of fodder at hand and then did some hasty repairs to the general store which had one wall pretty well blown out, but most of the roof was still intact. A few hours' work had the place reasonably weather-tight and a fire was burning in the iron pot-belly stove. They settled in.

"Well, Sarge, this worked out a lot better than I hoped!" said one of the soldiers, Urbaniak, Becca thought; she was slowly learning all their names.

"Yeah," said Dolfen. "We were lucky. Now we have to stay lucky. Once the snow stops I want lookouts posted where they can see anything approaching. We are gonna pack up all the canned stuff so that we can take it with us. We'll live on fresh beef and any other perishable stuff we find here. But we have to be ready to move at a moment's notice."

"Right, Sarge."

But the snow didn't stop. Not that day, or that night. By the time it finally let up the next day, there was nearly two feet on the ground. The white blanket concealed most of the destruction and the town looked almost normal. Lookouts were posted as Sergeant Dolfen had ordered, but aside from checking on the horses from time to time, everyone stayed inside. At first it was nice to be able to rest or sleep or eat as they pleased after their desperate flight, but by that evening they were all getting a little bored. One of the soldiers had a deck of cards and soon a poker game broke out. Becca watched for a while and when one of the soldiers had to go on lookout duty, she decided she would take his spot. The soldiers seemed surprised, and then amused, and after a while, a bit chagrinned when she turned out to be a pretty good (and pretty lucky) poker player. Of course, they were only playing for matchsticks, so it didn't really matter. Sergeant Dolfen didn't play, but he watched at a distance and made sure his men watched their language around her.

The following day was clear and very cold with a brisk wind blowing. No one argued with the Sergeant when he said they would stay where they were for a while. Becca felt sorry for the soldiers on lookout duty atop the tallest building in town.

But it was a good thing they were up there, because around noon came the cry they'd all been dreading: *Martians!*

Sergeant Dolfen ran to where the lookout was posted, and for some reason she couldn't define, Becca ran after him. Well, she couldn't exactly run, but she shuffled through the knee-deep snow as best she could. She scrambled up a ladder that gave access to the roof of the lookout building and found Dolfen already up there with one of his men.

"Where?" he was demanding.

"Out that way," said the soldier, pointing to the southwest. "Wasn't sure at first, but when I was, I gave a shout." Becca looked and saw a cluster of objects in the far distance. "They look like they are getting closer, but I can't really tell if they are coming directly this way."

"Damn," said the sergeant. "Wish I had a pair of field glasses!"

"My rifle has a scope," said Becca. Dolfen whipped his head around to look at her in surprise.

"What are you doing here?" he asked sharply. "You should have stayed inside!"

"I wanted to see!" she insisted. "My rifle has a scope. You want me to get it?"

"All right. Be careful on that ladder."

Becca snorted. "Yes, Uncle Frank." She turned and went back down. She heard the soldier chuckling and Dolfen swearing. She hurried to the stable and opened up the padded pocket in the saddle holster and took out the small telescopic sight and then returned to the lookout post. She handed it to Dolfen.

"Could have sworn that rifle of yours was an old Henry."

"It is."

"Huh, never saw a Henry with a scope."

"It was my Grandpa's. He brought it home from the war. He had it modified special to take a scope. He and my Pa taught me to shoot."

Dolfen took off the protective lens caps and then turned the scope on the distant Martians. He watched for a while, muttering to himself. "Ten... Eleven... damn, fifteen of the stinkin' things! And four others that are different!"

"They coming this way, Sarge?" asked the soldier.

"No, I don't think so. Anglin' off to the northwest, I'd say. They ought to pass a few miles west of us."

"Well, that's lucky!"

"Can I see, Sergeant?" asked Becca.

He handed the scope to her and she squinted through it. The indistinct shapes sprang into sharp focus and she swallowed down a lump of fear in her throat. A swarm of the tall three-legged machines strode across the snowy landscape. Several other machines accompanied them. They were lower and longer and seemed to have more legs. They might have been bigger overall, but it was hard to tell. It felt very strange to be able to watch the monsters without an urgent need to run away,

"Have you seen any of those other machines before, miss?" asked Dolfen.

"No. I only saw the tall ones. But the others ones might have been down inside the holes Pepe and I saw at San Augustin."

"Huh, wonder what they are?"

They watched the Martians until they were out of sight. Becca breathed a sigh of relief once they were gone.

"So what are we gonna do, Sarge?"

"Well, we're sure not going to try and follow that mob!" replied Dolfen. "At least not right away." He looked around the ruined town. "I guess we'll stay a while."

* * * * *

DECEMBER. 1908, ALBUQUERQUE, NEW MEXICO TERRITORY

The army had nearly moved out three times by Andrew's count. Orders had been issued, the troops had been assembled, trains loaded, and then… nothing. The orders had been cancelled and the troops sent back to quarters. Everyone was getting pretty frustrated—and the cold, snowy weather hadn't improved things. The only good thing about the delays had been that it had allowed Sergeant McGill to collect all the rest of their equipment, horses, and wagons.

And some other stuff. Andrew had seen the requisitions that he had signed and McGill had used and there were definitely things on the forms that were not on his master list! He had no idea what McGill was doing with the other stuff, and some instinct told him it was probably smarter not to ask.

Then, two days before the New Year, a garbled message had arrived from Fort Wingate. A report of Martians attacking the fort and the nearby town of Gallup. Shortly after that the telegraph line had gone dead and no further contact with the fort or points west could be made. Presumably the rail line had been cut as well.

This had galvanized General Sumner into action. New orders were issued and the army prepared to move once again. Andrew hurried to pass the word to his men.

"Get ready to move, men!" he ordered. "This time it's for real!"

CHAPTER SIX

CYCLE597,843.4, NORTH OF LANDING SITE 32

Qetjnegartis powered down the heat ray; there were no more targets in evidence. All the structures in the vicinity were either burning or reduced to rubble. Hundreds of the prey-creatures had been slain and the rest scattered. There had been little resistance. Its subordinates had reported that they had destroyed what appeared to be a military installation of some sort further to the east, but that resistance there had also been negligible.

It released the controls and contemplated the situation. They had driven north from the landing site a considerable distance, destroying and driving all before them. Communications from the other landing sites reported similar occurrences. Nowhere had the prey-creatures been able to mount significant resistance.

But the planet was vast; even with three-quarters of its surface covered by water, it still had as much land area as the Homeworld. The colonization force, as massive an effort as it was, could not begin to conquer, let alone control, so huge an area. So the word had gone out from the Conclave: consolidate, construct holdfasts, and bud off a new generation. Qetjnegartis and its subordinates had already begun the budding process, but a holdfast would be needed before they came to term.

All during the journey north, Qetjnegartis had been evaluating possible locations to build a holdfast, but nothing had suited. A good source of raw materials was required and none had presented themselves. This settlement was the largest so far encountered; surely these prey-creatures also needed raw materials; perhaps they could be found in this area. The part of the landing force left behind would arrive in two of the local days, bringing fifteen more fighting machines and the four constructors. Was this the place to build the holdfast?

As it pondered, one of its subordinates requested Qetjnegartis to attend it, as it had made a significant discovery. It moved its war machine to the indicated location. Sitting there was a large metal device of some sort. It had been smashed and its function could not be determined, but the amount of metal was substantial. Of even more interest were two parallel sets of metal tracks leading out of sight in both directions. They appeared to be mostly iron. The alloys used by the Race for the fighting machines contained relatively little iron, but it was still a necessary component, and many other vital devices used it in great amounts. This was indeed interesting…

"Commander, something comes."

Looking to the west, Qetjnegartis saw a large object, spewing smoke and approaching rapidly. It was throwing up a cloud of the frozen water on each side of its path. What was it? They had encountered nothing like this before. It alerted the others and ordered them to converge on the intruder. It sent power to activate the heat ray.

As the thing came nearer, Qetjnegartis realized that there were a whole series of objects trailing the first and that it appeared to be following the set of metal tracks. It thought of the destroyed machine it had seen earlier and concluded that this new machine was of the same sort. A primitive transport device, apparently.

The machine suddenly gave off a loud, shrill noise and began to decelerate rapidly. But it had realized its danger too late. Five heat rays fired, almost as one, and the machine exploded in a blast of molten metal and steam. The following objects left the track and tumbled on their sides or end over end and also burst into flames as the heat rays swept along them. A few of the prey-creatures escaped from the objects but were immediately annihilated. In just a few moments the entire assembly was destroyed.

Qetjnegartis moved to examine the remains. Yes, a transport system which moved on the metal tracks. The first expedition did report such devices in use. Not unlike the systems built on the Homeworld after the canals ran dry. These prey-creatures must use it for similar purposes.

If this was a major route of transport then perhaps this was not the best location to build a holdfast. The prey could use the system to mass its warriors. But no, why should there be anything to fear? These creatures were nearly helpless and posed little threat. And time was running short. There was no need to look for a new location.

"Begin salvaging this metal," it commanded. "We will construct the holdfast here."

* * * * *

JANUARY, 1909, WASHINGTON, D.C.

The President's annual New Year's Day reception in the White House was in full swing. Every year since he took office, Roosevelt had insisted on personally greeting members of Congress, the Supreme Court justices, his Cabinet, the diplomatic corps of foreign embassies, the military, and every private citizen who cared to brave the long wait in winter weather. Two years ago the weather had been so beautifully pleasant that the line to get in had stretched for many blocks and the President had spent hours with the crowd even though he was one of the fastest handshakers alive.

This year the weather was not nearly so pleasant, with a blustery wind and occasional flurries of snow and sleet. And the mood was nearly as different as the weather. For the world was at war—most of the world, anyway. Europe alone had been spared the attention of the invaders, but every other continent was under attack and the reports of defeat and depredation were becoming alarming. The security in the White House was heavier than anyone could ever remember—as if Martian assassins might try to sneak in. The President's two oldest sons, Ted and Kermit, newly minted officers from the Plattsburg Camp, stood near their father in uniform and never strayed far.

Some had suggested that Roosevelt cancel the reception, or severely scale it back, but he had refused, of course. It was not in the man to retreat from any challenge, even an invasion from Mars. Others had felt differently and attendance was down more than could be blamed merely on the weather. But those who had shown up were all greeted personally with a handshake, and many received his legendary grin and trademark 'Dee-lighted!' Leonard Wood watched from across the Blue Room and marveled at Roosevelt's stamina. Two years ago, the ushers had calculated that the President had shaken over eight thousand hands in the course of four or five hours. There wouldn't be so many today.

But while the preliminaries were much the same as previous years, what followed was not. Usually the visitors and well-wishers were simply ushered past the President and then back outside again where they dispersed. And while that was still true of the ordinary citizens, this time, many of the important persons—particularly the foreign diplomats—hung on, hoping for some more substantive conversation with Roosevelt.

The President clearly wasn't too happy with this change in tradition; he usually spent the rest of the day with his family in private celebration; but short of ordering the Secret Service to toss the visitors out, there was no avoiding them. He did, however, move to the downstairs reception space, which, although as magnificently renovated by Edith Roosevelt as the rest of the White House, was also extremely difficult to heat properly during the winter. Perhaps he felt a need to cool off after all the handshaking, or maybe he hoped the cold would drive away some of the hangers-on.

Once in the large hall, the crowd began to coalesce into groups. Many sought out the Russian ambassador, Baron Roman Rosen, to try to get confirmation of a persistent rumor that one of the Tsar's armies had been badly defeated in Kazakhstan. The stoic Russian would neither confirm nor deny the rumor, but the expression on his face did not inspire confidence.

Many more congregated around James Bryce, the British ambassador. The British, with their huge overseas empire and communications links had, perhaps, the best information on the scope of the Martian invasion. And the information which had been released was not good. As Wood had feared, the Martians had descended in remote locations where they would not be disturbed, and were now pushing outward into more settled regions. The British colony in South Africa was under attack, as was the German colony in East Africa. The French holdings in North Africa were reporting war machines moving north out of the Sahara. More of the tripods were in Australia and the Ottomans had sightings in Arabia. While nothing had been seen so far in the Himalayas, the British were understandably worried about India's northern border. Word out of China and the Far East could only be described as *confused*.

Of all the Great Powers, only the Austro-Hungarians were completely unconcerned, having no overseas possessions. The Japanese were also complacent, being secure on their islands and worrying only about their relatively small enclaves on the Asian mainland.

But the biggest crowd that afternoon was surrounding Theodore Roosevelt. The diplomats from South and Central America were most in evidence. Early hopes that the Martians would ignore the Western Hemisphere had foundered as reports began to stream in from Caracas, Buenos Aires, Rio de Janeiro, Santiago, and Mexico City. The ambassadors from Paraguay and Bolivia were especially agitated since all communications from those countries had been cut off abruptly just two days earlier. All of them were asking—or sometimes demanding—American aid. Roosevelt had words for all of them, often speaking in Spanish, although he resorted to French with the Brazilian ambassador as his Portuguese was fairly non-existent. Sadly, words were about all he could offer. The United States' military resources were already sorely stretched, and the mobilization of new forces was going painfully slow. Congress was still dragging its feet on a conscription act, although that wasn't a huge concern yet; volunteering was still strong, and the shortage of weapons and equipment and training camps meant that they couldn't use a bigger influx of recruits anyway. American industry was still gearing up to produce what was going to be needed. At least the War Bond Act had been passed to raise the necessary funds to pay for it all. J.P. Morgan had bought a hundred million the very first day they were available to pave the way.

But the diplomats weren't satisfied with excuses, they wanted assistance—now. Wood moved closer, eavesdropping, and heard the Argentine ambassador threatening to refuse coaling rights to the warships Roosevelt was sending to the west coast of Panama unless aid was forthcoming. The Chilean ambassador seized on the idea and made similar threats. Voices started to be raised, both around Roosevelt and also the British ambassador. Wood shook his head, thinking about how little cooperation or interest those same men had showed during the months leading up to the invasion.

He could also see that the President was becoming uncomfortable. He'd always loved being the center of attention, but not of this sort! Mobs, even mobs composed of distinguished diplomats, made him uneasy, and when attacked, either physically or verbally, his nature was to strike back. Wood had seen him knock a man to the ground over some rude remark. What would he do now?

It went on for a few more minutes and then Roosevelt raised his hands and called for calm. He stepped up on a chair and from there, a table, his hands still raised. Every eye turned toward him and the noise began to die away.

"Gentlemen!" he cried in his high-pitched voice. "Gentlemen!"

The noise stopped entirely and the men began to gather around the table on which stood Theodore Roosevelt, President of the United States. He wasn't a particularly tall man, although his barrel chest and heavily muscled arms made him look larger than he was. Elevated on the table, he seemed to tower over them all.

"Gentlemen," he said again after a long pause. "We—and when I say we, I mean all of humankind— are facing a new and unprecedented challenge. And if I may be permitted to paraphrase Lincoln for a moment: as our case is new, so we must think anew and act anew. We must disenthrall ourselves and then we will save our planet!" He paused and looked over the assembly; his eyes gleamed and it was as if he was addressing each man separately. Wood found himself smiling. This was Theodore at his best!

"We each knew the danger, we each were warned, and we each knew that the threat affected every nation, every people. And yet we each acted alone, seeing to our own defense and ignoring what our neighbors were doing—or failing to do. We acted as we always had: as Americans, or Englishmen, or Frenchmen, or Argentinians! Gentlemen, we acted like the Greek city-states awaiting the arrival of the Persian hordes! That will not do anymore!

"We must put the past behind us and move forward together. We must consolidate our forces and coordinate our efforts. We must work together for the greater good! And together we will gain victory!"

The applause that followed started out as polite and then grew to enthusiastic. But Roosevelt waved it away. "Mere words are not enough, gentlemen! Action is what is needed! And act we will!" He looked around the crowd. "Root! Root, get over here!" He beckoned Elihu Root forward. "You all know my Secretary of State; in the following days he will organize a great international conference to analyze the situation and determine our best course of action, and how we can best use our resources for the common defense."

The look on Root's face made it clear to Wood that this was entirely new to him; Theodore probably came up with the idea just minutes ago. And what an idea! Military cooperation on a world scale. Nothing like this had ever been contemplated before. Had Roosevelt overreached? But then, just last year, he had organized an unprecedented conference with all 46 state governors and hundreds of other experts to discuss the conservation of natural resources. The man had a way of making the outrageous seem completely reasonable. Maybe he could make this work, too.

Secretary Root managed to catch the ball Roosevelt had so unexpectedly thrown him and discussions immediately began on locations and timing. A beaming President slipped out the door, covered by the distraction.

* * * * *

JANUARY, 1909, ALBUQUERQUE, NEW MEXICO TERRITORY

"We finally goin' t'move, sir?" asked Sergeant McGill.

"I think so," replied Andrew Comstock. "Better warn the men to get packed—again." He couldn't keep the exasperation out of his voice. They'd been told almost ten days ago that they'd be moving out immediately, and here they were still in Albuquerque. Oh, the army had *started* moving out immediately, but they were moving by rail and there was a strict order of priorities. First had gone the cavalry, to create a scouting screen in front of the army. This made sense, of course, since they had no real idea just where the Martians were. They couldn't risk trying to steam straight into

Fort Wingate on a train! Then had come artillery and infantry and all the supplies for them and a hundred other items; all deemed vital by someone. Major Comstock's little band of Ordnance people had a priority so low he hadn't been sure that they'd ever be allowed to go. He'd been tempted to try to go by road, but it was fifty miles in a straight line just to the first assembly point in Laguna and then another hundred to Wingate. His batch of novice riders and teamsters would never make it; not in this weather. Better to wait for a spot on the trains.

"Yes, sir," said McGill. "We're not waitin' for the tanks, sir? They're just up the tracks in Santa Fe, aren't they?"

"Yes, and God only knows when they'll get the clearance to come forward! No, we've got a spot on one of the trains this afternoon and I'm not going to pass up on that. The tanks can follow when they can."

"Yes, sir. I'll get the lads movin'."

"Right. I'll get my own stuff together."

"You sure you don't want one of the men to act as your batman, sir? T'ain't right for an officer to be doin' his own chores, sir."

"I can manage, Sergeant. I was a second lieutenant not that long ago. And the men have other things to do."

"If you say so, sir." He didn't look convinced, and as Andrew made his way back to the boarding house, he had to admit that a major really did have an image to uphold. With all his prior duties since graduation, he had people to take care of those things: restaurant waiters, hotel valets, boarding house washwomen, even Victoria or Mrs. Hawthorne if he had a tricky bit of clothing repair. But now, he was going to be out in the field for days and weeks and if he didn't have one of the men do it, he'd have to do it himself. Not just his laundry, but fixing meals, saddling his horse, and all those other little chores. Of course, he'd done all that stuff while he was a cadet and he remembered how much time it took away from more important things. Yes, maybe he ought to take McGill up on the offer. Whatever man he chose probably wouldn't mind, since he'd get paid for the extra duty, and Andrew had a stipend in his pay to take care of exactly those sorts of things.

The town was still bustling, but it was impossible not to notice that there were far fewer people around. Thousands of troops and their officers had already departed and many more were preparing to go. Of course, new units were arriving, too; the force which had been assembled at Albuquerque was just the vanguard of a general redeployment of the army westward. Trains carrying more forces were backed up to the Mississippi. All the more reason to get out now, while they could.

Andrew reached his boarding house and went up to his room. Packing didn't take long since he hadn't really unpacked from the last false alarm. He did have to search out the landlady, Mrs. Muntz, and get a few bits of laundry he'd left with her and pay her for it. He was paid up for his room through the end of the week, but he didn't feel inclined to argue with her for a refund on the days he wouldn't be here. "I don't know when I'll be coming back this way," he said. "If any mail should come for me, please leave it with the provost office here."

"All, right," she replied. "You be careful with those Martians! And don't you be letting any of 'em to come here, will you?"

"Don't worry, ma'am, you'll be safe here." He said it automatically, but he wondered if it was really true? The force being sent out to Fort Wingate was large, but not all that large. Two brigades of infantry, one understrength cavalry brigade, and eight batteries of field artillery; maybe 12,000 men all told; not counting all the supply and support troops and the various other hangers-on that are attached to any army—like Andrew and his men. The Martians, as far as could be determined, were landing in groups of five cylinders. If there were three of the war machines in each cylinder, as had been the case in the first invasion, then they might have fifteen of the war machines. Could General Sumner's force handle fifteen tripods?

He finished his packing and then headed for the rail yards. It was crowded there but eventually he found his men, along with their baggage, two wagons, and thirty horses. He felt a bit guilty that he and his twenty men were going to need no less than six railway cars to move everything. No wonder it was taking so long to move the army! It was early afternoon before they were directed to a siding where they could begin loading and it was nearly dark before they were done and the cars hitched to the other cars of the train. His men were stuck in one box car with all their gear, the horses took up four more and the wagons were lashed to a flat car. There were several dozen other cars making up the train, but he wasn't sure what they were all carrying. A regular passenger car was attached just ahead of the caboose and that was where all the officers congregated. Andrew climbed aboard just before the whole thing lurched into motion.

A quick look around revealed that he was the senior officer present; all the others were captains or lieutenants. He picked a seat next to a captain with Signal Corps insignia, stuffed his valise in the overhead rack, and sat down. The man looked at him with interest.

"Evening, sir."

"Evening."

"I'm Tom Selfridge, Army Aeronautical Division."

Andrew's eyebrows went up. "Really? I met one of your fellows last year at the Wrights' place in Ohio. What the hell was his name…?"

"Lahm? Frank Lahm?"

"That was it! He actually took a ride in the contraption. Braver man than me."

"Oh, they aren't that bad—most of the time."

"You've ridden in one of them?"

"Better than that, sir! I'm a pilot myself!" Andrew stared at him and decided that he wasn't pulling his leg.

"Really? What are you doing here?"

"Hunting Martians. We've got my flier and mechanics packed up in one of the box cars."

"I'll be damned. I've seen the machines flying around Fort Myer, I guess one of them must have been yours."

"Probably; there were only a half-dozen of us then. Did you see my crash?"

"Uh, no…"

"Came within an inch of cracking my fool skull open," said Selfridge with an obvious tone of pride in his voice. He pointed to a pink scar on his forehead. "Smashed the hell out of the machine though," he added sadly.

"And yet you went back up again."

"Of course. They promoted me to captain, so how could I refuse? Although if I'd known they were going to pack me up and send me out *here*…" He grinned.

"I know what you mean," said Andrew, smiling in turn. "A few months ago I was snug and warm back in Washington."

"Ordnance, eh? What are you doing here, sir? Seeing what our guns do against the Martians?"

"Yes. That and how the new tanks do—if they can ever catch up with us."

"Tanks? Oh, you mean those steam-gun-tractors things they've been talking about? You have them here?"

"Trying to get them here. They're stuck at Santa Fe right now. Hope they can join up with us before the fighting starts. But I'm also here in hopes of salvaging any wrecked Martian equipment that we might capture in the course of things."

"Ah! A treasure hunter! Well good luck! I'll tell you what: I'll find 'em, your tanks can smash 'em, and then you can go sweep up the pieces!"

They both laughed and shook hands. He decided he liked the crazy pilot. A little while later he liked him even more when he produced a bottle from his bags and shared it. This attracted some of their fellow passengers and more introductions were made. Most of the other officers were with the Quartermaster Corps and they seemed quite envious of the dashing Selfridge and even— to his surprise—himself. Apparently quartermaster work was *really* boring.

They had a jolly time for a while, but eventually things quieted down and they all tried to get some sleep. The train rattled and lurched through the night with frequent stops. They travelled about twenty miles south to the town of Los Lunas where the line branched off to the west. Morning found them well short of the assembly point at Laguna. Dozens of trains were blocking the track ahead of them. Andrew was impressed to see railroad work gangs actually laying track to create new sidings.

During one of the innumerable stops, a man got aboard their car. He was dressed in a heavy civilian overcoat with a broad-brimmed white hat. He glanced around and then came over to where Andrew and Selfridge were sitting. "You in charge here, Major?"

Andrew shrugged. "Seem to be. Can I help you?"

"Was wondering if I could ride with you folks?"

"Uh, this is a military transport train," said Selfridge. "I don't think we're taking paying passengers."

"Oh, I'm not paying!" snorted the man with a grin. He looked to be in his forties and was carrying a large valise. "I'm a newspaperman, White, Bill White, *Emporia Gazette*." He held out a thick-fingered hand and Andrew automatically shook it.

"There's a mob of other reporters with the general's headquarters, oughtn't you be with them?"

"No doubt! But I just managed to catch up with this travelling circus! Wasn't easy! Been riding in box cars and such for the last three days. Then I saw you fellows and thought that this might be a bit more comfortable! D'you mind?"

"Not at all. We've got room. Make yourself at home."

"Many thanks!" White crammed his valise into a rack and then sat down next to them.

"Emporia? Where is that, if I may ask?"

"Kansas. And you?"

"Well, the last posting for both of us was Washington. But now we're here. And you're here to report on the army?"

"The army, the Martians, anything worth reporting about! My readers are tired of all the rumors and guesses and half-truths being bandied about. And so am I! I'm here to get some facts!"

"Well, if you find any, be sure to share them with us, will you?" said Selfridge. "We probably know about half as much as your readers right now."

White laughed. "I guess that's the way the army operates, isn't it? But I've learned that people usually know more than they realize." With that, the newspaperman proceeded to squeeze both of them dry of everything they knew about the current situation. White seemed genuinely interested in everything they had to say and took copious notes. He spent more time on Selfridge's glamorous job as a pilot, but he showed real interest in Andrew's mission, too. Neither officer felt any inhibitions about talking—it wasn't as if the Martians were going to be reading the *Emporia Gazette* and learning secrets!

"Glad I bumped into you young fellas," said White after a while. "I don't think most folks realize just how big a thing this all is. My paper reprints stories from overseas telling how the Martians are landing all over the place, but it doesn't seem to make much of an impression. Deep down, I think most folks just don't believe there is a big wide world out there, so anything happening there isn't real, either. All they're worried about is new taxes and the possibility of a draft. Hell, some of the damn fools still believe that this is all a hoax to get Roosevelt a third term!"

"That *did* bother a lot of people," said Selfridge. "Some felt that two terms was written in stone even though it isn't written in the Constitution. Like that lunatic, Schrank who was planning to shoot him at the inaugural next month. Thank God they caught him before he could!"

"True," said White, "it did bother me a bit, too. But in a real crisis, there's no one I'd rather have at the helm!"

"He's an amazing man," said Andrew.

"Have you met him?" asked White.

"I've been at meetings where he was present. Read a few reports with him listening, but I've never really spoken to him."

"I've known him for years," said White proudly. "And you are right: he's amazing. A bit strong-willed for peacetime, but in a real war, he's just the man we need."

"Well, it looks like we may have a real war," said Andrew.

"Yes. And that's why we're all here, isn't it?"

The train slowly moved along. During the stoppages, they got off to stretch their legs. The very cold weather of the previous week had subsided a bit, but it was still damn cold. The snow on the ground was only a few inches deep and melting, but he could see that the mountains to the south and west were heavily shrouded in white. He had expected the southwest to be warm and sunny, but he hadn't allowed for the much higher elevation. They had winter here just like home!

Eventually they made it to Laguna, which wasn't much of a town compared to Albuquerque, and unloaded. Mr. White went his way and Selfridge went his, but they promised to stay in touch. Andrew found that he liked both men quite a lot. A new tent city had sprung up on both sides of the tracks and small mountains of supplies were growing hour by hour. Andrew checked in at headquarters and learned that the cavalry was already fifty miles farther west, near the town of Grants, probing to find the enemy. Some of the infantry and artillery was preparing to move out on foot to follow.

Andrew was very happy that Sergeant McGill had been able to acquire all that field gear when he discovered that tiny Laguna couldn't provide housing sufficient even for the army headquarters, let alone all the other officers who were arriving. The wall tent McGill had for him was only slightly warmer than being outside, but wrapped in his overcoat and a few blankets he was able to survive the nights. McGill did assign him a batman, a corporal named Kennedy, who was nearly as accomplished a scrounger as McGill himself. By the second night he had a tiny coal stove in his tent, which made a huge difference.

They waited and shivered for a few days, but then word came back from the cavalry that they were encountering civilians fleeing east. They reported that Martians had attacked them. The next day, a dozen miles west of the town of Grants, which was deserted but undamaged, they encountered a single enemy war machine which retreated when it saw them. Pursuing for a few miles they discovered that the railroad had been torn up beyond that point. Not just torn up, but completely destroyed; the ties burned to ash and the metal rails missing entirely. A few ranches in the area had also been destroyed.

General Sumner concluded that the destruction of the railroad was to hinder the army's approach and that the Martians feared an attack. Emboldened, he ordered the army to push forward as quickly as possible. With the rail line near at hand, the infantry didn't need to carry a lot of supplies on their backs and could make good speed along the road that paralleled the tracks. They managed ten or fifteen miles a day despite the muddy conditions, and made it to Grants near the end of January. There they halted to let everyone else catch up. From there they would resume the drive to Fort Wingate.

Andrew and his men made it to Grants a few days later than the infantry and artillery. Even mounted, it was a difficult journey for inexperienced men. Many of the riders were still very green and the teamsters were still learning how to drive the wagons. They frequently had to pull off the road to let faster units pass. But they did get there. Grants was little more than a whistle stop on the railroad, so another city of canvas quickly arose. Even General Sumner was in a tent now. Andrew bumped into White from time to time but the newspaperman could provide little except the gossip he picked up around headquarters—which was little different from the rumors floating through the camps. He tracked down Tom Selfridge and watched him and his men assembling his flying machine. He still felt that a man would have to be crazy to go up in one of those things. Like the one he'd seen in Dayton, this was a two-seater and Selfridge had a sergeant who would fly with him when they went up.

The cavalry was still catching occasional glimpses of Martian machines off to the west, but they were not making any attempt to engage them by themselves. Although no definitive information had been received, it had to be assumed that the scouting force of the 5th Cavalry which had gone south from Fort Wingate had been destroyed or scattered. Unsupported cavalry couldn't be expected to hurt the enemy war machines.

So it would be up to the infantry and artillery. Andrew wasn't exactly sure what the infantry could hope to accomplish since, with the exception of a few machine guns, they were armed exactly like the cavalry. But the artillery could certainly hurt the Martians! The British had managed to destroy several of them during the first invasion with standard field guns. The American guns ought to be able to do as well. *Assuming the Martians haven't improved their machines…*

And they only had eight batteries of artillery; thirty-two guns in total. If the Martians had fifteen war machines as they were expecting, that was only two guns for each machine. Not a very good ratio. A nagging feeling that this ratio wasn't going to be good enough began to grow in Andrew. It became so strong that he actually worked up the nerve to suggest to General Sumner, during the last meeting before the final advance was ordered, that perhaps they should wait for the tanks.

"T-they have over fifty 3-inch guns between, them, sir," he stuttered. "It could make a big difference."

"If they could actually bring them to bear," snorted Sumner. "From what I've heard, the damn things can barely move under their own power. The one thing we do know for sure about the enemy is that their machines are highly mobile. I will not have my army tied down to a lot of dead weight! If your tanks can catch up and get into the fight, all well and good. But I will not wait for them. We will start our advance in the morning as scheduled!"

He could see that there was no use in further argument, so he shut up. He left the meeting feeling depressed. He'd spent the last two years helping the Army get better weapons to use against the Martians and yet now, on the eve of battle, they were using exactly the same weapons they'd had years ago.

Well, that wasn't entirely true. The Army did have six armored cars. The stop-gap program that had been started to provide something to fill in until the tanks were ready had yielded some results. After a lot of shopping around, the Army had selected the bizarre eight-wheeled 'Octoauto' made by the Reeves Pulley Company in Indiana to be the basis of the design. They had added an armored cabin on top of the chassis and put mounts for two machine guns. The result was a very strange beast, indeed. But the Reeves Company had built several other autos and the Octoauto had a reputation for ruggedness and the mere fact that all six were still with the Army showed that the reputation was merited.

A strange, but oddly familiar roar, suddenly reminded him that there was another new thing. Tom Selfridge had his flying machine unpacked and assembled! He followed the noise over to an open field west of the town in time to see the ungainly contraption take to the air and circle once before heading west.

"How far can he go?" he asked one of the mechanics.

"His record is about forty miles and back, sir."

"Eighty miles without landing?"

"Yes, sir." Andrew whistled in appreciation. He continued to watch until the machine was a tiny speck in the distance. He decided to wait until it returned and have a word with Selfridge.

He was still waiting two hours later, long after the machine would have run out of fuel.

* * * * *

CYCLE597,843.4, HOLDFAST 32-1

Qetjnegartis regarded the constructor in operation. Some of its manipulators were drawing raw materials into one end, while finished parts were emerging from the other. A second constructor was taking those parts and using them to assemble an excavating machine. One excavator was already at work, shoving mounds of dirt into a wall to create the holdfast's ramparts. The inner surface would be vitrified while the outer side would be left as rubble to impede the movement of any intruder. That was the first step; the wall would protect the inside of the holdfast from observation or direct attack. Then defensive weaponry would be installed along the rim of the wall, relieving the war machines from protective duty.

Once the defenses of the holdfast were complete, the real work would begin. Burrowing machines would carve out the underground chambers where the mines, refineries, and manufacturies would be created. Storerooms for raw materials; holding pens for food animals; feeding chambers; laboratories for research; in time it would resemble a holdfast on the Homeworld.

Budding would take place and then the buds would have buds. The population would grow and then new expeditions would embark to secure more areas and create new holdfasts. Step by step the planet would be conquered.

A shuddering vibration from its side made Qetjnegartis pause and look to examine the bud growing there. The lump was quite large now, being over halfway to the time it could detach. Distinct features like the manipulating tendrils could be discerned beneath the protective flap of skin. It now seemed certain that the bud would be a new being rather than a replacement for Qetjnegartis' body. There was still no sign of infection among any of its group. The new techniques were proving effective. It had been thousands of cycles since the last time it had been permitted to bud off a new being. It was an interesting experience and it looked forward to doing it again.

A signal from one of its subordinates demanded its attention. "Commander, I have urgent information."

"Report."

"The prey-creatures are continuing to mass to the east. There are now many thousands of them and they are clearly warriors. They appear to be preparing to advance against us. Also, I have just now observed and destroyed a flying machine operated by the prey-creatures."

Qetjnegartis twitched in surprise. Nothing of this nature had been reported by the first expedition. "Are you certain? There are flying animals on this world, could that be what you saw?"

"No, Commander, it was clearly a machine of some sort. There is no doubt. I will transmit a recorded image." It did so and Qetjnegartis had to admit that it was certainly as its subordinate had reported: an artificial construction which could fly. The fact that a mere brush of the subordinate's heat ray had set the thing ablaze and caused it to tumble from the sky did not diminish the fact that this was an unexpected and unsettling discovery. The planned defenses of the holdfast were not designed for defense against things which could fly. Still, the image showed a device which appeared incredibly fragile and clumsy. Perhaps it posed no real threat.

This mass of prey-creatures to the east was another matter.

Qetjnegartis briefly considered just letting them come on and destroying them near to the holdfast, but quickly discarded that plan. With the defenses incomplete, there was too much danger of the prey-creatures slipping past them and attacking the construction machines. They were not designed for combat and could be easily damaged. That was to be avoided if at all possible.

So, they would give battle farther east. One war machine would be left here for security and to oversee those activities which could continue without supervision. The other eleven would advance and deal with this situation.

Qetjnegartis issued its orders.

CHAPTER SEVEN

JANUARY, 1909, RAMAH, NEW MEXICO TERRITORY

"Well somebody has to pay for all this!"

Sergeant Frank Dolfen wearily stared at the angry shopkeeper and restrained himself from shooting him. They had been stuck in the town of Ramah for several weeks now and some of the missing townfolk had begun to return. Many people had been killed when the Martians had swept through, but others had managed to flee into the surrounding hills and hide. Now they were coming back to try to pick up the pieces of their lives. Unfortunately, one of them was the man who owned the general store where Dolfen, his men, and the other refugees had set up their quarters. He didn't seem happy that they had not only helped themselves to his place of business, but also to the goods which the business held.

"Sir, there happens to be a war going on. My men, and these other people we are protecting, need food and a place to stay. I'm sorry about it, but that's just the way things are. If you make up a list of what's been taken, I'm sure the government will repay you for your losses."

"The government! The government! That could take months! If it ever happens at all!" He turned and waved his hands around his shop, which was currently filled with people and bedrolls. "And how long are you going to stay? How can I run my business with you people camping out in here—eating my food and drinking my liquor?"

"Your business?" snorted Private Urbaniak. "Who you doin' business *with*? The Martians? Ain't no one else around now." Some of the men laughed.

"Hey, Sarge," said Private Cordwainer, "isn't trading with the enemy treason or something? Maybe we ought to confiscate all these here goods."

"I'm not trading with the Martians!" sputtered the shopkeeper. "But this is all my property! A man has to make a living!"

"A living! A living!" cried Rebecca Harding, suddenly a few feet away from the surprised man. "How dare you worry about making money when people are dying? My whole family was killed and my home destroyed by the Martians! These men saw all the rest of their regiment killed by the Martians! And you stand here begrudging them a roof over their heads and a few sacks of flour! How dare you!" The fury on the girl's face shocked everyone into silence.

The man took a few steps backward until he bumped into a barrel. He looked from face to face. "That true?"

"Yeah," said Urbaniak, every trace of humor gone from his face. "And Miz Gordon there and her boy and Mister Kershaw lost their homes, too. Hell! What about your own neighbors, man? You're doin' pretty well compared to some, so count your blessings and stop actin' like a damn fool."

The man's face turned red and he muttered something inaudible and then he stomped outside into the snow. Apparently he had a house somewhere else in town. The tension in the room vanished and the men started making jokes again. The girl looked a little embarrassed by her explosion of anger, but then smiled and sat down.

A little while later Urbaniak came over to him. "So what do you think, Sarge?"

"About what?"

"About us getting moving. The snow's been melting a bit and we've been here over three weeks now."

"Really?" He'd sort of lost track of the days. "Can't be that long!"

"S'true. It'll be February on Monday."

"I'll be damned. Guess we were getting a bit too comfortable, weren't we?"

"Yeah. But I'm wonderin' what's going on out there. Back at Wingate and all. Can't stay here forever."

"No, you're right. Looks like it's gonna rain tomorrow, but maybe we could get moving after that clears out."

"Sounds, good, Sarge. Wouldn't want to leave any sooner or it would look like the old pinch-purse drove us off!" The both laughed.

So that became the plan. The soldiers would get moving, and somewhat to his surprise, the civilians said they wanted to go, too; even some of the townspeople—although not all. He hadn't counted on that, but he could hardy refuse to take them. So the civilians would come—including Rebecca Harding.

Lately, the girl was following him around like a puppy. She'd even started cooking meals for him. Well, she and the other woman, Mrs. Gordon, were cooking meals for everyone, but somehow Becca always had a plate made up special for him. He found the situation irritating. The last thing he needed was some infatuated girl latching on to him! It was ridiculous, he was old enough to be her father! And what would Stella think when they got to Wingate? *If she's even still alive...*

The thought of what might have happened at Wingate and the nearby town of Gallup was spurring the sudden urge to move. The forces they'd left behind there would have no more hope of stopping the Martians than the regiment had had four weeks earlier. He could only hope that those couriers the colonel had sent off had gotten there and spread a warning. Maybe Stella had gotten out in time. *Time to find out.*

It did rain hard the next day, but stopped by nightfall. They decided to wait one more day to let the ground dry and then they would go. That morning, Dolfen was taking a turn at the lookout post when the girl climbed up the ladder with a cup of hot coffee for him. "Good morning, Sergeant," she said, handing him the cup.

"Morning. Thanks."

"So we'll be leaving tomorrow?"

"That's the plan."

"And we're going that way?" she pointed to the northwest.

"Yeah. About the only way we can go. South's no good if that's where the Martians are comin' from. If we could head east we could get to Albuquerque, but there's no getting over those mountains." He pointed to the imposing mass of Mount Sedgewick and the adjoining ridges; high, rocky, and deeply buried in snow at the moment. "Goin' west would just take us through a lot of very empty miles all the way to Flagstaff. So if we can go northwest we can see what's happening at Fort Wingate and Gallup. If things… if things aren't good there, we can still get past these mountains and turn east and head for Albuquerque."

"I'm glad you're leading us, Sergeant."

"Hmmm. We'll see."

"You've been in the army for a long time?"

"Quite a while, yeah."

"I wish I could join the army."

"What in blazes for?"

"So I can fight. Pay them… pay them back for what they did." The girl was staring out over the plains with a frightening intensity. *No teenage girl should ever look like that!*

"Well…" Dolfen didn't know what to say. "You ought to be getting back to…"

A low rumble that actually shook the building they were on slightly jerked both of them around. It was coming from the north, the mountains, and it didn't stop. It just went on and on.

"Is… is that thunder?" asked the girl.

"No! That's artillery! A lot of it!"

"What's happening?"

"A fight's goin' on beyond the mountains. A big one!"

"The army?"

"Well, it sure can't be the navy! God, I wish I knew what was happening!"

"Are… are we still leaving tomorrow?"

"Yes! We need to get moving!"

*****

FEBRUARY, 1909, THOREAU, NEW MEXICO TERRITORY

"Looks like this is the real thing, sir."

Major Andrew Comstock nodded his head. "It sure does, Sergeant. And it's gonna be a hell of a show."

The army had advanced from Grants and had now reached the even smaller hamlet of Thoreau. But it appeared that this was as far as they were going to go without a fight. Cavalry scouts had reported ten or twelve of the Martian war machines coming this way at a rapid pace. So the infantry was shaking itself out into a battle line and the artillery was taking up firing positions.

The army was facing almost due west in a flat valley between two lines of mountains. Several miles to the north was Mount Powell, which consisted of a series of very steep escarpments almost a thousand feet higher than the valley, their sides glowing with a red sheen in the morning light. To the south, the mountains were closer. The land did not rise as sharply there, but it continued in a series of slopes and mesas up and up to a formidable, snow-covered ridge that stretched completely across the southern horizon; the north faces still in dark shadow. Andrew's map said that one of the peaks was called Mount Sedgwick, but he wasn't sure which one. Directly to the front, the ground sloped up very gently to a low rise about a mile and a half away. They couldn't see anything that lay beyond, although they had cavalry scouts well in advance of that. The position had been deliberately chosen with a restricted view. There was no hard information on the effective range of the Martian heat rays and they didn't want to risk being caught in a situation where the enemy could hurt them without the artillery being able to hit back. So if the Martians came close enough to fire at the army here, the guns would definitely be in range. It was a classic 'reverse slope' position like he'd read about at West Point.

General Sumner had set up his command post on the flat roof of one of the buildings in Thoreau. Andrew had parked his detachment nearby in hopes of getting a good view, and perhaps news of any destroyed enemy machines that he might try to salvage. The place, like the other habitations they'd passed through, was deserted; the residents fled east. Andrew idly wondered if the place was named for the famous poet and naturalist and how that had come about?

The troops had been deployed in an entirely conventional formation, one infantry brigade to the north of the road, and the second to the south. Each brigade had its two regiments lined up side by side, each with two battalions forward and one in reserve. The battalions had two companies deployed in extended order on the firing line with the other two companies acting as supports. Andrew noted that it played out just like the 1904 Drill Regulations he had used at West Point. The cavalry were on the flanks and the artillery batteries were spaced fairly evenly along the whole line, although several hundred yards behind the infantry. A scattering of machine guns were also sprinkled along the line with the infantry. Three of the armored cars had been placed on each flank. The whole thing was about three miles long from end to end. Some of the infantry and guns were digging in, but most were just watching and waiting. Andrew noticed that none of them appeared to be wearing their breath masks. He looked down at the canvas bag hanging from the strap looped over his neck. His own breath mask was in there. He was already wearing leather gloves against the cold and his leather riding boots should give as much protection as the men's leggings. The black dust the Martians had used in England was lethal if inhaled, but it could also poison a man just by contact with the skin. He hoped they wouldn't use the stuff today.

He looked up as Bill White, the newspaperman, rode up. Not only had he acquired a horse, he also had a breath mask. They exchanged greetings. "It appears we are about to have a battle, Major."

"Yes," agreed Andrew. "And soon."

"Mind if I tag along with you?"

"Suit yourself, sir. But you'll probably learn more if you stay with the general."

"Too many of my esteemed colleagues hanging around headquarters; like a flock of vultures. Whatever I see there will be reported by dozens of others. But if you are successful in your mission, Major, I might get a unique view of some Martians, close up."

"If we're lucky."

"Speaking of luck, it's a damn shame about Selfridge, isn't it?"

"Yes, he was a good man. I wonder what happened?"

"We might never find out, I suppose."

They had been waiting nervously for over an hour when a strange buzz-saw sound came to their ears from off to the west. Corporal Kennedy was just handing him a cup of coffee he'd boiled up and he jerked around, slopping half of it on the ground. Andrew thought he saw a flicker of red light reflecting off the still-shadowed hillsides to the south, but he wasn't sure. After a few minutes, a smudge of dark smoke wafted up in the distance but quickly dissipated. Only a short while later, the buzz-saw snarled twice more, louder than before.

"Gettin' closer," observed Sergeant McGill.

"So it seems."

"Wish we knew what was comin'!"

"Yes. We could really use Selfridge and his damn flying machine today!"

106

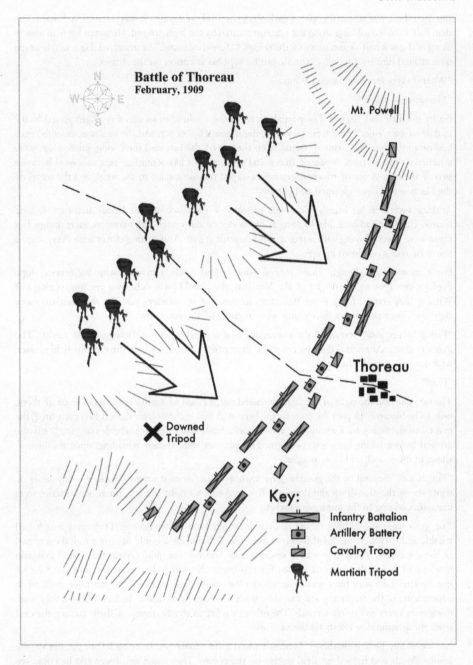

Battle of Thoreau
February, 1909

Mt. Powell

Thoreau

✗ Downed
Tripod

Key:

Infantry Battalion
Artillery Battery
Cavalry Troop
Martian Tripod

"Look!" said Bill White, pointing. A swarm of cavalry appeared on the crest of the far rise. Andrew took out his field glasses and focused in on them. The first of the riders appeared to be moving at a brisk trot. But as more of them topped the rise, the followers were moving faster and faster. The last of them were riding at a full gallop and one man turned in his saddle and fired back the way he'd come.

But then there was something else, a dark object beyond the cavalry. It was just a curved shape, less than half a circle, bobbing along the horizon created by the high ground. He swept his field glasses along and saw a half-dozen more of the things. "Here they come," he muttered. He could hear the men around him start to talk excitedly, but he kept his attention on the shapes.

"What do you see?" demanded White.

"Martians—I think."

Bit by bit they rose higher. The partial circles became whole ovals and a red light glared in the middle of each one. There were eleven of them now. Higher yet, and the oval was mounted on a box or a cylinder. Two arms sprouted from the top of the box and three long, jointed legs were attached to the bottom. A pair of thin metal arms, almost like tentacles, were mounted between two of the legs. A ray of morning sunlight escaped the mountains to the south and the metal of the Martian machines gleamed and glittered.

Andrew sucked in his breath. He'd seen pictures of the machines the British had captured, of course. But that had been like looking at the bones of dinosaurs: old, harmless, inert things. But these were alive! Moving with a strange and unsettling gait. And getting closer with every step; a shiver of fear went down his spine.

For a moment he thought that General Sumner had made a mistake with his reverse-slope deployment. Due to the height of the Martians, they could look right over the intervening hill! What if they started firing now? Were they in range of the artillery yet? But the Martians came right on; closer and closer. Surely they were in range of the guns now…

"Firing by section!" screamed the commander of a nearby battery. "Range, 2,500 yards!" The gunners clustered around their pieces while their officer stood, looking through his field glasses, with one arm raised. "Ready!"

"Fire!"

The two guns on the right of the battery roared out, a cloud of smoke billowed in front of them, only to be blown back past the guns by the breeze. A few seconds later the left two guns fired, the gun tubes slamming back against the recoil mechanisms and lifting the wheels completely off the ground before falling back into position. The gunners were already reloading; open the breech, shove in the round, and close it again.

"Fire at will!" Several of the gunners gave a whoop and the men went to work; a steady series of shots shook the air. All up and down the line to Andrew's right and left, the other batteries were firing too, adding to the impressive racket.

The guns were the M1897 model, a French design built under license. They were tough and reliable and they were intended for rapid fire. A well-drilled crew could fire off a round every two or three seconds. These crews were veterans and Andrew was quite certain they could maintain that rate of fire if they wanted to. But for this battle they needed accurate fire, not just a lot of fire. So after each shot there was a pause to let the smoke clear and then the gun-layer made a few adjustments to the traversing and elevating wheels before firing again. Andrew guessed they were firing once every five or six seconds. The other men kept a steady stream of shells coming forward from the ammunition chests on the caissons.

But were they hitting anything? Andrew trotted a few dozen yards to his left to get out of the smoke clouds and trained his field glasses on the enemy. They came into focus and he could see gouts of smoke and dust that were bursting up well behind them, but he couldn't tell if any of them had been hurt. The gunners were firing directly at them rather than in a barrage, so any shell that missed would fly hundreds or thousands of yards beyond them before bursting. The noise of the exploding shells merged with that of the barking guns to produce a continuous roar.

"God! What a racket!" shouted White. "But is it doing anything to them?"

"I don't know... I can't see..."

"There! Over there!" cried Kennedy, barely to be heard above the din. "They hit one of the bastards!"

Andrew lowered his glasses and looked to where Kennedy was pointing: down toward the left end of the line. He brought the field glasses back up to his eyes and trained them on one of the Martians. The tripod-machine had stopped advancing and was staggering around in a circle; smoke was streaming from a part of the thing's body. As he watched, another shell hit it and one of the arms went tumbling away. It lurched to a halt and the batteries down on the left zeroed in on it. Two more hits in rapid succession slammed the thing backward and it crashed to the ground, a smoking heap of twisted metal.

Hurrah!

A cheer went up from all along the line; thousands of men shouting in triumph. Andrew realized he was shouting himself. We hurt them! But what will they do now? Would the Martians be enraged? Would they come charging forward, heat rays blazing?

"Look! Look!" shouted someone nearby. Andrew twisted his head from side to side. What? What was happening?

"They're running!"

He stared, scarcely able to believe his eyes. It was true! The Martians were retreating! Falling back!

As the men realized it, they jumped up and began waving their helmets and hats and cheered all the louder. The artillery continued to hammer away and Andrew thought at least one more of the tripods suffered a hit, but soon they all disappeared behind the high ground. The artillery was ordered to cease fire and the gun smoke slowly drifted away. But the men kept cheering.

"Well, that was easy," said McGill. "Cowardly set o'gits, aren't they?"

"I wonder if they are going to use their black dust weapons," said Andrew uneasily scanning the skies. "They used them against the British artillery the first time." His hand brushed the canvas bag on his chest to make sure it was still there.

But minutes went by and nothing more happened. A short while later, some riders began leaving General Sumner's headquarters and galloped up and down the lines. *The army will advance!* they cried. *General pursuit!* The infantry formed up and started moving forward; the horse teams came forward and the gunners hitched their guns to the limbers. The cavalry, which had retreated back behind the lines during the fighting, were now sending out scouts toward the high ground. Andrew looked to his men and grinned.

"Well, gentlemen! Let's get the wagons and go claim our booty! Coming, Mr. White?"
"Oh yes! Wouldn't miss it for the world!"

* * * * *

CYCLE597,843.5, EAST OF HOLDFAST 32-1

Qetjnegartis considered the situation with irritation and no small measure of alarm. One of the war machines destroyed and its operator killed. Two other machines lightly damaged. This was entirely unexpected. The reports from the first expedition, while fragmentary, indicated that the weapons of the prey-creatures were largely ineffective. There had been a warning to avoid large bodies of water because the creatures did possess vessels of impressive size that could be quite dangerous, but their land armies were discounted, although one report did admit to a war machine being destroyed by a random shot from one of the large projectile weapons.

109

Nothing had prepared it for what had just happened. The prey, instead of being demoralized by the appearance of eleven war machines, had stood their ground and opened a heavy fire with over thirty of their projectile throwers. The things seemed ridiculously primitive, relying on an explosive chemical to hurl metal objects. But hurl them they did, and with considerable force and accuracy. Franjandus' machine had been hit seriously, and before it could withdraw to safety had been hit several more times and wrecked. All contact with Franjandus had been lost and it was assumed to be slain.

And while every member of the Race was completely expendable for the common good, the situation here was different. There were still so few of them on this world. None could be spared until more buds were created. The loss was so surprising that Qetjnegartis had ordered a retreat to consider the situation and make new plans. They had put the high ground between themselves and the prey and were safe for the moment.

What to do? To attack again would expose all to more of the enemy's fire. The effective range of their projectiles was well in excess of the heat rays—another surprise! They would have to pass through that gauntlet before they could get close enough to strike back. More machines and their drivers might be lost and they could not afford that.

The first expedition had carried a toxic particle weapon delivered by a long range rocket. It could cover a large area with a lethal cloud. It would be perfect for this situation. But the Conclave that planned this second venture had considered the weapon wasteful of resources and unnecessary. None were included in the current expedition. The devices could be manufactured, of course, but not in time for the current engagement.

So what was to be done? Maneuver against the prey? They were deployed in a long, straight line. Perhaps turn a flank; hit them from a direction where only a fraction of their large weapons could fire? Reduce the risk and concentrate against a smaller number? But there were swarms of individual prey there, too. Did they pose a threat? It seemed unlikely, but unlikely things were already happening today. Qetjnegartis felt the weight of its responsibilities as never before. A serious error could see its whole command wiped out. That must not be allowed to happen!

Retreat? Fall back to the Holdfast? Its defenses were still almost non-existent. Could they be put into any sort of shape before the prey came and launched their own attack? To have the Holdfast overrun now, to lose the constructor machines, would be a disaster. No, retreat was not a good option. They had to fight. But what was the optimum…?

"Commander! The enemy advances!"

Qetjnegartis regarded the images being relayed to it by one of the other war machines. It had raised a vision pick-up just high enough to see over the ridge. Yes, the prey were coming toward them. But wait, look how the large projectile throwers were moving! They had been connected to some sort of vehicles being hauled by draught animals. How incredibly primitive! More importantly, they clearly could not be operated in that position. They were vulnerable. How long would it take them to become operational again? If they could just be drawn in close enough…

"All attend!" Qetjnegartis commanded. "Lower your machines to the loading position."

"But commander…" protested Hlaknadar.

"Obey! They will not see us here until it is too late!"

* * * * *

FEBRUARY, 1909, THOREAU, NEW MEXICO TERRITORY

"Come on! Get that thing moving!" Andrew shouted at one of his wagon drivers. The man was still so clumsy with the vehicle he didn't deserve the honorific *teamster*. The whole army was on the move now—forward in pursuit of a beaten foe. The mood of the men around him was just incredible. There had been a tension in everyone for weeks that only grew with each mile they advanced. The fear of the unknown. How powerful was the enemy? How bad would the fight be? Could we really win? But now! Victory! They had hurt the enemy and they were on the run! It was hard to believe, but it was true. The army had done a wonderful job.

But now it was time for Major Andrew Comstock and his little band to do their jobs! He was leading his detachment through the swarms of troops toward the still smoking remains of the downed Martian machine. They had to get there and secure it before any souvenir-hunters made off with something important. He also wanted to get some photographs of the untouched wreck so they could try to document the exact effect of the artillery fire on the machine. He had a Kodak Brownie camera for the job. He also had some sketch paper. He was a fair draftsman and wanted to make some diagrams with notations. He was already mentally composing his report for General Crozier.

"Didn't even need none o' them bloody tanks," said Sergeant McGill.

"No," agreed Andrew. "The general will probably be disappointed about that. But we only actually destroyed one of them, remember. We might need the tanks later. See to the wagons, Sergeant, I'm going on ahead." He spurred his horse into a canter and guided it toward the wreck. Bill White, the reporter, followed along. As he got close, the horse became increasingly skittish and he was obliged to stop about thirty yards away and dismount. A couple of his men, including Corporal Kennedy, had accompanied him and he handed off his reins to him. White did likewise, staring intently at the wreck.

"Careful, sir," cautioned Kennedy.

"Right." He unsnapped the flap on his pistol holster and advanced cautiously on foot. Up close, the machine actually appeared smaller than it had from a distance. Sort of like those spiders that looked so enormous, but then shriveled into a tiny ball once you squashed them. Andrew shivered; he hated spiders and he wished his imagination hadn't come up with that particular comparison. He drew his revolver. He was surprised to notice that White had a pistol as well.

"You might want to stay back a bit, sir," he said to him.

"Not a chance, Major! This is news!"

"All right, let's take a look."

The machine's 'head' appeared to be the main part of it. It was basically spherical in shape, but squashed down so that the sides bulged out in a projection that formed a lip or rim that nearly circled the head. In the front, there was a flat area that formed a sort of face with a central hub surrounded by small recesses and projections. The central hub was where the red light had been. But the light was dark now and Andrew could not see where the light had been coming from; there was a spot in the exact middle, but it appeared to be metal just like the rest of the machine. He'd been expecting it to be glass or something transparent. The whole head was about fifteen feet in diameter. The boxy structure underneath was only about seven or eight feet in each dimension. The top part of it actually was a box, but the bottom was nearly a cylinder. The two thick arms he had seen were mounted to the box, just below the head. One of those arms had been torn off by a shell. A few wires and tubes protruded from the stump. He saw now that there were three of the smaller tentacles rather than two as he'd first thought. The three legs and the three tentacle-things were all attached to the lower cylinder. He was reasonably certain that this was not an exact duplicate of the ones the British had captured. There were differences. *An improved design?*

He'd have to have the men find the missing arm. But the other arm was still there and it was the one holding the heat ray device. He looked at the deadly thing closely. It was about six feet long and three feet tall and two feet thick. It looked rather like his Brownie camera of all things. The legs were as thick as a man and about twenty-five feet long, not counting the odd 'hip' mechanism.

111

Walking slowly around the machine, he saw that it had been hit at least a half-dozen times by the artillery. In addition to the lost arm, there was a gaping hole in the head from which a gray smoke was wafting. There were several other gashes in the head's metal where shells had hit but not penetrated. And one of the hips had been shattered, nearly severing the leg. Only a few cables still connected the pieces together. That must have been what brought the machine down in a heap.

"The artillery really blasted it, eh?" said White.

"Yup, did a good job on them."

A glittering of sparkly dust on the ground caught his eye and he squatted down to see what it was. It turned out to be hundreds and hundreds of tiny pieces of metal. He picked one up and saw that it was a perfect hexagon, about the size of the nail on his little finger. It was as thin as a piece of paper and he gasped when he actually cut himself on the edge of it. What the hell was it? Looking up, he saw that one of the gouges in the metal head was just above the glittering pile and that more of the pieces were scattered nearby. Closer inspection showed that at the point of impact there were many more of the little hexagons exposed. There were layers of them, one on top of the other, almost like the scales on a snake or other reptile, but only around the gouge. Farther away, they merged into a seamless whole with no individual hexagons visible at all! This was amazing, but there had not been a word of anything like this in the British reports. Was this new, or were the damn British just keeping it a secret?

"What have you got?" asked White.

"Not sure. Seems like the metal is made up of these little pieces that somehow combine to make a whole. Not a big metal casting like we'd do. Beats me how it holds itself together, though."

"Well, this one didn't hold itself together, did it?"

"No. It looks like a big impact—like a shell hitting—will cause it to come apart. Boy the scientists are gonna have a lot to study on this thing!"

"But this head is way too big to fit on your wagon, Major. Unless you figure out some way to take it all apart."

"We might have to be content with the smaller pieces. Maybe when we repair the rail line up to here we can figure a way to get it aboard a rail car."

"Anyone home, sir?"

Andrew looked over his shoulder and saw that McGill had arrived with the wagons and the rest of the men. The army was moving past the site and many of the men were pausing to point and gawk at the wreck, despite the shouts of their officers and sergeants to keep moving. A limbered battery of artillery was struggling up the slope, the drivers whipping the horses on; he could see that the cavalry was nearing the crest of the rise. A couple of the armored cars chugged by, backfiring noisily.

"You mean inside here? Not sure. But the thing's other arm is over that way somewhere; have a couple of men try to find it."

"Yes sir." He passed on the order and three men set out. Andrew turned back to the machine. It may have been wrecked, but McGill was right: what about the Martian inside? Was it still alive? To capture a live Martian would be a real feather in his cap! Although the thought of having to somehow restrain—and care for!—one of the hideous creatures had him hoping the thing would be dead. He looked into the hole that had been blasted into the face of the machine, but could not see anything. Searching further he discovered a place which seemed like it might be a door or hatch. But how do get it open?

"Sergeant, see if we have a pry bar among the tools. I think we can…"

Several bugle calls sounded off to the east, but they were instantly cut off by the buzz-saw snarl they had heard earlier. Andrew whipped around to look up at the ridge line. At first he couldn't see anything except lines of troops silhouetted against the sky. But then smoke started billowing up and red light was flickering off it and the buzz-saws went on and on. The troops on the ridge halted and then started falling back. Some of them were shouting and waving.

"What's happening now?" asked White.

"Got a bad feeling about this, sir," said McGill.

Then the cavalry came galloping back over the rise. Some of the horses didn't have riders and a few of them seemed to be on fire. Officers were shouting and more bugles rang out. An armored car appeared on the crest, its eight wheels throwing up dust as it tried to retreat. An instant later it exploded. The nearby battery halted and the gunners started to unlimber their pieces.

"Oh God!" cried Kennedy. "There they are!"

Tall gray shapes were emerging from the smoke. *Martian tripods! They're attacking again!* They came on with a terrible speed and were on the ridge in a moment, only four or five hundred yards away. They raised their arms and the heat rays lashed out with that buzz-saw shriek. Men and horses flashed to puffs of smoke and steam as the rays swept over them. The ray appeared to consume them completely, leaving nothing behind!

Some men tried to fight back and a crackle of rifle fire erupted, but it had no visible effect on the foe and the heat rays exacted a terrible price for the men's bravery. Hundreds died in seconds and a few, only grazed by the rays, ran back screaming, wrapped in flames, or rolled on the ground trying to put out the terrible fire. Ten of the machines now stood at the crest of the rise, killing countless numbers with each ungodly buzz. Andrew stood there, gripping his useless pistol and stared, frozen in place. He could hear Bill White saying: "Oh God! Oh God! Oh God!" Over and over.

The battery in front of him was swinging its guns around, but far too late. The two nearest Martian machines turned their rays on the battery and in a moment explosions shook the ground as the ammunition caissons exploded, throwing men and debris skyward. Andrew was knocked backward by the concussion and nearly fell. But he couldn't tear his eyes away. The wooden gun carriages burned up like straw and the gun tubes, glowing a dull red slumped down amidst the ashes. The men who had hoped to work those guns, and the horses who had pulled them, were obliterated, just... wiped away.

All along the line it was the same awful story. The Martians concentrated their efforts against the artillery and in minutes all eight batteries had been destroyed. Andrew didn't think any of them had managed to get off a single shot. The cavalry was already running to the rear as quickly as their horses could carry them and now the infantry line was collapsing. Their rifles apparently useless, the troops had no alternative but to fall back. But the Martians were faster than they were and the retreat almost instantly became a rout. The men threw away their weapons and ran.

"Sir! We gotta move!" It was McGill, he was pulling him by the arm, back toward their horses; shaking him out of his stupor. "Mount up! Let's move!"

But it was already too late. The nearest tripod was striding down the slope and it was sweeping its heat ray in their direction.

"Cover! Take cover!" he screamed. He pulled McGill and White back in the direction of the wrecked machine and they flung themselves into the covered space behind it. Some of his men did the same. Others found cover behind rocks or in depressions in the ground. Some tried to run. The horses broke loose and galloped madly away, except for those harnessed to the wagons; they were trapped.

The ray passed over all of them, men and horses alike. The prairie grass blazing up wherever it touched, but the wrecked tripod shielded them. Choking smoke swirled around Andrew and he coughed and gasped for breath. Behind him he heard screaming men and screaming horses. Beside him, McGill was shouting something in Gaelic; cursing probably. White had curled into a ball with his face pressed against the ground.

And then it was past. He looked out from the lee of the wreck and saw the tripod striding on down the slope, pursuing the ruin of the army. He watched it, slaughtering more men at every step, until it was a half mile away.

"Sir... sir, we better get outta here. If they come back, we're cooked for sure."

"Yeah... yeah... get the men up..." he was so dazed it was hard to think straight. A few minutes ago he was part of a victorious army and now... now... a nightmare.

He looked around. The two wagons were just piles of burning wood; lumps of ash showed where the horses had been. Had anyone been in them? Men were emerging from their hiding places. At least some of them were. Andrew looked back down the hill; all the Martians were still moving east. But they were bound to come back here to check out their fallen comrade. He and the others had to get out before they did. White was still on the ground and he had to physically drag him up to his feet. The man seemed dazed.

"Ready, sir," said McGill.

"How... how many are hurt?"

"Well, no one is *hurt*, sir. Looks like we lost six men killed. An' all the horses is gone. Dead or run off." The stunned survivors were huddling together behind him. "Gotta move sir. Which way?"

"Uh... well, east's no good, that's where they all are. West's where they came from. South... south, I guess, up into the hills there."

"Sounds good, sir. Least there'll be cover there. All right! You heard the major! Get moving!" The thirteen stunned survivors turned and started walking and Andrew followed. Step by step they went south, climbing over progressively rougher terrain as the mountains drew nearer. Everyone was constantly looking back to see if the Martians were coming, but they were still getting farther away and the rasp of their heat rays was fainter now. After an hour or so they had put a few miles between themselves and the wreck and climbed at least three or four hundred feet in elevation. They paused for a rest and Andrew pulled out his field glasses and looked on the scene of the disaster. His hands were shaking so badly he could barely hold the glasses steady.

He couldn't see any details at this distance and that was probably just as well. Dozens of black pillars of smoke rose up as things burned. Houses from the little town, wagons, piles of supplies, everything was on fire. The smoke merged into one big cloud which the wind blew east, smudging the clear blue sky. The Martians could still be seen, striding back and forth. From time to time he would see a flicker of the heat rays and a new column of smoke would appear. There was no sign at all of any resistance.

"Bad as it looks?" asked McGill quietly. Andrew just nodded.

"How... how could this have happened?" asked White.

"We saw how it happened," said McGill. "But, we better keep going, sir. Another mile or two and it looks like we could find some cover."

"And then what?" cried one of the men. "What are we gonna do?" Some of the others added their voices to the question. A few looked close to panic.

Andrew stood up, a strange feeling of dread and rage mixed within him.

"The first thing we are going to do," he said sternly, "is stay alive."

* * * * *

CYCLE597,843.5, EAST OF HOLDFAST 32-1

Qetjnegartis looked on in satisfaction. Victory. The prey-creature army had been annihilated. All the large projectile throwers had been destroyed and many thousands of the creatures as well. As it had hoped, the large weapons could not move and fire at the same time. The sudden counterattack had caught them unprepared and they had all been destroyed before they could fire at all. Once that was done, it had simply become a matter of exterminating the rest of them.

Many had escaped, it was true, but the survivors were no longer any threat and would serve to spread panic among the others. Qetjnegartis continued the pursuit until there were no large groups of the prey left in sight and then ordered a halt.

Yes, this was excellent. The prey's army had been utterly smashed. The threat eliminated. They could now return and finish work on the holdfast and complete the budding process. When the buds had matured sufficiently to operate the extra war machines, they could set out again; making new conquests; linking up with the other landing groups.

But a great deal of energy had been expended. They would all need to feed soon. And a store for future needs should be accumulated. Fortunately, there was a good supply close at hand.

"Begin the harvesting," it commanded.

CHAPTER EIGHT

FEBRUARY, 1909, SOUTHWEST OF THOREAU, NEW MEXICO TERRITORY

"The damn things are roamin' all over the place to the east o' us, sir," said Sergeant McGill. "No good tryin' to head that way while they're there."

Andrew Comstock nodded grimly. "I think you are right, Sergeant. But I don't like the idea of just sitting here. There's not enough cover. We need to get farther up into these hills and find somewhere to hole up for a while; until the Martians clear out."

"Yes, sir—assumin' they *do* clear out."

"One step at a time. It will be getting dark soon and it's going to get damn cold tonight, as clear as it is. We've lost nearly all our gear and we don't dare build a fire out here. Up in the hills, maybe we can find a cave where at least we can have a fire. Let's get moving."

"Yes, sir." McGill shouted at the men to get on their feet and was answered by a chorus of groans and curses, but the men started to move. Bill White still seemed dazed, but Andrew gave him a shove and he moved along with the rest.

The disastrous day was nearly at an end. It still seemed like a bad dream. The battle, which had started so well, had dissolved into flames and death. The army smashed to flinders before his eyes. There were undoubtedly survivors—like him and his men—but nothing like an organized military force remained. Fugitives—especially the cavalry—would be fleeing back along the rail line, spreading word of the defeat to all those still following. What would they do? Could they organize a defense before it was too late? Or would the Martians just keep advancing and smash every attempt? If that were the case then Andrew and the others were in truly a mess. Where could they go, on foot and with no supplies?

No supplies and nearly no weapons. Andrew and McGill each had a revolver, but none of the men had anything at all, and White seemed to have dropped his pistol somewhere along the way, so that was gone too. Their rifles had been on their horses or the wagon and they were all gone. They'd seen some stray horses wandering around; they'd have to try and catch some of them if they could. Not just for transport, but in hopes that there might be food or weapons attached to the saddles.

But no horses came close enough to grab before it was completely dark. Fortunately, the moon was nearing full and it gave enough light to see by as they scrambled higher into the hills. They were getting up into some much more rugged terrain, but despite being exhausted and chilled, Andrew drove them on until they found a really sheltered spot. Not a cave, but enclosed enough that they dared risk a fire. They collected fuel and soon had a blaze going. They huddled around it and tried to get warm. Their canteens were empty or nearly so and they didn't have a scrap of food. Unlike the infantry, they hadn't kept their haversacks on their persons. Most quickly fell

117

asleep despite their parched throats and growling stomachs. Andrew dozed off quickly too, but didn't stay asleep for long at a time. He woke up frequently, frozen on the side that was away from the fire. He'd twist around, check the position of the moon and then sleep until he woke up shivering again. The damn moon didn't seem to be moving at all and the night lasted about a thousand years.

Morning eventually came and brought at least a small improvement in their situation. A few horses, apparently attracted by the fire, or at least the smell of it, were standing around nearby, glumly nibbling at the shriveled winter grass. They had cavalry markings on their saddles, but more importantly, they still had their saddlebags and those bags had some food in them. Even better, one of them had coffee. A quick look around their campsite revealed a small stream trickling down from the mountains. So they filled their canteens, boiled some coffee, and ate the rations for their breakfast. It wasn't much, and there was barely enough left for a meager lunch, but it still raised all their spirits. Bill White was in much better shape than he'd been the day before and even cracked a few jokes. Andrew had been afraid he'd be saddled with an addle-wit, but thankfully, that wasn't the case—although a few of his troops still seemed pretty rattled.

Andrew still wasn't satisfied with their location. It was too exposed, especially from anyone looking down on them—like from a forty-foot high Martian tripod. So he got the men moving and continued heading south, up the slopes of the mountains. McGill insisted he ride one of the horses and they put the two men in the worst shape on the other two.

After about a half hour, they encountered what looked like a road. Or a path, anyway. It was unpaved—like all the roads in this part of the country—but there were some wagon ruts evident and just as importantly, no sign of the Martians. While investigating the wrecked machine yesterday, Andrew had noticed that the sharply pointed feet of the tripod would sink a foot or two into the dirt, leaving a distinctive triangular hole behind. There were no such holes to be seen here.

"So what do you think, sir?" asked McGill.

"Well, we don't want to go that way," he replied, pointing north. "That will just take us back toward the main road where the Martians are. But this must lead somewhere in the other direction. Let's go see where."

So they followed the road up into the hills. It was easier going than off the road, but still pretty steep. By mid-morning the slopes of the mountains were looming over them. There were patches of snow on the ground in the shady spots and the mountains themselves were still heavily covered.

"Hey! There's a shack up ahead!" cried the man who was in the lead. "A couple of shacks!"

They hurried ahead and indeed, there were several crudely built structures standing in a little canyon that reared up on three sides. Off in the distance there was a dark opening in the rock wall, and a mound of broken rock piled off to one side.

"Looks like a mine, sir," said Corporal Kennedy.

"Yes," agreed Andrew. "Take a look around, but move carefully and make plenty of noise. If there are any miners still here, they might be a bit jumpy. *And probably better armed than we are!*

His men spread out and Andrew followed the group heading for what looked like the living quarters. It was just a box with sheet metal walls and roof. But a stove pipe stuck up through the roof and that looked promising! He sure didn't want to spend another night clustered around a campfire!

Several of the men pushed through the door and almost immediately one of them shouted: "Hey! There's someone here! A soldier!"

Andrew came to the front and found a man in an army uniform lying on a cot. No one else seemed to be there. Looking closer, he saw that the uniform had scorch marks on it and the man's face had a nasty burn on one side. The eyes were closed at first, but then he groaned and they opened. He stared for a moment and then focused in on Andrew.

"Comstock," he muttered. "About damn time you got here."

"Selfridge!"

* * * * *

FEBRUARY, 1909, WASHINGTON, D.C.

"And this has been confirmed?"

"I'm afraid so, Mr. President," said Major General Leonard Wood.

Roosevelt grimaced. "When you start calling me that in private, Leonard, I know the news has to be bad. And Sumner? He's really dead?"

"Things are still pretty confused, Mister… Theodore. But it seems likely. The accounts we have said he was right there in the center, leading the army forward when things went to hell. There's certainly been no word of him since then."

"Yes, that would fit Sumner: leading from the front," said Roosevelt, shaking his head sadly. "A fine soldier. Remember when he was commanding the First Brigade of the Cavalry Division in Cuba? While you had the Second? Those were the days!"

"That they were," agreed Wood. "But we have a hell of a situation to deal with right now, Theodore. The army we had out there in New Mexico hasn't just been defeated, it's been destroyed."

"We have more forces in the region!" protested Roosevelt. "Just the other day the General Staff was complaining about how all the rail lines were clogged with troops and supplies!"

"That is true. But they are all reinforcements for Sumner's army. Sumner's army is gone, so all those reinforcements are just random units of infantry, cavalry, and artillery. They have no higher leadership or organization. Not an army. We need to build another one. We'll need a commander for it and he'll need a staff. And we need them quickly. Right now, the Martians could push right through to Albuquerque and even Santa Fe if they wanted to. Without firm control, all those reinforcements on the rail lines would just be lambs to the slaughter. You remember what it was like trying to get the ships loaded to go to Cuba?"

"Yes," growled Roosevelt. "Pure chaos. We practically had to hijack a ship to get out of there…"

"We *did* hijack a ship."

"Yes, we did, didn't we? And the 71st New York never forgave us for taking theirs. And all during that mess, six determined Spaniards with pop-guns could have routed the lot of us." He took in a breath and straightened his back. "So we need a new commander out west. Who do you think General Bell will recommend?"

Wood sighed and shook his head. "That's the other thing, Theodore. I… General Bell isn't taking this well."

"Well that's to be expected! *I'm* not taking this too well!"

"That's not what I mean. Theodore, the Chief of Staff of the United States Army is not taking this well!"

"You mean he's cracking up?"

"Yes, I'm afraid so. He's been under tremendous strain for a long time, Theodore. This may have been the straw that broke the camel's back. I've just been to the War Department and things are… well, things are like they were on that dock back in Key West in '98."

119

"Damnation. So we are going to need a new chief of staff, too."

"Yes. Now, my personal recommendation would be Bliss. He did see some action in the last war and he's an able administrator."

"Leonard…"

"Or Scott might not be too bad. He's the commandant at West Point at the moment, but I'm sure we could pry him out of there without too much trouble. Unless you'd rather go with Wotherspoon…"

"Good God, no! He's practically at retirement age—and he's been acting like he's already retired for the last decade! We need someone younger, someone with some fire in his belly! And…"

"Well then, I'd stay with Bliss—unless you want to go with someone much younger, but there'd be a lot of grousing if you jumped someone that young over all those officers senior to him."

"Leonard," said Roosevelt, fixing him in his gaze. "You're overlooking the obvious choice."

"Oh? Who?"

Roosevelt snorted like a bull. "Why yourself, of course! There's no one better qualified!"

Wood had known it would come to this, indeed, he'd been counting on it, but the forms had to be followed. "But Theodore! You can't pick me."

"And why not? You have seniority."

"Well… well, I'm not a West Pointer. I came into the army as a contract *surgeon*, for God's sake!"

"And since then you've fought Indians, helped track down Geronimo, raised the regiment of Rough Riders, commanded a brigade of cavalry in Cuba, commanded a division fighting insurgents in the Philippines…"

"But…"

"And you have a Medal of Honor—something I never got." The sour look on the President's face told Wood that he still hadn't forgotten or forgiven the political opponents who had kept him from receiving that much-deserved medal. "You've earned this, Leonard."

"But we're friends!"

"Indeed we are," said Roosevelt, smiling at him fondly. "Why should that disqualify you?"

"People will say it's favoritism! The 'spoils system' at its worst! Congress will never approve!"

"You let me worry about Congress. I am the Commander in Chief after all; I ought to be able to pick my own chief of staff." He paused and his gaze became piercing. "You are confident you can do the job, aren't you, Leonard?"

Wood stared back at his old comrade. Somehow the man had the ability to make the most outrageous idea seem completely reasonable. Like when he convinced him to help raise the Rough Riders. And once you agreed to do what he wanted, the notion of then failing the man was simply unthinkable. It was a gift that few men had, but Theodore Roosevelt had it in spades. Yes, he had no doubt that Roosevelt could bend Congress and the public to his will on this—just like when he fought to get him his second star. And the truth was that he did want this very much. All those years of having the West Pointers look down their noses at him… Vindication!

"Well?"

Wood jerked his head in an awkward nod. "I can do it, Theodore; it would be my honor."

"Good! Now who are you going to replace Sumner with?"

"Fred Funston."

"'Fearless Freddy'," said Roosevelt nodding. "He was fighting in Cuba before any of us! Competent man, but doesn't know when to keep his mouth shut. I had to reprimand him back in '04 for that.

120

Ha! Talk about the pot calling the kettle black, eh? And he's not a West Pointer, either, Leonard."

"No, but he's got enough fire in his belly for any two men. He's in charge of the Service School at Fort Leavenworth right now, but I know he'd give his right arm for a combat command."

"Well, by all means then, let's give him one!" said Roosevelt, smiling broadly. "Of course, I am commander in chief, maybe I should go myself!"

Wood realized that—for once—he was joking. "Theodore, no president has commanded an army in the field since Madison tried it at Bladensburg. I don't need to remind you how well *that* turned out."

Roosevelt laughed. "No you don't! All right, all right, I'll stay here and be good! Now go across the street and send Bell over to see me. I'll let him down gently and find some safe posting for him—if he still wants one. Then you get to work and clean up the mess out in New Mexico."

"Yes, sir." He turned to go.

"Oh, Leonard, wait a moment," said Roosevelt. He was looking very serious now.

"Yes?"

"You know that both of my older boys, Ted and Kermit were commissioned months ago. They've both requested postings to line regiments, but for some reason their transfers have been hung up in red tape. I've refrained from interfering in internal army affairs like that, but this has gone on far too long. Can you break the log-jam and get things moving?"

Wood stared at his old friend and forced himself not to shake his head in disbelief. Most fathers would be asking him to find some safe spot, far from the fighting, to put their sons. But not Theodore! In his mind this was the ultimate test of manhood. He'd been ashamed his whole life that his own father, a pacifist, had stayed out of the Civil War. And Theodore had pulled every string imaginable to make sure he got *into* the war with Spain. Now, here he was, making sure his sons had the same opportunity. *Not everyone is indestructible like you, my friend.* He sank into the chair facing Roosevelt.

"You... you're sure about this, Theodore?"

"Of course! They nag me about it every time they see me! Just itching for a fight! And in just a couple more years Archie and Quentin will be nagging me, too! Although God willing, this will all be over before they are old enough. You'll take care of it, won't you?"

"Certainly, Mr. President."

"Oh, and let's try and keep things quiet as long as we can, eh? About the bad news from New Mexico, I mean."

"That might take some doing."

"Yes, well, let's try anyway."

"Yes, sir."

Wood got up from his chair, took a deep breath, and made his way out of Roosevelt's office. Part of him was still shaken by this turn of events, but another part was looking forward to the challenge ahead. The idea of actually being in charge was a seductive one.

He passed out the gate and started across the street toward the State, War, & Navy Building, mentally composing what he was going to say to General Bell. A newsboy was standing on the corner and shouting:

"Extra! Extra! Army destroyed in New Mexico! Martians on the march! Extra! Extra! Read all about it!"

*****

121

FEBRUARY, 1909, SOUTHWEST OF THOREAU, NEW MEXICO TERRITORY

"Didn't have any trouble finding 'em," said Captain Tom Selfridge. "Or finding one of 'em, anyway. The things are tall as a windmill and all metal and you can spot 'em ten miles away."

"Yeah, we've seen them, Tom," said Andrew. The pilot was sitting up on the cot and looking considerably better than when they'd found him the day before. The burn on his face looked painful, but not dangerous. He had another burn on one of his hands, but that was bandaged up now. It was impossible to ignore the fact that they'd found Selfridge alone. The other man who had gone up with him had not been there. Bill White was sitting on another chair with a pencil and note pad. "So, I assume they hit you with a heat ray?"

"Yeah, like Icarus. Got too close to the sun and it melted my wings," he said sadly, shaking his head. He took a sip of coffee. "When we first spotted it, I swung wide to the north to keep my distance. It clearly saw us, but just watched as I went on west; to see if we'd spot any more. But we didn't see anything except the torn-up railroad. I was running low on fuel so I had to turn back. Then I made the mistake of passing by the Martian to the south this time. There was a strong cross-wind coming off the mountains that pushed us north—right toward it. Nothing I could do. I got too close to the damn thing and it fried us."

"You're lucky to be alive. The men I saw hit by the heat ray were consumed completely. Just burned up to nothing in an eye-blink." Andrew shuddered. The sights and smells of the battle were coming back to him. It was odd: during the fight, he couldn't remember smelling anything, but now he found the stink of burning flesh was in his clothing; the clothing of all the other men…

"I am, yes, but poor Gundersen, my observer, well, I think we must have been at the extreme range of the thing," said Selfridge. "It swept the ray over us and I could feel the heat on my face." He gingerly touched his left cheek. "I could feel the heat through my clothes, through my flying helmet. I guess my goggles saved my eye. But it wasn't much worse than being too close to a bonfire. I think… I think Gundersen must have shielded me from the worst of it, 'cause he started screaming. But at the time, I didn't really notice that; I was a lot more concerned about the fabric of my flier. That caught fire almost at once. Not all of it fortunately, or we would have dropped like a stone. But enough that I knew we was going down. I somehow managed to crash it, more or less in one piece. I got clear of the wreck, but Gundersen didn't move. I went back for him, but there was nothing I could do. His whole left side was all charred. Burned my hand trying to pull him out but…" He shook his head. "Then I ran because I saw the Martian heading my direction. Managed to make it into some rocks and get away. The thing seemed more interested in the wreck than in me. Good thing, too, 'cause I was pretty beat up. Hid in the rocks that night; damn near froze to death. The next day I found the road and came here. Heard all the firing the other day. The next thing I remember is seeing you."

Selfridge stared at Andrew for a moment. "So the army's really wrecked?" They'd given him a brief account yesterday and he'd taken things pretty well.

"For now, I think. Plenty more troops back up the line if they can get organized. I don't know if they can."

"Damn. Lucky you got away."

"Yeah. Lucky."

"So what's the plan now, Major, sir?" He grinned, although only the right half of his mouth curled upward.

"Get ourselves back to join up with the others. Not much else we can do. I've sent out some men to scout around. Hopefully, the Martians will move on and we can get out of here." He patted Selfridge on the knee and stood up. "But you rest up for now. It'll probably be a day or two before we go. And you'll have a horse to ride."

"That would be good. And thanks, Major."

Andrew nodded and left the shack. Yeah, they'd been lucky so far. Most of them were still alive and they were out of immediate danger. The miners' shack had been well stocked with food and the stove kept the place pretty warm. It wasn't really built to accommodate fifteen men, but it could in a pinch.

So what the hell do I do now?

The answer he'd given Selfridge about future plans had come out of his mouth automatically, but was that really what he was going to do? He was in command. It was his decision and his responsibility. But what was he *supposed* to do? He walked slowly around the small canyon and eventually sat down on a barrel to think.

He'd been given orders; he had a mission. Several missions, actually. His mission to observe the Martian machines and their capabilities was accomplished—all too well! He'd seen them in action and saw what they could do. So he ought to get back and report what he'd seen. Of course, anyone who had survived the battle could report exactly the same thing. Not much of a success to bring back.

His mission to collect any salvaged Martian equipment was now out of the question. He did have a few of those fascinating hexagonal metal flakes, but there was no hope of hauling away anything else. Even if they could get back to the wreck unseen and undisturbed, the wagons were gone and they couldn't hope to carry much of anything on their backs or on their few horses. His camera and his sketching tools had been on his horse and he had no clue where that was, even if it had survived. So all he had was what he could remember. Again, not much of a success.

One last mission was to observe how the new tanks performed in action. Well, they hadn't been in action yet—as far as he knew. Perhaps they were back up the line this very minute preparing to go into action. Or maybe they were already burned-out hulks, destroyed by the Martians. No way to know until he got there to see. Okay, there was a mission he could still carry out. And fortunately, the only way to carry it out was also the only sensible course of action anyway: move east and link up with what was left of the army.

Andrew let out a long sigh and felt a little better. Decision made; now he just had to carry it out somehow. Well, they wouldn't be moving today in any case. He had to wait until the scouts got back, and besides, they could all use another day of rest.

"Major?" He turned and saw McGill coming up. "The boys found somethin' interesting."

"What?"

"Come take a look, sir." The sergeant led him to a small shack, about the size of an outhouse, tucked away in a corner of the canyon. Several of the men were standing there, looking in the door. They parted to make room when Andrew got there. Inside were a stack of wooden boxes. The label on the side read:

"Dynamite. For the mine, I guess."

"Detonators an' fuses, too, sir. I'm thinkin' this might make more of an impression on those tin giants than rifles and pistols, sir."

Andrew blinked. "Yes, I suppose it would. You're thinking about making bombs, Sergeant?"

"That was my thought, yes, sir. Some of the lads have experience with explosives. If we can attach a bundle o' these to one of the thing's legs, maybe we could bring it down."

"Take a hell of a good man to get close enough to do something like that, Sergeant."

"Good or lucky, that's for sure. Still, it's better than nothing."

"No arguing with that. Fine, get to it."

"Very good, sir!" They started hauling out the boxes and breaking them open like kids with their Christmas presents. Well, maybe these kids could come up with something useful. He left them to it and headed back toward the shack. He idly wondered what had become of the miners who owned the place.

Before he got there, he heard the sound of a lot of hooves approaching; the clatter of horseshoes on rock echoed off the canyon walls. Cavalry? Some detachment that had escaped? But no, a single rider—one of the scouts he'd sent out—came into view and he was towing a long line of horses all tethered together. The noise attracted all the other men and they gathered to secure the beasts.

"Where'd you find all these?" demanded Andrew.

"They were all clustered around a little pond, drinking, sir. They seemed glad to see me! I figured we could use them, so I brought 'em back."

"Good thinking. And good work! With this lot we've got nearly enough for everyone."

"All cavalry mounts," said McGill, looking them over.

"How'd the horses all escape if the riders… if the riders are gone?" asked another man. The image of a heat ray sweeping along, too high to hit the horses, but just low enough to decapitate the riders, came to Andrew's mind.

"Poor sods probably dismounted to try and fight on foot," said McGill. "When they got burned, the horses probably bolted."

"Yes, that seems likely," said Andrew, shaking the image from his mind. "No rifles on any of these. The troopers took them with them."

"How we gonna feed 'em, sir? Not much to graze on up here."

"No. But we aren't going to be staying here much longer. Once we hear from the other scouts we'll get moving tomorrow. So be ready to move out."

This brought a general brightening of faces. He knew the men were worried; hell, he was worried, too! But the thought that they'd soon be back in friendly territory was exactly what they wanted to hear. Now if they could just get there! He left the men to their packing and their bomb-making and went back in the shack to see Selfridge. He was now in one of the chairs and White was curled up on the cot, sleeping.

"So, what's the situation?" asked the pilot.

"Looking better. We've got enough horses for everyone now, so we ought to be able to make good time. We just need to scout out a route that will let us slip by the Martians and link up with friendly forces. Are you going to be able to ride?"

"Oh, sure. Just tie me to the beast if you have to. Anything to get out of this dump!"

"Yeah. But you're sure, Tom? We may have to ride like hell if they spot us."

"Given the choice of riding like hell or staying here, I'll ride like hell, Major!"

"Good man. And when we're alone, you can call me Andrew. Still not used to this 'major' business."

Selfridge chuckled. "All right, Andy…"

"*Andrew*. I hate 'Andy'."

"Oh, okay. But how far do you think we'll have to go to get to friendly territory?"

Andrew shrugged. "No idea. The Martians pursued the wreck of the army as far as we could see them the day of the battle. No telling where they went after that. Hell, they could be in Albuquerque by now if they just kept moving."

"Damn, that's scary. How'd it come to this? Were we that arrogant? That overconfident?"

"I don't know. We *did* hurt them. We destroyed one of their machines with the artillery. But then they suckered us into chasing them and they turned on us and destroyed the guns before they could fire again. Maybe if we'd just stayed put, let them come to us…"

"They're not stupid, Andrew."

"No, they saw what we were doing and adapted to it. If we'd stayed put, they'd probably have tried to flank us or something. Still, they aren't invulnerable. Our weapons can kill them. We just need to adjust our tactics to match the situation. And there are a whole lot more of us than there are of them! We just need to bring our numbers to bear. We can still beat them."

"Right! And we need more aircraft! If I'd still been around during the battle, I could have warned you of their trap. I need to get back and into another flier!"

Andrew stared at the man in wonder. "You'd actually do that? Get into one of those contraptions again? Even after what happened?"

"Of course! This wasn't my first crash, you know! Now that I know what those heat rays can do, I'll stay well clear next time!"

"Tom, you're crazy—but I'm glad we've got you. Now all we need to do is…"

"Major! Major!" Andrew jumped as McGill crashed through the door into the shack. White jerked awake with a grunt. "Major! Beasley's back and he says there's somethin' coming!"

Andrew leapt up and hurried out. Beasley was another one of the scouts that had been sent out, and now he was back, on a lathered horse. "What did you see?" he demanded.

"At least five of the things, sir!" gasped the man.

"Coming this way?" He looked around him and the only way out of the canyon was into the mine.

"Uh, no, I don't think so, sir. They're following the railroad—or where the railroad used to run— but, sir, there's something else with them!"

"What?"

"I couldn't get very close, but it looked like a bunch of people!"

"People? With the Martians?"

"That's what it looked like, sir. Maybe… maybe you can see more with your field glasses, sir. They're not movin' very fast. Probably be a half hour before they're even with the road leadin' up to this place."

"Well," said Andrew. "Then let's go have a look. Sergeant, get me a horse, will you?"

"Sir, do you think it's a good idea to…?"

"We were sent out here to learn what we could about the Martians, Sergeant. I want to see what this is all about. But we'll be careful."

"Yes, sir."

"Mind if I come along?" It was White, looking fully awake now.

Andrew hesitated. Did he want the civilian with him? What if he panicked and gave away their position? Still, the man had an eye for detail. Maybe he could dictate any observations he made to him. "All right, let's go."

He, White, and McGill mounted up and then followed Beasley back the way he had just come. They went along the road and then out into the more open spaces. Beasley led them to a little rise where they dismounted and cautiously walked up to a spot where they could see out to the north.

"There, sir. Do you see them?" said Beasley, pointing.

Andrew could see them; five Martian tripods, just as he'd said. They were four or five miles away at least and there did seem to be something moving along with them. Andrew took out his field glasses and focused on them. It was hard to see clearly, but there was definitely something there. Maybe they were people...

"I want a closer look."

"Sir..." said McGill.

"If we head down that way, into that big rock pile, we'll have some good cover and they should pass right by us, no more than a mile away. Now let's go, before they get closer."

His two men clearly didn't like the idea, but Andrew was determined to get a close look at what was going on. People? With the Martians? What did that mean? They mounted up again and moved quickly down the slopes, being careful to keep higher ground between them and the Martians, until they reached the cluster of rocks he had seen earlier. They tied their horses in a sheltered spot and then worked their way through the rocks until they found a place where they could see without exposing themselves. Andrew edged forward until he could spot the Martians. They were much easier to see now, although a fold in the ground blocked everything except the upper parts of the Martian machines. Whatever had been moving with them could not be seen from here. But they were moving west, slowly, and if they kept going as they were, he'd get a good look at them and whatever was with them as they went by.

They waited. The Martians got closer. Andrew suddenly felt very exposed, but it was too late to pull out now. Then, finally, the Martians moved past the ground that obstructed the view and Andrew saw what was moving along with the tripods.

"Damn," he hissed.

"What is it?" asked White.

"People. Soldiers. Prisoners, I guess."

"Prisoners?" gasped Beasley much too loudly. "I thought they just killed everyone!"

"Our men, for sure, sir?" asked McGill.

"Quiet, both of you. Yeah, I can see the uniforms. Too far to make out any faces, but—Damn!"

"What?"

"One... One of the men fell and he couldn't get up and... and they just burned him." Andrew's eyes were glued to his field glasses and he couldn't look away. There appeared to be several hundred men in the group and they were being herded along like cattle. The five Martian machines ringed them in, waving their long, thin tentacles at them. Any man lagging was given a nudge, but if they fell and didn't get up... Many of the men were being helped by their comrades.

"What would they want prisoners for, sir?" asked Beasley. "What are they gonna do with them?"

"I don't know..."

"There were some rumors," said White. "From the first invasion in England, I mean. One man claimed that..."

"I've seen the reports!" snapped Andrew. "It was dismissed as the ravings of a madman!"

"But there were other..."

126

"Mister White, *shut up!*" He looked back and fixed the newspaperman in his gaze. Then he flicked his eyes toward Beasley. The soldier was clearly close to panic. He was pretty close to panic himself. He *had* read the reports, and they were conclusive.

White blinked, caught on, nodded, and then shut up.

"So what do we do, sir?" asked McGill. "Those are our 'mates.'" There was a strange expression, an anger, on the man's face that Andrew had never seen before.

"We're not exactly in shape to mount a rescue, Sergeant."

"No, but we gotta do something… sir."

"Yes we do." He thought for a moment and then nodded his head. "The Martians are clearly taking them *somewhere*. We need to find out where that is. It's important. And if we know where our men are being held, maybe we can come get them when the army regroups. So as for what we are going to do… We're going to follow them."

* * * * *

CYCLE597,843.5, EAST OF HOLDFAST 32-1

This is highly inefficient, reflected Qetjnegartis. The prey-animals were moving in the desired direction, but at a terribly slow pace. Unfortunately, there seemed to be no way to speed them up. Their legs were only a tiny fraction of the length of those on the fighting machines, and they could only move so fast in this miserable gravity. And while that made them very easy to catch, once caught, you were left with the problem of getting them where you wanted them. Qetjnegartis was coming to regret giving the order to start harvesting in the aftermath of the battle.

At the time, it had seemed a reasonable decision. Sustenance was needed and much was close at hand. The areas around the new holdfast were nearly barren, with all the prey-creatures destroyed or fled. It did not seem wise to pass up such an opportunity. So its subordinates had encircled a large group of fleeing prey, and using warning blasts of the heat rays, herded them into a compact group. The bipedal prey seemed to comprehend what was wanted of them, and it took only a few demonstrations of the penalty for refusing to comply to get them all moving in the proper direction. The four-legged ones were not so quickly trained and nearly all tried to flee. Many were destroyed before Qetjnegartis ordered a stop to that. The creatures were no threat and might be harvested at some later time.

So the prey had been herded toward the holdfast. At first they had moved at a reasonable pace, but this had gradually slowed as the creatures became fatigued. Finally, after nightfall, the entire lot of them had fallen to the ground as a group and refused to move, even after several had been destroyed as a warning. Clearly, the things were incapable of moving farther without rest. Several of Qetjnegartis' subordinates had urged that the entire group be destroyed so they could keep moving, but it had refused that course of action. There was no immediate urgency. The enemy army had been destroyed and it was unlikely that any new threats would arise for some time. Besides, despite the inconvenience, it was finding a certain fascination in observing the actions and reactions of these creatures.

The first expedition had had no opportunity for any detailed study of them. This time they would have to make the effort to learn about them so that they could be better controlled—or better destroyed if necessary. Qetjnegartis did agree, however, that all ten war machines were not needed for this task. It sent five back to the holdfast with orders to scour the entire area and make sure it was secure. Interestingly, some of the prey-creatures seemed to take this lessening of the guard as an opportunity to escape. None had succeeded and the others gave up the attempts. Apparently they did have some limited ability to reason.

The next day they continued, allowing the creatures brief stops for rest. Again, with the coming of darkness, the prey refused to move further. And again Qetjnegartis' subordinates made their frustration known. "Commander, each of us can carry three or four of the creatures. Let us do that and destroy the rest. This world is teaming with them; we will have ample opportunities to collect more. This is a serious waste of time."

"I disagree," countered Qetjnegartis. "The area around the holdfast will soon become deserted of prey as they learn to avoid it. With the arrival of our new buds, much sustenance will be needed. And we must begin a detailed study of these creatures as soon as practicable. Many samples will be needed. In any case, these are my orders."

The others obeyed, of course. The genetic links of descent were unbroken, and obedience was automatic. Still, a wise leader took the opinions of others into its calculations. "But, we can make use of this waiting time. I fully agree that the methods we are using are inefficient. In the future we will need new machines, better suited to this task. Let us spend this time to consider what changes will be needed to best meet our future needs."

* * * * *

FEBRUARY, 1909, NEW MEXICO TERRITORY

Becca Harding had no idea where they were. They'd left the town of Ramah three days earlier and had ridden northwest, just as Sergeant Dolfen had said they would. But this was a part of New Mexico completely strange to her. Fortunately, the way had been fairly easy. A road of sorts followed a long narrow valley between the tall mountains to the east and a lower set of hills to the west. Pine trees covered the lower slopes of both and provided concealment, firewood, and a break from the chill winds. It was still very cold, although something in the air spoke of the coming spring.

But what sort of a spring was this going to be? Any normal spring would see her helping with the plantings, and much more fun: helping with the new foals that would be born. Of course, this spring would have been different in any case. She'd have been fretting about her mother's plot to send her to that school back east and trying to figure out how to foil it. But there wouldn't be any planting this spring, no new foals; and even the removal of the threat of school couldn't lighten her heart. Her whole world had been destroyed, burned up. Gone.

What was she going to do? The sergeant had talked of getting her back to her aunt and uncle in Santa Fe and she supposed it was inevitable that she would end up there. They weren't going to let a young girl go wandering around in the middle of a war. War. That's what this was now, wasn't it? When she'd been very young there had still been some troubles with the Indians in the region and there had been a few raids and some fighting. But nobody called it a war. A few years later there had been a war with Spain, but that was so far away and so brief than few people paid it any real mind. And then there had been the Civil War. That was a real war! Her grandfather told many stories about it, even though this far west there hadn't been much more than a few skirmishes, although her grandfather made them sound like great battles.

But now, here, where she lived, there was a real war. Not a skirmish, not a raid; an invasion. The Martians were destroying everything, killing everyone, and there didn't seem to be any way to stop them. Sergeant Dolfen had been very excited by the sound of the cannons the other day and felt sure that the army had stopped the Martians or at least hurt them badly. How he could tell that just by some distant noise, she didn't know. Becca was far less confident. She had seen the horrible Martian machines close up—far closer than any of these soldiers—and she couldn't see how anything could stop them. She supposed they would be stopped eventually. This was America, after all, and any problem could be solved! But how long would it take? How much fighting? How many more people were going to get killed? What could she do to help?

That was the question she'd been asking herself. How could she help beat the Martians? She desperately wanted to help beat the Martians! She was sensible enough to realize that she wasn't going to be able to personally wreck their machines and kill the things driving them, but there must be all sorts of people needed to help and support the men who actually would do the wrecking and killing, such as cooks and laundresses and nurses. Could she be one of them? Would they let her? She was very certain that her oh-so-proper aunt in Santa Fe would not let her do any such thing! She still might even send her off to that school in Connecticut! So what could she do?

As they jogged along the road, she pondered the problem. There were sixteen of them in the party now; the eight soldiers, Mrs. Gordon and her boy, Mr. Kershaw, four new people from Ramah, three men and a woman who had decided to join them—and Becca. They had managed to find enough horses for all of them and even two extras to carry supplies. Becca rode Ninny, of course; the animal seemed to have recovered completely from his ordeal. She was still thinking about her problems when they reached a spot where the sergeant decided they would camp for the night. As always, they put the fire in a place where the light would not carry far, and they huddled around to cook their meals.

"Okay, tomorrow we will be getting pretty close to Fort Wingate and Gallup," announced Dolfen. "No telling what we might find there, so we're gonna have to be real careful. Hopefully some of our people will be there, but that still means we gotta be careful. I know we don't look anything like a Martian, but if they've been through here, our men are going to have jittery trigger fingers. Wouldn't do to get shot by our own side!"

This left everyone very thoughtful and there wasn't much talk before they all turned in. The next morning they had their breakfast and got moving again. The easy path through the long valley soon ended in a jumble of rocks and hills. The mountains off to their right petered out here, sloping down toward the flatter ground, but there still were foothills and outliers that thrust to the west. They spent most of the morning climbing up and over them. Just before noon, they caught a view of the flat lands stretching north and west. The sergeant stopped there a while, trying to catch a view of the town of Gallup, but it was hazy and too far to see anything, even with the scope from Becca's rifle. They started down the other side and stopped for lunch in a little canyon.

"So what do you think, Sarge?" asked Private Urbaniak. "Should we head for the fort, or the town? The town's farther, but the ground's a lot easier." From what Becca had been able to understand from earlier conversations, Gallup was down on the flat, but Fort Wingate was up in the foothills farther to the east. An area of rough ground lay between it and where they were now. They would have to go over or around that if they were going to go to the fort.

Sergeant Dolfen was silent for a while and then said: "I think we're gonna split the difference. Head north to the railway. Once we get there, we can get a look at both the fort and the town and see which looks better. If the fort's okay, we'll go there first and report in. But it's still another twenty miles at least. We won't get there today." This brought some moans of disappointment from the civilians. Another night out in the cold.

They were just getting up from around their tiny cook fire when the man on guard gave a strangled shout: "*Hey! Hey!* Look out!"

Becca sprang up, but it was already far too late. One of the Martian machines was coming around the end of the canyon, not a hundred feet away! She stood frozen for an instant and then turned to run.

But there was nowhere to go.

The sides of the canyon were too steep and the Martian was at the lower end. The upper end was where the horses were, but they were already bucking in terror and dragging their picket pins out of the ground. Anyone trying to go that way would risk being trampled. But that was still better than being burned up! They all ran in that direction, but a moment later Becca heard that horrible sound, the sound of the Martian heat ray.

She expected to die. She expected one instant of unbearable agony and then oblivion as she was burned to nothing. Just like Star, just like her mother and grandmother. Then she felt the heat, she saw a dazzling light from in front of her...

But she didn't die.

The heat ray passed over her head and struck the ground between the people and the horses. It swept in a line from one wall of the canyon to the other, burning a glowing trench in the ground. Then it swept back again, coming a bit closer as it did. Ninny and all the other horses broke free and galloped off, screaming as terrified horses do. She heard gunfire, shouts, and human screams from behind her, but she just stared at the vanishing horses and waited for death.

Someone bumped into her and nearly knocked her down. Only then did she turn around. The Martian was only about fifty feet away now, towering over them. Its single red eye seemed to be staring right at her. The soldier who had been on guard was working the bolt on his rifle and pulling the trigger again and again, but the gun was empty and all it produced was a click. Sergeant Dolfen had his pistol drawn, but wasn't firing. The others were all in a clump pushing slowly back.

Suddenly one of the soldiers, Private Johnson, screamed and ran. He leapt over one of the smoldering trenches, but before he could go another dozen paces, the heat ray blasted him to a cloud of smoke.

"Stand your ground!" shouted Dolfen. "If it wanted to kill us, we'd all be dead now!" Everyone huddled behind the Sergeant, staring at the machine. What was happening? Why hadn't it killed them? Becca squeezed in behind Dolfen, trembling like a leaf.

The thing just stood there, like some ancient god deciding on what doom to pronounce for the puny mortals at its feet. The seconds ticked on and on for what seemed like hours. Mrs. Gordon was whimpering and her boy was crying. "No one move!" hissed Dolfen.

Finally, the giant stirred. It took a few steps backward on its long, spikey legs. Was it leaving? But then the heat ray lashed out again. For an instant Becca thought the god had decreed death. But the ray passed over them like before. Looking back, they saw the ray was again sweeping between the walls of the canyon, but now on each sweep it was coming closer and closer!

"Move!" cried Dolfen. "Forward!"

There was no choice. Step by terrified step, they stumbled forward, toward the Martian. It continued to retreat before them, just as the heat ray continued to advance behind them. They were forced to follow the machine down to the end of the canyon. Becca glanced to her left and saw that there was a second canyon that came down out of the hills; that was how the Martian had gotten so close unseen.

As they came out into the open and were no longer hemmed in by the canyon, one of the men from Ramah tried to run for it, but he was destroyed just like Private Johnson had been. He didn't get twenty feet.

"Stay together, dammit!" snarled Dolfen. "We can't escape like this! Not now! We'll wait for a better chance!"

The two deadly examples were enough. No one strayed far from the sergeant. Once the Martian had them in the open, it used the heat ray and its long thing tentacles to herd them forward, with it following behind.

"Where's it taking us?" whispered Becca.

"It looks like we're going northwest—toward Gallup."

"What's it going to *do* with us?" whimpered Mrs. Gordon.

The sergeant didn't answer.

CHAPTER NINE

FEBRUARY, 1909, NEAR FORT WINGATE, NEW MEXICO TERRITORY

"What are they going to do with them, sir?"

Andrew cut short an angry reply. This was at least the twentieth time one of his men had asked that question. He and his troops had been shadowing the Martians and their captives for two days now and every day someone—usually half a dozen someones—asked him the question. *How the hell should I know?* Except that he *did* know. The classified reports from the first invasion in England said that the Martians fed themselves by draining the blood out of animals. Out of people. *We're just food to them.* It was a horrifying, infuriating notion. How dare they? How dare they treat people as food? Okay, they had heat rays and big war machines and they could travel between the worlds. But humans hadn't done too badly, either! *We've built big cities and the pyramids and railways and we're digging a canal across Panama! We're clearly intelligent beings!*

His thoughts went back to a long-ago conversation he'd had with Colonel Hawthorne where he'd compared the Martian invasion of Earth with the European's invasion of the Americas. Yes, the Europeans had ignored the accomplishments of the Aztecs and Incas and killed and enslaved them. But they didn't eat them!

Maybe it wasn't as bad as it seemed. Maybe the incidents in England had been acts of desperation. Maybe the Martians had lost their own food supplies somehow and had to prey on humans or starve. Maybe they didn't eat people as a routine. *If that's the case then what are they going to do with the prisoners?* Slaves? Laboratory animals to be vivisected? Zoo exhibits? Not comforting thoughts, to be sure, but better than being eaten. Well, vivisection would be about as bad, he supposed. Worse, maybe.

"Runnin' out o' cover up ahead, sir. What do we do?"

Andrew jerked out of his dark thoughts. Sergeant McGill had come up next to him and was pointing ahead. Yes, it was true. They had been following the Martians on a parallel course, keeping to the cover of the foothills so they wouldn't be seen. But up ahead, the land was flattening out and if they kept going, they would be spotted for sure. There were just twelve of them now. They'd left one man back at the mine with Captain Selfridge. They had two extra horses they were using to carry the supplies they'd found. A small party, but still too large to escape being seen out in the open.

"We could swing further south, up that way," he said. "More cover there."

"But we'd probably lose sight of them if we did that, sir."

"Yes, but they've been following the path of the railway without deviating a bit, Sergeant. After all this time, I think we can assume they'll keep doing so. If we pick up our pace and swing wide to the south, we can get ahead of them and then wait for them to catch up again."

"Very good, sir."

Andrew looked closely at McGill. He still wasn't quite sure what to make of the man. He was always perfectly courteous with his *yes sirs* and *no sirs*, but every now and then he'd throw in a *very good sir* when it seemed like he truly agreed with one of Andrew's decisions. He was pleased when he got one of those, but it also made him wonder what was really going on in the Scotsman's head when he just got a *yes sir.*

He gave the order and they turned further south. As McGill had said, they quickly lost sight of the Martian machines and their captives. There weren't so many captives anymore and that was weighing on his mind as well. More and more of them were dropping and unable to get up again. Neither the threat of instant incineration nor the entreaties of their comrades could rouse them. Once or twice he'd seen men who were still on their feet refusing to leave a fallen comrade and both men had died. Clearly, the captives were getting weaker and weaker. They did have some food in their haversacks—or they did when they'd started, it was probably all eaten by now—and they'd passed over several creeks where they'd filled their canteens, so they hadn't gone completely hungry or thirsty, but surely they couldn't go much farther without more rest. Did the Martians realize this? Did that mean they were getting close to their destination? Or perhaps they didn't care—although it seemed foolish to take all this time to herd their captives along, only to destroy them all anyway.

"Where do you think they're headed?" asked Bill White. He got asked that question a lot, too. The newspaper man had insisted on coming along. He'd tried to convince him to stay back at the mine with Tom Selfridge, but here he was.

"I'm guessing Fort Wingate or Gallup," he replied. "The men can't go much farther than that."

"And what do you think is there?"

"No idea. Maybe the Martians are setting up some sort of base."

"I suppose that would make sense. If they are really planning to conquer the Earth, they'll need to permanently occupy places to operate out of. They can't hope to control everything from their original landing sites."

"No, that's true, especially when those sites are so far away from our cities and all. You're quite the strategist, Mr. White."

"Just common sense."

"At the Academy they taught us that common sense is one of the most important things a good commander can have."

"Really? Do you suppose that General Sumner skipped class the day they taught that?"

Andrew was silent for a while before he answered. "He... he didn't do too badly considering the situation."

"He got his whole army destroyed! How could he have done worse?"

Andrew shrugged. "It's a whole new type of warfare. No one's ever had to deal with something like this before. An enemy whose entire force is composed of highly mobile, heavily armored, heavily armed machines? A lot of the old rules just don't apply anymore. Tactically, anyway. Strategically? I'm not sure. But I think you're right that they'll need to build outposts and fortresses and bases of operation. As powerful as their machines are, they've only got a limited number of them. We estimate that two hundred cylinders landed. If each one has three machines in it then that's only six hundred spread over the whole world. If they really do mean to conquer us, they will have to build bases where they can dig mines and build factories so they can build more machines." He lowered his voice. "And they'll need food. Or places to store their food, anyway. Maybe that's where they are taking our men."

White nodded. "So the rumors are true, eh? But you were right to tell me to shut up, Major. It's a damn scary idea, isn't it?"

"Yes, sir. Damn scary."

The conversation died and they concentrated on making their best time through the rugged terrain along the base of the mountains. The mountains themselves had dwindled considerably as they proceeded west. There were now just some ridges only four or five hundred feet higher than the plains to the north. But most of the slopes were steep and covered with pine trees. It was slow going, but Andrew was confident they were still moving a lot faster than those poor devils being herded by the Martians.

Around noon, a strong smell of smoke filled the air. They proceeded cautiously and soon came around the curve of one of the hills to see Fort Wingate spread out in front of them. Or what was left of it. The place looked to have been about two dozen large wooden buildings enclosing a big parade ground on three sides, with many more, smaller buildings scattered about. Now, all those structures had been burned to the ground. Some were just blackened rectangles on the ground, but others had sizeable piles of debris remaining. A few of those were still giving off thin clouds of smoke. Smaller black patches showed where men had died. Andrew had become all-too familiar with the looks of those.

They studied the place for a while, but there was no sign of any Martians in the vicinity, so they rode down and took a closer look. No one had any doubt what had happened, but there were hundreds of the triangular holes in the ground that the feet of the tripods made if any confirmation was needed. The destruction was nearly total, although ironically, the fort's flag pole was untouched, and the Stars and Stripes rippled gently in the breeze. They spotted a few charred bodies in the piles of debris, apparently men killed by the burning buildings rather than the heat rays directly. Someone suggested burying them, but there clearly wasn't time and Andrew said no, even though it hurt to do so. The smell was becoming overpowering, so they didn't want to linger long. They were just about to press on when a cry brought them to a halt.

"Hey! Hey there! Wait!"

Andrew looked around for the source and then spotted a lone figure running out of the woods that covered the ridge to the south. He was waving his arms and shouting. They turned their horses and trotted toward him. As they got closer they could see that the man was wearing a soot-covered uniform; his hands and face were also blackened with soot. He stopped and waited for them, gasping for breath.

"Oh, thank God! Thank God! I didn't think anyone was ever gonna come!"

"Were you part of the garrison here, soldier?" asked Andrew, reining his horse to a stop. "What's your name?"

"Yes... yes, sir. 5th Cavalry. Name's Flanagan, sir."

"What happened?" It was a stupid question: there was no doubt what had happened. But he wanted to hear it from the man.

"Martians, sir! Just like everyone was talking about! Big as life! Have you seen 'em?"

"Yes. But what happened here, Private? Can you tell me?"

"Yessir, it was... I dunno, a few weeks ago. Lost track of the days, sir. A day or two after those messengers from the colonel came back. I was on watch one night. There was this bright red glow from off toward Gallup. A fire for sure. I told the sergeant of the guard and he sent me to tell the officer of the day. I hadn't but got to his office when those... things came busting into the fort! It was hell sir, pure hell. Everything on fire, people running and screaming. I emptied my rifle into one of them giants, but it didn't do no good! After that... after that, there wasn't nothing to do but try to get out. What else could I do, sir?" The man looked at him beseechingly, like he was expecting Andrew to grant him absolution for surviving. "What else could I do?"

"Nothing, Private, nothing at all. You did right to stay alive so you could report."

The look of relief on the man's face made Andrew want to weep. He and all his men were alive only because they'd gotten out. So they could report. Yeah, so they could report. "Did anyone else get away?"

"Yeah, yeah, there were about a dozen of us that got up into the hills."

"They still up there?"

"No, well, there's Lieutenant Davis. He was hurt bad and couldn't move. I stayed with him. Couldn't just leave him there. But the others, they wouldn't stay. They left after a couple of days. But I couldn't leave the lieutenant. Have you got a doctor with you?" He looked around, his eyes searching. "When's the rest of the relief getting here? They'll have a doctor, won't they?"

An uneasy silence settled over the group. Finally, Andrew said: "They're still a ways off, Private. We were just scouting ahead. Might be a while before they get here. But can you take us to your lieutenant? We might be able to do something."

"Sure, sir! Follow me!" His face lit up like a puppy invited for a walk. He turned and went back the way he had come, past the burned-out buildings, and then up the hill to the south. The way was steep and they were all forced to dismount to follow the path. After perhaps a quarter of a mile they came to a little hollow in the hillside where a crude lean-to had been constructed out of pine branches. Someone was lying under it. "There he is!" pointed Flanagan. "Sir! Sir! I've brought help!"

The figure didn't move and there was a smell in the air that made Andrew cringe. McGill went forward and knelt down for a moment and then shook his head. He got up and came over. "Been gone a while, sir. At least a few days." He sniffed. "Maybe more."

Flanagan was still talking excitedly about help arriving. Andrew took him by the arm. "Soldier... Soldier! Your lieutenant's dead. I'm sorry." The man reacted like he'd been punched in the belly. He looked at the body and then and Andrew and back again. Then he collapsed to the ground and started crying.

"Poor blighter," said McGill.

"Yes, but what the hell are we going to do with him? I hate to just leave him here, but there's no question of taking him with us."

"No, that's true, sir. We could send him back to the mine where we left Captain Selfridge. The pack horses are carrying half loads now, we could put everything on one and give him the other."

"He'd never find it on his own."

"No, but if we sent someone with him..."

"We can't really spare anyone, Sergeant."

"I know sir, I know, but... well, I'm worried about Lansing." McGill jerked his head toward one of the men.

"Lansing? What's the matter with him?"

"Not sure, but he's been acting a bit quirky lately, if you take my meaning, sir. His pal got killed during the fight and he's taken it hard. And this... uh, mission you've got us on, I'm afraid it might be more than he can take."

"I... see," said Andrew slowly, trying hard not to stare at Private Lansing. His voice fell to a whisper. "Is there anyone else?"

"Don't think so, sir. Most of the lads are fine. Scared, sure, but eager to do something that could hurt those bastards. Lansing is just… well, he needs to go back, I think."

"All right. We'll send him with Flanagan."

"Yes, sir."

"And Sergeant? Thanks for noticing that. I should have seen it myself."

"My job, sir. You've got other things on your mind."

They buried Lieutenant Davis as quickly as they could and sent the two men back the way they'd come. Lansing protested at first, but quickly gave in and then looked relieved. Yes, better not to take him along. He tried to convince Mr. White to go with them, but the newspaperman insisted on continuing. So Andrew and the ten others moved out and put as much distance between Fort Wingate and themselves as they could before nightfall. They stayed up on the ridge, among the trees, as much as they could and it wasn't until the sun was going down that they got a clear view out to the west. The town of Gallup ought to be off that way… but…

"What the devil is that?" said McGill.

"What? Oh!" A half dozen miles out onto the plain there was an odd line drawn across the ground. It seemed to bend toward them and then away again before vanishing in the evening mist. Andrew pulled out his field glasses.

"What is it, sir?"

"I think it's what we've been looking for."

"Sir?"

"It's some sort of embankment, an earthen wall that's been piled up. Around the town, I guess. It looks to be a huge circle, a few miles in diameter at least."

"See any of the Martians?"

"No… no, I don't see any of the tripods, but there are several dust clouds rising up from behind the embankment. This has got to be some sort of base or fort!"

"It's enormous," observed Bill White. "Why would they need something so large?"

"I don't know. Maybe we can find out."

The men got very quiet at that and dispersed to make camp. McGill came up to him later. "Are you really gonna try to get into that place, sir?"

"I don't know. I'd love to be able to get up on the embankment and at least get a look inside."

"Pretty damn risky, if you don't mind my saying so."

"I know, I know and I don't intend to commit suicide, Sergeant. But I at least want to scout around and see if there's any way I could get up close to it. And I won't need everyone for that."

"Begging your pardon, sir, but it seems to me that we've completed our mission. We've found their base and we know they are herding prisoners in there. Anything more we could learn wouldn't balance the risk of gettin' killed and not gettin' the word back."

"I'm at least going to take a look around in the morning."

McGill sighed. "If you say so, sir."

Andrew frowned as his sergeant moved away. Was he being stupid here? What McGill said was correct: it probably was an unjustifiable risk. But to turn back now when they were this close to maybe actually learning something useful? *'Maybe' being the operative word!* If he was sure there was something important he could learn then, yes, it would be worth the risk. But he was just hoping.

Could he risk himself—and maybe everyone else—on a maybe? Maybe he should sleep on it…

"Sir! Sir!" one of the men hurried up. It was Beasley, he'd been on lookout.

"What?"

"I spotted what looks like a campfire, sir! Maybe three or four miles off to the southwest!"

"Really? Show me!" He followed Beasley, stumbling over tree roots in the dark, until they reached a spot with a view. Sure enough, there was a faint speck of light off in the distance. He looked through his field glasses and there was no doubt that it was a small fire. Most everyone in the group else had trailed along and they started talking.

"What d'you think it is, sir?" asked Corporal Kennedy.

"Well, people, probably," he replied.

"Really careless people," said another man.

"Yeah, if we can spot them, any Martians around probably can, too."

"Maybe they don't know," said White.

"How could they not know?"

"I imagine the newspaper deliveries have been rather irregular around here of late."

"Quiet, all of you," ordered Andrew.

"What do we do, sir?" asked McGill.

Andrew sighed. "Let's go find out who they are. If they're people trying to get away, we can have them douse that fire and direct them back the way we came. If they aren't… well, they might even be survivors from Fort Wingate or the rest of the 5th Cavalry. They were supposed to be scouting around here. If that's the case we can add them to us. McGill, Beasley, come with me. The rest of you stay on alert. We'll be back soon."

They wearily re-saddled their weary horses and headed off toward the light. It wasn't easy going in the dark and Andrew nearly changed his mind about the whole venture. His irritation increased when he discovered that Bill White had joined them. "What are you doing here?" he demanded.

"Just being nosey. I'm a reporter, remember?"

They covered a couple of miles and slowly approached where they thought they'd seen the fire. They'd lost sight of it a number of times as they moved over the rough ground, but always spotted it again. They had to be getting close. Just who were these idiots? By all the accounts Andrew had heard at General Sumner's staff meetings, the Martians must have swept through this area to have reached Fort Wingate and Gallup. How could any people still in the vicinity not know about that? And not have the sense to keep their fires concealed? Andrew peered through the dark, trying to see. There! He saw the fire again. It was only a few hundred yards away; they'd come farther than he'd thought. Wait… what was….?

"Halt!" he hissed. "Stop!"

"What is it…?"

"Quiet! Don't move!"

Heart pounding, he slowly drew out his field glasses. The light from the fire showed a group of people clustered around it, but it had also reflected off something else… something big… It was almost invisible in the dark, but then it moved slightly and he was sure.

"A Martian! There's a tripod there! To the right of the fire!"

"Bloody hell!" whispered McGill. "Let's get out of here!"

"It hasn't seen us! No sudden moves! But there are people around that fire!" He continued to stare through the glasses.

"More prisoners? Blokes from the 5th, you think?"

"Yes, I think… *Oh God!*"

"What?"

"Women! At least two women and a kid, I think."

"Saints preserve them," hissed McGill. Beasley cursed.

A chill passed through Andrew. Somehow, amidst all his nightmare thoughts and speculations on the eventual fate of the captured soldiers, he'd never really considered this possibility. Despite all the evidence he'd seen of the Martians' utter ruthlessness, he had still thought about this in conventional military terms. The invaders might slaughter or enslave or feed upon or vivisect soldiers they captured, but civilians? Women and children? Hundreds, probably thousands of women and children had been killed in the first invasion in England, but he'd still thought of that as the unfortunate, but inevitable fate of people caught up in a raging battle. It hadn't been deliberate, had it?

Yes it had.

The full realization came to him like a thunderbolt: the Martians didn't care. They might not even know that humans had a distinction between soldiers and civilians, but they wouldn't care, even if they did. No more than an average person would distinguish between a soldier ant and a worker ant. *We're all the same to them: things to be killed! Things to be eaten!* This war would be one without mercy.

On either side!

A burning anger began to grow inside Andrew. They had to be stopped! These monsters had to be stopped! Before they could do this to more people. To people like his landlady back in Albuquerque, or to Victoria back in Washington!

"Sir? Sir!" McGill had grabbed his arm and was tugging at him. "Women, sir! We can't let those devils have 'em! What do we do?"

Andrew stared McGill in the eyes.

"We stop them."

* * * * *

FEBRUARY, 1909, WASHINGTON, D.C.

Major General Leonard Wood, Chief of Staff of the United States Army, looked down at his left foot and cursed. The damn thing was twitching again and the tingling was spreading all along his left side. The fingers on his left hand were numb and he could barely move them. Damnation! This wasn't the time for this! A half-dozen years earlier he'd been forced to have an operation on his brain for a tumor that was growing there. It had been a risky thing to do, but the results had been miraculous and he'd had no more troubles for years. But now they were coming back again. There was no time for another operation! What was he going to do? If any hint of this got out, there would be calls for him to step down, and he was not going to do that!

He jerked erect when he heard Theodore Roosevelt boom a greeting to his aide in the outer office. A moment later the President strode through the door. "Morning, Leonard! Morning!"

"Good morning, Mr. President," he replied, awkwardly getting to his feet. He shrugged his left hand into the pocket of his tunic. "How are you today?"

"Splendid! Splendid! That message you sent me last night from Funston was just what I needed. Slept like a baby!"

"Theodore, all it said was that he had reached Albuquerque and had taken command of the forces in the region."

"Yes, but the mere fact that he was in Albuquerque and not the Martians is good news, eh? Yesterday you were worried that if the Martians just kept advancing they would roll right over everything before a defense could be organized."

"True, and we've been very lucky—so far. The Martians have made the classic mistake of not pursuing a beaten foe to its destruction. If they had just kept advancing we could have been in serious trouble."

"Good to know that they do make mistakes, isn't it?"

"Very, but it doesn't begin to make up for the huge mistake we made in our own planning," said Wood. "Theodore, we have a hell of a task facing us and it's getting worse day by day."

"What do you mean? Something new has happened?"

"Yes. I'm afraid that the rumor of another landing in Idaho has finally been confirmed." He shoved a paper across his desk at Roosevelt. "It would appear that they landed in a very desolate area in the southeast part of the state. We've received word that they have now cut the east-west rail line near the town of Pocatello. No idea where they might move from there, but we have nothing nearby to stop them no matter which way they go."

Roosevelt consulted one of the many maps hanging on the wall. "Hmph!" he snorted. "Not that far from Yellowstone. I've been through that area, and yes, not many people live there. Doesn't seem like an immediate concern, Leonard."

"Perhaps, perhaps not. Theodore, there are six major transcontinental railroad lines. We have already lost the Southern Pacific from Santa Fe to Flagstaff. Now we've lost the Union Pacific line through Idaho. If that force at Pocatello moves south, we'll lose the other Union Pacific route that goes through Salt Lake City. That will leave us only the other Southern Pacific line that runs through El Paso and along the border with Mexico and the Northern Pacific and Great Northern lines in the far north. As we've heard, the Mexicans are already in a very bad way and the Canadians are nearly certain now that there is also a landing in Alberta. If so, we could lose all three lines in the next few months."

"Which would cut the country in half." The president looked properly sobered now.

"Yes, just as we foresaw months ago, and if they tear up the rail lines like we know they were doing in New Mexico, it will make it very difficult for us to launch any sort of counterattack against them. At least in the short term."

"That will make the canal all that more critical. It will be the only practical way of staying in touch with the west coast. Reminds me, when is that division going to embark for Panama?"

Wood suppressed a sigh. Roosevelt's obsession with the canal in Panama could be irritating at times. Not that he wasn't right about its importance. "They should be departing within the week. Of course, with this development in Idaho, we could really use them out west."

"One division in all that emptiness, Leonard? It might not make much difference out there. But the Isthmus is only twenty miles across and half of that is blocked by Gatun Lake. One division guarding ten miles could make all the difference."

"True, but I'm already getting frantic messages from the governors of Idaho, Montana, Wyoming, and Utah to send every man and gun I have to guard their territories. When they hear I'm sending troops to Panama instead, they are going to howl."

"Let them howl," snorted Roosevelt. "I'm used to howling. I've got the ambassadors from nearly every country in the Western Hemisphere howling outside my door right now."

"Which is why you're over here with me?" asked Wood, with a smirk.

"Of course! Of course!" replied the President with an answering grin. But the smile quickly faded. "I wish there was something we could do to help the poor devils. It's really starting to look like everything south of Texas is going to be overrun, except for Panama."

Wood consulted another map and then rifled through a sheath of papers, using only his right hand. "Most of the big coastal cities are holding out, from what we know, although La Paz seems to have fallen. But the interiors of all of the South American countries are in chaos. Still, that's mostly wilderness. If the cities can be defended, there may be some hope."

Roosevelt shook his head. "They don't have anything to hold with. Most of their armies are like something from a Gilbert and Sullivan operetta. And they have very little heavy industry to produce armaments. They import most of their weapons."

"Well, what about the Europeans? We talked about that before, and I know how much it irks you to bring them in after all the trouble we've gone through keeping them out, but it may be the only hope. Is this grand world alliance you're trying to build making any progress, Theodore?"

The President growled and shook his head. "Not enough. Those who need the help are the most enthusiastic and those who ought to be providing the help are the least. Everyone is paying lip service to the idea, but real, material aid is not forthcoming. The French and the Germans are the worst, blast them! They've got the most powerful armies on the planet and so far they've refused to send a man beyond their borders—even though no Martians have landed in Europe!"

"Any idea why? I'd think the Kaiser, in particular, would be eager to get involved. I met him back in '02 and again in '08 and you could see he was so damn proud of his army. You'd think he'd want to show what it could do—unless he's afraid of getting it banged up."

"Yes, you'd think so, wouldn't you? I really have no idea what Willy is up to. The times I've met him, you could tell we was just itching to expand his empire and prove that Germany really is a Great Power—as if any more proof was needed!" Roosevelt paused and then shook his head. "Honestly, I think he and the French are holding back to see just how badly the invasion hurts the British. They're both terribly jealous of the Brits, you know. Of course it hasn't helped that the British have been so stingy about sharing what they've learned from the Martian machines they captured. The French and Germans have been terrified that England will use their new knowledge to dominate the whole world."

"So they'd rather see the Martians dominate the world? I can't even think of a word to describe insanity like that!"

"I can think of a few, but I won't use them here," said Roosevelt. Wood nodded, the man almost never resorted to profanity, although he had the widest range of insulting non-profane vocabulary to describe people he disliked that Wood had ever encountered. "I'm hoping that they will come around once they see how serious this is. The Martians are going to be on the southern shores of the Mediterranean soon and coming over the Urals. The Tsar's armies have gotten themselves rather badly chewed up from what we're hearing."

"Hopefully that will bring them to their senses," said Wood. "But in the meantime we have to figure out how to defend our own territory."

"Well, we will be giving you the tools to do it soon enough, Leonard. The Conscription Act will be on my desk by this afternoon and I'll sign it at once. We'll have a million new men in uniform for you by the end of the year and another million every six months for... well, for quite a while."

"We need more than just men in uniforms, Mr. President. The reports from the battle indicate that small arms are useless against the enemy machines. We are going to need artillery in unprecedented amounts and in larger calibers—and the men trained to use it. We are going to need heavier machine guns—and a lot more of them—and we are going to need to develop weapons and tactics that can make infantry effective again—or all those millions of men in uniform are just going to be lambs to the slaughter."

"I know, and we are working to get you what you need. New contracts are going out every day. We're getting industry converted to war production and General Crozier's people are rushing the new weapons into service. We'll get you what you need. In the meantime, is there anything else I can do to help?"

Wood frowned. There was one thing he really wanted, but he wasn't sure he should ask. *Why not? I'm the Chief of Staff, damn it!*

"Can you get rid of Ainsworth for me?"

"Is he giving you trouble again?"

"Yes, to put it mildly. Despite my gentle, and not so gentle, reminders that the General Staff Act strips the Adjutant General of nearly all his old powers, he refuses to cooperate. Theodore, he simply has to go if I'm going to do my job."

Roosevelt scratched at his mustache, adjusted his pince-nez on his nose, and then nodded. "All right. I'll take care of it."

"Thank you, sir," sighed Wood in relief.

"You are welcome." Roosevelt straightened up and turned toward the door. "All, right, I'll leave you to it." He paused, turned back and eyed Wood closely. "Are you all right, Leonard? You don't look well."

Wood straightened up and put back his shoulders. "I'm fine, Theodore, just fine."

* * * * *

FEBRUARY, 1909, NEAR GALLUP, NEW MEXICO TERRITORY

Sergeant Franz Dolfen, 5th US Cavalry, watched the coming dawn, fingered his revolver, and tried to figure out the best way to make his death mean something. He was going to die; of that he was absolutely certain. The questions were: when and how? Part of him regretted not getting himself killed when they first saw the Martian machine. It would have been quick and easy and he wouldn't have any decisions to make now. But he hadn't. The presence of the girl and the other civilians had forced him to... to surrender.

Technically, he supposed he was a prisoner of war, even though he still had his pistol and two of his men had their rifles. Hell, even Becca was armed; her fool horse had bolted with the others, but the critter had come trotting up to their campfire during the night and he still had that old Henry in the saddle holster. The Martian didn't seem to object to the horse or their weapons. *It knows we can't hurt it.*

But he knew full well that the Martian didn't consider them prisoners of war. It wasn't going to treat them by any civilized rules based on tidy agreements between nations, even though it had allowed them to rest after a grueling day of marching. He'd heard the rumors about what had happened in England and he was quite certain this thing wasn't herding them along to some prison camp. He wasn't exactly sure where it was taking them, but he was certain it was somewhere he didn't want to go.

So he needed to arrange an escape.

An escape—not his escape.

There was no way they could all escape, but maybe some of them could. The ones who weren't going to escape needed to buy time for those who could. He looked around at the others. Most were still huddled around the fire trying to keep warm. They'd lost nearly all their blankets when the horses ran, so it had been a very miserable night. Miserable and terrifying. The Martian had loomed over them the whole time, never straying far even when it appeared to be walking a perimeter around them.

"Everyone, listen to me," he said in a low voice. Some of the people stirred, but some didn't. "Hey! Wake up! We'll be moving soon, I guess, and we need to make plans!" The rest finally turned and he could see everyone looking at him in the pale light. "We need to plan an escape. We don't want to go where this thing is taking us. We have to get away."

"It'll kill us with that ray it has!" protested one of the men from Ramah. "We won't get twenty yards!"

"If we all run in different directions, it won't get all of us. Some of us will get away."

"Are you crazy? You wanna die?"

"No, but unless we do something, that's what's going to happen to all of us! This thing isn't taking us wherever it's taking us for some damn tea party!"

"I'm with you, Sarge," said Private Urbaniak. "A quick death's better than whatever these monsters have in store for us. But why not do it in the dark?"

"The thing seems to see in the dark better than we do. In daylight at least we can avoid falling down when we run."

"Yeah, makes sense. So what's your plan?"

"I was watching it yesterday and it generally kept about fifty yards behind us. That's no good for us to try anything. But sometimes if we slowed down or we hit some rough ground it would come up right behind us to hurry us along. Today when that happens again, I'm gonna make a break and run right under the thing and back the way we came. It'll have to turn to go after me. When it does, that will be the signal for the rest of you to scatter."

There was a long silence and then Becca Harding said: "You're going to be killed, Sergeant."

"Does sorta put you right on the bull's-eye, Sarge," said Urbaniak.

"Maybe," said Dolfen, "but if the two of you with rifles take a pot-shot or two as you run, we might be able to get the thing turning in circles and not know where to shoot. But you have to move fast! Scatter and keep moving until you can get away clean or find some good spot to hide. Miss Harding, you get on that fool horse of yours and ride hard and don't look back! You hear me, girl?"

She didn't answer, but Mrs. Gordon was quick to ask her to take her boy with her and the boy immediately insisted on staying with his mother; the girl offered her horse to the two of them and some of the other civilians started objecting to the whole plan. Dolfen let it go on for a minute but then cut them all off.

"Shut up! All of you! We are going to do this, so be ready! If any of you don't want to run, that's your choice, I can't force you. But the rest of you all have to go in a different direction and here is what we'll do." He assigned a different direction by compass point to each of the people and hoped they wouldn't clump up into easy targets. He wasn't sure the girl was going to do what he told her, but there was no more time to argue. The Martian had become aware of their movements and apparently decided if they were rested enough for that, they were rested enough to move. It hooted at them and moved in, waving its tentacles. Dolfen was half-tempted to try the plan right then, but no, the thing was on alert. They needed to wait.

141

So they got to their feet and started moving. His legs and feet were aching and stiff with cold. He was cavalry, dammit, not infantry! Another reason not to try it now: he needed to get his muscles warm and stretched out before he tried any running. They stumbled along as the sun came up, all of them looking at him every few seconds until he told them he'd give them warning before he gave the command to run. After a while, the girl, leading her horse which she refused to ride, came up next to him.

"I don't want you to die, Sergeant."

"Well, I don't want me to die, either, but we have to try something."

"But why do you have to be the decoy?"

"I'm in command. It's my job."

"Maybe if you took my horse you'd have a better chance."

Dolfen snorted. "That critter won't leave you, Miss. I try taking him and he'll circle back to you and get all three of us killed."

"Then let me be the decoy. I can move a lot faster on horseback."

He sighed. He had known it was going to come to this. "No. It's my job. You just run and keep running."

"But…"

"Hey, what's that?" Private Cordwainer was a little in front of the rest. He stopped and pointed off to the northwest.

"What?" For a moment he was afraid that the man had spotted another Martian and that would totally ruin any escape attempt, but no, he didn't see any of the towering machines. What was… Oh.

The nearly level rays of the sun were lighting up a strange line across the horizon. It stood out brightly against the darker sky beyond. His eyes suddenly picked out a few familiar landmarks and he realized where they were except…

"Gallup is just over there, maybe six or seven miles, but what the hell is that?"

"Looks like some sort of wall…"

"But where's the town? We ought to be able to see it from here!"

But they couldn't see it. The mysterious wall blocked off the view. What was it? Something the Martians had built? Why? And what was left of the town behind?

They had all stopped, and now the Martian machine was close behind and hooting at them to move. "Let's go," said Dolfen. "There's a gully up ahead, I think. When we hit that be ready to run!"

There were no arguments now. The wall in the distance seemed more ominous than the machine right behind them. The people all clustered together until he ordered them to spread out a bit. The more dispersed they could be right at the start, the better. But the damn girl stayed close to him. Was she going to mess this all up by trying to help him? What could he do to give her the best chance? He really didn't want her to get killed…

He saw the gully about a hundred yards ahead. "All right, get ready! When we get to the gully, you all cross on over. I'm going to hold back and then reverse direction. When you hear my pistol, run like I told you!"

Dolfen was as frightened as he'd ever been in his life. It felt like there was a block of ice in his stomach. But he pulled out his pistol and held it against his chest so the Martian couldn't see. *For all the good it will do! Might as well throw rocks. But maybe it will get its attention.*

They reached the gully. It was only about eight feet deep, but the sides were fairly steep. They scrambled down into it and then the others went up the other side, the girl tugging on her horse's lead. Dolfen stopped at the bottom, took a deep breath, turned and...

What the hell?

There was a man. A man crouched in a little crevice in the side of the gully. He must have walked right past him without seeing... But he was holding something... something smoking. "Keep going!" the stranger hissed, waving with his free hand. Dolfen stumbled backward to the far side of the gully, just as one of the metal feet of the Martian machine stepped down into it.

The man leaped out of his hiding place and looped what he was holding around the ankle joint just above the foot. Two bundles, connected by a rope; bundles of... *dynamite!*

"Run, you idiot!" screamed the man, who instantly took his own advice and dashed away, down the gully. Dolfen gawked for a moment and then clawed his way up the other side and flung himself flat on the ground. An explosion slammed him even flatter; it felt like a horse had landed on him, knocking the breath out of his lungs. A cloud of smoke and dust enveloped everything. *Get up! Move!* He hauled himself to his feet, gasping and coughing.

The Martian was right there.

As the wind blew the smoke away, he found himself staring right into the red, glowing eye of the Martian, not ten feet away. Two of the machine's legs were still on the far side of the gully, but the foot of the third leg had been blown off by the explosion and the whole thing had stumbled forward. One metal arm was braced on the lip of the gully and the head was almost on a level with him. He stood there frozen as the two far legs stepped down, one after the other, and then the machine straightened up. The other arm, the one holding the heat ray device, swung up and out and a horrible buzzing filled the air.

But then there were other noises: shouts and screams and rifle shots, and he saw more men, men in uniform, appear from along the gully, charging toward the Martian. Another explosion slammed into him and he nearly fell. But so did the Martian. A cloud of smoke billowed up from the rear of the machine and it staggered a few steps to the side, jerking awkwardly with its truncated leg. Dolfen scooped up his pistol from where he'd dropped it, but what to do now? Run? Attack?

The heat ray shrieked to life and a blast of fire struck the ground thirty yards to his left and then swept toward him, incinerating everything it touched. He flung himself forward and leaped back into the gulley, and tumbled down the slope until he was nearly under the machine. He could feel the heat through his uniform. He scrambled along on hands and knees until he was behind the thing before he stood up.

A soldier appeared next to him swinging two bundles of dynamite connected by a rope as if it was a bolas. He let go and it soared up and up...

...and bounced off the Martian and fell almost at Dolfen's feet.

He stared at the smoldering fuses on the dynamite and then at the Martian which was turning his way, heat ray still blazing. Without thinking, he grabbed the rope and flung it upward with all his might. The dynamite bundles spun in a lazy arc... and then wrapped themselves around the arm holding the heat ray.

The incandescent trench had almost reached him when the other man tackled him, knocking him aside and sprawling them both on the ground. An instant later, the dynamite exploded, again punching the air from his lungs. The roar was deafening and the smoke blinding, but the heat suddenly cut off and a moment later the heat ray device, as big as a steamer trunk, thudded to the ground a few feet away from him, the metal claw still clutching it.

Ulla! Ulla! Ulla!

A call, like an undulating siren, rang out. Dolfen's stunned ears could only hear it faintly, but he could feel the vibrations it made deep in his chest. He twisted around, still half-pinned by the other man, and saw the machine drag itself out of the gully and start to limp away. Smoke was trailing from a spot near one hip, and sparks were spitting out of the stump of its arm.

More troops with bombs were converging on it. Ants attacking an elephant. *But these ants can sting!* Another explosion and the machine staggered again. Dolfen struggled to his feet and then climbed to the top of the gully. The Martian had lost another foot from the last bomb. It was trying to run, but it nearly fell.

Ulla! Ulla! Ulla!

The thing spun in a circle, its smaller tentacles lashing out wildly. One man was hit by them and went flying. But another closed in from behind and his bomb tangled on the already damaged hip joint. The blast rent the air and the entire leg was torn off, fragments tumbling away in all directions. The Martian made one last futile attempt to keep its balance and then came crashing down to the ground. It lay there for a moment as if stunned, but then its remaining limbs started thrashing about. A man dashed in and tossed another bomb onto the thing's head. The explosion didn't rip anything off this time, but the machine finally stopped moving and an eerie silence fell as the smoke cleared.

Dolfen stood there gawking, He fumbled out his canteen, but his hands were shaking so badly he could barely get the cap off and take a drink. Only then did he realize his mouth was full of grit. He choked and spat before taking another swig.

"Nice throw, Sergeant. I thought we were both dead."

He looked and saw the man who had tackled him and was surprised to see major's leaves on his tunic. "Uh… well, thank you, sir. If you an' your men hadn't come along I think we were all gonna be dead. How… how'd you manage…?"

"We were, uh, scouting. Spotted your fire last night. Saw you folks were in trouble and decided to do something about it. You're 5th Cavalry, Sergeant…?" The man was shouting and Dolfen realized that he was, too. They were both half-deaf from the explosions.

"Dolfen, sir. Yeah, we're with the 5th. Got the holy hell beat out of us a few weeks back. Me an' some of the others an' some folks we picked up were trying to get back to Wingate." He gestured at the wall in the distance. "What's going on, sir? What's that? Where's the rest of the army?"

"My name's Comstock, and well, the situation is a bit complicated…" The man had been grinning with a lunatic grin, but now he wasn't. "The army…"

"Hey, Major!" called one of the new men. He was standing close to the Martian machine and waving. "Something's happening here!"

Major Comstock immediately sprinted toward the machine. Dolfen followed more slowly. His legs were still shaking. As he walked, he saw that there were only eight or nine men with Comstock. And one of them was dressed in civilian clothing; he was scribbling furiously in a small notebook. Dolfen's own people had scattered as he'd ordered, but they were all drifting back in now. He breathed a sigh of relief when he saw the girl on her horse, holding Mrs. Gordon's boy.

He reached the group that had clustered around the machine's head. The thing didn't look nearly so large now, smashed and beaten, but it was still pretty big. And he immediately saw what had attracted everyone's attention. A round door or hatch had opened up in the side which was about five feet off the ground. Some smoke was drifting out of it.

"Can you see anything inside?" asked one man.

"No, it's too dark—wait! There's something movin'!"

Everyone stepped back. Those who had weapons raised them. Dolfen squinted, trying to see into the dark hole, but the bright morning sun, reflecting off the metal skin of the machine, made it impossible to see anything. At least at first. But after a moment it was clear that something was, indeed, moving and it was trying to get out of the hatch. Dolfen watched in revulsion as several thin, gray, snake-like things emerged from the darkness and gripped the edges of the opening. Several more appeared and then there was a burbling hiss from inside the hole and a larger gray lump heaved into view. A Martian. The Enemy.

Dolfen swallowed uneasily as the thing came into view. There was no doubt it was hideous. A cluster of the tentacles surrounded a parrot-like beak which must be the thing's mouth. Two dark, bulbous eyes glittered wetly in the sunlight, but it was impossible to tell where they were looking; there were no whites surrounding them. A smell like rotting fish filled the air and he nearly gagged. The thing pulled again with its tentacles and tumbled forward, out through the hatch, and fell to the ground. All the watchers stepped farther back.

The thing hit the ground like a soggy sack of grain. It didn't seem to have any bones to give it shape and it just sagged and oozed. It gave off another burble and its tentacles waved feebly. In spite of Dolfen's revulsion and anger, he couldn't help but feel a touch of pity for this awful thing. So ugly, so helpless without its machines. It wasn't even very large. Not the least bit threatening now.

"Damn," said Major Comstock. "I'd love to take this thing back with us as a prisoner. Sergeant, is there any way we can rig something to carry it in?"

For an instant Dolfen thought the Major was talking to him, but then he saw another man with chevrons on his sleeve.

"Bloody hell, sir," answered the man with a noticeable Scottish burr in his voice. "I don't know as we'll even be able to carry all of us, let alone this monster!"

"Well, send someone for the horses and we'll see what we can…"

The roar of a gun from close behind sent everyone scattering. Another shot and then another and another. He looked back and to his astonishment there was Becca Harding. She had the Henry against her shoulder and she was working the lever-action and firing again and again.

Into the Martian.

The bullets tore into the soft flesh of the creature making terrible wounds from which poured a dark liquid. The thing was waving its tentacles franticly and giving off an awful wail, but then the limbs fell limp and the noise stopped.

And still the girl kept shooting, a terrifying look of rage on her young face. She emptied the rifle, all sixteen rounds, into the thing and then kept working the action and pulling the trigger, even after the gun was empty until Dolfen gently took it away from her. The girl's face was streaked with tears, and those hate-filled eyes turned to look at him.

"It's dead, Becca. You killed it. Good job."

The civilian with the notebook stepped over to the girl and asked: "What's your name miss?" and he wrote it down when she told him. Who was that guy?

"Well, saves us a bit o' trouble," said the other sergeant. "Unless you want to take this mess with us." He rolled his eyes. "Sir."

The major sighed and walked over to the oozing remains. "No, no, the British already have dead samples and I doubt we can learn much from this." He put his boot against the Martian and gave it a little shove. It rolled over with a ghastly squish and everyone froze as a new horror was revealed.

145

"God in Heaven!"

On the newly turned side of the Martian there was a translucent sack, and inside was... *Another Martian?* It must be. It was a miniature version of the larger one. Eyes, beak, tentacles, all the same except it was only the size of a small dog. Its tentacles seemed to be pushing against the side of the sack that held it. The major came up and squatted down to look closely at it.

"It's... ah... reproducing," he declared. "Now *this* would be valuable if we can preserve it somehow. Sergeant, where are those horses? See if we've got something we can put this in."

"Sir?" said the other sergeant, grimacing, who then sighed. "Yes, sir."

"Y-you mean it's a baby?" gasped Becca Harding, the color draining from her face. "I... I didn't know she was... pregnant!"

Comstock stood up and shook his head. "It's not like that, Miss. The Martians don't have males and females. They reproduce by fission, like some lower forms of life here on Earth. Don't... trouble yourself over this." Harding nodded, but didn't look convinced.

"Looks like the thing's in trouble, sir," said one of the men. The little horror was growing agitated. Its tentacles were waving around wildly. Then it began to tear at the sack with its beak. Eventually it managed to rip it open and spilled itself and a puddle of liquid out on the ground. But its movements were getting weaker and weaker and finally stopped altogether. One of the men suddenly made a strangled sound, turned away, and vomited. Dolfen felt like doing that himself.

"Couldn't survive on its own yet," muttered Major Comstock. "Well, it's small enough, we'll take it with us."

"And we better get moving, sir," said the sergeant. "Can't believe those things won't come to investigate what we've done here."

"Right. Ah, here are the horses." Two men came riding up, towing ten other horses. "Some of us are going to have to ride double, I'm afraid. Thirteen horses and ... uh... twenty-three of us? Is that right?"

"I think so, sir. Oh, and I think Private Ogileavy's got a broken arm from when that thing hit him."

"Damn. Well, get him fixed up as best you can and on a horse. Try to even out the loads as much as possible. Sergeant McGill, I'm turning things over to you for the next few hours. Head back the way we came. I'll catch up as soon as I can. If I don't... you get back to the mine, collect the others and try to link up with the army."

"Sir? What are you talking about, sir?"

Comstock pointed toward the wall in the distance. "I'm going to try and get a look at what's on the other side of that."

"Alone, sir?" The man was aghast.

"Only takes one, Sergeant."

"I'd like to go along," said the civilian.

"Not this time, Mr. White!" snapped the major.

"But..."

"No!"

"But you can't go alone!" insisted McGill. "Dammit, you shouldn't be going at all!"

"We need to know what's going on. It's important, Sergeant."

"Then let me come with you!"

"No, I need you in charge here."

McGill snarled in exasperation. "At least let me send one of the lads with ye!"

"No, Sergeant, there's no need for anyone to…"

"I'll go with you, sir," said Dolfen. The man's eyes turned to him.

"What? Why?"

Good question. He wasn't sure why he'd made the offer. It was just… "I know the place, sir. Got some friends there. I'd like to know what happened." Comstock opened his mouth but then hesitated.

"Yes!" snapped the one named McGill. "Sir, if you're gonna be a fool, beggin' your pardon, don't be a *damn fool!* Take the sergeant!"

"Come on, sir," said Dolfen. "Time's a-wasting."

"All… all right, let's go."

They quickly mounted two horses and turned them toward the mysterious wall. Only then did the girl, busy with her horse, notice what was going on. "Sergeant! Where are you going?"

"I'll be back! Go with the others! Don't worry!"

"But… but why?"

He kneed the horse into a canter to follow the major. He turned his head and called: "I'll be back!"

I hope.

CHAPTER TEN

CYCLE597,843.5, EAST OF HOLDFAST 32-1

The distress signal took Qetjnegartis by surprise. They and their captive prey-animals were within a day's travel of the holdfast. The others it had sent back earlier were sweeping the surrounding area for any wandering prey and all appeared to be well. By all expectations once they returned, work could resume on the holdfast at maximum effort, the buds could finish maturing, and preparations could be made for future expansion.

But now there was an emergency call for aid from Kravnijuntus. It said only that it was under attack and then the signal had cut off abruptly. No attempt to reestablish communications had been successful. What did this mean? Under attack? By the prey-creatures obviously, but how many? What sort of weapons did they have? More of those large projectile throwers? The location indicated was already dangerously close to the holdfast. If it was a substantial force, this could turn into a major setback.

Qetjnegartis checked the location of the other war machines and was dismayed to see that none were in position to quickly investigate. Kravnijuntus had been the only one to the south of the holdfast since that area had already been swept when they had come through earlier. The others were all out to the north and west. Zastranvis was minding the constructor machines and closest to the scene of the attack, but Qetjnegartis did not want to leave those invaluable machines unguarded.

It considered the situation and made a swift decision. Of paramount importance was the safety of the holdfast. It would order all the others on patrol to converge there. It would meet them there personally and then move south to investigate. The ones herding the captives would continue to do so. Yes, this was the most reasonable course of action.

Qetjnegartis issued its orders.

* * * * *

MARCH, 1909, GALLUP, NEW MEXICO TERRITORY

Major Andrew Comstock urged his horse onward. The sergeant from the 5th—what was his name? Dolfen?—was right beside him. The wall in the distance got closer at an excruciatingly slow pace. It had only looked to be five or six miles distant and he'd thought the horses would get him there in just a few minutes. But it was taking longer and the Martians would certainly respond soon. Maybe this hadn't been such a good idea after all.

"What are you looking for, sir?" asked Dolfen. He seemed much more at ease in the saddle than Andrew. A veteran cavalryman, surely. A lot older, too. It still made him a little uncomfortable ordering around men twice his age.

"Whatever's there. Anything and everything. No one's ever seen something like this before." He paused and then asked: "What are you looking for?"

"I don't know, sir. I just wanted to see... if anything's left."

"You have friends in Gallup? Family?"

"No family. But there's a woman..."

"Oh? I thought that girl with the others was... she seemed very worried about you."

"Just a kid we found on the way. She thinks... not sure what she's thinking, sir. But what about the army? What's going on?"

Andrew hesitated for a moment, but then he told him. Everything.

"Damn," said Dolfen when he'd finished. "When I heard the guns from across the mountains. I'd hoped... As bad as that. Sir?"

"'Fraid so. But the Martians didn't follow up. There are still a lot more troops moving this way. If they can get organized, things might not be as bad as they seem."

"And you came all the way out here with just a dozen men? What for?"

"I wanted to find out what they were doing. That was my mission. Now I just need to get a look behind that wall and we can all go home."

The miles had gone by much faster while he was talking. The wall loomed up in front of them and they slowed as they reached its base. It was thirty or forty feet high, and while the slope wasn't impossibly steep, it was all dirt and loose stones. He didn't want to try to take the horses up that. If one of them got hurt or lamed, they'd be stuck here. So they dismounted and tied the horses' leads to rocks to keep them from wandering. Then they began the climb to the top.

It wasn't easy and he tried not to think about what would happen if a tripod suddenly appeared at the top. They didn't have a clue what was on the other side and it could easily be sudden death. But they struggled on, shins and knees bruised, and hands scraped raw. They finally neared the top and then slowed to a crawl. Very carefully, they poked their heads up above the edge.

Nothing immediately fatal was waiting for them. Indeed, there wasn't that much to be seen at first glance. Looking to the left and right along the curve of the wall, he could see that the inner face was much steeper than the outer face, but he couldn't see what was keeping it from collapsing; although the surface had a strange almost glassy look to it. The wall curved around in a circle and the far side was at least three miles away, although there was a cloud of dust coming up from there—was it still under construction on that side? There were ramps leading up to the top of the wall at intervals.

"Where... where's the town?' asked Dolfen from beside him. It was true: the inside of the ring had been scraped clean. If the town of Gallup had once stood here, there wasn't a trace of it to be seen.

"I... I think it must be part of the wall now," said Andrew. "I'm sorry, Sergeant."

"The bastards!" hissed the man. "But what happened to all the people who were here?"

Andrew didn't answer; he didn't know if all the people in the town had been killed in the first attack or if they'd been... collected, like the troops they'd seen. Even if he had known, he wasn't about to say anything to Dolfen. Instead, he pulled out his field glasses. A glint of sunlight on metal had caught his eye. He focused and saw that close to the eastern side of the wall there was some sort of activity going on. He sucked in his breath when he saw at least a dozen tripods standing in the shadow of the wall. They weren't moving, but still looked very menacing. But somewhat closer at hand there were several other machines at work. They were unlike anything he'd ever seen before. What were they? What were they doing? It was too far away to tell.

"There's something over there," he said. "I need to get closer."

He expected an immediate protest from Sergeant Dolfen, so when he didn't get one he lowered his glasses and turned to look at the man. He was staring back with a strange expression, his fists clenched.

"You think... you think that what you learn could help beat them?" he asked, talking slowly. Andrew suddenly realized that the man was close to the edge. He had talked about 'going home' earlier, but this had been Dolfen's home. Gallup and Fort Wingate and the 5th Cavalry. All gone. Destroyed by the Martians.

"That is my hope, Sergeant," he replied, speaking very carefully. "That's what I was sent out here for: to learn what we need to beat these things. And right now I could use your help."

"You've got it, sir. Let's go."

They scrambled back down to the horses and then rode as quickly as they could along the base of the wall, heading east. Andrew had briefly considered sending Dolfen to bring the horses while he made his way on foot along the top, but this was clearly better. If they encountered the enemy now, they could still run for it. If he'd been up there, he wouldn't have a chance. They hurried along and he found himself looking at the tumbled pile of stone and dirt that made up the wall. In spite of himself, he was looking for bricks or beams or broken roof tiles—or blackened bones; some trace of the town of Gallup. But there was nothing.

After riding about a mile, they halted again and made the same painful trip up the wall. They were even more careful about poking their heads up this time. When they were just below the apex, he noticed a series of metal objects topping the wall farther to the north. They stood like the crenellations on a medieval tower and he was afraid that they might also be serving some sort of defensive purpose. He didn't want to get close to them and fortunately there were none on this section.

Peering down inside, he saw that they were much closer to the strange machines now; perhaps just a half mile away. He took out his field glasses again and looked. The dozen tripods were still standing in a row just as they had earlier. But the other machines... he could see them much more clearly. Instead of standing tall like the tripods, these things were long and low, supported by eight metal legs. Each one had a forest of tentacles and arms sprouting from the top and sides that all seemed to be moving and doing things. But what? "Strange looking things," he muttered.

"Sir?" said Dolfen. "I think we saw those things, the ones with all the legs, I mean, a few weeks ago when were holed up in Ramah. They were heading this way in a group."

"Really? They must have come from the original landing site to the south!"

He stared for a while, trying to interpret what his eyes were showing him. There was one machine that wasn't moving much and two others that were working at either end of it; but what were they...? "Oh My God," he whispered.

"What is it, sir?" asked Dolfen.

"They... they're factories! They're building things!"

"Oh. Well, I guess that makes sense..."

"No! You don't understand! Those machines, *by themselves*, are making things! The one in front is loading stuff—they look like rails from the railroad—into the one in the middle and other things—finished parts!—are coming out the back! The third one is assembling them into something. It looks like one of those things along the wall. Yes, it's finished it and now it's going up the ramp with it!" He looked on as the machine scuttled up the ramp with surprising speed and placed

151

the object—it looked like a cylinder with some strange projections—onto the wall maybe fifty yards from the next one over. It came back down to where a small pile of new parts was already waiting for it. As he watched, there was more movement and something emerged from a hole in the ground that he'd seen earlier; it was another one of the machines! It walked over to the middle machine and poured something into a hopper on the top.

"Oh," breathed Andrew. "This is bad. Really bad!"

"What do you mean, sir?"

"I… we… the high command, I mean, we always assumed that if the Martians got a foothold on Earth that they would try to establish themselves and gather resources and build factories so they could increase their strength. That's certainly what we'd do in their place. But we assumed it would take time! Months and years! They'd have to dig mines and build refineries and smelters to extract the ore and only then could they start building the factories to produce new war machines. Years! But they've only been here a few weeks and they're doing it already! And if those new Martians mature rapidly… This changes everything! I've got to get back to Washington and warn them!" He'd hoped to find something worthwhile on this trip, but he never dreamed it would be anything like this!

"Well, it's time to get moving, that's for sure! Look, sir!" Andrew looked where Dolfen was pointing and saw four dust clouds off to the north and west. His binoculars revealed them as tripods walking rapidly their way.

"There's another one!" cried the sergeant. "It's a lot closer!" And it surely was: this machine was just reaching the top of the wall only a little ways beyond where the construction machines were at work, not a mile away.

"Right you are! Let's go!" They jumped, tumbled, and slid down the slope as quickly as they could, mounted their horses, and galloped off to the southeast.

* * * * *

CYCLE597,843.5, HOLDFAST 32-1

Qetjnegartis looked down upon the mangled remains of Kravnijuntus and was filled with an entirely unfamiliar sensation. When Franjandus had died in battle it had been regrettable, but still a worthy sacrifice for the good of the clan and the race. And an honorable death. But this, this was different somehow. Clearly, Kravnijuntus had been slain after its machine had been rendered inoperable. It had exited and then been… slaughtered. Such a waste.

And how had it been done? Explosions had torn off some of the limbs of the fighting machine, but the damage was different from what it had observed on Franjandus' machine after the battle. Was this some new weapon? And there was no trace of any of the prey-creatures to be found. Had none been slain in carrying this out? A pair of the creatures, riding draught animals, had been observed fleeing the vicinity of the holdfast a short while ago, but no others. Surely, those two could not have done this alone!

Looking closer it discerned the empty bud sac on Kravnijuntus' side. Where was the bud? There was no trace of it close by. Had it freed itself from the sac or been… taken? Qetjnegartis probed its own bud. It did not appear to be sufficiently developed to survive on its own yet, but buds did develop at different rates. Could the prey-creatures have taken it alive? The thought was more disturbing than any Qetjnegartis had had in a very long time.

"Commander? We have surveyed this location and find only imprints of the prey-creatures and their draught animals, and only a small number. There is no sign of any vehicles, such as those that pulled the projectile throwers. The imprints appear to go off to the east."

Qetjnegartis acknowledged this report, but it did not make the situation any clearer. So, what to do? There apparently was no large force poised to threaten the holdfast. But the two creatures seen earlier, had they gotten close enough to see inside the holdfast? Had they recognized the status of its incomplete defenses? And what had slain Kravnijuntus and destroyed its machine? An earlier report from it had indicated it was bringing prey back to the holdfast. Those prey had clearly escaped and no doubt accounted for the imprints in the ground. But how had they freed themselves?

"Commander, what are your orders?" Its subordinates were waiting.

What was the proper course? With the loss of Kravnijuntus, it had only ten war machines in operation. Twelve more were ready but had no operators. *There are too few of us here; the next landings must bring more personnel and less equipment.* And the first layer of defenses for the holdfast was still at least twelve days from completion. What to do? Remain here and defend the holdfast and wait for the buds to mature? That might be prudent. But what had those two creatures learned? What might they learn from the captured bud? Qetjnegartis was beginning to have serious doubts about some of the reports from the first expedition. The prey-creatures were not, it seemed, so easily demoralized. They would continue to struggle even after a defeat. What if they returned in strength before the holdfast was secure? It needed to know what was happening out there.

"We will pursue these creatures. Six of us will go. The other four will defend the holdfast. We begin immediately."

* * * * *

MARCH, 1909, NEAR FORT WINGATE, NEW MEXICO TERRITORY

Rebecca Harding shifted in her saddle and pulled Timmy Gordon a little closer. He'd finally stopped whining about not being able to ride with his mother and now it seemed like he was dozing off. She was ready to fall asleep herself. The events of the last two days seemed like one long drawn-out nightmare which had left her exhausted. Sleep was the only way to escape this nightmare.

But she couldn't sleep, they had to keep moving. They had been riding as hard as the horses could stand since the rescue that morning. The rescue! She still couldn't believe it. She'd been convinced that they were all going to die in some especially awful fashion. Even the presence of her faithful Ninny was no comfort—he would just die, too. And then Sergeant Dolfen came up with his crazy plan to sacrifice himself to try to let the rest of them escape. It wasn't going to work; she could see that as clearly as everyone else. But since they were all going to die anyway, she'd gone along.

And then, then men had appeared from nowhere, throwing bombs, and before she could even try to get away, the huge Martian machine was lying on the ground, wrecked and helpless. It had seemed impossible. They had been running from these things for weeks and they had been unstoppable. And yet this one had been stopped by a handful of men!

She'd dared to come back for a closer look and then that awful... *thing* had appeared! She'd suddenly been filled with an all-consuming rage. Somehow she'd never been able to feel anything but fear for the machines. They'd been like some elemental force. What point was there getting angry with a thunderstorm or an avalanche? But the machines had been driven by those horrible little things! *Those* she could hate! Without a conscious thought she'd pulled out her grandfather's rifle and emptied it into the Martian. She could still remember how... *good* it had felt to do that. They could be killed! And even after she saw the little one attached to the bigger one, it hadn't dampened her hatred. Hideous creatures! They should all be killed!

But they couldn't stay to admire their handiwork. More Martians would be coming and they had to run again. The men had used up most of their bombs and they all admitted that they'd been very lucky their ambush had worked once. It wasn't likely they could do it again. So they had to run.

But Sergeant Dolfen hadn't come with them! He'd gone off with that other man, the major. She still didn't know why. But the big, gruff Sergeant McGill had taken charge and he'd driven them onward. She didn't think she liked McGill, but she was too tired to really tell.

They'd ridden all day to get back to the hills. Nearly all of them were riding double so they couldn't push the horses very fast, although they had the luck to find two of the horses that had originally been with them before they were captured. That had helped. Even so, they had to dismount and walk frequently, and once they'd put some miles between them and the ambush site, they had stopped to rest a few times. By afternoon they'd reached the comforting concealment of the forests which covered the lower slopes of the mountains. Looking back, some of the sharp-eyed thought they could see some Martians out on the plain, but they couldn't be sure. Even the telescope on her rifle didn't show much. She'd seen no sign of Sergeant Dolfen or the major. She hoped he was all right.

"Come on!" snapped Sergeant McGill. "We have to keep moving!" Rebecca sighed, shifted the boy a bit, and rode on.

Just before nightfall they came to the ruins of Fort Wingate. There wasn't much left and Private Urbaniak and the others from the original group of soldiers were visibly upset. This had been their home, she gathered. She tried to remember her own home by the lake, but the only image that came to mind was a raging fire. They moved on another couple of miles to the east before finally stopping. Their horses couldn't go any farther today and it would be too dark to keep moving through the wood in any case. From what McGill had said, they had another fifteen or twenty miles to go tomorrow to reach some mine where more of their men would be waiting. Sergeant Dolfen would be heading there, too.

They found a sheltered spot to build a fire and make a meal. They had recovered some of their 'requisitioned' foodstuffs from the store in Ramah on the stray horses and the soldiers had some stuff from the mine, so they ate pretty well. There was a bit more talk around the campfire that night than normal. The two groups had much to tell each other. A lot of it was grim telling: the destruction of towns, the slaughter of the 5th Cavalry, and the even greater slaughter of the main army. But the fact that they had destroyed a Martian machine—something it had taken a whole army to do—buoyed their spirits considerably.

"It's just a matter of figuring out how to beat those bastards," said one of them. "And we're learning that now!" The others agreed heartily.

"And that was some mighty good shooting, Miss!" said another.

Rebecca blushed, but smiled. "Nothing to it. Close range and it wasn't moving. My grandmother… anyone could have done it. You fellows did the hard work." They all laughed at that.

"And I am going to have one hell of a story to file when I get back," said the newspaperman, who had come with the new batch of soldiers. "You boys—and girls—are all heroes!"

In spite of their exciting day, everyone was soon ready for sleep. The poor soldier who had the broken arm was already asleep, although he seemed to be doing well. They were still short on blankets, so Rebecca found herself teaming up with Mrs. Gordon and her boy. But they had barely gotten themselves settled when the man on sentry duty called out: "Hey! Hey, look over there!"

The sky to the west, glimpsed through gaps in the trees, was a bright red. For a moment Rebecca thought it was just the sunset, but no, that had disappeared an hour ago. In an instant she realized what it was: "Fire!"

"The forest is on fire!"

"And the wind is blowing it this way! Smell the smoke?"

"Get up! Get your horses saddled!" shouted McGill. "We have to move!"

"They've barely had a chance to rest! Can they make it?"

"No choice! Get moving!"

They hastily packed up their meager belongings and saddled the horses. It was awkward and clumsy doing it in the dark and the horses clearly weren't happy. Ninny looked at her with reproach. But then they were off.

On foot.

There was no possibility of trying to ride in the woods in the dark. Or at least no sane person would try it. Becca had done it with Ninny when they fled her burning home, but she hadn't been quite sane at that point. But now they led their horses, and in a long line made their way through the trees.

Becca looked back from time to time. The red glow seemed to be getting brighter and she assumed that meant it was gaining on them. The smell of smoke was getting stronger too, and from time to time some glowing embers would float down around them. Sergeant McGill shouted something about breaking out of the forest soon, but to Becca it seemed endless. And their going was slow. Several times they came upon ravines too steep for the horses and they had to double back to find a new route. Once, the rear part of the group got separated from the rest, and precious minutes were lost linking up again. All the while the fire was getting closer, although without the light from the fire, the going would have been impossible.

Then, off to their left, to the north, they heard that awful sound—the sound of the Martian heat rays. They weren't terribly loud, so they must be a good distance away, but shortly after, the red glow of fire was on their left as well as behind.

"They're setting fire to the forest!" cried someone.

"Really? You think so?" replied someone else sarcastically. "Keep moving!"

They struggled onward, stumbling over rocks and tree roots. The horses were frightened and agitated, but at least they kept moving. Becca had been worried that they'd be too exhausted, but the fear of the fire drove them onward. But how long could they keep it up? Horses and humans were nearing their limits. The new fires to the left didn't seem to be getting any closer. The wind was from the southwest, so even though it was driving the original fire behind them onward, the new fires to their north weren't spreading their way.

Suddenly there were shouts from the front of the column. Becca wondered what new disaster had arisen, but she was too tired by now to really care. Except the shouts didn't seem to be shouts of alarm… She caught up with the others and gasped.

Two men were sitting on rocks. A quivering, foam-flecked horse stood behind them. In the wavering red light she could see that they were all blackened with soot. One of them grinned, white teeth standing out in the black face.

"What kept you?" he said.

"Sergeant Dolfen!"

* * * * *

CYCLE597,843.5, EAST OF HOLDFAST 32-1

The fire was… amazing. Qetjnegartis had noted the phenomenon before, but most of the earlier fires had been relatively small. The one they were setting now was enormous by comparison. Vast stretches of the tall native vegetation were engulfed in flames. It was spreading on its own with no further assistance from the heat rays; driven by the wind. Reports indicated that much of the planet was covered with vegetation similar to this. How did the prey-creatures avoid having their whole world burn up? Well, no matter; if it all burned, so much the better. Qetjnegartis swept its machine's heat ray over another stretch and felt a sense of satisfaction as the tall central stalks exploded and the branches erupted in flames.

"Commander, the prey-creatures have surely been destroyed." One of its subordinates was clearly growing impatient with this exercise.

"Nevertheless, we will continue. The creatures have been using this sort of growth to conceal their movements from us. We must eliminate any such approach to the holdfast."

"As you command."

* * * * *

MARCH, 1909, NEAR FORT WINGATE, NEW MEXICO TERRITORY

"I'm so glad you're safe, Sergeant!"

Frank Dolfen looked at the girl and shook his head. "Is that what you call this?" He had to shout to be heard above the roar of the fire. The reunited party was making its way through the woods as quickly as it could, but Dolfen was afraid it wouldn't be quickly enough. The fire was close behind and it looked as though there was fire ahead of them now, too.

"You know what I mean!" said Becca Harding. "I was afraid I'd never see you again, the way you rode off!"

"Had a job to do."

"How'd you manage to get ahead of us like that?"

Wouldn't the girl ever shut up? His mouth was parched, the smoke was getting thicker, and he didn't feel like talking. "We were following you," he rasped. "But the Martians spotted us and chased us into the woods. The trees were too close together for them to get through, so they just started burning everything. We couldn't make very good time through the trees and we were afraid they'd get ahead of us moving in the open and all and cut us off. So we headed north to the edge of the trees and made a break for it. Ran the one horse into the ground and then we had to ride double. Just barely made it back into the woods before they caught us. But we'd covered a lot of ground and figured we'd gotten ahead of you. So we waited. Couldn't have gone any farther on that horse anyway."

"What... what was behind the wall?"

"Ask the major when you get a chance. Now save your breath and keep moving!"

She finally stopped talking and Dolfen moved ahead of her on the narrow path they were following. He was towing the horse he'd shared with the major, who was up ahead with Sergeant McGill trying to spot any familiar landmarks. Apparently they'd come through here on their way west. Of course it hadn't been on fire at that time. They struggled on for perhaps another half-hour and then the front of the column stopped and the rest all straggled up to join them. The fire was maybe a half-mile behind them to the west, but it looked to have already crossed their path ahead of them. Off to the southeast there was a faint light of dawn in the sky. *The whole night gone?* When had he last slept? He couldn't remember. He caught up with Comstock and McGill, who were standing on the edge of a deep ravine. It crossed their path, running down to the northeast.

"I think this is the way we came," said Comstock.

"Are you sure, sir? I don't remember anything this steep," replied McGill.

"We probably got out of it lower down than this. But it's going the direction we want to go and there's hardly any undergrowth that will burn in it. We can use this as a safe road out of here!"

McGill seemed skeptical, but then he looked around and nodded. "No other way to go—unless you want to head up higher into the mountains."

"All right! Everyone, down into here!"

Getting the horses down the slope was difficult, and there was no way in hell they'd get them back out again. If this didn't lead anywhere, they'd have to abandon them. They continued single-file for a mile or so and Dolfen was having doubts about the choice of routes. The smoke was very thick and fire seemed to be all around them now. A wall of flames was catching up to them from the west and people began shouting that they needed to turn some other direction.

But the major and McGill insisted they keep following the ravine and they put Dolfen at the rear to make sure everyone kept moving. The roar of the fire became almost deafening and the smoke stung his eyes and choked his throat. The heat on his left side seared any exposed skin. He pulled his hat low and turned up his collar despite the fact he was sweating. Burning branches started falling among them and the horses were getting difficult to control as embers burned them. One of them broke loose and scrambled up the side of the ravine, which wasn't so steep anymore, and galloped off—directly into the approaching fire.

The trees just to their left, up on the edge of the ravine, were burning now and Dolfen was sure they were done for, when suddenly the fire was diminishing; the trees on either side were just smoldering pillars, blackened trunks with most of the branches burned off. The fire had already passed by! The fire they were fleeing had been chasing them for miles, but the Martians had gotten ahead of them and set fires which had burned out, providing a safe path for them!

Safe, but still not easy. There were some small fires and burning branches in the bottom of the ravine and the smoke was still thick. Twice, entire trees had fallen into or across the ravine and they had to struggle up out of it, and then back down on the other side. The horses were getting balky and they were all exhausted.

But finally they got near the edge of the forest and found a covered spot where they could stop and rest. A tiny creek was at the bottom of the ravine now and the horses—and the humans— were able to drink a little and clear the soot out of their throats. They peered out from the refuge from time to time, looking for Martians machines, but they saw nothing. Had they given up? It was fully light although the sun was hidden by the clouds of smoke from the fire, which was still burning on the higher slopes. They decided to rest for a while, and nearly everyone was soon asleep.

Dolfen woke up a few hours later, coughed and spat, and painfully got to his feet. *Gettin' too old for this sort of thing.* The sun was visible as a hazy orb seen through the smoke; it looked to be a couple of hours before noon. The only other one awake was McGill. Dolfen went over and sat down next to him. "Where do we go now?"

"If we hug the edge o' the hills we ought to get to the mine about dark. There's food and shelter and hopefully four more men there. We'll need to rest up a few days after all this, but then I guess we'll head east and try to join up with whatever's left of the army. The major says he's got stuff he needs to get back to Washington."

"He's quite the pistol, that one, isn't he?" Dolfen gestured to where Comstock was sleeping. "How'd you end up with him?"

McGill shrugged. "After fifteen years in the infantry—not the US Infantry, mind you—I felt I'd done enough marching for one lifetime. Once I got into the American Army, I wiggled my way into the Ordnance Department; figured there would be more paperwork and less marching. Turns out I was right—until the bloody Martians showed up. The major's some bright young sprout that the top brass wanted to go have a looksee at the critters, and yours truly got the job o' lookin' after him." McGill paused and the expression on his face grew softer. "He's all right, though. There's been a few times where a real idiot could have gotten us all killed, but here we are."

157

"Yeah, here we are," said Dolfen, looking dubiously at their surroundings.

McGill laughed. "Could be worse! But it's time to get moving. We've been lucky so far and we wouldn't want to press our luck." He got up and started nudging the sleeping people with his foot. There were many groans and curses and a few protests, but the people got up. This was no place to stay and they all knew it.

The horses were still in a bad way so they made no attempt to ride them. At least not yet. If they had to make a run for it, they would save the horses for the end of the race. They left their shelter and wound their way out of the last of the still smoking trees. The ravine petered out about the same time the trees did and they bent their course to the east, staying as close to the foothills as they could manage. Looking back, Dolfen could see mile after mile of charred forest; only the trees on the higher slopes had escaped the flames.

They proceeded for a couple of hours, making more stops to rest than Dolfen was comfortable with. He felt terribly exposed away from the trees, but they could only push themselves and the horses so hard. They stopped around noon for lunch and finished off the last of their meager rations. Dolfen hoped McGill was right about there being food at this mine place. He wasn't sure what they'd do for the horses' fodder.

They pushed as hard as any of them could manage, but they were still far short of their goal when darkness fell. Comstock half-heartedly tried to convince them to make one last push to reach the mine, but none of them had any push left. So they found a concealed spot in the rocks and collapsed for the night. They hadn't seen or heard any sign of the enemy that whole day.

The next morning Dolfen was so stiff and sore he could barely move, and he could tell that everyone else was in the same state. But they had to move and since they had no food left to make breakfast, they didn't even have an excuse to delay a few minutes. There were still no threats in sight so they continued on foot to spare the horses. They had only been going a few minutes before it became clear that Mrs. Olsen's feet were so badly blistered from yesterday that she couldn't keep up, so she was allowed to ride. The sky was clouded over and it looked like it could rain. The wind was still southerly and it brought a welcome warmth. Winter was nearly over, but what sort of spring would it be?

They hadn't gone far when they started finding the triangular holes that the Martian machines made when they walked. So they had been through here, and while that was no surprise, it still felt ominous. They kept a sharp lookout in all directions. After an hour or so, one of Comstock's men pointed out that the bundle with the little Martian's body was starting to ooze and drip a bit, smelling truly awful, but the major wouldn't let him dump it.

An hour or so later they were curving their path back toward the southeast. McGill told him that there was a path not too far ahead leading up into the hills where there was a small mine. "With any luck we can rest for a couple of days and then get moving east again."

But just then, their luck ran out.

"Look!" shouted Private Urbaniak, who was bringing up the rear. "There they are!"

* * * * *

CYCLE597,843.5, EAST OF HOLDFAST 32-1

What does it take to kill these things? Qetjnegartis looked at the prey-creatures through the magnifier and had to conclude that there was sufficient probability that these were the same ones it had been chasing to warrant further pursuit. It had just given the order to return to the holdfast mere moments before when a subordinate had spotted them. It seemed impossible that anything could have survived the inferno they had created the previous day, and yet here they were, still fleeing east. The first two, and in all probability the others who had slain Kravnijuntus.

But now they were out in the open, only five telequel away. They would not escape again.

* * * * *

MARCH, 1909, SOUTH OF THOREAU, NEW MEXICO TERRITORY

Andrew looked over his shoulder; the Martians were definitely closing on them—fast. They were maybe three miles behind at the most. Another fifteen minutes and they'd be in range of the heat rays. And there wasn't a damn thing they could do about it. Riding double on the nearly exhausted horses, they weren't moving much faster than a walking pace. And even if they split up, there were six of the enemy machines and they'd probably be able to run them all down. Damn! They were so close to getting away!

But they kept moving; to do anything else was death, either immediately by heat ray, or later as food. The entrance to the passage through the hills crept closer; the enemy would keep chasing them through it, but if they could only get into the mine! He doubted the Martians could follow them there! But it was just too far…

"We'll never make it, sir," said McGill, coming up beside him. "What do you think we should do? Scatter?"

"Probably wouldn't make any difference," he gasped. "Too many of them."

"But you need to get back, sir. Tell 'em what you saw. Maybe the rest of us can draw 'em off. Give you the freshest horse and you might make it to the mine."

"I'm not going to run off and abandon all of you!"

"Sometimes… sometimes you have to leave a rear guard, sir. So the rest of the army can live. It's hard, but it's a part of soldiering."

"I can't do that!"

"Then we'll all die for nothing, sir! If you can get back then at least our deaths will mean something!"

Andrew stared at his sergeant in dismay. He was right; there was no arguing that. But how could he run and leave the others—women and children—and save himself? He'd never be able to look himself in the mirror again.

"Whatever we're gonna do, we gotta do it quick, sir. Not much time left."

He was right again. But what could they do? Scattering seemed the only possible option. But he was damned if he was going to take the freshest horse or ask the others to cover for him! They'd all take the same risk and have the same chance. If he made it, well and good, but if he didn't…

"All right! Listen up!" he shouted.

But he'd barely gotten the words out when there was a sound, a sound that he never expected: a bugle call! He jerked his head around and there! Half a mile ahead, just emerging from hills was a group of horsemen; thirty or forty at least. Cavalry!

"That way! As fast as you can!" They spurred their poor animals and they, perhaps sensing some sort of safety with a larger herd, managed almost a trot. But the cavalry had spotted them and a group broke away and galloped toward them. They closed the distance rapidly and Andrew spotted a lieutenant in the lead. To his surprise the man shouted: "Major Comstock?"

"Yes! How'd you know?"

The lieutenant reached him and turned his horse to follow alongside; no one even considered stopping. "Lieutenant Kenshaw, 7th Cavalry, sir. Friend of yours, Captain Selfridge, told me this was probably your party."

"Selfridge is with you? And my other men?"

"Yes, sir, found them at that mine up in the mountains, but if you don't mind my saying, we really

159

better get the hell out of here!"

"No argument! But our horses are done. Can yours take us riding double?"

Kenshaw looked doubtful. "Dunno, sir. Our horses are pretty fresh, but I don't know how far they could go and still stay ahead of those things."

"We just need to get to the mine!"

"The mine, sir? I'd think you'd want to get back to the army."

"Army? What army?"

"General Funston, sir. He's got quite a force, eight or ten miles east of here."

"I'll be damned!" Andrew looked back at the Martians, they were closer than ever. Run for the mine? Run for the army? The mine might be closer, but it was still a trap with no way out. If they could reach the army! "But can we stay ahead of them that long?"

"We can try, sir!"

"All right, but I won't leave anyone behind!"

"Right! Sandusky!" Kenshaw shouted to one of his men. "Get back to the troop and tell them to drop all their gear! And I mean everything! We'll be taking passengers!"

"Yes sir!" The man kicked his mount into a gallop and raced off. The rest of them followed more slowly.

"Everyone, listen!" Andrew shouted to his own party. "We'll be doubling up with the cavalry! There's no time for any nonsense! As soon as we join them, just get off your horse and get on another! We've got to move!" A chorus of excited replies came back. They had all sunk into despair, but now, now hope was rekindled. He just prayed it wasn't a fool's hope.

The cavalry were jettisoning the last of their gear as they rode up. Everyone jumped, or more accurately collapsed, out of their saddles and the troopers helped them all mount up. Andrew found himself riding behind Lieutenant Kenshaw. They immediately took off at a brisk trot.

"You must have made them mad, sir," said the lieutenant. "To chase you all this way, I mean."

"Maybe so. But tell me about General Funston's army. What's he got?"

"He's got the bit between his teeth, is what he's got, sir! He only showed up the day before yesterday and Good God what a difference! Before that we were just milling around like a flock of chickens. The trains kept bringing in more troops and more supplies but no one was in charge. Or I should say the brigade commanders were arguing about who ought to be in charge! Then General Funston arrives and within a few hours we were on the move! He sent us out to reconnoiter and we happened to bump into those two men you sent back and they led us to the mine where Captain Selfridge was."

"But what sort of force does he have with him?"

"A couple of short infantry brigades, a few batteries of guns, and us and the 10th Cavalry. I think that's it, sir."

Andrew frowned. Not even as powerful as the force General Sumner had gotten slaughtered. True, there were only six tripods this time, but he didn't see how Funston could...

"Oh, and there's a few dozen of those steam-powered gun tractor things. Crazy-looking contraptions! And they scare hell out of the horses!"

"The tanks?" cried Andrew in delight. "The tanks are finally here?"

"Is that what they're called? Yes, they're clanking round, trying to keep up with the rest."

"Thank God! Now we've got a chance!"

"You really think they can do anything, sir?"

"I hope so! Lieutenant, send a man ahead! Have him tell Funston that we are bringing six Martians right to him! Have him get ready to give them a proper welcome!"

"Yes sir! Sandusky! Got another job for you!"

CHAPTER ELEVEN

CYCLE 597,843.6, EAST OF HOLDFAST 32-1

Qetjnegartis looked on as the first group of prey-creatures joined a second, larger group. They were all riding the draught animals and apparently these were not as fatigued as the first batch. They were now maintaining their distance and even pulling ahead slightly. Experience had shown that they could not maintain this pace indefinitely, but it could now be a significant amount of time before they drew close enough to use the heat rays. Was it logical to continue the pursuit? The time already used was becoming excessive. The machines back at the holdfast required supervision to operate at full efficiency. Perhaps it would be better to abandon this effort and turn back.

Still, there was the matter of what the creatures had learned at the holdfast, or could learn from the dead bud. Most of Qetjnegartis' compatriots would have scoffed at the notion that these creatures were capable of learning anything, but that was self-deception. The entire strategy for this second expedition was based on the premise that the creatures *had* learned from the first invasion and would be better prepared for a landing near their major cities. To assume that they were incapable of learning anything more was illogical. All but the most primitive animals were capable of learning to some degree; it was an essential survival skill.

The prey-creatures had already demonstrated that they could be dangerous. And the more they learned, the more dangerous they would be. It was a very simple equation and with a straightforward reciprocal: the less they learned, the less dangerous they would be. Therefore, the pursuit would continue until these were all destroyed.

But it was still tedious. These draught animals gave the prey an unexpected mobility. In addition to machines which could more efficiently harvest the prey, the Race needed machines which were *faster*.

* * * * *

MARCH, 1909, NEAR THOREAU, NEW MEXICO TERRITORY

"Y'know, Sarge, I'm getting really tired of running from these damn things!"

Frank Dolfen snorted and grinned. Private Urbaniak, clinging to the back of one of the 7th's troopers—just as Dolfen was—had come up abreast of him. "Yeah, I know what you mean. But maybe we won't have to run much longer. From what I overheard from the major, we've got friends up ahead."

"So we're leading these bastards into an ambush?"

"Seems like that's the idea."

"I'd pay good money to see that!"

"With any luck you'll get to see it for free." *If we can actually pull this off!*

They had been running for over an hour since meeting up with the boys from the 7th and so far they were staying ahead of the Martians. But he wasn't sure how much longer they could maintain the pace. Or how much longer they would *have* to maintain the pace. All anyone could tell them was that the army was off to the east somewhere. The cavalry had been sent out here to scout with the promise that the rest would follow, but where they were by now remained to be seen. The major had sent a courier racing ahead to spread the word and give them time to prepare.

The group had come down out of the hills to get on the flatter, smoother ground near where the railroad used to run. They could make better time there and it was easier on the horses. The rough ground didn't seem to bother the Martians any, so there was nothing to be gained by staying in the hills. He glanced around to make sure none of his people were lagging. The girl was riding with a trooper a few dozen yards away, and incredibly, that crazy horse of hers was keeping pace even though all of their other exhausted mounts had just wandered off when they abandoned them.

As they rode, Dolfen realized they must be backtracking the path the Martians had taken with their prisoners going the other way. The major and his men had told him all about that horror. A few blackened patches of ground marked where men had been unable to keep up. What had happened to those men? Had they been delivered to whatever fate awaited them behind the great wall raised around where Gallup had once stood? And what had happened to Stella? Was there any chance she'd escaped?

He jerked himself out of one set of awful thoughts to be confronted by another nightmare scene. They were riding through where the big battle had been fought. The major's men and the men of the 7th had already seen it, but it was new to Dolfen and his people. It was... strange. He'd seen the old photographs taken after Civil War battles; the fields littered with hundreds of bodies; both men and horses. But here there weren't any bodies—or hardly any. Just vast areas of scorched earth, like the remains of the burned forest they had fled through. And yet he could feel the sense of death all around. Men had stood and died here. A few half-melted field guns and some overturned wagons which had somehow escaped the flames were the only real evidence that a battle had been fought here.

No, as he looked closer he could see that there was some other evidence. A man caught fully by the heat rays was just... gone. Nothing left but ash. But someone only caught by the edge of the ray, then there were remains. Dolfen spotted the blackened bones of men and animals along the route they were riding; even a few bodies that were more or less intact. Perhaps they'd only been close enough to have their clothes catch fire. There was a strong smell of burning, but it wasn't much different from the forest fire. There had been a small town here, but it was just rubble and charred timbers; the destruction was much more thorough than at Ramah. *If we don't stop them, then every town is going to look like this...*

"Come on! Come on!" cried a sergeant in the 7th. "Keep going!"

But the horses were definitely slowing. He looked back and the Martians were still there, two miles back. And closing? He couldn't be sure. He looked ahead and for a moment he thought he saw some movement on the next ridge line a couple of miles to the east. He rubbed his eyes on his dirty sleeve and looked again. No, he didn't see anything now. Maybe he'd imagined it. But if they didn't reach help soon, they were going to be caught. Where the hell was the damn army?

Halfway to the next ridge they had to cross a stream. The bridge was no longer there, so they had to go down the bank on one side, splash across, and then up on the other. As they did so, a rider who had been concealed behind the bank mounted up and joined them. It was the man the officers had sent ahead earlier.

"Lieutenant! Sir!" he cried.

"Sandusky!" shouted the lieutenant commanding the detachment from the 7th. "I hope to hell you haven't been lollygagging here all this time! Report!"

"No sir! I made it back to the army! They're just ahead; the other side of the ridge! I found the colonel and he took me right to the general! They're getting everything ready and they sent me to find you and tell you to just come straight on! Try and sucker those things right in if we can!"

"Good! Good!" exclaimed the major. "That's exactly what we'll do!" This brought a cheer from the men of the 7th, but everyone else, including Dolfen, was too tired to do anything but mumble prayers of thanks. Were they actually going to get somewhere safe? Did such a place even exist anymore?

Instinct told him to go faster, get to the army as quickly as possible, but to nearly everyone's dismay, Major Comstock actually forced them to slow down. "We're bait!" he explained. "If we get too far ahead they might give up. We need to wiggle on the hook a little!"

"Damnation! The man's a maniac!" muttered Urbaniak.

"It's all right," said Dolfen, not at all sure that it was. "We'll save the horses for a race to the finish."

They slowed to a walk and the Martians were catching up. How far could their heat rays shoot? How close did they dare let them get? Comstock had been here for the first battle and it was his job to evaluate the capabilities of the enemy's weapons, but Dolfen hoped the man knew what the hell he was doing! Two miles… a mile and a half… They sent the men carrying the civilians on ahead, but the rest of them maintained the walking pace. A mile and a quarter… they were getting close to the crest of the ridge…

"Okay!" shouted Comstock. "Let's reel them in!"

The riders gave the spur to their mounts and the tired beasts surged ahead. They couldn't gallop, not with each horse carrying two men, but they managed a fast trot. They reached the top of the ridge, which was barely tall enough to merit the name, and started down the other side. For an instant Dolfen thought they were the victim of some cruel joke, because there was almost nothing to see. A long shallow valley sloped away from them for a couple of miles and it looked nearly deserted. But no, there were things there! A large cluster of wagons milled about in the far distance and he could see the black smoke of train engines. Closer at hand he could see what must be the infantry, but they were all hugging the ground, mostly concealed by the scrub growth and depressions in the earth. Suspicious lumps behind the center of the line must be the artillery, but they'd had things thrown over them. It wouldn't fool any human looking at them, but perhaps it might fool a Martian.

They trotted down the slope and caught up with the others, all the while looking nervously behind them. They lost sight of the Martians for a while, but then the bulbous heads of the machines reappeared as they marched up the ridge. Dolfen and the others passed through the lines of infantry, all the men clutching their rifles and watching them pass. They seemed incredibly vulnerable. It was a damn shame they didn't have any of those dynamite bombs like the Ordnance men had made.

Looking back again, he saw that the enemy machines were at the top of the ridge and still coming on. *Not long now!* They shifted their course a bit to the south to clear the front of the disguised artillery ahead of them. A good thing, too, because only moments later the gunners sprang up and threw off the things covering their guns. The battery commanders raised their arms and then…

"Fire!"

* * * * *

CYCLE597,843.6, EAST OF HOLDFAST 32-1

Something slammed into Qetjnegartis' machine and smoke momentarily obscured its view. What? But then it saw the clouds of smoke in the distance and realized what had happened. More of the large projectile throwers! Another prey-creature force! Even as it processed this information, hundreds more of the creatures rose from the ground and began firing their small weapons. A strange rattling, like what might be heard in a strong sandstorm on the homeworld, filled the control cabin as the projectiles bounced off the armor.

Messages began pouring in from its subordinates, reporting the obvious and asking for orders. But what to do? This appeared to be a trap—and it had walked right into it. Perhaps the sensible thing to do was to walk right out of it again. Could it get the prey to pursue as they had done in the first battle? Destroy their dangerous weapons while they moved and then crush the rest of the force? *They are capable of learning...*

But then the large weapons fired again and Qetjnegartis counted only eight of the smoke clouds. There had been thirty-two in the first battle. *Only a small force?* Perhaps this was the last of the prey's reserves, scraped together and committed in desperation. If they could be crushed it might break their last resistance. Yes.

"Press forward! Ignore the individual creatures and destroy the large weapons!"

* * * * *

MARCH, 1909, WEST OF PREWITT, NEW MEXICO TERRITORY

Major Andrew Comstock gave a whoop as the guns opened fire. He twisted around to look back; several explosions blossomed on the ridgeline behind the Martians and it looked like at least one hit on one of the machines. But where were the tanks? He'd seen the disguised field guns even before they revealed themselves, but he couldn't see the tanks anywhere. Without them this was going to be another slaughter!

"I need to find the general!" he shouted in the ear of the lieutenant he was clinging to.

"Might not be easy in all this mess, sir!"

"He'll be somewhere with a good view! See any place like that?" He was turning his head from side to side trying to spot something that looked like a headquarters; signal flags, clusters of horses or vehicles, something...

"Maybe over there, sir?" The man pointed at a little hill with a cluster of stunted trees. There seemed to be some activity there.

"All right, we'll give it a try. Go that way."

"I need to see to my troop..."

"Then give me your damn horse! That's an order!"

He ruthlessly evicted Kenshaw from his horse and trotted off toward the hill. The artillery was still banging away and a sudden cheer made Andrew look back. One of the tripods was staggering from a hit. It was turning in circles, smoke seeping out of it. But the others were still coming on fast. They'd have the artillery in range of their own weapons any second.

Andrew faced forward again and saw a man on a horse galloping straight toward him. The man rode up and reined in his mount.

"You Comstock?" he demanded. He was only a captain, but if he was on the general's staff he'd act like he was a general himself.

"Yes!"

"Well come on, the general wants to talk to you!"

He kneed the beast into the best speed it could still manage and followed the captain. They reached the little grove of trees just as the first shriek of heat rays was heard. Andrew winced as a loud explosion immediately followed. The guns weren't going to last long and once they were gone…

The captain led him to a cluster of officers. He didn't have any trouble recognizing Frederick Funston. A little chubby and fully bearded, Funston had made headlines a few years before with his handling of the aftermath of the great earthquake in San Francisco. He was said to have ice-water in his veins and despite the chaos all around him today, 'Fearless Freddy' appeared totally unruffled. He was giving an order to an aide as Andrew rode, up, but he immediately turned his attention to him.

"Comstock?"

"Yes sir."

"You're one of Crozier's men, aren't you?"

"Yes sir,"

"What the hell were you doing out there?"

"Uh, I was with General Sumner's army with orders to observe. When the army was destroyed, me and my men were cut off. We trailed a group of Martians back to their base and I saw…"

"Yes, yes, we can talk about that later. Right now I need to know: are those six the only ones I'm facing right now?" He pointed toward the Martian machines.

"Yes, sir! They've been chasing us for over two days, but there are only the six. But sir! I was told that the tanks are here! Where are they? Without them the Martians are going to break right through your center!" He pointed to where the tripods were blasting the artillery—half the guns were gone already.

Incredibly, Funston was smiling. He turned slightly and called to one of his aides. "Now, Lieutenant. Send up the signal."

"Yes sir!" cried the officer. A Signal Corps officer. "Sergeant! Now!" With a roar and a trail of smoke, a rocket leaped skyward.

Almost immediately, clouds of black smoke belched up from the right of the line and the left and from almost directly behind them. As Andrew looked on in delight, a dozen huge metal boxes lurched forward from the gully they'd been hiding in. *The tanks!*

Funston looked back at him. "You're a West Pointer, aren't you, Major? Surely they taught you about the Battle Cannae!"

* * * * *

CYCLE597, 843.6, EAST OF HOLDFAST 32-1

The heat ray swept across another of the large projectile throwers and the thing's chemical ammunition exploded, throwing the prey-creatures who had been serving it in all directions. The draught animals to the rear of it fled in panic. Qetjnegartis looked on in satisfaction. Yes, this had been the right decision. Although Purlintas' war machines had been badly damaged, the other five had only suffered minor hits and were now in position to finish off the enemy's heavy weapons and then the slaughter could commence. Perhaps this would crush the last resistance in this…

"Commander! Beware! Some… some things are approaching!"

Qetjnegartis quickly scanned its surroundings looking for threats, but there was nothing that… What are those? Thirteen strange objects had appeared to the front. They were nearly trapezoidal

167

solids in shape with odd projections at front and rear. The projections at the rear of each were spewing clouds of black smoke. Magnifying the image it could see that there were moving traction belts on each side that were pushing or dragging the objects across the ground. Vehicles of some sort?

"More are coming from the right and left, Commander!"

Qetjnegartis shifted the view and indeed, twelve more were coming from the north and fourteen from the south. The two new groups were still some distance away, but the first group was quite near. What were they? Nothing like this had been encountered by any of the invasion groups. Did they pose any sort of threat?

As if in answer, the group to the front suddenly halted and puffs of smoke appeared at the front of each. An instant later, Qetjnegartis' machine suffered a heavy impact that drove it backward. The feedback from its controls did not indicate any significant damage to the machine's systems, but a sparkling cloud of metal flakes blowing past the cockpit indicated at least some of the armor had been stripped away. Three of its subordinates reported that they too had sustained some damage. *More of the projectile throwers! Mounted on moving platforms!*

"Destroy these things! Quickly!"

Following its own order, Qetjnegartis swept its heat ray across the three nearest platforms. Smoke flashed off of them, but they did not explode the way the other projectile throwers had. Were they destroyed? No! The things fired their weapons again and another blow struck its machine, and this time the information flowing through its tendrils told it that there was a breach in the lower body. No critical systems were damaged, but it was now vulnerable.

"These vehicles are armored! Concentrate your fire until they are destroyed!"

It aimed the heat ray at a single vehicle and fired, leaving the beam on the target. The thing began to glow. First a dull red and then brighter and brighter until it suddenly exploded in a flash of light and a cloud of smoke and steam. Yes! They could be destroyed. Two more of them erupted in flames as Qetjnegartis' subordinates followed its example.

But it took time and the prey-creatures made use of the time. They fired again and now more fire was raining down as the two flanking forces converged. Ridnapadge suddenly called for assistance, but before any could be rendered, its machine crumpled to the ground, hopelessly wrecked. The odds were shifting rapidly...

Qetjnegartis' own machine shuddered again and this time the damage was severe. The heat ray was disabled!

This is no good. Over thirty of these new devices and only three of us still fit to fight. If we stay, we will be destroyed. We can't even use the same tactic as we did to win the first battle; these things can move and fire at the same time.

It rankled, but there was no choice.

"Retreat. I command again: retreat."

* * * * *

MARCH, 1909, SOMEWHERE IN THE NEW MEXICO TERRITORY

Rebecca Harding tried to watch what was happening without losing sight of Sergeant Dolfen, or losing her grasp on Ninny's reins. After the mad run to reach the army, they had been deposited by the cavalrymen who had saved them and left to fend for themselves. The major had ridden off in a hurry and his men tried to chase after him on foot. Sergeant Dolfen had gathered his men and the civilians and led them toward the rear. To safety? With the cannons roaring and the heat rays shrieking and the men yelling, no place felt safe. No place in the whole world.

Dolfen led them to a small gully a few hundred yards behind the line of cannons, but it seemed to Becca like a singularly unsafe place to stop. The Martian machines were coming right after them and started destroying the cannons. She looked on in horror as the brave, brave soldiers kept loading and firing right up until the heat rays found them, turning them to flame and blowing up their cannons. The horses that pulled the cannons bolted and fled, some with burning tail and manes. Smoke drifted back over her and that awful and all-too familiar smell of burning flesh nearly made her gag.

"We can't stay here, Sarge!" shouted one of the men. "They'll walk right over us!"

"I know! I know! Come on, let's go that way!"

They were all gasping and exhausted, but they realized they had to move. They stumbled farther to the rear, dodging stampeding horses and around supply wagons, all the while the sound of the heat rays was getting closer.

But then there was an odd whooshing noise and Becca looked up to see a red rocket, like an Independence Day fireworks, streak up into the sky and burst. What was that? Some signal to retreat? But almost immediately, there was a roar from just ahead and clouds of black smoke jetted up, seemingly from out of the ground. Moments later, a dozen incredible things pulled themselves out of a gully and rumbled toward them!

What were they? Not Martians surely! They might be made of metal like the Martian machines, but they were painted green and covered with rivets and streaks of rust marred their sides; nothing like the gleaming, perfect machines of the invaders. Each one had a boiler on the back with a tall smokestack, belching black clouds. Some sort of rotating belts on the sides, making terrible squeaking sounds, were pulling them forward and what looked like a cannon stuck out from the front. On a few of them, men were sticking out of hatches on the top. Soldiers! These must be some sort of army war machines!

"Holy shit!" cried Sergeant Dolfen. "We'll be caught right between them and the Martians! Turn! Go left!" He reached out and grabbed Becca's arm and dragged her after him. Ninny was squealing in fright.

Boom! Boom! Boom!

The cannons on the front of the machines suddenly fired and she was nearly knocked down by the blasts; and almost losing hold of Ninny. She struggled upright, kept moving, and then felt that awful heat from the Martian ray. It wasn't aimed at her, but it passed over her to wash across the strange army machines. She expected them to blow up, just like everything else, but was astonished when they continued to fire their cannons, apparently unharmed except for scorched paint!

But the rays lashed out again, focusing on individual machines, and this time they did explode. Bits of debris rained down around them, but the smoke was blown the other way. In spite of this, a cheer went up and looking back, she saw one of the enemy machines come crashing down. *They killed one!*

Sergeant Dolfen hauled her down into a ditch and they huddled there, gasping for breath and watching the battle. And it really was a battle, not just some slaughter. The Martians seemed confused by the appearance of the new army machines—and there were two more groups of them closing in from the sides now, too! They turned this way and that, firing off their rays in different directions. But shells continued to burst around them and on them and they were being hurt. One machine in the distance was jerking around in awkward little circles, a closer one was wrecked, and the remaining four looked like elks worried by a pack of dogs. Becca wished she still had her grandfather's rifle so she could shoot, too, but she'd been forced to abandon it during the last mad scramble to get here.

The fight went on and an alarming number of the army's machines seemed to be burning, but then one of the closest Martians was hit and some large piece of it flew off. It stood there for a moment and then turned around. An instant later the others did as well. They were moving away!

"They're running!" she screamed.

* * * * *

MARCH, 1909, WEST OF PREWITT, NEW MEXICO TERRITORY

Andrew wanted to get close to some tanks. Once released from General Funston's scrutiny, he had no actual orders other than the ones he'd been operating under all along: observe the enemy, observe the tanks, report back. Well, he had a hell of a lot to report! But there was no way he was going to leave while this battle was going on! The tanks were finally in action and he was damn well going to see what they did!

And so far they seemed to be doing pretty well.

One of the Martian machines was down and the others were all taking damage. Andrew had held his breath when a heat ray swept across several of the tanks, and then cheered when they had survived. The armor worked! Or at least it worked for a while. A longer exposure melted right through the armor and destroyed the tank, but they could still survive a lot longer than field artillery.

And now the tanks were closing in on three sides and the Martians were retreating! Somehow, Andrew could sense that this wasn't some phony retreat to get the humans to pursue into a trap; no the Martians were running—running for their lives!

"Looks like they're beat, Major!"

Andrew turned to see who had spoken and was stunned to see that it was Lieutenant Robert Frye, the man he'd detached way back in Illinois to shepherd the tanks forward! He'd completely forgotten about him! "Frye! You made it!"

"Sure did," replied the lieutenant, grinning. "Hell of a job, but we got here. I saw you there watching, but I hardly recognized you, sir, what with that growth of beard and all. Guess you and the others had a bit of an adventure, too."

Andrew ran a hand over his unshaven face. "Yeah, a bit. But where are the other tanks? I only count about forty of them."

Frye shrugged. "Broken down getting here. The trains could only get us to about ten miles away and they had to come the rest of the way under their own power. We were lucky to only lose a third of them, sir." Frye looked a little hurt.

"Yes, I'm sure. But good job, Lieutenant! A great job! You'll have to tell me all about it… later."

"Yes sir… *Oh!* Look at that!"

The Martians were falling back, up the long slope, but the two flanking tank forces were closing on them like the jaws of a trap. Two of the Martian machines had stopped to face the northern wing. They had destroyed three of the tanks, but were getting pounded in return. Suddenly, one of the machines was enveloped in a crackling web of blue lightning bolts that looked for all the world like Dr. Tesla's bizarre contraption out on Long Island! An instant later the thing disappeared in an eye-aching blast of light. A colossal *boom* rolled across the landscape, shaking the ground, and when Andrew could see again, there was no trace of the first machine and the one which had been close by had been smashed to junk.

"Wow!" cried Frye. "That got 'em!"

* * * * *

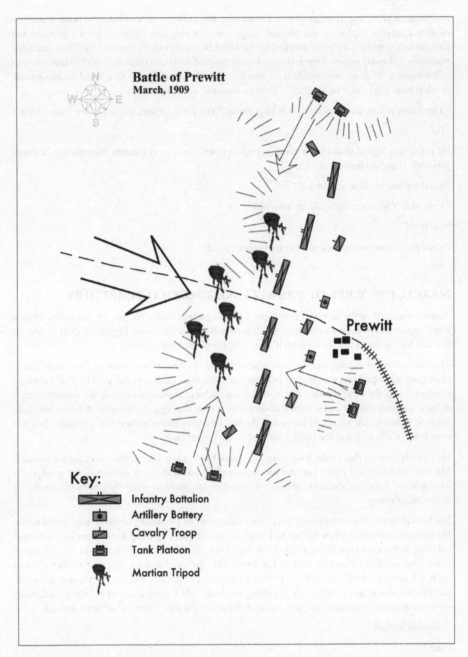

Battle of Prewitt
March, 1909

Prewitt

Key:

Infantry Battalion
Artillery Battery
Cavalry Troop
Tank Platoon
Martian Tripod

CYCLE597,843.6, EAST OF HOLDFAST 32-1

Qetjnegartis was looking right at Gndercal's machine when it exploded. *The power cells*. Each fighting machine was powered by two enormously efficient power cells. A single charging could power a machine for nearly a quarter of a cycle of normal activity. They had numerous safeguards to harmlessly discharge them into the ground in the event of serious damage. No system was foolproof and if the damage was catastrophic, the cells could discharge instantaneously—causing a massive explosion like had just happened. Not only had Gndercal been vaporized, but Javlnadrap's machine had been wrecked by the blast. No matter that several of the prey-creatures' machines and many more of the individual creatures had also been destroyed in the blast, this was still a disaster. With its own machine weaponless and Purlintas' unable to control its movement, that left only Hlaknadar fit for battle—and its machine was damaged too.

"This battle is lost, Commander," said Hlaknadar. "You must escape. We will cover your retreat."

"But…"

"It is the only logical choice! But you must move now!" As if to emphasize the message, another projectile slammed into its machine.

And there was no denying the logic.

"Very well. Your memories will be honored."

"Go now!"

Qetjnegartis sent its machine west at maximum speed.

* * * * *

MARCH, 1909, WEST OF PREWITT, NEW MEXICO TERRITORY

Andrew watched as the last tripod collapsed to the ground under the fire of the tanks. Only a single tripod had managed to escape, scuttling over the ridge like some frightened crab. It was far too fast for the tanks to catch—even if they could avoid breaking down.

The firing slowly died away but the cheers went on and on. The infantry rose up from their hiding places and whooped and tossed their helmets and even their rifles into the air. The tank crewmen climbed out of their metal boxes and stood on top and waved their arms. Only the cavalry seemed to have any business left and several squadrons went over the ridge in pursuit of the lone survivor. Andrew remembered what had happened the last time they thought they'd won a battle, but this time it was really true and the cavalry did not come fleeing back.

He numbly realized that he did have things he ought to be doing. He needed to secure the wrecked Martian machines and check for any survivors, collect any important wreckage and arrange for its shipment, interview the tank crewmen to get their impressions while they were still fresh… a dozen other things.

But he was so tired he could barely keep from falling out of the saddle of his requisitioned horse. He couldn't remember when he had last slept. So he sat there, ignoring Lieutenant Frye's excited babbling as his eyes kept trying to close of their own accord. He was only able to rouse himself when Sergeant McGill and the rest of his men slowly gathered around. Sergeant Dolfen showed up, too, leading his small band of troopers and civilians. The girl still had her crazy horse, he noted, but Bill White was gone; off to file his story, no doubt. He looked down at his exhausted, filthy men and realized he couldn't ask any more of them for this day. They had all done enough.

"Sergeant McGill."

"Sir?"

"Let's find some food and a place to sleep, shall we?"

"Very good, sir!"

CHAPTER TWELVE

APRIL, 1909, WASHINGTON, D.C.

"So, you are all convinced that this is not some new landing, gentlemen?" asked General Leonard Wood, Chief of Staff of the United States Army. He looked around at the other officers in the meeting room.

"Yes, sir," replied his senior aide. "While the cylinder was largely intact, there was damage to the exterior that could not be reconciled with its landing. Some of the scientists are suggesting that it was caused by a collision with a meteorite in space. This may have knocked it into a new elongated orbit which only brought it down in Tennessee. So the consensus is that this is some errant cylinder from the main invasion, not something from a new wave. No other new landings have been reported in that region or anywhere else, sir."

"I see. And the contents of the cylinder?"

"Also largely intact, although all three of the Martians were dead and much of the equipment inside was damaged. Still, our people ought to be able to learn quite a lot from it."

"Good, good," said Wood. "But the main thing is that we don't have to deal with a new landing. We have a big enough job with the ones we already have." He sighed and briefly closed his eyes. That was an understatement if ever there was one! While the New Mexico landing seemed to be contained for the moment, the one in Idaho was wreaking havoc in the northern Rockies and there was now no doubt of the existence of the long-suspected one in Alberta. Only one rail connection to the west coast was still open, the Southern Pacific line along the border, and considering the news coming out of Mexico, Wood doubted it would be open much longer. All of Mexico had been overrun except for a few cities along the coasts, and the invaders were moving into Central America. The news from South America wasn't much better. American troops and ships had secured the Panama Canal construction area, but the place was being overrun by refugees from north and south. Many had been put to work on construction jobs, both for the canal and the new defenses being built, but thousands more were just in the way and they all needed to be fed. Some suggested they be transported to the Caribbean islands, particularly Cuba, but those places were already being deluged by waves of people escaping the mainland in any boats they could find.

Refugees were starting to be a problem here at home, too. People from Idaho, Montana, and the Dakotas, as well as Wyoming and Utah were starting to drift east. It was only a trickle, so far, but unless a solid line of defense could be established, the trickle could quickly become a flood. And creating that defense line wasn't going to be easy.

Huge numbers of newly drafted men were reporting to the training camps and many thousands had already passed through those camps and reported to their units. Wood had close to half a million men ready or nearly ready to deploy. But they were terribly short of heavy weapons and the recent battles had shown that men without those weapons were useless against the Martians.

And even if they had the weapons, the problem was getting them to where the Martians were. The vast regions of the American West had few roads worthy of the name and only a few navigable rivers. Transporting and supplying armies could only be done where there were railroads. And the Martians were destroying the railroads wherever they went.

There was some debate about whether this was a deliberate strategy or whether the enemy was using the metal in the rails as a source of raw material. But whatever the case was, it made operations against the Martians incredibly difficult. Funston had tried to follow up his recent victory, but the 'tanks' which were so vital could only move short distances without rail transport. Funston had tried to attack the Martian fortress without them and had been bloodily repulsed. He was now waiting on crews of railroad men to repair the tracks, but the civilian workers were leery of getting too close to the Martian stronghold. In fact, the railroad men were turning out to be a damn uncooperative bunch. Roosevelt was considering reinitiating the US Military Railroad system which had worked so well during the Civil War, but it hadn't happened yet.

So Funston was stuck and the other forces which had been sent west had accomplished very little, and the Martians from the Idaho landing were getting bolder and bolder, sending a raiding force as far east as Rawlins. Wood was beginning to think that he would have to form his defensive lines in Nebraska—or even farther east. That would not sit well with a lot of people!

He checked his pocket watch and saw that he was due at another meeting. He dismissed his staff and headed for another part of the huge State, War, & Navy Building. He had only gone a few steps down the hall when his left knee nearly buckled. *Damn!* Fortunately, there was no one close by to see. Pulling himself upright, he backtracked to the small washroom attached to his office. Alone, he pulled a small bottle of chloroform out of his pocket and dabbed a small amount on a handkerchief and inhaled the fumes for a moment. The dizziness this produced passed quickly, but unfortunately the numbness in his leg was almost unaffected. Cursing again he put the bottle away. *One day someone is going to catch me.* The symptoms were getting worse and the chloroform treatments weren't working anymore. He needed the operation, but when could he possibly have it done? He had a war to fight! If he became incapacitated, even his friendship with Roosevelt couldn't prevent him from being replaced.

Splashing some water on his face he drew himself up and slowly but deliberately made his way to the next conference. This was to hear a report from the Ordnance Department. Entering the large conference room, he was cheered by the conspicuous absence of Fred Ainsworth. The former Adjutant General was finally gone. Or almost gone. He was still hanging around Washington, agitating with political enemies of Wood's trying to get his old position and power back. But while that might have borne him some fruit in peacetime, in wartime, few people had the patience for it. Ainsworth wouldn't be back.

All the officers present rose to their feet at his arrival and he shook hands with the ordnance chief, William Crozier. "Well, Bill, I understand you have quite a little tale to present to me today!"

"Yes, sir, quite a tale indeed! But I won't be doing the telling. It's Major Comstock's story and I'll let him tell it!" He gestured forward a very young man wearing major's leaves who came to attention and saluted.

"At ease, Major, at ease." He shook the man's hand. "Let's all sit down and hear this story."

The man looked nervous, but sat and began to speak. He had a stack of notes with him, but didn't seem to be referring to them. "I had been sent west to join General Sumner's army to observe the Martian machines and also the performance of our new tanks. When the battle near Thoreau began I was behind the center of our lines and..." Wood leaned back in his chair and listened as the young man's story unfolded. He had read a short summary, so this wasn't entirely new, but even so, he was amazed and impressed with what he heard. It took nearly half an hour, with no interruptions, for Comstock to finish. "After that, I returned to Washington, arriving yesterday."

"Well!" said Wood clearing his throat. "That's extraordinary! Well done, Major, well done!" The young man blushed and mumbled his thanks. "I'm very impressed that after the battle was lost you decided to press on with your mission instead of retreat. That sort of gumption and initiative is all too rare."

"Thank you, sir, but honestly, there didn't seem to be much choice. The area to the rear was swarming with the Martians. Going back seemed more dangerous than going ahead. And once we spotted the prisoners... well, turning back just didn't seem right."

"But a dozen of you taking on—and destroying!—one of the enemy machines," Wood shook his head. "The idea of the dynamite bombs was sheer genius; General Crozier, we must take thought about arming all of our infantry with such weapons! Right now they aren't even cannon fodder, but with something like this, they could be effective again!"

"Yes, sir," replied Crozier. "We are already working on it. We ought to have something in a few months."

"Why so long? We have dynamite in abundance, don't we?"

"Yes, we do, sir, but the crude dynamite bombs that Major Comstock and his men made could be just as dangerous to our own men as the Martians, right, Major?"

"Uh, that's true sir, I very nearly blew myself to bits when we attacked the Martian. It was a miracle none of us were killed."

"We are exploring several different approaches which will be safer to use but still effective," said Crozier.

"I see. Well, don't take too long; we will have need of them very shortly. But what was this other thing you said, Major, about ways to make the infantry rifles more effective?"

"Well, you see, sir, it took about a week to get back to Washington, and I spent a lot of that time examining the remains of the Martian machines we brought with us on the train. The metal protecting their machines seems to consist of millions of tiny pieces of a hexagonal shape. They interlock into a mesh somehow, giving them great strength." Comstock interlocked the fingers of his hands in demonstration. "I could see from the bullet spalls on the metal that our rifle and machine gun bullets were just bouncing off harmlessly. But in the spots where an artillery projectile had struck, the pattern of the mesh had been broken, which not only gouged out a section of the armor, but weakened the surrounding structure." He twisted his hands and pulled his fingers apart. "I could see that there were smaller gouges surrounding the main gouge. I believe that these small gouges were caused by rifle fire. It appears that once the armor has been damaged, it becomes vulnerable even to the weaker weapons. Of course, those are just my own observations, sir. I'm sure our experts will have much more to say."

"Yes," continued Crozier. "We are already looking at increasing the power of our rifle cartridges and producing hardened, armor-piercing bullets for our 1903 Springfields. In addition, we are looking into a new type of heavy machine gun with a point-five inch caliber."

"That sounds excellent, General," said Wood. "But hurry it along! We have no time to spare!"

"Uh, sir?" said Comstock. "I want to reemphasize the danger revealed by what I saw inside the Martian fortress. These construction machines of theirs mean that instead of having to create an entire industrial base from scratch, they've brought one ready-made with them! Their ability to increase their strength is far greater than we ever..."

"Yes, Major," said Wood, "I fully realize that. And that's why we have to be able to strike and strike hard at the earliest possible moment!" Without thinking, he made to thump the table with his left fist, but the hand just flopped against the top like a dying fish. None of the others seemed to notice, but Wood twisted his shoulder to drag the hand back under the table. Damn! "Uh, but I'm afraid that's all I have time for today, gentlemen. General Crozier, if you could have a full report delivered to me as soon as possible."

"Certainly, sir, but there were several other items I wanted…"

"We'll have to schedule another time, General. Oh, and Major Comstock, let me congratulate you again on your amazing accomplishments. I think there might be a medal in this for you."

"Thank you, sir, but…"

Wood raised his right hand to silence the boy and carefully stood up and walked slowly out of the room, trying not to limp. *I'm going to have to talk to Theodore. He'll understand.*

* * * * *

APRIL, 1909, SANTA FE, NEW MEXICO TERRITORY

"What will you do now, Sergeant?"

Frank Dolfen turned his head to look at the girl walking beside him down the streets of Santa Fe. After the battle he and the other survivors of the 5th had been sent back to Albuquerque and then on to Santa Fe. The girl had somehow managed to come along—even finding space on the train for her horse. The other civilians had remained behind.

"There's a camp north of the city I have to report to. They're sending all the survivors from the first battle there to reorganize. Word is that there are more than they first thought, even more men from the 5th. Don't know what they'll do with us. Probably use us as cadre to rebuild the regiments."

"What's a… cadre?"

"Like a foundation you can build on. Veterans who know how things are done and who can show the new recruits the ropes."

"Oh, I see. I bet you will do a great job, Sergeant. None of us would have made it but for you." A motorcycle roared past them, throwing up dust. "I don't like those things, they're so noisy and they scare the horses."

Dolfen smiled. "But they don't get tired or scared, either. Keep 'em filled with gas and they'll go on and on. Think how much trouble we would have been saved if we'd had motorcycles instead of horses." *Yeah… Motorcycle cavalry…*

"Maybe, but I'll stick to horses, thank you."

"Glad you could keep yours. He seems real attached to you. Hope that livery stable you put him in takes good care of him."

"If they don't, they'll answer to me!"

"And considering you're the only girl in America to have killed a Martian, I can't imagine they'll want to get you riled up."

"Now you're makin' fun of me, Sergeant."

"That I am not, young lady! You're a pistol and that's for sure!" He paused and looked at her. "You going to be all right here? You still have the money the boys collected for you? You've got the address of your aunt and uncle here, don't you?"

"Yes," she said and sighed. "I'll go and see them a little later. God only knows what they'll think, me looking like something the cat dragged in. I just… I just wanted to say good-bye to you first."

Dolfen looked at her and sincerely hoped that she wasn't going to do something stupid like tell him she loved him or something like that. But when she didn't, he found himself strangely disappointed. *Don't be a fool!*

"Uh... well, you know where I'll be."

"Think you'll be there long?"

"Hard to say. The rumors have been flying. Seems General Funston is waiting for heavy artillery before he tries to crack the Martian fort at Gallup. But other are saying there's trouble up in Wyoming or the Dakotas and they may send us there. Probably won't know until they start loading us on trains."

She handed him a slip of paper. "This is my Aunt's address. You could write to me."

"I'll try."

"Thank you for everything, Sergeant." She came over, stood on tip-toes and kissed him on the cheek. "Goodbye."

"Goodbye, Miss. Take care."

She nodded, but didn't smile and then turned and walked off down the street.

* * * * *

APRIL, 1909, SANTA FE, NEW MEXICO TERRITORY

Rebecca Harding forced herself not to look back—at least until she got to the end of the block. But when she did look, there was no sign of Sergeant Dolfen. *What? Did you think he would come running after you? You're just a silly little girl and he's a grown man!* And quite a man he was, too! She often thought that her father and grandfather were tough men and she supposed they were, but she'd never met anyone like Sergeant Dolfen. She'd be long dead but for him.

She shook her head and continued on her way, asking a woman who was sweeping her stoop how to get to the part of town where her aunt lived. The woman looked at her very oddly, but told her what she needed to know. It was quite a walk, which gave her time to think. Part of her very much wanted to go to her aunt's house. A place with a door where she could shut out the world. A place with a bath! Hot food! A soft bed! She was sure it would be very pleasant—at first. But then what was she going to do? What would her aunt and uncle let her do? They would be her legal guardians and have exactly the same authority over her as her parents had had. They could send her to school in Connecticut, they could make her sell Ninny, they could make her do anything they wanted!

But what do you want to do, girl?

She didn't have an answer for that. Well, she knew what she *really* wanted to do: fight the Martians. She wanted to be a soldier and fight Martians. But they didn't have women soldiers. Even though she had killed a Martian face-to-face, they wouldn't let her be a soldier. To even suggest it would bring laughter and mockery. If she really tried to insist, it could get her locked up in the attic of her aunt's house like some senile old woman. So of the options *possible* for her, what did she want to do? She had no answer.

Her path took her past the railroad station. The tracks were filled with trains. Some taking troops and supplies to General Funston's army, others going the other way carrying... carrying what? She stopped and watched one train where there were many people clustered about and lots of small enclosed wagons with big red crosses painted on the sides.

Wounded. Trains full of wounded.

The Martian heat rays didn't leave many wounded, but she supposed there must be some. And with any large army there would be men hurt in accidents or men who got sick. Apparently they were being brought here, to Santa Fe.

Rebecca moved closer and saw men carrying the wounded out of the train on stretchers and putting them in the wagons, the ambulances. But there were women there, too! Women wearing what looked like uniforms. They had khaki tunics just like the men and long khaki skirts. They had white aprons and white hats and armbands with the red crosses. Nurses!

She came right up behind one of the women and watched as she helped settle one of the wounded men. The man had bandages over most of his face and he was moaning quietly. The woman finished and suddenly turned, almost colliding with Rebecca. "Oh!" she exclaimed. "Watch out, girl!"

"I'm sorry," said Rebecca.

"What are you doing here? What do you want?"

Rebecca looked her up and down.

"I want to help."

* * * * *

APRIL, 1909, WASHINGTON, D.C.

Major Andrew Comstock walked down E Street toward the bridge leading back to Fort Myer and his quarters. Colonel Hawthorne walked along with him. It was as beautiful a spring morning as you could ask for, which is why they hadn't taken a car, but Andrew didn't notice the flowering trees or the birds singing. "Colonel, I don't think General Wood really understood what I was saying about the Martian construction machines."

"Well, he has an awful lot on his mind, Andy."

"But this is so important, sir! The moment I saw what was happening I knew I had to get the word back! *You* understand, don't you, sir?"

"Yes, I think I do. It does change the equation quite a lot. Remember that conversation we had a long time ago about the Indians and the Europeans?"

"Yes I do, sir. I think about it often."

"I said if the Indians had simply worked together, gathered their tribes into a huge force, they could have wiped out each tiny colony as they appeared. But if those colonists could have been building muskets and cannons and machines to build forts as soon as they stepped off their boats. Well, I'm not so sure about the Indians' chances."

"Yes! Exactly! So what do we do, sir?"

"That's the question, isn't it? But honestly, even if Wood fully appreciated the danger, understood it all as you and I do, what could we do that we're not already doing? Destroying the enemy bases would still be a priority even if they didn't have the construction machines. You've been away for a couple of months, Andy, you haven't seen what's been happening around here."

"What, sir?"

"People are waking up to the fact that this is all for real. Some still don't believe it, but more and more do. The country is mobilizing its strength like it never has before. Men being trained, factories working around the clock; even the Civil War is going to pale next to this sort of effort. We're a strong country and we will be putting all our strength into this."

"I hope you're right, sir."

They walked in silence for a while. Andrew looked around and had to admit that there had been changes, even in the time he'd been away. There were men in uniform everywhere; the streets were filled with them. When his train had arrived in the city he had passed through lines of fortifications under construction and there were huge military camps everywhere. There were even posts with men and weapons right here in the city. Field guns guarded the bridges and machine guns were posted atop many of the buildings.

"Victoria missed you terribly while you were gone, Andy," said Hawthorne suddenly. "She was disappointed that you went right to headquarters without even stopping to see her."

"I… I needed to report in," he replied, suddenly flustered. "I'll go see her as soon as I can get changed. With your permission, sir."

Hawthorne chuckled. "You always have that, son. And we'll expect you for dinner tonight."

"Thank you, sir." The desire to see Vickie suddenly grew very strong in him. And was Hawthorne hinting that if he did ask her, he would have his blessing? Sure sounded like it… "What… what do you think I'll be assigned to next, sir?"

"Do you mean will you be staying in Washington for a while?" said Hawthorne, grinning. "Hard to say. Of course just writing your report ought to keep you here for a month! And if I haven't said so before, that was a hell of a job you did, Major! I think you'll be getting that medal Wood mentioned."

"I lost some of my men, sir; saw an awful lot more get killed. Somehow medals don't seem quite so important as they used to."

"That is the way of it, isn't it? Well, in any case, I think we'll be able to find you some work that will keep you back east for a while. It's clear the tanks need improvements if they're to be of any use in offensive operations. Guns need to be improved, we need to get Tesla in gear on his contraptions, and the Wrights need to improve their flying machines. Oh yes, they'll be plenty of work."

"Yes, sir. But I'm still worried about what the Martians are doing. If they can build more of their tripods as quickly as it seems they can…"

"It's a worry for sure," agreed Hawthorne. "But the one hopeful thing I see in your report was those dozen tripods you saw just standing in a row inside the fortress. Why weren't they out doing things?"

"Uh, I was assuming it was because they were for the new offspring the Martians were growing."

"Yes, that was my thought, too. And if that is the case then we may be in better shape than we think. Every destroyed tripod we've been able to examine has had a Martian in it. They have to have an operator for each one! They can't operate automatically."

"There were dozens of those heat ray towers on the wall of their fortress," Andrew pointed out. "The ones that hurt General Funston's army when they tried to attack. They must have been under some sort of automatic control, sir."

"True, but that's a different situation. The immediate threat is their tripods. Every cylinder that's been found, the ones in England and the errant one that fell near Memphis a few weeks ago, they all carried only three Martians. If it takes a Martian to control a tripod, then the defining factor of their strength is not how many machines they can build, but how many Martians there are to run them."

"Yes, sir. It's a shame there was so little left of the one we captured by the time we could get it on ice. We need to know how long it takes to grow a new Martian and how long it takes them to mature to the point that they can control a machine."

"Yes," agreed Hawthorne. "If we were dealing with humans, we wouldn't need to worry. Nine months to be born and then a dozen years at least until they could fight. But with the Martians, who knows? If they can produce a new one every six months and if the thing can fight in a year or less then… well then we may be looking at a very long war, Andrew."

"Yes, sir. A very long war."

EPILOGUE

CYCLE 597, 843.7, HOLDFAST 32-1

Qetjnegartis watched as the bud pulled itself free of the growth sac and flopped on the floor of the birthing crèche. Of necessity, the crèche was a crude place, tunneled out of the rock beneath the holdfast and, for the moment, lacking in most of the usual facilities. Still, it would do.

It was a long time since it had done this and it was an interesting sensation. The new member of the Race had been given the basic set of knowledge during its final days of gestation and its intellect, which had been rudimentary up until then, had expanded enormously in just that short time. Communication between the bud and Qetjnegartis had not only become possible, but nearly incessant during that time.

Leaving the growth sac had severed that communications and clearly the bud was distressed by this. It stretched out its tendrils toward Qetjnegartis and it reached down and grasped them, re-establishing the link.

Where are we?

On a new world which the Race has marked for conquest. There is much work to be done.

Can I help?

Indeed yes. You were created to help.

That is good, is it not?

Yes.

This bud and the others were essential. The unexpected losses both in battle and on the still missing cylinder had put the group at considerable risk. Only five of the original fifteen members remained. While the holdfast's defenses had been improved to the point that they could repel a minor attack, they were far from complete. The war machines were essential to the defense, and it would be at least a quarter cycle until the new buds would be able to pilot them. Even then, there would only be ten instead of the expected thirty.

Worse, Zastranvis was exhibiting the first signs of the microbial infection which had destroyed the first expedition. The new drugs were keeping it in check, but its next bud would have to be a replacement body for itself instead of a new member. None of the others had shown any symptoms yet, but it was inevitable that they all would. This would lead to additional delays in expanding their strength.

Fortunately, Group 33 to the north was still at full strength and would soon have thirty war machines in operation. The Conclave had given it orders to drive south and link up with Qetjnegartis' group. If no major attack came between now and the link-up, they should be safe.

And overall, things were going well. The lands to the south had been nearly overrun. Large sections of the land in the opposite hemisphere had been subdued as well. And nowhere—except here—had any significant setbacks been experienced. Much remained to do, but the next wave of cylinders was due to be launched soon. When they arrived, a large offensive could start which would break the last resistance. Yes, success seemed certain.

Qetjnegartis moved toward the door and pulled gently on the bud's tendrils. *Come, you must be hungry. We shall visit the feeding chamber. After feeding I will show you the rest of the holdfast. We have great tasks ahead of us.*

THE END

MARTIAN INTERLUDE ONE

CYCLE 597,843.8, GUERKADAN

Valprandar of the Bajantus Clan watched through the viewport in the observation blister as the high-altitude winds dispersed the propellant gases from the muzzles of the colossal launching guns built into the side of the ancient volcano. After the blindingly bright initial flash, the gas clouds had glowed in interesting colors before fading and finally disappearing against the background of the dark sky.

The last shot of the ten-shot salvo had been fired for the day. Ten new transport pods had been sent on their way to the Target World. Ten had been launched the previous day and ten more would be launched tomorrow. A total of one hundred transports would be launched in this wave. Only half as many as in the initial assault, but five of them were being sent to Group Commander Qetjnegartis and the members of the Bajantus Clan already on the Target World. There was a desperate need for reinforcements following the reverses suffered in the recent battles.

"It is quite a thing, is it not?" asked a voice from beside it.

Valprandar turned and waved its tendrils respectfully at the one who had spoken. Galdan was the fourth-most senior member of the clan. A being of immense age and wisdom and the actual leader of the clan. The senior-most member of the clan, Baj, along with two others nearly as old, could no longer command in anything except ceremonial functions. They were members of the revered *Ancients* who had survived since almost the beginnings of the Race. The *Ancients* could still bud off replacement bodies and sustain their lives, but the replication errors which had accumulated over the eons had left them with damaged and diminished faculties. It was a fate which awaited anyone who lived so long apparently, but Galdan's faculties were still unimpaired.

"Yes it is," replied Valprandar.

"So huge an effort. Such a spending of rare resources. Nothing like this has happened since the cities were moved underground. Many question the wisdom of it," said Galdan.

"And yet it is necessary if we are to survive. A new world, young and rich. We must seize it and make it our own. The Council of Three Hundred has so ruled."

"Yes, that is what was agreed. Take the third planet and slowly relocate the Race to it. Leave our dying world for another. At the time, it seemed the alternative with the least negatives. But with these recent reverses, Some are having second thoughts."

"Chance has not favored us, it is true," said Valprandar, carefully choosing its words. It did not know what Galdan was suggesting, nor what the proper response should be. "Overall the invasion is going well. The Race has seized large areas and most of their holdfasts are secure. Even with our misfortunes we will still have vast holdings once the prey-creatures are subdued."

"Assuming the prey-creatures are subdued."

"Surely there can be no doubt of that. They are primitives. Vastly inferior. Given time, our victory is assured." The words came automatically, but the notion that the clan leader had these doubts was… disturbing.

187

"We can hope so, but there have been disquieting signs. Reports from the Target World which could indicate that they are not quite so inferior as we had been led to believe."

Valprandar was shocked by such a statement and glanced around at the other people who had come to watch the launchings. The Guerkadan facility was neutral ground and members of many different clans were present. Had any of them overheard? Galdan noticed and said, "Walk with me." It turned its travel chair and moved away from the observation viewport and into one of the elevators. Valprandar followed. The elevator took them down to a central concourse and they directed their chairs toward the quarters reserved for the Bajantus Clan.

The spaces in the facility were utilitarian. Not belonging to any specific clan, there had been little effort spared for aesthetics. The tiled floors and walls were perfectly constructed, of course, but utterly lacking in any ornamentation. In truth, few members of the Race were aesthetically inclined. But those few who were, having hundreds of thousands of cycles to do their work, had left their mark on most clan facilities. Valprandar had to admit that such efforts did often result in pleasing effects and since the expenditure of vital resources was minimal, it could be tolerated.

Once inside the secured quarters, Valprandar turned its chair to face Galdan. "You do not believe that our victory is assured?"

The commander waved its tendrils in a non-committal fashion. "Few things in life are completed assured. I did not mean to alarm you. I simply mean that the prey-creatures appear to have more intelligence and resourcefulness than the report from the first expedition had indicated. Our forces are encountering weapons and devices which were not observed previously. Whether this is just a matter of chance and these devices existed but were simply not seen in the small area explored, or, if they have been created in the interval between expeditions specifically to fight our forces, is unknown. In the latter case, what other innovations can we expect to face as things progress?"

"It would be a matter of concern," admitted Valprandar. "But I suppose that since a primitive species has so much yet to learn, it's not unreasonable that they might learn quickly."

"You mean more quickly than we do, now that our knowledge is so vast?" Valprandar looked sharply at Galdan. Was it speaking in jest? Perhaps partly, but there was truth in what it said as well. The Race had reached such a level of perfection that new advances were indeed a rare thing. The devices and machines used now had not changed significantly in many thousands of cycles. Indeed, the great launching guns and transport pods were the first new things in a very long time.

"And if the prey-creatures do possess their equivalent of scientists and engineers," continued Galdan, "one would expect them to be located in the larger cities - areas which we deliberately avoided attacking."

The notion of a prey-creature *scientist* was so absurd as to be laughable, but Valprandar kept its response as level as possible. "The strategy of landing in remote locations was agreed upon by all. And it seems to have served its purpose. None of the landing sites was disturbed,"

"True. But as of yet, none of the larger prey-creature manufacturing—and the presumed engineering and scientific facilities—have been disturbed, either. Who can know what they are doing there now?"

"With this next wave of transports and the natural growth of our strength on the Target World, we shall soon be able to attack and destroy those areas," said Valprandar. This discussion was becoming more unsettling by the moment. Did Galdan have some point it was trying to make? Or was this conversation simply rhetorical?

"So we can hope. But I do not like relying upon hope. Although, truth to tell, I would not be saddened if some other clan were to suffer a serious reverse in the near future. Qetjnegartis' clumsy handling of events has made us an object of derision among the clans."

Ah! Now we come to it!

"While there is no doubt that some of the reverses we have suffered were due to mischances which no one could have predicted or prevented, I am having serious doubts about Qetjnegartis' judgement. In light of the increasing difficulties which it may soon face, leaving it in command may be a mistake."

Valprandar's attention was completely focused on Galdan. "What can be done over so vast a distance?"

"To attempt to oversee activities from the Homeworld would be difficult and probably counterproductive. Therefore a new commander shall be sent to the Target World. You shall go with it when the next wave is launched."

Valprandar had expected nothing like this when Galdan ordered it to accompany it to the launching. This was a great honor, an opportunity to increase its status—and a daunting responsibility. But to leave the Homeworld—forever! Still, there was only one reply possible. It waved its tendrils in submission. "I shall do my best for the sake of the Race and the Clan, Commander."

"Good."

"What about Qetjnegartis?"

"You are senior to it and it will obey you, of course." Galdan paused and then went on. "If there is any difficulty, you are free to act as you see fit."

"I understand," said Valprandar.

BREAKTHROUGH!

PROLOGUE

CYCLE 597, 843.7, HOLDFAST 32-1

"Controlling our machines is little different from controlling our own bodies," said Qetjnegartis. "Grasp the controls with your tendrils and let your awareness flow into the machine as you would let it flow through your body. Go ahead, try it." The rapidly maturing bud, who had been designated Davnitargus, did as it had been directed, extending two of its manipulating tendrils and wrapping them around the control rods of the training machine. A third tendril continued to clutch one of Qetjnegartis' to maintain the neural link. "Do you feel it?"

"I... believe so," replied Davnitargus. "At least I feel... something."

"Excellent. Do not be alarmed or discouraged at the crudity of it. No machine can match the perfect melding of minds that our links provide. It is but a substitute, just as spoken words are a substitute for direct communications when distance prevents a physical link: inferior, but necessary."

"I understand. How do I make this machine respond?"

"Let your awareness explore the structure of the machine. It will feel very strange at first, but try to find the way to the center light of the three that sit atop it." Qetjnegartis could sense the bud's fumbling attempts—and its frustration—but was pleased when it finally succeeded. "Good. Now turn on that light."

"How?"

"Trace the circuits back to the power supply. Find where the switch controlling the power to the light is located and close it." This proved much more difficult for the bud, but it applied itself with a determination which Qetjnegartis found very commendable. After a considerable time the light came on. Davnitargus was pleased and Qetjnegartis complimented it on the success. It had been over a hundred thousand cycles since Qetjnegartis had last instructed a new bud, but the perfectly preserved memories of that event included the same sense of satisfaction as it was feeling now. *And with the conquest of this new world, this will become common!* On the exhausted and dying Homeworld, a new bud was a rare thing. But here! Here the Race could grow and grow and grow!

"This seems very inefficient," observed the bud. "Why not simply have a mechanical switch where it could be operated with my tendrils?"

Qetjnegartis radiated amusement. "In some situations you would be correct. But for more complex machines that would not be practical. The construction and fighting machines will require you to carry out scores, sometimes hundreds, of operations simultaneously. Physically manipulating switches would not be possible. But do not be dismayed! You have just begun to learn the process. Soon, turning on this light will be as easy—and as automatic—as breathing. Later, operating complex machines will become just as easy."

"If you say so," said Davnitargus. It still seemed dubious, but it proceeded with the exercise and before long was able to turn the central light on and off at will. Qetjnegartis was just starting it on controlling multiple lights when a deep rumble shook the underground chamber, bringing down a small cloud of dust from the ceiling. Almost immediately came a communications from one of its subordinates.

"Commander, the prey-creatures have commenced a heavy bombardment. I believe that a major attack may be intended."

"Understood. I will come directly." Qetjnegartis turned its attention back to Davnitargus. "I must go. You shall remain and continue to practice as I have shown you."

"The prey-creatures are attacking again? They have done this many times before and failed each time. Why do they persist?"

"I do not know. Perhaps they believe they have grown strong enough to succeed this time. Now, I must go."

"Can I help in the defense?"

"Not yet. You must master controlling our machines first. That is what these exercises are for."

"I understand."

Qetjnegartis left the chamber and pulled itself into one of the travel chairs which were necessary due to the strong gravity of the target world. It set it in motion toward the main control center, its metal legs clicking and scratching on the stone floor. The corridor was just a crudely cut tunnel through the rock. There had been no time to smooth the walls or line it with tiles as was proper. The demands of defending the holdfast precluded such niceties.

The rumbles were more frequent now and Qetjnegartis twitched in annoyance as several drops of water splashed on it. The roof was leaking—again. The amount of uncontrolled water on the planet was almost beyond belief. In addition to the oceans, which covered three-quarters of the surface, there was water almost everywhere else, too, and it was proving a serious difficulty. Precipitation from the atmosphere turned the surface into sticky morasses, often immobilizing the fighting machines. Water vapor in the air reduced the range of the heat rays and caused corrosion of delicate equipment, and water in the ground seeped into the chambers of the holdfast, despite repeated vitrification of the walls. The effort required for basic maintenance was exceeding predictions by a factor of three, and this was mostly due to moisture. *We must change our methods.*

Qetjnegartis reached the control center and stopped its chair next to that of Zastranvis who had the watch. "Status?"

"A very heavy bombardment from the prey-creature's projectile throwers has commenced in Sector 9, Commander. Three of the defense towers have already been put out of operation. Many of the prey and their vehicles are massing opposite the bombardment area. I predict they will attack once enough of the defense towers have been destroyed."

"That has been their pattern in the past. What steps have you taken?"

"I have ordered the constructor machines to deposit spare defense towers in the area to the rear of Sector 9 to create a secondary line outside the bombardment zone. I have alerted the others to prepare their fighting machines for combat."

"Very good," said Qetjnegartis. The reply was automatic, but in fact, the situation was not very good at all. Zastranvis' reference to 'the others' meant the three other surviving members of the group. There had been fifteen of them to start, select members of the mighty Bajantus Clan. But one of the five transport capsules had been lost on the journey to the target world and against all expectations seven more members of the clan had been slain in battle after arrival. Only five remained; a dangerously small number. True, all five had spawned off new buds, but it would still be another eighth of a cycle before they were matured enough to operate the machinery effectively. No matter that more than a score of new fighting machines had been constructed, there was no one to operate them.

And the holdfast was under siege.

The stunning defeat in a battle off to the east had forced Qetjnegartis and the others to take refuge in the partially-finished holdfast. If the prey-creatures had been able to follow up their victory with an immediate assault, they might well have overrun the holdfast and killed them all. But the large weapons, on which they depended, could only move slowly and it had been many days before they had reached the base. Qetjnegartis had put the time to good use, and while the defenses were far from complete, they had proved sufficient to repel the first few attacks.

From that point it had become a race to see who could build up their strength the fastest. The prey-creatures had rebuilt their crude transport system and used it to bring forward warriors, large projectile throwers, and more of the armored vehicles which had proved decisive in the battle. Qetjnegartis and the others had used the constructor machines to add more defense towers to the ramparts which had been thrown up around the holdfast. The defense towers held heat rays as powerful as those carried on the fighting machines and could obliterate an attacking force with ease—if they could survive.

Unfortunately—and unexpectedly—the weapons of the prey-creatures could actually throw their projectiles farther than the effective range of the heat rays. They could stand off and safely shower the holdfast with their explosive shells and there was little that could be done about it. The projectile throwers were protected by thousands of warriors and a hundred or more of the armored vehicles, and scores of smaller projectile throwers. No sortie from the holdfast to destroy the heavy weapons could be safely attempted. Only the extremely poor accuracy of the prey-creatures' weapons had allowed the defenders to survive so far. The prey-creatures had to fling hundreds of projectiles for every one of the defense towers that they destroyed. Since they seemed to be unable to sustain their bombardments, Qetjnegartis and the others were able to replace the destroyed towers during the lulls.

But now they were attacking again and it was the heaviest bombardment yet seen. Obviously the prey-creatures had brought up more of their heavy weapons. The barrage went on for some time and one defense tower after another was destroyed along the section of rampart facing the enemy. Qetjnegartis made no attempt to replace them while the attack continued. The possibility of losing one of the precious constructor machines was too great to risk. Instead, a secondary line of defense towers was erected well to the rear of the rampart. If the enemy tried to penetrate into the holdfast once they had created a breach in the outer defenses, they would be met with scores of new heat rays.

And that, indeed, did seem to be their intent. The bombardment had begun before dawn, and by shortly after midday, over twenty of the defense towers had been destroyed, creating a gap in the coverage. The enemy could now approach the rampart without being fired upon. The fire of their projectile throwers, which had been concentrated on the rampart, now split into three groups. Two groups continued to fire on the rampart and the defense towers, but to either side of the gap, apparently in hopes of widening the hole. Then a third group began throwing their projectiles beyond the rampart. Qetjnegartis observed this in growing concern. The prey-creatures had not done this before. This did not pose any great threat to the holdfast itself since it was all deeply underground, but if the secondary line of defense towers was also breached, it could become a major danger.

Fortunately, the enemy was firing blindly. The high rampart, a thick wall of stone and rubble, blocked their ability to see beyond. The projectiles rained down randomly and while a few came close to the secondary line of towers, none did any significant damage. And shortly after, the entire bombardment began to slacken.

"They are massing to attack, Commander," observed Zastranvis.

Yes, it was true. Swarms of the prey-creatures were emerging from their trenches and forming up; others, riding draught animals, were moving forward, and the boxy, smoke-spewing, armored vehicles were dragging themselves into position on their bizarre rotating tracks. "They will attack soon," said Qetjnegartis. "I will take a fighting machine and join the others. You will direct the fire of the defense towers from here."

"Yes, Commander."

Qetjnegartis moved his travel chair quickly through the corridors to the main hanger where the fighting machines were kept. Most of the machines were standing erect on their three long legs, but several were lowered into the loading position and Qetjnegartis maneuvered below one of them where the access hatch was open. Pulling itself aboard against the heavy gravity was awkward, but it had done this many times and was soon in the pilot's seat. It grasped the control interface and activated the machine, along with five of the others. Using those others in battle was beyond even Qetjnegartis' capacity, but they could follow along in slave-mode. They would be kept as a reserve in case any of the piloted machines became damaged during the coming fight.

As it guided the machine up the ramp to the surface, Qetjnegartis evaluated the situation. Not the immediate tactical situation, but the overall situation, and there was no denying that it was unsatisfactory. Almost a half-cycle ago the great expedition to conquer the target world had begun. Two hundred transport cylinders, in forty groups of five, had landed. The previous, failed, expedition that was launched four cycles earlier had landed in a densely populated region and with the benefit of surprise had inflicted great damage on the prey before any resistance could be mounted. But the Council of Three Hundred had decided that with surprise no longer possible, a repeat of this strategy could lead to disaster. Each transport cylinder carried three fighting machines, but they had to be assembled after landing. This created a serious window of vulnerability. If the prey-creatures attacked quickly, the landing forces could be overwhelmed before they could defend themselves.

To avoid this, the landing sites of the second expedition had been deliberately selected to be as far from the major population centers of the prey-creatures as possible which allowed them enough time to assemble the fighting machines before the prey-creatures could respond. The plan had worked perfectly and not one of the landings had been disturbed. The machines had been assembled and when the time was right, the attack was launched.

Overall, this initial assault had gone very well. Vast stretches of the planet had been overrun. And while it was true that a mere six hundred fighting machines could not hope to actually control so much territory, they had smashed the local resistance to the point that there would be no trouble securing those regions when the following generations of buds had matured. Three of the southern continents, numbers 2, 4, and 6 as the Race had designated them based upon their size, were mostly subdued except for some of the coastal cities. The south polar region, continent number 5, had proved completely unoccupied by the prey-creatures. The central part of the largest continent, number 1, had been swept of most resistance. Heavy fighting was expected in the western and eastern parts of that continent, but those regions would be left for later. This was also the case on the other northern continent, number 3—the continent where Qetjnegartis' group had landed. Five groups had descended on the sparsely populated central regions and the continent had been nearly cut in two. The eastern and western regions would be attacked later, when all was ready.

In addition, one of the most vital parts of the invasion plan was working: the measures taken to counter the contagions which had wiped out the first expedition. Procedures which kept exposure to possible sources of infection at a minimum were proving effective. Only a few members of the Race had developed symptoms so far, and drugs had kept them in check long enough for the victim to bud off a replacement body which, as expected, proved more resistant.

Yes, everything was going very well—except for here.

Of all the landing groups, only this one, Group 32, had run into serious difficulty. Other groups had taken casualties, of course. There had been some serious fighting on the largest continent and the occasional fighting machine had been destroyed. And this planet was fraught with dangers. More losses had occurred due to mishaps than to the actions of the prey-creatures. Group 39 on the south polar continent had lost three machines and their pilots at a blow when an ice sheet had collapsed into the ocean.

But none of the other groups had suffered the sort of setbacks as Group 32. Even before the landing, something had gone wrong and one of the transport cylinders never arrived. Twenty percent losses right from the start. At the time it had not seemed critical, but Qetjnegartis sorely missed those clanmates now!

The landing site for Group 32 had proved to be in a region poor in resources, so Qetjnegartis had decided to move northward in search of a better location. They had swept all of the prey-creatures before them, slaying and destroying their habitations at will until they found a suitable location here. Construction on the holdfast had begun. But then, against all expectations, the prey-creatures had massed powerful forces in the region and despite a first crushing defeat, they had come on again and lured Qetjnegartis and six others into a trap. The armored gun-vehicles, nothing of which had been seen before, attacked in large numbers and only Qetjnegartis had managed to escape. One more clanmate had been lost in a still unknown fashion. It was then that Qetjnegartis and the other four survivors had taken refuge in the holdfast.

It was an unacceptable situation. Not only were they in danger of annihilation, but their status among the other clans had dropped drastically. Qetjnegartis had been forced to ask—plead!—for aid from Group 33 to the north. And while the aid had been promised, it had not so far materialized. Even when it came, Qetjnegartis was uncertain what the end result would be. Would the leader of Group 33 demand to take charge of Group 32? It was a distinct possibility.

The fighting machine reached the surface and Qetjnegartis pushed those distant problems to another compartment of its mind and focused on the immediate problem. The other three machines, piloted by Ixmaderna, Namatchgar, and Utnaferdus, were waiting and they all moved off toward Sector 9, the spare machines in tow. The rampart in that zone was wreathed in a cloud of smoke and dust. Explosions erupted from time to time, but it was clear that the prey-creatures' bombardment was tailing off. This was the usual pattern: fire until a gap had been created and then send forward the warriors. It didn't understand why the prey-creatures didn't continue their bombardment while the attack took place. Perhaps for fear of hitting their own warriors? That was a possibility, but it made little sense to Qetjnegartis. They had so many warriors, why would they worry about sacrificing some? The behavior of these creatures was still a mystery. No matter. If they chose to make it easier for Qetjnegartis to defend the holdfast, so be it! They reached the new line of defense towers and halted to wait developments. They were not long in coming.

"The prey-creatures are advancing," reported Zastranvis. "Swarms of the foot warriors in front and the gun-vehicles following. Commander, some of the vehicles look different than the usual ones."

"Relay the image to me." Its subordinate complied and Qetjnegartis studied the information that one of the surviving defense towers was gathering. For the most part the attack was developing just as the previous ones had, but as Zastranvis had said, there were some unusual vehicles following along behind the main line. It was difficult to see clearly through the smoke and dust, and Qetjnegartis could not determine what function the vehicles served. They appeared similar to the armored gun vehicles, but they had no obvious weapons mounted on them, although one had some strange device projecting from the front. They would have to be watched carefully when they got closer.

The prey foot-warriors neared the base of the ramparts and passed out of sight of the defense towers. This blind spot was annoying, but it was assumed that the enemy would begin to climb the slope. The outer face had deliberately been left a jumbled mass of loose rocks to make this as difficult as possible. The armored gun-vehicles could not negotiate the slope at all, and halted farther away where they could still be seen. But those other, strange vehicles continued onward until they too, disappeared into the blind spot beyond the curve of the ramparts.

"Ready the defense turrets in the second line to fire as soon as any of the prey appear," commanded Qetjnegartis. Zastranvis confirmed that all was ready.

A considerable time passed, but nothing appeared on top of the ramparts. "What can they be doing?" asked Namatchgar.

"I do not know," replied Qetjnegartis. "But it is important to find out. Ixmaderna, you will take your machine and cross the rampart. Cross in Sector 11, well away from their heavy weapons, and then move south and east until you can get a clear view of the outward face of Sector 9."

"At once, Commander."

"Take no risks. If you cannot reach a good position in safety, return. You cannot be spared."

"Yes, Commander." Ixmaderna moved off immediately, the long legs of the fighting machine carried it quickly, and before long it mounted one of the ramps leading up to the rampart; then it vanished beyond.

"In the meantime, Namatchgar, use the eradicator against the area where they are massed."

"Yes, Commander, but it is unlikely to have much effect; the prey creatures have developed measures to protect themselves."

"I know, but it may interfere with whatever they are doing." The eradicator was a toxic chemical weapon which the first expedition had developed. Initially it had been quite effective, but the prey-creatures now had protective garments which mostly nullified its effects. Still, it was the only weapon they had which could hit targets which were out of a direct line of sight. Namatchgar readied the weapon, which was an unwieldy tube carried by its fighting machine, and then fired it off. The projectile flew in a shallow arc and disappeared behind the rampart. A moment later a black cloud billowed up and then slowly dispersed.

"This situation of not being able to observe parts of our defenses is unacceptable," said Qetjnegartis. "We need to take thought about inconspicuous vision pick-ups which could be planted beyond the rampart in places unlikely to be bombarded."

"Or pick-ups mounted on some sort of flying device," said Utnaferdus. "It is intolerable that the prey-creatures are able to fly and we are not."

"No doubt they were inspired by some of the flying creatures native to this world," said Namatchgar. "The Homeworld's air is too thin for such things."

The suggestion took Qetjnegartis by surprise. While it was true that the prey-creatures possessed some crude and flimsy flying devices, it had never occurred to it to try and produce ones as well. But before it could pursue the thought further, a report arrived from Ixmaderna. "Commander, the prey have directed some of their fire against me and sent some of their vehicles and animal-riders in my direction. So far I am in no great danger, but I do not know how long I will remain so."

"Understood. Can you see what the prey-creatures are doing?"

"They are clustered around the base of the rampart, but I cannot… wait, they are moving away… retreating!"

"That is very odd. Why would they…?"

A sudden eruption of smoke, dust, and flying debris from beyond the rampart cut Qetjnegartis' question short. A moment later a strong concussion slammed into its fighting machine.

"They are trying to breach the rampart!" exclaimed Utnaferdus.

And so it appeared to be. Once the smoke had cleared and the dust settled, Ixmaderna was able to transmit a clear image of what was happening. Fortunately, despite the size of the explosion, only a relatively small crater had been blasted in the outer face of the rampart in Sector 9. But the prey-creatures were swarming over the area again, probably planting more of their chemical explosives. If they were permitted to do this repeatedly…

"Commander, if they can create a passage through the rampart for their armored vehicles, this could be very bad," said Utnaferdus. "We must prevent it!"

"Yes, that is so. The explosives they are using must be held in those new vehicles. If we can destroy them, it will foil their plans. Ixmaderna, you will make a feint toward the enemy's large projectile throwers and try to draw off some of their forces. Again, you are to take no undue risks. Zastranvis, you will have two of the constructor machines bring defense towers into a ready position. If the prey-creatures' bombardment on the rampart ceases you will have them start repairing the gap in the defenses. The rest of us will move to the top of the rampart and destroy those new vehicles."

Everyone acknowledged the orders and began to move. Qetjnegartis advanced, flanked by Namatchgar, and Utnaferdus. The five slaved machines followed along—they would probably be needed. They reached the base of the ramparts and paused to position themselves. The inner face of the rampart was steep, but in addition to ramps at intervals, there were carefully designed steps which would allow a fighting machine to move to the top very quickly. Speed was going to be critical.

"Very well. Attack."

Qetjnegartis piloted its machine to the top and the prey-creatures' army was spread out before it. Thousands of the creatures on foot or riding animals and scores of vehicles covered the ground beyond the rampart. A number of the riding animals were lying dead, victims of the eradicator, no doubt. Close by, the vehicle with the mysterious projection was revealed to be some sort of drilling machine. It was working in the crater the first explosion had created, black smoke pouring from the tube on its back. Drilling a hole for more explosives! The other different vehicles were, as it had suspected, transports to carry the explosives. Some stood with open doors and their cargoes being unloaded by the creatures.

Almost instantly, the prey began to fire their smaller weapons and the steady rattle of impacts on the skin of Qetjnegartis' machine filled the control chamber with noise. "I will destroy the drill. You two fire at the cargo vehicles." Three heat rays lashed out almost simultaneously. The two firing at the explosives produced huge balls of flame, but oddly, no explosions—had it been wrong about what these were? No matter. They must destroy all that they could. Namatchgar and Utnaferdus turned their rays against several more of the cargo vehicles which were still closed. Qetjnegartis' own ray was focused on the drilling machine and quickly burned off anything flammable. The metal underneath began to glow, hotter and hotter.

A heavy impact slammed into the fighting machine causing the ray to swing off target for a moment. The enemy gun vehicles were firing now and it was only a matter of time before they caused serious damage. This needed to be finished quickly so they could retreat behind the rampart again.

The boiler, which provided the steam to power the drill vehicle, ruptured and a cloud of steam enveloped it. The steam would disperse the energy from the heat ray, but the machine was clearly disabled. Qetjnegartis turned its attention to the remaining enemy. What else needed to be done to stop their attack?

At that instant, two massive explosions ripped through the packed enemy warriors. The cargo vehicles were carrying explosives and they had finally been detonated by the heat rays. Two columns of smoke and flame climbed skyward. Moments later there were a series of new detonations as the other cargo vehicles exploded, too.

Qetjnegartis looked on in satisfaction until it noticed a large piece of one of the vehicles tumbling end over end directly toward it. It tried to dodge aside, but it was too late. The wreckage slammed into the fighting machine and despite all Qetjnegartis' efforts it lurched backward and fell off the rear of the rampart. Even with the padding in the control cabin, the impact was enough to stun it momentarily. Most of the machine's systems suddenly ceased responding.

"Commander! Are you injured?"

Taking a quick internal check of its body, Qetjnegartis, replied in the negative. "However, this machine is disabled. I must transfer to one of the others. Stand ready to carry me." It pulled itself toward the hatch, hampered somewhat by the fact the machine was now horizontal rather than vertical. The main power had failed, but the emergency batteries were enough to open the hatch at a touch of its tendril. It pulled itself into the opening and then waited for Utnaferdus to move into position to grab it with the manipulators on its machine.

Before it could do so, there was a sudden clatter of projectiles bouncing off the sides of the fighting machines. Something struck Qetjnegartis a stinging blow. "Beware! The prey are on the rampart!" exclaimed Namatchgar. Qetjnegartis tried to look in that direction, but the too-bright sunlight was blinding and an instant later Utnaferdus unceremoniously seized it with the manipulators, snatching it into the air.

Disconnected from its machine, Qetjnegartis could relay no orders, but its subordinates took the initiative admirably. Namatchgar fired its heat ray in a long sweep across the top of the rampart and a moment later Zastranvis, from the main control chamber, activated the secondary line of defense tower as well. Qetjnegartis could not see the results, but the enemy fire diminished noticeably.

They reached one of the spare fighting machines and Qetjnegartis awkwardly pulled itself aboard. It examined itself and determined that the wound was superficial. It wrapped its tendrils around the control interface and activated the new machine, but before it could take any further action Ixmaderna reported. "Commander, the enemy is retreating from the ramparts! I believe they have given up."

Qetjnegartis permitted itself a long slow exhalation. "Excellent," it said. "Continue to observe, to make sure they plan nothing else, and then return to the holdfast. Zastranvis, begin repairs on the defenses. You others shall safeguard the construction machines."

Its subordinates began carrying out their orders, but Qetjnegartis remained immobile, thinking. *That was far too close! The prey get more aggressive and more innovative day by day. How many more attacks can we survive?*

CHAPTER ONE

JUNE 1909, SANTA FE, NEW MEXICO TERRITORY

First Sergeant Frank Dolfen, 5th United States Cavalry, led his detail through the streets of Santa Fe, heading for the rail yards. It was a typical late-June day in New Mexico, which meant it was hot as blazes and dry as dust. Dolfen had spent most of his adult life on one western army post or another and the weather, hot or cold, wet or dry, didn't bother him anymore. The same could not be said for many of the people crowding the streets. Most of them were in uniform and they looked like they were going to melt right out of them. Either that, or pass out from the high altitude of Santa Fe. *Easterners.*

Dolfen had been an easterner once himself. Born in the coalfields of Pennsylvania, he'd joined the army and headed west almost twenty years earlier. The heat and the altitude didn't bother him, but the crowds did. The wide-open—and empty—spaces of the west were what he loved, but sleepy Santa Fe was mobbed. The town of five thousand, bypassed by the main railroad lines, had been slowly dwindling away despite it being the 'capital' for the territorial government, but that was before the Martians had landed in New Mexico.

Albuquerque to the south, larger and on the main railroad line, had become the central assembly point for the army besieging the Martian stronghold in what had once been Gallup, off to the west. The influx of men and materiel had quickly overwhelmed that town, so Santa Fe had been pressed into service as a rear staging area. Huge camps had grown up all around, right up to the towering Rockies just to the east. The army personnel now outnumbered the local inhabitants by at least ten to one and it seemed to Dolfen that every one of them was here, blocking the street.

"Make way!" he growled, urging his horse forward. While no one paid any heed to his command, they couldn't ignore the horse and slowly he pushed his way through, followed by the other eight men of the detail.

The nearer they got to the rail yards the more crowded it became. Trains were arriving constantly and troops were debarking, forming up, and marching off to camps outside of town. At least most of them were. Some who arrived were not part of any unit; they were replacements for existing units. Those were the ones Dolfen was coming to get.

The 5th Cavalry had the dubious honor of being the very first American soldiers to meet the invaders in battle. It had not gone well. The Martian fighting machines with their deadly heat rays had proved more than a match for lightly armed cavalry. Most of the 5th had been wiped out. Dolfen and only a handful of others had managed to escape and then only because they'd been ordered to escort a civilian to the rear.

Not the whole regiment had been there, luckily. There was still enough of a cadre left to rebuild around, and that was what was happening now: rebuilding. Dolfen had orders to collect a new group of replacements and escort them back to the regiment's camp north of town. This wasn't Dolfen's first trip to the replacement camp.

"Hey, Sarge!" called Corporal Jason Urbaniak from behind him. "Ya suppose any of this new batch o' sods will know how to ride?"

"None of the last batch could, that's for sure!" added Private Callahan from further back.

Sadly, that was the truth. Despite the fact that the mass mobilization of manpower was pulling millions of men into the army, and surely there had to have been a lot of men with riding experience among them, most of the men being sent to the 5th had never had their legs across a horse before. Turning them into useful cavalrymen was proving a challenge.

They finally reached the rail yards and the replacement camp that had been set up next to it. The place was an absolute pigsty and Dolfen wrinkled his nose in disgust. The men unfortunate enough to be dumped here didn't belong to any unit and whoever was in charge of the place obviously was making no effort to instill discipline in his temporary charges. Of course, it may have been a deliberate strategy: make being a replacement so awful that once a man reached an actual unit he'd be so relieved that he'd make no trouble for fear of being sent back here. An interesting theory.

There were a couple of dispirited sentries wilting in the heat standing by the gate in the fence that encircled the camp. The sentries were there to keep the men in, rather than an enemy out. One of them grumpily took the list Dolfen handed him off to the headquarters tent, and after quite a delay returned to announce that the men would be rounded up and delivered. Having gone through the routine before, Dolfen knew it could easily be an hour or more before the men could all be found. He dismounted and all his troopers did likewise, flopping on the ground in the little shade their horses could provide.

Dolfen sat at his ease, sipping from a small metal flask he always carried and watched the bustling rail yards. Most of the arriving trains carried either troops or the supplies for them. There was very little heavy equipment in evidence since most of that was sent straight to General Funston's army at Gallup, but there was one string of flat cars on a siding that were loaded with the new steam tanks. They were strange-looking metal boxes on caterpillar tracks with a cannon mounted in the front and a boiler in the back. They had proved decisive at the battle of Prewitt, and from what Dolfen had heard, they were the only weapons the army possessed that could face the Martian war machines on anything approaching equal terms. But these tanks wouldn't be matching themselves against anything for a while. They were all scorched and charred, with broken tracks or holes melted through them—casualties from some fight with the enemy. There was a repair and salvage yard in Santa Fe and they were clearly destined for it.

A loud and long whistle blast announced the arrival of another train. It was answered by a loud clatter of hooves and the rattle and creak of wagons. But rather than cargo wagons, these were enclosed and had large red crosses painted on their sides. The arriving train must be carrying casualties of the flesh-and-blood variety. Dolfen perked up and tried to catch a glimpse of the people riding the wagons, but they were too far away.

He got to his feet. "Urbaniak, take charge. I'll be over there if our new lambs arrive."

"Sure, Sarge," replied the corporal, not stirring from his spot.

Dolfen walked toward the siding where the train had stopped. Every one of the cars was painted the standard Army Green with 'U.S.M.R.R.' stenciled in white letters on the side. The government had finally gotten fed up with the chaos in the private railroads and reinstituted the United States Military Railroad system, last seen during the Civil War. Dolfen couldn't say that he'd noticed any marked improvement, but he supposed it was a start.

Swarms of ambulances were pulled up all around the train and already stretchers were being carried off and placed inside. The people doing the carrying were all men, but there were also a good number of women there too, most wearing the uniforms of the Army Nurse Corps. Dolfen was looking for one particular nurse. There was no guarantee she would be here; she might be in the large hospital that had been built to the east of town, but he was willing to bet otherwise.

He walked down the line of ambulances, looking at the faces of the women. Most of them were much older than the one he was looking for and all seemed harried and tired. From what he'd heard, the army at Gallup was having a hard time of it, and while the Martian heat rays didn't leave many wounded, there were still plenty of other ways for a man to get hurt or get sick. The nurses would have plenty to do.

He was nearing the end of the line and was afraid she wasn't here when he spotted her. Rebecca Harding was a tall, solid young woman with a deep tan and a dusting of freckles on her round cheeks. Her dark blonde hair was tied up and barely visible under her nurse's hat. She wore a uniform not all that different from the one he was wearing: wool tunic and trousers and leggings, all far too hot and heavy for this climate. Add in her calf-length skirt and the white apron and it was a wonder she wasn't on one of those stretchers with heatstroke, but she was a native of the climate and Dolfen had seen her riding and walking in far worse situations.

She was standing next to one of the train cars and copying down the information for the patients as they were unloaded. Each man had a paper tag on a string around his neck, presumably with his name, rank, unit, nature of his injury, and all the other things that followed a man around in the army. Becca, as she liked to be called, peered at the tags and quickly scribbled in a ledger she was carrying. The bureaucracy at work.

He stood a few yards away and just stared at her with a faint smile on his face. He remembered the first time he'd ever seen her, a worn-out scarecrow on an exhausted horse, fleeing from the Martians who had destroyed her home and killed her parents. A lesser person might have fallen apart, but not her. With just a little rest she'd given a good account of what had happened to her and the very next day, when they'd been forced to flee, she'd kept up and never complained despite the grueling pace. Then what happened later… yeah, she was a quite a girl.

When the last stretcher was unloaded, she continued to write for a moment and then glanced around. When she caught sight of him her face broke into a huge smile. "Sergeant!" she cried.

"Hi, Miss Becca."

She dodged around a pair of stretcher-bearers and came up to him and gave him a brief hug. "It's so good to see you again! How have you been?"

"Oh, fair to middlin'. Just came into town to pick up some more replacements. Saw all the ambulances here and thought I'd see if you were with them."

"Well, I'm so glad you did! It's great seein' a friendly face!"

"Are you still stayin' with your aunt and uncle?"

The girl's face fell and she frowned. "Yeah, for the time being."

"They still givin' you trouble about bein' a nurse?"

"Yeah. My aunt says it's 'not proper' for a young lady! *Proper!* How can she not understand what's happening? We all have to do our part! The Martians don't care about proper!"

"Some people just can't see a thing until it's starin' them in the face," said Dolfen sympathetically. "I… I don't think I really believed in the Martians 'til they started murderin' the 5th." Becca's face grew even grimmer at that. She'd been right there and seen it, too.

"Harding! What are you doing?! Get over here!" A sharp female voice made them both jump. One of the other nurses, a hard-looking woman with graying hair was looking sternly at Becca and pointing a finger at the ground in front of her.

"Gotta go. You take care of yourself, Sergeant." She turned and scurried over to the woman, who glared at Dolfen, too, for good measure. He returned the glare for a moment and then turned and headed back to the replacement camp. As he neared the gates, he saw a body of men, loaded down with gear, being herded through. Corporal Urbaniak and the other troopers were pushing them into some semblance of a formation.

"Oh, there you are, Sarge!" said Urbaniak, looking relieved. "I was just going to send a runner to find you."

"Everyone accounted for, Corporal?"

"Forty-eight men on the list and forty-eight here. All the names match, too."

"Well, that's a small miracle." He walked up and down the line of men, looking them over. They were young and most seemed fairly excited. He wondered how long they had been stuck in the camp. Oh well, he'd turn them into cavalrymen. He stepped back and loudly said, "All right gentlemen, welcome to the 5th Cavalry."

* * * * *

JUNE 1909, SANTA FE, NEW MEXICO TERRITORY

Becca Harding watched Sergeant Dolfen walk away while dutifully nodding her head as Miss Chumley berated her for fraternizing with soldiers. She hadn't been fraternizing with soldiers! She'd been saying hello to one specific soldier! Sergeant Dolfen was a friend, and he'd saved her life—several times. Chumley had never had anyone save her life. Chumley had probably never had a friend, either!

Finally, she was released from the scolding and climbed aboard one of the ambulances as the convoy headed back to the hospital. One of the other nurses, Alice Findley, sat beside her. "What did you do to tick off Ol' Iron-Corset?"

"Oh, nothing," replied Becca, not wanting to explain. "It doesn't take much."

Alice laughed. "That's for sure! But we might not have to put up with her for much longer."

"Really? Why?"

"They're saying that they may open up a forward field hospital much nearer to the fighting. A hospital with nurses. And Chumley would be in charge of them—God help 'em!"

"Huh," said Becca, several thoughts popping into her head simultaneously.

"They're only taking volunteers," continued Alice, "but who's gonna volunteer when they find out they'll be under *her* command?"

Becca didn't reply and the pair lapsed into silence, listening to the rattle of the wagons, the clip-clop of the horses' hooves, and the groans of the wounded. When she had first started helping here, those groans had been like knife stabs to her heart, but after three months of it she had become numb to those feelings. She still tended the men with the same devotion and care as before and there were days when something would leave her in tears, but it was impossible to maintain the same sensitivity day after day without going mad.

They reached the hospital, and she performed the exact same duty she had at the railroad, checking each man off her list as they were transferred from the ambulances into the wards—as if they could have lost any of them on the way here! After that it was back to her usual routine: assisting the doctors, changing bandages, cleaning up the messes, and generally doing whatever she was told. She was slowly learning some basic medical skills, but she was still a junior member of the team and that meant she got the worst jobs. It was hard, often disgusting, work, but she told herself that she was helping in the fight against the Martians. She wished she could really fight them, but no one was letting women—or girls—fight Martians.

Of course, she *had* fought them, even killed one of them, during that desperate flight from her lost home. That was more than all but a few of the men had done, but no one here would believe her if she told them that, so she'd never tried.

Eventually her shift ended and she walked back to her aunt and uncle's house. The other nurses slept in a tent, but she could go to a fine home with soft beds and indoor plumbing. She'd prefer the tent.

The residential area of Santa Fe hadn't been touched much by the war. A few high-ranking officers had established quarters in some of the fancier homes and as a result sentries had been posted to keep the other soldiers out of those areas. The sentry at the end of her street knew her and gave her a friendly 'good evening' as she passed. She trudged up the steps of the house, feeling very weary. It was a nice house, a veritable mansion compared to what she was used to. Apparently her uncle was pretty well off, although she had no idea how he made his money.

They had a maid, too, and the woman relieved her of her tunic and tsk-tsk'd at the spatters of blood and—other things—that had escaped her apron. She went into the parlor and slumped down on one the chairs, too tired for the moment to go up the stairs to her room. Her aunt called out something from the kitchen, but she merely grunted in reply.

After a while supper was ready and she roused herself and went into the dining room, realizing that she was actually quite hungry. Her aunt frowned and made some comment about the fact she hadn't changed out of her uniform yet. The maid served the food and it was good. Becca felt a bit guilty about eating so well when the soldiers, the wounded, and her fellow nurses were living primarily on army rations. Her aunt complained about the rising cost of food in the town but then nattered on for the rest of the meal about some exhibit of Indian artifacts that the local School of American Research was putting on.

"That nice Dr. Hewett put it together and they say it's wonderful. We'll have to make time to go see it," she declared. "Especially since you won't have time to do it later, Rebecca." Becca looked up sharply to see her aunt smiling.

"What do you mean?"

"Just that I've finally gotten a reply from that school in Connecticut where your mother enrolled you! They still have a spot for you. You leave in two weeks!" Becca stared at her aunt for a long moment and then resumed eating.

"No."

"What do you mean, no?"

"I mean no, I'm not going."

"You most certainly are! Your uncle has agreed to pay for your tuition in the future."

"Thank you, but I'm not going. I have a job here."

"We will have no more of that talk, young lady!" snapped her aunt. "And as for that 'job' of yours, I did a little checking and I found out you told them you were sixteen! You're only fifteen!"

"I'll be sixteen next week."

"That doesn't matter! Your uncle has filed all the paperwork and we are now your legal guardians. You are going to school, and that's that!"

Becca looked from her aunt's face to her uncle's and struggled not to explode. She remembered when her mother had told her about the school almost exactly a year ago. Arguing then hadn't done any good and she could see it wouldn't do any good now, but she couldn't stop herself.

"Aunt Rosilee, Uncle Albert, there's a war on! I have to help."

Her aunt made a sound of exasperation. "The war! I'm sick of that being an excuse for every outrageous thing people do around here! This used to be a nice town! A town with culture! Look at it now! It's just a huge army camp filled with rabble!"

"*Rabble?!* They're soldiers! They're here to protect you and this fine house! The Martians are out there! They killed my father and my grandmother and my mother—your sister!—and burned my house to the ground! The soldiers are the only thing keeping them from coming here and doing the same thing!"

"Martians!" snorted her aunt.

"I've seen them! Seen what they do!"

"No more of your wild stories, young lady! And I'll have no more back talk! You are going to that school and that's that!"

Her uncle had not said a word, but she could see she'd get no help from him. She got up from the table and went upstairs to her room. A year ago she might have thrown a tantrum and cried herself to sleep. But a year ago she'd been a different person. Well, maybe not that different. She'd gone and found the Martians in spite of her parents' commands. She'd done what was right instead of what she'd been told. It hadn't done any good then, but it had still been right. She had no doubt what was right now. She began gathering her things.

Miss Chumley will be looking for volunteers.

* * * * *

JUNE 1909, WASHINGTON, DC

"The wedding is going to be lovely. I just wish we had more time to make all the plans!"

Major Andrew Comstock smiled at Victoria, his fiancé, and put his arm around her. "More time?" he said in mock dismay. "I wish we could have it tomorrow!"

Victoria looked scandalized for a moment, but then she smiled and snuggled closer in the back of the carriage. "So do I," she giggled. The mere fact that they were alone together—well, except for the driver—showed what a difference being engaged was from courting. Just a few months ago, before he proposed, there was no way this would have been allowed. Sadly, the carriage was taking him to the railway station for the start of another inspection tour instead of some secluded romantic location. Philadelphia to talk to Baldwin Locomotive about plans for new steam tanks and then Niagara Falls to see Nikola Tesla. And then, hopefully, back to Washington. The carriage was approaching the Capitol Building and would soon turn left on Louisiana Avenue and the station was just a few blocks from there. Not much time.

"I'll be back as soon as I can," he said. "And then I'll help with the wedding plans."

Victoria gave a snort of not-quite laughter, making her dark curls bounce. "You men have it so easy! You and Papa can just wear your uniforms! No decisions at all!" She paused and brushed a hand across the chest of his tunic. "But you do look so splendid in your uniform. Mama heard some rumors that they may give you the Medal of Honor for what you did out west. That will look fine on your uniform!"

Now it was Andrew's turn to snort. "Well, if they do they better cut it into four or five pieces! I didn't do it alone!" Involuntarily his thoughts turned back to the nightmare that Victoria couldn't begin to understand. The destruction of General Sumner's army, the desperate flight of Andrew and his surviving men, stumbling on the Martian stronghold, destroying one of the tripods with dynamite they'd found at a mine, and then running again, and only by accident leading their pursuers into a trap which became a 'great victory'. None of it seemed especially heroic to him. They were just trying to stay alive, but his superiors had been pleased. They'd made his brevet promotion to major permanent and given him new responsibilities. Most importantly, his immediate superior, Colonel Hawthorne, had given him permission to marry his daughter. Everything seemed to be moving so quickly—and he was only twenty-three!

The carriage reached the station and slowly made its way through the mobs of people there.

Washington was the heart of the war effort and the number of people coming and going was immense. Andrew thought fondly back to his first summer here, just after he graduated from the Point—and before the Martians arrived—when Washington became a ghost town during the summer heat. Congress and the President retreated to cooler refuges until the fall. No more! The country—indeed, the entire world—was at war. Now, the city never slept.

They got as close to the station building as they could and then Andrew debarked and helped Victoria down. The driver put his valise beside him and then retreated to give them as much privacy as the crowds would allow. Andrew didn't give the crowd the slightest heed and kissed Victoria.

All too soon they had to pull apart. "I have to go, Love. I'll write. And I'll be back soon." Victoria nodded and tried to smile, but she didn't say any more. He picked up his valise, leaned forward to kiss her for a moment more, and then headed for his train.

* * * * *

JUNE 1909, WASHINGTON, DC

"How are you, Leonard? You don't look well."

General Leonard Wood, Chief of Staff of the United States Army, looked across the desk at his old friend, Theodore Roosevelt, President of the United States, and decided he would lie to him—again. "I'm fine, Theodore, it's just this heat."

"Yes, it's especially bad this year, isn't it? But ha! Listen to the two of us! It's not half as bad as Cuba in '98! Now *that* was hot! We sound like a couple of old men!" The President flashed his famous grin.

We're not as young as we were in Cuba. Wood was only 49 years old and Roosevelt two years older, but the truth was that Wood was not a well man. He had a brain tumor and needed an operation. Only he and his doctor knew this and he was determined that as few others as possible found out. He'd been named Chief of Staff only five months earlier and if it became known how ill he was, he could lose that and it would probably be the end of his career. *I can still do my job! I just have to be careful.*

"But as we were saying," he said, trying to turn Roosevelt's attention back to business, "Funston feels that he only needs to make one more big push to capture the Martian fortress near Gallup. We need to give him as much support as we can."

"It seems to me that he made that same claim just before the recent debacle," grumbled Roosevelt.

"True, but this is the only place where we can get at the enemy in strength. We still don't even know the exact position of their landing site in Idaho and they've torn up the railroads for a hundred miles or more in every direction. Without the railroad it's impossible to supply a significant force in that territory. Hell, when I was chasing Geronimo in Mexico we could barely keep a couple of companies supplied with wagons and pack mules."

"I know, I know. I've been through that area myself, you know. Up near Yellowstone. Beautiful, and amazingly rugged. But the governors of Idaho, Utah, Wyoming, and Colorado are screaming for help. Salt Lake City has been overrun and there have been reports of sightings near Denver. There's even word of Martians moving down into Montana from Canada!"

"I've seen the reports, Theodore. You get them from my people, after all."

"Yes, yes, but that doesn't change the fact that several million people are under direct threat. Thousands—tens of thousands—are fleeing their homes. And from their point of view, we aren't doing a blessed thing to help them!"

"Mr. President, we have a division in Denver, another in Cheyenne, two divisions in Bismarck, and several more headed west. But you know as well as I that simply sending troops isn't enough. Men with rifles and bayonets have no chance against the Martians! They need artillery and the steam tanks to have a real hope of beating them. Those things are in short supply. And even when we have them, trying to keep them supplied is a nightmare. The tanks burn coal and use up water at a frightful rate. Funston's siege at Gallup is using artillery ammunition in unprecedented amounts and in that semi-desert region we are having to ship in water—all along a single rail line."

"You're talking logistics, Leonard," replied Roosevelt. "Your average man, Great Thunder, your average senator, doesn't know logistics from Adam! They see the enormous training camps, men flocking to the colors by the millions, factories working round the clock, and they want to know why none of that huge strength is being put to use."

"Because all that strength is stuck here in the east. Moving it west is the problem."

"We have to do better, Leonard."

"We will, we will."

"But speaking of moving troops, how are the shipments to Panama going?"

Wood restrained a sigh. Roosevelt's obsession with Panama and the canal could be trying at times. "The 27th Division will be leaving this week. The 4th is already there."

"But what about the heavy guns? And the emplacements for them?"

"Six more of the twelve-inch disappearing guns and eight of the ten-inch mortars will be going on the same ships with the 27th. With no immediate threat to the east coast, we are diverting a lot of the heavy ordnance from the forts here to Panama. They are pouring as much concrete for the fortifications there as they are for the locks, Theodore. And there hasn't been a Martian sighted within a hundred miles of the canal. Stop worrying."

"It's only a matter of time before the Martians realize how important the canal will be to us once it's open. With every major rail line between east and west cut except for the Southern Pacific, it might well become the only way to keep the country united. We have to be ready for when the inevitable attack comes!"

"We will. But what about the French and the Germans? Are they really coming?"

"Yes, at last," said Roosevelt, frowning. "The French plan to land a corps in Veracruz by early August. The Germans say they will have forces in Venezuela about the same time—although they don't say how much. I can't say I'm all that happy about having them here in this hemisphere, but since there's no hope of us sending more significant expeditions south, it's better than nothing. Anything to get them involved!"

Wood nodded. With no direct threat to their homelands at the present, the French and Germans had been terribly laggard in supplying help to anyone else. The British were fighting desperate battles to protect their far-flung colonies, the Russians had lost control of Siberia, the Ottomans, most of Arabia, and the word out of China was confused to say the least.

The French were fortifying their colonies in North Africa, so at least they were doing something. But Germany, with the most powerful land army in the world, had so far done nothing. They had seemingly written off their colony in East Africa, and unsurprisingly they had ignored Russian pleas for help. But now they were sending troops to Venezuela. In 1902, the United States had come within days of going to war with Germany over a similar plan during a debt crisis, but now they were coming again with America's, if not blessing, acquiescence.

"Oh, and that reminds me," said the President, "We may need to send some troops to Cuba. Maybe Haiti, too."

Wood frowned, his eyebrows scrunching together. "You just said we wouldn't be sending more expeditions south."

"I meant expeditions to fight the Martians. This would be different."

"Ah, the refugee crisis?"

"Yes, people are fleeing from Mexico, Central America, and South America in fleets of small boats. Some are coming here, of course, but Cuba and the Caribbean islands are being overwhelmed. Cuba's government is on the verge of collapse—again. They're asking for help. Can we send anything?"

Wood thought for a moment. "Yes, maybe. Fortunately, unlike the Martians, this is a problem that *can* be dealt with using just rifles and bayonets. I have some units which are pretty well trained, but lacking heavy weapons. I'll draw up a proposal. Anything else, sir?"

"No, I think that's all for now. Thank you, General." Roosevelt got to his feet and without thinking, Wood automatically tried to do the same. His left leg buckled and he collapsed back into his chair with a groan. *Damn!*

Roosevelt was at his side in an instant. "Leonard! What's wrong? Do you need a doctor?" He turned to call for his adjutant.

"Wait!" cried Wood. "Wait, Theodore."

"What is it? Are you ill?"

"Theodore… Theodore, we need to talk."

CHAPTER TWO

JULY 1909, SANTA FE, NEW MEXICO TERRITORY

"No! No! Your *other* left, you stupid sods!"

First Sergeant Frank Dolfen looked on in exasperation as the troop disintegrated into a milling throng of men and horses. It had been a simple maneuver, *By Fours Left*, but some of the new recruits had tried to turn right instead and the march column had turned into a mob. Well, at least none of them had fallen off their… No, wait, there was a man on the ground over there, so even that silver lining was snatched away.

"The horses are smarter than they are," observed Corporal Urbaniak. "You could see *they* knew which way to turn and would have without those idiots sawing on the reins."

"Yeah, maybe we should just tie them to the saddles and let the horses be in charge." He threw up his hands and snorted in disgust. "Well, get them sorted out and we'll try it again."

An hour later, Dolfen grudgingly admitted that they had made some progress and decided to call it day—for the sake of the horses if not the men. Of course, then there was another hour of horse and equipment care before the men could be dismissed and Dolfen could relax.

Except that he couldn't really relax. Being the First Sergeant of the squadron involved vastly more work than he'd had when he was just a section leader. Paperwork! Good God, the paperwork! There was a clerk who did most of the actual writing and filing and such, but Dolfen still had to oversee it all; especially since Captain DeBrosse was almost as green as those recruits he was trying to train. The enormous expansion of the army was calling for huge numbers of new officers. West Point couldn't begin to supply them all so there were dozens of new training schools to turn bright young sprouts into officers. DeBrosse had some experience in the Illinois National Guard and at least he knew how to ride, but he had a long way to go in learning how to run a cavalry squadron! The fact that he was barely half Dolfen's age didn't help.

He walked into the large tent that was being used for the squadron headquarters. He had planned to check with the clerk and take care of any new paperwork that might have arrived, but DeBrosse was there at a desk and he couldn't just ignore him. "Afternoon, sir," he said.

"Oh, Sergeant," said the Captain, looking a little startled. "How did things go? Are the new recruits shaping up?"

"Yes, sir. Slowly. A bit at a time. No casualties today, anyway. Another month and we'll be in tolerable shape."

"A month? That long, you think?" DeBrosse looked nervous, but then he always looked nervous.

"Yes, sir, at least. It's going to take another coupla weeks before the new ones can even control their horses and do the basic squad maneuvers. And a good third of 'em don't even speak English. Italians and Poles for the most part. The recruiters are scooping 'em up as soon they fall off the boat, I'm guessing. And once they do learn the basics, there's still section and troop drill, dismounted drill… lots more things before they'll be ready. Oh, and that reminds me, sir, any word on when we'll be getting those new dynamite bombs they're giving the infantry? We'll all need some training with those."

"Uh, I hadn't heard anything about those, Sergeant. I'll ask the major next I see him."

"We really need those, sir! Our rifles ain't gonna be worth spit if we come up against the Martians!"

"They have given each troop two machine guns…"

"Only those cast-off thirty-calibers from the infantry!" said Dolfen forcefully. "They fire the same ammo as our rifles and won't do much more! Now if we could get some of those new fifty-caliber Brownings they're giving the infantry…!"

"I haven't heard anything about that, either," replied DeBrosse. "Those are very heavy, I understand and…"

"We need something, sir! I've seen what happens when men try to go up against one of their machines with nothing but rifles! It's a massacre!"

"Our job will be to scout, not to fight, Sergeant. Find the enemy and report back."

"That was our job the last time! And half the 5th was wiped out anyway!" Dolfen could feel himself losing his temper. DeBrosse was cringing back away from him and he forced himself to calm down. "Sorry, sir," he muttered.

"That's… that's all right, Sergeant. I know you survi-… uh, veterans had a hard time of it and we newcomers should learn from your experience. But tell me, is it really true you destroyed one of the tripods? I've heard some of the stories in camp and…"

"I… was involved, sir. It was really those ordnance guys. They had the bombs. I just… helped out a little. But sir, that's why we need to get some bombs of our own!"

"I'll… I'll see what I can do. But Sergeant…" DeBrosse rummaged around on his desk and pulled out a piece of paper. "I'm afraid we aren't going to have that month that you want. We've got orders to move out in just five days."

* * * * *

JULY 1909, PHILADELPHIA, PENNSYLVANIA

"This all looks very impressive, Mr. Schmidt—on paper. But are you actually going to be able to build any of these things? Build them and get them to work? I recall how much trouble you had with the Mark I steam tanks," said Andrew Comstock, giving the Baldwin Locomotives man the best scowl he had learned from his boss, Colonel Hawthorne.

"We have learned a great deal from the Mark I, Major," said Schmidt. "The Mark II, which is in production now, was another step forward. We are confident that we can accomplish what we are proposing."

Andrew grunted noncommittally and returned his attention to the drawings spread out on a large table in a Baldwin conference room. They showed a number of proposed designs for new war machines. They ranged from sensible to… ridiculous. He pointed to one of the more sensible ones. "This 'Mark III' tank, would you really be able to mount three cannons on it?"

"As you can see, it is just a modification of the Mark II," said Schmidt. "We add these two side sponsons with a gun in each. Not much different from how the secondary guns on a warship are mounted. The sponsons are detachable for rail transport. We hope to have a prototype ready for testing before the end of the year."

"But what about the extra weight? You already upped the gun from a 3-inch to a 4-inch on the Mark IIs. Can the engine and drive train handle it? And what about ammunition storage? Will there be room for a loader for each gun? That would push the crew up to what? Nine? Where will they all fit?"

"We are calculating eight with two loaders for the three guns. Not ideal, but the best we can do. The extra weight should be manageable; as I said we've learned a lot from the earlier models. As for ammunition storage, yes, the three guns will reduce it to about twenty rounds per gun, but…" Schmidt paused and looked sheepishly at Andrew. "From reading your own report of the action in New Mexico it seems likely that most battles will be decided one way or the other before ammunition supply will become a critical factor."

Meaning if they haven't killed the Martians by then, they'll probably be dead themselves! Schmidt's evaluation angered him, but he couldn't deny the probable truth of it. At the Battle of Prewitt, the tanks and the Martian machines had squared off and blazed away like gunfighters in a western dime novel. It had all been over in just a few minutes. Still, the cold-blooded calculations of the engineer bothered him. Instead of giving rein to his feelings, he picked up another sheet of drawings. "And what about this? This 'Mark IV' tank? If I'm reading the scale properly, it's about twice the size of a Mark III—in every dimension! How in the world would we even transport it? It's over twice the width of a railway car!"

"The design takes that into consideration, Major," said Schmidt proudly. "The side sponsons, the caterpillar tracks, and the main turret are all separate assemblies. The Mark IV can be shipped in manageable pieces and quickly assembled once it reaches its destination. The gun in the turret would be a 5-inch, possibly even a 7-inch. It's clear that the smaller caliber weapons can only harm the enemy machines with massed fire. We think it likely that larger weapons will be called for in the future."

Andrew shook his head in doubt. The tank was a monster, with guns bristling in every direction. He'd be tempted to call it a 'land battleship', except the next set of drawings had already laid claim to that title. Looking at them he recalled a conversation he'd had with Colonel Hawthorne almost two years earlier where he'd jokingly suggested putting wheels on navy warships so they could fight the Martians on land. But this was—apparently—no joke. It looked like a small cruiser, or perhaps a coast defense monitor, which had been mounted on two enormous sets of caterpillar tracks. A massive turret was situated near the front mounting, according to the notes, a 12-inch naval rifle. A half-dozen other turrets mounted smaller guns and even smaller ones along with machine guns poked out of ports here and there. A large smoke stack and what Andrew could only call a conning tower added to the impression of a land-going warship.

"You're really serious about this?"

"Why wouldn't we be?" replied Schmidt, looking puzzled. "You folks were the ones who asked for it."

"We did?"

"Yes indeed." Schmidt rummaged through a folder and eventually pulled out several sheets of paper and handed them to him. The top sheet was a letter from the Ordnance Department dated November of 1907 and signed by Major Anthony Waski, an ordnance officer Andrew bumped into from time to time—although he was a colonel now. The letter called for Baldwin to investigate the possibility of constructing a machine based on the attached drawing. The second sheet proved to be a crudely hand-drawn sketch of a battleship on wheels. Andrew had to restrain himself from laughing. Now he remembered a frantic conversation between General Crozier, the head of the Ordnance Department, and Colonel Hawthorne and Major Waski with himself a silent witness. They'd just left a conference with their counterparts in the navy ordnance bureau where they'd proposed just such a thing. Crozier was adamant that the army have a comparable proposal. Andrew had completely forgotten about it—but here it was!

"Could such a thing be built?"

"Well, we believe we can make the tracks work. We don't have the facilities to build the upper portions, so we contacted William Cramp & Sons down at the shipyard and what would you know? They were getting ready to contact us! It seems the navy wants something just like this! Cramp can build the upper portions—they build battleships, after all—but they had no clue how to build the tracks! So we've been working together to develop this."

"How… how would it be transported to the front? Even disassembled, the pieces would be too large for rail cars."

"Yes, that would be the real trick, wouldn't it? But the navy proposal calls for a screw propeller which would run off the same drive as the tracks. The design as proposed here doesn't displace enough water to float, so there would be detachable flotation modules which would allow it to sail—or be towed—by water to as close to the action as possible. Then it could move out of the water on the tracks into battle."

Andrew continued to study the drawings and despite his skepticism had to admit that the idea was enticing. The thing was far larger than the Martian tripods and the notion of the enemy suddenly being the David facing a towering Goliath instead of the other way round as it had been so far was very satisfying—as long as you didn't take the analogy all the way to its conclusion. "This… this could be very useful attacking the Martian strongholds. It's tall enough to look right over the rampart walls and it might even be able to move over them on its tracks."

"That was our thought, too," said Schmidt.

"But how much would such a thing cost?"

"Probably not much more than a warship of comparable size. We hope to have some more accurate figures for you soon."

"And you say the navy is planning to build these?"

"That's what they have said."

"Huh." If the navy was going to build them, it was inevitable that the army would want them, too! "Can I have copies of these to show General Crozier?"

"Certainly. We have them all ready for you, Major. Oh, and by the way, we will be moving our planning and development offices to our new facility in Eddystone over the next several months. We'll have a lot more room there—and if your bosses approve these new designs, we'll certainly need it!"

They provided him with a bundle of documents and he thanked them and stepped outside into the stifling heat. It wasn't quite as bad as Washington, but the air was filled with smoke and coal dust. Washington hadn't acquired much industry yet, but Philadelphia had been a major manufacturing center even before the war and now was second only to New York. Hundreds of tall chimneys spewed their black clouds into the mid-morning sky. He looked back at the Baldwin facility, which covered over eight city blocks, and admitted that there wasn't much spare room for building enormous tanks. Their new facility in Eddystone, just south of Philadelphia, was on the Delaware River, which would prove convenient if those land battleships had to be transported by water.

Broad Street was as busy as ever, but many of the people were wearing uniforms like himself. On one street corner, a military band was blaring patriotic music and a recruiting stand had been set up. A small crowd had gathered, but it didn't look like the recruiters were doing much business. The initial wave of volunteering had dwindled as more and more men took up the good paying factory jobs that were appearing due to the massive armaments programs. Congress had just approved a conscription bill to help make up the deficiency. Just as had happened during the Civil War, some men were volunteering to avoid the stigma that went with being a draftee.

Andrew swung aboard a south-bound street car that carried him down to the enormous Broad Street Station which dominated the center of the city. It had been built by the famous Philadelphia architect Frank Furness in a Gothic style which didn't really appeal much to Andrew. The upper floors held the office of the Pennsylvania Railroad and a tower reared up from the top floors that rivaled that of the much more attractive city hall two blocks away. Swarms of people milled about the street level entrances. Again, a lot of the men were in uniform. As he walked toward the entrance, Andrew was interested to see several men with signs protesting the new U.S. Military Railroad that had been put into effect. The big railroad owners, men like J.P. Morgan, were not happy with the measure, which not only created an actual branch of the army with its own trains and personnel, but also gave the government enormous control over the civilian railroads and the prices they could charge. Even so, it was surprising to see a protester here. So far, the USMRR trains were only being used in the areas close to the Martians; Andrew had yet to see one this Far East.

Inside the station, he retrieved his valise from the baggage room and headed for the platform where his train would arrive. Pausing, he managed to stuff all the documents Baldwin had given him inside his bag without rumpling them too much. He really ought to get an aide to carry things. *I'm a major now, after all!* As a lieutenant fresh from West Point he'd been assigned as Hawthorne's aide when his future father-in-law had only been a lieutenant colonel. Perhaps he could get a lieutenant of his own…

As he crossed the crowded lobby, he noticed a small commotion; a man and two women were being escorted out by police. With a start, he realized they were more protesters, although of an entirely different sort than the ones outside. The man carried a sign which read: *The Wages of Sin is Death!* One of the women began shouting: "This is God's punishment of a sinful world! Repent or die in the flames of the Martian rays!"

Andrew stopped to watch as the trio were ejected. He'd read in the papers about some religious zealots claiming that the Martian invasion was a judgment from God, but this was the first time he'd encountered such people himself. Were they actually serious? And if they were, did they think the Martians were God's righteous agents? Was it therefore a sin to fight them? Did they think that if everyone did cleanse themselves and turn to God that the Martians would miraculously vanish? Andrew's thoughts went back to the day he saw the Martians slaughter General Sumner's army. A lot of those men had probably been praying for God's help—seconds before they were burned to ash. *I bet if Martian tripods were marching down Market Street those people would be screaming for the army instead of praying!* But the bottom line, as far as Andrew could see, was that they were telling people to pray for help rather than help themselves.

Shaking his head in disgust, he trudged up two flights of stairs to the elevated platform in the great train shed. Colonel Hawthorne, who held the most amazing store of facts and figures in his head, had once told him it had the largest open span—over three hundred feet—of any train shed in the world. Looking at the graceful iron trusses, Andrew felt a small thrill of pride. Humans could do some amazing things. Suddenly the notion of building land-going battleships didn't seem so outrageous after all. *We can, we really can do this!*

The place was bustling with trains arriving and leaving almost constantly. His own train arrived only a few minutes late and he climbed aboard the second class car and found a seat next to the window. The breeze would feel good once they got moving. The car was crowded and a family of what he assumed were Mennonites, straw hats, old fashioned bonnets and all, took several of the seats across the aisle and apologetically plunked a little girl down on the seat next to him. She appeared to be about six and she looked at him with curious eyes. Andrew wasn't comfortable around children, but he forced himself to give her a friendly smile.

"Are you a soldier?" she asked.

"Yes, I am."

"What's your name?"

"Andrew. What's yours?"

"Rachel. Do you fight the… the M-Martians?"

"Well, yes, that's part of my job."

"Are they around here?" She looked about as if one might spring out of the woodwork.

"No, no, they are out west, a long ways away. You don't have anything to worry about."

"My pa can't fight, my brothers neither. It's against the Book."

"Well, not everyone needs to fight. Your pa and brothers grow food and that's important, too. Soldiers need to eat."

"I guess that's right, isn't it? But why…?"

"Rachel! Leave the poor man alone!" scolded the child's mother suddenly. "Mind your manners!"

"Yes'm," said the girl, inching away from Andrew and staring down at the floor of the rail car. Andrew looked at the mother and was about to say that it was all right, but the stern expression on the woman's face made him decide to leave well enough alone. He looked out the window instead.

The train lurched into motion and was soon chugging down the enormous viaduct that the locals called the 'Chinese Wall' until it reached the bridge over the Schuylkill River. Usually when Andrew passed through Philadelphia he'd be taking the line south back to Washington, but today he was heading west. The train was switched onto what was called the Main Line and soon left the city behind. As the train picked up speed the breeze felt wonderful despite the occasional bits of coal smoke and embers that found their way in along with it. Ahead lay a series of fashionable suburban towns where many of the city's well-to-do had estates. Wynnewood, Ardmore, Bryn Mawr…

They weren't quite so fashionable now as they once were, of course. The train had barely left the city behind when they passed through the muddy and overgrown remains of the fortifications that had been hastily thrown up in the first panic after the launch of the Martian cylinders in '07. When the Martians had all landed out west, work had been halted. One line of earthworks went right through what had once been a golf course. Further on, there were tent cities and drill fields; training camps for the army that, unlike the fortifications, were in full use.

More camps were scattered on either side of the tracks as they moved out into the Pennsylvania countryside. Once away from Philadelphia, the landscape became a patchwork of farms and small towns. The corn was nearly head-high and the wheat turning gold. It looked like it would be a good harvest this year. The train stopped a number of times, and the Mennonite family got off at Lancaster. Andrew watched the little girl walk away and he pondered what it would be like to have one of those. Marriage tended to lead to children after all. He had trouble picturing himself as a father.

They reached Harrisburg in the early afternoon and Andrew bought a newspaper from a boy on the platform. He breezed through the national news since it was mostly about the war and he had much better information from his own briefings. He was more interested in the international situation, and there were a number of stories from foreign press services. Overall the news was pretty bad. The Martian strategy of landing in hard to reach areas, then expanding out from there had worked perfectly. Central Asia, north of the Himalayas, had been lost; South America, Mexico, most of Australia, all gone.

Africa, south of the Sahara, had been mostly overrun—at least it seemed to have been; how could you really tell? Only a few coastal towns were still in human hands and these were being flooded by waves of refugees from the interior who spoke of metal giants killing everything in their path. Capetown and a fair chunk of Britain's South African colony were being held stubbornly, but there were rumors that no more troops would be sent there because they were needed to defend Egypt and the Suez Canal. So far, British gunboats on the Nile along with a mixed army of regulars and colonial troops had been able to keep the Martians at bay. There were frustratingly vague mentions in the paper of 'new' British weapons being used, but no details.

Andrew frowned. The damn British! They had been jealously guarding the Martian machines they had captured in the first invasion and sharing almost nothing with anyone else. And one of the few things they had been willing to show to outsiders, a power generator of some sort, had exploded disastrously in Liverpool, killing over a thousand people—including Andrew's father who was there to observe the test. But apparently they *had* learned some things from their captures and were now putting them to use—and still not sharing anything!

Well, we have our own captured equipment now! We don't need help from the damn Limeys!

While he read and fumed, the train turned north and wound its way along the Susquehanna River, through tidy Williamsport, charming Lock Haven, and then on toward Buffalo. Andrew was, in fact, on his way to see for himself what had been learned from some of the equipment that had been captured in New Mexico.

North of Lock Haven the countryside changed dramatically. He was in the heart of coal country now and it looked little different than the blasted landscape the Martians had made around Gallup. The hills and ridges had been denuded of trees, new hills of tailings had grown up around every mine head. Lifeless ponds, black and greasy, seemed to soak up the last rays of the setting sun, and streams choked with trash trickled forlornly toward the Susquehanna. Andrew looked in revulsion as lines of figures, as black as the mounds of coal, trudged away from the mines, toward ramshackle homes, while other lines of not-quite-so-black figures trudged the other way. The mines were working around the clock these days. Three shifts a day. Over and over.

A different group caught his eye: men in uniform, leaning on their rifles. Soldiers. A few years back, before the new invasion threat, there had been strikes and disruptions in coal country. That couldn't be allowed to happen again.

The train rolled on; past villages and towns and mines, and always there were the lines of trudging figures with the change of shifts. And some of those figures were far too small. Just boys. Andrew thought of the little girl on the train. Her older brothers were about this size. They were lucky to have a farm to work instead of a mine. What sort of a future did these boys have? *Well, if we don't win the war, they won't have any future at all.* The country ran on coal, so Andrew couldn't see anything for it. He pulled the newspaper out again and stopped looking out the window until it was too dark to see.

It was after nine by the time he reached Buffalo and then another hour to get the train for the short run to Niagara Falls. He could hear the roar of the falls from his hotel. He fell into bed, exhausted, but mused for a few minutes until sleep took him. Niagara Falls was a favorite spot for honeymooners. Would he and Victoria even have time for a proper honeymoon? Maybe they could come here…

The next morning he was pleased and a little surprised to find a motor staff car waiting for him, exactly on time, outside the hotel. The private driving it looked very young and even though he knew how to operate the vehicle, he was very sketchy on military courtesy. Instead of getting out and opening the door for him, he just yelled: "You Major Comstock? Well, hop in!" The kid had probably been in the army about six weeks, so he decided not to make an issue of it.

"I'm taking you to Fort Niagara, right?" asked the driver as he pulled away from the hotel with a lurch.

"That's right. You know the way?"

"'Course I do! Just came from there!" The driver made several turns and then they were on a road leading north out of town. The falls were behind them now and Andrew could catch glimpses of the Niagara River far below to the left. The road was following the river down to Lake Ontario, but it could not make the drop of one hundred and seventy feet in one leap the way the river could, so there were several switchbacks and a few hair-raising slopes on the way. The paving stopped only a mile or two north of the town and they were on rutted dirt after that.

"You here to see them fire the Martian ray?" asked the driver after a while.

Andrew jerked upright. "What?!"

"The ray! The thing they captured out west. That Doctor Tesla fella has been playing with it all week! Helluva thing!"

Andrew forced himself to close his mouth. This was supposed to be a secret! And Tesla was supposed to have waited for Andrew to get here before he made the first test firing! Blast the man! But he supposed he should have expected this. He'd met Tesla a number of times and it was clear that he had no respect for any authority but his own.

Still, once they started firing tests there would be no keeping the secret. The army would have preferred to do this in some location away from prying eyes, but the device required such an enormous amount of electrical power that there were few places which could supply it. The hydroelectric plants at Niagara along with the open waters of Lake Ontario made this the best location available.

They finished the long descent and after a few more miles came to a tall fence with a gate in it. A large sign proclaimed it to be Fort Niagara with the familiar flaming bomb emblem of the Ordnance Department on either side. Soldiers were guarding the gate and to Andrew's surprise there was a small crowd of civilians just outside. Reporters, from the look of them.

The auto stopped just outside the gate and a sergeant demanded Andrew's identification. He produced it, and while the sergeant was examining it, the reporters crowded around the car and began shouting: "Is that Comstock?" "Yes, I think that's him!" "Major! Is the ray device here the one you captured in New Mexico?" "How soon until we can make rays of our own?" "How long will your tests continue to interrupt the local power supply?"

Andrew didn't reply. After a moment, he had his papers back and the guards let the car pass through the gate. The reporters continued to shout at him until he was out of earshot. The driver looked back at him with a strange expression. "*You* captured the ray gadget?"

"No, we couldn't carry the one *we* captured. This is one that they captured at the Battle of Prewitt."

"Huh, I'll be damned."

To the left, the land sloped up to a rocky prominence where the Colonial-era fort that gave the place its name was situated, but Andrew's destination was the cluster of newly-constructed wooden buildings and sheds along the low ridge that overlooked the lake. The driver deposited him at the headquarters building, but he was informed by a clerk that everyone was down at the testing range by the lake.

Just then, the electric lights in the building flickered and dimmed down to a faint glow. At the same time, Andrew heard that awful buzz-saw snarl of a Martian heat ray. Even though he knew it was just the captured device, it set every nerve tingling as he gritted his teeth and clenched his fists. Images of men and horses being burned to ash flashed through his mind. The screams... the smell... The noise cut off and he breathed again.

"Sir? You all right, sir?" He looked and saw the clerk eyeing him with a worried expression.

"What? Oh, sure." He unclenched his fists, but his hands were shaking. He put them behind his back. "How do I get down to the firing range?"

"Just follow the road to the right. It will take you there."

He nodded and made a hurried exit. The road was as described and in a few moments he was past the buildings and on the edge of the low bluffs above the lake. There were several trucks and a crowd of people on the beach and they were all looking at a cloud of mist—steam?—drifting above the lake a few hundred yards off shore. He hurried down and soon recognized the tall, gangly shape of Nikola Tesla in the midst of the crowd, which was gathered around the heat ray device. As always, Tesla was impeccably dressed, even his knee-high rubber boots were custom made.

Tesla was grinning like a loon and somehow his smile grew even broader when he caught sight of Andrew. "Ah! Captain Comstock..."

"It's major, Mister..."

"...you just missed it. Beautiful! Such amazing power! But do not worry. After it cools down for a few minutes I will show you. Gentlemen! Gentlemen! This is Captain Comstock, the man who so kindly provided us with this magnificent device! I'm sure you've read about his heroics in the papers." Everyone turned to face him and he had to resist the urge to smile and wave. Tesla had a well-known aversion to shaking hands, so Andrew didn't offer him his.

"Uh... Doctor Tesla, I'm very surprised that you have been firing this device when we had agreed..."

"Ah!" Tesla waved his hand dismissively. "We were ready, so why wait? So much to learn! But here, let me introduce you to my assistants." He reeled off a string of names but Andrew had no hope of matching them to the men standing there. Almost as an afterthought he introduced the commander of Fort Niagara, an ordnance officer named Thompson wearing captain's bars who must have been twice Andrew's age. The man frowned at him, but nodded.

"So you have been able to get this to work?" asked Andrew pointing at the machine. "Your last telegram only said you hoped it would be possible."

"Yes, yes! The method by which the Martians control the device is still a mystery—but I will solve that. When I attempted to feed power to it I determined that a mechanism which I must describe as a switch—although unlike any switch I have ever seen—was blocking the flow. Unable to close it, I decided to simply remove it and use my own switch. That proved the key. It works! Here, I think it has cooled enough. Let me show you."

At that point, a man who had been standing to the side came forward. He was older and wore a conservative and well-made business suit. "Nikola," he said, "how many more firings do you plan to do today? I really need to know."

"What? Oh, a dozen more, I suppose," replied Tesla. "Ah, Captain! I forgot to introduce Mr. Harper. John Harper, the chief engineer of the magnificent hydroelectric plant which provides the power for these experiments. I met John back when I was working with Edward Dean Adams to build this place, and we have worked together from time to time. He and the owners have graciously agreed to help."

"Our patriotic duty, Major," said Harper proudly. "But taking the plant out of service for this is quite a hardship for our customers."

"It requires the whole plant?" asked Andrew.

"Almost the entire capacity of Plant Number One, Major. Nearly fifty thousand horsepower."

"Yes!" said Tesla. "An amazing amount, isn't it? We had to lay a whole new set of lines from the plant to here. Look at the size of the busbars we needed!" He gestured to the heat ray. Looking closer, Andrew saw that the device had been fitted to what he recognized as the mount for a coast defense mortar. It could be elevated and depressed by a hand-wheel connected to a set of gears and traversed by another—just like an artillery piece. Although with the two massive cables attached to the back of the ray, it was obvious the thing could not be traversed very far. The cables were connected to the busbars Tesla had boasted of and then more cables ran back across the beach to disappear into the bluffs. One of the buildings on top of the bluff had dozens of heavy wires strung from it to a series of poles that marched off to the south, apparently connected to the power plant along the Niagara. *Fifty thousand horsepower!* It was amazing, but also daunting. A power plant the size of a city block to supply just one ray device; somehow the Martians did it with something a tiny fraction of the size…

"Oh! And that reminds me, Captain," said Tesla wheeling to face him, his expression stern and unsmiling now. "I have been informed that you have delivered several of the Martian power generators to Edison! Why were they not given to me?"

"That was General Crozier's decision, Doctor. With so much to examine, he decided the task should be split up. You got the heat ray, Edison and… several others were given the power devices. Metal samples were sent to…"

"Bah!" snapped Tesla angrily. "Edison will learn nothing! He is a good man, don't mistake me; he helped me so graciously when my laboratory burned down. But his grasp of the electrical forces is rudimentary. He will not discover the Martians' secrets. Give them to me, Captain, and I shall!"

Andrew, used to Tesla's tantrums, replied levelly. "That's not my decision, Doctor, but I will pass along your request to the general. Now, can I see the demonstration of the ray?"

The man fussed for a few seconds more, but then seemed to forget about it entirely and was snapping out instructions to his assistants. Two of them shooed the spectators back from the ray device while another got on a telephone, apparently connected to the power plant. Tesla stood next to a large electrical switch mounted to a table a dozen yards to the rear. "Is all ready?" he demanded to know, and his men acknowledged with quick nods of their heads. "Very well! Stand by!" Andrew retreated another dozen yards behind Tesla. He found that he was beside Captain Thompson.

"This fellow is mad as a hatter, you realize," said the captain none-too quietly.

"Yes, but he is brilliant."

"Firing… *now!*" cried Tesla, and he threw the switch.

Prepared for it this time, Andrew managed not to flinch, although the noise still set his teeth on edge. The ray, not terribly visible in the bright morning sunlight, blasted outward and struck the surface of the lake a few hundred yards away. The water instantly exploded into steam that erupted up and out in a thundering white cloud. He was surprised that there was almost no heat to be felt from where he was standing. He remembered what it was like when a ray came close and he'd assumed it would be like that even standing behind the device. But it wasn't. Apparently all the heat was going the other way.

After boiling Lake Ontario for a few more seconds, Tesla opened the switch again, and ray and sound ceased. The scientist came bounding over, the lunatic grin back on his face. "Well? Well?" he shouted. "What do you think?"

"Uh… congratulations, Doctor, on getting it working. It looks and sounds exactly like what I saw in New Mexico."

"Ah! But of course! I was forgetting that this is nothing new to you. But to a man of science like myself this is nothing short of astounding. To take electric current and convert it into a focused beam of raw energy like this opens up a whole new realm of research!"

Captain Thompson noisily cleared his throat and stepped forward, holding up a file folder. "Yes, Doctor, and according to this set of orders I was given, there is a great deal of research which we are supposed to be doing today. I've had my men working for the last three days preparing the targets listed here. Can I suggest that we leave the poor lake alone and get to work?" He gestured down the beach to the east.

Looking that way, Andrew saw that there were groups of men with piles of… he wasn't sure what they were piles of, spaced a few hundred yards apart stretching for a mile or more until the beach ended where the bluff curved out to the lake. Ah, yes, he remembered now. Assuming Tesla could get the ray working, they were to test the effect of the ray on various materials at various distances.

"Yes, of course, Captain," said Tesla. "Now that we know the ray is working properly, we can begin the tests."

"Very well. Sergeant, signal the men." One of Thompson's men pulled out a green signal flag and waved it briskly. The groups down the beach went to work. The first test was to try and determine the effective range of the ray. Some people—like Andrew—had seen the Martian weapon in action and lived to tell the tale, but no one really had the time to take any precise measurements. So now, the teams of men were setting up mannequins dressed in full combat gear in a precise line laid out by army engineers at intervals of five hundred yards. Meanwhile, several men were swinging the heat ray around on its mount to aim exactly down that line. Every bit of information was important, so two other men were recording the air temperature and pressure, humidity and wind speed.

As each group was ready, they waved a flag. Thompson was watching them through field glasses. "We should have laid some telephone lines," he muttered. Finally, he was satisfied and his sergeant waved a red flag. The work parties scampered off to sandbagged sanctuaries well out of the line of fire. "All right, Doctor, you can fire when ready." Tesla's people called the power plant and after a few moments he stepped up and threw the switch.

The heat ray stabbed out again and a series of smoke clouds exploded down the beach. After a moment, Tesla shut off the ray. Andrew had his own field glasses out and when the smoke cleared he trained them at the targets. Or where the targets had been. The first and second ones were gone completely. The third also appeared to be gone, but it was a long way off and it was hard to be sure. Beyond that he couldn't see clearly, although something appeared to be burning near the end of the beach.

"Well, let's go have a look, shall we?" said Thompson. He and Andrew climbed into the cab of one of the trucks, with Thompson's sergeant driving. They chugged down the line of targets, looking at each in turn. The men who had set them up had come out of their refuges and were writing down their observations.

As he expected, the first and second targets had been completely obliterated. There were just some scorched marks on the sand and a few clumps of ash. The third target, at fifteen hundred yards, wasn't completely destroyed; there looked to be a few melted bits of metal—buckles off the equipment, Andrew guessed—and the barrel of the rifle was clearly identifiable, even though it was twisted and blackened.

The one at two thousand yards showed the first significant change. The mannequin was not totally destroyed. There was a sizable lump of remains, with bits of uniform and gear only scorched. The metal helmet sat on top of the pile and the rifle was almost intact with wisps of smoke still curling up from the wooden stock. Still, if it had been a real person, it would be very dead.

The next target, the one at twenty-five hundred yards—the beach was longer than it had looked—wasn't in bad shape at all. It still stood on the pole that held it erect. The uniform was charred and blackened on the side facing the ray, but the other side was untouched. "If the fellow could find any cover at all, he would probably be all right," observed Andrew.

The last target, at three thousand yards, was barely touched. A little charring to the uniform, but not much. "You wouldn't want to expose bare flesh to it, I don't imagine," said Thompson, "but with the anti-dust gear, the mask, gloves, and leggings, you'd probably be okay for a while."

"Yes," agreed Andrew. "So, against infantry, the thing is lethal to two thousand yards and then its effect tails off sharply after that. Horses would probably do badly out to three thousand." He walked around the mannequin wondering if there was any change that could be made to the uniform or gear which would increase the survivability of the infantry. "You know, if we were to…"

The sudden noise of the heat ray blotted every thought from his mind except to take cover. He flung himself down to the sand and covered his head with his arms.

"What the hell…?" he heard Thompson say. "God *damn* the man!"

When he felt no heat, Andrew dared take a look. The heat ray was firing, but it was aimed out at the lake again. "What…? What's he doing?"

"Playing with his toy again!" snapped Thompson. "I swear he's like a child!"

The ray switched off and Andrew got to his feet, dusting sand off his uniform. "We better get back there before he does anything else!" They climbed into the truck and drove back to where Tesla and the ray device were waiting. The scientist seemed completely oblivious to the fact that he'd nearly given Andrew a heart attack. "Just checking on something," he explained.

"Doctor Tesla," said Thompson. "There are basic safety regulations which must be followed on a firing range—any sort of firing range! From now on, I will have a man posted by the firing switch and he will not allow you to operate the device unless an officer is present."

Tesla just waved this off and asked: "What were the results?"

Andrew gave him a brief, and stiffly worded, report on what he'd seen, trying to keep the annoyance out of his voice. "So what's next? Tests against metal plates?"

"Yes," said Thompson. "The men are setting up frames to hold sheets of metal right now. It might take a while—those sheets are heavy. Do you want to come back to my office for some coffee?" Tesla accepted, but Andrew begged off.

"It's such a beautiful day, I think I will stay out here," he said. But in truth, he was still shaking inside from the incident with the ray. He needed to walk it off. He wandered east along the lake shore again, pretending to watch the work parties. *My God, what's the matter with me?* He hadn't fallen apart like this out in New Mexico. He dodged Martians and their rays for a week or more, helped blow up one of their tripod machines, and come home a hero. And now the mere sound of a heat ray set him quivering and running for cover!

And there were the nightmares. Not every night; sometimes weeks would go by without one. But still far too often. They were always the same: he'd be standing there and a heat ray would be swinging along, burning a glowing trench in the ground. However, it was never coming at him, it was always coming at someone else: Victoria, his mother, Colonel Hawthorne, Sergeant McGill, that Harding girl, someone he knew. And they'd be oblivious to it, unaware of their peril. He'd try to warn them, pull them aside, but he'd be frozen in place, dumb and paralyzed—until it was too late. He'd wake up quivering and dripping with sweat. He shivered, despite the July sun overhead, and shook his head. *Some hero I am!*

But as he stood there, looking out on the lake, the fit passed and he breathed easier. With any luck he'd never go through anything like that again. He wasn't a line officer, after all!

A noise drifting across the water caught his attention. A boat had come into view from around the headland and he realized it was full of reporters, probably the frustrated ones from the gate. Captain Thompson had posted several guard boats to keep anyone from drifting into the firing area on the lake and one of them was moving to intercept the intruders. The sightseers withdrew, but stayed in sight. It didn't really matter, he supposed. The whole world knew the Americans had captured some Martian devices—and it wasn't like the Martians were going to be reading the newspapers!

Eventually Thompson and Tesla returned and the work parties finished getting things set up. "If the last test was any indication," said Thompson, "I doubt the ray will even make it all the way to the last target."

"Yes," agreed Andrew and a sudden impulse took him. "I think I'll observe from down range. Between targets two and three."

Thompson's eyebrows went up. "All right, Major, but do stay well back from the line of fire."

"Of course."

"We'll hold our fire until you are in position." He glanced at Tesla and frowned. Andrew turned and walked off. He wasn't exactly sure why he was doing this. Just to prove to himself his courage? Maybe. Probably.

It was the better part of a mile from the ray device to where he wanted to go and he was sweating by the time he got there. Once in position—about a hundred yards uphill of the firing line—he got out his field glasses and then waved his hat back at Thompson. After a few seconds, the heat ray fired. He had his glasses trained on the first target and he was seeing it from the side opposite that the ray struck. For an instant, there was a bright glow all around the edges of the metal plate. Then, almost immediately, a spot in the middle turned red, then orange... yellow... white. From start to finish it couldn't have been more than a second, and then the gobs of molten metal were flying in all directions as the ray burned through.

He immediately shifted his field glasses to the second target. The glow around the edges seemed brighter but the red spot was longer in coming. He counted seconds as the metal went from red to white and he was all the way up to six before the ray blasted through. Again he shifted his focus, now to the third target, and he was seeing it from the front. The whole plate slowly turned a dull red, but there was no hot spot like before and then the ray shut off. The plate quickly cooled to a dull gray.

He walked down to inspect it, but didn't get too close. He could feel the heat radiating off it. But there was no burn through and no obvious damage. He was still looking when Thompson arrived in the truck. "So! At fifteen hundred yards the metal will stop it, eh?"

"Stop it, yes. But if this had been the front of a steam tank, the crew probably would have been roasted alive. It got damn hot! But the ray definitely starts to spread out with distance. Still, this plate was only subjected to the ray for a short while before we had to shut it off. If it had hit this one first without wasting seconds on the first two plates..."

"Yes, well, let's take down what's left of the first two and try it again on this one."

So they did that, but the third plate survived again, although it was glowing orange and there was a bit of melting in evidence. After that they took the plate down and shot directly at the one at two thousand yards. Andrew moved down to stand close to it and was pleased that he wasn't shaking at all. When the ray fired, the plate didn't even get hot enough to change color, although it was far too hot to touch. They didn't bother firing at the last two.

After a break for lunch they did some more tests against different types of materials. First was an invention that some engineers and metallurgists at the Massachusetts Institute of Technology had come up with which sandwiched a layer of asbestos between two thin sheets of steel. At five hundred yards, the ray blasted through in only a slightly longer time than against the solid metal sheet. But at a thousand yards it took significantly longer, and at fifteen hundred it couldn't get through at all and the plate on the side away from the ray did not get terribly hot. Andrew felt that this approach had some potential.

The last series of tests were against slabs of concrete six inches thick. Interestingly, the concrete proved more resistant to the heat ray than anything else. The slab at five hundred yards eventually cracked and crumbled, but the farther slabs were barely touched. "I doubt we can build tanks out of concrete," said Andrew, "but perhaps a layer on the front."

"Yes," agreed Thompson. "And thick concrete walls should be able to resist the rays indefinitely. Fortification constructed of concrete should be most effective."

It was late afternoon by the time they finished their tests with the concrete and Mr. Harper, manager of the power plant, insisted they cease for the day. Everyone was tired, so there was no argument.

"A most successful day, Captain," said Andrew to Thompson. "I'll be sure to mention your efficiency to my superiors. And you'll forward your official report as soon as possible?"

"Certainly, Major, and thank you. And there will be more reports to follow. We need to run more tests under different weather conditions. I suspect the ray will be much less effective in the rain."

"Yes, we've already received reports to that effect from the front." He pulled out his pocket watch and checked the time. "Well, I think I'll be on my way."

"And you will see about getting me some of those Martian power units, won't you Comstock?" cooed Tesla, smiling the way he did when he wanted something. "I simply must have some of those!"

"I'll see what I can do," said Andrew, making his escape as quickly as he could. The same driver took him back to the hotel.

"That's a helluva thing, ain't it?" he said. "Watched it from up above. Sure wouldn't want to get caught by that!"

"No, you surely wouldn't," replied Andrew.

He slept like the dead that night and was on an early train back to Washington the next morning. He alternated between napping, daydreaming about his fiancé, and working on his own report. At Harrisburg he changed trains and went south through Baltimore, arriving in Washington in the early evening. He'd wired ahead with his arrival time to have a car waiting, so he was surprised to see a carriage waiting, and even more surprised that Victoria was there with it. She ran to him, skirts and curls bouncing. She had an enormous grin on her face. "Oh, Andrew! Andrew! I have the most marvelous news! You'll never guess! Never!"

"No, I don't suppose I will," he said, catching her up in his arms. "What is it?"

"Oh, Andrew! The President! The President is coming to the wedding!"

CHAPTER THREE

JULY 1909, NEAR FORT WINGATE, NEW MEXICO TERRITORY

Army nurse Rebecca Harding couldn't sleep. She should have been exhausted after a long day, but the incessant rumble of the artillery and the flickers of the gun flashes against the canvas of the tent kept her awake. She tossed and turned in her cot, but eventually sat up and ran her hands through her dark blonde hair and rubbed her eyes. Everyone else in the tent seemed to be asleep. She got into her uniform as silently as she could and then slipped outside.

Technically she was violating orders by being away from her quarters after dark, but it wasn't the first time. Sometimes after working the night shift she would go off to be by herself for a while. She felt that need again tonight. There was a sentry near the entrance to the nurses' camp, but since they hadn't built any sort of fence around the tents, she just went the other direction until she was out of his sight. The sentry was there for the nurses' protection, but Becca was perfectly capable of taking care of herself. Miss Chumley had obtained service revolvers for all the nurses and Becca's was in her pocket.

The camp and the field hospital that it served were built near the ruins of Fort Wingate. The Martians had destroyed the place on their first sweep through the area and all that remained were burned piles of debris. Becca turned away from the fort and started to climb a low hill to the west. The hill had once been covered by trees, but the Martians had destroyed them, too. She had been here when that happened. She had been fleeing the Martians with Sergeant Dolfen and a batch of other survivors, and the enemy had tried to kill them by burning down the forest around them. They'd nearly succeeded.

It was wonderfully cool in the clear night air. Downright chilly even, and she was grateful for the wool uniform that she cursed in the heat of the day. Making her way around the blackened trunks of the trees was difficult in the dark, but eventually she reached a point where she had a clear view of the army's siege lines around the Martian fortress. Hundreds of campfires stood out against the dark plain; tiny pinpricks of light in an arc that stretched for miles. Beyond them, barely visible in the distance, was a circular ridge from which no lights shone. The Martians had built a high wall all around their base made of piled up stone and dirt. It encircled the place where the town of Gallup had once stood. Not a trace of it remained now. They had devices all along the top of the wall which could fire their dreaded heat rays. No one knew what they were doing inside those damned walls.

Becca had very nearly come to know what was going on in there. She and Sergeant Dolfen and a dozen others had been captured by one of the Martian machines and they had been herded toward the fortress. They'd only been a few miles away from it when they were rescued by Major Comstock and his men who destroyed the machine with dynamite bombs. She was so glad she'd never seen the inside of the fortress. There were rumors about what the Martians did with their captives...

Well, perhaps they would all learn what was going on in there soon—and live to tell about it. A major attack was supposed to start sometime in the coming days. Several batteries of guns were firing at the place—they fired around the clock now. She could see the flashes and hear the reports much more clearly from her vantage point than back in the camp. The explosion of the shells was farther off, but each thump and crump was like music to her. Yes! Hurt them! Hurt the monsters!

She hated the Martians like she'd never hated anything in her short life. They'd killed her mother and her father and her grandmother and her friend Pepe. They'd burned down her house, destroyed the ranch, her neighbors' homes, the town. They'd killed so many other people and driven her screaming into the night. They'd destroyed her world and now they were trying to destroy everyone else's, too. They had to be stopped! And she wanted to help stop them! She clenched her fists and exulted in the sound of the guns. She wished she was one of the people firing those cannons. She wanted to fight! But they didn't let girls fight. So she'd be a nurse instead. At least it got her near the fighting. Maybe the chance would come. It wasn't going to come if she was in Santa Fe—or Connecticut!

Three weeks ago she'd simply waited until her aunt and uncle were asleep and then walked out of the house. She'd gone to the hospital, found a cot to sleep on for a few hours until dawn, and then seen Miss Chumley and volunteered for the forward field hospital. Chumley had seemed surprised, but had accepted her gladly. She'd spent the next few days in terror that her aunt would show up with the sheriff and drag her off, but that hadn't happened. And then the new unit had moved out on the train and now she was here. Her only real regret was that she'd had to leave her beloved horse, Ninny, back in Santa Fe. Somehow he'd survived all their earlier adventures, but there had been no way to bring him along now. She hoped her uncle would take care of him properly.

She stood and watched for a while and then found a rock to sit on. It was still a long time until dawn and she felt sleep creeping up on her. She should head back to the camp before someone noticed she wasn't there...

"Miss Harding, what are you doing out here?"

Becca yelped and jumped to her feet. A dark shape had snuck up on her. But the shape's voice...

"Miss Ch-Chumley?"

"Yes. And I ask again: what are you doing out here? You are violating regulation, you know."

"I... I couldn't sleep."

"And you felt it necessary to come way out here? Why?"

"I wanted to see what was happening." She gestured toward the artillery and then braced herself for the inevitable dressing down that Chumley would give her.

But to her amazement, Chumley just nodded. "It is quite a thing, isn't it?"

"Ma'am? Yes, ma'am."

The older woman was silent for a moment and then said: "I've been doing this for over ten years now. I was hired as a civilian nurse for the army back in '98 during the Spanish War. I figured I would be treating wounded men, but I never saw one. What I saw instead were men dying from malaria and yellow fever and dysentery. You're too young to remember, but that was a very bad time. They crowded the volunteers into camps all along the Gulf Coast without a thought about sanitation. Far more men died of disease than from Spanish bullets. It broke my heart to see those boys, so eager to fight, struck down that way. They were so brave... That sort of bravery deserves... I don't know how to say it. So when they created the Nurse Corps in '01 I joined up. I wanted to go help the boys fighting the Insurrection in the Philippines, but I got sent to Cuba instead. A lot of sick men there, too. I wanted to help. I *needed* to help." She paused and looked straight at Rebecca. "Just like you." The firing had stopped and it was dead silent on the hilltop.

"Yes, ma'am."

"It seems I was wrong about you, Miss Harding."

"Ma'am?"

"When you first showed up in Santa Fe, I thought you were just some flighty young girl who thought that nursing would be *glamorous*. So I gave you all the worst jobs thinking you'd give up and run along home. But you didn't. You did every job well and never complained. And when you volunteered for this posting, again I was expecting you to go running back to your fine house in Santa Fe after a few weeks in a tent. But you surprised me again. You didn't run, you didn't complain, and you knew what to do."

"I've been working outdoors my whole life," said Becca. "I'm not from Santa Fe."

"Yes," said Chumley. "I did some checking, asked a few questions. A friend showed me a newspaper from six months ago. You've been here before, haven't you? And you really killed a Martian? Like the paper said?"

"Yes, ma'am. Right over there a few miles." She pointed out to the dark plain where a new battery had just opened fire. "'Course it wasn't such a big thing. The soldiers had already wrecked its machine."

"Why didn't you ever tell me?"

"Would you have believed me? My aunt and uncle in Santa Fe didn't."

"No, I don't suppose I would have. Seems pretty incredible."

"It seems like a dream now. A nightmare, I guess."

"And you want to keep fighting the Martians?"

"No one will *let* me fight the Martians!" she said bitterly.

"We're all fighting the Martians, Becca. Every one of us. The men manning those cannons, the riflemen in their trenches, the generals back in Washington, the stevedores loading the trains... and us. All of us. Each one doing their part. Not everyone can fire a gun—like you did—but we can all do our bit."

"I... I guess I never thought of it that way..."

"Well you should. You're doing an excellent job here. Oh..." There was a sound of rustling paper and Chumley held something up. "This arrived today. It's from the provost officer back in Santa Fe."

Becca sucked in her breath.

"He wants to know if you are here with us. And if you are, he directs that you be sent back to Santa Fe."

"I won't go back!" She retreated a step, but then clenched her fists, and looked defiantly at Chumley.

"I'm not asking you to."

"You're not? But... but the order..."

"What order?" There was a sound of tearing paper. "You know how unreliable communication with the rear is."

"Oh! Oh, yes! Thank you, ma'am!" Becca gasped in relief.

"You're welcome. Now come on, we can still get a few hours of sleep before reveille."

* * * * *

227

JULY 1909, BALTIMORE, MARYLAND

"Mr. President," said Leonard Wood. "If… if anything should happen…"

"Now none of that sort of talk, Leonard!" boomed Roosevelt. "You are going to be fine, just fine! They say that your doctor, this young Cushing fellow, is a genius, an absolute genius. You'll be up and about and back to work in no time!"

Wood sighed. Theodore's enthusiasm and optimism, while heartening, could also be exasperating at times. True, it had been invaluable when he'd finally been forced to tell him about the brain tumor. Roosevelt had never for a moment considered replacing him as Chief of Staff as Wood had feared. No, instead he'd moved heaven and earth to find the very best surgeon and whisk Wood off to the hospital at Johns Hopkins for the operation. So here he was, sitting up in a bed in a rather palatial suite with Roosevelt, his son, Ted, and a half dozen other officers and assistants trying to get a few last things done before the doctors came to get him. With luck, he *could* be back to work soon, and this Harvey Cushing was supposed to be the best. Still, there was a very real possibility that he wouldn't wake up from the anesthesia…

"Theodore, we have to face facts. And the fact is I might not recover. In that case, you must have a replacement ready to step in. There is too much at stake to leave the post vacant for any length of time. Now my staff can keep things going for a couple of weeks, but if it's any longer, you are going to have to name someone else. Now I've given you my list of possible…"

"Yes, yes, I've read it. Now MacArthur might do in the short term, but the last thing I want is another Civil War veteran running the army! Arthur is what, sixty-five? You remember the problems we had with Nelson Miles! That boy of his, though, Douglas, he's got some potential. We need to find a command for him."

"Yes, you're right. But we have more urgent matters to deal with. Funston will be launching his final assault very soon. If it succeeds as he's promised, you can't let him rest on his laurels. We need to turn him north and see if he can do to the same thing to any Martian fortresses in Idaho—or wherever else they might have built them. We need to keep pushing and…"

"We will, Leonard, we will," assured Roosevelt. "But what do you think of this latest proposal by the Germans? First they were just talking about landing a corps at Caracas in Venezuela, but now they want to land what sounds like a whole army in Brazil!"

"Well, they do have some legitimate concerns in Brazil. Over 300,000 Germans live there. Or lived there. God knows what's going on there now. But there's no way we can send an expedition, so we should be glad they are willing to."

"Yes, I suppose. I hate to toss the Monroe Doctrine out the window, but if this gets the Germans into the fight, I suppose it's worth it. We might have the Devil's own time getting them out again once this is all over, though!"

Wood smiled in spite of himself. Leave it to Theodore to be thinking about afterward. Privately Wood doubted whether either of them would live to see an afterward. This was going to be a very long war, he feared. "And the French are landing their own corps at Veracruz next month?"

"So Ambassador Jusserand says. And in this case I'll welcome them with open arms! If the Martians come boiling up out of Mexico, we've got almost nothing to stop them. The Rio Grande line only exists on paper and Governor Campbell has been screaming his head off for troops."

"He's got troops, what he doesn't have is equipment—just like everyone else. With no industry at all down there—they have to import small arms ammunition, for God's sake—there's no hope of them making artillery or tanks. It all has to come from back east and there is too much demand elsewhere."

"True, but we need to do something. Right now the only rail connection we have with the west coast, the Southern Pacific line, runs through Texas and we need to keep it open. If we lose that, California, Oregon, and Washington will be in peril."

Wood couldn't argue with that, but as a general and as a former surgeon he knew that sometimes you had to make difficult choices. Roosevelt was in love with the American West. After the death of his first wife he had spent several years ranching in the badlands of the Dakotas and he often talked about how the experience had transformed him. Ever since, he made periodic trips to the west for his health, both physical and mental. He would never voluntarily abandon the land or its people to the Martians. But sentimentality didn't win wars. The hard truth was that in this war the west didn't matter that much. Nearly all the country's industry was in the east. The coal fields, the iron mines, even most of the oil was in the eastern states. Industrial production, making the guns and tanks, was going to be the key to winning. Defending the production centers had to take top priority. Which reminded him…

"Mr. President, if those astronomers are right, then we need to start forming a reserve in case…"

The door to the suite opened before he could continue and a small mob of doctors, orderlies, and nurses swarmed into the room. "Oh dear, already?" said Roosevelt. "Well, Leonard, I will see you later, God bless you." The President and the other military men withdrew, leaving Wood facing a far more formidable host.

* * * * *

CYCLE 597, 843.8, HOLDFAST 32-1

Qetjnegartis helped Davnitargus into the control cabin of the fighting machine. The bud was maturing rapidly but was still too small to reach the grab bars on either side of the hatch. Once it had hold of them, however, it pulled itself the rest of the way with no problem. It seemed unusually strong for its size and age, perhaps an adaption to the stronger gravity of the target world? The ability of the Race to make changes to their bodies in response to environmental conditions was not entirely voluntary or deliberate. Unexpected things did sometimes occur.

Before following inside, Qetjnegartis looked down the long row of gleaming fighting machines parked in the hanger. They would be more than enough to drive off the enemy besieging the holdfast if only they had the people to pilot them. Reinforcements were due to be launched from the Homeworld very soon, but they could not possibly arrive in time. So there was no choice but to instruct the buds how to operate them, even though they were not ready for such a challenge. No, no choice at all. It heaved itself into the cramped space behind the pilot's position.

"Position yourself on the pad there and grasp the control rods," said Qetjnegartis. "The interface works exactly like the other machines you have been training on, although as you will find, this machine is far more complex. Do not be concerned about errant actions, the machine is on safe mode and will not actually execute any command you might give it."

Davnitargus did as directed but it was clear that it was having some difficulty reaching the controls. "Progenitor, this is… awkward," it said. Qetjnegartis was pleased that the bud sometimes called it *progenitor* instead of by name. It was a sign of respect.

"Yes, this machine was designed for someone who is full grown. We did not anticipate young buds needing to use them."

"And we are doing so because of the prey-creatures' attacks?"

"Yes," replied Qetjnegartis, both pleased that Davnitargus had deduced the reason and annoyed that the reason existed. "We believe that a very serious attack will happen soon. We may need you and the other buds to repel it."

"Then I shall learn to operate this machine despite the awkwardness."

229

"Excellent. We shall begin with something simple. Now grasping the rods, let your awareness…"

They worked together until Davnitargus was showing clear signs of fatigue. "You did well, very well. Now, let us feed and rest for a while. We can work more later."

Qetjnegartis helped the bud out of the cabin and into a travel chair that moved them from the hanger into a corridor. The faint rumble of the enemy bombardment came through the walls. It was a constant feature these days. It rarely stopped or even slackened. They were concentrating on Sector 9 of the rampart again and a continuous rain of projectiles was making it difficult and dangerous to replace the defense towers, or even repair the outer face of the rampart. After their last failed attempt to breach the rampart with buried explosives, they now seemed intent on simply pounding their way through with their projectiles. And if not interrupted, their attempt might succeed; a dangerous gap was beginning to appear and an attempt to make repairs had led to the near destruction of one of the work machines. Even without a complete breach in the rampart, the outer face might be leveled sufficiently for the enemy vehicles to reach the top—which would be equally dangerous. Things were reaching a critical point and Qetjnegartis felt the burden of command as never before. Still, even simple tasks like feeding needed to continue.

It guided the travel chair to one of the lower levels of the holdfast. The captive prey animals were held there. One large chamber held the intelligent ones while several others held various types of non-intelligent creatures. There was also an extraction chamber, feeding chamber, and a laboratory. Qetjnegartis was not surprised to find Ixmaderna in the laboratory, examining the remains of one of the non-intelligent creatures. Ixmaderna had a great interest in biology and spent any time it was not required elsewhere here, continuing its studies. "Greetings commander, greetings Davnitargus. Have you come to feed?"

"Yes. How go your investigations? You continue to concentrate on the lesser creatures?"

"It seemed the wisest course, Commander. Other holdfasts which are not… which have more resources to devote to study have spent so much effort on the intelligent creatures that it is unlikely I could add anything. But the lesser creatures appear to be restricted by type to specific geographical areas. Many of the ones we are capturing here have not been reported by any of the other holdfasts."

"I see. This does seem wise," replied Qetjnegartis, choosing to ignore the clumsy attempt to conceal its comment on the dire situation *this* particular holdfast found itself in. "But there are not many of any type left in the pens. How much longer can we sustain ourselves?"

"Unless we are able to venture outside the holdfast and gather more, I estimate only another twenty days, Commander. We have no food supply for the prey we capture so I am forced to feed the herbivores to the carnivores to keep them alive for our use."

"That should be sufficient. If relief does not arrive to lift this siege long before that, food will be the least of our worries."

"Indeed? And is the relief force on the way?"

"So I have been promised. I am scheduled to converse with Commander Braxjandar in less than a tenthday so I must feed now and be ready."

"I understand. Allow me to prepare one of the prey for you." Ixmaderna transferred the controls from the detailed manipulators it had been using for its examination to the larger ones used to deal with the captives. To reduce the chances of infection, the animals were all kept in strict isolation. Speaking of which…

"How is Zastranvis? Is its infection under control?"

"For the moment," replied Ixmaderna. "The drugs retard the pathogen's progress, but cannot eliminate it. Given time, it will surely kill Zastranvis, but it should have a replacement bud ready before that happens, and tests have shown that the infection has not transferred to the bud."

"That is good. It is unfortunate that its new bud will be a replacement body for it rather than a new being, but we knew this would be the case." It glanced down at its own new bud. As soon as Davnitargus had detached itself, Qetjnegartis had started growing another bud. They had to increase their numbers as quickly as possible. It hoped that this one would also become a new being rather than a replacement.

While they talked, Ixmaderna used the manipulators to seize one of the prey-creatures. The thing tried to escape while making a series of loud noises. Some of the others tried to grab hold of the manipulator or pull the caught one free and Ixmaderna was obliged to use a second manipulator to brush them loose. But finally the selected prey was carried through into the processing chamber. A restraining device held it immobile while the liquefying fluid was fed into its body through a number of tubes. The creature gave off one final burst of noise and then was still.

While the fluid did its job, Qetjnegartis and Davnitargus moved into the feeding chamber. The young bud moved close to the transparent barrier and examined the prey creature closely. "They do have some measure of intelligence, do they not?" it asked.

"Yes, to some small degree. They are able to construct tools and machines. They have some sort of society which permits them to cooperate."

"And they must communicate with each other somehow."

"It must be assumed so. Perhaps those noises they make."

"Would it be possible for us to communicate with them?"

"To what end? They can never be anything but prey to us."

Davnitargus fell silent and Qetjnegartis made no attempt to continue the conversation. The young bud would come to realize that only the Race mattered. After a short while the extractor signaled it was finished. The prey-creature's body was now little more than its outer hide stretched over its skeletal structure. They each inserted a feeding tube into their mouths. The nutrient solution which had been created was fully sterilized and Qetjnegartis ingested it with no pleasure. The entire process was much different than the normal methods used on the Homeworld. It wondered what the bud thought of it since it had never experienced the old ways but did carry some of Qetjnegartis' memories of them.

When they were finished Qetjnegartis said: "You should rest now. I must converse with Commander Braxjandar. When I have finished, we will resume your training." The bud acknowledged the command and Qetjnegartis took the travel chair to the command center. On the way there it passed a maintenance machine patching yet another leak in the corridor walls.

It reached the command center and after a brief status update from Namatchgar, who had the watch, it moved to the communications station. It positioned itself in front of a large display screen and grasped the control interface. It sent out the signal requesting contact and then waited. And waited. The agreed upon time came and went and still it waited. There was no doubt that the signal was getting through…

Braxjandar deliberately makes me wait. It is trying to establish its dominance.

After another moment an answering signal was received and contact was established. The image of Braxjandar appeared on the screen—but it said nothing. Qetjnegartis was irritated, but there was nothing it could do—it was indeed the supplicant here. "Greetings Commander Braxjandar of the glorious Mavnaltak Clan," it said. "Many thanks for this meeting."

"Greetings Qetjnegartis of the *mighty* Bajantus Clan," came the reply. "What assistance can we render to you?"

More insults. It knows perfectly well our situation!

"We are under attack by very strong forces of the prey-creatures. We need your assistance or we may be destroyed. The Colonial Conclave has already agreed that you should render us this assistance. I need to know when the assistance will arrive."

"Yes, the Conclave's directive," said Braxjandar. "We have received it and of course we shall obey. However, that directive also acknowledges that we are not required to take any action which would put our own... interests in peril. Considering how *very dangerous* you have proven the prey creatures to be, I am not sure how much force I dare send so far into *your* territory. What if we are suddenly attacked while our rescue force is off assisting you?"

"Have you discovered strong enemy forces moving against you?" demanded Qetjnegartis.

"No, not at present, but I would hate to find myself drawn into a trap—as you were."

"Then the sooner you assist us here, the sooner your forces can return to your own territory."

"Perhaps. But it is a great distance. If the distance were less, perhaps..."

Now we get to it.

"What do you want, Braxjandar?"

"I believe that moving the boundary between our territories south five hundred telequels would be sufficient to address my concerns."

"Five hundred!" exclaimed Qetjnegartis. It had been expecting a demand of this nature, but not that large! "That would make your territory nearly twice as large as mine!"

"Our clans' territory," corrected Braxjandar. "Surely you are not claiming the territory for yourself, Qetjnegartis?"

"No, of course not. But five hundred..."

"You are having such difficulty defending what you currently hold, it would be illogical to burden your clan with more. I am quite certain the Conclave would agree."

Qetjnegartis hesitated. Did that mean the Colonial Conclave had already agreed in secret? Prior to the launch of the expedition there had been extensive negotiations in the Council of Three Hundred about where each clan would land and where the boundaries of its territory would lie. The powerful clans laid claim to what they thought would be the most desirable areas. But it was acknowledged that these boundaries might need to be adjusted once the actual conditions on the planet were discovered. They had devised a Colonial Conclave whereby the clans on the target world could coordinate their efforts. Its authority did not supersede that of the Council back on the Homeworld, but it could not be ignored, either.

"If you do not agree," continued Braxjandar, "you can wait for the reinforcements which will soon launch from the Homeworld. But of course they will take an eighth of a cycle to get here and if they arrive too late, then in all probability the Conclave would direct me to take charge of all the territory once assigned to the Unfortunate Bajantus Clan. Tragic, but necessary."

Qetjnegartis' tendril clutched the interface more tightly. Braxjandar held every advantage and they both knew it. If Braxjandar failed to render assistance it might face the criticism of the Conclave, but that would not change the fact that Qetjnegartis and the others, along with the Bajantus Clans' presence on this world, would be no more. As a further reminder, a strong tremor ran through the control center as another prey-creature projectile struck overhead. No, there was no choice.

"Very well. I agree to these conditions. When can your assistance arrive? And how much will you send?"

"Excellent," said Braxjandar and there was no mistaking its satisfaction. "I knew that you could be counted on to act wisely, Qetjnegartis."

"When?!"

"Patience. I will send fifteen fighting machines—my entire reserve. They will arrive in between five and ten days. The area between us is unexplored so it is impossible to precisely predict the travel time. Can you hold out that long?"

"We shall have to."

* * * * *

AUGUST 1909, BALTIMORE, MARYLAND

"Ah, he's waking up, I think."

"He woke up earlier today, but wasn't really coherent. He should be doing better now that the fever's broken."

Leonard Wood could hear the voices. He'd been hearing voices on and off for what seemed like ages, but they had never been this clear. He could understand them now. One sounded very familiar…

"Come on, Leonard, open those eyes. You've been sleeping long enough!"

Roosevelt.

He made an enormous effort and cracked open one of his eyes. The room seemed dazzlingly bright, but one enormous figure was standing at the foot of the bed and slowly came into focus. Yes, it was him, huge teeth revealed in an equally huge grin, bristly mustache above, and two eyes crinkling in delight behind the pince-nez glasses. "Well! There you are!" he boomed. "Welcome back to the land of the living! You gave us a nasty scare there, you know?"

"What… what happened…?" he managed to croak. "How long…?"

"Almost two weeks! You go off and leave me to run the war all by myself, Leonard! Not at all fair!"

"Two weeks? But the doctor said…" His eyes drifted across the other figures in the room and finally came to rest on Doctor Cushing.

The man shrugged. "The operation itself went fine, but you came down with a bad infection afterward. As the President said, we nearly lost you. How are you feeling now?"

"Tired. But all right I guess." He paused and wiggled his hands and feet under the sheets. "No numbness, no tingling. A definite improvement."

"I'm not surprised. It was a sizeable tumor and pressing on the brain significantly. With its removal your symptoms should not recur."

"When… when can I get out of here?" Two weeks! He didn't want to even think about the amount of work that must have piled up!

"With anyone else I'd want them to remain here for another week. But I know perfectly well that you won't agree to that, General. So, if you continue to improve, I can release you in two days. But you *will* have to take it easy for a while."

"Yes, and you need to rest now," said Roosevelt. "I just wanted to drop in and see you for a bit. We'll talk again once you're back to Washington."

"Theodore… Mr. President, wait," said Wood reaching out his hand. "What's been happening? Has Funston launched his attack?"

Roosevelt looked to Cushing who shrugged in resignation and said, "Just a few minutes, if you please, sir."

"Very well then," said Roosevelt, taking a chair, reversing it, and sitting down next to Wood.

"Funston hasn't attacked yet, but he promises that he will in just a few days. He's very confident of success."

"Good, good. Has anything else critical happened?"

"Oh, there're mountains of things for you to go through when you're up and about, but… only one thing that's really critical." The President paused and his face grew serious.

"What's happened, sir?"

"Well, Leonard, just as we feared, with Mars approaching opposition, they've started launching cylinders again."

"Dear God. How many?"

"Three salvos of ten so far. They started three days ago and naturally we don't know how many more they plan to launch."

"And they'll be here in four months?"

"It seems likely. The astronomers mostly agree and it's what some of them predicted."

"So we need to get ready for another invasion."

"Yes. Get well soon, Leonard. We need you."

CHAPTER FOUR

AUGUST 1909, WASHINGTON, D.C.

Andrew Comstock ducked his head slightly to pass beneath the arch of crossed sabers held by a dozen fellow officers. Victoria, clutching his arm and pressed close, didn't have to worry. The look of absolute delight on her face filled him with a matching joy. The addition of the President to the guest list had transformed their wedding from a modest thing that was to be held in the Fort Meyer's chapel to a gala event held in St. John's Episcopal Church on Lafayette Square just a block from the White House. The church had been designed by the noted architect Benjamin Latrobe and had been used by every president since Madison. But it wasn't a huge church and much of the crowd of guests, onlookers, and newspaper men had spilled out onto the sidewalks and across 16th Street.

Beyond the rows of officers were more well-wishers, many of them friends of Victoria, who threw handfuls of rice at them. Andrew had always thought this a rather stupid tradition, but the barrage largely bounded off his tightly buttoned dress blue uniform. Victoria's frilly wedding gown had vastly more nooks and crannies to catch the grains and he imagined she would be picking rice out of her dress for weeks. Perhaps tonight he'd help her with that...

They were quickly past the rice-throwers and saw their carriage waiting for them at the curb. President Roosevelt and his family were also waiting, Roosevelt beaming as though it was his daughter who was getting married. His own carriage waited just behind the one for the new Mr. and Mrs. Comstock. Andrew helped his bride aboard and seated himself beside her, and after a moment they were off. A squad of cavalry preceded them and another brought up the rear, behind the President's carriage. Quite a mob of people were lining the streets, waving and cheering. The whole thing was beginning to feel like a fairy tale.

Andrew had to remind himself that this wasn't really for Victoria and himself—or at least not completely. Colonel Hawthorne, his father-in-law—that would take some getting used to!—had explained that the President's advisors felt that this would be a good boost to public moral. After so much bad news from around the world, the sight of an army hero getting married would be a welcome change. He still had trouble thinking of himself as a hero, but if this could help the effort against the Martians, why not? And Victoria was certainly enjoying it!

"Quite a day, isn't it, Mrs. Comstock?" He had to nearly shout to be heard.

"Oh, it's so splendid, Mr. Comstock!" she shouted back. "Something to remember always!"

The ride was short, just a turn around Lafayette Square and then into the grounds of the White House—where the reception was being held. Mrs. Roosevelt loved to entertain, he'd heard, and apparently she wasn't passing up this opportunity. He vaguely remembered all the hoopla when her step-daughter, Alice, had gotten married back in '05—before the Martians returned.

Unfortunately, before they could retreat to the cooler confines of the White House, photographs were demanded outside and this required nearly half an hour in the sweltering heat and humidity of August in Washington. Andrew could feel the sweat dripping down inside the wool of his coat. But finally they were released and the President escorted them inside where they were offered ice water before being forced to stand in a receiving line for another hour.

He only knew a handful of people who came past them for handshakes. The vast majority were there for Roosevelt; senators and congressmen (despite Congress being out of session for the summer), judges and cabinet members, foreign ambassadors and diplomats and high-ranking military personnel. General Wood, the Chief of Staff, his head bandaged from a recent operation, was allowed to jump to the head of the line. "Congratulation, Major," he said shaking his hand. "Oh, I have something for you and…"

"Now, now, Leonard!" interrupted the President. "Don't spoil the surprise! That will come later!"

Wood smiled and rolled his eyes. "Very well, Mr. President. We all know how you love surprises." He kissed Victoria's hand, and moved on.

"What was that all about?" whispered Victoria.

He shrugged and shook his head. He had no idea.

Eventually, they had greeted everyone and moved into the East Room for the reception. The huge room was breathtaking with its cream walls, four marble fireplaces (thankfully unlit), parquet floors, and three immense crystal chandeliers. They were seated at the head table, of course, along with Victoria's parents and Andrew's mother who was still wearing the look of stunned astonishment that she'd had ever since she'd been told what was going to happen today. He was glad she had been able to come. She'd been a virtual recluse ever since his father's death. Victoria's maid of honor was there, too, but Roosevelt had rather ruthlessly supplanted Andrew's best man, an old Academy friend, from his traditional position. Hawthorne said it was probably because the President had something important to say.

And so it proved. They hadn't been seated more than a few minutes and the waiters had barely been given time to fill the champagne glasses of all the guests before Roosevelt got to his feet. The man's commanding presence got him almost complete silence in just a few moments. "My friends!" he said, his high-pitched voice carrying easily to every corner of the large room. "My friends, I have three things to say to you today. First, of course, is to wish the new Major and Mrs. Comstock a long life, children, health, and happiness!" He raised his glass and everyone else did likewise in the toast. Victoria was blushing and Andrew knew that he was, too, but fortunately, he wasn't expected—or given the opportunity—to say anything in reply. Roosevelt was already moving on. "Secondly, I want to acknowledge an American hero! Most of you have heard of the exploits of Major Comstock in the recent campaign. Caught up in the disaster of General Sumner's army, instead of fleeing like most men would, he rallied his command and pressed on to carry out his mission. Armed with little more than his wits, he destroyed a Martian tripod, learned vital information about the enemy's activities, and then led an enemy force into an ambush masterfully set by General Funston. Such heroism must be recognized!" The guests broke into spirited applause and Andrew was blushing again.

"In the past," continued the President, "the only award we had for heroism was the Medal of Honor. This had to be approved by Congress. But the war we now find ourselves in will produce heroes in such numbers that I fear Congress, with its already so busy schedule, will find itself overwhelmed!" Roosevelt grinned and the crowd laughed. They knew that he was getting in a dig at the legislative body for taking the summer off.

"So! Working with the Secretary of War and the Chief of Staff, we have devised a new set of awards which can be given out by the army without legislative approval. I'm pleased to announce that the very first of these, the Distinguished Service Cross, will be bestowed on Major Comstock today!"

More applause, and Andrew was in a daze. He found himself propelled forward to where General Wood was waiting. Wood already had a Medal of Honor for his own exploits in tracking down Geronimo. He held up a bronze medal on a blue ribbon with red and white stripes on the edges. The medal was indeed cross-shaped, with an eagle with outstretched wings in the middle. Wood pinned it to his tunic and said a few words, which Andrew entirely failed to hear. He mumbled something back but could never remember what. More applause and eventually he was back in his seat with Victoria clutching his arm. She squealed in delight, but Roosevelt was speaking again.

"Finally, I want to announce some other very good news. After months of preparation, tomorrow General Funston will launch his final attack to destroy the Martian fortress in New Mexico!" This brought cheers, not just applause. Many people got to their feet and shouted in joy. "Yes, we are at last to see the turn of the tide! Up until now the enemy has had it almost entirely their way. They overrun our lands, destroy our cities, and kill our people. And let's be honest: other countries have suffered far worse than our own. The Martians have seized vast stretches of our world and while we have at some points checked their advance, at no point have we managed to roll them back—until now! The destruction of the New Mexico fortress will be a sign to all—human and Martian alike!—that Earth shall not fall to the invader! Yes, we've all heard that more of the weasels are on the way, but the Martians can be beaten and we will beat them!"

The room erupted and Andrew and Victoria joined in the cheers. The President surely knew how to inspire a crowd! But as he'd been warned by his father-in-law, sometimes he didn't know when enough was enough. The President went on for at least another twenty minutes with his inspiring oratory, even though everyone could see the waiters clustered nervously in the doors, unable to serve the food while Roosevelt was speaking. But eventually he did finish up and sit down and things proceeded more or less normally from there, although the first two courses were cool and a bit congealed.

Still, it was all splendid and many toasts were drunk to all sorts of things. Later, members of the Marine Corps Band provided music for dancing. Victoria and Andrew danced first, of course, but then she danced with her father and Andrew danced with his mother—although he practically had to drag her out onto the floor. After that, more couples spilled out onto the floor and things became very merry.

At one point, Andrew, to his surprise, found himself dancing with the President's oldest daughter, Alice Roosevelt Longworth. The woman had been a famous beauty in her early days in the White House and was still very attractive. She seemed to be looking him over with a keen eye. "The medal suits you very well, Major," she said.

"Uh, thank you, ma'am. It was quite unexpected."

"I'm sure it was, but it does suit you. Very well indeed. A shame we are both married," she ended with a slightly wistful sigh.

"Uh, I, uh, don't think it's a shame at all," Andrew choked out.

Mrs. Longworth laughed. "No, I suppose not. But the thrill will wear off, believe me!" The dance finished and Andrew fled back to Victoria.

The wonderful day drew on and people started to leave, but Roosevelt pulled him aside. "So Major, it's none of my business, but what sort of plans do you have for your honeymoon?"

"Oh, well, we have a room booked at a hotel here in town for tonight. But that's about all, sir. What with my duties and all we couldn't plan for anything longer. Maybe someday we'll go up to Niagara Falls—assuming Tesla hasn't burned the place down."

Roosevelt guffawed and actually slapped his thigh. "Ha! I hope you can get there! But I'm thinking I can do a bit better by way of a wedding gift!"

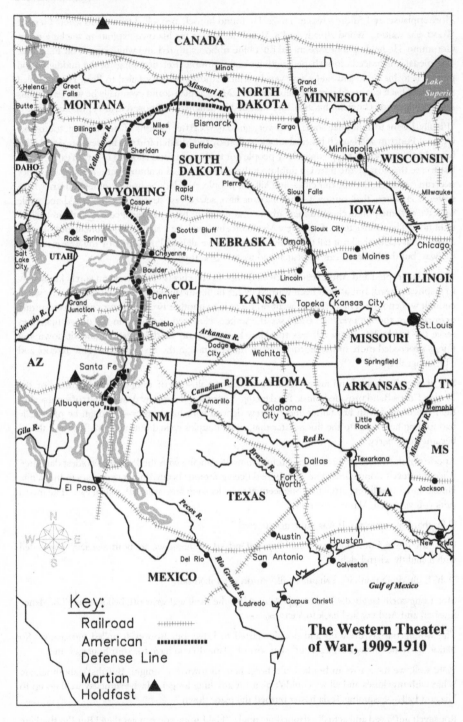

Key:

Railroad +++++++++++

American ••••••••••
Defense Line

Martian ▲
Holdfast

The Western Theater
of War, 1909-1910

"Sir?"

"I'm off to Panama next week to inspect the work there. I asked General Crozier for a man to look at the fortifications being constructed and he gave me several choices." He looked at Andrew with a shrewd eye. "How would you and your lovely bride like to take a little honeymoon cruise?"

"V-Victoria, too?"

"Of course! Wouldn't be much of a honeymoon without her, would it? But we'll be going on the *Mayflower*. She's got plenty of accommodations for women. Edith and I have taken several cruises aboard her. We won't be gone long, maybe three weeks. So what do you say?"

What *could* he say? "I... uh, we would be honored, Mr. President!"

"Bully! Bully!"

* * * * *

AUGUST 1909, NEAR FORT WINGATE, NEW MEXICO TERRITORY

The bombardment started before dawn.

The steady rumble and flicker of the guns, which had been a constant presence for weeks, suddenly became a roar, an earthshaking noise that went on and on without pause. The light on the outside of Rebecca's tent was almost continuous, like the worst lightning storm she'd ever seen—except even worse.

She'd been waiting for this—everyone knew it was coming—and she was already dressed. The other nurses and Miss Chumley were awake and ready, too. They drifted out of their tents without a word and walked toward the guns. Becca led the way to her hilltop vantage point and the others followed. From there they could see everything. The artillery positions were already wreathed in clouds of smoke which slowly drifted east in the still air. As each gun fired, the smoke around it lit up like a lantern—and a dozen guns were going off every second. The light was bright enough to cause the women and the tree stumps to cast distinct shadows. The noise was even louder here, the concussions thumping against her chest and making her ears ring. Some of the shells shrieked like banshees as they wailed away from the guns.

But Rebecca was more interested in where the shells were *going*. The Martian fortress was looming darkly in the distance and it, too, was blanketed in smoke as the rounds slammed down and exploded with more flickers of light. Most of the flashes were muted by the smoke but sometimes they were clearer and sharper. After watching for a while there was suddenly a much brighter flare; an eye-aching blaze of brilliant blue light which lit up the entire countryside for a moment and left an after-image throbbing in Becca's sight.

"What was that?" cried one of the nurses.

Becca remembered how one of the Martian tripods had exploded with a flash just like that during the Battle of Prewitt. That ordnance officer, Major Comstock, had said something about the power supply shorting out. Perhaps the same thing had happened here to one of the Martian defense towers. She didn't really care so long as it was hurting the enemy.

"Dear God," said another woman, pointing to the barrage, "I wouldn't want to be under that!"

"The *Martians* are under that!" she said fiercely.

The tableaux was mesmerizing; flash, flash, boom, boom. Rebecca felt she could watch it forever. But time was passing and she slowly realized that the darkness was receding. She glanced behind her and saw the mountain peaks to the southeast were touched with pink. The plain in front of her was no longer a featureless black. The lines of trenches could be seen now; the dozens and dozens of steam tanks in rows behind them. The guns were still barely to be seen in their smoke clouds, but from time to time a gun or a crewman or a truck carrying ammunition would become visible.

The wind was starting to freshen and some of the gun smoke was reaching her on the hill. The acrid metallic smell and taste of cordite and gun cotton tickled her nose and throat. It wasn't pleasant, but right now she'd choose it over the finest perfume.

With a start she discovered they weren't alone. Off to her left, just thirty yards away, was an observation post. Four men with field glasses and a telegraph. They'd been there all along and in the dark she hadn't seen them. They must be spotting for the artillery.

As the sky started becoming blue she heard a new sound, a strange drone coming from behind her. Turning, she saw not one, but two flying machines. The flimsy canvas and wood contraptions had been flying around the camps occasionally for a few weeks, but she'd never seen them venture near the enemy fortress. Were they going to do so now? At the moment they were actually below her, but cruising in lazy circles higher and higher. Eventually they were well overhead and the pair straightened out and headed west—toward the enemy.

"Oh! I think something's happening!" cried someone.

Becca quickly looked toward the army and yes, things were starting to move. Thousands of troops, just a brown mass from this distance, were emerging from the trenches, puffs of black smoke were coming from the stacks of the steam tanks and the metal boxes started to lurch forward. The assault was beginning!

The troops formed into a series of thin lines which marched forward, followed by the tanks which maneuvered through gaps in the trench lines. One of them broke down and momentarily blocked the passage of several others until it was ruthlessly pushed aside to clear the way. All the while the artillery kept firing. During previous attacks, the cannon fire slacked off when the assault began, but not this time; the firing maintained its same furious rate. Only when the troops and tanks neared the cloud of smoke and dust that marked the edge of the enemy fortress did the fire falter and only for a moment as the gunners switched to more distant targets.

The soldiers disappeared into the smoke. Becca wished she was with them.

"Come on ladies," said Miss Chumley, barely to be heard in the din. "We need to get back. The wounded will be coming in soon."

Becca didn't want to leave, she wanted to watch. But she had a job to do. She turned and followed the others, casting back one last glance at the scene of battle.

* * * * *

CYCLE 597, 843.8, HOLDFAST 32-1

The floor of the corridor was actually shuddering with the enemy bombardment as the travel chair carrying Qetjnegartis and Davnitargus moved quickly toward the vehicle hanger. Bits of debris were falling from the ceiling almost continuously and several bounced off them.

"This is by far the worst yet," observed Davnitargus, using its tendrils to flick away a fragment of rock.

"Yes, the enemy is committing all their strength against us. Clearly they hope to destroy us with this assault."

"Can they succeed?"

"If no help arrives I believe so. Or at least they may well destroy the holdfast. We must all be prepared to flee. That is why you will accompany us. You and all the buds."

"I understand," said Davnitargus, "but I fear that I may prove of little use in the coming battle. My mastery of the fighting machines' controls is far from complete."

"You underestimate yourself," replied Qetjnegartis. "You have made great progress in just the last few days. I am confident you will do well."

They reached the hanger and saw that the others were already there. The survivors of the Bajantus Clan on the target world: five adults and five buds. Zastranvis was there although its illness had become worse recently. It would be far better off in the main control chamber controlling the defense towers and the construction machinery, but if they were forced to flee it would be trapped. It would have to do its job from inside a fighting machine.

Qetjnegartis helped Davnitargus into a machine and then boarded its own. It quickly powered up the machine and checked its function. All was well, of course. It then activated the long-range communicator. "Commander Braxjandar, please reply, this is Qetjnegartis."

Unlike their last conversation, the reply came almost immediately. "Yes, Qetjnegartis, what do you want?"

"The enemy has launched its attack and I see little hope of resisting it. When can I expect your arrival?"

"We are fifty telequel northwest of your position. The terrain is quite difficult. I estimate two or three tenthdays to cover it."

Qetjnegartis had feared that this would be the case. "I do not know if we can hold out that long."

"Make your best effort. If you are forced to abandon your holdfast we will rendezvous with you, and if the situation permits, a counterattack can be launched. I can promise no more."

"Very well, Commander, we will hold out as long as we can. When you near our position, please contact me again. I may be able to help with your tactical dispositions."

"I understand, Qetjnegartis," replied Braxjandar. There was nothing more to be said and the connection was broken.

Qetjnegartis switched the communicator to connect with the other nine members of the clan. "Now we must fight. Help is coming, but it will not arrive for some time. We must delay the enemy as long as possible without sacrificing ourselves needlessly. Follow me."

It turned its machine and headed up the ramp to the surface. The others followed.

* * * * *

AUGUST 1909, NORTH OF FORT WINGATE, NEW MEXICO TERRITORY

First Sergeant Frank Dolfen was riding north in the darkness when he suddenly saw his own shadow flickering on the ground in front of him. Twisting around in his saddle, he looked back and saw the southern sky lit up with an amazing glow. Without a word of command, the entire troop came to a halt. After many long seconds a low rumble rolled across the prairie like distant thunder—except once started it never stopped.

"God!" exclaimed Corporal Urbaniak. "Will you look at that!"

"Really pulling out all the stops, ain't they?" said Private Cordwainer. "Damn! Wish they'd let us stay back there so's we could watch!" Some of the new recruits were chattering excitedly in Polish or Hungarian.

"All right! All right! Quit gawking and move out!" said Dolfen. "We've got a job to do!" The column lurched back into motion.

In truth, Dolfen was wishing the same thing as Private Cordwainer. The big attack was finally underway and here they were being sent off in the opposite direction! But orders were orders. A few frantic refugees had come into the camps yesterday babbling about Martian machines off to the north. The army had been scouting in all directions, of course, but none of the patrols had reported anything. But apparently the refugees had been convincing enough that the generals wanted to be sure. So the 5th had been ordered out. They had left in the middle of the night and were already fifteen miles north of where Gallup had once stood, passing through the tiny towns of Gamerco and Ya-Ta-Hay. Twin Lakes was just ahead. The aptly named Big Rock Hill was looming off to the right and Chuska Peak, barely visible in the dark, off to the left. They were to push north all the way to Newcomb, another thirty-five miles.

The regiment was following what passed for a road in these parts and it led steadily upward to a high plateau. Dolfen snuck a few looks back to watch the bombardment. It still seemed as intense as ever, although the flashes were being washed out by the growing dawn. *Surely we'll win this time!*

The last attack had nearly worked from what he'd heard and this attack was going to be a lot stronger. The trains had been bringing in more big guns and ammunition week after week. He'd heard some officer say that it was going to be the heaviest bombardment ever fired in North America, outdoing anything in the Civil War. From what he was seeing and hearing, he could believe it.

But he wished he could be there to see it close up. The Martian stronghold ringed what had once been Gallup, New Mexico. It was the nearest town to Fort Wingate, where he'd been stationed before this all began. There'd been a bar in the town... a woman who ran it. What had become of her? From what he'd seen when he climbed the wall that had been raised, there was nothing left of the town, not a stick left standing—not even any ruins. But what had happened to the people? Had any gotten away? Had any been captured? Were any left alive there inside the enemy fortress? He wanted to find out. Well, maybe he'd get the chance later, after they took the place.

The column passed through Twin Lakes, but the two-dozen adobe houses were dark and empty. At this point the regiment started to split up. The second squadron veered east and the third west, while Dolfen, with the first squadron and the regimental headquarters, stayed on the road north. This would allow them to scout the widest possible front. The 5th had done a similar thing off to the south back when they weren't sure if any Martians had even landed. He didn't like to think about how that had turned out.

It was full light now and they were on the flat plateau. The battle around Gallup was lost to sight except for the cloud of dust and smoke hanging overhead, although they could still hear it. He looked around, gauging wind and sky. There was a line of clouds off to the west and he suspected they might get a storm by afternoon. A flash of red on the ground caught Dolfen's eye in the bright morning sunshine. He looked closer and cursed. It was a small patch of that stuff, the 'Red Weed'. Back during the first invasion, the one in England, huge clumps of it had grown up and then mostly died off again. The experts said it was some sort of plant native to Mars which had come along with the invaders. No one knew if it was a deliberate thing or if it had come accidentally with the Martians. In any case, it was an invader, too.

The stuff had been showing up here and there recently. It didn't seem to grow nearly so fast in New Mexico's climate as it had in England, but the order had gone out to destroy it wherever it was found. The areas around the army's encampment had been pretty well scoured, the weed ripped up and burned—and oh how it stank! Farther out, ranchers said that their livestock wouldn't eat it or even go near it, but they feared it might crowd out the native grass they depended on. They were doing what they could to get rid of it, but how could they clean up hundreds of thousands of square miles? Dolfen suspected that once the army destroyed all the Martians, they might still be facing years of 'weed patrol'.

But first things first: they needed to destroy the Martians. There was no time for gardening now!

"Come on you lunks! Pick up the pace! We've got a long way to go!"

* * * * *

CYCLE 597, 843.8, HOLDFAST 32-1

"Some of them are across the ramparts, Commander."

"Yes, that was inevitable," said Qetjnegartis. "More will follow. Zastranvis, direct the secondary line of towers to fire."

"Yes, Commander, but so far they are making poor targets."

Qetjnegartis and the others were waiting just behind the defense towers which quickly began firing their heat rays, sweeping them across the face and top of the ramparts. It was hard to see if they were doing any damage. So far only the foot warriors had shown themselves, but their vehicles were sure to follow soon. Enemy projectiles started to fall all around them now. One of the defense towers was hit and stopped firing. One of the spare fighting machines also took damage.

"Perhaps we should fall back," said Ixmaderna. "Their fire will grow increasingly accurate and we have little opportunity to strike back from here."

"Yes, soon. Let them waste time aiming their weapons here and then we will move."

"As you say, Commander."

Qetjnegartis could not tell if his attempt to appear calm and confident was working, but his subordinates were obeying and that was what mattered. But things were not going well. The prey-creatures' bombardment had been truly devastating. The line of defense towers on the outer rampart in Sector 9 and the two adjacent sectors had been obliterated in a shockingly short time. Now the fire had shifted to the secondary line of towers inside the ramparts and unlike during previous attacks this was not poorly aimed or sporadic. It was intense and well directed—perhaps by the two flying machines that circled the holdfast. The enemy's ability to fire in an arc from long range made the standard defensive tactics almost useless. It required a prodigious expenditure of resources, of course, tens of thousands of projectiles were needed, but the prey-creatures seemed to have the resources to spend.

One by one the defense towers were destroyed and when one of the spare fighting machines was crippled Qetjnegartis decided it was time to retreat. In the past few days they had constructed a small redoubt in the center of the holdfast. It was a circular rampart less than half a telequel in diameter with more defense towers on the parapet. The fighting machines quickly made their way there and took refuge inside. Qetjnegartis was pleased at how the buds were able to keep up. They were doing very well in piloting the machines. How they would do in combat remained to be seen. Once inside the redoubt they were free from the bombardment for a while—but the enemy attack continued.

"There are enemy vehicles on top of the outer rampart," reported Zastranvis. "And more foot warriors inside of it."

Shortly after that the enemy projectiles began to pummel the redoubt. Only a few at first, but then more and more. One of the spare fighting machines was destroyed and then Namatchgar's machine was so badly damaged it had to transfer to one of the other spares.

"This is no good, Commander!" said Ixmaderna. "We're crammed into this small space and the enemy fire is even more concentrated!"

It was true, instead of the redoubt being a refuge, it was a death trap. But what to do? Help was still at least a tenthday off, maybe more. Commander Braxjandar's predictions about their arrival time were alarmingly imprecise. Retreating again seemed the only wise choice, but it rankled to be driven like prey! Qetjnegartis longed to strike back, but to attack now into the massed strength of the enemy would be suicide. Each member of the Race was expendable—but only if their death accomplished something!

"The defense towers on the rampart in Sector 4 are still intact, Commander," said Zastranvis. "Perhaps we could fall back to them." Yes, the side of the holdfast directly opposite where the enemy attack had been concentrated had not been bombarded at all.

"Very well," it said. "We will make our stand there and hold until help arrives." They moved out immediately and quickly fell back to the far side of the redoubt. This appeared to catch the enemy by surprise because once they were out of the deadly trap no more fire bothered them for some time. They reached the rampart in Sector 4 and stopped there to await developments. Unfortunately, something developed almost at once.

"Commander," said Zastranvis, "I have been monitoring the internal vision pick-ups inside the lower parts of the holdfast."

"And?"

"Commander, the enemy is inside."

* * * * *

AUGUST 1909, NORTH OF FORT WINGATE, NEW MEXICO TERRITORY

The noise of the battle could still be clearly heard even though they were almost thirty miles away now. Dolfen remembered talking with a Civil War veteran when he was a new recruit; the man had told him that he'd been able to hear the great bombardment before Pickett's Charge at Gettysburg while he was in Lancaster—over fifty miles away. *They can probably hear this in Albuquerque!*

The column was just north of Tohatchi, a village that was part of the Navaho reservation. They were passing small groups of Indians fleeing south. When asked what they were running from, they just said trouble. The answers sent a chill through Dolfen. They'd gotten exactly the same answers from the Indians they'd encountered in that disastrous expedition south last fall. He exchanged looks with Corporal Urbaniak—he'd been there, too.

"Got a bad feelin' about this, Sarge."

"Yeah." He nudged his horse into a faster pace and caught up with Captain DeBrosse. "Captain? If we do run into those bastards—and it seems like we might—we gotta be ready."

"We will be," replied DeBrosse immediately. But then he paused, looked uncertain, and said: "Uh, do you have any suggestions, First Sergeant?"

"If there are a lot of them we need to be ready to run and run fast, sir. Their damn machines aren't quite as fast as a horse, but they don't get tired. Given time, they can run us down. Our horses are already tired and…"

"Our job is to scout, First Sergeant. If a strong enemy force is moving against General Funston's flank, he needs to be warned."

"I understand that, sir, and it was a good idea of the colonel's to drop off squads along the way behind us to rest their horses so they can relay messages back at a gallop, but that won't do the rest of us any good if we're caught out here."

The captain was silent for a few moments. "What can we do that we're not already?"

"We should stop the squadron here and let our scouts get farther ahead, sir. With the pace we've been pushing, they're scarcely a mile in front of us—hell, I can see them from here! We need to rest our horses a bit so if we have to run we can do it."

"I… I'll suggest that to the colonel. Thank you, First Sergeant."

"But…"

"*Thank you*, First Sergeant."

244

Dolfen realized there was no point in arguing further. He nodded to DeBrosse and then fell back.

"Well?" asked Urbaniak when he drew abreast.

"The Young Napoleon is gonna talk with the colonel."

Urbaniak snorted and then spat. "Think he'll listen?"

"He might." The colonel of the regiment was new, too, but at least he was a regular. As he watched, DeBrosse rode to where the colonel and his staff were clustered. They appeared to be talking, but there was no way to tell what was being said. But after a minute or two a bugler sounded the halt.

"Well I'll be damned," said Urbaniak.

"Yeah. I'm surprised that... hey... wait..." There was a sudden flurry of activity around the command group. What was going on...?

"Sarge!" cried Urbaniak. "Look out there! To the right of those cliffs! Are those...?"

"Oh, hell!" Some objects had moved into view from around the edge of Chuska Ridge. They looked way too familiar. Dolfen fumbled out a pair of field glasses he'd bought for himself when he became first sergeant. He trained them, focused them, looked. "Hell!" he said again.

"Martians?"

"Yeah." He licked his suddenly dry lips and resisted the urge to reach for his canteen—or the flask he always carried.

"How many?"

He was counting. *Seven, eight, nine...*

"Fifteen."

"Oh, shit!"

* * * * *

AUGUST 1909, NEAR FORT WINGATE, NEW MEXICO TERRITORY

"It's just some cracked ribs, Private," said Rebecca Harding. "You're going to be fine. We'll get you wrapped up. How'd this happen?"

"Ooh," groaned the soldier. "M'own damn fault, miss, didn't get out of the way quick enough and the recoil caught me."

"Artillery?"

"Yeah, 104th Field Artillery. Damn, what a stupid thing t'do! Beggin' your pardon, miss."

"Don't worry about it," said Becca. She wrapped the bandages around the man's torso and then sent him off to one of the wards. She looked around for new patients, but there weren't any at present. So far things had been pretty quiet in the hospital. The guns continued to roar in the distance, but casualties had been light and almost entirely accidents involving the artillery. The men tried to fire the big guns so quickly—sometimes too quickly. Aside from the cracked ribs, they'd had two broken arms, a dislocated shoulder, and one poor guy who'd lost three fingers to a howitzer's breech block. About average, really.

But it was only a matter of time before a lot worse started coming in. She wasn't sure which she hated more, the burns or the dust casualties. A person caught fully by a heat ray was reduced to ash and was beyond any help, but sometimes a man would only be grazed by the ray. An arm or a leg would be burned—sometimes burned completely off—or the man's clothing would catch fire producing less severe burns, but all over. They were awful for the victim and difficult to treat effectively. Burn patients filled entire wards back in Santa Fe. But if the man managed to survive for a week or two they usually recovered.

245

Dust casualties, though…

The black dust the Martians sometimes used was fiendish. A man who inhaled a lot of it was dead in minutes and never reached the hospital. Someone who breathed in just a few grains was just as dead, but it could take them days or weeks to die. The stuff literally dissolved the victim's lungs and no one ever recovered. She remembered one man back in Santa Fe who looked like he was going to be the exception. He'd been brought in and put in the special ward for dust casualties and after nearly a month he appeared to be recovering. And then one afternoon he suddenly started coughing up blood and was dead in an hour.

Getting the stuff on your skin wasn't quite so deadly, but it was far more ghastly. It dissolved skin and muscle just like it would dissolve lungs. A single grain would start burning its way into a person and left untreated it could melt a chunk the size of a fist. And that was just one grain. A lot of them could burn off an arm or a leg or a face in short order. The best treatment, oddly enough, was alcohol. Pure grain alcohol would dilute the dust and it could be sluiced away. But it took quite a lot because just a little only liquefied the dust into a solution which still worked like acid. There had been attempts to supply the troops with alcohol for first aid, but inevitably it had found its way into the soldiers' stomachs instead of onto dust wounds. If no alcohol was available, then heat would also work. Steam or fire would stop it—but obviously with serious pain and damage to the patient. Water could wash the dust away, but only if used instantly. Once the grains started burning into you, water was useless.

The soldiers—the nurses, too, for that matter—had been equipped with dust masks to protect the face and lungs, and gloves and leggings to keep the dust off their skin. But they were only partially effective at best. A person caught full in a dust cloud would be so covered with the stuff that it was nearly impossible for them to get out of their clothes without getting some of it on them—or in them. They had set up a facility where soldiers could be cleaned off with controlled blasts of steam, but it didn't seem to work all that well. And a dust-covered soldier was a menace to everyone around them. Becca had heard stories of men being shot by their own friends—whether out of mercy or fear, she wasn't sure.

The only bright spot about the dust was that once exposed to air and sun it did seem to break down pretty quickly. After a few days an area which had been covered in it wasn't dangerous anymore. Sometimes badly covered soldiers could just sit down and wait it out. And the Martians didn't seem to be using it so much lately; maybe they were running out. She hoped there wouldn't be any dust victims today.

Confirming that there was no immediate work to be done, Becca went outside the tent and looked to the west. The guns were still firing, perhaps not quite so quickly as before, but the sun was well up in the sky now and it seemed like they'd been firing forever. She walked over to one of the ambulance drivers, a man she knew named Simms, and asked: "Any word about what's happenin'?"

"I heard some rumors that our troops are over the walls and inside."

"They never managed to do that before, did they?" asked Becca. "So we're winnin'?"

"Sure seems like it! I've been here since the beginning and every other time we never got past the outer wall. Maybe we can beat these sons-o-bitches this time!" He glanced at her and added, "Sorry."

"Cuss 'em all you like! I sure do!"

Simms laughed but then straightened up and pointed. "Looks like you've got some customers." Sure enough, an ambulance was approaching, a motor-powered one; they didn't use horse-drawn ones near the front lines because of the dust problems. Becca didn't like to think about what the black dust did to horses. It pulled to a stop outside the big receiving tent. Becca ran over to see if they needed help.

The doors opened and she could hear shouting. One voice was high-pitched and unintelligible. Several others, however…

"Hold him down!"

"Trying to, dammit! He's strong!"

"Well tie him to the stretcher if you have to!"

Several more Medical Corps men crowded into the vehicle and after a bit unloaded a stretcher with a patient on it. Becca had expected it to be some poor fellow, frantic with terrible burns, but she was surprised that there didn't appear to be any burns on his uniform. A dust victim, perhaps? But wait… the uniform was in tatters and incredibly filthy. The man had long shaggy hair and a thick beard—both against regulation. A puff of wind brought an awful stench to her nostrils. What in the world…?

The man caught sight of her and tried to lurch upright on the stretcher, but his arms were tied to the poles and he couldn't. He started to scream, "Run girl! Run! Don't let 'em get you! They eat us! *They eat us!*" His voice rose to a shriek.

Becca stood there, frozen in horror, as the man was carried away.

"Saints preserve us!" said Simms coming up next to her. "What happened to that poor devil?"

"I don't know," she whispered, but she was afraid that she did.

A moment later another ambulance arrived, this one carrying an infantryman with a badly broken leg, and Becca shook off her shock and went to work. It was a compound fracture with the bone sticking out through the skin. She helped one of the surgeons work on it. The man was in a lot of pain and she tried to distract him. "How'd this happen, soldier?"

"Fell off the wall," he replied through gritted teeth.

"Inside the fortress? Our troops are inside?"

"Yeah… yeah… got a little too excited, I guess… tripped and fell and… but the others are in."

"Good, good! Well done, soldier!"

"Dunno about that… *this* sure wasn't well done!" He gestured to his leg.

"Don't you worry! We'll get you fixed up and…"

Before she could go on, an officer dashed into the tent and shouted: "Drop whatever you're doing and get ready to move! Right now!"

The man turned to leave, but one of the surgeons stopped him. "Move? Why? What's happening, Lieutenant?"

"Martians! There's a bunch of 'em coming down from the north and they're headed straight for us!"

CHAPTER FIVE

CYCLE 597, 843.8, HOLDFAST 32-1

Qetjnegartis' machine shuddered with another near miss. There didn't seem to be any damage from it, but it was only a matter of time until something did hurt it critically. The situation was growing increasingly desperate and it knew it would have to make some serious decisions very soon.

The respite they had gained from retreating to the far side of the holdfast had lasted longer than Qetjnegartis had expected. First, the enemy had spent time to destroy the defense towers on the redoubt, even though they didn't really matter anymore. Then, it seemed that the move had put them out of range of the smaller projectile throwers and only the very largest ones had been able to reach that far. Unfortunately, the fire soon became heavier again. The enemy was moving the smaller weapons forward and the bigger ones were finding the new range.

Enemy vehicles and foot warriors were inside the ramparts now and advancing across the open ground toward them. Others were sweeping around the top of the ramparts in both directions, destroying the defense towers one by one. It wouldn't be long before they were attacked on three sides.

Braxjandar was close now, but unless relief arrived very soon, it might well be too late. What was the proper course? Fighting to destruction would achieve nothing. But if the holdfast was lost with its construction machines, factories, and all their equipment, it would also be a disaster. The prey-creatures had gotten inside the underground sections, but so far had not penetrated to the vital areas. Given time they no doubt would.

The fighting machines had a limited self-repair ability, but they were not capable of constructing other machines. And without access to the holdfast's central generator, they would eventually become immobilized as their power was exhausted. Forced to flee into the wilderness, the clan would have little hope of building a new holdfast. Even the reinforcements on the way from the Homeworld would be of little help when they arrived since they were carrying primarily people rather than equipment. At best, the Bajantus Clan would have to indenture themselves to some other clan, losing their independence and all prestige. It was a fate little better than destruction.

"Progenitor, the enemy comes within range," said Davnitargus over the communicator. "May I fire at them?"

What the bud had said was true, foot warriors were getting close and some of the self-propelled projectile throwers not far behind. "Yes. Fire at anything that gets close enough."

Almost instantly a heat ray leapt from the projector on Davnitargus' machine. But it was poorly aimed and shot harmlessly into the sky. The bud brought the ray down but was soon blasting the ground far short of where the enemy was moving. "Carefully!" cautioned Qetjnegartis. "And fire in short bursts. If you fire for too long you could overheat the projector."

"I understand, Commander." It could sense the bud's frustration, but Davnitargus ceased fire, waiting for a moment, and then fired again. This time its aim was better, but still not very good. All the others were firing now, too, and the adults swept their rays across the lines of foot warriors. Some were slain and the others dove for the cover of the rocks. The defense towers on the rampart started to fire too, and the area to their front soon became an inferno.

But the enemy was firing back. Small projectiles from the foot warriors were bouncing off the machines' armor and the larger weapons on the enemy vehicles joined in. The distant projectile throwers rained down in a growing storm. One of the defense towers right behind Qetjnegartis collapsed in ruin and the others were taking damage. Not being able to move like the war machines made them particularly vulnerable.

Despite its warning, Davnitargus managed to overheat its ray projector and had to cease fire until it cooled. Two of the other buds had done the same and all three fell back behind the adults.

Explosions to the right and left revealed that the enemy forces moving along the top of the ramparts were closing in. They only had to engage a single defense tower at a time and could quickly overwhelm it.

A heavy blow made Qetjnegartis' machine stagger back as a projectile struck it. One of the enemy vehicles had moved in closer through the smoke. It focused its heat ray on the machine and left the beam firing until the enemy exploded. But more vehicles were coming forward.

Suddenly, Zastranvis gave a strange, inarticulate shout over the communicator and its machine charged forward, directly toward the enemy. Its bud followed along, stumbling awkwardly. Qetjnegartis instantly ordered them to come back, but neither obeyed or even responded.

"What is happening?" asked Utnaferdus. "Why don't they obey?"

"It must be the illness," said Ixmaderna. "It had been getting worse and the strain of battle may have unhinged it."

The pair advanced so quickly that the prey-creatures were taken by surprise. The war machines were in among them before they could react. Heat rays stabbed out and one vehicle after another was destroyed. Six of them were left burning in moments. But then the enemy recovered and fire hammered the two machines from all sides. Even the foot warriors were emerging from their hiding places and hurling explosive bombs. The bud's machine fell first, its inexperience with controlling the machine making its situation hopeless. An explosion blew off one of its legs and it toppled over with the other two limbs flailing helplessly. More explosions ripped through the control cockpit and the machine disappeared in a cloud of smoke.

This seemed to send Zastranvis into an even greater frenzy. It spun about, the heat ray blasting in all directions, its manipulator tendrils seized prey-creatures and flung them into the air. But more enemy vehicles and warriors were closing in.

"Can we not help it?" asked Namatchgar.

"We would only share their fate," said Qetjnegartis sternly. In truth it wanted to help, to charge after Zastranvis, but duty demanded it not give in to those feelings.

Zastranvis continued to fight, but its machine was being heavily damaged. The heat ray stopped firing and one of the manipulator tendrils was torn loose. Suddenly the machine was enveloped by a crackling blue globe of energy which was followed by an enormous explosion.

The power cells! Was that due to damage, or did it do this deliberately?

The blast engulfed everything for a hundred quels in every direction, consuming vehicles, foot warriors—and Zastranvis.

When the smoke cleared there was a burned and blackened circle on the ground and the half-melted remains of enemy vehicles. Several more vehicles outside the circle were burning, too.

Other transports and swarms of foot warriors were drawing back, but more were still advancing in the distance. Zastranvis' sacrifice had won them a respite, but it wouldn't last long. *And there are only eight of us left now…*

"Commander Qetjnegartis, respond at once."

The voice coming over the communicator was so unexpected, Qetjnegartis froze for an instant. *Braxjandar!*

"Yes! This is Qetjnegartis! Commander Braxjandar, where are you?"

"We have arrived. We are on the high ground north of your holdfast. I can see that you are under attack. How can we best assist you?"

The immediate instinct was to have Braxjandar bring its forces directly to where Qetjnegartis and its people were huddled. But was that the wisest course? Bring them into this cauldron of fire? No! It was the enemy's long range projectile throwers that were the biggest danger!

"The prey-creatures have a large number of projectile throwers positioned to the east of the holdfast. They are all pointed against us here. If you could move on them quickly you may be able to destroy them before they can turn to face you. Once they are destroyed you can come into the holdfast to assist us further."

"Very well, Qetjnegartis," replied Braxjandar. "We shall do this."

"My thanks. But move quickly before the enemy can redeploy to face you."

"Understood. Moving now."

Qetjnegartis felt a relief pass through it unlike anything it had ever experienced before. Perhaps they would not die today after all.

"Progenitor, are we saved?"

"We can hope so, Davnitargus. But we must hold here for a while longer."

* * * * *

AUGUST 1909, NORTH OF FORT WINGATE, NEW MEXICO TERRITORY

"Crap!" snarled Sergeant Frank Dolfen. "The idiots haven't even turned the guns!"

"There's gonna be hell to pay now, Sarge!" said Corporal Urbaniak.

"What the hell have they been doing? The couriers should have been here at least half an hour ago!"

Dolfen was sitting on his exhausted horse staring down at what could soon become a disaster. Off to the right was the enemy fortress and it seemed to be completely wreathed in smoke. Masses of troops and horses and vehicles were milling around the outside and he could catch glimpses of more up on the walls or even down inside. They had finally managed to break through the defenses—but at the worst possible time.

The 5th had spotted the Martians two hours ago and almost thirty miles away. Couriers had been sent back with a warning immediately and then the rest of the regiment deployed to delay the enemy to give the army time to get ready.

Unfortunately, the Martians refused to be delayed.

Against a human enemy, cavalry was just the thing to delay them. They could dismount and form a skirmish line across the enemy's line of march. The enemy might outnumber the cavalry a hundred to one, but they still couldn't ignore them and just keep marching or the cavalry would pick them off like rabbits. No, the enemy would have to deploy troops to deal with them and that

251

would take time. And as soon as they got too close, the cavalry could hop on their horses and ride away—and then do it all over again a few miles down the road. It was a tried and true tactic which had been used for centuries.

The 5th Cavalry tried it today. A skirmish line was formed with two paces between each trooper, every fourth man holding the horses of the other three a hundred yards to the rear, the machine guns set up at intervals. All by the book. But the Martians hadn't read the book. They just kept coming. The 5th fired away with their rifles and machine guns, but the bullets merely bounced off. The ungainly-looking tripods with their strange but surprisingly fast gait simply walked right through the 5th's line without a pause. Oh, they'd fired their heat rays as they moved and a number of men had died, but the Martians paid them no more heed than a man swatting gnats as he walked. If they'd only had some of those dynamite bombs! They punched through the line and left the cavalry behind. All the cavalry could do was mount up and follow.

Last winter, Frank Dolfen had been chased over half the territory of New Mexico by Martians, so it was novel to be doing the chasing for a change. But it didn't alter the fact that the cavalry had failed in its mission. Instead of giving the army hours or days warning of the enemy's approach, all they were going to be able to give was minutes. And looking down now from the ridge, it seemed that even what little warning they had been able to give had been for naught. The army's attention seemed totally focused on the Martian fortress—not the new enemy coming down on their flank.

The fifteen tripods paused for a moment and then headed down the slope. Not toward the fighting going in and around the fortress, but toward the army's rear area. "The bastards are going for the guns!" cried Urbaniak. And so they were. The army had amassed a huge collection of artillery, everything from the standard three-inch field guns to huge eight and ten-inch monsters that must have been stolen from the Coast Artillery. They, and all their support equipment and ammunition stores, had been set up in a long arc behind the trench lines which paralleled the east side of the enemy fortress.

But they were all facing west and the enemy was coming from the north.

Some of the field guns could be turned quickly enough and Dolfen could see that many of them had already been moved from their revetments, apparently to get them closer to the fortress. They were out in the open field with their horse teams at hand, they were fairly mobile. The heavier guns, though, they would take a lot more time to be turned. And they weren't going to have that time.

The field guns got off a few scattered shots and to Dolfen's delight, one of the tripods actually went down. But the rest kept moving and then the Martians were in range and the heat rays began to stab out. Immediately, explosions erupted as ammunition caissons blew up. Gun crews scattered and horse teams broke loose and bolted. The tripods kept on moving, right into the mass of guns, killing and burning as they went. The artillery couldn't shift its aim quickly enough at such close quarters and shots went screaming off in wild directions. A round whistled over Dolfen's head and exploded a few hundred yards behind him.

"Where are the damn tanks?" cried Urbaniak.

"All inside the fortress, I guess."

"God have mercy. What do we do, Sarge?"

What *could* they do? The regiment was all scattered after the pell-mell pursuit. He didn't know where Captain DeBrosse had gotten to—or if he was even still alive, for that matter. Dolfen had a dozen troopers around him and there were a lot of others in the vicinity, but what could they hope to do now that they hadn't already tried to do before?

"If… if this gets as bad as it might, the army is going to have to retreat. Maybe we can help cover it." He looked around and spotted what he was looking for. "Bugler! Sound the rally! Come on! Follow me!"

* * * * *

AUGUST 1909, NEAR OF FORT WINGATE, NEW MEXICO TERRITORY

"Hurry up! Get those stretchers aboard!" A dozen voices all seemed to be shouting the same thing. Rebecca Harding didn't need to be told! Ever since the warning about the approaching Martians, all the medical personnel, including the nurses, had only thought of one thing: get the wounded out! There hadn't been any great influx of new wounded yet, but the tents had several hundred others from earlier mishaps and skirmishes. They needed to be moved out. They pulled the walking-wounded from their cots and sent them off on foot toward the railhead. The others were put on stretchers, almost heedless of their injuries, and bundled aboard ambulances, wagons, or anything else with wheels and followed those on foot.

Fortunately there were several trains with steam up on the sidings; the army's insatiable demand for supplies and ammunition meant that trains were coming and going almost constantly. Unfortunately, the trains currently there were meant for cargo and not wounded. No matter! Crates were ruthlessly dumped out if the cars weren't already empty and the stretchers loaded aboard. Box cars, flat cars, it made no difference; every square foot of space was taken up with this new, groaning cargo.

One train was filled and moved out, east toward Albuquerque. Becca looked in disgust as dozens of able-bodied men jumped on board as it gathered speed. She helped put another stretcher onto the second train, but that was the last of this first load and there was still plenty of room on the train for more. "All right!" cried Miss Chumley, "Back to the hospital! There are still some men there!"

"Wait!" said one of the surgeons, a captain. "Nurse, maybe you and your ladies should get aboard this train now… just in case."

Chumley was having none of that. "Doctor, you are going to need every hand. Come on, girls!" They boarded the ambulances and wagons and turned them around. Becca leapt up and took the reins of one of them; she'd been driving wagons since she was a child. Another nurse, Clarissa Forester, climbed up beside her.

As they headed west, through the enormous stacks of supplies around the railhead, they began to encounter men, individuals and small groups, heading the other way. Some of them shouted when they saw the nurses and urged them to turn around. *The Martians are coming!* they cried. But most said nothing.

Far ahead of them the roar of battle continued and the clouds of gun smoke still drifted overhead. But now the cannon fire seemed to take on a more frantic note and it was punctuated by louder explosions and new columns of smoke rose up, tinged with flame. And then she heard it: that awful, awful sound of the Martian heat rays.

"There they are!" shouted one of the ambulance drivers, pointing. Becca looked and yes, there, maybe a mile off, a dark nightmare shape stalked through the smoke. A heat ray stabbed out like a striking snake, staining the smoke clouds red, and another explosion billowed up, bits of debris spinning off in all directions. The smoke thinned for a moment and she could see a half-dozen others farther away. Some of the ambulance drivers reined in their teams.

"Come on!" screamed Becca. "Come on!" She lashed her own team and the wagon rumbled forward. Most of the others followed—but not all.

More men were streaming to the rear now. Suddenly one of them jumped up next to her and tried to grab the reins. "Yer goin' the wrong way, girl! Turn round!" Three others clambered in the back.

"This is for the wounded!" she snapped.

"T'hell with the wounded! Turn round!" He jerked the reins out of her hands.

Without a thought, her revolver was out of her pocket, and the barrel shoved into the man's face. She thumbed back the hammer. "Get off! Get off or you'll die right here!" The man was so startled he slid sideways on the seat and fell off the wagon and landed on his back in the dirt. She swung the pistol around at the other men. "Get off!" None of them even had a weapon. They goggled at her for a second and then bolted. The other man scrambled up and ran after them.

"God in Heaven!" gasped Forester. "Would you really have shot him?"

"Damn right I would!" Becca recovered the reins and the horses moved out. A few minutes brought them to the hospital. They posted some guards to make sure their vehicles didn't get taken and the others, men and women together, ran into the tents and brought out the rest of the wounded. Becca helped carry one stretcher and then went back for a second. The noise of the heat rays was getting closer. She deposited the second man and then ran back to look for more. Clarissa screamed at her: "Hurry! For God's sake hurry! They're getting closer!"

Becca dashed into one tent, but it was empty. She moved on to another. It was empty, too. Wait! What was that? Someone—or something—was screaming, it was an animal howl of sheer terror. Where...? Then she noticed an area at the back of the tent that had been screened off with cloth drapes. The noise was coming from there. She ran over and yanked the drapes aside.

A man—*that man*—was lying there, still tied to the stretcher. He was thrashing frantically, trying to get loose and howling. When he saw her he stopped and cried: "Please! Don't let them get me! *Not again!*" He resumed his thrashing.

"Calm down! I'll cut you loose!" She had a small pocket knife and she pulled it open and slashed the ropes holding him. "Come on! We have to go!" The man lurched up but immediately fell. He got up, staggered a few yards and fell again. Becca grabbed his arm and pulled it over her shoulders and hauled him to his feet. They emerged from the tent—and froze.

A tripod was there. It was two or three hundred yards away, but to Becca it looked like it was standing right over her. The man's legs gave way underneath him and he slumped to the ground, whimpering. Then the Martian fired its heat ray and it swung the beam of destruction in an arc that started to her left and moved toward her. Tents and stacks of supplies dissolved in flames that leapt skyward. The ray came within fifty yards of her and she could feel the heat on her face, but then it swung on past and receded again, leaving a blazing ruin in its wake.

"*Rebecca!*" shrieked Forester. "*Come on!*"

She couldn't seem to force her limbs to move. But then the Martian machine turned and started to move away. She sucked in her breath and pulled the man to his feet again. They stumbled toward the wagon and dragged themselves aboard. The man tumbled into the back among several of the wounded and she let him lie. Forester was staring to the west, her eyes wide. "They... they're going away! Why?"

Becca grabbed the reins and turned the wagon around. She glanced back at the retreating Martians. No, they weren't retreating. "They're going after the rest of the army."

The wagon lurched and rumbled along, trying to catch up with the ambulances, but they only caught up when they reached the railhead.

The empty railhead.

"They left without us!" cried Forester. It was true, the other train was gone. "What do we do now?"

Rebecca was too dazed to think. But Miss Chumley was there and she instantly took charge. "All right! There's no train so we'll have to use the wagons! We might be out here a few days, so we need some supplies. You girls look through those stacks of crates and find some rations. Find water, too. Move!"

It was done quickly and fortunately everything they needed was close at hand. Within five minutes they were on the move again. There were crowds of fleeing soldiers all around, but the nurses kept their pistols drawn and no one tried to commandeer their vehicles.

Becca looked back from time to time, but all she could see was the burning camps and supply dumps. She kept expecting to see Martians in pursuit, but there was nothing but the smoke. After a while the road passed around an out-thrust spur of the mountains to the south and the camps were lost to sight.

"Where are we going now?" asked Forester.

"Albuquerque, I guess."

*****

CYCLE 597, 843.8, HOLDFAST 32-1

Qetjnegartis switched off the heat ray as the prey-creature vehicle exploded in a cloud of smoke and steam. It looked for new targets but didn't find any. Was that the last of them?

"Progenitor, is the battle over?" asked Davnitargus. Qetjnegartis was very pleased that the bud had survived.

"I believe so. You performed very well."

"Did I? I tried my best, but I fear I contributed little."

"Compared to the adults, perhaps not, but that is to be expected. For one so inexperienced in so desperate a fight, you did well."

"It is unfortunate that Zastranvis and its bud were slain. We have suffered much loss."

"Yes." Much loss indeed. Two members of the clan slain, another wounded, and a dozen fighting machines destroyed or damaged. And the holdfast badly damaged. How badly remained to be seen. And if the prey-creatures were still loose inside the underground chambers…

"Something approaches!" said Davnitargus urgently.

Qetjnegartis tensed and prepared to activate the heat ray. More of the miserable creatures? How much longer would this go on? But then it checked the tactical display and relaxed. "They are friends."

Through the clouds of smoke that still rolled over the area, six fighting machines appeared. They walked up to Qetjnegartis and halted. The communicator came to life and Braxjandar spoke. "So you still live, Qetjnegartis?"

Greetings, Commander Braxjandar, with your help we have won a victory this day."

The prey-creature army has been broken. All the large projectile throwers and all their fighting vehicles have been destroyed. Several hundred of the creatures have taken refuge in the small redoubt in the center of your holdfast. I have posted guards so they cannot escape."

"They will provide useful sustenance," said Qetjnegartis. "My thanks."

"The rest of them are fleeing east. They should trouble you no more."

"The prey-creatures have shown surprising resilience. They recover from defeats quickly. If reinforcements arrive for them, they may be back. Perhaps if you would pursue them for a time…"

"Pursue them!" said Braxjandar, anger in its voice. "I have lost two of my people killed today! Another very badly wounded! Four of my machines were wrecked and all the rest damaged! And now you plead with us to pursue!"

"Then you can now see how dangerous these creatures are. We should not underestimate…"

"I have saved you from shame and destruction this day, Qetjnegartis! You dare ask no more. My people and I will remain here for one day and then depart. We have affairs of our own to attend to. Reinforcements are on the way from the Homeworld. If you cannot defend yourself until they arrive then perhaps you don't deserve to survive! I have nothing more to say to you." Braxjandar turned its machine and strode away.

"So be it," said Qetjnegartis, spreading half its tendrils in resignation.

* * * * *

AUGUST 1909, NEAR OF FORT WINGATE, NEW MEXICO TERRITORY

First Sergeant Frank Dolfen guided his weary horse through the remains of the army's encampments. There were still fires burning, but the first drops of rain from the storm he'd seen building earlier were starting to fall. The smell of burned canvas, burned wood, and burned flesh was everywhere. There weren't many bodies; the heat rays didn't leave much in its wake, but the smell told that there had once been living bodies here.

In fact, there were still some living bodies here. Men who had somehow escaped the disaster kept emerging from hiding places or drifting back from the direction of the Martian fortress. There had been thousands streaming to the rear in the beginning, but it had dwindled to just a trickle now. Dolfen told each one he encountered to just keep moving.

"Not much more for us to do here, I'm thinking, Sarge," said Corporal Urbaniak. "Still no sign of the lieutenant or the captain. Guess that means you're in charge."

"They'll probably turn up. Everyone's scattered to hell and gone. But it doesn't look like the Martians are going to come after us." *Not that there's anything we could do if they did.* The cavalry's utter impotence—again—was like a heavy weight on him.

"Wonder why? They've got us beat."

"I don't know. But I'm not going to look a gift horse in the mouth. Come on, let's get moving." They called in the other men of the troop, who had been spread out as a rear guard, and then headed east. Their path took them through the field hospital. The tents were still standing but the place was deserted. *Sure hope Becca got out okay.*

As they neared the railhead they disturbed groups of men who were breaking open crates and boxes. Looters? *What in the world could they possibly find that would be worth anything now?*

"You idiots better get movin'!" shouted Urbaniak. "Nothin' between you and the Martians now!" Some took his advice, others kept looking.

Dolfen found that he was bone-weary. It had been a very long and very bad day. Even if his equally weary horse had been capable of any pace faster than a walk, he didn't think he was. The rain was heavier now and he pulled his gum blanket out of the saddle bag and wrapped it around him. Flickers of lighting lit the sky, but the following thunder seemed puny compared to the roars that had filled the day earlier.

"So now what, Sarge?" asked Urbaniak. "What th'hell do we do now?"

"Dunno. Guess we go back, refit the army, and try again."

CHAPTER SIX

SEPTEMBER 1909, 70 MILES EAST OF ISLA DE COZUMEL

The *U.S.S. Mayflower* was a commissioned warship in the United States Navy. She was 273 feet long, 36 feet wide, displaced 2,700 tons, could cruise at 17 knots, mounted a half-dozen six-pound cannon, and had a crew of about 170. But she was also the President of the United States' yacht. She boasted two white and gold reception rooms, a wine cellar, silk paneled walls, a galley fit for a gourmet chef, and a solid marble bath. When the President and his entourage were aboard the compliment would swell to two hundred.

Two hundred and two.

Andrew Comstock carefully slipped out of bed without waking Victoria. His bride had been having trouble with seasickness and this had been the first night she'd slept soundly. He quickly dressed in his lightweight tropical 'whites' and went out the bedroom door. He could still hardly believe that he was here on the *Mayflower* or that the President had given Victoria and him the large cabin he would normally occupy! That solid marble bath was theirs for the journey, not his!

A set of double doors opened out onto the rear area of the ship. He guessed it was technically called the 'poop deck' or some such thing. He was still a bit confused by naval terminology. It was enclosed with polished brass railings and the American flag—the ensign—was on its pole at the stern, flapping in the breeze caused by the ship's passage. The upper deck, which was also the roof of their stateroom, ended just behind him and a six-pounder cannon was mounted on each corner, the brass fittings on the guns polished as brightly as everything else on the ship.

It wasn't quite dawn yet; they were as far west as Chicago and he was still on Washington time. The eastern horizon was glowing pink and he was interested to see that it was off to the left side of the ship. The last two days the dawn had been almost dead astern. They must have rounded Cuba and turned south during the night. The ocean was smooth as glass and he hoped Victoria's seasickness would be better today. The last three days they had passed through the remnants of a large storm which had struck the coast of Florida. The seas had been very rough and the small ship had been tossed around on the waves. It had made both of them wish they were aboard one of the battleships, even if there would be no marble bathtub.

Turning the other direction, he saw one of those battleships looming like a gray mountain half a mile away. It was the *Delaware* fresh from the builder's yards, completed almost a year ahead of schedule and off on her maiden voyage. Looking about, he spotted several of the escorting cruisers farther away. The ships were all painted a gray color and difficult to see. The *Mayflower* was still sporting her peacetime colors: white hull and tan upper works.

A twittering of the bosun's pipes caught his attention and he saw crewmen assembling on the upper decks for their morning roll call. He climbed the ladder up to the same level and watched the proceedings. It wasn't much different from the army he decided, and after just a few minutes

257

the men dispersed to their duty. Every man was spotlessly dressed so he guessed the ship's 'black gang', the men who shoveled coal and worked the engines, had stayed below. Those who had to be seen by the President and his guests were probably all picked men.

The eastern horizon was very bright now and it was already getting warm. It was going to be a hot day. He leaned on the rail and watched the sun come up. He'd never been out to sea before and he had to admit it was an amazing experience.

"Good morning, Major."

Andrew turned at the voice and saw that it was the President's oldest son. He was named Theodore like his father, but went by 'Ted'. He was wearing whites just like Andrew and had captain's bars pinned to the collar. "Good morning, Captain. Up early, too?"

"Yes, gets to be a habit." He joined him at the rail. "How are you and your wife getting on, sir?"

"Please, call me Andrew."

"All right, if you'll call me Ted. But are you enjoying the voyage?"

"Oh, absolutely! Still totally flabbergasted at being here. At least I am. Victoria thinks this is all some fairly-tale-come-true. I don't know how to thank your father."

Ted laughed. "Don't even try! He takes those things as such a matter of course that he's surprised when people try to thank him."

"He's an amazing man."

"No argument there. He can still amaze me."

Andrew hesitated but then went on. "To be honest with you, I'm most amazed that any of us are here. What with all that's happened."

"You mean the setback with General Funston's army?"

"Yes. I would have thought the President would want to stay in Washington to deal with the situation."

Ted laughed again. "You don't know my father!"

"No, not yet."

"My father never—*never*—backs down. Not to anyone for anything. Well, except to my mother now and then."

"That doesn't count," said Andrew with a smirk.

"No, it doesn't. But he had publicly announced that he was going to make this inspection trip to Panama. Nothing, not even the defeat in New Mexico, is going to make him change his plans. It's just not in him."

"I'd think he'd want to be back where he can keep a closer watch on what's happening."

"Oh, I'm sure wants to be there! God in Heaven, he wants to be everywhere! Everywhere at once! If he could split himself into a dozen men it wouldn't be enough to suit him. But General Wood is back on the job and my father trusts him like he trusts few other men. They fought side by side in Cuba and he'd trust him with his life—or the life of the country."

"I see…"

"Of course he *is* keeping tabs on things. The poor wireless operators are working in shifts." Ted shook his head. "It's just a damn shame Funston didn't attack a day sooner."

Andrew snorted. "It seemed like half the battles we read about at the Point were decided because this guy didn't move fast enough or that guy overslept or so-and-so took the wrong road and arrived late. Funston seemed like a real fire-eater when I met him. I'm sure he felt he needed the extra equipment or ammunition that caused the delay."

"True. It's always easy to criticize from a thousand miles away. Still…"

"Andrew? Oh there you are!" He turned and saw his wife coming up the ladder he had used earlier. She was wearing a white dress with blue trim and a broad white hat held on against the wind with a wide blue ribbon that went under her chin. She looked absolutely beautiful. "I couldn't find you and I got worried," she said taking his arm.

"Well, I could hardly have gone far. It's not that big a ship."

"You might have fallen overboard!" She looked past him and said: "Good morning, Captain Roosevelt."

Ted came to attention and bowed. "Good morning, Mrs. Comstock. I trust you're well this morning."

Victoria blushed and giggled the way she still did when anyone called her Mrs. Comstock. "Oh yes! Much better today, thank you! The ocean is so smooth!"

"Yes, we've left the rough seas behind, I think. At least for a while."

"Going to be a hot day, though," said Andrew.

"Well, we'll have shade," said Ted, pointing to where crewmen were rigging awnings for that very purpose. "Ah, father's up." Indeed, the senior Roosevelt emerged through a door out onto the deck. He immediately spotted them and came over wearing his trademark grin.

"Morning! Morning!" he boomed. He was dressed all in white like the rest of them with a straw boater clapped on his head with one hand. "How is everyone this fine day?" The trio all responded with assurances of good health. Roosevelt nodded and looked past them out to sea, putting his other broad hand on the railing.

"So! We leave the Gulf behind and head into the Caribbean. The captain tells me we passed two French cruisers during the night."

"Heading for Veracruz, sir?" asked Andrew.

"I imagine so. Wish we could swing by and see how they are doing there. But it would add over a thousand miles to the trip and we haven't the time."

"They've really landed an army in Mexico?" asked Victoria.

"So they say. But the trick isn't landing the army. The trick will be keeping it there."

"Do you think the Martians will mass their forces and try to throw them out?" asked Andrew.

"I certainly would if I were them, but we haven't figured out how they think yet, so who knows? If I'd commanded the force that beat back Funston, I would have pursued our army to destruction. But instead they just let us go. As bad as it was, we mostly lost materiel rather than people. So there's no telling how they'll react to the French in Veracruz or to the Germans in Caracas. They might just ignore them."

"Oh! What are all those little boats over there?" asked Victoria, pointing off to west. Andrew looked and saw that the dawn was reflecting off dozens of sails in the distance. All four of them walked over to the other rail. "Heavens! There are more of them! Look there!" Indeed, there appeared to be a hundred or more sails visible now with specks at their sides which might also be boats. An armada of the things.

"The fleet Agamemnon sent against Troy must have looked like this," said the President.

"But what are they all doing?" asked Victoria. "They surely aren't all fishermen are they?"

Roosevelt looked from the boats to Victoria and actually seemed uncomfortable—the first time Andrew had ever seen an expression like that on the man's face. "I… I expect they are people trying to get away from the Martians, my dear."

Victoria's face went very serious. "Oh… oh dear. Those poor people. The Martians are over that way? Really?" She pointed west.

"Yes, Yucatan is just sixty miles over the horizon. Cuba's only about forty miles to the east. People in Mexico are fleeing to the coast and finding boats to cross over."

"Are we doing anything to help them?"

"Well, as you know, we are running things in Cuba again—at their request. We've been setting up camps in the west of the island to take in the refugees."

"Oh, good!"

"Still, a hundred and fifty miles of open ocean in little boats like that can't be easy," said Ted.

"Er, no," said the President, still looking anxiously at Victoria. "But breakfast must be nearly ready. Why don't we go below and see what the cooks have prepared?"

"Are you hungry, dear?" asked Andrew.

"Yes, I am. I hadn't felt like eating much the last few days with the sea so rough. But now that we have this lovely calm I think… *Oh!* Oh my God!" She gasped and went white as a sheet and stepped away from the rail.

Confused, Andrew looked at the sea and then saw it. A body in the water, drifting past the ship. It was small, a child perhaps. Victoria was frozen like a statue and Andrew went and gathered her in so she couldn't see it anymore. She was trembling.

"Perhaps you should take your wife back to your cabin," suggested the President.

He did as directed and soon had Victoria lying on the bed, propped up with pillows. "I'm sorry, love," he said. "Are you going to be all right?"

Her expression of shock had given way to one of disgust, even anger. "Yes, yes, I'll be fine. I shouldn't have acted that way! I'm the daughter of a soldier and a soldier's wife for heaven's sake! It was just so… so unexpected."

"I wasn't expecting it, either. I… saw worse in New Mexico, but there I was expecting it. This had seemed like… like…"

"Like some honeymoon cruise? Yes. But we were both wrong, weren't we? This is a military expedition into a war zone, isn't it?"

"Yes, I guess it is."

"And we will both be prepared from now on, won't we?" She raised her chin, looked into his eyes and didn't blink.

He smiled. "Yes, I guess we will."

"Good! Now you go back to the President. I will be along in a few minutes and we'll have breakfast!"

He found the two Roosevelts where he'd left them. The President looked grim. "Sorry about that, Comstock. Is she all right?"

"Yes. She's almost completely recovered. In fact, she'll be joining us for breakfast in a few minutes."

"Bully!" cried the President, brightening. "Stout lass you've got there!"

"Yes, I think so."

"Still, I should have thought of this. We've been getting some very sad reports about the refugees. They've been grabbing anything that will float to escape and tragically, some of the things they're grabbing won't float very far. But I've sent word to the admiral to give us a closer escort and if they spot anything too awful we'll change course to avoid it."

Andrew glanced out to sea and indeed, two of the cruisers were closing in on the *Mayflower*. He noticed lookouts were climbing the masts to the crow's nests. "Thank you, sir, I appreciate that."

"Ah! Here's your lady now!"

Victoria was on deck again and only looking a little pale. They followed the President down to the dining salon and had a nice breakfast. Victoria didn't eat much, but the President made up for it. Andrew had never seen such an appetite. He ate enough for any two men and while he was a bit fat when compared to the famous photos of him as a Rough Rider, he was still very fit. Andrew had seen him racing Ted up the shrouds to the crow's nest on their first day out.

And despite him shoveling down ham, eggs, bacon, melons, a chicken leg left over from last night's dinner, and cup after cup of coffee, he also talked enough for any two men. And such a talker! Andrew was amazed at the range of his conversation. From Thucydides, to Shakespeare, to Bacon, to a half dozen historians and writers Andrew had never heard of, the President had quotations and facts enough for an encyclopedia. And there was no doubt where he got all of those facts: the man was always reading. He usually carried a book with him and any time he wasn't involved in something else, he had his nose pressed in it. He was talkative at every meal, but this morning he steered the conversation away from any further mention of the war, no doubt for Victoria's sake. Instead he spoke of the avian and botanical wonders waiting for them in Panama. The President was a noted wildlife expert with several books on the subject to his credit—he wrote books, too!—and he talked about the birds he had seen on his first visit to Panama in '06.

After breakfast, Victoria took a nap and the President went to the wireless room to answer messages. Andrew found himself at the rail with the younger Roosevelt again. He was only two years older than Ted and Andrew decided that he liked him quite a lot. They watched in silence as the ships passed through flotillas of small boats, all crammed with refugees. The people cried and screamed as they passed, but there was nothing they could do to help.

"Not an easy thing seeing a dead man for the first time," Ted observed.

"No."

"I suppose you saw quite a few in New Mexico."

"Some. The heat rays don't leave much if they hit a man directly. But sometimes they just graze them. What about you? Seen many?"

"Uh, aside from funerals, which don't really count, just one. An hour ago."

"Oh. Sorry, didn't know."

"Don't worry about it. It's something I need to get used to, too. When I finally get a real posting I expect I'll see a lot more."

Andrew looked at Ted in surprise. "A real posting? You won't be staying on as your father's aide?"

"No, I'm supposed to be assigned to the 26th Infantry once we get back from this trip."

"Well, that's wonderful, congratulations. I had just thought that your father would want to keep you with him."

Ted was silent for a long while, staring out at the blue waters, before he answered. "I suppose most parents would, but you need to understand my father. For him, combat is the ultimate test a man can face. He's never been able to forget that his own father was a pacifist and stayed out of the Civil War. And as proud as he might be of being President, it's nothing compared to how he feels

261

about his service in Cuba. That 'crowded hour', as he puts it, is the thing he's most proud of. The stories he used to tell us! And the games we'd play. My God, we must have captured San Juan Hill a thousand times there in Oyster Bay!" He was silent again for a while and then added: "So you see he'd never stand in the way of my experiencing the same thing."

"And is that what you want?"

Ted laughed. "Of course! I'm Teddy Roosevelt's son! My brother Kermit is already with an artillery unit. Archie is terrified the war will be over before he finishes at Groton and gets a chance to fight. Quentin is much too young, but even he's hoping to get into it. He keeps reminding father of all the drummer boys they had in the Civil War and he even got hold of a drum to practice. Yes, I'm afraid that all the Roosevelt boys have war fever."

Andrew wasn't quite sure if Ted was joking, but finally decided he wasn't. They parted company and he went to be with Victoria.

The next day there were fewer small boats to be seen as the coastline swung westward creating the Bay of Honduras. But on the following morning they sighted land a little off to the right. It was the so-called Mosquito Coast where Honduras bordered with Nicaragua. The squadron would follow the coastline from this point on down to Panama, looking for signs of the Martians.

Andrew left the looking to others and instead began studying what they had come down here to see: the transoceanic canal at Panama. Of course, he'd read a great deal about it. The newspapers had been full of the stories when the United States had bought out the failed French attempt and then not-so-secretly backed the Panamanian independence movement which split their province off from Columbia. And now that the canal was well under way there were more stories about the vast size of the endeavor. The largest construction project in the history of the world! Enough rock and earth excavated to build a thousand Great Pyramids! And when you counted the concrete for the great locks, enough to build a few dozen more! The raw numbers were staggering.

But as he looked over the drawings he became even more impressed. The design itself was true genius. An artificial lake filled by rainwater would cross half the isthmus and then locks on the Atlantic and Pacific side would complete the canal, raising ships up to the lake and then back down to the oceans. The water in the locks would come from the lake and always flow downhill. Just open or shut the right valves and gravity would do the rest. No pumps needed! The only motors would be the electric ones opening and closing the great lock gates or running the locomotives which would guide the ships through the locks. And the electricity was generated by a hydro-electric plant at the dam forming the lake. It was very nearly a perpetual motion machine. Just add rain water—which Panama had in abundance.

Of course, Andrew wasn't here to inspect the canal, he was here to inspect the fortifications being built to defend the canal. Before the Martian threat arose, the fortifications planned were to defend the canal from attack from the sea—by humans. Several powerful batteries of guns at each end were all that was thought necessary. But now the canal needed to be defended against attack from the land. This would require a vastly greater system of forts stretching completely across the isthmus—and looking in both directions.

Compared with the engineering drawings for the canal, the plans for the defenses still seemed a bit sketchy. Part of that was because there was still some uncertainty about where the final shoreline of the artificial lake would run, but mostly it was because the experts were unsure of the best sort of defenses to build against the Martians. There were to be several meetings when they arrived to discuss that very topic. Andrew didn't know if his opinion would be asked for, but he wanted to be ready if it was.

The next few days saw intermittent showers. It was still the rainy season in this part of the world and they could see huge banks of clouds building up over the land and then moving out to sea. The rains rarely lasted long, but they were incredibly intense when they came—so hard Andrew had never seen anything like it. It pounded the canvas awnings with a roar like drums—or artillery—and ran off into the sea in rivers. And then it would be over and the sun would come out and the humidity would leave the people dripping like they'd been standing in the downpour.

There were still swarms of boats sailing west—and still bodies in the water—but now they were also seeing a few direct signs of the Martians. The east coast of Central America did not boast any big cities—those were all located on the more temperate western coast—but there were many small villages. Some of them had been burned to the ground, while others had not been touched. There didn't seem to be any pattern to the destruction. But at every village—even the destroyed ones—there were people. People packing into boats, people building them, and people just waiting for another boat to show up. When they saw the squadron they waved and shouted. Some pushed off on rafts or even swam out into the surf, even though the ships were a mile or more off shore. They couldn't stop, of course.

One morning they saw a thick cloud of smoke ahead on the shoreline. When they reached the spot—a place called Tuapi on the charts—they found fires still burning, but no visible Martians. No visible people, either.

As they proceeded south, the destroyed villages grew fewer and then stopped altogether. The one major town they saw, Limon in Costa Rica, was unharmed, and its fine harbor was choked with boats and the waterfront crowded with people. But now they saw that the boats were no longer heading east, out into the Caribbean, they were sailing southeast along the coast. "Where are they going?" asked Victoria.

"Panama," answered the President.

The next day they reached their destination. The Atlantic end of the canal, which everyone automatically called the 'eastern' end was, due to the odd way the isthmus was shaped, actually the western end; but whatever you called it, it was packed like New York Harbor. Dozens of large ships were there unloading cargo and hundreds of smaller boats were milling around, trying to unload people. Navy torpedo boat destroyers were dashing around like sheep dogs keeping the small boats out of the way of the big ships. Farther out to sea was the main naval squadron, there to guard the canal. The battleships which had accompanied them on their voyage veered off to join them.

Navy ships cleared a path for the *Mayflower* to tie up to a long pier that projected from the waterfront of the city of Colon, which was situated just to the east of the canal terminus. An escort of U.S. Marines with a brass band, along with a crowd of dignitaries, was there to greet the President. The leader of the delegation was Colonel George Washington Goethals, the chief engineer of the canal. Goethals was tall and thin, his hair and mustache almost completely white despite being barely fifty. He wore a civilian suit instead of a uniform and welcomed Roosevelt without much warmth, Andrew thought.

The ceremony was cut short by another one of those incredible downpours and Andrew, Victoria, the two Roosevelts, and Goethals were all bundled into a carriage which carried them through the town to the rail station. A train whisked them past scenes of astonishing construction work too quickly to take in and then on to the famed Culebra Cut where Goethals' residence was located. There was a reception that evening where they met most of the high-ranking men working on the canal project. Victoria was tickled that people kept thinking she was Roosevelt's daughter Alice. Andrew repeatedly assured her that she was far prettier. And she was. That night it felt a little odd to sleep in a bed that wasn't moving. Several times they were awakened by loud rumbles that shook the whole house. They didn't seem like thunder…

The next morning the inspection began. The train took them back to the Atlantic end where they toured the construction site for the enormous Gatun Locks. Work on the locks had begun only a few months earlier and had not progressed far, but the scope of the project could be clearly seen. Three sets of double locks, each one over a thousand feet long and a hundred feet wide, would raise a ship eighty-five feet to the future level of the lake. Massive steel forms on railway tracks were being filled with concrete continuously by an ingenious set of overhead cableways that carried an endless stream of gondolas, each holding six cubic yards. The iron support towers soared overhead and from their observation point, the men working there seemed like ants. Andrew looked on in awe. *Even a Martian tripod would look like an ant next to this!*

"It's so complex!" gasped Victoria. "How on earth did you ever figure this all out?"

"Major Sibert, here, is in charge of the Atlantic Division," said Goethals, indicating one of their escorts.

Sibert came forward and explained how it all worked. "They're using a slightly different system on the Pacific locks," he said in conclusion, "but the goal is the same: to keep the concrete flowing to avoid any delays."

"Which reminds me, Mr. President," said Goethals, "with the additional fortification called for, we are going to run short of cement unless more is sent to us. We stockpiled a good amount prior to the start of construction, but we are running through that quickly. I've sent repeated requests for more, but the deliveries aren't keeping up. We can secure the sand and other aggregates locally, but we can't make the cement here."

"Yes, yes," growled Roosevelt, "the demand is enormous. We're building new fortifications all over the country, you know. And until just a few years ago we imported more cement than we made ourselves. But new plants are opening up all the time. You'll get your cement, Colonel, have no fear."

From the locks they moved to Gatun Dam, which would create the artificial lake. It was a huge earthen dam that stretched across the path of the Chagres River. Like so many things connected with the canal, it was the largest in the world. "The river was always the biggest challenge," said Goethals. "The French tried to build a canal at sea level, but they never figured out how they would handle the enormous flow of the Chagres, which was right in their path. When we decided to build a lock canal and the lake, the river became an ally instead of an enemy. We will be closing the gates in the dam and start filling the lake soon."

The tour continued and the train took them back to Culebra Cut. Here the work, instead of building something new, was to take away something old—an eight mile long cut through the continental divide. The work dwarfed even the construction of the locks. A hundred or more enormous steam shovels dumped loads of earth and rock onto waiting railroad cars which carried it away to dump sites or to add to Gatun Dam. Like the bucket system at the locks, the idea was to never waste a moment. The shovels were in constant use and the trains shuttled in and out over a vast rail network.

"My predecessor, John Stevens, was a railroad man," explained Goethals. "He set this system up, and while we've expanded and improved on it, it's still his basic design. We do most of the blasting at night and then spend the day carrying away the spoil."

"Ah, so that is what that noise was!" said Andrew. "We wondered about it."

"What are all those people up on the hills doing?" asked Victoria, pointing to the slopes of the mountains on either side of the cut, where swarms of men were at work.

"Yes," said Roosevelt, "I don't remember this from my last visit. What have you got them doing, Colonel? By thunder, there certainly are a lot of them!"

"Yes, Mr. President," said Goethals. "That's one of the things I most wanted to talk to you about. Those men are almost entirely refugees who have fled from the Martians. They are coming here in huge numbers. A year ago I had thirty-five thousand men working here. Today I have over a hundred thousand."

"A hundred thousand!" exclaimed Roosevelt. "But I know you don't have that many on the payroll! Congress would have had a fit!"

"I'm not *paying* them sir, just feeding them. And in return they are working. Up there where we can't get the steam shovels. One of the biggest challenges we face is the landslides. We excavate in the Cut and then the rains come and the mountains start sliding down on us. The big slides kill men, wreck equipment, and force us to re-dig everything. For a long while we thought we'd just have to keep digging and endure the slides until the mountains finally reached the proper angle of repose. That could take years. But with all this extra manpower…" Goethals shrugged. "A Bucyrus steam shovel can move the same amount in a day as three thousand men with picks and shovels, but if I have a Bucyrus shovel and three thousand men, I'd be a fool not to use both."

"Very wise. And you are making progress?"

"Yes, sir, we are. The number of slides has been reduced—although we'll never be completely free of them—and we are ahead of schedule."

"But when will it be complete?"

"The original completion date was 1915 or 1916. Even before the Martians arrived, we had that cut back to 1913. With the extra resources you've sent us and the extra manpower, I'm hoping we can be open for traffic by the summer or fall of 1911, sir."

"So, two more years?" Roosevelt frowned and his pince-nez nearly popped off before he could grab them.

"Yes, sir, I'm afraid that's the best we can hope for. However…"

"What, Colonel?"

"The refugees, sir. As I said, I am feeding them, but I'm not sure how much longer I can do that. Including the women and children there are over two hundred thousand of them and thousands more coming through the jungle or by boat every day. We've cleared jungle areas to set up camps for them and we have the women and older children planting crops to help feed themselves, but it isn't enough. I've tried to import more food from some of the Caribbean islands, but they are facing their own refugee crises and food prices are going up fast. Unless I can get more from back home we could facing a major problem here, sir. I'm grateful for the divisions of troops you sent, we might need them if food starts to run out."

Roosevelt frowned, and to Andrew's surprise instead of reassuring Goethals that all would be well, simply said: "I'll look into it." Andrew glanced over at Ted who seemed surprised himself.

They had lunch at Goethals' house and then finished the day by looking at the Pacific end. More locks were under construction there along with a massive breakwater meant to deal with the Pacific's large tides. "Almost no tides in the Caribbean," explained Sydney Williamson, the head of the Pacific Division and the only high-ranking civilian on the team, "but on this side, the ocean can rise and fall twenty feet."

A quick tour through Panama City completed the day. There were no crowds lining the streets or cheering the President. In fact, most of the people looked rather sullen. "The locals aren't happy with all the refugees coming in," said Goethals. "The Panamanians are becoming a minority in their own country—and it's only going to get worse."

They had dinner that night with Goethals and his top subordinates, some of the senior military officers in Panama, and their wives. A number of things were discussed, but it was Dr. William Gorgas who had the most to say. He was an army doctor who had worked miracles in eliminating

Yellow Fever and dramatically cutting down on Malaria in Panama. When the French were trying to build a canal, a thousand men a month were dying from the twin tropical scourges. By fully embracing the theory that the diseases were transmitted by mosquitoes and then setting up programs to eliminate them, he had cut the death rate from thousands to less than a dozen a month from Malaria and to none at all from Yellow Fever.

"But now, with all these new people swarming in," said Gorgas, "I'm fearful that we may see a resurgence. We've got tens of thousands living in close proximity to swamp areas where the mosquitoes breed. I don't have the manpower to drain or treat those swamps with oil. And I certainly don't have room in our hospitals to handle the thousands of new patients which could result."

"So what are you suggesting, Doctor?" asked the President.

"More supplies in the form of quinine, wire screens for windows, netting for beds, mosquito traps, and oil for the water. But primarily I need manpower to distribute the supplies and see that they are used."

"What about the refugees, themselves? Couldn't they supply the manpower?"

"Perhaps in time if we can make them understand the necessity. But please understand, sir, we tried that here when we first took over. It didn't work. The natives have lived this way for generations. They saw no need to change. It wasn't until we supplied our own men—at least as team leaders—that we started to make progress."

"William, you can't seriously suggest that we divert workers from the canal for this project of yours," said Goethals. "We can't afford it. Not just the time, but every damn mosquito you kill will cost the government ten dollars!"

Gorgas smiled. "But think if one of those ten dollar mosquitoes bit you, George. What a loss to the country that would be!" Goethals snorted, but Gorgas went on. "Actually, I wasn't suggesting that any of the canal workers be taken for this."

Well, who then?"

We have two infantry divisions stationed here now. I haven't noticed them doing much of anything lately, Mr. President."

"What?" exclaimed General Thomas Barry, commander of the XI Corps, the senior army commander in Panama. "You can't be serious! They're here to defend the canal from the Martians! Not mosquitoes!"

"I understand that, General, but as far as we can tell, the Martians aren't anywhere close at the moment, but the mosquitoes are. And I wasn't suggesting that all your men be put to this task. Perhaps one regiment from each division on a rotating basis."

"But…"

"Doesn't seem unreasonable," said Roosevelt. "Keeps the men busy, let's them get familiar with the surroundings, saves lives."

"But, *sir*!" said Barry.

"Draw up a proposal, Doctor."

"Thank you, sir," said Gorgas.

The following day was the meeting Andrew was there for, the one to discuss the defenses of the canal. They met in a brand new headquarters building on a hill overlooking the Gatun Dam. Victoria was off on an outing with Mrs. Goethals, but the President and Ted came with Andrew; indeed the meeting was for the President's benefit, not Andrew's. General Barry was there with a few of his staff, along with a navy commander, named 'Blue' who represented Admiral Hugh Rodman, commander of the Atlantic naval squadron, but most of the men in attendance were from the Corps of Engineers led by Colonel William Bixby, the man charged with building the fortifications. They had maps and diagrams and a huge sand table showing the entire canal area in marvelous detail.

Bixby started things off with a general overview of the situation and the challenges facing them. "Mr. President, as you can see from the maps, we have a massive undertaking facing us. We have an isthmus approximately thirty miles wide in a straight line with the canal running through it which we must defend against attacks coming from either direction. It won't be possible to run our defenses in a straight line, so we are probably looking at nearly a hundred miles of defenses at a minimum. Much of the ground, like near the Culebra Cut, is extremely difficult and even in the flatter areas we need to deal with the jungle.

"However, we also have some advantages. The very jungle which will make construction difficult will also serve to protect us in the short term. The Panamanian jungle, which stretches along the isthmus fifty miles or more on either side of the canal, is as thick and as nearly impassable as any in the world. From what we know of the Martian machines, they will find it extremely difficult going, perhaps even impossible. Of course they could probably burn their way through using their heat rays, but that will take a great deal of time and give weeks of warning of what they are trying to do.

"Another advantage is that once the Gatun Lake is filled, it will create a barrier across nearly half of the isthmus. This will relieve us from having to fortify the entire length of the line immediately."

"Excuse me, sir," said Andrew, getting up the nerve to speak. "While the evidence we currently have indicates that the Martians do not like large bodies of water, there is no conclusive proof that they can't cross them. For all we know, their machines might even be able to operate underwater like a submarine. The lake might not prove to be the barrier that you hope."

Bixby didn't appear the least put out being questioned by a man half his age. He simply nodded. "Yes, that's certainly true, Major. But we must accept the fact that there is no possibility of instantly constructing an impregnable line of fortifications—two lines of fortifications, actually. It is going to take time. Possibly a length of time comparable to the construction of the canal itself. That being the case, we must concentrate our efforts on the most vulnerable spots first. Those areas are clearly the ones nearest to the coasts, where the Martians can move most easily."

"Of course, sir."

"Later, if we are given the time and resources, we can extend the defense lines to enclose the lake and give us continuous defenses. I might add, that once the lake is filled and the Atlantic locks completed, we will be able to move warships onto the lake to bolster our defenses in that area."

"Uh, sir," interjected Commander Blue, "the admiral instructed me to remind you that he objects to employing his ships in such a fashion. The restricted waters of the lake and the likely short ranges at which the Martians would have to be engaged could prove extremely hazardous. He feels that any support the army requires can be provided just as effectively by ships on the open ocean."

"Yes, Commander, the admiral has already made his views known to me," said Bixby.

Roosevelt cleared his throat and leaned forward. "Commander, please let Admiral Rodman know that I expect him and the navy to give whatever support is required to defend the canal. If that means bringing his ships up onto the lake, then that is what he will do!" Blue nodded nervously. "But, do continue, Colonel. You say your initial efforts will be concentrated near the coasts?"

"Yes, Mr. President." He walked over to the model and took up a long pointer. "We propose to construct a string of concrete forts from the oceans to the shoreline of the lake. The Atlantic side is by far the easiest job since the lake will be closer to that coast. On the west side of the canal we will build five forts following the line of the Media River. On the east side, about three miles from Colon, we will only need two forts. These forts will be constructed with all-around defense in mind and mount heavy guns. Initially, we can connect the forts with trench lines dug and manned by the infantry. Later, when we have time, we can replace these trenches with concrete." Bixby pointed to the locations on the model.

Walking around to the other side he continued. "The Pacific side is going to be far more work, I'm afraid. The two lines will each be over twenty miles long and some of it through extremely rough territory. Just as we don't know if the Martian machines can negotiate deep water, we also don't know how well they handle mountains. So we've had to make some assumptions about what will or will not prove to be impassible to them. We realize this is a risk, but we really have no choice at this time." The pointer touched a long string of tiny forts leading from the Pacific coast, up over the mountains, and then to the lake. Andrew could see just what a daunting task it would be to build them. "We are hoping that fire from the forts and other supporting guns and ships will be able to close off any pathway that we can't physically block."

Bixby moved over to one of the large wall maps. It showed the isthmus and had it divided into a grid pattern. "In fact, controlling the artillery will be the key to the defense. Ultimately, we will have hundreds of guns in place here and we plan to create a system using observers with telephone lines, combined with a central plotting facility to allow us to concentrate their fire against any point of the defense." He pointed from the forts to various squares on the map. "Assuming the Martians don't hit us everywhere at once, we should be able to smash any attack as it occurs."

"That's very good, Colonel," said Roosevelt, nodding. "But suppose…"

He was interrupted by a nervous-looking corporal who came in and handed a note to Commander Blue. The man quickly read it and then looked up in surprise.

"Trouble, Commander?" asked Roosevelt.

"Uh, I'm not sure, sir. This is a message from Admiral Rodman. He says that there is a German light cruiser, the *Emden*, approaching at high speed. They have signaled asking if you are here and if so, if one of their officers might meet with you as soon as possible?"

"Indeed? Well, certainly, let him come."

"Yes, sir!" Blue hurried out.

"It will probably take him a few hours to get here, sir," said Bixby. "Shall we continue?"

"Of course."

From the general overview they proceeded to specifics, principally the construction of the forts. "We plan to construct them of concrete, of course. From what we've heard, that has proven to be a material very resistant to the Martian heat rays."

"I believe that Major Comstock can comment on that," said the President. "Right, Major?"

Andrew, surprised and pleased that the President seemed to know about his trip to Niagara Falls, nodded. "Yes, sir. The Ordnance Department has recently completed a series of tests using a captured Martian heat ray and concrete has proven to be the best material we've found to defend against it. A slab only six inches thick was able to resist the ray for some time at five hundred yards with only some cracking and crumbling. At longer ranges the ray had very little effect at all. When we consider that the heat ray has almost no physical impact like an artillery shell, it ought to be possible to build defenses with concrete much thinner than commonly in use."

"If that's true, this is excellent," said Bixby, clearly impressed. "Current fortifications need concrete walls ten or twenty feet thick to resist the impact of heavy shells. But if we could reduce that to five feet or even less it would be a huge saving in time and materials!"

The discussion went on to cover the sort of guns which would be mounted in the forts.

"Disappearing mounts are falling out of favor for coast defense," said Bixby. "The much longer ranges now possible mean the incoming shells are traveling in a much higher trajectory and could land behind the wall shielding the guns. But if the Martian heat ray travels strictly in a straight line, a disappearing gun might be the ideal weapon. Would you agree, Major?"

Andrew looked at the diagram Bixby pushed toward him. It showed a typical twelve-inch disappearing gun mount. The idea was very simple: the gun was mounted on a carriage which could raise and lower it using a counterweight. In the lowered position it would be below the top of the fortification's parapet and safe from enemy fire. The gun could be loaded and even aimed in that position. Then, when all was ready, a lever would release the counterweight; the gun would rise up above the parapet and already be trained on its target. The gun would immediately be fired and the recoil would drive the gun back down into the loading position. The gun would only be exposed for a few seconds.

At the turn of the century, the range of naval guns had only been a few thousand yards and a shell fired at a coastal fort would travel in almost a straight line. The shell would either hit the face of the fort's walls or fly over the parapet for long distances and explode harmlessly. Only an incredibly lucky hit against a gun in the firing position would do anything. This made the disappearing mounts very effective. But as Bixby said, recent developments in gunnery had increased the range of guns enormously. Shells flung from twenty thousand yards would come down in a steep arc and could land just behind the parapet, damaging the guns and killing their crews. But the Martian rays…

"The heat rays travel in a precisely straight line, like light, sir. They do not follow a ballistic path. The disappearing mounts would appear to be an ideal weapon. Of course their black dust projectiles do travel in an arc, but with their wide area of dispersal they would be dangerous even if they traveled in a straight line, too. The gun crews will need dust protection just like the other troops."

"Damn uncomfortable in a climate like this!" said General Barry.

"Pretty damn uncomfortable to have your lungs dissolved, too, General," said Roosevelt.

"Very good," said Bixby. "We'll employ as many disappearing mounts as possible."

They discussed a few more things, like ammunition supply and storage, but by then it was nearly noon and they stopped for lunch. This was served in a dinning hall with large, screened-in windows, by white coated stewards. Andrew sat next to Ted.

"Hope you weren't bored," said Andrew

"Not at all. It was very interesting and it seems like a lot of progress was made."

"I suppose. But maps and models won't stop the Martians. There's a hell of a lot of work to do to make all this planning a reality."

"True. And a lot of folks back home are going to ask why all that work is being done here instead of there?"

It was an awkward question that Andrew had no intention of trying to answer, so he changed the subject. "Hmmm. I wonder what the Germans want with your father?"

"I think we're about to find out. Look." Ted raised his chin and jerked his head toward the windows.

Andrew turned to look out and saw several American army officers, and Commander Blue escorting another man in a foreign naval uniform. They hurried up the steps to the building, and a few moments later they entered the dining room. The new man had a mustache and small chin beard and his face was ruddy and sweat-covered. He was brought over to where Roosevelt was seated. He came to attention, clicked his heels together and bowed stiffly from the waist. But before he could say anything, Roosevelt addressed him in fluent German.

Andrew didn't know what the President had said, but the man looked surprised, and then smiled and answered in accented, but understandable English. "Thank you, Your Excellency! You are most kind. I am Korvetten-Kapitan Hans Zenker, aide to Vizeadmiral Hubert von Rebeur-Paschwitz, commander of His Imperial Majesty's Caribbean Squadron."

"Ah!" exclaimed the President. "How is old Hubbie? I knew him when he was Willie's naval attaché back in Washington!"

"So the admiral said, sir. He hoped you would remember him."

"I do! I do! But what brings you here in such a hurry?"

The German became serious and formal again. "Sir, as you know, the Kaiser has seen fit to land a force in Caracas, Venezuela to save the local people from the depredations of the Martian invaders."

Roosevelt's easy manner dropped away, as well. "Yes, I was aware of that, sir, please go on."

"Of course, sir. We have secured the city and beaten back several small attacks by Martians moving up directly from the south. But now our scouts have detected a much stronger force which has descended from the mountains to the coast several hundred miles to the west. We believe they intend to march on Caracas from there. The Admiral plans to intercept them with his squadron two days from now. He has sent me here to inquire if any of your forces would be interested in participating in the operation?"

The light that appeared on Roosevelt's face was like a tropical sunrise. He broke out in an enormous grin and slammed his fist on the table. "By thunder we certainly would!" He jumped to his feet and turned to face Bixby and Barry. "Sorry gentlemen, you'll have to go on with your meeting without me! I need to join Admiral Rodman on his flagship!"

The German officer's eyes grew very wide and his ruddy complexion turned pale. "Uh, Your Excellency! Admiral von Rebeur-Paschwitz did not mean that you should come yourself!"

Somehow the President's grin grew even wider. "What? And miss out on all the fun? Ted! Andy! Don't just stand there! Get moving! There's not a moment to lose!"

CHAPTER SEVEN

SEPTEMBER 1909, FIVE MILES SOUTH OF CURACAO ISLAND

The battleship *Michigan* rolled gently in the swell as it cut a creamy wake through the calm waters. Just astern of her was the battleship *Delaware*, and just ahead the armored cruiser *Pennsylvania*. Two more big cruisers, the *North Carolina* and *Tennessee*, trailed behind. Several smaller cruisers prowled on the flanks. They'd lost sight of the speedy *Emden* the day before as she went ahead to tell her fellows the Americans were coming.

Major Andrew Comstock stood on one of the platforms that projected off to the side of the main bridge. There was probably some sort of nautical name for it, but he didn't know what it was. Navy crewmen were moving to and fro or climbing the ladders up through the odd cage-masts to the soaring lookout platforms far overhead. Thick black smoke poured from the funnels of the ships as they tore through the water at nearly their top speeds.

The American squadron had been charging eastward for almost two days. President Roosevelt had dragged Ted and Andrew away from the conference, down to the harbor, and into a motor launch which took them out to Admiral Rodman's flagship, pausing only long enough for a steward to transfer a few bags of clothing from the *Mayflower*. In truth, Andrew was excited about going, he just hoped someone had gotten his message to Victoria—and that she wasn't too angry with him when they got back.

The President was tremendously eager to join in the fray and Andrew remembered his earlier words with Ted. Was the President determined to get in another 'crowded hour' while he could? Admiral Rodman had seemed reluctant at first, but quickly caught Roosevelt's enthusiasm, even to the point of leaving the older and slower warships behind.

They had sailed through one night and then a second. If the Martians were where the Germans said they were, they ought to see them today.

The President's arrival had caused more than a little disruption aboard the *Michigan*. Admiral Rodman had been forced out of his cabin, which forced the ship's captain out of his, which had forced the first officer out of his... and so on. Andrew and Ted were sharing a cabin formerly occupied by a pair of lieutenants. He didn't know what had become of them.

Glancing over his shoulder he noticed the President and his son coming up the ladder. The elder Roosevelt waved a cheery good morning and then went onto the bridge with Ted. Andrew followed. Admiral Rodman was already there. "Good morning, Mr. President," he said. "I trust you slept well?"

"Well enough! Well enough! Always a bit restless before a battle. Will it be today, do you think?"

"It will depend on how fast the Martians have been moving east, sir. The Germans seem to think it will be today, but if the enemy has moved faster than expected, we might not catch up with them until tonight—in which case I'd prefer to wait until tomorrow morning to engage."

"Yes, certainly. Better gunnery in daylight," said the President nodding.

"We are about twenty miles off the coast of Venezuela right now, sir. I have the *Birmingham* sailing closer inshore scouting for signs of the Martians."

"Bully!" said Roosevelt. He peered out the right-hand windows on the bridge and squinted. There wasn't anything to be seen.

"A bit hazy this morning," said Rodman, "but it will burn off soon. Should have good visibility for shooting, sir."

"Good! But tell me, Admiral, at what range were you planning to engage the beasties?"

Rodman's eyebrows went up. "That's a good question, sir, and I've been discussing it with my officers. Closer will increase accuracy, but we must consider the safety of the ships—and our passengers." He stared pointedly at Roosevelt.

"Ha! It won't be the first time I've been shot at! But seriously, I don't think you have much to worry about, right Major?" He looked at Andrew.

"Uh, yes, sir. I mean no, sir, if you keep even a moderate distance you ought to be safe. We did tests of a heat ray against armor plates and at two thousand yards it barely burned the paint off the steel. Flammable items—and people—could be vulnerable out to three thousand. Four thousand for a long exposure."

"Four thousand yards? Really?" Rodman snorted. "I doubt I'd risk the ships much closer than that to the shore even without anyone shooting at us! Quite a few rocks along this stretch of coast. At four thousand yards we are going to have a duck-shoot, Mr. President."

"I hope so, Admiral, although keep in mind your targets will be smaller than a warship." Roosevelt stepped out onto the bridge wing—wing! That's what they were called!—and looked forward and then aft. They all followed him out. "It's quite a force you have, Admiral, and yet only a small fraction of our navy. When I see our fleet I sometimes wonder what Isaac Hull or Oliver Perry would think if they could see this?"

Rodman smiled and nodded. "I've read your book, sir. It's required reading at Annapolis now."

"*The Naval War of 1812*? I wrote that when I was younger than Ted, here."

"It's still the standard work on the subject."

"I sometimes think I should do a new edition. While it's fine when it comes to describing the ships and the battles, I realize now—have realized for quite some time—that there's no context to what I wrote."

"Sir?"

"Context, Admiral! I wrote about ships, the men who manned them, and about the battles they fought. But scarcely a word about the strategic decisions which brought those battles about. I wrote a book about the War of 1812 and never once even mentioned the president or the secretary of the navy!"

"I... I can't say I noticed that, sir."

"Well, I didn't either at the time—not having met any presidents or secretaries of the navy yet."

"So when you write the history of this war, sir," said Ted with a strange smile on his face, "what will you say about the strategic decisions which brought about the battle we'll be fighting today?"

"What? Do you mean will I include the fact that the President caused it so he could watch a sea battle?"

"Something like that, sir."

They all laughed and then the admiral excused himself to attend to his duties. The three of them, having no duties at the moment, leaned on the rail and watched the ships and the sea. As the admiral had said, the mist disappeared as the sun got higher and the *Birmingham* and the coast of Venezuela appeared. It was hard to see anything from this far out, but they could tell that some substantial mountains rose up beyond the coastline. They stood in silence for a while and then the President turned to him.

"So, Major, as our most recent combat veteran and the only man in the fleet who's seen a live Martian, do you have any advice for dealing with them?"

Andrew pondered that for a moment and then said: "Hit them with everything we've got, sir. Oh, and if they retreat, don't try to follow them up into those hills."

The President laughed. "No, I don't imagine Rodman will be tempted to make Sumner's mistake." He paused and his smile faded. "Not funny, is it? I forgot that you were there with Sumner at Thoreau. Must have been terrible."

"I suppose any battle is terrible, sir. But I think the worst was when I realized we'd been beaten and there wasn't anything anyone could do about it."

"Praise God that I've never had to experience that, Major."

"And you won't have to today, sir. We're going to beat them for sure!"

"That's the spirit! We'll beat them here and we'll beat them everywhere!"

They parted company and Andrew wandered around the ship for a bit. The admiral had given them a complete tour yesterday, but there were a few places he wanted to look at in closer detail. In particular, he was interested in the system which aimed the big guns. He finally tracked down the assistant gunnery officer, a lieutenant commander named Smith, who was willing to spare him a few minutes to explain it all.

"Well, believe it or not, as recently as the Spanish War we were still aiming our guns the same way Drake did against the Armada," said Smith. "We'd peer out along the gun barrel and when we thought it was lined up on the target we'd pull the lanyard and hope for the best. Against a big, slow-moving target we might hit it at two or three thousand yards." Andrew nodded, he knew that.

"But in the last few years we've made all sorts of advances. Those British fellows, Pollen and Dryer, led the way, but we're not far behind now. For accurate fire at long ranges you need to know how your own ship is moving, you need to know what direction the enemy is moving and how fast, and above all you need to know the range. Not just the approximate range, but the actual range to within a hundred yards or so or you are going to miss."

Smith pointed upward. "So, we have trained men in the flying bridge up there and the other one astern and they have special telescopes and instruments which can tell us all those things. They send all the information down to the plotting room, which is about four decks below us here, where they take it all and come up with a firing solution. That's sent to the gun turrets and at the proper moment the guns fire."

"Interesting. So do you think you'll be able to hit something the size of a railroad locomotive at four thousand yards?"

"Ought to be able to get pretty darn close, Major! And we won't need to score a direct hit; a twelve-inch shell makes a helluva bang!"

"I bet it does. I'm looking forward to seeing one." He thanked Smith and went in search of lunch. He'd been dining with the Roosevelts at every meal for days now and he decided to try something a little less frenetic. Some looking led him to a mess compartment for junior officers. It seemed appropriate since his major's rank was only equivalent to a navy lieutenant commander. The food wasn't nearly as elaborate as what he'd been getting lately, but it was still good. His army uniform got him some odd looks, but no one spoke to him, which was fine. He needed to think.

Combat. He was going into combat again. As a spectator. Again.

He hadn't stayed a spectator very long the first time, but he said a silent prayer that this time would be different. He was a little ashamed of himself for being afraid, but eventually he realized he wasn't worried about his own safety—well, maybe a little. No, it was like he said to the President: that awful awareness that the battle was lost; he never wanted to experience that again.

And I won't! I mean what can go wrong? Aside from a Martian heat ray finding its way into the ship's magazine and blowing us all to Kingdom Come?

That seemed very unlikely—unless the Martians had some new trick up their non-existent sleeves. *Stop worrying! They're not omnipotent!* No, they weren't; humans had tricked them and beaten the hell out of them at Prewitt, and they'd do it again today.

He was just getting up from the table when gongs rang through the ship, calling the men to their battle stations. Andrew hurried up to the bridge and got there just as the Roosevelts arrived. "What's happening, Admiral?" demanded the President.

"A signal from the *Chester*, sir," said Rodman with a look of satisfaction on his face. He gestured to where the scout cruiser was visible about twelve miles ahead. "They report that they've made contact with the German squadron and that Admiral Rebeur-Paschwitz's flagship is flying the 'Enemy in Sight' signal."

"Bully!" cried Roosevelt. "So it will be today!"

"So it would seem, sir. Now if you'll excuse me, I need to get things sorted out."

But it didn't appear that very much sorting out was needed. The heavy ships of the squadron were already in a very tidy line-ahead formation, with only the *Chester* and *Birmingham* detached as scouts. There was a great deal of rushing around on the bridge with messengers coming and going, but Andrew wasn't sure what it was all for. Crewmen went around the bridge, unlatching all the windows, so they wouldn't be shattered by the concussion of the guns.

After about a half hour there were some shouts and shortly after that the masts of the German ships were visible on the horizon. Andrew had been lent a very powerful set of navy binoculars and he trained them where everyone else was looking and yes, he could see the tops of the German ships. Minute by minute, they crept above the horizon and eventually he could see their hulls, too. They appeared to be headed right for the American ships.

"Mr. President," said Rodman appearing with a scrap of paper in his hand, "we've identified the German ships. There are three battleships, the *Westfalen*, *Schleswig-Holstein* and *Lothringer*. The *Westfalen* is larger and…"

"She mounts twelve eleven-inch guns, although she can only bring eight of them to bear in any one direction," interrupted Roosevelt. "The other two are older ships with only four eleven-inchers apiece in their main batteries. But do go on, Admiral."

Rodman paused and then smiled and shook his head. "Yes, sir. There are two armored cruisers, the *Roon* and the *Yorck*; and two light cruisers, *Emden* and *Kolberg*. They also have four torpedo boats."

"So, not as powerful as your squadron then, wouldn't you say, Admiral?"

"It would be a close match, sir, but we do have the edge. But we're here to fight Martians, not Germans like we almost did in '02, correct, Mr. President?"

"Oh surely! Forgot you were here with Dewey for that one! And where are the Martians?"

"Signal from *Birmingham*, sir!" shouted an ensign. "Enemy sighted, south-southeast!" A dozen sets of binoculars swung off to the right. Andrew scanned the distant coastline, but didn't see—wait! Sunlight reflecting off metal drew his eyes back and there they were! Tiny shapes moving in the distance, barely to be seen.

"How many do you think?" asked Roosevelt.

"Hard to say at this distance, sir," said Rodman. "I'll signal *Birmingham* to make a count. But sir, we've got two independent squadrons here and we don't want them running into each other. How are we going to organize our attack?"

"Good question, Admiral. What would you suggest?"

But before Rodman could reply, another signal was received, this time from the German admiral. Rodman took it, read it, and smiled. "He says: *'Believe Roosevelt senior officer present. Do lead on, sir'*.

"Ha!" cried Roosevelt. "All right then! Would having the Germans fall in astern of us and extending our line of battle be appropriate, Admiral?"

"Entirely, Mr. President. I will see to it at once."

The American ships turned slightly more toward the coast while the German ships adjusted their course to pass the Americans to seaward. The distance was closing at almost forty miles an hour so they didn't have to wait long. As the German ships came abreast, about five hundred yards away, Roosevelt stepped out onto the left bridge wing and doffed his hat as the German flagship sailed past. A small figure aboard the *Westfalen* did likewise. Andrew studied the German ships as they passed. They were broader and lower and, in Andrew's opinion, distinctly uglier than the American ships. The American armored cruisers, in particular, were some of the most elegant warships he'd ever seen. When the leading German ship neared the end of the American line it put its helm over and turned sharply to follow along. Each of the other ships did the same thing, one after the other. Finally, both squadrons were in a single long line, except for a few of the smaller ships out on the flanks.

"Nicely done," said Rodman. "Von Rebeur-Paschwitz has a well-drilled command."

They stepped back inside the main bridge and were met by several sailors carrying life jackets and steel helmets. Andrew took his and so did Ted, but the older Roosevelt waved them away. "I don't need those!"

"Sorry, Mr. President," said Rodman, putting his own on and then taking a set and personally offering it to Roosevelt. "Regulations, sir. If you refuse, I'll have to ask that you go below."

The President stared for a moment and then laughed and put them on, tucking the strap on the helmet under his chin. Andrew looked and blinked. For some reason, Roosevelt wearing the bulky life jacket and helmet made him look just like an old salt-shaker his mother owned. He shook his head to get rid of the image.

"You'll also want these," said Rodman offering wads of cotton. "It's going to be very loud, sir." Everyone stuffed the cotton in their ears.

"Range to the enemy eight thousand yards, sir," said the captain of the *Michigan*, speaking very loudly because of the cotton. "When do you want to open fire?"

"Don't shoot too soon," cautioned Roosevelt. "Don't want to spook them like a flock of quail!"

"I believe we will commence firing at five thousand," said Rodman.

The Martians were clearly visible now, even without binoculars. With them, Andrew could see the machines marching eastward along the shore. They seemed oblivious to the approaching warships. The Martians were moving about ten miles an hour according to the gunnery officer, so the warships were slowly catching up and closing on a converging course. The lookouts on the ships had counted twelve of them. Seven thousand, six thousand, the range fell and fell. Almost time...

"Mr. President," said Rodman suddenly becoming very formal. "Would you care to give the command to fire?"

"Why yes," said Roosevelt, with a large grin. "I'd be dee-lighted to..."

"Father! Get down!" Suddenly Ted grabbed the President and dragged him below the level of the bridge windows. Almost immediately the bridge was filled with a bright red light and Andrew felt heat, like that of an open oven, on his face. People cried out all around him and he ducked down to get out of the light.

The awful red glow persisted for a few more seconds and then faded as the ray swept sternward. Andrew dared to pop up and look. The Martian machines were now spraying their heat rays out to sea. But the range was too long.

"Mr. President! Are you all right?" asked Admiral Rodman.

"Fine! Just fine!" cried Roosevelt, rising to his feet. "But by all means fire! Shoot the scalawags!"

"Very good, sir! Signal to squadron! All ships commence firing!"

There was a moment of intense activity with, it seemed, everyone shouting orders at once. Andrew peered out the window at the pair of immense turrets near the front of the ship. They swung slightly to the right and...

Boom!

An enormous concussion thumped into him as flame and smoke blossomed out from the muzzles of the guns. A huge roar rattled the bridge windows—and his teeth. A few seconds later there was a lesser noise as the ship's secondary batteries fired. He trained his binoculars at the beach, but at first he could see nothing as the smoke from the guns swept back over the bridge. But then it cleared and he could see the Martians. Or he could see where they had been. They too, were now wrapped in smoke. An instant later there was a gentler double concussion as *Pennsylvania* and *Delaware* fired their broadsides. Seconds passed and then large explosions erupted on the shore in the midst of the smoke. Some bit of something went soaring skyward, tumbling end over end. An arm? A leg, perhaps? He couldn't tell.

More rumbles as the fire passed down the line. *North Carolina* and *Tennessee* and then the German ships. The roar became continuous. He was almost taken by surprise when Michigan let off another salvo and he nearly dropped his binocular. Smoke blotted out his view again and he dared to look away. There was the President, binoculars pressed to his eyes with one hand, but his other was balled into a fist which he was slamming rhythmically against the window frame. Other officers around him were cheering.

He looked at the beach again and the storm of shells continued to churn up the landscape. The smoke drew aside for an instant and he thought he saw one of the Martian machines, but it vanished again as more explosions erupted. What looked like heat rays stabbed out now and then, but they were at random angles, hitting nothing. *Michigan* fired off a third salvo—or was it the fourth?—but her guns were now turned distinctly toward the rear. They had passed the Martians and were drawing ahead.

"Stand by to reverse course to starboard in succession!" shouted the admiral. They were going to turn around and hit them again. Several minutes went by before all the ships had acknowledged the signal. When all was ready, Rodman commanded: "Execute!"

The little *Chester* was now in the lead and she turned sharply to the right until she was going the other way and passing down the line of ships in the opposite direction. *Pennsylvania* followed and then it was *Michigan's* turn. The ship heeled noticeably as she swung around and Andrew had to brace himself. Then she straightened out and was heading west; *North Carolina* thundering past to the right, preparing to turn.

A thrill passed through Andrew. The power, the… *majesty* of this was unlike anything he'd ever experienced. He looked toward the shore, where the Martians were still wreathed in smoke. *You sons-of-bitches think you can build war machines? Well take a look at these!*

While the ships turned, the fire had fallen off to almost nothing. The front of the line was re-aiming its guns to the opposite side and the rearward ships couldn't fire because the leaders were now in their way. The smoke on shore was dispersing and Andrew tried to see what had been done to the Martians.

It was hard to tell. There was still smoke and flames and mangled shapes on the ground that he hoped were Martian tripods. But there were two—no three—machines still on their feet. *Not for long!*

"Signal the squadron to resume firing as their guns bear," said Rodman.

"Sir! Wait!" cried another officer. "Look!"

"What? Why…? Oh for the love of God! What's that idiot think he's doing?"

"What is it, Admiral?" asked Roosevelt.

"One of the damn German torpedo boats! It's charging the Martians!"

Every eye turned to look toward the rear of the line. Sure enough one of the small sleek craft was knifing through the water toward the shore. A small gun on its bow popping away.

"Wants to get his licks in, I guess," said Roosevelt.

"He's going to block our fire!" snarled Rodman.

"And he's getting way too close to the Martians!" exclaimed Andrew. "They aren't all out of action!"

"Signal the Germans to get him the hell out of there!"

As Andrew watched through his binoculars, one of the Martians fired its heat ray. He didn't see any damage to the ship, but the men manning the gun disappeared and a few puffs of smoke appeared only to be whisked away by the wind. But whoever was in command seemed to get the message because it started to turn away. The tiny vessel swung its bow away from the shore and back out to sea.

But then the Martians fired again.

Not a heat ray this time, but some sort of projectile flew away from their machine in a lazy arc through the sky. Andrew feared he knew what it was. "Turn you idiots! Turn!" They tried, but the projectile arced back down and burst a hundred yards in front of them. A black cloud billowed up and the German ship charged right into it. It emerged again a few seconds later and continued its turn out to sea.

But it kept right on turning.

It moved in a long arc that barely missed colliding with the tail end of the German line and them it curved right around and headed toward shore again. But at least it was out of the line of fire.

Rodman muttered a curse and then ordered the ships to open fire.

The guns roared out again and the Martians disappeared under a whirlwind of flame and smoke. The long line of ships steamed past the point of land where the enemy was clustered, each vessel in turn pounding away with every gun it had. Andrew expected to see Martians trying to escape, but if any did, they were concealed by the smoke. After the second run, the scouts signaled that they could not see any more of the enemy and the combined squadron drew off-shore to about five miles and most of the ships stopped their engines and dropped anchor. The unfortunate torpedo boat circled several more times and then ran aground, its engines still going at full speed.

Then, to no one's surprise, Roosevelt insisted on going ashore.

For form's sake, the admiral tried to talk him out of it, but it was clear he realized it was a lost cause. He did at least get the President to agree to allow the marines to go in first to secure the area.

Andrew, daring to tread even where Admiral Rodman had feared to go, also made some demands on the President. "Sir, we know the Martians had at least one of their black dust weapons. If they had any more and they were broken open by our bombardment, the area could be covered with the stuff. You—and any men we send ashore—must be wearing appropriate clothing and no one should try to pick up anything at all they find there until we can confirm that there is no dust present." Roosevelt grumbled, but when Ted sided with Andrew, he gave way. Tall rubber boots were found and handed out.

Every Leatherneck in the squadron was assembled and put into boats and sent ashore. Fortunately, the standard marine equipment now included the same anti-dust gear as the army. The Germans did the same with whatever passed for marines in their fleet. Altogether there were nearly five hundred men. They landed without incident, except for one boat which capsized in the surf, and spread out to scout the area. It was two hours before they signaled the area was safe—two hours with an increasingly restless Theodore Roosevelt pacing the bridge.

But eventually they were allowed to go ashore. Roosevelt tried to jump out of the boat into the surf, but Andrew stopped him. There could be dust floating in the water despite the fact the marines had found none so far. So they waited until the boat was pulled up onto the beach and they debarked dry-shod.

The beach and the land behind it had been blasted to bits. There were craters everywhere. Craters overlapping craters, craters inside other craters, and scattered inside the craters were bits and pieces of the Martian machines. Andrew had seen a number of wrecked tripods in New Mexico and except for the one which had been vaporized when its power plant exploded, they had all been more or less intact. Not this time. The machines had been… shredded, smashed, ravaged… Andrew searched for the right word and finally settled on pulverized.

There were a few small items he recognized from the other wrecks he'd seen, but very few. The majority of the debris was unrecognizable. And the whole area was glistening with millions of those little metal hexagons that were left behind when the Martian armor was pierced. He didn't see anything even vaguely like a Martian body. The tripod's crews had been completely destroyed. He'd hoped to be able to determine how many tripods had been destroyed by checking the remains, but he saw that would be impossible. It would require a complete inventory and there was no time for that. *Leave it to the Germans; it's their problem now.*

"Well, we certainly took care of these rascals, didn't we?" said the President after he'd walked around for a while.

"Yes, sir," said Andrew. "It's a great victory." And it was. They had surely hurt the Martians in this part of the world badly today. Now they just needed to do the same thing in a hundred other places—places where the navy couldn't reach.

There wasn't much of a breeze on the beach and they were soon all sweating rivers. Despite this, Roosevelt insisted on hiking down to where the German torpedo boat was grounded. There was a crowd of Germans already gathered there. The ship had hit a rock about fifty yards offshore and that had flooded it sufficiently to drown the engine so it was just sitting there, rocking gently in the waves. There was no sign of anyone on board. No bodies, nothing. Some of the Germans were shouting in hopes of hearing a response, but there was none.

"Beastly stuff, that dust," said Roosevelt.

"Yes, sir," said Andrew. "And we are very lucky they only had the shorter range version of it here today. If they had any of the long-range rockets like they used in England, half our ships might have ended up like this. I should have insisted that we engage at a longer range."

"All's well that ends well, Major. But yes, I need to talk to the admiral—and the Navy Department as well—to see what we can do to protect our ships from this sort of thing."

Finally even the President had seen enough and they returned to the *Michigan*. They cleaned up, put on fresh clothes, and then were all taken over to the German flagship for a celebratory dinner. There were many toasts and Roosevelt and the German Admiral talked for hours in English and German. Their hosts had a small group of musicians to provide entertainment and they even played Sousa's new march, *The Glory of the Yankee Navy* to honor their guests. Andrew was so tired he nearly fell asleep.

The long, long day came to a close and they headed back to their own ship. The President came over and sat next to Andrew and Ted and said quietly: "Gentlemen, thank you for indulging an old man's follies. I can't begin to tell you how much I appreciate it."

"It was an honor to serve under your command today, Mr. President," said Andrew, and he meant it.

Roosevelt chuckled, leaned forward, and slapped Andrew on the knee. "But it's time to go! Come, Major, let's collect your pretty bride and go home! We have a lot of work waiting for us!"

CHAPTER EIGHT

SEPTEMBER 1909, WASHINGTON, DC

Leonard Wood, Chief of Staff of the United States Army, strolled east along F Street; the huge bulk of the State, War, & Navy Building was directly in front of him, silhouetted by the rising sun. A storm had blown through the previous night and he luxuriated in the cool morning air. It was a taste of fall, but he was sure the humid Washington summer wasn't quite through with the city yet. He loved this time of day and always came in early to get some real work done before the inevitable interruptions found him.

He bought a copy of *The Washington Post* from an urchin on the corner and trotted up the steps to his office on the third floor. His doctors probably would have scolded him for not taking the elevator, but to hell with them! It was so good to be well again! Aside from a fading scar on his head, there was nothing to show that anything had ever been wrong. He could walk or even run without a problem. He took a deep breath as he threw open the door to his office and said good morning to his aide, Captain Semancik. A steward had already brought coffee and he took a cup and went into the inner office.

The headline on the paper—as he'd expected—proclaimed: *'President Defeats Martians in Naval Battle!'* The letters were so big they took up half the front page. Wood smiled and shook his head. Leave it to Theodore to turn an inspection trip into the biggest victory so far won against the invaders! He was going to be absolutely insufferable when he got back. A damn shame that it helped out the Germans more than the Americans. Still, every Martian killed was a gain. And good news—any good news—was big boost for the morale of the country.

And they needed it. The defeat of Funston in New Mexico had come as a huge shock. Everyone was expecting a victory. They had one now, even though it wasn't the one they'd been expecting, and hopefully it would help calm things down. Putting the newspaper aside, he took up the messages which had arrived overnight. Semancik had already put them in what he thought was order of importance, and he was usually right.

As he'd expected, the first half-dozen in the pile were all from Funston or members of his staff demanding reinforcements and supplies. Wood had been truly relieved that Fred Funston had survived the battle. Even though he'd lost, he still had a better grasp of the situation than anyone who might have replaced him. And he was still a fine commander. He'd made a mistake, no doubt, but he would learn from it and not make the same mistake again.

And he'd managed to salvage most of his army. Most of the men, anyway. He'd lost all his tanks and most of his artillery and a lot of his supplies, but when things had gone to hell, a surprising number of the men had managed to make it out. Funston was assembling them, along with whatever reserves he'd had and reinforcements already *en route*, into some semblance of order back near Albuquerque. Once again, the Martians had failed to follow up on a victory. But Funston needed a massive influx of weapons and equipment to make his army effective again.

And Wood had nothing to send him.

Oh, the factories were churning out tanks and guns in unprecedented numbers. The Baldwin works were in full production turning out steam tanks, American Locomotive in Schenectady was getting geared up, too, and that Henry Ford fellow out in Michigan claimed he could out-produce both with a new production method. Other arsenals were making cannons, still others aeroplanes. From rifles to belts, blankets, and boots, American industry was producing the sinews of war. Troops were pouring out of the training camps and new regiments and divisions were becoming combat-ready. The army was stronger than ever before.

But Leonard Wood couldn't send these hosts to Albuquerque. Not for a while, anyway.

The Martians had launched a new wave of cylinders in July and all the experts claimed they would be here sometime in November. Thankfully, there were only half as many as the first time, but just like after the first launch, there was no way of knowing where they would land, so they had to plan for the worst. The worst would be for them to land in the east, where most of the people and most of the factories were located. As long as the factories and mines kept working they could win this war. But if production was disrupted, things could get very bad.

So the east had to be defended, even if that meant hanging the west out to dry. Wood didn't like it, but there wasn't any choice. The new formations were being placed in strategic regions east of the Mississippi, locations from which they could quickly reach any new landing area. It was the same strategy they had used back during the first landings. A vast system of observers were in place to watch for falling cylinders. Each lookout post had telephone or telegraph communication to central command centers. If a cylinder was observed falling, it would be reported and, if confirmed, army units could be on the way to the location in a matter of hours.

It took time—days or even weeks—for the Martians to assemble their fearsome war machines after they landed. If troops could reach them before they could do it, they could be wiped out before they became a serious threat. But if they were given the time… That's what had happened back in '07. The Martians landed in out of the way places the army couldn't reach quickly. And while they hadn't threatened any big cities or mines or factories, they'd been able to assemble their machines and come out fighting. No one knew what they would do this time. Land in the east in hopes that all the troops and guns were out west? Reinforce the Martians in the west? Land in some other place entirely? Until they knew, Wood had no choice but to concentrate his forces in the east.

He had been able to send at least some things Funston's way. A few guns, a few tanks, ammunition and explosives, but not nearly as much as the man wanted—or needed. If he was attacked again before December he was going to be in trouble. All Wood could tell him was to dig in and wait. That's what he was telling his other western commanders, too. There was a corps in Wyoming, another in eastern Colorado, and several divisions and brigades posted in the Dakotas, Nebraska, and Kansas. They were short on tanks and heavy artillery, but they all had been preparing to advance when Funston took the Martian fortress at Gallup. Now all they could do was dig in where they were and wait.

Sighing, Wood took out a pen and started writing out quick replies to each of the communiques. Semancik would turn his chicken-scratches into intelligible messages. He sometimes wondered how many messages never even reached his desk. Semancik was very capable.

He worked through the stack as the morning wore away until Semancik stuck his head in the office. "Just wanted to remind you that the British Military Attaché will be here soon, sir."

"Ah, right. Thank you." He checked the time and saw that Major Vernon Kell was due in just fifteen minutes and the man was always exactly on time. He got up and stretched, freshened up a bit, and had another cup of coffee. He was curious about what Kell wanted. He'd said it was important but refused to elaborate.

Exactly on the tick of the hour Semancik ushered Major Kell into Wood's office. The Englishman was a bit younger than Wood, a bit taller, but sported a very similar mustache. He was stylishly dressed in civilian clothes rather than in uniform. They exchanged pleasantries, Kell giving his congratulations on Roosevelt's victory, and then they sat down. "So what can I do for you, Major?"

"Ah, well, General, I hope it is a matter of what we can do for each other," replied Kell. "I have been directed by His Majesty's Government to make certain information available to you."

"Really? Such as?"

"Well, there are several different items. Let's start with the strategic, shall we?"

"As you please," said Wood, wondering where this was going.

"Excellent. Several important decisions have been made recently. The first, sad to say, is the decision that Australia cannot be defended and must be considered lost."

Wood sat forward, startled. "Really? I mean I can understand the decision, but the British position had been so steadfastly in favor of holding onto every bit of the Empire that this comes as quite a surprise."

"It was not an easy decision, I'm told," said Kell stiffly. "But as Frederick the Great said: 'He who tries to defend everything defends nothing.' The vast distance and the considerable strength of the Martians—we now know that they made at least three and possibly four separate landings there—makes a defense impractical. Our forces in the area are now in the process of evacuating all those we can to India, New Zealand, or Tasmania."

"Makes sense," conceded Wood, wondering how this affected the United States.

"In addition, our attempts to counterattack in our South African colony have been suspended. For the immediate future we will restrict our activities there to the defense of the region around Capetown." Wood nodded, again, this was of no great concern to him. "And finally, the last bit of bad news: the situation in Canada is becoming serious."

"We were of the opinion that it had been serious right from the start," said Wood. All right, now this was relevant.

Kell shrugged. "Yes, of course. But now it is more serious. The Martians who landed in Alberta initially moved south where they cut the railway to the Pacific, but now they have turned east. In addition, we have confirmation of a second landing site on the border with Alaska..."

"We had suspected that," said Wood.

"Yes, but now they are moving east and south. Lastly, the Danish government has confirmed that there was a landing in Greenland. And our reconnaissance indicates that they may attempt to cross over to the mainland when the Davis Straight freezes over this winter."

"That makes sense," said Wood. "There can't be much to interest them in Greenland. But that means you have three forces converging on eastern Canada."

"Yes, and just as is the case with your country, the east is what really matters. Nearly all the people and industry are in Ontario and Quebec. The western provinces are virtually uninhabited. Therefore, due to this threat and our lessened commitments in Australia and Africa, the General Staff has concluded that a major expedition be sent to Canada."

Wood sat up. Now *this* was important! He and his people had been very worried by the lack of defense to the north. If Canada fell, the Martians would threaten the whole northern border. "When? How large a force? Where do you plan to deploy it?"

"Nothing is going to happen until after the next wave of landings, I'm afraid," said Kell. "We have to plan for the worst—just as we know you are doing—and not leave the home islands unprotected until we know there will be no landings there. But assuming there are none, come November, we will start moving troops across the Atlantic. Just a few divisions to start, but if all goes well, more will follow. As for where they will go… that's less certain." Kell got up and walked over to one of the maps on the wall of Wood's office. "The layman might well say we should build a line from Lake Superior northeast to Hudson's Bay. Looks fine on the map, doesn't it? It seals off all the Martians to the west from coming east. But the reality is that this is all an absolute wilderness. No railroads, no roads of any kind; really, only a scattering of tiny villages. Trying to supply an army in this area—especially in winter—would be utterly impossible. And it wouldn't even do the job if we could. In winter the Martians could just cross James Bay and outflank the whole line."

Wood nodded patiently, this was all entirely obvious. "So where…?"

"Initially, we plan to build a line from Georgian Bay across to the St. Lawrence below Kingston." Kell drew a line on the map with his finger. "That would safeguard London, Toronto, and a good chunk of territory. We'll also build defenses around Ottawa, Montreal, and Quebec City—and support them with the navy. Eventually, if we're given the time, we hope to create a continuous line north of the St. Lawrence all the way to the sea. We realize that this plan effectively abandons ninety-five percent of the country, but there's nothing else we can do."

Wood studied the map. It probably did make sense, but he couldn't help but notice the enormous empty space from Lake Superior all the way west to the American units in North Dakota. It was every bit of five hundred miles with nothing to prevent the Martians from sweeping down through Minnesota into the rear. He realized it was unrealistic to expect the British to fill that gap and he was grateful he wouldn't have to worry about the Martians wading across the St. Lawrence into New York or Vermont, but still…

"It will certainly be good to have you here, Major," he said. "Frankly, sir, there has been a great deal of grumbling about the lack of English cooperation."

Major Kell looked like he had swallowed something very sour. But whatever angry reply he might have wanted to make, he swallowed that down, too. "Yes, we are aware of that, General. But we have been quite busy elsewhere, you know. In fact, were it not for several recent successes in Egypt and India which turned back Martian offensives, we wouldn't be able to even undertake this much. However…" he paused and walked over and opened the office door. "I am pleased to inform you that His Majesty's Government pledges its full cooperation from this point on." He gestured with his hand and two men came in, rolling hand trucks stacked high with large leather-bound books.

"What's all this?"

Kell picked up one of the volumes which was at least two inches thick and obviously quite heavy and put it down on Wood's desk. He flipped open the pages and Wood saw that it was crowded with text, mathematical equations, and engineering diagrams. "These sir, are the complete collection of everything our scientists have discovered from the Martian devices we captured after the first invasion. We are confident you will find them useful."

* * * * *

SEPTEMBER, 1909, ALBUQUERQUE, NEW MEXICO TERRITORY

First Sergeant Frank Dolfen's horse splashed across the Rio Grande and then struggled up the far bank. The town of Albuquerque lay just ahead. There was a bridge over the river, but it was jammed with wagons and he was in no mood to wait. The long retreat from Gallup was nearly at an end—or at least he certainly hoped so. They hadn't seen any sign of the Martians since the day of the battle and that was a damn good thing. The mass of refugees which escaped the disaster had eventually sorted themselves out into some semblance of an army, but without artillery or tanks they would have been helpless if attacked. The cavalry, as always, was tasked with covering the retreat—not that they could have done a blessed thing if the Martians had showed up.

The retreat had been all of a hundred and fifty miles and he swore he could feel every inch of it in his aching arms, legs, and backside. Of course he should feel grateful he didn't have to march the whole way like the infantry, but in fact, most of the infantry got picked up by trains as they retreated. The railroad was still working along the whole route and several times a day there would be a train there to deliver food and pick up people and what little equipment that had been salvaged. The army shrank and shrank as it retreated—but the cavalry still had to cover whatever was left. And what was left was a large mass of wagons and horses; slow and vulnerable but too valuable to simply abandon.

The only bright spot in the whole mess was that his friend, Becca Harding, was driving one of those wagons. Somehow in the rush to escape she'd ended up with a wagonload of wounded. Those in her care had eventually been transferred to a train, but she'd volunteered to continue with the army to help any men who'd become sick or injured on the way. Dolfen had found excuses to check on her frequently during the march. She was up on the bridge right now with her rig and he waved to her and she waved back. He didn't know if he'd have a chance to see her again and that saddened him. She was a great kid—and a good friend.

A provost officer was directing traffic up ahead. "What unit?" he demanded as Dolfen and his following troopers approached.

"5th Cavalry."

The man checked a sheet of paper and then pointed. "Your camp's up that way, about two miles."

"Right. All right, you lunks! Almost there! Follow me!" He turned them north along the river, and the depth of their weariness could be gauged by the fact that there were hardly any answering comments, complaints, or jokes. Everyone was beat. Except for Jason Urbaniak, of course. The man seemed capable of talking no matter how tired he was. Now he moved up next to Dolfen.

"So whaddya think's gonna happen now, Sarge?"

"Looks like we're digging in," he said, pointing to groups of men who were working with picks and shovels on trenches on the east side of the river. "Guess that means we'll be stayin' a while."

"Sure hope you're right! I could use a rest!"

"Yeah. And we need to get the regiment organized again. A lotta boys still missing and I don't think they were all killed." The 5th had been badly scattered on the day of the fight and Dolfen hadn't seen more than a hundred or so during the retreat. But they couldn't all be dead.

"Still no sign of the captain," said Urbaniak.

"Probably up ahead at the camp they've set for us."

"Hope they got tents and gear for us."

"Don't hold your breath."

As they rode along, they did see quite a few proper camps with the tents set in a regulation pattern. But as Dolfen had feared, the camp for the 5th was little more than a dusty rectangle marked in the dirt. There were a few dog tents already there and a heartening number of horses in a roped off area, but not much more. A corporal met them and directed them to their spot, assuring them that tents and supplies were on the way. They stiffly dismounted and saw to their horses.

"Oh, brother," said Urbaniak. "They better get us our stuff quick or there's gonna be hell to pay!"

"What do you mean?"

"Look who our neighbors are."

Dolfen glanced where Urbaniak was pointing and stiffened. Next door was a very proper and well-equipped cavalry camp. But the troopers…

"10th Cavalry," said Dolfen. "Yeah that could be awkward." The 10th was one of the army's colored regiments. They were good troops, no doubt, and most of the white regiments didn't give them any trouble—as long as they kept their distance. But to have them right there, with all the stuff the 5th lacked, oh yeah, that was sure to lead to trouble! "I better go find the captain and have a word with him."

But the captain was nowhere to be found and no one had seen him since the fight near Gallup. That was not good. Eventually he found the regimental adjutant, a first lieutenant named Siganuk, sitting under a tent fly. "Ah! Frank! I was just going to send for you!" he said.

"Really, sir? Have you seen Captain DeBrosse?"

"No, and no one else has seen him, either. I'm afraid we're going to have to assume he was killed. A damn shame."

"He was a good man," agreed Doflen. "So who has the squadron now, sir?"

"Lieutenant Pendleton is senior and is being brevetted to captain and will take over. But that means we need a new commander for C Troop—and that's why I wanted to see you."

What? No! He can't mean…

"Congratulations, Lieutenant, you have C Troop." Siganuk got up from his stool and slapped him on the shoulder.

"Sir! You can't do that! I'm no officer!"

"The colonel says you are, Frank, and these days that's all it takes."

"But… but… I can't be an officer! I've got no education, no…"

"You're one of the most experienced men in the regiment. The men look up to you. Don't worry, you'll do fine."

"But… but…" Siganuk's smile was starting to become a frown.

"No more arguments, Dolfen! We're in a war and everyone has to do everything they can! We need a lieutenant to run C Troop and you… are… it! Now shut up and go do your job!"

"I… uh… yes sir." He saluted and stumbled away.

An officer! How the hell could he be an officer? Officers were gentlemen, how could he be a gentleman? Of course, most officers were also idiots and he certainly knew how to be that! On the other hand, there must be some advantages to being an officer…

"Did you find the captain?" asked Corporal Urbaniak.

"No, found the adjutant, though."

"What'd he say?"

Dolfen straightened up and looked around. "Round up a detachment. We're going to go find ourselves some gear. And we're gonna find some of those dynamite bombs! We are not getting stuck like that again!"

"Sounds good to me," said Urbaniak. "But you got authorization for all that?"

"Yes I do. Now hop to it, Sergeant!"

Urbaniak turned away and then spun around on his heel.

"Huh?"

* * * * *

SEPTEMBER, 1909, ALBUQUERQUE, NEW MEXICO TERRITORY

Rebecca Harding shook the reins and shouted at the horse team. "C'mon you nags! Just another mile or two and we're done!" The worn out horses didn't answer, but kept plodding along, which was all that mattered. Albuquerque, the long retreat was at an end. Or at least she sure hoped it was. All the rumors said the army was going to make a stand here and from what she could see as she crossed the bridge indicated that for once, the rumors were true. Cities of tents stretched in all directions and swarms of soldiers were digging trenches along the river bank. This time of year the Rio Grande was little more than a stream, but in many spots the banks were pretty steep; maybe they'd be hard for the Martians to get across.

She was with the last of the wagons to arrive. The cavalry rearguard had already passed them and she'd waved to Sergeant Dolfen. It had been very reassuring to know he was close by during the retreat. But now they were here. She could deliver the last of the injured to the hospital and then join up with the other nurses. She didn't know if they'd be staying here or going back to the big hospital in Santa Fe. She glanced back to check on her passengers. There was a guy who had taken a fall and broken his ankle yesterday and another man who was sick with something and too weak to walk.

And then there was Sam.

That was what he called himself and he refused to give a last name. He was sitting there in the wagon like he'd been since that day when she'd first seen him. He was looking—and smelling—a whole lot better than he had then. He'd gotten a wash and a shave and a fresh uniform borrowed from one of the ambulance drivers, which made him look little different from any of the other men—except for the hollow, *hunted* look on his face. She guessed he was in his twenties, dark hair, brown eyes, and rather scrawny. There didn't seem to be anything physically wrong with him, but he refused to stray far from the wagon and refused to say anything about what had happened to him. Becca had expected Miss Chumley to tell him to go find his unit or just chase him off, but instead she pretended he wasn't even there.

But now they had reached their destination and she had to do something with him.

An officer was at the edge of town and he gave them directions how to get to the main hospital. She looked back at Sam. "We'll be there soon. What are you going to do then?" He stared at her but didn't say anything. "Maybe you can find your unit." She'd suggested that several times, but he'd never answered—until now.

"They're all dead."

"You don't know that," she replied, pleased that she'd gotten a response. "A lot of men got away from that first battle."

"All dead," he repeated.

"Well, even if they are, you have to do something. You're still in the army, you can't just walk away." She wished she'd taken a closer look at the collar disk on his uniform when she first saw him. That would have told her his regiment. But that was long gone and the borrowed tunic he was wearing now had a Medical Corps disk.

"Maybe I can stay at the hospital. Help out there."

This was the closest thing to a conversation she'd managed with Sam and she didn't want to risk shutting it off. "Well, maybe. We can always use help." But she doubted they'd just let him sign up without knowing who he was. They drove on in silence for a while and then she decided to take a chance. "You were in there, weren't you?"

She looked back at him and he had pulled his knees up to his chest and wrapped his arms around them. His eyes were almost shut. "So the Martians caught you and took you there. I'm sorry. They caught me, too, you know." His eyes widened slightly, but he frowned and looked skeptical.

"It's true. I was with a dozen others and one of their war machines trapped us in a canyon. It was herding us toward their fortress, but we managed to escape before we got there."

"Escape?"

"Well, we were rescued, actually. Some other soldiers with dynamite bombs ambushed the Martian and wrecked its machine and we got away."

"You were lucky."

"I know. And you weren't. I'm sorry. But you're free now. And you can fight again. And I'm sure the generals and scientists and all will want to hear about what you saw in the Martian fortress! You're really very important, you know!"

Sam glanced at the other two men in the wagon, but they were both asleep. "Put me in a cage."

"I'm sorry the Martians put you in a cage, Sam. But you're free."

"No. Generals'll put me in a cage."

"What? The generals won't put you in a cage!" Was the man becoming delusional?

"They'll keep me somewhere. I'll be a sideshow freak. Never let me go."

Becca opened her mouth to issue a denial, but then she stopped. Sam was staring at her with an unreadable expression.

"The Martians put us in a cage, but I'll never be in a cage again."

* * * * *

CYCLE 597, 843.9, HOLDFAST 32-1

"I'm sure that's the last of them, Commander," said Ixmaderna.

Qetjnegartis sincerely hoped its subordinate was correct. In the wake of the battle, the most difficult thing to deal with had not been the repairs to the holdfast, or the casualties, or even the arrogance of Commander Braxjandar. The worst thing was the fact that the prey-creatures had gotten inside the underground sections—and they might still be down there.

It was an entirely unsettling thought.

There was no doubt that they had been there, vision pick-ups had clearly shown them in some areas, and after the rest of their army had been routed, glimpses were seen of creatures who had been left behind. But the pickups did not have even close to complete coverage and there could be hundreds of places where the creatures could be lurking. Aside from the main hanger, the fighting machines would not fit through the corridors. The travel chairs could be fitted with weapons, but they were not designed to be used for fighting and would be vulnerable even to the small weapons the prey-creatures carried. No one wanted to go down there and search for them.

They could simply wait them out, of course, since eventually they would run out of food. But that could take many days and there was no time to waste. Much work needed to be done and they had to get back inside the holdfast to do it.

Several plans were considered, including flooding the entire holdfast with the eradicator dust. But in the end it was a simple plan, suggested by Davnitargus of all people, which had proved the most practical: turn off the lights.

It had long been known that the prey-creatures did not see well in even semi-darkness and could not see at all in a complete absence of light. So they had shut down all the lights remotely and waited. In ones and twos the creatures had made their way back into the light, some burning things to produce light. They had been allowed to go unmolested—at first—for fear that the sound of the heat rays might drive the miserable things back down inside. But several fighting machines had waiting in ambush farther away and it was not thought that any of them had escaped.

So now work could start again. Anything down below that the prey-creatures might have damaged must be repaired. The holdfast walls needed to be repaired and the defense towers needed to be replaced. Over five hundred of the prey had been trapped inside the inner redoubt. These needed to be secured and an enlarged holding pen inside created. One very important thing had been discovered: huge mounds of the food they ate had been left in their camps. This could be transferred to the holdfast and the prey could be kept alive until needed.

Then, once all that had been done, they could get back to work constructing new fighting machines. The reinforcements from the Homeworld were on the way and they would need them.

"Come," said Qetjnegartis, "let us proceed."

CHAPTER NINE

OCTOBER 1909, WEST ORANGE, NEW JERSEY

"We have discovered some truly amazing things from the power generators you've sent us, Major, truly amazing!"

Andrew regarded the legendary Thomas Edison from across a long table filled with papers, drawings, and piles of... *stuff* he couldn't begin to identify, although he was fairly certain some of them were of Martian origin. Edison's laboratories in West Orange, while not as well-known as his original labs in Menlo Park, were considered to be the best equipped facilities of their kind in the world. They covered several city blocks and reputedly held samples of over eight thousand chemical compounds as well as tools, nuts, bolts, electrical components, and a thousand other things from Elk horn to Shark's teeth. Everything and anything that might become useful for Edison's work. The man was often referred to as the 'Wizard of Menlo Park' and even though it was now in West Orange, the place did have the look of some fairy tale wizard's workshop.

The man himself, on the other hand, looked rather ordinary. Short and a bit stout, wearing a conservative suit and vest, his hair was mostly white with a bald patch on top. He looked the part of an elderly professional in his sixties. But behind that ordinary veneer was one of the most creative and imaginative men in the world. Two other men were with him, William Hammer and Frank Sprague, both electrical experts. Andrew had met all three on prior visits.

"First and foremost," continued Edison, "we discovered that the units you gave us are not power plants! They don't produce power, they store it."

"Really, sir?" said Andrew casually. "Do go on."

"We started with the assumption that they *were* power plants of some sort, of course. First of all, you told us they were, and second, there didn't seem to be any other source of power for the Martian machines, based on the drawings you provided. So with that in mind we proceeded with extreme caution. We didn't want another Liverpool explosion!"

Andrew stiffened. Edison was referring to a disastrous accident in Liverpool, England where apparently while experimenting with a similar unit, a massive explosion had killed several hundred people—including Andrew's father who had been invited to observe. "No, certainly not," he said quietly.

"We did every test we could think of without actually opening up the device. From magnetometers to galvanometers; we even set up a calcium tungstate screen to check for X-rays or Becquerel Rays. Nothing. The thing seemed inert. So, we took the risk and opened it. Not here of course! We trucked it thirty miles out into the Pine Barrens and fortunately—as you can see—didn't blow ourselves to bits."

"The nation is certainly glad that didn't happen, sir," said Andrew. Off to the side, Sprague was pointing at Edison and silently mouthing: *He didn't go!*

"Once we had safely opened the thing, we brought it back here and went to work, and I can tell you we were surprised by what we found! Or I should say: what we *didn't* find. There were a number of small mechanisms which we believe are for regulating the flow of power—things we did expect to find—but the rest of the cylinder was filled with this." Edison reached to the table and picked up something between his thumb and forefinger and held it up. Andrew leaned forward and saw a long strand of what looked like golden human hair. It was so thin that if it hadn't caught the light he would have been barely able to see it.

"Wire," said Edison. "Miles—we estimate thousands of miles—of this wire. It was wrapped in coils which filled the entire cylinder—which you'll recall was three feet in diameter and over eight feet tall. But that's all. Nothing which could have produced energy, unless by some system which is totally beyond our science. A possibility we did not discount, of course.

"Having nothing else, we set to work studying the wire. A chemical analysis produced an interesting mixture of elements; copper, silver, gold, molybdenum, and quite a few others. The wire has a surprisingly high tensile strength which exceeds that of steel. But its most amazing characteristics were electrical. Bill? Could you explain?"

Mr. Hammer nodded. "When we ran current through the wire we were astonished to find that there was no electrical resistance at all. I mean none. An Ohm meter attached to the wire registered zero. We still don't know how this is accomplished. There is a Dutchman, Heike Onnes, who has been working on this phenomenon, but his research has involved materials cooled to very low temperatures. This wire behaves as it does at room temperature!"

"And because of this lack of resistance," said Edison, "a coil of this wire would be able to store an astounding amount of current, like an impossibly efficient dry-cell battery! We tested this out by taking a small amount of the wire—just a dozen yards or so—and winding it in a coil and then applying current. It just soaked it up! We fed current in for an entire day and it probably could have held more. Then we connected the coil to a bank of incandescent lights. They were still burning a month later!

"So, Major, it is our conclusion that the Martians must have some sort of central power generating station—don't ask me how *that* works!—and this charges up these power storage units which the Martian war machines use. Of course we have no way of knowing what the power demands of the machines are, but considering how much power just one of these units must be capable of holding, I would guess that the machines could operate for months between chargings."

"I should add," said Mr. Sprague, speaking for the first time, "that if something were to disrupt the ability of the wire to store power, the unit might discharge itself all at once. This could produce a large explosion. That might explain the Liverpool disaster and the explosion that consumed one of the Martian machines at the Battle of Prewitt."

"Yes," said Edison. "And until we determine just what it takes to cause such a disruption, we must proceed with caution." He paused and looked closely at Andrew. "Pardon me for asking, Major, but do you understand what we've been telling you here? Your lack of... well... *astonishment* had been noticeable, and in my experience that means the person really doesn't understand what he's being told."

Andrew sighed. "Well, sir, I can't say that I begin to understand all the technicalities of it, but I do, in fact, understand the gist of what you are saying. Forgive me for not looking astonished, but... I think this will explain." He opened up his briefcase and took out a very thick bundle of papers and laid it on the table in front of Edison.

The man looked at the pages and slowly began to turn them. Hammer and Sprague crowded in to look over his shoulder. The expressions of all three men took on the astonishment which apparently Edison had been expecting from Andrew. "What... what is this?" demanded Edison.

"And look at this!" cried Hammer, snatching a sheet away from his boss.

"Where did you get these?" added Sprague.

"Well, Major? Explain what this is!" Edison's face was turning red.

Andrew took a deep breath. "First, gentlemen, let me congratulate you. Based on the very fine presentation you just gave, I would estimate that you've managed, in just six months, to unravel mysteries which took the British several years."

"The British! Is this their work?"

"Yes and…"

"If you had this, why in the world did you let us waste our time on…?!" Now his face was very red.

"Sir, please! We only received this a few weeks ago. Our *esteemed* allies have finally decided to share what they know with us." He gestured at the stack of papers. "This is only a fraction of what they sent us. We are making copies of it all as quickly as we can and you will receive a complete set within the month. Forgive me for not telling you as soon as I arrived but, frankly, I wanted to compare what you've told me with what's in these documents."

"I see," said Edison, some of the color leaving his face. He sighed deeply, rubbed at his nose, and sniffed. The side of his mouth bent up in what could have been a smile. "So tell me, Major, how did we do?"

"As I said: you deserve to be congratulated. Given the same evidence, you've arrived at the same conclusion—and in a fraction of the time. But tell me one thing. This wire: do you think you can produce it yourselves?"

Now the faces of the three men fell. "No," said Edison immediately. "Certainly not right now. As I told you we have learned the chemical composition of the wire, but simply mixing together the same elements in the same proportion does not produce the same results. The alloy we've been able to create has none of the physical properties of the original. Clearly there are steps in the manufacturing process that we do not understand."

Andrew nodded. "The British say the same thing."

"Even so," said Sprague, "we have thousands of miles of this wire from captured machines. We've seen that even small amounts of it can store large amounts of power. The potential for us to create compact storage batteries and powerful electric motors is very great. Have the British been working on those ideas, too?" He started rummaging through the stack of paper.

"Yes, I believe they have," replied Andrew. "They've also been working on some other things—with considerable success." He leaned across the table and flipped through the papers until he found a page he'd marked by folding the corner. "Are any of you gentlemen familiar with the concept of a 'coil gun'?"

"Uh, there was a Norwegian fellow…" said Hammer.

"Yes, Birkeland, Kristian Birkeland," said Edison. "He received a patent on the idea back in '04 or '05. Some sort of electromagnetic gun, as I recall."

"Yes, exactly," said Andrew. "A series of electromagnets accelerate a projectile to very high velocities. The British have already created, and are using, such weapons—using this wire. The Ordnance Department is very interested in building our own version. I believe the plans are in these documents. We'd like to have a test model ready before the end of the year."

Edison rubbed his chin. "Might be doable. We'll get to work on it." He picked up the strand of wire again and looked at Andrew. "We're going to need as much of this as we can get. And right now you fellows in the army are the only ones who can get it for us."

"Yes," said Andrew. "We're working on it. Well, sir, gentlemen, I have to be going. Please keep us appraised of your progress."

He took his leave and walked down to the train station, which was only a few blocks away. He caught a train to nearby New York City where he changed trains for Boston. In the middle of the day, it wasn't too crowded. At least half the other passengers were in uniform. Once in a seat, he closed his eyes. He'd only been back for a little over a week and the 'honeymoon' cruise seemed like a dream. He had a huge amount of work to do and had only spent one night with his wife since they returned.

The great victory on the coast of Venezuela was still a major news story, but it couldn't crowd out the fact that the second wave of Martian cylinders was due in less than two months. The level of activity had increased, just in the time he'd been away, to amazing levels. The fortifications around the cities, which had been all but abandoned after the first landing, were being worked on again at a frantic pace. And now they weren't just ditches in the mud. Concrete was being poured and guns mounted. The train passed fort after fort as it moved north.

Military camps were everywhere, too, and now they weren't just for raw recruits. The men were organized in functioning military units, ready for combat. Tank production had reached a level where a new battalion was finished every week. Camp Colt at Gettysburg had been tripled in size to train the crews. Heavy artillery, too, was being turned out in unprecedented amounts. His train passed sidings jammed with flat cars carrying tanks and guns, ready to move. If the Martians did try to land in the east, they were going to be in for a rude surprise!

It was mid-afternoon by time he reached Boston. He took a trolley car to the campus of the Massachusetts Institute of Technology. He had to ask direction to find the Metallurgy Department which was in a building on Garrison Street, some distance from the rest of the campus.

As he was about to go up the steps to the main door of the building, someone was suddenly shouting. "Major! Major Comstock?" He looked back the way he had just come and saw two men. One was fairly dashing toward him while the other was following at a more sedate pace. He paused on the steps and the leading man stopped on the sidewalk a few feet away, gasping for breath. "Major Comstock?" he said again.

"Yes. What is it?" He stared at the man and saw that he was about his own age, although he had already lost most of his hair. He had a small mustache and was wearing a rather cheap-looking suit of clothes with a crumpled hat clutched in his hand. The second man walked up and he was much older, fairly stout, and also sported a mustache.

"Oh, thank goodness we spotted you," said the younger one. "A friend of mine here at MIT told me you were supposed to be here today and we wanted to take the chance to see you!"

"Excuse me, sir, do I know you?" Andrew was fairly certain he'd never laid eyes on either one of the men before.

"No, no, we've never met, but please let me introduce us. My name's Goddard, Robert Goddard, and this is Charles Munroe."

"Pleased to meet you. But why did you want to see me? And why did you need to run me down on the street?"

"Well, you see, we know you work in the Ordnance Department—there were those stories in the newspapers about what you did out west—and that you're involved with developing new weapons to use against the Martians."

"Yes, that's true, although all I really do is see what other people have come up with and then report back to my superiors in Washington. Coordination, that sort of thing."

"That's perfect," said Goddard, "because Charles and I have an idea for a new weapon which we think will be very useful against the Martians!"

Oh dear... Since the start of the war, the army had found itself under an increasing flood of suggestions for 'great new weapons'. Most came from well-meaning citizens who had come up with some idea which they felt would help win the war. Most often the ideas were completely unworkable and could be disregarded instantly. Other times the ideas sounded reasonable enough that some investigation was warranted. Andrew had gotten stuck with a few of them and in each case they had proved to be impractical if not unworkable. The worst were the ones which had some sort of high ranking backer, like a senator or governor, working on behalf of some friend. Letting those people down softly was a job for a diplomat, not a major in ordnance. On very rare occasions, the idea had some real merit. Back in Washington, there was a whole office with a lieutenant and a half-dozen men who sorted through these ideas full-time to see what category they fell in. Andrew was grateful he'd gotten promoted soon enough to have avoided *that* duty!

But this was the first time he'd been hunted down in the street by idea bearers!

"Uh, there is an office at the Ordnance Department where you can send your ideas, gentlemen, I can give you the address. Right now I have a..."

"We've tried that route, sir!" interrupted Goddard. "If you could just give us a moment of your time, you'll see that we're not a pair of crackpots! Charles here is an engineer with the US Naval Torpedo Station in Newport!"

That got Andrew's attention. Munroe, Munroe, hadn't he heard that name before? He checked the time and saw that he had a few minutes. He came down the steps to stand with them on the sidewalk. "Mr. Munroe, if you work for the navy, why haven't you tried them?"

"I have tried. I'm afraid that they showed little interest."

"They said the 'Munroe Effect' had no application in naval ordnance!" said Goddard indignantly. "No application!"

Munroe Effect? Ah! That's where he knew the name from! "You, uh, you've done work with explosives, as I recall?"

"Yes, Major. It's a proven phenomenon that high explosives, if formed in certain shapes, will direct a significant portion of their force in a controllable direction. This would allow a charge of a given size to penetrate an object more deeply than a non-directional charge of the same size."

"Right, right, I remember now. It does seem as though such a thing might have some uses."

"Like penetrating the armor of a Martian machine!" said Goddard. "My friend told me you were here today to see some tests on the Martian armor. That's why we thought you might be interested."

"And what is your, ah, interest in this Mr. Goddard?"

"Well, you see, I've recently been doing some work in the field of rocketry..."

"Rocketry?"

"Yes, sir. A sadly neglected field! Rockets have been used by armies and navies for centuries, but there hasn't been any real progress in ages. I have some ideas which will make rockets far more reliable and far more accurate."

"I see."

"Rockets have the advantage that they don't need heavy metal gun tubes to launch them. They are much cheaper and much lighter—and thus more mobile—than conventional artillery."

And much less accurate, thought Andrew.

"But against the Martians, a standard shrapnel warhead would probably do them little harm. Based on the reports we've seen, the Martian armor must be struck a very heavy impact to suffer damage. Typical rockets would be unable to do that. I couldn't see any way a lightweight rocket would be much use.

"But then when I read about Charles' work I realized we had the answer! A shaped charge warhead delivered by a rocket could do the trick!"

"Perhaps it would," said Andrew, impressed in spite of himself. "But we have conventional artillery in ever-growing amounts."

"Yes, and I'm not proposing that our rockets would replace the artillery, Major! But it's obvious from the newspapers and military journals that our infantry is terribly vulnerable to the Martian machines. Even the hand-thrown dynamite bombs are extremely dangerous to use and force the infantry to close to suicidal ranges."

That's for sure!

"Rockets would give the infantry a real chance!"

"You think you could develop an effective weapon light enough to be carried by infantry?"

"It's possible! All we ask is a chance to try!"

Andrew checked the time again. "I have to go. But here is my card. If you can send me a written proposal, I will see what I can do."

"Thank you, sir!" cried Goddard, snatching the card and then vigorously pumping Andrew's hand. Andrew disentangled himself and retreated up the steps. That had been awkward, but who knew? Perhaps something useful would come of it.

Inside the building, which appeared to be a converted warehouse of some sort, he was directed down to the basement where he was met by Henry Howe, head of MIT's Metallurgical Department. He had two other men with him, Radclyff Furness and Nathanial Keith.

"Welcome, Major," said Howe. "Good to meet you at last. Nice to put a face to someone I've been corresponding with. I must say these samples you've sent us have posed a pretty puzzle!"

"That seems to be what everyone I send things say, sir. Have you managed to solve any of it?"

"We've certainly accumulated some fascinating data and observations, but I'm not sure we've solved anything. But here. Let me show you." He led the way through a maze of machines, cabinets, and work tables to an area that had been fenced off. He produced a key to unlock the door. "Need to keep these secure," he explained. "Can't afford to let the students take any souvenirs!"

At one end of the space was an enormous power-hammer. The rest was filled with cabinets, work benches, microscopes, vises, chisels, wrenches, saws, files, and a multitude of other tools. On many of the benches were sections of Martian machines which had been salvages after the Battle of Prewitt. One piece had been clamped beneath the power-hammer.

"Here, I want to show you this first, Major," said Howe, handing him a large magnifying glass. "Take a look at the section of metal right under the hammer." Andrew took the glass and did as instructed. All he saw was a uniform gray-silver surface. "Nothing to see, right? No sign of those hexagonal flakes?"

"No, none," said Andrew. The Martian armor seemed to be composed of a multitude of tiny metal flakes in the shape of a hexagon. Andrew had seen how they came loose when damaged.

"All right, now stand back please." Andrew did so while Howe made some adjustments to the power-hammer. As he waited, Andrew took a closer look at the actual hammer.

"Is that a three-inch artillery round?"

"A mock-up of one," said Howe. "No explosive charge, of course, but the same size, shape, and material as one. We have other heads for four-inch, five-inch, and seven-inch. We can adjust the force of the hammer to approximate the impact of the actual projectiles."

"Ingenious," said Andrew, very impressed.

"Beats the hell out of lugging these things out to an artillery range," said Furness.

"Okay, here we go," said Howe, flipping a switch. The hammer moved upward and then suddenly smashed down on the metal plate with a ringing crash. He flipped another switch and the hammer drew upward a little and stopped. "Take a look now."

Andrew picked up the glass and again inspected the surface. This time he saw a web of hexagonal-shaped cracks radiating out from the point of impact. He'd seen similar things on the wrecked Martian machines. "No loose flakes, though," he said looking around.

"No, through many tests we've been able to find just the right force to produce the cracks, without knocking anything loose."

"Okay, so what am I looking for?"

"Actually, nothing just at the moment, but remember how the pattern of cracks look." Andrew took another look and then handed the glass back to Howe.

"While we're waiting…"

"Waiting for what?"

"You'll see. While we're waiting, let me tell you a bit about what else we've learned. Naturally, the first thing we did was test the metal itself. Tensile strength, compression strength, malleability, melting point, they were all very high compared to any alloy we're familiar with. The melting point, especially; we had to use our hottest arc furnace to melt a sample. The chemical composition was quite unusual, too: titanium, aluminum, iron, copper, calcium, and a host of rare earths; an unexpected mix of elements. Mostly titanium and not all that much iron, so it has very little magnetic attraction. And using the exact proportions we found in the sample we tried casting our own pieces and…"

"Let me guess," said Andrew, "the results were different from the samples."

"Yes! How did you know?"

"I met with Edison this morning and he had some Martian electrical wire which did the same thing. As he put it: 'Clearly there are steps in the manufacturing process that we do not understand'."

"That about sums it up, yes," said Howe.

"So there's no way to produce this stuff ourselves?"

"Not at this time, no. Perhaps as we learn more. But to be honest we have a lot more to learn than just how to produce the alloy itself." He checked his pocket watch and said: "Should be long enough. Have another look at the sample, Major." Again he proffered the magnifying glass.

Andrew went back to the power hammer and looked at the metal plate. What was he supposed to…? He looked closer and the web of cracks was much smaller than before! When he first looked, the pattern was as large as his hand. Now it was about the size of a silver dollar! And squinting, he focused on one single crack at the edge of the pattern and saw that it was slowly closing up! After another few seconds it was completely gone! "It… it's healing itself!" he cried.

"That's a good way of putting it," said Howe.

"But how is it doing this?"

"Good question, I wish I had the answer."

Andrew glanced at his briefcase. There was another thick bundle of papers he'd brought for Howe, but unlike the one he gave to Edison, he hadn't had a chance to even browse through them. Did the British have any answers to this mystery? Somehow he doubted it.

"There are a few things we do know, however," continued Howe. "One is that prior to the healing process finishing up, the area around the damage is significantly weaker. I read the report you wrote after the battle in New Mexico and your hypothesis that damage can weaken the surrounding structure is exactly correct. That was some fine reasoning, Major."

"Uh, thanks…"

"Also, we've found that if the damage is enough to knock some of the hexagonal flakes loose, it will still heal, but with 'divots' where the missing flakes were, again weakening the structure in proportion to how big a 'divot' it was. And it should be noted that once a flake is knocked loose, it loses whatever this mysterious property is. We tried immediately putting the loose flakes back into their proper position on the plate, but they were not reattached."

Howe went over to a shelf and pulled down a box and opened it. Inside was a mound of the hexagonal flakes. "We also discovered that if a plate is smashed down to small enough fragments it loses its ability to hold itself together completely and simply falls apart."

"So," said Andrew, "at present your best recommendation for dealing with the Martian armor is to do as we have been: just keep pounding them until they fall over?"

Howe smiled grimly. "Yes, I'm afraid so. Of course the more force you can hit them with, the greater the damage—but that's nothing new."

Andrew nodded, thinking about the coil gun idea. Those should supply more force! He thanked the men and gave them the bundle of British document. They were just as scandalized as Edison had been, but when he left they had their noses pressed to the papers.

He stepped out of the building and saw why the street it was on was named 'Garrison'. There was a large brick armory on the next block and a swarm of men in uniform were assembling there. Walking over he realized that they were MIT students undergoing training. Yes, nearly every college and university in the country now had compulsory military training, hoping to turn out the educated officers that would be needed for the vastly expanded army.

The long day was drawing to a close. It was nearly dark by the time he got to the railroad station. He'd take the night train back to Washington where Victoria—and more work—awaited him.

* * * * *

CYCLE 597,843.9, HOLDFAST 32-1

"You are certain?" asked Qetjnegartis.

"There is no doubt, Commander," replied Ixmaderna, looking up from its instruments. "You have been infected. But there is no need to be concerned. Our drugs are quite capable of keeping it in check until your new body is grown. It is less than a tenth of a cycle until it matures."

"But we are so much in need of new individuals right now. To be forced to use this as a replacement is most inconvenient. The drugs will not suffice until I can grow the next bud?"

"That would be a very great risk, Commander. It would be over a third of a cycle before the next bud could mature. If the contagion grew suddenly worse, you would perish. Remember what happened to Zastranvis."

"Yes, you are correct. Very well then. But now I must go." Qetjnegartis left Ixmaderna's lab and returned to the control center. This latest development was annoying, but it was more than balanced by the good news which had come from the Homeworld. Not only were the transports which were soon to arrive carrying mostly personnel as Qetjnegartis had suggested, but five of them had been allocated here! With only half as many transports being launched as the first time, Qetjnegartis had only been expecting two or three. But the Council had allocated them based

298

upon need and few clans on the target world were as needy as the Bajantus! So, no less than fifty new clanmates were on their way. Added to the eight already here it would be a significant force.

Assuming they had fighting machines.

Prior to the enemy assault, there would have been no difficulty in supplying the newcomers. But after the battle, they had only ten still in good order. Five more could be repaired, but that still left forty-three new machines which would need to be constructed in less than a tenth of a cycle. Added to the necessary repairs to the holdfast, itself, it was going to be very difficult deadline to meet. Of course, assuming there was no new attack on the holdfast it made little difference if another ten or twenty days were needed to finish them—except for the embarrassment.

While the news about the reinforcements was very good, it was also an obvious rebuke to Qetjnegartis for needing those extra reinforcements. Only two other clans were receiving so many. It did not know what sort of concessions the clan leaders had to make to the Council to receive this boon, but they were probably substantial and the clan leaders would not be pleased to make them.

Of course it could be much worse. The three groups that landed on the south polar continent had found so little in the way of resources or food that they were being abandoned altogether. No reinforcements were being sent to them and unless they could discover some way to move to one of the other continents it was likely that all would perish. But they were all from minor clans with little influence in the Council—which is why they'd been assigned those landing sites to begin with.

And the commander of Group 30 on the continent to the south had recently suffered a major defeat, losing no less than twelve fighting machines—along with its own life. So yes, Qetjnegartis was not the only one to have reverses. Still it was irritating.

It reached the control center and took charge of one of the construction machines. There was much work to be done.

* * * * *

NOVEMBER, 1909, WASHINGTON, D.C.

Leonard Wood had moved operations from his office to the largest conference room which could be found in the State, War, & Navy Building. Huge maps were draped on the walls and tables had been pushed together in the center of the room to support the biggest map of all. Wooden counters representing military formations had been placed all over it and men with long poles were ready to move the counters around as necessary. Dozens of men, and a few women, packed the room, ready to process information as it arrived. Next door there was a fully staffed communications room with telegraph and telephone operators standing ready to receive the information.

They were waiting for the Martians.

According to the experts, they should be arriving very soon. None of them could predict the exact date, but they were sure it would be the last week or two in November. So the vast observation network had gone on full alert, the troops were ready to move and this headquarters in Washington was waiting to learn where to send them. Wood had been anxious, and nearly sleepless, for several days, and the President would show up here at all hours, clearly just as restless as everyone else. The tension seemed worse than during the first landings.

A cry from across the room caught everyone's attention, but it was just one man protesting that his papers were being blown around when another man dared to open a window to let in some air.

Wood was about to retreat to his office, where he'd had a cot set up, to try and grab a nap, when Roosevelt showed up again. He felt obliged to at least say hello, even though he'd just seen him a few hours earlier. "Good evening, sir. Nothing to report, I'm afraid."

"No, no, I wasn't expecting anything—you'd have sent word. But Edith was complaining that I'm wearing a hole in the carpet with my pacing."

"So you came over here to wear a hole in *my* carpet, eh?"

"Exactly! Exactly!" said Roosevelt with a grin. The grin quickly faded. "I've always hated waiting."

"Really? Who would have guessed, sir?"

They both laughed and then slowly strolled around the room, looking at the maps and the troop dispositions. "I keep asking myself if there is anything that I can do that hasn't been done," said Wood.

"Yes, I know what you mean. But you've really done a magnificent job, Leonard. The observation network is much denser than the first time. If anything comes down we ought to get word of it right away."

"Thank God we've still got communications with the west," said Wood, tracing his finger on a map along the line of the Southern Pacific Railroad. This utterly vital artery ran along the southern border of Texas and then west into New Mexico, Arizona, and California. "If they had cut that we'd have no way of knowing what was happening out there."

"I wonder why they haven't cut it?" said Roosevelt. "We've had sightings of the Martians on the other side of the Rio Grande. And there's nothing much to prevent them from coming north."

"Well, we can hope they are stretched thinner than we are. And they clearly use wireless telegraphy; they might not realize how dependent we are on wires strung on poles."

"The wireless sets—some are calling them *radios* now—are getting better."

"But they're not good enough yet for cross-country communications."

They continued to make everyone in the room nervous for another hour or so before Roosevelt went back across the street to the White House and Wood went to his cot.

It was an hour before dawn when Captain Semancik shook him awake. "We've got sightings coming in, sir."

"Where?" demanded Wood, shoving himself upright.

"Arizona and Nevada so far."

"Nothing in the east?"

"Not so far, sir."

"Get word to the President."

"A messenger is on his way, sir."

"Good." He pulled on his boots, buttoned up his tunic, and headed for the command center. The scene that met him was far different from the one he'd left hours earlier. Everyone seemed to be talking at once and people were running here and there. Messengers were bringing in reports from the communications room almost continuously.

He went over to a table where several ballistics experts were plotting the sighting data on maps. Wood looked over their shoulders but didn't ask any questions. They'd tell him when they had anything. Roosevelt arrived a few minutes later, wearing an overcoat and carpet slippers. "So what have we got?"

"Sighting from observers in Arizona and Nevada, sir. Bright shooting stars heading east."

"But nothing actually in the east?"

"Not yet, no."

They watched as the experts drew line after line on their maps and then yet more lines as new reports came in. There were a few errant lines, but the majority seemed to intersect in northwest New Mexico and in an area close to where Utah, Colorado, and Wyoming met. Dawn was creeping in the windows by the time they stood back from their work.

"So that's it?" asked Wood. "These two areas?"

"Based on the current sighting, yes, sir," said the senior officer.

"It appears they are reinforcing their existing forces rather than making new landings," said Wood.

"Yes. So what do you plan to do?" asked Roosevelt.

"We'll wait a few more days to make certain this is the lot of them," said Wood. "And if it is, we start sending our boys west."

CHAPTER TEN

CYCLE 597,843.9, HOLDFAST 32-1

Qetjnegartis carefully piloted its fighting machine over the holdfast's wall and headed west. The seven other clan members followed. The transport capsules bringing reinforcements from the Homeworld were about to arrive. Indeed, they were already entering the target world's atmosphere and decelerating after their long journey. It was a relief to know that fifty more beings would soon be defending the holdfast—even if there were fighting machines available for less than half of them. It would be enough to safeguard the place until the other machines were ready. It had been a harrying time after Braxjandar and its people had left. If the prey-creatures returned in force it was doubtful the holdfast could have survived another assault.

But there had been no sign of them. Scouts had been sent out and by all the evidence which could be found, it seemed that the prey-creatures had fled the vicinity. As an extra precaution, Qetjnegartis had ordered that the transport lines they used be destroyed for almost forty telequel to the east. The enemy had missed their chance and they would not be given another one again.

"Progenitor, I see something," said Davnitargus.

Qetjnegartis looked and saw what the bud was referring to: a bright light in the west. Instruments in the control cockpit confirmed that this was one of the transport capsules—not that any confirmation was necessary. The landing site was calculated to be two telequel to the northwest—very good navigation!

"Should we proceed to the site?" asked Davnitargus.

"Patience. We shall wait until all five have landed. It is possible that one or more of the capsules will land in some dangerous location and need immediate assistance. We will wait until all have landed before proceeding. In any case, it will take some time for the passengers to come out of hibernation."

"I understand."

The light was growing brighter and spurts of flame jetted off to the sides as the landing brakes came into play. It appeared to be coming almost directly at Qetjnegartis, but then, at the last moment, it became clear that it was coming down a distance away. The fireball slammed into the ground with a force that was actually quite shocking. *We survived that? I am glad I was still in hibernation!*

The impact threw up a cloud of dust and debris as the capsule plowed a long trench in the ground. It finally came to rest almost completely concealed by a mound of soil and rock piled up around it. The dust slowly settled and wisps of steam rose from the capsule.

"A second one comes," said Davnitargus. "It appears to be coming down farther away."

"Yes, but not too far." The second transport landed twelve telequel to the north. Qetjnegartis could not see it once it was down, but the telemetry indicated there were no problems. The third landed nine telequel to the south and the fourth flew directly over the holdfast and landed amidst the remains of the enemy's camp. The fifth came down between the first and the second. All were within easy reach. The operation had been executed very well.

Qetjnegartis dispatched four of its clanmates toward the first transport, while it and the other three proceeded to the next closest. Each of the fighting machines carried a basket capable of holding three people to bring the newcomers quickly back to the holdfast. Construction machines would later salvage the transports themselves for resources.

By the time they reached the transport, the occupants had awoken from hibernation and opened the vessel. They quickly climbed or were helped into the baskets and carried away. The newcomers were eager and excited to be on the new world, although all were having difficulties with the thick air and high gravity, but that was to be expected. One thing immediately caught Qetjnegartis' attention: the newcomers all had well-developed buds attached to them.

"You carried buds through the voyage?" it asked one of them.

"Yes, one of the other clans did so in the first wave and there was only a fifteen percent loss rate. It was deemed worth the risk to have a new batch available more quickly."

"Interesting. I hope it works out as expected."

Collecting all of them took almost half a day, but at last, everyone was safely in the holdfast. When the last group was delivered, Qetjnegartis parked its machine, lowered it to the loading position, and then debarked. Everyone, new arrivals and old, gathered round. It would address them all, welcoming them here and outlining the tasks ahead…

"Qetjnegartis."

Someone called to it and the voice sounded familiar. It looked as one of the newcomers pushed through to the front. "Qetjnegartis," it said again.

With recognition came surprise. "Valprandar… what are you doing here?"

"I would think that would be obvious, Qetjnegartis: I am here to take command."

* * * * *

NOVEMBER, 1909, ALBUQUERQUE, NEW MEXICO TERRITORY

"Frank, what the hell are you doing?"

Second Lieutenant Frank Dolfen turned to see his commanding officer, Captain Lou Pendleton, standing behind him. "Uh, I'm training my men, sir."

"Is that what you call it? What the devil is that thing?"

The *thing* the captain was referring to was a collection of lumber, telegraph poles, and various bits and pieces of wrecked railroad locomotives which Dolfen's men had found (or stolen) and then hammered together under his direction. "It's supposed to be a Martian tripod, sir."

Pendleton opened his mouth, closed it again, scowled, and then slowly walked around the object. It was nearly forty feet tall and was located in an empty field to the north of town. Finally, the captain stopped and scratched his head. "I'll be damned. It does sort of look like one, doesn't it?"

"That was the idea, sir." He gestured toward where the men of his troop were waiting. "I was thinking that we could get the men—and the horses—used to the damn things. And practice using the dynamite bombs."

"Wouldn't that sort of blow the thing to bits the first time?"

"We wouldn't use the real bombs, sir. For practice we'll use duds. Get the boys used to throwing them and getting them attached to the right places. Although I'd sure like to let the men set a few of them off. To get them used to lighting the fuses and the noise they make and all. Be good for the horses, too."

"I'll be damned," said Pendleton again. "Where'd you get the idea?"

"Dunno, sir. Just came to me. Seemed to make sense." Frank paused, but then went on. "To be honest, sir, me and a lot of the boys are gettin' damned tired of having to run away—or chase—these bastards without being able to hurt 'em. We need to figure out some new way of fighting."

"Can't argue with that," growled Pendleton. "Well, let me know how it works out. We may have to build some more of these things and train the whole squadron this way. Carry on, Lieutenant."

Dolfen acknowledged the order and Pendleton walked off about fifty yards, but didn't leave. Quite a few other people, attracted by the fake Martian, had gathered to watch. Frank didn't like that; it made him nervous. But he called his men to attention and explained what he wanted them to do. At first it was just riding around the Martian and then underneath and between its legs. They did it at a walk to begin, but then they increased the pace to a trot, and then finally did it at a full gallop. It was simple stuff and they did it well—even the men who had been raw recruits just a few months earlier. Then he had each squad come in at a different angle. This was harder since they had to avoid running into each other as well as the Martian. There was some confusion at first but eventually they got the hang of it.

Then it was practice with the bombs. The standard bomb being issued to everyone consisted of four sticks of dynamite arranged in two pairs. Each group of two was held in a waterproof canvas bag. The two bags were connected by a three-foot long leather strap. This allowed them to be wrapped around the target or thrown like a bola which would hopefully entangle some part of the enemy machine and hold the dynamite close until it went off. There was a fifteen second fuse which was ignited by a friction igniter attached to a ring. The whole thing would be stuffed into a bag which could be worn around the waist or over one shoulder. So, the drill was: pull the bomb out of its bag, light the fuse, and then throw or somehow attach the thing to the Martian—and then run like hell.

Frank had taken a few dozen bombs and had the dynamite and fuses replaced with wood to give the same weight but eliminate any risk of explosion. So the afternoon was spent on having men on their horses, pull the damn things out, get the strap untangled, pull the ring, and then throw it—all without falling off. It wasn't easy. The only good part of it was that the work kept the men warm. A sharp breeze had come up and the sun was clouding over and it was getting cold. Winter was on the way.

During a break, Jason Urbaniak—who was adapting to his new rank a lot more easily than Frank was—came over to talk. "Making some progress... sir."

"Yeah, a bit."

"But I hear the boys talking. Some of them are askin' what's the point? The damn Martians will just burn us up before we ever get close enough to throw the stupid bombs. Gotta admit I can see their point."

"Yeah, it's true. That's why were gonna do dismounted drill tomorrow."

The next day was even colder and everyone was bundled up; which made handling the awkward bombs all the more difficult. Some of the men were complaining. "If you can guarantee the Martians will wait until spring to attack then we'll skip it," said Frank, acting more like a sergeant than a lieutenant. "No? All right, snap to it!" He had them ride up close to the fake Martian and then dismount. Every fourth man rode off with the horses of the other three, who were obliged to crawl across the frozen ground until they were close enough to throw their bombs. By the lunch break everyone was tired, dirty, and thoroughly disgusted.

"Why we wasting our time with this?" said one trooper, not caring that Frank could hear. "They'll still burn us to a cinder before we can get close enough!" He didn't answer the man directly, but called them all to attention again.

"Okay, I know this might seem pointless to some of you, but the problem with our training is that our wooden Martian can't move. Out in the field I won't expect you to ride right up to it and dismount! That would be crazy. But what I *will* want you to do is get yourselves in its path—a good distance ahead—and then dismount. You'll find a good spot to hide and then let the bastards come to you. But they might not come directly to you. You need to be ready to move—to crawl— to a better spot to make your attack. When they get close, you pick yourselves up and use your bombs." Dolfen paused and looked his men over. "If the ground allows it, what I'd like to do is to dismount half the men and when they attack, the Martians will be so distracted that the other half can ride in and finish the job."

The men looked thoughtful but one of them said in thickly accented English: "Lot of us still get killed, zir."

Frank walked up to the man and stared him right in the eyes. "You're right: a lot of us *will* get killed. But if we can kill some Martians, it will be worth it." He swept his gaze across all the men. "Get used to that! This is a different kind of war we're fighting! It's not like old time *European* wars! We aren't gonna fight a couple of battles and then the one king decides he's had enough so he makes a treaty with the other king and gives him a couple of towns and some gold, shakes hands, and waits ten years to fight again. The Martians aren't here to take our towns or our gold, they are here to kill us! All of us! If we run away, they'll follow. They'll burn our towns and kill our wives and our kids. The only way to stop them is to kill them! So that's what we're doing: training how to kill them!"

The eyes of his men were wide, but after a moment Frank realized they weren't looking at him. He turned around to find that Colonel Berg, the regimental commander, and a small group of other officers were standing behind him. Frank came to attention and saluted. Berg returned it and stood there staring at him.

"Lieutenant," he said finally.

"Sir?"

"I want you to go and see the adjutant. Tomorrow is soon enough. I want you to describe this training program you are using and have him write it up."

"Uh, yes, sir."

Colonel Berg turned to the other officers.

"I want the whole regiment doing it this way as soon as possible."

* * * * *

NOVEMBER, 1909, SANTA FE, NEW MEXICO TERRITORY

"Good thing you showed up, miss," said the owner of the livery stable. "Your uncle stopped paying me two months ago and I was gettin' ready to sell him off. The army is paying good money for horses these days."

Rebecca Harding smiled as she ran her hands down Ninny's neck. Her horse looked to be in good health and there was no doubt he was glad to see her, too. He'd whinnied and nickered when their eyes met and he seemed very excited now. "Thank you for taking such good care of him, Mr. Dawkins. How much do I owe you?"

"Well, seein' as how you're in the army, I can give you a break. For two months board and feed... twelve dollars."

She almost gave him an argument. Twelve dollars was nearly a dollar and half a week. Didn't seem like much of a break to her. Her salary as an army nurse was only ten dollars a month. Dawkins clearly saw it in her face because he added: "The army is buying up all the feed, too. Price has almost doubled since last year."

"I understand," she said, digging the money out of her pocket. She paid the man and saddled up Ninny and rode off. The joy of being on her favorite horse immediately drove away the annoyance of what she'd had to pay to get him back. It was worth it! She'd been so glad when Miss Chumley had pulled the strings necessary to get permission for her to keep the horse at the hospital. Of course she'd have to share his use with some of the others, but he'd be hers to take care of—and at least the feed would be free.

They had shifted the nurse detachment back to Santa Fe, and her path to the hospital took her past her aunt and uncle's house. She didn't stop. She'd made one short visit when she got back, to let them know she was still alive, but her aunt had been so difficult she left after just a few minutes. The woman seemed unable to grasp what was going on. She'd railed at Becca for running off and threatened to get the sheriff and have her locked up so she couldn't go back to the army. Becca fled before she had to draw her pistol.

The weather had been turning colder, and this high up in the mountains there would be snow soon. But today was a fine sunny day and she nudged Ninny into a fast trot just because she could. He seemed to enjoy it, too. She knew she was taking a risk 'volunteering' him for the army, but he probably would have ended up there anyway, and now she could look after him. "Well, we've survived worse adventures, haven't we?" She patted his neck.

She arrived at the hospital and put Ninny in the pen they'd built for him. Then it was back to work. There weren't all that many wounded left in the wards almost three months after the battle, but with the cold weather they were seeing more cases of pneumonia and influenza, and as with any large grouping of people, dysentery and even typhoid. They were kept busy.

When her shift ended she went to the mess hall, which was the warmest place around. They were slowly replacing the tents with wooden buildings, but most of them still had canvas roofs and they got very chilly at night. The mess hall had a real roof and several large iron stoves for heat. She got her dinner and found a place close to a stove to eat it.

Week by week and month by month she'd become friends with the other nurses and orderlies. The shared experiences of work and battle and retreat had forged a real bond between them. She was the youngest of them, but they treated her like an adult instead of a child and she liked that a lot. There were times when she'd think about her father and mother and grandmother and that place she'd called home before this all happened, but the memories were becoming distant. She had a new family now who seemed much closer than the old one she'd lost.

She finished eating and then sat down with Clarissa Forester. The woman was probably the closest in age to Becca, although she was still quite a bit older. They chatted about the day's work and also about the arrival of Ninny. They shared some gossip about another nurse and the orderly she was supposedly carrying on with and both ended up giggling. "So have you found a boyfriend?" asked Clarissa, smirking.

"Me? No! Not yet, anyway."

"Really? What about Sam Jones? You seem to talk with him a lot. Good looking fellow even if he is a little odd."

"Sam? No, no, we're just friends. And he's not odd, he's just... shy."

"If you say so. Well, I'm going to get some sleep. See you later, Becca." She got up and left.

Clarissa's comment left Becca puzzled. Why in the world would she think she was sweet on Sam?

He'd made up the name of 'Jones' to use officially and he was now one of the hospital's orderlies. Becca would talk to him from time to time, but neither had ever done the slightest thing that would make anyone think they were anything but casual acquaintances. Had they? If Clarissa could think so, were others thinking it, too? Would Miss Chumley hear about it and object?

As she sat there, Sam came in and got his dinner. He glanced at her but sat down at a different table. Becca had wanted to talk to him, but now, she felt incredibly awkward doing so. Still, it was important. She forced herself to get up and sit down next to him. "Hi, Sam. How are you doing?"

"Okay."

"Sam, I've been thinking." She paused to let him ask thinking about what? But he said nothing and kept eating. "Sam, you need to tell someone about what you saw in the Martian fortress." She was whispering now.

"No."

"Sam! It could be important! The generals need all the information they can get to beat them!"

"No."

"What if I could arrange it so they wouldn't know who you were?"

"How could you do that?"

"Last winter I met a major in the Ordnance Department. He and his men were the ones who rescued me. It's his job to find out stuff about the Martians. He's a good man. If I explained the situation maybe he could come here and talk to you alone. Once he had what you could tell him, he'd leave you be. I'd suggest just writing everything down and sending that to him, but I'm sure he'd have questions."

Sam frowned and stopped chewing. He sat there for a long time. "Gotta think about this."

"Okay, Sam, okay. Take your time."

* * * * *

CYCLE 597,843.9, HOLDFAST 32-1

"Why are you no longer in command?" asked Davnitargus. "You have explained this to me, but I do not comprehend."

Qetjnegartis regarded the nearly-grown bud with concern. "Truly? You cannot sense it?"

"Sense what?"

"Valprandar's dominance."

Davnitargus was silent for a long time, but then said: "No. Or at least I sense nothing I can identify as such. I clearly sense your dominance and that of the other three adults who were here when I came into being. I sense the... submission of the other three buds to me. But the newcomers..."

"Yes? What of the newcomers?"

"They are... indistinct. Different."

"In what way?"

"I... cannot describe it."

Qetjnegartis' concern multiplied. Was there some defect in the bud? The hierarchy of dominance and submission within the clan was the fundamental pillar in the Race's social structure. Each member instantly knew its position within the hierarchy and obeyed those above it and commanded those below it. To not be able to sense this was... very disturbing. It thought back to its first *awakening*, had there been any uncertainty such as Davnitargus described? No, it could remember nothing like that.

"The other buds report similar experiences," said Davnitargus.

"You have discussed this among yourselves?" asked Qetjnegartis in surprise.

"Yes, the others are as confused as I. Can you explain the system again, Progenitor?"

"Very well. Each bud owes obedience to its progenitor. But this extends beyond the immediate generation. You owe obedience to me, and I to my own progenitor. But you also owe obedience to my progenitor, and its progenitor. Any bud you might have in the future would owe its obedience to you, to me, and to my progenitor, and so on up and down through the generations. Do you understand?"

"Yes, this much is clear."

"The link of obedience thus runs through the generations. But it also runs *within* the generations and this is based upon the order in which the buds were created. For example, I was the third bud of my progenitor. Thus I owe obedience to the first and second buds of my generation and *all* of the buds of prior generations within the clan."

"So then all of the Race owe obedience to the very first member of the Race?" asked Davnitargus. "Does such a one exist?"

"Not anymore," replied Qetjnegartis. "Whether any such individual ever did exist is a matter of much speculation and debate. No one knows if all of the Race is descended from one individual or a group of individuals. This would have happened long before any history was recorded."

"Is not our history recorded within each of us?"

"Within limits, yes. But over so vast a time, things have become lost. For while we have the means of prolonging our existence indefinitely by budding replacement bodies, we may still be slain through mishap or violence. The Race has fought wars against itself many times."

"If there was a single leader, who all must obey, how would it permit such a thing?"

"Any such leader was lost long ago. For while the link of obedience through the generations is strong, the link within the generations weakens with the time between individuals. So while the five hundredth bud of an individual would have a strong link to its progenitor, the link of obedience to the first bud of that same progenitor might be very weak. If the progenitor was slain, and perhaps many of the intervening buds of that same generation, the link between first and five hundredth could be broken. That is how the different clans came about. Gaps appeared in the chain of obedience which could not be filled."

"I think I see," said Davnitargus. "So you and Commander Braxjandar of Clan Mavnaltak might have once had some link of obedience to a common ancestor, but those links became broken and the separate clans were formed?"

"Yes, although these breaks happened very long ago. The exact details are now lost."

"And your relationship to Commander Valprandar?"

"It is from the prior generation of our clan, the same generation as my progenitor, although fourteen buddings separated in time. I must obey it and so must you. You truly cannot sense that?"

"No, I cannot. But I will obey as you direct. But the other forty-nine newcomers, I do not wish to make any errors in dealing with them. Can you explain their relationship to me?"

Qetjnegartis did so, even though it took quite some time. All the while it pondered this mystery. How could all four of the new buds lack this basic sense of order? And yet Davnitargus said that its sense of hierarchy among the surviving eight members of the first wave was intact. The hierarchy was affected by the generations and it was also affected by time. Could it somehow be affected by *place*? Would the fact that the buds were created here on the target world instead of the Homeworld be having an effect? It seemed unlikely, but it could not be discounted. And the consequences were very disturbing. If all the new buds created on this world felt no ties of loyalty to the clans on the Homeworld, what would be the result? With time they would outnumber the ones created on the Homeworld by a factor of thousands…

When it finished it added: "It would be best if you and the other buds did not discuss this with anyone."

"As you wish, Progenitor."

"Good. Now, we must go to the meeting chamber. Valprandar has scheduled a meeting of us all and it will begin shortly." They mounted a travel chair and went from their work area to the meeting. As they went, Qetjnegartis felt the new bud on its side moving. It was nearing maturity and soon the transference must begin. There were still no gross effects of the contagion in its existing body and it was very tempting to allow this bud to become a new individual, but no, the risk was too great. Qetjnegartis would transfer to a new body.

They reached the chamber where all the others were gathered. Valprandar was on a raised platform where it could address them. "New instructions have been received from the Colonial Conclave," it said. "In recent days we have suffered a number of serious setbacks. In the northern part of Continent 4, the northern and southern areas of Continent 2, and in the mountainous southern regions of Continent 1, our forces have been defeated with heavy losses." It paused and looked at Qetjnegartis. "And here on Continent 3 we have also had setbacks. In each case the defeat was the result of an ill-considered attack with inadequate forces against a prepared force of the prey-creatures. This cannot be permitted to happen again.

"Therefore, for the immediate future, no additional major attacks will be undertaken. We shall concentrate on repairing the holdfast, producing enough war machines for ourselves and the next generation of buds, and preparing for future offensives. Is this understood?"

All answered in unison: *Yes Commander!*

CHAPTER ELEVEN

DECEMBER, 1909, WASHINGTON, D.C.

Major Andrew Comstock took a seat at the conference table and marveled at how far he had come in just a few years. From a nervous second lieutenant whose duties were little more than carrying papers and serving coffee, he had become an important part of General William Crozier's Ordnance Department staff. His opinion carried weight and important men sought it out. He was quite sure that part of that was due to President Roosevelt taking a shine to him, but only part. He did his job and did it well.

There was a cold wind rattling the windows and clouds of snowflakes whipped by. In three days it would be Christmas and he still needed to find the right gift for Victoria. They were living in Colonel Hawthorne's house and Mrs. Hawthorne had gone all out decorating for the holiday. He wished they had their own place, but he was gone so often it was better for Victoria to have her parents close by.

The rest of the staff, including Colonel Hawthorne, came in and found seats as Crozier called the meeting to order. "Well, gentlemen," he said, "we are making progress on several fronts, but there are a lot of people asking why we aren't making more. What do we have and what can we expect for the new year? Colonel Waski, can you start with your report on the land ironclads?"

"Yes, sir," said Waski. "Baldwin and William Cramp have got their plans nearly completed for a prototype machine. The upper works are actually very straightforward and it would be constructed like a navy warship. The difficulty—as we expected—is the caterpillar tracks which would allow it to move on land. They are an order of magnitude larger than anything even conceived of before." He paused and rummaged through his papers until he found one and pulled it out of the pile. "Well, that's not exactly true, sir," he said, looking at the paper. "Years ago there was a proposal to use similar vehicles to transport ships across the Isthmus of Panama and avoid the need for a canal. But it was nothing but a pipe dream."

"We can't afford pipe dreams, Colonel," said Crozier. "We need a working vehicle."

"Yes, sir. Baldwin is working on it around the clock, but they are having a lot of trouble with how to take the power from the engines and transfer it to the tracks." Waski paused and took another batch of paper out of his folder. "And we received this the other day from George Westinghouse in Pittsburgh. He's suggesting a radical alternative where we would eliminate the direct mechanical transfer of power and instead incorporate a set of steam turbines in the main hull which would produce electricity which would then be used to run a set of induction motors in the tracks themselves."

"Could that work?"

"Baldwin is skeptical, but they are looking into it."

"Any estimate on when they can have this prototype ready?"

"They are hoping for the end of 1911, sir."

"Two years? That's much too long. Have them hurry it up."

"Yes, sir. Oh, and Baldwin has submitted this proposal for an interim design. They say they could have it working in a year." Waski slid a sheet of paper across the table to Crozier who looked at it and then passed it around to the others. When it got to Andrew he saw what looked like a miniaturized version of the land ironclad; a single large turret and instead of caterpillar tracks, four huge wheels. "They are calling it 'Little David' and it would be a way to deploy a very large mobile gun on the battlefield. They want permission to go ahead."

"A year?" asked Crozier. Waski nodded. "All right, tell them to go ahead. But what else is Baldwin up to? Ben?" He looked at Hawthorne.

"Sir, they are producing the Mark II and Mark III steam tanks on three shifts. They hope to have a working prototype of the Mark IV by early next year. American Locomotive has also begun production of the Mark II. Ford has won a contract to start production on both models, but won't be able to deliver any until next spring. We have also asked Baldwin to supply designs for other vehicles using the Mark II as a basis. These include self-propelled artillery, ammunition, fuel, and water carriers, and lightly armed transports for infantry. They believe they can meet our needs quickly. They are also working on a design for an armored train."

"Good, good. And I understand that the new high-velocity field gun will start deployment this month, correct?"

"Yes, sir, although on a makeshift carriage. As you know, the one that was designed for it has failed almost every test."

"Yes, bad business that. When can we expect a proper carriage?"

"Probably not for six months, sir."

Crozier frowned but didn't pursue the subject. Instead he turned his eyes on Andrew. "So, Major? What have you to report from our pack of geniuses?"

"Well, sir, for the most part they are still in the process of absorbing all the information the British gave to us. They have a lot of catching up and cross-checking to do before they can really start moving forward again."

"Yes, our British allies should have come forward years ago!"

"Yes, sir, I surely agree. But it seems that our own scientists anticipated quite a lot of what the British gave us, so the catching up ought to go pretty quickly."

"Good! But do any of them anticipate any usable developments in the near-term, Major?"

"The most concrete development, sir, is that Tesla has four of the captured heat rays functional. As you know, we have captured the remains of seven of the Martian machines. One was completely destroyed in the battle and two more of the heat rays were too badly damaged to function. But the remaining four could be used if given a sufficient power supply. Tesla was working on developing a smaller and more portable power sources, but..."

"But what?"

"When he was given his copy of the British records, he, well, he became a bit distracted. He's easily distracted, sir."

"So I've heard!" said Crozier. "Well get him undistracted!"

"We'll try, sir, but he's gone back to his Wardenclyffe Tower on Long Island. Claims he's on to a great discovery. It may be hard to pry him out of there."

"Do your best. What about Edison and his crew?"

"They have high hopes for the special wire from the Martian batteries, sir. They are pursuing quite a few ideas, including our own version of the British coil gun. But I wouldn't expect anything before next summer. The folks at MIT have pretty much given up on trying to duplicate the Martian metal. Considering that the British haven't made any real progress on that over a far longer period, that's not surprising. On the other hand, their 'sandwich' armor of steel and asbestos is already in use as a shield on the new high-velocity field guns and they are coming up with other applications." Andrew paused and looked at Crozier. "And that reminds me, sir, did you get that letter I forwarded from Goddard and Munroe? They buttonholed me up in Boston and I must say their proposals do seem to have some merit."

"I glanced at it," replied Crozier. "Rockets, eh? Might have some use. I sent it on to young Frederick to look it over. That's his job, after all, to look over crackpot ideas, eh?"

"Yes, sir," said Andrew.

General Crozier leaned back in chair and glanced out the window. It was snowing harder and the light was fading as the short winter day came to an end. "I think that will do it, gentlemen. Good job, all of you. Our next meeting won't be until after the New Year, so I'll wish you all a Merry Christmas right now."

Everyone returned the gesture and gathered up their papers before leaving. Andrew had a few things he wanted to deal with before he left, so he returned to his office. He actually had a real office! With a real orderly! He sent off some letters and organized a few other things and then sorted through his in-basket. Most of it was routine stuff he could do in the morning, but one letter caught his eye. It was an ordinary envelope, but it was dirty and battered. It was addressed to him, but there were stamps from military post offices in Washington, Chicago, St. Louis, and Santa Fe. It had apparently followed quite a route to get to him. There was no return address.

Curious, he opened it up and started in surprise. He read it through—three times. After sitting and thinking for a good five minutes he got up and walked next door to Colonel Hawthorne's office and poked his head in. "Sir? Have you got a minute?"

"Sure, come on in Andy," said his father-in-law.

He did so and shut the door behind him. "Thank you, sir. I just got a rather…"

"Andy, you know when we're alone, you can call me Ben—or even 'Dad' if you prefer."

"That's going to take some getting used to, si—er, Ben," said Andrew with an awkward grin.

"Work on it. But sit down. What's on your mind? That was a good report you gave the general, by the way."

"Thank you… But the reason I came over is that I just received a rather strange letter. Do you remember that girl in my report? The one who was with the group of people we rescued from the Martians?"

"The spitfire with the rifle? Hard to forget her!"

"Yes, sir, that's the one. Well, she's an army nurse now in Santa Fe. She was with Funston's army during the recent defeat at Gallup."

"Indeed? She seems to have knack for getting into tight places! But she obviously got out all right."

"Yes, she did. But in her letter she told me that when our people broke into the Martian fortress some of them actually got down into the underground areas and…"

"Really? She said that?" interrupted Hawthorne. "How does she know? We got some reports to that effect, but no one who was actually in there has turned up. If it really happened, they must not have survived the retreat."

"I guess not, Ben, but Miss Harding says that during the fighting there was a man who was delivered to her hospital unit who had been a prisoner inside the fortress."

"What? Someone from General Sumner's army?"

"Yes, or I suppose it might have been someone who was at Fort Wingate."

"Didn't she ask? And why hasn't this man come forward? He might be able to tell us a lot!"

"Well, you see, sir, that's the whole point of Miss Harding's letter. Apparently this man—she doesn't give a name—has recovered physically, but she says that he's very 'skittish' and nervous. Doesn't want to talk about what happened to him."

"Understandable; it must have been awful. But if we could get him back here I'm sure we could..."

"That's the thing: he won't come back here. Harding says he's convinced that if we get hold of him we'll lock him away because of what he knows."

"That's ridiculous! And in any case this man is still a soldier and he has a duty to talk to us! We need to wire Funston and have him send a provost detail to secure this man!"

"Uh... Ben, it might be hard to find him. Miss Harding didn't precisely say so in her letter, but it sounded to me as though this man is on a hair-trigger and could run for it if he even suspects we might try something like that. And it also sounded like she'd help him get away."

"Well, then why the devil did she even bother writing to you?" Hawthorne was visibly angry.

"She says that she's convinced this man that I am someone who can be trusted. She suggests that if I go out there alone she can set up an interview with him where he'll tell me everything he knows. I have to agree to not try and take him away afterward."

Hawthorne frowned and drummed his fingers on the desk. "Don't like it. But I suppose we'll get more out of him if he does it willingly." He frowned for a while longer and then stood up. "Let's go talk to the general."

* * * * *

CYCLE 597,844.0, HOLDFAST 32-1

Qetjnegartis opened its eyes. It had not expected to have another *awakening* so soon. Little more than a cycle had passed since its last one. It regarded its old body with something like regret. Not that it was anything more than dead organic material now, but there were no outward signs of the contagion which had forced it to abandon it so soon. Well, what was done was done.

It went through the same routine it always did after an *awakening*, exercising its limbs, checking the internal organs, and exploring the depths of its memory. All seemed to be in order, although its limbs seemed stronger than normal; an adaptation to this world's gravity?

"Progenitor? Are you functional?"

Davnitargus was looking at it. The bud had not witnessed an awakening before and had expressed much interest in the process. Remembering an earlier, and alarming, conversation with the bud it now turned its thoughts to the chain of dominance and subordination which it had always had since its first awakening. Had anything changed?

No... no... all seemed to be as it was. Valprandar was in command and it must be obeyed. The Clan elders on the Homeworld... Yes, everything was in order. Then a new thought struck and it looked at Davnitargus. "Am I still your progenitor?"

"Yes." The bud seemed surprised.

"And you will obey me?"

"Of course. Why do you ask such a question?"

"Never mind. Come, let us return to our work."

* * * * *

DECEMBER, 1909, ALBUQUERQUE, NEW MEXICO TERRITORY

"Merry Christmas, Lieutenant!"

Lieutenant Frank Dolfen turned and saw Sergeant Jason Urbaniak and a half-dozen other NCOs from the squadron staggering down the street. They'd clearly been drinking for a while, and there was nothing Frank would have liked better than to join them. But he couldn't. He was an officer now and it just wasn't done. He was with a few officers, himself, looking for just the right Albuquerque establishment for a Christmas celebration.

So instead of joining the sergeant's group, he simply nodded in their direction and murmured a 'Merry Christmas' in reply and moved on. He knew Urbaniak wouldn't be offended. He was an old veteran and knew how things worked as well as Frank did.

The other officers, young lieutenants from the 1st and 2nd squadrons, were an okay bunch. They didn't seem to resent the fact that he had once been an enlisted man, although they were clearly a little intimidated that he was old enough to be their fathers.

The streets of Albuquerque were mobbed with soldiers looking for a good time. With the front lines now on the doorstep, there were more troops stationed in the area than ever before, and those businesses which catered to their entertainment had grown enormously. Most of them were in the section known as Old Town and Dolfen imagined that was where Urbaniak and his gang had come from (and probably where they would return), but there were more respectable places in the newer sections of town. More respectable, but still offering the same services if you knew where to look.

They found one, a place called *The Silver Swan*, for no reason Dolfen could see, and went inside. It was plush, had a piano and someone who could actually play it, and a number of pretty girls who would serve drinks, dance, and presumably provide other entertainment upstairs. The regiment had just been paid so Dolfen had a pocketful of money, although the crinkling of greenbacks was nowhere near as pleasant as the clink of gold. Just like during the Civil War, the government had run out of cash and was now running on paper money and war bonds. Oh well, they were accepting the greenbacks here so what difference did it make?

Dolfen found a comfortable chair, paid for a few drinks, listened to the piano, and watched the flames in the fireplace. It was cold outside, but thankfully there hadn't been much snow yet except up in the mountains. Despite the panic when the second wave of Martian cylinders landed, there hadn't been any sign of them in weeks. One cavalry patrol had pushed all the way back to the siege lines around Gallup without finding anything. He was glad he hadn't pulled *that* duty!

Some of the officers were dancing with the girls and periodically a pair would disappear upstairs for a while. His thoughts went back to that saloon in Gallup. He'd spent a lot of time there. For the thousandth time he wondered what had happened to Stella. His hopes that she'd somehow escaped had long since faded. She surely would have turned up by now—especially since he owed her money.

"Merry Christmas, Lieutenant. Care to dance?"

He looked up from the fire to see a pretty, but overly made-up, woman standing beside his chair. She smiled at him. His immediate impulse was to send her away, but he didn't. She was being friendly and it *was* Christmas, and it had been a long time…

"Sure, why not?"

* * * * *

315

DECEMBER, 1909, WASHINGTON, D.C.

I should have burned that damn letter!

Andrew Comstock stood on the train platform with snow swirling around him. He turned up the collar on his greatcoat, but it didn't seem to do any good; it was still freezing. He stamped his feet and waited for his train to arrive. He was heading west again, to where the war was waiting. General Crozier was determined to get the information out of this mysterious acquaintance of Rebecca Harding and Andrew was the one to do it. He'd agreed not to order any attempt to take the man into custody—technically he was a deserter since he had not tried to rejoin his own unit—unless Andrew became convinced the man was holding back information.

At least the general had had the charity to allow Andrew to wait until after Christmas, but Victoria had been very unhappy at this sudden separation. Particularly because on Christmas Eve she'd told him that she was expecting a baby. Andrew's shocked response: *'What? Already?'* had not done anything to endear him to her. She hadn't come to the station to see him off and that was probably just as well.

He wasn't the only grumpy person on the platform, either. He'd been given permission to take a couple of men with him and he'd managed to pry Sergeant McGill out of his comfortable desk job and Corporal Kennedy to act as his batman. Both had been with him on that first trip out west, and neither one had been the least bit pleased at being dragged out there again during the holidays—or at any other time, he suspected.

"We goin' out there lookin' for souvenirs again… sir?" asked McGill.

"No, there's a system in place now where any Martian artifacts which are captured will automatically be shipped to us. We don't have to try and grab them first anymore."

"Then what are we goin' for?"

"To observe the new tanks and the new high-velocity gun in the field." That was the official reason for the trip—and Andrew would, in fact, do that while he was there. He hadn't mentioned the other reason for going to McGill.

"And you really need me along to do that?"

"No, Sergeant," said Andrew. "You are coming along to keep me out of trouble. The general was so impressed with the job you did last time, he insisted you come again."

McGill snorted and then looked thoughtful. "He didn't really say that, did he, sir?"

"No, I just made that up."

"Thought so."

"But you did do a good job and I'm glad to have you along."

"Oh, it's my pleasure, sir!" said the Sergeant, but then he muttered: "My bloody, stinkin' pleasure."

Train whistles cut off any further conversation and a pair of trains chugged into the station. One was the express that Andrew would be taking, but the other was a troop train. Just as it squealed to a halt, a column of soldiers came marching up in formation, obviously destined for that train. Unlike the trio already on the platform, they seemed in high spirits. They were singing a song which had been written years earlier for the war with Spain:

> *I have come to say goodbye, Dolly Gray,*
> *It's no use to ask me why, Dolly Gray,*
> *There's a murmur in the air, you can hear it everywhere,*
> *It's the time to do and dare, Dolly Gray.*

The British had appropriated the song for their own use during their war with the Boers in South

Africa. But now the Americans had taken it back again and it had gained new popularity.

> *So if you hear the sound of feet, Dolly Gray,*
> *Sounding through the village street, Dolly Gray,*
> *It's the tramp of soldiers true, in their uniforms so blue,*
> *I must say goodbye to you, Dolly Gray.*

Andrew, McGill, and Kennedy boarded their own train, but they could still hear the troops singing:

> *Goodbye, Dolly, I must leave you, though it breaks my heart to go,*
> *Something tells me I am needed at the front to fight the foe,*
> *See - the boys in blue are marching and I can no longer stay,*
> *Hark - I hear the bugle calling, goodbye, Dolly Gray!*

* * * * *

JANUARY, 1910, WASHINGTON, D.C.

The President's New Year's gala was very subdued this year. The weather was terrible and only a few thousand people braved it to line up and have their hands shaken by Theodore Roosevelt. They had come and gone before the afternoon was half over. The foreign diplomats had not lingered much longer, and Roosevelt was free to retire to the family quarters for dinner much earlier than most years. In an unusual move, he had invited Leonard Wood to join him. Since his wife, Louise, was visiting relatives, he had accepted.

The usually jovial Roosevelt, indeed, the whole Roosevelt clan, seemed more somber than usual today. The two oldest boys, Ted and Kermit, were both missing from the gathering. Ted had gone off to join the 26th Infantry and Kermit's artillery battalion was already on its way west. Ted's position as his father's military aide had been taken by a tall, personable captain with the unfortunate name of Archie Butt.

Dinner had been consumed and Wood found himself sitting near Roosevelt, staring at the roaring fireplace. They'd been sitting there for quite a while before the President broke his unusual silence. "So, Leonard, what do you think the new year will bring? Are we finally going to start driving those devils back? We've poured so much into this already, the people have made so many sacrifices. They deserve a victory."

Wood paused for a while before answering. "I don't know, Theodore. By spring we will have moved a huge number of men and equipment west; far more than Funston had when he launched his attack. And we'll be preparing to move on multiple fronts. Evidence suggests that the force that counterattacked Funston came down from the batch which landed in Idaho. If we can attack on that front and in New Mexico, they won't be able to help each other. Of course, they've been reinforced by the new landings, but still, I'm hoping for the best." He paused and looked at his old friend.

"But I'm afraid that you and I were spoiled by the Spanish War. That 'Splendid Little War' was over before it had barely begun. Three months from start to finish. We've been at this one in earnest for a little over a year and I don't see it ending any time soon. Consider the Civil War: the first year was mostly spent getting ready, along with a few missteps, and it wasn't until well into the second year that big things started happening."

"And it took four years to finish it," nodded Roosevelt. "Do you think it will take us that long?"

"We might be able to finish it here in America in four years—if we are lucky. But consider how much of the world is in the Martians' hands already. It might take us decades to be rid of them entirely."

"Yes, I suppose that's…"

"Father! That means I'll get a chance to fight!" The sudden shout from behind them made both men jump. Wood looked around the back of his chair and there was Roosevelt's youngest son, Quentin, sitting on the floor, with a huge grin on his face. The boy had just turned twelve and Wood knew he was as eager as—well, as eager as his father had been—to get into the war. "Will I get a chance to fight? Mother says it will all be over before I have the chance, but if it goes on for decades—that's ten years, right?—I'll surely be old enough!"

The elder Roosevelt reached back and pulled the lad forward. "Eavesdropping, eh? That's not polite, you know."

"But you and General Wood were sitting here talking! It's not my fault I could hear you!"

"No, I suppose it wasn't."

"But is it true the war could go on for years and years and I'll have a chance to fight?"

"Well, maybe, but no one can know that, can they? Let's keep that our secret, eh? A real military secret! If you're going to be in the army you need to be able to keep a secret! Can you keep it a secret? Even from your mother?"

"From Mother, too?"

"Wouldn't want to worry her, now, would we? She worries about your brothers, you know. Let's keep it a secret, eh?"

"All right, Father, I shall!"

"Bully! Good for you! Now go and play with your Christmas gifts, while I have a chat with the general!" The boy got up, a sly smile on his face, and ran off. Wood wondered how long that particular secret would remain one.

Roosevelt was looking thoughtful. "I suppose the blasted thing could go on for ten or twenty years, couldn't it, Leonard?"

"It could, I'm afraid."

"Then maybe we really should keep that a secret."

* * * * *

JANUARY, 1910, ST. LOUIS, MISSOURI

"Taking near as long to get there as it did last time, sir. Even without the bleedin' tanks draggin' along behind," said Sergeant McGill.

"At least we're warm and dry while we wait, Sergeant," replied Andrew. "Could be worse."

"Aye, sir, a lot worse, and that's the truth!"

They were sitting on a bench in the very crowded and rather palatial Union Station in St. Louis, waiting for their train to get clearance to move. Between some very bad weather and the army's massive redeployment to the west, train service was a frightful mess. It had taken them almost two weeks just to get here and by all indications it might take another two weeks to get to Santa Fe. They'd slept several nights on the train and several more in stations along the way. The rest of the time they'd managed to find a hotel when they knew the train was going to be delayed long enough not to leave without them. Andrew wasn't sure what it would be tonight.

"I'm going to get a drink, Sergeant, hold on to our spot here," he said suddenly, getting up.

"Yes, sir," said McGill.

"I'll bring back something for you and the corporal."

McGill's face brightened. "Very good, sir!"

He made his way through the crowd to the station's bar. This was even more crowded, but he eventually made it to the front and bought a bottle of whiskey. He took it and a glass, thinking to head back to the bench, but then he spotted a table which had just opened up and he took a seat before anyone else could grab it. McGill was a fine fellow, but just now he wanted to be away from him for a while. He opened the bottle and poured himself a glass. It wasn't the best whiskey he'd ever had, but it wasn't bad, and felt soothing after the days of frustration. He'd drink a glass or two and take the rest back for McGill and Kennedy.

"Excuse me, Major, is this seat taken?"

He looked up and saw a tall, solid-looking second lieutenant standing in front of him and pointing to the empty chair opposite him.

"No, help yourself, Lieutenant." The man sat down, draping his greatcoat over the chair back. He was a good-looking fellow, with a long straight nose and sharp eyes. Looking closer, Andrew noted that his uniform wasn't standard issue, it had been privately tailored and fit the man perfectly. He clearly had some money besides his army pay. Then he noticed the Tank Corps collar disk.

"On your way to the front, Lieutenant...?"

"Patton, George Patton, sir. And yes, I'm to join the 326th Tank Battalion. They're assembling near Kansas City."

"Pleased to meet you. I'm Comstock." He offered his hand and Patton took it in a very firm grip.

"Ordnance Department?"

"Yes, I'm heading to Santa Fe to observe some new equipment—including the tanks. How did you happen to end up with them?"

"Well, sir, I just graduated from the Point last spring and it seems like they're the wave of the future. I applied and was accepted. Just finished my training at the camp in Gettysburg."

Andrew looked closer. Patton seemed a bit old to be a freshly graduated cadet, but perhaps not. "Well, at least they have their own branch now. The last time I was at Camp Colt, the cavalry and the artillery were fighting over who would control them."

"Yes, and they both lost, didn't they?" Patton grinned.

"I guess so. Drink? Sorry, I don't have another glass."

"Thank you, sir," Patton took the bottle and drank from it.

Just then Corporal Kennedy ran up. "Major? They just announced our train will be moving in ten minutes. Better get going, sir."

"Right," he stood up, stoppered the bottle, and handed it to Kennedy. "Give that to the Sergeant. Lieutenant? Nice meeting you. Good luck with your unit."

"Thank you, sir. Good luck to you, too."

* * * * *

CYCLE 597, 844.0, HOLDFAST 32-1

Qetjnegartis watched as the excavator dumped its load into the processor. The crushed rock and soil was sucked inside to the separator and smelter. The crust of the target world held a higher percentage of the useful elements than did that of the Homeworld. Still, the total amount was generally small. Until a more thorough survey could be done to locate denser deposits, they would have to be satisfied with what could be extracted from digging locally. Fortunately, Element 22, which was used in large amounts, was proving quite abundant. And Element 26 was available in huge quantities from the metals salvaged from the prey creatures and could be substituted for Element 22 in many applications. Elements 42 and 79 were proving scarce so far, but other clans had reported finding significant amounts of the latter among the prey-creatures. The power elements, 90 and 92, had only been found in a few locations, but the Race was well supplied with that until local deposits could be located.

An ingot of metal emerged from the processor and another machine transported it to one of the construction machines. Qetjnegartis followed along in its travel chair to the main manufacturing chamber. Here, dozens of the newcomers were at work, guiding the machines. The five transport vessels had not been able to carry much equipment in addition to the passengers, but each carried a constructor machine and now those five and the other four were working continuously to produce the fighting machines the clan needed. Not just the machines for the fifty newcomers, but for the forty-six buds which had recently been detached. In less than a quarter cycle they would have over a hundred fighting machines ready for action.

One of them here was almost complete. It was a new design, brought from the Homeworld. It was slightly smaller than the standard model. It had a weaker heat ray and thinner armor, but it was considerably faster. No longer would those beast-mounted prey be able to outrun them.

Qetjnegartis' body was maturing rapidly. Soon it would be fully functional. The plentiful food supply was letting all the buds grow more quickly than usual. Those of the first group were nearly adults now and able to contribute in almost every way. Another quarter cycle and they could begin producing buds of their own. Yes, the holdfast was secure and the clan was strong.

Not as strong as some, though. The Mavnaltak Clan to the north was not only stronger but now had three holdfasts securing their large holdings. Valprandar was determined that once offensive operations were permitted again that the Bajantus Clan should create new holdfasts as well. It was a logical move to control such vast areas.

"Qetjnegartis, report to the command center at once." The order came over the communicator in its travel chair and it acknowledged immediately. It moved through the corridors, noting that the freezing temperatures had put an end to the leaks which had been such a nuisance. No doubt they would return when this hemisphere's spring came, unless some permanent solution could be found.

As expected, it found Valprandar waiting for it in the command center. "Yes, Commander? You wished to see me?"

"Yes, Qetjnegartis. New orders have come from the Conclave. We are to resume our attacks against the prey-creatures."

"So soon? We have fighting machines for only half our..."

"Large scale attacks are still not permitted. But it has been observed by other clans, elsewhere on the planet, that fast-moving raids, deep into the enemy's territory, can produce great disruption of their operations. In particular, destruction of their transportation system can cripple their ability to resist. We are ordered to begin such operations here very soon."

"This sounds like a wise course of action, Commander."

"It is good that you approve, Qetjnegartis. For you will be leading a major part of our forces."

"Indeed, Commander?" Its tendrils twitched at this unexpected news.

"You appear surprised, Qetjnegartis. Why?"

"The fact that you were sent to take command indicated that the clan elders were not pleased with my performance here. I did not expect to be given further responsibilities."

"This is true," said Valprandar. "And I was given authority to terminate you if I thought it necessary. After being here, observing the situation, and conferring with the other survivors I determined that while you did make errors, your judgment is not completely flawed. It would be an error on my part to not make use of your experience and abilities.

"Therefore, in ten days you will depart with a force of fifteen war machines. You will travel northeast and once through the mountains you will split into five groups of three."

"Commander, that will take us very close to the border with the Mavnaltak Clan."

Qetjnegartis could sense the amusement in Valprandar's reply. "Yes it will, won't it? Another similar group will be sent to the south. So far there have been no prey-creature forces contacted to the west, so we will only send a small scouting force in that direction. I and the rest will remain here and complete work on the holdfast and continue construction of more war machines. Your mission is to destroy everything you encounter, but you will not put your forces at risk. Understood?"

"I understand, Commander. We will destroy everything."

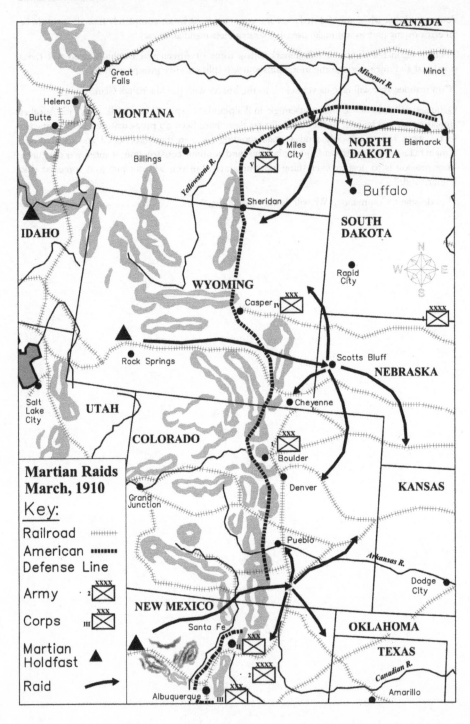

Martian Raids
March, 1910

Key:

Railroad
American
Defense Line
Army
Corps
Martian
Holdfast
Raid

CHAPTER TWELVE

JANUARY, 1910, SANTA FE, NEW MEXICO TERRITORY

Rebecca Harding *tsk-tsked* over the soldier's frostbitten fingers. "You need to take better care of yourself, soldier. You're probably going to lose some skin from the tips, but you were lucky this time. Make sure you wear your gloves!"

"Was wearin' gloves, miss! Just mighty darn cold out there!"

"Yeah, I can't argue with that. Still, try to be careful, keep your hands in your pockets as much as you can."

"Hard to do that when you're standin' guard duty and carryin' a rifle!"

"Got an answer for everything, don't ya?" said Becca, smiling. "Well, be as careful as you can. You can go back to your unit now."

"That's all? Don't I get no medicinal spirits or anything? The boys said they gave that out here!" The man looked indignant.

"Oh! So that's why you're here! Sorry, soldier, we only give out spirits for frostbite if bits of you are falling off. Move along." She smiled so he'd know it was a joke.

"Uh, how big a bit?"

"Git!" She swatted the man and laughed. He grinned back at her and went out, letting in a blast of icy air before the door was shut. But at least they had doors now. The tents had all been replaced by wooden huts with sheet metal roofs. There were big iron stoves in every building and it wasn't too bad most of the time.

The Martians seemed to have gone into 'winter quarters', too. There'd been no sign of them for several months and the only casualties they'd had to treat had been the usual sort any army in winter had to deal with. There were still quite a few men in the wards, but it was a lot different from when combat was going on.

Becca finished her shift and went to the mess hall. It was a while until the next meal, but it was where everyone came to socialize. She exchanged greeting with some of her friends and got a cup of coffee and sat down. She chatted with a few people, but then there was a commotion by the door and a number of people cheered when it turned out to be an orderly with the mail. Eager people clustered around the man as he handed things out. Becca didn't go over because she never got any mail from anyone. Well, every now and then she'd get something from Frank Dolfen, but the man was terrible at writing letters and she didn't expect anything.

So she was surprised when the orderly called her name. Maybe Frank had written to her! She jumped up and went over and took the envelope. It had her name on it on careful block letters, but no return address. What was this? She tore open the envelope and extracted the paper inside.

Her eyes grew wide.

> *Dear Miss Harding,*
>
> *I have received your letter and I wish to inform you that I am in Santa Fe. I would very much like to talk with your friend. I will accede to whatever conditions he might demand and will make no attempt to identify him or remove him against his will. Please arrange a meeting. You can contact me at the address given below.*
>
> *Your Obedient Servant,*
> *Major Andrew Comstock*

She looked around, but Sam wasn't in the mess hall. Would he really agree to a meeting? She'd practically had to twist his arm just to get permission to send that letter to the major. He probably didn't think he'd ever reply. Well, Becca hadn't really, either. But he had and he was here! So what should she do? She couldn't just walk up to him and say that the major was here, Sam might bolt.

She was going to have to do this very carefully.

* * * * *

CYCLE 597, 844.0, NORTHEAST OF HOLDFAST 32-1

Qetjnegartis carefully led the way through the mountain pass. The footing for the fighting machines was difficult and treacherous. Loose rocks, hidden under quels of frozen water, might shift or slide when stepped upon. One of the newcomers, still not fully accustomed to the heavier gravity of the target world, had fallen earlier that day and so badly damaged its machine that it could no longer operate. Qetjnegartis had been forced to have one of the others carry it back to the holdfast. Fortunately, along with the design for the smaller, faster fighting machines, the newcomers had also brought plans for a collapsible transport pod which could be attached to the rear of them. It was far better and safer than trying to carry someone with the manipulating tendrils.

But the incident left Qetjnegartis with only thirteen fighting machines for this important mission. They had left the holdfast the previous day and moved north and east through regions unfrequented by the prey-creatures and then up into the mountains to the north of the enemy's main defenses. They had initially been divided into five groups of three. Each group had one of the first wave in it to lend experience. In addition to Qetjnegartis, there was Ixmaderna, Namatchgar, Utnaferdus, and Davnitargus. The bud, now nearly an adult, seemed excited to be included.

Their goal was to penetrate beyond the enemy defenses and destroy as much as possible in their rear areas. It had become clear that the prey-creature armies were dependent upon a continuous influx of supplies and reinforcements to remain effective. Those supplies were moved by the transport vehicles which in turn were dependent upon the metal rails they ran upon. If those could be destroyed, the enemy armies might be seriously affected. At least that was the hope. There was still so much about the prey-creatures that was not known.

Qetjnegartis passed around a large outcrop of rock and saw a vast sweeping vista stretching away to the east. The horizon on this large planet seemed an immense distance away, and yet the sight reminded it of the Hadjnapnar Mountains near the clan's main holdfast on the Homeworld. The colors were all wrong, of course, and the frozen water rarely ever fell there anymore, but there was still a similarity.

And I shall never see it again.

Those coming to the target world realized that it was almost certainly a one-way journey. There would be no reason to ever return. That thought had not disturbed it in the slightest when it had been selected to lead the first wave of the Clan's expedition. It had been a great honor and a great opportunity. But lately… lately it had begun to have strange thoughts.

Is it simply because I am no longer in command?

Now that was a disturbing thought! That it would begin to doubt the mission simply because of its… its… It had to dredge up an archaic word from the depths of its memory to even put a name to it: its vanity. Unacceptable! Was there something wrong with it?

No, this was foolishness! It was still serving the clan and the Race and no one could ask for more. And Valprandar still trusted it enough to give it an important task. It had the authority to terminate Qetjnegartis if it thought necessary and it had not done so. For sometimes it was necessary. An individual with a record of failure and poor decision-making could not be left in a command position. But due to the instinctive chains of command and obedience, such an individual could not simply be pushed aside either. It had to be removed. And on rare occasions, an individual of extreme age might become erratic or even insane. The scientists believed that repeated buddings over many cycles could introduce errors in the genome. When that happened, the individual had to be terminated for the good of the Clan.

But I shall not be removed!

The way ahead was now downhill. The enemy was there and they would soon feel the might of Clan Bajantus! "Forward!" it commanded. "We shall crush the prey-creatures!"

* * * * *

JANUARY, 1910, SANTA FE, NEW MEXICO TERRITORY

"It will be all right, Sam," said Rebecca Harding. "Nothing bad is going to happen. He just wants to talk to you." Sam was sitting on a stool in a curtained-off area of one of the wards. He'd insisted that Rebecca wrap his head with bandages so only his eyes and mouth showed.

"He tries to take me, I'll fight," said Sam.

"He won't try to take you! I have his promise and he won't break it. Now you stay here and I'll go get him."

Two days ago she'd sent a message to Major Comstock where he'd been staying and yesterday they'd met in town to work out the details. Now he was waiting at the hospital administration building for Rebecca to take him to Sam. She made her way along the paths tramped down in the snow and found the major where she was expecting. "He's ready, sir," she said.

"And he's willing to talk?"

"I don't know how willing. He's willing to meet with you. I guess he'll say something. This way, sir."

"Please call me Andrew, Miss Harding."

"All right. And it might reassure Sam if you don't come across as an officer… Andrew."

They retraced her path and entered the ward. Becca had halfway expected to come back to find Sam gone, but he was still there, sitting on the stool. Comstock waited at the door until she waved him over. "Sam, this is Andrew, he'd like to talk to you." Sam's eyes glinted through the gaps in his bandages.

"All right. Have him sit there." He pointed at another stool. Comstock sat down. He had a pencil and a thick pad of paper.

"Maybe I should leave you two alone?" ventured Becca.

"No!" cried Sam. "You stay!"

"All right, all right, I'll stay. Let me get another stool." She pulled one over and sat down a little behind Comstock, pulling the curtain nearly closed behind her.

325

Comstock stared at the man for a few seconds and then rocked back on his stool, looking casual and relaxed. "Hello, Sam," he began. "I understand you spent some time with the Martians?"

Sam was utterly still and didn't say a word.

"Well, I almost had the same pleasure myself," continued Comstock. "I was with Sumner's army too, you know. I'd been sent there to observe the Martians and try and get hold of any wrecked machines. If you were there, you must have seen how the artillery knocked out one of the tripods down on the left. Did you see that?"

Sam nodded his head a tiny bit.

"Yes, and when it went down, me and my men—there were twenty of us—dashed over there, thinking to grab it. But then it all went to hell. Nearly got killed right there when the bastards came charging back over the ridge. Would have died except we hid behind the wreck. I guess you were caught out in the open, right?"

"Yeah."

"It was a hell of a mess. But the Martians went right on past us. I guess they were after you fellows. I probably wouldn't even be here except for that. I owe you my thanks."

"They were killing everyone," said Sam.

"Yeah, it sure looked that way from where we were. But we didn't stick around to watch. We skedaddled up into the hills to find cover. You poor sods had nowhere to go, did you?"

"Everything was burnin'. Ran an' ran until I couldn't run no more."

"Yeah, I'll bet. Then I guess the Martians rounded you up like a bunch of sheep, right? There were a few hundred of you, I'll bet?"

Sam nodded. "Me an' a few buddies were still alive from my company, but then all these other guys got herded in with us. Hundreds."

"We saw them driving you along the next day from up in the hills. We followed along and..."

"Why?" Sam leaned forward on his stool.

"I guess it does seem like a damn fool thing to do, doesn't it?" replied Comstock. "Not sure why. I had orders to learn as much as I could and I guess I wanted to know why they hadn't killed you. What they wanted with all of you. So we followed."

"Never saw anyone. We were all alone."

"We were staying well hidden. And we'd found some horses, so we could take roundabout routes. We saw... what they did to those of you who couldn't keep up." Sam's face scrunched up beneath the bandages.

"I... they kept forcing us to... they burned anyone who fell. My buddy... I tried to help him but... he fell and they..." Suddenly Sam was sobbing. He put his face in his hands and wept. "I tried, but I was so tired! I couldn't!"

She and Comstock sat in silence, neither one of them saying anything or making any move. Becca had learned this from dealing with scores of hurt or terrified soldiers. Let them cry it out. It was what they needed and you had to let them do it. She didn't know where Comstock had learned it, but she was glad he had. He was handling Sam just right. Finally, Sam stopped crying and wiped his eyes on his sleeve. The bandages under his eyes were wet.

"It's hard," said Comstock. "Six of my men got burned up when the Martians counterattacked. You can't help but wonder why them but not you? It's hard."

"Yes, sir," whispered Sam.

"We ran out of cover after the second day," continued the major as if nothing had happened, "and we had to ride on ahead and hope to pick you up again later. But we weren't able to. That night we ran into Miss Harding and her friends and we got a trifle distracted. Has she told you about that?"

Sam nodded. "She said you rescued her."

"Well, me and all my men. We'd found some dynamite and made some bombs. We got lucky—real lucky—and destroyed the Martian machine that had captured Miss Harding's party. Did she tell you that she killed the Martian driving it with her rifle?"

Sam looked at her in surprise. "No. She never said."

"Well she did. Emptied all sixteen rounds from her Henry into it. Made a helluva mess." He smiled at her.

"I was so mad at it. They killed my ma and my pa and my grandma. Couldn't help myself."

"My boss yelled at me for letting you do it. He wanted a live Martian—as if we'd have had any way of getting the damn thing back with us!"

"Oh dear! I'm sorry!"

Comstock laughed. "Don't worry! He couldn't have been too mad: he let me marry his daughter!"

Becca giggled but then covered her mouth and looked at Sam. What was he thinking of all this? But Comstock went on.

"So we lost track of you and the others, Sam. I rode up to the walls of their fortress and peeked over, but I couldn't see much. I guess you got a closer look, eh?"

Sam was silent for at least a minute, but then he nodded. "Yeah… I did."

"Can you describe what you saw?" Comstock took up his paper and pencil. "I'd really like to know."

Sam sat and wrung his hands and was silent for a long time, but at last he spoke. "They drove us up the big wall. A few of the guys were so scared at the sight of it… they tried to run… but they didn't get twenty yards. The rest of us they forced to climb over… guess there wasn't any gate. They didn't need a gate with those tripod things they drive; they just climbed right up like it was nothing. Some of the others couldn't make the climb, but instead of burnin' 'em the Martians picked 'em up and carried them over. Guess they figured we were so close to the end it would be a waste to burn' em now." Sam shook his head. "The ones they burned were the lucky ones."

"And once you were inside? From where I looked in, it didn't seem like there was much inside the walls."

"No, there wasn't much. Some machines standing around, but not much else. It was all underground. They marched us to a big ramp leading down. It was pretty steep and a lot of the guys fell."

"How wide was the ramp? How tall? How deep do you think it went?"

Sam went silent and Becca was afraid that Comstock's questions had shut off the sudden flow of information. But he was just thinking, she guessed, because after a moment he answered. "Maybe forty or fifty feet wide… I guess it was maybe fifty feet high once you got down in it—higher than the tripods, anyway. It went down, I don't know a hundred feet, maybe more."

"And at the bottom?"

"There was a real big open space down there. Hundreds of yards in each direction. There were some things way off in the distance, but I couldn't tell what they were."

"Where was the light coming from?"

"There were round balls up on the ceiling. They glowed like Edison bulbs. They were kind of dim, though, not like those arc lights they have in the cities."

"Where did you go from there?"

Step by step, Comstock guided Sam through his journey, getting descriptions of the Martian fort. How high? How wide? What were the walls and floors made of? He wrote it all down and a few times even paused to make a sketch based on Sam's description. He'd show it to Sam and make corrections if something was wrong.

But then Sam stopped talking. She was surprised to see that he was staring at her.

"Then where did you go?" asked Comstock. Sam didn't answer. "Sam?"

"I don't want her to hear the next part," said Sam.

"Oh, well, I guess…"

"Not proper for a woman to hear. Go away, Becca."

She looked from Comstock to Sam and back again. "Should I…?"

"It might be better," said Comstock. "Why don't you sit over there where you can still see?"

Becca stood up, part of her indignant. Did they think she wasn't tough enough to hear Sam's story? She had no doubt it was a horrible story, but it couldn't be any more horrible than seeing a man with his face burned off by the black dust! Could it? But if Sam was more comfortable talking just with another man… well, she could hardly argue. "All right." She took her stool and went to the other side of the room, leaving the curtain open. Sam and Comstock continued talking.

They talked for the better part of an hour. Sam seemed to be folding up inside himself and Comstock kept moving his stool closer so he could hear him. Eventually their heads were almost touching. Comstock scribbled furiously on his papers. Part of Becca wanted to know what Sam was saying—and part of her did not. She kept seeing him on that stretcher, bearded, long haired, wild eyed…*They eat us!* No… no, maybe she didn't want to know.

"Rebecca! What's going on here?"

She nearly jumped off her stool. Miss Chumley had come up behind her noiselessly. "Oh! Uh… you see, ma'am…"

"Who is that officer and *who* is the man in all those bandages? We don't have any patients here with those sort of injuries!" She started to step toward the pair.

"Miss Chumley!" hissed Becca, grabbing her arm. "Please! Don't interfere!" Becca was half a head taller than her boss and she firmly pulled her around.

Chumley pursed her lips, arched an eyebrow, and looked at Becca and then down at where her hand was clutching her sleeve. Becca sheepishly let go. "Please, ma'am! That's Sam with all the bandages on!"

"Sam Jones? What's the matter with him?"

"Nothing! Well, maybe something. But he… he knows some things the generals ought to know. I convinced him to talk to an officer I met. But he doesn't want the major to know who he is. He's scared!"

"Anyone looking at him knows that! The man's afraid of his own shadow! What could he possibly know?"

Should she tell her? She thought she could trust Chumley, but she'd promised Sam not to tell anyone. What should she…? But then she saw that Comstock had stood up. He was shaking Sam's hand! Then he walked right over to her.

"Thank you, Miss Harding. I think I have everything I need." Comstock's expression was very stern and his face quite pale. "The army is grateful for your help." He nodded to her and then to Chumley and made his way out. She looked after him and when she looked back, Sam was gone.

Chumley stood there frowning. "Miss Harding, someday I expect you to tell me what this was all about!"

* * * * *

JANUARY, 1910, SANTA FE, NEW MEXICO TERRITORY

Major Andrew Comstock made his way back to the tiny boarding house where he had a room. The streets were crowded, but he didn't see the people. Men saluted him, but he didn't return them. He bumped into things and murmured apologies. He staggered up the narrow steps to his room and threw open the door. McGill and Kennedy where there; rooms were so scarce the three of them had to share one.

"Ah, there you are, sir!" cried McGill. "Was startin' t'think you got yerself lost! Did you get what you were after?"

He didn't answer but he took out the sheaf of papers and carefully packed them in his valise.

"You all right, sir?" asked McGill, squinting.

Andrew looked at the pair and said: "Get your coats. I need a drink."

* * * * *

CYCLE 597, 844.0, EAST OF HOLDFAST 32-1

"All units prepare to attack!" commanded Qetjnegartis.

The force had made it through the mountains with no further casualties and descended onto the plain that lay beyond. Qetjnegartis knew precisely where they were located on the surface of the planet, but it had no idea what, if any, significance the settlement they were about to destroy might have. The one thing the expedition was lacking was truly accurate maps. Observations from the Homeworld had produced maps which could identify oceans and mountains and the larger rivers of the target world. Even some of the cities could be seen. But things as small as the prey-creatures' transportation system or small settlements could not be seen at such distances. The only way to map the surface was to go there.

There were about thirty structures just ahead and more could be seen in small groups farther away. This appeared to be a junction of two of the transportation lines and some of the vehicles which ran on the rails were stopped there. And there appeared to be some prey-creature warriors defending the place. They had encountered a few of them riding draught animals earlier that day and a few had escaped. Perhaps they had spread a warning, because as soon as they drew near, fire erupted from several small, low structures, which appeared to be more heavily constructed, and then from inside some of the larger ones. None of the weapons were the large projectile throwers fortunately, but there were at least two weapons which fired very rapidly; and from the impacts Qetjnegartis feared that they might possibly be able to do damage if given the chance.

"Destroy those weapons first!"

The thirteen fighting machines strode forward, heat rays blazing. Where the rays hit the ground, the frozen water exploded into clouds of steam. Where they hit the prey-creatures' structures, they exploded into balls of fire. Four machines concentrated their rays on the low structures where the heaviest fire was coming from and in moments they were obliterated. Then more rays swept across the other structures, turning them into infernos.

They didn't pause, and soon swept into the midst of the settlement. Prey-creatures were emerging from the burning structures, trying to escape. They were blasted down as they ran. One of the transport vehicles attempted to move away, black smoke puffing out of a cylinder on top, but it did not get far. Namatchgar led its group at top speed to get ahead of it and destroyed the rails it ran on. When the vehicle reached that spot it was disabled and then easily destroyed. Several of the box-like vehicles in the string exploded violently when the heat ray struck them.

The settlement was completely in flames now and smoke drifted high into the sky. Uncontrolled fire was still a novelty to Davnitargus and Qetjnegartis found it stopped near a particularly large conflagration. "It is fascinating, is it not?" asked the bud.

"Yes, but you will see much more of it soon. Much more. But come, we must not tarry." Qetjnegartis summoned everyone together and then said: "At this point we must split into groups. Ixmaderna, you will take your group south following this transport line. Destroy as much of the rails and supports as you can without seriously delaying your movements or depleting your energy reserves. Namatchgar, you shall go north with the same instructions, and Utnaferdus, you will take your groups along the transport line to the northeast. I will take my group and Davnitargus and travel due east.

"I emphasize again, that our mission is to cause confusion among the prey-creatures and do as much damage as possible without risking ourselves in a pitched battle. If you encounter serious resistance, you are to withdraw. Is that understood?"

"Yes, Subcommander!"

"Very well, you will proceed as instructed until you receive orders to return. If your energy reserves fall to twenty-five percent you will contact me for instructions. Carry out your orders."

The other three groups turned and began the operation. Heat rays blasted the transport lines as the fighting machines followed along them. Clouds of smoke and stream billowed up marking their route even as they dwindled in the distance. Qetjnegartis watched for some time and then addressed the three still with it. "Let us proceed."

They moved east.

* * * * *

FEBRUARY, 1910, WASHINGTON, D.C.

"How much of this has been confirmed, Leonard?"

The concern on the President's face was quite plain as he leaned over the huge map. It showed the western United States from the Mississippi almost to California and from Mexico to Canada. The temporary arrangement which had been set up during the watch for the second wave of Martian cylinders had proved so useful that Wood had ordered a permanent one to be created by demolishing a half-dozen offices in the basement of the huge State, War, & Navy Building.

The map was as detailed as could be accomplished, showing railroads, towns and roads, mountains, rivers, and swamps. Painted wooden blocks representing military units were scattered all over the surface showing how the army had been deployed. Men around the edge of the map had long poles to push the blocks around if necessary since the map was much too large to be able to reach the center. There were red blocks representing the enemy. Most of them were in clusters off to the west of the blue ones, but there were also some showing up in areas to the *east* of most of the blue ones. Those were the ones Roosevelt was staring at.

"Some of this we have confirmation for, Mr. President," replied Wood. "More information is coming in all the time." He swept his arm around, indicating the dozens of officers and enlisted men sitting at desks along the walls. Most were on telephones and writing down information on paper. "But we know for sure that the report from south of Pueblo is real. A dozen tripods smashed the railroad depot there and then split up and went off in four different directions. The attack on Scott's Bluff is also definite. Another large force, fifteen of them or more, blasted the town to bits. But the garrison there put up a good fight and when reinforcements from the 89th division arrived, the Martians pulled out. But they didn't retreat west, they split into four or five groups and headed in easterly directions. We lost sight of them in a snowstorm and we aren't sure where they are now. The sightings in Montana and North Dakota are not confirmed, but a number of telegraph connections have gone dead."

"So, do you think that these are raiding parties rather than a major attack?" asked Roosevelt. "Like Forrest and Mosby and Grierson during the Civil War? Strikes against our railroads and supply depots?"

"It could be, sir."

"But how did they break through our lines so easily, Leonard?" He pointed at the string of blue blocks stretched along the eastern side of the Rocky Mountains.

Wood snorted. "Maps are deceptive, Mr. President. Our 'line' is almost thirteen hundred miles long—and that doesn't even include the borders with Canada and Mexico. Our troops can't begin to create a solid defense line over a distance that vast." He picked up a long wooden pointer. "We've been reorganizing things since the movement west began. The First Army under General Bullard is responsible for the front from Great Falls, Montana, all the way down to Pueblo, Colorado. He's got three corps with a total of fifteen divisions. That's maybe 200,000 actual combat troops. Sounds like a lot, but spread out over seven hundred miles it comes to one man every six yards…"

"I understand that, General," said Roosevelt. "But a lot of that line is rugged mountains, we don't have to guard every foot of it."

"And we're not, we've concentrated our forces at the most critical points." His stick began jabbing at wooden blocks. "I Corps at Denver, IV Corps at Casper, V Corps spread out up in Montana trying to look west and north. But they can't hope to defend every pass over the mountains. The enemy machines are incredibly mobile and since they aren't tied down by supply trains, they can cross at points that no human army could even attempt. That leaves a lot of weak points in our line."

Wood shifted his pointer. "Only Funston's Second Army has been able to create a really solid line, but he's only covering the distance from Santa Fe to Albuquerque, a mere eighty miles or so. Even that takes two strong corps, and the enemy can slip around either flank."

"Which they are obviously doing," said Roosevelt. "So what do we do about it?"

"We have Third Army assembling around St. Louis, with a corps at Omaha. We can start pushing them forward to try and engage these raiding parties before they can do too much damage. But it's the dead of winter and our troops are not going to be able to stray far from the railroads. Might be hard tracking them down."

"Well, if they are after the railroads, they may come to us."

"Maybe. But if they can do a lot of damage to the tracks we could be in real trouble. All those troops at the front need supplies and there's not much they can hope to get locally. Do you realize that there are more soldiers in Montana right now than there are Montanans?"

Roosevelt sighed and Captain Butt brought him a mug of coffee. He took a sip and looked at Wood. "So what do you need, Leonard?"

Wood shrugged. "Everything. Men, tanks, guns, airplanes, ammunition, food. The list goes on and on."

"You'll get it," said Roosevelt. "The American people and American industry will give you what you need to win."

"Thank you, Mr. President. And in the meantime I'll get what troops we've got into motion."

* * * * *

FEBRUARY, 1910, NEAR SANTA FE, NEW MEXICO TERRITORY

"Damn! It's cold!"

Lieutenant Frank Dolfen looked at his sergeant and couldn't deny his statement. It *was* cold. *Damn cold*. But despite the cold, the 5th Cavalry, the 10th Cavalry, and two batteries of artillery were riding out of their warm and cozy camps in Santa Fe and up into the Glorieta Pass southeast of the town. The pass was the most direct route across the Sangre de Cristo Mountains and then down to the plains which lay beyond. But the top of the pass was at almost eight thousand feet and was choked with snow except where the trains had plowed a path. The artillery was being carried on a train, but no one knew how far they'd be able to go.

The word had come that the Martians had made it across the mountains farther to the north and were now raising Cain to the east. Somebody had to stop them and this scratch brigade was among the poor sods to have drawn the short straw.

"Cheer up Sarge, if we catch some Martians I'm sure they'll be happy to warm you up."

"Oh, very funny, sir! Very funny!"

"Maybe, but if we do catch the bastards, this time the joke's gonna be on them!"

CHAPTER THIRTEEN

FEBRUARY, 1910, ALBUQUERQUE, NEW MEXICO TERRITORY

Major Andrew Comstock looked at the telegram and frowned.

"So what's the verdict, sir?" asked Sergeant McGill.

"Looks like we're stuck here, Sergeant. At least for the foreseeable future."

"The railroad south's still open. We could get back through Texas."

"Yes, I know. And General Crozier knows that, too. But he thinks that since we're here anyway, we may as well stay and see how the new weapons perform. So he wants me attached to General Funston's staff."

"Oh joy. So what's my job, sir? Kennedy's your batman, but what do you want me to be doing?"

"Same as before, Sergeant: keep me out of trouble."

"A pleasure, sir."

Andrew nodded and then paused to consider the situation. He'd completed the interview with the mysterious and rather disturbing Sam. He still needed to write up a report based on the furious scribblings he'd made. He typically did things like that on the long train journey home from wherever he'd been, but if he was going to be here a while, he'd better do it soon while it was still fresh. He didn't think there was anything of critical importance in what Sam had told him, but every scrap of information they could accumulate about the Martians was valuable. And it was pretty damn disturbing information. They already knew the Martians fed off humans, but what Sam had experienced in the Martian fortress was just... obscene.

After the interview he'd gone on with his secondary mission: observing the new tanks and guns. He'd traveled up and down the Second Army lines between Santa Fe and Albuquerque, stopping in at units which had received the Mark II and Mark III tanks and the High-Velocity Field Gun— which the troops were calling the 'Anti-Tripod Gun'. Since there was no fighting going on, all he could observe were the drills the troops were doing and watch how well things went.

The Mark II Steam Tank was a significant improvement over the Mark I. Baldwin had made it two feet longer which not only gave the crew more room, but helped with the balance. The Mark Is had been very nose heavy and on any significant downgrade they could tip forward and bury the gun muzzle in the ground. The Mark IIs didn't have that problem despite carrying a heavier four-inch quick-firer in the nose. They were much more reliable mechanically, too. They still couldn't stray far from a rail line which was necessary for any sort of long-distance move, but they didn't break down every five minutes and the crews claimed they were a lot easier to fix in the field. Or maybe it was just that the crews were better trained. In any case, the men seemed to like them.

The verdict was still out on the Mark III. There was no doubt that it looked impressive, with a gun in the nose and two more sticking out from the side sponsons, but it had the same chassis and engine as the Mark II, which meant that it was overloaded and underpowered. The two extra guns also meant that it was very crowded inside. Andrew had squeezed himself inside one of them with its crew and there was scarcely room to turn around. Still, the crews he'd talked to were enthusiastic about all the firepower they commanded. He'd bumped into that Lieutenant Patton again, his battalion had been moved from Kansas City to Santa Fe, and the man seemed thrilled with the platoon he commanded.

Finally, there was the anti-tripod gun. The army had wanted something which could seriously hurt a Martian machine. The three-inch and four-inch guns in common use had proved incapable of punching a shell through the enemy's armor. Concentrated fire could eventually batter holes in the machines, but getting multiple hits on the agile Martian tripods wasn't easy. It was hoped that the new guns could kill the enemy with a single hit. The gun was only a 3.7-inch bore, but the barrel was over twice as long as a typical field gun, giving it an unprecedented muzzle velocity. That combined with the specially case-hardened projectiles made it a powerful weapon. Test firings had looked good.

The problem was the carriage. A modified version of the standard field carriage had been designed for it, but it had proved an utter failure. The massive recoil of the gun had literally shaken the carriage to pieces after just a dozen shots. Attempts to reinforce the carriage had not worked satisfactorily and it was determined to design a new one from the ground up, but it wasn't ready and the generals were demanding that the gun get into action right away. So they had taken the carriage from a much older siege gun and modified it for the anti-tripod gun. It was sturdy enough but the results looked… ridiculous. The thing had massive spoked wheels twice as tall as a man which lifted the gun up so high the crew had to stand on boxes to reach the breech and aiming controls. In addition, the gun also sported a massive shield to protect the crew made from that sandwich armor of steel and asbestos that the folks at MIT had developed. Put together, the contraption looked like a child's idea of a toy cannon. It was hard to move and difficult to operate and the crews hated it. Andrew had watched them doing practice firings and had to agree that this stop-gap design was of questionable value.

After finishing his observations, he was ready to head back to Washington. But then came word that the Martians had sent raiding parties through passes in the mountains into the army's rear and the rail lines had been cut. At least the most direct routes east were cut. As Sergeant McGill had pointed out, they could still go due south to El Paso and then try to make their way east through Texas from there. But General Crozier seemed to think that these raids might presage a new Martian offensive and if that was the case, he wanted him here to observe.

Yeah, I really should have burned that letter from Harding!

* * * * *

MARCH, 1910, SANTA FE, NEW MEXICO TERRITORY

"You really ought to talk to them, Rebecca."

Becca Harding looked at Miss Chumley and sighed. "They aren't going to listen to me. They've never listened to me. My aunt still doesn't believe that there are any Martians!"

"Well, you should at least try. Even if they refuse to listen, you can go away with a clear conscience. If you don't try and then something happens, you'll be second-guessing yourself for the rest of your life. Trust me, I know." Rebecca looked into the older woman's eyes. Against every expectation, she had come to think of Chumley as a friend. Someone she could confide in and someone she could trust. She'd trusted her enough to tell her the whole story about Sam and she hadn't betrayed that trust. Eventually she nodded.

"I guess you're right. I suppose I could try to go see them tomorrow…"

"Go now. Things are quiet for the moment; no telling what it might be like tomorrow. Take your horse and go, Becca."

She looked at her a moment longer and then smiled. "Yes, ma'am." She got up, put on her overcoat, and went to saddle up Ninny. She didn't have much hope that she could do any good, but as Miss Chumley had said, she had to at least try.

Word had come down from headquarters the previous week that the Martians were rampaging behind the army to the east, cutting the rail lines and doing untold damage. There were also signs that there might be a direct assault on the defenses of Albuquerque and Santa Fe. General Funston was urging the civilian populations of both towns to evacuate. It wasn't an order—not exactly—but with the warnings and restrictions that went along with it, it might as well have been an order. Martial Law had been declared and strict rationing of food and coal was in effect. Empty supply trains were being made available which would take people south to Texas. So far, a lot of people had left, but Becca was fairly certain her aunt and uncle were not among them. She needed to convince them to go.

Ninny carried her from the hospital to the quiet street where they lived. The place looked lonely and deserted. Handbills announcing the evacuation lay in the gutters or drifted along the sidewalk in the breeze. Some of the houses had actually had their doors and windows boarded up as if that would keep the Martians—or looters—out. But her aunt and uncle's house wasn't sealed up and a curl of smoke drifted out of the chimney. Becca took Ninny around to the back where he wouldn't be too noticeable and then she went and knocked on the front door.

She had to knock twice, but eventually her uncle opened the door. His eyebrows went up. "Oh, it's you," he said.

"Hello, Uncle Albert. I... uh, I wasn't sure if you'd still be here."

"Go away!" Her Aunt Rosilee screamed from somewhere in the house. "Leave us alone! We are not leaving!"

Uncle Albert glanced behind him and then back at her. "Soldiers have come by a few times telling us to pack up and go. She probably thinks you're another one." He turned and called: "It's Rebecca."

There was a long silence and then her aunt said, "What does she want?"

"I want to talk to you, Aunt Rosilee."

"We are not leaving!"

"Please, Aunt Rosilee, it's important."

There was no answer, but her uncle ushered her in and closed the door. He led her down the hall to the kitchen. Her aunt was there, dressed in a dark, severe dress as if she was already in mourning. But there was no one else there; had their maid already fled? Her aunt looked up and her eyes were red like she'd been crying. When she saw Becca, her expression became one of fury. "How could you! How could you! How could you take our home from us?"

"Rosie, stop it!" snapped her uncle. "Becca didn't do anything!" Aunt Rosilee rocked back as if she'd been slapped. Becca was shocked, too. She had never heard her uncle raise his voice to his wife or contradict her in any way. "It's not her fault!"

The woman put her face in her hands and began to cry. It was impossible to get any sort of reply out of her and Uncle Albert took Becca into the parlor. "She's been like that for a week." He looked at Becca. "So you think we should go?"

"It might be for the best. If the Martians cut the rail line to El Paso, things could get very rough here. And if the Martians attack the city..."

335

"Could that happen?"

"It could," she said firmly. "The army will do everything it can to stop them, but they might still break into the city. If they do... anything could happen."

Her uncle turned away and looked out the window. He started talking and she wasn't sure if it was to her or himself. "How can we go? So much of our money is in the house... the banks are closed and won't give us anything... the army says we can only take what we can carry... we'd be like vagabonds... living on charity... How can we do that?"

"You'd be alive. I came here with nothing but the clothes on my back. *Things* don't matter, Uncle Albert, *lives* do."

He turned back and looked at her like she was a crazy person. "Thank you for coming, Rebecca. You better go."

"You'll think about it?" she persisted. He nodded but didn't say anything. "Don't think too long." He escorted her out and closed the door. She stared at the door for a minute, briefly considered hammering on it and then hammering on them to try and knock some sense into them, but finally decided it wouldn't do any good. She went and got Ninny and rode back to the hospital. Her conscience wasn't exactly clear, but she did feel better with herself.

* * * * *

MARCH, 1910, NORTHEAST OF SANTA FE, NEW MEXICO TERRITORY

"They can't be too far away, sir! Ashes are still hot!"

Lieutenant Frank Dolfen acknowledged the report of his scout and then sent a courier with the information back to the squadron headquarters: another burned-out farmstead. They'd encountered dozens of them, and a few small towns, since beginning the mission two weeks ago, but so far they hadn't actually seen any Martians. The trail was getting hot—literally. If they could just catch up with the bastards!

At least moving was a bit easier. There had been a thaw, which had melted most of the snow, and then a hard freeze which had solidified the mud. The horses had an easier time of it and even the artillery could almost keep up. The guns had moved by train until they were about thirty miles east of Glorietta Pass when they encountered the first overt sign of the enemy: wrecked railroad tracks, rails half-melted and twisted, and ties burned to cinders—for miles. Repair gangs had followed, but it would take weeks to put the tracks in order, and the artillery had been forced to dismount and follow the cavalry overland.

They'd run into refugees, too. Men, women, and children; sometimes in wagons, sometimes on foot. They'd all told the same story: Martian machines striding across the plains like giants, burning anything in their path. The ones who'd escaped were the ones who took little or nothing. The ones who tried to take more, well, Doflen and his men had found their ashes piled near the ashes of their homes. They gave the survivors rations and directed them to link up with the railroad gangs and try to get to Santa Fe.

"No good, us just following these guys," said Dolfen in frustration. "Somehow we gotta get ahead of them!"

"Yeah, that's the Lord's truth," said Sergeant Urbaniak, riding next to him. "But they're so damn fast! And they don't seem to stop at night. Don't they ever get tired?"

"Their machines don't. Maybe the Martians don't, either."

"So all we can do is try to guess where they'll go and then get there first."

"Or get lucky. I'll take luck any day."

But they didn't get lucky that day, or the next. On the evening of that second day, the colonel called a meeting of his officers. Frank still had to be reminded that meant him, too. The regimental HQ had been set up in a little grove of trees near another destroyed farm. The trees were all still bare and didn't provide much shelter. Colonel Berg welcomed them, coffee and some whiskey was passed around, and then they got down to business. The colonel spread out a map of the area, but unfortunately it did not show a lot of detail.

"Gentlemen," said Berg, "so far this has been a fool's errand, and I damn well don't like playing the fool! The enemy is out there and we need to find a way to bring them to battle. So, it is time to take some risks. Instead of just following their trail of destruction, we are going to split up and send out forces to locations we think they might attack. Once contact is made, we will concentrate to destroy them."

"That *will* be risky, sir," said Major Campos. "Our detachments might be destroyed individually before the rest of us can arrive to help them."

"I know that, Paul, but there isn't any choice if we are going to hurt these scum. So, here is what we are going to do." He pointed to the map. "The Martians we're after were first sighted up north near Pueblo in Colorado. But then at least some of them followed the railroad south all the way down to where we first encountered the wrecked tracks at Tipton. From there they turned almost due east and we've been chasing them. We know they've hit the towns of Albert, Baca, and Garcia." His finger traced a path on the map. "Now, I believe that when they moved south along the railroad to Tipton, they must have seen the Union Pacific line that branches off at Trinidad and goes to Texas. I think they are now heading that way to destroy that line as well. If that's true, they will hit it somewhere around Clayton." He pointed to a town northeast of where they were now.

"If we just follow along behind them, all we're going to find is more wrecked track and burned towns. But if we assume that they will follow the railroad, then they will turn either northwest or southeast."

"Or both, sir," said Campos. "We don't know how many of them there are."

"True," said Berg, nodding. "So, I've conferred with Colonel Thaxton of the 10th and we've decided that I will take the 5th, and one battery, almost due north and reach the railroad near Felacen. Thaxton will take the 10th and the other battery and go east toward Clapton. With any luck that will allow us to get ahead of them as they destroy the track and set an ambush. But as I said, we will split up to allow us to cover more area and hopefully find them. Questions?"

There were a few, mostly involving certain logistical issues, which were quickly dealt with. Dolfen didn't have any questions and he thought it a good plan. A damn sight better than just following and never catching up! So the next morning, they turned their path north.

* * * * *

MARCH, 1910, WASHINGTON, D.C.

Leonard Wood stared at what everyone called the 'Big Map' and tried to find some sort of inspiration. The situation which was developing had all the marks of a major disaster. Wood wasn't a West Point graduate, he hadn't taken courses in military history, but he had years of actual experience in military operations under a wide variety of conditions, and his instincts told him that there was real danger here.

The Martian raiding parties were playing absolute Hob in the army's rear areas. Railroad tracks, rolling stock, and supply dumps were being destroyed all across Kansas, Nebraska, and the Dakotas. Dodge City, Scott's Bluff, Rapid City, and Bismarck had all been raided, if not destroyed, and nearly every line of supply to the front had been severed. Only Funston's Second Army still had an open, if roundabout, rail connection with the east. A few of the telegraph lines were still in operation and they had intermittent wireless contact with the main headquarters. Thankfully, the reports indicated that so far there had been no major attacks against the troop concentrations.

But that wasn't going to last.

The Martians wouldn't be doing this except to disrupt and soften up the armies in preparation for a major attack. But the question was what to do? Attempts to destroy the raiding groups had been almost entirely unsuccessful. The enemy had lost a few tripods, but more to mishap than combat. They'd found one abandoned where it had broken through a frozen lake, and another near Cheyenne which had apparently fallen off a cliff. But for the most part the enemy went where they would, destroying everything they found. If they ran into a garrison powerful enough to give a good fight, the Martians bypassed it and went somewhere else. The steady trickle of refugees heading east had turned into a flood. Feeding and caring for them was becoming a major challenge, and Wood didn't like to think about the hundreds—or thousands—who must have perished in the freezing weather before they could reach safety.

"So what do you think, sir?" asked Colonel MacArthur. The man was now Wood's new aide and was proving to be very able in that position. Wood had recommended his promotion to brigadier general, but that needed to be approved by Congress.

"I think that we have a hell of a mess, Colonel. These monsters have a greater mobility than any human army in history. No supply lines! Nothing to tie them down. Even the famous cavalry raiders in the Civil War had to return to their bases frequently. Only the Indians or the Mongols could move like they do!"

"There may have been a few others, sir, but yes, you are correct. So how do we respond?"

"I've been asking myself that and I'm not coming up with any good answers. The keys are the railroads. Somehow we have to protect them."

"Not going to be easy, sir. Even if we abandon the branch lines, we are still talking about a couple of thousand miles of track to keep all of our troops supplied. To build forts which are strong enough to drive off a raiding party along all those miles would tie down three-quarters of the army."

"In the Civil War, the North used the rivers instead of railroads wherever they could," said Wood. "You can't burn a river. But out where our troops are, there aren't any navigable rivers within five hundred miles."

"But just patrolling the rail lines won't do any good," said MacArthur. "Not unless the patrol is very powerful. Small patrols will just be killed like those cavalry we lost out near Minot."

"It's just too great a distance," muttered Wood. "We can't support armies that are that far away. They have supplies stockpiled for a month or two, but we may have to pull them back."

"Would the President approve of such a move, sir?"

"He'd fight like the devil to avoid it," replied Wood nodding. "The notion of abandoning six or eight entire states would stick in his craw—hell, it sticks in *my* craw! The political consequences would be enormous, too. But losing those armies *and* losing the states anyway would be even worse."

"Have you even discussed the possibility with him?" asked MacArthur.

"No, and I won't be able to until he gets back." Roosevelt was in New York, watching a parade. The British had finally sent their promised expeditionary force. Most of it had gone directly to Canada, but a division had disembarked in New York to make a symbolic show of support for their American cousins. It would encourage the people, and that was important, of course, but the

British troops would march through the city and then boards trains which would take them on to Canada. The British arrival would do nothing to help the looming debacle in the American west.

Wood looked at his aide. "Start making plans for a general withdrawal."

* * * * *

MARCH, 1910, NEAR EMERY GAP, NEW MEXICO TERRITORY

"There they are! There they are!"

The cry caused Frank Dolfen to jerk his head around and look south. At first he didn't see anything, but then he noticed what looked like smoke to the southwest. He pulled out his field glasses and focused in. Yes! Six or eight miles away there was definitely smoke, and tall objects moving in front of it. Three of them.

"Is it them?" asked Sergeant Jason Urbaniak.

"Sure is, and heading this way!"

"Never thought I'd say this, but thank God!"

"Yeah. But we gotta get ready. Looks like there's a cut through some higher ground about a mile north. Let's set things up there. And get a courier to the captain, he can't be more than a couple miles over that way."

"Right!"

Dolfen set the troop in motion and headed for the high ground. It was the fourth day since the colonel's plan was put into motion and now it looked as though it might pay off. They'd ridden north and reached the railroad, but to their dismay the Martians had already been there. The little town of Felacen had been reduced to rubble, but there were a few survivors who said the Martians were following the tracks north and couldn't be more than a few hours ahead of them. Chasing them didn't seem like it would be any more productive than before, until the colonel noticed that the railroad on his map made a great loop to the west. If the regiment went straight north they might be able to get ahead of them—and so it had proved.

But Dolfen's troop had been in the lead and everyone else was straggling out behind them. He didn't know how many more could join them before the Martians got here. And sixty men against three tripods was pretty poor odds. They reached the high ground and saw that it was just a low ridge, not more than fifteen feet high. But the southern side was steep and rocky and a cut had been made through it to allow the tracks to pass. Fifty yards south of the base of the ridge a small stream had cut a gully which the railroad crossed on a wooden bridge.

"Best place for an ambush I've seen all week," said Urbaniak. "Plenty of hiding places and if they want to destroy the bridge they'll have to come to us."

Dolfen agreed and he sent the troop through the cut and had them dismount on the other side to stay out of sight. He used his glasses to check on the enemy. They didn't seem much closer, although he knew that was deceptive. But there were definitely only three. Maybe, with help, they could handle three. Then he swung them to the east and was elated to see the rest of the squadron riding up. He went forward to meet with Captain Pendleton. "Looks like this is the spot," said his commander.

"I thought so, sir."

"Right! Okay, Frank, your men have the most training on making a mounted attack on these critters, so I want you to keep your troop on the other side of the cut. I'll deploy the rest in that gully. When they get close enough, we'll give 'em what-for and then you charge in and finish them off. Understood?"

"Yes, sir," said Dolfen, thinking that it wasn't going to be nearly that easy.

"The colonel will bring up the rest of the regiment and the guns and we can crush 'em in between us!"

"We'll sure as hell try, sir."

The other troops sent their horses to the other side of the cut and then took cover in the gully. Their single fifty-caliber Browning was set up in a clump of rocks on top of the ridge. Frank called his men together. "All right, we win the prize," he told them and then explained what they were expected to do. Some looked eager, some looked scared, most looked determined. The weeks of destroyed homes and burned bodies had grown a real hatred for the enemy in the hearts of most. "This isn't going to be easy, but the others are going to be counting on us to finish the job they start. So, look for my signal. I know I can rely on each and every one of you."

"Yu kin count on uz, zir!" said one of the men in a thick accent.

"I know I can. Now, check your weapons, check the fuses on your bombs—don't blow yourselves up, please!—and get what rest you can. I'm guessing we have about an hour." They did as he ordered and he had to force himself to sit down by his horse and munch down a piece of hardtack and accept a cup of coffee which someone had brewed, even though his stomach was in knots. *Have to look calm...* He pulled out his pocket watch and checked it a half dozen times, but the minutes passed very slowly. He checked his Colt revolver and he checked the one bomb he was carrying. When the fight started he had no intention of holding back. The only order he'd need give was *charge*. After that it would be each man trying to get his bomb delivered to its target.

Finally, he couldn't stand it any longer so he got up, took a piss, and then carefully went up to the top of the little ridge, crawling the last few yards. Urbaniak followed along. Everything seemed unnaturally quiet. From his position just below the crest, he peered out. The Martians were there, no more than a mile away, following the tracks and destroying them as they went.

They'd noticed, while following them, that they didn't destroy every bit of track. Rather, they'd destroy a few dozen yards and then leave an equal length untouched and then destroy another section. Watching them in action here, Dolfen could see why that was. The leading tripod would halt and use its heat ray to wreck a section of track while the other two kept moving. Then the new leader would stop and do the same thing. Leap-frogging forward in this fashion they smashed the railroad to uselessness, without significantly slowing their pace. No wonder they hadn't been able to catch them.

"Gonna be here soon, Lieutenant," said Urbaniak.

"Right. Tell the boys to get ready, but don't mount up until I signal them."

"Yessir!" Urbaniak scrambled down the ridge. As he went down, a courier from Pendleton came up.

"Lieutenant?" said the man. "The captain says for you to wait until you hear the bugle sound the charge."

"Okay, we'll do that. Where is the captain?"

"In the gully by the bridge, sir." The man ran off.

Dolfen turned his attention back to the Martians. They were about a half mile away now and still destroying track. Had they seen any of the troopers? They had to know that there were pursuers after them, didn't they? Who could tell what was going on inside their minds?

Half a mile, a quarter mile. Getting close now. Pray to God no one opened fire early. Let them come, let them come! Three hundred yards, two hundred... they were still burning the tracks... one hundred... *Bang! Pow!* A couple of shots rang out and Dolfen cursed. The Martians paused and the heads of their machines swiveled back and forth. But there was no more fire and the lead machine went back to wrecking the rails. The second one in the line advanced toward the bridge. They would no doubt want to destroy that. Fifty yards... another few seconds and the Martians would be able to look down into the gully. A few more and they might spot Dolfen's troops beyond the ridge.

A bugle blared, sounding *commence firing*. An instant later, fire erupted all along the gully and the Browning opened up. Dozens of men leapt out of the gully and charged forward, some of them shouting at the top of their lungs. The Martians were clearly taken by surprise and critical seconds went by before they reacted. The closest one finally fired its heat ray and burned a trench across the ground to the left, claiming the lives of a half-dozen men. But this allowed more to close in from the right. Dolfen saw one dynamite bomb go soaring up only to bounce off and fall to the ground. Several more did the same and then a series of explosions shook the air and the tripod disappeared in a cloud of smoke and dust. Some of the men had probably been killed by their own bombs, but everyone knew that was a possibility.

The other two tripods began firing, killing more men. Still more charged out of the gully to join the fray. A few fleet-footed (or foolhardy) souls were running toward the more distant targets. The Browning kept firing and Dolfen could see sparks on the armor of the one it was hitting. The sharp smell of cordite and hot brass mixed with dynamite, dust, and burning bodies.

He realized that the moment to charge was fast approaching. He leapt down the slope to where his horse was waiting. He led the troop forward a few dozen yards to the edge of the cut. He could hear the shriek of the heat rays, the stutter of rifle fire, and the *crump-whump* of the dynamite bombs. All that was needed now was the bugle call to bring him forward.

But it didn't come. Seconds ticked by and there was no bugle. Perhaps the bugler had been killed. He edged his horse forward so he could look through the cut. But the fire was dying down! What was happening? He stared as the wind blew the smoke aside and he could see that the three tripods were in full retreat, pulling away with their long strides. *Damn!* They'd lost their chance!

But one of the enemy machines had been hurt. It was definitely limping and lurching awkwardly. Now the bugle did sound, but instead of the charge, it was sounding recall. The men still out in the open fell back into the gully. Dolfen dismounted and trotted through the cut in search of the captain. He found him by the bridge. "Frank! Sorry about that. But they turned and ran so suddenly I didn't want to end up with you out there all by your lonesomes chasing those bastards."

"I appreciate that sir. So what now?"

"Well, I doubt they'll come straight on again. If they veer off, I guess we go back to chasing them and..."

A distant boom cut him off. They looked out, past the Martians, and saw a puff of smoke. An instant later, a small fountain of earth rose up between the Martians and them with a muffled explosion. Three more puffs came in rapid succession, followed by two more fountains and one solid bang on one of the tripods.

"The field guns!" cried Dolfen. "They made it!"

"Look! There's the regiment!" Dolfen whipped out his field glasses, trained them in the direction the captain was pointing, and sure enough, there was a long line of men on horseback. They were deployed in an arc that was coming up behind the Martians and stretching out well to the east and west to cut off other lines of retreat. "They're coming on! Gonna drive 'em right to us!"

And so it seemed. The Martians turned around again and were coming at them. "They're gonna try to bust right through us, sir."

"Well, they'll have to pay the toll if they want to get by!"

"Yes, sir!" Dolfen ran back to his command. "All right!" he shouted. "It's not over yet! Get ready!"

He kept the men mounted and positioned himself so he had a good view through the cut. The Martians were approaching quickly, pursued by artillery shells and the regiment on horseback. They were back in range of their heat rays with shocking suddenness. All three blasted out and swept across the landscape. Frank realized he was right in the open and reined his horse backward just in time as a beam stabbed through the cut right in front of him. Steam boiled up from the ground and small bushes burst into flame.

"Dammit, Lieutenant!" scolded Urbaniak, "That was a fool thing to do!"

"Yeah, yeah, I know!"

But now he couldn't see. The Browning on the ridge opened up again and there was a crackle of rifle fire. Shouts and screams drifted back from the other side of the ridge. There was a cry from above and he looked up to see the machine gun crew outlined in a dazzling red glow before they disappeared in a gout of flame. Bombs started exploding and an errant shell from the guns shrieked overhead to detonate far to the rear. Smoke was billowing up beyond the ridge.

And then there it was: a bugle calling the charge! It sounded once and then was suddenly cut off, but Frank had already risen up in his stirrups and waved his arm. "Come on! Follow me!"

His horse knew what to do and sprang forward. In a few yards he was at a full gallop, thundering through the cut. A tripod was right there, crossing the little bridge only fifty yards away. The other two were right behind. He fumbled out his bomb and realized it was already too late to try and throw it at the first one. He'd go for one of the others. The tripods were spraying fire to the right and left as the dismounted troopers attacked, but they hadn't been ready for this sudden attack from straight ahead. The men on the ground were still throwing bombs, and an explosion nearly knocked him off his horse as he rode right between the legs of the first enemy machine.

The second tripod was looming up over him as he yanked out the arming pin on his bomb. He swung and threw it upward with all his might, but couldn't stop to see where it went. He rode between its legs as well, suddenly realizing he hadn't a clue about what to do next.

That decision was taken out of his hands when a series of new bomb blasts erupted right behind him. His horse screamed and they were both going down. The ground came up and slammed into him hard, knocking the wind out of him. But his horse was thrashing in pain and Frank had the wits to pull himself free before the beast rolled on him.

Gasping for breath, he scrambled away and then looked back. Two of the tripods were already through the cut, but the third was still on this side and clearly in trouble. Smoke was pouring from its body and one leg was missing a foot. It staggered toward the bridge with an awkward motion.

Men on foot and men on horseback were swirling around it, shooting rifles and flinging bombs. More explosions erupted, killing men and further damaging the machine. But it was still fighting back. The heat ray incinerated men and its smaller tentacles swatted troopers away like flies.

Frank pulled himself to his feet and stumbled back toward the fight, his pistol in his hand, fully aware that there wasn't a blessed thing he could do. The Martian reached the bridge and stepped across the gully. Another man on horseback rode toward the thing, swinging a pair of bombs on their strap. Even from fifty yards away, Frank could see who it was: *Urbaniak!* His sergeant brought his horse to within ten yards and then flung his bomb. It soared upward spinning end over end and then caught on the Martian's hip joint. *Yes!*

But as Urbaniak turned away, the enemy's heat ray swung in his direction. "Jason!" screamed Frank. But there was nothing he could have done even if he'd heard him. The ray passed over horse and rider and in a blast of smoke and steam they were gone.

An instant later, the bomb exploded and the machine's leg was torn off and flung away in one direction. The rest of the machine toppled over the other way and crashed to the ground with an impact Dolfen could feel. The thing's remaining legs and arms thrashed impotently. More men were flinging bombs and explosion after explosion tore at the downed monster. Finally, the machine stopped moving and an echoing silence fell over the field of battle. Dolfen caught a glimpse of the other two Martians dwindling in the distance.

He limped up to the wrecked tripod. He glanced around in spite of himself, trying to catch some glimpse of Urbaniak's remains, but there were dozens of scorched patches of earth and mounds of ashes all around. No way to tell which one had been his friend. He stood there feeling utterly drained. Alone.

"Hey! Hey, sir!" cried someone. "It's opening up!"

Shaken back to his senses, he dragged himself over to where a small group of men were standing. A hatch had opened in the head of the machine. Smoke was pouring out of it and as he watched a cluster of gray snake-like tentacles emerge and grasped the sides of the hatch. These tensed and a moment later the body of the Martian emerged and tumbled to the ground. It lay there gasping and burbling like some mangled set of bagpipes.

"God! Sure is ugly, ain't it?"

"Filthy monster! It killed my pard!"

"Not so tough without its fancy machine, is it?" One trooper stepped forward and gave it a kick. No, just like the one Dolfen had seen outside Gallup, the thing looked pathetic rather than menacing. It was just a shapeless gray sack, smaller than a man, with two large black eyes, a parrot-like beak for a mouth, and a swarm of tentacles of various sizes and lengths waving feebly.

"What do we do with it, sir?" The men looked to him.

Dolfen glared down at the thing which had killed *his* pard. "A very wise young lady once showed me *exactly* what to do with one of these!" He raised his pistol and emptied it into the thing.

* * * * *

CYCLE 597, 844.1, EAST OF HOLDFAST 32-1

"I regret that I have failed to carry out your instructions, Subcommander. I allowed us to become surrounded by the enemy, and in breaking free, Kanastrad was slain. Jalnadnar's fighting machine was so badly damaged it had to be abandoned later. I have Jalnadnar in a transport capsule now and am proceeding north."

Qetjnegartis listened to Ixmaderna's report. This was not good, but it could have been worse. "Understood. Proceed to the rendezvous point at your best speed." It cut the communications link.

The loss of Kanastrad was annoying. They were still at a stage where personnel were precious. But so far, that had been the only such loss during the operation. One other machine had been crippled and its pilot transferred to a capsule, but of the fifteen fighting machines Qetjnegartis had started with, ten were still available.

But it was time to report in to Valprandar. It established the communications link and relayed the facts. "In summation, we have covered a great deal of territory and done much damage, Commander. The transportation system in this entire region will be unusable for some time."

"You have done well, Qetjnegartis," replied Valprandar. "The forces of Clan Mavnaltak to the north have suffered far worse. But now it is time to move on to the next phase of the operation. All the evidence suggests that our raids have left the enemy confused and in much disorder. There are reports from Commander Braxjandar that the prey-creature army it faces is beginning to withdraw and retreat east. It plans a major offensive against these forces, hoping to catch them on the move and annihilate them. Braxjandar has requested that Clan Trajnavzin to the north of them and our clan to the south launch simultaneous attacks in support of them. The Colonial Conclave has agreed and those are our orders."

Qetjnegartis twitched in surprise and alarm. "Have any of your scouts reported similar withdrawals of the enemy in our area, Commander?"

"No, but once they see their allies to the north of them in retreat they are sure to follow. They will not risk being cut off."

"I am not sure I agree with this line of reasoning. Were we not commanded to refrain from frontal attacks against strong…"

"No matter! I have my orders and I will obey them. Your orders are to reassemble your detachment and stand ready to strike the enemy from the rear."

Qetjnegartis did not agree with this action, but it had no choice. "Very well, Commander. We will be ready."

CHAPTER FOURTEEN

MARCH, 1910, WASHINGTON D.C.

"Leonard, you can't be serious!"

General Leonard Wood sighed. He'd known this was going to be a difficult confrontation and Roosevelt had wasted no time in confirming it would be. Wood wasn't happy that it was going to take place in front of such a large audience. In a one-on-one meeting with the President he might have been able to convince him, but word of the proposed withdrawal—*Retreat! Don't mince words!*—had leaked out and in addition to Roosevelt, Henry Stimson, the Secretary of War, Elihu Root, the Secretary of State, and a small crowd of aides and other interested parties had all gathered in the room with the Big Map. Even more had wanted to be here, including representatives and senators from the affected states, but Wood had put his foot down on that.

"I'm sorry, Mr. President, but I can't see that there is any choice. The situation is quickly becoming untenable."

"Untenable? You have half a million men out there and you're telling me they can't run down a handful of enemy tripods?"

"The Martians' mobility is unprecedented, sir. Except in a few cases where we've been able to lure them into an ambush, they have simply run away from any attempt to engage them. Or, if we attempt to engage them with too weak a force, they just destroy it and move on. The space involved is too vast, sir. We can neither garrison nor patrol the railroads in sufficient strength to keep them safe. Right now, the First Army is virtually cut off. If we don't withdraw it, and do that soon, we could be facing a major disaster. I'm sorry, sir, but those are the facts."

Roosevelt scowled ferociously and then turned to study the map. Wood had been studying it for days, but there were no good answers to be found there. "You said you were able to restore a rail connection from Topeka to Denver?"

"Yes, we were able to repair a short section of track and then use a branch line to open up a path. But there's no telling how long we can keep it open."

"Couldn't you do that elsewhere, too? Create rail repair units with a strong escort and drive along, repairing the track?"

"We have tried that in several locations, sir," explained Wood patiently. "The Martians simply side-step the repair party and destroy the track again in their rear. As I said, there's too much room out there."

"There must be *something* we can do! How can we just abandon Montana, Colorado, the Dakotas, Wyoming, Nebraska, and Kansas?!"

Wood refrained from mentioning that if things got as bad as he feared, they might have to give up Minnesota, Iowa, and Missouri as well. "Every day we delay depletes the supplies the armies have on hand, sir. General Bullard reports increased scouting activity by the enemy forces to the west. They may be planning a major attack. If we wait until the situation becomes truly desperate, we might not get any of those men back." He didn't add that two of those men were the President's own sons, both attached to First Army.

"What about Third Army?" demanded Roosevelt, pointing to a cluster of blue blocks back near St. Louis. "Can't you push them forward? Create a sort of fortified corridor to protect the railroads all the way to the front?"

"Mr. President, it's eight hundred *miles* from St. Louis to Denver. Third Army doesn't have nearly the strength for that. If we deployed them as you suggest, we could well lose them, too."

"What about Funston's Second Army, do you propose to pull them out, too?"

"Not at this time, sir, although they, too, have reported increased activity on their front. But they still have a rail connection to the rear through Texas and more defensible lines of retreat if they do need to fall back."

Roosevelt's expression grew even darker. He turned to look at Stimson. "Henry? Do you agree with this?"

Stimson, a thin man about Wood's age with a small mustache, looked troubled. He was ostensibly Wood's immediate superior, but the pair had worked as a team since Stimson replaced Taft a little over a year ago. Stimson was a lawyer and a politician and he had ably taken over the administrative end of the War Department, dealing with budgets, suppliers, and politicians. He'd gladly left Wood to deal with the military issues. But now the President was asking him a military question. "I... Uh, I would hesitate to disagree with General Wood's analysis of the situation on a strictly military basis. But it's also clear that there are issues here that go beyond the military, Mr. President."

"Yes," said Elihu Root, pushing into the conversation. "Like the fact that these states you are so blithely planning to abandon are full of people—American citizens! By the last census there are more than five million people out there! And you propose to leave them to those monsters! Do I need to remind you what would happen to them under the Martians?"

"The people would need to evacuate as well..."

"You expect them to just pack up and leave their homes at the drop of a hat? In winter? How many would survive?"

Wood had considered all this and the notion of the civilians trying to flee east through bad weather, with Martians marauding everywhere, had given him nightmares. But if the armies were destroyed that would happen anyway and then there might be nowhere to flee to. "Winter is nearly over, Mr. Secretary. And if we lose those armies, there would be little to stop the Martians from continuing east for as far as they wanted to go. Even all the way here."

Roosevelt turned away from his advisers and looked at the map again. He stared at it a long time. Finally, he said: "Leonard, where would you want the troops to fall back to?"

"I'm proposing that First Army pull back to a line along the Missouri River from Bismarck down to Kansas City. Third Army would be split, some going north to extend First Army's line from Bismarck back to Lake Superior to guard the northern flank. The rest would form a new Fourth Army and create a line from Kansas City to Wichita and then along the Arkansas River to where it can link up with Funston."

"That's a much longer line that we currently have!" objected the President.

"Yes, but with rivers to defend I'm hoping that we can prevent the Martian raiding parties from getting into our rear. Once we've established a strong defense, we can think about taking back the lands we've given up."

The President shook his head. "I'm sorry, Leonard, I can't approve of this. At least not until we can get the people out. Start evacuating everyone you can. And then we'll talk again about pulling the armies back."

Wood bowed his head. He'd been expecting this to be Theodore's answer. He'd had contingency plans made in case of this. It would take at least a month to even begin any meaningful evacuations and then only God knew how long to move that many people over the wrecked rail lines and through rampaging Martians. But he would put those plans into operation and pray for the best—while expecting the worst.

"Yes, Mr. President. I'll see to it at once."

* * * * *

MARCH, 1910, ALBUQUERQUE, NEW MEXICO TERRITORY

"And there's no doubt they're coming on in strength?"

"Uh, yes sir, the cavalry scouts report at least… at least forty tripods and they say there may have been more behind them. They had to withdraw rather quickly."

"Forty!" exclaimed someone.

"But there were at least a dozen in those raiding parties in our rear!" said another. "How could they have that many?"

"We don't know for sure, but that's what they've reported. I tried to get the aeronautical corps people to send one of their planes, but they're overhauling their engines and won't be ready until tomorrow."

Andrew Comstock watched General Funston's staff react to the news that had arrived. The general had given him permission to attend staff meetings as a courtesy, but he was normally there as an observer rather than a participant. The meeting was taking place in the very same mansion which the ill-starred General Sumner had occupied when he'd been here over a year ago. The place was looking considerably worse for wear, with much of the original furniture piled in a corner to make room for the large map table around which they were meeting.

The others were continuing to argue about the reliability of the scouting report, but to Andrew it seemed like many of them were trying to wish away the bad news. He decided it was time to add his own voice to the discussion. "General? May I say something?"

The debate died down and Funston turned his eyes to Andrew. "Yes, Major? You have something to add?"

Andrew straightened up and cleared his throat. "Yes, sir. As most of you know, I had the opportunity to take a look inside the Martian fortress at Gallup…"

"A lot of us got a look inside during the siege, Major!" snapped one of the other officers; a lieutenant colonel.

"Uh, yes sir, but when I saw it, I believe that the Martians had not yet built their underground facilities and their operations were taking place out in the open."

"Your point, Major?" asked Funston.

"Yes, sir. I was able to observe that their manufacturing operations were already well-established even at that early date. They appeared to be largely automated and they were building defenses and tripods. That being the case, the limiting factor on their strength was not the number of war machines they had, but the number of Martians available to drive them."

"Yes, go on."

347

"Many people have assumed that the recent landing of the second wave of Martians was identical to the first in what it carried. We know from the off-course cylinder that we captured that in the first wave each cylinder carried only three Martians and a lot of equipment. So we assumed that this second landing of five cylinders near Gallup would only carry fifteen Martians and more equipment. With the losses we've inflicted on them, we should only be facing twenty or twenty-five of the enemy now. But what if these new cylinders carried more personnel and less equipment? If they knew that the Martians in the fortress could build all the tripods they needed, what if they sent ten or twenty Martians in each cylinder instead of just three? We could be facing a hundred or more enemy war machines now."

Funston looked very serious. "You think this is possible, Major?"

"Yes sir. I... I, uh, tried to warn General Wood about their production capability after I got back from here last year, but I'm not sure he understood."

Half the people in the room started talking at once, some strongly disagreeing with Andrew's conclusions, others apparently accepting it, but not at all happy. Funston let it go on for a few moments and then silenced it. "Gentlemen, whether we are facing twenty tripods or a hundred, our task remains the same: defend this position. That is what we must do and that is what we will do. Now, based upon this scouting report, how quickly could they attack us here?"

The same lieutenant-colonel who had snapped at Andrew, Funston's intelligence officer, looked at the map spread on the table and calculated for a moment. "Well, they were spotted near the village of San Rafael. The patrol rode back to the telegraph at McCartys. Considering how fast they move... well, they could be here in a few hours."

"Very well then. Put all units on alert. Warn them they could come under attack at any moment."

As Funston's staff scrambled to comply, Andrew studied the map. Funston's army consisted of two corps; the II Corps under General Menoher was holding the line around Santa Fe, while the III Corps under General Wright was defending Albuquerque. Altogether there were nine infantry divisions plus a swarm of supporting units. Each division had a battalion of steam tanks and an attached brigade of heavy artillery, in addition to their organic contingent of guns. The corps had additional tanks, artillery, cavalry, and engineers at their disposal. With the influx of units from the east, it was a vastly more powerful force than the one which had been besieging the Martian fortress near Gallup.

Even so, the total defense line enclosing the two cities on the south, west, and north was nearly a hundred miles long. Both ends of the line were anchored on the towering Rockies to the east. It was well dug-in with trenches for the front line infantry and log and earth bunkers for machine guns and artillery. The steam tanks mostly were kept in reserve, ready to shore up any point which might be threatened. On paper it looked like a strong defense. But would it be enough?

The meeting broke up and Andrew headed back to the tent he'd been given a block from headquarters. A small park had been taken over for the overflow of staff people. Fortunately, the weather was moderating; it was almost spring. He collected McGill and Kennedy and then rode to the western edge of town. One very welcome privilege he'd gained from being part of Funston's staff was access to horses. Earlier, he'd found a good observation point on the roof of one of the taller buildings. If the Martians were going to attack today, he wanted to be able to watch.

As he neared his objective, a shout came from behind him. "Major? Major Comstock!"

He reined in his horse and turned to look back. A man was trotting down the street toward him. He was in civilian clothes with a tan overcoat and a black felt hat. He had a small bag over one shoulder on a strap. Who was this?

But as he got closer Andrew suddenly recognized him. "Mr. White? Bill White?"

"Yes! Yes, it's me!" gasped the man, coming up to stop beside him. And it was him, the Kansas newspaperman who had shared some of his adventures the last time he was out this way. He was the same red-cheeked, slightly pudgy man, bright-eyed and perpetually interested in everything and everyone around him.

"What are you doing here?"

"Oh, same as before: reporting on the war. Came down here to check out the situation and then got stuck here. I know I could get out if I wanted to, but only by traveling halfway around the world, so I decided to stay. Just heard you were here and thought I'd track you down. You make for good stories, Major! I won a lot of praise for the last story I got by following you!"

Andrew chuckled at that. "Well it's good to see you again!" He dismounted and shook White's hand.

"So, from all the bugles sounding and the way the place looks like an upturned anthill, I'm guessing something's about to happen? Am I right?"

"Maybe. The scouts report a large Martian force headed this way from the west. We don't know what they intend, but we need to be ready."

"And where are you going?"

"Right over there." Andrew pointed to his destination. "There's an observation post on the roof of that building. It's got a good view to the west."

"Mind if I tag along?"

"Not at all. Glad to have you."

They moved to the building, Andrew leading his horse so he could walk with White. The streets were bustling, but everyone was in uniform. The civilian population was mostly gone now, evacuated south. The building was a tall one, right on the edge of town at the corner of Gold and Bareles Streets. They left Kennedy with the horses in the alley behind the brick structure and then climbed four flights of stairs to the roof. There was already an observation post up there; a half-dozen men with binoculars and a field telephone commanded by a lieutenant. Andrew nodded to him. "Seen anything?"

"Nothing so far, sir," the man replied. "But from all the bustle around here, I guess maybe I should expect to."

"Those are the rumors. Keep your eyes peeled." The lieutenant, Conner, was his name if Andrew remembered correctly, dutifully picked up his field glasses and scanned the western horizon. Andrew and White went over to the parapet which surrounded the flat roof and looked in that direction as well. It was an hour or so after noon on a bright, brisk day. The wind was from the northwest and rather chilly. Tomorrow was the first day of spring, but you wouldn't have known it on that rooftop.

The view from there showed the Rio Grande River about a mile to the west. Despite the chill, the spring melts had begun and the river was rising. It was maybe a hundred and fifty feet wide, although Andrew suspected it wasn't very deep. The banks were fairly steep and about another ten or fifteen feet high. The eastern side was lined with trenches, but the other bank just had some brush and small trees. He doubted the river would present much of an obstacle to any tripods determined to cross. Past the river, there were a few clusters of buildings and the land rose gradually to a ridge about five miles away. Beyond that, the ground fell, creating a dead zone, until it rose again to a much higher ridge ten or twelve miles off. With his field glasses he could see that distant ridge clearly enough that any tripods cresting it ought to be easily visible.

The town was built in a long bend in the river, which curved back east to the south of them where there was one of the two bridges across the river. The trenches followed the river for a mile or two, but when it turned due south again, the trenches continued on east until they ended on the lower slopes of Cedro Peak. To the north, where the second bridge was, the bend was more gradual and the river and the trenches eventually faded out of sight to the northeast toward Santa Fe. To the east of Andrew's position was the town itself, which was bisected north to south by the tracks of the Atchison, Topeka and Santa Fe Railroad. About a half mile to the east of the railroad, the town petered out and beyond that the ground rose sharply up to the Sandia Heights. There was a narrow pass there in a gap between it and Cedro Peak.

And everywhere there were the signs of the army. The trenches filled with infantry, bunkers housing machine guns and small field guns. He noticed a few larger positions with the new anti-tripod guns. The section of the line at this point was being held by the 33rd Infantry Division. They weren't regular army, but they had been in service for over a year and Andrew hoped they knew their business. To the rear of the trench lines were revetments with more field guns and also the larger howitzers and siege guns. There were the tank parks, now all a-bustle with black smoke puffing out of the stacks of the vehicles as they fired up their boilers. And to the rear of that, it seems like every open space was filled with tents and shacks to house the troops. More men were still forming up in some of them, reserves to be sent forward as needed.

"A hell of a lot more strength that we had at Prewitt," observed White. "We ought to smash the devils."

"I hope you're right, Bill. I really do."

They watched for a while in silence. One of the enlisted men had a portable camp stove which ran on kerosene. He brewed up a pot of coffee and Andrew gratefully took a cup. The building also had indoor plumbing and Andrew went downstairs to make use of the facilities. It was nearly three o'clock now and he chatted with White.

"Oh, by the way, congratulations on the wedding and your medal," said the man. "Read about it in the paper."

"Thanks. Both came as quite a surprise."

"The wife know what you're up to here?"

"I write to her. She's... she's expecting."

"Really? Well congratulations again!" He stuck out his hand and Andrew shook it.

"I hope she's all right."

White laughed. "You're standing on the edge of a battlefield, waiting for the Martians to attack, and you're worried about her?"

Andrew smiled and shrugged. "Guess that's what it means to love someone."

"Yeah, I guess it does. Sallie will probably have some words for me when I get home." He paused and frowned. "I hope she's all right, what with the Martians running around in our rear."

"Emporia's near Topeka, right? There aren't any reports of anything nearly that far east. I'm sure she's fine."

"Yeah. Well, as long as we stop 'em here, they shouldn't..."

"Sir? Major! I see something!" The cry from Lieutenant Conner spun both men around. The young officer was pointing. Andrew brought up his own field glasses and trained them where Conner was indicating. He swept the view across the far ridge... stopped... focused.

"Yeah... yeah, there they are." A group of dark objects had appeared along the crest. As he watched, more and more joined them. One, two, five, nine, ten... He counted, lost count, started again. It was hard because they kept moving—and because more kept appearing.

"How many, do you think, sir?" asked Conner.

"At least fifty. Probably more."

"Fifty!" exclaimed White.

"Definitely more. Better get that off to HQ, Lieutenant."

"Yes, sir!" Conner got on the telephone. Bugles were ringing out from below. The word was spreading fast and the troops were taking their positions.

The first batch of tripods crested the ridge and started down the other side. More were following. Seventy at least. But they were starting to spread out. Some were angling north, and others south, creating a long line. After a few minutes they disappeared behind the nearer ridge. There were cavalry patrols on that ridge and it wasn't long before he could see them mounting up and falling back, toward the town.

"Looks like they're coming on," said White, sounding nervous.

"Yup, shouldn't be long now."

But it actually was a while, nearly twenty minutes, before the Martians re-appeared. When they did, however, they were now in a long thin line that stretched for at least five miles. In that formation it was easy to count them. "Seventy-three," announced Andrew. "Unless some are waiting in reserve behind the ridge."

"Why... why aren't we shooting at them?" asked White.

"Must be seven or eight thousand yards to that ridge. Out of range of all but the heaviest guns. Wait a few minutes."

But only a moment later some of the big guns did begin to fire. A battery just a few hundred yards south of their position opened up with a roar. More guns along the line joined them. Puffs of smoke began to rise up among the Martians where the shells struck. But there weren't any hits that Andrew could see. The enemy closed rapidly. And soon the lighter guns were firing too, and the noise became almost continuous.

"Now the fun begins!" shouted Andrew.

* * * * *

MARCH, 1910, SANTA FE, NEW MEXICO TERRITORY.

Rebecca Harding heard the guns. They were a long way off, but she could hear them distinctly despite the northwest wind blowing the sound away. Guns down around Albuquerque, she guessed. The word had come that morning that an attack might be in the offing. Everyone had been scrambling since then to get ready. The hospital was quickly in order and soon treating a few men who'd managed to injure themselves in their haste.

But that only demanded the attention of a few people. The rest could only wait for the inevitable influx once things got going. From the sound of it, that was going to happen soon.

"Did your aunt and uncle get out?"

Becca turned and saw that Sam had come up beside her. The man had been in an absolute funk for days after he talked with Major Comstock and Becca was worried that he'd run off, but he seemed to be better now. Still quirky, like a spooked horse, but able to do his job.

"I don't know. I got a message from my uncle, but it was hard to know what he meant. Readin' it one way it sounded like they were goin' to leave. But it could've meant just the opposite. I haven't had time t'go check the house."

"I hope they made it."

"Yeah, me, too."

"All the firing seems to be away south. Nothing close at all to here."

"Not yet."

"Wonder what they're up to?"

* * * * *

MARCH, 1910, ALBUQUERQUE, NEW MEXICO TERRITORY

"What are they up to?" demanded Bill White.

"Looks like they're just probing our lines," answered Andrew, still needing to shout to be heard above the roar of the artillery. "Testing our defenses, I guess." He looked closer. "Huh, I'd swear that some of those tripods are smaller than the others. Hard to be sure at the distance, though. I hope we can get a closer look at them after this is over."

"After they're dead, I assume?"

"That would be best, yes."

It had been nearly an hour since the 'attack' began, but so far the Martians had just made tentative advances against the army's lines and then fallen back again. The sun was well to the west now.

"But we are hurting them, right?"

"Yes."

And indeed they were. At least two of the enemy tripods had collapsed in ruin when lucky shots had hit them. Many others had taken at least a hit or two but with no obvious ill-effects.

"They're pin-pointing the position of our guns," said Andrew. "I'm worried that they're getting ready to use some of their long-range black dust rockets like they used against the British in the first invasion. Keep your mask handy!" There had been no evidence of that weapon being used during the current war, but Andrew was very worried about the possibility. Unlike the smaller version they used from time to time, which could blanket an area about a hundred yards across, that other weapon could cover miles of territory with a terrifying lethal cloud. Despite their precautions, such a thing could take half their force out of action.

"Looks like they're advancing again, sir!" cried Conner.

Andrew took up his field glasses and yes, another batch was moving closer. They'd been dancing around at the extreme range of the field guns, but from time to time a group would come closer. If they did like before, they'd come in and then fall back. These did exactly that, but as they turned to withdraw…

"We got one! Hey! We got one!" One of the observers shouted and pointed. Yes! A tripod was spewing smoke and turning in circles. The guns started zeroing in on it and explosion erupted all around the stricken machine. The other Martians turned back and…

"Hey! Look out! They're firing!"

A dozen heat rays stabbed out and swept across the defenses and across the buildings. One struck the next block and swung toward them. "Get down, sir!" shouted McGill.

It's got to be every inch of six thousand yards. It can't hurt me. It can't hurt me.

He stood his ground, hands clutching the parapet as the ray passed over him. It wasn't any worse than standing a few yards away from a fire in a fireplace, a breath of heat on the skin of his face. It actually felt good after the cold breeze he'd been standing in all day.

And then it was gone. The others got up and stared at him like he was a crazy man. But he just said: "Looks like we've got that one." The guns hadn't stopped and they had the crippled tripod ranged in now. In rapid succession a half dozen shells plowed into it and it crashed to the ground in pieces. He could hear some of the gunners cheering.

"Looks like they're giving up!" exclaimed White.

Andrew looked out from the vantage point. The setting sun was almost directly in his eyes now so it was hard to see clearly. But, yes, it wasn't just the group which had advanced that was falling back. The entire line was retreating, marching west, up the near ridge. They reached the crest and then went down the other side, the red sun glinting off the metal of the machines. In ten minutes they were all gone.

The cheers of the gunners who had killed the tripod were now swelled as men all along the defense lines joined in. The artillery fell silent, which made the cheers seem all the louder. But Andrew wasn't cheering; he took his glasses again and focused on the ground leading up to the farther ridge. It was empty. And it stayed that way.

Bill White was scribbling down some notes on a pad and then he came over and slapped Andrew on the back. "Well, that was easy! Guess we were too tough for 'em, eh?"

"I don't know. They're still out there, behind that ridge. They aren't leaving." He lowered the glasses and then shaded his eyes against the sun. The red disk was just touching the distant hills.

"I don't think they've given up at all. And it will be dark soon."

* * * * *

CYCLE 597, 844.1, EAST OF HOLDFAST 32-1

"Subcommander Qetjnegartis, we have begun our attack on the southernmost enemy habitation," said Valprandar. "We have probed their defenses and we shall begin the final assault in approximately one tenthday."

"I understand, Commander," replied Qetjnegartis. "What do you wish us to do?"

"I expect to crush the defenses here and then drive north to attack the other habitation. From what our scouts have discovered of the landscape, if your force were to travel southwest you will be able to cut off the prey-creatures' retreat and complete their destruction. Those are your orders."

"I will obey, Commander."

"Very well." Valprandar cut the communications link.

Qetjnegartis consulted its map. It was still frustratingly incomplete, but it could see the route Valprandar expected it to take. Qetjnegartis' raiding force had reassembled about a hundred telequel south of where it had first split up. An enemy force riding draught animals was nearby, but had made no move to attack. They would have to bypass that force and move quickly toward the mountains and the route into the enemy rear. It was clear that Valprandar was expecting heavy combat to occur and if the enemy was desperate to escape along the route that Qetjnegartis' force was blocking…

"Attention, all units. We have our orders." It activated the communicator to all its subordinates. "We will proceed southwest and engage in battle. However, I do not wish to needlessly endanger the two of us in the transport capsules. Both pods will be attached to Davnitargus' machine. Davnitargus, you will take these two back to the holdfast by the same route we used to reach this point. Understood?"

They all acknowledged the order. But a moment later, Davnitargus contacted it on a private circuit. "Progenitor, I do not wish to be separated from you."

"Your wishes are irrelevant. You shall do as I command."

"But could not one of the others take the capsules…?"

"Davnitargus! You will obey! I find your behavior very disturbing!" There was a long pause and then Davnitargus replied.

"I am sorry, Progenitor. I will obey."

"Good! Now let us all carry out our orders."

* * * * *

MARCH, 1910, NEAR WATROUS, NEW MEXICO TERRITORY

"They're movin' southwest again, sir," reported the scout. "All of 'em, and movin' fast."

Lieutenant Frank Dolfen sat in Colonel Berg's tent with the 5th's other squadron commanders and also with Colonel Thaxton, commander of the 10th Cavalry. A scout had just come in with some alarming news.

Dolfen was still having trouble adjusting to the fact that he was the acting commander for the 1st squadron. After that awful fight at the bridge he was the only officer left who could still ride. Captain Pendleton had been killed, as had Lieutenant Ingram of B Troop. The other two troop commanders had been badly injured. He'd expected the colonel to appoint some officer with higher seniority from one of the other squadrons to take command, but so far he had not. Of course maybe it was the fact that the 1st Squadron was little bigger than a troop now. They'd lost a hell of a lot of good men there—including Jason Urbaniak. The loss of his sergeant—and his old friend—was hard.

After the fight, they'd waited for the rest of the regiment to catch up and then they'd trailed the surviving Martians. They'd found a second machine abandoned with a smashed leg a dozen miles further on and that had made everyone feel good—they had really hurt the bastards. There had only been one left and if they could just catch up with it…

But then two days later, they saw that their quarry had been joined by four other machines. Five was a much more difficult proposition than one! So they'd waited for the 10th to catch up. But by the time they did, five more Martians had arrived and that was far too big a force for them to deal with. The Martians had spotted them and suddenly the hunters had become the hunted and the brigade was forced to retreat south. They'd managed to stay ahead of them, although they'd had to abandon one of the field guns when it broke its axle. Then a day ago, the enemy had stopped chasing them. The cavalry had made camp twenty miles farther south and sent out scouts to keep an eye on them.

"They're coming toward us?" asked Colonel Berg.

"Uh, no sir, not directly anyway. They're following the tracks—and not stoppin' to wreck 'em, neither."

Berg chewed on his lower lip. The faint rumble of guns they'd been hearing on and off that afternoon from the southwest had finally died away, but what that meant, no one knew. But it had been clear that a hell of fight had been taking place somewhere along the Santa Fe-Albuquerque line. And now the Martians here were headed in that direction in a hurry.

"Do you think they're trying to hit our folks from behind, Phillip?" asked Colonel Thaxton.

"Sure looks like it. If they came down through the Glorieta Pass, into the rear, it could really raise hell."

"So I guess we need to do something about that, eh?" Thaxton grinned. He'd been peeved to have missed all the earlier fighting and looked eager.

"Yes, yes, but this isn't the spot. Not on this flat ground and sure as hell not in the dark! We need to stay ahead of them and pick our ground. Maybe in the pass itself. If we ride like hell we can get there by dawn. Might be able to find some help there, too. But we need to get moving—now!"

The meeting broke up and Dolfen ran back to his camp. The bugler was already sounding 'boots and saddles' and the men were scrambling up from their cook fires and rolling up their blankets.

"Come on!" shouted Dolfen. "We've got a hell of a fight waitin' for us!"

* * * * *

MARCH, 1910, ALBUQUERQUE, NEW MEXICO TERRITORY

The light was nearly gone, but Andrew still waited on the rooftop. It was getting colder, despite the wind having died almost completely. Down below, the troops were coming out of the trenches and revetments and building up their fires to cook dinner. McGill was muttering something about finding dinner themselves.

"What are you looking for, Major?" asked Bill White.

"Not sure. They're still over there, just beyond the first ridge. Damn, I wish we had a way to drop some artillery on them!"

"Can't the big guns shoot that far?"

"They can, but they'd be firing blind. They'd have no way of knowing if they were even close to the enemy. If we had some observers with a line of sight and a telephone line, we'd be able to correct the fire, but we don't."

"So you think they'll attack? At night?"

"They aren't stupid, Bill. By now they have to know we can't see that well in the dark. They've already pinpointed our guns. And they have to be waiting for something. Thank God we've got a good moon tonight." He looked over his shoulder. The moon was five days from full and shining brightly in the clear sky.

"I sure hope you're wrong!" The newspaperman peered out into the dark. The last glow of the sun was fast fading away.

But nothing happened for quite a while and McGill had Kennedy forage some food for them. The men in the observation post were relieved with a new group, who Andrew ordered to keep a sharp lookout. Eight o'clock came and Andrew was starting to suspect that he'd been wrong after all. White was ready to leave and McGill was getting cranky. Maybe they should head back to their tent... or maybe just find a spot in this building. It would be warmer...

"Hey! Hey! I see something!"

Andrew popped up and ran to the parapet. Off in the distance, dark shapes were moving on the ridge in the moonlight. And there were red, glowing lights in the center of each of them. He grabbed his field glasses and looked again. Yes, tripods, a lot of them, all in a group, and they appeared to be heading almost directly for him! He tried to count them by the red lights, but it was impossible with the machines passing in front of each other and blocking the view. But one thing was certain: the Martians were now all in one huge mass instead of spread out in a line, miles long. "My God," hissed Andrew.

"What? What's happening?" asked White.

"They aren't attacking all along the line like before! They're in a flying wedge! They must be trying to smash a hole right through us!" He put down his glasses and snatched up the field telephone the observer team was using. "Get me General Funston! Yes, dammit! This is Major Comstock! I'm on his staff! Get him on the phone!"

355

There was an infuriating delay and all the while the Martians were getting closer. Others had obviously noticed because there were shouts and bugle calls, and before long some of the guns were firing again. Bright flashes, like heat lighting, lit up the landscape as guns blazed and shells detonated. If the Martians had presented a concentrated target like this earlier, in daylight, with the guns ready, they might have taken dreadful losses, but now it didn't look like they were being hurt much at all. No, wait, there was one going down, but the rest were coming on at top speed. The lighter guns were opening up now too, and even some machine guns.

The noise was becoming so loud he almost didn't hear when he got through to Funston's headquarters. "What? Yes! It's Comstock! I need to talk to the general! What? Yes, I know he's busy, but I need to tell him what I'm seeing! Yes, I'm at the OP on Gold and Bareles Street! What? All right, all right! Just tell him the Martians are all in a clump! Yes, one big mass! They are coming straight on, a little north of me! I think they'll hit the river near the northern bridge. They're gonna smash right through our lines! Have the general move all his reserves to that point! Yes! By the bridge! Hurry!"

The rip-saw shriek of the heat rays wrenched his attention away from the telephone. Damn, they were in range already? Beams of destruction lashed out from the leading face of the wedge, flaying the trenches and bunkers. Then, in the garish red light, he saw objects fly off from some of the tripods. Black dust!

"Get your masks on!" He dropped the phone receiver and fumbled for his in the bag hanging around his neck.

But the projectiles weren't targeted on him; they arced off and came down on the artillery revetments. Clouds of black smoke appeared, which were so utterly dark, reflecting no light at all, that they looked like holes in his vision. *They knew just where they were.* The guns stopped firing immediately. Even if their crews survived, they couldn't see their targets. Andrew could barely see, himself, through the grimy glass eyepieces in his dust mask.

The Martians came on. They were less than a half-mile from the river now and they seemed to cross that distance incredibly fast. Dozens of heat rays were blasting the trench lines and some were now striking the buildings on the edge of town five or six blocks north of Andrew's position. Flames erupted from windows and rooftops, adding to the hellish glow that seemed to be enveloping the world.

Now a new noise reached his ears, a noise he knew very well: the huff and puff of steam tanks. He looked over the parapet and there were a column of tanks heading up the street just below him, a cloud of coal smoke enveloped him for a moment as they chugged past. He leaned out and caught a glimpse of the pennant on one of the command tanks. Yes, it was the 304th tank battalion; they were attached to the 33rd division. If Funston could get the tanks from the 5th division just to the north to come south and then send in the corps reserve, maybe they could catch the Martians in a crossfire and shoot them to bits. But damn, they were going to have to move fast. The things were almost here!

They were going to hit the line maybe a half-mile north of where he was. He raised his field glasses and cursed when they clunked into the eyepieces of his mask. He tore it off and stuffed it back in its bag. There was almost no wind and the dust was heavier than air. None of it should be up this high. Using his glasses again, he could see that the Martians had reached the river by the north bridge. As he'd feared, it wasn't proving any obstacle at all. The enemy machines were wading right across it and up the eastern bank. Their heat rays were still sweeping everything in front of them. Explosions began to erupt as they hit some of the battery sites. Stacked ammunition popped sharply like giant firecrackers, while loaded caissons blew up with roars that shook the air. The nearest buildings were all engulfed in fire, the flames leaping into the night sky.

He saw a tripod at the top of the river bank go tumbling backward into the water as something hit it, but all the rest that he could see, in one huge mass, were soon across and in among the trenches.

More explosions echoed through the town, but Andrew wasn't sure what was blowing up. The enemy was now so close, right in among the defenders, that not much artillery was going to be able to hit them. Infantry bombs, maybe? But the infantry in the trenches to either side of the breakthrough were now flanked. The Martians could fire right down the line of trenches. Some men were already pulling out, starting to run.

The 304th was deploying off the street now, forming a line a few hundred yards to his north on the open ground leading down to the river. The sharp bark of their three and four-inch guns started to compete with the general roar.

The Martians were milling around their crossing point, but some were moving east and he lost sight of them behind the burning buildings. A large group of them, thirty at least, were now turning south, toward the tanks—and toward him.

The tanks halted and fired. The tripods fired and kept right on moving. The 304th had about thirty tanks. At the Battle of Prewitt, thirty tanks had virtually annihilated the Martian force. But then there had been only six, and now there were dozens. Tanks began to explode as the heat rays cut through their armor. Two tripods went down under the concentrated fire, but by that time half the tanks were flaming wrecks. These odds were simply impossible and within minutes most of the tanks were gone. Some of the crews of the remainder abandoned them and tried to flee on foot. They didn't get far. The tripods kept advancing, those near the river blasting the trench lines, those closer to the town fired at the buildings.

"Time to go sir!" shouted McGill grabbing his arm. "Let's get the hell out of here!" The buildings in the block to the north were being turned into an inferno. They would surely be next.

"Everyone out!" cried Andrew, waving to the observation team. They leapt down the stairs three steps at a time and burst out into the alley. He was slightly amazed that Kennedy and the horses were still there. He jumped into the saddle and pulled White up behind him. "Go! Back to headquarters!"

They turned onto Gold Street and galloped east. Andrew didn't look back until they had gone at least three blocks. When he did, he saw a tripod marching south right across the end of the street. He didn't look again until they'd reached the railroad tracks in the center of town.

There were mobs of soldiers, mostly quartermaster people, running in all directions. A few trains on sidings were getting steam up but Andrew didn't think they would have anywhere to go. He and McGill and Kennedy threaded their way through the crowd and then broke free of them to gallop the rest of the way to Funston's headquarters on the eastern side of town. The noise of battle was dwindling, but the glow of the burning buildings was growing.

"Wait here and don't lose those horses!" he ordered as he dismounted. He ran up the front steps of the big house and through the doors which were standing open. He found Funston in the same room where he'd last seen him, leaning over a map with a half-dozen staff members talking at him all at once. Andrew threw protocol to the wind and pushed right up to the general, ruthlessly elbowing senior officers out of his way.

"Sir! They've broken through!" he shouted in Funston's ear. "They're across the river and through the lines by the north bridge!"

"Who? Oh, it's you, Comstock. Yes, I know, I've sent tanks to seal up the breach…"

"The tanks are *gone*! I saw the 304th wiped out in about five minutes. The Martians have got so much firepower on such a narrow front that nothing's going to stop them! The whole west side of town is on fire and they're rolling up the 33rd in both directions!" He stabbed his finger down on the map by the bridge and then drew a large circle. "They've used the black dust to silence all the guns in the vicinity and they're chewing up your reserves as they arrive! General, you have to start withdrawing—*right now!*"

"Don't be ridiculous, man!" snapped Funston. "It's not nearly as bad as…" His voice trailed off as he looked at his staff officers. They all looked as grim as death. One stepped forward with a note in his hand and said.

"I'm afraid it is, sir. The 317th is gone—just like the 304th. It's like the major says: they're just smashing whatever we send at them. There's just too many in too small an area. If we don't pull back to regroup, we're going to lose everything."

Just then, General William Wright, commander of the III Corps, hurried into the room. "General, my lines are crumbling. I don't know how much longer they can hold. What do you want me to do?"

Andrew had to give Funston one thing: it didn't take him long to make up his mind. He wasn't a ditherer. Give him the facts and he'd give you his decision. "Very well," he sighed. "Bill, everything you've still got south of town, fall back along the railroad. Try to get word to the 78th to head north to Santa Fe and link up with Menoher. Anyone who can't go north or south will retreat through the gap due east. Get someone up there right now to form a rear guard."

His staff all gave relieved acknowledgments and went to work. Funston turned to his communications officer. "Steve, get a message through to General Menoher and…"

"Sir, I'm sorry, but the telegraph north has been cut."

"Damn, what about the radio?"

"Sorry, sir, it's out, too."

"Damnation." He looked around the room and spotted Andrew. "Comstock, you seem to have an uncommon gift for delivering bad news. I want you to get yourself to Santa Fe and let General Menoher know what's happening here. Tell him I give him full authority to withdraw his corps or stay in place as he sees fit, but that I recommend he withdraw. You got that, son?"

"Yes, sir!"

"Then get moving before the road's cut!"

"Yes, sir!" Andrew turned and dashed from the room. McGill, Kennedy, and White were where he'd left them. Somehow, White now had a horse of his own. "How'd you get that?" he demanded as he mounted up.

"Amazing what a twenty-dollar gold piece can accomplish," he replied. "I had a hunch we'd be on the move again soon and I wanted to be prepared."

"Well, I'm headed to Santa Fe. You coming?"

"Wouldn't miss it! I don't think Albuquerque's going to be a pleasant spot much longer."

"All right then! Let's go!" They trotted out of the headquarters area and Andrew took the first street heading north.

"We gonna be able t'get through that way, sir?" asked McGill.

"We'll find out. Come on." He tried to sound confident, but the flames which had engulfed the west side of town looked to be spreading across the north end—and the wind wasn't blowing that way.

More soldiers were in the streets now and many were infantry or artillery rather than quartermasters. The lines clearly had broken and apparently the morale of many of the men had, too. Some were running in abject panic, weaponless and witless. Others were much more deliberate and still had their rifles. A few eyed their horses enviously. Andrew unholstered his revolver to dissuade them from any funny business. The others did so as well, even White had a small pistol. At first the flow of men had been from west to east, right across their path. But as they neared the north edge of town, the flow was now southward—not a good sign.

Suddenly there was a bright flash followed a few seconds later by an enormous explosion which shook the whole town. Andrew had to haul back on the reins to keep his horse from bolting. The animals all squealed in fright as a mammoth fireball boiled up off to their left. "Ammunition dump!" shouted Andrew. "Keep going!" Another few blocks brought them to the north edge of town.

There were Martians there.

The extensive camps which had been constructed beyond the town limits were in flames and silhouetted against the glare were a dozen enemy machines, maybe five hundred yards away.

"No gettin' past them, sir!" said McGill. "We'd better turn east!"

Andrew looked off that way at the tall mountains, rearing up against the dark sky. From what he'd seen earlier, the ground there was very rough and he wasn't at all sure there was any way to go north once you were up in the foothills. And if they got carried through the gap in the mountains it could take days to reach Santa Fe.

"No! I need to go north!"

"I think the sergeant is right, Major!" said White. "Look! The things have turned this way!"

And indeed they had. They'd formed a skirmish line with a hundred yards or so between them and were heading due south, right toward the town. *Damn! If they keep coming there will be one of them on every street!*

But *only* one on every street…

A plan suddenly materialized in his head. "Fall back to the next block! Sergeant! I need a half-dozen of the infantry bombs!"

"Sir! Are ye outta yer bleedin' mind? The four o' us canna take on one o' those devils!" McGill's Scottish brogue came out full force as it always did when he was angry.

"We're not! We're going to take on one of the *buildings*, Sergeant!"

McGill's face suddenly lit up. "I'll be damned! Kennedy! With me!" He turned his horse and galloped off, followed by the corporal. Andrew followed with White to about halfway down the next block. The Martians were still approaching and their heat rays had turned the northernmost buildings into torches.

"What are you going to do?" demanded White.

"We're going to use the bombs to collapse one of the buildings—right on that tripod!" He pointed at the one now lined up with the end of their street.

White looked appalled. "McGill is right! You are out of your mind!"

"Hey, you were looking for a story. If you don't want it, you're free to ride east."

White muttered something which Andrew couldn't catch above all the other noise, but he didn't leave. McGill and Kennedy were back very soon. There was no shortage of men in the streets and they were probably happy to be relived of those burdens. "Got 'em, sir! Where d'you want 'em?"

"Third building down from here on the right. The four story one. Here, give me a couple." He reached for the bombs McGill was carrying, but the man pulled them away.

"Oh, no, sir! Not a proper job for an officer at all!" He swung out of the saddle. "You take the horses and we'll take care of that blighter!"

"It's setting the buildings on fire, you maniacs!" screamed White. "You'll burn!"

"It's only setting fire to the upper stories as it moves!" Andrew pointed down to the next block. "It doesn't want to collapse the buildings on itself!" He looked back at McGill. "All right! Go ahead, but remember the fuse is only fifteen seconds. You gotta set them and get the hell out! We'll be back in that alley."

"Right, sir!" McGill and a much less enthusiastic Kennedy ran down the block and disappeared inside the structure he had indicated. Andrew and White led the other two horses to the narrow alley. Andrew dismounted and peered around the corner. The Martian machine was at the other end of the block and as he'd said, the heat ray was just blasting the upper floors, setting them afire; confident, no doubt, that the whole building would burn eventually. Much of the town was burning by this time and clouds of smoke rolled past, stinging his eyes and making him cough.

Step by step the machine came down the street. It was almost up to the building the men had gone into. "Come on! Come on!" hissed Andrew.

Suddenly McGill and Kennedy burst onto the street and ran toward them. The Martian moved abreast of the building...

"It's seen them!" cried White.

The heat ray swung in their direction and Andrew held his breath. Then the lower floor of the building exploded outward hitting the tripod's legs. The second floor collapsed on top of the first, and the then the third and fourth floors tilted and fell outward into the street—right into the Martian.

The impact slammed the machine sideways into the building on the opposite side. The facade collapsed inward and the head of the machine was embedded in it. Its legs were buried in the rubble of the first building. It thrashed one arm and a tentacle, but it was clearly stuck.

"*Sine Fine!*" cried McGill as he came up to them and looked back, shaking his fist.

"We still can't get through that way!" said White in exasperation.

"We're not going that way," said Andrew calmly.

"What?"

Ulla! Ulla! Ulla!

The Martian distress siren was shockingly loud—just like it had been when they wrecked the tripod near Gallup. It sounded three times and then—just as Andrew had hoped—another tripod emerged from the side street to the right. It advanced and tried to help its comrade get free. "All right! This way!" Andrew led them down the alley to the next street over.

The street that was now empty of Martians.

Of course it was also still on fire...

They mounted up and rode down the street at a full gallop. The heat from the buildings burning on both sides was terrific, and burning embers stung Andrew's face, but they kept going and emerged into the fields beyond the town. The fires in the camps there had mostly burned down, but there were clouds of smoke drifting upward everywhere. Andrew lashed his horse onward and didn't stop until they were at least three miles down the road. Then he halted to let his poor beast rest for a bit. He looked back...

Albuquerque was burning.

The entire town was on fire now. An angry red light lit up the landscape and reflected down from the immense cloud of smoke that was blotting out most of the sky. Tall dark shapes stalked through the inferno. There were still some distant explosions on the far side of town and at least one clump of Martians was working its way north along the river bank.

"Looks like the bloody gates 'o Hell," said McGill.

"My God," breathed White.

"Yeah," said Andrew. "We can't stay here. Oh, by the way, that was a good job, Sergeant, Corporal."

"Our pleasure, sir," said McGill.

"Yeah, our bloody, stinkin' pleasure," said Kennedy.

"Come on, it's a long way to Santa Fe."

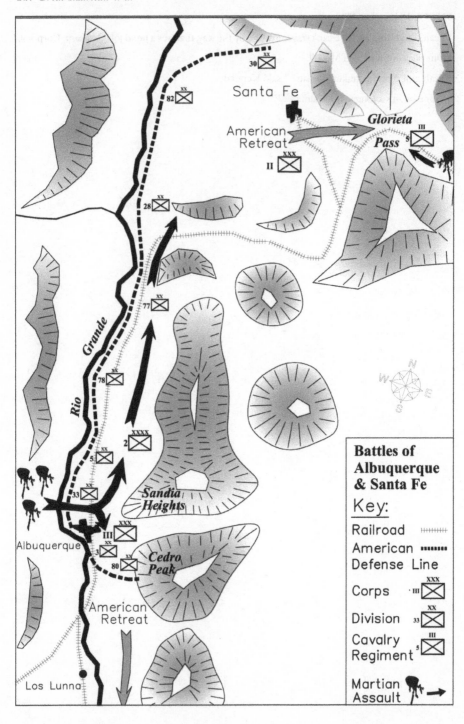

CHAPTER FIFTEEN

MARCH, 1910, SANTA FE, NEW MEXICO TERRITORY

The rumbles started up again a little after eight o'clock. The wind had died so they seemed louder than before, and after a while there were some even louder blasts that actually shook the ground a little. Rebecca hoped those were Martian machines exploding, but she feared they were not. An awful red glow started to fill the southern sky. It reminded her of the forest fire the Martians had set to try and kill her and Sergeant Dolfen and Major Comstock and the others when they were fleeing for their lives. Thankfully it was much farther away.

"That has to be Albuquerque," said Sam. She was getting used to Sam following her around when they weren't on duty. Miss Chumley had told her she would get Sam transferred to another hospital unit if he bothered her. He did bother her, but not that way. He was just an unsettling character. In the middle of a sentence he would suddenly switch off, like an electric light, and just sit there for minutes without moving before he'd come back on and act like nothing had happened. Part of her wished he would go away, but she knew he would have far more trouble with a group of strangers, so she put up with him.

"If the Martians attacked the town, some of it would catch fire for sure. Doesn't mean we're losing." She wasn't sure who she was trying to encourage, Sam or herself.

Shortly after that there was some activity in the surrounding camps, but no new orders came for them. The army had been on alert for most of the day, but nothing had happened except for the distant noises. She watched for a while longer and then turned away. "We should get some sleep. Could be a long day tomorrow."

She went back to her quarters, but sleep was a long time coming.

* * * * *

MARCH, 1910, NEAR GLORIETA PASS, NEW MEXICO TERRITORY

"Halt! Who goes there?"

The cry came out of the darkness so unexpectedly that Frank Dolfen was taken by surprise. He automatically flung up a hand and shouted: "Squadron…Halt!" The long, ragged column behind him stumbled to a stop.

"Who's there? Answer or I'll shoot!" came the voice again. It sounded very young and very nervous.

"Who d'you think?" someone further back yelled in reply. "We're sure as hell not Martians!"

"5th Cavalry!" said Dolfen. "Who are you, soldier?"

"I…uh, Ralph Prince, sir. Company L, Hundred'n Ninth Infantry." After a brief pause, he shouted again: "Sergeant of the Guard! Post Four! Come quick!" The last part wasn't exactly part of the regulations and it produced a tired chuckle from some of his troopers. The nervous soldier came forward close enough to see and Dolfen dismounted.

By the time the sergeant arrived, and he in turn summoned his officer, the strung-out column of cavalry was catching up with Dolfen's vanguard. Colonel Berg was called for and while he waited, Dolfen looked to the rear. There was a tiny glimmer of dawn in the east, but it was very dark, the moon having set several hours earlier. He couldn't see any of the red, glowing 'eyes' of the Martian machines, but he knew they were back there somewhere. They'd been running in front of them the whole night. Mile after weary mile had passed by and somehow they'd stayed in front. All the artillery had been forced to turn aside—they couldn't keep up—but the cavalry was all still here. Most of them anyway.

Colonel Berg arrived and found Dolfen and the infantry officer—a captain. "What's your situation, Captain, uh...?" demanded Berg.

"Greene, sir. I have two companies from the 109th, sir. We were sent out here yesterday afternoon with orders to defend the pass. Seems like there's a hell of a fight going on down by Albuquerque. Or there was, it's quieted down for the most part now." Dolfen could see the man peering anxiously into the dark. "Uh, what's going on, sir?"

"We've got nine Martian tripods a half-hour behind us. They're coming this way fast. I'm sure they want to get through the pass, but we are going to stop them, Captain. What sort of support do you have?"

"Uh, a couple of heavy machine guns, but that's all, sir. Nine?"

Berg cursed. "You'd think they'd have sent *something* to...! Oh well, we'll do it with what we have."

While they were talking, the squadron commanders came up and then Colonel Thaxton of the 10th with several of his staff. Berg addressed them all. "Gentlemen, we have arrived. The Martians will be here presently and we must arrange a warm welcome for them. The road leading up to the pass is narrow and will provide us with many opportunities for ambush. There's no room to deploy all of us at once and frankly we wouldn't want to even if there was. So we are going to establish a string of squadron-sized roadblocks from here up to the pass.

"Colonel Thaxton, you and your troopers have been belly-aching for the last two weeks about not getting a crack at these bastards, well, you're going to get your chance! You'll be in front, Captain Greene and his men will be next, and then the 5th, understood?"

Everyone answered in the affirmative. "Captain Greene, do you have communications with the rear?"

"There's a telegraph, sir, but the folks back in Santa Fe don't seem to answer very much. Busy with all the other things goin' on, I guess."

"Well, get on the wire and demand they send us some help. Use my name."

"Yes, sir!"

"Okay, we don't have much time and we've got to do this in the dark. Get to it and let your people know we must hold the pass!"

The officers headed back to their commands. Berg came over to Dolfen. "Frank, your squadron's the most experienced but also the most beat up. I want you as our last reserve. Take your men up to the top and wait there."

Dolfen wasn't even tempted to argue. "Yes, sir."

"And let's pray we don't need you today."

* * * * *

MARCH, 1910, SANTA FE, NEW MEXICO TERRITORY

Major Andrew Comstock reined in his horse and looked back. There was just enough light seeping over the eastern mountains to finally see something. What he saw didn't look good. Santa Fe was almost two thousand feet higher than Albuquerque so he was presented with a commanding view of the disaster.

That was the only word for it, really.

They had galloped like hell away from the dying town, through the fragments of the disintegrating 5th Division. Men and horses were streaming east and north, trying to get away from the Martian tripods, some of which, were actively pursuing them. The 5th was made up of regular army units, but they ran just the same as National Guard or new volunteers. Andrew couldn't really blame them; trying to reform a line to face this unexpected threat, *in the dark*, would have broken just about anyone.

So they'd kept riding. Andrew had been hoping to find a telegraph station which still had a connection to Santa Fe, but the next division in the line, the 78th, was in nearly as great a state of confusion as the 5th. The Martians hadn't hit them yet, but someone had seen what was going on and issued orders to pivot the line back to face south. No one Andrew asked could tell him where division headquarters was, so they'd continued north.

It wasn't until they crossed the corps boundary and reached the 77th Division that they found any sort of order. The division headquarters was still there and they had a telegraph to General Menoher in Santa Fe. He'd composed as succinct a message as he could manage and sent it off with a postscript that he would continue on to Santa Fe himself. He had no idea if it would get through or if anyone would pay attention to it if it did, and he didn't wait around to find out. He gave his opinion of the situation to General Duncan, commander of the 77th, got fresh horses, and set out again.

The next division in line was the 28th. They were up and alert, but didn't seem to have orders to do anything. Going to their headquarters would have meant a detour of several miles, so Andrew just kept heading north. It was all steeply uphill now and they had to go slowly to spare the horses. He would have abandoned them for a train if any had happened by. They'd been following the tracks since leaving Albuquerque, but the rails were strangely deserted.

And all the while the noise from behind was building again. After the absolute bedlam in Albuquerque, things had seemed almost silent; but now the sounds of combat were growing and Andrew stopped to look back.

From this height, the battle looked to be a considerable way off. There was a long, low cloud of smoke punctured by flickers of light fifteen or twenty miles away. He guessed that was the new position of the 78th. Or perhaps they'd already been destroyed and it was the 77th he was seeing, he couldn't tell. Closer, he could see troops moving from west to east in an orderly fashion. He was pretty sure that was the 28th. Maybe his message to Menoher had gotten through and orders had gone back out to get the troops moving.

"Are they still coming on?" asked Bill White.

"I'm sure they are. The bastards don't seem to get tired." Unlike us. He hadn't slept in a day and half and he'd just ridden fifty miles through the night. So had McGill and Kennedy. White, too, he guessed. They were all ready to fall out of their saddles.

"Not sure how many of them are comin' this way. There were seventy-three at Albuquerque that I counted. Or was it seventy-four? Can't remember, but a lot. Don't know how many we killed, but I'd bet ten or twelve, at least. So let's say sixty left. Some will be chasing Funston and whatever he's got left. If we're lucky, they split evenly and we're only facing thirty now. But maybe they're convinced Funston's beat and they're sending most of their strength against us. Could still be fifty of them comin'. The 78th can't stop that by itself—not in the mess they were in. The 77th and 28th might be able to slow them down. I don't know, maybe in daylight…"

"Come on, sir," said McGill. "No use sittin' here guessing. Let's get to headquarters and tell our tale and maybe we can sleep for a bit."

"The sergeant knows what he's talking about," said White. "Let's go." Andrew nodded and kicked the horse into motion. His backside and legs were really starting to hurt.

It was nearly full light now, and as they reached the outskirts of Santa Fe they could see that the place was all stirred up. If there was any concerted or deliberate action in the works it wasn't readily apparent. Andrew knew where Menoher's headquarters were and he managed to reach them without any real problems. Getting into the building wasn't quite so easy and he had to put all his best growling into play before he managed it.

But once he was inside and identified, General Menoher latched onto him like a leech, trying to drain information out of him like blood. He described what had happened in Albuquerque as best as his sleep-deprived brain could manage. "And then General Funston instructed me to contact you," he concluded. "He wanted me to apprise you of the situation and tell you that he gives you full authority to withdraw your corps or stay in place as you see fit, but that he recommend you withdraw."

"He actually said that?" demanded Menoher.

"Uh, yes, sir, that's pretty much an exact quote except for a few of the pronouns." He blinked and tried to stay alert. He was starting to babble.

Menoher frowned and turned away, his hands clasped behind his back. But his chief of staff, a colonel named Hinckley, who had been listening to Andrew intently now, started speaking. "There, sir, you see that you do have permission to withdraw. You should give the order immediately!"

The general turned back. "Trying to funnel the entire corps and all its support through that pass is going to be a nightmare, Colonel. It might be better if we stabilize our position and then see about doing this in an orderly fashion."

"Sir! You heard what Comstock said about what happened in Albuquerque! The reports from the 77th indicate at least fifty tripods coming our way. They are going to do just what they did there: punch through our lines and then chop us up piecemeal! Right, Major?" Hinckley turned to face him.

He was deathly weary and didn't want to get involved in this, but what choice was there? "I think the colonel is right, sir. Our current tactics just aren't able to cope with these mass attacks the Martians can launch. No army in history has been able to concentrate so much fighting power on so narrow a front. I'm afraid if you try to hold here the same thing will happen as did at Albuquerque."

"And we're already cut off from supply here, sir!" continued Hinckley. "Even if we did manage to beat off this attack, our situation is only going to get worse. If the 77th can hold for a while and the 28th form a rear guard, we can get everything else through the pass and away. We ought to be able to hold them at the pass for long enough for us to withdraw east. But only if we act now!"

Menoher wasn't particularly old, but he looked very old at that moment. Finally he nodded his head. "Very well, issue the orders."

The headquarters exploded into action and under that cover Andrew withdrew. He found McGill and the others. "We're done for now. The army's pulling out, but it will be hours before they really start moving." He pointed to an empty tent. "I don't know about you, but I'm going to get some sleep."

* * * * *

366

MARCH 1910, SANTA FE, NEW MEXICO TERRITORY.

The guns were much nearer now. The rumor was that the Martians had broken the lines at Albuquerque and were now moving north against Santa Fe. Some said the army would retreat, others said they were going to stay. All Rebecca knew was that wounded were starting to come in now in much larger numbers. Clearly, there was heavy fighting going on somewhere. It was mid-morning and she'd been at work since dawn.

A new load arrived and she helped sort them and forward them to the proper place. There were the usual burn casualties, men who'd been brushed by a heat ray but not incinerated, but they were starting to see a much greater number of men with injuries caused by the bombs the infantry were now carrying; lacerations, broken bones, shrapnel wounds. The bombs could hurt a Martian machine, but often the men using them were caught in the blast. The troops seemed to think the risk was worth it. At least it gave them some chance to fight back.

She finished writing down the information for this load on her lists when a new load arrived. The first man carried out of the ambulance was very tall and rather thin. Some might have called him handsome except he had half his face burned off. Becca looked closer and saw that the damage hadn't been caused by a heat ray—at least not directly. There were bits of metal mixed in with the burns. And small burns all over his uniform. Then she spotted the tank corps insignia on his collar. Ah, right. He'd been in a tank when a heat ray had burned through it. Hot steam and melted metal flying everywhere.

One of the doctors made the judgment that the man might recover and Becca opened his collar and pulled out his identity disk. Not all the soldiers wore the disks, but it made her job easier when they did. She wrote his name down on her list: *Patton, George S.*

He was carried away and she started on the next one, but then there was shouting and an officer came up. "All right! We're pulling out! Get those wounded ready to move!"

She'd been half-expecting this, but it still came as a shock. The hospital erupted in activity with everyone scrambling to secure transport of the patients, load food, water, and medicine to get them wherever they were going, and make sure everyone was accounted for.

"Haven't we gone through this before?" asked Clarissa Forester.

"Well, at least this time the Martians aren't already in the camp!" replied Becca. She stopped and looked nervously over her shoulder. "They're not, are they?"

"I think we would have heard something. Here, give me a hand with these boxes."

"No time for chatting, girls!" said Miss Chumley. "We'll get everyone we can aboard the trains. We'll keep as many wagons and ambulances empty as we can to pick up others en route. Miss Harding, you'll ride that horse of yours to carry messages or whatever else we might need. Understood?"

"Yes, ma'am!" said Becca, delighted she'd be with her beloved Ninny.

"Snap it up! We haven't got much time!"

* * * * *

MARCH, 1910, GLORIETA, NEW MEXICO

"What are they waiting for, sir?"

Lieutenant Frank Dolfen lowered his field glasses and shook his head. "I don't know, Sergeant. Nine of the damn things and they're just standing there."

"Maybe they're scared of the darkies," snorted First Sergeant Barton.

Dolfen scowled. He didn't particularly like the man who was now his senior NCO. Hell, but he

367

missed Urbaniak! "The colored troops are damn fine soldiers, Sergeant. And if they can scare off the Martians, then we need a lot more of them."

Barton shrugged and spat, but didn't answer. Dolfen got the impression the man didn't much like him, either.

But what *were* the Martians waiting for? It was now nine o'clock and the cavalry brigade had deployed to guard the eastern end of Glorieta Pass which was the only practical route in or out of Santa Fe from the east. A battle had been fought here during the Civil War, which turned back the Confederacy's attempt to seize New Mexico and points west. Would another battle be fought here today? Would the Martian's attempt to hit the army in the rear be turned back, too?

Dolfen looked around with nervous energy. He ought to be taking this time to sleep a little after the all-night ride to get here, but he couldn't. He was sure there was going to be a fight today. Was there anything he'd left undone?

The pass itself was well-suited for defense, that was for sure. The land was very rugged and mostly covered with pine trees, which even the Martian tripods would have trouble getting through. The trees were dripping wet, too, from the melting snow and maybe that would help keep them from burning. The only easy path was the one followed by the road and the railroad, which ran side by side; the road to the north of the railroad by a few dozen yards. From the east, the direction the Martians would come from, the path traveled northwest, rising nearly a thousand feet. At the top, there was a broad horseshoe turn that sent the road and rails back to the southwest where they descended about three hundred feet and then curved off to Santa Fe. The path varied in width from a few hundred feet to just fifty or so in spots.

Colonel Berg had deployed his brigade in a series of strongpoints leading up the road. A squadron or so was at each, dug-in as best they could in the rocky ground, with machine guns positioned and the men's bombs ready. The 10th held the first four strongpoints, then the two companies from the 109th, and then the three intact squadrons of the 5th. Dolfen's troop-sized squadron was the final reserve, positioned maybe a half-mile downhill from the top of the pass. The tiny town of Glorieta was just to his left rear, nestled in a small valley adjoining the pass.

There was a telegraph there and Dolfen saw Colonel Berg returning from it. He saluted as Berg came up to him. "All ready, Frank?"

"I think so, sir. So what's happening back there?" he motioned to the west where the sound of artillery had been growing by the hour. "We gonna get any help up here?"

"It's on its way. Or I should say the whole army is on its way. As near as I can make out, Funston got the holy hell beat out of him yesterday and what's left will be coming through the pass here soon. They say they are sending some guns up to help us clear the way."

"So we might end up attacking down instead of defending up, sir?" asked Dolfen in surprise.

"We can hope. But if help doesn't arrive and they attack first, we must keep them from getting past us. Even a couple of those devils in position just below the top of the pass could bottle up the entire army for hours. If they are being pursued from the other side it would be a disaster."

"I understand, sir. We'll hold 'em."

"I know you will." Berg slapped him on the shoulder. "Good luck to you."

* * * * *

CYCLE 597, 844.1, EAST OF HOLDFAST 32-1

"You will attack immediately," said Valprandar, its voice coming over the communicator.

"Yes, Commander," replied Qetjnegartis. "But the enemy holds a very strong position. We may take heavy loses."

"Your losses are immaterial!" said Valprandàr sharply. "We have already lost fifteen of our people dead and another ten wounded in this attack! But if you seal off the enemy retreat it will be worthwhile. If we can complete the destruction of this army all these lands will be ours for the taking. Attack at once!"

"Yes, Commander, at once."

* * * * *

MARCH, 1910, SANTA FE, NEW MEXICO TERRITORY

"Sir? Wake up, sir!" Someone was shaking Andrew and talking much too loudly.

"Wha? Wuzzat?" He tried to struggle awake, but his head seemed stuffed full of cotton. McGill was standing in the tent, next to the cot he'd commandeered.

"Here's some coffee, sir. Wake up, that colonel wants to talk to you." A hot tin cup was pressed into his hands and he gulped down a couple of mouthfuls of a bitter black brew.

"What colonel?" he coughed.

"The general's chief of staff, Hinckley. Says he's got a job for us."

That got through and Andrew came awake. "What time is it?"

"A little after nine, sir. Looks like things are happening."

Andrew struggled to his feet and grabbed his hat. Colonel Hinckley was waiting outside the tent. He looked very busy, very harried. Why'd he want to see him? He saluted. "Sir?"

"Comstock, we're pulling out. The 30th and 82nd, which are north and west of town, will go first. They're already on the move. The service units will go next and then the 28th and 77th—if there's anything left of them—will form the rear guard. The enemy is hitting them hard and we're not sure how long they'll be able to hold."

"I understand, sir."

"But…" Hinckley frowned. "We've gotten word that there's a Martian force on the other side of the pass—the damn report was hours old before it got to us! We're not sure how many, we think it's just a small raiding force, and we've got a brigade of cavalry in place to hold them back. But we need to clear them out so they don't delay our withdrawal. We've managed to scrape together a small force, including a battery of those new anti-tripod guns, and put them on a train to send to the pass. You're in Ordnance, right? You know about those guns, don't you?"

"Uh, yes, sir, I'm familiar with them, but…"

"Good! We're short-handed here, so the general wants you to see that those guns get up there and do the job! Can you do that?"

Andrew's head was spinning. A combat command? Was he crazy? But his mouth said: "Yes, sir. I'll take care of it."

"Good man! The train will be ready in just a few minutes. Get over to the depot and make sure you're on it!"

"Yes, sir!" Andrew saluted again and Hinckley was gone. He looked at McGill and Kennedy and Bill White, who was still there. "Well, gentlemen, we have our orders. Let's get to it. Where are the horses?"

* * * * *

369

CYCLE 597, 844.1, EAST OF HOLDFAST 32-1

Qetjnegartis swept the heat ray across the group of prey-creatures and watched as they were consumed. Their destruction was satisfying, but there didn't seem to be any end to the miserable creatures. It and its fellows had attacked one group of them and wiped them out, only to encounter a second group a half telequel farther up the pass. This too had been destroyed, but now here was a third!

And each new group seemed undismayed by the destruction of the previous group. They attacked with a fanaticism Qetjnegartis had not encountered before. Experience from the first invasion, and again in the second, had shown again and again that if the prey-creatures were subjected to sufficient violence, if enough of them were slain, then the remainder would succumb to their animalistic instinct for self-preservation and flee. They had shown none of the Race's willingness to make whatever sacrifice was necessary for the good of the group.

But the ones they were fighting now were nearly at that point. True, some would flee, but the rest were hurling themselves into battle with an almost complete disregard for their losses. And the close-quarter nature of the current fight was allowing them to use their numbers to good effect. The narrow passage, with the jumbled rocks and close-set plant-growth, provided many hiding places from which they could spring. And while they did not have any of the large projectile throwers, most were carrying the explosive devices which had proved very dangerous. Qetjnegartis' own machine had suffered minor damage and two of the others in the group had been so badly damaged as to be unusable.

They moved forward another hundred quel, only to encounter more of the creatures. They emerged from some of the tall plants and threw their explosives. Qetjnegartis and the others burned them down, but the charges detonated and debris rattled off the skin of its machine. The plants provided concealment and despite repeated attempts to set them ablaze, they appeared so sodden with moisture that they would only burn as long as the heat rays were trained on them. The fires would not spread or continue on their own.

They killed this newest batch and continued up the pass. Qetjnegartis caught a brief glimpse of the top, still five or six telequel away, and urged its force onward. Valprandar had said it would drive the enemy army into this narrow pass and Qetjnegartis was to block it from this side, trapping the enemy. But if the prey-creatures got over the pass in strength while Qetjnegartis was still on the lower ground it might prove impossible to hold them. If they had room to deploy their large projectile throwers up there, out of range of the heat rays, it could be very bad. "Move quickly!" it urged. "We must advance faster!"

They broke through another line of prey-creatures and then reached a section of the pass where the rock walls closed in on the north side. Suddenly, Qetjnegartis saw movement. "Cablantna! Beware!" It sent an urgent message to one of its subordinates, but it was too late. Ten of the prey-creatures launched themselves off the top of an outcropping toward Cablantna's fighting machine. Half of them missed or bounced off and fell to their deaths, but four managed to grab hold. It was inevitable that they would have the explosive devices!

Qetjnegartis activated its heat ray and swept it over Cablantna's machine. They had learned in earlier battles that by reducing the power of the ray and widening the focus, it was possible to produce a ray which, while still more than capable of destroying the prey-creature foot warriors, was weak enough to pose no threat to a fighting machine for a brief exposure. The beam was also wider and thus able to hit more targets. Qetjnegartis' ray set three of the enemy ablaze and they fell off like tiny meteors. But the fourth was on the other side—outside the reach of the ray! "Cablantna! Turn your machine around!"

But it was too late. The last creature leapt off and an instant later an explosion tore loose one of the machine's legs and it toppled over and crashed to the ground. Instruments said that Cablantna was still alive, but there was no possibility of transferring it to a transport pod. The entire way up the pass they had been under fire from prey-creatures with their small projectile throwers. While they were of no threat to a fighting machine—unless it had sustained previous damage to its armor—there would be too great a risk for Cablantna to emerge from its machine under these conditions. They would have to rescue it later.

"Continue forward!" it commanded. *Only six of us left! Can we reach the objective?*

* * * * *

MARCH, 1910, GLORIETA PASS, NEW MEXICO TERRITORY

"Gotta hand it to them darkies: they put up a helluva fight!"

Frank Dolfen glared at First Sergeant Barton, but then nodded. "Yeah, they sure as hell did. Took out three of the bastards." The 10th Cavalry had held the Martians for an hour, but they'd paid for every minute. He didn't think there were many of them left.

"Now it's our turn. Think we can stop 'em, sir?"

"We're sure as hell gonna try!" He looked back toward the top of the pass. They'd been promised help, but the road and the tracks were empty.

* * * * *

MARCH, 1910, SANTA FE, NEW MEXICO TERRITORY

The train depot was bedlam. There were at least twenty trains on sidings being loaded and huge crowds of people swarming around them. Becca guided Ninny through the throng, keeping pace with the ambulance wagons. It wasn't complete chaos, there was still some sense of order—unlike that frantic retreat from the siege at Gallup. Provost officers and their men directed traffic and kept things moving, albeit at a slow pace. Nearly everyone she saw was a soldier, but there were a few civilian mixed in and Becca suddenly wondered if her aunt and uncle had made it out. If she saw them now, she'd find room for them on a wagon, but she did not; although a few made her take second looks. Thankfully she didn't see any children, she wouldn't be able to ignore those.

They finally made it to the trains which would carry the wounded. She helped move them from the ambulances, keeping a close watch on Ninny where she'd tied him. Despite the seeming order, she wouldn't put it past someone to try and steal him. "Come on! Hurry it up!" cried one of the medical officers. "We need to get out of here!"

They finished the transfer and then the horse-drawn traffic was directed onto a road leading to the pass over the mountains. The hospital trains were left sitting on their sidings as other trains were sent out first. Becca saw that the lead train was carrying artillery on flat cars and she was angered at the thought that mere equipment was being given priority over wounded men!

The medical convoy started and stopped and inched forward. She could see columns of troops and wagons and guns ahead on another road that merged with the one she was on. There were more provost men at the intersection deciding who would be let through and in what order. The sounds of battle to the south were getting closer and closer. She nervously waited for their turn, and envied the streams of individuals who were ignoring the rules and sneaking past on the edge of the road.

Finally, they reached the intersection and after waiting for a brigade of infantry to pass, they were allowed into the column. The road turned southeast and started up the long slope to the pass. There seemed to be a hundred voices all shouting the same message.

"Close it up! Close it up! Keep moving!"

* * * * *

371

MARCH 1910, WEST OF GLORIETA PASS, NEW MEXICO TERRITORY

The train's locomotive belched thick black smoke as it labored on the upgrade. Andrew and his comrades were in a passenger car right behind the coal tender with some of the men of the anti tripod gun battery. Behind that were four flat cars, each one carrying a gun and its limber. The guns were all pointing backward, with the limbers just in front of them. Two more flat cars held caissons and then there were more carrying the horses to pull the guns. The rear of the train had a few more passenger cars carrying a company of infantry to support the battery.

Behind them, a quarter mile back, was another train carrying a railroad repair crew with lots of equipment and three steam tanks which had been modified as work tractors, although they retained their guns.

And to his amazement, Andrew was in command of the whole shebang.

It still seemed slightly crazy to him, but it was true that a small grouping of a gun battery and an infantry company like this didn't fall into any normal table of organization. The anti tripod guns weren't even in the normal divisional TO yet, they were just an attachment. The infantry company had been detached from a battalion of the 28th Infantry Division which was being used as a corps reserve. So there was no officer to whom a command like this would normally fall. It was completely ad hoc and any officer the higher command chose to assign to it would be 'normal'. Andrew assumed Hinckley had chosen him simply because he couldn't spare anyone else.

The battery was a unit from the Missouri National Guard commanded by a lieutenant named Truman. He wore thick glasses and seemed very nervous. This was clearly his first time in combat. "What do you think we'll be asked to do, Major?"

"All I've been told is that there's a cavalry brigade holding back a small Martian force on the other side of the pass. We need to kill them or drive them off so the army can get through. How much practice have your men had with those guns, Lieutenant?"

"Uh, mostly just dry-firing, sir. We go through the motions, but haven't been allowed to fire many live rounds. But they're good men. We had the old M1897s before they gave us the new ones and my men were right sharp with them!"

Andrew nodded. That was about typical for the other batteries he'd inspected. But it wasn't good. Hitting a small target a mile away wasn't easy and it took practice. These boys hadn't gotten that practice it seemed. He tried to remember what the ground on the other side of the pass looked like. He'd come through that way two different times, but all that came to him was a long uphill climb with rocks and trees on either side and a road on the northern side of the tracks. He wished he had a map, but he didn't.

"I'm hoping we'll have room to deploy your guns where we'll have a good field of fire looking down on them. If the cavalry can hold them, maybe you can pick them off like clay pigeons."

"That's a very appealing picture, Major," said Bill White. "I much prefer it to dropping burning buildings on them."

"Amen to that!" said McGill. Truman looked between them, apparently trying to determine if they were joking.

"Can't see a damned thing from in here," said Andrew. "I'm going back to one of the flat cars to get a better look. We may have to unload and go into action quickly." He led the way to the rear of the car and opened the door. The transfer to the flat car involved a gut-churning jump, but he and the others made it. From there he could lean out and get a better view.

The first time he'd come this way had been in '08 and the railroad had gone southwest from the pass, by-passing Santa Fe completely. You had to take a branch line back north to get there. But since then they'd built a connection directly from Santa Fe to the pass to try and reduce congestion on the tracks. It was good thing, too; Andrew suspected that that other line which went toward Albuquerque was probably in the middle of a battle right now. There was a cloud of smoke rising to the southwest and the sound of the guns could be heard above the puffing of their locomotive.

Leaning out and looking forward, he could see they were still a couple of miles from the top of the pass. But was that smoke he could see rising up from beyond? The others saw it, too.

"What are we runnin' into here, d'you think, sir?" asked McGill.

"I don't know, but we'll find out soon enough."

* * * * *

MARCH, 1910, GLORIETA PASS, NEW MEXICO TERRITORY

"Here they come! Get ready!"

"God help us!" said First Sergeant Barton.

Frank Dolfen took one last look at the top of the pass and snarled, "Looks like He's the only one who will today!"

"Maybe we ought to think about gettin' out of here, sir!" said Barton. "The rest of the regiment couldn't hold those bastards and there's still five of 'em left! What can we do with fifty men?"

The sergeant was probably right, it probably was hopeless. The enemy had smashed their way through the 10th, and then through the two companies of the 109th, and then through two squadrons of the 5th. They were in the process of smashing the third squadron and then it would be their turn.

"Run if you want to, Barton. I won't stop you." The sergeant cursed vilely, but stayed there behind a boulder with Dolfen.

Dolfen clutched his pistol in one hand and a bomb in the other. He doubted he'd live to see the end of this day, but he was determined to make his death count for something. The Martians were still slaughtering the third squadron in line, but that wouldn't take much longer. Then they'd march right up here and finish the job. Damn! If they'd just gotten any sort of help at all!

But the third squadron wasn't quite finished. As Dolfen looked in delight, a half-dozen bombs exploded. Not on the Martian machines, but on a stand of tall pines right next to the road. The branches of the trees were already on fire, but the thick trunks were intact and now three of them leaned outward and then toppled over, right onto one of the enemy tripods! The first tree made it stagger and then the other two knocked it right over and pinned it on the ground. Several other tripods came over to it and dragged the trees off their comrade, but after several attempts to get it on its legs again failed, they left it and continued on up the pass—right toward Dolfen and his men.

"Only four left now!"

"Shame there aren't any big trees here close enough to the road to do that again," said Barton.

"Nope, we'll have to do it the old fashioned way. Get ready!"

Dolfen had positioned his forces near the little village of Glorieta, but he hadn't put any of his troops in the building. They were mostly flimsy shacks for one thing which would provide little protection. But he was also hoping that the Martians would be distracted by those buildings, and while they were busy burning them he and his men might be able to hit them unexpectedly. "Keep down until you get the signal!" He had their remaining bugler nearby and the man nodded nervously.

The enemy was getting closer, only a few hundred yards away now. Rifle bullets were still pinging off the machines; there must be hundreds of survivors from the smashed units who'd fled up into the hills on either side of the pass. Some of them were still fighting. None of them had any chance of stopping them.

As if we do!

Closer and closer they came. Two hundred yards, one hundred yards, fifty yards, the first machine in line stomped past Dolfen's hiding place—and then turned toward the houses. The other three joined it and they all opened fire at once on the buildings, which exploded into flames.

"Now!" The bugler sounded the charge.

Dolfen sprang up from his spot and sprinted toward the nearest Martian. The rest of his men were doing the same, screaming battle cries as they came. Barton held back for a moment and then came forward, too.

But the Martians were on alert and noticed the attack immediately. The heat rays swung around and men started dying. Barton vanished in a flash of smoke and flame with three other troopers.

The distance was down to a few dozen yards and Dolfen, screaming with all the rest, pulled the ring on the fuse of his bomb. Smoke spurted out as it burned. He swung his arm back to throw and...

An explosion—someone's bomb—blew up right in front of him. The blast flung him through the air and he landed among some very hard rocks. Pain shot through every part of him. Stunned, he tried to pull himself up, but a second explosion—probably his own bomb—slammed him flat and consciousness fled.

* * * * *

CYCLE 597, 844.1, EAST OF HOLDFAST 32-1

Qetjnegartis looked around and switched off its heat ray. *Is that it? Have we destroyed them all?*

Nothing, except for a few scattered prey-creatures, were in evidence now. The way to the top of the pass seemed clear. But it had seemed that way several times before this day and it hadn't been true. And what was waiting on the other side? It activated its communicator. "Commander Valprandar, please respond."

The response was quite some time in coming, but at last it did. "Qetjnegartis, where are you?"

"Nearly at the top of the pass. I have only four functional fighting machines left. What is your situation?"

"The enemy fights with unusual vigor. We kill them in huge numbers, but I estimate we are still at least a tenthday away from your position. The enemy forces are attempting to escape. You must stop or at least delay them."

"We shall try. But if our situation becomes impossible, do I have your permission to withdraw?"

"If you position yourself properly, your situation will not become impossible! I am very busy here. Carry out your orders!"

"Yes, Commander." Qetjnegartis broke the connection and addressed its subordinates. "Continue the advance. Help is coming."

They pushed on up the pass and nothing else attacked them. Perhaps that was the last of them. But as they neared the top, one of the others gave a warning: "Beware, Subcommander! Something approaches!"

* * * * *

374

MARCH, 1910, GLORIETA PASS, NEW MEXICO TERRITORY

The train was barely moving five miles an hour as it neared the top of the pass. But as the slope leveled out, it picked up speed. Andrew leaned out from the flat car and tried to look ahead, but there was a lot of smoke and some tall trees blocking the view. What had been going on here? Was there anyone in command of that cavalry brigade he could talk to? Maybe he should tell the engineer to stop…

Suddenly the locomotive's whistle screamed out a shrill note that just went on and on. The train's brakes slammed on and Andrew had to grab something to keep from falling. An instant later there was a bright red flash and the locomotive exploded in a blast of flame; the boiler ruptured and a huge cloud of steam billowed out in all directions. The cars derailed and Andrew found himself tumbling off into a ditch as the flat car lurched one way and he went the other. Everything rumbled to a stop amid the sounds of screeching metal, shouting men, and screaming horses.

And the buzz-saw snarl of heat rays.

They're here? Right here? Oh God! Oh God!

They were supposed to be reinforcing some cavalry, not leading a charge! Andrew tried to clear his head and saw that he was in a ditch on the right side of the train. The cars were tilted over to the left, so the wheels on the flat car's trucks were right over his head. One of the gun limbers had broken loose and was in the ditch just a few yards ahead of where he was sprawled. The road that paralleled the tracks was somewhere over to the left, on the other side of the train. Just to his right was a steep ravine that went down fifty feet or more. He tried to struggle to his feet, but McGill was there and pulled him back. "Stay down, sir! They're right there!"

The heat ray fired again and the passenger car behind the locomotive erupted in flames. Burning men came tumbling out of the doors and windows, screaming horribly. He lay flat in the lee of the car as the rays swept quickly down the line and he could hear several of the limbers' ammunition explode.

Something tall loomed up out of the smoke—a tripod walking past. More heat rays and the caissons farther back blew up. And then it was on to the cars carrying the troops.

"Oh God! They're destroying everything!" moaned White, who was just beyond McGill. Lieutenant Truman was there, too, with several of his gunners. Andrew sat there, frozen in horror as three more of the tripods stalked by. *Four of them? Right below the pass? They'll bottle up the whole army!* But that seemed to be the last of them. No more came past and Andrew started crawling under the car to the other side of the train.

"Where are ye goin' ya bloody fool?" McGill tried to hold him back, but he slipped free and squirmed under and through.

"I want to see!" He heard McGill cursing in Gaelic as he made it through to the other side. He looked downhill and didn't see anything but the burning locomotive and cars. No other tripods were in sight. He looked uphill and there were the four which had wrought such destruction. Right in front of him was one of the anti tripod guns which had broken loose from the ropes securing it to the flat car and was lying almost on its side. Andrew scrambled forward to get behind its oversized gunshield. He'd be out of sight there. The whole gun was still warm from where the heat ray had washed over it. His heart was pounding and he was gasping for breath. He looked back and there were McGill and Truman, just poking their heads beyond the side of the car.

What to do? What to do? Things were going to hell in a handbasket. The guns were wrecked, the troops scattered. The repair train would be coming over the rise any moment and once it was destroyed, the rail line would be hopelessly blocked. All Andrew had was his revolver. What the hell could he do? He stared through the gap between the gun's barrel and the gun shield and one of the Martians was right there, maybe two hundred yards away. He stared at it down the length of the gun…

Believe it or not, just a few years ago we aimed our guns the same way Drake did against the Armada...

Commander Cushing's words came back to him out of nowhere. *We just looked along the barrel and when we thought we were lined up on the target, we pulled the lanyard and hoped for the best.*

He jerked his head around and shouted: "Get me some shells! From that limber!"

"What?" cried McGill. "Are you out of yer mind?"

"Just do it! Get them and bring them here! Truman! Get me those damn shells!" The pair disappeared and Andrew moved back and wrestled the breech of the gun open. Then he flung himself to where the hand wheels that aimed the gun were located. When the anti tripod guns were set up, they had a small telescopic sight mounted for aiming, but during transport those were stored elsewhere to keep them safe. Andrew looked along the barrel of the gun and spun the wheels. The barrel moved, but it couldn't move far lying on its side like this. But one of the tripods was right there.

He heard movement behind him. "Load!" he screamed without looking back.

"Yer gonna get us all killed, sir, you know that?"

"I know! I know! Load, dammit! Before it moves!"

There were several loud clanks and then Truman said, "You're loaded, sir!"

"Take the lanyard! Fire on my command!"

"Yes, sir!"

He spun the wheels some more until it looked like he had the gun pointing at the tripod. It was the last one in line as they slowly moved up the pass. He made one final adjustment, then he prayed and cried:

"Fire!"

He leapt back as Truman pulled the lanyard. The gun roared and jumped backward savagely. If he hadn't gotten out of the way it would have crushed him. Heedless of everything else he stood up, and as the smoke blew away he saw his target lurch, stumble, and fall forward as one leg was sheared off above the thing's knee joint.

"Yes! Load! Quickly!" McGill, Truman, and another man went to work. He saw White emerge from under the car with another shell cradled in his arms.

He went back to the aiming wheels and looked down the barrel. The other three tripods had turned back to see what had hurt their comrade. It wouldn't take them long to figure it out. He'd get off one more shot if he was lucky. Could he take out another one of them? He spun the wheels but then cursed when they stopped and wouldn't move any farther! He'd traversed it as far as it would go and it wasn't pointing at any of them! *Damn!*

"You're loaded!" shouted Truman.

Loaded but with no targets!

Except for the one that's already down...

He'd studied the drawings he'd helped make of the Martian tripods. Studied every part of them. Knew them like the back of his hand. The one that was down, it was lying there and he was staring right up its underside. From there he could see... *Yes!* He spun the wheels the other way.

"What are you doing?" demanded McGill. "They're over to the right!"

"I'm not firing at *them*! Ready, Truman?"

"Yes, sir!"

"Ready…" he moved the wheel a tiny bit. "Fire!"

The gun jerked backward again and he barely escaped it this time. He heard a loud impact and then through the smoke there was a blue glow.

"Everyone get down!" He screamed it with all his breath and then tackled Truman and McGill.

An enormous explosion blotted out everything; sight, sound, feeling. Andrew was slammed to the ground and blacked out for a moment. When he came to, there were blue spots floating in front of his eyes and a ringing in his ears. McGill, Truman, and White were struggling up and someone gave Andrew a hand and hauled him to his feet, too.

"Saints preserve us!" said McGill. It sounded like a whisper, but Andrew realized he'd actually shouted it.

He looked where McGill was staring, and the place where the tripods had been was just a scorched and blackened patch of ground. Andrew painfully hauled himself up on the flat car and looked around. The rear part of the train had been reduced to flinders. There wasn't a sign of the Martians. Oh wait, what was that? Down in the ravine there was a mound of wreckage, the remains of something Martian, but it surely was no threat now.

A train whistle drew his attention to the top of the pass. The repair train was just coming over the rise and slowing to a stop. Andrew got down from the flat car and limped forward, dizzy and barely able to keep upright. Behind him he heard McGill say: "Where t'hell's Kennedy gotten himself to?"

Bill White answered: "I think that's him pinned under the car."

"Damn," said McGill.

Yeah, damn…

He met the boss of the repair gang and motioned to the wreck. "How long to fix that?"

The man looked skeptical. "Oh, two or three hours at least… First we gotta use the tractors to push the wrecked cars down into that ravine and then…"

"In two hours the Martians will be here!" He leaned forward until his face was nearly touching the face of the startled man. "You've got forty-five minutes! Now get to it!" The man blinked, looked at Andrew, looked behind him and then looked at Andrew again.

"Yes, sir!"

* * * * *

MARCH, 1910, WEST OF GLORIETA PASS, NEW MEXICO TERRITORY

The trains had quickly outdistanced them at first, but then they suddenly stopped, and those on foot and in wagons and on horses caught up and began to pass them by on the parallel road. There were still the usual starts and stops you'd have in any army column, but in general they kept moving forward. Not nearly fast enough in Becca's opinion. The fighting was clearly catching up with them, and they could see that parts of Santa Fe were now burning.

More alarming was the fact that they started to encounter small groups of men and individuals coming *down* from the pass who claimed that there were Martians up there, too. But a little later there was a dazzling blue flash from up ahead and an enormous *boom* rolled down the valley. Becca knew what it was and smiled. And the column kept moving; that was the surest sign that the scaremongers had been exaggerating.

It was well after noon by the time the ambulances and Becca got to the top of the pass and started down the other side. There were signs of destruction everywhere and a repair gang had just finished fixing a section of track. The locomotive whistles blew and the trains started moving again. Maybe the fleeing men hadn't been exaggerating all that much after all.

But they *were* moving and that was good. Except that now they were finding wounded men along the road; a lot of them, and more were being dragged down out of the hills. They loaded them into the ambulances and wagons as best they could and kept moving. As they came upon the remains of a little town, a soldier who looked like a cavalryman, waved and shouted: "Hey! Can you help? I've got a wounded officer here!"

She rode over and halted Ninny next to a man lying on a blanket. He looked badly battered, but not badly burned. There was a bandage on his head and one leg had been crudely splinted with some sticks. She bent over and looked closer…

"Sergeant Dolfen!"

"He's a lieutenant, Missy," said the man sternly. "And he's hurt! He needs help!"

"And he'll get it! Clarissa! Bring your wagon over here!"

* * * * *

CYCLE 597, 844.1, EAST OF HOLDFAST 32-1

Qetjnegartis came to its senses and immediately realized it was badly injured. It wasn't certain how badly, but badly enough. It also realized that its fighting machine was a complete wreck. Nothing was working and the only light was from a jagged hole in the hull of the control cockpit. What had happened? One of the fighting machines had been damaged. They went to investigate and then… then it had regained consciousness here.

It managed to shift itself enough that it could see out the hole. It appeared to be lying at the bottom of a steep slope. But at the top there were prey-creatures. A lot of them. No sign at all of its subordinates, just a seemingly endless column of foot warriors, draught animals, and equipment marching past from west to east. Some of the transport vehicles on rails moved by at intervals as well, filled with equipment, large projectile throwers, and the fighting vehicles.

Clearly, the attempt to block the prey-creature's line of retreat had failed and they were escaping through the pass to the east. This went on for a very long time, and the day was nearly over before the flood dwindled to just a few. And then there was nothing moving at all until it was nearly dark.

Finally, there was movement again and Qetjnegartis was relieved to see fighting machines at the top of the slope. Eventually someone came down and found it. It was transferred to a transport pod and carried up the slope where Valprandar was waiting.

"You still live, Qetjnegartis," it said. "This is good. We have found three others of your group who also live."

"Good news, Commander, but the prey-creatures have escaped in large numbers, you must begin the pursuit immediately."

"There will be no pursuit. Our losses have been heavy and our expenditure of energy extreme. Most of my force needs to return to the holdfast to recharge their power cells. Many, like you, need medical attention. We will repair and heal ourselves and begin the pursuit when we may."

"The enemy may escape us, Commander."

"If that is true, so be it. We have done all we can for now and even the Colonial Conclave cannot ask for more. This is still a great victory."

"As you say, Commander."

CHAPTER SIXTEEN

APRIL, 1910, WASHINGTON, D.C.

"You were right and I was wrong, Leonard."

General Leonard Wood knew Theodore Roosevelt well enough to realize just how hard it was for him to make that simple statement. He didn't want to make him feel any worse—but he wasn't going to let him off the hook, either.

"That doesn't matter, Theodore, what matters is what we do about it."

"And what *do* you plan to do about it?" Roosevelt was sitting behind his big desk in the White House. Wood had requested that this meeting take place in private.

"We are going to have to fall back to the Mississippi…" he raised his hand to cut off the President's inevitable protest. "There simply isn't any choice, Theodore." He got up and moved to one of the maps Roosevelt kept in his office. It wasn't as big or detailed as the Big Map, but it would do. "We've been hurt too badly to make a stand anywhere further west. The V Corps up in Montana and the Dakotas has been all but wiped out. They were too scattered, trying to cover too much ground, and the Martians just encircled each division and chopped it to bits. If we try to form a line at the Missouri River, the enemy will only outflank us to the north. They could be in Minneapolis before we could even get a line formed."

"But, their sacrifice wasn't in vain. The rest of First Army, I and IV Corps, have successfully pulled back and should be able to make it back to the Mississippi. Your two boys will be okay, Theodore." Roosevelt made a strange jerking motion with his head in acknowledgment. "Combined with Third Army and the other new forces we're activating, we should be able to form a solid line along the Mississippi and over to Lake Superior. The navy is sending what shallow draft vessels it has up the river and they are starting construction of a powerful flotilla on the Great Lakes. Given the time we should be able to build a very strong line along the river. Naturally, we will hang on to any towns like St. Louis which are on the west bank of the river."

"What about Funston's forces?"

"I'm going to leave him and his Second Army headquarters in Texas. What had been his II Corps, however will be reattached to First Army and fall back to the Mississippi. We'll have to send Funston whatever troops and equipment we can spare to hold Texas and Arkansas."

The President shook his head. "What a mess! Good God, what will the country say?"

Wood was silent for a moment. Yes, the country was going to be mad as hell. Explanations for the cause of the defeat, and the sound military logic for the retreat, was not going to satisfy the man in the street. The people would want simple explanations and the assurance that someone would pay for the disaster. Some people were already demanding payment; congressmen from the abandoned states, and men looking to take advantage of Roosevelt's misfortunes. Some, like retired General Nelson Miles, were hinting they would challenge him for the presidency in 1912.

Finally, Wood nodded and said: "Let's be honest, Theodore, the country is going to want someone's head to roll for this. We can't do without your head, but I'm prepared to resign if that's what's necessary. There's no denying that a great deal of this is my fault, too."

"No," replied Roosevelt firmly. "I need you and the country needs you. I'm not about to start shooting my generals to *encourager les autres!* We made mistakes, we both made mistakes. But we'll learn from them and By Thunder we'll beat these rascals yet!"

"Yes we will, Mr. President, yes we will."

* * * * *

CYCLE 597, 844.1, HOLDFAST 32-2

Qetjnegartis observed the excavator pushing debris to form the rampart around the new holdfast. It was being constructed in the area between the two prey-creature cities which had been destroyed in the recent battle. Surveys had confirmed a good supply of resources in the region, including the huge amounts of materials which could be salvaged from the cities and the wrecked equipment of the enemy army.

It was a good location, and best of all it would not be in any danger of attack. The remains of the enemy armies were still in retreat and now hundreds of telequel away. Observations from the Homeworld had detected a very large river to the east. The plan was to drive the enemy beyond it and use it as a buffer to prevent any incursions until the new holdfasts could be completed and more buds grown to replenish the clan's strength.

This would be a vital task. The clan had taken very heavy losses in the recent battles. Many of the newcomers had been slain and of the original twelve who had come in the first wave, only Qetjnegartis and Ixmaderna remained. Ixmaderna had been even more seriously injured than Qetjnegartis and was now growing a replacement body for itself. Still, if any major combat could be avoided for a cycle or two, the clan's strength could be rebuilt many fold.

As it observed the construction operations, Valprandar arrived at the head of thirty fighting machines. It came up to Qetjnegartis and halted. "Greetings Commander, you depart in pursuit of the enemy?"

"Yes, Subcommander. How do your injuries fare?"

"They are healing well. Another tenthcycle and I will be restored."

"That is good. We should be back by then to assist with the construction."

"I trust your endeavors will meet with success. But be wary, the enemy has much resilience. They are not fully defeated yet."

"So I have seen," said Valprandar. "But do not be concerned. We will not bring on any great battle. We shall simply harry them, destroying any stragglers or easy targets, and continuing the destruction of their transport systems. Once they have been driven beyond the river we will scout a location for the next holdfast and then return."

"Excellent. I shall await your return."

Valprandar led its force away and was soon out of sight. Qetjnegartis hoped the mission would be as simple as Valprandar seemed to think it would be.

* * * * *

APRIL, 1910, WASHINGTON, D.C.

"Welcome back, Major, it's good to see you again." Major General Crozier extended his hand and Andrew shook it.

"Thank you, sir, it's good to be back." And it really was. His reunion with Victoria—now very obviously expecting—had been tearful, but very, very nice. He felt guilty about racing ahead and leaving the remains of II Corps behind to make its long retreat, but he needed to get back here to tell what he had seen.

"I've read your report," Crozier went on. "Well done, very well done. I've put in for another brevet for you to lieutenant colonel, and I'm sure it will approved. You might get another medal out of this, too."

Andrew was surprised, Crozier had never paid much attention to him and certainly had never spoken to him like this before! "Th-thank you, sir. I had a lot of help."

"No doubt, no doubt! But come on, the meeting is about to start and they'll have a lot of questions for you. Don't be nervous, just speak your mind."

They were back in the familiar confines of the State, War, & Navy Building and about to attend a meeting of the General Staff. They walked into the big conference room where Andrew had spent so many hours as a young lieutenant, holding papers and serving coffee. But now he was seated beside the head of the Ordnance Department and expected to participate as an almost-equal. Many of the bureau chiefs were there, too. General Wood was not there, however, but his chief assistant, Brigadier General Douglas MacArthur, was sitting in for him.

The meeting was called to order and one of the officers gave a brief summary of the overall situation in the west. It was not good. Most of the troops west of the Mississippi were still retreating east as fast as they could, sometimes with Martian forces in hot pursuit. Reserves were being assembled as quickly as possible to shore up a defense line along the great river. There were serious doubts that a secure line could be created in time to keep the enemy from getting across. When the officer finished, MacArthur stood up.

"Thank you, Colonel. Gentlemen, our purpose here today is not to evaluate the strategic situation, but to look at the tactical problems which the latest campaigns have revealed. It has become shockingly plain that out methods and techniques are inadequate to deal with the capabilities of the Martians. You are all aware of the general course of events which took place at Albuquerque and Santa Fe, but we have here an eyewitness to those events, Major Andrew Comstock. Major, would you be kind enough to tell us what you saw and what conclusions you've drawn?"

Andrew stood up and looked over the faces which were staring at him. They were all older—in many cases a *lot* older—but he had gotten used to that. He nodded to MacArthur and began. "Of course, General. I had been sent to New Mexico to make some observations on equipment in General Funston's army and I was there in Albuquerque when the Martian attack began…"

He went on to describe everything he had seen there. What the Martians had done, how the army had responded, and the consequences of what had happened. There were numerous interruptions for questions from the listeners and most of the morning was gone before he got to the end of it. "It became plain to me that the Martians have two strengths, mobility and unprecedented firepower, which give them a large advantage over us. Their mobility and their independence from a line of supply give them the ability to perform raids deep into our rear areas, disrupting communication and our supply lines. This became evident very quickly during their recent offensive. But what came as a surprise during the battles at Albuquerque and Santa Fe was their ability to use that mobility to concentrate their forces on such a narrow front that they could overwhelm our defenses in a matter of minutes, break through our lines, destroy our reserves, and then proceed to defeat our forces in detail. We expected them to fight like a human army, spread their forces to match ours, and fight it out in a more or less conventional fashion. When they did not do this, we were caught off guard and unprepared. Unless we can adjust our tactics, we could face the same thing in future battles."

"Thank you, Major. I should add that what reports we've been able to get from survivors of the debacle suffered by the V Corps in Montana indicate that this is exactly what happened to them as well. Major, do you have any suggestions for how we should adjust our methods to meet this?"

"I gave it a great deal of thought on the journey back, sir, and I believe there are certain things we should do as quickly as possible. On the tactical level there are four measures we can take to improve our defenses. First, we need to restrict the mobility of the Martians. Their ability to quickly concentrate against a small section of our defense lines must be countered. There are several ways we can do this. One is to make better use of the terrain. We have observed that the enemy machines have difficulty dealing with dense forests and with swampy ground. We should make use of such terrain where it is available. Where possible we can try to create swampy ground by intentionally flooding areas near rivers. We can also create artificial obstructions. I have heard suggestions of trying to create 'Martian-sized' barbed wire entanglements, but I am skeptical of their utility. While barbed wire was used effectively during the Russo-Japanese war, I'm afraid that the Martians could quickly burn through any such obstructions with their heat rays. Concrete walls twenty feet high or higher could completely block their movements, but obviously this would only be possible in areas where we have the time and resources to construct such things. But another method I would advise is to create pit-fall traps in front of our lines. Not a hole big enough to hold an entire tripod, of course! Just a hole in which a tripod's leg might get caught. The nature of the Martian tripods is such that if even one leg can be immobilized the machine becomes trapped. Soldiers could dig deep holes and then camouflage them. Perhaps some sort of mass-produced 'bear trap' device could be manufactured to be put at the bottom to grab the tripod's leg when it falls in the hole. The best thing about this type of trap is that the soldiers can create them themselves on the spot. If even a portion of an attacking force could be immobilized it could seriously interfere with their plans." He paused, took a deep breath and continued.

"Second, we need to reorganize our artillery. At Albuquerque our guns did the best they could, but each battery or even each gun was firing at whatever target happened to come in front of them. There was no overall plan of action. When the Martians attacked at night and when they used their dust weapons, the effectiveness of our guns dropped dramatically. When I was down in Panama, the engineers there had an excellent plan to coordinate all of their artillery and create a system where fire from guns all over the isthmus could be called down on any area they chose on very short notice. If such a system could be adapted for use by field armies, then every gun within range could be used against an enemy target whether the gunners can see it or not. At Albuquerque, if General Funston had been able to direct all of his guns against the large concentration of Martian machines, the results of the battle might have been much different."

"Major, you are talking about two very different situations!" said one of the officers. "At Panama they will have months or years to set up a system like that. Trying to do the same for a moving field army on just hours' notice would be impossible!"

"It would be difficult, sir, but I don't believe it would be impossible." He paused. "And since it seems likely that for the near future our armies will be on the defensive, we might have more time to prepare than you suggest." There was some rumbling from the audience as they took this in, but then MacArthur told Andrew to continue.

"Third, we need to dramatically improve our ability to fight at night. The Martians seem to have realized that this is a weakness we have and are taking advantage of it. Part of our response will need to be in training. Soldiers need to be able to move and follow orders in the dark. When the lines broke at Albuquerque, the men were unable to reform them and dissolved into a mob. We need to train them how to avoid this. We also need to develop means of lighting up the battlefield. There have been experiments done in the past with rockets or other types of munitions which can use burning chemicals to produce a very bright light. We need to pursue this line of research and deploy something as soon as possible. Electric arc searchlights will also be needed. The navy already has such devices on some of their ships. We need something similar with portable power supplies.

"Fourth, we need better weapons and equipment. The steam tanks, our most effective counter to the tripods, are still too slow, too lightly armed and armored, and too mechanically unreliable. Improvements must be made. We need to improve our artillery, too. More powerful guns which are more accurate and easier to move. We need better anti-dust clothing and equipment. We need better airplanes which can fly longer distances at higher altitudes and which can carry radios. And above all we need better weapons for our infantry. The bombs they have been equipped with, while far better than nothing, still require a level of courage to use which not every soldier can supply. And those that do are often killed in the attempt. We need to develop new weapons which make our infantry effective, but which don't demand they sacrifice themselves to use!

"Finally, we need to make all of our people know what we are facing. Let them know what's at stake. I don't know how many of you have read the report I sent from an interview I had with a soldier who had actually been captured by the Martians, but I assure you that they will show us no mercy at all! We have to be ready to make any sacrifice necessary to stop them!"

Andrew's words were becoming animated and even heated. But when he suddenly realized he had gotten to the end of his presentation, he became self-conscious and embarrassed. "Uh, that's all I have to say, sir," he ended awkwardly.

"Thank you, Major," said MacArthur. "An excellent presentation. You have given all of us a lot to think about. General Wood asks that you all consider these issues and create a set of recommendations on how best to respond to them. We'll take this up again next week when General Wood can be here."

The meeting broke up and Andrew felt drained. General Crozier came over to him and put an arm around his shoulder. "A fine job, Andy! Really first rate!"

"Thank you, sir. I hope I didn't shock too many of them."

"They needed to be shocked, son! You don't get people to change a lifetime of thinking by serving them chamomile tea! They needed a real dose of castor oil and you gave it to them! Colonel Hawthorne would be proud of you."

"I'm surprised he wasn't here today…"

"Oh, didn't he tell you? He's with Wood at the Capitol today testifying before that damn new House Committee on the Conduct of the War. Damn busybodies think they know how to run things better than we do. Wood wanted someone who could answer technical questions, and I sent Ben."

"I see. I guess General Wood is getting a lot of criticism for what happened out west, isn't he? But it's not his fault. No one knew what we were really up against and…"

"Don't you worry about Wood! He can take care of himself. And as for you, *Colonel*, you need to take care of yourself! I can see you're still exhausted from your adventure. Go home! And say hello to that pretty wife of yours!"

"Yes, sir! That's the best order I've ever gotten!"

* * * * *

383

MAY, 1910, HETH, ARKANSAS

Lieutenant Frank Dolfen tentatively put his right foot in the stirrup, then stood up and swung his left leg over the horse's back, and thumped down onto the saddle. He winced in pain as his left leg banged against the side of the horse. He'd only had the splint off for two days and it still hurt like hell.

"Frank! What in blazes do you think you're doing?"

He turned and tried to smile as Rebecca Harding came running up. "What's it look like I'm doing, Becca? I'm stealing your horse!"

She laughed. "I should have sent you back on the train with the rest of the wounded!"

"So why didn't you?"

"There wasn't any room."

He nodded even though they both knew that wasn't strictly true. He'd expected to wake up dead, but instead he'd awakened in a lurching, shaking, bouncing wagon with terrible pains in his head and left leg, and slightly less terrible pains pretty much everywhere else. But Becca had been there, along with several other nurses and a doctor and quite a crowd of people, all moving northeast along the railroad tracks as fast as they could manage.

Despite his failure to stop the Martians at the pass, somehow the army—or what was left of it—had managed to break through and was fleeing. Everyone was expecting the Martians to appear on their tails at any moment, but for no reason anyone could fathom, they did not. Time passed while the host slowly crawled along as the track crews repaired the rail lines in front of them.

After a few days they turned southeast on that very line where Urbaniak had been killed. Frank's injuries were healing under Becca's stern orders and eventually the only thing really wrong with him was his broken leg. That was going to take some time to heal.

When they reached the cut and the little bridge where the fight had occurred, to his amazement that ordnance major, Andrew Comstock, had appeared to insist that certain parts of the two wrecked tripods be taken along. Becca told Frank that she'd seen him in Santa Fe before the battle. He had that same Scots sergeant with him and even that same newspaperman! Dolfen had asked him if ordnance majors were issued their own personal reporters. He'd just laughed.

The army lurched slowly forward as the tracks were repaired. Those on foot or horseback could have moved faster, but most of the food was on the trains and if they were left unprotected... the fear of an imminent attack never left them. They scavenged coal from wrecked depots and water from streams to keep the locomotives fed.

Then, about two weeks after leaving Santa Fe, they reached the end of the Martians' destructions and the rails were clear to the east. The trains carrying the wounded—and the major's booty—sped ahead, leaving the others behind. Frank might have gone with them, but Becca didn't suggest that he go and he did not. Major Comstock did go after a hasty good-bye. The newspaperman, White, went, too. Word had reached them that the whole army was pulling back to the Mississippi and he wanted to get to his family somewhere in Kansas.

They had hopes that once they reached undamaged rail lines that the army might be shuttled east by the trains, but that proved to be impossible. With the whole army on the move along the entire front, there was a shortage of rolling stock. And there was also the mass exodus of the civilian population. Everyone was trying to get out. And so those trains which did arrive, carrying food, made the return journey carrying women and children instead of soldiers. Their group actually got bigger instead of smaller as thousands and then tens of thousands of civilians joined the march.

They came in wagons and buggies and on foot. They carried what possessions they could and vast herds of cattle were driven along as well. Understandably the civilians were not a happy lot. They blamed the army's failure for their plight and there was no way to argue with that. Morale in the II Corps was rock bottom and the officers and NCOs struggled to maintain discipline. The only bright spot was that the spring weather was mild.

The month of April was spent in crossing the Texas panhandle, Oklahoma, and then on into Arkansas. The horde grew and grew and the generals worried that if the Martians did come after them, there could be an incredible slaughter. The civilians outnumbered the soldiers by several times and it would be impossible to protect them. Becca and the other medical people spent most of their time treating civilians rather than soldiers. At night the prairie was lit by thousands of campfires.

Eventually they reached Little Rock and there they found that the city was not going to be abandoned. The Arkansas River flowed through the town, and since it was navigable much of the year, the place was being converted into a fortress which could be supplied by boat. Some of the civilians decided to stay there while others continued on by water. The remainder all spent a week there resting. When they resumed the march, the 77th Division was left behind to bolster the garrison. Their destination was Memphis, a hundred and thirty miles away.

And so now they were camped at the little whistle stop of Heth, Arkansas. The river and Memphis were only twenty miles off. Everyone was hoping they would get there today.

Frank and Becca were on a first name basis now and she was standing next to him with her fists on her hips. "I ask again: what are you doing on Ninny, Frank? Your leg's not full-healed and you know it!"

"Just seein' if I remember how," he sighed. "I haven't been off a horse for this long since I joined the army."

"Well, I guess I can forgive you—if you get down right now." He slowly swung out of the saddle and she helped him down to avoid jolting his leg. On the ground, they stood there very close together, looking at each other. She had grown an inch or two since he'd first met her and her face had matured. She wasn't a girl anymore…

"Becca? Thanks for not sending me back with the wounded." She blushed very red in the dawn light and turned her head. But she didn't step away. "When… when I woke up, I knew the 5th was gone. The regiment had been my only home for near twenty years and I saw them die in that pass. Near all of them. The first thing I thought about was what the hell I was gonna do. But then I saw you there and, well, you're the only friend I have left." He clapped his mouth shut, amazed that he'd dare to say any such thing.

She turned her face back to him and opened her mouth to say something. But just then the buglers started sounding reveille and the moment was lost. They stepped apart and Becca took Ninny's reins and Frank picked up the crutch he'd been using. The camp was stirring all around them and people were hurrying to get their breakfasts and pack up the camp. Everyone was anxious to get moving. Perhaps today the long journey would finally end.

Less than an hour later they were on the move, which was little short of a miracle for a mob that large. Or it was more accurate to say that the army was on the move. The civilians tended to straggle along on a looser schedule. Frank was now driving one of the medical wagons while Becca rode nearby on Ninny. There wasn't anyone in the wagon right now. A train had delivered supplies yesterday and taken away all the sick and injured they had on hand. But there would probably be more before the day was over. The march was hard on people.

The spirits of everyone were good with the end so close, but there was a tension, too. The last couple of days they had noticed black smoke on the horizon behind them and to the northwest. It didn't necessarily mean anything, of course. There had been a heat-lightning storm the other night and the smoke could be from a lightning strike. And there were plenty of stragglers all around and maybe some of them had gotten careless with their campfires. Even so, there was no doubt that everyone was also thinking it could be the Martians.

"I still can't get over how *flat* the land is," said Becca. "You can see forever and ever here!"

"Yeah, nothing like the mountains you grew up in."

"The world is so big! I'd never been out of New Mexico before all this happened. I've looked at maps, of course, but they don't really tell you what things are really like. Have you really been across the ocean, Frank? All the way to the Philippines?"

"I was there for a year fightin' the insurrectionists. And believe me, you aren't missin' anything. I *hate* the jungle! I'll take these wide open spaces any day, Martians and all."

"What was the ocean like? I can't imagine so much water!"

"That… was impressive. The Pacific just went on forever. But wait 'til you see the Mississippi! Nowhere near as big as an ocean, but still pretty damn big."

"Think we'll see it today?"

"Actually, I think I can see it right now. Look over there." He pointed off to the right.

"Where?" Becca turned her head and rose up in her stirrups. "I don't see anything! Are you playing a joke on me, Lieutenant Dolfen?"

"No, I'm not," said Frank with a chuckle. "Way over there. See that line of trees? Just beyond. See the sunlight reflecting off the water?"

"Oh! Yes! I see it!" She paused and then sounded a little disappointed. "Doesn't look all that big."

"Wait until we get closer. It'll be big enough for you."

But it didn't get closer very quickly. Frank remembered from a map he saw that the railroad was heading northeast and the river was also bending that way, so they were almost paralleling it right now. Later, it would swing around the other way, almost across their path, and that's where the bridge to Memphis was.

Other people had spotted it, too, and there was a palpable feeling of excitement sweeping through the huge column. The pace grew quicker as everyone began to move faster. By noon they were much closer to the river. It was just a couple of miles off to their right and Becca was properly impressed. "It is big! Look at that, it must be almost a mile across! And look at all the boats on the river! Dozens of them!" There were a lot boats and barges and larger ships there, spewing smoke from their stacks. Several of them were painted gray and Frank guessed they might be navy ships.

A rider came down the column and announced that the front of the army had reached the bridge, but warned them that with the huge numbers involved it was very likely they would not all get across today, so they should be prepared to camp out for another night. This brought a groan, but they perked up when they were told that the citizens of Memphis had made preparations to greet them and that there would be hot food and cold drinks waiting for them.

"Hard to believe we really made it," said Frank. "Never thought I'd get out of that pass alive."

"Thank God," said Becca.

"Well, thank someone. Can't say I'm all that well disposed toward the Almighty these days."

"Don't let Clarissa hear you talk that way. She's been getting all Bible-reading and Bible-thumping lately. This is all God's will according to her." Frank grunted. He'd noticed that a religious revivalism seemed to be sweeping through the army, but it held no appeal for him.

They were getting quite close to the river now. There was a small town, West Memphis, if he remembered the map correctly, on the west side of the river and it looked as though it was being fortified. Large earthworks were being raised on either side of the railway. The ones on south side went right down to the river. The ones on the north side curved out of sight. The column was being funneled through the gap and progress was slowing down.

Suddenly there was commotion behind them. They looked back and there was a sort of ripple passing through the crowd, like waves on a pond. A growing sound of voices filled the air and some of those voices sounded almost like screams…

"What's happening?" asked Becca, looking around in confusion.

"I don't know." Frank stood up from his driver's seat on the wagon and looked west. West was the only direction that mattered right now. "Oh God, no!"

The land wasn't quite flat here and gently sloped down to the river. There was higher ground to the west and on that high ground stood at least twenty familiar shapes.

"*Martians!*" cried a thousand voices, almost in unison. "*Run! Run!*"

The shapes on the rise began to move. Frank could see that there were now at least thirty of the terrible things. Their red eyes blazed as they came forward.

In a flash, panic swept through the column. People began to run, riders and drivers lashed their horses, and any sort of order or discipline vanished. The mass surged forward toward the bridge, still miles away. Bugles began blaring and there was movement around the earthworks. In the column, officers tried to get their men to halt and turn around, but few listened. II Corps began to disintegrate.

They'll just walk right down here and slaughter us all!

"Becca! Go on! Ride ahead! Get across the bridge!"

"No! I'm not leaving you!"

"Go, dammit! You can get away!"

"No!"

Frank cursed and lashed at the horses pulling the wagon in hopes of forcing a way through. If he could get through then Becca would get through. But it was hopeless, the mob was being compressed into a nearly solid mass; there was no way to move quickly and soon it might not be possible to move at all. People were already being trampled. If this went on, the Martians wouldn't even need to do anything!

Was there any way out? What if he managed to turn aside and make for the river? Maybe one of the boats could pick them up! He looked toward the Mississippi. It was crowded with ships and boats of all kinds. He was looking right at a low gray ship when it suddenly erupted in flame and smoke!

A loud *boom* shook the air and simultaneously there was the sound of a runaway freight train roaring overhead. Frank's head twisted around to follow the noise as it shrieked toward the Martians.

Later, Frank revised his opinion of the Almighty because there wasn't any doubt that He—or someone—was guiding the hands of the gunners aboard USS *Amphitrite* that day. One of the ten-inch shells squarely hit the head of the leading tripod; an absolute bull's-eye, that blew the thing to smithereens, the now-unconnected legs flying off in three different directions.

The Martians must have been as stunned as Frank, because they stopped, appeared to stare for a few moments, and then all of them turned and went back the way they had come!

The whole terrified, scrambling mob came to a halt and watched them go. Then people began to cheer and the cheers swept along the column as quickly as the original panic had. The tripods disappeared behind the high ground and were gone. Only the smoldering remains of their unlucky comrade proved that it hadn't all been some sort of mass delusion.

It was almost an hour before the part of the column where Frank and Becca were stuck started to move again, but once it did, it moved along rapidly. Maybe the Martians were gone, but no one wanted to wait to see if they would come back. Even so, it was sunset before they reached the bridge. It was a long iron structure that amazed Becca and impressed Frank. Wooden planks had been put down over the railroad tracks to make it easier for people, horses, and wagons to cross. Memphis glowed pink and welcoming on the far bank.

"Safe," said Becca. "Are we really safe?"

"Yes, I think we are."

She twisted around in her saddle and looked back toward the setting sun. "But someday we'll go back. Someday we'll go back and kill those things."

"Yes, we will. And we'll take back what's ours."

EPILOGUE

CYCLE 597, 844.3, HOLDFAST 32-2

"You understand the orders of the Colonial Conclave, Qetjnegartis? Offensive operations are to be halted, new holdfasts constructed, and our numbers built up until such time as the Conclave decides new offensives are warranted. Minor local offensives to maintain the security of your holdfasts are permitted, but nothing larger."

"I understand Coordinator Glangatnar. This course of action seems wise."

"We are *pleased* that you approve," said Glangatnar. "This is a decision of the entire Conclave. The prey-creatures are on the defensive almost everywhere. We will take this opportunity to consolidate and prepare for the future."

Qetjnegartis could sense the sarcasm in the coordinator's voice even over the long-distance communicator. "I understand and will obey," it replied although privately it wondered who this respite would benefit more. The Race grew stronger, but so did the prey.

"Very well," said Glangatnar. "And Qetjnegartis, I trust you have recovered from your wounds sufficiently to assume command of the Bajantus Clan?"

"I am completely recovered and fully capable of carrying out my duties. I have done this job before."

"Yes, that it true. Most unfortunate for Valprandar to have been slain as it was at the very end of the offensive."

"Yes, most unfortunate," said Qetjnegartis. Glangatnar cut the connection and Qetjnegartis turned away from the communicator. Davnitargus was there watching it.

"I could be wrong," said Davnitargus, "but I sensed a lack of sincerity in your last statement, Progenitor."

"Really?" replied Qetjnegartis. "Sometimes your perceptions can be *too* accurate, Davnitargus."

* * * * *

JUNE, 1910, WASHINGTON, D.C.

Leonard Wood stubbed his toe on the nightstand and muttered a silent curse as he slipped into bed. As usual, he was trying not to wake his wife and as usual, he failed. Louise rolled over and murmured, "What time is it, Leonard?"

"Almost midnight," he lied. It was well after midnight.

"You are working too hard, dear. It's been less than a year since your operation, you shouldn't push yourself so hard." This was a nightly ritual, too.

"It can't be helped. There's so much going on; cleaning up the mess out west, trying to guess what the British are going to do now with Edward dead and George the new king..."

Louise was silent for a few minutes but then said: "Did you see the letter from Leonard Junior? I left it on the kitchen table."

"No, I didn't. I'll read it in the morning. What did he have to say?"

"He mostly talked about the changes to the curriculum at West Point. Is it really true he'll be graduating in only two and a half years instead of four?"

"Yes. They've done away with everything except the purely military subjects. We need professional officers and we need them quickly."

"So you knew all about it and didn't tell me." It wasn't a question.

"I didn't want to worry you."

There was another long silence and then she said: "I'd hoped that with him there for four years the war would be over before he graduated. But now, with it only being two and half years it probably won't be, will it?"

"Probably not." He didn't add that it probably wouldn't be over in four years, either.

"But what about Ozzie? He's only thirteen! Surely it will be all over before he's old enough!"

"God willing."

She didn't say any more, but Wood was a long time falling asleep despite his exhaustion.

God willing.

* * * * *

JUNE, 1910, MEMPHIS, TENNESSEE

Lieutenant Frank Dolfen strolled down the street in Memphis and glanced from time to time at the pretty girl in the nurse's uniform walking next to him. He wanted to smile at her, but he knew she wasn't in a smiling mood. "So, there's no word about your aunt and uncle?"

"Nothing that I could find," she replied. "That doesn't mean anything, of course. If they didn't check in at the refugee camp in El Paso there wouldn't be any record. They might have gone on somewhere else." She chuckled sourly. "I can't see my aunt putting up with a refugee camp! And since they have no way of knowin' where I am now, any message they might try to send would have to work its way through the whole army bureaucracy to find me."

"Yes, that could take a while, Becca. Don't give up hope."

"And that's only if they even *try* to get a message to me. They might not bother."

"I'm sure they will, you're family after all."

"Yeah, I'm family. But if they didn't make it out..."

"Have you got anyone else?"

"I suppose I do, but I don't know who or where. Back east I suppose. I never paid much attention to the things my folks said about their relations since I didn't figure on ever meeting them. Any records are burned up now, I guess. But what about you, Frank? You must have some relatives beside that regiment of yours. You said you were from back east, right?"

"Yeah, Pennsylvania. I had a brother and a sister so I suppose I must have nieces and nephews by now. But anyone else would be back in Germany."

"You never tried to keep in touch?"

Frank shrugged. "Not really. Writing's a chore. But how are you doing here? The new hospital all set up?"

"Pretty much. It's big and looks to be permanent. From what we're hearing it doesn't look like we'll be moving west anytime soon."

"No, we took a licking and that's for sure. Got to raise more troops and re-equip the ones already here. And we need to figure out how to beat those bastards in the field. Right now they're too fast and too tough. We need to get faster and tougher, too."

"What will you be doing? Are they going to rebuild your regiment?"

"Not sure. I'm supposed to meet with some officer a little later today and find out what my assignment's gonna be."

"Well, I'm sure they'll give you something important. You've got a lot more experience fighting them than most." Becca paused and frowned. "At least you will be fighting them."

"What you do counts as fighting, too, Becca."

"Do you know how many times I've been told that?"

"Uh, about as many times as you've complained about it?"

Becca snorted in exasperation and her expression grew angry. But then she laughed. "I reckon that's about right! But all day long I patch up men who do fight them and I'm getting tired of it. I want to fight them, too!"

"Well, maybe there's your chance," he said pointing to a handbill which had been tacked to a post. It had a drawing of woman in a fanciful buckskin outfit with a skirt pointing a very long rifle. The words said: *Memphis is in Danger! Women of spirit needed for the Memphis Women's Sharpshooters!* And then there was an address. "You're certainly a woman of spirit, Becca!"

Becca glanced at the handbill and scowled. "Yeah, I've seen those before. I can just imagine what they do: tea socials and sewing bees to make their pretty costumes! I doubt any of them would even know how to hold a gun!"

"No, you are probably right. I'm sorry I don't have a better suggestion." Actually he was very glad he *didn't* have a better suggestion! The thought of Becca *deliberately* putting herself in harm's way chilled him to the bone. In spite of every effort, she had become important to him. This was getting awkward, so he checked the time. "I really need to get going, Becca. It's been very nice talking with you."

"And you. I guess if they send you off to a new assignment we probably won't see each other. So you take care of yourself! I might not be around to patch you up next time! And try to write—if it's not too much a chore."

He reached out and took her hand and she didn't pull it away. "I'll try. And you take care of yourself, too. I'll miss you, Becca."

She came closer and kissed him on the cheek. They squeezed hands and then she turned and walked away. He watched her go and then turned himself and went down the street, telling himself he was being stupid. He was twice her age after all. *It's war! People do stupid things in wars!* He wasn't sure if that was a justification for… well, for anything, but who knew? Maybe it was. The only thing he was sure of was that she was a hell of a girl and that he cared about her.

But for the moment he had other things he had to do. Memphis was now a garrison town and though it might have been ten times the size of Albuquerque or Santa Fe, it was coming to look like them: soldiers and the establishments which catered to soldiers everywhere. Enormous supply dumps and vast canvas cities on the outskirts. And the war was right across the river—at least potentially.

There were refugee camps, too, but they were being emptied out as quickly as possible. Most of the refugees were farmers or ranchers and they were in great demand. With the loss of the Great Plains, the country was facing a food shortage, so these men and women were being put to work on new farms being carved out of the forests east of the great river.

The fragment of Funston's Second Army which had made it back had been reorganized, reinforced, and deployed to defend a long stretch of the Mississippi north and south of Memphis. Frank had been told to wait for new orders and now it looked as though he was finally going to get them. He made his way through the streets and then out into the camps until he found the place he'd been told to go. To his surprise, the sign outside the large wooden building said: HQ 1st Cav. Div. A whole division of cavalry? In his experience, cavalry came in regiments and sometimes brigades. This sounded interesting.

He went inside, identified himself and then waited for nearly an hour until someone came to get him. He was led into an office where a major was sitting at a desk. "Ah, Dolfen, is it?" He stood up and they shook hands. "I'm Major Snyder, the personnel officer for the division. We're trying to put this thing together and I can tell you we need experienced officers! I'm told you were an acting squadron commander in the 5th."

"Yes, sir, for about a week."

"Yes, that was a tragedy out there in New Mexico. But I understand your boys did a hell of a job. We are going to rebuild the 5th, but it's not going to be anything like the old 5th."

"Really, sir?"

"No, I don't think I need to tell you that basic horse cavalry is finding it very tough going against the Martians. They have good mobility, but little real punch. Well, we're going to change that. We'll still have some horses, but in addition, we'll have armored cars, motorcycles, and some motorized artillery. When we come up against a Martian we'll have the means to hurt the sons-of-bitches." He looked at Frank. "You interested, Lieutenant?"

Frank smiled. "Yes, sir, I sure am."

* * * * *

JUNE, 1910, MEMPHIS, TENNESSEE

Rebecca Harding turned to look back a few times, but Frank Dolfen was soon lost to sight in the crowd. She liked him. She liked him a lot. She'd liked him from when they'd first met near her home in central New Mexico, and she'd grown to like him even more on the long retreat to Memphis. He was strong and capable and he cared about the people under his command—or in his care. He'd saved her life and he didn't seem to resent the fact that she might have saved his.

But he was going off to fight—and she would be left behind again.

I'm tired of being left behind!

She was tired of her nursing duties, too. And she was getting tired of the people she worked with. Miss Chumley was being given greater responsibilities in the expanding medical corps and had little time for Becca these days. Clarissa Forester was impossible to talk to since she did nothing but quote scripture anymore. And even Sam was gone. He'd vanished once they reached Memphis and she had no idea if he would ever be back.

She should go back to her camp, but she didn't want to. Instead she walked back down the street to that post and ripped the handbill off its tack. She looked at the ridiculous drawing and then she looked at the address. She folded the paper and stuffed it in her pocket.

Maybe it's time for a change!

* * * * *

JUNE, 1910, WASHINGTON, D.C.

Lieutenant Colonel Andrew Comstock looked in awe at the face of his infant son. He was the most amazing and wonderful thing he'd ever seen. So little! Little tiny hands and little tiny feet and wide blue eyes when he wasn't sleeping. He sat in a chair next to the bed where Victoria was dozing and held their son. It hadn't been an especially difficult delivery according to the doctor and Victoria's mother, but the noises coming through the door had been more terrifying than a Martian heat ray.

But everything was fine now. The baby was healthy and the mother was healthy and Andrew was a father. *A father!* It didn't seem possible. He had to admit that he hadn't been terribly enthusiastic at the notion, but now, with this tiny miracle nestled in his arms, he couldn't imagine how he'd ever doubted that this was a good idea.

Victoria stirred and then yawned and stretched. "Hi there, Mommy," said Andrew, grinning ear to ear.

"Hi, yourself, Daddy," she replied, smiling in turn. They both giggled and then instantly hushed as the baby made a little sound. It was just a sound, but it delighted both of them. The tiniest thing delighted them now. It was like being drunk. Drunk on love.

"How are you feeling?" he asked.

"Tired and a little sore. But fine."

"You look beautiful. Just like him."

"So are we settled on the name?"

"Arthur Benjamin Comstock. It has a nice ring to it. My father and your father. Of course it does give the poor little fellow the initials ABC. He'll get kidded about it in school."

"Well, that's a few years off yet."

"Yes."

They watched the baby sleeping for a while and Victoria dozed off again. Andrew felt like he could sit there forever in perfect bliss. But that wasn't possible. He'd been given a few days leave, but soon he'd back to work. Trying to figure out some way to win this war. He looked at his son.

And I will figure it out! Me or someone else or all of us working together! The war will be over long before you ever have to worry about it!

I promise.

THE END

MARTIAN INTERLUDE TWO

CYCLE 597,844.8, JAKALDAR

Tanbradjus sat in the visitor's gallery of the great conference chamber and watched the clan representatives slowly maneuver their travel chairs toward the exits. It had been a long and contentious meeting and it felt certain that very few of the representatives were entirely satisfied with the results.

Tanbradjus certainly was not satisfied.

Not that it had any say in the matter. It was a senior member of the Bajantus Clan, but not nearly senior enough to have a place in the Council of Three Hundred. Galdan, leader of the clan, and two close subordinates had represented the clan at this meeting. Tanbradjus had been allowed to observe, but nothing more. What it had observed had shaken it to the core of its being.

If anyone lives to record the story of our race, will they point to this moment and say: this was the beginning of the end?

Decisions had been made this day. Decisions which set the Race upon a road from which it would be difficult, perhaps impossible, to deviate. Tanbradjus strongly disagreed with those decisions, but naturally it would obey the commands of the clan leaders and if they had decided to follow the decisions of the Council, then so, of course, would it.

Tanbradjus noted Galdan heading for an exit and moved to join it as it had been directed. When it arrived, it was startled to see a crowd gathered there and even more startled when it realized the reason for the crowd. There were scores of waiting travel chairs and they all mounted weapons! They were guards, guards for the Council delegates. There were clan sigils painted on the chairs and as each delegation exited, their guards moved in to accompany them.

Tanbradjus was stunned. Nothing like this had happened since the end of the last major conflict, thousands of cycles ago. It stopped its chair a distance away and waited until Galdan and its party emerged from the chamber, collected its two guards, and moved away. Tanbradjus then approached and after being recognized by the guards, allowed to join the group as they passed into a major concourse and headed for the clan compound.

"Ah, Tanbradjus," said Galdan, "there you are. What did you think of the meeting?"

"A momentous occasion, Commander."

Galdan waved its tendrils in amusement. "Always careful with your words. Well, in these times, that is a true virtue. We must all be careful with our words."

"And apparently careful in matters beyond simple words," said Tanbradjus, indicating the guards. "Are things truly so dire?"

"Do you mean are we on the verge of starting a new war? It might have come to that, I suppose. The meeting was contentious and several delegates, fearing assassination for their views, insisted on bringing guards. When word of that got out, others decided to bring them as well. Ultimately nearly all did. But I think their presence shocked almost everyone as much as it clearly has you.

That may have helped in reaching a consensus. Every member lived through those times and they have no wish to repeat them."

"Is it truly a consensus, Commander?"

"Does it matter? The dissenters have been silenced and the majority will act. There will be grumbling, of course, but any who go beyond mere grumbling will be crushed. That was made very clear, I thought."

"Yes, very clear."

They reached the entrance to the clan compound and Tanbradjus was startled to see more guards. There had been none there when it had left to observe the meeting. Perhaps they were a reasonable precaution at that. While it was clear that Galdan—and thus the Bajantus Clan—would obey the decision of the Council, Galdan had argued strongly against the measures which had been decided upon. In the eyes of some that could mark them as a danger to the common good. In the past, clans had been exterminated for 'the common good.'

Once the gates were sealed behind them and their chairs parked, Galdan declared that it needed sustenance after the long meeting and invited Tanbradjus to join it. They proceeded to the feeding chamber. This was a circular space with padded, reclining benches along the walls. The draining device was in the center and a food animal was brought through a door leading from the holding pens. It was one of several different species used by the Race as food. This particular one was a quadruped and it moved readily into the draining device, which had been designed to look like the food distribution devices in the holding pens. All the food animals had been bred over many thousands of cycles for maximum productivity and docility. The creature barely responded when the device restrained it and the feeding probes entered its body.

"A shame that the prey creatures on the Target World are not so easy to handle," said Galdan before inserting the feeding tube into its mouth.

"Eventually they shall be, Commander," said Tanbradjus before inserting its own tube. "As I recall, even these beasts had to be domesticated in the far past."

Galdan waved a few of his tendril in acknowledgement and continued to ingest the beast's circulatory fluid. Tanbradjus did the same, reflecting on the sensory input the fluid provided. On the target world, the risk of the local contagions had required that the fluids taken from the local animals be processed and sterilized. Reports indicated that it changed the experience significantly. Still, it was necessary; the idea of being stricken down by some microscopic creature was actually quite horrifying.

When they had finished, the carcass was removed for reprocessing. Galdan leaned backward in its couch and regarded Tanbradjus for a long time before speaking again. "So you disagree with the decisions made today?"

"It is not my place…"

"I'm not asking about your place, Tanbradjus. I'm asking if you disagree. Answer my question."

There was no choice but to reply. "Yes, Commander, I do disagree. I believe the decision to be an error."

"A grave error?"

"Yes."

Galdan became silent again. Tanbradjus grew nervous. Had it made an even worse error?

Finally the clan leader stirred. "No matter how much we might disagree with this decision, we *shall* carry it out."

"Of course."

"However… it might not be as simple as that."

"Commander?"

"You observed the conference, but you no doubt noticed that several delegates made statements calling into question whether those on the target world would obey the new directives."

"I did and must confess that they confused me. How could they *not* obey?"

"How indeed. There have been reports from the target world. Reports of a most disturbing nature. I shall make them available to you. But to summarize: there could be those on the target world who might not obey."

Tanbradjus waved its tendrils in confusion. How could such a thing be possible?

"Therefore," continued Galdan. "I am going to dispatch you with the next wave of transports to ensure that the new directives are carried out."

"You are sending me to the target world, Commander?"

"I just said that, did I not?"

"Yes, Commander."

"Very well then. Make your preparations for departure."

Scott Washburn

COUNTERATTACK!

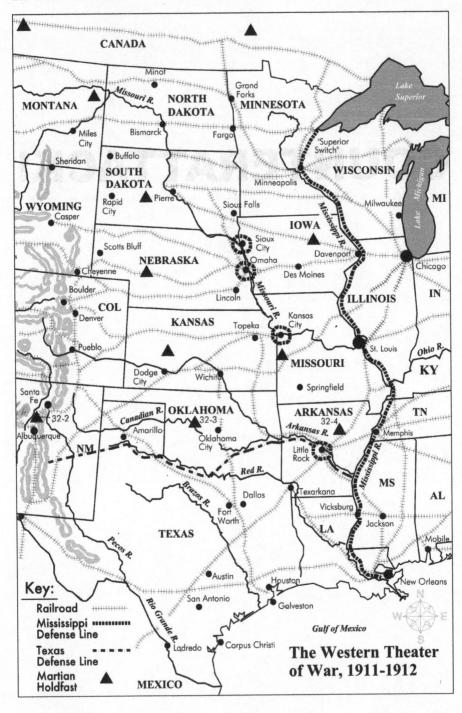

**The Western Theater
of War, 1911-1912**

Key:

Railroad ┼┼┼┼┼┼┼

Mississippi ▪▪▪▪▪▪▪
Defense Line

Texas ▬ ▬ ▬
Defense Line

Martian ▲
Holdfast

PROLOGUE

CYCLE 597, 844.7, SOUTH OF HOLDFAST 32-4

"Subgroup 2-3, destroy that weapon emplacement to your left. We will be enfiladed by it if it is not neutralized."

The subgroup leader acknowledged the command and Qetjnegartis looked on in satisfaction as the three war machines of the unit concentrated the fire from their heat rays to obliterate the prey-creature heavy projectile thrower. The clan was launching an attack to destroy a fortified prey-creature city which had resisted several lesser attacks in the past. Nearly all of the vast, flat plains between the mountains to the west and the large river to the east had fallen to the Race during the great offensive a half-cycle ago. But several cities, located on rivers, and thus not dependent on the enemy's usual—and vulnerable—transport system, had held out and fortified themselves. Qetjnegartis' clan, busy constructing new holdfasts and increasing their numbers, had not had the means to reduce these irritants until now.

At the end of the long advance, Qetjnegartis had questioned the decision to suspend offensive operations and consolidate, but it had to admit that the vastly increased strength of the clan was a comfort. They now had three fortified holdfasts, with a fourth nearly completed, and over two hundred members. In less than two-tenths of a cycle that number would swell to over three hundred as a new generation of buds matured. Qetjnegartis briefly regarded the pulsating sack on its side where its own bud was growing.

What a difference from those perilous days, a cycle ago, when the Bajantus Clan had been reduced to just eight individuals, clinging to a half-ruined holdfast! Extinction had been a real possibility, but the prey-creatures who inhabited this world had not taken advantage of the clan's weakness and the danger had passed.

Qetjnegartis hoped that the Race, here on the target world, had not made that same mistake.

While it was true that the clan and the Race were stronger, the evidence indicated that the prey-creatures had grown stronger, too. Warriors in huge numbers were massing on the far bank of the great river. Unlike the earlier armies, these new forces seemed well supplied with the heavy projectile throwers and the armored gun-vehicles which had proved alarmingly effective against the Race's fighting machines. In addition, they were building strong defensive works incorporating a cast stone material which was very resistant to heat rays.

Fortunately, the place they were attacking now had few of them. Most of the defenses were simply heaped piles of dirt and loose stones. Even though this bolstered the prey-creatures' defenses significantly, it was not as effective as the stone.

"The enemy fire has been nearly suppressed, Commander," reported Fadjnadtur, the second-in-command. "Shall we advance?"

Qetjnegartis evaluated the information coming to it over the tactical network. Brief but repeated thrusts against the city's defenses appeared to have destroyed most of the heavy weapons on this side of the perimeter. Projectiles were still falling periodically from more distant weapons, but not in great numbers. Had the enemy been weakened enough to permit a final assault? It had no wish to risk heavy casualties here. Every member of the Race was expendable, of course, but only if the objective was worth the cost. The clan had grown strong, but not so strong that it could throw away lives frivolously. This prey-creature enclave was an annoyance, but nothing more.

Still, the information indicated that an assault might succeed without unacceptable loss. Experience had shown that once the fighting machines closed with the enemy, the prey-creatures often lost cohesion and would flee. Although not always; Qetjnegartis' thoughts went back to a savage fight in a mountain pass where the prey had fought to the last and inflicted terrible casualties - nearly slaying Qetjnegartis in the process.

"Commander?" prompted Fadjnadtur. "A decision is required."

Qetjnegartis was annoyed. Fadjnadtur had arrived with the second wave of transports and was a close bud-mate to Valprandar, who had taken over from Qetjnegartis and been in command until it was slain at the end of the great offensive. It was clear that Fadjnadtur was not pleased that Qetjnegartis was back in charge again and had shown this sort of disrespect on several occasions.

"And a decision you shall have, *subcommander*. All groups, concentrate for an attack on area twelve."

With the great increase in the strength of the clan, its fighting forces had been organized along traditional lines. Three fighting machines constituted a subgroup commanded by one of the three; three subgroups made up a group with a separate commander in its own machine, and three groups, a total of thirty machines, plus a machine for the commander, made a *battlegroup*. Qetjnegartis had a full battlegroup with it today and now all its machines - plus the command machines of itself and Fadjnadtur - were concentrating against a single portion of the prey-creature's defenses.

This tactic had been used with great success before. The majority of the prey-creatures' forces - the foot-warriors, the heavy projectile throwers, and the armored gun-vehicles - could not match the speed and agility of the Race's fighting machines. Therefore, the Race would begin an attack spread out along the prey's lines, probing and doing what damage they could without risking heavy losses. Then, once the enemy had been weakened and the location of its major weapons mapped, the attack force would concentrate against a single spot and break through before the prey could react. Qetjnegartis hoped to do the same thing now.

The machines swept in from right and left into a tight grouping and then advanced at full speed. The ground they passed over was mostly flat, featureless, and easily traversable. Fortunately, there had been no inclement weather for several days and the soil was firm. After a period of the heavy precipitation—so common on this wet, wet world—the soil could become a soft and sticky mass which would slow or even immobilize a fighting machine. There were no such troubles today and they quickly closed on the enemy defenses.

The fire from the prey-creatures intensified as they drew near, but it was not severe. The larger weapons on the line had been destroyed by the earlier forays and the long-range fire couldn't adjust for their rapid movements quickly enough to be effective. There were several groupings of larger projectile throwers in trenches close behind the main line and Qetjnegartis ordered these to be blanketed with the toxic eradicator dust. They ceased firing almost immediately. The remaining fire was mostly from the smaller, portable weapons carried by the foot-warriors, although there were still some of the slightly heavier, rapid fire weapons. Those could be dangerous and heat rays stabbed out to silence them as the range decreased.

As they neared the line of trenches, the fire had almost ceased. The enemy works were blackened and burned by the extreme temperatures the heat rays produced. Clouds of smoke wafted skyward from fires which burned in many places. Beyond the trenches lay fields strewn with wreckage, and beyond those were the structures of the city itself. Many of the closer ones were ablaze. Not a living foe could be seen…

Suddenly, one of the lead fighting machines lurched forward and came to a halt in a strange bent-over position. Had it been hit? Perhaps a limb damaged? Qetjnegartis had seen no explosion from a projectile thrower. Another machine moved to assist and then it too stumbled and nearly fell. It staggered backward and then stood upright again.

"Report! What is happening?" demanded Qetjnegartis.

"There are pits in the ground, commander. Hidden pits. If we step upon them, the limbs of our machines will crash through for half their length. Jandrangnar's machine is stuck, and mine nearly became so."

The entire advance had stopped and enemy projectiles from distant throwers were starting to find their range. "Spray the ground with your heat rays! Uncover these traps! The attack must resume at once. Madgprindle, assist Jandrangnar."

Immediately heat rays blasted the ground in front of them. Qetjnegartis had no idea if this would reveal any of the pits, but there was no other option. The advance resumed and only one other machine encountered a pit before they were across the line of trenches. There, they paused to regroup.

The enemy fire was almost entirely stopped now, except for a few projectiles still falling around Jandrangnar's machine. And there were no prey-creatures to be seen anywhere. This was unexpected. During one of the great battles of the past offensive, the clan had smashed through the enemy lines and were immediately confronted with masses of fleeing prey and a few disorganized counterattacks by reserves rushed to the scene. But here there was… nothing.

"Group 1, turn east. Group 2, turn west, Fadjnadtur accompany them. Follow the line of entrenchment. Destroy all you encounter. I will take Group 3 into the city." The battlegroup split into three segments as directed and went in search of the enemy. They surely had not destroyed all of them.

The city to Qetjnegartis' front had been badly damaged by earlier attacks and the structures closest to the defense lines had been reduced to piles of blackened rubble. The smaller structures used by the prey were often constructed of flammable materials and would be completely consumed by the heat rays in this oxygen-rich environment, leaving little behind. But the larger structures were made of sturdier materials and their destruction produced large mounds of debris—treacherous footing for the fighting machines. That was the case here and few easy paths forward could be found.

Despite this, the leading machines of the group advanced, firing into structures which had not yet caught fire. Occasionally there would be returning fire from prey inside the structures, but their weapons did no damage. Qetjnegartis followed along behind the rest. The lack of significant resistance was… unsettling.

"Fadjnadtur, report your situation."

"We are proceeding as you ordered, Commander," came the immediate reply. "The trenches are mostly unoccupied. Very little resistance. We seem to have broken them."

"Do you see any of the prey fleeing?"

"Only a few. The rest must have fled already." Qetjnegartis checked with the commander of Group 1 and it reported the same thing. Had the prey-creatures truly all fled?

Its attention was brought back to the situation at hand when a building collapsed right across the path the group was taking. Flames from it leapt skyward and it was apparent the path would be blocked for some time. Qetjnegartis hesitated for an instant and then commanded, "Split up. Subgroup 3-1, go right, the rest of us will go left. We will reassemble on the other side of this." Three of the machines turned and went down the passage as directed. The others turned left.

The structures were taller here, higher than the fighting machines, and closely spaced. They could only proceed single file and they were closed in on either side like they were in a mountain pass.

"Commander!" a sudden communication came from Fadjnadtur.

"What is it?"

"We are being attacked! Prey-creatures are emerging from underground chambers! Hidden heavy projectile throwers are firing at us! They are behind us, too! We are being attacked from all sides!" A moment later the commander of Group 1 reported the same thing.

"Can you defeat these attacks?" asked Qetjnegartis.

"Unknown," replied Fadjnadtur. "More of the enemy are arriving and we are taking damage."

This had all the marks of an ambush. The prey-creatures had feigned weakness to draw them in! As if in confirmation, an explosion billowed up nearby, shaking Qetjnegartis inside its machine. "Commander! We are under attack!" exclaimed the leader of Group 3.

Prey-creatures were appearing from the buildings and out of the rubble. Some were firing weapons, others were throwing explosive bombs. Several of the rapid-fire weapons began firing from the upper floors of the structures and more bombs were thrown down from the rooftops. One bounced off the cockpit of Qetjnegartis' machine and exploded an instant later, slamming the machine sideways. Smoke engulfed it, blocking vision.

A flood of information came over the tactical net, too much for even Qetjnegartis to process immediately. Subgroup 3-1, which it had sent off alone, was under heavy attack both by the foot-warriors and by armored gun-vehicles, which had appeared from between the buildings. Group 1 had encountered more of the pit traps and had been attacked while they were trying to extricate themselves. Fadjnadtur and Group 2 were in a crossfire of heavy weapons which had been concealed in the rubble. All were taking damage and the actual strength of the enemy was still unknown. The situation was degenerating at an alarming rate and even Fadjnadtur's plaintive, *Commander, what should we do?* was no consolation.

"All groups withdraw," it commanded. "Fall back to our starting positions. Leave no one behind!" A chorus of acknowledgments came in reply.

Qetjnegartis turned its machine back the way it had come, spraying the tops of the buildings around it randomly with its heat ray. It paused to allow one of the others to lead the way and then followed. The structures on both sides were burning, but enemy fire came from them, too—the creatures were risking immolation to carry out their attacks. It ordered its subordinates to increase their speed.

Suddenly, the machine in front of it, piloted by Sladgenupral, went tumbling forward, to crash in a heap on the ground. Its legs were tangled in a heavy cable and thrashed futilely, unable to get free. Qetjnegartis was quite certain that no cable had blocked the passage when they came the other way. Instantly, swarms of the prey-creatures erupted from the buildings and, seemingly, from the ground itself to attack the downed machine.

Qetjnegartis knew that these enemies would be carrying their explosive bombs and try to place them on the vulnerable parts of Sladgenupral's machine. It activated its heat ray on the low-power, wide-angle mode and swept it across the prey-creatures and the crippled fighting machine. At this reduced power, it would not harm Sladgenupral, but it would still be lethal to the enemy. Score of the miserable animals were slain in moments, but not before some had achieved their purpose. Five or six explosions hammered at the machine, sending bits of it hurtling skyward and filling the space between the buildings with smoke and dust.

It continued to sweep the heat ray into the smoke and was soon joined by a subordinate who came up beside it. The smoke dissipated and they could see that the fighting machine was badly damaged. Telemetry indicated that Sladgenupral was alive, but injured. Qetjnegartis moved forward to extract it, while its subordinate deployed a carrying pod. Some fire was still rattling off the skin of its machine, but the main enemy attack had been destroyed. Qetjnegartis reached the wreck and used its manipulators to pry open the hatch.

"Commander! Beware!"

Almost simultaneous with the warning came a heavy blow to its machine. An enemy vehicle had emerged from gaps between the buildings and opened fire. Another trap! Qetjnegartis brought up its heat ray, reset it to maximum power, and then fired at the vehicle. Another impact, even more powerful than the first, struck and sent Qetjnegartis staggering back. To its dismay, daylight was seeping in through a hole in the cockpit! It twisted the machine sideways to turn the vulnerable spot away from the enemy and continued to fire the heat ray. The enemy vehicle exploded, and the immediate threat was eliminated. But how many more were still waiting?

"Commander, are you all right?"

"Yes, but this machine is damaged. Quickly, recover Sladgenupral, and let us leave this place."

This was done, and the group managed to break clear of the structures and into the open. The other two groups were gathering along the enemy trench line to provide covering fire. Qetjnegartis noted that three of their machines were missing. The battlegroup reassembled and quickly fell back until they were out of range of the enemy weapons. There they halted to evaluate the situation.

One of them dead, three injured, four machines destroyed, and half the rest damaged; and the enemy city still there. Not a good result at all. Qetjnegartis was not pleased.

This is intolerable.

* * * * *

JUNE, 1911, FORT MYER, DISTRICT OF COLUMBIA

Brevet Colonel Andrew Comstock sat down at the breakfast table and picked up the morning edition of *The Washington Post*. The headline story celebrated the recent victory at Little Rock. Andrew already knew the full details from his military briefings and chuckled in amusement at the paper's fanciful descriptions of the 'gallant defense'. Well, it had been pretty gallant, and he had to hand it to the troops who had succeeded in beating off the Martian attack. Andrew had seen for himself the consequences of an unsuccessful defense and he could imagine the chaos inside Little Rock once the enemy had pierced the defensive lines. That the men had not panicked, but instead had stuck to their posts and then struck back, spoke well of them - very well indeed. Most of the garrison was made up of the 77th Division which had survived the long retreat from Santa Fe last year. Veterans for sure! Andrew had shared part of that journey with them.

His wife, Victoria, swept into the room with little Arthur on her hip and a cup of coffee in her other hand, which she gracefully slid onto the table next to him. "Good morning, dear," she said, smiling. "Breakfast will be ready in a little bit."

"Thanks."

She disappeared for a moment and then came back and sat down at the table with her own cup. Arthur tried to grab it away from her when she took a sip, but she fended him off successfully. "What will you be doing today, dear?"

"Oh, the same as always," he replied absently, still paging through the paper. "Reading reports.

405

Writing replies. That sort of thing."

"Will you be taking any of those inspection trips again soon?"

"I'll be going to Aberdeen, Philadelphia, and then up to Long Island in a couple of weeks, why?"

"I was... I was hoping we could look for a house soon." Andrew put down the paper and looked at his wife. She was smiling faintly as she bounced the baby gently in her arms.

He glanced around at their comfortable surroundings. Since their marriage, a little less than two years ago, they had lived with Victoria's parents in their cozy home at Fort Myer, just across the Potomac from Washington. His father-in-law, Brevet Brigadier General Hawthorne, was also his boss at the Ordnance Department. They got along well and the house, which was government property, was more than big enough for all of them - and a couple of servants, too. He was perfectly happy staying here.

But Victoria had been hinting at getting their own place for a while now. Her mother was a delightful lady, but Andrew had noticed a growing tension between her and her daughter. Victoria clearly wanted to be the mistress of her own home...

"You're getting the salary of a full colonel now, dear," she said. "We should be able to afford it."

"My permanent rank is only major. If the war should end, I'll go back to that quicker than..."

"And how likely is that?"

"It'll end eventually..." he said lamely.

"Not any time soon," she countered. "I've heard you and Dad say so a dozen times when you thought I couldn't hear."

There was no answer to that, but fortunately, the maid chose that moment to come in with their breakfast, so he didn't have to. He busied himself with his food, but he could sense his wife's gaze on him. Yes, the war was not going to end any time soon. The Martians had landed in 1908 and things were still going their way. They had occupied nearly all of the Great Plains from Canada down to Texas and from the Rockies to the Mississippi. Except for the path through Texas, the country was cut in two.

Andrew had been an eyewitness to much of it. He'd been with the army when it first encountered the Martians in strength. He'd been through defeats and victories, he'd sat in on conferences with the President and high-ranking generals, and he'd conferred with brilliant scientists and engineers trying to devise better weapons to fight the merciless foe. And at age twenty-five he was a bird-colonel drawing the amazing amount of $333.33 a month, plus allowances. Even his permanent rank of major paid $250.00. Yes, they probably could afford a home of their own, even with the money he sent to his widowed mother.

"There are no empty residences left here at the fort," he said, not quite ready to give in. "And have you seen the prices in the city? Every decent place has been snapped up by generals, congressmen, diplomats, or lobbyists." It was true: the wartime expansion of the military and the government had swelled the city's population to the bursting point. There was a serious housing shortage.

"They are building a lot of nice new houses in Alexandria," said Victoria, teasing the baby with a piece of bacon. "Electric lights, indoor plumbing..."

"How would I get to work from way out there?"

"We could buy an automobile."

"If we could find one! All the auto manufacturers are building vehicles for the army these days, you know."

"Well then we might still find a place closer by. With all the comings and goings, surely some houses become vacant. We can at least try. Please, dear?"

He realized this was one battle he couldn't win. "Of course, love. Perhaps this Saturday."

"Thank you, Andrew! Oh, it will be lovely!"

"Uh, huh," Andrew went back to his paper. He snorted when he saw the article on page four mentioning that the Panama Canal was scheduled to open in a few weeks. In normal times that would have been the headline story on the front page.

But these weren't normal times.

* * * * *

JULY, 1911, PANAMA CITY, PANAMA

Lieutenant Commander Drew Harding sprawled on his bunk aboard the battleship *USS Minnesota* and tried to ignore the heat. It wasn't possible, of course; it was well into the rainy season now and even when it wasn't raining, it was terribly humid. The steady breezes off the Pacific would bring some relief, but little of that could find its way into the steel bowels of the large warship. Harding was wearing nothing but his underwear, but he was still dripping with sweat. He was tempted to go up on deck to get some of that breeze, but that would mean putting on his uniform. He gave up on that idea and closed his eyes. His next watch wasn't for a few hours and perhaps he could sleep for a while.

He was just dozing off when the door to his quarters banged open, bringing him awake again. It was his roommate, Hank Coleman. "Wake up, sleepy head!" cried the man with appalling cheerfulness.

"Why?" growled Harding.

"Mail boat! You've got a letter!"

That brought him more fully awake. Mail delivery to Panama was pretty regular, but he didn't usually get anything. His mother wasn't much of a writer, his father was too busy, and his girlfriend had broken things off when he'd opted for sea duty. He rolled over and put out his hand. "Gimme."

"Looks important!" continued Coleman. "From Washington! Maybe it's your promotion to admiral!" Even more interested, he sat up and looked at the letter. It was from Washington, but then he recognized the handwriting.

"Nope, it's from a friend of mine in the Army Ordnance Department, Andy Comstock."

"What're you doing hanging around with the army?" asked Coleman.

"Oh, we used to meet a lot when I was on Admiral Twining's staff on the Ordnance Bureau. There were all these meetings to discuss new weapons and such. I was just an ensign then and he was a second lieutenant and all we did was fetch coffee for the brass and clean up afterward. Well, it wasn't all drudgery, they'd have these really fine dinners after the meetings at the officers' club, and we got to tag along. Twining didn't skimp on the liquor and we'd get pretty potted by the end of 'em. Comstock was a good guy and we've stayed in touch." He tore open the envelope.

"And now you're the gunnery officer on a battleship," said Coleman. "Bet he's jealous."

"Ha! Don't bet on that. He's a full bird-colonel now!"

"Really? I know they're promoting everyone right and left these days, but a colonel? Wait, you mean he's *that* Comstock? The one who did all that stuff out west when the war started?"

"None other."

"And you're friends with him? Wow, how about an autograph? Can I touch you?" Coleman leaned over and poked him in the shoulder.

"Beat it, you goof!"

Coleman smirked and strolled off, banging the door shut behind him. Harding snorted. Hank was okay, but he could be a jerk at times. He pulled Andy's letter out of the envelope and unfolded it. It was dated almost two weeks earlier, but that was about normal for mail delivery. It started off in the usual fashion: *how are you? I'm fine, etc. etc.* Then there were several paragraphs describing Andrew's infant son. Drew had little interest in children and the man he remembered hadn't either, so the proud gushing was both boring and a little surprising. He'd noticed the same phenomenon with his older brother and a cousin. *The little imps do something to our brains...* He resolved to continue avoiding them.

The next page was more interesting. Andrew's description of a recent joint meeting between the army and the navy ordnance staffs, like the ones Drew had just mentioned to Coleman, had him laughing with a few sarcastic comments about people they both knew. But then he wrote: *The big topic for the meeting was that the stand-in for the land ironclads has started testing. I'll be going up to Philadelphia to see it in a few weeks.* Ah, Drew had been wondering how those projects were going. Both the army and the navy were developing enormous war machines, commonly called 'land ironclads'. They were going to be like warships on caterpillar tracks. But constructing and perfecting machines of that size was proving very difficult and they were still a long way from being ready. So a smaller and simpler version was being built as a substitute. He was pleased that they were into the testing phase already.

But enough about me, continued Andy, *what have you been doing? Enjoying your exotic location? Entertaining the lovely señoritas? And what about the canal? They say it's about to open, have you been through it yet?*

As a matter of fact, Drew had been through the canal, just the previous week. The *Minnesota* and a dozen other ships had been among the first to make the passage. It had been as impressive as all get-out. The enormous concrete locks had lifted the ships up to the level of Lake Gatun and then back down to the Pacific on the other side of the isthmus. It had seemed almost miraculous; the *Minnesota*, all sixteen thousand *tons* of her, raised eighty-five feet simply by opening some valves to let water into the locks, and then set back down again, gently as a feather, by letting the water out of the other set of locks. The cruise along the lake, artificially created by a dam, had been impressive, too, especially the enormous excavation at the Culebra Cut, which sliced right through the Continental Divide.

It had been a little scary, too. The Cut was still very unstable and there had been swarms of workers still moving earth there as they cruised past. Drew had seen stones and even large boulders tumble down the slopes into the water. A few small rocks had actually bounced off the ship. It wasn't safe, but the rush to get the canal open had overridden safety concerns. The Martians were starting to move south from Mexico and until the army could get its forts built, the navy was the canal's primary defense. They needed to get more ships on the Pacific side and the long haul around Cape Horn was very difficult these days with most of the old coaling stations in Martian hands—er, tentacles.

But now there was a strong fleet on both sides. Drew was glad to be with the Pacific Fleet. It was a bit cooler on this side and Panama City was far more pleasant than the city of Colon on the Atlantic side. Not all that pleasant, though, and the *señoritas*, Andy mentioned had been noticeably absent.

The fact of the matter was that Panama had been turned into an enormous refugee camp and construction zone. Huge numbers of refugees, hundreds of thousands of them, had fled to Panama from both north and south to escape the Martians. Most had been put to work building the canal and their added labor had gotten it open far ahead of schedule. Many of the rest—mostly women and children—were growing the food needed to feed all the workers and themselves. Vast cities of tents and shacks had been erected to house them, although many simply slept in the streets of Colon and Panama City. More people were coming in all the time and the refugees now far outnumbered the native Panamanians. The locals didn't like that at all and they had turned sullen toward all foreigners, including the *Norteamericanos*. Fortunately, the army had plenty of troops here to keep order. Few people—even the Panamanians—even bothered to pretend that the United States wasn't running the place now.

But everyone was wondering if they had enough troops to defend the canal in the event of a serious attack. The construction crews which had built the canal were now working full steam on building concrete fortifications, but they weren't even close to being finished. It was probably going to be up to the navy for the near future. Drew was hoping to get a crack at the beasties at some point.

Andy finished up his letter with the expected best wishes, but there was a postscript after his signature: *I've been meaning to ask you and I finally remembered to put it in this letter. Do you have any relatives out west? I met a girl on my first trip out there named Rebecca Harding. Same last name as yours. Her family was killed in the first Martian attack. She had an aunt in Santa Fe, but God knows what's happened to her. I was just wondering if maybe you are related.*

Drew's eyebrows went up. He had a passel of grandparents, aunts, uncles, and cousins, but as far as he knew, they all lived in the Albany region, where he had grown up. Still, if anyone knew, it would be his grandmother. He hadn't written to her in ages. He checked the time and saw he still had a while until he had to get ready for duty. He rolled out of his bunk and sat down at the tiny desk the cabin boasted and pulled out a sheet of paper.

* * * * *

AUGUST, 1911, MEMPHIS, TENNESSEE

Captain Frank Dolfen took a tight hold on the reins of his horse as one of the roaring airplanes flew overhead a little too close for comfort - for both man and beast. "Damn it!" he muttered as his horse shied.

"By Jove!" cried the rider next to him. "Those blighters should be more careful!"

Dolfen regained control of his mount and glanced at the man. He was British, which could be instantly discerned from his accent, and almost as instantly from his uniform. This was nearly the same shade of khaki as the one Dolfen wore, but it was cut differently and had a number of small bits of decoration you would never find on an American uniform. And there was his hat; he wore a distinctly British, off-white pith helmet with a gleaming brass regimental badge on the front. The man's name was George Tom Molesworth Bridges, but as he was quick to inform everyone, he went by the name of 'Tom'. He held a brevet rank of major.

"Yeah, they should," agreed Dolfen. "But you know fliers."

'Not really, old man. Are they all like that?"

"Pretty much, from what I've seen. All as crazy as jack rabbits. 'Careful' doesn't seem to be in their vocabulary."

"And you say we'll be working with them?"

"That's the plan. Don't know if it will really work. Come on, the headquarters tent is over there." He turned his horse toward a large tent on the edge of the field the fliers had turned into an aerodrome a half-dozen miles north of the city of Memphis. As they got closer, they saw a large sign erected in front of the tent proclaiming it to be the headquarters of the 9th Air Group. It had an insignia with a red '9' and a yellow lightning bolt going through the hole in the 9. There were a number of men in the area of the tent along with a couple of women in dresses and a scattering of children, too. With the huge refugee camps in the area, the military posts were a magnet for people looking for work or extra food. It was like that back at Dolfen's own camp, too.

They dismounted, and Major Bridges bent to give one of the kids a coin to hold both of their horses. "Whew!" he said straightening up and pulling out a handkerchief. "Hot as India! Is it like this all the time?" He mopped sweat off his face.

"For another coupla months. Summers are hell, but the rest of the time it's not bad." Dolfen led the way into the command tent, past a sentry who came to attention for Dolfen, but looked in puzzlement for Bridge's rank. Technically, as a major, the Britisher rated a present arms, but the sentry obviously didn't know what he was. Until a few hours ago, Dolfen hadn't either.

Things were bustling inside the tent. Orderlies were moving to and fro with papers in their hands, clerks were hammering away on typewriters, and there were several people talking on field telephones. Electric lights hung from the canvas roof. Dolfen identified himself to a harried lieutenant who led them to, and then without ceremony, abandoned them with the group's commanding officer. This was a lieutenant colonel named Selfridge. His first name was also 'Tom' and Dolfen had briefly met him in the first days of the war. He was a good looking fellow, and like most of the officers these days, very young in Dolfen's eyes. The skin on the left side of his face had a smooth and shiny look to it—compliments of a Martian heat ray. Selfridge held the dubious distinction of being the first American pilot to be shot down by the Martians.

Selfridge popped to his feet when he saw them and greeted Dolfen enthusiastically. "Hello, Captain! Good to see you again! Come up a bit in the world since our last meeting, eh?"

"We both have, sir," replied Dolfen. Selfridge had been a captain and Dolfen just a sergeant when they'd met during a desperate retreat to get away from pursuing Martians. "This is Major Bridges, compliments of the 4th Queen's Own Hussars."

"Ah! Our British liaison!" exclaimed Selfridge. "I'd heard rumors we'd be getting one, but I wasn't sure I should believe it. Glad to meet you, Major!" He extended his hand and Bridges took it without hesitation. Dolfen had heard tales that Englishmen didn't like to shake hands, but he'd noticed no such reluctance with Bridges.

"A pleasure to meet, you, Colonel," replied the major. "Of course I'm technically a liaison to Captain Dolfen, here, but I'm sure we'll all be working together."

"That is the point, isn't it? To coordinate our ground and aerial forces?"

"Yes, sir," said Dolfen. "And my commander wants to send out my squadron the day after tomorrow. Are your fliers going to be ready to support us?"

"Yes indeed! My boys are champing at the bit to get out there!" replied Selfridge enthusiastically. "We've been restricted to training flights on the east side of the river and I can tell you that we're getting tired of that! But come on, let me show you around!" He grabbed his cap and led the way out of the tent back into the bright sunshine.

"I have four squadrons in the group," said Selfridge, waving his hand to take in the whole operation. "With four flights of four aircraft in each squadron, that makes for sixty-four altogether. Of course that's on paper. There are always aircraft out of service for maintenance or repairs due to accidents - always having accidents. On any given day we can usually put fifty in the air."

"Now that I take a closer look at these machines," said Bridges, "they seem more familiar. I do believe we have something rather like them."

Selfridge laughed. "I'm not surprised, Major! This is a British design we are building under license. They're Burgess-Dunne D.8s, to be exact. A nice aircraft! Faster and a lot more stable than the old Wright Flyers I cut my teeth on. Very easy to fly. We've modified them to make two-seaters out of them. We have a gunner in the front with his machine gun and the pilot sits behind him. It can carry a hundred-pound bomb, too."

Dolfen studied one of the aircraft sitting close by. It was the same horribly flimsy-looking wood, canvas, and wire contraption like others he'd seen, but the crewmen, instead of being completely in the open, sat inside an enclosed area, like some oversized bathtub or canoe. The motor and propeller was at the rear, right behind the pilot's seat. But the biggest change from the other models was the fact that the wings were angled back on each side of the center. So instead of just being long rectangles, the wings were shaped like an arrow, or a military rank chevron. It made them look like they were moving fast even when sitting on the ground.

"How far can they fly, Colonel? How long can they stay in the air?"

"With extra fuel instead of a bomb, they can go about three hundred miles and stay in the air almost five hours."

Dolfen frowned. "So assuming you want to get back, you can't go more than a hundred and fifty miles from here? That's going to limit how deeply we can penetrate into enemy territory, sir."

"True, although we do have a forward airfield on the other side of the river, so staging from there would give us a few more miles. But, Captain, me and my staff had an idea the other day that I want to run by you."

"Sir?"

"Well, as I understand it, your squadron isn't just horse cavalry anymore, is it?"

"No, sir. We have one troop on horses, one on motorcycles, and a troop of ten armored cars. We'll also have a battery of field guns towed by motor trucks attached to us most of the time."

"Good! So that means you'll also have some supply trucks along? To carry ammunition and food, and gasoline for those motorcycles?"

"A few…" admitted Dolfen, not much liking where this seemed to be going. Cavalry was supposed to be light and mobile. If you started loading it down with a big supply train…

"Well, we were thinking that if we sent along a few trucks carrying gasoline and maybe a few spare parts and a mechanic or two, we could set up temporary airstrips wherever there is a flat field to land on…"

"Plenty of them over there, sir. Flat as a griddle cake all the way to the Rockies."

"Exactly!" said Selfridge, smiling. "That way we could follow along with you out to the maximum range of our planes. You could set up a strip and we could land and refuel."

"I guess that could work, sir. As long as the trucks don't break down. Nothing but dirt roads out that way and not very good ones."

"Communications will be a critical factor, Colonel," said Bridges. "How will we coordinate our movements?"

"A good point, Major. But thanks to you British, that should not be a big problem."

"I don't follow you, sir."

"Those wonderful radio transmitters you've supplied us with, Major."

"Oh, those things. Can't say I know much about them, Colonel."

"They're marvelous! They have a range of hundreds of miles, batteries which last almost forever, and they don't weigh ten pounds. We've got one for each flight leader and more back here at headquarters. You have some with your squadron, too, don't you, Captain?"

"A few, yes, sir. We're still learning how to use them properly. I've only got a few men who can send and understand the Morse."

"True, they're just spark-gap transmitters, but with practice we should be able to tell you what we can see and you should be able to call us when you need help. And that's what this first mission is going to be, isn't it? Just practice?"

"More than that, sir," said Dolfen. "We'll be out there in territory where there are Martians. My orders are that if we find the enemy and have a reasonable chance of beating them, we are to attack."

"Well that sounds like fun, Captain! My boys are itching to take a crack at the bastards."

"Pardon me for asking, Colonel," said Bridges. "But do you really think these machines can survive to get close enough to hurt a Martian tripod? I've seen them in action and they're not easy to destroy."

"I guess we'll find out," replied Selfridge. Some of the joviality left his face and he nodded. "A lot of us are going to get killed, I'm sure. But if we can take some of them with us, it will be worthwhile, right, Captain?"

"Yes, sir. And I'm thinking that if we can coordinate what we do, my troopers attacking at the same time as your fliers, we might give them so much to worry about that they can't stop us."

"Yes. That was exactly my thought, too. I was there at the Battle of Prewitt, just like you, remember. The enemy tripods are nasty customers, but they can only fire at one thing at a time. If they are engaged with your cavalry and armored cars and field guns and then my boys come flying in, well, we could overwhelm them."

"Sounds good… in theory, Colonel," said Bridges.

"Well, that's what we are here for, isn't it? To put the theory into practice? Let's go back to my office and we'll take a look at the maps and plan out our operation."

* * * * *

AUGUST, 1911, MEMPHIS, TENNESSEE

"All right, let's try it again. Slowly let out your breath and then squeeze the trigger." Rebecca Harding stepped back and watched Abigail LaPlace struggling with her rifle. The weapon, a Springfield 1903, was really too large and heavy for the girl, but when Becca had been put in charge of the marksmanship instructions, she'd insisted that they use the standard army rifles. Abigail shifted the sling on her arm and took aim. Becca gritted her teeth at the way the rifle's muzzle was drifting around. It settled down to near-immobility and Becca's hopes rose, but then the girl's whole body seemed to twitch and the gun went off with a bang. Becca didn't need to use her field glasses to check the target to know it had been a clean miss, but she said: "Better. Keep at it." Actually it *had* been better, at least the girl had kept her eyes open this time.

Abigail, and all the other women around her, were part of a 'militia' organization which styled itself the 'Memphis Women's Volunteer Sharpshooters'. While they were from Memphis, and they were women, and they were surely volunteers, they had a long way to go, in Rebecca's opinion, to earn the 'sharpshooter' part of their title. Their unofficial nickname was the 'Memphis Belles' and that seemed a far more accurate description to Becca. Theoretically, there were over a hundred members of the company, most from the finest families of Memphis, but it was rare for more than thirty of them to show up at a meeting at the same time. There were about that many here today.

She walked down the firing line to where the next shooter, a much older woman, was methodically working the action of her rifle. Loading and firing with confidence, a considerable pile of empty brass was accumulating around her feet. "You're doing well, Mrs. Halberstam."

"Please, Becca, you can call me Sarah," said the woman, opening the bolt and lowering the rifle so the butt was on the ground. "And thank you."

"You've obviously done a lot of shooting, ma'am."

"Some. Bird hunting, mostly. Never with one of these, though," she said, waving a hand at the Springfield. "It's got quite a kick."

"Yes, but we need some real power to hurt the Martians."

Halberstam smiled skeptically. "Not going to hurt one of those tripod machines, even with one of these from what I've heard."

"No, probably not," admitted Rebecca. "So what're you doin' here?"

"What are you?"

She shrugged. "Felt like I needed to be doin' *something!*"

"You're a nurse aren't you? That's surely doing something."

"I guess, so. But after two years of it, it doesn't seem... enough."

The older woman nodded. "You want to hit back at 'em. Hurt them yourself."

"Yeah."

"Killing one wasn't enough?"

Rebecca winced. She wished she'd never shown anyone the newspaper clipping she'd gotten from a local paper which recounted her exploits back in the first days of the war when she'd killed the pilot of a wrecked Martian tripod. But without that she'd never have been let into the group. It was for the upper crust and Becca was literally from the wrong side of the tracks these days. But the newspaper had done the trick and the group's leader, a formidable woman named Theodora Oswald, had been overjoyed to welcome Becca into the organization. She was the uppermost of the upper crust in Memphis, it seemed, and clearly her family had a lot of money. They owned a huge estate outside of town and it was now the headquarters for the sharpshooters. There was a shooting range and a drill field set up and plenty of colored servants to provide drinks when necessary. And she - or perhaps her husband - clearly had political pull, too. The fact that a hundred Springfields and fifty thousand rounds of ammunition had magically appeared at her mansion proved that.

"One was just a start," said Becca eventually. "We need to kill 'em all."

"Yes, it surely seems that way. Well, back to work." Halberstam raised the rifle and slid a cartridge into the breech. The Springfields had a five round magazine, but for safety reasons, Rebecca insisted that they load and fire individual rounds.

She continued her inspection of the shooters. Some, like Halberstam, weren't bad, and some, like Abigail, were probably hopeless, and most - as she'd feared when she first heard about this group—thought it was some sort of social club rather than a military organization. They clearly took far more interest in their sporty uniforms than they did in drill or marksmanship. The uniforms were ridiculous: buckskin jackets with a dangling fringe on the bottom and down each arm, billowy pantaloons tucked into calf-high boots, and a jaunty hat with a feather. Becca refused to wear it and stuck to her nurse's uniform.

She reached the end of the firing line and looked over to the 'parade ground' where Sam Jones was teaching the other half of today's group the rudiments of the manual of arms and the basic marching steps. Or trying to, anyway. His charges showed all the discipline of a flock of chickens. Sam was an enigma to her. When she'd first seen him, he was a bearded, raging scarecrow, rescued from the Martian fortress near Gallup, New Mexico. He'd been a part of General Sumner's army and was captured when it was destroyed in the first battle with the invaders. Rescued, he'd refused to go back with the army - or give his right name - and had attached himself to Rebecca's hospital unit. He was nervous like a skittish horse. But he had volunteered to help her out here and his

413

knowledge of the drill showed that he'd probably been with an infantry unit. He would disappear for days at a time, but so far had always come back.

She turned to go back down the line, when Mrs. Oswald appeared with several servants bearing pitchers of lemonade. She declared the day's efforts at an end and called all the ladies together for refreshments. Becca shook her head; they hadn't been at this for more than an hour. Of course, it was very hot. The women and girls clustered around... chattering about nothing in particular as far as Becca could tell. They seemed like nice people, but few of them appeared to have a clue of what the war was really like or about.

Oswald made some sort of speech and blathered on for quite some time before Becca could make her escape. She promised to come again next week. She rode her horse, Ninny, back toward Memphis, Sam walking beside her. "So how'd they do today?" she asked. "You able to teach 'em anything?"

"Not really. Like tryin' to herd cats. Pointless."

"So why you bothering?"

"Same reason as you: beats sitting around doin' nothing during our off-hours. Gets me out of camp. And some of 'em are kind of cute."

Becca chuckled. "Can't say I noticed. But yeah, it probably is pointless. In a fight, none of them will be worth spit."

Their way took them along the river where thousands of men were at work constructing fortifications. The Mississippi Line, as it was being called, had been little more than the river itself when Becca and the battered remains of the army's II Corps - plus a huge number of refugees - had straggled across the bridge into Memphis fifteen months earlier. They'd marched all the way from Santa Fe, each day fearing that the Martians would appear to finish them off. But they'd made it across the river – barely - and the Martians had pretty much left them alone ever since.

No one could explain why the enemy had gone dormant for so long, but no one was really complaining. The respite had given them a chance to build some real defenses along the river. They'd started with the cities and towns; places like New Orleans, Baton Rouge, Natchez, Vicksburg, and Memphis. Then on up the river to Cairo, St. Louis, Davenport, and Minneapolis. Each place had been turned into a fortress bristling with cannons. At first these had just been in earthworks, but now those were being replaced with massive concrete walls high enough that a Martian machine couldn't get across. More and bigger guns were being mounted, too. And now they were extending the concrete walls, creeping along the river, north and south from each fortress. Given time, they could link them all together in a – hopefully - unbreakable barrier.

"Those monsters are gonna have a heck of a time getting across here!" said Becca, pointing at the works.

"The river is over a thousand miles long, Becca," replied Sam. "It'll take years to make it all look like this."

"Maybe so, but there's a lot of swampland along it too. And they've got gunboats patrolling. We can hurt 'em anywhere they try."

"I hope so."

But Becca wasn't all that interested in the *defenses*. Just holding them back wasn't good enough. They needed to be driven out! Driven back! Wiped out! No one seemed to be saying much about that.

"Someday," she muttered to herself. "Someday we'll kill them all."

* * * * *

AUGUST, 1911, ROCK CREEK PARK, MARYLAND

"Come on, Leonard! This is bully, isn't it?"

Lieutenant General Leonard Wood, Chief of Staff of the United States Army, watched the President of the United States disappear around a bend in the trail ahead of him and spurred his horse to catch up. He glanced behind and saw that the President's military aide, Major Archie Butt, and the squad of escorting cavalry had fallen far behind.

Wood had spent a large chunk of his youth riding in far more rugged locations than Rock Creek Park, so galloping at full speed down the easy paths here didn't bother him. The object of his pursuit, Theodore Roosevelt, was an equally experienced horseman and was probably in no danger, but the thought of some freak accident befalling the President sent a chill down his spine in spite of the summer heat.

He sighed in relief when he caught sight of Roosevelt again and saw that he had reined in his horse and was halted next to the creek, in a little glen. Wood slowed as he came up beside him. "You shouldn't ride off alone like that, Theodore," said Wood, knowing his scolding was pointless.

"Oh, I know, Leonard," laughed Roosevelt. "The woods are just crawling with Martian assassins!" He waved his hands at the luxuriant greenery. Shafts of sunshine penetrated the canopy overhead, producing shifting patterns of light and shadow. It was a beautiful spot.

"There aren't any Martians around here," admitted Wood, "but there could be assassins of the two-legged variety."

"Oh, tosh! Who would want to kill me?"

Wood didn't answer, but the tiny twitch in the President's eye told him that he knew that there were lunatics around who did wish him harm. Prior to the Martian landings, Roosevelt had been one of the most popular Presidents in American history. In the immediate aftermath of the invasion the people had rallied around him and his popularity rose to new heights. But that was nearly three years ago, and the war was going on and on. There had been terrible defeats and damn few victories. Millions of Americans had been driven from their homes and even those who had not been directly affected were being asked to make more and more sacrifices. Yes, there were people angry enough, or crazy enough, to do the unthinkable. After all, Roosevelt had first become President because of an unthinkable act—in a time of peace and prosperity.

Major Butt and the escort finally caught up and formed a perimeter around Wood and Roosevelt. The President dismounted and gave the reins of his horse to one of the troopers. He stretched and strolled toward the creek. Wood groaned silently. *He's not going to…? Yes, he is. Damn it.*

"Come, Leonard, it's so blasted hot, let's take a dip."

There was no escaping it, so Wood swung off his horse and followed. Roosevelt was stripping off his clothes and dropping them on the bank of the creek. *Well, at least it's not November!*

Roosevelt's excursions to Rock Creek were famous - or infamous in some circles. In the early years of his presidency he would lead parties of senators, congressmen, ambassadors, and just about anyone who wanted to talk to him out here and then, in all weather, strip buck naked to wade or swim in the creek and climb the cliffs on the opposite bank. People wanting to gain his ear - and his respect - had little choice but to follow suit. Wood had managed to avoid most of those trips, but he did remember one frigid March day where there was ice floating in the creek…

He peeled off his sweat-soaked uniform and followed his leader into the water. He had to admit that it did feel good on a day like this. Major Butt was standing on the bank looking very uncomfortable. The man watched Roosevelt, looked back at the smirking cavalrymen, and then shrugged and started unbuttoning his coat.

"Oh, this is splendid!" said the President, submerging himself up to his chin. "It's been too long since I've done this!"

"We've all been a trifle busy," said Wood. "I'll be up until midnight catching up from this little jaunt."

"Don't try to make me feel guilty, Leonard! It won't work!"

"Oh, I know it won't. Never has."

Roosevelt laughed and rolled over on his back in the water. "But you know, the idea of Martian assassins sets me to thinking."

"Oh?"

"Well, sometimes I wonder just how much they know about us. Do they have any notion about how our governments work? Who our leaders are? If they ever had the opportunity to assassinate me - or the Kaiser, or the Tsar - would they even go to the effort?"

"Well, they surely must know that we are organized in some fashion. We have cities and armies and navies. Things like that don't just happen spontaneously. And they must have some sort of government of their own."

"True, true, but they might think themselves so superior that they don't even consider how we do things. I mean do we worry about who is the leader of a herd of cattle or a flock of chickens? To us they are just a resource to be exploited."

"Hmm…" grunted Wood, not much liking the comparison.

"And their complete refusal to try and communicate indicates the Martians feel the same way toward us."

Wood had to admit that it certainly could be true. There had been some attempts to communicate with the invaders. All had failed - often with fatal consequences to those making the attempt. Parties advancing under flags of truce had been reduced to ash. There was a report out of Russia of a group of Orthodox Bishops, marching forward with icons held high, being vaporized. More cautious attempts, using blinking lights from a distance or the new radio signals, had been ignored. It was plain that the enemy had not come to talk.

"So, it will be a war of extermination."

"From our point of view it will have to be," said Roosevelt. "There's no choice. But from their point of view…" he shrugged. "If they do just think of us as cattle…"

Both men fell silent. There was no longer any doubt that the Martians did feed upon humans— and other large warm-blooded animals. But whether that was just an expediency forced upon the Martians during the initial phase of their invasion or a long range policy was unknown. Although reports from scouting missions into Martian held territory in Asia and Africa told of huge pens holding human captives, far more than would be needed for immediate food supplies. It was an unsettling thing to think about.

Major Butt joined them in the water. "You do have a reception tonight, Mr. President," he said diffidently.

"Yes, yes, I know. We'll be back to the White House in plenty of time, Major."

"Well, at least the Canal is open," said Wood, trying to bring up something good.

"Yes!" replied Roosevelt, brightening. "Wish I could have been there. Just so blasted much work here, I can't get away." His expression quickly darkened again. "And not just running the war; the politics have become downright suffocating!"

416

Wood nodded. Yes, the massive wave of patriotic fervor in the first year or so, when Roosevelt could get anything he wanted out of Congress, Wall Street, or the people had long since disappeared. When it came to wars, Americans were notoriously impatient. They didn't balk at making sacrifices or risking death on the battlefield, but they wanted to *get on with it!* Get it done with so they could go back to their regular lives. They wanted 'splendid little wars', like the ones with Spain or Mexico. When they got a long, bloody one, like the Civil War - or this one - they tended to get angry and lose confidence in their leaders.

As they were now. Millions of people had been forced to flee the states and territories in the heartland. Except for a few fortified outposts in places like Little Rock, Kansas City, Omaha, and Sioux City, which could be supplied by river, the Great Plains had been overrun. The farms which had produced such bounty were abandoned and food prices were soaring. Mines and factories were working around the clock, so everyone had a job and wages were also on the rise, but everything cost more and wartime necessity had seen many of the worker safety and child labor laws, championed by Roosevelt in his early years, suspended. Conditions in some places were very bad. More and more women and children were being pulled into the workplace as the men were sent to the army. The factory owners were making fortunes, but the new taxes needed to pay for the war were mostly falling on the middle class. The fabric of American society was being strained as never before.

The American people had the grit to take all of that, of course, but only if they could see that their efforts were paying off. At the moment, the payoff was hard to see. Discontent was rising and the congressmen and senators were listening to their constituents. Committees had been formed to look into how the war was being handled - Wood himself was spending an inordinate amount of time on Capitol Hill answering congressmen's questions these days. Everyone had ideas on how it could be done better. Roosevelt was not getting his way nearly as often as he wanted and it only looked to get worse.

And next year was an election year.

1912 could see the most important presidential election since 1864. Maybe the most important ever. Roosevelt's third term in 1908 was unprecedented. A fourth term in 1912 might prove unacceptable. The opposition was already on the move.

"Did you see that letter of Miles' in the *Post* yesterday?" asked Roosevelt suddenly - as if he was reading Wood's mind.

"Yes. Yes, I did," replied Wood. General Nelson Miles had been a hero in the Civil War and more recently had been the Commanding General of the U.S. Army. Roosevelt had forced him to retire in 1903 so that the post of Commanding General could be abolished to make way for the current system with the Chief of Staff in charge. Miles had never forgiven Roosevelt and had tried to win the Democratic nomination for President in 1904. He'd lost that fight, but now he was back and with much wider backing. He'd written a letter that was savagely critical of Roosevelt - and Wood - and the way the war was being run. It was being reprinted in papers all over the country.

"His hat is in the ring for sure now," said Roosevelt sullenly. "You'd think he'd be too old for this sort of thing. He's what? Seventy-two?"

"Seventy-one, I think," said Wood. "Still hale, though. Remember when he rode ninety miles in one day just before you retired him to prove he was up to the task?"

"Yes, the show off. But he'll be the Democrats' choice for certain. I mean who else do they have? Bryan's been a pacifist his whole career and Wilson doesn't have any military credentials at all. They need a fighter."

"Well, he's certainly that."

We've got a fighter - what we need is a victory!

417

"By George! Look at that!"

Wood spun around, but saw nothing. Butt was looking for assassins and reaching for the pistol on his hip—only to realize it was on the pile of clothes on the bank.

"What?"

"I think I saw a cave swallow! They're rare in these parts. I think it landed somewhere on the cliffside. They sometimes make nests in crevasses."

Wood relaxed. Roosevelt and his damn birds! He was a noted expert on them and had written several books.

"Let's take a look, shall we?" The President paddled toward the far shore.

Wood sighed and followed.

A victory, we need a victory - and soon.

CHAPTER ONE

CYCLE 597, 844.8, HOLDFAST 32-2

Qetjnegartis found Ixmaderna where it had expected: in its laboratory. While Ixmaderna never balked at any task assigned to it, construction, combat, or production, it had always been clear to Qetjnegartis that its greatest interest was scientific in nature. Now that they had the time to build a proper holdfast, with a well-equipped laboratory, and that every clan member was not so urgently needed for other tasks, Ixmaderna had the freedom to indulge its interests.

"Greetings, Commander," it said when it caught sight of Qetjnegartis. "It is a pleasure to see you again."

"As it is you." Ixmaderna was unfailingly courteous and Qetjnegartis often found itself mimicking the behavior. "I have just arrived back from Holdfast 32-4. Is all well, here?"

"Yes, it is. Resource gathering is going as planned, and production is at nearly full capacity. There have been no attacks on this holdfast and our scouts report no significant prey-creature military forces within three hundred telequel." It paused for a moment and then continued. "I have heard the news of the attack you led against the prey-creature city, Commander. An unfortunate setback, but hardly critical."

"No," said Qetjnegartis, "But it is still irritating. Attacking the enemy in one of their cities which they have had the time to fortify is much more difficult than in the open field. I am concerned because our observations indicate that the cities are far more numerous - and far larger - the further east we advance. We are going to need new techniques to overcome this problem."

"New techniques and new equipment, Commander," said Ixmaderna. "We are not the first clan to encounter these difficulties. Others have reported the same thing, and the engineers on the Homeworld have been working to develop machines which may help us overcome them."

"Indeed? Have they come up with anything?"

"We just received a transmission today. It contained the construction template for an interesting device. Here, let me show it to you." Ixmaderna moved to a large display screen and activated it. The image which appeared was very similar to a machine commonly used in mining, but with some significant modification. Qetjnegartis immediately noted the scale and realized the size of the device.

"It is not piloted?"

"No, it is far too small for that. It would have to be controlled remotely. There are also instructions for adding the necessary devices to our fighting machines—or the holdfast controls—to do that."

Qetjnegartis considered this. "It will take training to employ these properly, but I can see how they could have been used to good effect in the recent battle. And being unpiloted, they would be completely expendable. We will need such devices in future operations. Very well, you have my authorization to begin construction. I will take thought on when and how to deploy them."

"Very good, Commander," said Ixmaderna, clearly pleased. "It shall be as you command."

"Are there any other things you wish to discuss?"

"Actually, yes, if you have the time, Commander."

"I do. Proceed."

"I have been studying the intelligent prey-creatures," said Ixmaderna.

"I thought you were focusing your studies on the non-intelligent creatures of this world?"

"So I was. But the life on this world is all of identical construction and there is little of significant interest at a strictly biological level—except for the dangerous pathogens, of course, but other groups, more capable than I, are pursuing those lines of research."

"You insult yourself, Ixmaderna, You are as talented a scientist as anyone I have met," said Qetjnegartis.

"You are kind, Commander. But in any case, I turned over the routine cataloging of the non-intelligent life to an assistant, and I began to explore ways of controlling the larger non-intelligent creatures which I thought might be of use as food-animals. I hypothesized that if we could develop ways of easily controlling these animals, we could dispense with any need for the intelligent prey-creatures in that role. We could exterminate them completely and rely solely on the non-intelligent beasts."

"An interesting idea," said Qetjnegartis. "Using the intelligent ones as a food source has always posed problems. If we simply confine them, as we did at first, then the challenge becomes one of feeding them until we require them. Unconfined, they are dangerous and will try to flee. Can what you suggest be done?"

"At first I was optimistic, Commander. We have observed the prey-creatures controlling large numbers of them seemingly with ease. My attempts have been far less successful. The non-intelligent creatures are panicked by the sight, sound, and smell of us and our machines. Some grow so terrified they injure or even kill themselves in their desperation to escape. Even ones born in captivity have proven uncontrollable. Perhaps with time that will change. But I have had some new thoughts and that brings us back to my study of the intelligent prey-creatures."

"Indeed?"

"Yes, I began studying their young ones and what I've found is truly remarkable."

"How so?"

"The prey-creatures reproduce sexually, as all the lower creatures do, of course. The embryos develop inside the female and are then expelled when sufficiently matured to survive."

"That is not remarkable, Ixmaderna, most lower creatures do the same."

"True, Commander, but what is remarkable is the length of time it takes these young creatures to fully mature. From my observations, it takes approximately fourteen of the local cycles for them to reach sufficient maturity to reproduce, and then another four to reach their adult size."

"Really?" asked Qetjnegartis in surprise. That was an extraordinarily long period compared to life on the Homeworld. "But how can you be sure of that? We have only been on this world for two cycles—four of the local cycles."

"That is true. I have not been able to observe any single creature grow from birth to maturity. But by dividing the creatures into groups, sorted by their size and weight and behavior, and then seeing how they develop over several of the local cycles, I have been able to extrapolate the total amount of time it would take one to go from the least developed group to the most developed. I may be in some small degree of error, but I am confident my observations are still valid."

"Why such a long time? Are all the creatures on this world like that?"

"That is the other odd thing. No, they are not. The non-intelligent creatures develop much faster. They are born with a basic set of abilities and just a few of the local cycles bring them to adulthood. But Commander, the thing of greatest import is the fact that the newly born intelligent prey-creatures appear to be completely ignorant of… well, everything."

"What do you mean?"

"Exactly what I said, Commander. As far as I can determine, the newborns have only their autonomic functions. They cannot move, feed themselves, or even communicate with their parent, except in the most rudimentary fashion. They are utterly helpless and would not survive without help. Everything must be learned as they mature."

Qetjnegartis was very surprised. When the Race reproduced, it did so by budding off a new being. It would grow in a sac on the side of the parent's body and when it had matured sufficiently, it would detach. Shortly before detaching, the parent would transfer a great deal of basic information to the bud. From the moment it detached, it was capable of routine functions. While its intellect and advanced skills would develop later, as it experienced new things, it was a useful member of the Race immediately. But if these prey-creatures were a hindrance rather than a help for such a long period… "How could such a species even survive, let along become the dominant one on this world?"

"It does seem unlikely, doesn't it?" replied Ixmaderna. "I can only speculate that any potential competitors were even more primitive."

"Extraordinary. If this is true, our conquest of this world seems assured. But how does this relate to your earlier statement about controlling the non-intelligent creatures?"

"I am only speculating at this point, Commander, but it occurs to me that if the infant prey-creatures are truly such a blank, then perhaps they could be trained—by us."

"Trained? To do what?"

"Well, anything, I suppose," replied Ixmaderna. "My initial thought was to use them to control the non-intelligent animals. Perhaps we could keep small numbers of trained prey-creatures to control large numbers of the non-intelligent animals. There might be other useful tasks they could be set to do, as well."

It took a few moments for the full implication of this to be processed by Qetjnegartis. "Could they be trained to fight other prey-creatures?"

"I… don't know, Commander. There may be some instinct against fighting their own kind, some sort of automatic loyalty…"

"The level of armaments the first expedition encountered would argue against that," said Qetjnegartis. "They reported warriors with weapons and powerful fighting machines on the oceans. Clearly they must wage war on each other."

"True," conceded Ixmaderna. "It might be possible. Of course, considering the very slow level of development, it will be three or four cycles—six or eight of the local cycles - before we would know if we've been successful."

"I understand. But this is significant enough that I believe it should be pursued."

"That is excellent… Of course to do this properly, I will need expanded facilities, a good supply of captured prey-creatures, perhaps an assistant or two…"

"I will order it done."

"My thanks, Commander."

"This has the potential of repaying the clan many-fold. No thanks are needed. But Ixmaderna... There is another matter I wished to discuss with you today."

"Yes, Commander? What matter is that?"

"You touched upon the subject, just now: instinctive loyalty."

"I see," said Ixmaderna, waving its tendrils in sudden understanding. "You are concerned about the buds."

"You have noticed this yourself?" Qetjnegartis was surprised.

"Yes. The buds created here do not have the automatic submission to the seniors who have arrived later. It is an interesting development."

Interesting! Ixmaderna's habit of understatement could be called 'interesting', but this was far too dangerous for that! The entire social structure of the Race was based upon the absolute submission of younger members to the older members within their clan. A member would submit to the will of its progenitor, or its progenitor's progenitor, or their bud-mates, up the line of ancestry for as far as it existed. But while the buds created on this world would submit to those who were here when they came into existence, they had no such submission to those still on the Homeworld or those who arrived from there after they were budded.

"I find it a very *alarming* development, Ixmaderna," said Qetjnegartis. "Since you have observed it, do you have any explanation for it?"

"Only an untested theory, Commander."

"Share it with me."

"If you insist. I'm reluctant to take a stance on something like this with no data to..."

"Share it with me."

"Very well. There are several theories that attempt to explain the known phenomena of our automatic dominance and submission. The most widely accepted - and the one I subscribe to - is that there is a mental link that exists between every member of the Race."

"I'm aware of that theory," said Qetjnegartis.

"Yes, it is theorized to be similar to the mental melding we can achieve when we grasp tendrils, but that it exists without physical contact and at a very weak - and hence subconscious - level. When a bud achieves consciousness, this subconscious link imprints the new being's place in the hierarchical structure of the Race. It instantly knows - and accepts - the dominance of all those there before it, and likewise its dominance of all who come after it. The problem in proving this is that no trace of this link has ever been detected even though reason dictates that it must exist within the electromagnet spectrum."

"Perhaps." Qetjnegartis had heard some lesser-accepted theories that postulated some entirely unknown method of transmission.

"If we accept that the link is electromagnet in nature," continued Ixmaderna, "then it must obey the inverse-square law. The strength of the link will weaken over distance. My theory is that the link is already very weak. It is strong enough to function within the relative small space of a single world, but too weak to function across interplanetary distances."

"Ah, I see," said Qetjnegartis. "To the buds created here, the others on the Homeworld would be too far away to detect and thus would not be included in their imprinted hierarchy."

"That is my theory, yes. Sadly there is no way to test it."

"Perhaps not, but it explains what we are observing." Qetjnegartis paused. "I need to consider the possible consequences of this. There could be some serious issues. Very serious issues."

"As you say, Commander."

"Ixmaderna, it would be best if we do not mention this to anyone else."

"I will obey Commander. But surely the other clans are noticing this, too."

"Perhaps so. But if anyone is going to raise an alarm, it will not be the Bajantus Clan.

* * * * *

AUGUST, 1911, SHOREHAM, LONG ISLAND, NY

Colonel Andrew Comstock breathed in the warm air and reflected that this was actually a rather nice place when it wasn't covered in snow. The other times he'd been here it had been in late fall or the dead of winter. He didn't need his greatcoat today! It would have been uncomfortably warm, in fact, if not for the breeze off Long Island Sound.

He was here to see the latest invention developed by the brilliant but erratic mind of Nikola Tesla. He'd met the man on a number of occasions and learned that the only thing you could predict about him was that he'd be unpredictable. Andrew glanced at the huge Wardenclyffe Tower, a metal monstrosity almost two hundred feet high, and was surprised to see that not only was it not, apparently, going to be in use today, but it looked as though some of it had been dismantled. When he'd gotten the message from Tesla that he wanted to demonstrate a new 'electric gun', he'd assumed it would be some improvement on the earlier adaptations he'd made to the tower. It appeared he'd been wrong.

He spotted Tesla in a nearby field, standing next to a strange device and surrounded by a group of men, some of whom he realized were newspapermen. "Blast him!" he snapped.

"Sir?"

He looked to the man accompanying him and raised an eyebrow. Lieutenant Jeremiah Hornbaker was his new aide and Andrew wasn't quite used to having him around. He'd been making inspection tours like this since before the war and almost always alone. But he was a colonel now and rated an aide. He'd actually rated one since he made major, but never got around to requesting one. Hornbaker was lanky, eager, and incredibly young - much like he'd been not so many years ago.

"Tesla!" he said jerking his head toward the tall, impeccably dressed figure. "He doesn't have the slightest regard for procedures or security. He probably invited those reporters before he bothered to inform the Ordnance Department he'd be making this test today!"

"I see, sir. But it seems as though he's built something, there."

Indeed it did, and unlike the Wardenclyffe Tower, this actually looked like some sort of weapon. There was a boxy structure about the size and shape of an automobile with all manner of pipes and tubes and wires spilling out of it. Above that, however was a long tapering cylinder, like a cannon barrel, mounted on a rotating mount. Cables came from the box and disappeared into the cylinder. There were thick rings of a white ceramic material at intervals along the length of the cylinder until at the end they stopped with a white ball where the muzzle should have been.

"Ah, Major Comstock!" cried Tesla when he caught sight of him.

"It's colonel…"

"So good of you to come! Gentlemen, this is Major Comstock from the Ordnance Department! He and I have worked together for years producing weapons for the war against the Martians!"

423

He grabbed him by the arm and displayed him to the group like some prize show animal. Andrew refrained from mentioning that so far, Tesla's work had yet to produce a single working weapon for the war effort.

Well, that wasn't entirely true. Tesla had managed to get a half-dozen captured Martian heat rays operational. They weren't terribly practical weapons, requiring enormous power generating plants to make them work. Five of them had been incorporated in the defenses of St. Louis, it being seen as the critical lynch-pin in the Mississippi Line.

"Mr. Tesla," said Andrew, "what have you built here?"

"Ah! Yes, right to the point! Good!" He turned and waved his hands at the contraption. "As I was explaining to these gentlemen, using knowledge gleaned from captured Martian machines, I have created the first electric cannon!" Andrew glanced back at the Wardenclyffe Tower and Tesla instantly noticed. "Yes! You were here for my first experiments, but I assure you that my new device is as far advanced beyond that as a machine gun is from a bow and arrow!

"Some of the problems with my first device - as you so ably pointed out, Major—was the short range, the difficulty in aiming, and the large power generators needed to operate it."

"And you have solved these problems, sir? I can't help but notice the cables leading back to your generator building," said Andrew, pointing to several cables as thick as a man's arm running to the large brick building at the base of the Wardenclyffe Tower.

"Ah! Yes, the device needs to be charged up by a significant source, but once charged, it is independent and can fire several times without recharging. You see, I have made use of that remarkable Martian wire which has no electrical resistance. Amazing!"

"Where did you get the wire?" asked Andrew sharply. The stuff was being strictly rationed, since the only source of it was from damaged Martian machines which had been captured. And even though each machine could yield thousands of miles of it, it was proving so useful for the new British-designed radio units and the experimental coil guns, it could only be acquired with Ordnance Department approval; and Andrew was damn sure none had been authorized for Tesla!

"Oh, I have my sources," replied Tesla with a smirk. "And I only needed a few hundred miles for this. But as I was saying, using the wire as a storage battery I have been able to accumulate an electrical charge of an unprecedented intensity. It can then be projected through this large tube, where I have additional coils of the wire. From there, the electric charge will leap to the target." Tesla pointed to an object in an adjoining field. It had to have been at least five hundred yards away.

"It can fire that far?" asked Andrew, surprised. The earlier demonstrations with the tower had only had a range of about fifty yards.

"Indeed yes! With future improvements I believe it can fire even farther. But here! Let me demonstrate! I charged the coils earlier today, so it is ready to fire!"

Andrew instinctively stepped back. The bloody thing was already charged? He'd seen what happened when one of the Martian storage batteries failed first hand and he had no wish to be close to some homemade copy of Tesla's! "Come on," he growled to Hornbaker, "let's move over there." He led the way to where a low stone wall provided a bit of shelter. Quite a few of the newspapermen followed him.

"Whenever you're ready, sir!" he shouted back at Tesla. The man waved and started fiddling with his device.

One of the newspapermen came up beside Andrew. "So, Colonel," he said, "you've been working with the doctor for a long time?"

"I wouldn't actually say working with him. I keep up to date with his activities—most of them anyway—and come to confer with him and observe demonstrations like this when events warrant."

"Is he as brilliant as they say?"

Andrew shrugged. "His mind works on a level I can scarcely conceive of, sir. If that's brilliant, then I'd have to call him brilliant."

"Some say he's a charlatan. Spending huge sums of government money and producing nothing."

Andrew wasn't touching that one! All he needed was to be quoted in the paper saying something bad about Tesla. "I guess we'll find out in a few minutes, won't we?"

Tesla waved again and shouted something Andrew couldn't quite make out. His hearing wasn't as good as it used to be. Getting caught on the edge of the blast of an exploding tripod last year hadn't helped. But he assumed Tesla was ready and that something would soon happen.

It did. A loud hum filled the air that got higher and higher in pitch until it faded from his ability to hear. Hornbaker groaned and muttered ow! Several of the other watchers were wiggling fingers in their ears. A moment later a blue glow appeared around the tube of the machine. It was the same color as a Martian tripod getting ready to explode and Andrew tensed to duck behind the wall...

Then sparks and crackling arcs of electricity were crawling up and down the tube, and an instant later a blindingly bright bolt of what could only be called lightning leapt away from the end of the tube and in an instant struck the distant target. The bolt persisted, connecting tube and target for a few heartbeats and writhing like a snake. There was a blast of flame from the target and then the bolt was jumping around the target, striking the ground in a dozen spots, almost too quickly to see. An enormous crack, like a thunderbolt, shook the air and then the light was gone. The boom rolled away across the landscape and out onto the Sound.

"God in Heaven," whispered the newspaperman. Except he wasn't whispering, he was shouting. Everyone's ears were stunned.

"I don't think anyone will be calling him a charlatan after this," Andrew shouted back.

The crowd pulled itself together and went back toward the cannon where Tesla was fairly dancing in delight. "Did you see? Did you see it?"

"Saw and heard! That was amazing, sir!" And it had been, it really had. The captured heat ray which Tesla had demonstrated had been impressive, but that was something which already existed. Tesla had only figured out how to make it work. But this! This was something totally new. "But what did it do to the target?"

"Let's go see!" Without further ado, Tesla skipped toward the target, leaving nearly everyone behind with his long, quick strides. Andrew hurried to catch up. He was sweating by the time they crossed the field. But the target was...

"Is that part of a Martian machine?"

"Of course! I had to make sure my cannon could actually damage one!"

"Where did you get it?" Andrew was sure Tesla hadn't been authorized this either.

"A friend supplied it. But look! Look what I did!"

The target had once been the curving rear plate of a tripod's head. Now it was a cracked and smoldering wreck. Black streaks marred the gleaming metal and there were holes in several spots. Thousands of the tiny hexagonal metal flakes that made up Martian armor were scattered all over. The thing had been propped up with several steel angles, but these were damaged, too, and the whole thing was leaning over drunkenly to one side. There were scorched patches on the ground all around, too. In a few spots the grass was still burning.

"Well? Well? What do you think?" demanded Tesla.

Andrew walked around, looking at the remains and directed Hornbaker to take some photographs with his Brownie camera. "You certainly did significant damage to it, sir." He put his hand through one of the holes, careful not to touch the edges—the thing was clearly still hot. "It would normally take a large caliber shell to do this sort of damage." It was impressive, but considering the size of the apparatus and the facilities needed to charge the thing, he was wondering if it was any improvement over conventional artillery. Then something else caught his eye. Just to the rear of the armor there was a… puddle of metal. Something had melted and then solidified again. It wasn't part of the armor; it had a golden color. "What's that, sir?"

"Ah! You have sharp eyes, Major!" said Tesla coming over next to him. "This is how I overcame the targeting problem!"

"And how did you do that?"

"The first few times I fired the cannon the electric charge would - as you'd naturally expect - simply jumped to the nearest object which would ground it out. The challenge was to get it to jump to where I wanted it to go."

"I can see that, sir." He remembered an early trial of the tower-device and how the bolt hit several unintended objects.

"Well, the breakthrough was when I discovered that the power, once stored in the Martian wire, took on a distinct and very unique frequency. You are familiar with electrical frequency, are you not?"

"In a general sort of way…"

"Good! Well, the frequency of the Martian current is quite unique. And I discovered that by attuning my projector properly, I could make the electrical bolt jump to a target that resonated at that frequency in preference of any other target! Brilliant, is it not!"

Andrew opened his mouth to agree and then stopped and looked at the puddle again. "So that's the Martian wire?" he said aghast. "Destroyed?"

"Only about a mile of it," said Tesla waving his hand as if it were nothing. The stuff was worth ten times its weight in gold right now! And melting would leave it useless. "I needed to make targets, you understand."

"Targets?" said Andrew weakly. "H-how many?"

"Oh, a dozen or so. I had to refine the technique, you understand. I really could use some more of it, now. Can you take care of that, Major?"

Andrew opened his mouth - he wasn't sure what was about to come out—but unexpectedly Lieutenant Hornbaker stepped in. "Excuse me, sir, but how did you prevent the bolt from jumping to the storage battery in your cannon? Seems like that would be the closest target."

Tesla spun around and stared at Hornbaker as if he'd never seen him before. "Who are you?"

"This is Lieutenant Hornbaker. He works for me," said Andrew.

"Ah, I see. Well, that is an *excellent* question, young man! And it took all of my inventiveness to find the answer!" He launched into a lengthy explanation of which Andrew could follow very little. The gist of it seemed to be that somehow Tesla had managed to alter the frequency of the current in his storage battery so that it would not attract the bolt.

"Doctor, so you are saying that your cannon will unerringly send its bolt to find a Martian power unit that's within range?" asked Andrew. "It will never miss its target?"

"That has been the result so far," confirmed Tesla. "At least within the effective range. If the range is too long, misses have occurred. But I should add that I believe the range will be determined by the *amount* of power stored in the target. The amount I could put in my little target batteries," he waved his hand at the puddle, "is tiny compared with what a Martian tripod must have. The effective range against one of them might be many times what it is here!"

Andrew took a deep breath and looked from the target to the cannon and then back to the target. Now this was something! A weapon which could wreck a tripod and never miss? The problems with the size of the device and the need for generators to charge it up seemed far less serious now!

"Mr. Tesla, I… well, first, sir, let me shake your hand!" He stuck his hand out, remembering too late that Tesla abhorred shaking hands. But to his surprise, the man took it and shook weakly. He quickly let go. "Congratulations, sir! This is an amazing achievement! Truly amazing! My superiors will be extremely interested in this. Can you provide drawings? Specifications? We will want to build a lot of these devices."

"My assistants are working on them now, Major," said Tesla beaming in delight. "Of course we will need a great deal of the Martian wire to build many of these."

"I'm sure we will get it." Somehow…

The reporters crowded in now and bombarded Tesla, and himself, with questions. Tesla was more than willing to talk about his genius, but Andrew had to temper his responses to avoid making any sort of statement he'd come to regret later. Eventually he broke free, and he and Hornbaker headed back to the train station.

"That was really something, sir," said the lieutenant.

"Yes, it was. And I still can barely believe it."

"Sir?"

"Oh, I've been coming to see Tesla for years and he's… well, as I'm sure you noticed, he's a bit of a blowhard. He promises the sun, moon, and stars, but up until now hasn't delivered much of anything. So for him to now come up with this. And he wasn't even *supposed* to be working on this, mind you. It's a surprise. A real surprise."

"But a pleasant one, surely."

"Yes indeed. I just hope I can get General Crozier to believe it. And use it."

"Will that be difficult, sir? I thought the general was open to new ideas."

"Oh he is. But I know he's skeptical of Tesla. He'll be cautious about committing a lot of resources."

"Maybe we should get him up here to see this."

"We might have to."

They reached the train station and Andrew found a telegram waiting for him. He read it and frowned. "Trouble, sir?" asked Hornbaker.

"It's from the Baldwin people. They'd like to put off the demonstration until tomorrow. Problems with their device apparently. I suppose we can just layover in Philadelphia…"

"Or we could go right on down to Aberdeen and see what Goddard has to show us, sir," suggested Hornbaker. "Then back up to Philadelphia the next day."

"Yes, yes, we could do that. Goddard is ready to go now from what his last message said. Good idea, Jerry. Check the train schedule while I send a wire to Goddard to get ready for this afternoon."

"Yes, sir."

The arrangements were made and soon the two of them were on a train heading south. Andrew immediately slumped down in his seat and pulled his cap over his eyes to try and catch some sleep. Hornbaker had his face pressed to the window of the car, taking in the sights. The young man was from some backwoods place in Kentucky or Tennessee and was still amazed by how built-up the east was. Andrew had seen those sights enough times not to need to do so again - although they did seem to change a bit each time he came through here.

America's mobilization to meet the demands of the war was changing the landscape and changing the society as well. New factories and smelters were springing up everywhere. Thousands of chimneys belched smoke into the skies and heaps of slag grew into small mountains. Winter time snows stayed white only a few hours before soot turned the drifts black. Vast marshaling yards were filled with tanks and guns waiting to be shipped to the front. Training camps turned out new soldiers, a hundred thousand each month. Women and children were working in those new factories so the men could go fight. Everyone was involved - everyone. Andrew's own wife was growing vegetables in a garden which took up nearly the entire back yard of her parent's house at Fort Myer and organizing the wives of other officers to do the same. With the loss of the Great Plains, there was a growing food shortage. It was finally sinking in that this was a war for survival. He dozed off thinking about the house and the garden.

Late afternoon saw them at the Aberdeen Proving Grounds in Maryland, north of Baltimore. The army had a large base there to test new weapons. Andrew had been here frequently over the last few years. In fact he'd been here just a month ago watching a field test on a new device which was hoped could help blast a way through the walls the Martians threw up around their fortresses. It had looked promising, although with the current state of the war, they were unlikely to need the thing for a while.

The weapon being tested today was one the army had great hopes for. The war against the Martians was unlike any ever fought by men. The enemy employed large, heavily armored war machines which were virtually invulnerable to the rifles and machine guns used by ordinary infantry. On rare occasions a damaged tripod might be taken down by some lucky fusillade of bullets, but that was exceptional. To make up for this, the infantry had been supplied with small bombs. These could wreck a tripod - indeed, Andrew and a small group of men had done exactly that a few years before - but it was difficult and incredibly dangerous. Not every infantryman had the nerve to make such an attack. And despite the tremendous output of America's factories, not every soldier could be supplied with a tank or an artillery piece. Somehow the masses of infantry which made up any army had to be made effective again.

What was needed was a weapon powerful enough to damage a tripod from a distance, and yet small and light enough that infantry soldiers could carry them into battle. A little less than two years ago, a young engineer named Robert Goddard had accosted Andrew on the streets of Boston and insisted he had just the weapon for the job. Andrew had been skeptical at first since the army was being flooded with 'great ideas' for winning the war - most totally impractical. But Goddard had been accompanied by Charles Munroe, an explosives expert who Andrew already knew of from his work in the navy's torpedo factory in Connecticut. The two of them together had proposed a shaped-charge explosive device delivered by a small rocket. Developing it had not been as simple or easy as Goddard had promised - but then few things were - but at last it looked as though the problems had been solved. Or Andrew surely hoped so.

Aberdeen was on a stretch of ground hugging the Chesapeake Bay. It was mostly low, flat, and in places, swampy. Scraggly clumps of trees grew here and there and swarms of mosquitoes everywhere. The weather was clouding over, but the wind had died and Andrew found himself sweating under his wool uniform. A motor staff car met them at the railroad station and carried them along dirt roads deep into the base. From time to time loud booms shook the air as artillery and explosives were tested. The car passed a few firing ranges where artillery of many types and sizes were being fired. They finally arrived at a secluded field where a small group of people were waiting for them. He spotted Goddard right away. The man, though little older than Andrew, was almost completely bald and never seemed to wear a hat.

Goddard trotted over to greet them, smiling broadly. "Welcome, Colonel! Glad to see you. As soon as I got your wire I had things set up here. Glad you could come today, it's supposed to rain tomorrow."

"Your weapon isn't affected by the rain is it?" asked Andrew.

"No, no! We've made it quite waterproof. We were told right from the start that whatever we came up with would have to be able to stand up to field conditions. I was just thinking that the demonstration would be a lot more pleasant if we weren't standing in the rain."

"Yes, I see. So, what do you have for us?"

"I hope I have the final prototype for the Anti-Tripod Rocket Launcher. We've been testing it almost non-stop for the last week. Over two hundred rounds fired with no serious mishaps."

"That implies some not-so-serious mishaps, Dr. Goddard," observed Andrew.

"Well, yes, there have been a few misfires and a few duds, but that's to be expected. There have been no injuries and no unintended damage. And the performance has been excellent. Here, let me show you." He led the way to where several tables had been set up. On one was sitting the launcher. This was little more than a piece of hollow tubing about three inches in diameter and about four and a half feet long. It had a crude aiming site, a curved wooden piece that would allow the operator to rest the tube on his shoulder, a pistol grip near the middle and another near the front, and a small box that was only a few inches square near the rear. The other table held a dozen of the rockets themselves. These were a little less than two feet long with a bulbous nose, a thin central section, and four guiding fins at the rear.

"Looks like a stovepipe," said Hornbaker.

Goddard chuckled. "Yes, that's what the men are already calling it. I imagine that will prove a lot more popular than the ATRL." He picked up the tube and handed it to Andrew. "About thirteen pounds, only a little more than a standard rifle, so the men should have no problem carrying them. The production model will have rings to attach a carrying sling. The rockets are a little over three pounds each, but a bit awkward for carrying. I've sent the specification to the Quartermaster Department, as you instructed. They are going to develop a carrying rig which will hold eight rockets and which can be worn like a back pack. I'm thinking that the weapon can be used by a two-man team. The rocketeer would operate the weapon and the other man could carry the rockets and act as the loader."

"The exact method of deployment is still being worked out," said Andrew. "Ideally there would be one of these for each squad, but it will be quite a while before they are available in sufficient numbers for that. For now, we'll try to get a few to each company. But show me how this works." He handed the tube back to Goddard and then nodded to Hornbaker, who got out his camera.

"It's very simple to operate, Colonel; come with me," said Goddard. He started walking out into the field, one of his assistants following with a rocket. Andrew and Hornbaker trailed along. When they were about a hundred yards from the tables, Goddard stopped and swapped the tube for the rocket. "The launcher is just a hollow tube to guide the rocket in the first moments of flight until its moving fast enough for the fins to provide stability. The loader inserts the rocket halfway into the rear of the tube." The assistant put the tube onto his shoulder and Goddard slid the rocket in. "This is the only tricky part. First, you pull out this pin, which arms the warhead. Then you tug loose this wire and wrap it around this little coil attached to the tube." He did so and slid the rocket the rest of the way in. A small click of metal indicated that it was somehow secured in place and wouldn't fall out if the tube was tilted. "Okay, it's ready to fire. If you'd move over here next to me—there's quite a back blast and you can't be right behind it when it fires." All three of them moved about a dozen yards to the side of the firer. "Whenever you are ready, George."

The man nodded and directed the tube toward a distant target about two hundred yards away. There was a moment as he adjusted his aim and then there was a loud roar and a blast of smoke from the rear of the tube. The rocket flew out the front and in a surprisingly short time crossed the distance to the target and exploded. The explosion wasn't particularly loud or impressive, to Andrew's disappointment. Goddard waved to the men around the table and one of them trotted forward with another rocket.

"The propellant in the rocket is very stable under normal conditions and has to be set off by an igniter," explained Goddard as he loaded again. "The ignition is electrical. We have a standard National Carbon zinc-carbon Leclanché dry cell in this box attached to the tube. It is good for a few dozen firings. I'm thinking that we could have a new battery included with each carton of rockets." He looked right at Andrew and pointed at the arming pin on the rocket. "However, once this pin is removed, the rocket is dangerous to handle. The firing pin is in the rear and the sudden deceleration of hitting the target will drive it into the explosive. Even simply dropping it could cause it to detonate. So the pin should only be removed just prior to firing."

Andrew frowned. "We'll need to hammer that into the men using it. Hornbaker, here, will be putting together the operating manual for this and he'll need your notes and any other useful advice you can give."

"My pleasure, Colonel." He finished loading and George sent another rocket against the target. "Would you care to give it a try, Colonel?"

Andrew blinked in surprise. "Uh, sure, why not?" Another rocket was brought forward and Andrew put the launcher up on his shoulder the way he had seen the assistant do it. Goddard loaded and patted him on the shoulder.

"You're ready, Colonel. Flip up the cover over the trigger and press it when you want to fire. Give us a moment to move aside."

Andrew shifted the tube so that his eye was close to the rear sight, which was nothing more than a metal tab sticking out with a small hole in it. He lined it up with another metal bar attached to the front of the tube. He could see several marking spaced vertically on it. "How is the sight calibrated?" he called.

"Oh, sorry!" replied Goddard. "The top mark is for one hundred yards, the second for two hundred, and the last for three hundred."

"Ah, I see. Okay, here goes." The range to the target looked about two hundred yards to him, so he lined up the second mark on the target. He flipped up the little cover over the firing button and gingerly pressed the button underneath it. There was an instant's delay when he heard a tiny crackling sound, then a loud whoosh, and he was engulfed in smoke. He heard the bang as the rocket detonated, but he couldn't see a thing until the smoke dispersed. The others walked over to him, Goddard grinning. "Did I hit it?"

"A little over, sir," said Hornbaker. "Close though."

"It does take a little practice, Colonel," said Goddard. "Of course a real tripod would be a much bigger target than what we have here."

"There's no recoil at all," observed Andrew.

"Of course not," said Goddard. "That's the nature of a rocket launcher."

"But what can it do to the target? Can it blast through the Martian armor? That's' the whole point after all."

Goddard's smile faded. "Let's take a look at the target, shall we? It's a piece of a Martian machine we were given for testing."

They walked down range to the target, which Andrew saw was the curving piece of the cockpit of a Martian tripod about six feet in height and width—not unlike the target Tesla was using that morning. It was rather badly battered with cracks and holes and divots taken out of the surface. But the holes and most of the divots had red paint dabbed on them. "We only had the one target," explained Goddard. "So after each series of tests we paint the hits so we don't confuse new hits with old. Here these are the new hits we made just now."

Andrew looked close and saw the newest divots in the armor. And that's all they were, divots. "We didn't penetrate."

"No, Colonel," said Goddard. "But this sample is from the most heavily armored part of a tripod. The drawings you've provided show that other areas are not so well protected."

"We need a weapon which can kill these things, Doctor!"

"Sir, I must remind you that even regular artillery usually requires multiple hits to destroy an enemy machine," said Goddard stiffly. "The rocket launcher has a similar destructive potential as a four-inch gun. To make it powerful enough to punch through the armor with a single shot would require a weapon far too large and heavy to be employed by ordinary infantry - although I would like to pursue the development of such a weapon. We were directed to create a weapon which infantry can use and this is it."

"Well, yes," said Andrew damping down his disappointment. "It's certainly safer than the bombs we've equipped the poor sods with, and far better than nothing. Sorry, Doctor, I suppose I let my hopes get away from me. But you say that this is ready to go into production?"

"Yes, Colonel. There are several facilities which are only waiting your approval to begin work."

"Very good. I'll talk to General Crozier and we should have that approval in a few days."

"Excellent!" said Goddard, recapturing his good humor. "I'll be involved for a few months getting the factories up to speed. After that, I'd like your permission to pursue a few new ideas I have concerning larger rockets and possible multiple launchers for a barrage system. Charles Munroe is already working on a larger shaped-charge warhead and…"

"I'll pass that along, Doctor, but for right now, please concentrate your efforts on production of your stovepipes. We need to get these into the hands of our troops as quickly as we can. The Martians may be quiet for the moment, but that won't last!"

CHAPTER TWO

SEPTEMBER, 1911, EAST OF AUGUSTA, ARKANSAS

"Where the hell are they?" growled Captain Frank Dolfen. "It's been three hours since we called for them!"

"Yes, and I don't know how much longer we can hang about here before those blighters notice us," said Major Bridges. The two officers were lying on their bellies on a small rise in the ground that passed for a hill on the flat eastern edges of the Ozark Plateau. They were seventy miles west of Memphis and about an equal distance northeast of Little Rock, staring at a new Martian fortress. Like the one Dolfen had spent weeks looking at near Gallup, New Mexico two years earlier, it was a ring of raised earth and stone about forty feet high and three miles in diameter. At the moment, there were two Martian tripods not a mile off, apparently on patrol. Clouds of dust in the distance hinted at others. Dolfen, Bridges, and a pair of troopers had snuck to this position during the night.

They were waiting for a group of Air Corps bombers to come and attack. Not Colonel Selfridge's planes, but a different group with much larger machines. They had attacked the place several times before, but reconnaissance from the air hadn't been able to determine what sort of damage was being done. So the request had gone out for some reconnaissance from the ground and Dolfen's squadron had been the lucky ones to get the job.

But the bombers were late.

"They better show up soon," said Dolfen. "Take a look at those clouds off to the west. A storm's coming for sure. A few hours off yet, but they sure won't want to be flying once it gets here!"

"Might be useful for us, though, old boy. Give us a spot of cover to make our withdrawal."

"True. I don't relish the idea of staying here until dark." He looked north. They had put the horses in one of the small gullies that crisscrossed the area, but once they mounted up they would be visible for miles.

They waited another half hour as it got hotter and hotter; it might be September, but summer wasn't over yet. "Maybe I should try the radio again."

"I'd advise against it. We found out in Afghanistan that those beggars can track our signals if we broadcast too much. Might lead them right to us."

Dolfen frowned, but the Englishman was probably right. Despite his foppish manner, Bridges did seem to know what he was doing. An experienced cavalryman and a good rider who had fought Martians himself, defending Britain's colony in India. They settled down to wait some more, but only a little while later Dolfen heard a faint buzzing. He rolled over on his back and swept the eastern sky with his field glasses. "I think I hear something."

"Yes, I do, too. Can you see them?"

"No, I... wait. There they are!" He pointed to a swarm of dark specks.

"I don't see... oh, yes, now I do. How many do you think?"

"Looks like about thirty to me..."

"They certainly are high up, aren't they? Can barely see them."

"They have to stay high to avoid the heat rays. The bastards can torch a plane two miles up, so they stay a bit higher than that."

"Can they even see the target from that high?"

"I sure hope so! Don't want them hitting us by mistake. But the walls of the fortress must look like a giant bull's-eye from above. They'd have to be blind not to see it."

The specks slowly crept across the sky. As they got closer, Dolfen could make them out clearly. They were twin-engine planes built by the Glenn Martin Company—or so Colonel Selfridge had told him; Dolfen had little interest in the nuts and bolts of aviation. Even so, he was impressed by the size of the bombers. He remembered the tiny and flimsy craft that were the best available just a few short years ago. *We're learning. We're learning fast.* But will it be fast enough?

"I looks like the Martians have seen them, too," said Bridges.

Dolfen redirected his attention from the planes to the enemy. The tripods, which had been striding back and forth, for all the world like human soldiers on sentry, had stopped. He half-expected them to lean backward to look up like a human, but they did not. They were faced in the direction of the oncoming planes, however, and they had raised their heat rays.

"Sure hope those blokes have their altitude right," said Bridges.

"Amen to that."

The planes were nearly overhead now and Dolfen flinched when the buzz-saw shriek of the heat rays pierced the air. On a bright day like this, the rays were hard to see, but they were clearly directed skyward. He looked up at the planes again and focused his glasses. The formation flew onward in a stately fashion, and to his relief, none of them burst into flames. Looking closer, he thought he saw small objects falling from them. "I think they just dropped their bombs!"

He tried to follow them down but lost sight of them. He lowered the glasses and looked out toward the enemy fortress. The seconds ticked by, and after a dozen or so, he thought he heard a whistling sound. A half-dozen more and suddenly geysers of smoke erupted from the walls. A heartbeat later, the deep rumble of the explosions made the ground tremble. More geysers and more booms but then it was over. The echoes died away and the smoke and dust from the bombs merged into a single huge cloud which slowly rose and drifted east. Dolfen eagerly brought the glasses to his eyes and scanned the fortress for damage.

"Anything?" asked Bridges.

"Not... not much, damn it. Maybe a couple of their ray towers wrecked, and a few craters in the wall. Nothing burning, it doesn't seem." He cursed again. "I suppose I shouldn't expect much. General Funston bombarded the Gallup fort for *months* without doing any serious damage. The reports we got from inside said that pretty much everything was deep underground. The only way to root 'em out is to go in there and do it ourselves."

"Pity," said Bridges. "Still, it can't hurt to let the bastards know we can hit them even at this distance."

"Yeah, I suppose. Seems like a lot of effort for little harm, though." He looked back up at the bombers and watched them turn east and disappear. Looking west, he saw the storm was still building and definitely closer. Another hour or so and they'd have a real gully-washer from the look of it. "I think we'll have all the cover we need to get out of here pretty soon." He told the two troopers to make sure the horses were ready.

He studied the fortress through glasses a while longer, making notes on a pad of paper. He was just putting away the glasses and his notes when there was a sudden commotion from the gully where the horses were being kept. Loud whinnying, followed by human cursing, and then to his dismay one of the horses bolted out of the gully into the open, dragging one of the troopers who clutched its reins.

He sprinted toward it, but Bridges got there faster and managed to halt the beast. Dolfen was there a moment later and between the three men they got the horse under control. "What the hell happened?!" demanded Dolfen.

"A goddamn jackrabbit, sir!" said the exasperated trooper. "I flushed it out of a bush by accident and this fool horse thought the thing was gonna eat him, I guess!"

"Oh, for God's sake! The damn thing ignores bombs and heat rays, but it's spooked by a rabbit?"

"Bloody hell," said Bridges. "The cad has gone and given us away, Captain. Look."

Dolfen spun around, and to his horror the two tripods he'd seen earlier were now heading their way! "Shit! Mount up! Ride!"

All four men jumped into their saddles and spurred their mounts into motion, leaving a fair amount of their gear lying on the ground. There wasn't a second to spare and they all knew it. Even the horses seemed to sense the danger, and being rested, they tore across the prairie as fast as they could.

Dolfen looked back and cursed. The Martians were far closer than he'd like, very nearly in heat ray range already. He probably had as much experience being chased by Martians as any man alive and he didn't like what he saw. A galloping horse could outdistance a tripod pretty easily, especially on flat ground like this, but a horse would get tired and the enemy machines never did. Worse, the two on their tails looked to be scouts. For the first few years of the war, the Martians had only had one type of fighting machine. They were powerful, tough to destroy, and while faster than a man on foot, significantly slower than a horse. But in the last year or two, they'd started to see other types. One was a bit smaller, less heavily armed and armored, but significantly faster. The army had designated the first types as 'attack tripods', and the smaller ones 'scout tripods'. Scouts still couldn't keep up with a galloping horse, but they didn't lose as much ground as an attack tripod, and when the horse had to slow down…

Bridges clearly saw it too. "Going to be a damn near thing to get back to your squadron before they catch us up, old man," he shouted. There hadn't been any covered spots close to the enemy fortress big enough to conceal the whole squadron so he'd left them about ten miles away and gone forward in the night with just Bridges and the other two. "Could you use the wireless to call them to us?"

"It takes five minutes to set up!" he shouted back. "Those bastards would have us before we could get the message off! Turn to the west!" he yelled to all of them. "Head for the storm!"

They veered to the left toward a wall of black clouds that was growing and building at an amazing pace. He could see flashes of lightning and gray sheets of rain connecting the clouds with the ground. It was a real squall line, and if they could get in there, they had a good chance of giving the Martians the slip.

A strong gust of wind suddenly hit them in the face and Dolfen's hat was torn away. Dust clouds were kicked up and stung his eyes. A few large drops of rain started hitting them, driven by the wind hard enough to sting. Glancing back, he could see that the Martians were coming on. If they could stay ahead of them for a few more minutes…

He heard the heat rays fire, but they were faint, barely to be heard above the wind. A sudden warmth on his back made him wince, but it wasn't bad, just like standing in front of a fire. They were still out of range. But the horses didn't like it and they put out a burst of speed. A moment later the heat cut off.

The rain was heavier now and the wind even stronger; bits of debris went flying past. They galloped across an abandoned wheat field and jumped the remains of a wire fence, the wreck of a farmhouse still stood in the distance.

"I say! What the devil is that?!" cried Bridges suddenly. Instinctively, Dolfen looked back at the Martians, but they were just as they'd been. What was the Englishman talking about?

"Over there!" The man pointed. Dolfen stared ahead and swallowed down sudden fear. Barely visible through the rain was a rotating column of dust and debris. It was dark, although slightly lighter than the clouds behind it, bits of stuff drifted around it and a roar like a freight train was growing.

"A twister!" cried one of the troopers.

"A what?" shouted Bridges.

"A tornado! A cyclone!" yelled Dolfen. It was almost directly in their path and seemed to be moving toward them and to the right, as though it would pass to the north of them. It was still a ways off, but it was moving fast. He stared at it a moment longer and then made his decision.

"Follow me! Head north!" He turned his horse to the right.

"But sir!" screamed one of the troopers. "It's headed that way, too! We should go south!"

"Better that than the Martians! Now come on!" he spurred his horse, although it hardly needed more encouragement to run. The tornado was now off to his left, but the distance was closing with terrifying swiftness. Would they be able to get past it? If he'd guessed wrong, it would herd them right back into the Martians' heat rays - if it didn't kill them outright.

Closer and closer the thing came. It was enormous, easily half a mile wide, maybe more. He had caught sight of a few small ones during his time in the army, but always from a safe distance. This close, the power of the thing was unbelievable. He shifted his course more to the east, trying to get around it.

The wall of darkness filled half the world now, blotting out everything to his left. Larger objects were hurtling past, but the wind was now coming from behind them, pushing them onward. Bridges came abreast of him, hat gone and mouth wide. He was shouting something, but the roar was all-encompassing; nothing else could be heard.

And then the noise and the blackness was more to the rear of them, the sky ahead was brighter. Had they made it past? He twisted around in his saddle and yes, the tornado was crossing behind them! Exhilaration filled him. They could swing west again and find cover before the Martians could…

The Martians!

He suddenly caught sight of one of the machines. The damn thing was standing right in the tornado's path! Didn't the fools know what it was - or what it could do? Apparently not, because the tripod was standing its ground and as he watched, it fired its heat ray right into the oncoming funnel-cloud.

The ray had no effect whatsoever. It did ignite some of the debris the tornado was carrying and for a moment streaks of red fire wrapped around the funnel. But then the edge reached the machine and it was lifted bodily into the air! Dolfen watched in wonder - and jubilation - as the enemy was carried up and up until it disappeared in the cloud. He continued to stare, hoping to see the tornado spit the bastard back out again and watch it smashed to bits on the ground, but there was nothing. Clearly it had killed the invader somewhere Dolfen couldn't see. Of the other tripod there was no sign; destroyed, too, or retreated, he didn't know.

"By Jove! That was really quite something, wasn't it?" said Bridges coming up beside him again, a lunatic grin on his face.

"Sure was! But come on, let's find some cover just in case the other one is still there after it passes!"

* * * * *

CYCLE 597, 844.8, HOLDFAST 32-4

Qetjnegartis was inspecting the damage from the prey-creature's aerial attack when the message from Xasdandar arrived. It and Faldprenda had been sent in pursuit of a small party of prey who Qetjnegartis suspected had some connection with the attack.

"Commander Qetjnegartis, respond please."

"Responding. Report."

"Commander, I regret to report that Faldprenda has been slain."

Qetjnegartis instantly focused its attention on this unexpected information. "How?" The most obvious answer would be some sort of an ambush. It prepared to order out a larger force to deal with it.

"It… it was destroyed by an… atmospheric phenomenon, Commander. I have never witnessed anything like it."

"Explain."

"We were pursuing the prey-creatures as you ordered. We encountered a storm and the prey attempted to take cover in it. We followed. But then we encountered a column of air which was spinning at very high speed. Faldprenda's fighting machine was caught in it."

"And this air was able to *destroy* its machine?" That scarcely seemed possible.

"Yes, Commander. It was so strong it lifted it off the ground and to a high altitude before dropping it again. It landed with such force, the machine was shattered in many pieces and Faldprenda was slain. I have recorded images I can send you."

"Do so." Its subordinate complied and Qetjnegartis watched the images with a sense of wonder. It was astonishing, but there was no doubt. "Amazing. There have been sightings of these phenomena by others, but no close encounters with them. We never suspected they could do such damage! We must take precautions to avoid them in the future."

"Yes, Commander."

"And what of the prey you were pursuing?"

"They may have been destroyed by the same phenomenon, Commander. I could find no trace of them once the storm had passed."

"Very well, return to the holdfast. I will dispatch a salvage team to recover the remains of the fighting machine. I am also concerned about this party of prey-creatures. They grow increasingly bold and I dislike their ability to spy upon our activities. There are also many of the non-warriors still at large in these regions. We must be more aggressive in our patrolling and harvesting."

"Yes, Commander."

Qetjnegartis issued the orders, but was disturbed by this senseless loss. The target world held many surprises, some of them deadly. *How many more will we discover to our loss? We had hoped that this place would be the salvation of the Race. Will it be the source of our destruction instead?*

* * * * *

437

SEPTEMBER, 1911, EAST OF AUGUSTA, ARKANSAS

"Well, that was bloody well amazing, Captain! Do you have things like that around here often?"

Frank Dolfen smiled at the Britisher and nodded. "This time of year? Yeah, I guess we do. Thunderstorms seem to cause 'em. Mostly in the flat lands, though. Kansas, Oklahoma, Iowa, parts of Missouri. Not quite so much down here in Arkansas, where it's not so flat, nor farther east or north. I spent years in the Dakotas and they were pretty rare up there."

"How on Earth do people manage to *live* in such a country?"

Dolfen shrugged. "I guess they're used to 'em. Most folks have storm cellars - sort of underground bunkers - to shelter in if one comes too close."

"That one definitely came too close!"

"Maybe so, but we were damn lucky it did. Come on, let's get out of here and back to the squadron."

They had found cover in a ravine to let the horses rest, but now they mounted up again and rode northeast toward where he had left the rest of the squadron. For a while he was concerned that the tornado might have rolled over them, the way it did the Martian, but the track of destruction veered off more to the east and was eventually lost to sight. They kept a careful watch to their rear to make certain there was nothing following them. The day was nearly over by the time they encountered the scouts and it was getting dark before he wearily dismounted, turned his horse over to a trooper, and stumbled into his tent. His orderly, Private Gosling, brought him coffee and some stew. He had to admit there were some advantages to being an officer!

"Sounds like ya had quite the adventure t'day, Cap'n!" Gosling, who everyone called 'the Goose', was an old veteran, even older than Dolfen, who himself had recently reached his twenty-year mark, and was not quite all there in the head anymore. Dolfen wasn't sure how he'd managed to find his way into the rebuilt 5th Cavalry, but he liked him and he did his job well enough.

"Yeah, damn near rode a twister home tonight."

"Saw the storm off t'the south of us. Looked like a bad one."

"Worst I ever saw. Glad it didn't get any closer to you."

"I remember one I saw when I was stationed down in Texas. We were near Pecos an'..."

"Goose?"

"Sir?"

"Have the officers join me in a half hour."

"Yes, sir. More stew?"

"No, this is fine, thanks." The man went out and Dolfen finished his supper and lay down on his cot for a few minutes. He didn't intend to sleep, but started awake when Gosling shook his shoulder.

"They're here sir."

He sat up, a little embarrassed, and went out under the tent fly. The lieutenants commanding the four troops of the squadron were there along with his aide, Lieutenant Lynnbrooke, and Major Bridges. "Evening, gentlemen, I trust you had a less eventful day than the major and I." This produced a small chuckle. His officers were all very young and seemed to treat him with the sort of automatic respect you gave a grandfather or elderly uncle; it was grating at times. There was also Lieutenant Abernathy, who commanded a battery of artillery which had been attached to the squadron. He didn't know the man well, but the mere fact that he'd managed keep up with the cavalry over sixty miles of dirt roads proved that he was no slouch.

"All right, we've accomplished the first part of our mission. We've observed the effects of the air attack on the Martian fortress. Tomorrow we get on with the rest of it. We will head northwest to hit the White River at Newport, then swing east to Jonesboro, then up to Paragould, and then back to Memphis. Our orders are to scout and lend assistance to any civilians we might find. This includes urging them to head east."

"Sir?" said Lieutenant Lynnbrooke. "We've already had a dozen or so people come in during the day while you were gone. A couple of families from near Beedeville. They're afraid to stay any longer."

"Are they on foot, or are they mounted?"

"Horses and wagons, sir. They have forty or fifty head of cattle, too, and don't want to abandon them."

Dolfen frowned. Escorting the civilians - and the livestock - was part of his job, but he'd hoped to do that on the way back. They were still outbound. "When we're done here, go tell them our route. They might not want to go with us to Newport. If they do, let them know that if we run into trouble they may have to abandon their goods and ride fast. If they don't want to go to Newport, tell them to head east as fast as they can and they should hit army patrols in forty or fifty miles."

"Yes, sir."

They clarified some questions about the departure time and order of march and then dispersed. Dolfen washed some of the dust off himself, pulled a spare hat out of his valise for the next day, and then went to sleep.

The next morning was refreshingly cool and crisp in the aftermath of the storm; a preview of fall. They took to the road - or what passed for a road in these parts. His squadron was a mix of new and old that Dolfen still found strange. A Troop was the usual mounted cavalry that he had spent twenty years with, but B Troop was all mounted on motorcycles, some single bikes and others with sidecars, some of which mounted light machine guns. C Troop was the biggest difference, it consisted of ten armored cars. These were strange-looking vehicles with eight wheels, each supporting an armored cab with a rotating turret on top. Some were armed with new Browning 50-caliber machine guns and a few had a two-inch quick-firing cannon. Just peashooters against a tripod, but still better than rifles. D Troop was also on horseback, but had pack horses to carry more of the 50-calibers and three of the new mortars that were just coming into service. Dolfen had no idea if they would be of much use. Still, the whole force was vastly more powerful than an old-style cavalry squadron. There was also a supply troop with motor trucks carrying food, ammunition, and gasoline. Abernathy's battery was all pulled by trucks and had four three-inch guns. In a fight, those guns might be the best weapons they'd have.

The column mostly stayed to the road, but he had a squad of horsemen scouting a couple of miles ahead and some of the motorcycles providing security on the flanks and in the rear. The bikes were too noisy to be leading the column. The civilians had decided they wanted to stay with the soldiers, so they trundled along just behind the supply trucks. This didn't really slow things down because with the condition of the roads, the motor vehicles had to take it slow anyway. They couldn't risk a broken axle here in enemy country.

The mere fact that they had to consider this 'enemy country' rankled Dolfen in the worst way. This was America, damn it! How dare some invader make parts of it enemy country! *We'll drive them out! We will!*

But there was no doubt that the Martians were here, at least for the moment. Every now and then they'd come across the triangular-shaped holes the enemy tripods made.

And there was the Red Weed.

Dolfen could see a few patches of the damn stuff here and there as they rode. It was a red plant which resembled Earthly lichen and clung to rocks and bare patches of ground. In the winter it only grew very slowly, but in warmer weather it would expand rapidly. Finally, it would enter a period of explosive growth with the patches able to cover acres under a thick mat in a matter of a few days. Then, the stuff would die off just as rapidly, turning brown and crumbling to powder. But during its brief period of life it would choke out the local plants underneath it and worse, it would leave seeds or spores or something which would begin the cycle all over again.

It seemed to appear close to the Martian fortresses. During the siege of Gallup, they had found it frequently and made a point of destroying it by burning. But now, with large regions under the Martians' control, no one was making the effort to get rid of it and it was spreading at a frightening rate. Even if they did drive the enemy out, would they have to deal with this awful stuff forever after?

They headed north until they reached a crossroad which led them to a ford on the Cache River. It wasn't much of a river this time of year, but the land on either side was thickly wooded and the locals had said this would be the best place to get across. They got there around noon and Dolfen called a halt to water the horses. It was a good place to stop; the trees gave them concealment. He posted pickets to keep a watch.

They hadn't been there long before civilians started appearing. Apparently there were dozens of them living in the woodlands. They'd refused to abandon their lands during the disastrous retreat of 1910, but after a year of precarious existence, always on the lookout for Martians, many of them were ready to call it quits before another winter arrived. The appearance of the soldiers and the hope of an escort to safety made up the minds of many of them.

Dolfen looked at these people with renewed anger. They were dirty, their clothes halfway to becoming rags, and there was a scared, hunted look in their eyes. The kids were very quiet, with none of the usual energy you'd expect. Oh yeah, the Martians were going to pay!

"What's it like across the river?" asked one woman, clutching a toddler to her. "Will we be safe? Where will we live?"

"You'll be as safe as anyone can be these days," Dolfen told her. "We're building some mighty powerful defenses along the Mississippi. You can live in the camps they've set up until they can resettle you. You're farmers, mostly, right?" She and some of the others nodded. "Good, we sure can use you! They're creating new farms by the thousands across the river. The country needs food. Don't worry, you'll get by fine."

"What about the weed, that red weed? Is it across the river, too? It keeps showing up here, choking out what crops we can plant!"

"No, there's none of it there." *Yet*.

This seemed to satisfy most of them, but one older man asked: "But when can we come back? When are you soldier-boys gonna drive these critters outta here? I've lived here all my life and I don't plan to die anywhere else!"

"The army will be back one of these days. I won't lie to you and say it will be soon. The truth is we took a licking last year and it's gonna take some time to build up our strength so we can beat these devils. But we will beat them! Not next week, and maybe not next year, but eventually we will. For the time being we need to get you folks to safety. So pack your stuff up and get ready to go. Those of you without horses can hitch a ride on the trucks." His speech didn't seem to encourage them very much, but they did as he told them.

It took longer than he wanted, but eventually they were on the road again and reached Newport - or what was left of it - before dark. It looked to have been a town of a few thousand before the Martians burned it. It was on the banks of the White River, which while bigger than the Cache, was still only knee deep in most spots during the summer. The ruins were an all-too familiar sight these days. There weren't enough of the Martians to occupy all the vast territories of the American heartland, but there were enough to make periodic sweeps and they routinely burned any structures they found. Single farms and tiny hamlets were sometimes overlooked, but all the bigger towns had been wrecked. And any human unlucky enough to cross the Martians' path would be scooped up and carried back to their larders.

The destruction in Newport looked nearly total, but despite that, they weren't there long before another group of civilians began to emerge from the ruins and gather from the nearby countryside. They were like the earlier group: full of questions, full of worry. It seemed like most wanted to go with them, but others, when they learned the soldiers weren't staying, wandered away, muttering.

They camped there for the night, Dolfen giving strict orders not to let any cook fires or lanterns show. On the relatively flat land, the light would carry for miles and they'd learned, to their cost, that the Martians operated night and day.

But nothing disturbed them and they were up early and on the road not long after dawn. They had well over a hundred civilians and twice that number of cattle with them now. The cattle were a nuisance, but they would be needed to help feed people across the Mississippi, and they shouldn't be left here to feed Martians. They were heading northeast now, toward the town of Jonesboro. It was over thirty miles away and they wouldn't get there in one day. They recrossed the Cache near a little village named Grubbs. The sign at the edge of town was still hanging on a post, but nothing else was left. They camped five miles short of Jonesboro; it wasn't a good day's march for cavalry, but not bad for the traveling circus Dolfen now commanded.

He and his officers gathered around a concealed fire that evening, sharing drinks and stories. As usual, Major Bridges had the most of both. The Britisher had been all over the world and had a seemingly endless supply of stories and tall tales. "I still can't get over how flat this country is," he said for at least the tenth time. "Parts of India and South Africa are pretty flat, but nothing like this!"

"You fought Martians in South Africa, sir?" asked Lieutenant Harvey Brown, commander of A Troop.

"Bless me, no! I was there in 1900, fighting the Boers! The ruddy Dutchmen didn't seem to want the honor of belonging to the Empire. We would have taught them the error of their ways if it hadn't been for the Martians arriving uninvited back home that spring. Threw all our plans into the midden heap, I can tell you! Kitchener was absolutely furious! Have I mentioned I've met the Field Marshal?"

"A few times…"

"Anyway, we had to call off that war, even though the Martians all died quickly enough. We couldn't be sure there weren't more on the way, so we had to bring the army home, just in case, you know. Gave the Boers their independence - for all the good it did them. Most of 'em are dead now, of course - or refugees at Capetown." He paused and took a drink from the bottle being passed around. "I fought the Martians in Afghanistan, of course." He chuckled. "For years the government was worried about the Russians trying to invade India, but when it finally happened it was the bloody Martians, not the Russians! But Afghanistan, as different a place from this as you could imagine; Mountains and more mountains. All up and down! A good thing, too! Their machines aren't too good at handling mountains and we stopped them in their tracks."

"They can do all right in the mountains," said Dolfen quietly. "I saw two regiments of cavalry wiped out trying to stop only six of the bastards at Glorietta Pass."

No one made a reply to that. None of them had been there, but they all knew the story of why the 5th Cavalry had been forced to rebuild yet again. Having succeeded in dampening the spirits of everyone, Dolfen turned in. *Gotta watch that, a commander can't afford to be pessimistic—it's contagious.*

He was awakened once during the night by a false alarm from a nervous sentry, but other than that and the arrival of a few more civilians, things were quiet. Gosling had his breakfast waiting for him in the morning, and he pushed his people to get ready to move as soon as possible. The empty, ruined land was getting on his nerves. He waited until they were almost ready to move out before using the radio to send a short message giving their location and situation. Bridges' warning that the Martians could track the radio signals had him worried, too.

They made it to Jonesboro in a couple of hours. It was a bigger place than Newport, but it had been just as thoroughly wrecked. They picked up a few more families who wanted to go, but they didn't linger long. They pushed on northeast, heading for the town of Paragould. With luck, they would get there by the next day and then they would turn back to Memphis.

It was about two o'clock when they spotted the Martians.

A man from B Troop roared up on a motorcycle to give the word: tripods sighted to the southwest. Dolfen took out his field glasses and climbed atop one of the armored cars and swept the horizon to their rear. At first he didn't see them, but then he realized that four tiny specks were not trees. He looked for a few more minutes, but there didn't seem to be any others. *Four, we might be able to take four.* Were they coming this way? Yes, no doubt. Coming fast, too…

"Lynnbrooke! Get on the radio. Tell Colonel Selfridge where we are and what we're facing. We've got a job for his flyboys!"

"Yes, sir!" replied his aide, who dashed off.

"Bugler! Sound Officer's Call." The tones rang down the length of the column and shortly, all of his officers arrived. He looked them over, still standing atop the armored car.

"Well, gentlemen, for the last eight months we've been training and drilling, and organizing. Today we'll find out if all that work was worthwhile. We've got four tripods on our trail, coming fast. We can't outrun them, not with all the civilians. And in any case, we're through running from these bastards. Today we are going to make *them* run! Harvey, you will detail one squad to escort the civilians and the extra supply trucks. Head due east toward the river. Forget about Paragould. Push them, you understand?"

"Yes, sir!"

"The rest of your troop will form a skirmish line across our rear, just like we've practiced. We will continue moving east, but slowly. I've sent for the aircraft, but God knows how long it will take them to get here. So we take our time engaging them. Wait for my signal to dismount. Bill, I want your bikes deployed per the plan: one squad with A Troop, another on either flank, and one more in reserve. Got it?"

"Got it, sir," said Lieutenant Bill Calloway, commander of B Troop.

"C and D Troop and Mister Abernathy's guns will maintain a position back near me until I decide how and when to deploy them. If we keep moving, it will probably be at least an hour before they catch up with us. With any luck, that's about when the aircraft will arrive. The key is to hit them with everything at once! Don't use up our men piecemeal!" He reined himself in. They all knew this. He'd been drilling them on it for months. "All right, let's get to it."

His officers dispersed to issue orders to their commands. Dolfen climbed down off the armored car, wincing as his feet touched the ground. He'd broken his leg at Glorietta Pass and it still bothered him at times. He got back on his horse. There were already shouts - and a few screams - from the civilians, but Harvey's troopers soon had them moving east as quickly as they could be made to move. Lieutenant Lynnbrooke returned to tell him that he'd gotten the message sent off and even received a reply. "Colonel Selfridge says to hang on, sir. He's on his way."

"Liar," said Dolfen. "It'll take him at least a half hour to get his crates in the air and another forty minutes to get here. Still, at least he's on the move."

"Yes, sir."

"And we need to get on the move, too." C and D Troop and the artillery started first, taking the same path as the civilians. A and B Troops waited until they were about a half mile ahead before following. The tripods were still six or seven miles behind them, but closing. They were probably the smaller and faster scouts. Well good; they'd be easier to kill.

An hour later there was still no sign of the airplanes, but the Martians had closed to less than three miles from the mounted screen. He'd have to make his move soon, airplanes or no airplanes. He waited a bit longer and then waved to Lieutenant Calloway. "Go to it, Bill!" Calloway waved back and then sent one of his bikers racing out to give the order to the skirmishers.

As soon as he got there, bugles started ringing out and immediately the squad of motorcycles who were with the horsemen roared off directly toward the Martians. They deliberately kicked up as much dust as they could. They closed on the enemy very fast and Dolfen was afraid they would get too close too soon. But they spun about and came racing back the way they'd come.

Meanwhile, three quarters of the cavalry dismounted, the men disappearing into gullies and patches of tall grass. The land was mostly flat, but it was cut up with numerous little creeks and ravines and there were plenty of hiding places for a man. The remaining quarter towed the empty horses back toward Dolfen. With any luck the Martians wouldn't notice all the men now waiting in ambush for them. *Luck. We're gonna need all there is today!*

While this was going on, Lieutenant Abernathy was getting his guns into battery, and D Troop was setting up their mortars and machine guns. The armored cars of C Troop were spreading out into a line facing the oncoming enemy. They were doing it like they were on the drill field and Dolfen looked on in pride and satisfaction. *Now if it just works!*

Abernathy came trotting up. "We're ready, sir. When should I open fire?"

"As soon as you've got even the faintest chance of hitting them, Lieutenant. We need to keep them as busy as possible."

The young lieutenant took a look through his glasses. "All right, sir, I'll open up at thirty-five hundred yards. Normally that would be a waste of ammo, but we might get lucky."

"Get lucky, Lieutenant."

"Yes, sir." The man dashed off. Lieutenant McGuiness came up just as the other man was leaving.

"Ready, sir," he reported.

"Good, have the mortars open up when the bastards are five hundred yards in front of our skirmish line."

"Yes, sir. What about my machine guns?"

Dolfen shook his head. "You can't use them with all of our troops out in front. I'm afraid they'll be our last ditch if they break through."

"I understand, sir." He saluted and went back to his men.

Dolfen looked around. Still no airplanes. Had he taken care of everything? Was there anything left for him to do? Was he going to get his command chewed to pieces yet again?

"Looks like the show's about to begin, old man, eh?" Bridges was there, looking through his field glasses. "Is there anything you'd like me to do, Captain?"

"Stay alive, Major, stay alive."

443

"Delighted, sir, absolutely delighted."

Four loud booms, so close together that they were almost one, made him jump. Abernathy's guns had opened up. He looked down range and thought he could see a few explosions far beyond the Martians. Yes, a direct hit at this range was very unlikely. After about thirty seconds they fired again, but this time each one in sequence. This was far below their maximum rate of fire, but the gunners were wisely taking their time with each shot.

The Martians continued to close, apparently undismayed by the artillery fire, although they started to zig-zag a bit to throw off the gunners' aim. "The beasties are learning," he heard Bridges say from beside him.

"Yes, damn them."

Closer and closer. The mortars opened fire and explosions started to erupt around the enemy machines. The mortars threw an explosive three-inch bomb high in the air which then fell down on the target. They didn't have nearly the impact of an artillery round, but they had a bigger explosive charge so maybe they'd do some damage. Their one advantage was that they made virtually no smoke when they fired. Maybe the Martians wouldn't know where they were.

The enemy was nearly up to where the line of dismounted troopers were hiding. The motorcycles were gathering to make their sprint. The field guns went to rapid fire and they were now cranking out a round every few seconds. "Hit them," muttered Dolfen. "Hit the damn things!"

He saw what might have been a hit on one of the tripods, but they kept coming, obviously trying to get close enough to the guns to take them out. Just another hundred yards or so...

The motorcycles of B Troop gunned their engines and he could hear them even from three-quarters of a mile away. They leapt toward the Martians just as the cavalry emerged from their hiding places, shooting rifles and throwing bombs. The armored cars of C Troop surged forward, their small guns popping away.

"Nicely done!" shouted Bridges.

Yes, it had been nicely done, exactly as they'd practiced. Everyone was hitting them at the same time, although D Troop had to cease fire with the mortars now that the enemy was mixed in with the men. But was it doing any good? The Martians had halted their advance and were now firing off their heat rays in all directions as they turned to meet the threats coming in all around them. Abernathy's guns kept firing, any misses would fly far beyond the other men before bursting.

Smoke, dust, and flames leapt up all around the tripods, but all four were still there, still fighting. "Come on! Come on!" said Dolfen, it was almost a prayer. His men were dying out there and he was just watching!

Suddenly one of the tripods staggered. It stumbled backward and then toppled, disappearing into the clouds of dust. Got one! A cheer went up along the line, but the other three continued to blast away with their heat rays. Dolfen stared through his field glasses, trying to see, but what he saw was men on foot and men on motorcycles emerging from the smoke, falling back. Two of the armored cars were burning, the others were pulling back...

We've shot our bolt... what the hell do I do now? Try to regroup? Hit them again?

A sudden roar made him flinch and he nearly dropped the glasses. Something passed low overhead. Then another and another. Dolfen looked up in astonishment as wave after wave of aircraft roared past. Dozens of them!

"Selfridge! He made it!"

Indeed he had. The airplanes, like some flock of impossibly large birds, threw themselves at

444

the enemy, machine guns blazing. They were on the Martians before they could react. Dolfen could see the sparks of fifty-caliber bullets hitting the armor. Bombs started exploding around the tripods, making the earlier artillery and mortar fire look like firecrackers. He prayed his men had been able to get clear.

But the Martians recovered immediately and shifted their fire. Airplanes burst into flames and tumbled from the sky as the heat rays washed over them. In moments a dozen blazing wrecks littered the ground. But the rest pressed on and the appearance of the fliers seemed to rally the spirits of the troops. Men were surging forward now instead of retreating.

Plane after plane made its attack, but were they accomplishing anything? Survivors were turning, circling around to attack again, but so many of them had already gone down. And still the tripods were fighting.

Abernathy's guns had ceased fire for fear of hitting the aircraft. Should he order them to open up again? So many planes were being destroyed already, maybe the risk would be...

"I say! Look at that fellow!"

Bridges' cry brought his attention back to the aircraft. A burning plane was diving right at one of the tripods! As Dolfen watched, the machine hit it head on and its bomb exploded. The blast blotted out plane and tripod in a flash and a cloud of smoke. When it cleared, neither one remained.

For a moment, the battle seemed to come to a halt; everyone, human and Martian alike, stunned by what they'd just seen. And then a great cry went up from Dolfen's soldiers. Men rose up and charged, motorcycles and armored cars rumbled forward. Abernathy's guns roared back to life.

And the Martians fled.

The two surviving tripods turned and ran as fast as their spindly legs could carry them. The planes and cycles pursued them for a few miles, but when two more planes were brought down, the rest turned back; after a while the motorcycles did, too. The enemy kept retreating until they were out of sight.

The aircraft regrouped and flew east. One came low and circled several times and waggled its wings. Dolfen guessed that was probably Selfridge and waved back. Then it turned and followed the others.

Dolfen let out a long sigh and ordered the buglers to sound recall. Slowly his men fell back to his position. He was heartened by how many there were. The losses weren't as bad as he'd feared. But he was sure they were bad enough. When they totaled it up they'd lost about forty dead and another dozen wounded. The crazy fliers had lost no less than seventeen of their aircraft and most of their crews died with them. They only pulled five men alive from the wrecks and one of them died within the hour. Damn, this was the part of being an officer that he really hated. All those dead men were acting under his orders. He'd sent them out there to get killed while he stayed safely in the rear. It was the way things worked, he supposed, but he'd never get used to it.

He ordered the artillery to limber up and get moving. The wounded were loaded up on a couple of the ammo trucks. D Troop followed immediately. It took a while to reorganize the others and Dolfen took the opportunity to ride out and inspect the remains of the battle. The one tripod which the plane had struck was just scattered debris, but the other one which had gone down was mostly intact, although its pilot was dead.

Dolfen had standing orders concerning downed tripods: salvage the power units if he could. They were bulky cylindrical objects mounted on the undersides of the tripods. Apparently they were valuable for some reason. He had some of the mechanics from C Troop take a look and they actually got one of the things detached and strapped to an armored car. But the other one would need a crane to get at and there was no time. He fully expected the Martians to come back in greater numbers and he wasn't going to wait for them.

"Okay, great job, everyone. Now let's get the hell out of here."

CHAPTER THREE

OCTOBER, 1911, EDDYSTONE, PENNSYLVANIA

Colonel Andrew Comstock looked at the behemoth towering over him and whistled.

"God in Heaven," said his aide, Lieutenant Hornbaker.

"Yes," replied Andrew. "If God were going to build himself a chariot, it might look like this."

"Impressive, isn't it?" Andrew turned to see the Baldwin Locomotive Works representative, John Schmidt, smiling broadly. They were standing in Baldwin's new facility in Eddystone, along the Delaware River just south of Philadelphia. With all the demands for war production they had outgrown their factory in the northern part of that city and built the new place here. Production lines were turning out dozens of steam tanks every day, but Andrew wasn't here to see the steam tanks. No, they were here to see something a great deal larger.

"Yes, it certainly is, Mr. Schmidt. But does it work?"

"Of course it works! That's why we invited you here today, Colonel. We've got steam up and we're ready to go."

"Well, by all means then, tell your people to get going."

Schmidt ran off to do that while Andrew continued to stare. They were here to see the tests of the new land ironclad. His thoughts went back to a conversation he'd had with General Hawthorne standing on the banks of this very river four years earlier. They'd been looking at the unfinished battleship Michigan and Andrew had quipped that it was a shame they couldn't put wheels on battleships so they could fight the Martians on land. It had just been a joke, but here was his joke made into reality!

Of course, the machine in front of them wasn't a battleship. Andrew had spent some time aboard real battleships and what they had here was only a fraction of the size. It was a little over a hundred feet long and about forty wide. The upper parts did look like a navy warship sitting out of the water like in a drydock. But that image was ruined by the two pairs of enormous caterpillar tracks on which the rest of it was sitting. Each track was about twelve feet wide, and twelve tall and maybe twenty-five feet long. A long angled bracket connected each track to the 'hull' of the vehicle. This was indeed shaped much like the hull of a ship and that was intentional. The only possible way to transport a monster like this would be by water and so the hull was watertight and able to float.

Well, almost. The hull didn't provide enough displacement to actually float, so when in transit, several detachable units would be fixed to the front and sides to provide the additional buoyancy. Or at least that was the theory.

"This thing can actually move, sir?" asked Hornbaker.

447

"So they claim. I guess we'll find out soon enough."

The upper parts of the vehicle were not finished yet. At the moment there was just a tall smokestack and a temporary control cabin. Assuming this test worked well, they would add the upper works and the armament which would be very formidable indeed. One large turret would mount a twelve-inch naval gun, while another mounted a seven-incher, and four smaller turrets would have five-inch guns. There were also a dozen or so mounts for machine guns. Heavy armor protected all the vulnerable parts and much of it was the metal-asbestos sandwich developed by the metallurgical lab at MIT. Tests had shown it to be extremely resistant to the heat ray, even at short range. Every opening could be sealed off on command to keep out the black dust weapon of the Martians. There was even an ingenious system to produce a cloud of steam around the machine which would reduce the effect of the Martian heat rays. In theory this thing could roll right into a swarm of tripods and smash them all. At least that was the theory. Another theory. The ironclads seemed to abound with theories.

Schmidt had climbed aboard the thing by way of a ladder which could be raised or lowered at need. He reappeared a few minutes later on the deck and waved to Andrew. The smoke coming from the stack thickened and then came billowing out in a steady stream. There was a sound of heavy machinery in motion and then the entire vehicle seemed to shudder. It jerked forward a few inches, stopped, and then lurched into motion, the massive tracks slowly rotating.

"It works!" cried Hornbaker.

"I'll be damned," said Andrew. "It really does." A small mob of workers had gathered and they began cheering.

At first it was moving very slowly, only a couple of feet per minute, but it gradually gained speed until it was moving at about a walking pace. The tracks crunched the gravel underneath them, but only sank a few inches into them. The thick iron plates were so broad they spread the weight over a large area.

"How do they steer it?" shouted Hornbaker.

"Same way as they do the steam tanks," said a nearby worker. "Make the tracks on the outside of the turn go faster. Look! That's what they're doing now."

Sure enough, the ironclad was slowly turning to the left. "If they want to do a really tight turn," said Andrew, "they can reverse the motion of the other tracks."

The huge machine swung around ninety degrees, reversed itself, and did the same thing until it was pointing in the opposite direction. After that, it halted and the ladder was lowered. Schmidt came to the edge of the deck and waved. "Come aboard!" he shouted.

Andrew eagerly climbed the ladder into the vehicle. The lower level was all hissing and clanking machinery and it was hot as hell, but a man directed him up another ladder to the deck. Schmidt was waiting for him and Andrew stuck out his hand. "Congratulations, sir! It really works!"

"Thank you, Colonel. I know it's been a long haul, but we have the measure of the thing now." He directed them over to the control station. "This is just temporary, of course. When we get the upper works finished, there will be something like the bridge of a ship where the commander and helmsman and all will be."

"Huh, I was expecting a ship's wheel," said Andrew. There was just a series of levers.

"Actually there will be a wheel eventually to control the rudder for when it's on the water," explained Schmidt. "These are the controls for the tracks. Would you like to try?"

Andrew smiled sheepishly and then allowed Schmidt to show him which levers to push to set the vehicle in motion. He gingerly slid a pair of them forward a notch and was delighted when they began to move! Another notch and they went a little faster.

"The real breakthrough was when we abandoned the idea of trying to make this like a traditional ship with the steam engine directly moving the tracks," explained the Baldwin man. "Trying to engineer a drive train from the hull down to the track assembly defeated us again and again. Just too much strain and the angles were all wrong. So we decided to put a British-made steam turbine in the main hull and use that to generate electricity. We use that to power Westinghouse electric motors down there in the track assemblies."

"Ingenious," said Andrew. "Uh, we seem to be about to ram that building up ahead." Schmidt laughed and took over the controls to bring them to a safe halt.

"So how long to finish this up? And how soon will you have more?"

"William Cramp & Sons is producing the upper works and gun turrets right now in Philadelphia. They're also building the flotation devices. Once those are done, we can move this up river to their yards and have the upper works and turrets installed. We hope to have this one finished by early next year. We've already started construction of the other five in the first run and they should be much faster to build. We ought to have the first squadron done by the spring."

"Another six months. A lot can happen in six months." He wasn't too happy about that and knew the generals wouldn't be either. "So what about the 'Little Davids'?"

"That's next on the tour, Colonel. Follow me, will you?" They went down through the ironclad and Schmidt led them to another part of the sprawling Baldwin works. Andrew pointed out an area where armored railroad trains were being built.

"Yes," said Schmidt, "we received a large order for those from the government last spring. We're just going into mass-production now."

"They would have been a big help back in 1910," said Andrew grimly. "Could have used one at Glorietta Pass, that's for sure."

They left the train sheds behind and came to another complex of buildings. Sitting outside were a number of huge... *things*. "There they are, Colonel, almost ready to send to the front."

They weren't nearly as big as the land ironclad, but they were still damn big. Four huge wheels, each twice the height of a man, were connected to a central hull which also held a boiler and smoke stack. Projecting above was the mount for a gun turret. The turrets held no guns as of yet, but from the size of the mount you could tell it would be a big one.

"The turrets are the same size and design as the main turret for the land ironclads," explained Schmidt. "It will hold a twelve-inch gun."

"There don't seem to be any other guns, sir," said Hornbaker. "And the boiler looks kind of vulnerable. Will they be adding more armor, sir?"

"No," said Andrew, who was familiar with the project. "These were designed as a fill-in until the land ironclads were ready. They are basically just a way to get a really big gun near the combat. With the range of the twelve-incher, they ought to be able to stay far enough back that the relative lack of armor won't be a liability. Or that's the theory." Turning to Schmidt, he asked: "Can they move?"

"Yes they can, Colonel. We have one with steam up over there." They walked over to one of the Little Davids which had smoke coming out of its stack. "Unlike the land ironclads these are powered directly from the steam engine. Only the rear two wheels have power. The front two are just for steering." He signaled the crew and shortly they had the thing chugging around the yard. While it would certainly be powerful once it had its gun, it seemed a poor substitute for the land ironclads, but Andrew didn't say so aloud. It was certainly far better than nothing.

"This looks good, Mr. Schmidt," said Andrew after they watched for a while. "When can you deliver them?"

"We'll need another few weeks to get them all operational and then the gun needs to be mounted. I understand you'll need to do some firing tests after that."

"Yes, we'll want them moved to Aberdeen for that. As I understand it, these can be disassembled for transport by rail. Correct?"

"Yes, Colonel, although I have to tell you it's a lengthy process both for disassembly and assembly again. It would be far better to put them on barges and ship them by water."

Andrew frowned. "That might be possible to get them down to Aberdeen, but I don't know where they'll be needed after that. You are going to have to train our men in the procedures."

"Yes. And we'll need you to send us the men you plan to use for the crews as soon as possible. Both for these and the land ironclads. They will have a lot to learn both to operate and maintain them."

"I'll talk to my boss. I understand there's some controversy about just where these monsters will fall in our organization charts - or who will be supplying the crews."

Schmidt snorted. "At least the navy doesn't have that problem!"

Yes, that was true. The navy was building its own version of the land ironclads. They were nearly identical to the army's, but apparently they had reduced the armor thickness and eliminated one of the smaller turrets to lighten the load and improve their sea-keeping characteristics. Andrew had heard that the navy was planning to attach them to their naval squadrons and use them to launch raids against Martian held territory that bordered the sea or large rivers.

"Oh, and that reminds me," said Schmidt. "There's one other thing."

"Really? What?"

"Have you decided what you are going to name these? They really ought to have names."

* * * * *

OCTOBER, 1911, TWELVE MILES WEST OF QUEPOS, COSTA RICA

"Main guns stand by, we're going to try and get a shot at them!"

Lieutenant Commander Drew Harding, gunnery officer aboard the battleship *USS Minnesota*, had been hoping to hear that order for over an hour. The *Minnesota* along with the *Connecticut*, *Virginia*, and a few cruisers had been patrolling off the west coast of Costa Rica when a scouting destroyer had reported seeing Martian tripods marching around the Gulf of Nicoya, about forty miles to the northwest. They had immediately changed course to intercept.

Drew and the squadron had been on a number of patrols since they arrived in Pacific waters back in July, and while they had seen the depredation of the Martians, this was the first time they'd spotted any live ones. Drew - and every man aboard - was itching to take a crack at them. This was especially true because the other half of the Pacific task force, who they alternated patrols with, had managed to engage the Martians twice and killed a few of them both times. They had made full use of their crowing rights in the bars and fleshpots of Panama City, and Drew and his comrades were heartily sick of it. Time to even the score!

At full speed they had closed the distance quickly, but then the scout reported that the Martians must have spotted their smoke and were now retreating back the way they'd come. It had become a stern chase. Drew was on the forward observation platform, high up on the cage mast. It had the best view on the whole ship and he'd been watching the Martians through a powerful set of binoculars. There looked to be six or eight of them and they were moving along the shoreline with the strange but rapid gait the tripods were capable of. Everyone was worried that they'd turn inland and disappear among the jungles that covered the mountains there. But the tripods didn't do well in thick jungles - or so they'd been told - and this batch seemed to prefer the much better speed possible along the shore. Mile by mile they had overhauled them and now they were nearly in range of the twelve-inch guns of the battleships. The cruisers could have closed the range faster, but the admiral didn't want them to spook the game before the big ships could get close.

And now the order had come to prepare to fire. Reluctantly Drew turned away and headed down the ladder. He enjoyed the status and responsibility of being the ship's gunnery officer, but there was one thing he hated about it: he couldn't see what was going on! In the old days, the gunnery officer would be right there alongside the gunners, directing their fire. They could see the target and see the effect of their shots. But these days, it was all different. Spotters up on the platforms would use precision optical instruments to observe the range, bearing, and speed of the target and pass that information down to a heavily protected compartment in the bowels of the ship. This was the Plotting Room and there, Drew and a team of highly trained officers and ratings, would take that information, add in further data about the course and speed of their own ship, and using an amazingly complicated mechanical calculator, rapidly determine exactly where to point the guns and when to fire them. This was sent to the gunners themselves who fired as directed.

And Drew never got to see a thing.

Information was already coming in when he arrived in the Plotting Room and his team was processing it and setting up shots even though they were still out of range. Before he could sit down, someone handed him a canvas bag which had the anti-dust mask in it. From time to time the Martians would use their toxic black dust weapon. The vessels had been fitted with shutters to try and keep the deadly stuff out, but on the older ships the attempts had not been entirely satisfactory and crews were given the dust masks just in case. Newer ships were being designed with anti-dust features right from the start. Drew looped the strap on the bag over his shoulder and then observed his people at work.

The distance was down to about twenty thousand yards and that was at the very edge of extreme range for the big guns. They really ought to try to close to fifteen thousand if they could. Minutes went by with everyone getting more and more anxious. Would they get a chance? They were setting up another shot when the telephone buzzed. Drew immediately grabbed and said: "Plotting Room."

It was the first officer. "Guns?" he said, using the traditional nickname for the gunnery officer. "The flagship just signaled commence firing. Give 'em hell, Drew!"

"Yes, sir!" He slammed down the phone and turned to his crew. "Stand by to fire! A Turret make ready!" Only the forward turret could be brought to bear with them chasing the enemy. Its two twelve-inch guns were already loaded and they'd been continuously aiming the guns based on the information being sent to them. All they needed was the command to fire.

Drew watched as the latest sightings were fed into the mechanical calculating machine and produced the new aiming directions. This was automatically relayed to the turret. He kept his eyes on the pitch and roll indicator and positioned his hand over the firing button. A green light burned next to it indicating the loaded status of the guns. The button would turn on a similar light in the turret and the commander there would pull the trigger. At just the right moment Drew pressed it.

Almost instantly a strong shudder passed through the ship. He couldn't hear the guns, but he could certainly feel them! A couple of the men gave a cheer before quickly going back to work. Drew picked up a different telephone and waited.

"Two hundred left, three hundred short," said a voice.

"Two hundred left! Three hundred short!" he shouted. His men fed those corrections into the machine. A new firing solution was produced and passed on. A few seconds later the green light went on and after a final check Drew pushed the firing button. Again the ship shuddered as another salvo was sent off.

451

"A hundred right, a hundred over," reported the lookout.

They had over-corrected. Drew passed on the new data and forty-five seconds later fired again. More corrections, more shots. But were they hitting anything? This went on for about ten minutes and then the order came to cease fire.

"Well?" he said to the observer. "Did we get any hits?"

"Hard to say, sir," came the reply. "A lot of shells fell right in their vicinity, but they've retreated into the jungle and we can't see them now."

"Damn."

A half hour went by and they were released from battle stations. Drew climbed back up to the observation platform and scanned the coastline with his binoculars. The squadron was circling off shore from the point of action. One of the destroyers got as close in as it dared while the rest stood by to support it if the Martians suddenly reappeared.

But they did not and the destroyer couldn't report any conclusive sign of damage to the enemy. The squadron drew off, feeling content with their actions, but disappointed by the results. When Drew came off watch he found his roommate, Hank Coleman, in their compartment. "Hey there, Guns! Get anything today?"

"Who knows? Don't think so. Scared the bastards though."

"Well, we'll get them next time."

"I hope so."

* * * * *

OCTOBER, 1911, WASHINGTON D.C.

Lieutenant General Leonard Wood found the President in his office having a shave. Roosevelt had the odd habit of shaving in the afternoon, after lunch. He said it just seemed like the best time to do it and Wood had never tried to argue the point. He was leaning back in his large desk chair, with a cloth covering him up to his chin and lather on much of his face. His barber was hovering over him, but when Roosevelt caught sight of Wood, he boomed out: "Leonard! Good to see you!" The barber stepped back with a snort of exasperation.

"Mr. President, I nearly cut you! Please stay still!"

"Sorry, sorry. But Leonard, sit down. Tell me what's happening while I stay still."

Wood nodded to Roosevelt's aide, Major Butt, and took a seat where Roosevelt could see him around the barber. "So, good news first or bad, sir?"

"Oh, the good to start! Tony, here, doesn't want me frowning!"

"Very well then. Good news. The lull in Martian attacks has allowed us to really build up our strength along the Mississippi. We're pouring concrete in record amounts and mounting dozens of large guns every month. There are scores of monitors and gunboats on call to move to danger points. We've got reserves on the east shore with large numbers of the steam tanks and armored trains. Many sections we can tentatively call secure from attack, allowing us to shift our mobile forces elsewhere."

"Nothing's ever really secure, Leonard. Funston thought his lines around Albuquerque and Santa Fe were secure and look what happened there."

"True, but we have to make some decisions about what we can live with. We've got over thirteen hundred miles to defend and we have to take some risks. We've fortified our most vital areas to withstand what we calculate as a worst case attack and are now working on less critical areas.

I'm particularly pleased with what we've accomplished on the Superior Switch." He got up and walked over to the big wall map and traced his finger on a line from Minneapolis to Lake Superior. "This is what I've been losing sleep over the most for the last year. The line along the river has natural strength, but the gap between it and the lake was wide open to be turned. If the Martians got around the river's headwaters to the north and flanked us, the whole line would have been in danger."

"But they didn't do that," said Roosevelt. "Glad I talked you out of building the line from Davenport to Milwaukee and abandoning the whole state of Wisconsin. We've given up too many states already."

"Yes we have, sir. But the Switch Line is very strong now and I'm no more worried about it than any other section. Currently 1st Army is holding the line from the lake to Davenport, 3rd Army has from Davenport to Memphis, and 4th Army the rest of the way to the Gulf. We've been adding divisions to each army as they arrive, but that's far too much territory for each of them, so I'm planning to split them in half to create three new armies and insert them into the line between the others. Each will have ten to twelve divisions, which is about the proper size."

"Sixty divisions, by God," said Roosevelt. "Over a million men."

"And that doesn't even include all the corps and army assets. Closer to two million right now."

"And all of them sitting on the defensive."

Wood restrained a sigh, knowing where Roosevelt was about to go with this. Fortunately, the barber was finishing up and plunked a hot towel over his face, cutting off anything further. Wood took advantage and plowed on with the news.

"We've got the defenses of St. Louis in good order. Seeing as how it's the largest bastion we still have on the west side of the river, we've put special emphasis there. In addition to regular artillery, we've installed all five of the captured heat rays that Tesla got working for us."

"Mmmph!" said Roosevelt, nodding his head.

"And speaking of Tesla, I've gotten a report from the Ordnance Department, young Comstock - you remember him - and he says that Tesla has really come up with something. A lightning gun of some sort which he thinks has real potential to be an effective weapon. I've given orders to proceed with development. We've also gone into full production of the new small rocket launchers. We'll be getting them to our infantry as soon as possible. We're hoping they will make a real difference. The land ironclads are in their final tests, and the Little Davids will be shipped to the front soon. I haven't decided where I'll station them, but I plan to keep them in reserve for now."

The barber removed the towel and smeared some scented lotion on the President's face.

"In other good news, the British defenses in Canada are shaping up well. They've repulsed a few probes near Montreal and Quebec, and their line from Georgian Bay across to the St Lawrence is a reality rather than just a line on the map. With luck, they'll secure our northern border."

"Oh, that reminds me Leonard," said Roosevelt, shooing away the barber and rubbing at his chin. "Bryce, asked me the other day if it would be possible for them to buy some of our steam tanks."

"What for? They make their own tanks. Probably better ones than ours."

"Well, he was saying that nearly all their tank production is going out to their regular forces. But the Canadians are raising a lot of provisional units and they don't have enough tanks to supply them, too. I was thinking that it might be a gesture of solidarity and good will. And it would strengthen our northern defenses."

"Hmmm, it might be possible. Production has been expanded enormously. I suppose I could divert some from the Ford plant in Michigan without causing any real problems. I'll have my staff look into it."

"Good! So, any more good news?"

"Not... really. We launched some bombing raids against several Martian fortresses, but the results have been minimal as far as we can tell. I don't think air attacks are going to accomplish much on their own."

"I got a letter from some lieutenant colonel in the Signal Corps the other day claiming exactly the opposite. He says we need more bombers, a lot more."

"What was his name?" asked Wood, scowling.

"Uh, Morgan? No, Mitchell, yes, that was it."

"Damn, I thought so. William Mitchell, he's made a pest of himself to me as well. Always demanding we build more planes - as if we didn't have enough demands on our resources. But blast the man! He had no business writing directly to you! He's a loose cannon."

"He also wrote that the air services ought have their own separate branch of the military."

"Yes, that's a hobby horse of his, too. I think he sees himself as the head of that new branch. Well, if he doesn't behave himself, he's going to find himself the head of some outpost in the Aleutians!"

"He's got spirit," said Roosevelt. "Got to hand him that. We need spirit."

"Yes, that's true. And aircraft have proven themselves useful. Just the other day a group of them helped destroy two tripods that were attacking a cavalry detachment in Arkansas."

"Bully! Well done!" The President shifted himself in his chair and put on his pince-nez glasses. "So what else have you got for me?"

Wood glanced at his notes. "Uh, work continues on the canal defenses. They are firming up. The navy reports that they are seeing more and more Martian scouting forces in the region, both north and south of the canal. They may be preparing for an attack."

"The canal *must* be defended," said Roosevelt sharply.

"And it will be, Theodore, it will be. Our defenses are already very strong and they get stronger every day. My analysts think that the German enclave in Venezuela and the French one in Mexico are proving to be real distractions to the Martians in those areas. They will siphon off strength from any attack on the canal."

"Well, that's good. The French and Germans surely haven't been much help otherwise!"

"We can use any help we can get. And I have to wonder if the French aren't doing more good than any of us suspect."

"What do you mean?"

"Well, I can't think of any other reason why the Martians down in Mexico haven't created more trouble for us in Texas, New Mexico, and Arizona. We are still wide open down there against a serious attack - which I guess brings us to the top of the 'bad news' list."

"Yes," said Roosevelt, nodding. "I'm getting telegrams almost every day from Governor Colquitt in Texas, and messages from their senators and most of their congressmen every week demanding more forces for Texas. I wish we could send more, Leonard."

"I wish we could, too. I'm meeting with General Funston later today. He's come up from Houston to plead his case. Uh... do you want to see him?"

The President frowned and shook his head. "No, you can handle him. I have meetings with the governors of Iowa and Kansas today wanting to know when in hell they can get their states back." He fixed his gaze on Wood. "What should I tell them Leonard?"

Now Wood did sigh. This was the perpetual question: when can we stop being on the defensive and start driving the invader back? "Mr. President, after our defeats last year, our priority has been to establish a secure line of defense for the eastern states…"

"And you just told me we have done so," interrupted Roosevelt.

"And as you just pointed out, sir, nothing is absolutely secure," countered Wood. "If we try to launch an offensive prematurely we risk disaster. Look at what just happened to the Russians: they had a fairly strong line along the Volga River but then tried to attack eastward. The Martians crushed their attack and then followed up with a counteroffensive of their own, and now the Volga's been breached and the Russians are in real trouble. They may lose Moscow before the winter. We can't risk the same thing happening here."

"No, no, of course not. But we can't just sit here forever! The people are demanding action. We've got five million refugees who want to go home."

"My staff *is* making plans, sir."

"I'd like to see them!"

"I'll arrange a presentation. But in brief, nothing will happen until we are certain the Mississippi Line is really secure - and frankly, sir, I'm hoping we can prove that by repulsing some serious Martian attacks and wear *them* down a bit. Once we are confident of our defense, then we can begin our own offensive.

"The whole key is the railroads, of course. The only way to supply our armies across the river is by rail, and as we found out last year to our loss, the railroads are just too damn vulnerable to fast moving Martian raiding forces. This means that any advance we make is going to have to be slow. We will have to push out from our fortified cities, like St. Louis and Memphis, rebuild the railroads for a dozen miles, and then build a heavily fortified outpost to defend the line. Push another dozen miles and do it again."

"Like an old fashioned siege with parallels and communication trenches," grumbled Roosevelt. "Those took a lot of time."

"Yes, sir, exactly like that, I'm afraid. But at the moment we have no choice. The Martian fortresses are too strong to be taken by a sudden rush and as far as we can tell, they aren't dependent on lines of supply like we are. Any attempt to bypass them will just leave our own forces in danger of being cut off and destroyed. No, our strategy will be to slowly approach their fortresses, protecting our own supply lines as we go, and then bring overwhelming force to bear to destroy them. I'm sorry, sir, but this is going to take time."

Roosevelt frowned and tapped his fingers on his desk. "Yes, yes, I can see that," he said after a moment. "But when can we start? Can I at least tell those governors that we'll be starting soon?"

"Not before next spring at the soonest, I'm afraid." *And maybe not even then depending on what the Martians do.* "And of course we need to wait until the next batch of enemy cylinders arrive, which are due in January." Yes, as incredible as it seemed, the dispatch of another wave of cylinders from Mars had now become almost routine. A hundred or so had been launched the previous month. Everyone was assuming they would be like the previous one: reinforcements for the existing Martian forces and not a landing in some new area. But they needed to be sure.

"So the spring, then," said the President. "Well, they won't be happy, but they'll have to accept it, I suppose. Hopefully we can make some real progress before the fall, do you think?"

Before the election you mean. Yes, that was the other thing weighing on the President's mind. There would be an election next year and there was some serious opposition to Roosevelt running for a fourth term—even from within the Republican Party. The Democrats were putting together their most serious threat in twenty years, and if the war continued as it was, there was a real danger that Roosevelt would not be reelected. Wood shuddered at the thought of trying to work with a President Nelson Miles! *Well, I probably won't have to—he's sure to fire me right off.*

Wood got up from his chair. "I have to be going, sir. Good luck with those governors."

"Thank you. And good luck to you with Funston. He's not the sort to take no for an answer!"

"Yes, sir, that I know!" Wood left the office, and slipped out a side door of the White House. He'd seen Governors Stubbs and Carroll waiting for their turn with Roosevelt when he'd come in and he didn't want to give them a crack at him. He walked across the street to the newly renamed War & Navy Building. It used to be the State, War, & Navy Building, but the vastly increased demands of the war effort had required more and more space until there just wasn't enough room for all three departments, even in that massive building. Wood had hoped to move the War Department to some location more remote from the center of Washington, but Roosevelt had insisted that the military departments be kept close by and Henry Stimson, the Secretary of War, had agreed, so the State Department's facilities were being moved to a new building under construction a block south. Wood appreciated the extra space for his operations, but they were still too close to Capitol Hill - and be it said, the White House - for comfort.

He trotted up the steps to his office and stopped short when he saw that Funston was already in the outer office. Damn, he wasn't due for another half hour! But it was too late to sneak away for a few moment's relaxation. Funston saw him and Wood had no choice but to go in and greet him. "Good to see you, Freddy! How was your trip?"

"Not too bad, Leonard, not too bad. More than the usual delays on the trains, though. Good God, but there's a lot of military traffic on the roads! Mile after mile of tanks and guns. Why in hell can't some of that be sent my way?"

Wood grimaced. Funston wasn't wasting any time! Well, in his place Wood wouldn't either. "Come into my office and we'll discuss it. I guess you've met my aide, Semancik, here?"

"Yes, and this is Captain Willard Lang, my aide. He's been with me since Albuquerque." They shook hands and then went into Wood's private office. Semancik served them all coffee and then withdrew.

"So, General, what's your situation?" asked Wood.

"I brought a detailed report, but in plain words, my situation stinks. You've given me an absolutely impossible task, General!"

"I know I have, but you're the best I've got, Freddy."

"Don't try to butter me up, Leonard! I learned all about impossible situations when I was a volunteer with the Cuban insurrectionists in '97. But we had it easy compared to this!" Funston was a round-faced, slightly portly man in his late forties with a full beard and a tendency to get red in the face when excited or angry. His face was pretty red right now. "I've got nine divisions of regulars and seven more of Texas Volunteers, and you expect me to defend a line two thousand miles long! You've got sixty divisions on the Mississippi to defend a line barely half that length!"

"And you know perfectly well why that is, General," said Wood softly.

"Because Texas doesn't matter to the stuffed shirts and millionaires back east!"

"I think it would be more fair to say that the east matters more, not that Texas doesn't matter at all."

"Fair?! *Fair!* When the Martians punch through my lines like they were tissue paper - and they will! - what am I supposed to tell my men and the civilians I'm defending? 'Yes, I know it's not fair, but Washington won't let me defend you'!"

"Freddy, calm down. I don't have to tell you the score. If we lose the east, it's the whole shooting match. I have to protect the cities and the factories. There's no choice, damn it!" Anger crept into his voice. Not at Funston, but at the whole situation.

Funston seemed surprise by Wood's outburst and got control of himself. His aide, Captain Lang, stepped into the silence. "We're well aware of the situation, sir. But unless you look at Texas as just a forlorn hope, we are going to need more equipment. Men we've got, but they can't fight Martians with nothing but rifles. If we can't be better supplied perhaps we should face facts and pull everyone back across the Mississippi rather than risk sacrificing them all."

Even Funston looked shocked at the suggestion. Abandon Texas? From a strictly military point of view it did make sense. Eliminate that enormous salient, bring the whole 2nd Army into the main defense line; yes, it would make sense.

But there was no way they could do that.

They'd lost other states, way too many, but they'd lost them after fighting for them. They'd lost a hundred thousand men fighting for those states. But give up the biggest one without a fight? And also give up the last rail connection with the west coast? No, Roosevelt would never agree and the country would go berserk. Funston knew it and he suspected that this Captain Lang knew it, too. The whippersnapper was just baiting him!

"We are sending you equipment," growled Wood.

"But not enough," countered Funston. "My regulars don't have half the artillery and tanks as your troops on the Mississippi, and the volunteers have got virtually nothing heavier than a machine gun. As Lang says, with all the refugees, we could field twice the number of volunteer organizations, but we don't even have rifles and machine guns for them!"

Wood nodded. It was true, and he felt guilty about making that promise to Roosevelt about diverting some tanks to the Canadians. And it was also true that Funston's defenses were hopelessly weak against a serious Martian attack. The only really strong part of his line was from Little Rock along the Arkansas River, down to where it joined the Mississippi. And except for Little Rock itself, even that wasn't terribly strong. Which was why he had the 4th Army defending the lower Mississippi line all the way from Memphis down to the Gulf, even though technically Funston's forces were blocking any Martian attack there. Theoretically, he could add 4th Army to Funston's defense, and push them forward, beyond the river. But if – when - Funston's line was breached, then there would be nothing to hold the Mississippi further south. No, he couldn't do it.

But he had to do something. He couldn't hang Funston - and Texas - out to dry.

"All right, Freddy, All right. I've got two new regular divisions, just completing their organization. I was going to send them to 1st Army, but I'll give them to you, instead."

"That would be wonderful, Leonard. But it's still not enough."

Wood held up his hand. "I'll also divert some tanks and artillery your way. There are a dozen train loads heading out to California, but things are still so quiet out there, I'll send them to you instead."

"That's good. I'll tell you I've been damn tempted to grab those trains passing west! Hard to see all that equipment and not get any of it."

"So far you've gotten two or three times as much as we've sent to the west coast. We can't totally ignore them, you know."

"They don't need as much with all those mountains protecting them. Most of my line is stark naked."

"I'm also going to give you another gift. You've probably heard that we're starting production of a small rocket launcher for use by the infantry…"

"I've heard. When can we get some?"

"I'll send you the first thousand that come out of the factories, the very first, Freddy. You have top priority."

"That's good, but what we really need is the ability to produce weapons right there in Texas. Can't anything be done?"

Wood shook his head. "Texas doesn't have the infrastructure for that sort of thing. We can't just pack up and send you a tank factory, Freddy. Well, we could, but it wouldn't do you any good because there are no steel mills or foundries or any of the stuff that you'd need to supply a tank factory. Texas has cattle and cotton and not a whole lot else."

"They've got oil."

"Yes, some. And I know there's the potential for a whole lot more, but you can't build tanks out of oil. It would take years to create the sort of industrial base you'd need. No, we can build the factories here in the east faster and easier and ship the tanks to you. It just makes sense." Funston snorted and frowned, but didn't argue that point.

"Well, if that's the best you can do…"

"Right now, it is. But, let me tell about our future plans. The President wants an offensive as soon as possible and…"

"I bet he does! Everyone does!"

"Yes. And we are drawing up plans for some very deliberate advances starting next spring. We will move along a few routes, heavily fortifying them as we go to protect our lines of communication. I'm going to urge that one of the routes start out along the Arkansas River. As we advance, we will take over the defense of that part of your line. Your forces can then be redeployed to reinforce other areas. That two thousand mile line of yours will shrink and shrink."

Funston considered that and then nodded. "That would help. But if the Martians strike us hard somewhere else, we will be in trouble."

"I know, I know. But we'll have to deal with that when it happens. Sorry, Freddy." Wood got up to signal the meeting was over. The visitors stood, and Wood shook hands with Funston.

"Thank you for your time, General," said Funston.

"Good luck, Freddy."

* * * * *

CYCLE 597, 844.8, HOLDFAST 32-4

"The successful launch of the next wave of reinforcements will allow us to resume offensive operations on all fronts. I shall summarize what we have decided to do during the next cycle."

Qetjnegartis observed the image of Coordinator Glangatnar, administrator of the Colonial Conclave, in the communications chamber of the holdfast. This same image was being broadcast to all the other clan commanders on the target world, as well as their chief subordinates.

"Continents Five and Six have been entirely subjugated and will receive no additional reinforcements. Clans in those regions will consolidate and concentrate their efforts on production and resource gathering."

Qetjnegartis reflected that the clans on Continent Five, the south polar continent, had managed to stave off starvation by the unorthodox method of harvesting warm-blooded creatures which lived in the surrounding seas. But that method was so inefficient and labor intensive, that no great increase in their population was proving possible. Little labor was available for resource gathering, and what resources that were there, were buried beneath telequels of ice. Continent Five would remain a minor area of operations.

"Continent Six," continued Glangatnar, "is located close to a number of large islands; consideration will be given to developing methods for crossing the oceans to reach those islands. However, this is not a top priority.

"The central regions of Continent Two have been secured, although due to the very dense plant growths in those regions, much of the area remains unexplored, although there is no evidence of large prey-creature concentrations and hence, no need for immediate operations. Prey-creatures still control the southern and northern areas and these must be eradicated. The southern area is the most lightly defended and this should be conquered first. Then all forces can be shifted north to take care of the other areas.

"Continent Four is also mostly subdued. Only two fortified regions remain in prey-creature control. However, these are very heavily defended and have the support of powerful sea vessels. Care must be taken in any attack against them. Also, it has been determined that an even more heavily fortified region has been constructed on the narrow isthmus connecting Continent Four to Continent Three. We do not know why this has been done. There is no evidence of any major habitations in that area. We speculate that it has been built specifically to prevent the union of our forces on the two continents. A similar zone is known to exist at the connection between Continents One and Two. Therefore we have decided that this region must be eliminated. The clans on both continents have been directed to cooperate in this endeavor."

Qetjnegartis considered this. Clan Bajantus had not been called upon to join in this operation and it was grateful for that. It would be the responsibility of the clans to the south to carry this out. It did not believe that this fortified zone of the prey-creatures was critical enough to justify such a major operation, but as long as its clan would not have to supply forces it did not really matter.

"Continent One is still a major center of operations The central northern portions have been subdued, except for small groups lurking in out of the way places. But the southern regions are protected by the highest mountains on the planet and so far no attempt to penetrate them have been successful. To the east and southeast are very densely populated regions, and even though their weapons are mostly crude, their vast numbers have slowed our progress. To the west lies a major prey-creature power. We have enjoyed several major successes there recently, but much work remains to be done. It is known that to the west of them lie major habitations and cities with significant power output. We can expect resistance to increase the farther west we go. Operations will be pressed on all of those fronts as much as possible. Half of the new transport capsules are being sent to Continent One.

"On Continent Three a major offensive shall take place," said Glangatnar. "It is here and in regions of Continent One that the most significant resistance has been met. The prey-creatures there have shown the most resilience and ability to adapt. They must be crushed before they adapt further. Clans Bajantus, Mavnaltak, Novmandus and Uxmatrais will all strike eastward and southward. They will each be allotted ten transport in this new wave. Clan Zeejvlapna will provide whatever support it can. Major water barriers exist, but these must be crossed and the populated regions beyond laid waste."

All right, this is what concerned Qetjnegartis. Definite orders to attack, which must be obeyed. And ten capsules! A hundred new clan members! This was good news indeed! It would probably take a tenth of a cycle to get the newcomers organized, but after that a major offensive could be launched.

"One final item," said Glangatnar. "Included with the wave of incoming capsules is an experimental device. Rather than land on this world, it will attempt to go into a stable orbit and become an artificial moon. The capsule will have no crew, but will contain observation equipment which will allow it to provide accurate maps of unoccupied regions and even supply us with intelligence about the movements of the prey-creatures. If the device is successful in achieving orbit, you will be instructed how to receive the information it gathers."

More good news! The lack of accurate data on this world was a serious handicap. Observations from the Homeworld had given a knowledge of the larger geographical features, continents, major rivers, and cities, but smaller features, and the positions of prey-creature armies, could only be learned by actual scouting. If this device worked, it would be a huge help in planning operations.

Glangatnar concluded the conference and the communications link was broken. Qetjnegartis reflected that there was much work to do.

CHAPTER FOUR

NOVEMBER, 1911, SOUTHEAST OF CHEPILLO ISLAND, PANAMA

Lieutenant Commander Drew Harding couldn't stand it anymore. For six hours he'd been stuck in the plotting room aboard the Minnesota, periodically firing salvos at grid coordinates on a map—and not being able to see a damn thing! He stalked around the compartment and it was clear that his people had everything under control. He turned to his second in command, Lieutenant Buckman, and said: "Take over, I'll be right back."

Buckman looked surprised, but nodded and said: "Yes, sir."

Drew climbed up three decks and into a tropical downpour. The rains in this part of the world were incredible and he was soaked to the skin in seconds, but before he was halfway up the mast the rain had stopped and the sun was out again. He reached the observation platform, which was actually a large compartment on top of the lattice mast, and pulled out his binoculars.

He directed them at the Panamanian coast. To the west he could see Panama City and the vast refugee camps which had grown up all around it. Swinging east he could see some of the fortifications the army had built, which stretched clear across the isthmus. As he watched, there was a flash and a billow of smoke. One of the army's big guns had just fired. He looked farther to the east but couldn't see where the shell had landed. There was already so much smoke in that area it just disappeared among the rest.

A loud rumble from behind him told of one of the other ships in the squadron firing. They were all firing slowly and deliberately at a force of Martians which had come up from the southeast. In the past few weeks, the Martians had been getting bolder and bolder, pushing forces through the thick jungle, and getting closer to the canal. They'd been coming from both the north and the south, too. Technically they were coming from east and west, since that was the way the isthmus ran, but the bottom line was that Martian forces from North America and South America were both converging on Panama.

Initially, they had tried to approach along the coasts where the terrain was far easier. But the ships of the fleet had punished them so severely in those attempts they had been forced to stay inland and try to push their way through one of the densest and most inhospitable jungles on the planet. It was slow going and the army and navy had been given plenty of warning. Between the clouds of smoke from where the enemy burned the jungle to the swarms of refugees - the last holdouts—fleeing in front of them, it was easy to see where they were.

Shelling them while they were further away could be done, but without direct observation it used up a lot of ammunition for questionable results. Aircraft from bases near the canal could do some spotting, but it was still pretty inaccurate. Closer to the canal, the army, working with the navy, had set up a very impressive system for calling down fire on an approaching enemy. The whole area was divided up into grid squares and both the army's fixed guns and the navy's mobile ones could

461

smother any spot on the grid with heavy shells on command. It was a great system—except that Drew still couldn't see anything.

Minnesota let off another salvo shaking the whole ship and surrounding the vessel with a thick cloud of cordite smoke for a few moments until the wind blew it away in a gray cloud that rolled off toward the coast. It blocked his vision and so once again, he couldn't see the results. Damn.

He really ought to get back to the plotting room, but he watched a little while longer. The ships and the forts were still firing and maybe he'd see…

"Wow!"

He gave off a cry when a there was a bright blue flash from inside the smoke cloud. He knew what that meant: the power units on a Martian tripod had exploded. It happened sometimes. After nearly a minute there was a strange crackling rumble that was different from the normal sounds of a bombardment. He didn't think the shell which had caused that had come from Minnesota, but it was still satisfying.

"Commander? Commander Harding?" He turned and saw that it was Seaman Baker, one of his spotters; he was holding a telephone.

"Yes?"

"Uh, it's Lieutenant Buckman, sir. He needs you back in Plot."

"Oh, okay, tell him I'm on my way."

He went down the ladder as quickly as he could, and then down three more decks to the Plotting Room. While he was on the way, the ship's gongs rang and the order to stand down from battle stations was given. Had the Martians been beaten back? He hurried into the compartment and looked around, but all seemed in order. His people were securing their equipment. Cromely spotted him and said: "Oh, there you are sir."

"What's wrong?"

"Oh, nothing, but the captain was just here and wondered where you were."

Shit.

"What did you tell him?"

"Uh, I wasn't sure where you went, so I told him I thought you were in the head. It had been six hours and maybe you had to go."

"What did he say?"

"Nothing."

"Okay, thanks." Drew stayed there and made sure everything was secure until the end of his watch, and then went to the officer's mess room and got his dinner. Most of the other officers were loud and boisterous after the day's gunnery. A few pessimists were grumbling that they'd no doubt spend the next day restocking the ship's magazines from a munitions ship. It was true that they'd used up a lot of shells and powder today. Afterward, he went up on deck to watch the sunset. More clouds were drifting in from the Pacific, but it wasn't raining and there was a pleasant breeze. Panama wasn't bad in the fall and winter.

While he was standing at the rail, a yeoman found him and told him to report to the captain's cabin. Oh crap…

He quickly found his way to the holy-of-holies on the ship and rapped on the door. "Come in," came the immediate answer. He went through and saluted Captain Gebhardt.

Gebhardt returned it from behind a table he was sitting at. "Ah, Harding, sit down." Drew plunked down on a chair, back ramrod straight. Was he in trouble?

"Sorry I wasn't in Plot when you were there, sir," he blurted. "I... I needed to get some air."

Gebhardt looked at him with a piercing gaze, bushy eyebrows arching up. "You happy here, son?"

Startled, Drew automatically answered: "Yes, sir!"

The Captain's mouth drew back in a smirk. "But not as happy as you might be, eh? You've done a good job here, Commander. The ship's gunnery has been excellent and your team is well trained and disciplined."

"T-thank you, sir."

"But I've noticed a certain... restlessness about you, son."

"Sorry, sir!"

Gebhardt, shook his head and made a little waving motion with his hand. "It wasn't a criticism, just an observation. But tell me: how is Lieutenant Buckman working out?"

"Sir? Uh, he's a good officer, sir. He knows the job and the men and..."

"Could he take over for you, do you think?"

"Sir? Uh, I suppose he could... but why...?" Drew was getting nervous - more nervous. Was the captain going to fire him? Take the gunnery position away from him? Turn him into the stores officer or something equally awful?

"Calm down," said Gebhardt, obviously noticing Drew's reaction. He picked up a paper from the table and looked it over. "I've noticed that you have a certain... itch to close with the enemy. We don't get many chances to do that here, as I'm sure you've noticed. How would you like the chance to do that somewhere else?"

"Sir? I don't understand, sir."

"This," he said holding up the paper, "is an order from the Bureau of Personnel at the Navy Department directing me to give up one of my senior officers and send him to take command of one of the new river monitors that's being built. Unless you have some serious objection, I'm planning to send you."

What?!

"I... uh... but I've never commanded a ship, sir."

"Yes, I know, so does the Bureau, but with the enormous expansion of the fleet we simply don't have enough experienced ship commanders, so we are having to make do. From what I've heard, they will probably give you an executive officer with experience on the rivers but little military experience. He should be able to help you over the rough spots. So do you want this assignment, Commander?"

A command of my own! His mouth babbled: "Yes, sir! Uh, what ship, sir?"

"One of the new Liberation class ships. The Santa Fe. She's finishing up construction in New Orleans right now. Not a sea-going vessel, but heavily armed. And on the rivers you'll get close enough to see the red of their eyes. Satisfied?"

"Yes, sir! Uh, thank you, sir." He could scarcely believe it.

"All right then. Get your bags packed and get yourself to New Orleans. Dismissed."

* * * * *

463

NOVEMBER, 1911, MEMPHIS, TENNESSEE

Captain Frank Dolfen led his command across the bridge into Memphis. He was tired and the cold was making his bones ache. He wasn't a young man anymore. He'd hit the twenty year mark in the army last month and that was when he'd hoped to retire. In addition to all the other stuff they'd done, the Martians had wrecked that plan, too. *The bastards really owe me...*

This was their second foray into Martian territory west of the river, but unlike the previous one, they hadn't accomplished much of anything. Last time they'd come back with two kills to their credit—three if you counted the one the tornado got - and a few hundred refugees returned to safety. This time they hadn't seen a single Martian and their tally of refugees could be counted on two hands. The lands over there were getting really empty. On the other hand, he hadn't lost any of his men this time and that was a blessing.

"Good to be back," said Major Bridges. The Britisher was still with the squadron and Dolfen was a bit surprised by that. He was attached to observe and learn what he could about American methods - and give advice about British ones - but Dolfen wasn't sure there was much more for either of them to learn at this point. Oh well, the Limey was a pleasant enough companion on campaign. Sometimes.

"Yeah," replied Dolfen, in no mood to chat at the moment. On the east bank, he turned the column north toward where their camp was located. The massive concrete fortifications to the left blocked out the view of the river. The walls were nearly thirty feet high with a ten foot ditch in front of them, and they were steep enough that - hopefully! - no Martian tripod could climb over them. Large guns on disappearing mounts were placed on platforms at intervals. There were metal gates protected by more guns in rotating turrets every block or so to allow access to the waterfront. The gates were set in recesses in the wall and at right angles so there was no direct line of fire at them. It was an amazing effort and stretched for miles north and south of the city. There were similar fortifications around other river cities like Vicksburg and Baton Rouge. And the workers weren't stopping; they were adding mile after mile of walls spreading north and south of the fortress cities. Dolfen supposed if the war lasted long enough, the walls would stretch the entire length of the Mississippi. The locals were happy to be protected, but they didn't much like the demolition that had been necessary to do it. Whole blocks of buildings had been leveled. But if nothing else, it gave the city the best protection against flooding it had ever had.

After going a few miles north through the city, they were met by a small ambulance train. These took charge of the refugees and Dolfen was happy to tell the officer in charge that there were no wounded to treat. He was even happier when he caught sight of Becca Harding. The nurse was there on that fool horse of hers which had somehow survived all of their earlier adventures. She smiled broadly when she caught sight of him and he couldn't help but smile back. She trotted over to him.

"Welcome back, Frank!"

"Howdy, Becca."

"No casualties?"

"Nary a one. We were lucky."

"Glad you're back safe."

"Me, too. How you been?"

"Oh, about the same. Not too much work these days, although there was a boatload of wounded that came in from Little Rock a week ago."

"Still working with your sharpshooters?"

Becca grimmaced. "Tryin' to. Pretty hopeless."

Dolfen forced himself not to smile. Becca desperately wanted to fight the Martians and the Memphis Lady Sharpshooters organization was about the closest she could get.

"But I've been thinkin'…"

Uh oh…

"'Bout what?"

"Well, when you fellows go out on these long scouting missions, you could use some medical people to go along with you, couldn't you?"

"We do have a couple of medics…"

"Which won't be nearly enough if you get into a serious fight! They weren't near enough after that last fight of yours, I hear. And then there are those civilians you keep picking up. Some of them need medical care, too. Women and kids. What you need is a team with a real doctor and some nurses!"

He couldn't deny it, but Becca was so obviously hinting that she wanted to go along, that he forced his face into complete immobility. "I have no authority to create anything like that," he said stiffly. The last thing he wanted was her out there in the same danger he had to deal with.

"I know that," she said. "But if someone else did, you wouldn't object, would you?"

He felt like he was facing a Martian heat ray. If he said that he did object, she'd get angry. But if he said he didn't…

"Some of the French regiments have women attached to them like that," said Bridges suddenly. Dolfen had forgotten he was even there. "Vivandières they call them, I think. They carry water, tend the wounded, things like that."

"Yes, exactly!" cried Becca.

Dolfen glared at Bridges and said: "Well, I don't know…"

"Couldn't you ask your superiors, Frank?" asked Becca. Her desires were so sincere and deep-felt there was no way he could bring himself to dash them.

"I'll… I'll talk to the colonel."

"Oh, thank you!" she squealed, face bright and smiling. He forced himself to smile, too. Hell, he'd ask Colonel Schumacher and that would be the last anyone would hear of the matter. The 5th's new colonel was a pretty good officer, but he didn't like disruption to the routine. He'd be as happy to have women attached to his command as he would to have an outbreak of hoof-and-mouth disease! It would be all right.

Becca babbled on for a few minutes, but then the ambulance train moved out and she was forced to say goodbye. His troops hadn't stopped when they dropped off the civilians, so he broke into a trot to catch up to the head of the column; Bridges paced him.

"Quite a lassie, that one," said Bridges. "A real spitfire."

"That she is," replied Dolfen, "that she is."

* * * * *

NOVEMBER, 1911, MEMPHIS, TENNESSEE

Rebecca Harding looked over her shoulder, but Frank was already riding off at a brisk pace and didn't look her way again. That was all right, he had so many responsibilities. But he'd said he would talk to his colonel! She realized it was a long shot that anything would be done and a longer one that she'd be allowed to go even if the idea was approved, but at least it was a chance. She tried not to get her hopes too high, but it was hard not to. She was getting so bored with her routine at the hospital. She felt guilty thinking that way; tending the wounded and sick was an important and honorable job. She should be glad she was able to do that much to help in the fight against the Martians.

She thought back to when it seemed like she wouldn't even be allowed to do that much. After fleeing from her home, her mother and father and grandmother killed by the Martians, she'd ended up in Santa Fe and technically the ward of her mother's sister and husband. They'd tried to bundle her off to a school for girls in Connecticut, but she'd escaped into the nurse corps, despite not being of legal age. Well, she was eighteen now and no one could tell her what she had to do.

And there probably wasn't anyone left alive who would even try. Had her aunt and uncle escaped from Santa Fe as she'd urged? She'd had no word from them since the city fell. If they did make it out, they would have had to go south into Texas. Was there any way she could find out about them? Did she even want to? She had no affection for them, but as far as she knew, they were the only family she had left in the world.

No, no one could tell her what she had to do - except for Chief Nurse Chumley, all the doctors, and any officers she met, of course - but there were still plenty of people who could tell her what she *couldn't* do. She couldn't be in the real army, she couldn't take up a weapon, and she couldn't fight Martians. And that's the one thing she really wanted to do!

The lady sharpshooter organization was better than nothing, but only just. It did allow her to do some shooting and even feel a little bit important. The group recently elected officers and NCOs. Mrs. Oswald, the organizer of the group, had been elected captain, of course, but to her surprise, the ladies had elected her to be the company's drill sergeant. She supposed it was an honor. They'd even tried to get her to wear one of their ridiculous uniforms, but she'd begged off.

The little convoy reached the hospital area and the refugees were turned over to the officer in charge of dealing with them. Some of the children were crying and they all wanted to know what was going to happen to them now. *You'll be given a job! These days, everyone has to have a job!*

The huge influx of people from across the river had been a major crisis when it first happened. In that awful spring of 1910, the Martians had broken through the army's defenses along the eastern edge of the Rockies and swept across the Great Plains. Utah, New Mexico, and Idaho had already been lost to the Martians, but now North and South Dakota, Wyoming, Colorado, Nebraska, Kansas, Minnesota, Iowa, most of Missouri, Arkansas, and Oklahoma had been overrun, driving millions from their homes.

They had flooded east to the hoped-for safety behind the Mississippi. At first camps had been set up for them, but it was quickly realized that the loss of the nation's breadbasket, the vast wheat and corn fields, and grazing land from west of the river, was going to create a huge shortage of food unless steps were taken immediately. The obvious solution was to put these displaced farmers to work on new farms. There was still plenty of arable land east of the river, not so good perhaps as the lost lands further west, but good enough. Abandoned land was put back into cultivation and new farmland cut out of the forests. A million acres were planted in time for the 1910 growing season and three million more by 1911. Of course, these were not the modest single-family farms and ranches the refugees came from - and like Becca had grown up on - they were huge plantation-style farms with hundreds of people on each of them working for wages. From what she had heard, the conditions were still pretty grim.

Not as grim as the camps had been at the start, though. She had arrived with the first wave; those who had been driven out of Albuquerque and Santa Fe and a hundred little towns between there and the Mississippi. More and more followed, and many needed medical help. The army nurses and doctors had been overwhelmed. Some of the refugees had been doctors and volunteers had arrived from further east to help, but that first six months had been very bad. A lot of people died. Children died. But bit by bit the refugees were moved out to their new homes.

After the initial shock had worn off and the families settled, most of the young men had joined the army in hopes of taking back their land west of the river. Many of the initial refugee camps were now army camps, filled with those same young men. She had met some of them and they burned to strike back at the invader with a passion that matched her own.

After securing the ambulances and taking care of the horses, Becca checked in with Miss Chumley and was told there were no immediate crises to deal with and she could go back to her normal schedule - which meant she was free until after dinner. She went back to her quarters, which were in a barracks-like structure where she had a bed and a footlocker and not a whole lot else. She lay down on her bunk, closed her eyes, and dreamed of riding with Frank Dolfen's cavalry out on patrol against the Martians. She was sure Frank would allow – insist - that she have a rifle. And if the opportunity came along to use it, well…

And being with Frank would be good, too. Of course, he would have his duties and she would have hers, but at least she'd see him from time to time. He was the best friend she had and she liked him a lot. And he wasn't married and he'd lost his girl to the Martians in the first days of the war. And he wasn't *that much older than her…*

"Hey, Becca!"

She opened her eyes and saw that it was Clarissa Forester who had called her name. Clarissa was one of the other nurses and they saw a lot of each other. Becca considered her a friend, although lately…

"What?"

"We're having a revival meeting! Come on!"

Becca forced herself not to frown. "No thanks. I'll pass."

Clarissa did frown. "You really ought to come. There'll be music and a good preacher and it's important."

"Just got back with some refugees and I'm worn out. Leave me rest."

"Becca, I'm starting to worry about you. I haven't seen you at church on Sundays, either. How are we going to win this war without God's help?"

"By killing Martians. And I haven't noticed God killin' any lately. Guess we gotta do it ourselves."

Clarissa's frown became fierce. "Don't talk like that! It's blaspheming! God will help us, but we've got to be worthy! If we purge our sins, God will help us!"

"Go 'way, Clarissa." Becca closed her eyes and rolled over. She heard Clarissa snort and stalk off.

Revival meetings!

They were becoming very common lately. A religious fervor was sweeping the country, including the army camps. More and more people were becoming convinced that the Martian invasion was some sort of punishment from God for the sins of the world. Becca didn't believe a word of it. *What sort of sins did Pepe - or me for that matter - commit to deserve what's happened?* And what sort of god would deal out so terrible a punishment? When she'd dared to voice such a question a few months earlier, she'd gotten such a rash of frowns and *Tsk! Tsks!* from the Bible thumpers, she'd resolved to stay out of such discussions in the future.

But they were thumping more than Bibles these days. Some were getting downright nasty and blaming the woes of the world - meaning their own woes - on the ones who didn't eagerly join them. Some of the really zealous ones were smashing liquor bottles, dumping beer barrels, busting up poker games, and a few weeks ago a notorious brothel in town had burned down under mysterious circumstances and several people had been badly injured. Naturally, a lot of the soldiers had gotten mad at such high-handed actions, robbing them of their few pleasures, and that there had been fistfights and worse. They'd had to treat some knife wounds in the hospital. Becca was afraid that there was even worse trouble brewing. *There are a lot of angry people out there looking for someone to blame!*

What if they decided to blame her?

She opened her eyes, all hope of sleep vanished. Some of the worst of the thumpers were spouting 'if you're not with God, you're against Him' nonsense, and others were starting to believe them. The last thing she needed was for people like Clarissa to turn against her. Maybe it wouldn't hurt to at least be seen at some of the meetings. And they usually did have pretty good music.

She sat up with a groan and left the barracks.

* * * * *

NOVEMBER, 1911, WASHINGTON, D.C.

Leonard Wood was working late - again. He and his new deputy, Colonel Hugh Drum, were seated at a table covered with maps and piles of papers working out the new table of organization for the US Army.

"If we added the 39th Division to the 4th Army, we could push their boundary up to Memphis, sir," said Drum.

"No, no, I don't want the inter-army boundary anywhere near a major fortress. Too much risk that both commanders will overlook a danger because they think the other commander is handling it. We'll put the 39th in 3rd Army and leave the boundary where it is."

"That will make 3rd Army substantially bigger than average, sir."

"So be it. Dickman is doing a good job as an army commander, he can handle things."

"Yes, sir. But it will also leave 4th Army very much below average, just six divisions. And 7th Army is the same."

Wood looked at Drum for a moment. He was damn young for his post, early thirties, already a colonel, and he would probably be a general before his next birthday. The incredible expansion of the army was creating an enormous problem in finding experienced officers to command the new formations. Training schools could turn out captains and lieutenants by the wagon load, but finding capable staff officers - to say nothing of division, corps, and army commanders! - was a daunting challenge. He'd been forced to give up his previous deputy, Doug MacArthur, so he could take command of a new division. He'd probably be a corps commander before long. But at least Drum did have some experience. Fought in Cuba - where his father had been killed—and then later had worked with Fred Funston on his staff before the current war. Still, he'd never had to handle forces of this magnitude - as if anyone in the US Army had!

"We're taking calculated risks here, Hugh. Even with sixty divisions we don't have nearly enough to cover the whole line adequately. More divisions are in the pipeline, but until they are ready, we have to protect the most dangerous areas and pray the other areas don't get hit."

"I understand, sir."

"And we've got eight more divisions which will be ready before spring. I'm keeping them in the east just in case the next wave of cylinders should land there. Probably won't, I know, but we can't ignore the possibility. Once we're sure, we can send them west, and some will go to 4th and 7th Armies."

"What about the two new tank divisions, sir?"

Wood scratched his nose and frowned. Yes, what about them? Major General Samuel Rockenbach was organizing two experimental divisions composed almost entirely of steam tanks at Fort

Knox, Kentucky. It was a revolutionary idea originated by an English officer named Fuller which had caught the attention of Roosevelt and Secretary of War Henry Stimson. Instead of infantry regiments with a few battalions of supporting tanks as was the norm in most divisions, these would have tank regiments with just a few battalions of infantry in trucks. Even the artillery would be carried in armored tractors. Wood had his doubts about the utility of the divisions considering the mechanical unreliability of the tanks, but perhaps they could be effective.

"I think we'll keep those in our back pocket for now. Maybe we can use them when we start our offensives."

"Yes, sir."

"Okay, we've got a basic outline here. But we need to find a few corps commanders. Let's start with the XV Corps, I think we'll promote Frederick Foltz and give that to him…"

They worked for another hour and made some good progress. Then, when they were both yawning, Wood sent Drum home to his wife, who was expecting, promising that he'd be going home himself soon. He organized their notes and left them on Semancik's desk, who he'd sent home hours earlier, for him to put into a formal set of orders in the morning. He was about to do the same and surprise his wife by being there before midnight for a change, but his eye caught sight of a stack of letters in the in-basket and couldn't resist paging through them - just to get a jump on tomorrow's work, of course.

He glanced at a few and then took them all back to his desk. These must have arrived from the mail room just before Semancik left because his aide was very good at sorting out the important items from the frivolous - and these clearly hadn't been sorted. Wood had wondered, from time to time, just what he wasn't seeing. A chance to find out. There were a half-dozen requests from rich or important people asking that sons or grandsons or nephews be given safe postings in the army's rear area. There were easily twice that many from rich or important people from the occupied states demanding to know when they could go home - one insisting that the army be careful not to destroy any of his property in the process - and several suggesting that sons or grandsons or nephews deserved promotions or medals. He could see why none of these ever reached his desk. His respect for Semancik - always high - rose another notch.

But then one letter, clearly written in a woman's hand, caught his eye. It asked – begged - for news of her only son, who had been part of 1st Army's V Corps during last year's disaster. She'd heard nothing from him and the Personnel Bureau could only tell her that he was 'missing'. Surely the Chief of Staff could tell her where he was? Wood had just spent part of the evening reorganizing the V Corps, but he knew full well this woman's son wasn't there anymore. He'd almost certainly died with the rest of the corps in North Dakota. He sat and stared at it for a long time. How many other letters like this had Semancik intercepted? He wasn't sure he wanted to know.

Sighing deeply, he paged through the rest of the stack. Here was a letter from that Goddard fellow who had designed the new rocket launchers. He had ideas for larger rockets which could replace conventional heavy artillery. But he didn't think he was getting sufficient support from the Ordnance Department, was there anything Wood could do? Here was another letter from that blasted William Mitchell! Demanding more bombers again, of course. Damn it, hadn't that reprimand for going direct to Roosevelt taught him anything? What was he going to do with him? *Maybe I will send him to the Aleutians!*

Near the bottom of the pile was the weekly plea from Funston for more troops. Or at least he assumed it was weekly. Perhaps they came every day and Semancik filed the rest. But they were all the same: Funston needed more tanks, more heavy artillery, more trained men - especially tank officers, and more supplies. Wood truly wished he could give Freddy what he needed, but he couldn't. Not only was the material needed more urgently on the Mississippi Line, but the hard truth was that even if he sent two or three times as much to Texas, it wouldn't make any difference.

Texas was free only because the Martians hadn't decided to conquer it yet. Once they did, it was doomed.

There was an old military maxim: *reinforce success, not defeat.* Every tank and gun he sent there would probably end up wasted. How could he justify it? The war would be won by the deliberate offensives he was now planning - not by trying to hang on to... what did Funston's aide call it? A forlorn hope?

But enough of this. Time to get home. It was nearly midnight - again. He was putting the papers back in order, in hopes Semancik wouldn't notice, when he heard someone in the outer office. Who could it be at this hour? The cleaning staff knew to wait until after he was gone to come in. "Yes?" he called. "Who's there?"

The door opened and a tall young man in a captain's uniform walked in and saluted. "General, I'm George Patton."

Wood looked closer and saw that the right side of his face was scarred and a black eyepatch covered the eye on that side. He'd been a handsome fellow before whatever had caused that. *Heat ray survivor probably...* "What in the world are you doing here, son? It's almost midnight!"

"I've been trying to see you for weeks, sir, but I can't get an appointment. I'd heard you sometimes work late and I thought I'd take a chance to see if I could catch you here without an army of damn clerks and secretaries blocking my path!"

A man with initiative... "All right, so you've caught me. What can I do for you, Captain?"

"I want an assignment, sir. I was wounded at Santa Fe and the goddamn surgeons won't clear me for active duty. That was a year and a half ago, sir! I'm fine! I was in tanks, sir, and I when I heard about the new tank divisions I went to see General Rockenbach, but he wouldn't take me without the surgeon's okay. I mean it's true I was down with pneumonia two or three times after I was wounded, but I'm all over that now. Please, sir! I need to get back into the fight against those goddamn..." Patton cut loose with a stream of profanity against the Martians that shocked even an old veteran like Wood.

"Calm down, Captain."

Patton got hold of himself. "Sorry, sir. I just want to fight, sir."

"I can see that, son. I don't suppose you'd accept a light duty assignment..."

"I've been on light duty, sir! You don't think I've just been sitting on my ass all this time, do you?" Despite Patton's impressive size, his voice was surprisingly high-pitched. Right now it was getting very high-pitched.

"No, no, of course not. But you want a combat posting, eh?"

"Yes, sir!"

"And you know tanks..."

"Inside and out!"

Wood looked at the sheaf of papers in his hands and flipped through them until he found the ones he wanted. *Goddard... Mitchell... Funston... maybe I can kill four birds with one stone here.* He stood up from his desk and looked Patton in the eye.

"Then I think I can help you out, Captain. Ever been to Texas?"

CHAPTER FIVE

DECEMBER, 1911, EDDYSTONE, PENNSYLVANIA

"I sure hope this goes better than yesterday, sir," said Lieutenant Jeremiah Hornbaker.

"Amen to that," replied Colonel Andrew Comstock. He glanced over to where Generals Crozier and Hawthorne - his bosses - were talking with John Schmidt of the Baldwin Company. They were all perched atop the USLI-001, the first army land ironclad. No one had agreed on a name for them yet. A cold December wind was flapping the skirts of their greatcoats and a few flakes of snow drifted by. There were still no guns or upper works on the immense vehicle, but everything else had been completed, including a screw-propeller and rudder for when the thing took to the water.

Which it was about to do.

They were parked at the upper end of a concrete ramp which led down into the Delaware River. Waiting for them in the water was a large U-shaped hull, held in position by cables and a pair of small tug boats. If all went well, the USLI-001 would drive down the ramp and into the open end of the 'U' where it would be secured in place. If all the calculations of the engineers were correct, then the land ironclad would transform itself into a sea-going (or at least a river-going) ironclad. It would be able to float. It would then sail under its own power up the river to the William Cramp & Sons shipyard in Philadelphia where the guns and upper works would be installed. There were five more of the ironclads being finished up in the Baldwin works, and if all went well today, they would follow along. Crozier and Hawthorne had come from Washington to see it happen.

But they had also been at the Aberdeen Proving Grounds to see the test firing of the Little David's twelve-inch gun the day before, and as Hornbaker had just reminded him, that had not gone well. Oh, the gun had performed spectacularly, going off with a huge roar and a blast of flame and smoke, and the shell had blown the target to very small pieces. The recoil mechanism on the gun had transferred the force to the vehicle, just as it was designed to do, lifting the front wheels completely off the ground.

That should have warned him.

Several more shots were fired and the generals were very pleased. But then Crozier wanted to see the thing move around a bit and fire some more. All went well until it tried to fire with the turret pointing to the left. This time the recoil lifted the wheels on the left side off the ground—way off the ground. Up and up and three seconds later, the Little David was lying on its side with the gun pointing straight up in the air. Fortunately, no one was seriously hurt. Andrew checked his watch. If they'd gotten the crane out to the firing range as they'd promised, the damn contraption ought to be upright again by now.

Crozier had not been happy. He didn't exactly blame Andrew - there were plenty of people there to blame - but Andrew did feel guilty that he hadn't thought of that potential problem. That was part of his job, after all, to ask the simple questions and find the obvious flaws that the scientists and engineers had overlooked. Up until now he'd been pretty good at that.

Baldwin was already at work designing a set of retractable braces which could be deployed from the sides of the vehicle to prevent that from happening again. But the Little Davids were going to be sent west without waiting for them, with strict instructions to only fire with the turret pointing forward.

Andrew sincerely hoped that today's test would go a lot better.

"All right, I think we are ready!" shouted Schmidt suddenly. "Let's go!" There was a flurry of activity around the controls and the vehicle eased into motion. Smoke billowed out of the stack and Andrew could feel the vibration of the steam turbine down below. It had an entirely different feel to it than the reciprocating engines of other warships he'd been on; just a steady vibration instead of the *thump, thump, thump* of enormous cylinders.

The USLI-001 headed down the ramp at far less than a walking pace. It could go faster, but they were taking this delicate operation slowly. While they waited, several enlisted men began handing out life jackets - just in case, they said. Andrew eyed the gray waters of the Delaware flowing past in the distance. A few chunks of ice were floating on the surface. He was slightly reassured by the lifeboats carried on the auxiliary hull unit up ahead. He sure didn't want to go into the water!

Crozier walked around the upper hull, peering over the railings to look down at the monstrous caterpillar tracks, slowly turning. "Hell of a thing, isn't it?" he remarked to no one in particular.

The forward pair of tracks reached the water and started down in. Another fifty or sixty yards and they'd reach the hull. Andrew wanted to see just how it would be attached and secured. He knew that it had been painstakingly engineered to avoid any possibility of it ripping loose even in rough seas. And yet it had to be easily detachable once the land ironclad reached its destination.

The tracks were nearly submerged when the vehicle suddenly stopped. A Baldwin worker on a telephone shouted for Mr. Schmidt who rushed over and grabbed it away from the man and listened for a moment and then cursed.

"What's wrong, Mr. Schmidt?" asked Crozier.

"Motor Room Number 1 is flooding! A bad leak! Reverse! Put it in reverse!" he shouted to the man at the controls, handing back the phone. Levers were thrown and the ironclad lurched abruptly backward, up the ramp. But they'd only gone a few yards when there was a sharper jolt and they started twisting to one side. There was a muffled screeching sound from up forward.

"It's shorted, sir!" cried the man on the telephone. "Track 1 is out!"

"Keep going! Get us out of the water!"

Andrew ran to the forward railing. Yes, the front track on the left side wasn't turning, it was just being dragged along by the other three. The ironclad pulled itself up the ramp, continuing to twist around a bit, despite attempts to use the other tracks to keep it straight. Finally, they were completely out of the water and Schmidt gave the order to halt.

Workers dashed here and there and disappeared below or arrived on deck to cluster around Schmidt. Through it all, General Crozier stood immobile in the center of the deck, a scowl on his face growing darker by the minute. Finally, Schmidt came over to him, and Andrew edged closer to hear.

"I'm sorry, General, the vibrations of moving must have worked loose some of the seams. Water got into the motor room of the forward left set of tracks. Fortunately, no one was hurt. But we'll have to replace the electric motors before we can try this again."

Crozier remained silent for a very long moment before replying. "This is unacceptable, Mr. Schmidt."

"Yes, sir, I know, and I'm sorry."

"Sorry won't kill any Martians. How long to fix this and how are you going to make sure it doesn't happen again?"

"Probably about a week to pull the motors and replace them. We can inspect the watertight housings at the same time and do what we need to do to make them secure."

Crozier's expression was darker than ever. He swiveled his head around like a gun turret looking for a target. Unfortunately, his gaze came to rest on Andrew. "Comstock!" he snapped.

"Sir!" said Andrew coming to attention.

"We need these things at the front," he said very slowly and very clearly. "I am putting you permanently in charge of seeing that it gets done - soon."

"Yes, sir. Permanently, sir?"

"Permanently, Colonel. You are now formally attached to the 1st Squadron of US Army Land Ironclads until such time as I reassign you. Stay here. Stay with them. Get them ready. Get them into action. Understood?"

"Yes, sir. Understood."

"Good. Carry on." Crozier turned away.

Andrew looked helplessly at General Hawthorne, his immediate superior - and his father-in-law. The man chewed on his lower lip for a moment and then said: "I'll tell Vickie to send you your things."

* * * * *

CYCLE 597, 844.9, HOLDFAST 32-2

Qetjnegartis sat in its travel chair inside the large underground machine hangar in the second holdfast. Several fighting machines stood nearby, but Qetjnegartis's attention was fixed on a score of much smaller machines arrayed in two rows. Ixmaderna, in its own chair, was speaking: "As you can see, Commander, the small drone fighting machines function very well. Each one has a scaled-down version of the heat ray, which although small, is still completely lethal against the prey-creatures - I tested it on some captives to make sure. It will be less effective against their armored vehicles, but given time or numbers, could also destroy them. They also have a manipulating tentacle which is equipped with a sharp blade to allow it to function as a weapon at close quarters."

"Yes, I see," said Qetjnegartis, "and they are small enough to fit into restricted spaces and dig out the prey-creatures. How vulnerable are they to damage?"

"Obviously we cannot armor them as heavily as our fighting machines, but they should be resistant against the weapons carried by the enemy foot-warriors. The prey-creatures' heavier weapons will be able to destroy the drones, but their small size will make them difficult targets."

"What about their speed and endurance?"

"They are necessarily slower than a fighting machine, but since these are intended for assaults rather than raids or pursuits, that should not be a liability. Their energy storage cells are also much smaller due to their significantly reduced power demands. Fully charged, they should be able to function for thirty rotations of limited action, and perhaps four rotations of intense combat. They also have a charging umbilical which will allow them to replenish their energy from other machines."

"That is all good. But what about controlling them? That will be the key, it seems, since they are not self-directing."

473

"They have a limited self-directing ability, Commander," said Ixmaderna. "They can be ordered to move in a certain direction or to a certain point, or to simply follow the controller's own machine and they will do so, adapting their movements to the terrain. There is no need for the controller to direct every aspect of the machine's motion."

"Similar to the mining and construction machines, then?"

"Yes, the same principles exactly."

"So basic movement, but not combat?"

"Combat will require a more active participation on the part of the controller, yes, although the cutter-blade can be set to an automatic pattern of movements which create a deadly zone around the machine if the operator's attention is needed elsewhere. But picking targets and firing the heat ray will require direct commands."

"How many drones could one of us control at once?"

"I have been conducting trials, Commander. With practice, an operator can control between five and ten of the drones simultaneously. Interestingly, I have found that our younger members, the buds who matured here, seem the most adept at this."

"That is interesting," agreed Qetjnegartis. "But I am assuming that when fully involved in commanding the drones, the operator would be less able to control its own war machine?"

"That is true, although depending on the tactical situation that might not be a problem. But allow me to demonstrate what we can do."

"Proceed."

Ixmaderna contacted the operators in the two war machines and they activated their drones. The machines, small and large, began to move and went up the ramp leading to the surface. Qetjnegartis and Ixmaderna followed in their travel chairs. On the surface, the drones fanned out and began firing their heat rays at various patches of ground and waving their manipulators around. There was a covering of frozen water on the ground which erupted in gusts of steam where the heat rays touched it. Then the drones repositioned themselves around the controlling machine and assumed different formations, moving precisely and in unison.

"Impressive," said Qetjnegartis. "Actually employing them effectively in combat will require practice, I am thinking."

"Yes, that is certainly true. Perhaps we can find some small group of prey to attack and test out our methods."

"Perhaps. But the Conclave has suggested that we not deploy the drones until we have them in sufficient numbers for a major attack so as not to give away the element of surprise and allow the prey to develop countermeasures."

"It is certainly true that the prey-creatures are adaptable. They have developed many new weapons and methods just in the short time we have been here," said Ixmaderna in agreement. "But perhaps we can improvise some training exercises in the ruins of the two nearby cities. At least get the drone operators used to moving and working inside the prey-creatures' habitations."

"That is an excellent idea, Ixmaderna," said Qetjnegartis. "Develop a proposal for my review." Holdfast 32-2 had been constructed in the area between the two prey-creature cities which had been overrun during the clan's great offensive almost two local cycles earlier. While much of the useful materials in those places had been salvaged, there were still substantial ruins which remained.

"I shall do so at once, Commander," said Ixmaderna, clearly pleased. "There is one other thing I would like to show you while you are here, Commander, if you have the time. I realize that with four holdfasts to administer, your time is precious."

"It is true that traveling between the holdfasts is time-consuming," said Qetjnegartis. "I hope that someday we can connect our holdfasts with an underground transport system such as we have on the Homeworld."

"It would be a massive undertaking, Commander, but surely worthwhile."

"Yes, but there is no hope we can divert the necessary resources to it while the struggle against the prey-creatures continues. But in answer to your invitation, I can certainly make time for whatever it is you wish to show me."

"That is most kind. Please, follow me." Ixmaderna turned its travel chair and led the way back down the ramp into the underground portions of the holdfast. As they did so, they found themselves following a harvester machine. This was a modification of the basic fighting machine, which was designed to capture and transport prey. While it did have a small heat ray for self-defense, it had additional manipulator arms to seize prey and a large detachable cage for storing them mounted to the rear of the cockpit. The cage on this harvester was only about half full.

"Hunting does not appear to be good," remarked Qetjnegartis.

"Well, it is the local winter," replied Ixmaderna, "and many of the creatures, both intelligent and non-intelligent, spend much time in sheltered locations, rather than venturing out. But you are correct, Commander, large creatures of all kinds are becoming rare in the areas close to the holdfast."

Qetjnegartis paused to watch the harvester being unloaded. It was spending most of its time at the new Holdfast 32-4 and none of the harvesters had been constructed there yet.

"If you please, Commander, move back a bit," said Ixmaderna.

"Why?"

"For your safety. I have received reports from clans on the First Continent that some of the prey have concealed chemical explosives on themselves and then detonated them when they are brought to the holdfasts."

"Indeed?" said Qetjnegartis, hastily backing off its travel chair.

"Yes. The reports state that the prey in the eastern regions of that continent are fighting with a fanaticism and disregard for their own self-preservation unlike anything seen before."

"There have been no incidents of this kind here, have there?"

"No... if one discounts the flying machine which crashed into Hablantar's fighting machine recently..."

Qetjnegartis contemplated that incident. It *could* have been an accidental collision... but perhaps it wasn't. "So what steps are you taking to safeguard against such an incident here?"

"As you can see, the prey-creatures are being stripped of all items they carry and their artificial coverings before being sent to the holding pens." Indeed, a manipulator machine was doing that now and the prey-creatures were making loud noises in apparent fear or protest.

"Why not do that upon capture instead of waiting until they reach the holdfast? Does that not put the harvester as well as the holdfast at risk?"

"We had been doing that, Commander, but it appears that the prey are not adapted to the low temperatures of their winter season. We did strip them in warmer temperatures, but when we tried that in lower temperatures, most of the them were dead by the time they reached the holdfast. Perhaps if we constructed heated holding cages we could solve that problem. Oh, pardon me for a moment, Commander, I will be right back." Ixmaderna moved its travel chair forward to converse with the one operating the manipulator and soon returned. "I noticed that one of the females had a young one and directed that they both be sent to my laboratory rather than the usual holding pens," it explained.

"And I assume that is what you wished to show me? Your experiments with the young prey?"

"Yes, indeed, If you'll come with me." It turned its chair and headed into the main corridor which circled the holdfast. Qetjnegartis followed. They went down several ramps to the lower levels and eventually reached Ixmaderna's labs. These were quite extensive now and had a number of people working there, Ixmaderna's buds, mostly, and buds of the buds. Four holding pens were located at the far end of the complex. One held five adult prey-creature females and nine of the very young ones. As they watched, the newly captured female and its offspring were deposited in the pen through the hatch in the roof. It was shrieking so loudly it could be heard faintly even through the thick transparency. The other females paid it little heed, except for one which went over to it.

"Due to the complete helplessness of the infant prey-creatures, it is necessary to keep a number of females to feed and care for them."

"The one on the left appears to be carrying an unborn bud," said Qetjnegartis, pointing at one of them. "Am I correct?"

"Yes, and from my observations it will probably give birth quite soon. It is an interesting process. I have a visual recording of another birth if you are interested."

"Perhaps at some other time. This next pen has somewhat older prey."

"Yes, in hopes of training these creatures to obey us, I wished to remove them from the influence of the adults at as young an age as possible to prevent them from learning anything from their parents which might contradict our training. Finding the proper age to do this has proved challenging and is largely a matter of trial and error."

This pen had fifteen of the little creatures. Some were just sitting or lying on the floor, but others were running around and interacting with each other, although the purpose of the interaction was not readily apparent. "What are they doing?"

"I'm not entirely sure," replied Ixmaderna. "They will do this at times, chasing each other, sometimes even striking each other, although not to inflict serious injury, I don't believe. But observe." It touched a control and a row of lights appeared along the rear wall of the pen. The prey immediately noticed and all of them, even the ones who had not been active, got up and ran over with the others. Each one positioned itself directly in front of one of the lights. There was some pushing and shoving but shortly there was one creature in front of each light. Then a small panel slid aside beneath the lights and the creatures grabbed something inside and put it in their mouths.

"You have trained them to respond by feeding them?"

"Yes, it works quite well. It accustoms them to respond to certain signals. This has proved useful in the next stage." It moved to the third pen. "Here we are training them to do more complex tasks in order to be fed. We are combining the visual signals of the lights with audible messages in our language."

"And they are responding to that?"

"Sometimes we use visual signals alone, sometimes audible ones alone, and sometimes together. They respond to the lights very well, the audible ones less so. It is difficult to judge how well their hearing organs receive our speech. Nevertheless, they are responding to our orders - at least in simple ways."

"And in the fourth pen?" asked Qetjnegartis.

"These are the oldest ones and the most advanced. Unfortunately, due to the short time I have been conducting these experiments, these creatures were taken from their parents at a much older stage than I would have wished, so it is impossible to know how much they might have learned from their parents and how that might taint our results. However, they do respond to orders very well. Notice the collars they are wearing. They can deliver a painful electric shock on our command, so we can use both positive and negative reinforcement to their behavior. Their comprehension of spoken commands appears to be growing as the training continues."

Qetjnegartis watched the creatures for a while. They were taking blocks of plastic and arranging them in different ways according to diagrams projected on a screen. Verbal instructions were being given at the same time. At one point, one of them made a mistake and knocked over a nearly complete construction. The bud overseeing the training issued a command and all the creatures twitched in apparent pain. Then, to Qetjnegartis' surprise, all the others struck the one who had made the mistake several times and knocked it to the floor. "What just happened there?"

"We have observed that punishing the whole group for the mistake of an individual results in improved performance for the whole group."

"Interesting. So what is your evaluation of this project, Ixmaderna? Do you believe success is possible? Can these creatures be trained to serve us?"

"All the data so far indicates that it may be possible. But there is still much work to be done and I cannot guarantee the results. There are still too many unknowns."

"Understood. But you shall continue with this project as your duties allow. Now I must go. The next wave of transports from the Homeworld will be arriving soon and I must make plans for the new offensives."

*****

DECEMBER, 1911, NEW ORLEANS, LOUISIANA

"Standby to launch!"

The cry was repeated down the length of the slipway and the construction teams leapt to their tasks. Drew Harding looked on in satisfaction and no small amount of nervousness as the *USS Santa Fe* - his ship! - was about to take to the water for the first time. Involuntarily, his eyes were drawn to the sleeves of his jacket. They sported a first, too: the three gold bands of a full commander. Along with a ship, he had received a promotion. It had amazed him; in peacetime he would have had to wait until he was well into his thirties to reach such a rank. But these days…

"Ever seen this done before?"

Drew turned and saw his executive officer standing beside him. Caleb Mackenzie must have been nearly twice Drew's age. He had a wrinkled face, browned by decades of work in the sun, and a perpetual squint, as if warding off light reflecting from the waters. There was no sun to bother him today, and in fact, a light rain was falling. He wore the uniform of a senior grade lieutenant about as naturally as Drew would have worn a pair of lady's knickers. Mackenzie was - as he'd proudly told Drew - a river rat, born and bred. He knew ships and he knew the river, but only the urgent needs of a country at war would have ever put him in the navy.

"Not a sideways launch like this, no. A couple of stern-first launches, though."

"No room for that here."

'Here' was the Ingalls Shipyard on the south bank of the Mississippi, just across from New Orleans. The yard was owned by the huge Bethlehem Shipbuilding Company and was brand new. There were several other new yards along this stretch of the river, but most of them were turning out wooden river barges or similar auxiliary vessels. Only the Ingalls yard was building armored warships. But Mackenzie was correct; despite the width of the river, there was no room to send a new ship rushing backward out into the ship channel. A sideways launch would keep the ship safely close to the shore.

One of the shipyard workers, a foreman named Andy Higgins, dashed up and said: "We're just about ready, sir! You should come up to the platform!" Higgins was even younger than Drew, but in the few weeks he'd been here, it was clear the man was a human dynamo. He'd been an enormous help in learning his way around his ship.

He and Mackenzie followed Higgins up to the bow of the ship, where a wooden platform had been erected for the launching ceremony. A small delegation from the local community was there, holding umbrellas, along with a much larger group of the construction workers and their families clustered around to watch. Drew went up the three steps to the platform, while Mackenzie and Higgins remained behind.

The manager of the shipyard was there, a harried-looking man named Wachman, along with his teenage daughter, who would do the actual christening. He introduced Drew to the other men who were local politicians; councilmen or aldermen or dogcatchers or some such. Drew smiled and shook hands and immediately forgot their names. Wachman made a mercifully brief speech, thanking the workers for their efforts; and the politicians made somewhat longer speeches, cursing the Martians, praising the navy, and reminding everyone to vote for them next November. The rain was much heavier now and turning cold.

Finally, it was Drew's turn and he simply thanked the workers and assured them that their efforts would soon result in dead Martians. They seemed to like that and applauded lustily.

The girl, whose bright dress and flowers were starting to wilt rather badly with the dampness, stepped up holding a bottle. The navy had used a lot of different liquids to christen their ships over the years, ranging from wine to water from lakes or rivers close to whatever state, town, or city the ship was being named after. In recent years Champaign had started to be used. Since no one had wanted to make a thousand mile round trip to get a bottle of water from the Rio Grande, Drew wasn't sure what was in the bottle the girl wielded. But she stepped up and said in a surprisingly strong voice: "I name this ship, Santa Fe! May God bless her and all who sail in her!" She whacked the bottle against the bow and it shattered as it was supposed to, but splashed liquid all over her arms, as it wasn't. The crowd cheered and the girl beamed and laughed at the mess.

Shouts rang out all along the length of the ship and the launch crew went to work, knocking away the last of the braces holding it in place. Then with a squeal and rumble, it was moving. It lurched sideways and rushed with frightening speed into the river, throwing up a huge splash of water. Heavy chains were attached to it and these rumbled out after the ship, slowing it down through weight and friction. After a moment, the *Santa Fe* was at rest a few dozen yards from shore. A small tugboat moved in to push it up against a nearby dock.

"Well, it didn't sink," he heard Mackenzie say to Higgins. "A good start."

Drew looked over his command and smiled in satisfaction. The Liberation class monitors were basically scaled-down versions of the old *Amphitrite* class. They were two hundred and twelve feet long, fifty-six feet in the beam, which made them considerably shorter than the *Amphitrites* but a little wider, giving them a rather pudgy look. But this allowed them to draw only about eight feet of water so they could go much farther up the tributaries of the Mississippi. Full load displacement would be about three thousand tons.

The ship's small size had allowed its construction to be nearly completed before launching. The superstructure was almost finished so all that was lacking was the mast and the armament. This consisted of four eight-inch guns in a pair of turrets mounted fore and aft, and four four-inch guns mounted singly at the corners of the superstructure. The *Amphitrites* carried ten-inchers, but Drew had been assured that the eights were more than sufficient to destroy a Martian tripod.

The ship's crew, which numbered one hundred and forty, would be arriving in the next few weeks. Aside from Mackenzie, Drew hadn't met any of them. He had no idea how much experience they would have. So the next few months would be a frenzy of work to get the ship fully operational and the crew trained to work as an efficient team.

He made his farewells to Wachman, his daughter, and the local dignitaries and went down the steps and over to his first officer.

"Well, let's get to work."

* * * * *

DECEMBER, 1911, NORTHWEST OF MEMPHIS, TENNESSEE

"It's no good, sir! We're gonna have to turn back!"

Lieutenant Harvey Brown, Commander of A Troop, practically had to shout into Frank Dolfen's ear to be heard above the howling wind. It was the fourth day after Christmas and the third day since the squadron had set out from Memphis on another scouting mission. The first and second days had been sunny and fairly warm, but by the evening of the second day there were some ominous clouds building to the northwest. A cold wind had been shaking the tents by midnight. In the morning, the first flakes of snow were whipping past and now, by midmorning, the storm had hit with all its fury.

"You think it's that bad?" he shouted back at Brown.

Brown just stared at him, only his eyes visible between his hat brim and a scarf wrapped around his face. It was a stupid question and they both knew it. Yeah, it definitely was that bad. He couldn't see twenty yards and the snow was already six inches deep on the ground. He'd seen some bad storms during his times in the Dakotas and he'd heard the old-timers' tales about the Winter of the Blue Snow in '86-'87. This one wasn't quite that bad, but it was certainly bad enough.

"If it gets much deeper, the vehicles are gonna get stuck!"

That was a fact. The horses and men might be able to push on, but with over half the squadron dependent on trucks and motorcycles... No, there wasn't any choice.

"All right! Pass the word that we're turning around! Make damn sure everyone gets the order, we don't want anyone getting lost!"

"Yes, sir!" Brown waved a gloved hand near his hat by way of a salute and spurred his horse toward the head of the column.

It took a while and there was a great deal of shouting and confusion, but eventually they were all turned around and heading southeast. This put the wind at their backs and everyone felt much better. Dolfen hated like hell to have to abandon the mission - especially since the Martians didn't seem to suspend their operations because of the weather. But to keep going wouldn't accomplish anything except probably lose a lot of horses and equipment to no good purpose.

They struggled on for a few more hours until they reached the ruins of Jonesboro, which was near where they'd spent the previous night. Dolfen ordered a halt and they drew up the vehicles in the spaces between the least damaged buildings to create a windbreak. The men and horses clustered in the lee and built fires and pitched tents as best they could.

The wind continued to howl all night.

* * * * *

DECEMBER, 1911, NEAR MEMPHIS, TENNESSEE

Rebecca Harding pulled her hat down to conceal her face as Captain Dolfen rode by. She couldn't imagine how he'd react if he discovered she had stowed away on this expedition. He'd be mad as hell, she knew that, but what he might actually do, she wasn't sure. She still couldn't quite believe that she was doing this. She'd asked Frank to talk to his colonel about taking nurses along on his scouting missions and he'd said that he had done so, but no decisions - or permission - had been forthcoming. Had he really asked, or had he just told her he'd done so to put her off? It hurt to think he'd do something like that. Of course with the army it could take months for even the simplest thing to get done…

But when she heard Frank was heading out again, she had acted on impulse - just like when she and Pepe had gone to find the shooting stars so long ago. She'd asked Miss Chumley for a leave of absence, and since she hadn't taken any time off in over two years, Chumley had granted the request without a problem. She'd found a man's uniform that fit her well enough, packed a medical kit, gotten her horse Ninny, and just sort of tagged along with the two regular medics when the squadron moved out. The medics had discovered that she was a woman the first day, but they just laughed and made no trouble for her - which was probably more luck than she deserved.

So they hadn't turned her in and she had managed to avoid Frank so far. Her original plan - as far as she had one - was that if and when they got into a fight and she had to tend wounded, by that time it would be far too late to send her back so it wouldn't matter if he found her out. And she'd prove she was so useful that he wouldn't get too mad and he'd allow her to stay. Simple, right?

But now, the terrible winter weather had forced them to turn back, and barring any serious cases of frostbite, she'd have no chance to prove her worth. So she had to keep hidden. Fortunately, that same weather made it entirely unremarkable for her to be so bundled up that no one could see who she was. She'd used a blanket to disguise Ninny, too. The snow had finally stopped falling, but the wind was still bitter.

They crested a tiny rise and there was the river laid out in front of them, the city of Memphis on the far shore. It was late afternoon and the sun peeked out for a moment, painting the buildings and the fortress walls a rosy pink. Frank came riding back and he shouted to the men: "Move it along and I'll have you back in camp in time for the new year!"

New Years! It was true, tonight was New Year's Eve. She'd completely forgotten. The Year of Our Lord, Nineteen Twelve. It didn't seem possible.

But what sort of a year would it be?

CHAPTER SIX

CYCLE 597, 845.0, HOLDFAST 32-2

Qetjnegartis watched as Tanbradjus maneuvered its travel chair into the consultation chamber and sealed the door. It had arrived the previous day with the new wave of transport capsules. It was senior-most of the newcomers, indeed, it was senior to all except Qetjnegartis. It said that it had important orders to relay from the clan leaders and the Council of Three Hundred on the Homeworld. Qetjnegartis had been speculating on what those order might be ever since it was informed. *Surely not orders to replace me, or they would have sent someone senior.* They both had the same progenitor, but Tanbradjus was far junior in order of budding. Even so, it was now the second highest member of the Bajantus Clan here on the target world.

"I trust you have recovered from your journey and the revival from hibernation?" asked Qetjnegartis once Tanbradjus was halted.

"Mostly, although this gravity is very irksome! How do you tolerate it?"

"One become used to it quickly. And after a transference or two, one hardly notices the difference."

"Indeed? I hope you are right. My next bud will be ready to detach soon, but I don't relish enduring this for another quarter cycle until I can transfer." It touched the sack on its side with a tendril.

"Hopefully, you won't need to transfer even then."

"Really? I had heard that to avoid the contagions which infest this place it is necessary to transfer on every other budding." Tanbradjus appeared apprehensive; was it that afraid of the local disease organisms?

"Every other, or every third, seems to be the average for a new arrival. But with time, the chance of infection grows less - just as our scientists had hoped. I have only had to transfer once so far. But do not worry, we can test you for infection at frequent intervals and there will be no danger."

"I was not worried."

"Of course not. But come, you spoke of a very urgent matter. What message do you carry that could not be transmitted directly?" Qetjnegartis could not fail to notice that Tanbradjus was not extending a tendril to allow a mental link. Why? What did it have to conceal?

Tanbradjus hesitated before answering. "This chamber is secure? From being overheard, I mean."

"Of course. But what secret do you carry that could be so dire?"

Tanbradjus looked from side to side and its voice sank so far as to be barely audible. "Qetjnegartis, I fear that our leaders have gone mad."

"What?! Why would you say such a thing?"

"Tell, me, why did we - I mean the Race - come to this planet?"

"Why? To avoid extinction, of course. The Homeworld is dying, all recognize that fact. To stay would mean the eventual death of the Race. We will conquer this world and relocate our people here. That was always the plan…" Qetjnegartis focused on Tanbradjus. "Are you saying that this has changed?"

"Yes, the Three Hundred debated this for half a cycle before this last wave was launched. Many objected to the new plan, but the vast majority endorsed it."

"What new plan?"

"There will be no relocation." Tanbradjus quivered in its chair.

"What? Then… then what are we doing here?" Qetjnegartis tried to conceive some logical argument to support this decision, but failed utterly.

"The new plan is that those of us who are here will send resources back to the Homeworld to stave off the long extinction."

"But… but that's…"

"Insane? Yes, just as I said."

"It's not practical!" said Qetjnegartis, not quite daring to use the word *insane*. "The launching guns would need to be impossibly huge to overcome this planet's gravity and we would be firing… *uphill*, outward from the sun, to reach the Homeworld! The payloads we could hope to deliver would be absurdly small!"

"Yes, so the minority argued. But the rest would not listen. The elders are unwilling to leave and they command the rest. The orders I carry - and the orders we must obey - direct us to finish this war with the prey-creatures as quickly as possible…"

"Which we are already directing all our resources to do," interrupted Qetjnegartis.

"Yes, but we must also – simultaneously - begin preparations for the new directive. We must scout out locations for the launching guns we must build and start preparing plans and gathering resources."

Qetjnegartis waved its tendrils in dismay. Tanbradjus was right: this thinking was insane! "Perhaps… perhaps once the Council sees how truly impractical this is, they will reverse their decision…"

"Unlikely, and they have already taken steps which will make re-adoption of the relocation plan more difficult."

"What steps?"

"They are creating new buds to replace those of us who have left to come here."

"Madness!" cried Qetjnegartis, truly shocked. "Even if we could somehow send significant resources home, it would still be vital to reduce the total population!"

"Yes, the opposition made that argument, but the majority simply said that if the dissenters refused to create new buds then the others would be glad to take their allotment. That silenced them."

Qetjnegartis could think of no reply. This was indeed madness. The plan - the plan agreed upon - had been to send people to the target world to carry out the conquest here and prepare the way for the rest of the Race to come also. It would take thousands of cycles to carry out, but each transport which left, each load of people moved, would make the resources left on the Homeworld last all the longer. Calculations indicated they would last long enough to complete the relocation.

But this! This was mass suicide! Even if the new launch guns could be built and loads of resources delivered, it would at best delay the inevitable for a few hundred or a few thousand cycles. Then when the collapse finally became unpreventable, there would be no time and no resources to attempt an evacuation.

"I think that many in the Council were worried about the length of time the original plan would take," continued Tanbradjus.

"All knew it was a long-term project!"

"True, but the worry was that those of us who were here would bud and bud and fill up this world before the transfer could be completed. And…" its voice fell again, "there have been some disturbing rumors about… differences in the buds created on this world."

Qetjnegartis stiffened, but did not reply. Rumors? Ixmaderna had said it was inevitable the other clans would notice the same phenomena. Apparently some had dared to report this home.

"So it is true? The new buds have no loyalty to the Homeworld?"

"Not in the direct fashion such as you and I have but they…"

"Is it true?"

"Yes. Buds created on this world have no instinctive submission to those on the Homeworld. But they do have submission to their progenitors!"

"I was afraid that this was the case. Others at home fear this new development greatly."

"I think they exaggerate the danger…" said Qetjnegartis.

"Do you? And what of our own clan here? Only you and three others remain from the original landing force. You four are your own buds' - and their buds' - only links of loyalty to the Homeworld! If you are killed in this war then there would be an entire growing group who could not be controlled! What of that? Our situation may be extreme compared with most, but the same danger exists with them, too."

"Perhaps, but the situation is what it is and we cannot change it. I will endeavor not to be slain and spare the elders from a crisis - and you from the burden of command."

"I am serious, Qetjnegartis!"

"As am I, Tanbradjus."

They stared at each other in silence for some time, but eventually Qetjnegartis stirred. "Well, no matter how much we might disagree, there is nothing for it but to obey our orders. I will direct Ixmaderna to give some thought to possible locations for a launch gun. It is entirely possible, you realize, that no suitable site might be found in our territory?"

"Yes, in that case we would be expected to assist those clans who do have suitable locations."

"Of course. But of immediate concern is the coming offensive. At least the Council does not see fit to interfere with that!"

"No. Indeed they insist it go forward with maximum effort on all fronts."

"The plans are far along. We need wait only for the buds you and the other newcomers bear to detach. This will also give us time to analyze the images being sent down from the orbiting artificial satellite. Those should prove extremely valuable."

"So it was hoped. We must also coordinate our activities with Group 33 to the north."

"Yes, Commander Braxjandar is arrogant and can be difficult to work with, but it is capable and aggressive. It has greater strength than we at the moment and I am hoping that its attacks will draw off the enemy's strength from our front."

"It still seems incredible that these primitive prey-creatures are able to mount so much resistance," said Tanbradjus. "The reports of the first invasion…"

"Were extremely incomplete!" said Qetjnegartis in annoyance. "Has no one on the Homeworld read the reports that we have sent? The prey are intelligent and innovative and very numerous. Their strength is far greater than our initial studies indicated!"

"Calm yourself, Qetjnegartis!" said Tanbradjus. "I am not criticizing your actions. But I fear that the elders do not appreciate the difficulties which you face. Perhaps I do not, either. Please instruct me."

"Very well…"

* * * * *

JANUARY, 1912, NEAR DONALDSONVILLE, LOUISIANA

"Damn," said Commander Drew Harding.

"Don't get your feathers ruffled," said Lieutenant Mackenzie. "Could happen to anyone. Hell, it's happened to me more times than I can count."

Drew was standing at the bow of his ship and staring down at the muddy waters of the Mississippi. "But we were in the channel! This should have been clear!"

Mackenzie chuckled in a fashion that Drew found infuriating. "River's different from the open ocean." He cleared his throat and spat. "Sand bars like this 'un move around all the time. By tomorrow it'll probably be gone - or moved somewhere else. But at least it's just sand. No leaks reported from below."

"Thank God for that. Can we get off?"

"I 'spect so. Put 'er astern and see what happens."

Drew frowned and spun on his heel and walked back to the bridge. *Astern! Hell, I could have figured that out! If Mackenzie's such a damn expert on the river, why didn't he keep us from grounding in the first place?* Drew's relationship with his executive officer had generally been satisfactory, but the man could be really irritating when he wanted. Still, there was no doubt he knew the river, and Drew had to admit if he'd been up on the bridge he might have spotted that sand bar before the Santa Fe stuck her bow into it. However, the man didn't know a damn thing about gunnery and Drew took some satisfaction in that.

The bridge of the *Santa Fe* was exactly that, an open platform sitting atop the tiny armored wheelhouse which projected far out to either side so that lookouts could spot things - like sand bars - in the river. There was a wheel and an engine room telegraph - duplicates of the ones in the wheelhouse - and the ship would normally be controlled from here except in bad weather or in combat. Drew nodded to the officer of the watch, Ensign Hinsworth, a very young man with the peculiar first name of Albustus. Alby, as he preferred to be called, was still learning his job and was obviously very nervous that he had the watch when this happened - even though Drew had been there on the bridge, too.

"All back one-third," he ordered.

"Aye aye, sir! All back one-third!" Hinsworth made fluttering motions with his hand at the man at the telegraph until he moved the handles to the proper position. After a moment, a bell rang from the telegraph.

"Engine room answers, all back one-third," said the man.

"Engine room answers, all back one-third, sir!" squeaked Hinsworth.

"Yes, ensign, I heard," said Drew with studied calm. Smoke puffed out from the stack just behind them, and the ship vibrated a bit as the engines went to work.

But the ship didn't move. Drew looked about, trying to convince himself that they were moving, but no, they were still stuck.

"All back two-thirds," he ordered and after another relay of orders and replies, Hinsworth told him they were all back two-thirds. But they still didn't seem to be moving. Drew walked out on the bridge wing for a better look. The water at the stern was boiling now, brown with stirred up mud. He put it at all back full, and even though the ship was vibrating strongly and smoke billowed out of the stack in a thick cloud, they still didn't move. Mackenzie arrived on the bridge and came over to him.

"Got a real suction there, Cap'n. Doesn't want t'let go."

"Any *suggestions*, Lieutenant?" Drew didn't quite snarl at the man.

'Have t'twist 'er loose, I think." He looked out over the river, squinting, checking for other traffic, Drew guessed. "Put the port screw back slow, the starboard ahead full and give 'er full right rudder."

Drew thought about that for a moment and realized what Mackenzie was trying to do; he nodded and gave the order. The engine room slowed the right-side propeller and then ran it in the opposite direction. The helmsman spun the wheel which controlled the rudder. "Hard over, sir," he reported after a moment. The ship had been given an oversized rudder to allow sharp turns in the constricted space of a river. Drew hoped it would do the job now.

The ship was shuddering and the water at the stern was churning, but the boil was off to the right now, instead of dead astern. Between the opposite thrustings of the propellers and the rudder diverting the flow from the right screw, the stern of the Santa Fe was being pushed strongly to the left. But was she moving?

Yes!

There was no doubt, the stern was swinging around! Degree by degree, the stern moved left and the bow twisted right. They were pulling free!

"Ease 'er off a bit," said Mackenzie. "Don't want t'run 'er up on the shore once we're loose."

Drew ordered reduced speed on the engines, but before the engine room even answered back, the ship lurched and then swung clear. "Rudder a-midships! All ahead one-third!" cried Drew. *Santa Fe* slowed, stopped, and then moved forward again as if nothing at all had happened.

"There y'go, Cap'n. Yer gettin' the hang of things."

* * * * *

FEBRUARY, 1912, SOUTH OF KANSAS CITY, MISSOURI

"Bloody hell, there's another batch of the blighters!"

Major Bridges' exclamation made Frank Dolfen whip his head around so fast it hurt his neck. "Where?" he demanded.

"Almost due west. Still eight or ten miles off, I'd guess. A lot of them, though."

Dolfen squirmed around on his belly in their hiding place and focused his field glasses to the west. He quickly saw what Bridges was talking about: a cluster of dark shapes on the horizon. Martian tripods. And yeah, there were a lot of them. He tried to count, but at this point they were just silhouettes and they kept moving in front of each other, confusing his count. There had to be at least thirty of them. He watched them for a while until he was sure they were heading for the nearby Martian fortress and not coming for them. Then he rolled over on his back and rubbed his eyes. Bridges kept watching.

"I count forty of them, I think. Mostly the regular ones, but a few of the smaller scouts. And most seem to be carrying stuff on their backs, too."

"Those cages they've been using for captives?"

"No, I don't believe so. They're different."

Groaning, Dolfen rolled back and looked through his glasses again. The Martians were a lot closer now, only three or four miles away. He saw what the Englishman was talking about, but he couldn't figure out what the tripods were carrying. "Cargo of some sort, I guess. I suppose they must need to move stuff from one fortress to another."

"You're probably right, old man. But forty more of the damn things! That's how many we've seen arrive so far?"

"Forty more would be... nearly two hundred." Dolfen whistled. "They must be planning something for sure!"

The 1st Squadron of the 5th Cavalry was a long way from its base in Memphis. Word had come down all the way from 3rd Army Headquarters that things were happening up north. The newly formed 6th Army near St. Louis couldn't get any scouts through a thickening screen of Martian pickets, and bad winter weather had grounded their aircraft for long periods. So they'd asked if 3rd Army could slip someone in from the south to have a look. Dolfen and his men, veterans of several missions into Martian territory, had won the prize. *The reward for a job well done: a tougher job!*

They'd started out at the beginning of the month and traveled well over three hundred miles to reach this position near a newly built Martian fortress. It was now the end of February and they'd been watching the place for over a week. There was no way the armored cars or artillery could make such a journey so they and the supply trucks and half the motorcycles had been left behind. They'd been forced to rely on pack horses just like the old days. But they'd made it undetected and Dolfen now had a half-dozen outposts around the fortress making observations. Still, he was worried about what would happen if they were forced into a fight. Without the armored cars or the artillery they could be in real trouble. They had been issued a few of the new rocket launchers, 'stovepipes' everyone was calling them, but he had no idea if they would be of any use. And with the weather and the distance, he couldn't count on any help from Selfridge or his aircraft. No, they had to avoid a fight if at all possible.

A gust of wind penetrated the thick clump of bushes they were using for cover and Dolfen shivered. It was almost March, but the winter still lingered here in the plains. They didn't dare to build a fire and he was getting chilled to the bone. He glanced at the sun, but there were still several hours until nightfall when their relief would arrive and they could retreat to where the rest of the squadron was waiting in the ruins of the town of La Harpe.

The Martian tripods disappeared inside the walls of their fortress off to the northeast and there was nothing more to see. Sometimes there were tripods walking sentry or out hunting, but today there were none in evidence. Dolfen put away his field glasses, wrapped a blanket around himself, and wished for coffee. He knew it was slightly stupid for the squadron commander to be out scouting in person, but there was still a lot of sergeant in him, and he hated being off in the rear while his men were out in front. Besides, this was still more interesting than doing paperwork.

"I say, old man," said Bridges after a while. "How much longer do you plan to keep us at this lovely exercise?"

"Our orders say to stay here until another unit shows up to take our place - as you well know. The 3rd Cavalry is supposed to be here in two days, but I've got no idea when they'll actually arrive."

"Or if they'll arrive, eh? Perhaps you could use the wireless."

"Weekly transmissions only, you know that. The Martians come after us the moment we start sending. I don't want to have to relocate the camp again. So we've got at least two more days."

"Very well."

Dolfen shifted, trying to find a more comfortable position and cursed when something sharp dug into him. He reached around and pulled out a rock. He was about to toss it away when he paused and looked closer. There was a red patch on the rock the size of a dime. Red Weed. *Damn.* He glanced around to make sure there was nothing which could see, lit a match, and toasted it. "You see much of this stuff in India, Major?"

"A bit, but the Martians never got a foothold in India proper. And the locals are very good about getting rid of it when they find it. They think it's some sort of devil weed - which I suppose is true, now that I think on it. But they're very protective about their farmland over there, y'know. They set the children to work rooting it out. It's worse up in the mountains, in Afghanistan and the Western Frontier, though. Fewer people and much rougher land. Still, they're probably better off than any poor blighters still trying to hang on in Siberia. I've heard tell that there are places there where it covers thousands of square miles."

"We can't let that happen here."

"Hard to do anything when there are Martians about, old boy."

"Yeah."

They, and the two troopers they'd brought with them, huddled there shivering until well after nightfall when the relief arrived. Then they stumbled back through the dark to the gully where the horses were kept. At least the hike got Dolfen's blood moving again, although his feet still felt like two blocks of ice. They mounted up and rode back to La Harpe, still keeping a careful watch for the enemy. Unlike them, the Martians had no issues with seeing in the dark.

They made it there without incident and gratefully accepted cups of hot coffee in the warm and cozy headquarters which had been set up in the basement of the ruined courthouse. His aide, Lieutenant Lynnbrooke, was there and Dolfen asked him for the status of the squadron.

"All good, sir. The men are staying out of sight and the pickets all have good positions. They're pretty bored, but I rotate the pickets frequently enough that they don't complain much."

"Good. Any messages on the radio?" While they didn't dare to transmit, they could pick up messages from outside.

"Just the usual traffic and confirmation that the squadron from the 3rd is still on its way and ought to be here to relieve us on time."

"Good, good. Anything else?"

Lynnbrooke hesitated and then said: "Uh, we did pick up a group of refugees today, sir."

"Really? Where are they from? Did you question them about enemy activity?" Dolfen was a bit surprised. They'd encountered no one so far on this trip. The land seemed empty.

"They said they were from Iola. Been hiding there for the last year. They saw one of our pickets and came here to check."

Dolfen nodded. That was only five or six miles west of La Harpe. "Did they say anything else? If they've been here this long, they must have seen something."

"Some of them were pretty sick, sir. I turned them over to... uh, to the medics. Figured we could question them later."

"Were all of them sick?"

"No, but they were worried about the ones who are."

Dolfen frowned. "I want to know if they've seen anything." He got up from his chair with a groan.

"Can't it wait until morning, sir? You must be tired."

"I'm up. It should only take a few minutes."

"But sir…"

"But what?" Dolfen turned to face Lynnbrooke. What was the matter with the man? Couldn't he realize that their safety here depended on having the best information possible?

"Uh… nothing, sir."

Dolfen turned and made his way up out of the basement and then gave his eyes a few moments to adjust to the darkness before making his way across the street to the remains of the town's small library where they'd put their medical section. The stairway down had two sets of blankets rigged to prevent any light from leaking out. As he passed the first one, he heard a child crying and a woman's voice trying to calm it. He paused for a moment. For some reason the voice sounded familiar…

He pulled aside the second curtain and looked around. Yes, there were about a dozen civilians here, and there were two medics, but who was that other soldier? Someone in a greatcoat was kneeling next to the child who was crying. He was a bit smaller than your average trooper and his hair, peeking out from under a cap, was definitely longer than regulation. He turned his head and…

"Becca!"

* * * * *

MARCH, 1912, SOUTHEAST OF LA HARPE, KANSAS

"So, did everyone in the squadron know except for me?"

"Not everyone, I don't think," said Rebecca Harding, trying hard not to smile. She was riding beside Frank Dolfen as the squadron headed south, back to Memphis. The relieving column had arrived the day before and they could go home.

"Well, those two blasted medics knew! And I'll eat my hat if Lynnbrooke didn't know, too! The way he was trying to keep me from going to see the refugees! He knew you were there!"

"Well, I guess there were probably a few…" She shrugged.

"What the devil were you thinking?"

"I was thinking that I could be more use here than back at the hospital." She carefully kept her voice level. There was no point in getting into a shouting match.

"Well you're …!" Frank stopped himself in mid-shout. Then he stared at her, snorted, and shook his head. "You're really something, y'know that, girl?"

Now she did smile and quirked an eyebrow.

"Guess it wouldn't do any good for me chew you out, would it?"

"Not one bit. If Miss Chumley can't scare me no more, no way you can, either, Mister Captain, sir."

They rode in silence for a while. There was a warm breeze coming up from the southwest. It would probably bring rain tomorrow, but right now it felt nice. Spring coming at last.

"I don't want you gettin' hurt," said Frank after a while.

"Doin' m'best not to."

"You know what I mean! It's *dangerous* out here!"

"I reckon I'm aware of that. I kinda figured it out when the Martians killed my friend… and my pa… and my ma… and my grandma… and tried to kill me a time or two. I'd a' thought you'd have figured it out when they killed all your friends the day after you found me." She let her voice go cold.

"Becca…"

"Frank?"

He snorted again and looked away. "Never mind."

She stared at him and wondered what he'd been about to say. But he spurred his horse to a trot and went to the head of the column. Blast the man! She had no doubt that he cared for her - just like she cared for him. Why couldn't he say it? *You haven't said it either, girl.* No she hadn't, had she? Why not? And why was she out here? To fight Martians like she'd always said? Or because of Frank? Did she love him? She wasn't sure. She was eighteen and most girls her age were already married or at least betrothed. But that was in a world where the parents arranged such things and good girls didn't go chasing after soldiers. That was in a normal world that hadn't been invaded by Martians. That world didn't exist anymore.

After a while he dropped back and she nudged Ninny up beside his horse. "So I guess you won't let me do this again, huh?"

"I didn't let you do it *this* time, but that didn't stop you."

"But you'll be lookin' for me the next time you go out. What'll you do if you catch me?"

"Damn it! I *did* talk to the colonel and he said he wasn't sending any nurses out here! And he's right! This is no place for women!"

"No place for men neither, but you go."

"I have to! You don't!"

"Yeah, you're ordered out here, so you go. But you can't tell me you don't want to be out here, fighting back. I do, too."

Frank scowled and didn't say anything for a while. But he didn't ride off this time. After a while he said: "Becca?"

"Yes, Frank?"

"You might want to spend more time with those sharpshooters of yours."

She snorted. "Why? What use are they?"

"Because we saw almost two hundred Martian tripods back at that fortress."

"Two hundred!" That was far more than she'd ever seen or what had fought in the big battles in 1910 from what she'd been told. "What are they doing?"

"They didn't tell me. But if they're massing like that, it must be for an attack. Kansas City, maybe even St. Louis. And I can't believe they'll leave Memphis alone for long. There's no need for you to come out here lookin' for a fight." He stared right at her.

"The fight's coming to you."

* * * * *

MARCH, 1912, WASHINGTON, D.C.

"Mr. President, I think the lull is over. They're preparing for a major attack," said Leonard Wood.

Theodore Roosevelt walked over to the huge map table and nodded. They were in the large situation room in the bowels of the War and Navy Building, which had become Wood's second home the last few years. Dozens of officers and men bustled about, but they gave the President and his Chief of Staff a little bubble of privacy. "Their new cylinders have arrived and now they go on the offensive again. Just like the last time. Are we ready for them?"

"I believe we are, sir. Our defenses along the Mississippi are very strong and getting stronger every day. But I'm concerned about Kansas City and Little Rock." He grabbed up a pointer and tapped it down near the two fortified cities well beyond the main lines of defense. "The reports from cavalry scouts and aircraft indicate that the main concentrations of the enemy are near to both of those places. They may try to wipe them out before attacking our main lines."

"Can they hold?"

"I don't know. It will all depend on how big a force they throw at them. I wish we could reinforce both those places but…"

"But what?"

"Well, there's a limit to how big a force we can keep supplied out there. And every man we send is one less we have to defend the main line. And… well, to put it bluntly, sir, if they are overrun, there's little hope for any sort of orderly retreat. Those garrisons would probably be annihilated and I don't want to send any more men than I have to into what might be death traps." Wood paused and looked at Roosevelt. "Unless we want to evacuate…"

"Can't do it, Leonard. We just can't do it. I agreed to let you abandon Sioux City and Omaha already, but no more! We've evacuated nearly all the civilians from Kansas City and Little Rock, but we can't abandon the cities themselves. No more than we can abandon Texas. It might make sense militarily, but there's a lot more to it than that."

Like your political future? The thought came to Wood instantly. He was being unfair to Roosevelt, but he couldn't help it. There was still a lingering bitterness about his refusal to allow him to pull back from the Rockies in 1910 because of political considerations. They'd lost a hundred thousand men and nearly the whole war when everything went to hell. But at the same time, Roosevelt was right. The string of defeats, the retreats, and the loss of the whole middle of the country had been a huge blow to the morale of the nation. To give up even more… no, it was time to make a stand!

And politics was important. In spite of the mistakes he'd made, Roosevelt was still the best man to lead the country; of that, Wood had no doubt. The opposition, led by Nelson Miles, was already campaigning fiercely in anticipation of the November election. The main plank of their platform was all that lost ground and the administration's failure to take any of it back. Yes, as cynical as it might seem, politics did matter.

"Well," said Wood, dragging his thoughts back to the problem at hand. "At the very least, Kansas City and Little Rock can act as advanced posts, breakwaters to blunt and disrupt the Martian attacks. Blood them as much as we can."

Roosevelt frowned. "What's the proper military term? A Forlorn Hope?"

Wood sighed. "Yes, I guess that's it. But I'll send them what help we can. Fortunately, we're right at the spring thaw and the rivers will be up. We can send gunboats and monitors to both places. And maybe other boats and barges in case we do need to make a run for it."

Roosevelt turned away suddenly and marched across the room and back again, his hands clasped behind his back. When he returned, he thumped a fist on the edge of the map table, making some of the wooden blocks on it jump. "What else?"

"Assuming they do make it past Kansas City and Little Rock, then we need to think about where they will go next. St. Louis and Memphis are the obvious targets. I plan to send most of our reserves to those areas."

"What about the rest of the line?" asked the President, sweeping his arm to indicate the entire vast stretch of the Mississippi defenses. "Any threats elsewhere?"

"Nothing that we've detected. Of course that could change on short notice considering how fast the damn Martians can move. They did try some probes around Lake Superior when parts of it was frozen during the winter, but they seemed to give up on the idea when we dumped a few tripods through the ice with artillery fire."

Roosevelt laughed. "Yes! They don't like the water - thank God!"

"Oh, and I got a report from Funston - not a demand for more equipment for once - saying that he's gotten word from the French down in Veracruz that the Martians there are using some sort of new machine. No real details other than it is a lot smaller than their tripods. We haven't seen any sign of such a thing around here yet, but I've sent out word to be prepared."

"I suppose it's inevitable that the Martians will invent new weapons just as we have. But what the devil is Funston doing dealing directly with the French? Why didn't this come through our normal liaisons?"

Wood shrugged. "You know Funston. But he is sort of dangling on his own down there. Oh, and the British are reporting activity on their front in Canada. But we are going to have to trust that they can deal with it. As for elsewhere… things on the west coast remain quiet, and we've beaten off every probe they've made toward the canal. General Barry is convinced that a major attack is brewing, but we're already giving him everything he can use and he should be able hold - although the refugee problem is becoming a real crisis."

"Yes, I know, I know…" Roosevelt's brow was creased in worry. He had a lot more than just the military situation to deal with. The international situation, the domestic situation, taxes, war bonds, finances, labor problems, food shortages, the list went on and on and mostly things Wood didn't have to deal with at all. He could see the toll this was taking on the man. Wrinkles on wrinkles and his hair and mustache all gray now with many white strands evident. *Just like you? Take a look in the mirror old man!*

"Those are all the main issues, Mr. President."

"Very good. Well, I have to go. Have to meet with Cortelyou about the damn campaign. Good God, but I hate politics!"

Wood smiled. That was like a fish saying it hated water. "Have a good afternoon, Mr. President."

Roosevelt left accompanied by the ubiquitous Major Butt, his military aide.

"That went pretty well, I thought, sir," said Colonel Drum coming up to Wood. His assistant had watched the whole interchange from a safe distance.

"Yes, I guess it did. But we have a hell of a fight coming up, Hugh. And this one we have to win!"

"Yes, sir." Drum gazed at the map. "St. Louis, sir. We must hold St. Louis."

"We have to hold *everywhere*. Any breach of the Mississippi would be a disaster, but, yes, you are right: St. Louis is the linchpin. We need to form a reserve behind the river at that point."

"Yes, sir. And it's a great location in any case. From there we could quickly reinforce the whole northern half of the line if they do strike elsewhere."

"True. But my gut tells me that the main blow will fall on St. Louis. I want more tanks in that area and I want every one of those Little David machines sent there."

"All of them, sir?"

"Yes, all of them. If we are going to use them, I don't want them wasted in penny-packets. If they hit us there, we'll hit back hard!"

"Very good, sir."

Wood got up, stretched, and walked around the room, looking over people's shoulders and making them nervous. He was tired, but restless. Damn, he'd been cooped up in this tomb for too long! He spun about. "Colonel!"

"Sir?"

"It's about time I made an inspection trip. I've had enough of maps and wooden blocks! I want to see what's really going on out there!"

"Uh, yes, sir," said Drum, startled. "Where do you plan to go?"

He pointed at the map.

"St. Louis."

CHAPTER SEVEN

MARCH, 1912, PHILADELPHIA, PENNSYLVANIA

"Lower away!" The cry rang through the dry dock at the William Cramp & Sons shipyard in south Philadelphia. Andrew Comstock looked up at the huge crane and the metal cylinder hanging from it which was almost directly overhead.

"Sure hope they know what they're doing," said Jerry Hornbaker from beside him.

"They build battleships here, Lieutenant. This is nothing new for them," replied Andrew, but privately he echoed his aide's sentiments. Considering how many things *had* gone wrong so far with this project, it wouldn't really surprise him if the crane failed and the main turret of the land ironclad came crashing down to crush everything.

But inch by inch, the turret, which was close to twenty feet in diameter and ten feet high, came down and down and eventually fit into the circular mounting ring on the deck as neatly as you please. The work crew gave a cheer and then began unfastening the hooks on the end of the chains. The crane drew them up and then swung around to pick up the twelve-inch gun which would fit inside the turret. Another team was already at work inside the turret hooking up the traversing and elevating controls.

"That went well," said a voice. "Starting to look like something at last."

Andrew turned and saw that Brigadier General William Clopton had come aboard without him noticing. Another officer, a major, was with him; he was looking around the ironclad with an inquiring eye.

"Yes, sir, we're making some real progress now."

"About time. I was afraid I was going to get stuck commanding a bunch of very expensive white elephants. Might still happen, I suppose. Oh, by the way, this is Major Harold Stavely, he'll be taking command of this contraption once it's finished. I'll expect you to familiarize him with things."

Andrew shook his hand and said: "Welcome aboard, Major, I'll help you out however I can."

"Thank you, Colonel. I commanded a steam tank company out west, so I have some experience with steam powered vehicles - but nothing on this scale. Quite a thing, isn't it?"

"The other five commanders will be here within the week," said Clopton. "You'll be expected to help all of them, Comstock."

Andrew nodded. "Yes, sir." Clopton had been put in command of the 1st Land Ironclad Squadron and it didn't seem to him that the man was all that happy about it. *Well, you aren't all that happy about being here either, are you?*

He'd only been 'permanently' attached to the squadron for about three months, but it seemed much longer. He was working very long days, pretty much seven days a week. He'd only managed one quick visit to Victoria during that time and he missed her and his son terribly. But they had made progress. The first land ironclad had been repaired and the leaking problem had been solved - they hoped! - by sealing all the seams with electric arc welding. The Baldwin people had felt that just doing it on the four compartments housing the motors for the tracks would be enough, but Andrew had insisted - and General Crozier had gratifyingly backed him up - on welding every single seam which would be under water when the ironclads were afloat. It had taken a month, and they were still working on the last two of the squadron, but the next time they drove out into the river, there hadn't been a drop of leakage. So one problem solved.

The next problem had occurred less than an hour later.

They attached the flotation module without a hitch and the USLI-001 had become a ship. Andrew had been most worried about that, but it had gone as smooth as silk. Then, when they engaged the screw propeller and moved out onto the Delaware for the trip up the river to the shipyard, they discovered that the propeller simply wasn't big enough to move the ship against the current of the river; not with the huge amount of drag created by the caterpillar tracks. They had sat there, chugging away like mad, but all they could do was maintain their position against the flow. They had called for a large tug to help tow them, but by the time it had arrived, the Delaware, which was a tidal river, had shifted its direction and was now helping them upstream instead of pushing them down. So they made it to the dry dock, but it was clear that for any long-distance travel by water, each ironclad was going to need a large ship to tow it.

And those were just the big problems. There were dozens of smaller problems plaguing the unique machines. Andrew had followed John Schmidt, the chief engineer, from top to bottom and front to back into every space, large and tiny, to track down troubles and get them fixed. Andrew had taken a few engineering courses at West Point, which had always emphasized the subject, but they had mostly dealt with civil and military engineering. Now he found himself becoming, if not an expert, at least very familiar with mechanical and electrical engineering. In the last few weeks he was fixing problems on his own without Schmidt's help.

"Another month or so, sir," he said to Clopton. "We should have all six ready to head to the front in another month."

"Well, I hope to God you're right, Colonel. From what I'm hearing, there is going to be a hell of fight out west this spring and I damn well don't intend to miss it!" The general turned away and walked aft, surveying what would be his flagship.

Flagship! You'd think we were in the damn navy!

It did seem strange using nautical terms, but there was no denying that the land ironclads were more like ships than vehicles. Each one had a crew of nearly a hundred men and more than half were involved with the boilers, steam turbines, and engines. They'd even recruited some men from the merchant marine with experience in those things to man the engine rooms. The vehicles had a bridge, conning tower, and an observation platform on a tall mast. The gunnery system was an exact copy of that used on navy warships, although the Coast Artillery used a similar system, and they were supplying the gunners.

There were some differences, of course. To avoid wasting space or weight, there were almost no living quarters provided. In the field, the crew would sleep wherever they could on board, or pitch tents on the ground if the ironclad was halted. There was a tiny galley which could provide rudimentary meals in combat, but again, the men were expected to form their own messes most of the time. And each ironclad would have a small fleet of trucks following it to provide supplies, spare parts, and ammunition and rations for the crew.

Just organizing them had forced the army to develop entirely new ways of thinking. Each ironclad was being treated effectively as a battalion and would be commanded by a major or lieutenant colonel. A hundred men was an awfully small battalion, but considering the firepower involved, it wasn't an unreasonable decision. The squadron was treated as the equivalent of a brigade, hence Clopton's exalted rank. Privately, Andrew suspected a bit of one-upmanship with the navy was also involved.

And there was no doubt that a rivalry was developing. The navy was building their own land ironclads and there was competition for funding and resources. Admiral of the Fleet George Dewey, the hero of the Spanish American War, was insisting that the navy ought to have priority, but so far the army was winning that battle, and their ironclads would be in service first. There was even a fight going on over the *names* of the damn things! The army wanted to name them after some of the cities out west they hoped to liberate, but the navy had already grabbed the most prominent ones for a class of river monitors they were building. His old friend, Drew Harding, had just taken command of the *Santa Fe* and there was also a *Denver*, *Wichita*, and *Salt Lake City*. The army had put its foot down and demanded - and got - *Albuquerque* for the USLI-001. But the remaining five were going to be named *Billings*, *Sioux Falls*, *Omaha*, *Tulsa*, and *Springfield*. There would even be a christening ceremony in the coming weeks.

Andrew, accompanied by Stavely and Hornbaker, wandered around inside and outside the newly installed turret, looking over the shoulders of the busy workmen, until they were forced to get out of the way as the gun was swung down through the open top. As he emerged, Lieutenant Hornbaker got his attention and said: "Look, sir, isn't that…?"

"Tesla! What the hell is he doing here?"

There was no mistaking the tall, thin figure of Nikola Tesla. He was standing on the deck and talking in an animated fashion with General Clopton. Andrew hurried over, but as Tesla caught sight of him, he turned his back on Clopton and broke into a huge grin. "Major Comstock! So good to see you again!"

"Good to see you, Doctor, but what brings you here?"

"Ah! I was just explaining to General… uh… General…"

"Clopton," said the general, frowning.

"Yes! General Clopton, here, I have the most marvelous idea for this amazing colossus you've built."

Andrew's heart sank. Something new? They had enough new things to deal with. "But… but, Doctor, aren't you supposed to be working on your new lightning gun?"

"Yes, of course! That's what I'm talking about!"

"You *know* Doctor Tesla, Colonel?" demanded Clopton, breaking in.

"Uh, yes, sir, we've worked on several different projects in the past…"

"And he's been an enormous help, General! I hope you realize how fortunate you are to have someone like Comstock here!"

Clopton's gaze focused on Andrew. "Indeed?"

"Uh, but, Doctor," said Andrew, "What does your gun have to do with the land ironclads?"

"Why, I want to mount one on them!"

"What?"

"Oh, it's quite simple, really. The construction of the electric cannon has proceeded splendidly, just splendidly, except for the power supply. The army wants the cannon to be mobile, so it needs to be carried on a vehicle of some sort. But no normal vehicle can also carry a generator which can

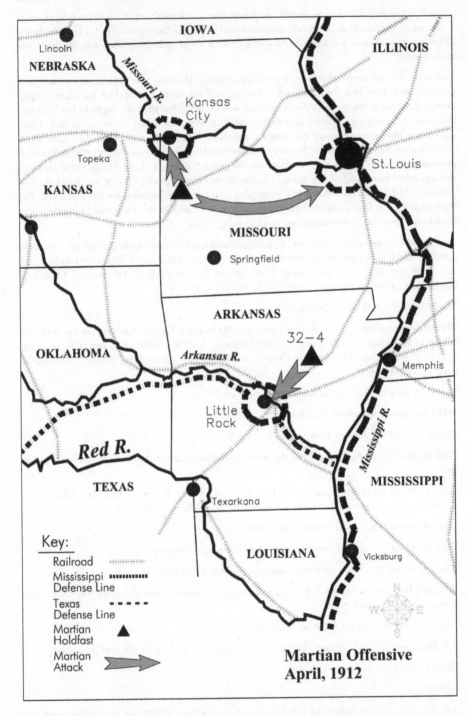

Key:
Railroad
Mississippi Defense Line
Texas Defense Line
Martian Holdfast
Martian Attack

Martian Offensive April, 1912

charge the capacitor quickly enough. They are working on some sort of auxiliary vehicle to carry the generator, but it could be many months before such a thing is ready. I don't want to wait!"

No, if Andrew had learned anything about Tesla, it was that he didn't want to wait for anything. "So then you are suggesting…"

"Yes! Exactly! I happened to bump into George Westinghouse last week and he mentioned the electric motors he was providing for the land ironclads. I asked how they were being powered and he said that each one had a steam turbine generator! Exactly what I need! Why in the world didn't you tell me, Major?"

"Well, I didn't think…"

"But it's perfect, can't you see? You could take the silly primitive cannon out of one of the turrets maybe the one they are trying to put in right now…" He pointed up at the crane.

"Not the twelve-incher!" cried Clopton.

"Well, one of the other ones then, and you could hook it up to the generator and there you would have it! Perfect! I can have the first one delivered here by next week!"

Andrew felt skeptical; Clopton looked skeptical. "What is this device you are talking about, Doctor?"

Before Tesla could launch into what was sure to be a long and nearly incomprehensible explanation, Andrew jumped in. "It's a new type of weapon, General, which fires something very much like a lightning bolt. I've seen it demonstrated and it does work—very impressively. I know the high command is eager to get it into action. Perhaps it could be mounted in the turret just forward of the twelve-incher…"

"We can't afford any more delays, Comstock!"

"Well, with Albuquerque almost finished up, we'll still have the other five to complete and that will take another few months, sir. That might give us time to install one of the cannons here."

"Yes! Yes!" cried Tesla. "We can certainly do that!"

"We'd need General Crozier's permission…"

"I'll get it! Now, I need to see the generator to work out the power runs!"

Andrew looked at Clopton, who shrugged. They found John Schmidt and sent him and Tesla below. When they were gone, Clopton rounded on him. "You really think this can work? I'm aware of Tesla's reputation; I'm quite an admirer, really, but in person he's a lot more… more…"

"Intense?"

"Yes, surely that, but also, more well, *eccentric*, than I was expecting. So, I ask again: can this contraption of his work?"

"It certainly worked in the test I saw, sir. It doesn't have the range of a conventional gun, but it does have the potential to affect multiple targets at once. It might be a worthwhile tradeoff to lose the forward seven-incher."

"Huh, and the Staff wants to see the thing in action… All right. Get Crozier's go-ahead and then go ahead! But I don't want any delay to prevent us from getting into action!"

"Yes, sir. No, sir, no delays." Clopton turned and left him. Andrew glanced at Hornbaker. "Well, Jerry, we have *another* job to do."

* * * * *

497

CYCLE 597, 845.1, HOLDFAST 32-4

"So we will attack?" asked Davnitargus.

"Yes," replied Qetjnegartis. "The Colonial Conclave has confirmed the orders and we shall commence the offensive in fifteen local days. But come with me and attend the briefing for our own people." Davnitargus activated its travel chair and fell in beside Qetjnegartis as they moved through the curving corridors of the clan's newest holdfast. Unlike the first holdfast, this one had been constructed without desperate haste and the corridors were properly tiled and leveled - and the roof did not leak! At least so far. As they moved, Qetjnegartis noticed the bud sack on Davnitargus's side. Its bud was going to have its own first bud.

"Your bud progresses well?"

"All appears as expected. It is an interesting experience. But you have gone through this many times, Progenitor."

"Yes, a great many over the long cycles. But only a few times was it for a new being, almost always it was a replacement body for myself."

"This world provides many opportunities not available on the Homeworld."

Qetjnegartis focused more attention on its offspring. Was there some subtle message in its statement? But a moment later it removed all doubt.

"It seems illogical for the others to remain on a dying world rather than come here, does it not? I fear I cannot understand this decision."

"It is not our place to questions the decision of the Council."

"Why not? If the decision clearly is incorrect, why should we not question it?"

"They are older and more experienced and wiser than we, Davnitargus. There may be more factors in their decisions than we know."

"Then why not share those factors with us and let us understand their reasoning? Blind obedience seems… illogical."

Qetjnegartis was becoming alarmed. On the Homeworld, any individual voicing such statements would be facing a quick termination. "Davnitargus… it would be best for you to not say such things."

"Even to you? I realize that those who have come here from the Homeworld are unsettled by the attitude of we young ones, but can I not discuss my concerns with the one who made me? I depend on you for guidance."

"And I am pleased to give it. But you must not speak this way in the hearing of others."

"As you command. I will not speak of this in the presence of those who came from the Homeworld."

Qetjnegartis halted its travel chair. Was this a deliberate prevarication by Davnitargus? Did it mean that it *would* discuss these matters with the buds created on this world? It had hinted before that there was some secret congress of the younger buds. But there was no opportunity to demand an explanation because at that moment Tanbradjus overtook them in its own travel chair. "Greeting Commander," it said. "We make our final attack plans, do we not?"

"Yes," replied Qetjnegartis. "We were just on our way to the briefing chamber." It glanced at Davnitargus and said: "we will finish our conversation later." It then put its chair in motion and they soon arrived where the other battlegroup commanders were waiting. The strength of the clan had grown significantly in the last half-cycle and could now field no less than twelve battlegroups, ten of which would be committed to this offensive - three hundred fighting machines and nearly that number of the new drones. Qetjnegartis relished having such strength and thought back to when the Clan's survival depended on a mere five machines!

It acknowledged the greetings of its subordinates and then activated a display screen which showed a map of the central portion of Continent Three. "Thanks to the artificial satellite, we now have detailed information on the topography of regions outside our control, as well as intelligence on the location and strength of the enemy forces," it began. "As you can see, the prey-creatures have set up a fortified line along the large river, which had been designated River 3-1." With the detailed maps had come the necessity of giving names or numbers to geographical features. For now, they used the number of the continent, as a prefix, and then numbered the features based on their relative size. It was imprecise, of course, but would suffice for now.

"While the pause in our operations has allowed us to build up our strength, it has also allowed the prey to do the same. This river defense line must be breached before it can be made even more formidable. However, before launching the main assault, there are two enemy fortress-cities west of the river which must be eradicated. One, City 3-20, is in the territory of Group 33 to the north, and the other is in our territory." The display zoomed in on the fortress-city which had so-far resisted all attempts to destroy it. The city was designated 3-118 and it lay along River 3-1.4, being a tributary of the large river.

"At the designated time, we will launch our full strength against 3-118 and destroy all defenders. From there we will move east to prepare for the assault across the river against City 3-37. Once we have a secure hold on the east bank, we can spread out to destroy the enemy's production facilities."

"Commander, will we employ the new drones in this attack?" asked Kantangnar, the leader of Battlegroup 32-4. "I had heard... rumors that they would be withheld."

"It had been proposed to withhold them until the primary attack across the river to achieve maximum surprise, but Group 33 wishes to use them in its attack on City 3-20. Also, Group 31 to our south has already deployed them recently, so the surprise value will soon be lost. Therefore we will use them in the assault on 3-118 to keep our losses to a minimum. Each group will have one of the controller machines and ten of the drones. With this added strength and flexibility, we should be able to overwhelm the defenders very quickly. From there we can move against the main objective along the river.

"Our attack will commence at night to reduce the effectiveness of the prey's weapons. The creatures have begun to use artificial illumination techniques to reduce their disadvantage, but it still exists and we will make use of that. Our main axis of attack will lie along this line…"

Qetjnegartis reviewed the battle plan and its subordinates asked their questions or made suggestions, and the plan was amended as necessary. Finally, all was arranged and it concluded the briefing:

"This stronghold must be destroyed quickly so that our larger operations can proceed. We will have one hundred spare fighting machines held in reserve. Each of our machines carries an emergency transport pod to rescue those whose machines are disabled. Those who are not injured will return to the battle as quickly as possible. There can be no acceptable outcome but complete success. Is this understood?"

"Yes, Commander!"

* * * * *

MARCH, 1912, MEMPHIS, TENNESSEE

Spring had finally arrived in Memphis. A warm wind from the southwest had driven away the last of the chill and the locals were certain that it would not return. Some of the trees were already in blossom and flowers were opening up in gardens. Becca Harding breathed in the fragrances as she walked up the drive of the huge Oswald estate.

"Jiminy! Willya lookit the size of this place!" exclaimed the man walking next to her. "The cap'in said it was the house of some rich old lady, but he didn't say how rich! Hooee!" He whistled.

"Uh, yeah, the Oswalds seem pretty well heeled," said Becca. She regarded the man. His name was Leonidas Polk Smith, although he went by 'Leo'. He was wearing a not-quite regulation army uniform with sergeant's chevrons on the sleeve. Above the chevrons there was a shoulder patch announcing that he was part of the Memphis Volunteer Militia. With the new Conscription Act, most men not doing absolutely vital jobs were being swept up - or in most cases shamed into enlisting—into the army. But there were some men who did have vital jobs who still wanted to serve. Smith, from what Becca was able to decipher through his thick southern drawl, worked at the local electrical generating plant when he wasn't with his militia company.

"And all the women in this here group of yours, are they rich, too?"

"Most of 'em seem to be. And it's not really my group."

"Heck! Shame I'm already married!" cackled Smith. "But if you ain't in charge, how come I was sent to see you about this company of wimmen?"

"Don't know," she said shrugging. It had come as a surprise to her when Smith had shown up at the hospital with an order signed by the adjutant of Memphis' garrison commander. It simply authorized the integration of the Memphis Women's Volunteer Sharpshooters into the city militia, and named her, Rebecca Harding, as the official liaison! She suspected that Mrs. Oswald, the group's leader, had somehow used her husband's political pull to get this to happen, but why had she been made the liaison instead of Oswald? Theories had swirled in her head, but the leading one was that Frank had been involved somehow. He knew she wanted to be more active in the war, but he didn't want her going out on his scouting missions - he was out there right now, blast him! - so maybe he'd pulled some strings to try and convert the Women Sharpshooters and Quilting Society (as Becca privately referred to it) into something more resembling an actual military unit. Just to please her? Or keep her out of trouble?

Or maybe Frank had nothing to do with it. As he'd warned her, the war seemed to be coming out of its long lull. Rumors were flying through the city and the army camps that a major battle was brewing. Everyone had their own prediction on what would happen: Memphis was the enemy's main target; no, they were going after St. Louis; no, they would attack Vicksburg just like the Yankees did in the Civil War; no they'd surely want New Orleans to block the whole river. It was the major topic of conversation in the mess tent at the hospital. The only thing that was certain was that the high command was putting everyone on alert and making every effort to bolster the city's defenses. Something was surely going to happen and maybe they even wanted the Women's Sharpshooters mobilized.

They reached the front door of the mansion and a colored servant directed them around to the back where they were told Mrs. Oswald was waiting. "We've got a rifle range back there," Becca explained to Smith. They rounded the corner of the house and found Mrs. Oswald waiting - along with about a hundred other women.

Becca's eyes grew wide. They were all wearing the unit's official uniform, buckskin jackets, pantaloons tucked into calf-high boots, and a hat with a feather, and holding their Springfield rifles. At the sight of her, Mrs. Oswald cried: "Oh, there they are! Attention, girls, attention!" The women shuffled into some semblance of formation with only a little bit of laughing and giggling. Oswald had a uniform like the others, but fancier with some gold braid on the collar, cuffs, and hem of the jacket and down the seam of the pantaloons. The feather in her hat was white instead of black like the others, and she had captain's shoulder straps. She also had a sword which she waved about dangerously.

Becca glanced at Smith, who was obviously trying very hard not to laugh. "Uh, here they are." She was amazed at the numbers. The group had over a hundred on its roster, but she'd never managed to get more than thirty to turn up at once.

"The gal with the sword is in charge?" asked Smith.

"Yup. I'll introduce you. C'mon." She led him over to where Oswald was waiting with a huge grin on her face. "Mrs... I mean Captain Oswald, this is Sergeant Smith of the Memphis Militia."

"Oh, Sergeant! So very pleased to meet you!" exclaimed Oswald, stuffing her sword under her arm and extending a gloved hand. To her obvious surprise, Smith grabbed it and shook firmly.

"Pleased to meetcha, ma'am. Captain Carstairs sent me to talk to you 'bout you folks fallin' in with us." He paused and frowned. "But he didn't say nothin' about you havin' rifles." He looked closer. "Hell, those're Springfields! My company's got nothin' but them old Krags!"

"Of course we have rifles!" said Oswald. "Some of the girls are fine shots! How do you expect us to fight without rifles?"

"Fight? The Cap'in jus' said you'd be with us to help out with coffee and rations and tendin' the wounded and all..."

"Certainly not, Sergeant! Wherever did he get such an idea? We are sharpshooters and we shall be fighting alongside you!"

"I'll be damned. Don't know nuthin' 'bout that. Well, I was just sent here, along with Miz Harding, to let you know where you're supposed to go if the alarm is sounded."

"And where might that be?" asked Oswald, no longer smiling.

"Oh, down by the river. Our assembly area's at Poplar and Front Streets."

"Near that lovely Riverside Park?"

"Well, t'ain't so lovely anymore, but yessum, that's the area. We're supposed to support a battery of big guns 'long the waterfront. I was supposed to take you and... uh, your NCOs for a tour... If you want."

"I can go with him, Mrs. Oswald," volunteered, Rebecca. "No need for you to go way down there, ma'am."

"Oh, but, Becca, dear, you can't go! Not yet, anyway! We have... well, we have a surprise for you, dear." She turned to Smith. "You can wait for a bit can't you, Sergeant?"

"Uh, for a little spell, but I gotta be gettin' back..."

"Splendid! Now, Becca, all the girls and I are so grateful for all the work you've done that we took a vote and decided that you should be second in command of the Sharpshooters!"

What?! She twitched and took a half-step backwards. She hadn't been expecting anything like this.

"Yes! You shall be our lieutenant! We even had a uniform made for you! Girls?"

To Becca's horror, several of the ladies came forward carrying another of the ridiculous sharpshooter uniforms over which they fussed so much. "I-I don't think... I can't..." she stuttered.

"Oh, don't worry!" said Oswald. "This is our gift to you! Doris, Abigail, take her inside and help her change!"

Becca's immediate impulse was to make a break for it, but she couldn't do that. This was clearly a sincere gesture by the women and she couldn't refuse. So she found herself decked out in the buckskin jacket, pantaloons, and boots and a large hat with a *red* feather. There were lieutenant's insignia on the shoulders. Then she was paraded back outside so the whole group could applaud.

She blushed pink and felt like a complete fool.

Smith was grinning ear to ear and she had to restrain herself from hitting him. "Whooee! Ain't you the sight!" he laughed. "But we got t'get goin' miss. If I show up any later, the Cap'n's gonna think I'm slackin' off!"

"Run along, Becca," said Oswald, fluttering her fingers. "I trust you completely to make the arrangements."

Becca started to turn away, but stopped herself, came to attention, and saluted the way she saw soldiers do. "Yes, ma'am!" The whole company laughed, but then cheered.

Becca spun on her heel and followed the sergeant.

* * * * *

MARCH, 1912, NEAR BEULAH, MISSISSIPPI

The *Santa Fe* slowly turned left into the mouth of the Arkansas River. Commander Drew Harding closely watched the surface of the river, the banks on either side, and the ship ahead of them. They were part of a small flotilla of supply ships, gunboats, and monitors heading up the Arkansas to Little Rock. Word had come that the Martians were preparing to attack that place, and the high command was sending reinforcements.

"Ya might want t'stay a bit further to the right, Captain," said Mackenzie. "The bend there can throw up quite a sand bar on the left."

Drew nodded and gave the order to the helmsman, and the ship swung a little bit wider in its turn.

"Gonna hafta stay on our toes," continued the first officer. "The Arkansas twists around like a snake most of the way to Little Rock. Lot narrower than the Mississippi, too. Good thing it's at flood right now."

"You've been along this stretch before, I take it."

"A dozen times at least. Not the worst bit of river I've traveled, but she's tricky. And I'm not jokin' about her bein' a snake! Probably ain't a straight stretch more than half a mile long. We're gonna need to relieve the helmsman every hour or so and the lookouts, too."

"What about you, Mr. Mackenzie? How often will you need relief?"

"Oh, I'll manage. Seein' as we're not first in line, we'll have it easier. And you're gettin' pretty good yourself at spotting trouble, you know."

Drew was surprised and pleased at the compliment but did his best to keep it off his face. "I'm sure between the two of us we'll manage."

Santa Fe eased into the channel and followed the other ships upstream. As Mackenzie had said, the Arkansas turned one way and then another, sometimes changing a hundred and eighty degrees and heading back the way they'd come before turning again. It seemed like they traveled two or three miles for every mile closer to Little Rock they got. Several times that day they had to crowd the shore dangerously to let vessels going the other way squeeze by. Most of those vessels were crammed with civilians, people trying to get away from the rumored attack.

After a few hours, Drew felt confident enough of the new routine that he decided to drill the crew on other matters. He was keenly aware of how green most of his men were. He had only a small cadre of experienced sailors, but far too many of the others were raw recruits, or men like Ensign Alby Hinsworth, who had gone through a hasty officers' school. Ever since Santa Fe was launched, he had worked the men ceaselessly to learn their jobs and become an effective team. He was proud of being the ship's captain, but there were times when he missed the veteran crew on the old *Minnesota*.

502

"Mr. Mackenzie, I'm going to bring the ship to battle stations. You and the bridge crew will remain at your posts and keep us from crashing into anything."

"All right," replied Mackenzie, "have fun."

Drew sighed, wondering if Mackenzie knew that there really was such a word as sir. He took the ladder down to the small pilothouse and flipped the switch that turned on the battle stations alarm bell. The shrill tone of the bell sent the men scrambling. There was far too much shouting, but at least they were moving. The realization that they were now west of the Mississippi and therefore in enemy country had spread through the ship and possibly some men thought this was the real thing. Well good, if they did, Drew wasn't going to do anything to disabuse them.

His yeoman appeared with Drew's helmet and anti-dust gear, and he dutifully put it all on; he had to set a good example. He waited while reports came from the various locations around the ship. Ensign Hinsworth shouted each one out: *Number Two four-inch, manned and ready! Engine room manned and ready! Number Three four-inch manned and ready! Sick Bay manned and ready! Turret Number One manned and ready! Magazine manned and ready! On and on until finally: All Stations manned and ready! The ship is cleared for action, sir!* Hinsworth saluted, banging his elbow against the side of the tiny pilothouse.

Drew returned the salute and checked his pocket watch; four minutes and thirty five seconds. It wouldn't have been bad for a battleship, but for a ship one sixth the size, it wasn't good at all. Still, it was the best they'd done so far.

He then proceeded to run them through as many drills as it was possible to do under the circumstances. Damage control and fire drills sent teams of men to various compartments to fight imaginary fires or plug imaginary leaks. The *man overboard* drill had them getting one of the ship's boats ready to launch. The casualty drill saw volunteer 'casualties' being taken to the tiny sick bay. The ship didn't rate an actual doctor, but there was a medical orderly trained in basic first aid. For the most part, the drills went pretty well.

But the thing nearest and dearest to Drew's heart – gunnery - couldn't be truly practiced in these circumstances. They could aim the guns, and he had them pick distant objects to act as Martian tripods, and they could bring up ammunition from the magazine and practice loading, but they couldn't actually fire the guns. After the commissioning, he'd had the opportunity to take *Santa Fe* down to a stretch of river where the shoreline was all swamp and no one lived, and shoot off the guns for a while. But it was completely inadequate in Drew's opinion. He was worried that if they did get into a fight, they wouldn't be able to hit a damn thing. He'd asked the captain in charge of this little convoy if once they got closer to Little Rock, they would be allowed to do some target practice. The reply had been evasive and non-committal. They'd have to wait and see.

It was getting on toward the dinner hour but there was one more thing he wanted to practice. Without any advanced warning, he reached over and flipped the Dust Alarm switch. There was a few seconds delay and then a siren began to howl with a shriek that would pierce almost any other noise. The men nearby stiffened and then exploded into action, some of them shouting *Dust! Dust! Dust!* Some pulled out the dust mask from the bag hanging around their necks, while others slammed closed metal shutters to seal off the windows in the pilothouse. The space suddenly became quite dark with only a few beams of light coming though the thick glass in narrow vision slits. If all was going well, then similar precautions were being made throughout the ship. Every hatch and porthole was being sealed to keep out the lethal black dust the Martians occasionally used. Even a few grains of the stuff inhaled was enough to kill a person, and contact with the skin could cause terrible burns.

"Engine room reports dust procedures in effect, sir!" shouted Ensign Hinsworth, his voice muffled by his mask. Yes, that was the real trick in protecting a ship from the dust. The fires for the boilers demanded a large and steady supply of air. Ships had ventilators to suck air down to them, but in a cloud of the black dust, that could be a fatal flaw which would hopelessly contaminate the ship. So the new ships had an air supply system which could channel the incoming air directly into the fires, theoretically destroying the dust before it could do any harm. The air intakes on the decks had filters, but this system took into account the possibility of battle damage destroying them.

Unfortunately, while the system might save the engine room crew from death from the dust, it might also kill them by heat stroke. A normal ship would suck outside air down to the engine room and *then* send it into the fire boxes. The air the crew breathed would be the same temperature as the outside. But under this system, the incoming air went through the fire first to destroy the dust. Some would then leak out for the crew to breathe. But it would be hot air - very hot.

The men could stand it for a few minutes, but no longer.

Drew looked out the view slit and saw that they had a relatively straight stretch of river ahead for a mile or so. "Prepare to release steam!"

"Steam lines ready, sir!" shouted Hinsworth.

"Release!"

The ensign threw a lever and a few moments later there was a loud hiss and a cloud of white steam enveloped the ship, released from pipes located all over the superstructure and upper decks. In theory this would destroy dust in the air and scour away any which had fallen on the ship. In an emergency, it could also blunt the effect of enemy heat rays. Drew could see nothing through the view slits. Mackenzie was piloting the ship from up above, but the steam would be blinding him, too. They couldn't sail like this for long.

"Secure steam!"

The hiss died away and the cloud dispersed. "Steam secured!"

"Engine room air to normal!" Hinsworth relayed the order and hopefully there would now be cool air flooding into the engine room. Whether it would also be dust-free, only the test of battle would tell.

Drew waited for a few minutes before he canceled the dust alert and a few minutes longer before letting the men stand down from battle stations. The shutters were swung up and latched, the hatch to the pilothouse propped open, and Drew breathed in the cool spring air. He turned to step outside and was met by a red-faced Mackenzie.

"Ya damn near scalded us to death, you know that?"

"Your dust gear should have protected you. Weren't you wearing yours, Lieutenant?"

The man's face got even redder. "Uh, well, no… it was just a damn drill and…"

"You know the procedures. Next time, wear your gear." Drew stepped past him and climbed up to the bridge, failing to keep a smile from growing on his lips. It was rare for him to get the best of his first officer.

He paced from one end of the bridge to the other, stretching his legs. He heard the off-duty watches being sent to dinner and it looked like the men were in good spirits. The day had gone well. The sun was westering and he thought he could make out the ruins of Pine Bluffs in the distance. They were making good time, despite the twisting river.

Morning should see them at Little Rock.

CHAPTER EIGHT

APRIL, 1912, WASHINGTON, D.C.

"It's confirmed, sir, they're hitting Kansas City in force." Colonel Hugh Drum met Leonard Wood at the door to the situation room and took his coat as he hurried in.

"When?"

"About an hour ago. I called you as soon as I was sure it wasn't a feint."

Wood rubbed at his eyes and then stared at the map. It was about four in the morning and Drum's call to his house had woken him out of a deep sleep. The map, stretching over thirty feet long, showed the whole Mississippi Line, but Wood's attention was drawn to one blue wood block sitting all alone west of the river. It represented the garrison of Kansas City. As he watched, an enlisted man with a long wooden stick pushed several red blocks up close to the blue one.

"Any estimate on strength?"

"No exact numbers, sir, but General Farnsworth is convinced that this is a major attack."

Wood nodded. Charlies Farnsworth was not one to panic, although after being stuck out on that limb for nearly a year, no man could be blamed for being skittish. But Wood had been sure this was coming for several months, so he had no doubt Farnsworth was right. The long-expected Martian offensive was starting.

And Farnsworth and his 37th Division were likely doomed.

"Any word from Little Rock? They will probably hit there, too."

"Nothing so far, sir," replied Drum. "But there was another message from General Funston just a few minutes ago. He says he can confirm a Martian incursion across the Rio Grande near the town of Hebbronville. That's about ninety miles west of Corpus Christi." Drum pointed to the far corner of the map where a new red block had appeared.

Wood frowned in concern. They didn't need this right now, but he supposed it was inevitable that the southern front couldn't remain quiet forever. It seemed like the French landings around Veracruz had distracted the Martians in Mexico, but perhaps that was coming to an end. "What sort of strength?"

"He isn't sure. It does seem to be localized and they haven't advanced any farther north, but Funston is requesting reinforcements."

"Of course he is. But there's nothing we can send until the situation along the Mississippi becomes clearer."

"Yes, sir. I'll ask him to get more information on the strength of the Martian force down there."

"Do that. But later. Are there any other reports coming in?" He waved his hand to take in the whole defense line.

"Nothing at the moment, sir. Farnsworth *is* requesting reinforcements."

Wood moved to the point on the table closest to Kansas City. There were swarms of blue blocks along the Mississippi, but none in easy supporting distance. In the last few weeks he had sent additional riverine forces up the Missouri, just as he'd sent them up the Arkansas to Little Rock, but there wasn't a great deal more he could do. Anything else he sent would probably be just more lambs to the slaughter. *A forlorn hope, just as Theodore - and Funston's aide - said.* Well, perhaps he could do something…

"Send a message to General Pershing to have the XV Corps send out as much cavalry as it can spare toward Kansas City. Maybe they can create a distraction - or at the least help to cover an evacuation."

"Yes, sir, right away. Uh, what about General Rochenbach's tank divisions, sir? Maybe they could…" He pointed at a blue block at the eastern edge of the table.

Wood looked at it and shook his head. "No, they'd never get there in time. And even if we had them at the front, they're too slow and too prone to breakdowns to send them out on a relief mission. Still… they've completed their training. Have the 1st sent to Cairo and the 2nd to Jackson. We'll keep them in a ready reserve."

"Yes, sir." Drum moved off to one of the multitude of communications stations arrayed around the perimeter of the room. Wood dragged a chair over to the table and sat down, after sending an enlisted man for coffee. God, he was tired. An ache was growing in his head and he firmly told himself it was just the stress on top of lack of sleep and not the damn tumor again.

He stared at the map. Outside, the morning was coming, but no hint of that reached the windowless situation room. Drum circulated between the communications operators and occasionally brought over items of interest. Wood continued to stare. He'd done everything he could to strengthen the defenses, but no line was impregnable. If the Martians hit somewhere that wasn't quite strong enough, got across the river in strength, and spread out to destroy the railroads as they had done out in Colorado and the Dakotas… it could be a disaster of incredible proportions. In his mind's eye he could see raiding forces sweeping through the army's rear areas, destroying supplies, scattering reserves, and then moving on to the cities where the factories were located. Smashing the means of production, interrupting the rail lines which supplied food and raw materials. Splitting the country into smaller and smaller chunks. No, he could not let that happen! Suddenly, just sitting there was intolerable…

"General?"

Drum had come up next to him and startled him out of his dark thoughts. "Yes?"

"A signal from General Duncan in Little Rock, they are under attack."

Wood nodded. Yes, the Kansas City attack wasn't just a lone operation; this was the great offensive, beginning at last. "Send a message to General Dickman at 3rd Army. Have the VII Corps send out its cavalry, same orders as the ones for Pershing."

"Yes, sir," Drum turned away.

"And Hugh?" Drum looked back.

"Sir?"

"Get a train ready. I'm finally going to take that trip to St. Louis."

* * * * *

APRIL, 1912, NEAR FORREST CITY, ARKANSAS

"Come on! Keep moving!" shouted Captain Frank Dolfen, 5th United States Cavalry. At times like this, the sergeant in him always came to the fore. He trotted his horse up and down the column urging his men onward. "It's a long way to Little Rock and those boys there need help! Move it!" A few of the men waved at him or made some sort of encouraging remark, but if any of them actually moved any faster, Frank couldn't see it. The main thing, he supposed, was to make sure none of them went any slower.

The word had come shortly after dawn: Little Rock was under attack again and this time the Martians really seemed to mean it. The whole regiment, not just Frank's 1st Squadron, was ordered to move out, and as they trotted across the bridge from Memphis, they were joined by the 9th Cavalry, creating a small brigade. When Dolfen had first reached Memphis after the long retreat, he'd been told that all the cavalry was being formed into an actual division, but up until now, the cavalry had all been used in small groups. This was more like it!

The 9th was a colored regiment and initially there were a few insulting remarks among the 5th, but when Frank heard one, he would stomp on the culprit making it. He'd seen the 9th's brother regiment, the 10th Cavalry, bleed to death at Glorietta Pass; and if anyone ever doubted the bravery of those colored boys, Frank could straighten them out!

They'd ridden hard all day, horsemen, motorcycles, armored cars, trucks, and all, but as night drew on they weren't even halfway to Little Rock. Forty miles was considered about as far as you could expect cavalry to go in a day. They'd gone farther than that, but they still had a long way to go. From time to time flights of aircraft had passed overhead heading west or coming back east. Dolfen wondered if any of them were Selfridge and his boys.

The Englishman, Major Bridges, wasn't with him this time. He'd gone to Washington to consult with the military attaché there and wasn't certain if he'd be back at all. Dolfen found that he missed the man's almost endless chatter.

The remains of Forrest City had disappeared in the darkness to the east when the colonel called a halt. Both regiments formed a defensive laager with the artillery deployed, pickets posted well outside the camp, and a quarter of the men on alert at all times. Once again they were in enemy country and there were too many of them to stay concealed, although campfires were all kept shielded to prevent their light giving them away. The shortest route from Memphis to Little Rock took them uncomfortably close to the Martian fortress. It was only twenty miles or so off to the north and they had encountered some very large patches of the Red Weed. When they moved on in the morning, the fortress would be in their rear. A ticklish situation for sure.

While he was munching on the dinner Private Gosling had provided, one of his sergeants, a man named Burk, came up to him. "Evenin', sir, got a minute?"

"Sure, what's on your mind?"

"It's those crazy new rocket launchers, the stovepipes. sir. We gonna get any more chances to practice with 'em? Ain't like shootin' a rifle! Gonna take more practice to hit anything with 'em!"

Ah, yes, the rocket launchers. A half-dozen had been delivered to the squadron three days ago. The officer who brought them had given a very brief explanation of how to use them. Some of the men had been given the chance to fire off a few rounds and that was it. "'Fraid not. At least not until we get somewhere safer then here. You'll just have to do your best, Sergeant."

"They aren't expectin' us to fire them things from horseback are they, sir? Critter won't put up with *that!*"

Dolfen chuckled. "No, I don't expect they will. Better tell the boys to dismount before trying to use the things."

"Yes, sir." Burk nodded and moved off.

After dinner, Colonel Schumacher, who was senior, called all the officers of both regiments together for a conference. "We just picked up a radio signal," he said. "Little Rock has been hammered hard all day, but they are still holding on. We have to get there and relieve some of the pressure on them. We'll sleep now and get on the move again at three."

"It's still at least another sixty miles, sir," said the colonel of the 9th. "We won't get there until dark and the men and horses will be worn out."

"I know, I know," said Schumacher, a tone of irritation in his voice. "But that's what we are going to do. See that your commands are ready, gentlemen!"

Dolfen made his way back to his own unit. Both of the colonels were right, he supposed. Getting there too late to help was pointless. But getting there too tired to fight didn't do any good either. And if they were too exhausted to escape if things went to hell, that was the worst of all. But he had his orders and passed them along to his troop commanders. Then he went to get some sleep.

Private Gosling had his bedroll all laid out, but the man was standing still as stone, looking to the west. Dolfen came up and asked: "What are you looking... oh!"

The western horizon was tinged with a red glow, bright flickers came at intervals like a distant thunderstorm. Dozens of his troopers were looking at it and there wasn't a sound in the camp.

"Looks like them boys in Little Rock are catchin' hell, sir," said Gosling.

"Yeah, it sure does."

* * * * *

CYCLE 597, 845.1, NEAR ENEMY CITY 3-118

"Report," ordered Qetjnegartis.

"Commander, the enemy's defensive fire is much reduced," said Kantangnar over the communicator. "I believe that the time has come to launch the main attack."

"Are you sure? The prey-creatures have tried to deceive us before, to lure us into a trap."

"There is no way to be certain, but we have verified the destruction of many of their heavy weapons, and we are pushing our drones very close to their trenches and they are encountering little resistance. The fire from the vessels on the river is much reduced; they may be running short on projectiles."

Qetjnegartis evaluated the situation. So far the attack had gone well. For over a day the clan's battlegroups had probed the enemy; advancing, doing damage, and then pulling back before the prey-creatures could do serious harm in return. Twenty-two fighting machines had been lost, but so far only two pilots had been killed and four wounded. The other pilots had been rescued, taken to the rear, and given reserve machines so they could return to the fight. Qetjnegartis was determined that losses be kept to an absolute minimum. This was just the first attack in the great offensive, after all. They would need all their strength for the attack across the large river. Over a hundred of the drones had been destroyed, but they did not matter.

Now the enemy's response was faltering. Had the probes done their job? Or was this a ruse to draw them into a killing zone? Qetjnegartis moved its machine forward to one of the hills which ringed the city to the north. It had a commanding view of the battle area. City 3-118 sat on both sides of River 3-1.4. The largest portion of the city was on the far side of the river, but once the northern bank was captured, the southern side would become untenable. On the western end of the city there was a tall hill, very close to the river, which dominated the entire area. The prey-creatures had heavily fortified it, but if it could be captured, their entire defense ought to collapse.

During the previous attack, Qetjnegartis had avoided the northern side specifically because of that hill and the low, swampy ground to the east of it. It had crossed the river, which could be waded

508

with little difficulty, and attacked the city from the south, thinking that their defenses would be weaker there. That had not proved to be the case and the attack had been repulsed.

We shall not be repulsed this time!

The clan had a vastly greater strength now, and while the enemy had improved its defenses somewhat, they could not possibly withstand what Qetjnegartis could now unleash. Still, it was cautious about simply relying on brute force. Victory was certain, but it could not afford heavy losses.

The hill was clearly the key to the enemy defenses. Taken, they could fire down on the prey-creature positions and then roll up the trench lines in both directions. It would not make the mistake of trying to penetrate into the built-up sections of the city immediately, as it had the last time. Once the main defenses ringing the city had been cleared, a more methodical approach could be taken to obliterating the central areas. Yes, the plan was a good one. It activated the communicator.

"Attention all battlegroups. We shall commence the main attack. Groups 32-2 and 32-6, you shall continue to probe along your fronts to distract the enemy. All other groups will converge on Sector Twelve. Groups 32-1, 32-4, 32-5, and 32-7 will attack the tall hill. All other groups will attack the low ground between the hill and the swampy area, penetrate the defense lines, and advance to the river. Avoid unnecessary losses, but press forward and do not stop until you have reached your objectives."

"Commander? Perhaps we should hold back a reserve?" It was Tanbradjus. "In case of emergencies?"

"No, there can be no half-measures now. We will attack and finish this!"

"As you command."

* * * * *

APRIL 1912, LITTLE ROCK, ARKANSAS

"Signal from Captain Gillespie, sir!" shouted Ensign Hinsworth. "He wants us to move upstream of Big Rock Mountain! The Martians are attacking there!"

"Acknowledged," replied Commander Drew Harding. "Helm, bring us about, ahead two-thirds." *Santa Fe* swung around to head upstream, following Captain Gillespie's ship, *Wichita*. The two smaller gunboats, *Evansville* and *Mount Vernon*, did not follow; apparently, they had different orders.

"Good God in Heaven, how much longer is this gonna go on?" Drew glanced at his executive officer. Mackenzie clutched the handrail and his face looked pale despite the smudges of coal and gun smoke on it. "They've been coming agin' an' agin' since yesterday mornin'! When's it gonna stop?"

Drew looked closer; the man was clearly near to the edge. Ever since he'd first met Mackenzie, Drew had been a little jealous of the man's superior knowledge of the rivers and resentful of his lack of military courtesy. He'd been hoping to have the chance to take him down a peg or two. But now, now that it was happening, he was sorry. Mackenzie had never seen combat and had been completely unprepared for the reality. Of course, there was a first time for everyone, and even Drew had never seen a combat like this one. Some men called up the courage to handle it. Other men... well, it looked like Mackenzie was one of the other men. But damnation, he *needed* the man!

"Lieutenant Mackenzie, we've been ordered upstream farther than we've gone so far. Is there any danger we could go aground?" No reaction. He reached over and shook the man's shoulder. "Mackenzie! Will we go aground?"

509

"Uh… uh, we should be okay," said the man, jerking in surprise. "With all the coal and ammo we've burned up, we're probably drawin' two feet less than when we set out. Should be okay…"

"Good! But could you check the coal bunkers and see how much we've got left?"

"Uh, yeah, yeah, right away… sir." Mackenzie turned and fled below. Drew couldn't help but smile at the sudden use of *sir*, but wondered if he'd come back.

"Mister Hinsworth, check the magazines. I want to know what we've got left there, too."

"Aye, aye, sir!" Hinsworth grinned and ran off. At least *he* didn't seem to be having any problems. Apparently, this was all some grand pageant to the kid. The ship completed its turn, heading upstream, and Drew looked at the sun, barely visible behind clouds of smoke; it wasn't quite noon yet.

The Martians had attacked in the dark of early morning the day before. He had been awakened and stumbled up on deck to see the northern sky a mass of red, the buildings of the town silhouetted black against it. The army's guns were already roaring and it wasn't long before the navy had been ordered to join in. They had been tied up along the waterfront, but quickly cast off and moved out into the main channel of the Arkansas. The flotilla was commanded by Captain Ernest Gillespie aboard the *Wichita*, a sister ship of *Santa Fe*. The two monitors, two gunboats, plus a half dozen converted riverboats of various sizes with improvised armor and armaments, completed the force.

At first they had just been firing at coordinates on the map, adding their metal to that of the army batteries. But as dawn came and the day went on, the Martians had become bolder and gotten close enough at times to be fired at directly. Drew thought that maybe they had destroyed one of them, but with all the smoke he couldn't be sure.

Night had fallen and by then the city north of the river - which someone told him was actually named Argenta, rather than Little Rock - was almost entirely in flames. Fortunately, the wind was from the southwest so the smoke was blown away and the buildings along the river had remained untouched But the Martian attacks continued. Drew had read stories - and Andrew's letters - about the night attack on Albuquerque, and he was happy to see that the army had learned from it. They now had rockets and artillery rounds which would burst into a bright flare which drifted slowly down by parachute, lighting up the surroundings marvelously. He'd heard that the navy was going to receive similar munitions, but so far none had materialized. Santa Fe and some of the other ships mounted powerful searchlights, though, and they had been in use almost constantly. From time to time they'd catch a tripod in their glare and pump off a few rounds, but he didn't think they'd scored any hits.

It had made for a very long night. He'd grabbed a few minutes sleep during a lull just before dawn, but for the most part he was running on coffee and sheer nerves. Now they were into the second day of the battle, and like Mackenzie, he wondered when it would end.

Hinsworth returned and saluted. "Fifteen rounds per gun in the forward turret, twenty in the aft turret, sir! The four-inchers have still got around a hundred per gun."

"Thank you, Ensign," said Drew frowning. He hadn't realized they used up so much of the eight-inch ammunition. They had a supply ship with more tied up at the docks, but there had been no opportunity to replenish. When they went back into action he'd have to…

"We should get a man at the bow with a lead once we're past the cliffs, Captain." Drew turned and was pleased to see Mackenzie was back. "An' we're down to about half of our coal, but nuthin' to worry about yet."

"Thank you, Lieutenant. Send someone forward with the lead."

"Right." Mackenzie left again.

Up ahead on the right was Big Rock Mountain. It wasn't all that much of a mountain as such things went, but it was all alone and reared two hundred and fifty feet above the river, making it look immense. It was some last outlier of the Ozark Mountains, off to the northwest, Drew supposed. The side facing the river was a stone quarry and had been carved into an almost perpendicular cliff. The opposite side, facing the Martians, was the west anchor of the defensive lines north of the river. It was studded with gun emplacements and on top was the main spotting post of all the artillery. If the enemy took it… things could get sticky.

They moved slowly past the mountain against the current, and the man in the bow was shouting out his soundings. It was almost impossible to hear him above the roar of the army's guns, so another man had to keep running back and forth between the bow and the bridge to relay the information. Since *Wichita* was leading the way and drew just as much water as *Santa Fe*, there wasn't much worry about running aground at the moment, but if they were forced to maneuver later on, it was good to have the system set up. Of course, if they came under fire, both the leadsman and the runner would be forced to take cover.

And coming under fire was definitely a possibility.

Wichita, two hundred yards ahead, suddenly fired its forward turret; a few seconds later the rest of her guns fired as well. Drew focused his binoculars in the direction they were shooting and tried to see the targets. The base of the mountain was shrouded in smoke, but he thought he could see some tall shapes moving there. The mountain itself blocked most of their view to the north where the attack would be coming from. They needed to go farther upstream, where the river curved a bit, to get a clear line of fire. He passed the word to the gunnery officer that they'd be going into action shortly.

As they moved, they were passed on their left hand side by one of the converted riverboats, the *Arkansas Queen*. She was a stern-wheeler and the paddle threw up a huge amount of spray. She'd once been a passenger and cargo hauler, but most of her upper works had been clad in sheet iron. Several modern field guns had been mounted, but she also carried an antique monstrosity on her foredeck which must have been a relic from the Civil War. Someone stuck his head out of the pilothouse and waved to Drew as they passed.

"What the hell's his hurry?" asked Mackenzie, who'd come back to the bridge.

"Guess he wants to get some licks in. Hasn't had much chance so far with all the long range fire we've been doing."

"Damn fool."

The *Wichita* moved ahead another half-mile and then signaled to hold station. Drew turned to Mackenzie. "What do you think, Lieutenant? About a hundred revolutions to hold against the current?"

Mackenzie studied the brown water flowing past. "Yup, about that. Maybe a hundred and five; the currents a bit faster this side of Big Rock." Drew sent the order down to the engine room and carefully judged the distance to the ship ahead to make sure they were maintaining their spacing; the thrust of the propellers balancing the river's current.

"I can see the enemy, sir!" cried Hinsworth, pointing. Drew brought up his binoculars. Yes, there were several dozen tripods moving forward, firing their heat rays against the defenders who couldn't be seen at all amidst the smoke and flames. He studied them in a sort of horrified fascination. They were nightmare things that moved with a gracefulness totally at odds with their appearance.

"Sir, can we open fire, sir?"

There was no use trying to direct fire against specific targets; the situation was changing too fast.

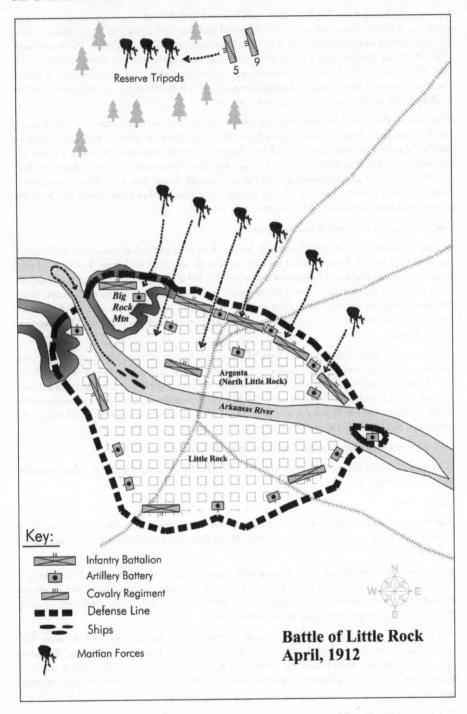

Reserve Tripods

5 9

Big
Rock
Mtn

Argenta
(North Little Rock)

Arkansas River

Little Rock

Key:

Infantry Battalion

Artillery Battery

Cavalry Regiment

Defense Line

Ships

Martian Forces

N
W   E
S

**Battle of Little Rock
April, 1912**

"Instruct the guns to commence firing, Ensign. They may choose their own targets."

"Aye, aye, sir!"

"Oh, and Ensign, tell the eight-inch crews to save five rounds per gun."

"Yes, sir!"

Wichita was already firing, and a moment later, *Santa Fe* joined in. The eight-inchers in the turrets shook the whole ship with deep, throaty roars, while the four-inchers in the casemate mounts made sharper cracks. Thick clouds of dirty smoke rolled away toward the shore to join the smoke already there. Rapid fire was impossible under the circumstances, and the gun-layers had to wait until they had a clear view before firing again.

A strange, almost bell-like sound made Drew turn his head. A new cloud was rolling away from *Arkansas Queen*, its antique had fired a shot. Not a chance in hell that it had hit anything. He turned back and studied the view through his binoculars. Were they accomplishing anything either? Hard to tell…yes! The smoke cleared for an instant and Drew saw a tripod suddenly topple over, a large chunk of it thrown skyward. "Got one!" he shouted.

"Did we? Did we get it?" asked Mackenzie.

"Sure did!" answered Drew, though in fact it might have been a shot from any one of the ships or even the army guns. No need to tell Mackenzie that, though. The success seemed to pump the man up.

They continued to fire for another ten or fifteen minutes. The forward turret reached its five round limit and ceased fire. The after turret fired a couple more times, but Drew couldn't see any targets now and stopped the fire of all the guns.

"What's happenin'?" asked Mackenzie. "Did we drive 'em off?"

"I don't know…"

"Sir! Sir!" cried Hinsworth. "Up there, sir!"

For a moment, Drew didn't know what the ensign was talking about, and then he saw it: up on top of Big Rock Mountain. Tiny figures were moving, right up to the edge of the cliff. Then, suddenly they were burning! Some dissolved in fire, but others, some of the others tumbled off the cliff, trailing flames all the way to the ground, far below. "Oh God!" groaned Drew.

"Is that…? Are they…?" Mackenzie gasped.

"Yes."

"Merciful God!"

And then there were other figures on top of the cliff. Much bigger ones. Heat rays stabbed out and buildings on the south shore of the Arkansas began to burn.

"Signal… signal from Captain Gillespie, sir," said Hinsworth. The boy's face was ashen. "Martians… the Martians are crossing the river south of Big Rock. We are to follow *Wichita* down to engage."

"But… but we'll have to sail right beneath those monsters!" cried Mackenzie. "Our guns won't even be able to point at them!"

"No they won't," said Drew grimly. "Helm! Prepare to come about and follow *Wichita*! Everyone else, get below! Get below and pray!"

* * * * *

513

CYCLE 597, 845.1, NEAR ENEMY CITY 3-118

"The hill is ours, Commander."

"Well done," replied Qetjnegartis. At last, the enemy's defenses were crumbling. It had cost the life of another clan member, three more wounded, and fourteen wrecked fighting machines, but resistance in the city on the north side of the river was all but destroyed. The prey-creatures' large projectile throwers there had been destroyed and the new drones were digging their foot-warriors out of their underground shelters and the above-ground buildings. The drones were proving extremely useful, although losses among them had been heavy. But that is what they existed for: to take losses instead of the large fighting machines and their valuable pilots.

"Continue the advance. Let none escape."

* * * * *

APRIL, 1912, NORTHEAST OF LITTLE ROCK, ARKANSAS

"Column… *Halt!*"

The command was passed down the long line of horsemen and vehicles. No bugles were used because they were getting close now. Very close. Frank Dolfen got down out of his saddle, more collapsing than climbing. Damn he was tired! It was almost twelve hours since they had set out in the dark of the wee hours. They had stopped from time to time, but not often and not for long. Little Rock was just ahead, just on the other side of a line of ridges.

If there was anything left of Little Rock.

While it was still dark, they could see the red glow ahead; and after dawn, the clouds of smoke. Now they could smell it, too. The smoke clouds were rolling by overhead, and sometimes ash would drift past on the wind. But the fight was still going on; the low rumble of artillery, which had been audible since mid-morning, was now a continuous roar.

With the habits of an old cavalryman, Dolfen looked over his horse before he saw to any comfort for himself. The beast looked to be in fairly good shape - no worse than Dolfen himself - but he doubted it was up to any major exertion - like a battle - without some serious rest. The horse didn't have a name; he'd stopped giving names to his horses years ago. Army duty was hard on horses and they rarely lasted all that long. No point getting attached to them. His tired brain suddenly thought about Becca and that crazy horse of hers. Somehow it had managed to last! *Thank God neither of them are here now!*

Or at least he sure hoped they weren't. He'd looked and looked hard, but he didn't think she'd been able to stow away again. The very short notice they'd been given to get moving made it unlikely she'd manage it, but that girl could be determined.

"So what now, sir?" He turned away from his horse to see Lieutenant Bill Calloway of B Troop standing there. "We gonna attack?"

"We didn't come all this way to just watch, Lieutenant. How's your troop?"

"Good, sir. Four of the cycles have conked out, but that ain't bad over a distance like this. The rest are ready to go - unlike your poor critters." He pointed at Dolfen's horse and grinned.

"Yeah, yeah, don't rub it in. Someday you'll run out of gas and then you try and feed your contraption on grass…"

"Scouts coming in, sir," said Calloway suddenly, all levity gone. "Looks like they're in a hurry." Dolfen turned and saw a half-dozen troopers galloping their way, whipping their tired horses.

"Trouble, you think, sir?"

"More than likely," said Dolfen "Better go see." He stiffly walked over to where he saw the colonel and his headquarters group. He got there about the same time the scouts did. The leader, a sergeant from one of the other squadrons, jumped off his horse, saluted, and said breathlessly: "Martians, Colonel! Just up ahead! A whole passel of 'em!"

"Calm down, Sergeant," said Colonel Schumacher. "Where are they, and how many?"

"Just up ahead, sir!" the man turned and pointed. "In a little valley, just the other side of those trees! Not two miles from here! An' there's gotta be at least fifty or sixty of 'em!"

A chill ran through Dolfen. Fifty or sixty? The brigade would be cut to ribbons—or burned to ashes more likely - by a force that size. Hell, the whole 2nd Army had been beaten by a force not much bigger than that back at Albuquerque! They were here to harry the enemy's rear, not take them head on!

"Sixty tripods?" asked Schumacher. "You're sure, Sergeant? Think, man, it's important."

"Sure as shootin', sir! I'm not some green recruit, sir! I counted an' there was at least fifty! You saw 'em, Hadley, didn'tcha?" He turned to one of the other scouts.

"Yes, sir!" said the trooper. "A whole herd of 'em, just like the Sarge said. All standin' there like the regiment on parade!"

"Damnation," muttered Schumacher.

"Hell, Colonel," said Major Urwin. "We can't take on a force like that! It'd be like the Charge of the Light Brigade—only worse!"

"No, no, you're right." He looked over the ground to the south and shook his head. "We'll have to swing to the left, give this batch a wide berth, and come on Little Rock from the east."

"It'll be dark by the time we can do that, sir…"

"Well what else can we do…?"

The command staff began to debate, and then had to do it all over again when the colonel of the 9th arrived with his own staff. Dolfen waited and listened, too tired to do anything else. But as he stood there, something the scout had said tickled an old memory. *Standin' there like the regiment on parade…* Standing there? Why would that many tripods just be standing there? Why weren't they in the fight around Little Rock? If they were there as a rear guard, why weren't they deployed for battle? It didn't make sense…

Suddenly the memory crystalized and he was back on the rampart of the Martian fortress around Gallup. Lying on his belly on the hard rock with Major Comstock, looking at… *Rows of tripods, standing like they were on parade!*

"Colonel!" The cry was wrenched out of his mouth.

Schumacher turned to him, a look of surprise on his face. "Yes, Captain?"

"Sir! I think… I think things might not be what we think!"

"What do you mean?"

"Sir, let me go take a look! I can be back in twenty minutes and you can all rest in the meantime! Please, sir! If I'm right, we may have caught the bastards with their pants down!"

* * * * *

APRIL, 1912, LITTLE ROCK, ARKANSAS

"Engine room! Give me everything you've got!" Commander Drew Harding shouted into the speaking tube and prayed that he could save his ship.

515

Santa Fe, which had already been vibrating strongly with the rapid motion of the pistons, took on a new feel, a new tone, as the engines turned the screws faster than they ever had before. Drew looked out the narrow slots in the armored shutters of the pilothouse, trying to gauge their speed. Fifteen, maybe eighteen knots… add in the current of the river and they were surging downstream at twenty-five miles an hour, maybe more.

But it wasn't going to be enough.

In his heart, he knew it wouldn't be enough. The Martians were on the cliffs, and as they passed beneath them, they could fire right down on them. Easy and effective range for their heat rays.

"It…It'll be like shootin' fish in a barrel," whimpered Mackenzie, huddled beside him in the cramped compartment. "We won't have a chance. We can't even shoot back!"

No, they couldn't. They were too close to the cliffs and the guns couldn't elevate enough to hit the Martians on top. "We'll have to try and get past them as quickly as we can."

"Why? Why don't we just stay where we were until…"

"Until what? The defenses of the city are collapsing, Lieutenant! We can't go up river much farther, and sooner or later they'd come and get us. Down river is the only way out. And in any case, this is the navy, mister! We've got our orders and we'll follow them!"

He turned away from the man in disgust and stared out the view slit. A moment later, *Wichita* fired her guns and Drew strained his eyes to see what she was shooting at. The message had said the Martians were crossing the river downstream from Big Rock Mountain; had Captain Gillespie spotted some of them ahead? But no, when the ship fired again, Drew saw explosions blossom out from the face of the cliffs.

"What're they shooting at, sir?" asked Hinsworth." Are they trying to collapse the whole cliff or something?"

That had been Drew's first thought, but no, it would be impossible. The huge mass of the hill looked like the Rock of Gibraltar. But as he watched, the smoke and dust from the explosions was wafted up the cliffside by the southerly breeze. Up and up until it swirled around the Martian tripods at the top. "They're trying to make some cover for us! Well, it can't hurt, I guess."

"Should we fire, too, sir?"

He thought about it. The only guns which could bear were the forward turret and the portside forward casemate gun. If they had to face more Martians downstream, he'd need the turret guns and they only had five rounds left… "Tell the Number One five-incher to join in, Ensign."

"Aye, aye, sir!" Hinsworth dashed away.

But before *Santa Fe* could open up with its single gun, there was more firing from close by. *Arkansas Queen* was shooting, and ironically, its two makeshift mounts using field guns could actually elevate enough to hit the top of the cliffs. A few puffs appeared near the tripods. The chances of three-inch shells doing anything was slim, but maybe they'd get lucky.

Closer and closer, the cliffs loomed up on their left and a half-dozen tripods stood there on top like executioners. One of them turned slightly and its heat ray lashed out to strike *Arkansas Queen*. The ship's improvised armor was pitifully thin and didn't even cover it completely. Almost instantly, fires erupted from a dozen points, and a moment later the ammunition of one of the field guns exploded, blowing the gun and its crew to bits. The ship turned away, toward the southern shore, but there was no escape. The fires spread quickly. A second tripod fired and the ray pierced through to the bowels of the ship and a huge gout of steam billowed up and out as her boiler exploded. Burning from stem to stern, it plowed into a mud bank and lurched to a halt. Drew saw a few men throw themselves into the water, but only a few.

We're next.

He looked toward *Wichita* and saw it engulfed in a steam cloud. Were the Martians using the black dust? He couldn't tell, but it didn't matter, the steam might provide some protection from the heat rays. He reached over and flipped the switch on the dust alarm. The howl of the siren was almost lost amidst the roar of battle, but everyone heard it and took the proper steps. Looking out again, he saw a heat ray strike the water just ahead and sweep toward them.

"Release steam!"

The view out vanished in a white cloud, but an instant later the cloud turned pink, and then a red glare blazed in through the view slits. Drew could feel the heat from it and put on his mask. The helmsman was clutching the wheel, Hinsworth was frozen like a statue, and Mackenzie had slumped to his knees.

Drew looked up and saw that the metal roof of the pilothouse was starting to glow red.

* * * * *

APRIL, 1912, NORTHEAST OF LITTLE ROCK, ARKANSAS

Captain Frank Dolfen stared through his field glasses and sucked in his breath. Sixty tripods, just as the scout sergeant had said. Dolfen and the sergeant, a man named Findley, had ridden to the edge of the little valley and made their way on foot through a line of trees to where they could see. It was a sight to chill the heart of any man. But the Martian machines were just standing there in three rows, not moving. No, wait, there were a couple of them which were moving. How many? He looked closer and he could only see three of the machines which were moving. They paced around the others, for all the world like sentries guarding a line of horses.

That's exactly what they are!

Yes, this was just like what he and Comstock had seen at Gallup. Tripods in storage, with no Martians inside. He remembered how the ordnance major had babbled on and on about the production capabilities of the Martians and how they could crank out machine after machine. *They have more machines than they have Martians to drive them!*

"Sir? *Sir!*" hissed Findley. "There's another one! Over there!"

Dolfen looked and indeed, a single tripod was quickly approaching from the south. It was carrying something, it looked like a metal egg the size of a man. It walked up to one of the motionless tripods and halted. He squinted through the glasses and could just make out what was happening. The egg opened up and inside was a Martian, a hideous, leathery sack with tentacles. It was lifted up to where a hatch opened in the lower part of the standing tripod. It disappeared inside and the hatch closed. A minute or more passed and then suddenly the tripod came to life. It and the other newly arrived one moved away, heading south, back toward the battle.

"I'll be *damned*," whispered Dolfen.

"What is it, sir?" asked Findley.

"It's an opportunity, Sergeant. The opportunity of a lifetime. Come on! We need to get back to the Colonel!"

* * * * *

CYCLE 597, 845.1, INSIDE ENEMY CITY 3-118

Qetjnegartis evaluated the reports and looked on the burning city with satisfaction. Victory. The prey-creature defenses were collapsing. Resistance in the northern half of the city was all but eliminated. War machines were crossing the river into the southern half and it appeared that resistance there was disintegrating. Yes, that was the usual pattern: the prey-creatures would fight tenaciously until the battle began to go against them. At that point, their baser instincts for self-preservation took hold and they would flee to save themselves. Qetjnegartis was determined that this time very few would succeed. It had the forces available to pursue the enemy to complete destruction. It would begin by destroying all the river vessels so that...

"Commander! Commander Qetjnegartis! Respond!"

The communication was so abrupt and so lacking normal protocol that Qetjnegartis paused a moment before replying. "Yes. What is it?"

"Commander! This is Galnandis! Powerful enemy forces have attacked us! They are in among the.... We need assist..." The circuit suddenly went silent.

Galnandis? It had been left with two others to guard... *The reserve fighting machines!*

An enemy force in the rear? A powerful force? How powerful? Scouting reports from yesterday had found nothing for many *telequel* in any direction. Where had it come from? The artificial satellite, while useful, was in an orbit too low and too erratic to provide useful real-time tactical information. Somehow something had eluded detection and was now attacking.

Qetjnegartis hesitated. The battle here was won, but if a powerful enemy was approaching, and it caught them up against the river and the remainder of the city's garrison... And even if it was not a large force, the reserve fighting machines were vital for the upcoming operations.

"Attention, all battlegroups. A new enemy force is in our rear. All groups halt in place. Groups 32-4, 32-5, and 32-9, move to the machine storage area and report on the situation there. Speed is essential."

* * * * *

APRIL, 1912, NORTHEAST OF LITTLE ROCK, ARKANSAS

"Charge!"

Frank Dolfen shouted as loudly as he could, waved his arm, and dug his spurs into his mount's flanks. The bugler immediately echoed his command and the 1st Squadron of the 5th US Cavalry surged forward. The other squadrons were doing the same thing, and a tide of horseflesh and machines swept into the west end of the little valley.

The 9th was also attacking from the opposite end. In fact, the colored troopers had jumped the gun and attacked a few minutes before the 5th was ready. No matter, it only added to the enemy's confusion. The three sentry tripods had turned one way to meet the first threat, but now they were literally turning in circles as foes came at them from all sides.

Colonel Schumacher had been wonderfully quick to understand what Dolfen had told him - and brilliantly decisive in risking his command by believing it. If Dolfen had been wrong, if all sixty of those tripods had been operational, then his regiment would be annihilated in moments.

But Dolfen wasn't wrong! The charge thundered forward and the rows of tripods stood there, just as immobile as before. The horses galloped between the standing giants and the troopers whooped at the top of their lungs.

Men on horses and men on motorcycles and men in armored cars converged on the three hapless sentries and hammered them with everything they had. Rifles and machine guns, light cannons and stovepipe rockets, bundles of dynamite and sheer human grit hit them, hurt them, and flung them to the ground in mangled wrecks. It was over in what seemed like seconds. It had cost three dozen men and horses turned to ash, and two of the armored cars burned fiercely, spewing black smoke into the sky, but still a bargain price for such a victory.

The soldiers shouted and cheered and tossed their hats in the air. Even the horses seemed to be exhilarated by what they'd accomplished. But there was no time to waste. Dolfen nudged his tired horse into motion and found the colonel.

"Dolfen!" he cried when he caught sight of him. "You were right! By God you were right!" Colonel Schumacher looked as giddy as his men.

"It won't take them long to find out what we've done, sir. We need to get explosives placed and blow these things to hell."

"You're right again! You heard him gentlemen! Get your men to work and finish the job!"

Scouts were sent out, the armored cars, along with them, machine guns and mortars formed a defense line facing south, but everyone else got off their horses and their motorbikes and began swarming over the immobile tripods, planting their dynamite bombs where they would do the most good. Fortunately, there was no shortage of explosives. Every man had at least one of the bombs and many had more than one.

Men climbed, or were boosted by their squadmates, up the legs of the machines to where the odd hip joints met the lower bodies of the tripods. The bombs were packed tightly into place anywhere it looked like they might do damage. The trick was going to be setting them off without getting blown up with them. The bombs issued to the troops had a friction igniter to light the fuse, but the fuse only had a ten second delay. Not much time for a man to get down and find cover.

But time was short and these men were used to facing sudden death. Some tried to rig up ropes to pull the pin on the igniters from the ground, but the bolder ones just said to hell with it, pulled the pins and jumped. *Fire in the hole!* they screamed and scattered in all directions.

The first explosion blew two of the legs off one of the machines and it toppled over with a crash. The men, unhurt, whooped and went back to work. Some went on to another machine, while others decided to go back and place more bombs on the relatively unhurt head of the downed tripod to see if they could wreck it some more.

One after another the tripods were felled like trees before lumberjacks. Dolfen looked on in exhausted satisfaction. But then a bugle sounded officers call and he moved over to where the colonel and his staff were clustered around a map.

"Gentlemen," said Colonel Schumacher when everyone was there. All the jubilation was gone from his face. "Our radio has just picked up a signal from the Little Rock garrison commander. The defenses have been breached and the city is going to fall. He's ordered everyone to try and retreat down river. Once we are done here, we will move east and try to link up with what's left of the garrison and cover their…"

For one instant, everything was lit up by a brilliant blue light, and then Dolfen was knocked to the ground and a roar shook the world.

He found himself lying on top of the colonel's adjutant and tried to push himself up. He could see the man with his mouth open, apparently shouting something, but Dolfen couldn't hear anything but a loud ringing in his ears. He twisted around and a huge billowing cloud of smoke was rushing toward him.

But before it reached him, there was another dazzling flash of blue, only slightly dimmed for being inside the smoke cloud, and an instant later another blow slammed him backward onto the unfortunate adjutant again. Smoke and dust swept over the tangled group of officers, choking and blinding them.

As he tried to struggle up, he felt rather than heard a heavy impact nearby. The ringing in his ears slowly faded, only to be replaced by a shrill noise close at hand. The smoke and dust cleared and he could see again. He staggered to his feet, coughed up a mouthful of grit, and tried to spit it out. Colonel Schumacher and some of the officers looked around in a daze, but the others were clustered around... what?

Dolfen moved over to them and discovered the source of the noise. A man was pinned to the ground by the severed leg of one of the tripods. It lay right across his torso and he was screaming, blood coming out of his mouth. Looking around, Dolfen saw bits of metal and wreckage scattered everywhere.

"What the hell happened?!" screamed someone in his ear.

"One of the tripods... two of 'em, must have blown up... Their power gizmos... I saw that happen at Prewitt... didn't think about that..." No he hadn't, had he? "Didn't think it could happen with the ones just standin' there..."

As the smoke cleared away, he saw a scene of devastation. The tripods, those that hadn't been blown completely to pieces, were scattered around the valley, smashed, torn apart, reduced to junk.

The two regiments of cavalry had been reduced to junk, too. Bodies lay among the wreckage; men and horses.

"Oh, God," groaned Dolfen.

Somewhere a bugler was blowing recall and men were picking themselves up off the ground, trying to catch panicked horses, tend to the wounded... what a mess. All the elation of what they had accomplished drained away.

Frank Dolfen limped away to try to find what was left of his squadron.

* * * * *

APRIL, 1912, LITTLE ROCK, ARKANSAS

The heat has almost unbearable and the roof of the pilothouse was cherry-red. Drew Harding was quite certain he was going to die. A loud concussion slammed the ship and he was thrown against the bulkhead. It had been strong but not strong enough to have come from his own ship. *Wichita, that must have been Wichita...*

"Oh, God! Let me out!" screamed Mackenzie. He surged up from his knees and started clawing at the pilothouse hatch. Hinsworth grabbed him to hold him back.

But then the red glare coming through the view slits faded away and the roof changed to a dull red and then back to gray metal. It was still hot as the gates of Hell, but what was happening? Drew went to the speaking tube and shouted: "Secure steam!" The hissing stopped and the white cloud outside dispersed, but the heat...

"Let me out!" shrieked Mackenzie.

"Let him out," gasped Drew.

Hinsworth let the man go and he flung open the hatch and staggered outside. Drew saw Mackenzie grab hold of the railing and then scream and fall back, his hands burned. He slumped to his knees and then screamed again as the hot metal plating of the deck burned through the knees of his trousers. He lurched up and Drew yanked him back into the pilothouse where he collapsed, sobbing. Pulling off his dust mask, Drew and the others went outside, careful to touch nothing. He could feel the heat of the deck through the soles of his shoes, but it didn't get too bad. Cooler air touched his face, and he sucked it greedily into his lungs. He looked up at the cliffs, but to his amazement, the summit was empty. The tripods were gone. Why? What the hell was going on?

"Sir!" cried Hinsworth. "Dead ahead!"

He turned about and saw that the noise he had heard had indeed been the *USS Wichita*. She lay, broken in half, both ends burning, just a few hundred yards ahead. Drew leapt back into the pilothouse and spun the wheel. They were already as far to the south side of the river as they dared, so there was no choice but to steer back into the center, closer to where the Martians had been. But the enemy was gone.

He looked for survivors in the water as they churned past, but there were none. *Wichita* had been battened down just like *Santa Fe*, and there would have been no way for anyone to get out. Only after they were past did he take a good look at his own ship. *Good God!* The mast and upper works were scorched and blackened and even partially melted in spots. The two wooden launches stored on the after deck were burning, as were some coils of rope. The upper mast with its observation platform was leaning precariously off to starboard, and the bridge railings were twisted all out of shape. The funnel had a hole in its side and the smoke billowed out of that as well as the normal opening on top.

"Sir? Sir, the radio is out," reported Hinsworth.

"Not surprised, the antenna's all melted. Check for damage below, Ensign."

"Aye, aye, sir!"

They were almost past the mountain now, and Drew looked ahead for enemies, but the river banks were strangely deserted. Where were the Martians? He could see some explosions of in the southern part of the city and still hear some artillery fire, so they weren't all gone, but he didn't spot a single one from where he was.

Mackenzie was slumped down on the deck, looking stupidly at his burned hands and whimpering. "Mister Mackenzie, go below and have those looked after. Go on, get below!" The man nearly crawled off.

Once fully beyond Big Rock Mountain, Drew could see tripods off to the north and some others in the southern part of the city, but none seemed to be coming his way. He reduced speed to spare the engines and searched for any sign of organized resistance. The waterfront on the south bank was empty of ships, even though the damage to the docks appeared minimal.

Finally, a couple of miles ahead, he caught sight of a cluster of vessels. He spotted one of the *Olmstead* class gunboats and steered for her. As he got closer, he saw that in addition to the remaining ships of the flotilla, every other ship, boat, or barge that had been at Little Rock - which was still afloat - had gathered near a small island in the river. The island had been fortified and it marked the eastern end of the city's defense lines. There were two forts on either bank and swarms of people, horses, and vehicles were crowded on the shores. Many appeared to be loading on to the ships.

"Looks like they're leaving, sir," said Hinsworth, who had just returned. "Oh, and there's no damage below, but everyone's near passed out from the heat." He looked aft. "Oh, and the flag's all burned up. I'll have another one rigged."

Drew reduced speed even more and pulled up close to the gunboat, it was the *Evansville*, and shouted across to her skipper, Lieutenant Commander Brighton. "What's happening? Our radio's out!"

"General Duncan's ordered a retreat!" Brighton yelled back. "Where's Gillespie?" he gestured up river.

Drew shook his head. "Sunk! I'm low on ammo! Did we save any?"

"*Pelée's* over there," replied Brighton, referring to the munitions ship. "But you're senior now, Harding! What do you want us to do?"

Drew's shoulders sagged. He was suddenly very, very tired and he didn't need anything else piled on him. What to do? He looked around at the barely controlled chaos.

"Load up everyone we can and then cover the retreat!"

CHAPTER NINE

MAY, 1912, PHILADELPHIA, PENNSYLVANIA

Colonel Andrew Comstock watched the train chug into the enormous shed of the Broad Street Station. He found that he was both nervous and excited. Victoria and his son were on that train. It had been three months since he'd last been home and he missed them terribly. But as glad as he was to see them, he dreaded telling his wife the news.

The train squealed to a halt and Andrew scanned the cars, looking for Victoria. There she was. He saw her leaning out one of the car windows and waving. He returned the wave and hurried over to where she was. "Hello!" he shouted.

"Andrew!" cried Victoria and then she held up young Arthur, who initially looked very uncertain about this new place he was in, but when he caught sight of him shrieked: *Da! Da!*

A warm glow passed through Andrew that had nothing to do with the spring weather. He stopped just below the window and stood on tip-toe to grasp the hands of his wife and son. "How are you? The trip okay?"

"Yes, fine. So good to see you, love. Can you come in and help with the luggage?"

"Sure! Be right there." He went to the end of the car, up the steps, and inside. He gave his wife and son a quick hug and then got the luggage out of the overhead rack. Before the war there would have been a dozen porters competing for the job, but nearly all of those men were in the army now. Andrew didn't mind carrying the bags at all, except… "Wow, what all did you bring? How long are you planning to stay?"

"Andrew! You've never had to travel with a baby. Almost all of this is for Arthur."

"Oh! Well, no matter, I can manage." He grabbed up the bags and trundled them off the rail car. The platform wasn't terribly crowded, unlike other times he'd been here. New regulations had gone into effect restricting 'unnecessary' civilian travel. It had been done to free up rolling stock for military use, but it was just another example of how the war was changing everyday life. There were still plenty of people, however, because there were always ways around the regulations. Andrew had had no problem getting a pass for Victoria and Arthur.

He lugged the bags down to street level and only had to wait a moment for his driver, who had been circling the block, to spot him and pull over. Being a colonel had its advantages: his own car and driver. The driver popped out and helped him load in the bags and then they were off. Andrew had reserved a room at a nice hotel down on 7th Street, and it was only a short drive on Market Street to get there. He was staying at a boarding house in Eddystone, but it was a dreary place and Eddystone, itself, wasn't much better; so he'd arranged for this hotel instead.

"How's your mother?" he asked.

"Oh, she's fine, fine. Worried about Dad - and you, too, of course." Her father, General Hawthorne, was technically Andrew's boss - or had been. He spent most of his time in Washington these days,

523

unlike when Andrew had first become his aide, before the war. They had never managed to find a house, so Victoria and Arthur were still living in her parent's home at Fort Meyer. He knew Victoria wasn't happy about that, but it was really the only practical thing to do.

"Is everything all right with your dad? You must see him nearly every day now that he's not traveling so much."

"Almost. But we do worry about him. He's sick a lot, though he tries to hide it. He works too hard."

"Everyone's working too hard."

"Like you."

The arrival at the hotel saved him from having to answer that one. They checked in, and his driver helped carry the bags again before he dismissed him. The room was nice enough, and they got settled before taking a stroll. It was a beautiful day, but Andrew noticed his wife wrinkling her nose. "What's wrong?"

"The coal smoke! It's so thick!"

"Really?" he replied, sniffing deeply. "All the new factories, I guess, I hardly notice it anymore."

"I guess it's because there aren't many factories in Washington that I notice it more."

"That's true. But Philadelphia is a huge manufacturing center. And now that you mention it, after one day last winter, the snow was gray, and by the next it had turned black. All the soot from the factories."

Their stroll took them past Independence Hall and there was a large crowd of people gathered in the open space in front of the old building. There was a band and many of the people carried signs and placards. As they got closer, Andrew realized that it was a political rally in support of Presidential-aspirant Nelson Miles.

A banner close to the building had a list of names of cities which had been lost to the Martians. *Salt Lake City, Denver, Bismarck, Omaha, Des Moines, Albuquerque, Santa Fe...* Andrew winced. The list went on and the last two names were in red: *Kansas City* and *Little Rock*. The banner than asked: *How Many More??????*

A speaker on the steps was shouting angrily. "... and Roosevelt has the gall, the unmitigated gall to ask the American people to give him another four years! Four terms in office? God in Heaven, Washington himself only wanted two! And Washington *won* his war! Roosevelt is losing this war! How many more cities will the Rough Rider lose? How many more of our precious boys will die? I say no to Roosevelt! He's had his chance! It is time for a change! A time for Nelson Appleton Miles! Miles for President!"

The crowd took up the chant: *Miles! Miles! Miles!*

The band struck up a patriotic march and the crowd cheered and chanted. Andrew steered his family onto 6th Street and away. Victoria looked back with concern on her face. "Do you think Miles will win?" she asked.

"Unless something changes, I'm afraid so," said Andrew. "Most people still don't understand what we are facing in this war. They hear about the defeats and the retreats and the cities lost and they can't accept the fact that it's because the Martians are more advanced than we are, and that we have a lot of catching up to do. They figure it must be because somebody made a mistake."

"So they blame the President? From what you and Dad have said - and from what I saw on the trip to Panama - if it weren't for him we would have lost the war!"

"You're right. But people don't listen to reason. And now General Miles comes along and his supporters are all but promising that he'll win the war and win it quickly if they make him President."

"What could he do that President Roosevelt isn't already doing?" snorted Victoria.

"Not much. But the people are tired of the war and I guess they think that any change is better than no change."

"*I'm* tired of the war! But it doesn't mean I'm going to vote against the best man! Not that I *can* vote, of course."

Andrew wasn't going to get drawn into that subject again. So he said: "Come, I didn't ask you here to talk politics! Are you hungry? There's a very fine restaurant a few block from here. It's called *Bookbinders* and General Clopton introduced me to it."

"Well, yes, I am hungry, but what about Arthur? He's being very good, but I don't know how long he'd keep that up in a restaurant."

"They have private rooms upstairs. We can get one of those. It's early yet and they should be available."

"All right."

They made their way to the restaurant and Andrew was pleased that it, indeed, was not crowded. The head waiter looked at Arthur doubtfully, but the boy was being on unusually good behavior and they were led upstairs to a cozy room that looked out on Walnut Street. Andrew ordered a bottle of wine and placed their orders. Arthur started getting fussy once they stopped moving, but the little fellow was so worn out by the trip that he soon dozed off in his mother's arms and they settled him down on a side chair.

They sat and held hands across the table and smiled at each other. "Missed you," said Andrew.

"Missed you, too." Victoria's smile faltered. "But where are you off to now?"

Andrew started in surprise. "What do you mean?"

"I mean that you obviously aren't coming home any time soon or why would you have sent for us? From your letters I know that the land ironclads are nearly complete and that ought to finish up your need to be here. So if you are not coming home, where are you going?"

Andrew sighed. Yes, Victoria was a smart woman. Too smart sometimes. "Yes, you're right, I have a new assignment and I will be gone for a while longer. I'm sorry."

"Where? What will you be doing? And for how long?"

"You know the old saying that the reward for a job well done is a tougher job?"

"Yes?"

"Well, it appears I did my job here too well. I learned about the land ironclads so well that General Clopton wants me to stay on as his second in command to make sure the darn things keep running properly. I'll be heading west with the squadron in a few days."

"West? You mean to the Mississippi Line?"

Andrew nodded.

"A combat assignment? But... but you're a staff officer!"

"The policy now is to rotate officers between staff and the line. So people don't get stuck in a rut and so each side understands the problems of the other. Clopton went straight to General Crozier and twisted his arm to get me. It's a compliment, really."

"But it will put you in combat."

"Being a staff officer hasn't been too terribly effective at keeping me out of combat so far."

"I know! Oh, Andrew!" She got up out of her chair with tears in her eyes. He automatically stood up and embraced her. At that moment, Arthur decided to wake up and start crying, and a few seconds later the waiter arrived with their food. They sprang apart, Victoria going for the baby, Andrew spinning to face the startled waiter. It took several minutes to get settled again, Victoria with Arthur on her lap and both of them seated again, picking at food they neither really wanted anymore.

"How long do you think?" she said quietly.

"How long until I go? We plan to make the first move down to Newport News next week. That will be the first real test of how the ironclads handle open water. If everything goes well - and I doubt it will - we'll work our way down the coast from harbor to harbor until we get to New Orleans. Then up the river to wherever they need us. If there are any delays at Newport News I might be able to get up to Washington for a day, but I don't know if…"

"I meant, how long until you come home?"

"Oh, well, there's no way to tell. All the brass are hoping that the land ironclads will be the spearhead for the offensives everyone is clamoring for. So they'll probably want us until… until…" He faltered and dropped his eyes.

"Until you win the war? That could be a very long time. Years."

"That's true for any soldier these days, love." He stared at his cooling lobster. "But if things work well, the army will be building more of the ironclads. Maybe they'll send me back here to work up my own squadron. I could be back east for months and months." He looked up and gave her as hopeful a grin as he could manage.

She answered with a tiny smile. "As it happened, I have some news for you, too, Andrew."

"Oh? What?"

In the half-second before she replied, he knew exactly what she was going to say.

"Andrew, I'm expecting again."

* * * * *

CYCLE 597, 845.1, HOLDFAST 32-4

Qetjnegartis stared at the image of Commander Braxjandar of Clan Mavnaltak in the communications display and tried to gauge its mood. The clan to the north had also fought a large battle recently and also gained a victory.

"My congratulations on your success, Braxjandar," said Qetjnegartis. "I trust your losses were not excessive."

"Excessive, no. But not inconsequential, either," it replied. "The prey-creatures learn quickly and fight with greater tenacity than ever. Do you not find this to be true?"

"Yes. I fear they are more intelligent than we first gave them credit for."

"All the more reason to crush them quickly and not give them the time to learn more," said Braxjandar. "I propose to attack City 3-4 in six days' time. Can I count on Clan Bajantus to attack City 3-37 at the same time to keep the enemy confused? This was agreed upon."

Qetjnegartis waved its tendrils in the negative. "I am afraid that will not be possible. Despite crushing the enemy at City 3-118, our force of reserve fighting machines was destroyed. It will be at least thirty days before they can be replaced. I cannot launch a major attack without them. Can you delay your assault for that long?"

526

"Destroyed? How could your entire reserve be destroyed?"

"An enemy raiding force attacked from the rear. Several of the reserve machines had their power supplies explode and the other machines were caught in the explosions. A regrettable setback."

"Did you not have a guard on them?"

"I do not have time to discuss my tactical decisions, Braxjandar! I can attack 3-118 in thirty days! Will you wait or not?"

"I will not, Qetjnegartis! The enemy is off balance and I will not give them time to recover. I will attack as planned. The Colonial Conclave will not be pleased to hear that you have failed to support me properly."

Qetjnegartis held back its anger. The loss of the reserve machines truly rankled and Braxjandar's arrogant attitude was not helping. Still, the opinion of the Conclave could not be ignored. "I and my clan face difficulties you do not. City 3-37 lies on the far side of the great river. Crossing it against the enemy defenses may be very difficult. We do not know the depth of the water, the strength of the current, or the condition of the bottom. Your next objective lies on this side of the river and can be attacked directly. Also, is not Clan Novmandus ordered to assist you from the north?"

Braxjandar waved its tendrils dismissively. "They are proving to be of little help. They have such a vast territory assigned to them, with almost no prey-creatures to contend with, that they are making little effort to construct an effective battle force. Their attention is on building new holdfasts to administer their territory. In time, of course, they may become very powerful, but for the moment all they can do is distract some of the enemy forces to the north. I understand that you have a similar lack of cooperation from the clan to your south."

"That is true, although they do have serious prey-creature forces to contend with, and I have heard that they are also suffering from… internal difficulties."

"Then it would appear that the conquest of this continent has been left to you and I, Qetjnegartis."

It was surprised by this statement. Was this a peace-offering of some sort? Perhaps some gesture in return was wise. "That may well be true. I regret my inability to launch a full-scale assault at this time. But I will agree to send raiding forces north and south along the large river. This may spread alarm and confusion among the prey-creatures. At the very least it will allow me to gather information on the enemy defenses. Perhaps a better attack site will present itself. And I promise that our main attack will commence within thirty days."

"Very well," said Braxjandar. "I will attack on schedule. Perhaps my attack will aid yours, if nothing else."

"So be it," said Qetjnegartis.

* * * * *

MAY, 1912, ST. LOUIS, MISSOURI

General Leonard Wood eagerly stepped off the train in the huge expanse of St. Louis' Union Station; Colonel Drum was right behind. Despite the top priority granted his train, it had taken three days to get here. There was a crowd of men in uniform waiting to meet him. Leading the group was John Pershing, commander of 6th Army. Pershing had briefly worked for Wood two years earlier as his assistant chief of staff, but the huge demand for officers with command experience had seen him made a division, corps, and now army commander. 'Black Jack', as he was sometimes called due to his time with a colored regiment, had grown into his new responsibilities well, and Wood was glad to be working with him. He returned his salute and stuck out his hand. "Hello, John, good to see you again."

527

Pershing took his hand and shook it firmly. "And you, sir. Although you've picked a hell of a time to make an inspection! I've got Martians not thirty miles from this spot!"

"I know, John, I know. That's why I'm here."

Pershing's welcoming expression turned to suspicion. "You're taking command here, sir?"

"Technically I was already in command. Here and everywhere else, John. But do you mean am I relieving you? No. I'm here to observe. And to get the hell out of Washington for a while."

Pershing smiled briefly but still looked wary. Wood could certainly understand the man's uneasiness. No commander wanted the boss looking over his shoulder, but that was just too bad. Wood was very glad that Congress had finally stopped dragging its feet about re-creating the four-star rank and giving it to him. During the Civil War, it had taken them two years to even allow three star ranks, and that had meant a horde of major generals commanding corps and armies and all squabbling over who had seniority. They had been facing the same thing in this war with the lieutenant generals. But now he had four stars on his uniform and there was no doubt who was in charge. Still, they had lieutenant generals at both corps and army level. Perhaps there needed to be a five star rank…

"I see, sir," said Pershing. He turned and gestured to several other officers with him. "This is my own chief of staff, Colonel George Marshall, and you know General Foltz, of course."

"Of course! How are you, Fred?" The commander of XV Corps, which was charged with the defense of St. Louis, Lieutenant General Frederick Foltz, stepped up and shook his hand. "Fred was indispensable helping me sort out that mess in Cuba after the war," said Wood to Pershing. "He was the supervisor of police and captain of the port in Havana, while I was the military governor of the island."

"And now we've got another mess to deal with, sir," said Foltz. "Scouts report I've got a couple of hundred tripods bearing down on me. They could hit us as soon as tomorrow."

"Right, and there's no time to waste. Let's dispense with the formalities and get to work. Take me to your headquarters and brief me on the situation."

Pershing nodded and they all made their way out of the station to the street where a group of staff cars awaited. They chugged off along streets almost devoid of civilian traffic, but crowded with military. "How has the evacuation proceeded?" asked Wood, nodding to the streets.

"Well enough, sir. Nearly all the women and children are gone, but there are still plenty of civilian workers in the factories and maintaining the utilities and other services. Still, the population is less than half of what it was."

"What were you able to save from the Kansas City garrison?" It was a question he'd dreaded to ask, but he needed to know.

"Not much, I'm afraid," said Pershing, frowning deeply. "The reports that made it back are sketchy to say the least. The enemy attacked in overwhelming strength and the defenses collapsed very quickly. Some of the riverine craft have made it back here carrying some survivors. Scouting aircraft report others on foot traveling overland. Whatever has made it out is no longer a usable military force - except for the ships, of course, I've added them to the city's defenses."

"Duncan?"

"No word."

"Damn. Well, hopefully they took some of the bastards with them. From the reports we're getting, the defenders at Little Rock made them pay."

"That's good to know, sir," said Pershing, "but it doesn't help us much here. Forgive me for asking, but can we expect any reinforcements besides yourself, General?"

Wood looked Black Jack in the eyes. "As a matter of fact, yes. I've had the 1st Tank Division sent to Cairo. They're on ships and I can have them sent wherever you like."

Pershing looked surprised. Clearly he hadn't been expecting anything. "That would be wonderful, sir. The steam tanks are the best things we've got to stop the tripods."

"Actually, we may have something better."

"Sir?"

"I'll tell you about it when we're inside." The motorcade had arrived at Foltz's headquarters which was located in the Hotel Jefferson, a fifteen story building which had a good view in most directions from its penthouse ballroom. The elevator took them up.

St. Louis had been identified as a strategic point almost from the start of the war, so plans for its defense had been worked on for years. Since the disaster in 1910, those plans had been put into effect with much greater urgency and had now reached a very sophisticated stage. The penthouse headquarters contained a huge and beautifully made sand table map of the city's defenses with hundreds of small blue flags stuck into it, which Foltz now explained in detail.

"We started with the defenses of the city, itself," he said, using a pointer to trace an egg-shaped oval which fit into a bend in the Mississippi. "A line of concrete walls with emplacements for heavy guns was constructed from the river on the south and then around to meet the river again north of the city, a distance of almost thirty miles. We've also built some substantial works along the waterfront, although we've always assumed we'd have support from the navy to defend that approach."

"Dangerous to make assumptions," muttered Wood, "but for the Martians to attack from the river side would mean they have already gotten across, and that would be a disaster in its own right. Proceed, General."

"Yes, sir. We did not wish to depend solely on a single line of defense, so once this main line was complete, we expanded our defense zones to provide a forward line. As you can see, the Missouri River comes in from the west and then turns to the northeast to join the Mississippi north of the city, forming a rectangular shape with water on three sides. The only landward approach is from the southwest." He traced the river with his pointer.

"To take advantage of this, we've constructed a line from this point on our main line up to the Missouri at the town of St. Charles, giving over two thirds of the main line an outer defense. This new line has a number of concrete forts connected with earthen trenches. We're calling it the Donnelson Line after an engineering officer killed in an accident during construction."

"That looks good, Fred," said Wood. "But it looks like you have an even more extended line further to the southwest." He pointed at the sand table.

"Yes, sir, we do. The Meramec River enters the Mississippi here, about ten miles south of the city, and provides a natural barrier almost halfway to the Missouri. At this time of year, the Meramec is deep enough to get some of the smaller gunboats almost ten miles upstream, so we've built a line of trenches and bunkers along its banks and then the rest of the way to the Missouri here."

"That line has to be what? Forty miles long?" asked Wood.

"About thirty-seven, yes sir. We realize it is far too long to defend with the troops we have, so this will just be a forward outpost line to force the enemy to deploy and reveal his intentions. The 58th Division is holding the position. And we have all the country registered for artillery fire. Our long-range guns can hit anywhere along this whole line. We've also dug thousands of pit traps to snare and immobilize their machines. Our intent is to hurt them as much as possible before they can even reach our main defenses."

"Just so long as your troops in the forward line don't get hurt too badly trying to fall back." The 58th was nearly a third of the whole garrison and they couldn't afford to have it destroyed.

"Yes, sir, we've given a lot of thought to that. As you can see from our table, there are a multitude of small streams which crisscross the area. We've seen how the enemy tripods have trouble with soft and marshy ground, so we've dammed up a number of these streams creating ponds and small lakes and a lot of flooded ground they will have trouble getting across. Each of our forward units will have designated fall-back routes to the Donnelson Line along dry ground through these areas which are already registered for our artillery. If the Martians follow those routes, they will be hammered by our guns. If they try some other route, they'll get stuck in the mud - and we'll hammer them anyway."

"You are aware that the enemy is now employing a smaller machine in conjunction with the tripods? What provisions have you made to deal with those?"

"Yes, sir. We've gotten reports on those. The men who have seen them are calling them spiders. They will make our trenches and underground bunkers less secure, but the reports also say that they aren't nearly as heavily armored as the big tripods. Rifles, machine guns, and the stovepipes can destroy them. Frankly, sir, our infantry are looking forward to facing something they can fight on more even terms. We'll handle them."

"What about ammunition? Particularly artillery ammunition? How are you supplied?"

"We believe we have a sufficient reserve for seven days of all-out combat, sir. We have eight different main dumps and twenty secondary ones closer to the front to assure rapid resupply to our units. If it goes longer than that…" Foltz shrugged. Yes, it would surely be decided one way or another long before that.

Wood nodded. "I'm impressed, gentlemen, very impressed. Oh, what about the captured heat rays we've sent you? Where are they positioned?"

"Well, General, we were constrained by the fact that the devices require a huge amount of electrical current to work. The local power plants can meet the demand, but obviously we need to get the current from the plant to the device, so we are limited to where we can deploy them. At first we simply picked five locations along the main walls with good lines of fire and then ran power lines to those locations. Later, the engineers realized that the devices themselves were not that large or especially heavy and could be moved quickly with the right equipment. So what they've done is to set up nineteen different locations along the walls and run power lines to each of them. We have the devices themselves on trucks and can move them to whichever locations seem threatened. We can then set up the devices and fire from there."

"That's ingenious, Fred. Good thinking."

"It was the engineers who thought of it, sir, I can't take any credit. But if the Martians get close enough, they are in for one hell of a surprise!"

Wood and many of the others there chuckled. "I sure hope we can give them one, Fred." He turned to face all of the assembled officers. "Gentlemen, you have done an outstanding job, but sometime in the coming days, all of your work will be put to the test. *St. Louis must be held!* At all costs! Not only is it vital to our overall defenses, but all of our future offensive operations depend on our ability to hold on to what we already have." He looked the men over and they seemed properly sobered.

"With this in mind," he continued, "we are giving you every bit of support we can. I've already told General Pershing that the 1st Tank Division has been put at your disposal. I've also alerted II Corps, to your south, to be prepared to take over the southern section of your line on the east bank of the river. So, if necessary, you could cross over the 42nd Division to reinforce your lines here." Foltz's eyebrows went up and many of the others nodded. XV Corps had five division, but only three were in the St. Louis lines. The other two extended the corps' lines north and south along the river.

"That would be excellent, sir," said Foltz. "I'll send General Hotchkiss the word to be ready to move."

"Finally, there will be several ships docking at your wharfs within the next few hours carrying our latest 'secret weapon'. They're called 'Little Davids' and they are a large steam powered vehicle mounting a twelve-inch gun in a rotating turret. Be advised that they are not tanks. Their armor isn't particularly strong and they carry no secondary weapons, so they aren't fit to get in close and mix it up with a bunch of tripods. They are only meant to be a means of moving a very heavy gun to where you might need one. There are six of the beasts and I leave it to you to put them to the best use."

"Thank you, General," said Pershing. "I've put all of 6th Army's reserves on call for XV Corps' use. This is primarily additional artillery, which I'm moving up on the east bank of the river for now." Black Jack looked at Wood. "Sir, I can guarantee you that St. Louis will be held to the last man."

* * * * *

MAY, 1912, NEAR MONTGOMERY ISLAND, ARKANSAS

Captain Frank Dolfen looked east and could see the glittering waters of the Mississippi in the far distance. *Thank God, we made it.* The retreat from Little Rock had not been nearly as long as the agonizing trek from Santa Fe two years earlier, but it had been bad enough. For one thing, the Martians had put on a much more aggressive pursuit - although not as aggressive as they might have.

Despite the disastrous explosion among the parked tripods, which had cost the two cavalry regiments five times as many men as the initial attack had, the sudden blow to the enemy seemed to have disorganized them. Precious hours had gone by before any serious response was made, and this allowed the cavalry to put itself back together, slip out to the east to make contact with the survivors of the Little Rock garrison, and retreat down river.

It wasn't until the next day that any real attacks developed. Even then the enemy seemed very cautious, perhaps because of the gunboats in the river. It was clear the Martians didn't like ships and the big guns they carried. Any time the ships pulled within range, the tripods would give ground and try to find cover. The retreating troops huddled close to the river whenever they could. Or maybe the enemy's caution was because they had no reserve tripods to replace losses. Dolfen liked to think that was the reason.

Even so, the Martians had hurt them. The damn things could move so fast they would dart in, blast away at anything they could, and then fall back again before the ships or any of the artillery could find the range. Only a few dozen of the steam tanks had escaped Little Rock, and on the road they broke down at an alarming rate; there were just a handful left now. Infantry - and cavalry - had to do far too much of the fighting and the dying.

Worst of all, their expected support had vanished.

They'd been told that as they fell back down the river, they would run into the forces of General Funston's 2nd Army which had been assigned to defend the south shore of the lower Arkansas. The surviving garrison could join up with them and make a stand somewhere. From what Dolfen had heard, there were supposed to be two infantry divisions stretched out along the south side of the river. That was a hopelessly inadequate force to guard a hundred miles of winding river, but it was still a lot better than nothing - and nothing was what they were finding. The 78th Infantry & 5th Texas Volunteers divisions simply were not there.

They found groups of Texas and Arkansas militia, poorly trained and lightly armed, but when asked where the army units had gone, they could only shrug their shoulders and say south. When they found out what was pursuing the Little Rock garrison, most of the militia had melted away. A few had joined in, but only a few.

So the retreat had to continue. There weren't enough of them left, and no good positions to defend, so it was keep running - all the way to the Mississippi. They did get some help; once they were further down river additional gunboats arrived, and when the water was deep enough, their old friend, the monitor Amphitrite with its ten-inch guns.

There were also Tom Selfridge's planes, and aircraft from other units as well. During the daylight hours they had planes overhead almost constantly; those gave them warning of approaching Martians and even killed a few of them, too. As a result, the retreat didn't become a rout - not quite.

And now they were here, at the Mississippi. The river was teeming with ships, both military and civilian. Dolfen could see that some were drawn up along the shore and appeared to be loading troops and vehicles.

"So what now d'ya think, Captain?" He turned in his saddle to see Private Gosling alongside. The Goose had managed to stay alive and even provide a few modest comforts during the retreat. If Dolfen had been forced to command his squadron and look out for himself, he would have gone hungry and slept in the mud. With Gosling's help, he'd done neither.

"No one's told me. Looks like they are shifting what's left of us to the east shore." He pointed at the boats.

"It'd sure be nice to put that big stretch o' water 'tween us and them bastards, an' that's the Lord's truth!"

"Amen." Dolfen glanced over his shoulder, looking west, to make sure the Martians weren't going to try and ruin things the way they almost did two years ago, but the horizon was empty. As he looked, he noticed one of his troopers riding past, carrying a strange object. It was a long pole, maybe twelve feet long, and on the end of it was... What the hell?!

"Trooper... Private, uh, King, what the devil have you got there? Is that a stovepipe rocket at the end of it?"

"Yes, sir!" grinned the trooper. "Can't fire one of them blamed things from horseback! So I figure I can just ride up to one of them tripods and jam this thing up its... well somewhere it'll hurt, sir!"

"That close and you're like to blow yourself up!"

King's smile faded and he shrugged. "Maybe so, sir, but no one can 'spect to live long these days. If I can take one of those devils with me, it'll be worth it."

Dolfen realized that the man was right. Hell, he'd been training his men for months with the idea that they were all expendable if they could hurt the enemy. This wasn't any more dangerous than using the dynamite bombs. Still... *Lancers! Rocket lancers! God help us!*

"Well, be careful how you use it, Private."

"Will do, sir!" King gave him a wave which wasn't quite a salute and moved on.

Dolfen watched him go and shook his head. He had a hell of a lot of brave men in his outfit. It broke his heart to see so many killed, but what else could they do? He sighed. So now what? Gosling's question was a good one. Stay here? Ride a hundred weary miles back to Memphis and rebuild the unit again? He'd lost nearly fifty men and all but two of the armored cars were gone— destroyed or broken down and abandoned. He'd have to...

"Captain! Captain Dolfen!"

He jerked in surprise at the shout. He'd been almost dozing in the saddle. He looked and saw a courier riding up. Now what? "Yeah?" he growled.

"Orders from the Colonel, sir! We are to proceed to the river, where we will be loaded on ships to take us back to Memphis!"

"Well, I'll be damned," he said. Private Gosling was grinning.

"Beats the hell out of riding, sir!"

* * * * *

MAY, 1912, NEAR OZARK ISLAND, ARKANSAS

Commander Drew Harding eased his ship out of the mouth of the Arkansas River into the much broader waters of the Mississippi and breathed a long sigh of relief. They had made it! The retreat from Little Rock had been hell, sheer hell. The army garrison had been a disorganized shambles and so it had been left to the navy to cover the retreat. Mercifully—and inexplicably—the Martians had left them alone for a few precious hours, allowing the boats and barges to get loaded and the armed vessels to replenish their magazines. But from that point afterward, the Martians had come again and again to try and finish the job.

Santa Fe, *Olmstead*, and the other gunboats had dashed back and forth, like sheepdogs protecting their flock from a pack of wolves. They hadn't saved all of the sheep, but by God, they'd done for some of the wolves! There wasn't any doubt this time that *Santa Fe* had gotten some of the bastards. Drew could still see in his mind the one that had taken two eight-inch shells square in the head. It had been torn to pieces in a glorious explosion.

It had gone on nearly without a pause for days as the footsloggers made their slow and agonizing way down the river. Drew had barely managed a few hours of sleep a day with the attacks coming frequently and Mackenzie useless. He'd pressed young Alby Hinsworth into service as his first officer, and the boy—he was all of five years younger than him - had done an outstanding job.

Speak of the devil, here he was. Hinsworth appeared on the bridge and saluted. "Pardon me, sir, but the radio is working again. Finally got the new antenna rigged."

"Good, good. Signal *Amphitrite* and let them know."

"Aye aye, sir." The lad disappeared again.

The only saving grace during the retreat was when Amphitrite joined them. Captain Jorgensen, the monitor's commander, was the senior by a dozen years, and Drew gladly turned command over to him. With only his own ship to be worried about, the load was merely crushing instead of impossible. Mile by mile they had fought their way along, and now they were here.

So now what? He was so tired he could barely frame the question, let along produce any answers. Well, he could just wait until someone told him…

"Signal from *Amphitrite*, sir!" said Hinsworth, bustling back.

"Sweet Jesus, now what?"

"We are to head to Memphis for repairs and await orders, sir!"

Drew clutched the railing, closed his eyes, and let out his breath. "Thank God. Mr. Hinsworth, you have the con. Carry out our orders, I'm… I'm going to my bunk for a while."

"Aye, aye, sir!"

CHAPTER TEN

MAY, 1912, ST. LOUIS, MISSOURI

It was still dark when Colonel Drum woke him up. The XV Corps staff had put Wood in a ridiculously luxurious suite in the Hotel Jefferson. Despite the clean sheets and tidy appearance, the place had obviously been recently occupied and probably by General Foltz. He'd been tempted to insist that there was no need to displace the corps commander, but he supposed if they hadn't done that for him, they would have felt compelled to do it for Pershing. Protocol; there was no getting away from it, even on the edge of a battle.

"Sorry to wake you, sir," said Drum, "but it's started."

"Where?" asked Wood sitting up and swinging his legs out of bed.

"They are getting reports from all along the outer western perimeter, sir. No major attacks yet, it doesn't seem." Drum handed him a cup of coffee and Wood slurped at it appreciatively.

"Probing us. Their standard tactic. But just on the landward side? Nothing along the rivers?"

"No, sir. At least not yet."

"Good." Not a crisis then. He could at least take time to shave and dress properly. "Tell them I'll be up directly."

"Yes, sir." Drum withdrew and Wood levered himself up and into the bathroom. It was so odd, he thought, as he lathered his face; a critical, perhaps decisive, battle would soon be fought and here he was in a fine hotel, calmly shaving! It didn't seem right, somehow. It was like something out of an earlier age. Wellington at the ball in Brussels on the eve of Waterloo. Something like that.

He shaved, took care of other necessities, and carefully put on his uniform. The elevator - a bloody elevator! - took him up to the command center. He paused in the lobby and peered out a window. There were flashes of artillery in the distance and he thought he could hear a low rumble.

He entered the penthouse and saw that everyone else had preceded him. Pershing and Foltz and all their staffs were clustered around the big sand table and the maps hung on the walls. Unlike his own situation room back in Washington, all the communications people were one floor down and messages had to be sent back and forth by runners. All eyes turned to him as he came through the doors.

"Morning, gentlemen," he said. "A very early good morning! So they're here? Show me the situation."

Pershing opened his mouth to say something, but then thought better of it and turned to Foltz. Yes, this was his command and he knew it better than anyone. Pershing looked like he hadn't been out of bed much longer than Wood, while Foltz looked like he hadn't been to bed at all. He stepped forward. "We have reports of the scout tripods all along our lines from the town of Drew, here on the Missouri, down to Fenton, about halfway to the Mississippi." Foltz used a pointer to trace along the defense lines from northwest to southeast. "The reports started first at Drew and then spread down the line, so it appears the bulk of them are following along the west bank of the Missouri. It's just probes so far for the most part. When we send up flares and try to range in the artillery, they pull back out of the light for a while and then try again at another point. They are clearly scouting out our defenses, sir." While the general was talking, a captain on his staff was sticking small red flags on pins into the map.

Wood checked the time and saw that it was after three. It would start getting light in a few hours. "Well, good, if they don't make a major push until daylight, it will be to our advantage. How are you responding?"

"Until they commit themselves, I don't intend to move our reserves beyond their forward staging areas, General. The navy is on alert and getting their ships on station. Naturally, all the men are up and anyone not on the front line is being fed. All the fliers are getting their aircraft ready, and as soon as it's light, they'll go up and get us a better idea of what we're facing."

"Have there been any reports from anywhere else along the Mississippi?" Wood directed this question at Pershing.

"No, sir, nothing."

"All right, then get your 42nd Division ready to cross the river. Drum, send word to II Corps to shift north to fill the gap."

"Yes, sir," said Pershing. "What about the 1st Tank Division? Can I commit them?"

"Where would you want them to go?"

Pershing hesitated. "Until I have a better feel for where the enemy is going to strike, I can't say. But I'd like their transport ships to get as close to here as they can so there will be as little delay as possible once I do know where."

"Makes sense. Drum, see to it."

"Yes, sir."

Wood looked over the map again, wondering if there was anything they'd forgotten. "So we wait."

So they waited.

Reports continued to come in, but they were always the same: Martian tripods spotted but then disappearing again as soon as the artillery opened up on them. "They're trying to spot the location of our guns, sir," said Colonel Drum.

"Yes, no doubt. They did the same thing at Albuquerque and apparently at Little Rock and Kansas City."

"We've kept that in mind, sir," said Foltz, overhearing. "Every one of our forward field gun batteries has at least two alternate firing positions. Just before dawn I'm going to order those that have fired to shift to their secondary sites. If the Martians try to smother them with their black dust, they'll hit a deserted location."

"Excellent, General," said Wood. Foltz really had done a fine job here, but Wood wondered just how much of that was his work and how much it was his staff—or oversight by Pershing? He'd have to make some inquiries. As the war went on, the army was going to get even bigger. He was going to need new army commanders and he was toying with the idea of a command level even higher than the army - a group of armies. If Foltz was capable of greater responsibility than a corps, he wanted to know it.

Orderlies circulated serving coffee, and the hotel's kitchen was able to supply food for those who wanted it. Wood nibbled on a bacon sandwich; he wasn't really hungry, but it helped him appear calm in the eyes of his subordinates. Every hour or so he'd check his watch to discover fifteen minutes had gone by. Dawn, he wanted the dawn.

Around five, the enemy probes started to become more frequent and they spread farther south along the outer line. Assault tripods as well as the scouts were being reported. *Soon, the real attack will come soon.* Wood got up from his chair to stretch and went over to the east-facing windows. Shading his eyes against the glare from inside, he searched the horizon for a hint of the sun…

"General!" Wood turned to see Foltz gesturing to him to come over to the map.

"What's happening?"

"We're getting reports from the 58th of the spider-machines. Here, here, here… and here." He pointed to four locations along the outer perimeter.

"Numbers?"

"Nothing definite yet. A few of the forward outposts have been forced to fall back, but there's no report of huge numbers." Foltz hesitated and glanced at Pershing. "I was just about to order the artillery to reposition, sir. Do you think I should go ahead?"

Wood raised his eyebrows. It was a good question, of course. The appearance of the spiders could presage the main attack, so repositioning the guns would be a smart move. But it would take time, and if the attack came while they were on the move, the 58th might not have its artillery at a critical time. But Foltz shouldn't be asking Wood—or Pershing for that matter. It was his corps and he should be making the decision. "Do as you think best, General."

Foltz hesitated a moment longer and then nodded and turned to an aide. "Tell General Kuhn to go ahead and move his guns."

The order was sent off and activity slowed again. Wood went back to the window and was pleased to see a faint streak of pink in the eastern sky. Minute by minute the pink crawled up the sky, but it was turning a deeper shade of red instead of shifting to blue. *Red sky at morning, sailor take warning?* They didn't want bad weather, even though rain would cut down the range of the Martian heat rays. They wanted good visibility to…

"I always hated this part the most," said a voice from beside him. He turned and saw Pershing standing there. "The waiting. When you knew there would be a fight today, but you had to wait. I just wanted to get on with it."

"Yes, like that day outside Santiago in '98. Lying there under the Spanish guns for *hours!* Waiting for someone to give the order to go."

Pershing made a sound which might have been a chuckle. "I was just a lieutenant in the 10th, but I remember you and Roosevelt prowling around like caged lions. And when the word finally came, Roosevelt and his Rough Riders were off like a shot."

"Theodore has always been a man of action." Wood fell silent, thinking of those days.

"And how could any of us have imagined that just fourteen years later we'd be in a war like this?" Pershing shook his head.

"A simpler time. A different world… when the only enemy you had to worry about were other men."

"Yes, sir." Pershing stood there a moment longer, seemingly lost in his own reminiscences, and then moved away, leaving Wood to stare at the growing dawn. *I should send a report to Theodore.* He'd surely know that Wood had slipped out of Washington by now and where he had gone. Hardly a day went by when he didn't stop by Wood's office, although that had dropped off in the last few weeks since the tragic death of his military aide, Major Archie Butt, who had drowned aboard the

RMS Mauretania when it struck an iceberg and sank the previous month with a great loss of life. Butt had been on a diplomatic mission to England, and Roosevelt was in mourning; his usually dynamic energy damped down. He'd bounce back, of course, he always did. Wood remembered his friend in Cuba where he'd weep over the death of one of his beloved Rough Riders and then the next day be out there leading more of them to their deaths. A complex man…

Wood's time as an army surgeon had stripped war of every vestige of glory and romance. When he saw men dying of pneumonia or dysentery on a daily basis, in addition to those mangled in actual combat, it gave him a different perspective on life and death. Yes, he mourned those lost and respected those who soldiered on and risked a death like that, but he'd put it all behind a glass wall to keep the stench of it from driving him mad. If he'd had to mourn each of the hundred thousand men he'd lost in 1910…

Am I going to lose another hundred thousand this week?

It could happen. There were no accurate figures on the losses at Kansas City and Little Rock yet, but they could total thirty or forty thousand. This fight for St. Louis could easily cost another sixty thousand - *even if we win.*

And if we lose…? If they lost, if the Martians got across the river and began to rampage across the east, the deaths would be in the millions. *Well, Leonard, you wanted this job. Now you've got to do it.*

He shook his head to clear out those disturbing thoughts and turned away from the window, back to the map. More messages had arrived and Foltz and his staff were pouring over them. Wood walked over to them. "Something new?"

"Yes, sir," said Foltz, "we've got reports of the spider-machines showing up in the 58th's rear areas. Not a lot of reports, but some. It appears they are slipping through our lines in the dark." Foltz frowned. "Our outpost line isn't continuous, it can't be with so few troops, but it was designed to spot the tripods, not these smaller machines."

"They might not be heavy enough to set off the pit traps we've dug, and they probably aren't as vulnerable to getting stuck in the mud, either," said Pershing. "Damn, some of my officers had suggested stringing barbed wire like the Russians and Japanese did in their war, but I said no because the tripods would just step right over it. Maybe I was wrong. It might stop *these* things. Or at least make them reveal themselves breaking through."

"The tactics keep evolving," nodded Wood.

More reports came in of the spider-machines. Several of the relocating artillery batteries had run into them and one had been routed and the others forced to flee further to the rear, some losing guns in the process. Some of the telegraph and telephone connections to the forward posts were being cut. The 58th was dispatching teams with the stovepipe rocket launchers to try and deal with the intruders. Wood tried to imagine the courage it would take to stalk such things in the dark.

But it wasn't all that dark anymore. The sun was not quite up yet, but there was more than enough light to see by. In addition to the rumble of artillery, he could now hear the drone of aircraft. A half-dozen airfields had been built in and around St. Louis, and with the dawn, the airmen were aloft. Some of the larger, multi-engined craft carried radios, and hopefully they would start sending back good information on the enemy's whereabouts and numbers.

Runners brought in more messages and one was handed to Foltz with special urgency. "Looks like they've stopped their dancing about, sir," he said after reading it. "A force of at least thirty tripods is attacking the outpost at Drew. Our artillery is hitting them, but they are coming on." New red flags were appearing on the sand table. After a few more minutes, another outpost farther south along the line reported the same thing. It looked like the main attack was beginning.

After Wood's brain surgery two years ago, his doctor had absolutely forbidden him to smoke again. He had obeyed, and for the most part he'd been able to resist the urge with no real problem. But nearly all the men around him were smoking like chimneys and suddenly he wanted a cigarette more than he could ever remember. Rather than give in - or stand there fidgeting - he turned and strode away, down the long penthouse ballroom, his hands clasped behind his back.

At the far end of the space was another big table which was covered with a more conventional paper map. This was the artillery plotting area. Between the artillery batteries organic to the infantry divisions, the attached corps and army-level batteries, the heavy guns built into the fortifications, and the weapons on the navy ships, there were close to a thousand artillery pieces arrayed for the defense of St. Louis. They were all coordinated from here. The map showed the artillery positions and the whole area was set out with an overlaid grid. The officers here could direct the fire of any gun to any location within its range. The men were very busy, getting reports on potential targets, receiving specific requests for fire, calculating which guns to use, and issuing the firing instructions. As Wood watched them, he heard the rumbles from outside grow louder. More and more guns, which had stood idle during the early skirmishing, were being committed to the fight.

As he studied their activity, Wood's admiration for the skill of the men grew. He knew the basic principles of what they were doing, but the actual mechanics of making it work were beyond him. These men were experts and he thanked God they were here. The artillery was their best hope to stop these monsters. The sun was fully up now, and though partially obscured by clouds, light was streaming in the eastern windows.

"General?" Wood turned and saw that Pershing was there.

"Yes?"

"Foltz is going to order the 58th to pull back. They've got as many as a hundred and fifty tripods hitting them at six different locations, and if they try to hold any longer, we won't get any of them back."

"All right, carry on." He followed Black Jack over to the sand table. There were a lot more red flags on it now. Foltz looked up as he approached.

"Aircraft are reporting several hundred additional tripods massing in this area, near Manchester, sir." He pointed to the table. "It looks like they are getting ready to do their flying wedge right through the line. My boys can't hold against that."

"No, best get them out of there," agreed Wood.

"Yes, sir, I'll have them fall back to the Donnelson Line northwest of the city. I'm hoping to draw the enemy in that direction. I just hope those damn spiders don't slow up the withdrawal." Wood looked at where Foltz was pointing and nodded. If they could get the Martians to hit the secondary line built between the city walls and the Missouri, perhaps they could get them to expend their strength there. Even if they broke through that - and he was sure they would - they would still have to attack the main defenses around St. Louis, itself. But if their line of attack went farther south, they'd hit the walls on the south side of the city and the defenses to the northwest would be wasted.

"General," said Pershing, "the 42nd is on the move, they'll start crossing the river into the city within the hour, although it will take the better part of the day to get them all here. I'd like to start landing the 1st Tank Division at the city docks as well."

"That's where you want to commit them, then? As a central reserve?"

"Yes, sir," said Pershing. He straightened up from the table, sighed, and rubbed his chin. "I had been thinking about using them in some grand outflanking movement by landing them down river, behind the enemy positions. Pull off a Cannae or an Austerlitz and get my name in the history books. Mighty alluring, but it just won't work. Without the docks and the cranes it would take a full day to land just the tanks, and once they were ashore they'd have to drive for miles through all the flooded ground we've created just to get into action. We'd lose half of them before they got close enough to shoot. No, I've got to play it safe with this."

Wood could fully understand Pershing's frustration. But he was right. To try something bold here might see the whole, very powerful force wasted. "I think you're right, John. We know the Martians are coming here. Let's give them a warm welcome."

Pershing and Foltz continued to issue orders and receive reports. The 58th Division was being hard pressed, but only in a few spots. Most of the troops and guns were falling back along their pre-planned routes, covered by artillery fire from more distant batteries. Air reconnaissance reported that things were very bad in those spots where the Martians were concentrating and losses were heavy there, the enemy advancing faster than the troops could retreat. But the aircraft were also reporting that significant numbers of tripods were blundering into swampy ground and getting stuck when they tried to pursue soldiers who fled off the roads. Artillery was zeroed in on the immobilized Martians, and a number of machines had been destroyed.

The morning dragged by and the blue flags from the forward lines moved back toward the Donnelson Line while several thick concentrations of red flags headed in the same direction. Toward noon, Wood and the other generals were becoming concerned that one large mass of red was drifting eastward toward the southern section of the city walls; but then fire from gunboats on the Meramec River started hitting them from the rear, and more ships on the Mississippi joined in, causing the Martians to veer westward again toward the Donnelson Line where they wanted them to go. They all breathed easier.

Noon came and Wood forced himself to eat something, although he had no appetite at all. As he chewed on a sandwich, he noticed a new officer arrive who almost immediately started arguing with Pershing. He recognized him as General Mason Patrick, the commander of the air forces in the St. Louis area. Wood got up and went over to the pair.

"General, my men are champing at the bit!" said Patrick.

"They're just going to have to champ a bit longer, Mase," replied Pershing. "They are doing a fantastic job with the reconnaissance and artillery spotting, but I'm not going to commit your bombers and attack aircraft until the right moment."

"But dammit, sir, there are hundreds of targets out there right now!"

Wood came up and both men turned to face him. "So, General Patrick, your men want to fight?"

"Yes, sir! We've been training for months, but except for dumping load after load of bombs on dirt mounds, we haven't been allowed to do anything!"

Wood bounced slightly on his heels and clasped his hands behind his back. "General, I can guarantee you that your men will be allowed to fight - and very soon. This battle has barely begun, and we are going to need every man to win it."

"But sir..."

"However, General Pershing is correct: the moment is not quite here. We all know how brave your men are, and the terrible losses they endure when directly attacking the tripods. We can't afford to waste them in random attacks. Use your bombers certainly - from a safe altitude - but the low-level attacks, they are the most effective and the most costly. We must save them for the proper moment: when the enemy is most concentrated and already heavily engaged with our ground forces. Patience, General, patience."

Patrick frowned and chewed on his lip, but eventually he nodded. "I understand, sir. But, sir, what if this 'proper moment' comes during the night? My boys won't hesitate to fly in the dark if they have to, but they won't be nearly as effective and I could lose half of them to accidents. And two of my airfields are up here, behind the Donnelson Line, and they could be overrun if we wait too long!" he pointed to the area in the northern bend of the rivers.

"A valid concern," conceded Wood. "But I'm confident we can hold them through at least one night. The crisis will be tomorrow, General. We'll need your boys tomorrow."

"If you say so, sir." Patrick clearly wasn't happy and Wood could understand. Holding back the planes was a risk, and he hoped he was making the right decision. Patrick saluted and left.

"Bit of a firebrand, isn't he?" said Pershing.

"Yes, but that's what we need for that sort of job." He went back to look at the sand table. The flags representing the 58th Division were being moved into their fall-back positions in the second line. More flags were being moved from the docks in St. Louis to the same area. These were the 42nd Division. It was quite a distance for them, but fortunately a railroad paralleled the defense line and they were making use of it. The flags already in the line were for the 19th Division.

They were taking a risk here with this redeployment. The 19th was holding the entire length of the line. Not knowing just how much of the 58th would make it back safely, it had been too dangerous to have the 19th only holding part of the line and praying that the 58th could fill in the unoccupied sections. So that meant that the 58th would be intermingled with the 19th along the line. And it was the same situation with the newly arriving 42nd. There was no section reserved for them, either, and it would have been crazy to put them into a totally new location in the middle of a battle anyway. All three divisions were going to be jumbled together and that was a recipe for confusion. But there was no other real choice. Trying to shuffle troops around so each division had its own section of the line in the face of the enemy was simply impossible. Each unit would have to dig in and hold where it was. General William Weigel, commander of the 19th Division, was being given tactical command of the line, although Foltz would be looking over his shoulder very closely.

More flags began to appear and these were the forces of the 1st Tank Division. Their ships were at the city wharfs and unloading. They would head out to form a reserve for the troops holding the Donnelson Line. Wood hoped they could get there in time. The red flags were getting close. Several other blue flags caught Wood's eye and he leaned forward to see what was written on them. He straightened up and looked sharply at Pershing.

"You've sent the Little Davids out beyond the walls?" Wood had assumed the six self-propelled twelve-inch gun vehicles would be kept as a last reserve.

"It seemed like the proper thing, General. As tall as they are, they aren't tall enough to fire over the city walls, at least not directly. They could fire indirectly, of course, but we have plenty of other heavy guns for that. They seem like ideal long range snipers to pick off tripods with direct fire. And with only one gate in the walls big enough for them to pass through, I felt that having them backing up the Donnelson Line was the best use for them. They can always fall back if they are threatened."

Wood scowled. What Pershing said was true, but they had spent so much time and money on the blasted things, he didn't want to risk losing them unnecessarily. Still, he'd given them to Pershing to use and it was Black Jack's command, so he just nodded and remained silent.

Damn, war was becoming so complicated! Wood had spent most of his career with just the traditional infantry, artillery, and cavalry. Even though he had no formal military training, he had caught on how to use them - and how to lead them - quickly. He'd gone from a contract surgeon to leading an ad hoc infantry formation against Geronimo, to colonel of a regiment of volunteer cavalry, to commanding a brigade, and then a division in Cuba. Each step up had been more complicated, but the cogs of the machine had been mostly the same. But now, now there were

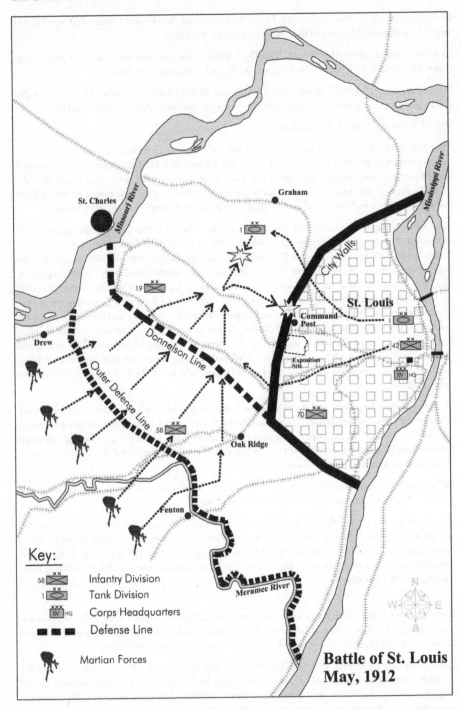

**Battle of St. Louis
May, 1912**

Key:

58 ⊠ ××   Infantry Division

1 ⬭ ××   Tank Division

XV ×××HQ   Corps Headquarters

      Defense Line

      Martian Forces

airplanes and radios and steam tanks and huge, clanking war machines, and God only knew what else to try and keep track of and coordinate.

But this was the only way they could hope to win.

The afternoon dragged on. The leading elements of the Martian forces reached the Donnelson Line and recoiled, hammered by masses of artillery. This new resistance seemed to surprise the enemy and they drew back, apparently to regroup. "Surely they didn't think the forward line was all we had," said Foltz.

"We have no idea what, or even how, they think," said Wood. "But this is giving us the time to get our forces in place, so let's be thankful."

"Yes, sir, except night's coming. I'd rather not fight these bastards in the dark if we can avoid it."

"I doubt we can avoid it. They know we're not as effective at night, so they'll probably wait. I'd expect them to do the same sort of probing attacks as they did on the first line."

"And they'll probably try to infiltrate those damn spider-machines again, Fred. Better alert your troops to keep a close watch tonight," said Pershing.

"Yes, sir, and this line is held strongly enough we ought to be able to stop them from sneaking through."

Wood nodded and then asked the question he always hated. "Any figures on losses? Ours and theirs?"

Pershing called over his intelligence officer, a colonel named Dowding. He wore spectacles and rummaged through a sheaf of papers. "Reports have been coming in, General, but it's too early to have really good figures."

"I know. But what's your best guess?"

"It seems like the 116th Brigade of the 58th took the brunt of things. Still, their losses don't look too bad. Maybe a thousand men lost, along with a dozen guns or so. The other brigade, the 117th, got off more lightly. Maybe five hundred men and only a few guns. As for Martian losses…" he rummaged some more. "Maybe fifty tripods destroyed. We don't have any good estimates for the spider-machines, I'm sorry, sir."

"Fifty? Out of how many? Do you have any figures on their total force?"

"It's hard to get a good count, since they can move around so quickly. Easy to count the same one twice, you know. But we are estimating a force of around five hundred tripods, sir. No idea on the spiders."

Wood suppressed a shudder. Five hundred tripods? It seemed an enormous force, far larger than the force which had routed the army in 1910. *We're a lot stronger now, too.* And they'd killed a tenth of this force before they even got to the main defenses… except…

"We've gotten reports that the Martians are recovering the pilots out of wrecked tripods and transferring them to spare machines so they can return to the fight. Your men need to make sure that they destroy the tripods completely and kill the pilots."

"Yes, sir," said Pershing. "We've instructed the men about that and we have teams with every company which have demolition charges - much larger than what the infantry normally carry—to go out and finish off the damaged machines."

"Excellent." He paused. "It will take good men for a job like that."

"Yes, sir, and we've got 'em. Damn good men."

The day drew to a close without a serious attack on the Donnelson Line. It appeared that the

Martians were calling up their own reserves and returning to the probing attacks they'd used before. Wood, guessing that they had a few hours before the next round would commence, went down to his own suite and lay down. Despite his exhaustion, it was hard to sleep, but he finally drifted off.

* * * * *

CYCLE 597, 845.1, EAST OF HOLDFAST 32-4

Qetjnegartis halted its fighting machine and looked out at river 3-1. The artificial satellite had provided exact measurements of the feature, but somehow it appeared far larger than expected. Qetjnegartis had not yet seen the planet's oceans, so it knew that there were bodies of water vastly larger than this river, but it had never seen so much water in one place before and it was impressive.

And daunting.

"Forcing a crossing will not be easy, Commander," said Kantangnar, leader of Battlegroup 32-4, which had escorted it here. "Preliminary reconnaissance has shown the river to be deep with a strong current, and a very soft bottom. It is not known if our machines can cross it at all. We have tried to send drones across, all have been lost, either swept away, or hopelessly stuck in the mire."

It used the magnifier in its machine to study the defenses of city 3-37 on the far shore. They were elaborate and formidable, using huge amounts of the cast stone material which was so resistant to the heat rays. There were also very many of the large projectile throwers, both on the shore and on vessels in the river. Some of them were firing the new flares which the prey-creatures were using to provide artificial light. The approach of the battlegroup had not gone unnoticed, despite the darkness.

The prospect of attempting to cross here was not a pleasant one. Losses could be extreme and victory by no means assured. But Group 33 to the north was launching a major attack at this very moment, and Group 32 would have to launch its own assault as soon as possible. Still, there was no absolute necessity to launch the attack at this exact spot...

"We cannot remain here long, Commander," said Kantangnar. "The enemy will concentrate its fire on this location if we do not move."

"Understood. I have seen enough."

CHAPTER ELEVEN

MAY, 1912, ST. LOUIS, MISSOURI

Wood had managed a few hours sleep, but he still felt very tired, his head full of fog. He yawned as he rolled out of the bed and took the mug of coffee Colonel Drum offered him. Had Drum slept? Probably not. As he drank, he went over to the western window in his room and looked out. The sky was dotted with tiny lights drifting slowly earthward. Star shells the men were calling them, but even from fifteen miles away, they were brighter than any of the true stars in the sky. Wood checked his watch and saw that it was still an hour shy of midnight when the waning moon was due to rise. With the clouds he'd seen at dusk, he doubted the moon would be much help.

There were plenty of other lights out there, too. With the enemy closing in on the main defenses, nearly all the artillery was coming into action and there was a constant flickering of the guns, most in the far distance, but some much closer by. Those nearer flashes tore away the night for an instant, lighting up the landscape and rattling the hotel's windows.

He went back up to the command center to see what was happening. The first thing he noticed was that Fred Foltz wasn't there. "He's gone out to a forward command post," explained Pershing. "With those three divisions mixed together he wants to make sure there are no foul-ups." Wood nodded. It was a good move; the last thing they needed now was the three division commanders arguing over who was in charge.

"So you'll command the rest of the corps from here," said Wood. It was a statement, not a question.

"Seems to make the most sense, sir." Pershing paused and then added. "I think the main attack will start very soon. The front line troops are reporting that more and more of the spider-machines and tripods are massing."

"How are the star shells holding out?"

"We've used a lot, but we've got at least enough for the rest of tonight. If it's not settled by tomorrow night… we may be in trouble."

"I'll have some shipped in from the reserve stocks of 5th Army."

Another hour of anxious waiting proved Pershing correct. The spider-machines began to overwhelm some of the forward strongpoints, despite scores of them being destroyed. Then three groups of tripods, each over a hundred strong, punched their way through the defense lines at different points. This was just what they had done at Albuquerque.

But unlike Albuquerque, the line did not collapse.

There were a dozen concrete forts, each studded with powerful guns, along the line and these served as anchors and rally points to the soldiers in the earthen trenches and bunkers. The troops on each side of the breaches folded back to the nearest fort and continued to fight. The forts were designed to fight in any direction, so their guns blasted away at the Martians moving past them, and many tripods turned to deal with the threat. This gave Foltz time to send his reserve tank battalions forward to counterattack the penetrations. The 1st Tank Division wasn't in position yet, but XV Corps had eight battalions of its own tanks, almost three hundred of them, on hand and they rumbled forward to engage.

Wood stared at the big sand table as red and blue flags were moved around and suddenly couldn't stand it anymore. Maps and models! He needed to see! He found some binoculars and dragged Drum up to the roof of the hotel. The horizon in every direction was a constant blaze of gun flashes. Guns in the city, guns north of the Donnelson Line, guns from the ships on the Mississippi, Missouri, and Meramec, and even a few long range guns from across the river in Illinois were firing as fast as they could. Out there on the open rooftop, the noise was much louder, a constant deep rumble, punctuated by sharp bangs from the closer batteries.

"God Almighty," whispered Drum, staring at the spectacle.

All that firepower was being directed against a few square miles of landscape about fifteen miles off to the west. Wood trained his binoculars that way, hoping to see the results of this incredible onslaught. Surely something was happening! There was smoke and flames and an almost continuous string of explosions, but it was all tiny and far away and impossible to interpret accurately. A westerly wind was coming up and a strong smell of burning was in the air.

Wood watched for a while, but he grew increasingly frustrated. "I need to get closer," he growled.

"I, uh, rather thought you would, General," said Drum. "I've located a secondary command post on the city walls which ought to have a better view. If you want, we can get there in half an hour, sir."

Wood smiled. "You're a good man, Hugh. Get a car ready. I'll tell Pershing what I'm up to."

"Yes, sir."

They went downstairs, Drum to fetch the car and Wood to confer with Pershing. Black Jack didn't seem surprised - or upset - that his senior would finally get out from underfoot. "I'll have any important news relayed to where you'll be, sir," he said. "That post has a full set of telephones."

"Thanks. I'll probably be back here before too long, John. Just need to stretch my legs a bit."

"I completely understand, sir. Be careful out there."

Wood took the elevator down to the sumptuous lobby of the hotel and then out the revolving doors onto the street. Drum was waiting there with a staff car and driver. For some reason the guns were even louder down here and the smell of burning even stronger. They got aboard and the car lurched into motion.

"Gonna have to take a few detours, sir!" shouted the driver. "The streets are fulla trucks 'n tanks 'n guns!"

And so they were. While the bulk of the 42nd Division's fighting formations had already reached the front, the division's logistical train was still moving through the city. Long lines of horse-drawn wagons and motor trucks heading west clogged many of the main streets. And on parallel roads were the tanks and vehicles of the 1st Tank Division, still moving up from the docks. Their driver was forced to take smaller side streets.

At one intersection, they had to wait as a column of steam tanks, smoke belching from their stacks, clanked past. They were mostly the newer Mark IIIs, with the side gun sponsons, but following along were several behemoths which were much larger.

"Good God!" exclaimed the driver. "Lookit those bastards!"

"The Mark IVs," said Wood, nodding. He'd seen drawings of them, but never in the flesh. They looked rather like the Mark IIIs, except they were about twice as large in every dimension. Easily thirty feet long, they sprouted guns from the hull, from side sponsons, and a big cylindrical turret sitting on top. They were so wide they nearly filled the street, and as he watched, a telephone pole was snagged by one of the guns and snapped off like a twig. He could feel the ground shuddering as they lumbered past.

The driver looked at the column nervously and when he saw a slightly longer gap between the tanks, gunned the engine and roared across the street to the other side. Wood gripped the armrest of his seat and winced. "Easy there!" shouted Drum. "Get us there in one piece, will you?"

"Sorry, sir. Thought we was in a hurry!"

They wove their way through back streets and eventually emerged near a large park. It had been the site of the 1904 Louisiana Purchase Exposition and many of the bigger exhibit buildings were still there. Millions of people had attended. Wood had missed the exposition, being in the Philippines at the time, but Roosevelt had come and described it to him several times. It had been a world's fair with all the most advanced technology of the time on display. Now, the park was displaying some of the world's most advanced weaponry. A dozen or more heavy artillery batteries had been sited on the open ground and were in full operation. The flashes of the guns lit up the classical facades of the buildings, and from the looks of things, had broken many of their windows, too.

The new city walls were just beyond the park. A line of concrete, gleaming white in the gun flashes, marched across the western skyline. The walls were a good thirty feet tall with higher towers at intervals. It looked for all the world like some ancient fortification like what Hadrian's Wall or the Great Wall of China must have looked like in their glory. *If only it was just barbarians we were trying to keep out.*

They drove to a spot a few blocks northwest of the park and stopped next to an especially large tower. An officer with the collar disks of the coast artillery was there to meet them. "General Wood!" he shouted above the roar of the guns. "I'm Major Bill Hase, I just received word you were coming!"

"Didn't mean to trouble you, Major. Just wanted to get a closer look. Can you see anything from up there?" He pointed at the tower.

"Hell, yes, sir! Helluva fight going on to the southwest! Come on! Take a look for yourself!" Hase led the way inside the massive concrete tower and up a flight of stairs. Just below the top, he paused at a landing and motioned. "Main command center for this section of the line is in there, sir." Wood peered inside and saw a dimly lit room with narrow view slits and a dozen men; spotters for the artillery, he assumed. "Better view from up top, though."

"Lead on."

They went the rest of the way up onto the roof. Wood was a bit winded after the five-story climb. There were a few men already up there, peering through binoculars and a small telescope. Wood went to the parapet and looked around. The tower was higher than the walls and projected out in front of them a bit so he could look along their length.

The walls were thirty feet high, but only about eight feet thick. Against rifled artillery, they would be breached pretty quickly. But the Martian heat rays had no impact like an artillery round and concrete had proved to be the perfect insulator against the high temperatures of the alien weapons. Eight feet of concrete could defeat the rays almost indefinitely. In front of the wall was a ditch about ten feet deep, although this one was full of water. The experts claimed that a tripod could not climb over the wall. Wood hoped they were right.

The top of the wall had a parapet tall enough for men to shield themselves behind and spots where they could fire out. There were a few machine gun teams at intervals but not many other troops. Wood hoped there were more in reserve somewhere. A few hundred feet to the north there was a broad platform behind the wall on which was mounted a large gun on a disappearing mount. In the loading position, the gun was completely concealed behind the wall. But once loaded and aimed, a counterweight would lift the gun up above the wall for a moment where it would fire. The recoil would drive the gun back down to the loading position. Done properly, it would only be exposed for a few seconds to return fire by the Martians. Wood could make out another platform farther along the wall, and maybe another one beyond that. In the flickering dark it was hard to tell. Walking to the other side of the tower, he could see a similar arrangement going in the opposite direction.

"Quite a set-up you have here, Major."

"Thank you sir. We're the 112th Coast Artillery. I've got six of these twelve-inchers under my command."

"The 112th? You were originally stationed at…?"

"Fort DuPont, sir. Well, our guns were mostly at Fort Delaware in the middle of the river, but we lived at DuPont."

"Oh yes, I remember," said Wood. He didn't add that he also remembered the 112th had the worst gunnery scores in the entire army. A report had crossed his desk several years earlier noting how they'd inadvertently fired a dud practice round into downtown Salem, New Jersey. Now that they'd been transferred to St. Louis, he hoped their gunnery had improved.

"I think we can see something from here, General," said Drum gesturing to him from the western edge of the tower. Wood moved over to join him, and Hase offered him a much larger pair of binoculars than what he'd been using. He brought them up to his eyes and focused on an area where there seemed to be a lot of explosions.

Between the larger binoculars, and being five miles closer, he could see quite a lot now. There were clouds of smoke, glowing red from raging fires, billowing up from several areas. Burning villages? Burning supply dump? Burning tanks? All three perhaps. And silhouetted against those clouds he could see tripods, still very small, even with the binoculars, but unmistakable. The light of the drifting flares reflected off others as they moved. Their heat rays stabbed out at intervals and new fires would erupt. From time to time, patches of inky darkness would appear in the midst of the battle, blotting out everything.

"What's that?" asked Drum. "Their black dust weapon?"

"Probably. They like to use it against our artillery and they must be in among some of the batteries behind the defense line by now." Wood didn't like to think what that horrible poison was probably doing to the men and horses out there.

But the Martians were being hit in return. Exploding shells burst around and sometimes on the tripods, obscuring them for a moment—or sometimes obscuring them permanently. Shells had to be raining down on them from almost every direction. Looking to where the Martians were firing their heat rays, he thought he could see small shapes firing back at them. Tanks or maybe field batteries, he couldn't really tell, but whoever it was, they were fighting.

"Looks like they are moving north, across our front, sir," said Drum. He had to shout because the noise here was much louder. "They'll run smack into the 1st Tank Division if they keep going that way."

"Good!" Or he hoped it was good. What if the tanks weren't ready yet? They needed to give them all the support they could. He looked north and south along the wall and then at Major Hase. "Your guns don't seem to be firing, Major."

"No, sir," said the young man, looking frustrated. "We've got orders not to."

"Why not? You've certainly got targets."

"Yes, sir, but we're not really set up to fire a barrage like most of the big guns. We can't lob a shell up in an arc so it comes down right on the bastards. We're designed to fire directly at them - like we would at a ship. And right now if we miss, our shells will fly for miles and probably land right in the midst of friendly troops. We've got orders to wait until they're closer - and for daylight." Hase seemed very eager. "Of course, if you ordered us to shoot…"

"I see," said Wood. Yes, that did make sense, but he shared Hase's frustration that these big guns were out of action. Still, he wasn't going to override whoever had given the order. He said no more and Hase went away disappointed. He watched for a while longer and then went down to the command post to see what he could learn about the big picture. *I should have stayed back at the hotel! What was I doing coming out here?*

The word from headquarters indicated that the eight tank battalions from the XV Corps had hurt the Martians significantly, but they had shot their bolt, taken heavy losses, and the survivors were falling back to join up with the 1st Tank Division, which was still assembling a few miles to the north. Fortunately, the Martians weren't pressing them closely. They still seemed distracted by the forts on their flanks and rear, although they had overrun two of them. It was now after two o'clock and it would start getting light around five. The aircraft could join in the fight then and gunnery would improve. Pershing had no good figures on how badly the Martians had been hurt, but it seemed plain to Wood that the battle was going to be decided, one way or another, in the morning.

They watched from the roof again and the fight was definitely drifting to their right, to the north. It had been off to the southwest, but now the heart of the battle was almost due west. Wood asked Drum to see if there were any similar command posts farther north along the walls in case he wanted to move to follow the action.

But as he continued to watch, it seemed the action had stalled.

There was still a hell of a lot of firing going on, but the Martians were no longer advancing. From what Wood could see, they were milling around in the same general area, shooting their heat rays from time to time and dodging fire, but they had stopped moving north. A trip down to the command post confirmed it. Pershing believed they were regrouping, massing their tripods and spider-machines. "They've pulled away from the forts along the Donnelson Line," he said over the telephone. "They're all assembling in that area near the town of Lackland."

"Regrouping," agreed Wood, "but to do what?"

"I guess we'll find out, sir."

He hung up and went back up to the roof. An hour went by and Drum found some coffee for them. Major Hase pleaded with him again to be allowed to open fire with his big guns, but Wood refused. The chance of a direct hit at this range was slim, and a miss could fly all the way to the Missouri. It would be a fine addition to the 112th's record if they sank a navy warship on the river!

More time passed and finally there was a faint glimmer in the eastern sky that wasn't caused by artillery. The sun was coming at last after what had seemed an endless night. But what sort of day would this new dawn bring?

What are you bastards up to? Wood stared through the binoculars and tried to force them to produce an answer. *They can't stay where they are. Given time, we'll pound them to pieces. If they go south, it will just be back the way they came; a retreat. To the north they'll hit the 1st Tanks and that will draw them further into the pocket with the navy on three sides of them. West will take them to the Missouri. That's no threat, but it could be another direction to retreat. The only other way they can go is…*

"General! Sir!" Drum was pointing. "I think they're moving, sir! It looks like they're… like they're coming…"

"East. Straight for us."

"Yes, sir. General, we better get back to the main command post," said Drum, gesturing toward the stairs.

"I'm staying here."

"But, sir!"

Wood stared right at Drum, the young man's face looked pale in the flickering light. "This is where we stop them, Hugh. I'm done retreating. We will stop them *right here!*"

Drum swallowed and then nodded. "Yes, sir."

"Get word to Pershing. Tell him what's happening. Have him concentrate his forces here. Get the 1st Tanks and the Little Davids on the move: hit them in the flank, by God. Get the planes in the air and send every man he's got to the walls."

"Yes, sir!" Drum dashed down the stairs to the command post. Wood turned to Hase, who had been hovering close by.

"Major, you may commence firing."

"Yes, sir! Thank you, sir!" Hase gave a whoop and he too disappeared down the stairs.

Wood went back to the parapet and raised the binoculars once again. Yes, the enemy had stopped their dithering and were on the move again - straight for him. The artillery was shifting its aim to follow them, but for a few minutes, the Martians outdistanced the fire and broke clear of the clouds of smoke and dust which had cloaked them. The growing light in the east was illuminating them better than the star shells now and they were painted in a pink glow. He caught his breath when the Martians crested a slight ridge and almost their whole force was put on display. There were more than he could count easily, several hundred at least, their metal legs bringing them closer and closer.

An old memory suddenly surfaced and he blinked. Years ago, when he was the military governor of Cuba after the war, one of the local officials had taken him on a trip to a remote area of the coast where a strange phenomenon occurred every year. Thousands, millions of land crabs emerged from the jungles to make a trek down to the beaches to lay their eggs. The land was absolutely carpeted with the things, their multiple legs moving with unwavering determination, even if some of their fellows were crushed by passing carts or human feet. They were driven by some irresistible instinct to make the journey no matter what. What Wood was seeing now seemed just like that - an unstoppable wave.

Not this time! This time we are going to stop them!

They were still at least five miles away, but Wood knew the machines could move very fast when they wanted to. They could be here in twenty minutes if they came straight on. But as he continued to watch, he realized that they were not moving all that fast, and then as the light grew, he could see why. At their feet was another swarm of smaller machines. Or so he assumed; at this distance he could see no details, just a mass of moving objects around the larger tripods. The spider-machines. Reports had said that they were slower than the big tripods, and it seemed as though that was true. Well, good! One of the chief strengths of the big tripods was their speed. If these little things slowed them down, it would be a big help—at least on the strategic scale.

Drum rejoined him on the roof top. "I told Pershing and he's directing all his reserves here, sir. He asked me if you'd be coming back to the main headquarters. He seemed a bit put out when I told him you were staying."

"I expect he would be. Well, so be it."

"I found these for you, sir. *Please* take them." He held out a steel helmet and one of the anti-dust kits. It consisted of a canvas bag holding the hood and mask with breathing filters and a pair of leather gloves to protect the hands. "I didn't bother getting the leggings since you already have your boots. Please, sir, we've seen them using the black dust."

"Very well," said Wood, looping the strap of bag over his neck, exchanging his hat for the helmet, and stuffing the gloves in his pocket. "Did you get a set for yourself?"

"Yes, sir. I have them right…"

A huge roar drowned out whatever else Drum was going to say. A moment later there was another roar and then a third. Wood walked over to the north side of the tower and saw clouds of smoke billowing up around the platforms for the disappearing guns. Hase hadn't wasted any time. He immediately turned and went over to the south side, just in time to see the other three go into action. One by one the big guns rose up on their carriages as the counterweights were released. Their muzzles poked over the top of the wall for a few seconds, then a blast of flame belched out, and the recoils drove them back down into the loading position. Three more crashes of noise left his ears ringing.

Impressive, but are they hitting anything?

He directed his attention back to the enemy, but he couldn't see any notable effect by the twelve-inchers. The other artillery was tracking the movement of the enemy force again and shell bursts were making it hard to see. Hard, but not impossible. A savage grin crossed his face as one of the tripods stumbled and then fell to the ground. *We're hitting them.*

A tap on his shoulder made him look aside and there was Drum again, holding out a small ball of cotton. He pointed to his ears. The roar of the big guns made it perfectly clear what it was for. Wood nodded, took the cotton, ripped it into two pieces and stuffed them into his ears. He picked up the binoculars again and continued to watch the unfolding battle.

The Martians were closing, maybe four miles away now, but they didn't seem to be advancing as quickly as before. Explosions continued to erupt around them, but they were shooting back at things Wood couldn't see. Infantry? Tanks concealed in gullies? He couldn't tell.

Drum tapped him again and pointed up. Aircraft were now overhead in growing swarms. Most of them were the smaller ones and at low altitude, but he spotted a few higher up. They were high enough to catch the sunlight which was not yet touched the dark landscape. There were two distinct groups of the small ones close by and he thought he could make out another group or two off to the north. They were circling, waiting, while others joined up with them; massing their strength before they attacked. Yes, the planes needed to attack en masse or they'd just be picked off before they could accomplish anything.

The enemy must have seen the aircraft, but they didn't pause, they kept on coming. Four miles, three miles, the smaller spider-machines were clearly visible now. Hundreds and hundreds of them, although from time to time Wood could see them - or bits of them - flung into the air by the exploding artillery shells.

"Sir? Maybe we should get back to headquarters." Drum had to put his mouth right next to his ear and shout to be heard. Wood just shook his head.

And then the aircraft made their attack. A swarm of at least a hundred swept by almost overhead, the noise of their engines even overpowering that of the guns. Three other groups came in from different directions.

Now the Martians did halt. They quickly formed several tightly-spaced concentric circles facing out in all directions. Wood realized what they were doing and groaned. *No! Break off! You don't have a chance against that!*

But the pilots, those brave, crazy pilots, kept right on going; and then the Martian heat rays lashed out, hundreds of them, and the sky was suddenly full of blazing aircraft and dying fliers. One group after another bore in against their target only to meet the same fate. A few made it through, close enough to fire their machine guns and drop their bombs, and Wood even saw a tripod go down here and there, but it was a feeble accomplishment against such a cost.

The survivors, only a few score of them, pulled out of range and tried to reorganize themselves. Wood prayed that they'd have the sense not to try again. *Damn, what a waste...*

"Sir! Look!" Drum was shaking his shoulder.

Explosions, huge explosions, far larger than artillery would cause, were suddenly erupting in and around the Martian formation! For an instant, Wood thought that perhaps they were from the big disappearing guns along the wall or perhaps some of the railroad guns from across the river, but no, there were far too many of them. He looked up and saw the bombers overhead, just small dots high up in the sky. Bombs!

The wave of explosions marched through the Martian circles and it was too late for them to spread out or avoid them. Tripods were torn apart and flung skyward. One of them blew up in a huge blue flash that left Wood's eyes dazzled. *That hurt them!* A loud rumble shook the tower to its foundation.

It was all over in a just a minute or two. The bombers flew on in a stately fashion and then turned to head back to their bases. As the smoke cleared, Wood could see ragged holes in the enemy formation. He couldn't tell how many machines had been destroyed, but a few dozen at least. Probably a lot of the spider-machines as well. The enemy was trying to reorganize itself, but the artillery, which had paused its fire during the air attack, was finding the range again. The Martians seemed to realize that they couldn't stay there and lurched into motion again.

But they hadn't gone more than a few hundred yards when something tore through them from right to left. In Cuba, Wood had seen rifle fire slicing through tall grass, clipping off stalks. It was just like this now. Several tripods had arms torn away or legs amputated beneath them, and one was shattered completely, its pieces spinning off like pinwheels. "What the hell was that?" he shouted.

"It came from over on the right..." said Drum.

Wood swung his binoculars that way. To the north, there was a bit of high ground and several dark shapes were perched there. As he watched, there was a flash from one of them and a cloud of smoke engulfed it. The smoke billowing up was suddenly turned from gray to white as the first level rays of the dawn touched it. A moment later, the light struck the hulking vehicle which had produced the smoke. A *Little David!*

The newly constructed war machines were there, on the high ground, firing into the massed Martians. And as the last of the night's shadows were swept away, he could see that they weren't alone. Dozens of smaller vehicles, each spewing clouds of black coal smoke, were trundling forward, down the slope, toward the enemy. Smaller puffs of white smoke came from their guns. The 1st Tank Division had arrived!

Once again, the Martians seemed confused by this new attack. They stood there for long moments as the fire tore through them. Machine after machine crashed to the ground. Finally, some sort of decision was made and the large mass split into two, half heading north toward the tanks and the Little Davids, and the other half heading east.

Toward him.

There were still at least a hundred tripods and God knew how many of the spider-machines in the group headed east. They seemed much closer now, no more than three miles away, maybe less. Drum looked from the enemy back to him. "Are you sure you want to stay here, sir?"

He almost answered automatically that he did. But did he? Really? He was the bloody chief of staff of the United States Army! Was he going to get himself killed over some point of honor? Instead, he took a deep breath and walked over to the north side of the tower and looked out.

What he saw surprised him. While he had been watching the battle so single-mindedly, much had happened. The areas behind the walls, which had seemed nearly deserted when they'd arrived, was now teaming with activity. Hundreds of soldiers were marching up or climbing on to the walls. Mortars were being set up behind the walls while machine guns and stovepipe teams took position along the parapet. Field guns were going into battery further back, and a few hundred yards away a crane was lifting something up to one to the towers. A platoon of steam tanks clanked along, looking for some place to deploy. The disappearing guns roared out another salvo and a freshening westerly wind blew the smoke clouds back across the troops. Wood made up his mind.

"I'll stay."

Drum looked exasperated. "Then *please* come down to the command post, sir! It's much better protected!"

"In a bit, in a bit. When they get closer." He went back to the western side of the tower and raised his binoculars again. The Martians were still coming on. The land west of the walls was mostly open, but there were patches of trees, some farms, and a few small clusters of houses. The invaders set them all ablaze as they passed, and the smoke from those fires joined that of the artillery bursts.

Those bursts were coming faster than ever as the word of the assault was spread to the batteries. Now their crews put forth the last of their strength. They'd been working their guns for over a day, but they knew this was the decisive moment and they held nothing back. The roar, which had rarely slackened, now became all encompassing. Geysers of earth and debris shot upward all around the tripods, and he lost sight of the other group which had turned to face the Little Davids and the 1st Tanks. No way to know what was going on over there. No matter, the battle was going to be decided *here!*

Two miles, one mile, the enemy continued to advance. But there were fewer of them now; they were paying for every yard. Wrecked machines littered the ground behind them. And still the artillery hammered the foe. The men at the plotting table back in the Hotel Jefferson were doing their job, calling in fire from every battery and ship within range. Wood suddenly wondered what their orders were for when the enemy got close to the walls? Cease fire? Continue firing despite the chance—hell the certainty—that some shells would land on friendly troops? He wished he'd asked. He instinctively glanced skyward, then looked to his aide.

"Hugh, why don't we go down to the command center?"

"Yes, sir!"

They went down the stairs, Wood giving a backward look at the men who remained behind. What orders did they have? The command center on the floor below was much busier than it had been before. The commanders of some of the newly arrived units had congregated there and they were clearly surprised to find Wood there, too. They snapped to attention when they saw him.

"Carry on, gentlemen. Carry on. We've all got jobs to do so let's do them." The men went back to work. Major Hase was looking out through one of the embrasures with a pair of binoculars in one hand and a field telephone in the other, apparently directing the fire of his big guns. A pair of infantry captains appeared to be arguing about where their men should be posted. Another officer with ordnance tabs was talking excitedly with one of the artillery officers. Other men, the spotters for the artillery, peered through other embrasures, feeding their observations back to those plotters at the Jefferson. Everyone had a task - except Wood.

He moved to one of the view slits, trying not to crowd the spotter, and looked out. The Martians were much closer now, a thousand yards or less. Their bulbous heads reflected the sunlight and their long spindly legs propelled them forward with a gait that simply looked *wrong*. And now their heat rays were firing again—firing at the walls. Blasts of pure heat leapt out from the devices they carried and sprayed across the human defenders.

The men at the embrasures cried out in alarm and began to slam closed the metal shutters. Nothing hit the command center yet, but the observers, and Wood, peered hesitantly through the small but thick quartz vision slit built into the shutters. Theoretically, they would protect a man long enough to duck, but as far as Wood knew, they had never been tested.

The urge to be able to see was irresistible and Wood squinted through the quartz. His field of view was narrow and the smoke was getting thicker, but he could still dimly make out the enemy in the distance. On and on they came. Five hundred yards, four hundred, and the smaller spider-machines - *God they do look like spiders!* - stayed with them, a horrifying mass of legs and waving tendrils.

Now some of the tripods came to an abrupt halt. One fell over completely, even though Wood had seen no shell strike it. *The pit traps!* Out in front of the walls, the men had dug traps to snare the legs of the machine. Skillfully hidden, the enemy hadn't seen them until it was too late.

"Yes!" screamed Major Hase. "Hit the trapped ones! Before they can get free!" Wood glanced aside to see the coast artilleryman shouting into a telephone receiver. He looked back at the Martians, and a moment later, one of them was blasted to fragments as a twelve-inch shell tore through it. After a few seconds, two more were destroyed. *Hit them! Hit them!*

Suddenly, the world turned red.

A blinding red glare filled his vision and a terrible heat seared his face. He flung up his arm, turned away, and ducked down. Around him, men were crying out, but Wood could see nothing but red, despite blinking furiously. *Damn!* Was he blind?

"General! Are you all right?" He heard Drum next to him and felt him grab his arm and drag him a few feet to one side. Tears were filling his eyes and streaming down his cheeks and he wiped his face with his sleeve. It hurt. He gasped in relief when the red faded and he could see blurry images in front of him. More blinking and wiping and the blur turned into the grainy concrete of the command center's floor. He could see! "General! Are you hurt?"

"I'm... I'm all right."

"Sir, your face is burned!"

Yes, he could feel the pain now. He imagined all the skin around his eyes had been burned. He touched it gingerly, but it didn't seem too bad. "I'm all right."

"I'll send for a medic."

"Later. What's happening?" He looked around and saw several other men who had been injured. The red glow in the vision slits was gone. He went over to the one he'd been looking through and swore. The quartz was cracked and discolored and not transparent at all anymore.

But the battle was going on. He could hear it and feel it. He needed to see it! He reached out to open the metal shutter but jerked his hand back. He could feel the heat radiating off the metal. No, he couldn't open them. He turned toward the door.

"Where are you going, sir?" demanded Drum.

"Up to the roof."

His aide swore a remarkable oath, but didn't try to stop him. Swaying on his feet slightly, he went into the stairwell and nearly collided with a man helping a badly burned soldier down the steps. "You sure about this, sir?" shouted Drum.

He wasn't really, but to stay locked up in that concrete box was intolerable. He went up the steps and then paused just below the opening to the roof. There was the noise of explosions and the shriek of the heat rays and the cries of men, but no blasts of heat were sweeping the rooftop just at the moment. He edged out, crouching low. The men who had been up here were all huddling below the parapet, bobbing up now and again to see. A headless body with a smoldering tunic lay sprawled on the concrete. Working his way to the north wall, Wood popped up to take a look.

The Martians had reached the wall.

Their machines were clustered in front of it and spread out for hundreds of yards to either side of Wood's tower. Some were down in the water-filled ditch, scrabbling and splashing futilely with claws and legs to pull themselves up and over it. Others stood back beyond the ditch, firing their heat rays against the wall or at any human bold enough to show himself above the parapet. Wood saw a ray swinging in his direction and ducked down as it passed. The top of the concrete glowed redly for a moment and he could feel the heat radiating off of it.

He dared to look again. The troops on top of the walls were tossing their dynamite bombs over the parapet and they were exploding among the Martians. One of the tripods had a leg blown off and it topped over into the ditch. Bolder men were rising up to fire off their stovepipe rockets. The disappearing guns still rose up to fire, but Wood wasn't sure what they were aiming at with the enemy so near. The scream of artillery shells was very close now and some were bursting just a few dozen yards beyond the ditch. The mortar crews down below were firing frantically with their tubes pointed almost straight up, trying to drop their bombs just on the other side of the wall.

He had to duck again as another blast of heat swept across the top edge of the tower. Fortunately, the tower was taller than the enemy, and they couldn't hit the men on top - unless they were foolish enough to expose themselves.

He looked again, careful not to touch the hot concrete, and saw a tripod pick up one of the spider-machines and fling it over the wall. It landed among the mortar crews and scrambling up on its metal legs, began firing a small heat ray and lashing out with a razor-tipped tentacle. Men screamed and began to run.

An infantry squad appeared, firing rifles into the horrid thing. It fired back with its ray, but a well-aimed Springfield shot shattered the device and the ray sputtered out. The Martian killing machine advanced on the troops with its red-stained tentacle flashing about in front of it, but then there was a whoosh and a cloud of smoke, and a stovepipe rocket exploded against it, blowing off a leg and tumbling it onto its back. A trooper ran forward, placed a bomb on the machine's belly, and then darted aside. The blast blew the thing to pieces.

But the other Martians had gotten the same idea and more and more of the spiders came flying over the wall. Some landed heavily and were damaged, but most sprang up and attacked. He saw one land among the crew of one of the twelve-inchers and the poor gunners didn't have a chance.

More troops came up to reinforce the line and some of the steam tanks as well. The noise of battle rose to a crescendo and Wood vaguely realized the cotton balls had fallen out of his ears somewhere. The melee behind the walls was mesmerizing. Men died and spiders were crushed. But this wasn't good. If the Martians could clear a section of its defenders, how long until they could rip open a hole they could get through? If the tripods and spiders got loose into the city…

"General! General Wood?" Someone was shaking him. He slumped back behind the wall and saw it was the ordnance officer he had seen earlier. "General! Do I have your permission to fire?"

"What?"

"General, can I open fire?"

"With what? What are you talking about, son?"

"The heat rays, sir! They're set up but I can't use them without an order from headquarters! I can't get through to General Pershing, but I was just told that you were here!"

"What?! You have them here?" A thrill went through him.

"Yes, sir! We've got them hooked up in five locations along this section of wall. But I can't fire them without your orders, sir!"

"Well God in Heaven, fire! Fire the damn things!" The man grinned and ran for the stairs.

Still the battle raged. More and more spiders were making it across the wall and they quickly proved that they could take out a steam tank if given the chance. Reserves in this area were getting used up and the tripods were hammering at the wall with their claws and starting to rip chunks of concrete loose. The artillery fire was slackening, too, out of shells or their crews exhausted.

A sudden commotion from the west parapet of the tower made him jerk his head around. A metal leg had appeared on the edge of the parapet. A second one joined it and they scrabbled to find a hold.

"A spider-machine, sir!" cried Drum. "We need to get out of here!" Drum hauled him up and dragged him toward the stairs. One of the observers grabbed a metal leg and tried to shove it loose, but the machine's tentacle came over the parapet, striking like a scorpion's stinger and skewered the poor devil. Wood stopped resisting Drum. Yes they had to...

The sound of a heat ray pierced the air. There were dozens of them already firing, but this one sounded different somehow. Looking north, Wood saw a ray stab out from one of the towers which had been built so they could enfilade the walls, firing down their length. The ray struck a tripod standing on the edge of the ditch, catching it at the narrow spot where the head met the strangely shaped hip joints. It flared brightly for a moment and burst into molten fragments, and the machine crashed to the ground.

The ray shifted to the next tripod in line.

The Martians did not react at first. Perhaps they thought it was some mistake, an errant shot by one of their own. Perhaps they just didn't believe it. But they hesitated for long fatal seconds as the ray claimed a second tripod and then a third. The ray ceased and Wood knew that it couldn't fire continuously without overheating. Finally, the Martians responded, turning toward where the ray had come from, but still they seemed confused.

"Look, sir!" cried Drum. He was pointing at the spider-machine. It had pulled itself up nearly over the parapet, but it had stopped, frozen in place. Not moving at all. Looking down, Wood saw that all the spiders had stopped moving. Soldiers stared at them for an instant and then attacked. Bombs and stovepipes and steam tank cannons ripped into them.

"Push that thing off!" shouted Wood. A half dozen men sprang into action. They grabbed the spider's legs and with brute strength toppled it off the tower.

The heat ray in the other tower blazed to life again, claiming another victim. The surviving Martians finally fired back, and after a moment there was an explosion in the tower, but not before a fifth tripod crashed to the ground.

There were still a half dozen tripods along this section of wall, and after a few more seconds the spider-machines, the ones which hadn't been wrecked, came back to life; but the tripods were backing away, not renewing the attack. As the wind blew a hole in the smoke, Wood could see out far to the north, and it looked as though the enemy which had turned that way were now heading south. Retreating?

Yes!

The ones in front of him turned and moved away as fast as they could. There were only a handful of the spider-machines with them and they were quickly left behind. Wood walked to the western parapet, stepping around the man who'd been gutted by the spider and looked out, fumbling for his binoculars. He brought them up, but his hands were shaking and he couldn't focus them. He gave up on that and just looked out. All along the walls, the Martians were falling back. At first, the defenders seemed as stunned as the Martians had been when their own heat rays had been turned against them, but they soon went back to work. The 112th's guns claimed at least three more of the tripods before they disappeared. Damn fine shooting.

The enemy drew off to the west and the south, pursued by the remains of the Little Davids and the 1st Tanks. And the artillery and the aircraft. Explosions and airplanes chased the enemy into the distance. Wood couldn't tell how many of the tripods had gotten away, but it wasn't nearly as many as had come in the first place. *We stopped them. They hit us with everything they had and we stopped them.* A wave of relief and exaltation swept through him.

He was very tired, he realized, and he didn't resist when Drum had a medic put some ointment on his burned face and apply some bandages; it was starting to hurt quite a bit now.

"We should get back to headquarters, sir," suggested his aide.

"Yes, yes, we should…"

But he couldn't leave until he'd thanked the men who'd won this victory. He wandered through the command center shaking hands, and then down to the ground level and along the walls, talking to gunners and tank crews and infantrymen. There were wrecked spiders everywhere along with wrecked tanks and a great many casualties. The spiders left a lot more wounded than the big tripods did. Ambulances were arriving near the wall now and doctors, nurses, and medics were working to save those who could be saved. Wood talked with the wounded and thanked the medical people.

It was nearly noon before Drum could stuff him into a staff car and head back to headquarters. On the ride back through the mercifully undamaged streets, Drum was babbling on about the battle, but Wood was trying to decide what to do next. The Martians had been hurt, hurt very badly, he believed. The obvious thing to do was to launch a counterattack. Could that be done? What forces did he have left? What forces could be brought up? What…?

"General? General, we're here."

Wood jerked awake and looked around in confusion. They were outside the Hotel Jefferson. Asleep. He'd fallen asleep. Shaking himself awake, he emerged from the car. There was a swarm of other cars on the streets and a large crowd near the entrance, talking excitedly. Wood slowly made his way through to the doors…

"Well, Leonard, I hope you've had your fun!"

A familiar voice drew him up short and he spun around. The crowd parted to reveal a very familiar figure. Eyes sparkling behind his pince-nez glasses, the mouth was drawn into a grin, exposing those enormous teeth.

"Not very fair to sneak off and direct a battle without me, you know. But well done, Leonard! Bully!"

Wood just gawked for a moment before he could find his voice.

"Roosevelt!"

CHAPTER TWELVE

CYCLE 597, 845.1, HOLDFAST 32-4

Qetjnegartis stared at the communications display and forced its tendrils into immobility. When the alert came from Clan Mavnaltak asking for contact, it had assumed it would be Commander Braxjandar, telling of its latest victory and demanding to know why Qetjnegartis had not launched its own offensive. But it had not been Braxjandar…

"This is truth? Braxjandar is slain? How did this come about?"

Kalfldagvar, one of Braxjandar's subordinates and now, apparently, the leader of Clan Mavnaltak on the target world, waved its tendrils in agitation. "A great calamity, Qetjnegartis. We launched our attack and all seemed to be going well. We crushed the prey-creature's outer defenses as we expected. They fought hard, but they could not stop us. But then there was another line of defenses, much stronger than the first. Their large projectile throwers were in operation in numbers never before encountered. Our losses mounted, but we breached the second line and pushed forward.

"We slew thousands of them, but then we encountered more of the miserable creatures and more of their armored vehicles. There seemed to be no end to the things! At that point we also saw that there was another defensive line constructed of the cast stone material. I… I advised Braxjandar that we should withdraw, but it was convinced that this line of defenses was the last, and if we could pierce them, the enemy would collapse. So we attacked. Braxjandar led it personally."

"And this attack failed?" asked Qetjnegartis, even though there could be only one possible answer.

"Yes. We took heavy losses just reaching the walls, and then we could not get over them quickly. We began to tear them down. The drones performed well and it looked as though victory could still be achieved but then… then…" Kalfdagvar faltered.

"Then what?"

"Something none of us thought possible! We were suddenly fired upon with heat rays! Our own heat rays! Firing out from the walls! A score of us were destroyed before we even realized what was happening. Braxjandar was among them."

Qetjnegartis was stunned. "How is this possible? Could you have been mistaken? Could it have been some new, primitive weapon of the prey-creatures which just had the appearance of a heat ray?"

"No! Analysis proved that is was identical to our own weapons. We speculate that they have somehow devised a way of using salvaged ray projectors, taken from destroyed war machines. Or at least we hope so. The only other possibility, that they have built these from scratch, is too terrible to contemplate!"

"Even the possibility that they have managed this much is terrible enough, Kalfdagvar! This would indicate a reasoning ability far above anything we credited them with."

"Yes. But in any case, with the loss of Braxjandar and the others, the attack faltered and I had no choice but to order a retreat. Less than fifty of us survived to reach the nearest holdfast."

Fifty! Braxjandar had boasted that its attack would have nearly five hundred fighting machines! Such a loss…

"What will you do now, Kalfdagvar?"

"I have reported this news to the Colonial Conclave. They have ordered that the offensive continue. Obviously it will be some time before my own people can attack in any strength. We shall make what small probes we can to keep the enemy off balance. The Conclave has demanded that Clan Novmandus to our north stir itself to make a major effort and they have agreed. But it is now more urgent than ever that you attack boldly Qetjnegartis. Surely the prey-creatures must have concentrated most of their strength against us to deal such a blow. The opportunity for you to establish a hold across the great river might never be better. You must attack!"

There is no evidence to back up your claim, Kalfdagvar, thought Qetjnegartis. But aloud it said: "We will do what we can. You have our condolences for your losses."

Kalfdagvar appeared to have no interest in condolences, but made no more demands and ended the communications. Qetjnegartis sat there for some time assimilating this new and unexpected information. The situation was very complex—and very dangerous.

Group 31 to the south was in disarray. They had been inadequately supported by their clans on the Homeworld and were now divided by the need to hold what they already had and to assist an offensive against a heavily fortified zone which separated the third continent from the fourth. There would be no help from there. The groups to the far north were only now beginning to render any real assistance.

And Group 33, the Mavnaltak Clan, was defeated. This was entirely unexpected. Up until now, Braxjandar had been the acknowledged leader on this continent. It had produced nothing but victory. Everyone - including Qetjnegartis - had expected this to continue to be the case.

But now, now the hopes for a final victory on the third continent were resting on Qetjnegartis. In some ways it was a very satisfying situation, especially after all of Braxjandar's condescending behavior. But in other ways it was very unsettling. The other clans were now expecting it to produce the victory they wanted.

Can it be done?

The news about the prey making use of captured devices was very alarming, but it made the need for a quick victory all the more vital. If the prey were so clever as to accomplish this, then they must be given no time to accomplish more. The river needed to be crossed and a new holdfast established as quickly as possible. But where? And how?

Qetjnegartis reactivated the communicator and contacted Kantangnar, commanding Battlegroup 32-4. It answered immediately. "Report your situation. Do you continue to advance unopposed?"

"Yes, Commander. Except for a few small garrisons and light scouting forces, we have encountered no significant resistance. We have advanced three hundred telequel south of the confluence of River 3-1.4 with River 3-1, destroying all that we have seen. Unless the situation changes, we could push all the way to the ocean."

"Have you discovered any locations where a crossing of the river might be easily done?"

Kantangnar hesitated for a moment. "None that seem exceptionally favorable, Commander. While it is true that the large cast-stone fortifications are fewer here than to the north, the river grows steadily wider as we progress and much of the land along it is very low-lying and saturated with water. Some areas have proven virtually impassable and we were forced to detour many telequel west to get around them. One city on the far shore stands on high ground and was very heavily fortified. Also, the enemy water vessels have been seen in great number and have been following us. Any time we get close to the river they fire upon us, and we have taken some minor damage. Attempting a crossing so far from our holdfasts would be… difficult."

"I understand," said Qetjnegartis. "Very well, continue as you have for as far as you can without putting your force in danger. Report to me regularly."

"Yes, Commander." The connection was closed.

Qetjnegartis considered the situation. Crossing the large river and establishing a strong holdfast on the far side was essential. The crossing itself would be difficult, but it seemed likely that establishing the holdfast would be even more so. The prey-creatures would certainly see the danger such a thing would pose to them and make every effort to prevent that happening. Up until now, every holdfast had been established either in a sparsely populated region or in areas which had been swept clean of prey-creature forces following a major victory. In each case there had been no immediate opposition. The construction machines were much more vulnerable to damage than the war machines, especially in the early stages of construction before the underground areas could be started. If the prey-creatures were to bring up powerful forces, especially their large projectile throwers, building a new holdfast might well prove impossible. Qetjnegartis recalled the siege of the first holdfast and how nearly it had been overrun. If the prey had brought such forces to bear earlier, it probably would not be alive contemplating the problem now.

So yes, we can probably force our way across the river, but then what?

It could see no easy answers. So, as it often did when in need of counsel, Qetjnegartis opened a communications channel to Ixmaderna in its lab in Holdfast 32-2. It was one of only two others who had arrived with the initial landing force and still survived. It was a being of long experience and considerable wisdom. Once the communications link was established, Qetjnegartis explained the problem, including the information from Kalfdagvar.

"I find it most interesting that the prey-creatures have learned how to make use of our technology, even in so simple a way as this," said Ixmaderna.

"You consider using our most potent weapon simple?" asked Qetjnegartis.

"As a device it actually is, Commander. A matter of supplying sufficient power and turning it on. Far less complex than operating one of the fighting machines. Even so, for them to have puzzled out all the particulars so quickly does come as a surprise. Although after working with their young, I suppose it shouldn't have been."

"You consider them intelligent, then?"

"More intelligent than we expected before coming here, surely. Still, it is not as if they constructed a heat ray on their own - or at least so we must hope."

"I find the situation very disturbing. Is there anything we can do to render our technology inoperable in the event it is captured?"

Ixmaderna waved its tendril in contemplation. "Perhaps. It may be possible with certain devices. I shall give it thought."

"And what about the strategic situation? What are your thoughts on that?"

"I see only two possibilities which give a great chance for success with an attack that must be launched soon. One is to somehow arrange for a battle which utterly devastates the enemy without ourselves suffering too great a loss in the process. We would then have the strength to defend the new holdfast before they could assemble a new attack force."

"If I had the power to guarantee such a result, we would not be in the present situation," said

561

Qetjnegartis. "The other possibility?"

"You must force your crossing in an area which is either so isolated that the enemy cannot quickly bring its forces to bear - such as was the case with our first holdfast - or an area which has naturally strong defensive features to give the construction operation protection from attack."

"And an additional factor is that the location cannot be too far from an existing holdfast," said Qetjnegartis. "After what happened to our reserve fighting machines during the attack on city 3-118, I am extremely reluctant to bring the construction machines along with the attack force. But to have to bring them from a holdfast later would take too much time if the distance was great."

"True," said Ixmaderna. "That limits the areas open to you - unless you found the ideal site and built a new holdfast in the vicinity on our side of the river."

"That would take too long. Our attack must come soon. And if the enemy guessed our plans, the ideal site could be fortified before we were ready to attack."

"That is also true. So your area of attack is limited to perhaps two hundred telequel of Holdfast 32-4. Do any locations recommend themselves?"

"No. The principle feature is city 3-37. But it is heavily defended with an outer fortress on the west shore connected by a bridge. Considering what happened to Braxjandar's forces recently, I am extremely reluctant to attack such a fortress."

"Then somewhere to the north or south of it?"

"It is mostly flat, wet country with no dominant features to prevent an enemy counterattack. It would also appear that the tracks of their transportation system are far denser on the east side of the river. This would allow them to assemble their forces quickly. And they can also transport their forces using the rivers. The only easily defensible locale would be..." Qetjnegartis paused.

"Yes?"

"The city itself. It is ringed on all sides with walls and obstructions to deter attack. If we could somehow manage to seize the place without sustaining ruinous losses, we could put those defenses to our own use. Not as effective as our own, but they might suffice until we can build more."

"An interesting idea, Commander. And with the entire city available to salvage, we avoid the danger of picking some unsurveyed spot only to find it completely lacking in necessary resources."

"Yes, that was another danger which concerned me."

"But it comes back to capturing the city. Can you do that?"

"A direct, frontal assault would be extremely costly, perhaps impossible with the river and the enemy water vessels to contend with. And yet clearly the prey-creatures fear exactly such an attack since they have constructed such formidable defenses. Perhaps if we made a feint, a diversionary attack against the section on the west shore to draw in their reserves, and then made a surprise crossing twenty or thirty *telequel* north or south of the city, and then quickly struck the city from the landward side. The defenses are not nearly so strong there. We could take the city, perhaps even capture the bridge across the river intact, and then move in our construction machines. Yes, if we could do this a success might be possible."

"The enemy water vessels could still pose a threat."

"Yes, we would need to establish very strong defenses along the river, north and south of the city to prevent their approach. Give some thought about how best to do that."

"As you command."

"The diversions can be done easily enough, but I am still very uncertain about the river crossing.

We shall have to make some trial crossings with just a few machines to see if it can be done at all. Perhaps I will have Kantangnar make some attempts and send another force farther north to do the same. This may also distract the enemy. But it is the drones that worry me most. They will be essential for taking the city, but I fear we will lose great numbers of them to mishap if we try to walk them across the river bottom."

"Yes, that is a great risk," said Ixmaderna. "But an idea comes to me."

"Yes?"

"We have seen that the prey-creatures are capable of making use of our own technology. Perhaps we should make use of theirs."

* * * * *

MAY, 1912, MEMPHIS, TENNESSEE

Things were busy again in the hospital. Wounded had started to stream in only a few days after the terrible battle at Little Rock, and the stream hadn't stopped for the two weeks that followed. Even now, nearly a month later, there were still a few new arrivals coming in as the survivors of the battle reached safety. Rebecca Harding looked at their newest patient. He was a middle-aged man with bandages on his hands and knees. His ID disk said his name was Mackenzie and he was with the navy. Probably off one of the gunboats, she thought.

"These burns, sailor?" she asked, pointing to the bandages.

"Yes'm," replied the man. He looked disoriented. She felt his head and it was feverish.

Frowning, she gently cut and peeled away the bandages. The man twitched and moaned as she worked. Yes, as she feared, the burns on his hands had become infected. The ones on his knees looked to be healing, but the hands… Looking closer she saw that the burns weren't actually all that bad, not like many she saw. Over the years she'd seen a lot of burns. These were probably secondary burns, made when the man touched something which was hot rather than as the direct result of a heat ray. Still, he was in danger. She cleaned up the wounds as best she could quickly and then called one of the doctors over to look at him.

The doctor, who looked as exhausted as she felt, examined the patient and just shook his head. "Finish cleaning up the wounds, get fresh sterile bandages on them," he said. "Then make sure he has food and water and rest. We'll just have it let this run its course and hope he can pull through."

Becca nodded and went to work. Sadly, there wasn't much that could be done for an infection like this. Either the man had the strength to fight it off or… he didn't. Becca was glad that this doctor wasn't one of the older ones who still prescribed bromine treatments. They were incredibly painful for the patient and didn't do any good that Becca had ever seen.

She spent nearly an hour using boiled water to clean out the wounds and then carefully covered them with gauze which had also been boiled. The patient cried out from time to time and she had to firmly hold on to his wrists when he tried to jerk away, but he seemed to be in a daze.

As she was finishing up, she heard a voice a few yards off asking: "Excuse me, miss, I'm looking for one of my men, Caleb Mackenzie. I was told he is here." Becca looked up and saw a man three beds down talking to Clarissa Forester. *Mackenzie?* She double-checked the ID disk and sure enough, it was him.

"Over here, sir," she called. The man's face brightened and he walked over to her. He was quite young, but he wore the uniform of a naval commander.

"Ah, there you are, Mr. Mackenzie!" he said. But when Mackenzie didn't answer, he frowned and looked at Becca. "Is he all right?"

"Uh, he's pretty sick, commander…?"

"Harding, Drew Harding, *USS Santa Fe*. But what's wrong with him? The burns weren't that bad, I didn't think."

"They've become infected. Are you his commandin' officer? When did these happen?" She eyed the man closely. He had the same last name as her…

"At Little Rock. I guess it was three, no, almost four weeks ago now. My ship doesn't have much of a sick bay. No doctor, either. We patched him up as best we could, but there was nothing else we could do for him. The medical services were overwhelmed so we just waited until we got here. But I didn't think… A few days ago it seemed like he was doing fine!"

"Burns are hard to treat. They can get infected days or weeks later, before the skin can finish healin'. I'm sure you did your best, sir."

"But he'll make it, right?"

Becca looked down at the man. No telling how much he was hearing. She got up and led the commander a few yards away. "We're doin' all we can do for him. If he's strong, he should pull through. That's all I can tell you, Commander."

The man frowned and chewed on his lower lip. "I see. Well, if there's anything I can do… Would you be kind enough to keep me informed, Miss…?"

"Uh, Harding, Becca Harding. I'll try to let you know how he's doin'. You said you are on the *Santa Fe*? Is it docked here at Memphis?"

"Yes, but… Harding? Rebecca Harding?" He was looking at her with a strange expression.

"Yes, that's right."

"Do you, uh, do you know a man named Andrew Comstock?"

"Major Comstock?"

"Well, he's a colonel now, but yes. You know him? You were the girl he met out west in the first days of the war?"

"Yes, that's right! You know him?"

"Yes, I knew him back in Washington when he was just a second lieutenant and I was an ensign. Staff duty, y'know. We've been friends since then and he, uh, he wrote me about you."

"About me?"

"He was curious if we were related, us both having the same last name and all. He, uh, he wrote me that your folks were all killed in the war and you might not have any family left that you knew about. He asked me if I could check into it."

Becca looked at him in shock. A relative? Family? "I… I… did you?"

"I wrote my grandmother, she's the expert on the family history. She's back with most of my other family near Albany. She wrote back, but mostly with questions for me to ask you - not that I ever expected to be able to do it in person! She mentioned a cousin… or was it an uncle? - I'll have to re-read her letter - who moved out west before the Civil War. Colorado, maybe? She said they lost touch with him."

"My grandfather fought in that war and then settled in New Mexico!" said Becca. "Do you think that could be him?"

"Maybe. Can you give me his full name? Any other details?"

"The name sure, it was…."

"Harding! Stop lollygagging! You've got a patient to tend!"

Becca looked and there was Miss Chumley with a stern expression on her face. Commander Harding looked sheepish. "Don't mean to get you in trouble, miss. Maybe you can write down anything you remember and send it to me? The *Santa Fe* will be docked for repairs for the next few days."

"All right. And thank you!"

"No, thank you - for taking care of Mackenzie. You will let me know if I can help in any way?"

"Yes, sir, certainly." He nodded to her and then left, nodding to Chumley as well as he passed. Becca hastily went back to work on Mackenzie. She got him bandaged up and made sure he had water and that the orderlies would feed him, but her mind was only half on what she was doing. Less than half maybe. The amazing conversation with Commander Harding kept crowding out her other thoughts. Family! She'd pushed the possibility that she still had family left in the world to the far corners of her mind. Her family was dead. And there weren't any more. None. But perhaps there were. And that Commander Harding seemed like a nice man; not like her aunt and uncle. But then he was from her *father's* side of the family, a group she'd never met or knew anything about. Maybe they were different - even if they were from back east. The thought of having someone was… exciting. She wished she could tell Frank about it.

Her shift ended but before she could slip off to the mess hall and then her bunk, Miss Chumley intercepted her. "I need to have a word with you, Miss Harding." Her formal tone meant she wasn't happy with something.

"I'm sorry about that, ma'am. The commander was concerned about one of his men and I…"

"That's not what I wanted to talk to you about. It's about that other preoccupation of yours."

"What? You mean the sharpshooters?"

"Yes, exactly. With things quiet here for so long I saw no harm in letting you indulge your interests. You worked hard and well and if that was your idea of fun, so be it. But now things are getting serious again. The rumors are that Memphis may be attacked soon. That will make the influx we had from Little Rock seem like nothing. And yet I've heard you talking about having a position you are supposed to defend with your sharpshooters. Which is it going to be, Rebecca? Are you going to take your gun and go fight, or are you going to stay here and help the wounded? You can't do both."

Becca stared at the woman and didn't know what to say. She'd been afraid that someday it would come to this, but she'd never figured out what she would do when it did. "I… I don't know, ma'am."

"Well, you need to make a decision - and soon. If my best nurse is going to run off and play soldier I need to know before the wounded start arriving in truckloads!" She glared at her in her best Chumley fashion and Becca instinctively nodded.

"Yes, ma'am. I'll… I'll let you know tomorrow."

* * * * *

MAY, 1912, HAMPTON ROADS, VIRGINIA

The *USLI Albuquerque* slipped its moorings and was slowly turned seaward by its towing ship, a freighter called *Monodnock*. Andrew Comstock held onto the railing of the superstructure to steady himself against the motion and looked back. The other five ironclads of the 1st Squadron were also leaving their docks and heading out. The sun was just peeking over the rim of the world to the east, there was a gentle westerly breeze, and it looked like it would be a fine day.

"Finally on our way," said Lieutenant Hornbaker, from beside him.

"I surely hope so, Jerry. And it's certainly about time."

"That it is, sir. I hope there are no more problems."

"Amen."

They had left Philadelphia two week earlier and made it - just barely - to the Norfolk Navy Yard. The voyage was supposed to have taken less than two days, but it ended up taking four. The ironclads with their towing vessels could do eight to ten knots depending on the wind and the seas; maybe two hundred miles a day - in theory. They made it down the Delaware River with no problems, but when they passed Cape Henlopen, at the mouth of Delaware Bay and into the open ocean, they discovered the sea-keeping characteristics of the ironclads with their big flotation modules was about as good as a large rock wrapped in a life jacket. They pitched and rolled, surged and sidled unlike anything ever seen - and the ocean was relatively calm.

The towing vessels struggled to keep their charges under control and on course. Their nice line-ahead formation was soon scattered over twenty miles of ocean and the two escorting destroyers were dashing madly about like overworked sheepdogs trying to keep an eye on everything. By the afternoon of the first day, things were settling down as the crews got used to handling the strange vessels. Then the tow cable on *Sioux Falls* broke. A few frantic hours followed as the ships tried to get a new cable strung. The others reduced speed to wait for them, and it was well after dark before they were on their way again.

An hour later, *Springfield* reported a serious leak in one of its floats. A destroyer had to come alongside and lend its pumps to get the flooding under control. It worked, but speed had to be reduced to just a few knots.

By the middle of the second day, all six ironclads were reporting strange and ominous sounds from where the floats were connected to their hulls. Was the motion of the voyage working them loose? If even one of them broke free, an ironclad would be on a quick trip to the bottom. The Baldwin engineers who were aboard scrambled around, inspecting every connection they could get to, and reported no obvious problems. But the naval captain in command reduced speed again and steered the ships as close to the shore as possible. Everyone was on alert and never took off their lifejackets. No one got much sleep that night.

The third day was much the same, although *Tulsa* began leaking, too; fortunately, not badly enough that its own pumps couldn't handle it. General Clopton was getting very annoyed and Andrew could scarcely blame him. He remembered the ordeal of getting the first batch of steam tanks to the front in the first year of the war. This was just like that - except then there had been little risk of drowning.

They finally made it into Chesapeake Bay and the safety of Norfolk. Repairs were made, and Clopton - and Andrew - had insisted on a complete inspection of everything involved with keeping the ironclads afloat; adding an extra week. Then a storm had blown up the coast and they hadn't dared to leave the refuge of the bay.

But it hadn't all been work and frustration. Victoria had taken a train down from Washington and they had a brief reunion and a last night together before saying goodbye again. Her pregnancy was starting to show a little. Would he see her again before the baby came?

Then, just before the storm arrived, came news of a great victory at St. Louis. The Martians had launched a huge attack there and had been stopped cold. Everyone was celebrating and every ship - and ironclad - in the bay had fired a salute. Good news at last!

Finally they were on their way again. Larger ships to do the towing had been found, heavier cables employed, and every flotation module had been triple checked and secured. Maybe this time there would be no mishaps. Their escort was much larger, too. There was now a destroyer assigned to each ironclad and the protected cruiser, Olympia, Admiral Dewey's famed flagship from Manila Bay, was leading the squadron, commanded by a commodore. The high command wanted the ironclads at the front and they wanted them there soon. Despite the victory at St. Louis, there were alarming rumors of new threats all along the Mississippi Line.

The squadron moved out into Hampton Roads, and to Andrew's surprise, they started getting salutes from the other ships anchored there. Mostly just horn blasts, but a few actually fired their tiny saluting guns. Olympia returned the salutes and many sailors came up on deck to wave.

"Are they only being friendly, or are they expecting us to win the war for them?" wondered Andrew aloud.

"Maybe they're just happy to get our ugly hulks out of their nice harbor," said Hornbaker.

Andrew laughed. "We're certainly a batch of ugly ducklings, aren't we?"

"You can say that again, Colonel."

Andrew turned at the new voice and saw that Lieutenant - junior grade - Jason Broadt along with Major Stavely, the ironclad's commander, had joined them. For the sea voyage, a naval officer had been assigned to each ironclad along with a few ratings to help the poor soldiers keep their contraptions afloat. Broadt seemed like he knew his business, but there was no doubt he considered this duty beneath him.

"Morning, Major, Lieutenant. Everything ship-shape today?"

"So far," replied Broadt. "Which is," he looked back at the docks, "about three miles. Only one thousand eight hundred and forty more to go to reach New Orleans."

"About two weeks, do you think?"

"If we're lucky. And luck isn't something we've had in abundance thus far, Colonel."

"Well, then we are due for a change."

"Two weeks?" said Stavely. "Oh, God…"

Poor Stavely seemed especially prone to seasickness, and even the four day journey from Philadelphia had nearly done him in.

"Maybe our good luck will include some calm seas."

"Let's hope so. Just get me on solid ground and let me fight is all I ask. See you later, Colonel." The two men went on up the ladder to the observation platform.

Andrew refused to let Broadt's cynicism infect him. They were going to make, it and when they went into action, they would make a real difference. The ironclads might look ugly and be cantankerous machines, but they packed enormous firepower and were armored heavily enough that even the Martian heat rays would find them a tough nut to crack. And speaking of firepower…

"Let's go check on how Tesla's people are making out today."

Tesla had gotten General Crozier's permission to replace the forward seven-inch gun on Albuquerque with his new lightning cannon, and a team of his people had been working to get it installed for over a month. They couldn't get it done before departure so they had come along.

Andrew, followed by Hornbaker, went down the ladder from the superstructure to the main deck, and then around the huge bulk of the twelve-inch turret to the smaller turret just ahead which now housed Tesla's latest invention. The snout of the device emerged from the front of the turret through the same embrasure the cannon would have normally used. It was a slightly larger version of what he'd seen on Long Island many months earlier: a long tapering cylinder, like a cannon barrel, with thick rings of a white ceramic material at intervals along its length, until at the end they stopped with a white ball where the muzzle should have been. He wondered how resistant it would be to a heat ray. The steel barrel of a large gun could take high temperatures pretty well, but what about this thing? It would be a shame to see it melted or shattered before it could fire a shot. Perhaps they should keep the turret rotated backward as far as it could go until they were ready to fire. He'd have to mention that to Stavely.

The hatch to the turret was open and he could hear men talking inside. He stuck his head in and saw a multitude of wires and cables and all manner of stuff he could scarcely recognize. During the construction of the ironclads he'd become very familiar with the basics of electrical wiring, but Tesla's devices were as far removed from normal electronics as the Martian devices were from human ones. But Tesla's assistants seemed to know what they were doing. Or at least he sure hoped so. They had installed some sort of transformer in the engine room attached to the output of the steam turbine generator and then run thick conduits through the ship up to here. Now they were hooking up the gun to its power supply.

"How are you making out?" he asked the foreman, a very young man named Edwin Armstrong.

"Oh, I think we've got her worried, Colonel," said Armstrong with a grin. "Another few days and we should have it all wired up. D'you think we could do some test firings?"

Andrew jerked in surprise. "Out here? But… but from what Doctor Tesla said, you need to have some of that Martian wire as a target or there's no telling where the lightning will go! Mightn't we hit one of the other ships - or ourselves?"

"I guess that could be a problem. We did bring a few test targets made with the Martian wire, but putting them on a raft or something might not be that good an idea at that. Maybe the next time we're near land?"

"I'll talk to General Clopton, but don't get your hopes up."

"All right, but I don't like the idea of taking this thing into combat without ever having tested it."

"Hopefully we won't go straight into a battle once we get wherever they send us," said Andrew. "Once we're ashore we can run some tests."

"I hope so. We still need to train your men on how to fire this beast."

"Yes, that's true. Well, I'll see what the general says. He's over on the Olympia for this stage of the trip."

"Better accommodations?" asked Armstrong with a smirk.

"Better chow, too." They both smiled. The ironclads only had the sketchiest bunk space and galley. For this trip, most of the crews were staying on the towing ships, but Andrew felt duty-bound to stay with the Albuquerque - which made him the ranking officer on board. He could deal with the Spartan accommodations and food - he'd certainly survived worse out in New Mexico - and they were scheduled for short stops in Charleston and Key West, so maybe he could at least a get a few decent meals.

"Well, I'll leave you to your work."

They withdrew and went up to the control center on the tall forward mast. Broadt was there and seemed satisfied with the way the vessel - he steadfastly refused to call it a ship - was handling. By mid-morning they rounded Cape Henry and turned south into the Atlantic.

"Well, we are on our way," said Andrew. "Next stop: the war."

CHAPTER THIRTEEN

JUNE, 1912, WASHINGTON, D.C.

General Leonard Wood bought a copy of the Washington Post as he did every morning on his way to his office in the War and Navy Building. It was barely six o'clock, but even at this early hour the streets were bustling with military men, and he was forced to return salute after salute. Not that long ago he could enjoy a few minutes of solitude on this walk from home, but no more.

Matters weren't helped by the fact that he was now being hailed as the 'Hero of St. Louis'. Newsboys shouted at him and total strangers stopped him on the street to shake his hand. No matter that Pershing and Foltz - and the tens of thousands of troops under their command - deserved the real credit. They were still out there, while he was here. It was flattering, of course, but he really didn't need the distraction.

And the total strangers were the least of it. He'd only been back in Washington for three days and he was already getting confidential messages from powerful people suggesting that perhaps he ought to challenge Roosevelt for the nomination at the Republican convention in Chicago next month! Most he hadn't even dignified with a reply, and for the few which he could not avoid answering, he'd made it quite clear that he had no interest. Damn fools! His loyalty to Theodore was absolute and even if it hadn't been, he firmly agreed with Lincoln's advice about changing horses in midstream. They'd started this war with Roosevelt and by God they'd finish it with him!

Or at least he surely hoped so. The victory at St. Louis had given the nation's morale a sharp boost, but would it be enough? While it was true they had inflicted heavy losses on the enemy, they had not retaken any of the lost territory. Many people were still predicting a victory for Nelson Miles in November.

He made it to his office with just another dozen salutes, said good morning to Semancik, and went to his desk to look at the latest dispatches. He had a meeting with the President in only an hour and he wanted to be on top of things. His aide had done his usual excellent job in arranging the dispatches in order of importance, and the first one on the pile was from the intelligence officer at 4th Army headquarters in Vicksburg. It told him exactly what he'd been expecting - and fearing. He read through it twice. "Damn him!" he growled. God *damn* the man!"

Precisely at seven o'clock he arrived at Roosevelt's office in the White House. The President was having a 'working breakfast' which meant that his desk was piled with dishes as well as paperwork. In spite of warnings from his doctor, he was still eating far too much. The remains of ham, chicken, and sausages as well as rolls and pastries littered plates stacked to each side. A tall pot of coffee sat within easy reach. A servant was trying to clean up, despite Roosevelt snatching a few last morsels before they vanished. Wood's eyebrows rose when he saw the uniformed man standing off to one side.

Roosevelt had a new military aide to replace the unfortunate Archie Butt who had drowned so tragically. The new aide, by coincidence, was also named 'Archie', but he had a far better last name.

It was Roosevelt.

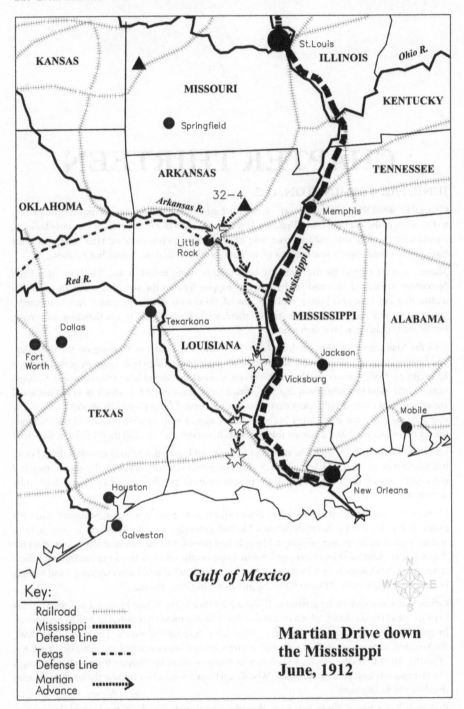

KANSAS

MISSOURI

Springfield

ILLINOIS

St. Louis

Ohio R.

KENTUCKY

ARKANSAS

32-4

TENNESSEE

OKLAHOMA

Arkansas R.

Little Rock

Memphis

Mississippi R.

Red R.

Texarkana

LOUISIANA

Dallas

Fort Worth

TEXAS

MISSISSIPPI

Jackson

Vicksburg

ALABAMA

Mobile

Houston

Galveston

New Orleans

Gulf of Mexico

Key:
Railroad
Mississippi Defense Line
Texas Defense Line
Martian Advance

Martian Drive down the Mississippi June, 1912

Second Lieutenant Archie Roosevelt snapped to attention when he saw Wood and gave him a parade ground salute. In spite of himself, Wood smiled as he returned it. "At ease, Lieutenant. Good to see you. How'd you like Plattsburg?"

"Very good, sir. They've compressed the course to just ten weeks. No Sundays off now."

"And he passed with flying colors, too!" boomed the elder Roosevelt after swallowing down a last mouthful. "Top of his class!"

"I wouldn't have expected any less," said Wood. The Plattsburg officer training school had been set up prior to the Martian invasion, but it had been expanded and was still turning out junior officers to supply the needs of the huge new armies which were being raised.

"Archie wants a combat assignment, like his brothers, but I thought I'd keep him here for a few months to get adjusted to military life. After that, well, we'll see." He shook his head. "Young Quentin is terribly jealous. He's demanding to go to Plattsburg, too, but fourteen is a bit too young."

Wood nodded, thinking that eighteen had been a bit too young, too, for Archie. Hell, he'd only been seventeen when he left for Plattsburg, and Wood had been forced to give him special permission. But there was no keeping a Roosevelt out of uniform when there was a war to be fought. "Mr. President, we have a very serious matter to discuss - several of them, in fact."

"I gathered as much from your message. So we can't even enjoy the laurels of the victory in St. Louis before the next crisis interferes?"

"I'm afraid not. Still, the victory was crucial. I liked your speech about it very much, by the way. One of your best."

Roosevelt waved that away. "Just words. We need action. What have you got for me, Leonard?"

"Problems. The biggest one comes from down south. I'm afraid that Fred Funston has run amok."

"What do you mean?"

"I mean that he's stripped his defense lines and gone hunting. I've gotten word that the troops we thought were guarding the lower Arkansas River have been withdrawn and there's nothing between the Martians and the Gulf of Mexico. They're streaming down the west bank of the Mississippi. They're halfway to Baton Rouge and still moving."

"Thunderation!"

"So far it looks like just a scouting force, but they are burning everything they encounter. If they keep going, we may lose our last rail connection west."

"How did this happen? Where are the troops who were supposed to be guarding that area?"

"That's the mystery, sir. I've managed to piece some of it together, but we are going to have to get the full story from Funston, himself." Wood sighed and took a seat opposite Roosevelt. He waited until the servant left with the breakfast cart before continuing. "I'd been getting some rumors that Funston was massing his forces for some sort of operation. I knew his defeats at Gallup and later at Albuquerque and Santa Fe were really eating at him. He was just itching to hit back somewhere. It appears that he was planning an attack against the Martian fortress near Albuquerque."

"Did he have the sort of strength needed for such an operation?"

"It's hard to say. Perhaps he felt that the fortress there, being in the rear area, would not be so heavily defended. But we'll never know if that was true or not. You recall how back in March, I think it was, we got word of some sort of Martian incursion across the Rio Grande near Corpus Christi?"

"Yes, we were worried that it was a major attack from Mexico. But then nothing much happened and you thought it was just a reconnaissance."

"Well, the word I've now gotten is that the Martians set up some sort of operation down there. It doesn't appear to be construction of a fortress, thank God, but they are up to something. Last month, Funston used those reserves he'd been massing to launch an attack against them. Nothing wrong with that, of course. But the attack failed and rather than inform us and wait for us to send help…"

"Not that we could have sent much," said Roosevelt. Wood shrugged, not disputing the statement.

"Even so, rather than work with us, he stripped out three divisions from the VIII Corps, the ones guarding the lower Arkansas, to reinforce his attack in the south. That was about a week before the enemy hit Little Rock. When our forces retreated along the river, they found nothing there but a few scattered militia companies. The Martians punched through them with ease and are now rampaging south."

"Is the Mississippi Line down there secure?" asked Roosevelt, clearly concerned. "If we stopped them at St. Louis, only to let them across the river further south…"

"As I mentioned, this seems to just be a reconnaissance in force, they've made no attempt to cross. Fortunately, there aren't any bridges below Memphis, just ferries. But that doesn't change the fact that our defenses down that way are very weak. We skimped on building up 4th and 7th Armies because we were depending on Funston's forces to at least delay any drive to the south. I'm afraid we cannot afford to skimp any longer."

Roosevelt drummed his fingers on his desk. "So the counterattack we were hoping to launch from St. Louis will have to be put off."

"Yes, I hate to do it, we have a real opportunity there, but the new divisions are going to have to go south. There's just no choice."

"Blast, and there's no other forces you can draw on? We really bloodied the Martians, and if we could just launch a serious follow-up, maybe we can start driving the devils back."

Wood shook his head. "I'm afraid not. The forces actually at St. Louis are badly battered. Foltz's corps is a shambles, and the 1st Tank Division, just an empty shell. To make matters worse, the enemy is finally stirring himself up north. Our scouts in 1st Army are reporting tripods massing north of the Superior Switch. We don't dare weaken that area at all. A breakthrough there would be a disaster."

"Surely, surely, but what about the 2nd Tank Division? You still have them in reserve, don't you? Couldn't something be done with them?"

"Possibly, but I'm worried about the Memphis area. The force that attacked Little Rock is still out there. The tripods that we've seen going south don't make up a tenth of it, and we need to see where the rest of it is going to strike. Of course, maybe they'll just send some of it north to reinforce what's left of the group that hit St. Louis, but we have no way of knowing for sure. I've ordered out more cavalry patrols and air reconnaissance in hopes of locating them. Until we do, I want to keep the 2nd Tanks in reserve. The navy is sending more ships to the Memphis area, too. And lastly some good news, the new land ironclads are on their way. They ought to be there in a few more weeks. Perhaps if we can clarify the situation, we can find a place to use them where it will do some good."

"Does Memphis have any of the captured heat rays? They really did the job at St. Louis."

Wood shook his head. "Four out of the five we had there were destroyed or damaged. We've captured dozens more, of course, but it will be quite a while before they are ready to be used. For the time being, Memphis will have to depend on the forces already there, and I want the 2nd Tanks available if needed."

Roosevelt frowned and took his pince-nez glasses off his nose, cleaned them with a handkerchief, and put them back in place. "I suppose that's the sensible course of action, but blast I hate to leave the initiative to those bashi-bazouks. I'd much prefer to take some bold action and force them to react to our moves."

"I understand, Theodore, and I share your feelings. But our position is still very precarious. We dare not make a major mistake. If they get across the river in strength, we could be in very serious trouble. We might even lose the war."

"Yes, yes, I suppose you are right. So is that all the bad news?"

"Almost."

"What else do you have?"

Wood got up from his chair and walked over to a window and looked out. The White House gardens were in full bloom, belying the dire situation the country was in. As he watched, young Quentin dashed by, pursued by a pack of boys his own age and several dogs. Wood turned back to face the President.

"We need to decide what to do about Funston."

*****

JUNE, 1912, MEMPHIS, TENNESSEE

"That should about do it, Commander."

Drew Harding looked over his ship and had to agree with the manager of the Memphis repair yard. *Santa Fe* was back in fighting trim. The damage they'd taken at Little Rock had been repaired. If you knew where to look, you could see the patches and new metal, but he could accept the cosmetic blemishes as long as his ship could fight.

And it looked as though another fight was in the offing. A huge battle had been fought - and won! - up in St. Louis, but the rumors were flying that an attack on Memphis would happen soon. The whole city was stirred up like a nest of bees as last minute preparations were made. The waterfront was crammed with ships, some bringing in supplies, some taking out civilians and wounded; and many were warships, some fresh from the victory at St. Louis, topping off their coal bunkers and magazines. Speaking of which...

"Mr. Hinsworth, how did you make out with the ammunition?" He turned to his newly promoted executive officer.

"Great, sir!" answered the young man with a grin. "The magazines are filled to the brim and I found room for an extra ten rounds per gun for the eight-inchers and twelve for the five!"

"Very good. I don't want to run short like the last time. The loaders understand they are to use the extra rounds first? We don't want them lying around outside the magazines any longer than necessary."

"Yes, sir, I told them."

"Good, good. Well, I have to get over to that big conference, so you are in command, Mr. Hinsworth. Try not to let her sink while I'm away."

"Right, sir," replied Hinsworth, still grinning. The kid was turning into a good exec, and Drew was determined to keep him in that position even in the unlikely event that Mackenzie ever returned. He left the bridge and walked up the gangway to the dock. Making his way around the work gangs, mostly colored men, stripped to the waist in the heat, he reached the gate in the huge concrete walls which ringed the city and passed through. A conference was being held by the local army commander, some general named MacArthur, to coordinate the activities of all the forces which had been massed to defend Memphis.

The conference was in a big hotel on Union Street, and even though it wasn't all that far, it was all uphill. Memphis was built on a string of bluffs along the river which were a good sixty or seventy feet above the water level. Drew was soon sweating like those stevedores under his heavy uniform coat. He was slightly amazed that he was being included in this meeting. MacArthur was a corps commander and the place would probably be swarming with generals. But the senior naval commander in the area, Commodore William Rush, apparently impressed by his performance at Little Rock, had made Drew a squadron commander, in charge of a half-dozen small gunboats, in addition to his own Santa Fe, and he'd been ordered to attend.

He reached the hotel, which was called the Peabody. The entrance had dozens of soldiers and a machine gun stationed there, protected by walls of sandbags. Drew had to present the written order he'd received to get in. From there, he was directed to the ballroom, which was crowded with other officers. Most of them were army, but Drew spotted a cluster of naval uniforms and made his way over to them where he found Rush, who greeted him.

"Morning, Harding. Ready for the circus?"

"Uh, yes, sir. What do you think the general is planning to talk about?"

"God knows. MacArthur has a reputation of being a bit of a showman."

"He's awfully young to be a corps commander, isn't he, sir?" asked one of the other naval officers.

"Yes, just thirty-two. But he's got connection, you know. He was Wood's chief of staff a few years ago, then was promoted to command of the 66th Division, which was the chief unit in the garrison here. Then he was given command of the whole garrison, and two months ago he was given command of the VII Corps when Clarence Edward was promoted and transferred to take command of 4th Army. A lot of promotions going on these days - but then I don't need to tell any of *you* that do I?" He smiled and most of the others did, too. Every one of them was holding a rank they never could have dreamed of just a few years ago.

Drew looked around and saw that some army junior officers were herding people toward the front of the room where there were two large objects - maps he assumed - covered by cloths standing on a raised stage. "Looks like the show is about to begin," said Rush. "Let's find our spots, gentlemen." They trailed along and stood at the rear of the army.

There they waited for a good ten minutes before there was a commotion around one of the side doors. An officer strode through and up the steps to the stage. He was tall, with black hair, a long, slightly curved nose, and a strong jaw. He was immaculately decked out with a Sam Browne belt, polished boots, and the widest set of Jodhpur trousers Drew had ever seen. He moved briskly to the center of the stage as someone shouted out for attention. The army people all instantly snapped to. The Navy people did so a bit more casually.

MacArthur looked over the assembly and stood with feet slightly apart and his hands on his hips. "Stand at ease, gentlemen," he said. "As you all know, we have a great task ahead of us: defending this city. We all know the Martians are coming, and coming soon, but we shall be ready for them and we shall defeat them!" He waved to an aide and the cover was pulled off one of the maps, revealing the city of Memphis and its defenses.

The city, itself, was on the east shore of the Mississippi and protected by the line of massive concrete walls which stretched north and south, eventually disappearing off the edges of the map. A secondary line, which Drew had been informed was not as strong as the main line, formed an arc around the city on the landward sides, meeting the main walls north and south of the city.

MacArthur grabbed a long wooden pointer and started calling out features on the map, but Drew was more interested in the river than the shore defenses. The Mississippi, close to three quarters of a mile wide in this area, came down from the north and then turned almost due east before swinging in a wide arc until it was heading in the exact opposite direction, slightly north of west, before turning south again. The wide loop to the east was where the city was located. He noted with interest that there was a small channel called the Wolf River which sliced northwest from the city to rejoin the Mississippi several miles above the first big turn, creating a sizable island, which was low and swampy. He wasn't sure if the Wolf River was navigable for his ship, but he intended to find out.

MacArthur paused in his lecture and then suddenly slapped the map to the west of the river. "Over here is West Memphis," he said. "My predecessors have regarded this area as expendable, a forlorn hope, an outer work which in the event of a serious attack would be abandoned, its garrison withdrawn over the bridge, which would be demolished after they passed. 'Defense Plan M' they called it. Gentlemen, I feel that plan to be defeatist and I will not endorse it! We will not give up any more ground! Not one inch! So forget Defense Plan M!" He had the attention of everyone in the room now and continued.

"Up until now, the West Memphis defenses have been held by a single regiment from the 66th Division along with some artillery and local militia. I plan to reinforce them with two brigades, one taken from the 29th Division and another from the 36th Division, to the north and south of the city."

This created a stir among the army officers and one asked, "Excuse me, sir, but won't that leave the defenses along the river in those areas rather weak?"

"A bit weaker, perhaps," replied MacArthur, "but not weak. The line of concrete walls extends farther and farther along the river every day. As they do, the heavy artillery takes up most of the load and the infantry can sidle north and south, strengthening their positions as they shorten. In the meantime, our friends in the navy can make sure the enemy stay on their side of the river, right, Commodore?" He looked at Rush.

"We'll certainly do our best, General," said Rush.

"Good! But as I was saying, West Memphis and the bridge will be held. Supported by our guns on the river and on the eastern shore, we shall crush the enemy attack and then we shall launch an attack of our own!" He waved to his aide and the man uncovered the second map. It showed a much larger area of Arkansas across the river.

"You've all heard of the big victory at St. Louis. I take nothing away from the brave men who fought there, but a huge opportunity was missed. With the enemy defeated, an immediate counterattack should have been launched. Push them and keep pushing! Kansas City might have been liberated and the enemy driven all the way back to their fortress!" He looked out at the assembled officers, his face stern, eyes blazing. "Gentlemen, we shall not make that same mistake!"

He pointed to West Memphis on the map and then drew a line across it, all the way to...

"Little Rock! That is our objective! Once we have crushed their attack we shall drive the enemy back and liberate Little Rock!"

Silence was the immediate reaction of the men in the room. Drew could only think that MacArthur was getting ahead of himself. Surely their immediate concern was defeating the Martian attack. Plans for the future were fine, but until they had won the immediate battle and then seen what they had left fit for duty, how could they know if such a counterattack was even possible?

One man finally broke the silence, an army officer with two stars on his uniform. "Uh, have you cleared these plans with Washington, sir?"

MacArthur waved his hand in casual dismissal. "Don't worry, Bill, when the time comes I'll make them see what needs to be done. But now, let's get down to brass tacks!" He turned back to the first map and began to lay out the basic plans for the defense of the city. Most of it was meant for the army and had little effect on the navy or Drew. Still, there was an overall plan for utilizing all the artillery in the region, along with the navy ships, which was of the same sort used down in Panama when he was aboard the old *Minnesota*. A junior officer circulated among the navy officers handing out folders with the details. Drew paged through while the general dealt with non-navy matters. Yes, he could handle this…

The meeting dragged on for another hour, but eventually wrapped up with another declaration of their inevitable victory by MacArthur. Then, to Drew's amazement, a group of newspaper reporters were called in and MacArthur made a prepared statement to them and posed for pictures in front of the maps. Commodore Rush decided they could excuse themselves and they escaped.

"God in Heaven!" said the captain of Amphitrite. "What a blowhard!"

Rush snorted, but didn't dispute the statement—or reprimand the man for having made it.

"If nothing else, he's certainly counting unhatched chickens," said another. "Little Rock! Is he serious?"

"I'm sure he is," said Rush. "He was born there, you know."

* * * * *

JUNE, 1912, NEAR KEY WEST, FLORIDA

Andrew grabbed the railing as the *Albuquerque* rolled sharply to the right. Salt spray lashed his face, only to be immediately washed away by the wind-driven rain. A weird wailing hum filled the air as that wind whipped through the rigging overhead. He was soaked to the skin, despite a rain slicker. He looked around, but the visibility was less than a quarter mile; he could barely make out the dark bulk of the Monodnock up ahead. The towing ship had a light on her stern which twinkled fitfully in the gray dimness of the storm. None of the other ships were in sight anywhere. The seas were mountainous, with the tops of the waves far above the main deck of the ironclad. They broke and crashed over the flotation modules, which creaked and groaned loudly enough to be heard over the storm.

"Dear Lord, how much more of this can we take?" shouted Jerry Hornbaker from beside him. "We're gonna break apart!"

Andrew didn't answer. He was wondering the same thing himself. The voyage from Norfolk had been going so well. The sea had been so pleasant that even Major Stavely had managed to throw off his seasickness. They made it past the legendary hazards of Cape Hatteras in a dead calm under sunny skies and paused for two days in Charleston to take on coal. General Clopton had held a wonderful dinner for all the senior officers, both army and navy at the city's best hotel. Then it was back to sea.

They had just rounded the tip of Florida when word reached them of a bad storm which had formed in the northern Gulf and was heading southeast toward them. Some had suggested turning back and going north along the east coast of Florida to try and find a sheltered harbor there, but the commodore in charge had insisted they could make it to the navy anchorage at Key West.

They almost made it.

They ran into the outer edges of the storm during the night and it built steadily in the hours before dawn. Any hope of sleep was long gone, and Andrew had donned his lifejacket and stared out of the pilothouse windows into the shrieking blackness for an eternity. He hadn't seen Stavely all night. Now that it was light, he wasn't sure that being able to see was better than being blind. He'd made it through one storm on that memorable voyage down to Panama with President Roosevelt, but it had been nothing like this.

"The commodore said we should reach Key West this morning!" said Andrew to Hornbaker, shouting to be heard. "But we probably lost time running against the storm. God knows where we are now!" He looked up to the observation platform. Perhaps he could see farther up there. But then the ship rolled again, the platform swung across the sky, and he decided he didn't want to see that badly.

So they clung to the rail as the rain poured down on them. From time to time they'd catch sight of other ships. Usually it would be their escorting destroyer, but sometimes the visibility would improve enough to see farther, and he thought he could see some of the other towing vessels.

Around eight o'clock, Lieutenant Broadt appeared, coming up the ladder from below. He saw them and paused. "Morning! Quite a little blow, ain't it?" The man was actually smiling.

"'Little blow'?!" cried Hornbaker. "Isn't this a hurricane?"

"This? Why, it's scarcely a breeze. A real hurricane and we'd be on the bottom already."

Andrew stared at the man, but then the vessel rolled sharply and even Broadt had to grab the railing. "You're kidding, aren't you?" asked Andrew.

"Well, a bit," admitted the navy man. "Still, this isn't a hurricane. A pretty strong gale, but not a hurricane."

"Are we gonna make it to Key West?" asked Hornbaker. Jerry was looking a bit green. Quite a few of the army crewmen were bent over railings and looking worse. Andrew had discovered the trick on earlier voyages to stare straight out at the horizon when he was feeling queasy - except today there was no horizon.

"We ought to see the lighthouse any time now."

"So we're not in any danger?" demanded Andrew. "The ships are holding up?"

"Can't speak for the others, but this bucket is doing okay. A few leaks, but nothing to worry about. Once we're in the anchorage, we'll be fine."

"And we should be there soon?"

"An hour or two, probably. The approach is going to be a bit tricky, the anchorage was chosen more with coming from the Atlantic in mind, but it should be okay." Broadt, nodded to them and then went up the ladder to the swaying observation platform as if it wasn't moving at all. Andrew and Hornbaker retreated inside the pilot house for a while to escape the rain and spray, but the enclosed space made their nausea worse and they soon went back out into the wind and water.

Suddenly, there was a shout from above and a horn blast from Monodnock. They looked around and spotted a dim light off to the north. It appeared and disappeared on a regular rhythm and they assumed it was the lighthouse Broadt had spoken of. And then, bit by bit, a shoreline appeared, although it was just a slightly darker streak of gray in the gloom. It grew more distinct as the blinking light slowly passed to the east.

A few minutes later, Broadt came back down the ladder. He grinned and pointed. "We're here. Told you we'd be all right."

"But where's the anchorage?"

"We'll be rounding the point in a little bit. You can just make out Fort Zachary Taylor over there. Then it's north a few miles and around another point, and we'll be there. Not an enclosed harbor like Charleston, you understand, but a safe anchorage."

He stayed with them as they, oh so slowly, made the turn to the north. The wind and seas seemed worse than ever there and Broadt confirmed that the islands had given them a little shelter which was now lost, but he seemed unconcerned. It was nearly another hour before they saw the second point. Even then they had to claw their way north another mile against wind and waves before they could make their turn. Then, with the weather behind them, they made what seemed like a mad rush into the lee behind the island into the much calmer waters of the anchorage.

The visibility improved a bit and Andrew breathed easier when he spotted three of the other ironclads and their tows and escorts already there. *Monodnock* stopped her engines and dropped anchor. *Albuquerque* followed suit and sat there rolling easily. Signal lamps started blinking, and shortly they received a message that the other ironclads were *Omaha, Tulsa,* and *Springfield.*

"I hope *Billings* and *Sioux Falls* are all right," said Andrew.

"They'll be along," said Broadt, and within a half hour, Billings indeed entered the anchorage. Noon came and Andrew was feeling well enough to go down to the galley and get some food. He'd eaten nothing since dinner the previous evening.

But he'd barely started on a sandwich when he heard a faint wailing from outside. It went on and on, and after a few minutes, his curiosity overwhelmed his hunger and he went back out on deck. Broadt was there, and this time there wasn't any trace of good humor on his face. He was leaning into the wind, looking northwest with his head cocked.

Outside, Andrew recognized the sound: a ship's steam whistle. Normally they came in short toots, but this one was continuous. Then, it was abruptly silenced and over the roar of the wind and seas came a low rumble which changed to a screech of metal before fading away.

"That... that surely can't be good," gasped Andrew.

"No," said Broadt, his face grim. "No it can't."

Nor was it. By late afternoon, the storm dwindled and died with amazing swiftness, and a few rays of sun peeked through the shredding clouds. Shortly, a steam launch put off from the *Olympia* and swung by *Albuquerque* to pick up Andrew. General Clopton and the commodore were aboard and the boat chugged out around the point. It didn't take long to see what had made that ominous noise.

The ship towing *Sioux Falls* had lost power just a mile from safety and been thrown up on the shore by the waves. She lay there, her back broken, like a dead leviathan. Amazingly, there had been no loss of life. Even more amazingly, *Sioux Falls* had also survived somehow. With its puny propeller, there had been no hope of fighting the seas, so its commander had turned directly toward shore. The moment its tracks touched bottom, he had jettisoned the flotation modules and lurched onto the shore with only minor damage. The navy men seemed to think it little short of a miracle.

"Miracle or not, it's still stuck here," said Clopton. It was true, the flotation modules had been smashed to bits on the rocks and there wasn't another set this side of Philadelphia. "Well, we aren't going to wait. Can we get going again in the morning, Commodore?"

The naval commander nodded. "Everyone else is in good shape. By morning, the storm should be completely out of our path and we can make a straight run to New Orleans. But for this evening, I'd be pleased if you and your staff could join me for dinner on *Olympia.*"

After days of the simple fare offered by *Albuquerque's* small galley, Andrew was more than willing to accept the invitation. But the launch took them straight back to *Olympia* and he was conscious of his still slightly damp service uniform. He hadn't brought a full dress uniform, but still...

Olympia was an old ship and had been one of the navy's first modern all-steel vessels. As such, she was a transition from the earlier ships. While she mounted her main guns in turrets fore and aft, her secondary guns were in an open gun deck reminiscent of those found on the old wooden ships. The commodore's cabin, along with the other officers', were also on this deck and several of the cabins had been temporarily dismantled to make room for the dinner. White-gloved steward guided Andrew to his chair.

The commodore was naturally at the head of the table with Clopton on his right and *Olympia's* skipper on his left. The navy officer ran down one side of the table and the army on the other.

Andrew sat next to Clopton, but directly across from him was an officer he'd never seen before, and with a start he realized what sort of a uniform he was wearing.

"Oh yes, I almost forgot," said the Commodore. "Let me introduce you all to Major Tom Bridges. He just arrived aboard a few hours ago. Came down from Washington to observe your crazy ironclads. He's British, as you can see, and we've been ordered to extend him every courtesy." Everyone rendered greetings and the tall, red-cheeked, and mustachioed man smiled and nodded to one and all.

"Thank you, sir," he said, his accent very distinct. "I spent a few months observing one of your cavalry units out west. I *thought* I'd be getting some leave back home, but when we found out that your new war machines are going to see action soon, I was ordered here. I look forward to working with you, General Clopton."

Clopton nodded, but didn't look too pleased. "I hope you find your stay enlightening, Major. But I'm afraid there won't be any room on *Springfield* where I'll have my headquarters. In any case, Comstock here knows more about these contraptions than anyone. You can accompany him."

Andrew was taken back, but Bridges grinned and reached across the table extending his hand. "Splendid! I couldn't be more pleased to serve with you, Colonel!"

There wasn't anything to do but to shake his hand. "Uh, glad to have you with us, Major."

* * * * *

JUNE, 1912, MEMPHIS, TENNESSEE

Becca Harding peered out over the top of the city wall and across the Mississippi. The sun wasn't quite up yet and there was a thin mist clinging to the river and the shore beyond. The enemy was over there somewhere. Everyone said that they were coming, coming to attack Memphis. The whole city was in a frenzy, with rumors of every sort flying as fast as loose tongues could spread them. Troops were moving into and through the city in large numbers. Even this early in the morning, she could see a column marching across the bridge into West Memphis. Train loads and ship loads of supplies and ammunition were pouring in. And people were leaving, too. The very young and the old were being moved out, by train and by boat. Others were slipping out, by horse or motor car. Becca turned and looked down from the wall and frowned at the campsite of the Memphis Women's Volunteer Sharpshooters.

It was nearly empty.

The word had come down three days ago that all of the local militia units were being mobilized to defend the city. There had been an initial wave of excitement among the women, and grand plans were made and the whole company assembled at the Oswald mansion. They had paraded through the streets to their assigned spot by the river. Becca had felt a thrill of pride to march as their lieutenant, and a surprising number of people came out to wave and give them a cheer.

But it had been a long march, and before they were halfway to their designated spot, Mrs. Oswald had pleaded exhaustion and went back to ride in the carriage which had been following the company, driven by one of her servants. Several other women had soon joined her, and by the time they got to the river, the company had dissolved into a long stream of stragglers - a few even gave up and went home before they got there.

They had pitched camp - fine new canvas tents, also provided by the Oswalds - in the muddy field which had once been a city park, amidst the equipment and supplies of the artillerymen who manned the big guns along the walls, and right next to the other – male – militia unit they were assigned to work with. Sergeant Leo Polk Smith, who she'd met earlier, had strolled over, looking just as amused as before, to make some suggestions on how to arrange things, and he'd been followed by a few dozen of his fellow militiamen. They'd laughed, hooted, and some made some very rude remarks, until one of their officers came over and herded them back where they belonged. That same officer had then posted sentries to make sure they *stayed* where they belonged.

By that time, many of the women were having second thoughts about the whole thing, and nearly half of them went to sleep in their own homes despite the fact that the tents were what an officer would normally rate with a cot and everything. A number of them had not come back the next morning.

Becca wondered if there would be anyone at all here today.

The artillerymen were up and so were the other militiamen, building fires and boiling coffee. It was an utterly familiar routine to Becca, and she moved to one of the ladders to climb down to ground level to get her own coffee started. A few of the gunners nodded or said good morning. None of them treated her as an officer, but at least they were treating her like a lady. Her hand brushed the lump in her pocket. She still carried the revolver Miss Chumley had given her back at Gallup, almost three years ago.

Even though it wasn't proper work for an officer, she stopped at a pile of shattered lumber which had once been a house before it was demolished to make way for the new walls. The soldiers were using it for firewood and she scooped up an armload. One of the campfires still had a few smoldering embers and she managed to coax it back to life and get a coffee pot hung over it.

By then, there were some moans and groans coming from a few of the tents, so she knew she wouldn't be totally alone. Of course, she wouldn't have been completely alone even if every last sharpshooter had deserted. She looked over to where Ninny was picketed and smiled. She'd managed to spirit her horse away from the hospital after she'd told Miss Chumley that she was leaving to join the sharpshooters full time. It hadn't been an easy decision, and she was wondering if she'd made a mistake. Chumley hadn't been happy, but she had no real means to stop her from leaving as all the nurses were volunteers and Becca had never signed any papers or sworn any oaths. She had told Becca that she could still come back if she wanted to.

A shout from across the way caught her attention. Sergeant Leo Smith was calling his own company together for morning roll call. She had been copying Smith's actions whenever possible in running the sharpshooters, so she got up from the fire and walked down the rows of tents, whacking the poles with a stick. "All right! Up and at 'em, girls! Wake up! Get up! On the street for roll call!"

More moans and groans answered her, but eventually about two dozen women were lined up in front of the tents. It was more than Becca had expected, but still pretty disappointing. The woman who was supposed to be the company first sergeant was among the missing, so she appointed Sarah Halberstam, one the most reliable people in the group, to fill in. She read off the roll, dutifully repeating the names of the absent twice, and then marking them as 'not present'. When she was finished, she saluted Becca and said: "Twenty-five present for duty, Lieutenant."

Becca returned the salute. "Thank you, Sergeant. Get the girls to breakfast. We'll police the camp afterward and then do some drill."

"Yes, m-ma'am." Halberstam, nearly twice her age, looked about as comfortable *ma'aming* her as Becca felt being *ma'amed*, and after a few seconds, they both grinned.

"Takes some gettin' used to, doesn't it?"

"You're doing fine, Becca. It's not easy for any of us, I guess."

"Yeah. But make sure the girls who are still here know how proud I am of 'em, okay?"

"The others will be back. Well, some of them, I'm sure." Halberstam smiled, but she couldn't keep the doubt out of her eyes. She nodded and went back to the rest to get breakfast cooking. At least they had some fresh stuff and weren't depending on hard tack and salted pork.

Becca went back to her own tent and washed her face with some water out of her canteen. Camping out seemed like second nature to her. As a child on the ranch, she'd done it all the time. Then there was the long months during the siege of the Martian fortress at Gallup. But most of the women in the sharpshooters were upper class ladies from Memphis' finest families. They'd lived in nice houses with servants their whole lives. This must seem like a real hardship to most of them. It was hard to blame them for slipping back home at night to sleep in a soft bed.

She was pleased that nearly a dozen of them did return before breakfast was over. They looked a little sheepish, but she decided not to make an issue of it. If she did, they might not come back tomorrow. The fact of the matter was that she had no real authority over them at all. They could walk away any time they wanted to. *Just like I walked away from the hospital.* That was a thought which was intruding more and more lately. She had left a job where she was undeniably doing good to take another job where she might well not do any good at all. Was her obsession about fighting just a childish tantrum? She'd get back to that question - after the battle.

She was just about to order the company to fall in when a carriage clattered up. She recognized it and the driver; they came from the Oswald mansion. Was Theodora coming today? She walked over to the carriage with Sarah Halberstam, but as she got closer, she saw that the driver, an elderly colored man named Moses, was alone.

"Hi, Mo," she said. "What brings you here?"

Moses climbed down from the carriage. The usually jovial man didn't look happy. "Mornin' Miz Becca," he said. "Got a message from Missus Oswald."

"Oh? What is it?"

"Well, she an' Mister Oswald took out real early this morning, fore it was even light, in their motor car. Took all sorts of bags and boxes with 'em. Wouldn't say where's they were goin', neither. But the Missus told me to tell you that she…" he hesitated as if recalling her exact words. "She has the… ut-most… con-fi-dence in your… ability to command the sharpshooters."

"Oh," said Becca. "I see. I guess… I guess she's not comin' back?"

"Didn't look that way to me, no ma'am," said Mo.

"Oh. Well, thank you for tellin' me, Mo. What are you goin' to do now?"

"Don't rightly know, Miz. They locked the house up tight a'fore they left. 'Cept the servant's quarters, of course. Guess I'll go back there an' see what happens."

"You're welcome to stay and help out here, if you want, Mo."

"Could I?" Mo's expression brightened. "The carriage would be good for haulin' stuff. An' I kin take care of your horse, too, Miz Becca."

"That would be fine, Mo. I can't offer you no pay, but you can eat our chow."

"Thank you, Miz! No pay is fine. I know how to shoot a rifle, too! If you can spare me one, I'll get me a Martian!"

Becca laughed. "I think we can scare one up for you, Mo. Why don't you park the carriage over there."

Mo bobbed his head and got back aboard the vehicle.

Becca looked at Sarah and the older woman was smiling. "Well, looks like you are in charge, Becca. Everyone knew that was the case all along. But now it's official, Lieutenant!"

* * * * *

581

CYCLE 597, 845.2, EAST OF HOLDFAST 32-4

Qetjnegartis maneuvered its fighting machine between the tall vertical columns of the native vegetation. It was almost completely dark beneath the dense foliage and it had to set the light-amplification on the vision pick-ups to nearly the maximum. The growths were of considerable height, and the main columns of the bigger ones were thick and strong enough to even block a fighting machine. In places where they grew closely together, it was impossible to find a path. Of course, it could simply use the heat ray to burn a way through, but the flames and smoke that would produce would be revealing - and that was to be avoided at all cost.

The long-planned attack was about to be launched and surprise was essential. For the last ten days, a screen of the smaller scouting war machines had spread out from the holdfast, driving back the prey-creature patrols. This would no doubt alert the enemy that something was going to happen soon, but there was no avoiding that, and indeed it could well prove to be an advantage - as long as they did not realize just *what* was about to happen.

The enemy's air patrols were a more serious problem. Every day in which the atmospheric conditions were not unfavorable, the prey-creature flying machines were in the air, sweeping across the landscape. Fortunately, they did not fly at night. The prey-creatures could not see well in the dark, and while they had started using artificial means of illumination on the battlefield, their flying machines had rarely been encountered after nightfall.

Qetjnegartis had taken advantage of this to move its forces. The areas of dense vegetation, usually an annoying hindrance to movement, were now proving valuable. The growths were tall enough to conceal a fighting machine, and this particular area was now concealing almost two hundred of them. Another area a score of *telequel* to the north held a like number. Over a thousand of the new drones accompanied each group along with the novel... *constructs* devised by Ixmaderna. A great deal - far too much in Qetjnegartis' judgment - was being staked on the success of these untested things. But there seemed little other choice. The attack must be launched and the river must be crossed.

It reached the main gathering point of the battlegroup commanders. Most of the commanders were older clan members who arrived in the second or third wave of transports, but a few were from the first of the buds to be created here on the target world. Qetjnegartis' own bud, Davnitargus, was in command of Battlegroup 32-8.

"The operation begins tonight," it announced. "Tanbradjus will lead the two battlegroups and the reserve fighting machines which will create the diversionary attack. This is beginning as we speak. We will remain here, out of sight until tomorrow night, when we shall commence the river crossing. Are there any questions?"

"Do you have any estimates on how difficult the physical passage of the river will be, Commander?" asked Gandgenar, commander of Battlegroup 32-12. "Our success will depend much on that."

"You are correct. Unfortunately, we have had no way to test the river bottom in the crossing area for fear that this will give away our intentions. Tests in other locations indicate that the conditions can vary significantly, so we will only know when we make the attempt. This is far from ideal, I know, but there is no other practical alternative. But whatever conditions we encounter, we must make every effort to overcome them and cross the river."

"I understand. We will not fail you, Commander."

There were no other questions. The plan had been worked out in detail, and they had all studied it. "Very well. For now we wait."

* * * * *

582

JUNE, 1912, NEAR EARLE, ARKANSAS

"They're comin' for sure, Captain! Thick as fleas on a dog's back!"

Captain Frank Dolfen looked at the face of the gasping scout in the light of a lantern.

"You're sure? It's not just another screen of their scouts?"

"No sir. There's enough moonlight to see by and there were swarms of 'em behind the scouts. Couldn't count 'em all, but three or four dozen at least!"

"And coming this way?"

"Coming this way fast, sir! Can't be more'n four or five miles off now!"

Dolfen nodded grimly. They'd been expecting this for days. The 5th Cavalry and two other regiments of the 1st Cavalry Division had been spread out to the west of Memphis to give warning of the impending Martian attack. They'd been skirmishing with the enemy scout machines, on and off, for nearly a week. There had been too many of them to engage in a pitched battle, and they'd been careful enough not allow any ambushes of smaller groups. So the cavalry had been forced back mile by mile until they were less than twenty miles from West Memphis. If this new report was correct, the attack would happen very soon.

"All right," he said, turning to his second in command. "Get the men up and ready to move. Get a messenger off to the colonel and another one straight back to headquarters. Tell them they're coming."

CHAPTER FOURTEEN

JULY, 1912, MEMPHIS, TENNESSEE

"Holy cow! Wouldja lookit that!"

Rebecca Harding stared out from the city walls with hundreds of other people. The dark western sky was lit up with a continuous flickering glow. Closer at hand, artillery was blasting away, adding to the flashes and producing a noise it was hard to hear over. Leo Polk Smith was standing next to her and seemed to think the tremendous display of firepower was some sort of Independence Day celebration come three days early.

She had to admit it was impressive and rivaled, or maybe even exceeded, the one she'd seen back at Gallup. She tried not to think about how that one had ended up. But things were going to be different this time. That time at Gallup, the army had been attacking the Martian stronghold, and just when it seemed like victory was in reach, a new enemy force had arrived by surprise and smashed into the rear area, destroying the artillery and throwing the army into confusion. That couldn't happen this time. The enemy was attacking the defenses of West Memphis across the mile-wide Mississippi. They had attacked the previous night and had been probing and probing all through the day, and now night had fallen again. The guns in the defenses, on the ships in the river, and the long-range guns on the eastern shore had hammered back, hopefully hurting the Martians.

Reinforcements had been streaming across the bridge into West Memphis all day. There had been rumors that the Women's Sharpshooters would be ordered across to join them, but Becca refused to believe that. Few people knew they even existed and fewer would deliberately put them in harm's way. She'd always known the sharpshooters would be keep in reserve and never be committed except as an absolute last resort. Before it had gotten dark, she'd seen some ambulances crossing the bridge in the opposite direction as the marching troops. They were bringing back wounded. Maybe she should have stayed at the hospital…

"Do… do you think the Martians will make it over here?"

Rebecca looked and saw that Abigail LaPlace had come up next to her. Abigail was the youngest of the sharpshooters, a few months younger than Becca. She was still amazed that her parents were allowing her to do this.

"Doesn't look like it," said Leo Smith, overhearing. "They've been attackin' all day and don't seem to be makin' much progress."

"Can't tell nothin' from that," said Becca. "They're just probing us. Testin' the strength of the defenses and locating our artillery. They did that at Albuquerque. Then they hit us all at once when it got dark. They might be fixin' to do that same thing here tonight."

Smith jerked his head back, face skeptical in the flickering light. "How d'you know all that?"

"I was there." It wasn't exactly the truth, she'd been further north in Santa Fe, but she had heard what happened from the other soldiers during the retreat. Smith snorted, shook his head, and turned away. He clearly didn't believe her, but she didn't care. She turned back to Abigail. The girl was in uniform and carrying her rifle but...

"Where's your dust mask, Private?"

"I... I left it back in my tent, ma'am."

"If the enemy is close by, never go without carrying it. I gave orders about that."

"Sorry, ma'am. But it's heavy and the Martians are way over there and..."

"That's no excuse. They move fast and they don't always give any warning. We have to always be ready." Becca looked out across the river. "This fight has just begun."

* * * * *

JULY, 1912, WEST MEMPHIS, ARKANSAS

"We will move out in one hour. We'll stay as close to the river as we can until we're past them, then we will turn northwest and head toward Clarkdale. Keep your advanced guard and flankers as close to your column as you safely can. We are to avoid all contact. It shouldn't be too hard, the enemy doesn't like our ships on the river and they've pulled in that flank. Once we reach Clarkdale, we'll send out scouts and see what we can see."

The assembled officers of the 5th Cavalry looked at Colonel Schumacher and listened gravely to his orders. The colonel had to almost shout to be heard above the nearby guns.

"What's our objective, sir?" asked Frank Dolfen. "The men and horses are still pretty tired." They'd been sparring with the Martian scouts for nearly a week and had finally fallen back inside the defenses of West Memphis. They were looking forward to a chance to rest a bit.

"Our objective?" replied Schumacher. He smiled. "Why, Frank, you shouldn't need to ask. The generals are hoping we can pull off the same miracle as we did at Little Rock: find the enemy's reserve tripods and destroy them. They're sending us and the 9th out to the north and the two regiments in the other brigade out to the south with the same mission."

The other officers began murmuring. One of them said: "Hopefully we can avoid blowing *ourselves* up this time, sir."

"Yes, let's extend every effort to avoiding that. But that is our mission and we will carry it out. Return to your commands and get them ready, gentlemen. That's all."

They all saluted Schumacher and he returned it. Then they dispersed. Frank was just nearing the area where his squadron was camped when the bugles started ringing out down the line sounding the assembly. If it had not been for the roar of the artillery, he was quite sure the bugles would have been answered by the moans and curses of the men, awakened from the first sound sleep they'd had in a week. The fact that they'd been able to sleep only a quarter mile behind the front lines in the middle of a battle showed how tired they were.

Tired or not, they got up. Dolfen passed on the orders to his own officers and in a commendably short time the troops commanders were reporting ready. Normally it would have taken longer in the dark, but there was an almost constant light from the flares and star shells the gunners were sending up. They were mostly a few miles away, but they were so intense they lit up the whole area brighter than a full moon. He hoped it wouldn't give them away to the Martians when they moved out.

There were the inevitable delays getting two regiments ready to move, but in only a little longer than the hour the colonel had given them, they were on their way. The 5th was leading the column, and as 1st Squadron, Frank's men were leading the 5th. He could tell they were tired by the general

586

lack of grumbling, but they were veterans and knew they had a job to do. He was still rather appalled by the number of men in A Troop carrying those damn rocket lances - long poles with stovepipe rockets fixed to the end of them. They were bloody suicide weapons and everyone knew it. Even a few of the motorcycle riders in B Troop were carrying them now, although the bikes with sidecars tended to have the passenger carrying an actual stovepipe launcher if they could get one. The launchers were still in short supply, but the army, in its infinite wisdom, was shipping twenty rockets with each launcher; as if there was any hope that a man would survive long enough to fire more than three or four of the things.

They slowly made their way down streets already packed with troops and wagons. The local commander, General MacArthur, had been pouring troops across the bridge into West Memphis all day. Dolfen had been based in this area for months, and they'd been told that the plan was that West Memphis would not be heavily defended in the event of a major attack; but it sure seemed like MacArthur was planning to hold the place now. Dolfen approved: they'd already given up too much ground. Still, he wondered where all these troops were coming from.

A staff officer had been assigned to show them the route out of town, and at first Dolfen wondered if the young man was lost, because he seemed to be leading them almost due east; but then he saw there was a method to his madness. The east side of West Memphis was protected from flooding by a stout levee, and the top was flat and wide enough for a column of cavalry. He led them up on to it and turned north. This let them pass through the defensive works with no trouble, the river on their right and the Martians – hopefully - well off to their left.

As promised, there were numerous warships on the river firing at the enemy, and their heavy guns did seem to be keeping the Martians away. Dolfen sent his scouts ahead, warning them not to go too far. He was a bit worried about being silhouetted on top of the levee, but a quick look at the ground on either side convinced him this was the only practical route. So they rode north with a grandstand view of the battle to the west.

The artillery was firing at a steady pace, and from time to time there would be a salvo from a ship on the river. He could see explosions where the shells hit and sometimes a tripod would be lit up, but they were too far off to tell if any damage was being done. Every now and then they'd see a heat ray being fired, but it looked as though the enemy was still just probing the defense lines. The main attack was still to come. Dolfen was actually glad to be out of there, now that he thought about it. A city fight was no place for cavalry.

They rode a few miles and got to the place where they were supposed to turn more to the west and head for the town of Clarkdale, but the scouts came back and reported that there was a solid line of enemy tripods blocking the path in that direction. "There's one of them bastards every four or five hundred yards across the line of march," said a sergeant. "No way we'll get past 'em without a fight, sir." Dolfen reported this to Colonel Schumacher.

"There's no point in us getting ourselves into a pitched battle here," he said. "Is the way along the levee still open, Frank?"

"Seems to be, sir. Although it swings in a loop off to the east, following the river."

"Well, so be it. We'll take a wider route up to Gilmore and see if we can get into their rear from there."

"That's gonna take a while. Might be dawn before we get there, sir."

"I know. We'll have to pick up the pace. Get them moving, Captain."

"Yes, sir." He gave the orders and the column lurched into motion again. The levee actually turned away from the direction they wanted to go for a mile or so, but then swung back to the northwest. It was also getting lower and lower and eventually stopped altogether. There was still a dirt road following the river, but it was overgrown and clearly hadn't been used for a while. Frank hoped it

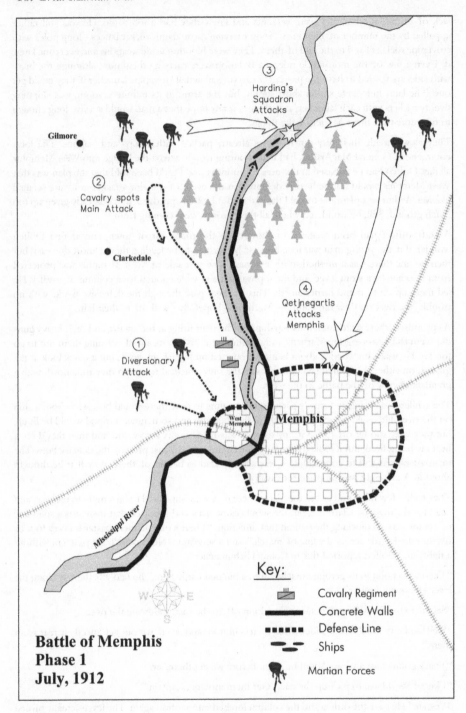

**Battle of Memphis
Phase 1
July, 1912**

Gilmore

② Cavalry spots
Main Attack

Clarkedale

③ Harding's
Squadron
Attacks

④ Qetjnegartis
Attacks
Memphis

① Diversionary
Attack

West
Memphis

Memphis

Mississippi River

Key:

Cavalry Regiment

Concrete Walls

Defense Line

Ships

Martian Forces

wouldn't just lead them into a swamp. Their staff officer had disappeared an hour earlier and he had no one familiar with the area. Except for the remains of one smashed tripod - killed by the navy apparently - they had left the battle behind. While they could still hear it, they were getting no light from the star shells anymore and it was very dark under the trees which lined the road.

It was about one in the morning when by dead reckoning they turned away from the river and headed for Gilmore. They broke out of the trees and found that the moon, just two days past the full, was now overhead and providing enough light to see by. They advanced a mile over abandoned fields and eventually stumbled on a road which appeared to be going the way they wanted. The battle was just a rumble now, and the noise from the motorcycles and armored cars seemed very loud in the warm, still night air.

The land sloped slightly upward away from the Mississippi. Another mile or two and it would flatten out with unobstructed views for miles. Once it was light, maybe they could get some aircraft spotting for them. They'd been a big help during the skirmishing in the previous week, although no attacks had been permitted. Apparently they were saving them for the...

"Captain! Captain Dolfen! Rider coming in!"

The shout wasn't loud, but it still made him flinch. He looked ahead and a man on a horse was galloping down the road as fast as the beast could carry him. Damn, they must have run into another Martian scout. The bastards were being a lot more careful after what had happened at Little Rock. Could they get around it somehow? If they lost the element of surprise...

"Martians! Martians, Captain!" gasped the man. As he reined in his horse, Dolfen saw that it was Sergeant Findley, one of the best scouts in the regiment. "A whole passel of 'em!"

"What? How many? Where?"

"Hundreds! Just the other side of that high ground! Hundreds of them heading east!"

"Get hold of yourself, man! Are you sure?"

"'Course I'm sure! They ain't a mile off and I can see 'em in the moonlight!"

Good God! Another attack force? Where had it come from? And where was it going? "Come on, show me!" The scout turned his horse around and they both headed back the way he'd just come. Dolfen shouted back at Lieutenant Lynnbrooke: "Halt the column! Get the colonel up here!"

Dolfen leaned forward and used one hand to hold his hat on as they galloped to the higher ground. Even before they reached the top, he could see the heads of the tall war machines bobbing along in the distance. The man had been right: there were a lot of them.

A *lot* of them.

He halted his horse and took in the horrifying sight. More tripods than he'd ever seen at once before. A hundred at least and maybe more, all striding from left to right across his path. Moonlight reflected off their skins like off the water in a flowing stream. The red lights which normally glowed from the middle of their 'faces' were all dark for some reason. Their thin, metal legs were moving with that bizarre, yet rapid gait that always gave him chills. It looked like some metal forest on the march. And all around the machines' legs...

"Are those the spider-machines they've been talking about?" whispered Findley.

"Must be," said Dolfen. They'd heard a lot of stories about them, but this was the first time he'd actually seen them. There looked to be hundreds and hundreds of them moving with the bigger machines.

"Dear Lord! There are more of 'em! Look, sir!" The trooper pointed and Dolfen saw that beyond the horde in front of him, there was another dark and glittering mass on a rise in the ground another mile or so off to the north.

"My God," gasped Dolfen. "This is bad, really bad."

"What's that noise, sir? That other noise?"

Dolfen cocked his head and heard what the man was asking about: a hissing, grinding sound like something big being dragged along the ground. He fumbled out his binoculars and looked. It was hard to see much, even with the moonlight, but after a moment he realized that broad rectangular shapes were being pulled by some of the tripods using cables. At first he couldn't grasp what they were but then it suddenly came to him.

"Boats! Damn, they've got boats!"

"To get across the river?"

"What else? We need to warn headquarters! Come on!" They turned their horses around and galloped back down the hill to where the head of the column had halted. As he'd hoped, Colonel Schumacher was there.

"What have we got, Frank?" he asked.

"Trouble, sir! Big trouble! There's two or three hundred tripods and God knows how many of those spider-machines, and they are all heading toward the river and they've got boats!"

"Boats?"

"Boats or rafts of some kind. They're dragging them along. Sir! They mean to cross the river north of the city!"

"You're right. No other possibility. We need to let MacArthur know. Is there a radio in one of your armored cars?"

"Yes, sir! Right back there."

"Sir," said Schumacher's adjutant, "we transmit this close to them, they'll hear for sure. They'll come after us and we can't fight three hundred tripods!"

"No choice, this can't wait," said the colonel. "Get that message off, Frank. The rest of you, get the column turned around and prepare for a fighting withdrawal!"

* * * * *

CYCLE 597, 845.2, WEST OF RIVER 3-1

"Commander, we have intercepted an enemy transmission. It is very close by. Two or three *telequel* to the south."

Qetjnegartis checked its own sensors and saw that it was true. "It is likely that we have been spotted. Tanbradjus 's forces were to have swept this area clear."

"It is a large battle area, Commander," replied the subordinate. "It is difficult to guard every approach and…"

"Enough! We must deal with the reality. Send one group to investigate and make sure no large force is preparing to attack. The rest of us will push on to the river with all speed. We must get across before they can shift forces or their watercraft can interfere."

* * * * *

JULY, 1912, MEMPHIS, TENNESSEE

The pounding on his cabin door yanked Drew Harding out of the first sound sleep he'd had in two days. "What? What now?" he snarled.

"Sir! Sir!" came a muffled voice he recognized as belonging to Lieutenant Alby Hinsworth. "Signal from the flag, sir! We need to get moving!"

590

Not quite awake, Drew sat up and swung his legs out of the bunk. "Move? Where?"

"Up river! There's word the Martians are trying to cross!"

Fully awake now, Drew grabbed his shoes and was grateful he hadn't bothered to undress. "Just us, or the whole - for God's sake open the door so I can talk to you!" The door swung open and Hinsworth looked in. "Just us or the whole squadron?"

"The whole squadron, sir! Commodore Rush wants us up there right away. Engage and report the situation. I've ordered full steam in ten minutes and we're getting ready to raise anchor."

"Good man!" Drew finished with his shoes, grabbed his coat and hat, and went out the door. It was still dark except for the gun flashes on the western shore. "What's the time?"

"A bit after three, sir." Drew was glad Hinsworth wasn't one of those who clung to the traditional navy practice of using 'bells' to tell time. Good, two hours and it would start to get light.

They reached the bridge and a signal rating was there with a scrap of paper. "Sir, *Evansville, Vanceberg, Manchester,* and *Louisville Star* have all acknowledged the order to move out. No reply from *Dixie Dancer.*"

It didn't surprise him. The first three were navy gunboats and the *Louisville Star,* one of the modified riverboats, had a good skipper. But *Dixie Dancer* was nearly useless, both the ship itself and the man in command. Drew wasn't going to worry about whether they came along or not.

He took up his binoculars and scanned the river for nearby traffic. The commodore had divided his forces into a number of squadrons which he had been rotating into and out of action during the attack so the army would have continuous support. Drew's squadron had been in twice and he'd hoped to be able to rest his men - and himself - for a few more hours before going in again. But it was not to be.

His squadron had been anchored near the eastern shore to keep them out of the way, and as far as he could tell, the route up river was clear. He turned to Hinsworth. "Signal *Evansville* to take the lead, we'll follow and then the rest. Did the commodore say how far north the enemy is?"

"No, sir. Just that they were crossing north of here."

"Well, they can't be crossing along the stretch where they've built the concrete walls. We'd see the flashes from the guns if they were. So they have to be at least ten or twelve miles up river. That gives us a while. Get under way, but don't order battle stations just yet. Tell the galley to feed the men as soon as possible."

"Yes, sir."

The anchor was raised and *Santa Fe* started moving. They slipped in a cable length behind *Evansville* and the engines were put full ahead. Going against the current, they could only do ten or eleven knots. It would be at least an hour or so before they could expect to run into the enemy. Drew rubbed the sleep out of his eyes and gratefully accepted a mug of coffee and a sandwich.

The battle around West Memphis was still going on, but after a half hour, he started seeing flashes from the north—almost dead ahead. Shortly after that, some of the big guns along the concrete walls on the eastern shore started firing, although he couldn't tell at what.

"Mr. Hinsworth, get the men to battle stations, clear the ship for action."

"Yes, sir!" The alarm gong rang out and the crew hurried to their posts. A rating appeared to hand Drew his life-jacket, helmet, and anti-dust gear. It was a warm, humid night, but he didn't hesitate to put them on. Reports quickly came back that all stations were manned and ready. His crew were veterans now.

The river was in a long shallow curve to the right, and Drew couldn't see that far ahead due to a thick forest on the eastern shore beyond the line of walls. But the flashes of guns flickered above the trees and the sound of explosions could now be heard. As he watched, a star shell burst in the distance and it was followed by a pair of rocket flares. Somewhere around the bend there was fighting.

"Signal *Evansville* to let us catch up. We'll go in in pairs. Have the others do the same. Use the signal light." The orders were given and the leading gunboat slowed to let *Santa Fe* draw abreast of her on the right. *Vanceberg* and *Manchester* were pairing up astern, and to his surprise he saw a shape which had to have been *Dixie Dancer* closing in on *Louisville Star*.

"Shall I send a message to the commodore?" asked Hinsworth.

"Let's wait until we have a better idea what's going on. This could just be a feint to draw our forces away from Memphis."

"Yes, sir."

But minute by minute he became convinced it was no feint. The flashes grew brighter and more numerous, and the roar of explosions even drowned out the rumble from the West Memphis fight, now ten miles astern. Finally, the river straightened out and he could look ahead.

"Good Lord, sir," said Hinsworth. "Look!"

Drew was looking. The river appeared to be filled with dark shapes and the western bank was a mass of flame and smoke. Geysers of water leapt up out of the river, and heat rays stabbed out from the shapes against the shore. He raised his binoculars and the shapes became distinct: tripods. A lot of them. Sweeping his view from shore to shore he saw that there were some tripods already climbing out of the water on the east side. There were no concrete walls here, just trenches. More tripods were wading into the river from the western shore, a seemingly endless horde, their metal skins gleaming in the light of the flares.

"Signal the commodore," said Drew. "Tell him that the enemy is crossing the river in great strength and that we need immediate reinforcements."

"Yes, sir!" said Hinsworth, who dashed away.

The squadron was still advancing at full steam and the range was closing quickly. What to do? Their guns outranged the enemy heat rays, so it would make sense to hang back - at least until reinforcements arrived. Charging right into that mass of tripods would not be a good idea. He turned to a signal rating and said: "Order to squadron. Hold position here and commence firing."

* * * * *

CYCLE 597, 845.2, RIVER 3-1

Qetjnegartis stood its machine on the western shore of the river and observed the situation with satisfaction. Despite being discovered by the enemy prior to launching the attack, it was clear that at least some measure of surprise had been achieved. No prey-creature water craft had been waiting and the defenses on the far shore, while substantial, were not proving to be especially formidable. This spot had been chosen because none of the cast stone walls had yet been erected, although there were some not far to the south whose weapons were within range.

Crossing the river itself was proving difficult, but not as bad as feared. A number of fighting machines had become immobilized in the soft bottom, and two had been swept away by the flowing water. But most were crossing with only minor problems. And the vessels Ixmaderna had designed were proving entirely suitable for transporting the drones across the river. Floating vessels had not been used on the Homeworld for many thousands of centuries, since the canals had dried up, but the principle was still understood. A hollow container made of light materials would, along with its cargo, displace a sufficient mass of liquid to balance the pull of gravity. Towed by a fighting machine, the vessel could transport the drones across the water safely.

Some of them had already reached the far shore and were in amongst the defenders there. The prey-creatures were fighting fiercely, but they did not seem to have substantial reserves and had only a few of the armored fighting machines. It appeared as though the feint against the city's outer defenses to the south had been successful in deceiving the enemy about the location of the main attack.

"Commander, enemy water vessels are approaching from the south," communicated a subordinate.

Qetjnegartis turned its attention in that direction and saw that six vessels had appeared from around a bend in the river. They were coming directly toward the crossing, but then turned slightly, slowed, and began firing with their large projectile throwers. Explosions began to erupt in the water, some dangerously close to the fighting machines. But there were only six of the vessels. Surely not a great threat.

"Proceed with the crossing," it commanded. "Ignore those vessels unless they come closer. Get across, destroy the defenders there, and push inland with all speed. We need to strike the defenses around the city before the enemy can redeploy."

Following its own command, Qetjnegartis moved its machine down the bank and into the water.

* * * * *

JULY, 1912, NORTH OF MEMPHIS, TENNESSEE

"The commodore says that help is on the way. Engage the enemy at your discretion, sir," said Ensign Alby Hinsworth.

"Very well," said Drew Harding. *My discretion! Yeah, right!* He *was* engaging the enemy. With long range fire. But he couldn't tell if he was doing anything. There seemed to be a constant flow of Martian tripods moving across the river from west to east. Shells from the squadron were falling among them, but it was impossible to tell if they were scoring many hits. What was evident was the fact that there seemed to be much less resistance on the eastern shore. There wasn't much fire coming from there anymore and the flares were fewer, Drew's ships were firing their own star shells now. Tripods were emerging from the river and moving ashore. They were getting across.

"Sir? Sir?" A rating was holding the intercom phone and calling to him.

"Yes?"

"Sir, the lookout up top says there's something going on you ought to see."

"What is it?"

"He's not sure, but he asks that you come up top."

"Very well. Mr. Hinsworth, you have the con." He went out the bridge hatch and then clambered up the ladder to the observation post on the mast. The observers for the guns worked there.

"Sir!" said the petty officer in charge. "Take a look, sir, they're up to something." He pointed to the very powerful set of binoculars mounted on a pintle. Drew leaned forward and peered through the device.

"What am I looking for, Chief?"

"It looks like the buggers are towing rafts, sir!"

"Rafts? What in the world would they be doing that for?" But looking closer in the erratic light from the star shells he saw what the chief was talking about: dark rectangles were moving behind some of the tripods, which were submerged up to their heads. What were they for? He swung the binoculars over to look at the eastern shore. There were dozens of the things drawn up on the bank. As he watched, another one was pulled up and as it was, a cluster of tiny shapes, just barely visible at this distance, clambered out and moved inland.

"Spider-machines! The damn rafts are full of their spider-machines!"

"That ain't good, sir! Whadda we do?"

"Our job is to keep them from getting across, damn it!"

"Aren't gonna be able to stop them from way back here, sir."

The man looked at him and as they locked eyes, Drew knew what had to be done; and the knowledge chilled him to the bone despite the warm air. Without another word, he went back down the ladder. The forward turret fired just then, the vibration nearly knocking him loose.

Back on the bridge, he looked at the men there. His next action could get them all killed, but there was no choice. No choice at all. The commodore and the reinforcements might take an hour to get here. By then it would be too late for them to do any good. All those tripods and all those spiders would sweep down on the city from the north and…

"Mr. Hinsworth, signal the squadron to advance and engage the enemy closely. Let the commodore know what we are doing. Helm, take us up river, full speed ahead."

To their credit, the men only hesitated for a moment before carrying out their orders. The engine room telegraph rang up full speed and the ship began to vibrate gently. Drew stepped out onto the bridge wing and looked off to the east. There was the faintest glow of dawn in the sky. Good. Hinsworth rejoined him after a few minutes. "All ships acknowledge, sir. No immediate reply from the commodore." Drew looked rearward and saw that the other five ships were following. In ten or fifteen minutes they might all be reduced to flaming wrecks, but they were following, by God. He rested his hands on the rail of his ship and looked up at the mast. An amazing calm filled him.

"Mr. Hinsworth."

"Sir?"

"I think this would be a good time to break out the battle ensign."

"Sir? The… the…?"

"The battle ensign. I know we have one. I think *Santa Fe* should look her best today, don't you? Get it run up, won't you?"

"Uh, yes, sir, right away."

Hinsworth disappeared and returned a few minutes later with two other men hauling a large bundle of cloth. In the days of sailing ships, they carried enormous flags called battle ensigns. They'd be flown during a fight to help identify friend from foe in the smoke and confusion of combat. The navy still carried them, but they were rarely flown anymore except in ceremonies. *Santa Fe*'s battle ensign was over twenty feet high and thirty feet long. There was barely enough room to fly it from the cables running up to the observation platform. It took all three men to haul it up. The wind generated by their speed caught the cloth and it billowed out behind them. The red and the blue looked almost black, but the white stripes and stars gleamed dimly in the waning night. Yes, it looked good. Right and proper.

"Ensign, turn on the searchlights and get the machine guns manned. Damage control parties stand ready."

"Yes, sir," gasped Hinsworth. Drew was running the kid ragged. But he got the job done. Beams of light blazed out from the ship and lit up the enemy, who weren't all that far off now. A little over two miles, Drew estimated. Men appeared to man the half-dozen machine guns mounted on the ship. There was one on the end of each bridge wing. The guns had small metal shields to protect the crews, but the men were still terribly exposed. There was nothing for it, however; he was going to need every bit of firepower they had very shortly.

Only their forward guns could shoot at the moment, but they were firing steadily now and it looked as though they were scoring some hits. They'd do better as the range dropped. Hinsworth was back and stood next to him waiting for the next order. Some of his usual bravado appeared to be missing. In fact, he looked scared.

"Mr. Hinsworth."

"Sir?"

"I've been meaning to ask: however did you end up with the name of 'Albustus'?"

"Sir?" The boy seemed startled and then laughed nervously. "Oh, uh, well, I guess it's a family tradition, sir. My father, my grandfather, way on back, all of them were named that. The first one fought in the Revolution, I've been told. He's buried in New Castle, Delaware, right next to George Read who signed the Declaration. Silly name, I guess, but it's tradition."

"Tradition," said Drew, nodding. He looked up at the huge flag. "Tradition. Well, we have some navy traditions to uphold today, Mr. Hinsworth. Let's get to it."

"Yes, sir."

They moved into the armored pilothouse. The shutters were closed, but they left the rear hatch open for the moment. "Course, sir?" asked the helmsman.

"Right into the center of them. If any get in your way, run them down. In fact, *aim* to run them down."

"Aye, aye, sir!" The man's face took on a wolf-like grin, baring his teeth.

Drew looked through the quartz block in the view slit. The enemy were still moving across the river, seemingly oblivious to the approach of the warships. In the growing light he could see that some of the tripods were almost completely submerged and were moving only slowly. The rafts were being towed by cables, but the current of the river was dragging them downstream, and some of their towing tripods looked to be having trouble controlling them. As he watched, a shell from one of the ships hit the water and exploded very close to a tripod; it must have severed the towing cable because one of the rafts was suddenly drifting loose and slowly spinning down the river toward them. A moment later, another shell hit the raft squarely, ripping it apart and sending spider-machines tumbling off in all directions. They splashed into the water and vanished immediately.

"Can't swim, can you, you bastards?" said Drew, grinning.

But now the enemy was starting to react. Most kept moving toward the eastern bank, but the ones closest to the ships began turning in their direction. Some heat rays stabbed out and he flinched back from the view slit as one swept across *Santa Fe*. But the range was still very long for the Martians and it did no damage.

Not such long range for the humans, though.

The light in the east was growing moment by moment and the searchlights and star shells were barely needed anymore. The gunners aboard the ships were finding the range now and hits were more frequent. A tripod off to the left suddenly blew apart as something tore through it. Another appeared to stumble, disappeared under the water, and didn't reappear.

Drew was briefly tempted to halt the advance and pound the enemy from a safe distance, but no, the bulk of them were still crossing unmolested further upstream. The range was still too long for really accurate shooting against such small targets. They needed to get in there and wreck as many as they could, slow them up, delay them until Commodore Rush arrived with more ships.

The range closed very quickly, as it always did. Ships or objects which seemed to hang in the distance forever without getting any closer were suddenly just *here* in what seemed an eye-blink. The guns were roaring continuously as their crews slammed shells and powder into the breeches as quickly as they could. The shriek of the heat rays filled the air and the rattle of the fifty-calibers on the bridge wings could be heard through the open hatch. Cordite smoke swept around them and made it very difficult to see. It was impossible for him to assign targets and the gunners were going to have to pick their targets as best they could.

The ship shuddered and that hateful red glow surrounded them. A heat ray was hitting them and he released stream to counter it. The stink of the cordite was joined by a different smell. His ship was on fire. But the guns in the forward turret roared again and the glow winked out. He looked out port view slit and a tripod, spewing smoke swept by, not two hundred yards away.

"Sir! Dead ahead!" Hinsworth was at the forward slit and shouting to him. He moved up beside him and looked out. The wind was freshening and it blew away the smoke for a moment. Right in front of them was a tripod, but it was submerged hallway up its bulbous head, the glowing red eye in the middle of the face even with the water.

"Ram it! Helm, steer straight for it!"

The Martian seemed to be stuck in the mud for it only made a few jerky attempts to avoid the ship bearing down on it. Suddenly the water just in front of it exploded outward in a billowing cloud of steam. *Its heat ray! It couldn't raise it above the water!* Drew found himself laughing out loud as *Santa Fe*, all three thousand tons of her, slammed into the enemy machine. There was a muffled clang and a slight lurch, but that was all.

Then the red fire was back - some other tripod firing at them - and an instant later an explosion slammed the ship and smoke blotted out everything.

"The forward turret! The forward turret is gone, sir!" cried Hinsworth,

But the aft turret was firing and all the casemate guns as well. They were in the midst of them now. Drew went to the bridge hatch and looked back. *Evansville* was off their port quarter, burning in a dozen spots, but her guns were still firing. A tripod looming next to her suddenly tumbled backward into the water and vanished.

Vanceberg and *Manchester* were following, not hit too badly yet, it didn't seem. But the two converted river boats, *Louisville Star* and *Dixie Dancer*, were both burning from stem to stern a half mile behind. Their improvised armor was just not enough against the Martian weapons. He glanced up and was saddened that the battle ensign was just a few scorched tatters.

Suddenly a rating appeared, climbing up the ladder from below. "Sir! Sir! Message from headquarters!" Drew pulled him into the pilothouse.

"From the commodore?"

"No sir, from General MacArthur's headquarters!" He held out a slip of paper and Drew took it. Read it.

> To *all commands: Defense Plan M now in effect.*

"What the hell?"

"What is it, sir?" asked Hinsworth.

"MacArthur's pulling everything back to Memphis."

Hinsworth looked around. "Bit late for us."

"Yeah." Drew crumpled the paper and threw it away.

The ship lurched again and there was a screech of twisting metal. They'd hit something. Another tripod? No heat ray was raking them just at the moment and he dared to step out on the starboard wing to take a look. There was nothing he could see at first. Smoke was billowing out of the forward turret and the charred bodies of the machine gun crew were sprawled at the end of the wing. A few tripods were in the river not far off, but they were ignoring Santa Fe at the moment. Many more were farther off and some were firing at the ships coming on behind. He couldn't see anything they might have hit. Perhaps they'd run down another Martian…

Something moving caught his eye.

A metal bar was hooked over the railing near the bow. It didn't belong there. Another one appeared. Then something the size of a cow heaved itself up and over. It was a metal egg about six or seven feet long, standing on three articulated legs. It had one arm holding something that looked remarkably like a human pistol and another with a long whip-like tentacle. As Drew looked on in horror, another one appeared farther aft. And another. They started scuttling aft.

He retreated into the pilot house and opened his mouth to shout an order he never expected to ever give.

"All hands! Prepare to repel boarders!"

Hinsworth leaned past him through the hatch, paused, looked, and then ran for the machine gun. Drew swung around, saw that the port machine gun was still in action, and the gunner was blasting away at something close at hand. He grabbed the man who had brought up the message and shoved him toward the ladder. "Go below! Have anyone you can find grab a weapon - axes, hammers, anything! - and get up here!"

He stepped out on the starboard wing again. Hinsworth was pouring fire into the spider-machines on the foredeck. One was already down and bullets were tearing through the second. The third one fired the pistol-thing, which was a miniature heat ray, but the flimsy gun shield was able to absorb it just long enough for Hinsworth to swing the gun over and bring it down in a shower of sparks. The boy had a lunatic grin on his face. "I got 'em! I got 'em, sir!"

Drew smiled a crazy smile of his own and stepped toward him…

… just as a metal monster pulled itself up on the bridge railing right behind Hinsworth.

"Alby! Look out!" Drew flung himself forward.

Before the boy could even turn, the long snake-like tentacle with a gleaming blade on the end of it flashed around, slicing Hinsworth's head from his body. Drew's momentum carried him toward the machine gun, but he knew he'd never reach it. The tentacle swung back. He was inside the arc of the deadly blade, but the tentacle slammed into him like a pile driver.

An agonizing pain blasted through his shoulder, and then he was flying through the air. He hit the river and the muddy waters of the Mississippi swallowed him up.

* * * * *

JULY, 1912, MEMPHIS, TENNESSEE

"Where'n hell's the commander of those damn lady sharpshooters?!"

For a moment the shout didn't register, but then Becca Harding suddenly jerked awake. *That's me!* She stood up, the blanket she'd wrapped herself in falling away, and looked down from her perch on the city wall. "Up here!"

"Well, git yerself down here! We've got orders!"

"Coming!" She made her way past some other soldiers who, like her, had decided to camp out on the wall where they could watch the battle, and let herself down an iron ladder attached to the concrete. It was still dark, although she could see the first glimmer of dawn in the east.

The man who had shouted was waiting for her. She saw that he was an officer with the militia so she came to attention and saluted. He didn't bother to return it. "Get your girls up and moving," he said. "They're shifting us to a new position."

"Where, sir?"

"Up on the north side of the city."

"What's happenin', sir?"

"Not sure. Looks like the fight over yonder was just a decoy. The Martians are over the river to the north and headin' this way fast. So get a move on! We'll be pulling out in ten minutes, you be ready to follow." He turned and walked away before she could even respond.

She ran back to her camp and started kicking tent poles and shouting for the girls to get up. The nearby militia company was already falling in. Old Mo came walking over. "What's all the fuss, Missy?"

"Get the horses and the carriage ready! We're movin' right away!"

* * * * *

CYCLE 597, 845.2, RIVER 3-1

Qetjnegartis looked back at the river. All six of the enemy vessels had been destroyed; the burning remains of several of them could still be seen. Their reckless charge had done an alarming amount of damage, but they we gone now and the crossing could be completed. But they must move quickly, the black smoke plumes of more vessels could be seen beyond the thick growths of vegetation to the south. They would be here soon, but they would be too late.

"Keep moving. We must strike the city before the prey-creatures can prepare."

* * * * *

JULY 1912, NEAR ROSEDALE, MISSISSIPPI

"Sorry to wake you, sir, but we just got a signal from General Clopton."

Andrew Comstock squinted at the light streaming in through the door of his tiny cabin. His aide, Lieutenant Hornbaker was standing there, silhouetted by the glare. "Is it important?"

"Looks to be. Memphis is under attack. A major attack. We're to proceed directly there at full speed."

"All right, all right, I'll be up in a minute."

598

CHAPTER FIFTEEN

JULY, 1912, WASHINGTON, D.C.

"Has there been anything more from MacArthur?" asked President Theodore Roosevelt.

"No sir," replied Leonard Wood. "Nothing since that 'Defense Plan M' message an hour ago. I've tried to get hold of him, but his aides just tell me he is 'indisposed'. I've been in touch with Dickman at 3rd Army headquarters, but he can't get through to MacArthur, either. All we know is that the enemy has crossed the river in great strength about fifteen miles north of Memphis."

The early morning light was streaming in the windows of Roosevelt's office in the White House. His son and aide, Archie, came in bearing a tray with a coffee pot and cups. The President filled one and walked over to one of the maps which hung on the walls. "Defense Plan M, that's the one that calls for concentrating everything inside the defensive works around Memphis, is it not?"

"Yes," said Wood, once again amazed by Roosevelt's memory. There were dozens and dozens of different plans for all the sections along the line; Wood, himself couldn't keep them all straight. "In recent weeks, MacArthur was becoming highly critical of it and kept asking for more and more materiel so he could take a more aggressive posture. But now he's fallen back on it."

"And the Martians are across the river, Leonard?" His finger touched a spot north of Memphis on the map. "I thought we had enough troops guarding that area."

"We had hoped that there would be, but we had to make our plans based on calculated risk. We couldn't possibly have enough troops everywhere, so we put what we hoped would be enough to hold until reinforcements arrived. We had the 29th Division in that area, but apparently MacArthur stripped a brigade away to reinforce West Memphis when the Martians made an attack there. What was left couldn't hold long enough."

"And he did that without clearing it with you?" Wood nodded. "Damnation! It's like Funston all over again! This could be our worst nightmare!"

"Well, the worst would be for them to get across and build a fortress on the eastern side. A raid, while bad, would not be a complete disaster so long as we can drive them back across the river."

"And can we?"

"We are certainly going to try. I've ordered Dickman to send everything he can to the Memphis area. The 2nd Tank Division is in Jackson, they will be moving within the hour, although I doubt they'll be able to de-train and get into action before tomorrow." He came over beside Roosevelt and traced his finger along the railroad from Jackson to Memphis. "And Clopton's land ironclads are coming up river. They're somewhere around here, a hundred miles or so from Memphis. I've ordered them directly there."

"Good... good. If we can hit the rapscallions hard, maybe we can drive them back."

"That's what I'm hoping."

Roosevelt frowned. "But what about MacArthur? Why isn't he answering us? Do you think there's something wrong - beyond the obvious, I mean?"

Wood shook his head. "I don't know. When he was head of my staff, he would draw up plans - good plans - but he would act as if they were immutable, like the results were set in stone and were bound to happen just as he'd intended. If anything happened to mess them up, sometimes he would go into a funk. Get all quiet and moody. I was never sure if it was just pique on being forced to change his plans or… or if it was something else. It didn't happen often, but almost always for big things."

"We can hardly afford to have him in a funk right now. He was my military aide for a few months when I first became President and he seemed steady enough then, but that was ten years ago. Do you think he should be replaced?"

"I'm going to order Dickman at 3rd Army to go have a look, but it will take him a while to get there. And I'm sure he'll be reluctant to take any drastic steps in the middle of a battle. MacArthur's got some good subordinates there. Let's hope they can take up the load until… until he's no longer 'indisposed'."

"I suppose you're right. We can't try and fight the battle from here."

"No, battles are fought and won by the men who are there where it's happening."

* * * * *

JULY, 1912, WEST MEMPHIS, ARKANSAS

"Come on! Move it! Move it!" Captain Frank Dolfen stood in his stirrups and tried to see what was holding up the column. All he could see was a solid line of troops and trucks jamming the sole bridge across the Mississippi. It was mid-morning and the battle was still raging. *Battles*, he should say, for there were two fights going on now. The first one, which was in its second day, was the fight around West Memphis; but everyone realized it had just been a diversion, a feint to draw strength away from where the real attack would come.

That was the attack he and the 5th had discovered last night. A huge force of tripods, pulling boats and swarms of the spider-machines all heading for a crossing point north of the city. They had sent the warning back by radio and that had drawn a dozen of the tripods down on them. Both regiments of cavalry had beat a hasty retreat back to the defenses of West Memphis. Dolfen didn't think they'd gotten hurt too badly, and somehow he'd managed to get his own squadron to safety more or less intact. The rest of the regiment had been more badly scattered.

They had barely been given time to catch their breath before the word reached them that the enemy had gotten across the river and was threatening Memphis from the north. The cavalry had been ordered to cross the bridge and get up there to do what it could. Unfortunately several brigades of infantry along with battalions of steam tanks and batteries of guns had been given the same order and there was only the one bridge.

Somehow, Dolfen had gotten 1st Squadron reformed and up to the approaches to the bridge ahead of most of the other troops, but it had still been a colossal traffic jam; and now, three hours after dawn, they were just starting to cross.

The column lurched into motion and they made it about halfway across before halting again. From the bridge, he could look to the north. There was a lot of smoke in that direction, but it still seemed pretty far off. Maybe the enemy wasn't in the city yet. The noise of the guns was all around and he couldn't tell if there was any noise coming from the north. In truth, ever since that explosion at Little Rock, his hearing wasn't as good as it used to be. And where was Becca in all this? Was she with her sharpshooters or back at the hospital? The hospital was on the north side of the city. He couldn't believe that in the midst of all that was happening, he was worrying about that girl - but he was.

There were dozens of boats, big and small, in the river below him. Some were heading north, but others were going south. He noted one coming down river which had smoke drifting off it from a dozen wounds. A navy warship, and it had clearly gotten the worst of a fight. The river was filled with floating wreckage, bits of wood, boxes, life rings... bodies. Yes, there were a few floating bodies, too.

"Navy couldn't stop 'em, I guess," said Lieutenant Lynnebrook.

"But it looks like they tried."

They started moving again, and to Dolfen's amazement, they actually reached the other side where provost officers shouted at them to keep going. Dolfen had lost all contact with Colonel Schumacher so he just picked a street going north and urged his men along it. They were all tired, but there was no stopping now. The Martians were trying to break into the city.

And they were going to stop them.

*****

JULY, 1912, SOMEWHERE ALONG THE MISSISSIPPI

Drew Harding's feet touched something solid and he opened his eyes. Bright sunshine dazzled him, but he saw something large and dark stretching out before him. After a moment he realized it was the river bank. With the sun in his eyes, as it was, it had to be the east shore. Thank God. The last he remembered, he was trying to reach the east shore. That was after... after...

After the USS *Santa Fe* blew up and sank.

My ship. I lost my ship.

The thought was numbing. Every captain's nightmare.

Those spider-machines. It had been them. Not even one of the tripods. They had collided with something, he remembered that. It must have been one of the rafts full of the spiders. They hadn't seen it in all the smoke and confusion. And then the things were everywhere. With *Santa Fe*'s low freeboard, they could climb aboard easily. They'd killed poor Alby and knocked Drew into the river. Hurt his shoulder. It was so painful, he couldn't use the arm at all; he'd have gone right to the bottom if he hadn't been wearing a life jacket. He'd bumped into some piece of drifting wreckage and clung to it.

When he looked back at his ship, he'd seen that the spiders had small heat rays and they were burning their way inside. The current took him farther and farther away, so he couldn't see much more, but then the ship exploded. One of the things must have gotten into the magazine. She broke in half and went down.

Then the river took him around the bend and out of sight of the fighting. He was nearly run down by the arrival of the rest of Commodore Rush's command surging up the river at full speed. He'd shouted and tried to wave with his good arm, but no one had seen him. Or they hadn't tried to help if they had.

He had kicked his legs and paddled as best he could toward the eastern shore, but he never seemed to get any closer. He kept trying until he was exhausted. At last he saw what he thought was the entrance to the Wolf River, that little channel which cut off the swampy island he'd been curious about earlier. He'd used his last strength trying to get into that, and looking around now, it seemed like he'd succeeded.

His feet touched the bottom again and he tried to stand. But there was no strength in his legs. All he could manage was to use his legs to push himself the rest of the way to shore. He abandoned the faithful bit of flotsam and dragged his sodden body up out of the water and collapsed on the muddy bank. The pain in his shoulder, which had subsided to a dull ache, returned full force and he groaned.

After hours in the water, he was chilled to the bone, but the bright morning sunshine beat down on his dark uniform, warming him. He tried dragging himself farther up the bank but made little progress. Then he heard some shouts and strong hands grabbed him and turned him over.

"Yeah, he's alive! Navy guy - an officer, too! Get the stretcher!"

* * * * *

JULY, 1912, MEMPHIS, TENNESSEE

"Becca! What are you doing here?"

Becca Harding turned at the sound of the familiar voice. There was Miss Chumley, the chief nurse of the hospital. In spite of the cloud they'd parted under when she'd told her she was choosing the sharpshooters over her nursing duties, she smiled when she saw the woman. Chumley had been very kind to her over the years and she still thought of her as a friend.

"Hello, ma'am. We were pulled out of our position along the river and sent up to the northern defenses. They shifted us around two or three times and then an officer told us to come back here an' guard the hospital. I'm sorta surprised you're all still here."

"We've been told to be ready to evacuate twice now, but we've gotten no orders to do anything. I've been getting the ambulances ready, just in case."

"Well, you've got thirty armed sharpshooters to make sure no one troubles you, ma'am." Her girls were marching up behind her; tired, but still enthusiastic, now that things were actually happening.

"Good, good. I hope we don't need you, but you remember the chaos when we pulled out of Gallup and again at Santa Fe. Pray God we won't have to do that again, but if we do, I'll be glad to have you around, Becca."

Yes, those had been real messes. At Gallup she'd been forced to draw her pistol to keep some men from stealing a wagon she needed to transport the wounded.

Chumley gave her an odd look. "And if you do have a spare moment, I'm sure we can find some work at your old job, Becca. We've gotten quite a lot of wounded here from the fight across the river. They're not sending us any more from there, but now we're starting to get men coming down from the north." She looked in that direction where the rumble of artillery was getting louder by the minute.

"Uh, we'll see, ma'am. I'm in charge of the sharpshooters now and I have responsibilities." For a moment she thought Chumley was going to remind her of the responsibilities here that she'd abandoned, but the older woman refrained and just nodded.

"I understand. Well, I'm glad you're here, Becca. I have to get back to work." Chumley turned and walked quickly back to one of the tents.

Becca had been leading Ninny, and when Moses came up with the wagon, she turned the horse over to him. She had organized her girls into four squads and she put one on sentry while the other three set up a camp in an open area. While she was getting things organized, she saw Sam Jones come up. The strange, quirky man who had been rescued from the Martian fortress at Gallup was still hanging around the hospital as an orderly. He'd clearly been in the infantry before that, but he'd refused to go back to his unit and was technically a deserter. But no one at the hospital had wanted to make an issue of it and so here he was.

"Hi, Sam," she said.

"Hi, Miss Becca. Looks like you might get that fight you've been lookin' for so long." He nodded his head in the direction of the gunfire. The man seemed nervous.

"Yeah, it seems so. What are you gonna do, Sam?"

He didn't answer, but his eyes took on that same look as they had when she's first seen him; a wild animal fear. As near as she could guess, he'd been captured and held with some of his comrades in a cage while the Martians ate them one by one. The attack on the fortress at Gallup, which had come oh, so close to victory, had managed to free him, but he was in mortal terror of ending up like that again. "I'll… I'll do what I have to," he said, finally.

"Well, take care of yourself, Sam."

"You, too." He turned and left, looking back at her once as he walked away.

"Was that Sam Jones?" asked Sarah Halberstam, coming up behind her.

"Yup."

"Is he going to be joining up with us?"

"Nope."

"Too bad, he worked so well with us, teaching us the drill."

Becca didn't answer, but Sarah stood in front of her, face worried. "Becca, what are we going to do if the Martians break into the city?"

She shrugged. "Fight."

"How? These rifles won't hurt one of those tripods and you know it. And we don't have any of the dynamite bombs or those stovepipe rocket-things like the real soldiers do. If a tripod comes walking up, what are we supposed to do?"

"I've heard that the spider-machines aren't as tough. That rifles can hurt them. Maybe we can deal with them while the other soldiers take care of the tripods."

"None of the other soldiers are even around!" It was true, they'd gotten separated from the militia company they'd been attached to.

"Then we help evacuate the wounded!" said Becca, growing annoyed. "We do what we *can*, Sarah. If that's not good enough for you, then maybe you should go home!" She immediately regretted her words. Sarah had been one of the most dedicated women in the group, making almost every meeting. "Sorry, sorry, I shouldn't have said that to you."

"It's all right, Becca," said Sarah, nodding. "All of us, all of us who are still here anyway, want to do something to help. But you're the one who made this all real, showed us how to do something that matters." She reached out and squeezed her arm. "Don't worry, we'll make you proud."

Becca blinked, sniffed, and then nodded. "I know you will."

* * * * *

CYCLE 597, 845.2, EAST OF RIVER 3-1

Finally, across the river! Qetjnegartis felt a distinct sensation of relief. The enormous body of water, which had posed such a strategic puzzle for so long, was behind them at last.

The challenge now is to stay here.

Yes, that was the next task. They were across the river and had done so with only moderate losses. Forty-seven fighting machines and two hundred and thirty drones had been destroyed or crippled or lost in the river while smashing through the defenses along the river bank or dealing with the group of water vessels which had attacked in the midst of the crossing. But it could have been far worse. A much more powerful water force had arrived, but only after the crossing was complete. Qetjnegartis had not tarried to fight those when there was no need. It had ordered its forces away from the river, southeast to strike the city, away from any interference from the river craft.

A large area of very dense vegetation lay off to the west along the river, and many of the prey-creatures who had held the defenses had fled there, but it was so dense it seemed unlikely that the enemy's armored gun vehicles could operate there. So the right flank was secure. To the east and south, the country was far more open, with crop lands and small habitation centers and roadways. They would have to be wary of possible attacks from those directions. The plan was to penetrate into the city as quickly as possible and use the enemy's own defenses to guard the rear.

The city was about ten *telequel* away and Qetjnegartis had dispatched a force of the fast fighting machines to scout ahead. They were reporting only a scattering of enemy forces, which they were destroying or driving off with ease. The main force with the slower-moving drones was following as quickly as possible. Qetjnegartis would have preferred to probe the enemy defense lines and then launch the main attack after nightfall, but there was no time for that. The attack must be made immediately.

As they got closer to the city, the projectiles from the prey-creatures' long range weapons started to fall more frequently. It appeared that the diversion and sudden crossing of the river had achieved the surprise that had been hoped for, but that surprise was now wearing off. The enemy was reorganizing and responding more forcefully. Some of the fire was coming from the vessels on the river, even though they had no direct line of sight. So far, most of the projectiles were doing no damage, but it expected that to change once they got closer to the defensive lines. Reports from the failed attack at City 3-4 indicated that the prey-creatures were becoming increasingly sophisticated and had devised a system where they could direct fire from widely separated weapons against a specific target many *telequel* away.

Images sent from the artificial satellite showed that the defenses on the landward side, while not as formidable as the cast-stone walls along the river, still could not be discounted. There were several small fortresses, which were made from the cast stone and mounted large weapons, and these were linked by trenches where the foot-warriors and the smaller projectile throwers could take refuge.

Tanbradjus reported that although it was continuing the diversionary attack, there was clear evidence that the enemy was moving forces eastward, back across the river into the city. Those forces would no doubt be moving to reinforce the northern defense lines.

"Commander, we are crossing one of the prey-creatures' transport tracks and a strange vehicle is approaching along it." The communication was from Battlegroup 32-6, on the left flank.

"Relay an image."

The subordinate did so and Qetjnegartis saw what at first appeared to be one of the steam powered transport engines towing a string of other vehicles, as was normal. But on closer examination it realized that all the vehicles were armored and many of them mounted weapons. Indeed, they began firing almost at once. The battlegroup responded immediately and the strange vehicle was quickly reduced to wreckage, but not before it had destroyed a fighting machine. The operator was rescued, but as there were no reserve machines available, it had to be kept in a transport pod in hopes that it would survive the battle. There was no chance of sending it to the rear, as there was no rear in this fight.

Some of the habitation centers they passed had prey-creature warriors inside them. These fired their small weapons, even though they had little hope of doing any damage. Qetjnegartis ordered that the structures be set afire from a distance and that no attempt be made to destroy every last creature. They could not afford the time. Soon, hundreds of burning structures marked their passage. Clumps of vegetation were similarly dealt with. The scouts had discovered and mapped areas where the ground was especially soft and these places were avoided.

Shortly after the encounter with the armored transport machine, Battlegroup 32-4 discovered a base for the prey-creatures' flying machines. Over fifty of the machines were lined up on the ground or preparing to take to the air. On the ground, the flimsy devices were completely defenseless and all were destroyed in moments. That was very good, although other flying machines were already in the air overhead, and there would certainly be more arriving if past battles were any indication. They needed to press on to the city before they did.

The pace of the drones slowed their progress and the sun was far up in the sky by the time the outer line of the city's defenses came into view. The scouts had done their jobs well and most of the heavy weapons positions had been plotted. Only two of the cast stone forts were on the northern side, and Qetjnegartis decided that the easternmost one could be ignored.

"Battlegroups 32-9 and 32-11, you shall engage the other fort and keep it occupied. Battlegroup 32-4, you shall protect our right flank. All other battlegroups will concentrate and strike in the area to the west of the fort. Any machine becoming immobilized or disabled shall be left behind, your orders are to press into the city as quickly as possible. Use the eradicator against the heavy weapons positions. Battlegroup 32-14 shall bring up the rear and assist those in need of help. Take up your positions and commence the attack on my command."

The components of the force moved into their spots quickly and precisely, with only the smallest amount of confusion with the drones. Not every drone operator was fully proficient yet, and it was as Ixmaderna had once said: the younger operators seemed to be the best at this. Even so, soon all was ready and Qetjnegartis gave the order to attack.

The battlegroups sent to engage the fort quickly had it so blanketed with the eradicator dust that almost no fire was coming from it, and they had only lost two machines in the process. A force of drones was sent to see if it could be silenced permanently. All the others, with Qetjnegartis following along, pressed ahead against the defensive lines. Projectiles fell all around them like one of the local precipitation storms, and a number of fighting machines and drones were destroyed. But the rest kept moving.

As it had feared, once they were within a *telequel* of the enemy positions, they began to encounter the pit traps set to snare the legs of the fighting machines. Most were cleverly hidden and constructed so that a drone or, presumably the prey-creatures themselves, could cross without triggering them. But when a fighting machine put its weight down on one, its leg would crash through and be caught. Qetjnegartis could not see any easy way of dealing with these, or at least none that would not delay an advance just as much as the traps themselves.

As it had ordered, those which became immobilized were left to fend for themselves, even though they became excellent targets for the enemy weapons. Assigning others to assist would just make both easy targets. The surest way to help them would be to destroy the prey-creature weapons as quickly as possible. This the attacking force did, moving forward and opening fire with their heat rays. Eradicator projectiles were fired against known weapon positions.

There were more traps immediately in front of the enemy trenches and a ditch filled with water. A score or more machines became trapped or mired in the mud at the bottom of the ditch, but the rest pulled themselves up and over, sweeping the defenses with their heat rays. A number of fully enclosed bunkers held out for a while, but those in the trenches were annihilated.

But not before they did considerable damage. The explosive bombs which the prey had been using for some time destroyed or damaged a number of machines, but perhaps more alarming was a new weapon, first encountered in small numbers at City 3-118 and in larger numbers by Clan

Mavnaltak at City 3-4. It was a small device, small enough that it could be carried by a single prey-creature. It appeared to fire some sort of rocket-propelled projectile which could explode with a force similar to those fired by the much larger weapons the enemy used. A single shot could rarely do serious damage to a fighting machine, but multiple hits were capable of bringing one down; and even a single shot proved sufficient to destroy the drones.

To Qetjnegartis' relief, there were none of the armored gun vehicles waiting in reserve as was so often the case. The prey had learned that the best response to an assault was to mass all of their vehicles for an immediate counterattack. But there were none here now, another success for the diversionary attack.

A half *telequel* of open ground lay ahead, between the defenses and the structures of the city. A few weapon positions and some fleeting prey could be seen, but little else.

"Continue the advance," commanded Qetjnegartis. "Drive through the city to the bridge over the river. Destroy everything you can, but do not delay your progress. We must move quickly."

* * * * *

JULY, 1912, MEMPHIS, TENNESSEE

"Rebecca, we've finally been given orders to evacuate. Can you and your girls help?"

Becca Harding had been staring north. The hospital had been built on the northern outskirts of Memphis and about a mile south of the defense lines. A stand of trees blocked a direct view to the north, but the sounds of fighting had been growing louder for the past hour, and clouds of black smoke had been billowing up above the trees for a while. The Martians were clearly there and getting closer. She turned and saw that it was Miss Chumley who has spoken.

"Well it's certainly about time! Those monsters could be here in five minutes!"

"I know, I know," replied Chumley. "We're loading the wounded into ambulances and wagons, but we could use some help."

"All right, you've got it. Sarah! Get the girls! We've got a job to do!" Sarah Halberstam, who was acting as her company sergeant, immediately rounded up the sharpshooters who had been watching the smoke just like everyone else. She brought them over to Becca. "Ladies, the hospital is being evacuated. We need to help load the wounded. And we'll probably be pulling out along with them, so keep all your gear handy. There's not much time, so move it!"

Rather than being annoyed or sullen, as Becca had feared, the women looked relieved and happy to have an actual task to do. They'd been ordered here, there, and everywhere with no apparent purpose so many times that a clear job was welcome. They stacked their rifles and went inside the hospital tents and buildings and started hauling out the wounded men on stretchers. It usually took four of them for each stretcher, but they did it and loaded the men into the ambulances.

It quickly became apparent that there weren't going to be enough vehicles for all the patients. They pulled aside those who were able to walk and made them do so, marching alongside the wagons. Becca spotted Moses with his wagon and waved to him. "Mo! We're gonna need you here!" The man jogged over to her.

"Yes, Miz Becca?"

"Dump all the junk you've got in the back! I need you to carry some wounded!"

"But that's all the ladies' things!" he protested. "Your tent, too."

"Dump it! There's more important things to carry."

Moses nodded. "I reckon you're right, miz." He pointed off to a column of smoke in the distance. "I'm guessin' that's the Oswald place. Nuthin' to go back to anyways. Only people matter now."

"That's right, only people." She hesitated. "When you go, take Ninny along with you."

Moses stared at her. "You sure 'bout that, Miz Becca?"

"Yeah. He's people, too. Keep him safe, will you?"

"Do my level best, Miz."

"Good. Take the wagon over there and load it up."

"Yes'm. Uh, where am I takin' 'em?"

"Just follow the others. Do what they tell you." Moses nodded and went back to his rig. Ninny was tied nearby and the man retied his lead to the back of the wagon. Becca wondered if she'd ever see him again. But he had no business here...

A sudden roar off to her left made her spin around. While she'd been working, an army field battery had unlimbered on some open ground just a hundred yards away and was now firing at something. She couldn't see what, but the noise of battle was closer than ever. They didn't have much time left.

While she was searching through the camp, looking for anyone who might have been missed, she saw a horse-drawn ambulance coming up from the west. She ran over to it. "The hospital's being evacuated! You have any room for more?"

"Yeah," said the driver. "Only carrying one guy. Where they taking the wounded now?"

"Not sure. Railroad depot, probably. Just head south into town as soon as we get you loaded. Sarah! We got room for a couple more here!" She went around to the back and opened the door. As the driver had said, there was just a single occupant; a young man with his arm in a sling and a grotesque lump on his shoulder. No, that was his shoulder. It had been dislocated and needed to be popped back into its socket. She could do that, but there was no time. "Sorry, but you have to move over, we need to get more people in here."

"R-Rebecca?"

She twitched and looked closer. Did she know this fellow? His face did look familiar, even twisted in pain and covered with dirt. Suddenly she recognized him. "Commander Harding! What are you doing here?"

"Don't know, 'cause I don't know where here is."

"You're at the general military hospital, but we're evacuating. How did you get here?"

"Lost my ship. Ended up in the river. Crawled ashore. After that, I don't know."

"Oh." She didn't know what else to say. Her girls were there with another stretcher. "Well, no time to talk now. We'll get you to someplace they can fix you up." She stood aside while the ambulance was filled up and then it lurched away.

"I think that's all, Becca." She turned and saw Sarah Halberstam. "They're all on their way, all the patients and staff are gone."

"Good. Let's grab our stuff and get along after them. We'll escort them all the way to..."

"Look! Oh God, look!"

Becca spun around and immediately saw what had caused the shout. Beyond the trees was a Martian tripod. No, two of them. Three. Maybe more. Still a quarter mile off, but heading this way. "Come on!" she shouted. "Move!" She led the way toward where their rifles and backpacks were stacked.

There was a mad scramble to grab all their stuff. Becca had left hers to the side so she had it immediately, but the others took precious seconds. She ran a few dozen steps to the south, looking for the best route of escape. The outskirts of the city started just beyond the hospital, but they were all low wooden houses. Not much cover, they'd have to…

The artillery battery off to the left roared again, and an odd, metallic sound made her look back. They'd hit one of the tripods! The closest one was staggering around, smoke pouring from its head, and then it fell with a crash, disappearing behind the trees. *That's gonna make them mad…* "Come on! *Move!*" she screamed.

The women came running and she let half of them pass before following along. "Just keep going! Straight for the town!"

A strange *wumpf* sound had her looking back again. Something flew from one of the tripods and soared over toward the guns where it burst in an inky black cloud. It spread out and the wind blew it in her direction. An icy chill spread through her despite the July heat.

"Dust! Black dust! Get your masks and gloves on!" She instantly tore open the canvas bag hanging from her neck. She pulled out the mask and hood, threw away her hat and pulled the apparatus over her head. The hood covered her head completely and extended down around her neck with a cinch-cord to close it tight around her collar. There were two round eye pieces to see through and a bulky filter to allow her to breathe. Two leather gloves, almost like a cavalryman's long gauntlets, completed the outfit. She looked down to make sure her trousers were tucked into her boots.

Then she looked up and the black dust was nearly upon them. A large hospital tent stood a dozen yards away. It would not provide complete protection, but it was better than nothing. "The tent! Get inside! Hurry!" She started pushing the women toward it.

"Abigail! Come on!" Sarah Halberstam suddenly looked back and shouted.

Becca turned and there was Abigail LaPlace standing frozen, hands clutching the unopened bag holding her dust gear, looking at the cloud of death sweeping toward her. She shoved Sarah toward shelter and leapt back to grab Abigail. The girl was as rigid as a statue; Becca hauled her to the tent.

But it was too late.

The dust, like some swarm of tiny locusts, swirled around them, so thickly she could barely see the tent only a few paces away. With one last surge she dragged them both through the flaps inside where the others were clustered. Abigail was screaming and fell to the ground.

Becca had seen dust victims before, but never like this. Anyone caught fully in a cloud with no protection never reached the hospital. Abigail had the dust all over her. On her clothes, in her hair, on her face, and hands. Tiny black specks like coal dust. She lay on the ground thrashing and shrieking, her eyes squeezed shut. Her hands came up and started to tear at her face.

Becca fell to her knees and grabbed Abigail's wrists, trying to keep her from hurting herself. But it was no use, the dust was starting to eat into the skin. Her screams were interrupted by gasping coughs, and foam, flecked with red and black, started spitting out of her mouth. Becca could hear more screams, muffled by dust masks and realized it was the other women.

"Do something!" shouted one of them.

But there was nothing that could be done. The horror went on for what seemed an eternity, but which probably wasn't more than a minute, until the girl suddenly went stiff and then collapsed. Not screaming, not breathing, her face a terrible mass of black and red.

Shaking, Becca stood up. The others were crying and sobbing and one of them was clawing at the tie holding her mask. "Leave that on!" she shouted. But the woman lifted it up far enough to vomit, before tugging it back into place. Becca grabbed a blanket off a cot and threw it over Abigail.

The shriek of a heat ray and a red light glowing through the tent's canvas reminded her where they were. "Come on! We can't stay here! Grab your stuff and let's go!"

"You've got dust all over you, Becca!" said someone, it sounded like Sarah.

"I know. I'll deal with that later! Come on!" She peered out of the tent and the black cloud was gone, blown along with the westerly breeze. There was dust all over the ground, but there was no choice. She hustled them out of the tent and saw a tripod not two hundred yards away. Its heat ray was sweeping across the first row of tents and shacks on the edge of the hospital, sending them up in flames. Becca turned in the opposite direction and they fled into the town.

* * * * *

JULY, 1912, MEMPHIS, TENNESSEE

"Looks like a helluva mess ahead, Captain!" Lieutenant Lynnbrooke turned in his saddle and looked back at Frank Dolfen. "Not sure we can get through here!"

Dolfen stood up in his stirrups and saw what his aide was talking about. The street ahead was jammed with wagons, trucks, and people on foot, all heading south. They might be able to get the horses and motorcycles through on the sidewalks, but the armored cars would never make it. They'd have to take a different route...

Wait a minute...

Squinting, he saw that some of the vehicles in the oncoming column had large red crosses on the side. Ambulances! Having no definite orders beyond heading north and engaging whatever enemy he found, he'd been deliberately leading his squadron in the direction of Becca's hospital in hopes that she might be there. He'd led them over to Ayres Street which went to the hospital, but it now looked as though the hospital was coming to him. He realized it was ridiculous to be worrying about one girl in all this madness, but he couldn't help it.

"Lynnbrooke! Take the squadron west a block or two and find a route north. I'll rejoin you up ahead."

"But..."

"Do it!" He spurred his horse onto the sidewalk and pushed his way through the people fleeing the other way. Some were walking wounded, and others were stragglers of one sort or another. There were also an alarming number of civilians. The city was supposed to have been mostly evacuated, but clearly a lot of folks had stayed behind—until the Martians arrived. But Frank wasn't paying much attention to them. He was scanning the hospital vehicles for any familiar face.

Amazingly, he found one.

There was Nurse Chumley, perched on one of the wagons. He'd met her a number of times when he'd visited Becca. At first, she'd made no secret of her disapproval of any soldier showing interest in one of her girls. That had changed a bit after he was made an officer, but she had remained a snappy old biddy. But she was there now and Frank was glad. He ruthless turned his horse across the traffic and pulled up beside the wagon. "Chumley! Where's Rebecca?"

The woman acted as though he'd grown up out of the ground. "Who...? Oh, Captain Dolfen! What are you doing here?"

"Comin' t'give the Martians a warm welcome. But is Rebecca with you?"

"She's with her sharpshooters," she said and Frank's heart fell. She could be anywhere then... "But they helped us evacuate. She ought to be bringing up the rear." She jerked her head backward.

"Thanks! Thanks a lot!" He turned his horse again.

"Be careful! Those devils aren't far behind!"

Yes, that was for sure. He could see smoke and flames ahead and not nearly far enough away. He couldn't see any of the tripods yet, but where there was smoke and flames, there were usually Martians. He reached the end of the block and looked west and he was gratified to see Lynnbrooke on the next street over urging along the squadron. Lynnbrooke spotted him, but Dolfen just waved him on.

He kept forcing his way through the people headed the other direction and saw that he was nearing the end of the line of wagons and ambulances. If Becca was bringing up the rear she ought to be around here somewhere. But all the people on foot he could see were walking wounded, retreating soldiers, or civilians. Did Becca still have that fool horse with her? She'd be easier to spot if she were mounted, but he didn't see any riders ahead.

A trooper caught up with him. "Captain! Lieutenant Lynnbrooke says that he can see Martians ahead! Do you want to halt and deploy?" Dolfen stared ahead and yes, now he could make out tall shapes, dimly through the smoke. Maybe a half mile ahead. But where was Becca? Could he have missed her in the crowd? Maybe just her, but there were supposed to be a group of them. Women in silly uniforms with rifles, he couldn't have missed seeing all of them. So were they still up ahead? Closer to the Martians? Maybe there had been stragglers with the wounded that they were helping. Damn, he couldn't just keep marching right toward the bastards, his command would be slaughtered. They'd have to deploy and hope Becca could get here ahead of the enemy. *If she's even out there. She might have taken some other street and I've missed her completely.*

"Yes. I'll come." He turned down a side street and made it over to where Lynnbrooke had the squadron. He signaled a halt as soon as he saw Dolfen coming. The squadron was still in pretty good order and the officers gathered quickly.

"All right," he told them, "we are going to set up a blocking position here, along this cross street." He spotted the street sign. "Along Jackson Avenue. We'll take position here and the next two main intersection to the east. This one… Manassas, the next one over is Ayres, and I don't know what the next one over is, but you can see that big red shop sign on the corner. The armored cars will wait in ambush along Jackson. You can pop out and fire down the streets at the tripods when they get closer and then scoot on across behind the buildings before you become a sitting duck. Understood?" Lieutenant Buckman, commander of the armored car troop nodded.

"A and B Troops will dismount three sections each and get them into the buildings on each side of the streets farther up the block. The rest will stay mounted and get into these alleys between the buildings, so that they'll be ready to come out and hit them while they're busy with the armored cars and the dismounted troopers. Gregory," he turned and looked at Lieutenant McGuiness, the commander of D Troop, "get your heavy machine guns set up inside buildings where they can support everyone else. As for your mortars, I leave that to you." He swept his gaze across everyone.

"We haven't got much time, but scout out routes to fall back along. We aren't going to be able to hold here very long, I don't think, and we will have to fall back from position to position. Our mission is to hurt and delay these bastards as long as we can without getting shot all to hell. There are reinforcements coming, we just need to buy time for them to come up.

"One last thing: the Martians have got those spider-machines with them, so be on alert. *But…* there are still people trying to get away out there! Be certain you don't kill any of 'em by mistake! Questions?" There weren't any and Dolfen nodded. "Okay, let's get to it."

His officers ran back to their men, and in moments the squadron was in motion. Horsemen, their mount's hooves clattering on the cobblestones, trotted off to take up positions. Some dismounted and had their horses taken to sheltered areas in the block south of them. Motorcycles, their engine roars echoing off the surrounding buildings, did the same, although there was no way to take the bikes to the rear; they were parked in alleys or on sidewalks. Troops scrambled into the buildings, all carrying bombs and some - not enough - with the new stovepipe rocket launchers. The armored cars formed three groups, near each of the intersections, ready to dart out at the right moment. The machine gun crews, straining under their heavy loads - the fifty-caliber Brownings weighed a hundred pounds even without their tripods or ammunition - as they lugged them into position. Dolfen didn't know how the mortars were going to be placed or directed, but he left that to McGuiness.

It was all done very efficiently and he was proud of his men, especially since this urban setting wasn't one they had trained for. But damn it, where was Becca? He pulled out his binoculars and looked down the street. The Martians were about four blocks away, at least four or five of them on Ayres Street; and from the smoke, at least that many on the parallel streets. Their heat rays were in almost constant use, blasting the buildings along the streets as they advanced. Most of the smoke was rolling to the east, but the smell of burning was heavy in the air.

Artillery fire was coming down around them intermittently, although he had no idea where it was coming from or who was directing it. There were aircraft circling far overhead, so maybe they were the ones calling it in. And speaking of aircraft, where the hell were Selfridge and his boys? He knew that several hundred aircraft had been assembled around Memphis to help in the defense. They would surely be a help now.

"Sir? Captain?" It was Lynnbrooke. "We're about ready, but our flanks are wide open. We're blocking three streets, but it looks like they're coming down every one of them from the north. They'll move right past us on the east and west, sir."

"I know, I know, but there's nothing we can do. There are more troops moving up from the bridge, we'll just have to hope they can fill in on our flanks. In any case we need to be ready to fall back on a moment's notice. We might be in a city, but we're still cavalry."

"Yes, sir."

The enemy drew closer and Dolfen cursed when he realized that they were simply setting fire to every building they passed whether there were any humans in evidence or not. His troops in the buildings here would have to evacuate or fry - and before they could hope to do anything to the Martians. *Unless we give them something else to worry about…*

The only thing he had to work with were the armored cars. Their guns, though small, had a range comparable to the heat rays. If they started shooting, maybe they could draw the Martians close enough for the others to strike. He ran over to where Lieutenant Buckman was standing atop his command vehicle. "Change of plans! We need to sucker them in to let the boys get a crack at them."

"And you want us to be the suckers, sir?"

"That's right. Move into the intersection, fire a couple of shots, and then run south to the next street. Take cover and then do it again. No more than three blocks, though. Got it?"

"Yes, sir, got it. Give me a minute to get it set up." Buckman sent a pair of runners off to relay the order to the more distant squads while he instructed the one that was with him. While this was being done, Dolfen peered down Ayers Street with his binoculars. The tripods were just two blocks away now and still burning everything along their path. If the armored cars weren't able to grab their attention and get them to chase them, he was going to have to pull his men out and… *wait!*

A sudden motion at the end of the block, caught his eye. A group of men were running down the sidewalk toward him. No, not men - women! It was Becca's sharpshooters, desperately trying to stay ahead of the pursuing enemy. Not that the Martians seemed to be chasing them in particular, but they'd be just as dead if they caught up.

And they *were* catching up.

The women were stumbling along, some supporting others, some had their dust masks on and others did not. But they were clearly exhausted and not moving nearly fast enough. He couldn't spot Becca among them, but she had to be there. *Come on girl, move!*

"Ready, sir!" shouted Buckman.

He looked back at the waiting armored cars and cursed. If he sent them out now and the plan worked, the Martians would increase their speed and walk into the trap he'd set - and Becca and the women would be caught right in the middle of it. But if he waited… the women *and* his men might all get fried anyway.

"Wait!" he commanded Buckman, holding up his hand. Then he ran out into the middle of the street, waving his hat and screaming at the women to hurry. They saw him and they did hurry up, Dolfen waited until they were halfway down the block, but he could wait no longer. He jumped back and told Buckman to go.

The gas engines of the armored cars roared and the balky machines lurched out into the open. The sharp crack of their two-inch guns seemed very loud despite all the other noise. They fired off three rounds apiece in just a few seconds and then they gunned their engines and raced south down the street, their turrets swiveling around to fire a few more parting shots.

Looking the other way, he was amazed to see the leading tripod stagger and come to a halt. A lucky shot hit something important? Another tripod maneuvered past it, but valuable seconds were gained. The armored cars made it down to the next intersection and the women made a last sprint to where Dolfen waited for them. "Quick! Get around the corner here!"

The women, about twenty of them, turned the corner and collapsed on the ground. He still didn't see Becca, but a number of them were wearing their dust gear and their faces were hidden. The shriek of a heat ray brought his attention back to the fight. He peered around the corner and grinned savagely. The plan was working, the fire from the armored cars had caught the Martians' attention and they were advancing down the street, firing back at them and no longer blasting the buildings indiscriminately. Just a little bit farther and…

A bugle rang out, its shrill tones audible above the roar of battle. Immediately, rifle fire and machine gun fire and stovepipe fire blasted out from the buildings along the street. Bullets sparked off the tripod's armor and the smoke trails of the rockets ended in small explosions, ripping at the machines.

The Martians, four or five of them, halted in mid-block and swung their rays across the buildings on either side; brick facades crumbled and flames erupted from the windows and burst through the roofs. Dolfen hoped his boys had the sense to get out before they burned.

But while the enemy was firing into the buildings, more troopers, men on foot, on motorcycles, and on horseback were emerging from the alleys between the buildings. Some were flinging dynamite bombs, others were firing stovepipes, and as he watched, half a dozen of those madmen with the rocket-lances galloped out around the legs of the enemy.

Explosions staggered the metal giants. Arms and legs were torn off, the lead machine crashing to the ground in a cloud of smoke. As Dolfen watched in wonder, a mounted trooper drove his lance into the knee joint of one of the tripods. The explosion blew the man off his horse, but it also blew the leg off the Martian. It swayed to one side, tried to regain its balance, and then toppled over right into the front of one of the burning buildings. The wall gave way and the machine crashed through, into an inferno, its remaining legs thrashing wildly.

"That's it! Burn you bastard!"

And then it was over, the remaining Martians retreated as quickly as they could, one limping noticeably.

"By God! By God, Captain! Did you see that?" Lynnbrooke had come up beside him and was pointing and almost dancing.

"I did, Lieutenant. But I hope the boys on the other streets did as well." He looked over the rooftops, but couldn't see much. At least no Martians were turning the corners at the other intersections - yet. "But we can't stay here celebrating. Look, they're regrouping and I think there are some of those spider-machines with them now. We can't stay here. Pass the word for the men to fall back four blocks south."

"Yes, sir!" Lynnbrooke dashed off. Private Gosling trotted up holding Dolfen's horse.

"We movin', Captain?"

"Yup. But we need to help these women, they're spent. Round up some more horses, or a truck if you can find one." He pointed to where the sharpshooters were huddled. Damn it, he still didn't see Becca! Had she made it...?

"Frank?" A muffled voice drew his attention to one of them. One of the women came forward. She was wearing her mask, but the height and build were about right.

"Becca?" He moved toward her, his hands out.

"Don't touch me!"

That wasn't the greeting he'd been hoping for. "Are... Becca, are you all right?"

"I'm covered with the black dust! Don't touch me!"

Instinctively he backed off, but a dagger of fear pierced him. Dust! An uglier death was hard to imagine. But wait, she clearly wasn't dying... "Did you get any on you?"

"Not so far, but it's all over me." He looked closer and yes, he could see black specks on her leather jacket and skirt. Not a lot, but it only took one. "I can't ride a horse, I'd kill the poor beast." She pointed at where Golsing was bringing up some horses.

"Well, we can't stay here! They're coming back."

"I know, I can walk. Let's go."

The men of the squadron—a gratifying number of them, too—were emerging from the alleys and heading south. The other women were loaded on horses or put behind some of the motorcycle riders. Frank remained on foot and motioned Becca to move. "Let's get out of here."

CHAPTER SIXTEEN

JULY, 1912, SOUTH OF MEMPHIS, TENNESSEE

"Looks like a hell of a fight going on, Colonel." Andrew Comstock glanced at his aide, Lieutenant Jerry Hornbaker, and then back at what he was referring to. The whole sky to the north was a mass of black smoke. Memphis was burning. The view from *USLI Albuquerque*'s observation platform was both exhilarating and daunting. The city was obviously in trouble.

But there was clearly a battle still in progress. The rumble of artillery could be heard clearly even from ten miles away. Ten miles; they had sailed all the way from Philadelphia, survived storms and river sand bars, and now here they were, only ten miles from Memphis. The five remaining units in the army's 1st Land Ironclad Squadron would soon enter combat for the first time.

He hoped.

The ironclads were still being towed, as their tiny propellers would have made little headway against the flow of the Mississippi. They had made it to New Orleans with no further mishaps, but then there had been an infuriating delay to find new towing ships since the vessels which had brought them from Philadelphia drew far too much water for the river. The ironclads themselves also drew too much water, but anytime they encountered a sand bar or mud bank, they could simply engage the caterpillar tracks and drive right over it. He'd lost count of the number of times they'd had to do that. But the towing ships couldn't do it so they had to be powerful enough to do the job, but with a shallow enough draft to avoid getting stuck. The vessels had finally been found and they set out, but it was slow going, maybe five miles per hour at most.

So, another two hours to Memphis. But what would they do when they got there? Where was the fight actually taking place? And would they be able to get from the river to the fight? He looked to the eastern shore and eyed the imposing concrete walls marching northward. They looked to be at least thirty feet high and with a ditch in front of them. There were gates at intervals, but there was no way a land ironclad could fit through them. If the fight was inside the city, they might be stuck on the wrong side of the walls. At least there were no cliffs along the shores like there had been at Vicksburg.

"It appears we are in for a bit of a party, eh, Colonel?"

The Englishman, Major Bridges, had climbed up into the observation platform and now crowded out Hornbaker from the viewport. Andrew hadn't been happy being made host for the man, and he found that he didn't like him at all. He was older, far more experienced in the ways of the world, and not shy about reminding everyone of the fact. He talked too much and too loudly, and laughed at his own jokes. The enforced close conditions of the ironclad didn't help matters. He wished that Bridges would have gone with Clopton, but Andrew got the impression that Clopton didn't like him, either.

"Yes," said Andrew shortly.

If Bridges sensed Andrew's dislike, he made no sign. "Any word from the general about what he plans to do?"

Clopton had made his flagship on the *Springfield* but ordered Andrew to remain with the *Albuquerque*. After what had happened to *Sioux Falls* in the storm, the general decided that it was too risky to put the commander and his second in command on the same ironclad. It was sensible, but it made consultation difficult.

"I imagine he'll keep his plans to himself until he finds out what the situation is. We've gotten damn little information from the people in Memphis."

"That's his prerogative, of course. Wellington - and Good God Kitchener! - always played their cards very close to the vest. A bit hard on their subordinates, of course."

"I'll be sure to mention that to the general next I see him," muttered Andrew. He mentally chided himself for being snippy, but the man just brought that out in him. And, of course, Bridges was right: a commander did need to confide his plans with the men who would carry out the orders he gave. How else could they act intelligently? And that was especially true for the second in command. What the hell would Andrew do if Clopton suddenly dropped dead?

Bridges looked to be about to say something else when Major Stavely joined them in the already crowded platform. He saluted Andrew. "Sir, the engineers who came with the Tesla cannon are asking if they should start charging up their capacitors? I wasn't sure what to tell them."

Yes, there was the new experimental lightning gun in the forward turret. They had managed to test it exactly once two days earlier. They had sent a boat ahead with one of the special targets and dropped it in the river, and then they'd fired at it when it drifted past. The gun had worked, sending out a spectacular lightning bolt to vaporize the target, light up a large patch of the river, and kill a few thousand fish which came floating to the surface. The rest of the vessels in the convoy had all signaled their approval with their steam whistles. It was true that the capacitors took several minutes to charge up, but there was no need to do it hours early as far as Andrew knew. Perhaps the engineers were getting anxious about the coming fight, too.

He looked at Stavely. The man was the commander of the ironclad and theoretically it was his decision. He could understand why he might defer to Andrew on the question this experimental weapon—Andrew had been the liaison with Tesla after all—but he seemed to defer to Andrew in an awful lot of other matters, too. Was he that intimidated by Andrew's rank? That might be possible, he supposed, because for once a junior officer wasn't years older than him. Stavely didn't appear any older at all.

"I'd advise them to wait a bit longer, Major. We're still at least a couple of hours away from the battle."

"Very good, sir." He saluted again and left.

"The waiting is always the worst, isn't it?" said Bridges.

"Yes," replied Andrew. "The waiting is the worst—except for what comes after."

* * * * *

JULY, 1912, MEMPHIS, TENNESSEE

The ambulance wagon rocked and swayed and rumbled its way down the street. Every jolt seemed to go directly into Drew Harding's shoulder. He'd never experienced this kind of pain in his life. A dislocated shoulder; he'd heard someone say that. Not all that serious and not all that hard to fix if he remembered correctly. Damnation, how much longer to get to a hospital?

And was there even any hospital to go to? The sounds of combat were growing louder behind him, not fainter. Were the Martians catching up? *Maybe it would be better if they did catch me...*

The pain in his shoulder was replaced by one in his heart, in his gut. He'd lost his ship. How many of his crew had survived? Surely some must have. Surely. Hinsworth hadn't. The crew in the forward turret hadn't. The machine gunners out on the wings… The image of the exploding *Santa Fe* was burned into his memory as if by a heat ray. It was entirely possible that no one had escaped. No one but him. How did you explain *that* to a board of inquiry? How did you explain it to the wives and parents of the men who died?

I should have just drowned…

No chance of that now, although the damned wagon might shake him to death, he supposed. His strength was slowly returning after the long time in the water and the death-like lethargy was leaving. Where were they? Somewhere in Memphis, but where? He supposed he ought to check in with someone, let them know he was alive; get word to Commodore Rush somehow. There was a little sliding hatch between the main compartment and the driver up front. Maybe he could ask where they were going.

Wincing with the pain, he slowly turned around, but couldn't reach the hatch. He'd have to stand up. He pushed himself up and reached for the wooden knob on the hatch. But just then the wagon hit some especially bad bump and he lost his balance. He twisted so as not to land on one of the other wounded men and ended up falling all the way to the floor of the ambulance. A terrible pain shot through his shoulder, but at the same time there was a loud pop, which went all the way through him. He lay there, gritting his teeth and drenched with sweat, but as the pain subsided, he realized that something had happened. His shoulder was back where it belonged! And the pain was not nearly as bad as it had been. It still hurt, but nothing like before. He struggled upright.

"You okay back there?" Drew looked up and saw that the little hatch he'd been trying to reach was now open the driver was looking through it.

"Yeah, yeah, fine. Where are we?"

"Stuck. Streets ahead are jammed with troops and tanks. We might be here a while, so relax." The hatch slid shut again.

Drew sat there for a minute or two and then got up and shuffled between the stretchers to the back of the wagon and looked out. The rear of the wagon was facing north and the whole sky was covered with black clouds of smoke. It looked like the city was on fire. Closer at hand, it was like the driver had said: the streets were packed with troops and tanks and artillery, trying to get to the fighting.

He flexed his arm and winced. It still hurt and didn't seem like there was any strength in it, but at least he could move around without the agonizing pain like before. He lowered himself down to the street and looked south, the way the ambulance was trying to go, and saw that there was little hope in getting through any time soon. What to do? He was still very tired, but somehow waiting in the ambulance was intolerable. Looking closer, he recognized where he was. That was Union Street up ahead and that meant that the tall building a few blocks west must be the hotel where MacArthur had his headquarters.

Making up his mind, he abandoned the ambulance and slowly made his way through the crowds of soldiers. The intersection at Union Street was filled with clanking, smoking steam tanks, and he was obliged to move down an alley between buildings to reach the next block. The rumbles from the north were getting louder. If the Martians arrived before the mob could get itself sorted out, it was going to be a slaughter.

He reached the hotel and saw that the chaos on the streets extended into the building as well. Or perhaps he had it backward; maybe the chaos in the hotel had spilled out onto the streets. Men were clustered around the front doors and being held back by a half-dozen sentries. Men emerged and made their way through the crowd to dash away on whatever mission they had, but no one seemed to be getting in. Drew looked down at himself. Someone had taken off his waterlogged tunic when they'd found him on the shore, and without that, his navy service dress had no rank insignia of any kind. They'd never let him in.

He stood there trying to decide what to do when one of the army officers at the edge of the crowd turned away and stomped in his direction, a look of disgust on his face. As he came up to Drew, he reached out to seize the man's arm. "What's going on?" he demanded.

The man, a major, pulled loose, but then paused to stare at Drew in puzzlement. "Who are you?"

"Commander Harding, US Navy. What's happening?"

The man shrugged. "I don't know! They're not letting anyone into headquarters and there aren't any orders coming out! Nothing since that 'Defense Plan M' message last night!"

"Yeah, I got that one. But what you mean there aren't any orders? What's MacArthur doing?"

"Nothing, apparently. Someone said he's down in the basement and won't see anyone!"

"What? So who's in command?"

The man shrugged. "No one, I guess."

* * * * *

CYCLE 597, 845.2, CITY 3-37

Qetjnegartis considered the situation. The plan appeared to be succeeding. They had broken through the defenses of the city on a wide front from the north. Two of the fortresses which were part of that line had been overrun and a third would soon fall. The main attacking force was driving through the northern parts of the city causing great destruction. Prey-creature resistance had been tenacious in spots and almost non-existent in others. A number of war machines had been lost and quite a few of the transport pods were now in use with rescued pilots. It might become necessary to set up some secure zone where they could be placed to avoid carrying them along into combat.

The most advanced elements were nearing the center of the city and resistance was stiffening. Enemy reinforcements were crossing the bridge from the western shore despite Tanbradjus's efforts to keep them occupied with the diversionary attack. But reports indicated that most of these forces were disorganized and not yet deployed for battle. If they could be struck before they were ready, they might be destroyed in detail.

"All units continue the advance," it commanded. "Drive through to the bridge and secure it. Victory is in our grasp."

* * * * *

JULY, 1912, MEMPHIS, TENNESSEE

"They're pushing through down that street on the left, Captain!" shouted Lieutenant Lynnbrooke. "If we don't pull back, they're gonna flank us!"

Frank Dolfen looked to his left and saw a steam tank at the next intersection on fire and infantry fleeing past it. Damn. After falling back twice, they'd found a good position which looked like they might be able to hold a while. The Martians had tried to break through twice, but three wrecked tripods were now forming a nice roadblock. The spider-machines were forcing their way through the wreckage, but the small machines were nowhere near as hard to kill as the big ones, and a dozen or more of them lay wrecked just beyond their larger brethren. The buildings here were mostly brick and concrete, and while they still had stuff inside which would burn, they were providing better defensive positions than before.

But if the Martians got past them on the left and curved in from behind, they were cooked. "All right, spread the word to pull back. We can move before they hit us again." Lynnbrooke ran to obey and soon the squadron was starting to move. He wasn't sure how many men he had left now. Half the armored cars had been lost and most of the men were on foot; horses run off and motorcycles abandoned. But they were still a cohesive combat force and they were fighting hard.

They weren't alone anymore, either. Fresh troops had come up and they only had to try and defend one street instead of three. But the boys on their left were getting pushed back and there was no choice but to retreat. He looked around and spotted Becca and her girls and waved to them to join the withdrawal. They were fighting hard, too. Or at least as hard as the men would let them. There was a natural instinct to protect them, so the women kept getting pushed back toward the rear and into areas where they would be safer. The women didn't seem to be all that upset about it, except for Becca who was constantly coming forward to take some pot shots with her Springfield. He thought he'd seen her take down one of the spiders with a great shot.

He was still terrified about the black dust on her. It was an incredibly ghastly way to die and it would only take a single inhaled grain to kill her. Sooner or later she had to get out of the dust gear, and unless she was very careful - and lucky - she would get some of the dust on her or in her.

But there was no time to worry about that now. They had to pull back and do it quickly. He herded the women across the street, onto the next block, and moved them down the sidewalk. One of the buildings was already on fire and they had to detour into the street to get around it. He looked back just in time to see one of the men in the rearguard be incinerated by a heat ray that came from off to the left. Yes, they'd pulled out just in time. Well, almost in time.

As they moved, the block was shaken by several explosions and debris rained down around them. It wasn't the Martians, it was 'friendly' artillery. Batteries from all over the Memphis area were being trained on the invaders, and some had either bad aim or bad spotters. Errant rounds kept falling among the troops. It was to be expected, and losing the occasional man was far, far better than having no artillery support. The big guns probably killed more of the enemy than any other weapon. Without them, they would have been overrun long ago.

They reached the end of the block and Dolfen was met by a major with engineer tabs. "Captain, pull back another block. We're going to bring down these buildings here to form a roadblock." He pointed at several tall buildings just to the south.

"All right, but they're coming down on the flanks." Dolfen pointed to the next street over.

"I know, but we've got teams over there, too. All along this line actually. We're gonna try to hold them here for a while."

"Sounds good, sir. We'll pull back." He waved to Lynnbrooke and got the men moving again. Looking back north, he saw that the Martians were now getting past the tangle of wrecked machines. It wouldn't be long before they were here. "Come on! I know you're tired, but keep moving!"

They made it to the next intersection and he was heartened to find three steam tanks waiting there, just out of sight around the corner. Some of the heavy stuff from across the river was finally getting through. He deployed his troopers into the buildings on either side of the street and put the armored cars in ambush just like the tanks. Becca and her sharpshooters slumped down on the sidewalk across from them.

He found a spot where he could see around the corner in relative safety. The enemy was coming on again. A half dozen of the tripods and a swarm of the spiders were at the end of the block, spraying the buildings on each side with their heat rays. The two buildings the major had pointed out were already in flames. He hoped the explosives and the detonator wires were somewhere they wouldn't burn.

Artillery fire started falling around the tripods and that got them moving forward. The spiders came first and then one tripod with the others following at intervals. He spotted the engineer on the other side, peering intently down the street. He slowly raised his hand.

The spiders and the lead tripod reached the buildings and Dolfen braced himself for the explosion, but it didn't come. Had it misfired? No, the major still had his hand raised. What was he waiting for? *Come on! Do it!*

But he waited a little longer, until the *second* tripod was between the buildings. Then he dropped his hand. Dust and smoke erupted from the base of both buildings almost simultaneously. The structures were five or six stories tall and they slowly bowed in toward the street. Then they were falling and disintegrated in a huge cloud of dust which enveloped everything, including the tripod in the lead. More explosions rumbled in the distance and he saw other dust clouds billowing up on the blocks to the north and south.

Moments later, the steam tanks started to move and they clattered, squeaked, and groaned their way around the corner to face down the street. The smoke and dust slowly cleared, and as soon as the lead tripod became visible the tanks opened fire. Two of the armored cars managed to find a spot where they could get a clear shot and joined in as well. Beyond the tripod, the street was blocked with a mound of rubble thirty feet high. Dolfen hoped that there was another tripod underneath it.

He ducked back behind cover as a heat ray swept across the steam tanks. Their armor started to glow red, but they fired off another volley of shots and the ray abruptly blinked out. Daring to look, he saw that the Martian machine had toppled backward against the piled rubble, a gaping hole in the front of the head.

A dozen or so of the spider-machines were in the street, but they were motionless. He'd seen that happen several times before that day. The spiders would be moving and firing and then suddenly freeze in place. Sometimes for just a few seconds and sometimes for longer. His troopers in the buildings wasted no time in taking advantage. Fire ripped at the spiders, puncturing bodies or blasting off limbs. A few shots from the tanks completed the destruction.

After a minute or two, a tripod's head appeared above the mound of rubble and it seemed to be trying to climb over the obstruction. But when a four-inch round from one of the tanks caromed off its armor, the thing disappeared again. Artillery continued to fall, and when some aircraft - finally! - appeared, their attacks and the answering heat rays looked to be several blocks further north.

"Have they given up, do you think, sir?" asked Lynnbrooke.

"I doubt it. But it may be a while before they attack again. Make sure the men take the opportunity to resupply with ammo. See if you can scrounge up any more bombs or stovepipe rockets. We're nearly out."

"Yes, sir." Lynnbrooke moved off. Dolfen pulled out a handkerchief and mopped his face.

"Frank? Frank?"

He turned and saw that Becca had come up behind him. "Are you all right?"

"Frank, can you help me take off this mask?" her hand came up to touch her dust mask.

"Becca, you've still got dust on you! You could die."

"I *will* die unless I get this damn thing off! I'm melting in here and I've got to have some water." She was swaying on her feet and grabbed a lamp post to keep from falling. Yeah, it was hot as blazes today and it must have been absolute hell under that mask. She had to take it off sooner or later. "Frank, please."

"All right, all right. Come over here. Let's take this real slow and careful." He moved her into the

620

doorway of a tobacco shop and looked her over. There were still some dust specks on her, but not nearly as many as when he first saw her. The ridiculous buckskin uniform she had complained to him about was finally proving its worth. The smooth, tanned leather provided little for the grains of dust to cling too. Unlike the wool uniforms the soldiers wore where the dust grains would get caught in the weave.

He was already wearing his gauntlets, so his hands were protected. He took his handkerchief and started brushing away the grains he could see, being careful to stand upwind of her. Shoulders, back, front…

"The mask, Frank, get the *mask* off!"

"Uh… right, right…" There wasn't much dust that he could find on the mask. It was a rubberized canvas material that was as smooth as the buckskin. He dislodged a few grains from the edges of the round eyepieces. He could see her eyes dimly through the glass, which was partially fogged up with moisture. He worked his way down to the neck area and grimaced. Where the cinch cord pulled the bottom tight around her neck were creases and folds that had caught a lot of the dust. "Hold still, this is gonna be tricky."

He brushed away as much as he could with the neck tight. Then he very carefully loosened the cord…

"Captain, I've got the men resting and…" It was Lynnbrooke.

"Lieutenant, are the Martians hitting us again?" He asked without looking away.

"Uh, no, sir, not yet."

"Then you can handle things for the moment. Leave us be."

"Uh, right, sir."

He loosened the cord and pulled the bottom of the mask out a little, revealing more grains of dust. He brushed them off and then repeated the process until he had the bottom as loose as it would go. "Ready?"

"More than ready! Do it!"

Okay, how best to do this? Slow or fast? Fast might dislodge any hidden dust, so slow. "Don't move and don't breathe." He grasped the top of the mask and slowly lifted it upward. Inch by inch he pulled it over her head. Every moment he expected her to start screaming as some grain he'd missed fell on her bare skin. But she didn't and finally the mask was clear. He moved it aside and tossed it away.

"Thank God!" gasped Becca. She started to reach for her canteen.

"Don't move, dammit!" snapped Dolfen. "I need to check around your collar."

"Well, hurry!" she snapped back.

"Yeah, yeah…" He looked closely around the collar of the jacket, but he didn't find anything. She reached for the canteen again, but he slapped her arm back. "Wait!" He inspected the canteen and frowned when he saw a few grains of dust on its cover. "Here, take mine." He gave her his own canteen and she gulped it down. Her face was a bright rosy red, covered with sweat, and beautiful.

"Oh… oh that's good," she gasped. "Thank you, Frank." She looked intently into his eyes. "*Thank you*, Frank."

He found himself blushing. "Uh, you're… you're welcome. But you've still got dust on you from the waist down. You need to be careful."

"I will be."

"And let me find you a helmet and another dust mask. They could use it again." It only took a short search to find what he was looking for. There was discarded equipment all over the place.

He found her a spare canteen and a rations pack as well.

He had just gotten her settled back with the other women when Lynnbrooke reported that the Martians looked to be forming for another attack.

"They're coming again?" asked one of the women, her face twisted in dismay.

"Yeah, ma'am, this ain't over yet."

* * * * *

CYCLE 597, 845.2, CITY 3-37

"Resistance has stiffened, commander. The direct routes to the bridge are blocked by fallen buildings and the prey-creatures are well dug-in among the ruins. It will take much time to fight our way through. Heavy losses are to be expected."

Qetjnegartis regarded the tactical display in his fighting machine and had to agree with the report of its subordinate. The attack had lost momentum and the enemy had managed to assemble enough force to block the direct route to the vital bridge. Perhaps they could just smash their way through, but at what cost? They had to have enough force left to hold the city once they took it. Reports from the battlegroups pushing along the eastern line of defenses indicated that a new enemy force was assembling in that area, and if it attacked while the bulk of Qetjnegartis' forces were still engaged in the city, the situation could become very precarious. They needed to finish things here as quickly as possible so they could redeploy to meet the new threat. But how?

An indicator light on its control panel notified it that Ixmaderna wished to communicate. This was hardly an opportune time, but Ixmaderna was well aware of the current situation; it would only try to communicate if it was an urgent matter. Qetjnegartis opened the channel. "Yes?"

"Commander, as you have directed, I have analyzed the images taken by the artificial satellite taken when it passed over your location a short time ago. I can transfer the data whenever you wish."

"Excellent, do so at once."

"Transmission commencing."

The data arrived and immediately the tactical display was updated. The images from the satellite were very detailed and Ixmaderna had been able to interpret them to give at least an approximation of the location of the prey-creature forces. The satellite only passed over any given location on the planet about once per local day. It was fortunate that it had passed over City 3-37 when it did.

Qetjnegartis studied the information and saw that the enemy's forces were still moving across the bridge from the fortified area west of the river. But as they arrived they were being fed directly into the areas under direct attack by the clan's forces. As its subordinate had reported, the direct routes to the bridge were filled with foot-warriors and machines. But to the east...

To the east, their line ended at about the same point as Qetjnegartis'. There was a gap of nearly three *telequel* between the end of the prey's line and the defensive structures guarding the eastern approach to the city. If it were to use the superior mobility of the war machines and suddenly shift the route of attack... Yes.

"Attention, all units. Battlegroups 2, 10, and 14 will maintain the pressure on our current front. Seventy-five percent of the remaining drones will assist. All other groups will immediately disengage and move east to the coordinates shown on your tactical map. From that point we will turn south and then west to outflank the enemy, surround them, and drive to the bridge. Speed is essential. Commence immediately."

* * * * *

JULY, 1912, MEMPHIS, TENNESSEE

"Well, we're here. Now what the hell do we do?" Andrew Comstock was speaking rhetorically, but naturally Major Bridges felt compelled to answer. He always felt compelled to answer.

"Bit of a sticky wicket, eh, old chap?" He pointed to the burning city. "The battle is over there, and you're on the wrong side of the wall. A pity there's no gate big enough to let you through."

"They didn't know about the ironclads when they built the walls, Major."

"There looks to be a big gate at the end of the bridge, there, but I'm damned if I can see any way for us to get up to it."

"No. I don't think it would be wide enough even if we could."

The 1st Land Ironclad Squadron had finally arrived at Memphis only to find an unholy mess inside the city and on the river as well. Dozens of ships and hundreds of smaller craft were clustered in the vicinity of the bridge that crossed the Mississippi. The bridge itself was crammed with men and vehicles, but they didn't seem to be moving at all. A few of the warships were lobbing shells into the city, but most of them were silent. In fact, many were tied up alongside other vessel, apparently replenishing their ammunition. If they'd been fighting for the last day, they were probably out.

The smoke from the city was a dense cloud drifting eastward and flames could be seen shooting skyward in many places. The land sloped up steadily from the river and it was possible to see things over the wall. What Andrew could see didn't look good.

"Sir," said Jerry Hornbaker. "General Clopton wants us to come alongside *Springfield* to confer with you. I've ordered our tow to bring us over there."

The squadron was loitering just south of the bridge, not wanting to get caught in the jam of vessels ahead. They slowly brought *Albuquerque* over next to the flagship. Clopton was on the bridge with a speaking trumpet. "What do you think?" he called over.

Andrew had his own trumpet. "The fight is over there, sir." He pointed to the city.

"How do we get there, Colonel?"

"Sir, those walls are only six or eight feet thick. Enough to stop a heat ray, but not a twelve-incher! I suggest we take the direct approach!"

Clopton was silent for a moment; surprised perhaps. But then he nodded vigorously. "Let's do it! The squadron will form line on the right! Let's get ashore!"

* * * * *

JULY, 1912, MEMPHIS, TENNESSEE

Becca Harding opened the bolt of her rifle and pulled a five-round stripper clip of ammunition out of her cartridge belt. She fit the clip in place and pressed the cartridges down into the magazine. She flicked away the empty clip and closed the bolt, loading a round into the breech. She'd done this what seemed like a thousand times in the last few hours. Only a couple of the other women were firing their weapons, but the rest were happy to keep Becca supplied with ammo from their own belts. She'd had to swap rifles a few times when hers got so hot the grease started dripping out of the stock.

She leaned around the corner of the building she was hiding behind, spotted one of the damn spider-machines, took aim, and fired. The bullet hit it, causing a visible spark, but not affecting it in any other way that she could see. It swung its small heat ray in her direction and she dodged back. The ray swept across where she'd just been and the edges of the brick glowed redly for a moment. Cursing under her breath, she worked the bolt, loading another round, and tried to decide if she

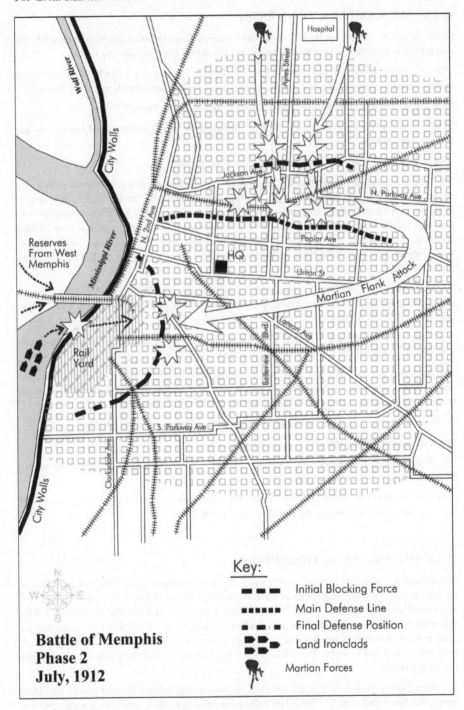

**Battle of Memphis
Phase 2
July, 1912**

Key:

▬ ▬ ▬ Initial Blocking Force

■■■■■ Main Defense Line

■ ▬ ■ ▬ Final Defense Position

Land Ironclads

Martian Forces

dared risk another shot. Sometimes the machines kept their weapon trained on the same spot, waiting for an unwary shooter to try again. She'd almost been killed several times that way, but so far she'd been lucky.

"Becca," called Sarah Halberstam. "The soldiers are waving us back again!"

All right, that decided the issue, she wouldn't chance it again. She turned and trudged along the alley, herding the women in front of her. She glanced back over her shoulder to make sure the spider wasn't following. They made it through to the next street unharmed and followed a corporal's direction to the new position.

Fall back, fall back. For the last two hours they'd been chased from one location to the next. They'd hoped that they could hold the strong position they'd built behind the collapsed buildings where Frank had helped her out of her mask. At first it seemed like the Martians had given up. They'd only probed half-heartedly with a few tripods and some spider-machines, which they'd beaten back easily. But then the word came that more Martians were attacking from the east, getting in behind the defenders; slaughtering them.

They had to retreat or risk being slaughtered, too. So the line bent back, swinging away from the Martians and toward the river. The Mississippi was at their backs now, only a few blocks away. She wasn't sure where Frank was; at first he'd hovered around her and the other women like some mother hen until she'd tartly told him to go take care of his *own* company. This one was hers. So he had and she had hardly seen him since. She hoped he was all right. Maybe she should have kept her mouth shut…

She and the others moved through another block of buildings and out onto a very wide street. In her fatigue, she stumbled over a set of railroad tracks and then looked around in surprise. The bridge across the Mississippi had been primarily for railroad traffic and there were several rail yards at its eastern end. In all the confused movements and retreats she'd lost track of where she was and didn't realize they were on the edge of those yards.

There were large sheds and engine houses and lots and lots of box cars and flat cars, some of them piled with supplies, lined up on sidings. There were also great crowds of troops and steam tanks and horses and guns all jammed up around the large set of gates leading to the bridge. She'd heard Frank say that a lot of the garrison's troops and equipment had been sent across the river to West Memphis because it seemed like the main enemy attack was going to be there. When the attack had really come from the north, they had to try and bring all those troops back across the river. She and the others had been fighting alongside many of those troops for the last few hours, but she knew from personal experience during the long retreat from Santa Fe in 1910 how long it could take to squeeze an army through a narrow choke point. It appeared as though an awful lot of those troops were still stuck on the bridge or on the far shore.

But at the moment it didn't look like these troops were trying to get through to the battle anymore. The battle was coming to them and they were trying to get themselves sorted out into some kind of combat formation. Officers were shouting directions and Becca finally spotted Frank. He talked briefly with one of those officers and then waved to his men to follow him. They were nearly all on foot; all the armored cars and most of the motorcycles and horses were gone. They were infantry now. As she and her girls followed along, she wondered what had become of Moses and Ninny. Had they found some refuge or had they been caught up in the fighting? Her horse had survived so much since that fateful trip down to see where the shooting stars had landed, it would be a shame for him to get killed now. *It would be a shame for you to get killed now, kid! Keep your mind on your business!*

Frank led them over to a position by some large piles of coal, stacked railroad ties, and gondola cars sitting on the tracks. They were south of the bridge now with their backs to the tall concrete walls lining the river. She saw some of the gunners on one of the platforms with a big disappearing gun. They had turned the weapon as far as it could, but it was just facing along the wall's length. It wouldn't turn far enough to shoot to the rear.

They found cover in and around the gondola cars and behind the stacks of ties. They were very conscious of the fact that the coal and the ties would burn very nicely when touched by a heat ray. But the cars were mostly metal and that would help. The cavalrymen's sole remaining machine gun was set up along with a pair of mortars. Becca found a spot under one of the cars where she had a good view to the east. Well, not a good view, but a clear line of fire extending a hundred yards or so. She scrounged a half-dozen clips of ammo from the other girls, who were mostly sheltered behind the big metal wheels of the cars, and tucked them into her belt pouches. Sarah Halberstam lay down under the car beside her. Frank came by, appearing very harried. He just looked over their position, nodded, and moved on.

Several of the steam tanks chugged up on their left and infantry clustered around and behind them. A squad of men came up, apparently thinking about occupying the spot Becca and her girls were in, looked at them in confusion, and then moved off to find a spot somewhere else. She had no idea what unit they belonged to, everything was all mixed up.

"How are the others holding up?" she asked Sarah.

"They're scared, Becca. Worn out and scared to death." She paused and then added: "So am I."

"Yeah, yeah, me, too."

"Really? You don't look it. You never look scared; you look angry."

Becca shrugged. "The mad hides the scared, I guess."

Sarah nodded and then looked around. "Well, I guess our retreating is over. Nowhere left to run from here."

"No, I reckon that's true." And it was; their backs were literally to the wall. "So we have to stop them."

"You think we can?"

"We can try."

Sarah smiled. "We did our best. So did you, Becca. You've done a great job. As the soldiers would say: it's been an honor serving under your command today, sir."

Becca blinked, her throat tight. "I... we are soldiers, Sarah."

"Yes, I guess we are, aren't we? - thanks to you."

"Not sure if that's a compliment, considerin' the circumstances."

Sarah laughed. "Well, it was meant to be. This is our home, Becca. We all ought to be willing to fight to defend it. You showed us how." She held out her hand and Becca leaned over and grasped it.

"Well, those monsters don't care that we're women. Let's show them what *humans* can do!"

"Yes... Oh God, here they come!"

The firing, which had died down a bit, suddenly rose to a high tempo again and the noise of the heat rays pierced the roar. Through the smoke she could see the dark shapes of the tripods stalking forward. She didn't waste her ammunition shooting at them, instead she squinted through her sights, looking for the spider-machines.

Cannons were firing and she saw one of the tripods fall, but then heat rays were sweeping across the area. Shooting down from above, they couldn't quite reach Becca where she was under the gondola, but the ground just in front of her blazed red, the far metal rail of the track turned a dull orange and the gravel gleamed like hot coals. She ducked her head to shield her face from the blast of scalding air which roiled around her. But then it moved on. Screams and an explosion came from her left where the steam tanks had been.

She looked up again, her eyes watering from the heat and the smoke. As she'd feared, the piles of coal were burning and she couldn't see more than a few dozen yards now. A puff of wind from the west blew some of it away, but it was still bad.

The air shook as artillery fell much too close for comfort. Stones rattled down around them, banging off the top and sides of the gondola. *This is it. Can't hold nothing back now!*

Squinting and coughing, she peered ahead looking for a target. Any target.

A shape materialized a little to her left and she swung the rifle toward it. A squat horror with multiple legs and arms was scuttling toward her. She aimed and fired and hit it. She worked the bolt and fired again. She thought Sarah was firing, too, but the noise had grown so great it was all mingled in one all-encompassing roar. She emptied the magazine and loaded in another clip. She fired again. The spider-machines had a small glowing red 'eye', just like the larger ones. She aimed at that and squeezed the trigger. The eye shattered and went out. The spider halted and seemed to turn from side to side as if blinded. Becca chambered another round and sent it through the hole where the eye had been. A few sparks shot out and the spider slowly leaned to one side and fell over.

"We got it! We got it!" screamed Sarah Halberstam, her voice just barely audible in the bedlam.

But then her scream became a wordless shriek and Becca turned and saw that the woman was on fire. A second spider had emerged from the smoke and turned its heat ray on Sarah. The small ray devices carried by the spiders weren't powerful enough to reduce a person to ashes, but they were still deadly. Sarah's clothes were burning and she rolled toward Becca trying to put out the flames. The spider was twenty yards away and followed her with the ray. Becca grabbed the woman and dragged her behind the wheel of the gondola, out of the line of fire for the moment. She beat on Sarah's clothes with her leather-gloved hands to try and put out the flames. She was still screaming and thrashing almost uncontrollably. Her left shoulder was a blackened ruin.

At last the fire was out and Sarah collapsed in her arms, moaning. Becca peered around the wheel and saw the spider moving forward, around the end of the car. In a moment it would have a clear line on them. She grabbed her rifle and worked the bolt, but the magazine was empty. She fumbled for a clip, but each pouch on her belt that her frantic fingers came to was empty, too. The spider was coming…

A massive rumble shook the earth beneath her and a loud explosion echoed across the rail yard. It came from the west and she tore her eyes away from the spider-machine for an instant to look that way. But all she could see were burning vehicles, dead men and…

…the city walls.

A cloud of smoke was rising up from just beyond a stretch of them, just to the right of the big disappearing gun. What was that? Some new Martian attack? The final blow? But when she jerked her head back to look at the spider-machine, it seemed to be as transfixed by this new development as she was.

Another series of explosions made her look at the walls again and new clouds were rising up and then… then a whole long section of the wall seemed to be leaning, leaning away, leaning outward. With a roar of shattering concrete they crumbled to pieces and fell in a huge swirling cloud of dust. What was happening?

She sat there, frozen, cradling Sarah Halberstam and her useless rifle in her arms, watching the dust. A dark form began to take shape within the cloud. At first all she could see was a dark mass atop long rods, and for an instant she was sure it was a tripod. But no, the shape on top was square, not round like a Martian machine, and it was perched on something even larger…

As she stared in astonishment, a huge green shape emerged from the cloud. It was bristling with guns and from a pole on the top flew the Stars and Stripes. In white letters across the prow was written the word:

Albuquerque.

* * * * *

JULY, 1912, MEMPHIS, TENNESSEE

Colonel Andrew Comstock whooped in delight as the section of city wall toppled outward into the ditch, disappearing in a cloud of dust.

"That did it, Major! Let's get moving!"

"Yes, sir!" said Major Stavely. "Driver! Full speed! Steer for the hole! All guns prepare to fire!"

The *Albuquerque* lurched into motion and rumbled its way up the bank and toward the gap in the walls. Andrew hoped they hadn't killed anyone in making that gap, but he supposed it was possible. Anyone looking out should have immediately understood what was going to happen and gotten the hell out of the way. But with the battle raging, maybe they hadn't looked out. Or were too confused to understand.

But there hadn't been any choice, none at all.

They had to get into the city where the battle was and the only way to do it that wouldn't include a thirty mile detour was to go through the walls. Against a fortification built to withstand an attack by humans it would have been hopeless. Walls thirty feet high would have also been thirty feet thick to resist the impact of rifled artillery. It would have taken them days to blast their way through. But the Martian heat rays had no impact when they struck. They burned or melted their way through objects, but concrete was the ideal material to resist the rays. Walls a mere six or eight feet thick had proved perfectly able to resist the rays. In the rush to build as many walls as possible, they were made as thin as practical to save time and materials. Which also meant they were vulnerable to heavy artillery.

The land ironclads had plenty of that.

They had turned toward the river bank, and when their tracks had touched ground they jettisoned their flotation modules and hauled themselves ashore. They had to crush or shove aside some wooden piers and a few small boats along the waterfront, but that didn't hinder them in the slightest. Some sheds and other buildings had to go, too. People were gathering all around waving. Whether in welcome of the ironclads or in protest of the property damage Andrew wasn't sure. The city walls, just ahead, had thick concrete platforms to mount the big disappearing guns built at intervals, and they didn't want to try and blast through there. Fortunately, the walls projected out at those points and they were easy to spot. Clopton directed the squadron to concentrate on a single one-hundred-yard section of wall about a quarter mile south of the bridge.

The first salvo, five twelve-inch, four seven-inch and ten five-inch shells, exploded all along the base of the wall. This close, they could aim very precisely. Huge chunks of concrete were gouged out and flew off in all directions. A couple of the twelve-inchers had punched all the way through. The five-inch guns got off a few more shots before the big guns were reloaded, but then they all fired off again.

The next salvo had brought the whole section of wall down, exactly as they had hoped. Not only did it open a gap in the wall, but the debris had nearly filled the ditch which lay in front of it. The path was now clear.

Albuquerque led the way with the others following close behind. The gap was probably wide enough to go two abreast, but they were going single file. None of them knew exactly what they'd be facing on the other side, but the smoke and flames and noise indicated that the fighting was very close. They had to be ready for anything as they drove into the cloud of dust.

The ironclad's huge tracks crunched over the rubble in the ditch and then climbed up over the broken-off stub of the walls. Andrew had to steady himself as the machine pitched and jerked over the uneven ground. The other people on the bridge, Stavely, Hornbaker, several enlisted men, and the inevitable Major Bridges did so as well.

Up, over, and through. The wind pulled the dust away like a curtain and they were in Memphis.

They were in what looked to be the rail yards. Tracks filled with cars, sheds, engine houses, mounds of coal, water towers, control towers, and all manner of other things covering several hundred acres. Most of the things seemed to be on fire. The open spaces were crammed with troops and steam tanks, wagons and horses. Many of them were on fire, too.

On the far side of the yards were what they had come for: Martian tripods.

A dozen at least were in sight, and from the heat rays emerging from the smoke in the distance, there were surely more coming. But the nearer ones were motionless, not moving, not firing. Why?

"I think we surprised the blighters," said Bridges.

"I think you're right! Well, let's take advantage of it! Major Stavely, fire at will!"

"Yes, sir! All guns, commence firing!"

The main turret swung slightly to the left, steadied, and then fired. A gout of flame and a cloud of black cordite smoke erupted from the end of the barrel. In the instant before the smoke hid the view, Andrew saw a tripod simply disintegrate; head blown to flinders, arms and legs flying off in all directions. A moment later, the five-inchers joined in, although he wasn't sure what they were firing at.

Albuquerque continued to move forward, clearing the way for the others to follow. *Tulsa* was behind them and swung out to the right, *Omaha* was next and would go left. By the time the twelve-incher was reloaded, the view had cleared enough to pick a new target; and a moment later, another tripod was annihilated. Hornbaker was shouting like it was a football game.

But now the enemy was beginning to react. Heat rays stabbed out to hit the ironclads and Andrew tensed. The forward armor ought to be able to stand up to them, but would it? The bridge shutters had been lowered and the steam lines pressurized if a defensive cloud needed to be released.

A ray blazed around the bow and another played along the main turret. But there were no explosions, no sudden alarms, and a moment later the guns roared out again and claimed the attackers. "No damage reported!" cried Stavely jubilantly.

"Looks like you've gotten their attention, though, old chap," said Bridges, pointing.

Andrew looked through the thick quartz view block and saw what the Britisher was talking about. Six tripods were moving into position in front of them. "Major Stavely, I think we have a target for Professor Tesla's cannon! Tell them to get ready!

"Yes, sir!"

* * * * *

CYCLE 597, 845.2, CITY 3-37

Qetjnegartis absorbed the status reports and was pleased. Victory was within its grasp. The flanking movement had succeeded perfectly. The prey-creature defenses had been thrown into confusion and they had retreated in disarray back toward the vital bridge. Now they were penned into a narrow space with the clan's fighting machines closing in from three sides. Once they were destroyed, the enemy on the bridge could be similarly disposed of. There were still the dangerous water vessels on the river, but the enemy's own defensive walls would provide cover for the war machines and they could be destroyed or driven off by heat ray fire from the shores. Other battlegroups could be sent to the eastern perimeter to deal with the new enemy force assembling there.

Losses had been heavy, but not so crippling that the city could not be held. Once a link-up with Tanbradjus' forces on the western shore was made, construction machines could be moved into the city and a proper holdfast constructed. The base on the eastern shore would be secured. Raiding parties could be sent out to disrupt the prey-creatures' transportation systems and the manufacturing facilities which surely must exist in the east. The way would be opened for the final conquest of this continent. Success. The Colonial Conclave and the elders back on the Homeworld would be pleased…

"Commander! Commander Qetjnegartis! Respond!"

It was Davnitargus, commander of battlegroup 32-8. It sounded very agitated. What could be wrong? "This is Qetjnegartis. What do you want?"

"Commander, we have reached the bridge, but are under attack by… by…"

"By what?"

"I do not know! War machines of some sort. Huge war machines! Much larger than ours! The heat rays seem to have little effect on them!"

"Relay an image."

The image was difficult to interpret. Smoke obscured much of the details, but it could see a very large object… no, several very large objects. They were somewhat similar to the armored gun vehicles the prey-creatures used, but much larger. Projectile throwers in rotating cylinders studded their surface. Other objects of unknown purpose projected above. As Qetjnegartis watched, a war machine's heat ray struck the forward surface with seemingly no effect until the war machine was destroyed by a single shot from one of the enemy weapons.

"Davnitagus, concentrate your forces against a single enemy and destroy it. I will be on the scene shortly."

"Understood," said the bud.

Qetjnegartis was not far off. It had followed along behind the main advance, coordinating activity rather than directly engaging in combat. Now it set its machine in motion and quickly came forward to a spot with a clear view. The tall buildings ended on the edge of a large open space filled with burning structures, prey-creatures, war machines, and the newly arrived devices.

Just as it halted, six of the war machines opened fire on the leading vehicle. The heat rays struck various locations on the thing with no immediate effect, but then all six rays converged on a single point at the front. The metal quickly turned bright yellow and started to melt. *Yes, this is the proper way to deal…*

A blindingly bright light sprang from one of the cylinders. It wasn't a beam of energy, like a heat ray, but a jagged, twisting blast like a static charge jumping from point to point. It leapt out and connected to the nearest fighting machine, but then jumped to the next and the next until all six were connected. The bolt writhed and twisted, and all the fighting machines jerked spasmodically as they sent out showers of sparks and gouts of smoke. After, a moment the bolt vanished and the six machines collapsed to the ground.

"Commander!" said Davnitargus over the communicator. "Did you see that?"

"Yes, I saw."

"What was that?"

"I don't know." It tried to formulate a more useful response but nothing came.

"What are you orders?"

Even as it tried to reach a decision, the enemy giants came forward. There were five of them, and their weapons smashed machine after machine.

"Commander?"

"Fall back. We must fall back and regroup so we can concentrate and destroy these things."

"Yes, Commander, at once."

* * * * *

JULY, 1912, MEMPHIS, TENNESSEE

Rebecca stared in wonder at the enormous machines. They were like ships mounted on big caterpillar tracks like the steam tanks used. They had guns, big guns, all over them. And they were olive drab and they flew the American flag.

"They're ours," she whispered. "They're ours, Sarah." She looked down at the woman in her arms. Her eyes were closed, but she stirred, moaned, and her eyes fluttered open.

"Look, Sarah, they're ours. And they're killing the Martians. Look!" As she sat there, soldiers were coming forward, shouting, faces twisted with some terrible combination of fear, joy, and anger. One of them ran up to the still frozen spider-machine, strapped a bomb to it, pulled the fuse, and ran off. He obviously hadn't even seen her there, only twenty feet away. She twisted around to shield Sarah as much as she could. The bomb exploded wrecking the spider. Some bit of shrapnel stung her cheek.

One of the colossal machines rolled by, not a hundred feet away, its massive tracks crushing everything under them. "Look, Sarah, can you see it? Can you see?"

Sarah Halberstam jerked her head in a tiny nod. Her mouth shaped *I see it, Becca*, but made no sound she could hear. They watched the behemoth pass by, its guns shaking the ground. Becca turned her head to try and see what was happening, but the gondola blocked her view. More troops streamed past. She couldn't keep sitting there. She needed to see what was happening and get medical help for Sarah. God only knew where the hospital people were now.

"Sarah? Sarah, we need to get you some help. Can you move?"

But Sarah Halberstam didn't move. Becca shook her gently, but she didn't move.

Her lips were quivering as she closed the woman's eyes and gently moved her aside so she could get up. She pulled her under the gondola car where hopefully nothing would disturb her.

She rubbed away her tears, grabbed her rifle, and went in search of ammunition.

* * * * *

JULY, 1912, MEMPHIS, TENNESSEE

"Major, there are men on the ground in front of us. What should I do?" The driver of *Albuquerque* looked toward his commander, seeking guidance.

Andrew looked forward as well as he could through the narrow view slit. The rail yards were a mass of train cars, steam tanks, men, artillery limbers, and horses. And there were men on the ground. Dead? Wounded? Stavely turned to look at him. "Colonel?"

He swallowed. "We have to pursue, Major, we can't let the enemy regroup. Keep going."

"When I was commanding a company of steam tanks, sometimes we had to…" Stavely grimaced, nodded, and turned back to the driver. "Keep going, Sergeant."

The man didn't look happy, but he said: "Yes, sir."

The ironclad continued to move at its top speed of about five miles an hour. Mercifully, it was impossible to see the ground directly in front of the machine, nor see what its huge tracks were rolling over. There were definitely crunching sounds coming from below, but Andrew told himself it was from empty wagons and rail cars and not human bones. *No choice. No choice.*

"Bloody sad thing, Colonel, but war is hell, as your General Sherman would say," said Major Bridges.

The enemy was retreating. Tesla's lightning cannon had worked beyond anything Andrew had hoped for. Six Martians destroyed with a single shot! Granted, it would be ten minutes before they could fire it again, but the Martians didn't know that. And it was clear that they had been shocked by what had happened. Just moments after it fired, the surviving tripods started falling back. General Clopton had ordered a pursuit and that is what they would do.

Beyond the rail yards, the larger buildings of the city took over, creating narrow canyons on either side of the streets. The bigger avenues were just wide enough for an ironclad to move along. Well, almost wide enough; the ironclad was snapping off lamp posts and electrical poles and projecting signs as it moved. Andrew wasn't sure if they could actually smash their way through a block of buildings, and hopefully they wouldn't have to find out. Albuquerque steered into one of the streets, while the four others each took parallel routes. The remains of the other army troops in the area were rallying and following along.

Most of the Martians, able to move much faster, had already retreated a half mile or more, but some of the spider-machines had been left behind. The ironclads had a dozen heavy machine guns able to shoot from armored mounts along the lower hull, and these were firing busily at them. Oddly, most that Andrew could catch sight of were just standing frozen as the bullets tore them apart. Some of them were simply crushed as the ironclad rolled over them.

Up ahead there was a crippled tripod, one of its legs blown off, trying to drag itself along with its arms and other legs. As the *Albuquerque* approached, it propped itself up and fired its heat ray. But the front of the ironclads were very heavily armored with the steel-asbestos sandwiches developed by the MIT engineers. The shoes on the caterpillar tracks were solid steel six inches thick and continually rotating to prevent a heat ray from being able to burn its way through. For a short exposure, there wasn't a thing the Martian could do.

"Run it down," Andrew said with grim satisfaction.

There was slight lurch and they crushed the thing flat. Only after they'd done it did Andrew wonder what would have happened if the tripod's power cells had exploded with them sitting on top of it. *Need to be careful about that…*

"Colonel, there are a bunch of them gathered up ahead. Seven or eight blocks away, there. Do you see?" Stavely pointed. Andrew squinted, pulled out his binoculars, cursed at the fuzzy image, and stepped out onto the bridge wing to get a clear view. Yes, three-quarters of a mile ahead there was a cluster of tripods milling about. A dozen or more of them.

"Do they think they're out of our range?" asked Stavely who had followed along.

"Let's enlighten them with the twelve-incher, Major. Give them a shot and tell the crew to make the next one armor piercing."

"My pleasure, Colonel!" said Stavely with a grin.

A moment later the big gun roared out, half-deafening Andrew. Through his binoculars he saw the shell burst among the tripods and at least one went down. Now, if the gunners could just reload before they had the sense to disperse. A well-drilled crew ought to be able to reload and fire in less than a minute, even with the thousand pound shells the big gun fired. He counted silently and had only reached fifty-two when they fired again.

The guns and the ammunition they fired were designed by the navy. An armor piercing round had a thicker metal shell and the fuse had a delay to allow it to smash its way deep into the vitals of a ship before exploding.

The tripods had far less armor than a battleship.

Even from that far away, Andrew could see the havoc the shell wrecked among the Martians. It tore its way right through their formation, arms, leg, heads, whole machines went flying before the shell finally burst. Andrew was reminded of the descriptions he'd read in history class at West Point about solid shot from artillery ripping through the close-packed infantry of a Napoleonic column.

"Wow!" cried Jerry Hornbaker.

"Yes, Lieutenant," said Andrew. "Wow, indeed."

* * * * *

CYCLE 597, 845.2, CITY 3-37

Qetjnegartis was thrown violently against the safety restraints as something large smashed into its fighting machine. The machine staggered and it was barely able to regain control to prevent it from toppling over. What had happened? It was at the rear of the formation? Had one of the high-angle projectiles landed on it?

No, as it looked around it realized that something else had happened. Four of the fighting machines had been wrecked and three others seriously damaged all at a blow. The impact on its own machine had actually been part of another machine which had been torn off.

"Commander!" said one of its subordinates. "These narrow passages are death traps. The enemy can fire right along them and we are easy targets."

"Yes, yes, you are correct. Quickly, let us move into the lateral passages, out of their line of fire."

The surviving machines moved into cover behind the buildings. They were safe for the moment, but what was to be done? Over half of the fighting machines which had crossed the river were out of action. Nearly eighty percent of the drones were gone. More and more prey-creature forces were gathering with the new giant machines. Was there any way to defeat them?

"If we stay in these side laterals until the large machines approach, perhaps we can ambush them, Commander," suggested Davnitargus. "If we are very close, perhaps their large weapons will not be able to bear on us."

"Perhaps. Very well, let us try." Commands were issued and on laterals adjoining each of the five passageways on which the enemy vehicles were approaching, fighting machines were gathered. Vision pick-ups were extended on manipulators to see the enemy. They were coming on slowly; perhaps this would work.

But flying machines were overhead, circling beyond the reach of the heat rays. They were clearly directing the fire of the long-range high-angle projectile throwers. Their shells were falling more and more frequently near the closely massed fighting machines. Could they warn the large machines as well?

They were nearly here. A bit closer and the trap could be sprung…

The machine stopped.

"Commander, they can see us!"

Qetjnegartis looked and saw that the tall tower on top of the enemy machine was higher than the intervening buildings. This close they had a direct line of sight to the tops of the fighting machines. They had detected the ambush. Should it still be sprung? They would have to emerge into the passageway and attack from the front. If that electric arc weapon was ready, how many machines could it take down?

The image from the vision pick-up showed the largest weapon turning to the left. What was it aiming at? The building was in the way. *Surely they aren't going to…*

The side of the building forty *quel* ahead of Qetjnegartis exploded outward and the fighting machine in front of it was torn to pieces. The prey had fired right *through* the building!

"This is no good, Commander!" said Davnitargus. "We must withdraw!"

Retreat meant failure. The only possible place to go was back across the river. The chance to establish a hold on the eastern shore would have to be abandoned. Was there anything that could be done to salvage the situation?

But then word came from the commander of the battlegroup on the eastern perimeter. The enemy force which had gathered there was now attacking. "There are over three hundred of the armored gun-vehicles, Commander," it reported. "We cannot stop such a force without immediate reinforcements."

To send the reinforcements would leave Qetjnegartis with insufficient force to deal with the current situation - if indeed there were sufficient forces now - but to ignore the request would mean the enemy would come driving in on their rear at the most critical moment. To stay could mean the annihilation of the entire force.

"Progenitor," said Davnitargus, "it was a noble attempt, a brilliant plan, but to stay here will mean our destruction; and with it, all hope for our clan on this world. We must withdraw."

Another projectile crashed through the building, but fortunately this time it did not hit any of the fighting machines. No, Davnitargus was right, to stay would mean destruction with no hope for any gain.

"Very well. All forces, this is Qetjnegartis. We must retreat. Disengage and move north. We will re-cross the river at the same point as we initially crossed. Speed is essential."

It received the acknowledgments almost immediately. Clearly all were expecting the order.

Turning its machine, Qetjnegartis fled the scene of disaster.

* * * * *

JULY, 1912, MEMPHIS, TENNESSEE

"They're retreating, Colonel, shall we pursue?" asked Major Stavely.

"By all means, Major," said Andrew. "I doubt we'll catch them, but let's make sure they don't stop."

"You're not going to wait for an order from General Clopton, Colonel?" asked Major Bridges.

"Any fool can see what needs to be done, Major, and Clopton's no fool. Let's drive these bastards into the river."

* * * * *

JULY, 1912, MEMPHIS, TENNESSEE

Drew Harding sat on the steps of the hotel, cradling his arm. He was filthy and utterly exhausted. A steady stream of men ran up and down the steps into the headquarters now. He looked up as the same army major he'd talked to earlier sat down next to him with a grunt. "So what's happening?" asked Drew. "Did we win?"

"Looks like it. Or it sure sounds like it if you listen to MacArthur. He's a pistol, isn't he?"

"I guess." In truth he wasn't sure what to make of General MacArthur. He'd been so absurdly confident at that meeting before the battle; pompous, even. And then during the crisis he was nowhere to be seen. His subordinates had been like a flock of chickens with all their heads cut off. With nowhere else to go, Drew had found a spot near the entrance to the hotel and dozed off. The fighting to the north didn't seem to be getting any closer, so it had seemed like a good idea.

Then, suddenly, everything was in an uproar. The sounds of battle were coming from the east instead of the north and they were getting close very fast. The headquarters staff had come boiling out of the building, carrying rolls of maps and stacks of paper and calling for vehicles to move it all. But before an evacuation could even get under way, the Martians were marching down the streets just a block away to the north. Everyone tried to find cover.

And into the midst of the chaos, MacArthur had suddenly appeared; he was immaculately decked out in his fancy uniform, decorations on his chest, and a riding crop in his hand. He'd walked through the mob like a large ship parting the waves, ignoring every shouted plea for orders. He'd strolled over to the intersection and just stood there, in plain sight, watching the Martian tripods moving past, not five hundred feet away. To Drew, it looked like he was trying to get himself killed. But no heat ray claimed him.

The sounds of fighting near the bridge grew to an uproar, and then to everyone's astonishment, the Martians had come back the way they had come, heading east, away from the bridge. A few minutes later they were followed by the most outlandish contraptions Drew had ever seen. He instantly knew what they were; he'd read about them and he'd gotten some letters from his friend, Andrew Comstock, who was helping to build them. But he'd had no idea they were ready for action or that they were coming to Memphis. They were, perhaps, the ugliest bits of machinery he'd ever seen, but at that moment they looked beautiful. Everyone stopped and stared.

MacArthur had stared, too, but then he stirred and came back to the entrance of the hotel. Everyone had gathered round. "A great victory is within my reach, gentlemen," he'd said. He didn't speak loudly, yet somehow everyone could hear him. "But now I need all your help to grasp it. Let's get to work." He'd walked back into the hotel, his staff streaming after him.

"So what are you going to do now?" asked the major.

He sighed. What he really wanted to do was to sleep for about twelve hours. "I guess I need to find Commodore Rush and get some orders."

* * * * *

JULY, 1912, MEMPHIS, TENNESSEE

Captain Frank Dolfen, 5th US Cavalry, stumbled over the rubble, back toward where he hoped his men were waiting. The sun was sinking toward the western horizon, although it could only be seen from time to time through all the smoke. Large sections of the city were still burning and he doubted that any of the fire brigades were still functional. They'd have to let it burn itself out, he guessed.

The smell of burning; burning wood, burning coal, burning flesh, was almost overpowering. It was odd: during the fighting he'd smelt nothing. But now he could smell everything. It was like that in every fight he'd ever been in. His senses narrowed down to sight and sound. Afterward he'd find himself covered with cuts and scratches and have no memory of how or when he'd gotten them. Like now. His uniform was torn and burned in a dozen spots, and he hurt in more places than that.

Most of them he guessed had come from at the end, during the fight in the rail yard. He'd been running from spot to spot, encouraging his men, trying to keep them fighting. Trying to keep them alive. Between dodging heat rays and dodging shrapnel from their own artillery, he'd spent most the time on his belly, crawling among the railroad cars.

He'd been quite certain they were all going to die. They were in a box with nowhere to run, and a swarm of the tripods were approaching from seemingly everywhere. A strange acceptance had filled him. It had been a good fight and they'd hurt the enemy a lot. *He'd* hurt the enemy a lot over the years. He'd been sad that the 5th Cavalry was going to die yet again. Sad that Becca was going to die, too. So young. No younger than many of his troopers, of course, but it was still a shame.

Then, those incredible, amazing... *things* had broken through the walls. Just smashed right through them, and blown the holy hell out of the Martians. Those big guns, that unbelievable magic lightning cannon, they'd simply wrecked the bastards. He'd heard rumors of the 'secret weapons' the army was building, but never really believed it. So far the only new weapons they'd seen were the airplanes and the stovepipe rocket launchers. Useful things, to be sure, but still kind of pathetic compared to what the Martians had.

But these! These things were enormous! Bigger than the tripods, big as buildings. He'd seen one of them knock a tripod over and then crush it flat under its tracks. It was *glorious*. Yes, glorious; not a word he'd had much use for in recent years, but that's what it was. He'd laughed and shouted and thrown his helmet in the air. And then the Martians were running; fleeing back the way they'd come. The troops had all cheered and come out of whatever hole they'd been cowering in to follow along behind the big green behemoths.

He'd waved to his men to come on. It was a pursuit, and that was what cavalry was for. Granted, they were all on foot now, but it still wasn't a chance to be missed. He'd shouted and led them forward.

For a couple of blocks.

The spirit was willing, but their bodies just couldn't do it. They'd been fighting or on the move between fights for a full day and a night. They had done all that could be expected of human flesh and blood. They'd tried, but eventually their pursuit had slowed to a crawl and then stopped altogether. Other troops had streamed past them, eager to finally get into the fight. Dolfen and his boys had been content to let them. Lynnbrooke had found him leaning against a wall, gasping for breath. He told him to gather the men and form them up back in the rail yard. The lieutenant, half his age, had smiled and done it. Dolfen had followed along a bit more slowly.

"Over here, sir," said someone. Looking up, he saw a cluster of men right at the edge of the yard. Somehow, they still had a guidon and the tattered red pennant with the white letters for the 1st Squadron fluttered fitfully in a weak breeze. He looked around, hoping to see others like it, but there weren't any, just a steady stream of men and vehicles moving up from the bridge and smaller groups filtering back in the opposite direction. He hadn't seen or heard anything of the rest of the regiment since they were separated at the bridge. He hoped that he and his men weren't all that was left.

And how many did he have left? He could see forty or fifty sitting or lying down. There could easily be some stragglers who had become separated during all the frantic repositioning. Maybe a few wounded who had survived and who might someday return to the ranks. But at least half were gone. Half of the officers, too. Buckman had burned up in his armored car, and he'd seen Gregory McGuiness cut down by one of the spider-machines while he was trying to clear a jam in his remaining Browning.

But it wasn't all bad news, there was Gosling, his orderly, miraculously coming up to him with a tin cup filled with coffee. Bless the man. He took it and gulped it down, realizing he was terribly thirsty. Hungry, too, as he hadn't eaten since dinner the night before. "Thank you, Goose," he said.

"M'pleasure, Captain. Helluva thing today, weren't it?"

"Yeah. A hell of a thing." He looked over his men and was pleased to see that most appeared to be in good spirits despite their ordeal. Or perhaps because of it. They all knew that they'd won a huge victory today. Maybe a war-changing victory. And his unit had played an important part. If they hadn't spotted the enemy's flank attack, hadn't delayed the Martians long enough for the new machines to arrive, if the Martians had overrun everything and been lined up along the walls waiting for them… things might have been much different. They'd done a hell of a job. And not just his boys… He looked around again, suddenly worried, but Gosling chuckled.

"She's over there with t'other ladies, sir. By the buildin' there."

He looked where he was pointing and breathed a sigh of relief when he saw the cluster of women. He handed the cup back to Gosling and walked over there as quickly as his aching legs would carry him.

Becca was standing apart from the others and he spotted her immediately. He came up to her and stopped. "Becca."

"Frank." She looked at him with eyes filled with pain and a bottomless weariness. He glanced at the other women. They had none of the jubilation that his men had. They seemed in a daze. *This was their first fight. They had no idea what to expect.*

"Are you all right?"

"Well enough. How are you?"

"Beat t'hell, but well enough." He looked toward the women. "How… how are they?"

"Beat t'hell," she said quietly. "Not sure how many we lost. I started the day with thirty. I've got twelve now. Four I know… four I know for sure were killed. Not sure about the others."

"There's bound to be some who got separated," said Frank, trying to sound reassuring. "Always happens in a fight. They'll turn up."

She nodded. "Yeah, I 'spect so. Some of the others probably just ran off to their homes. They all live nearby and they might have gone there."

"Yeah, probably." He paused. "It's a hard thing, Becca. Nothing can prepare a person for it."

"It's not my first battle, Frank."

"No, but it was theirs. And you brought them through it."

"Some of 'em."

"You can never bring all of them through. Believe me."

"No, I believe you. Don't make it any easier though."

"No."

"Frank, I need your help."

"Sure. What do you need?"

"Come with me." She led him through the smashed door of a dry goods store along the street. There was a stack of clothes on the counter. "I've still got some of the black dust on me. With all the dirt and soot and coal dust I've picked up, there's no hope of getting it all off the way we did with my mask." She looked him right in the eyes.

"Frank, help me get out of these clothes."

He blinked. "Becca. Maybe some of your girls can help…"

She stepped forward, grabbed him by the tunic, went up on her toes and pressed her lips against his. His eyes got wide, but he didn't pull away. She tasted of smoke and sweat but still very good. He probably tasted the same to her. After a minute or so she stepped back.

"Frank Dolfen, *help me get out of these clothes.*"

He took a deep breath.

"Yes, ma'am."

CHAPTER SEVENTEEN

JULY, 1912, WASHINGTON, D.C

"We've won two tremendous victories, Leonard," said Theodore Roosevelt. "St. Louis and Memphis will go down in history with Gettysburg and Marathon. But they were both defensive victories. We can't stand on our laurels or rest to lick our wounds. That was the error so many generals have made down the centuries. We need to counterattack! And right away!"

"Yes, Mr. President," said Leonard Wood. Both men were in high spirits and the light streaming in through the windows of Roosevelt's White House office seemed brighter than it had in years. "I fully agree, but the question is where?"

"Indeed it is," rumbled Roosevelt, getting up from his chair and walking over to a map hanging on the wall. He poked a thick finger against a spot in western Missouri. "I have a lot of people urging me to liberate Kansas City."

"Yes, I know, Mr. President," said Wood, frowning. Senators and representatives from Missouri and Kansas had been bombarding him with pleas, just as they had Roosevelt.

The President turned and looked at him closely. "But you don't agree?"

"No, sir, I don't. Kansas City would be a great prize, no doubt, but another error that past generals have made is to overreach themselves after a victory. Kansas City is too far from our nearest base in St. Louis. The forces there were badly battered and are still recovering from the fight there. And the Martians might be able to call on reinforcements from their forces up north facing our 1st Army."

"Pershing says he can do it."

"Only with massive reinforcements. That will take time and we could miss our opportunity."

"So you favor what MacArthur is clamoring for? A drive on Little Rock?"

"Actually, sir, I favor a drive on the Martian fortress to the northeast of Little Rock. The fortresses are the key, sir. Not the cities. The cities are just piles of rubble now. Their strategic value is minimal."

Roosevelt snorted. "Don't say that to anyone outside this room!" He glanced over at his son, Archie, and raised an eyebrow to make sure the boy understood that meant him, too. He nodded. "While you are no doubt correct, the people want their country back. To even hint that we don't care about that would be... a very serious mistake."

A political mistake as well as a military one, eh? The election was fast approaching. The latest victories had pushed things slightly in Roosevelt's favor if the polls were to be believed. But only slightly. They needed more and this could be it. Still, to make military decisions for political reasons rankled Wood.

"I know that, Theodore. But to take the country back we must destroy the enemy strongholds. We do that and we automatically take the country back, too." Wood came over to the map and pointed to the spot where the fortress in question was located. "We've never yet captured one of their fortresses—anywhere—but at this moment, this is the most vulnerable one. It's relatively close to Memphis and that's where we have the forces to strike. The land ironclads are there, and 2nd Tank Division was barely scratched in the battle and it's there, too. To move them up to St. Louis for a drive on Kansas City, or even the Martian fortress that's closest, would take weeks, giving the enemy too much time to get ready. We can strike here! Now!" He thumped his fist on the map.

Roosevelt took a turn around the room, then halted next to Wood and slapped him on the back. "Thunderation, but you are right! We'll do it. Send the orders right away." He paused and then said: "You have no problems with putting MacArthur in command? I've heard a few… disturbing things about what went on during the battle."

"Yes, so have I, but he seems to be back in control now and there's no denying his energy. General Dickman will be in overall command, of course, but I think MacArthur will have to be the one to command the assault."

"All right, I accept your recommendation. Get them on the move, Leonard!"

* * * * *

AUGUST, 1912, NORTH OF MABERRY, ARKANSAS

"Well, there it is, Gentlemen," said Colonel Andrew Comstock. "Our objective."

He was standing on the bridge of *USLI Albuquerque*, as it rumbled its way toward the walls of the Martian fortress in the distance. With him were Major Stavely, commander of *Albuquerque*, his aide, Jeremiah Hornbaker, the British observer, Major Bridges, and his old friend Drew Harding.

Poor Drew had lost his ship at Memphis and gotten several broken ribs and a dislocated shoulder in the process. He was currently on convalescent leave, but still faced an official hearing about the loss of his monitor. He was clearly very worried about that, although Andrew couldn't see that he had much to be worried about. From what he'd heard, Drew and his command had done a lot of damage and slowed the enemy down. But you could never tell about the navy, they were so damned touchy about their ships. The army was so much more forgiving. Lose a tank, lose a gun, they just gave you another one with no fuss. Of course, no one had lost a land ironclad yet…. When he'd heard about Drew's situation, he'd invited him to come along on *Albuquerque*. The man had accepted at once.

"It'll be dark soon," he said pointing toward the setting sun. "We'll attack first thing in the morning."

"With just the three ironclads?" asked Bridges. "Do you think that will be enough?"

"It will have to be. And we're hardly alone." He tried to sound confident, but in truth he was worried. All five of the land ironclads had survived the Battle of Memphis with relatively little damage, although he had cringed when he saw the spot on the front of *Albuquerque* where the combined heat rays had come within an inch of burning their way through. A heavy patch had been welded over the spot, but it was still a weak area. All five had started out on the offensive to capture the Martian stronghold, but only three had made it, *Albuquerque, Springfield,* and *Omaha. Billings* had broken down the first day out and *Tulsa* the day after. Both were being worked on, but neither would be here in time for the attack. Even the three which had made it were making some unpleasant sounds when they moved, and the engineers were worried about how much longer they could go without a major overhaul. The sad fact was that the ironclads were mechanically unreliable. Any hopes that they could just roll all the way to the Rockies were pipe-dreams.

Sioux Falls was on its way, too. A set of the flotation modules from one of the other ironclads, no longer needed once they had crossed to the west side of the Mississippi, had been sent to Key West. But it would be another week arriving and would not be here for the attack, either.

Still, the ironclads had a lot of support. The 2nd Tank Division was with them, although a third of their tanks had broken down on the way. There were also the equivalent of two infantry divisions - although cobbled together from about four different division—along with all the artillery, cavalry, and supply units that could be assembled in the short time they had. More troops were being brought into Memphis by rail to replenish the garrison and keep an eye on the force of Martians which had driven south along the river, breaking the connection with Texas and points west.

A signal went up from *Springfield* and the ironclads creaked to a halt. They were about five miles from the enemy stronghold, a long rampart encircling an area about three miles across. Some of the tanks and infantry pushed on another mile or so to protect the artillery, which would be spending much of the night getting set up and ready for the bombardment which would start the show.

"Excuse me, sir," said Stavely, "I'm going below to check on the machinery." Andrew nodded to him and the man left. Bridges decided he wanted a view from the observation platform while there was still light and climbed up there. Hornbaker went off to see about dinner, leaving Andrew alone with Harding.

"So what do you think of it?" asked Andrew, waving his hand to take in the ironclad. "I asked you that when we started out, but what do you think now that you've had a chance to look at it?"

Harding, whose left arm was in a sling, looked around and smiled sheepishly. "Well, sir," he began - there were a couple of enlisted men in earshot, so he didn't call him by name, "she - it's - a hell of a beast. When I first saw them in Memphis, they were a sight for sore eyes, but now that I've spent a few days aboard one, I'd be lying if I said I'd fallen in love with it."

Andrew chuckled. "Even so, you almost called it a she. What's with you navy guys and your boats?"

Drew shrugged. "Beats me. Tradition, I guess. But seriously, while there's no denying the effectiveness of the things, mechanically speaking they're a nightmare. Our ships can sail around the world with just onboard maintenance. You've lost forty-percent of yours trying to go seventy miles. Still, it's all brand new. With some improvements they might be what can win this war."

"The navy is building their own version, y'know. A little bigger than these to improve their sea-handling. Maybe you should see about getting command of one." Andrew knew it was a mistake the instant he said it. His friend's face fell and he shook his head.

"Assuming the navy still wants me to command anything after this."

"Drew, if we'd lost the battle, you might have something to worry about. They'd be looking for scapegoats. But we won the battle. Everyone's going to be a hero. So stop worrying."

He smiled and nodded. "Thanks for letting me come, sir. I would have gone crazy just sitting around back there."

"Glad to do it."

"So, are we going to win here tomorrow?"

"Damn right we are. So get some rest. It's going to be a long day."

* * * * *

CYCLE 597, 845.2, HOLDFAST 32-4

"Commander, the enemy is taking up positions about six *telequel* to the south. There are three of the large new war machines, over two hundred of their usual armored gun vehicles, several hundred of the projectile throwers, and many thousands of their foot-warriors," reported Tanbradjus.

"Their flying machines have been seen in considerable numbers."

Qetjnegartis regarded its sub-commanders gathered in a conclave room in the holdfast. Although none were grasping tendrils to form a link, there was no ignoring the great sense of tension.

"Only three of the new machines? Five were reported advancing in this direction. What has become of the other two?"

"They have halted in two different location. We do not know why."

"We have observed that the prey-creature machines are very crude and unreliable," said Davnitargus. "Perhaps they have broken down. Several tens of their smaller vehicles have halted along their route as well."

"But even with those losses, it is still an immense force," said Tanbradjus, the second in command. "Considering our own weakened state and having found no response to the new enemy machines, perhaps we should consider abandoning this holdfast and regrouping farther to the west."

"We defended the first holdfast against a heavy assault with fewer than ten war machines," said Qetjnegartis. "We still have seventy machines in operation here, plus several hundred drones, and the fixed defenses. We cannot give up this place so easily. It would be a huge blow to our strategic capabilities and the prestige of the clan."

"But you received reinforcements at a critical moment that first time. What reinforcements can we expect?"

"Nothing for at least three days," said Davnitargus. "Holdfasts 32-2 and 32-3 are sending what they can, but it totals less than a full battlegroup. Kantangnar is returning with its battlegroup as quickly as it can from the south, but it will not be here for at least two days; and we have reports that the prey-creatures are sending water vessels up the river to the ruins of city 3-118. Kantangnar may have to make a wide detour to reach here."

"Can we delay the enemy attack?" asked Qetjnegartis. "Perhaps a sortie during the night?"

"The prey are taking full precautions against such a thing, Commander. Their forces are concentrated and they are sending up the artificial illumination munitions at frequent intervals. It is doubtful that any damage we could do would balance the losses we might take in the process."

"So you see, Qetjnegartis," said Tanbradjus, "We shall be overwhelmed before any help can arrive. We should withdraw this night."

"I think you are too quick to give up," replied Qetjnegartis. "If we abandon this one, we will be reduced to a mere three holdfasts. The enemy will be emboldened and we might soon find ourselves facing this same situation at Holdfast 32-3!"

"And if we try to stay here and are annihilated?" retorted Tanbradjus. "The other holdfasts will have little defense left at all!"

"It is a risk," admitted Qetjnegartis. "But if we succeed, the enemy will be forced to withdraw and we can rebuild our strength here."

"Also," added Branjandus, "if we are to withdraw immediately, there will be little time to destroy this facility. The prey-creatures have shown the ability to learn from our own devices they have captured. What might we learn from this place?"

A silence fell in the chamber. Clearly no one had given thought to this. Qetjnegartis had not and it was impressed that Davnitargus had done so.

"We... we can set the main reactor to overload," said Tanbradjus. "The melt-down would destroy much of the holdfast."

"Much, but not all."

"It is still better than...!"

"Enough," said Qetjnegartis. "I have decided. We shall defend this place. Return to your posts and make ready." It could sense disagreement from some, but there was, of course, no further argument. The others began moving out of the chamber.

"Davnitargus, remain a moment."

When the others had left and the chamber had sealed, Davnitargus looked to Qetjnegartis. "Progenitor?"

"I want to defend this place if at all possible. But we should also be prepared for a rapid evacuation, for it is entirely possible that Tanbradjus is correct."

* * * * *

AUGUST, 1912, NORTH OF MABERRY, ARKANSAS

"The bombardment will commence at first light," said Colonel Schumacher. "It will be a short one because we have no huge stockpile of ammunition. The primary targets will be the Martian defensive towers. About one hour after the start, the artillery will pause to allow the bombing aircraft to make their attack. Following that, the land ironclads will use their big guns to try and pick off any towers which have survived. Once that's done, the artillery will resume firing to cover the attempt to breach the enemy's walls."

The colonel paused and looked over the faces of his officers by the light of the lanterns hung around his tent. Frank Dolfen returned his gaze steadily. He was glad Schumacher had survived the fighting at Memphis. He was tired of breaking in new colonels. Almost a third of the men hadn't survived, but the regiment was still an effective fighting force. There had been no time for much in the way of replacements of men or equipment, so they only had a handful of armored cars in the whole regiment. Many of the motorcycle riders were either now on horses or had been left behind. But from the sound of things, they would be fighting as infantry in this next battle anyway.

"How are they gonna breach the walls, Colonel?" asked a lieutenant from the third squadron. Frank had been wondering that himself. "I've heard tell that it's a lot easier said than done."

"I don't have the details," replied Schumacher. "It's some device they've cooked up for the land ironclads is all I know. But while they are doing that, we, and the bulk of the infantry, are going to close up on the walls and climb to the top. Exactly where we'll do that will depend on how well they've destroyed the defensive towers. We'll try to go up where they ain't." That got a chuckle. Trying to scale the outer face of those walls with the heat ray towers shooting down on them would be suicide.

"They are going to send a few of the tanks along to support us and take out any surviving towers, and we'll just have to see how well that works. But in any case, we will get up on the walls somewhere. Once on top, we take cover and wait for the breaching. The brass seem to think that all of the enemy tripods will concentrate opposite where the breach is going to be made. We can hope they are right, but we need to be prepared to take on any that don't cooperate.

"Because our job is to get inside that fortress, gentlemen. We're to leave the tripods to the ironclads and the tanks. The infantry - and us - are to take out any of the spiders we might see, but then find a way down inside and take the place! We don't know what we'll find down there, but we have several directives from on high.

"One is to free any captives we might find. We have good reason to believe that there are a lot of our people down there. We're to rescue them. Second, we're to secure any machinery and equipment that we can. The eggheads back east want to get their hands on it. Maybe it will help them build more things like those ironclads."

Schumacher paused, took a breath and then went on. "Lastly, we've all been told in the past to try and kill any of the Martians we can find. We know that they can make machines faster than they can make more Martians. So our orders have been to finish off any downed tripods. Make sure the pilot is dead. That made sense when we were on the defensive; we didn't want any of those bastards to be rescued and come back to fight another day. But the situation has changed. We are on the offensive now. And the ground we take we are going to keep! So this time, we are going to try and take prisoners. As far as we know, no one has taken a live Martian captive. But this time we are going to try. The brass wants to have a little word with them, I guess. So tell your men. No itchy trigger fingers. Fight when you have to, but if the opportunity comes to take one of them alive - do so!" He looked around. "Any questions? No? All right. Go brief your men and then try to get some rest. We form up at three. Dismissed."

The meeting broke up and Dolfen headed back to the camp to have the men assembled. Men - and one woman. Becca was here; there had been no stopping her. Not after what had happened in Memphis. After all that had happened in Memphis. He still wasn't quite sure he understood everything that had happened, but when the new offensive had been announced, Becca had simply shown up, said that she was coming along, and that was that. Technically, she was a medic, and she did have the knowledge and the equipment to fill that role, but she carried a rifle and clearly intended to use it. He saw her standing there at the rear of the formation. She was making no attempt to conceal her gender this time and the men seemed to accept her. He wasn't sure how many of the men knew about the... change in his relationship to her, but no one had said anything to him—not that any of them would.

He passed along the information from the colonel and dismissed the men. Some bedded down immediately, but others drifted back to their campfires, probably too nervous to sleep. They were all veterans, but the battle tomorrow would be different than anything they'd faced before. Becca waited until all the others had moved off and then came up to him. "I'll be coming along tomorrow," she said.

"I know."

She stared at him and cocked her head with a strange look on her face.

"What?" he said.

"Is that all? 'I know'? You're not gonna try and talk me out of it or anything?"

"Would it do any good?"

"Nope, not one bit."

"So I won't waste my breath. I'll need it for tomorrow." He reached out and touched her arm. "But promise me one thing?"

"What?"

"That you won't get yourself killed."

"I won't if you won't."

"It's a deal."

"Good. Now let's get some sleep. We're gonna need it."

* * * * *

AUGUST, 1912, NORTH OF MABERRY, ARKANSAS

Commander Drew Harding woke up with the bugles that echoed throughout the army. He'd spent a terrible night, just like the other ones since leaving Memphis. His shoulder ached and his ribs, too, making it very hard to get any sleep. At least he rated a cot rather than sleeping on the ground like most of the other men. The army's land ironclads had so little living space that nearly everyone had to camp out on the ground when they stopped for the night. The navy's versions were going to be large enough for bunk space, from what he'd heard.

It was still dark, without even a hint of dawn in the east. But there were plenty of campfires and lanterns around and a number of electric lamps shining from the towering *Albuquerque*, along with the blue-white glare of the welders. There was a party of engineers welding something to the bow of this ironclad and the *Omaha*. He'd asked Andrew what it was, but he'd just grinned and said that he'd see when the time was right.

He pulled on his clothes, stumbled out of the tent, and found coffee waiting for him around the fire. Several of the land ironclad's junior officers were there, along with Major Bridges. He found he liked the Englishman; he was witty and had an endless store of tales from his adventures in the far-flung corners of the Empire. "Morning, Commander," he said. "I trust you slept well?"

"Not so well, sad to say. I miss my nice comfy bunk. You?"

"Oh, slept like the dead, old boy. I've got the happy knack of being able to sleep anywhere. In the mud, on rocks, even slept up in a tree a few times in South Africa. Lions, you know."

"Really. Is the colonel about?"

"Over at *Springfield* conferring with General Clopton, I believe. Bacon?" He offered a plate and Drew took it. He sat, slurping coffee and munching the bacon with some hard bread. He missed the good food from a ship's galley, too. *Definitely made the right choice when I went to Annapolis.*

Bridges was staring at him. "I understand you've known Colonel Comstock for quite some time, Commander."

"Oh hell yes. We go way back. Before the war, I was in the navy's ordnance bureau while he was with the army's ordnance department. There were a lot of inter-service meetings there in Washington and we saw each other quite a bit. Became drinking buddies. A good man."

"He certainly seemed glad to see you. I was just wondering why he treats me like a pound of week-old kippers. I pride myself in being able to charm everyone - damnation I even managed to make Kitchener laugh once - but I can't seem to break through his armor. Any idea why?"

Drew frowned and chewed on his lip, unsure if he should say anything. As he sat there, a gun went off and a few seconds later a star shell burst in the direction of the Martian fortress. They'd been doing that all night to keep an eye on the enemy. Bridges looked at him curiously in the flickering light. "Well... It's probably because you're English."

"You don't say?" said Bridges, looking surprised. "What? Did my great granddad kill his great granddad at Lexington or something? I thought we'd gotten past all that rubbish."

"No, it's more recent history than that, I'm afraid. You remember that big explosion you folks had in Liverpool back in oh-seven?"

"I do. What a bloody mess. I was in India at the time, but it was in all the papers. But what...?"

"His father was killed in the blast. He'd been invited there to observe whatever it was your scientists were trying to do."

"And he holds me to blame for *that*?"

"It hit him hard. And he wasn't even out of West Point when it happened. I guess he needed someone to blame."

Bridges nodded. "Yes, some people deal with grief that way. I've seen it in others. Well, it's a shame, but I guess there's nothing I can do about it, eh?"

"I suppose not. Just don't judge him too harshly. It's not personal."

"He certainly seems competent enough. And I guess you Yanks don't hand out the decorations like he's got for nothing."

"No, we don't. He's earned every one of them."

By this time, the whole army was stirring; companies of infantry falling in, steam tanks firing up their boilers, gunners screwing fuses into their shells. *Albuquerque* gave a short toot on its whistle to tell its crew to pack up and come aboard. Drew went into the tent he'd been given and packed up his valise. Fortunately, someone else would pack up the tent and the cot.

As he came out, he saw Andrew returning and they exchanged greetings. "Morning, Drew. Ready for the big day?"

"Ready as I'll ever be, I guess. So this is it?"

"Yup. The weather is looking good and we've gotten a radio message that the aircraft will be leaving on time. That was the only thing that might have delayed us. But it won't, so we go on schedule. The artillery will start shooting at first light. But come on, let's get aboard."

There was a movable gangway which could be lowered down from the ironclad allowing access, but it was very steep. With him carrying his valise in one hand and his other in the sling, it was awkward getting up.

"Here give me that," said Andrew, reaching down and taking the valise. With a hand free to clutch the rail, Drew could pull himself up.

"Thanks."

They made their way up to the bridge but then went out on the port wing to give Major Stavely room to get his vehicle in order. Bridges and Hornbaker joined them and Drew found himself acutely aware of Andrew and Bridges. He'd noticed the coolness between them before, but now every little glance and motion seemed to send signals. *Stop it, it doesn't matter right now.*

"Is General MacArthur going to be aboard *Springfield* for the battle?" asked Bridges.

"Yes," said Andrew.

"Well then, I'm glad I'm over here," said Drew. "With his staff, there won't be room to swing a cat over there!"

"He only had two people with him. I think most of his staff will stay on the ground to carry out his orders while he takes a look from up close."

"He does seem to be the fearless sort," said Drew, remembering him standing there in the middle of the street as tripods walked past.

"It's a good plan," said Andrew, "and I understand he devised it himself."

"Brilliant and brave," said Bridges. "Sounds like a dashed good combination."

"Well, he was brave at Memphis," said Drew. "Not so sure about the brilliant part."

"I guess we'll find out soon enough," said Andrew. With that, the conversation lapsed and they waited in the darkness until a faint blue line could be seen on the eastern horizon. A few minutes later, a white signal rocket soared into the sky and it was immediately followed by three quick shots from some field guns. Drew caught his breath and then the world was lit up with the fire of nearly two hundred guns.

* * * * *

AUGUST, 1912, NEAR THE MARTIAN FORTRESS

Rebecca Harding looked on happily as the artillery opened fire. It was beginning! They were going to assault and capture the enemy fortress. They were going to kill the monsters, drive them away, and take back part of the land. She reminded herself that she'd heard that kind of talk before. At the Martian fortress where the town of Gallup had stood out in the New Mexico Territory. Not far from where she had once lived. They'd been supposed to capture the fortress there, too, but that had not happened. Instead, they'd been beaten and forced to flee. Step by step they'd fled all the way back to the Mississippi.

That's not gonna happen again today!

No it wasn't; today they were going to win. Today they were going to start on the long road back.

The guns hammered away, their flashes still overpowering the slowly growing dawn. Explosions sparked along the wall of the enemy fortress. There was too much smoke and dust to really see what effect it was having, but it seemed well-aimed to her with most of the shells landing right on top of the ramparts, where the enemy heat ray towers were located.

Her horse shied a bit at one especially loud bang, and she patted his neck to calm him. She had been so happy when Moses had come up, driving his wagon with her beloved Ninny in tow. She had had no idea if either of them had survived the battle, but Moses acted as though it had just been a Sunday drive in the park. Even so, he'd had no desire to come along on this new adventure.

Neither had any of the Memphis Women's Sharpshooters. One battle had been more than enough for them. Indeed, after the fighting was over, they had nearly all melted away, back to their homes - or what was left of them. A few had said goodbye to her and thanked her, but most acted as though it had all been a really bad idea and the sooner it was forgotten, the better. Oh well, they'd done more than she'd expected.

And now she was part of the real army. Sort of. She was traveling with the army, she planned to fight with the army, and no one seemed to be trying to stop her. She wasn't trying to disguise herself like the last time, and many of the men, including some of Frank's superiors, had seen her and not said anything. Of course, she hadn't signed any papers or sworn any oaths, and she doubted she would be paid like the other soldiers, but none of that mattered to her. She was here, with Frank.

Frank. She wasn't entirely sure what those moments they had spent together in the abandoned dry goods store really meant. They had both been exhausted, filthy and smelly - not exactly the sort of thing girls dreamed about. But they'd smiled at each other afterward. It had to have meant something...

A bright blue flash from inside the smoke and a long rumbling boom that competed with and won against the other noise caught everyone's attention, and a small cheer went up. One of the heat ray tower's power thingy had blown up as they sometimes did. The guns were hitting things.

It was nearly dawn now and the troops were moving into their assault positions. The 5th rode a mile or so around the eastern side of the fortress and then halted again. The sun peeked over the edge of the world; long black shadows stretched out in front of them and the face of the enemy ramparts glowed pinkly—they were covered with that damn red weed. The artillery wasn't hitting this part of the fortress as heavily, and further to the north there was little smoke and Becca could see some of the towers were still intact on the wall. They wouldn't be going that way.

The bombardment was slowly dying and after a few more minutes it stopped entirely. The wind carried off the smoke and dust and revealed what the artillery had done. As everyone expected, the walls themselves were intact. But it looked like all the towers on the southern half had been destroyed. There might have been one or two which had escaped, and Becca could see officers peering intently through their binoculars. There was Frank a few dozen yards away looking and pointing and talking with his officers.

Off to her left she spotted the three huge land ironclads moving forward, their tall smoke stacks spewing black clouds into the morning sky. They moved up to a position only a few hundred yards short of the wall. Then their big gun turrets swiveled and fired a few times. Explosions blossomed atop the wall. They were picking off any towers which looked like they might still be able to work. When they were finished, they reversed and backed off a bit.

"Are they retreating?" asked a trooper close by.

"No, you idiot!" replied another. "Weren't you listening to what the captain said? The bombers are on the way and they probably don't want to be too close. Those crazy fliers aren't particular where they drop their bombs!"

"Hey! Yeah, look! There they are!" shouted a third cavalryman. He was pointing skyward and everyone looked up.

At first, Becca couldn't see anything, but then she spotted a swarm of dark specks off to the east. They approached at what seemed a crawl, but within a few minutes they were nearly overhead.

"Want to look?" Becca started at the voice at her elbow. It was Frank offering his binoculars. He was smiling at her.

"Why, thank you, Captain," she said, taking the binoculars and looking up again. The specks now revealed themselves as airplanes. Large airplanes with two engines. There looked to be hundreds of them, flying in tight formations. As she watched, tiny black shapes started falling off them. "They've dropped their bombs, I think," she said. She handed the binoculars back to him.

"Okay, hang on to your hats and pray they didn't drop them short!" he said.

She'd lost track of the bombs when she looked away, tried to find them again, and then gave up and just looked toward the Martian fortress. After what seemed like far too long a time, there came a shrill whistling sound and then geysers of earth suddenly leapt up a few hundred yards in front of the walls, and then marched forward to engulf it. The roar from the explosions made the previous bombardment seem tranquil by comparison. The earth shook and Ninny snorted and shied, veteran though he was of things unnatural.

A half-mile wide section of the walls and the area to the front and rear was hammered by bombs, rocks the size of steamer trunks were tossed in the air to come crashing down again. The very air was shaking.

And then it was over. After a minute or two, the artillery started firing again, but her ringing ears could barely hear it. The ironclads started forward once more, and then Frank was shouting to get ready.

"It's our turn now!"

* * * * *

CYCLE 597, 845.2, HOLDFAST 32-4

Qetjnegartis felt the impact of the explosives even in the deeply buried command chamber. It was annoyed when the tactical status display showed that four fighting machines had been destroyed and their operators slain. When the bombardment by the projectile throwers had ceased and the large new machines of the prey-creatures had come forward, it had assumed some attempt to breach or scale the walls was about to occur, and it had ordered the fighting machines forward to oppose it. But then the flying machines had appeared with no warning and there had not been time to pull the fighting machines back. So far, between this and the earlier bombardment, it had lost ten machines and six pilots slain or wounded. The other four had been carried back and transferred to new machines.

But what was happening now? The large machines were coming closer again and the bombardment had resumed. And this time it was not aimed at the defensive towers on the walls, it was landing in

648

an arc behind the ramparts, apparently in an attempt to seal off the area where the large machines were gathering. Were they going to attempt to breach the walls at that point? What was the proper response?

At the same time, thousands of the prey foot-warriors were scaling the walls to either side of that area. They were taking cover on top. Meanwhile, groups of the armored gun vehicles were moving along the walls attacking the remaining defensive towers one at a time. The tactics of the prey were becoming increasingly sophisticated. Qetjnegartis dispatched six fighting machines to each side of the holdfast to oppose the vehicles attempting to destroy the towers. It was tempted to send more machines or perhaps drones up on to the walls to attack the foot-warriors gathering there. But no, hundreds more of the armored vehicles were poised to support them, and any fighting machine on top of the walls would instantly be brought under heavy fire. The losses could not be sustained and the foot-warriors were of little danger in an open battle like this.

The critical point would be the place where the enemy intended to make the breach. Whatever they planned, they could only make a narrow entrance. If enough power could be assembled opposite that point, then anything attempting to enter could be destroyed. Yes, that was the proper response.

It issued its orders.

* * * * *

AUGUST 1912, THE MARTIAN FORTRESS

"All right, Major, bring us forward," said Andrew Comstock. "Stop about fifty yards short of the wall."

"Right, sir," said Stavely. He gave the order and *Albuquerque* squealed into motion. Yeah, he didn't like the noises the thing was making these days…

"Slowly. Line it up just like I said."

"Yes, sir."

The land ironclad inched toward an apparatus that the company of engineers had just set up against the forward face of the wall around the Martian fortress. Andrew had been very impressed at how quickly they'd accomplished it. The captain in charge said they'd been practicing for months. Andrew had known about this unit for many months and even seen them demonstrate their equipment at Aberdeen one time, but he hadn't really paid all that much attention to them. At the time, there seemed little likelihood that they'd have any opportunity to try it out against a Martian fortress.

But then this offensive had been decided upon and a frantic message had gone out to get the 187th Engineer Company and all its gear up to the front immediately. By some miracle, not only had they made their way through the clogged railway system to Memphis, but then they'd been able to catch up with the assault force and arrive in the nick of time.

Just ahead of *Albuquerque*, there were two metal chutes erected on small scaffolds to hold them about fifteen feet off the ground. One end was positioned against the face of the wall and the other was pointed at the approaching ironclad. The chutes were a little over a foot in diameter. Resting in the chute was a section of metal pipe. The end facing the wall was pointed like a javelin. The other end was open and had a socket-like connection. Andrew knew that the hollow inside of the tube was packed with explosive. An identical set up had been arranged for *Omaha*, which was coming up alongside them with only a yard or two between their mammoth set of caterpillar tracks.

An engineering officer had come aboard and was standing at the very front of the ironclad, looking down and using hand signals to tell the driver what to do. A little to the left, a little right, slow down, and finally stop. Andrew decided to go and take a look for himself. He left the bridge, followed by Drew, Hornbaker, and that blasted Englishman. They came up behind the engineer, who was a first lieutenant. "How's it going?" asked Andrew.

The man glanced back, a look of annoyance on his face, but he said: "Well enough. We'll be ready for the first section in a minute."

It was longer than that, but eventually, he gave the signal for slow ahead. Andrew went up to the rail and looked down. The apparatus which had been welded to the front of *Albuquerque* during the night was a pair of push rods which could be lined up with the end of the explosive packed tubes. Now, using the immense mass and power of the ironclad, the tubes were slowly pushed into the wall of the Martian fortress.

The walls were simply a big mound of rock, earth, and rubble which had been piled up by the alien machines. The outer face was steep and treacherous with loose stones. Andrew had climbed the one near Gallup and knew how difficult it was. They were completely impassible to vehicles. But being loose stone rather than something truly solid, the tubes could be pushed right into them.

They crawled forward about twenty feet and then the engineer waved them to stop and then to reverse. As soon as they had pulled back, two new ten foot sections of pipe were lifted up by a crane mounted on a truck and lowered into each chute. They were then fitted into the sockets at the rear of the leading pipes. When all was ready, the process was repeated, pushing the pipes deeper into the wall.

"We'll be lucky if those pipes don't buckle," said Drew.

"The walls of the pipe are an inch thick. And they are packed full so they are nearly solid. This has been tested, and if we come straight on, it should work."

"Damned ingenious," said Bridges.

"What happens if the Martians suddenly pop up on the wall and start shooting at us, sir?" asked Drew.

Andrew glanced up at the top of the wall. The barrage was supposed to discourage the enemy from doing that, but it was still a good point. The explosives in the tubes *shouldn't* explode just from heat, but you never knew. And of course all of *them* were standing right here in the open. They'd be incinerated in an instant. All the gunners were on alert, of course, and *Springfield* and a hundred steam tanks were ready to provide covering fire if necessary; but none of that would do any good for those of them standing where they were, unprotected. *I'm not necessary here, I should go back inside.* But instead he stayed.

"That's why we need to hurry."

A third set of pipes were pushed in, and then a fourth. As the fifth pair were set up, a man dashed up to Andrew. "Sir, we just got a signal from *Springfield* that the artillery is running low on ammunition and the second wave of aircraft will be here soon. We need to finish this now."

Andrew looked to the engineer. "Will this be enough?"

"This will make two one-hundred foot lengths for us and the same for Omaha. That will be close to ten tons of explosives. It should do the trick, sir."

"All right then! Get this last set pushed in and we'll pull back. The rest of us better get up to the bridge."

As the ironclad moved forward once more, the rest of them retreated back, past the main turret, and then up a ladder to the bridge. Major Stavely met them at the pilothouse door. "That's it, sir, the charges are placed."

"Excellent. Pull back three hundred yards and we'll wait for the fireworks!"

* * * * *

AUGUST, 1912, THE MARTIAN FORTRESS

"Keep your fool heads down—all of you!" shouted Frank Dolfen. His troops, already lying on their bellies atop the wall, tried to flatten themselves down a little further. A couple peered at him from under the brims of their helmets, their expressions seemed to say: *okay, but what about you?* Dolfen was kneeling next to the wreckage of one of the heat ray towers rather than lying down. Well, rank had its privileges.

They'd made the climb up to the top of the wall without much problem beyond scraped hands, bruised knees, and uniforms stained red by the Martian weed that was everywhere. It would have been a terrible thing to try and do if someone was shooting at you, but today no one was. He thought back to the time - the two times - he'd done this before, back at Gallup. That time, it had just been him and that Major Comstock. This time, he'd brought a whole army with him.

He swept his binoculars in a long arc, taking in the view. A half-mile to his left, the big land ironclads were doing something very close to the face of the wall, and a large number of steam tanks were also drawn up close by. A half-mile to his right, a dozen more tanks were dueling with one of the heat ray towers, and as he watched, they took it out. A similar duel was taking place on the other side of the fortress, beyond the land ironclads. Given time, they would destroy all the remaining towers.

Behind the wall and opposite where the ironclads were at work, there was a thick wall of dust and smoke where the artillery was concentrating its fire. It was in a half ring, touching the wall not four hundred yards away and looping around to touch the wall on the other side of the ironclads. Two hundred guns were banging away as fast as they could and the explosions were nearly constant.

He could catch glimpses of Martian tripods standing or moving about beyond the wall of smoke. They seemed to have gathered, ready to oppose the attempt to break through the wall. He couldn't tell how many, but if there were a lot of them, they were going to make it very rough on whoever went through the gap first. He was glad he and his men wouldn't be involved with that. He glanced over to where Becca was laying flat. He wished she wasn't here. He'd had some hopes that maybe he could convince her to stay with the horse holders down at the base of the wall. Maybe the presence of her fool horse would make her want to stay with him. No hope there. She'd just left her horse with Private Gosling, who was holding all the officers' horses.

Lieutenant Lynnbrooke crawled over to him and said: "I went up to the edge of the wall, sir. I couldn't see anything, no tripods or spider-machines waiting for us."

"Good."

"But it's very steep. There are a few ledges here and there, but everywhere else it's almost vertical. The rocks seem all fused together, too. Not many handholds. There's a ramp about two hundred yards off to the right, but there's a whole regiment of infantry waiting to use it."

"Send back to the horses for some ropes. We'll let ourselves down that way."

"Right, sir." He crawled away.

Things were going to happen soon, he expected. And once it did, he and his men were going to have to come down off the wall and deal with whatever they found inside. He lifted his binoculars and scanned the inside of the fortress again. It was basically an empty circle three miles wide. There were some lumps and bumps here and there, but no obvious entrances to the underground parts. He'd heard that at Gallup some troops had found ways to get in. Hopefully they'd be able to it again here.

A shrill noise caught his attention and he looked over to his left. The three land ironclads were all sounding their steam whistles. He could only assume that something was about to...

He'd never seen a volcanic eruption except in drawings in the newspapers, but what happened now matched his mental image of what one must look like. The section of wall in front of the ironclads... *erupted.* The top part of the wall lifted up into the air, almost in a single piece, while two huge clouds of rock, dust, and smoke blasted out from the front and rear sides of the wall, spewing debris for hundreds of yards. Then the upper part disintegrated into another boiling mass of flying junk. Boulders tumbled end over end and came crashing down again. Smaller rocks were flung great distances, a few thudding down only a hundred yards away.

The wall beneath him was shaking and the clouds of dust all merged into one and drifted slowly eastward. The noise blotted out all other sound, even the artillery bombardment. He knelt there staring as the dust slowly settled. The artillery fire died away and the cloud from that dispersed as well.

What was revealed was a huge ditch blasted through the wall. All the rocks and dirt from a big section had been blown in all directions. He couldn't see down into it from where he was, but the land ironclads were starting forward, so apparently they thought they could make it through. The Martian tripods had stood as still as everyone else during the explosion, but now they started forward, too, directly toward the ironclads. Could they get through and deploy before they were overwhelmed?

But then a buzzing reached his stunned ears and it quickly grew to a roar of another sort. Looking back he saw a swarm of aircraft coming right at him. They were flying scarcely higher than the walls, and a moment later they swept over him so close he felt he could reach up and grab one. Hundreds of them! *Selfridge and his boys must be with them.*

Lynnbrooke was back tugging at his sleeve. He pointed toward the edge of the wall. The men were getting up from where they lay. Dolfen wrenched his attention back where it belonged. He shouted at his bugler: "Sound the advance!"

* * * * *

AUGUST, 1912, THE MARTIAN FORTRESS

As the dust and smoke gradually thinned, Andrew Comstock tried to see what the explosion had done. Had it cleared a path which the ironclads and the tanks could traverse? It was essential that the tanks could make it, too. General Clopton had convinced MacArthur that as impressive as the ironclads might be, they couldn't win this battle by themselves. They needed the tank support, so they had to get inside the fortress.

Slowly, slowly the air cleared and revealed what the engineers had wrought. An enormous divot had been made through the wall. The upper half had been gouged out for a width of perhaps fifty feet - barely wide enough for an ironclad. Just as importantly, the displaced dirt and rock had been scattered on either side and formed what looked like a passable ramp up into the breach. There was no way to tell if there was a similar ramp down on the other side, but there ought to be.

Only one way to find out!

A toot from *Springfield* indicated that Clopton agreed. Forward!

Albuquerque would lead the way and Major Stavely got it up to full speed as quickly as possible. The British-designed steam turbine spun, the electricity it produced powered the big Westinghouse motors, and they turned the Baldwin-built caterpillar tracks. Human ingenuity on the move! They reached the edge of the debris field and started up the ramp, crushing down the rocks and boulders and hopefully creating an easy path for the tanks to follow. He was able to see through the gap now, and what he saw put a lump of fear in his throat. A seemingly solid phalanx of tripods was coming the other way, maybe a half-mile in the distance. Swarms of the spider-machines were all around them. Could they get through the hole before the Martians put a stopper in it?

"Sir! Here come the aircraft!" Hornbaker shouted at his side. Andrew looked through the rear door of the pilothouse, and to his relief, the promised air support had arrived. Squadron after squadron of the small attack planes swept in at low altitude, spread out over a wide arc. Past the ironclads, over the walls, and straight against the enemy, closing in on them from three sides.

"Right on time!" cried Drew Harding. "First the bombers and now these. They taught us at Annapolis that no battle plan ever works right."

"Taught us the same thing at the Point. Guess there's a first time for everything, eh?"

The aircraft bore in on the Martians, machine guns chattering. The tripods halted and formed a tight mass, facing outward. Their heat rays lashed out and the formations of planes were turned into balls of fire. Dozens fell in the first seconds. More followed. Flaming wrecks fell to the earth everywhere. Only a few made it close enough to drop their bombs. Fewer still hit anything, and only a couple of hits were on tripods. Andrew felt sick to his stomach.

But the sacrifice of the fliers had bought precious seconds. *Albuquerque* crested the top of the gap and headed down the other side and onto the flat ground inside the fortress. *Omaha* was right behind and swung right, *Springfield* swung left. Twelve- and seven- and five-inch guns roared out and shells tore through packed enemy machines. A dozen tripods went down in seconds. The ironclads reloaded and fired again, smashing more of the hated foe.

With most of the aircraft destroyed, the Martians now turned against the new threat. Dozens of heat rays stabbed at the metal giants and Andrew ducked away from the red blaze that came in through the quartz blocks in the pilothouse view slits. The guns on the ironclads roared out again, and some of the deadly rays were silenced. But they were under the concentrated fire of the whole Martian force now and damage reports were coming in as some of the rays cut through the armor in spots. Major Stavely ordered steam to be released to lessen the effects. A hissing cloud engulfed them.

They were blinded now and the steam would only help them for a few moments. "Maybe we should turn!" cried Drew Harding. "Show them some undamaged armor!"

"Worth a try," said Andrew. "Stavely bring us left!"

The major gave the orders, but a moment later he shouted: "Track number two is out! We can only turn right. Turning now!" The ironclad shuddered and groaned as it dragged itself around sideways. After a few seconds, it lurched to a halt. "Number four is out, too! We're stuck!"

"Damn!" Blind and immobilized, they were sitting ducks.

But then the red glare faded completed and a host of new sounds filled the air. Cannon fire. Smaller cannons to be sure, but a lot of them. Andrew poked his head out of the pilot house, and when the wind pulled the steam curtain away for a moment he saw dozens and dozens of tanks pouring through the gap in the wall, their guns blazing. The 2nd Tank Division was charging into action.

"Secure steam!" gasped Stavely. The hissing died away, and after a moment they could see again. There was *Omaha*, off to the right, its guns still firing, still killing Martians. To the left was *Springfield*; Andrew was dismayed to see black smoke boiling out of a hole in its side, and its observation platform gone. But some of the guns were still firing. And all around were steam tanks. Mark IIs with their single guns and Mark IIIs with three of them. Even a few of the large, but notoriously unreliable Mark IVs had made it through. All were firing steadily at the enemy. There didn't seem to be all that many of the enemy left now; maybe thirty or so.

"Sir! Look there!" Hornbaker pointed.

"What?"

"Spider-machines! A whole bunch of them! I think they're going after *Springfield!*"

Andrew looked through smoke and saw: a moving carpet of the smaller machines, and yes, they looked to be heading directly toward the flagship.

"That's how they sank my monitor, Andrew," said Drew Harding urgently, his face twisted with remembered anguish. "They got aboard and down inside and blew up the magazine."

Andrew turned to Major Stavely. "Major, can you put some fire on those things? The machine guns, maybe?"

"I can do better than that! Doctor Tesla's cannon is still undamaged. It's ready to fire!"

Andrew's face lit up. They'd been too far away to use it at first, and with all the damage he'd assumed it was out of action. But it wasn't! "Yes! Tell them to fire at the spiders!"

Stavely passed along the order and just a few moments later the turret with the Tesla Gun swung around and the blue-white lightning burst forth. It leapt to one of the spider-machines and then another. And then another, more and more, a dozen, two dozen. They writhed and shuddered, and many of them exploded in a display that to Andrew looked like kernels of corn on a frying pan. When the lightning winked out, the field was littered with wrecked spider-machines. Many of the survivors stood frozen while fire from the tanks picked them off.

"Sir? Sir?" said Stavely. "I think the rest are pulling back."

Andrew looked out and indeed some of the remaining tripods seemed to be retreating.

"Looks as though you've broken their back, old boy," said Major Bridges.

"Yes, yes, I think you're right!"

* * * * *

CYCLE 597, 845.2, HOLDFAST 32-4

"Qetjnegartis, we must retreat! This fight is lost!"

Qetjnegartis listened to the message from Tanbradjus and then looked with growing dismay at the tactical display in the command center. Everything was happening so fast. The attack of the prey-creatures had been more relentless and devastating than anything it had encountered before. It had been expecting a slow and methodical attack such as it had faced at the first holdfast. A step by step assault with time to react. But this! The large projectile throwers, the heavy flying machines, the explosion which breached the wall, and then the onslaught of the lighter flying machines, the huge vehicles and the smaller ones. All one right after the other with no pause.

They had less than thirty fighting machines left, and while they had disabled two of the large prey-creature machines, they were still firing their weapons and were supported by nearly two hundred of the smaller vehicles. At the same time, thousands of the foot-warriors, many carrying explosives, were roaming inside the holdfast's walls. Some were attempting to blow open some of the small access doors, clearly trying to get inside. How long before they succeeded?

"Qetjnegartis, I am ordering the fighting machines here with me to retreat," said Tanbradjus. "If I do not, we will all be destroyed."

Qetjnegartis's tendril stiffened on the interface rods. Was this a deliberate challenge to its authority? It doubted that Tanbradjus would be able disobey a direct order if given one, but this was still a breach of protocol.

Perhaps the circumstances warrant it.

Yes, there was no doubt the battle was lost. Further resistance would only mean needless losses, which they could not afford. Losing the holdfast was a severe setback, but losing it and all the defenders would be immeasurably worse.

"Very well, all units will retreat to sector 3-28-243. We will reassemble and then head west."

"At once, Commander," said Tanbradjus. "A wise decision."

The communications link was broken. Qetjnegartis looked to the other two clan members in the control chamber. "Go to the hanger at once. Rendezvous with the others. I must set the reactor to melt down."

"But Commander, that can only be done manually. You may be trapped here. Let one of us do it."

"You have your orders. Carry them out."

"Yes, Commander." The two transferred into travel chairs and moved out. As Qetjnegartis was about to do the same, a message arrived from Davnitargus.

"Commander, I will bring the remains of my battlegroup to the hanger exit to cover your retreat."

"No, I may be delayed. You shall retreat with the others. I will join you later."

"But, Commander..."

"Obey me, Davnitagus!"

There was short delay, and then the bud responded. "I obey, Commander."

Qetjnegartis transferred into a travel chair and headed for the reactor chamber.

*****

AUGUST, 1912, THE MARTIAN FORTRESS

Captain Frank Dolfen led his men across the flat central area of the Martian fortress, looking for some way to get in. Off to the south there was still a hell of a fight going on and he could not help but think that if that fight was lost, all the people on foot were going to have a hell of a time getting out of here again. Coming down those ropes had been quick and pretty easy. Going back up them would not be.

That wasn't his concern at the moment, however. His job was to find some way inside the enemy fortress. He spotted other groups of men clustered around some of the lumps and bumps he'd seen earlier. Sometimes an explosion would erupt from one of them. Were they blasting their way inside? He couldn't tell. Colonel Schumacher had split up the squadrons to cover more ground, and to Dolfen it almost seemed like he considered this some sort of contest. Who could get in first and start capturing great stuff?

They came across a few wrecked tripods but the Martians who had piloted them were either dead or gone. They also found some of the spider-machines, still very much alive. One killed two of his men before they took it down with massed rifle fire. Several others were frozen in place and they just slung bombs on them and blew them up. He guessed they were supposed to capture those, too, but he'd seen the frozen ones come back to life before and he wasn't about to take chances with them.

Becca was still with them and still unharmed.

They reached the center of the big flat plain and Frank tried to decide where to go next. Further north there were still a few of the heat ray towers functioning on the walls and he didn't want to tangle with them. Best leave those things to the tanks.

"Sir! Over there!" Lynnbrooke grabbed his arm and pointed. About a hundred yards away, a tripod seemed to be climbing out of the ground.

"Down! Everyone take cover!"

The men hit the dirt and brought up their weapons. But the tripod was facing away from them and rapidly moved off to the north. A few shots from distant guns burst around it, but it kept moving. Dolfen quickly looked around to make sure there weren't any others coming out of different holes. There weren't, but he saw that twenty or thirty tripods a half-mile to the south were also moving quickly away from where the battle had been going on. Steam tanks appeared to be in pursuit. Had they won?

"Another one!" hissed Lynnbrooke. A second tripod appeared in the same spot as the first. It too moved rapidly away.

"Looks like we've found a way in," said Dolfen. "On your feet! Let's check it out!" They advanced warily, and as they got closer, they discovered a ramp leading down into the earth. It was a big ramp, obviously designed for the Martian tripods. At the bottom there was a huge metal door, but it was wide open.

"Somebody forgot to lock up when they left," said Lynnbrooke.

"Well let's get down there before they remember! Send out a few runners. Find the colonel and tell anyone they meet to come over here." There were bands of troops all over the place and it shouldn't take long to find reinforcements. The rest of them moved to where the top of the ramp merged with the plain and then started down, weapons ready. They had a few of the stovepipe launchers in addition to a machine gun and their bombs, but they really didn't want to take on anything tougher than a drone if they could avoid it.

They reached the bottom and found themselves on the edge of a huge underground space. It was dimly lit, but they could see rows of tripods standing near the far wall. All the men tensed and crouched down, but Dolfen looked at them closely through his binoculars.

"I think they're empty. Like those once we saw near Little Rock. Spares, I guess."

"If they're not, sir," said a trooper, "an' we go out there, we're cooked for sure."

"If they have Martians in them, they'd be outside fighting. Now come on."

"What about the doors, sir?" asked Lynnbrooke. "Wouldn't want to get trapped down here."

Dolfen looked over his men. "Sergeant… uh, Wilkerson, stay here with your squad and see if you can find something to jam the doors with. Blow 'em up if you have to, but keep them open."

"Yes, sir."

Leaving the squad behind, the rest of them, about a hundred men, started across the open space. As their eyes adjusted from the bright sunshine outside, they could see well enough. Near the parked tripods, there were a number of smaller three-legged machines. Bigger and differently shaped than the spider-machines, they were as silent and inert as the bigger ones. Nonetheless, none wanted to linger in the vicinity and they were nearly jogging by the time they reached a set of smaller doors on the far side.

The doors led to a corridor which went off in both directions. Dolfen looked one way and then the other; they were empty. The corridors curved slightly so he couldn't see very far. But the one to the right was sloping slightly down, while the left-hand one sloped upward. Part of him really wanted to go back up, but something told him the things they were probably looking for were farther down. Some faint noises made him look back the way they had come and he saw more troops coming down the ramp. Good, they weren't on their own anymore. Making up his mind, he went down the corridor to the right.

The corridor was about twenty feet wide and twenty feet high. But the walls curved inward toward the top making it a sort of flat-bottomed tube. There were doors at intervals set into the walls, but they were all sealed and he didn't want to waste time trying to blow his way into them. Clearly this place was going to take a lot of time to explore, but he wanted to try and find the main parts of it as quickly as possible.

Down they went and then they found an intersection with one ramp going to the right but more steeply downward, and another to the left leading upward. After a little thought, he took the one leading down. It went down about thirty feet, he guessed, and then got broader. A set of heavy doors were standing open and he sent some men ahead, while he followed more slowly with the rest.

Now they came upon some sections where there were windows in the sides of the corridor. Looking through, there were rooms filled with what looked like machinery and perhaps laboratory equipment. He remembered a photo in a newspaper of Thomas Edison's lab and it was kind of like that - only different.

"Looks like we're finding the stuff the generals want, Captain," said Lynnbrooke.

"Yeah, looks like. But I have no idea…"

"Captain!" One of the men he'd sent ahead was running back, he looked… upset.

"Trouble?"

"Uh, no, sir, no Martians, anyway. But… but we found something…"

"What?"

"Uh… people, sir, but they're… they're…" The man swallowed and turned away.

Suddenly Frank knew exactly what they'd found. He'd heard rumors… He gritted his teeth. He didn't want to see this, but he had to. But Becca was back there and she *didn't* have to see this. She was tough as nails, he knew, but she still didn't have to see it. He turned to Lynnbrooke and said loudly: "Lieutenant, I'm concerned about our rear. Take a squad back to that intersection and stay there." And then more softly: "And take Miss Harding with you. Don't take no for an answer, you understand?"

"Uh, yes, sir." He moved toward the rear. He thought he heard Becca say something, but he couldn't catch it and she didn't speak again. When he glanced back, he saw her going with Lynnbrooke and the others. Good.

He led the way forward, further down the corridor. There were more chambers with the windows. Big ones. And inside…

"Oh, God…"

* * * * *

AUGUST, 1912, INSIDE THE MARTIAN FORTRESS

Becca Harding looked back several times, but all she saw was the tail end of the group of troopers heading the other way, and they were soon lost to sight around the curve of the corridor. She had a good idea of what was back that way. Holding cages. Holding cages for the people the Martians used as food. Sam Jones, the soldier who had been rescued from the Gallup fortress, had spoken of them - shrieked about them, actually. *They eat us!* She didn't want Frank coddling her, but somehow this time she had no real desire to fight him over it. She followed Lieutenant Lynnbrooke.

They went back to the intersection and waited. She'd seen more soldiers following them down the ramp into the fortress. They ought to see some of them soon. Had they won? It had looked like it. They were inside the enemy's stronghold and the few remaining ones they'd seen outside were all running away. They'd done it! Captured one of the fortresses, liberated some of the land. For the first time all day she started to relax…

"I hear something, sir," said one of the men. They all paused and listened. At first she couldn't hear anything but her own breathing, but then she heard something else. A clicking sound. Metal on stone maybe. Not leather boots, surely. But where was it coming from? Four corridors went off in different directions and the sound was echoing off every wall. She raised her rifle. One of the men had a stovepipe launcher and he made sure it was ready. The lieutenant had his pistol out.

The sound was definitely coming closer. Becca turned this way and that, but she saw nothing. The lieutenant sent a man down the way they had just come - the only direction the noise couldn't be coming from - to tell Frank what was happening and to get some more men.

Suddenly the sound was clearer and coming from the ramp leading up. They spun to face that way, just as a machine came into view. It was a medium-sized tripod machine, not a spider and not one of the big ones; it was like one of the parked ones they'd seen earlier. The top was open and she glimpsed part of a Martian inside.

She fired her rifle, but the bullet bounced off the metal skin. Two others fired as well, but with no more effect than her shot. The stovepipe man was raising his weapon when flame burst from the machine. A small heat ray blasted out and swept across the group.

"Look out!" cried Lynnbrooke. He flung her down to the floor and shielded her with his body. A half-dozen screams filled her ears. She landed heavily and Lynnbrooke was on top of her for a moment before he rolled away, his clothes burning.

She twisted around, expecting the next blast to kill her. But the machine had already turned away and was heading down another corridor. She'd dropped her rifle, but then she saw the stovepipe launcher lying on the floor. The man who had carried was lying dead beside it, his head a smoldering mess.

She leapt to her feet, scooped up the stovepipe and pointed it at the retreating Martian. She'd insisted that the troopers show her how it worked and with an odd calmness and clarity, as though she had all the time in the world, she placed the tube on her shoulder, aimed, and pressed the firing button.

There was a loud *whoosh* and the rocket sprang from the tube and hit the machine, blowing off one of its legs. The thing crashed to the floor and skidded along for a few yards. The grey shape of the Martian tumbled out and rolled up against the wall and laid there.

There were shouts and the sound of feet pounding up the ramp, but she didn't turn to look. Instead, she picked up her rifle and walked toward the Martian.

* * * * *

CYCLE 597, 845.2, HOLDFAST 32-4

Qetjnegartis had been surprised and horrified to encounter the prey-creatures inside the holdfast. So soon? They were inside already? It was on its way to the reactor room when it ran right into a group of them. The travel chairs had all been fitted with the same sort of heat rays as the drones carried, but it had never expected to need it. But it had and it fired at the prey and thought it had brought down them all. But then something had struck the travel chair and now it was lying on the floor, stunned.

It heard a noise approaching from behind and pulled itself around to see one of the prey-creatures approaching with a weapon. Qetjnegartis was unarmed. There wasn't a thing it could do to defend itself.

The creatures halted a few *quel* away and aimed its weapon.

Well, the disaster is now complete. The clan had been dealt a devastating blow. There were scarcely a hundred adults left on the planet and only the three holdfasts. It would take several years to rebuild their strength to even what it was a few days ago. Would they be given those years? It seemed doubtful. The prey-creatures grew ever stronger, ever more resourceful. *And they will have this entire holdfast to study.* It would not be able to melt down the reactor and the place would remain intact.

There were still many other clans on the target world and most were in far better shape. Eventual victory might still be possible, but the Bajantus Clan would play little if any part in it. Command would fall to Tanbradjus, and it had serious doubts about its wisdom. *It was wiser than me on the question of defending this place.* Perhaps things would work out.

The wait for death seemed interminable. What was this creature delaying for?

* * * * *

AUGUST, 1912, INSIDE THE MARTIAN FORTRESS

"Becca!"

She heard Frank's voice from behind her, but she didn't take her eyes off the hideous creature lying before her. Her rifle was pointed straight at it and all she had to do was squeeze the trigger.

"Becca, they want us to take prisoners. This one's helpless."

Still she didn't turn. The hate in her was a boiling acid, searing her soul. These awful things had come here, killed her parents, her grandmother, her friend Pepe, destroyed the farm, her whole world, killed countless others, and would kill her and Frank if they weren't stopped. Why should she spare any of them?

"Becca, you've already killed one of them face to face like this. That's more than most people. And if you kill it, this one will just be another dead Martian. We've gotten plenty of those in the last few weeks. A live one might help the scientists learn better ways to kill the others. Don't do it, Becca."

Her hand tightened on the stock of the rifle.

"I want to kill it, too, Becca, believe me. After all I've seen, I want to kill them all. But if we can learn anything from this one, we should. And frankly, girl, after the scientists get their hands on it, this one might wish you'd killed it."

That got through the wall of hate in her brain. Yes, shooting it now was just a quick death. But life for this thing as a laboratory animal. Poked and prodded and given electric shocks just to see how it reacted. That would be punishment for its crimes that went on and on and on. So no, not mercy, not mercy at all.

She lowered the rifle and she heard Frank sigh.

She spun around, brought the rifle up to her shoulder and said: "It's all yours, sir."

* * * * *

AUGUST, 1912, THE MARTIAN FORTRESS

Colonel Andrew Comstock leaned against the rail of *Albuquerque*'s bridge. It was slightly deformed thanks to a heat ray, but it had cooled off now and he rested his weight on it. The whole front half of the ironclad was looking a bit deformed and decidedly shabby. All the paint had been burned off and the metal underneath was discolored in those strange patterns that extreme heat could cause. Half the guns were out of action and with the two right side track units damaged, it wasn't going anywhere any time soon. Repair crews were looking things over, but he suspected it would be weeks - or maybe months considering the lack of facilities - before it was ready for action again.

Andrew felt pretty much the same as the ironclad. He was exhausted and he could feel his muscles quivering. The non-stop action of the last few weeks, getting to Memphis, fighting the battle there, getting here, and the fighting today, had worn him out.

But at the same time, an exhilaration filled him. They had done it! They had beaten the Martians in an open battle, driven them off, and captured their fortress. Reports that were coming in said that the whole thing was intact and that they had even captured some live Martians. This was the victory everyone had been hoping for.

They'd paid a price for it, his eyes went out to look at the still smoldering wrecks of the aircraft which had provide the vital, but so costly, diversion which had allowed the ironclads to get inside. A lot of other men had been killed, too, but nowhere near as many as in past battles. Yes, it was a great victory.

"Quite a thing, wasn't it?" asked Drew Harding, coming up beside him.

"Yes, quite a thing. What do you think of the ironclads now?"

Drew nodded his head. "They won this fight for sure. They may be what we need to win the war."

"We're building more of them. A lot more. This was just the beginning. The first step on the long road back."

A shout from above made them look up. A man - a braver man than Andrew - had shinnied out on the pole which stuck out from the side of the observation platform forty feet overhead, and attached a new line to a pulley mounted there. The heat rays had burned away all the old lines. He threw the line down to two men waiting below and they attached it to the pulley there. Then they hooked something to the line. There were more shouts and then one of the five-inch guns on *USLI Albuquerque* boomed out with a blank charge.

All around them on the vast round plain of the captured enemy fortress, men stopped whatever they were doing and looked that way. A bugler started playing *To The Colors*, and a dozen more joined in, the sweet sound echoing off the walls. The men at the line pulled and the flag ran upward.

Andrew and Harding came to attention and saluted. Thousands of other men did as well.

The flag reached the top and the breeze caught it and displayed it. The Stars and Stripes gleamed in the afternoon sunshine, waving over land that was America once more.

EPILOGUE

NOVEMBER, 1912, WASHINGTON, D.C.

"The results have come in from Ohio," said George Cortelyou. "You are reelected, Mr. President. Congratulations, sir."

A cheer went up from the crowd in the East Room of the White House. Theodore Roosevelt's campaign manager shook his hand and then gave way to let all the others do so as well. General Leonard Wood fell in near the rear of the line.

There was quite a crowd here tonight, far larger than past elections. Roosevelt usually disdained this sort of thing, but it was clear that tonight he was in a far more ebullient mood than in past years.

That was probably because this had been the toughest election he had ever faced - and the President loved a political fight. And also because the war was going far better than anyone could have hoped just a few months ago.

The huge defensive victories at St. Louis and Memphis had been followed up with the capture of the Martian fortress near Little Rock and the liberation of that city. Then the enemy had evacuated and destroyed their fortress near Kansas City, and another near Des Moines, and abandoned all that ground without a fight. To all appearances, they were falling back toward the Rockies.

The news had electrified the country. The peoples' confidence in Roosevelt had been restored and Nelson Miles' single-issue campaign based solely on the lack of military progress lost ground steadily.

Still, it had been a near run thing. The Supreme Court's ruling that the refugees from the overrun states could cast absentee ballots from those states had seemed sure to give the election to Miles. But the victories had caused a dramatic shift to Roosevelt as those people felt there was hope they might see their homes again soon after all.

Wood hoped that they wouldn't be disappointed.

The road back was going to be long and not nearly fast enough to suit most people. Wood was determined that they not make the same mistake as they had in 1910 and leave their lines of communications vulnerable to enemy raids. The armies were not going to just rush forward to the Rockies. The railroads would have to be rebuilt and powerful fortresses were going to be constructed every twenty or thirty miles along them to keep them safe. That was going to take a lot of time and a lot of effort. Wood secretly doubted they would be ready for a final assault on the remaining enemy fortresses before the 1916 election.

And it might not happen at all depending on what happened to the north. In September, there had been a serious attack along the Superior Switch defense line. 1st Army had very nearly been forced back. Only by sending every man he could lay hands on to help had the line been held. The British in Canada were reporting alarming concentration of enemy forces along their front.

The north was Wood's biggest worry now. They knew that the strength of the Martians was determined by how many Martians they could produce, not how many machines. They'd killed a hell of a lot of Martians from the two landing groups in the United States and both groups were weak now. But they knew that there were at least two more groups in Alberta and Alaska, and one more in Greenland. None of those had been involved in much fighting. How strong had they grown? Would he awake one morning to find news that ten thousand tripods were coming down from the north? If even a tenth of that number appeared, it could derail any plans for a drive on the Rockies. Still, the recent victories gave them a chance even if the worst happened.

"Good evening, Leonard."

The voice at his elbow made him turn and there was Elihu Root, the Secretary of State. "Good evening, Mr. Secretary, how are you?"

"Well enough, well enough. A great night for sure. And you? How goes the war?"

"As well as can be expected, sir. We'll be consolidating for the winter, but building up for offensives in the spring. How's the rest of the world?"

Root shook his head. "Confused is the only word that comes to mind. The British are holding on all their various fronts. The Japanese have occupied a lot of China's coastal cities and are holding them. China is a mess, as always. We're getting some very strange rumors from Russia. They've lost Moscow but seem to be holding on to Ukraine and the areas around St. Petersburg. And Poland is in revolt. We aren't sure what the Kaiser is up to in South America, he's playing things very close to the vest there. And the French... well, that's why I wanted to talk to you. What are you hearing from Funston down in Texas?"

Wood stiffened. Fred Funston was a very touchy subject these days. Roosevelt and he had secretly decided to relive him once the election was over. "He's destroyed a small Martian stronghold down near Corpus Christi and stabilized his lines. We still don't have reliable rail connections with him. We're hoping to rectify that in the spring."

Root frowned. "The reason I ask is that we've been getting some rather... disturbing rumors about diplomatic agreements being made directly between the French and Governor of Texas."

"Supposedly there were some French troops involved with the attack on the stronghold..."

Root's voice fell to a near whisper. "And have you heard that there was a referendum on the ballot down there? A referendum, which if approved, would give the state legislature the power to secede from the Union?"

Wood snorted. "Didn't they try that once already? Didn't work out so well as I recall."

"It's no laughing matter, Leonard! If they throw in their lot with the French, it could be a real mess. Other western states could get the same idea."

"Well, the surest way to avoid that is for us to reopen the railroads and give them the support they need." Wood didn't mention the fact that he had argued strongly against giving them the support they needed, nor that it had been the right decision at the time. "We'll be making that a top priority next year."

"Next year might not be soon enough. Isn't there anything you can do...?"

"Elihu! Leonard! Good to see you!" Without his noticing, the line had advanced and they were now at the head of it. There was Roosevelt beaming and booming. He grabbed their hands and shook vigorously.

"Congratulations, Theodore," said Root.

"Congratulations, Mr. President," said Wood.

"And congratulations to both of you! We wouldn't be here but for all of your hard work! You both have my thanks."

"There's a lot more hard work ahead," said Wood.

"True! True! But tonight at least we can relax and pat ourselves on the back. The work can wait until tomorrow!"

* * * * *

DECEMBER, 1912, WASHINGTON NAVY YARD

"And it is the unanimous finding of this inquest, that the loss of *USS Santa Fe* was due to enemy action in the course of carrying out its assigned duties. No blame for her loss can be assigned to any person. This proceeding is concluded."

Commander Drew Harding let out the breath he'd been holding. He sprang to his feet as the panel of officers left the room and then accepted a handshake and congratulations from the lieutenant who had acted as his counsel for the hearing.

That hadn't been nearly as bad as he'd feared. His friend Andrew had been right: with the war going well, no one needed to look for scapegoats and they'd been willing to give him the benefit of the doubt. Still, it was a hard thing. He'd lost his ship and no one would ever forget that. Nor that somehow he'd been the sole survivor. And even if everyone else did forget, he wouldn't. He'd been writing letters to the families of his men for weeks.

He left the hearing room in the big headquarters building and headed toward the personnel offices which were in a wing on the opposite side and two floors up. He trotted up the stairs, not at all troubled by his shoulder or his ribs; they were all pretty well mended. He walked down a hallway to a specific room and rapped on the frame and then went in.

Inside he found a navy captain at his desk. The brass plate on it said: *Winthorpe*. He looked up and smiled. "Well, Harding! Good to see you. I assume all went well?"

"Yes, sir. As well as could be expected."

"I assumed that by the fact that you are here and not in the brig," Captain Winthorpe laughed. The smile faded. "So now you come to me looking for work."

"Yes, sir, I need a new assignment."

"Well, you had your own ship, so I can't very well assign you to another one in a subordinate role. But we don't have any ships in need of a captain just at the moment. In a few months something might turn up. In the meantime, I can give you a desk assignment somewhere. You were in the ordnance bureau a few years back, weren't you? Maybe I can find a posting there."

"If that's all that's available, sir." He didn't much like the idea and it must have shown on his face.

"Or…" said Winthorpe slowly, "there is another possibility."

"Sir?"

"I understand you got a close up look at the army's land ironclads out at Memphis this summer. What did you think of them?"

"They're small, cramped, and mechanical nightmares. But there's no denying their effectiveness, sir." Where was Winthorpe going with this?

"Well, as it happens, the navy is building its own version of the contraptions."

"So I'd heard, sir."

"And we need commanding officers for several of them. It's proving hard to find men willing to take the posts."

"Really? After Memphis and Little Rock, I'd have thought they'd be lining up for the positions."

"Ha! Well you'd be wrong. Too new, too different, the experienced officers are afraid of what a posting like that might do to their careers. And I'll be honest with you, Harding, taking command of one of these things might be a bad career move. If the war ends soon, you'll be in command of a white elephant which nobody wants."

But I'll be in command of something. Something that can hurt the enemy.

"I understand, sir, but I think I'll take my chances with that. If the position is available, I'd like it very much."

* * * * *

CYCLE 597,845.5, LOCATION UNKNOWN

Qetjnegartis watched the prey-creature writing mathematical equations on a black panel with some sort of white stick which left marks on it. It had taken only the briefest amount of study to realize what the marks meant: basic numbers using symbols for one, two, three, and so forth. Surprisingly, the creatures used a base ten system just as the Race did. The operational symbols had taken a bit more study to unravel: addition, subtraction, multiplication, division. They had used actual objects to make the connection between the symbols and what they represented.

More difficult to puzzle out was just why they were doing this. Eventually, the only answer Qetjnegartis could arrive at was that they were trying to communicate with it.

When it had first been captured, it had expected a quick death, either deliberately or accidentally, as these creatures experimented on it. But they had been very careful, and while some of the examinations had been unpleasant, none had proved lethal. Five other clan members had been captured along with it on that disastrous day at the holdfast. Three had been badly wounded and died within days. One of the others had clearly become mentally unhinged by the ordeal. It had stopped eating and died soon after. The last one had been taken elsewhere after twenty days and it had not seen it since.

Qetjnegartis had been alone after that with little to do but contemplate its fate and watch the prey-creatures make their symbols. They were feeding it; blood from some non-intelligent animal it assumed. But it wasn't being filtered, and between that and the close contact it was having with the prey-creatures, it expected to become ill with the local pathogens sooner or later. A bud was growing in the sack on its flank, and if it lived long enough to do so, it planned to transfer its consciousness to the bud at the proper time. It had no intention of creating a new member of the Race under these circumstances.

Another option was to cease eating and simply die as the other one had done. There were certain attractions to that path, and it would remain open, but it would not take it yet. It supposed that this could be considered a chance to learn about its captors. *A shame Ixmaderna isn't here instead of me. It would have welcomed the opportunity.*

It wished it knew what had happened to the others. Had they escaped? Were the other holdfasts still surviving? How was the overall course of the war going? The reverses suffered by the Bajantus Clan did not mean the war was being lost on all fronts. But there was no way to find out. It was completely cut off and isolated. It was very unsettling to be kept in such ignorance.

It was also becoming boring. Boredom didn't come easily to the Race. With memories stretching back thousands of cycles, there was always something of interest to contemplate. Even so, the enforced inaction was difficult. The desire to work was an integral part of every individual.

The prey-creature was standing very close to it now, holding out the white stick and shaking it. Was it annoyed at the lack of response? Qetjnegartis looked at the black panel. The creature had wiped away all the other writing and only one equation remained. It recognized the symbols from earlier sessions:

$$1+1=$$

The Race did not make a lot of use of written records. The perfect memory of each member and the ability to pass on information and even memories to new buds meant that nearly everything of import was remembered by multiple individuals. There was a written language, too, and all items of basic knowledge had been recorded in the event of some great catastrophe, but it was rarely necessary to refer to those records.

But for these prey-creatures, such record must be utterly necessary. It remembered Ixmaderna's lecture about the short lives and inability to pass on information to offspring and their long maturation period. To them, these written symbols were vital.

The prey-creature came closer. At first they had kept Qetjnegartis at bay and sometimes even restrained, until they realized how physically helpless it was. Now they simply placed it on something flat. There were always armed warriors present, of course.

The prey-creature was making noises. They were always making noises and this was clearly how they communicated with each other. Qetjnegartis doubted that it would ever be able to decipher whatever passed for a language, and was certain it could not reproduce the noises. But communication through symbols, that might be possible.

Possible, but was it desirable?

What can I learn from them? More important, is there anything they can learn from me?

That was clearly why they were doing this: in hopes of learning something useful. But they could only learn things of use if it decided to give them to them. *I control that.*

So there seemed to be no harm. And the boredom was becoming intolerable.

Qetjnegartis reached out a tendril and wrapped it around the white stick. The action seemed to surprise the prey-creature because it jumped back and made a loud noise. Qetjnegartis ignored it and dragged itself closer to the black panel. Remembering the proper symbol, it took the stick and awkwardly scratched:

2

* * * * *

CYCLE 597,845.5, HOLDFAST 32-3

"The prey-creatures are not pursuing us, Commander," said Davnitargus. "I have led scouting expeditions as far east as City 3-118. The prey-creatures are there in considerable strength and they have their own scouts sent out nearly to the mountains, but there is no evidence they are preparing for a major expedition westward."

"That is very odd," said Tanbradjus. "They must surely know they hold the advantage. Why do they not exploit it?"

"The local winter is coming on," said Davnitargus. "The prey-creatures have difficulty functioning or feeding themselves in low temperatures. Experience shows that they probably will not attempt any major operations until warmer weather returns."

"That is good to know. It gives us a chance to rebuild our strength." Tanbradjus paused and then went on. "I am relying on those of you with experience on this world to guide me when necessary. With the regrettable loss of Qetjnegartis, I will be relying on you in particular, Davnitargus."

It regarded the new commander closely. Was this some veiled statement that it doubted its trustworthiness? "I serve the clan and Race, Commander," it replied.

"As do we all. But I shall speak plainly, Davnitargus."

"That is usually best."

"It is known that those budded on this world lack the inherent submission to superiors that exists on the Homeworld."

"Indeed?"

"Yes. Some find this extremely disturbing. But the situation is what it is. You are the senior most of all those budded on this world. I will expect you to keep the others in line. Can I trust you to do that Davnitargus?"

"Of course, Commander."

For now.

* * * * *

DECEMBER, 1912, LITTLE ROCK, ARKANSAS

"Merry Christmas, Becca."

"Merry Christmas, Frank."

They didn't have champagne, they didn't even have wine. They were forced to clink tin cups half-filled with bourbon, but neither one minded. They were alive and together and nothing else really mattered. The 5th Cavalry was stationed in the remains of Little Rock now. The town was slowly being rebuilt and refortified. The rail connection east had been repaired and concrete fortresses were being built all along its length. Two divisions of infantry were defending the place along with four battalions of steam tanks and a lot of artillery.

The cavalry had been conducting scouting missions west all through the fall to keep an eye on the Martians, but aside from small scouting parties, they hadn't seen much. Half of their job had been to turn back parties of civilians who somehow thought the recent victories meant they could go home again. It wasn't easy convincing them that it would be a very bad idea. Becca had gone along on those scouts and no one had complained.

"Remember our first Christmas together?" asked Becca.

"The one in the Pueblo cliff-dwelling?"

"Yes, we didn't even remember it was Christmas until the day was nearly over. No tree, no presents - no bourbon."

"I've spent nicer ones, that's for sure. I wonder whatever happened to those people," said Frank. "The civilians we picked up who wouldn't go on to Ramah with us."

"Dead probably." She got up and went over to the fire and poked at the logs and threw another one on. The army had taken over a lot of the abandoned property in the town - the buildings which hadn't been too badly damaged. Frank's captain's rank had rated him a modest town house with a nice parlor. There was no electricity or running water, of course, but they made do.

They made do. They were sharing the house and no one said a thing. Becca's mother - or her aunt - would have been absolutely scandalized, but neither one of them gave a damn about such things. Frank had asked to marry her, and she'd said yes, but then when they checked the regulation, they found that as a married dependent she'd technically be barred from serving with the 5th out in the field. But as a camp follower, well, the regulations were reassuringly vague about it. So they'd let things be.

"Oh, speaking of presents," said Frank. "I have something for you. Came last week, but I've been saving it for today." He pulled a sheet of paper out of his tunic pocket and handed it to her.

"What is it?"

"Read it."

She unfolded it and held it so the firelight fell on it. She squinted, frowned, and shook her head. "It's written in *army*, Frank, what does it mean?"

He laughed and took it back. "Congress recently approved a bill to give veteran army nurses officer's rank. So they could boss enlisted men around, I guess. When I heard about it, I had a little talk with Colonel Schumacher. He pulled some strings and this, young lady, is your commission as a second lieutenant in the Army Nurse Corps."

"Really?" She snatched it back, a look of delight on her face. "A lieutenant? Me?"

"Sure enough; you'll get the pay, too. 'Course you already were a lieutenant with your sharpshooters."

She snorted. "A make-believe rank for make-believe soldiers."

"You sell yourself - and all your girls - short, Becca. They fought and some of them died. Nothing make-believe about it."

"No. you're right. Some of them were good soldiers, too." She held up the paper. "But this is for real? I'm a lieutenant?"

"Well, in the nurse corps you are. You can't really command troops in a combat situation."

"That's all right, don't really want to. As long as it means I can keep comin' along and fightin', I'm content."

"As long as Schumacher is colonel that's what it means."

"Then we'll have to make sure he stays alive!" She held up her cup. "To Colonel Schumacher!" They clinked them together and drank.

"So what happens now?" she asked.

"Well, I was thinking we'd get drunk and then go to bed." He reached out a hand and pinched her.

"I meant with the war, you goof!"

"I doubt much will happen during the winter. They'll want to get everything fortified and set up for a spring offensive."

"So we'll be movin' west in the spring?"

"Seems likely."

"Good," she said. "We took some of ours back this year. But we ain't gonna stop until we have it all."

"Amen to that."

* * * * *

JANUARY, 1913, WASHINGTON, D.C.

"Happy New Year, dear," said Andrew Comstock. He took his wife in his arms and kissed her.

"Happy New Year, love," replied Victoria. She smiled, but he could see that she was troubled. The birth of their daughter three months earlier had gone well. Little Arthur and Elizabeth were sleeping soundly despite the noise of the revelers roaming the streets of Fort Myer. So that wasn't the problem.

"I'm sorry about the new assignment, but it will be months before they're ready to take the field. We'll see a lot of each other."

"But then you'll be going back to the war."

"I'm a soldier. It's my job."

"You had a job in the Ordnance Department. Not a combat command."

"My Ordnance job didn't exactly keep me out of harm's way."

"No, it didn't! But why do you have to be in the front lines? Just the other day you told me that that pilot friend of yours…"

"Tom Selfridge?"

"Yes, him. You said he'd been taken off flying duty and sent back to train new pilots. Why can't you do something like that?"

He shook his head. "Piloting is the most dangerous job there is, love. They have about a seventy-percent casualty rate. Tom barely survived the battle at the Martian fortress. The high command thought he had taken enough risks. But my job is different; the land ironclads are the most powerful and safest combat command I could have. We took on seventy tripods with only three and won. I'll be commanding a whole squadron. Six of them. I'll be as safe as any soldier can be."

She sniffed and turned away. "How much longer will this go on?"

"It is going to take a while to clear the Martians all out. But we will."

"We're really winning? There are all these statements from the President, from the government, but I don't know what to believe."

"Yes, we are winning. We hurt them very badly this year. We'll hurt them even worse in the spring. Someday the war will be over and we are going to win."

She moved into his embrace again. "You promise?"

"Yes, I promise."

THE END

Scott Washburn

NOTES ON THE HISTORICAL CHARACTERS IN THE BOOKS

In my books I make use of a large number of actual people who were alive at the time the stories take place. Some are well-known people, like Theodore Roosevelt, while others are more obscure, like Tom Selfridge. What follows are short biographies of some of those characters. They are presented in alphabetical order.

Sir George Tom Molesworth Bridges, KCB, KCMG, DSO
(August 20, 1871 – November 26, 1939)

A British Army officer with a distinguished career. He graduated from the Royal Military Academy in 1892 and joined the Royal Artillery, serving in India and Nyasaland. He saw action during the Boer War. In 1909 he transferred to the 4th Queen's Own Hussars. He served as military attaché to Belgium, Holland, and Scandinavia between 1910 and 1914. He fought in the early battles of World War I and gained fame when he rallied two demoralized infantry battalions, who were on the verge of surrender and led them to safety. Soon afterwards he was sent to Antwerp to help coordinate the defense there. He was given command of the new 19th Division which saw action at Loos and later at La Boiselle. In 1917 he was sent on a mission to the United States to help coordinate their integration into the Allied war effort. He returned to France and lost a leg at Passchendaele, but quickly recovered after a brief period of work under Churchill in his Ministry of Munitions. Before the end of the war he was sent on missions to the United States, the Balkans, and Russia. Between 1922 and 1927 he served as the governor of South Australia.

James Bryce, 1st Viscount Bryce, OM, GCVO, PC, FRS, FBA
(May 10, 1838 – January 22, 1922)

Bryce was an English lawyer and academic who became a member of Parliament and later the ambassador to the United States. Educated in Germany he became a great admirer of both German and American culture and believed that the three countries should be natural allies. In America he became personal friends with Theodore Roosevelt and worked hard to improve Anglo-American relations. He wrote several books on American institutions and culture.

Archibald Willingham DeGraffenreid Clarendon Butt
(September 26, 1865 – April 15, 1912)

As a young man, Archie Butt had a brief career as a newspaper reporter. He then served for two years in the American embassy in Mexico. During the Spanish American War he joined the army, was commissioned as an officer, and served in the Quartermaster Corps where his work with animal husbandry drew some attention. In 1901 he was commissioned in the regular army. After short postings in Cuba and Washington, D.C., he became the military aide to President Theodore Roosevelt. He later served President Howard Taft in the same role. Returning from a vacation in Europe in 1912, he died when the RMS Titanic struck an iceberg and sank.

George Bruce Cortelyou
(July 26, 1862 – October 23, 1940)

An American politician who held many important posts, including Secretary of Commerce and Labor 1903-1904, Postmaster General 1905-1907, and Secretary of the Treasury 1907-1909. He was Chairman of the Republican National Committee and a close confidante of Theodore Roosevelt. Cortelyou managed Roosevelt's presidential campaign in 1904.

William Crozier
(February 19, 1855 – November 11, 1942)

William Crozier was the son of a US Senator from Ohio. He graduated from West Point in 1876 and served with the 4th Artillery for several years on the western frontier. He then taught mathematics at West Point for five years. In 1888 he was sent to Europe to study new developments in artillery. Upon his return he went to work for the Ordnance Department and designed a new type of gun and the Buffington-Crozier disappearing gun carriage. During the Spanish American War he was in charge of inspecting American coast defenses. He later served in the Philippines and in the Relief Expedition to Peking during the Boxer Rebellion. In 1901 he became the Army's Chief of Ordnance, a post he held until 1917. During his tenure he oversaw the development of a number of classic weapons such as the 1903 Springfield rifle, the 1911 Colt automatic pistol, the Browning Automatic Rifle (BAR) and the M1917 light machine gun. He retired from the Army in 1918.

Hugh Aloysius Drum
(September 19, 1879 – October 3, 1951)

Drum was born into a military family and at age 19 was directly commissioned into the United States Army as a lieutenant because of his father's heroic death during the Spanish American War. Drum saw service in the Philippines before attending the Army Command and General Staff College. Drum later served as chief of staff for General Frederick Funston during the Veracruz operation and also during the 1916 expedition against Pancho Villa where he gained the favorable attention of General John Pershing. During World War I Drum became the chief of staff of the US First Army. Between the wars Drum served on a number staff assignments, including as assistant to Douglas MacArthur. He was also involved in the movement to prevent the establishment of a separate US Air Force. He was passed over for promotion to become Chief of Staff of the US Army and was later embarrassed during the Carolina Maneuvers just prior to World War II by being captured by the enemy force. This probably prevented him from receiving a combat command during World War II and Drum was forced to retire in 1943.

Thomas Alva Edison
(February 11, 1847 – October 18, 1931)

Thomas Edison was an American businessman and inventor. He is credited with no less than 1,093 US patents and is best known for his inventions of the phonograph, the motion picture camera, and the first practical electric light bulb. He was also instrumental in the development of electric power generation and distribution. He was sometimes known as the "Wizard of Menlo Park", the location of one of his laboratories. Edison is credited with the first industrial research laboratory which turned out inventions and products by mass-production techniques. Edison was largely self-educated and his successes were due to his ability to see the practical application of science rather than through traditional scientific research methods.

Frederick Funston
(November 9, 1865 – February 19, 1917)

Frederick Funston, "Fearless Freddy", failed the examination to enter West Point and dropped out of college without graduating. He then had a number of jobs including newspaper reporter and a surveyor for the Department of Agriculture in Alaska. Eventually he joined the Cuban revolutionaries fighting for their independence from Spain. He became seriously ill there and returned to the United States. When America declared war in 1898 he became a colonel of volunteers from Kansas. He was sent to the Philippines and fought the insurrectionists there, winning the Medal of Honor for heroism under fire. He was awarded a commission in the regular army. Returning to the United States, he was in command of the Presidio in San Francisco at the time of the great earthquake in 1906. He took charge of the city and was instrumental in bringing the fires under control. He also ordered his troops to shoot looters. His actions were both praised and criticized. He later held various commands both in America and the Philippines. He commanded the forces occupying Veracruz in 1914 and was involved in the operations against Pancho Villa in 1916. President Wilson was considering Funston for command of the American Expeditionary Force to France in 1917 when Funston died from a heart attack at age 51.

Robert Goddard
(October 5, 1882 – August 10, 1945)

Robert Goddard was an American inventor, physicist, and engineer. He is credited with building the first liquid-fueled rocket. During World War I he worked on a small man-portable rocket for use by the infantry. Although the end of the war curtailed further development, Goddard's concept was revived and became the famous Bazooka rocket launcher widely used in World War II. Many of Goddard's inventions became the foundation for later rockets used by the military and NASA.

Andrew Jackson Higgins
(August 28, 1886 – August 1, 1952)

Andrew Higgins was an American businessman in the lumber and boat-building industry. He is best known for developing and building the Landing Craft Vehicle Personnel (LCVP) commonly known as the "Higgins Boat" which was used in almost every amphibious operation in World War II. Dwight Eisenhower once referred to Higgins as 'the man who won World War II for us".

Douglas MacArthur
(January 26, 1880 – April 5, 1964)

Douglas MacArthur was born in Little Rock, Arkansas into a military family (his father won the Medal of Honor during the Civil War) and spent his early years on various military posts throughout the west. He graduated the top of his class at West Point. He took part in the occupation of Veracruz, Mexico in 1914 where he was nominated for the Medal of Honor after a risky (and unauthorized) reconnaissance mission. During World War I he served with the 42nd Division and was noted for his reckless bravery, accompanying his men on nighttime patrols and daytime assaults, wearing no helmet and armed with nothing but a riding crop. He was decorated no less than nine times during that war and rose to the rank of brigadier general. After the war he was superintendent at West Point, served for several years in the Philippines, and was president of the US Olympic Committee for the 1928 Olympics. In 1930 he became Chief of Staff of the United States Army. He retired from the army in 1937 and became the chief military advisor to the Commonwealth Government of the Philippines. Recalled to active service in 1941, he became commander of the US Army forces in the Far East. His conduct during the Japanese attack on the Philippines has been a matter of controversy ever since. Ordered to Australia, MacArthur built up a powerful force and conducted what many consider a brilliant campaign, fighting his way through New Guinea, the northern Solomon Islands, and ultimately back to the Philippines. He became the military governor of Japan after the war and then commander of the United Nations forces in Korea in the early stages of the war there. After several controversial actions he was ultimately fired by President Truman and forced to retire. MacArthur was known for his personal courage, flamboyant and imperious style, and reluctance to share public fame with any of his subordinates.

Nelson Appleton Miles
(August 8, 1839 – May 15, 1925)

Nelson Miles was an American military officer who served with great distinction in the American Civil War and later in the wars on the frontier. He rose to the rank of Commanding General in the US Army before being forcibly retired by Theodore Roosevelt in 1903. Miles made an unsuccessful bid for the presidency in 1904.

John Joseph Pershing
(September 13, 1860 – July 15, 1948)

Pershing graduated from West Point in 1885 and was soon assigned to the 6th US Cavalry. With this regiment he served in a number of campaigns on the frontier. In 1891 he was promoted and transferred to the 10th Cavalry, which was a unit of "Buffalo Soldiers" with black enlisted men serving under white officers. It was here that he got his nickname "Black Jack". He served as an instructor at West Point before returning to the 10th for the Spanish American War. Pershing served bravely at the Battles of San Juan Hill and Kettle Hill in Cuba. It was here that he came to the attention of Theodore Roosevelt. Pershing served in various occupation duties in Cuba and the Philippines before returning to the United States. Roosevelt, president by this time, tried to advance Pershing's career, but was thwarted several times by the Army bureaucracy. Pershing served in several staff positons before being sent to the Far East to observe the Russo-Japanese War. On his return, Roosevelt finally succeeded in promoting him to brigadier general—jumping him three ranks in the process. Pershing then held several more staff positions and also went to the Balkans to observe fighting there. In 1913 he was given command of an infantry brigade in San Francisco and in 1915, while Pershing was away, his wife and three children were killed in a fire at their home. In 1916 Pershing led an expedition into Mexico to try to capture the revolutionary leader Pancho Villa. The expedition failed. In May, 1917 Pershing was made the commander of the American Expeditionary Force sent to France during World War I. Pershing is credited with turning the huge American force of raw recruits into an effective army. He resisted the attempts of the British and French to use the Americans as replacements for their own depleted units and insisted that the Americans fight as a coherent force. After the war Pershing became Chief of Staff. He retired from active service in 1924, but remained active in many veterans organizations until his death.

Theodore Roosevelt Jr.
(October 27, 1858 – January 6, 1919)

Theodore Roosevelt was the 26th president of the United States and one of the most remarkable public figures in the country's history. Born as a sickly child he built up his health through a rigorous program of exercise and outdoor activity. He was home-schooled and then attended Harvard College. His interests were wide-ranging including history and the natural sciences. Due to his poor eyesight he had extremely acute hearing and became an expert on bird songs. He had thoughts of becoming an historian or scientist but very quickly became fascinated with New York politics (much to the horror of his family). He was elected to the New York State Assembly in 1882 and gained a reputation as a progressive in the mostly conservative Republican Party. The death of his first wife, Alice, and his mother within hours of each other in 1884 plunged Roosevelt into deep grief. He dealt with it by fleeing to North Dakota where he bought a ranch and learned the cattle business. His experiences among the cowboys of the region created a love for nature and the rough outdoors that he retained throughout his life. He returned to New York in 1895 and was elected as President of the New York City Board of Police Commissioners. He began a campaign to weed out corruption and crack down on crime in the city that won the admiration of many people, but the ire of the bosses of the city's political machine. He married Edith Carow in 1886. In 1897 President McKinley appointed him Assistant Secretary of the Navy. Roosevelt was an advocate of naval power and as a college student wrote a book on the naval aspects of the War of 1812 that became the standard work on the topic. Roosevelt applied his usual energy to the job and since the Secretary, John D. Long, had little interest in naval affairs, Roosevelt had a free hand. When it became clear that war with Spain was inevitable, Roosevelt made sure the fleet was ready for action. He issued the orders which sent Commodore Dewey's squadron to Manila on his own authority. With the coming of war, Roosevelt was determined to get into combat. He believed that war was the ultimate test of manhood. When the government authorized the raising of volunteer regiments, as had been done for the Civil War, Roosevelt resigned his position and received authorization to raise a regiment of cavalry. He convinced his friend, Leonard Wood, to be the colonel of the regiment while he was the lieutenant colonel. The regiment, the 1st United States Volunteer Cavalry, was composed of an amazing cross section of American society, from Manhattan dandies to Wild West cowboys and cattle rustlers. Wood and Roosevelt whipped them into shape in an amazingly short period of time and saw them dispatched with the expedition to Cuba. The "Rough Riders" as they were called, first saw action at a place called Las Guasimas in late June 1898. Roosevelt came under fire several times. On July 1st Roosevelt, now in command of the regiment since Wood had been promoted to command a brigade, led the famous charge up Kettle Hill and later attacked San Juan Hill. Roosevelt, conspicuous on horseback, was utterly fearless as he led the way. He was recommended for the Medal of Honor for his actions, but enemies in Congress denied him the medal. (It was awarded to him posthumously in 2001). By the time the war ended, Roosevelt was commanding a brigade of cavalry, which included the Rough Riders, and led them back to Long Island where they were mustered out. Roosevelt was now nationally known and he easily won the governorship of New York in 1899. In that position he once again came into conflict with conservative Republicans who controlled the political machinery. In an effort to drive him out of any position of real power, they schemed to get him nominated as McKinley's running mate in the 1900 presidential election. Roosevelt felt he could not turn down the honor, although he understood it would probably be the end of his political career. The expectations of everyone were confounded when McKinley was assassinated in 1901 and Roosevelt became president. As president he championed many progressive ideas including his "Square Deal" to give ordinary citizens a fair chance to succeed. He worked to break up business monopolies and establish fair labor laws and ensure safe food and drugs. His great love of the outdoors led him to create many new national parks and monuments and safeguard vast stretches of wilderness areas. He was a great believer in American 'Manifest Destiny' and made the building of a canal between the Atlantic and Pacific a priority. He conspired with Panamanian revolutionaries in achieving independence from Columbia and then negotiated a treaty to give the United States the rights to build a canal across the Isthmus of Panama. In 1905 he negotiated an end to the Russo-Japanese War and this won him the Nobel Peace Prize in 1906. Refusing to run for a third term in 1908, Roosevelt turned the presidency over to his friend, William Taft. Roosevelt had always been a prolific reader and writer. He was capable of reading and remembering a book in a single day. He wrote many books and magazine articles on history and wildlife. In 1909 he led an expedition to Africa sponsored by the Smithsonian Institution where he acquired many animal specimens and wrote articles and books about the journey. Afterwards he toured Europe and was the guests of kings and princes. He gave many speeches and it would be no exaggeration to say he was the most famous man in the world. Unfortunately, back in America his friend, Taft, was proving to be untrustworthy when it came to protecting many of Roosevelt's progressive accomplishments. Determined to correct this, he tried and failed to secure the Republican nomination for the 1912 election. He then formed an independent party which came to be known as the "Bull Moose" party. It was a contentious campaign and Roosevelt was shot, but survived an assassination attempt. Roosevelt came in second, but by splitting the Republican vote it gave the election to Democrat Woodrow Wilson. Retiring again to private life, Roosevelt was asked to lead an expedition into the upper reaches of the Amazon River. Hoping to recreate his triumphant African expedition, Roosevelt accepted. The expedition was a disaster. A number of the party died and Roosevelt was carried home on a stretcher, near death. He recovered, but he was never the healthy, robust man he had once been again. When World War I broke out, Roosevelt believed that the United States would inevitably be drawn into it and should prepare. He was highly critical of President Wilson for failing to do so. When America did enter the war, Roosevelt hoped to be given command of a division, and while many people, including the British and French, thought that was an excellent idea, Wilson, remembering Roosevelt's criticisms, prevented that from happening. Roosevelt spent the war raising bonds and making speeches, but never reached the front. All four of his sons, however did serve in France. His oldest son, Ted, fought with the 26th Infantry Regiment. Kermit

Roosevelt, as eager as his father to fight, did not wait for America's entry and joined the British Army, seeing action in Mesopotamia before rejoining the American 1st Division in France. Archie Roosevelt also fought with the 1st Division being wounded severely. The youngest son, Quentin, served as a pilot and was killed in action in July of 1918. Quentin's death devastated the elder Roosevelt. After the war Roosevelt considered running for president again in 1920, but his health, never really recovered from the Amazon fiasco, deteriorated sharply and he died in January 1919 at the age of 60, one of the most popular presidents in American history.

Elihu Root
(February 15, 1845 – February 7, 1937)

Elihu Root was a successful lawyer whose connections with influential people took him into politics and government service for much of his life. He became the US Attorney for the Southern District of New York for several years and was then made Secretary of War in 1899 by William McKinley. He continued in this role when Theodore Roosevelt became president. As Secretary, Root presided over a massive restructuring of the US Army, transforming it from a chaotically administered frontier constabulary force into a modern and professional military. In 1905 Roosevelt named Root to become Secretary of State. In 1909 Root was elected to the US Senate from the state of New York. Root won the Nobel Peace Prize in 1912 for his work to use arbitration and cooperation to settle international differences. After leaving the Senate he continued to advise many government officials. He favored the United States' entry into World War I and campaigned for preparedness. He led a delegation to Russia in 1917 to try to establish relations with the revolutionary government there. He supported the US joining the League of Nations. He was a member of the 1922 Washington Naval Disarmament Conference.

Thomas Etholen Selfridge
(February 8, 1882 – September 17, 1908)

Thomas Selfridge was a lieutenant in the US Army Signal Corps Aeronautical Division where he had the dubious distinction of becoming the first person killed in an airplane crash when he and Orville Wright were making a demonstration flight at Fort Myer, Virginia in 1908.

Henry Lewis Stimson
(September 21, 1867 – October 20, 1950)

Henry Stimson was an American statesman, lawyer, and politician. During his career he served as Secretary of War under William Taft (1911-1913), Secretary of State under Herbert hoover (1929-1933) and Secretary of War under Franklin Roosevelt and Harry Truman (1940-1945).

Nikola Tesla
(July 10, 1856 – January 7, 1943)

Tesla was a Serb, born in the Austro-Hungarian Empire. He showed an early interest in physics and engineering. He was a brilliant but undisciplined student and never completed his formal schooling. He drifted from job to job, mostly working with electrical equipment like telegraphs, until he moved to Paris and went to work for Thomas Edison's Continental Edison Company which was involved in installing electric lighting in the city. Tesla learned a great deal about the industry and soon came to the attention of the manager who brought Tesla back to the United States with him in 1884. Tesla remained with the Edison Company only 6 months, resigning after not receiving bonuses he believed he was owed. He soon set up his own company and received several patents. But he while he was a brilliant inventor and designer, he was not much of a businessman and soon lost the company—and his patents—to the investors he had taken on. After working at odd jobs for a time he began work on an electric induction motor running on alternating current. This ultimately brought him to the attention of George Westinghouse who was in a fierce competition with Edison and several other companies in the electrification of American cities. This brought Tesla into the great 'War of the Currents' debate between Alternating Current and Direct Current supporters. Westinghouse and the AC supports eventually prevailed and Tesla made a great deal of money from his patents and was able to pursue his own personal research interests from that point on. In the following years he produced a staggering number of new inventions in a variety of fields, concentrating on items he could patent and market. Among these were mechanical oscillators/generators, electric discharge tubes and X-ray imaging devices. He developed a radio-controlled boat and experimented with ideas for wireless lighting and power transmission. He became well known as an inventor and famous for his eccentric showmanship at public lectures. Not all of his attempts were successful, however, like his expensive Wardencliff Tower on Long Island which was intended to provide radio communications across the Atlantic. Tesla eventually fell into relative obscurity and lived quietly until his death.

Harry Truman
(May 8, 1884 – December 26, 1972)

Harry Truman served in the Missouri National Guard and saw action during World War I in an artillery unit. He worked in a clothing store after the war until he was elected as a county official in 1922. He spent the rest of his life in public service, becoming a US senator and then vice president in 1944. The death of Franklin Roosevelt in 1945 made Truman president. Truman was a central figure in the post-war world, implementing the Marshal Plan for the rebuilding of Europe and developing the strategy of containment which ultimately won the Cold War.

William Allen White
(February 10, 1868 – January 29, 1944)

William White was a life-long newspaperman and political commentator and activist. He bought the Emporia Gazette in Emporia, Kansas in 1895 and became the editor. He was a progressive conservative and championed the ideals of small town America. He was personal friends with both Theodore and Franklin Roosevelt. He helped Theodore in his 1912 Bull Moose campaign and later helped FDR awaken American to the perils of fascism prior to World War II.

Leonard Wood
(October 9, 1860 – August 7, 1927)

Wood received a medical degree from Harvard College and became a surgeon with the US Army under contract in 1886. He served with the 4th US Cavalry in the campaign against Geromino. Even though he was not technically a line officer, he took over command of a detachment from the 8th Infantry Regiment which had lost all of its own officers. He also rode over 100 miles through hostile territory to deliver dispatches. For these actions he received the Medal of Honor and was given the rank of Captain in the regular army. Stationed in Washington, he became the personal physician to President McKinley and made the acquaintance of Theodore Roosevelt, who was the Assistant Secretary of the Navy. At the outbreak of the Spanish American War, Roosevelt was determined to raise a regiment of volunteer cavalry, but recognizing his own lack of military credentials, convinced Wood to act as the colonel while Roosevelt was the lieutenant colonel. Deployed to Cuba, Wood was quickly promoted to command of a brigade and later a division. He participated in all of the major land battles of the campaign. After the war he was appointed the military governor of Santiago from 1899 to 1902 and made a number of important reforms to improve the health of the population there. He was promoted to brigadier general and sent to the Philippines in 1902. He commanded a division there and later the whole department. Despite accusations of unnecessary violence against the insurrectionists and civilians, he was promoted to major general. In 1910 President Taft, who had worked with Wood in the Philippines, appointed him Chief of Staff. In that position he worked to establish ROTC programs in the United States and pushed for military preparedness. This put him at odds with Woodrow Wilson, who dismissed him in 1914. Wood continued to push for preparedness and when the United States entered World War I Wood was considered for command of the American Expeditionary Force. However, he was thought to be too politically controversial and John Pershing was given the command instead.

Wood spent the war training new military formations. He made an unsuccessful run for president in 1920. In 1921 he was made Governor General of the Philippines. His tenure there, until 1927, was marked by considerable tension and animosity between him and the local Filipino leaders. Wood returned to the United States in 1927 due to a brain tumor which had bothered him on and off for a number of years. He died during surgery. Wood was married to Louise Adriana Wood (Condit-Smith) (1869-1943), and they had two sons, Leonard Jr. (1892-1931) and Osborne Cutler (1897-1950) both of whom served in the US Army.

ABOUT THE AUTHOR

Scott Washburn is an architectural designer by profession,
an avid reader of military history as well as long time re-enactor
and wargamer. He has written several SF&F books that
are being published by Zmok Books